THE GIRL WHO KICKED THE HORNETS' NEST

Also in the Millennium Trilogy and published by
MacLehose Press, an imprint of Quercus

The Girl with the Dragon Tattoo
The Girl Who Played with Fire

Stieg Larsson

THE GIRL WHO KICKED THE HORNETS' NEST

Translated from the Swedish by

Reg Keeland

MACLEHOSE PRESS

QUERCUS · LONDON

First published in Great Britain in 2009 by

MacLehose Press
an imprint of Quercus
21 Bloomsbury Square
London
WC1A 2NS

Originally published in Sweden as *Luftslottet Som Sprängdes*
by Norstedts, Stockholm, in 2007.
Text published with agreement of Norstedts Agency.

A CIP catalogue reference for this book is available
from the British Library

ISBN (HB) 978 1 906694 16 6
ISBN (TPB) 978 1 906694 17 3

10 9 8 7 6 5 4 3 2

Typeset in Monotype Sabon by Ellipsis Books Limited, Glasgow

Printed and bound in Great Britain by Clays Ltd, St Ives plc

THE GIRL WHO KICKED THE HORNETS' NEST

PART I

INTERMEZZO IN A CORRIDOR

8 – 12.iv

It is estimated that some six hundred women served during the American Civil War. They had signed up disguised as men. Hollywood has missed a significant chapter of cultural history here – or is this history ideologically too difficult to deal with? Historians have often struggled to deal with women who do not respect gender distinctions, and nowhere is that distinction more sharply drawn than in the question of armed combat. (Even today, it can cause controversy having a woman on a typically Swedish moose hunt.)

But from antiquity to modern times, there are many stories of female warriors, of Amazons. The best known find their way into the history books as warrior queens, rulers as well as leaders. They have been forced to act as any Churchill, Stalin, or Roosevelt: Semiramis from Nineveh, who shaped the Assyrian Empire, and Boudicca, who led one of the bloodiest English revolts against the Roman forces of occupation, to cite just two. Boudicca is honoured with a statue on the Thames at Westminster Bridge, right opposite Big Ben. Be sure to say hello to her if you happen to pass by.

On the other hand, history is quite reticent about women who were common soldiers, who bore arms, belonged to regiments, and played their part in battle on the same terms as men. Hardly a war has been waged without women soldiers in the ranks.

CHAPTER 1

Friday, 8.iv

Dr Jonasson was woken by Nurse Nicander five minutes before the helicopter was expected to land. It was just before 1.30 in the morning.

"What?" he said, confused.

"Rescue Service helicopter coming in. Two patients. An injured man and a younger woman. The woman has a gunshot wound."

"Alright," Jonasson said wearily.

He felt groggy although he had slept for only half an hour. He was on the night shift in A. & E. at Sahlgrenska hospital in Göteborg. It had been a strenuous evening. Since he had come on duty at 6.00 p.m., the hospital had received four victims of a head-on collision outside Lindome. One was pronounced D.O.A. He had treated a waitress whose legs had been scalded in an accident at a restaurant on Avenyn, and he had saved the life of a four-year-old boy who arrived at the hospital with respiratory failure after swallowing the wheel of a toy car. He had patched up a girl who had ridden her bike into a ditch that the road-repair department had chosen to dig close to the end of a bike path; the warning barriers had been tipped into the hole. She had fourteen stitches in her face and would need two new front teeth. Jonasson had also sewn part of a thumb back on to an enthusiastic carpenter who had managed to slice it off.

By 12.30 the steady flow of emergency cases had eased off. He had made a round to check on the state of his patients, and then gone back to the staff bedroom to try to rest for a while. He was on duty until 6.00 in the morning, and seldom got the chance to sleep even if no emergency patients came in. But this time he had fallen asleep almost as soon as he turned out the light.

Nurse Nicander handed him a cup of tea. She had not been given any details about the incoming cases.

Jonasson saw lightning out over the sea. He knew that the helicopter was coming in in the nick of time. All of a sudden a heavy downpour lashed at the window. The storm had moved in over Göteborg.

He heard the sound of the chopper and watched as it banked through the storm squalls down towards the helipad. For a second he held his breath when the pilot seemed to have difficulty controlling the aircraft. Then it vanished from his field of view and he heard the engine slowing to land. He took a hasty swallow of his tea and set down the cup.

Jonasson met them in the emergency admissions area. The other doctor on duty, Katarina Holm, took on the first patient who was wheeled in – an elderly man with his head bandaged, apparently with a serious wound to the face. Jonasson was left with the second patient, the woman who had been shot. He did a quick visual examination: it looked like she was a teenager, very dirty and bloody, and severely wounded. He lifted the blanket that the Rescue Service had wrapped round her body and saw that the wounds to her hip and shoulder were bandaged with duct tape, which he considered a pretty clever idea. The tape kept bacteria out and the blood in. One bullet had entered the outer side of her hip and gone straight through the muscle tissue. Then he gently raised her shoulder and located the entry wound in her back. There was no exit wound: the round was still inside her shoulder. He hoped it had not penetrated her lung, and since he did not see any blood in the woman's mouth he concluded that probably it had not.

"Radiology," he told the nurse in attendance. That was all he needed to say.

Then he cut away the bandage that the emergency team had wrapped round her skull. He froze when he saw another entry wound. The woman had been shot in the head and there was no exit wound there either.

Dr Jonasson paused for a second, looking down at the girl. He felt dejected. He had often described his job as being like that of a goalkeeper. Every day people came to his place of work in varying conditions but with one objective: to get help. It could be an old woman who had collapsed from a heart attack in the Nordstan galleria, or a fourteen-year-old boy whose left lung had been pierced by a screwdriver, or a teenage girl who had taken ecstasy and danced for eighteen hours straight before collapsing, blue in the face. They were victims of accidents at work or of violent abuse at home. They were tiny children savaged by dogs on Vasaplatsen, or Handy Harrys, who only meant to saw a few planks with their Black & Deckers and in some mysterious way managed to slice right into their wrist-bones.

So Dr Jonasson was the goalkeeper who stood between the patient and Fonus Funeral Service. His job was to decide what to do. If he made the wrong decision, the patient might die or perhaps wake up disabled for life. Most often he made the right decision, because the vast majority of injured people had an obvious and specific problem. A stab wound to the lung or a crushing injury after a car crash were both particular and recognizable problems that could be dealt with. The survival of the patient depended on the extent of the damage and on Dr Jonasson's skill.

There were two kinds of injury that he hated. One was a serious burn case, because no matter what measures he took it would almost inevitably result in a lifetime of suffering. The second was an injury to the brain.

The girl on the gurney could live with a piece of lead in her hip and a piece of lead in her shoulder. But a piece of lead inside her brain was a trauma of a wholly different magnitude. He was suddenly aware of Nurse Nicander saying something.

"Sorry. I wasn't listening."

"It's her."

"What do you mean?"

"It's Lisbeth Salander. The girl they've been hunting for the past few weeks, for the triple murder in Stockholm."

Jonasson looked again at the unconscious patient's face. He realized at once that Nurse Nicander was right. He and the whole of Sweden had seen her passport photograph on billboards outside every newspaper kiosk for weeks. And now the murderer herself had been shot, which was surely poetic justice of a sort.

But that was not his concern. His job was to save his patient's life, irrespective of whether she was a triple murderer or a Nobel Prize winner. Or both.

Then the efficient chaos, the same in every A. & E. the world over, erupted. The staff on Jonasson's shift set about their appointed tasks. Salander's clothes were cut away. A nurse reported on her blood pressure

7

– 100/70 – while the doctor put his stethoscope to her chest and listened to her heartbeat. It was surprisingly regular, but her breathing was not quite normal.

Jonasson did not hesitate to classify Salander's condition as critical. The wounds in her shoulder and hip could wait until later with a compress on each, or even with the duct tape that some inspired soul had applied. What mattered was her head. Jonasson ordered tomography with the new and improved C.T. scanner that the hospital had lately acquired.

Dr Anders Jonasson was blond and blue-eyed, originally from Umeå in northern Sweden. He had worked at Sahlgrenska and Eastern hospitals for twenty years, by turns as researcher, pathologist, and in A. & E. He had achieved something that astonished his colleagues and made the rest of the medical staff proud to work with him; he had vowed that no patient would die on his shift, and in some miraculous way he had indeed managed to hold the mortality rate at zero. Some of his patients had died, of course, but it was always during subsequent treatment or for completely different reasons that had nothing to do with his interventions.

He had a view of medicine that was at times unorthodox. He thought doctors often drew conclusions that they could not substantiate. This meant that they gave up far too easily; alternatively they spent too much time at the acute stage trying to work out exactly what was wrong with the patient so as to decide on the right treatment. This was correct procedure, of course. The problem was that the patient was in danger of dying while the doctor was still doing his thinking.

But Jonasson had never before had a patient with a bullet in her skull. Most likely he would need a brain surgeon. He had all the theoretical knowledge required to make an incursion into the brain, but he did not by any means consider himself a brain surgeon. He felt inadequate but all of a sudden realized that he might be luckier than he deserved. Before he scrubbed up and put on his operating clothes he sent for Nurse Nicander.

"There's an American professor from Boston called Frank Ellis, working at the Karolinska hospital in Stockholm. He happens to be in Göteborg tonight, staying at the Radisson on Avenyn. He just gave a lecture on brain research. He's a good friend of mine. Could you get the number?"

While Jonasson was still waiting for the X-rays, Nurse Nicander came back with the number of the Radisson. Jonasson picked up the telephone. The night porter at the Radisson was very reluctant to wake a guest at that time of night and Jonasson had to come up with a few choice phrases about the critical nature of the situation before his call was put through.

"Good morning, Frank," Jonasson said when the call was finally answered. "It's Anders. Do you feel like coming over to Sahlgrenska to help out in a brain op.?"

"Are you bullshitting me?" Ellis had lived in Sweden for many years and was fluent in Swedish – albeit with an American accent – but when Jonasson spoke to him in Swedish, Ellis always replied in his mother tongue.

"I'm sorry I missed your lecture, Frank, but I hoped you might be able to give me private lessons. I've got a young woman here who's been shot in the head. Entry wound just above the left ear. I badly need a second opinion, and I don't know of a better person to ask."

"So it's serious?" Ellis sat up and swung his feet out of bed. He rubbed his eyes.

"She's mid-twenties, entry wound, no exit."

"And she's alive?"

"Weak but regular pulse, less regular breathing, blood pressure is 100/70. She also has a bullet wound in her shoulder and another in her hip. But I know how to handle those two."

"Sounds promising," Ellis said.

"Promising?"

"If somebody has a bullet in their head and they're still alive, that points to hopeful."

"I understand . . . Frank, can you help me out?"

"I spent the evening in the company of good friends, Anders. I got to bed at 1.00 and no doubt I have an impressive blood alcohol content."

"I'll make the decisions and do the surgery. But I need somebody to tell me if I'm doing anything stupid. Even a falling-down drunk Professor Ellis is several classes better than I could ever be when it comes to assessing brain damage."

"O.K. I'll come. But you're going to owe me one."

"I'll have a taxi waiting outside by the time you get down to the lobby. The driver will know where to drop you, and Nurse Nicander will be there to meet you and get you kitted out."

Ellis had raven-black hair with a touch of grey, and a dark five-o'clock shadow. He looked like a bit player in *E.R.* The tone of his muscles testified to the fact that he spent a number of hours each week at the gym. He pushed up his glasses and scratched the back of his neck. He focused his gaze on the computer screen, which showed every nook and cranny of the patient Salander's brain.

Ellis liked living in Sweden. He had first come as an exchange researcher in the late '70s and stayed for two years. Then he came back regularly, until one day he was offered a permanent position at the Karolinska in Stockholm. By that time he had won an international reputation.

He had first met Jonasson at a seminar in Stockholm fourteen years earlier and discovered that they were both fly-fishing enthusiasts. They had kept in touch and had gone on fishing trips to Norway and elsewhere. But they had never worked together.

"I'm sorry for chasing you down, but . . ."

"Not a problem." Ellis gave a dismissive wave. "But it'll cost you a bottle of Cragganmore the next time we go fishing."

"O.K., that's a fee I'll gladly pay."

"I had a patient a number of years ago, in Boston – I wrote about the case in the *New England Journal of Medicine*. It was a girl the same age as your patient here. She was walking to the university when someone shot her with a crossbow. The arrow entered at the outside edge of her left eyebrow and went straight through her head, exiting from almost the middle of the back of her neck."

"And she survived?"

"She looked like nothing on earth when she came in. We cut off the arrow shaft and put her head in a C.T. scanner. The arrow went straight through her brain. By all known reckoning she should have been dead, or at least suffered such massive trauma that she would have been in a coma."

"And what was her condition?"

"She was conscious the whole time. Not only that; she was terribly frightened, of course, but she was completely rational. Her only problem was that she had an arrow through her skull."

"What did you do?"

"Well, I got the forceps and pulled out the arrow and bandaged the wounds. More or less."

"And she lived to tell the tale?"

"Obviously her condition was critical, but the fact is we could have sent her home the same day. I've seldom had a healthier patient."

Jonasson wondered whether Ellis was pulling his leg.

"On the other hand," Ellis went on, "I had a 42-year-old patient in Stockholm some years ago who banged his head on a windowsill. He began to feel sick immediately and was taken by ambulance to A. & E. When I got to him he was unconscious. He had a small bump and a very slight bruise. But he never regained consciousness and died after nine days in intensive care. To this day I have no idea why he died. In the autopsy report, we wrote brain haemorrhage resulting from an accident, but not one of us was satisfied with that assessment. The bleeding was so minor and located in an area that shouldn't have affected anything else at all. And yet his liver, kidneys, heart and lungs shut down one after the other. The older I get, the more I think it's like a game of roulette. I don't believe we'll ever figure out precisely how the brain works." He tapped on the screen with a pen. "What do you intend to do?"

"I was hoping you would tell me."

"Let's hear your diagnosis."

"Well, first of all, it seems to be a small-calibre bullet. It entered at the temple, and then stopped about four centimetres into the brain. It's resting against the lateral ventricle. There's bleeding there."

"How will you proceed?"

"To use your terminology – get some forceps and extract the bullet by the same route it went in."

"Excellent idea. I would use the thinnest forceps you have."

"It's that simple?"

"What else can we do in this case? We could leave the bullet where it is, and she might live to be a hundred, but it's also a risk. She might develop epilepsy, migraines, all sorts of complaints. And one thing you really don't want to do is drill into her skull and then operate a year from now when the wound itself has healed. The bullet is located away from the major blood vessels. So I would recommend that you extract it . . . but . . ."

"But what?"

"The bullet doesn't worry me so much. She's survived this far and that's a good omen for her getting through having the bullet removed, too. The real problem is here." He pointed at the screen. "Around the entry wound you have all sorts of bone fragments. I can see at least a dozen that are a couple of millimetres long. Some are embedded in the brain tissue. That's what could kill her if you're not careful."

"Isn't that part of the brain associated with numbers and mathematical capacity?" Jonasson said.

Ellis shrugged. "Mumbo jumbo. I have no idea what these particular grey cells are for. You can only do your best. You operate. I'll look over your shoulder."

Mikael Blomkvist looked up at the clock and saw that it was just after 3.00 in the morning. He was handcuffed and increasingly uncomfortable. He closed his eyes for a moment. He was dead tired but running on adrenaline. He opened them again and gave the policeman an angry glare. Inspector Thomas Paulsson had a shocked expression on his face. They were sitting at a kitchen table in a white farmhouse called Gosseberga, somewhere near Nossebro. Blomkvist had heard of the place for the first time less than twelve hours earlier.

There was no denying the disaster that had occurred.

"Imbecile," Blomkvist said.

"Now, you listen here—"

"Imbecile," Blomkvist said again. "I warned you he was dangerous, for Christ's sake. I told you that you would have to handle him like a live grenade. He's murdered at least three people with his bare hands and he's built like a tank. And you send a couple of village policemen to arrest him as if he were some Saturday night drunk."

Blomkvist shut his eyes again, wondering what else could go wrong that night.

He had found Salander just after midnight. She was very badly wounded. He had sent for the police and the Rescue Service.

The only thing that had gone right was that he had persuaded them to send a helicopter to take the girl to Sahlgrenska hospital. He had given them a clear description of her injuries and the bullet wound in her head, and some bright spark at the Rescue Service got the message.

Even so, it had taken over half an hour for the Puma from the helicopter unit in Säve to arrive at the farmhouse. Blomkvist had got two

12

cars out of the barn. He switched on their headlights to illuminate a landing area in the field in front of the house.

The helicopter crew and two paramedics had proceeded in a routine and professional manner. One of the medics tended to Salander while the other took care of Alexander Zalachenko, known locally as Karl Axel Bodin. Zalachenko was Salander's father and her worst enemy. He had tried to kill her, but he had failed. Blomkvist had found him in the woodshed at the farm with a nasty-looking gash – probably from an axe – in his face and some shattering damage to one of his legs which he did not trouble to investigate.

While he waited for the helicopter, he did what he could for Salander. He took a clean sheet from a linen cupboard and cut it up to make bandages. The blood had coagulated at the entry wound in her head, and he did not know whether he dared to put a bandage on it or not. In the end he fixed the fabric very loosely round her head, mostly so that the wound would not be exposed to bacteria or dirt. But he had stopped the bleeding from the wounds in her hip and shoulder in the simplest possible way. He had found a roll of duct tape and this he had used to close the wounds. The medics remarked that this, in their experience, was a brand-new form of bandage. He had also bathed Salander's face with a wet towel and done his best to wipe off the dirt.

He had not gone back to the woodshed to tend to Zalachenko. He honestly did not give a damn about the man. But he did call Erika Berger on his mobile and told her the situation.

"Are *you* alright?" Berger asked him.

"I'm O.K.," Blomkvist said. "Lisbeth is the one who's in real danger."

"That poor girl," Berger said. "I read Björck's Säpo report this evening. How should I deal with it?"

"I don't have the energy to think that through right now," Blomkvist said. Security Police matters were going to have to wait until the next day.

As he talked to Berger, he sat on the floor next to the bench and kept a watchful eye on Salander. He had taken off her shoes and her trousers so that he could bandage the wound to her hip, and now his hand rested on the trousers that he had dropped on the floor next to the bench. There was something in one of the pockets. He pulled out a Palm Tungsten T3.

13

He frowned and looked long and hard at the hand-held computer. When he heard the approaching helicopter he stuffed it into the inside pocket of his jacket and then went through all her other pockets. He found another set of keys to the apartment in Mosebacke and a passport in the name of Irene Nesser. He put these swiftly into a side pocket of his laptop case.

The first patrol car with Torstensson and Ingemarsson from the station in Trollhättan arrived a few minutes after the helicopter landed. Next to arrive was Inspector Paulsson, who took charge immediately. Blomkvist began to explain what had happened. He very soon realized that Paulsson was a pompous, rigid drill sergeant type. He did not seem to take in anything that Blomkvist said. It was when Paulsson arrived that things really started to go awry.

The only thing he seemed capable of grasping was that the badly damaged girl being cared for by the medics on the floor next to the kitchen bench was the triple murderer Lisbeth Salander. And above all it was important that he make the arrest. Three times Paulsson had asked the urgently occupied medical orderly whether the girl could be arrested on the spot. In the end the medic stood up and shouted at Paulsson to keep the bloody hell out of his way.

Paulsson had then turned his attention to the wounded man in the woodshed, and Blomkvist heard the inspector report over his radio that Salander had evidently attempted to kill yet another person.

By now Blomkvist was so infuriated with Paulsson, who had obviously not paid attention to a word he had said, that he yelled at him to call Inspector Bublanski in Stockholm without delay. Blomkvist had even taken out his mobile and offered to dial the number for him, but Paulsson was not interested.

Blomkvist then made two mistakes.

First, he patiently but firmly explained that the man who had committed the murders in Stockholm was Ronald Niedermann, who was built like a heavily armoured robot and suffered from a disease called congenital analgesia, and who at that moment was sitting in a ditch on the road to Nossebro tied to a traffic sign. Blomkvist told Paulsson exactly where Niedermann was to be found, and urged him to send a platoon armed with automatic weapons to pick him up. Paulsson finally asked how Niedermann had come to be in that ditch, and Blomkvist freely admitted that he himself had put him there, and had managed only by holding a gun on him the whole time.

"Assault with a deadly weapon," was Paulsson's immediate response.

At this point Blomkvist should have realized that Paulsson was dangerously stupid. He should have called Bublanski himself and asked him to intervene, to bring some clarity to the fog in which Paulsson was apparently enveloped. Instead he made his second mistake: he offered to hand over the weapon he had in his jacket pocket – the Colt .45 1911 Government model that he had found earlier that day at Salander's apartment in Stockholm. It was the weapon he had used to disarm and disable Niedermann – not a straightforward matter with that giant of a man.

At which Paulsson swiftly arrested Blomkvist for possession of an illegal weapon. He then ordered his two officers, Torstensson and Ingemarsson, to drive over to the Nossebro road. They were to find out if there was any truth to Blomkvist's story that a man was sitting in a ditch there, tied to a MOOSE CROSSING sign. If this was the case, the officers were to handcuff the person in question and bring him to the farm at Gosseberga.

Blomkvist had objected at once, pointing out that Niedermann was not a man who could be arrested and handcuffed just like that: he was a maniacal killer, for God's sake. When Blomkvist's objections were ignored by Paulsson, the exhaustion of the day made him reckless. He told Paulsson he was an incompetent fool and yelled at him that Torstensson and Ingemarsson should fucking forget about untying Niedermann until they had called for back-up. As a result of this outburst, he was handcuffed and pushed into the back seat of Paulsson's car. Cursing, he watched as Torstensson and Ingemarsson drove off in their patrol car. The only glimmer of light in the darkness was that Salander had been carried to the helicopter, which was even now disappearing over the treetops in the direction of Göteborg. Blomkvist felt utterly helpless: he could only hope that she would be given the very best care. She was going to need it, or die.

Jonasson made two deep incisions all the way down to the cranium and peeled back the skin round the entry wound. He used clamps to secure the opening. A theatre nurse inserted a suction tube to remove any blood. Then came the awkward part, when he had to use a drill to enlarge the hole in the skull. The procedure was excruciatingly slow.

Finally he had a hole big enough to give access to Salander's brain. With infinite care he inserted a probe into the brain and enlarged the wound channel by a few millimetres. Then he inserted a thinner probe and located the bullet. From the X-ray he could see that the bullet had turned and was lying at an angle of forty-five degrees to the entry channel. He used the probe cautiously to prise at the edge of the bullet, and after a few unsuccessful attempts he managed to lift it very slightly so that he could turn it in the right direction.

Finally he inserted narrow forceps with serrated jaws. He gripped the base of the bullet, got a good hold on it, then pulled the forceps straight out. The bullet emerged with almost no resistance. He held it up to the light for a few seconds and saw that it appeared intact; then he dropped it into a bowl.

"Swab," he said, and his request was instantly met.

He glanced at the E.C.G., which showed that his patient still had regular heart activity.

"Forceps."

He pulled down the powerful magnifying glass hanging overhead and focused on the exposed area.

"Careful," Ellis said.

Over the next forty-five minutes Jonasson picked out no fewer than thirty-two tiny bone chips from round the entry wound. The smallest of these chips could scarcely be seen with the naked eye.

As Blomkvist tried in frustration to manoeuvre his mobile out of the breast pocket of his jacket – it proved to be an impossible task with his hands cuffed behind his back, nor was it clear to him how he was going to be able to use it – several more vehicles containing both uniformed officers and technical personnel arrived at the Gosseberga farm. They were detailed by Paulsson to secure forensic evidence in the woodshed and to do a thorough examination of the farmhouse, from which several weapons had already been confiscated. By now resigned to his futility, Blomkvist had observed their comings and goings from his vantage point in Paulsson's vehicle.

An hour passed before it dawned on Paulsson that Torstensson and Ingemarsson had not yet returned from their mission to retrieve Niedermann. He had Blomkvist brought into the kitchen, where he was required once more to provide precise directions to the spot.

Blomkvist closed his eyes.

He was still in the kitchen with Paulsson when the armed response team sent to relieve Torstensson and Ingemarsson reported back. Ingemarsson had been found dead with a broken neck. Torstensson was still alive, but he had been savagely beaten. The men had been discovered near a MOOSE CROSSING sign by the side of the road. Their service weapons and the marked police car were gone.

Inspector Paulsson had started out with a relatively manageable situation: now he had a murdered policeman and an armed killer on the run.

"Imbecile," Blomkvist said again.

"It won't help to insult the police."

"That certainly seems to be true in your case. But I'm going to report you for dereliction of duty and you won't even know what hit you. Before I'm through with you, you're going to be celebrated as the dumbest policeman in Sweden on every newspaper billboard in the country."

The notion of being the object of public ridicule appeared at last to have an effect on Inspector Paulsson. His face was lined with anxiety.

"What do you propose?"

"I don't propose, I *demand* that you call Inspector Bublanski in Stockholm. This minute. His number's on my mobile in my breast pocket."

Inspector Modig woke with a start when her mobile rang at the other end of the bedroom. She saw to her dismay that it was just after 4.00 in the morning. Then she looked at her husband, who was snoring peacefully. He would probably sleep through an artillery barrage. She staggered out of bed, unplugged her mobile from the charger, and fumbled for the talk button.

Jan Bublanski, she thought. *Who else?*

"Everything has gone to hell down in Trollhättan," her senior officer said without bothering to greet her or apologize. "The X2000 to Göteborg leaves at 5.10. Take a taxi."

"What's happened?"

"Blomkvist found Salander, Niedermann *and* Zalachenko. Got himself arrested for insulting a police officer, resisting arrest, and for possession of an illegal weapon. Salander was taken to Sahlgrenska with a bullet in her head. Zalachenko is there too with an axe wound to his skull. Niedermann got away. And he killed a policeman tonight."

Modig blinked twice, registering how exhausted she felt. Most of all she wanted to crawl back into bed and take a month's holiday.

"The X2000 at 5.10. O.K. What do you want me to do?"

"Meet Jerker Holmberg at Central Station. You're to contact an Inspector Thomas Paulsson at the Trollhättan police. He seems to be responsible for much of the mess tonight. Blomkvist described him as an Olympic-class idiot."

"You've talked to Blomkvist?"

"Apparently he's been arrested and cuffed. I managed to persuade Paulsson to let me talk to him for a moment. I'm on my way to Kungsholmen right now, and I'll try to work out what's going on. We'll keep in touch by mobile."

Modig looked at the time again. Then she called a taxi and jumped into the shower for a minute. She brushed her teeth, pulled a comb through her hair, and put on long black trousers, a black T-shirt, and a grey jacket. She put her police revolver in her shoulder bag and picked out a dark-red leather coat. Then she shook enough life into her husband to explain where she was off to, and that he had to deal with the kids in the morning. She walked out of the front door just as the taxi drew up.

She did not have to search for her colleague, Criminal Inspector Holmberg. She assumed that he would be in the restaurant car and that is where she found him. He had already bought coffee and sandwiches for her. They sat in silence for five minutes as they ate their breakfast. Finally Holmberg pushed his coffee cup aside.

"Maybe I should get some training in some other field," he said.

Some time after 4.00 in the morning, Criminal Inspector Marcus Erlander from the Violent Crimes Division of the Göteborg police arrived in Gosseberga and took over the investigation from the over-burdened Paulsson. Erlander was a short, round man in his fifties with grey hair. One of the first things he did was to have Blomkvist released from his handcuffs, and then he produced rolls and coffee from a thermos. They sat in the living room for a private conversation.

"I've spoken with Bublanski," Erlander said. "Bubble and I have known each other for many years. We are both of us sorry that you were subjected to Paulsson's rather primitive way of operating."

"He succeeded in getting a policeman killed tonight," Blomkvist said.

Erlander said: "I knew Officer Ingemarsson personally. He served in Göteborg before he moved to Trollhättan. He has a three-year-old daughter."

"I'm sorry. I tried to warn him."

"So I heard. You were quite emphatic, it seems, and that's why you were cuffed. You were the one who exposed Wennerström last year. Bublanski says that you're a shameless journalist bastard and an insane private investigator, but that you just might know what you're talking about. Can you bring me up to speed so that I can get the hang of what's going on?"

"What happened here tonight is the culmination of the murders of two friends of mine in Enskede, Dag Svensson and Mia Johansson. And the murder of a person who was no friend of mine . . . a lawyer called Bjurman, also Lisbeth Salander's guardian."

Erlander made notes between taking sips of his coffee.

"As you no doubt know, the police have been looking for Salander since Easter. She was a suspect in all three murders. First of all, you have to realize that Salander is not only not guilty of these murders, she has been throughout a victim in the whole affair."

"I haven't had the least connection to the Enskede business, but after everything that was in the media about her it seems a bit hard to swallow that Salander could be completely innocent."

"Nonetheless, that's how it is. She's innocent. Full stop. The killer is Ronald Niedermann, the man who murdered your officer tonight. He works for Karl Axel Bodin."

"The Bodin who's in Sahlgrenska with an axe in his skull?"

"The axe isn't still in his head. I assume it was Salander who nailed him. His real name is Alexander Zalachenko and he's Lisbeth's father. He was a hit man for Russian military intelligence. He defected in the '70s, and was then on the books of Säpo until the collapse of the Soviet Union. He's been running his own criminal network ever since."

Erlander scrutinized the man opposite him. Blomkvist's face was shiny with sweat, but he looked both frozen and deathly tired. Until now he had sounded perfectly rational, but Paulsson – whose opinion had little influence on Erlander – had warned him that Blomkvist had been babbling on about Russian agents and German hit men – hardly routine elements in Swedish police work. Blomkvist had apparently reached the point in his story at which Paulsson had decided to ignore everything else he might say. But there was one policeman dead and another severely wounded on the road to Nossebro, so Erlander was willing to listen. But he could not keep a trace of incredulity out of his voice.

"O.K. A Russian agent."

Blomkvist smiled weakly, only too aware of how odd his story sounded.

"A *former* Russian agent. I can document every one of my claims."

"Go on."

"Zalachenko was a top spy in the '70s. He defected and was granted asylum by Säpo. In his old age he became a gangster. As far as I understand it, it's not a unique situation in the wake of the Soviet Union's collapse."

"O.K."

"As I said, I don't know exactly what happened here tonight, but Lisbeth tracked down her father whom she hadn't seen for fifteen years. Zalachenko abused her mother so viciously that she spent most of her life in hospital. He tried to murder Lisbeth, and through Niedermann he was the architect of the murders of Svensson and Johansson. Plus, he was behind the kidnapping of Salander's friend Miriam Wu – you probably heard of Paolo Roberto's title bout in Nykvarn, as a result of which Wu was rescued from certain death."

"If Salander hit her father in the head with an axe she isn't exactly innocent."

"She has been shot three times. I think we could assume her actions were on some level self-defence. I wonder . . ."

"Yes?"

"She was so covered with dirt, with mud, that her hair was one big lump of dried clay. Her clothes were full of sand, inside and out. It looked as though she might have been buried during the night. Niedermann is known to have a habit of burying people. The police in Södertälje have found two graves in the place that's owned by Svavelsjö Motorcycle Club, outside Nykvarn."

"Three, as a matter of fact. They found one more late last night. But if Salander was shot and buried, how was she able to climb out and start wandering around with an axe?"

"Whatever went on here tonight, you have to understand that Salander is exceptionally resourceful. I tried to persuade Paulsson to bring in a dog unit—"

"It's on its way now."

"Good."

"Paulsson arrested you for insulting a police officer . . ."

"I will dispute that. I called him an imbecile and an incompetent fool. Under the circumstances neither of these epithets could be considered wide of the mark."

"Hmm. It's not a wholly inaccurate description. But you were also arrested for possession of an illegal weapon."

"I made the mistake of trying to hand over a weapon to him. I don't want to say anything more about that until I talk to my lawyer."

"Alright. We'll leave it at that. We have more serious issues to discuss. What do you know about this Niedermann?"

"He's a murderer. And there's something wrong with him. He's over two metres tall and built like a tank. Ask Paolo Roberto, who boxed with him. He suffers from a disease called congenital analgesia, which means the transmitter substance in his nerve synapses doesn't function. He feels no pain. He's German, was born in Hamburg, and in his teens he was a skinhead. Right now he's on the run and he'll be seriously dangerous to anyone he runs into."

"Do you have an idea where he might be heading?"

"No. I only know that I had him neatly trussed, all ready to be arrested, when that idiot from Trollhättan took charge of the situation."

Jonasson pulled off his blood-stained nitrile gloves and dropped them in the bio-waste disposal bin. A theatre nurse was applying bandages to the gunshot wound on Salander's hip. The operation had lasted three hours. He looked at the girl's shaved and wounded head, which was already wrapped in bandages.

He felt a sudden tenderness, as he often did for patients after an operation. According to the newspapers, she was a psychopathic mass murderer, but to him she looked more like an injured sparrow.

"You're an excellent surgeon," Ellis said, looking at him with amused affection.

"Can I buy you breakfast?"

"Can one get pancakes and jam anywhere round here?"

"Waffles," Jonasson said. "At my house. Let me call my wife to warn her, then we can take a taxi." He stopped and looked at the clock. "On second thoughts, it might be better if we didn't call."

Annika Giannini woke with a start. She saw that it was 5.58 a.m. . . . She had her first client meeting at 8.00. She turned to look at Enrico, who was sleeping peacefully and probably would not be awake before 8.00. She blinked hard a few times and got up to turn on the coffeemaker before she took her shower. She dressed in black trousers, a white polo neck, and a muted brick-red jacket. She made two slices of toast with cheese, orange marmalade and a sliced avocado, and carried her breakfast into the living room in time for the 6.30 television news. She took a sip of coffee and had just opened her mouth to take a bite of toast when she heard the headlines.

One policeman killed and another seriously wounded. Drama last night as triple murderer Lisbeth Salander is finally captured.

At first she could not make any sense of it. Was it Salander who had killed a policeman? The news item was sketchy, but bit by bit she gathered that a man was being sought for the killing. A nationwide alert had gone out for a man in his mid-thirties, as yet unnamed. Salander herself was critically injured and at Sahlgrenska hospital in Göteborg.

She switched to the other channel, but she learned nothing more about what had happened. She reached for her mobile and called her brother, Mikael Blomkvist. She only got his voicemail. She felt a small twinge of fear. He had called on his way to Göteborg. He had been tracking Salander. And a murderer who called himself Ronald Niedermann.

As it was growing light an observant police officer found traces of blood on the ground behind the woodshed. A police dog followed the trail to a narrow trench in a clearing in a wood about four hundred metres north-east of the farmhouse.

Blomkvist went with Inspector Erlander. Grimly they studied the site. Much more blood had obviously been shed in and around the trench.

They found a damaged cigarette case that seemed to have been used as a scoop. Erlander put it in an evidence bag and labelled the find. He also gathered samples of blood-soaked clumps of dirt. A uniformed officer drew his attention to a cigarette butt – a filterless Pall Mall – some distance from the hole. This too was saved in an evidence bag and labelled. Blomkvist remembered having seen a pack of Pall Malls on the kitchen counter in Zalachenko's house.

Erlander glanced up at the lowering rain clouds. The storm that had ravaged Göteborg earlier in the night had obviously passed to the south of the Nossebro area, but it was only a matter of time before the rain came. He instructed one of his men to get a tarpaulin to cover the trench and its immediate surroundings.

"I think you're right," Erlander said to Blomkvist as they walked back to the farmhouse. "An analysis of the blood will probably establish that Salander was buried here, and I'm beginning to expect that we'll find her fingerprints on the cigarette case. She was shot and buried here, but somehow she managed to survive and dig herself out and—"

"And somehow got back to the farm and swung an axe into Zalachenko's skull," Blomkvist finished for him. "She can be a moody bitch."

"But how on earth did she handle Niedermann?"

Blomkvist shrugged. He was as bewildered as Erlander on that score.

CHAPTER 2

Friday, 8.iv

Modig and Holmberg arrived at Göteborg Central Station just after 8.oo a.m. Bublanski had called to give them new instructions. They could forget about finding a car to take them to Gosseberga. They were to take a taxi to police headquarters on Ernst Fontells Plats, the seat of the County Criminal Police in Western Götaland. They waited for almost an hour before Inspector Erlander arrived from Gosseberga with Blomkvist. Blomkvist said hello to Modig, having met her before, and shook hands with Holmberg, whom he did not know. One of Erlander's colleagues joined them with an update on the hunt for Niedermann. It was a brief report.

"We have a team working under the auspices of the County Criminal Police. An A.P.B. has gone out, of course. The missing patrol car was found in Alingsås early this morning. The trail ends there for the moment. We have to suppose that he switched vehicles, but we've had no report of a car being stolen thereabouts."

"Media?" Modig asked, with an apologetic glance at Blomkvist.

"It's a police killing and the press is out in force. We'll be holding a press conference at 10.oo."

"Does anyone have any information on Lisbeth Salander's condition?" Blomkvist said. He felt strangely uninterested in everything to do with the hunt for Niedermann.

"She was operated on during the night. They removed a bullet from her head. She hasn't regained consciousness yet."

"Is there any prognosis?"

"As I understand it, we won't know anything until she wakes up. But the surgeon says he has high hopes that she'll survive, barring unforeseen complications."

"And Zalachenko?"

"Who?" Erlander's colleague said. He had not yet been brought up to date with all the details.

"Karl Axel Bodin."

"I see . . . yes, he was operated on last night too. He had a very deep gash across his face and another just below one kneecap. He's in bad shape, but the injuries aren't life-threatening."

Blomkvist absorbed this news.

"You look tired," Modig said.

"You got that right. I'm into my third day with hardly any sleep."

"Believe it or not, he actually slept in the car coming down from Nossebro," Erlander said.

"Could you manage to tell us the whole story from the beginning?" Holmberg said. "It feels to us as though the score between the private investigators and the police investigators is about 3–0."

Blomkvist gave him a wan smile. "That's a line I'd like to hear from Officer Bubble."

They made their way to the police canteen to have breakfast. Blomkvist spent half an hour explaining step by step how he had pieced together the story of Zalachenko. When he had finished, the detectives sat in silence.

"There are a few holes in your account," Holmberg said at last.

"That's possible," Blomkvist said.

"You didn't say, for example, how you came to be in possession of the Top Secret Säpo report on Zalachenko."

"I found it yesterday at Lisbeth Salander's apartment when I finally worked out where she was. She probably found it in Bjurman's summer cabin."

"So you've discovered Salander's hideout?" Modig said.

Blomkvist nodded.

"And?"

"You'll have to find out for yourselves where it is. Salander put a lot of effort into establishing a secret address for herself, and I have no intention of revealing its whereabouts."

Modig and Holmberg exchanged an anxious look.

"Mikael . . . this is a murder investigation," Modig said.

"You still haven't got it, have you? Lisbeth Salander is in fact innocent and the police have violated her and destroyed her reputation in ways that beggar belief. 'Lesbian Satanist gang' . . . where the hell do you get this stuff? Not to mention her being sought in connection with three murders she had nothing to do with. If she wants to tell you where she lives, then I'm sure she will."

"But there's another gap I don't really understand," Holmberg said.

"How does Bjurman come into the story in the first place? You say he was the one who started the whole thing by contacting Zalachenko and asking him to kill Salander. Why would he do that?"

"I reckon he hired Zalachenko to get rid of Salander. The plan was for her to end up in that warehouse in Nykvarn."

"He was her guardian. What motive would he have had to get rid of her?"

"It's complicated."

"I can do complicated."

"He had a hell of a good motive. He had done something that Salander knew about. She was a threat to his entire future and well-being."

"What had he done?"

"I think it would be best if you gave Salander a chance to explain the story herself." He looked Holmberg steadily in the eye.

"Let me guess," Modig said. "Bjurman subjected his ward to some sort of sexual assault . . ."

Blomkvist shrugged and said nothing.

"You don't know about the tattoo Bjurman had on his abdomen?"

"What tattoo?" Blomkvist was taken aback.

"An amateurish tattoo across his belly with a message that said: *I am a sadistic pig, a pervert and a rapist*. We've been wondering what that was about."

Blomkvist burst out laughing.

"What's so funny?"

"I've always wondered what she did to get her revenge. But listen . . . I don't want to discuss this for the same reason I've already given. She's the real victim here. She's the one who has to decide what she is willing to tell you. Sorry."

He looked almost apologetic.

"Rapes should always be reported to the police," Modig said.

"I'm with you on that. But this rape took place two years ago, and Lisbeth still hasn't talked to the police about it. Which means that she doesn't intend to. It doesn't matter how much I disagree with her about the matter; it's her decision. Anyway . . ."

"Yes?"

"She had no good reason to trust the police. The last time she tried explaining what a pig Zalachenko was, she was locked up in a mental hospital."

*

Richard Ekström, the leader of the preliminary investigation, had butterflies in his stomach as he asked his team leader Inspector Bublanski to take a seat opposite him. Ekström straightened his glasses and stroked his well-groomed goatee. He felt that the situation was chaotic and ominous. For several weeks they had been hunting Lisbeth Salander. He himself had proclaimed her far and wide to be mentally imbalanced, a dangerous psychopath. He had leaked information that would have backed him up in an upcoming trial. Everything had looked so good.

There had been no doubt in his mind that Salander was guilty of three murders. The trial should have been a straightforward matter, a pure media circus with himself at centre stage. Then everything had gone haywire, and he found himself with a completely different murderer and a chaos that seemed to have no end in sight. *That bitch Salander.*

"Well, this is a fine mess we've landed in," he said. "What have you come up with this morning?"

"A nationwide A.P.B. has been sent out on this Ronald Niedermann, but there's no sign of him. At present he's being sought only for the murder of Officer Gunnar Ingemarsson, but I anticipate we'll have grounds for charging him with the three murders here in Stockholm. Maybe you should call a press conference."

Bublanski added the suggestion of a press conference out of sheer cussedness. Ekström hated press conferences.

"I think we'll hold off on the press conference for the time being," he snapped.

Bublanski had to stop himself from smiling.

"In the first instance, this is a matter for the Göteborg police," Ekström said.

"Well, we do have Modig and Holmberg on the scene in Göteborg, and we've begun to co-operate—"

"We'll hold off on the press conference until we know more," Ekström repeated in a brittle tone. "What I want to know is: how certain are you that Niedermann really is involved in the murders in Stockholm?"

"My gut feeling? I'm 100 per cent convinced. On the other hand, the case isn't exactly rock solid. We have no witnesses to the murders, and there is no satisfactory forensic evidence. Lundin and Nieminen

27

of the Svavelsjö M.C. are refusing to say anything – they're claiming they've never heard of Niedermann. But he's going to go to prison for the murder of Officer Ingemarsson."

"Precisely," said Ekström. "The killing of the police officer is the main thing right now. But tell me this: is there anything at all to even suggest that Salander might be involved in some way in the murders? Could she and Niedermann have somehow committed the murders together?"

"I very much doubt it, and if I were you I wouldn't voice that theory in public."

"So how *is* she involved?"

"This is an intricate story, as Mikael Blomkvist claimed from the very beginning. It revolves around this Zala . . . Alexander Zalachenko."

Ekström flinched at the mention of the name Blomkvist.

"Go on," he said.

"Zala is a Russian hit man – apparently without a grain of conscience – who defected in the '70s, and Lisbeth Salander was unlucky enough to have him as her father. He was sponsored or supported by a faction within Säpo that tidied up after any crimes he committed. A police officer attached to Säpo also saw to it that Salander was locked up in a children's psychiatric clinic. She was twelve and had threatened to blow Zalachenko's identity, his alias, his whole cover."

"This is a bit difficult to digest. It's hardly a story we can make public. If I understand the matter correctly, all this stuff about Zalachenko is highly classified."

"Nevertheless, it's the truth. I have documentation."

"Could I see it?"

Bublanski pushed across the desk a folder containing a police report dated 1991. Ekström surreptitiously scanned the stamp, which indicated that the document was Top Secret, and the registration number, which he at once identified as belonging to the Security Police. He leafed rapidly through the hundred or so pages, reading paragraphs here and there. Eventually he put the folder aside.

"We have to try to tone this down, so that the situation doesn't get completely out of our control. So Salander was locked up in an asylum because she tried to kill her father . . . this Zalachenko. And now she has attacked him with an axe. By any interpretation that would be attempted murder. And she has to be charged with shooting Magge Lundin in Stallarholmen."

28

"You can arrest whoever you want, but I would tread carefully if I were you."

"There's going to be an almighty scandal if Säpo's involvement gets leaked."

Bublanski shrugged. His job was to investigate crimes, not to clean up after scandals.

"This bastard from Säpo, this Gunnar Björck. What do you know about his role?"

"He's one of the major players. He's on sick leave for a slipped disc and lives in Smådalarö at present."

"O.K. . . . we'll keep the lid on Säpo's involvement for the time being. The focus right now is to be on the murder of a police officer."

"It's going to be hard to keep this under wraps."

"What do you mean?"

"I sent Andersson to bring in Björck for a formal interrogation. That should be happening . . ." – Bublanski looked at his watch – ". . . yes, about now."

"You *what?*"

"I was rather hoping to have the pleasure of driving out to Smådalarö myself, but the events surrounding last night's killing took precedence."

"I didn't give anyone permission to arrest Björck."

"That's true. But it's not an arrest. I'm just bringing him in for questioning."

"Whichever, I don't like it."

Bublanski leaned forward, almost as if to confide in the other man.

"Richard . . . this is how it is. Salander has been subjected to a number of infringements of her rights, starting when she was a child. I do not mean for this to continue on my watch. You have the option to remove me as leader of the investigation . . . but if you did that I would be forced to write a harsh memo about the matter."

Ekström looked as if he had just swallowed something very sour.

Gunnar Björck, on sick leave from his job as assistant chief of the Immigration Division of the Security Police, opened the door of his summer house in Smådalarö and looked up at a powerfully built, blond man with a crewcut who wore a black leather jacket.

"I'm looking for Gunnar Björck."

29

"That's me."

"Curt Andersson, County Criminal Police." The man held up his I.D.

"Yes?"

"You are requested to accompany me to Kungsholmen to assist the police in their investigations into the case involving Lisbeth Salander."

"Uh . . . there must be some sort of misunderstanding."

"There's no misunderstanding," Andersson said.

"You don't understand. I'm a police officer myself. Save yourself making a big mistake: check it out with your superior officers."

"My superior is the one who wants to talk to you."

"I have to make a call and—"

"You can make your call from Kungsholmen."

Björck felt suddenly resigned. *It's happened. I'm going to be arrested. That goddamn fucking Blomkvist. And fucking Salander.*

"Am I being arrested?" he said.

"Not for the moment. But we can arrange for that if you like."

"No . . . no, of course I'll come with you. Naturally I'd want to assist my colleagues in the police force."

"Alright, then," Andersson said, walking into the hallway to keep a close eye on Björck as he turned off the coffee machine and picked up his coat.

In the late morning it dawned on Blomkvist that his rental car was still at the Gosseberga farm, but he was so exhausted that he did not have the strength or the means to get out there to fetch it, much less drive safely for any distance. Erlander kindly arranged for a crime scene tech to take the car back on his way home.

"Think of it as compensation for the way you were treated last night."

Blomkvist thanked him and took a taxi to City Hotel on Lorensbergsgatan. He booked in for the night for 800 kronor and went straight to his room and undressed. He sat naked on the bed and took Salander's Palm Tungsten T3 from the inside pocket of his jacket, weighing it in his hand. He was still amazed that it had not been confiscated when Paulsson frisked him, but Paulsson presumably thought it was Blomkvist's own, and he had never been formally taken into custody and searched. He thought for a moment and then slipped it into a compartment of his laptop case where he had also put Salander's D.V.D. marked "Bjurman", which Paulsson had also missed. He knew that technically he was withholding evidence, but these were the things that Salander would no doubt prefer not to have fall into the wrong hands.

He turned on his mobile and saw that the battery was low, so he plugged in the charger. He made a call to his sister, Advokat Giannini.

"Hi, Annika."

"What did you have to do with the policeman's murder last night?" she asked him at once.

He told her succinctly what had happened.

"O.K., so Salander is in intensive care."

"Correct, and we won't know the extent or severity of her injuries until she regains consciousness, but now she's really going to need a lawyer."

Giannini thought for a moment. "Do you think she'd want me for her lawyer?"

"Probably she wouldn't want any lawyer at all. She isn't the type to ask anyone for help."

"Mikael . . . I've said this before, it sounds like she might need a criminal lawyer. Let me look at the documentation you have."

"Talk to Erika and ask her for a copy."

As soon as Blomkvist disconnected, he called Berger himself. She did not answer her mobile, so he tried her number at the *Millennium* offices. Henry Cortez answered.

"Erika's out somewhere," he said.

Blomkvist briefly explained what had happened and asked Cortez to pass the information to *Millennium*'s editor-in-chief.

"Will do. What do you want us to do?" Cortez said.

"Nothing today," Blomkvist said. "I have to get some sleep. I'll be back in Stockholm tomorrow if nothing else comes up. *Millennium* will have an opportunity to present its version of the story in the next issue, but that's almost a month away."

He flipped his mobile shut and crawled into bed. He was asleep within thirty seconds.

Assistant County Police Chief Carina Spångberg tapped her pen against her glass of water and asked for quiet. Nine people were seated around the conference table in her office at police headquarters. Three women and six men: the head of the Violent Crimes Division and his assistant head; three criminal inspectors including Erlander and the Göteborg police press officers; preliminary investigation leader Agneta Jervas from the prosecutor's office, and lastly Inspectors Modig and Holmberg from the Stockholm police. They were included as a sign of goodwill and to demonstrate that Göteborg wished to co-operate with their colleagues from the capital. Possibly also to show them how a real police investigation should be run.

Spångberg, who was frequently the lone woman in a male landscape, had a reputation for not wasting time on formalities or mere courtesies. She explained that the county police chief was at the Europol conference in Madrid, that he had broken off his trip as soon as he knew that one of his police officers had been murdered, but that he was not expected back before late that night. Then she turned directly to the head of the Violent Crimes Division, Anders Pehrzon, and asked him to brief the assembled company.

"It's been about ten hours since our colleague was murdered on Nossebrovägen. We know the name of the killer, Ronald Niedermann, but we still don't have a picture of him."

"In Stockholm we have a photograph of him that's about twenty years old. Paolo Roberto got it through a boxing club in Germany, but it's almost unusable," Holmberg said.

"Alright. The patrol car that Niedermann is thought to have driven away was found in Alingsås this morning, as you all know. It was parked on a side street 350 metres from the railway station. We haven't had a report yet of any car thefts in the area this morning."

"What's the status of the search?"

"We're keeping an eye on all trains arriving in Stockholm and Malmö. There is a nationwide A.P.B. out and we've alerted the police in Norway and Denmark. Right now we have about thirty officers working directly on the investigation, and of course the whole force is keeping their eyes peeled."

"No leads?"

"No, nothing yet. But someone with Niedermann's distinctive appearance is not going to go unnoticed for long."

"Does anyone know about Torstensson's condition?" asked one of the inspectors from Violent Crime.

"He's at Sahlgrenska. His injuries seem to be similar to those of a car crash victim – it's hardly credible that anyone could do such damage with his bare hands: a broken leg, ribs crushed, cervical vertebrae injured, plus there's a risk that he may be paralysed."

They all took stock of their colleague's plight for a few moments until Spångberg turned to Erlander.

"Marcus . . . tell us what really happened at Gosseberga."

"Thomas Paulsson happened at Gosseberga."

A ripple of groans greeted this response.

"Can't someone give that man early retirement? He's a walking catastrophe."

"I know all about Paulsson," Spångberg interrupted. "But I haven't heard any complaints about him in the last . . . well, not for the past two years. In what way has he become harder to handle?"

"The police chief up there is an old friend of Paulsson's, and he's probably been trying to protect him. With all good intentions, of course, and I don't mean to criticize him. But last night Paulsson's behaviour was so bizarre that several of his people mentioned it to me."

"In what way bizarre?"

Erlander glanced at Modig and Holmberg. He was embarrassed to be discussing flaws in their organization in front of the visitors from Stockholm.

"As far as I'm concerned, the strangest thing was that he detailed one of the techs to make an inventory of everything in the woodshed – where we found the Zalachenko guy?"

"An inventory of *what* in the woodshed?" Spångberg wanted to know.

"Yes . . . well . . . he said he needed to know exactly how many pieces of wood were in there. So that the report would be accurate."

There was a charged silence around the conference table before Erlander went on.

"And this morning it came out that Paulsson has been taking at least two different antidepressants. He should have been on sick leave, but no-one knew about his condition."

"What condition?" Spångberg said sharply.

"Well, obviously I don't know what's wrong with him – patient's confidentiality and all that – but the drugs he's taking are strong ataractics on the one hand, and stimulants. He was high as a kite all night."

"Good God," said Spångberg emphatically. She looked like the thundercloud that had swept over Göteborg that morning. "I want Paulsson in here for a chat. Right now."

"He collapsed this morning and was admitted to the hospital suffering from exhaustion. It was just our bad luck that he happened to be on rotation."

"May I ask . . . Paulsson, did he arrest Mikael Blomkvist last night?"

"He wrote a report citing offensive behaviour, aggressive resistance to police officers, and illegal possession of a weapon. That's what he put in the report."

"What does Blomkvist say?"

"He concedes that he was insulting, but he claims it was in self-defence. He says that the resistance consisted of a forceful verbal attempt to prevent Torstensson and Ingemarsson from going to pick up Niedermann alone, without back-up."

"Witnesses?"

"Well, there is Torstensson. I don't believe Paulsson's claim of aggressive resistance for a minute. It's a typical pre-emptive retaliation to undermine potential complaints from Blomkvist."

"But Blomkvist managed to overpower Niedermann all by himself, did he not?" Prosecutor Jervas said.

"By holding a gun to him."

"So Blomkvist had a gun. Then there was some basis for his arrest after all. Where did he get the weapon?"

"Blomkvist won't discuss it without his lawyer being there. And Paulsson arrested Blomkvist when he was trying to hand in the weapon to the police."

"Could I make a small, informal suggestion?" Modig said cautiously. Everyone turned to her.

"I have met Mikael Blomkvist on several occasions in the course of this investigation. I have found him quite likeable, even though he is a journalist. I suppose you're the one who has to make the decision about charging him . . ." She looked at Jervas, who nodded. "All this stuff about insults and aggressive resistance is just nonsense. I assume you will ignore it."

"Probably. Illegal weapons are more serious."

"I would urge you to wait and see. Blomkvist has put the pieces of this puzzle together all by himself; he's way ahead of us on the police force. It will be to our advantage to stay on good terms with him and ensure his co-operation, rather than unleash him to condemn the entire police force in his magazine and elsewhere in the media."

After a few seconds, Erlander cleared his throat. If Modig dared to stick her neck out, he could do the same.

"I agree with Sonja. I too think Blomkvist is a man we could work with. I've apologized to him for the way he was treated last night. He seems ready to let bygones be bygones. Besides, he has integrity. He somehow tracked down where Salander was living but he won't give us the address. He's not afraid to get into a public scrap with the police . . . and he's most certainly in a position where his voice will carry just as much weight in the media as any report from Paulsson."

"But he refuses to give the police any information about Salander."

"He says that we'll have to ask her ourselves, if that time ever comes. He says he absolutely won't discuss a person who is not only innocent but who also has had her rights so severely violated."

"What kind of weapon is it?" Jervas said.

"It's a Colt 1911 Government. Serial number unknown. Forensics have it, and we don't know yet whether it is connected to any known crime in Sweden. If it is, that will put the matter in a rather different light."

Spångberg raised her pen.

"Agneta . . . it's up to you to decide whether you want to initiate a preliminary investigation against Blomkvist. But I advise that you wait for the report from forensics. So let's move on. This character Zalachenko . . . what can our colleagues from Stockholm tell us about him?"

"The truth is," Modig said, "that until yesterday afternoon we had never heard of either Zalachenko or Niedermann."

"I thought you were busy looking for a lesbian Satanist gang in Stockholm. Was I wrong?" one of the Göteborg policemen said. His colleagues all frowned. Holmberg was studying his fingernails. Modig had to take the question.

"Within these four walls, I can tell you that we have our equivalent of Inspector Paulsson, and all that stuff about a lesbian Satanist gang is probably a smokescreen originating mainly from him."

Modig and Holmberg then described in detail the investigation as it had developed. When they had finished there was a long silence around the table.

"If all this about Gunnar Björck is true and it comes out, Säpo's ears are going to be burning," the assistant chief of the Violent Crimes Division concluded.

Jervas raised her hand. "It sounds to me as though your suspicions are for the most part based on assumptions and circumstantial evidence. As a prosecutor I would be uneasy about the lack of unassailable evidence."

"We're aware of that," Holmberg said. "We think we know what happened in broad outline, but there are questions that still have to be answered."

"I gather you're still busy with excavations in Nykvarn," Spångberg said. "How many killings do you reckon this case involves?"

Holmberg rubbed his eyes wearily. "We started with two, then three murders in Stockholm. Those are the ones that prompted the hunt for Salander: the deaths of Advokat Bjurman, the journalist Dag Svensson, and Mia Johansson, an academic. In the area around the warehouse in Nykvarn we have so far found three graves, well, three bodies. We've identified a known dealer and petty thief who was found dismembered in one trench. We found a woman's body in a second trench – she's still unidentified. And we haven't dug up the third yet. It appears to be older than the others. Furthermore, Blomkvist has made a connection to the murder several months ago of a prostitute in Södertälje."

"So, with Gunnar Ingemarsson dead in Gosseberga, we're talking about at least eight murders. That's a horrendous statistic. Do we suspect this Niedermann of all of them? If so, he has to be treated as a madman, a mass murderer."

Modig and Holmberg exchanged glances. It was now a matter of how far they wanted to align themselves with such assertions. Finally Modig spoke up.

"Even though crucial evidence is lacking, my superior, Inspector Bublanski, and I are tending towards the belief that Blomkvist is correct in claiming that the first three murders were committed by Niedermann. That would require us to believe that Salander is innocent. With respect to the graves in Nykvarn, Niedermann is linked to the site through the kidnapping of Salander's friend Miriam Wu. There is a strong likelihood that she too would have been his victim. But the warehouse is owned by a relative of the president of Svavelsjö Motorcycle Club, and until we're able to identify the remains, we won't be able to draw any conclusions."

"That petty thief you identified . . ."

"Kenneth Gustafsson, forty-four, dealer, and delinquent in his youth. Offhand I would guess it's to do with an internal shake-up of some sort. Svavelsjö M.C. is mixed up in several kinds of criminal activity, including the distribution of methamphetamine. Nykvarn may be a cemetery in the woods for people who crossed them, but . . ."

"Yes?"

"This young prostitute who was murdered in Södertälje . . . her name is Irina Petrova. The autopsy revealed that she died as a result of a staggeringly vicious assault. She looked as if she had been beaten to death. But the actual cause of her injuries could not be established. Blomkvist made a pretty acute observation. Petrova had injuries that could very well have been inflicted by a man's bare hands . . ."

"Niedermann?"

"It's a reasonable assumption. But there's no proof yet."

"So how do we proceed?" Spångberg wondered.

"I have to confer with Bublanski," Modig said. "But a logical step would be to interrogate Zalachenko. We're interested in hearing what he has to say about the murders in Stockholm, and for you it's a matter of finding out what was Niedermann's role in Zalachenko's business. He might even be able to point you in the direction of Niedermann."

One of the detectives from Göteborg said: "What have we found at the farm in Gosseberga?"

"We found four revolvers. A Sig Sauer that had been dismantled and was being oiled on the kitchen table. A Polish P-83 Wanad on the floor next to the bench in the kitchen. A Colt 1911 Government – that's the pistol that Blomkvist tried to hand in to Paulsson. And finally a .22 calibre Browning, which is pretty much a toy gun alongside the others. We rather think that it was the weapon used to shoot Salander, given that she's still alive with a slug in her brain."

"Anything else?"

"We found and confiscated a bag containing about 200,000 kronor. It was in an upstairs room used by Niedermann."

"How do you know it was his room?"

"Well, he does wear a size XXL. Zalachenko is at most a medium."

"Do you have anything on Zalachenko or Bodin in your records?" Holmberg said.

Erlander shook his head.

"Of course it depends on how we interpret the confiscated weapons. Apart from the more sophisticated weaponry and an unusually sophisticated T.V. surveillance of the farm, we found nothing to distinguish it from any other farmhouse. The house itself is spartan, no frills."

Just before noon there was a knock on the door and a uniformed officer delivered a document to Spångberg.

"We've received a call," she said, "about a missing person in Alingsås. A dental nurse by the name of Anita Kaspersson left her home by car at 7.30 this morning. She took her child to day care and should have arrived at her place of work by 8.00. But she never did. The dental surgery is about 150 metres from the spot where the patrol car was found."

Erlander and Modig both looked at their wristwatches.

"Then he has a four-hour head start. What kind of car is it?"

"A dark-blue 1991 Renault. Here's the registration number."

"Send out an A.P.B. on the vehicle at once. He could be in Oslo by now, or Malmö, or maybe even Stockholm."

They brought the conference to a close by deciding that Modig and Erlander would together interrogate Zalachenko.

Cortez frowned and followed Berger with his gaze as she cut across the hall from her office to the kitchenette. She returned moments later with a cup of coffee, went back into her office and closed the door.

Cortez could not put his finger on what was wrong. *Millennium* was the kind of small office where co-workers were close. He had worked part-time at the magazine for four years, and during that time the team had weathered some phenomenal storms, especially during the period when Blomkvist was serving a three-month sentence for libel and the magazine almost went under. Then their colleague Dag Svensson was murdered, and his girlfriend too.

Through all these storms Berger had been the rock that nothing seemed capable of shifting. He was not surprised that she had called to wake him early that morning and put him and Lottie Karim to work. The Salander affair had cracked wide open, and Blomkvist had got himself somehow involved in the killing of a policeman in Göteborg. So far, everything was under control. Karim had parked herself at police headquarters and was doing her best to get some solid information out of someone. Cortez had spent the morning making calls, piecing together what had happened overnight. Blomkvist was not answering his telephone, but from a number of sources Cortez had a fairly clear picture of the events of the night before.

Berger, on the other hand, had been distracted all morning. It was rare for her to close the door to her office. That usually happened only when she had a visitor or was working intently on some problem. This morning she had not had a single visitor, and she was not – so far as he could judge – working. On several occasions when he had knocked on the door to relay some news, he had found her sitting in the chair by the window. She seemed lost in thought, as listlessly she watched the stream of people walking down below on Götgatan. She had paid scant attention to his reports.

Something was wrong.

The doorbell interrupted his ruminations. He went to open it and found the lawyer Annika Giannini. Cortez had met Blomkvist's sister a few times, but he did not know her well.

"Hello, Annika," he said. "Mikael isn't here today."

"I know. I want to talk to Erika."

Berger barely looked up from her position by the window, but she quickly pulled herself together when she saw who it was.

"Hello," she said. "Mikael isn't here today."

Giannini smiled. "I know. I'm here for Björck's Säpo report. Micke asked me to take a look at it in case it turns out that I represent Salander."

Berger nodded. She got up, took a folder from her desk and handed it to Giannini.

Giannini hesitated a moment, wondering whether to leave the office. Then she made up her mind and, uninvited, sat down opposite Berger.

"O.K. . . . what's going on with you?"

"I'm about to resign from *Millennium,* and I haven't been able to tell Mikael. He's been so tied up in this Salander mess that there hasn't been the right opportunity, and I can't tell the others before I tell him. Right now I just feel like shit."

Giannini bit her lower lip. "So you're telling me instead. Why are you leaving?"

"I'm going to be editor-in-chief of *Svenska Morgon-Posten.*"

"Jesus. Well, in that case, congratulations seem to be in order rather than any weeping or gnashing of teeth."

"Annika . . . this isn't the way I had planned to end my time at *Millennium.* In the middle of bloody chaos. But the offer came like a bolt from the blue, and I can't say no. I mean . . . it's the chance of a lifetime. But I got the offer just before Dag and Mia were shot, and there's been such turmoil here that I buried it. And now I have the world's worst guilty conscience."

"I understand. But now you're afraid of telling Micke."

"It's an utter disaster. I haven't told anybody. I thought I wouldn't be starting at *S.M.P.* until after the summer, and that there would still be time to tell everyone. But now they want me to start asap."

She fell silent and stared at Annika. She looked on the verge of tears.

"This is, in point of fact, my last week at *Millennium*. Next week I'll be on a trip, and then . . . I need about a fortnight off to recharge my batteries. I start at *S.M.P.* on the first of May."

"Well, what would have happened if you'd been run over by a bus? Then they would have been without an editor-in-chief with only a moment's notice."

Erika looked up. "But I haven't been run over by a bus. I've been deliberately keeping quiet about my decision for weeks now."

"I can see this is a difficult situation, but I've got a feeling that Micke and Christer Malm and the others will be able to work things out. I think you ought to tell them right away."

"Alright, but your damned brother is in Göteborg today. He's asleep and has turned off his mobile."

"I know. There aren't many people who are as stubborn as Mikael about not being available when you need him. But Erika, this isn't about you and Micke. I know that you've worked together for twenty years or so and you've had your ups and downs, but you have to think about Christer and the others on the staff too."

"I've been keeping it under wraps all this time – Mikael's going to—"

"Micke's going to go through the roof, of course he is. But if he can't handle the fact that you screwed up one time in twenty years, then he isn't worth the time you've put in for him."

Berger sighed.

"Pull yourself together," Giannini told her. "Call Christer in, and the rest of the staff. Right now."

Malm sat motionless for a few seconds. Berger had gathered her colleagues into *Millennium*'s small conference room with only a few minutes' notice, just as he was about to leave early. He glanced at Cortez and Karim. They were as astonished as he was. Malin Eriksson, the assistant editor, had not known anything either, nor had Monika Nilsson, the reporter, or the advertising manager Magnusson. Blomkvist was the only one absent from the meeting. He was in Göteborg being his usual Blomkvist self.

Good God. Mikael doesn't know anything about it either, thought Malm. *How on earth is he going to react?*

Then he realized that Berger had stopped talking, and it was as silent as the grave in the conference room. He shook his head, stood up, and spontaneously gave Berger a hug and a kiss on the cheek.

"Congrats, Ricky," he said. "Editor-in-chief of *S.M.P.* That's not a bad step up from this sorry little rag."

Cortez came to life and began to clap. Berger held up her hands.

"Stop," she said. "I don't deserve any applause today." She looked around at her colleagues in the cramped editorial office. "Listen . . . I'm terribly sorry that it had to be this way. I wanted to tell you so many weeks ago, but the news sort of got drowned out by all the turmoil surrounding Dag and Mia. Mikael and Malin have been working like demons, and . . . it just didn't ever seem like the right time or place. And that's how we've arrived at this point today."

Eriksson realized with terrible clarity how understaffed the paper was, and how empty it was going to seem without Berger. No matter what happened, or whatever problem arose, Berger had been a boss she could always rely on. *Well . . . no wonder the biggest morning daily had recruited her. But what was going to happen now?* Erika had always been a crucial part of *Millennium*.

"There are a few things we have to get straight. I'm perfectly aware that this is going to create difficulties in the office. I didn't want it to, but that's the way things are. First of all: I won't abandon *Millennium*. I'm going to stay on as a partner and will attend board meetings. I won't, of course, have any influence in editorial matters."

Malm nodded thoughtfully.

"Secondly, I officially leave on the last day of April. But today is my last day of work. Next week I'll be travelling, as you know. It's been planned for a long time. And I've decided not to come back here to put in any days during the transition period." She paused for a moment. "The next issue of the magazine is ready in the computer. There are a few minor things that need fixing. It will be my final issue. A new editor-in-chief will have to take over. I'm clearing my desk tonight."

There was absolute silence in the room.

"The selection of a new editor-in-chief will have to be discussed and made by the board. It's something that you all on the staff will have to talk through."

"Mikael," Malm said.

"No. Never Mikael. He's surely the worst possible editor-in-chief you could pick. He's perfect as publisher and damned good at editing articles and tying up loose ends in work that is going to be published. He's the fixer. The editor-in-chief has to be the one who takes the initiative. Mikael also has a tendency to bury himself in his own stories and be totally off the radar for weeks at a time. He's at his best when things heat up, but he's incredibly bad at routine work. You all know that."

Malm muttered his assent and then said: "*Millennium* functioned because you and Mikael were a good balance for each other."

"That's not the only reason. You remember when Mikael was up in Hedestad sulking for almost a whole bloody year. *Millennium* functioned without him precisely the way the magazine is going to have to function without me now."

"O.K. What's your plan?"

"My choice would be for you, Christer, to take over as editor-in-chief."

"Not on your life." Malm threw up his hands.

"But since I knew that's what you would say, I have another solution. Malin. You can start as acting editor-in-chief as from today."

"Me?" Eriksson said. She sounded shocked.

"Yes, you. You've been damned good as assistant editor."

"But I—"

"Give it a try. I'll be out of my office tonight. You can move in on Monday morning. The May issue is done – we've already worked hard on it. June is a double issue, and then you have a month off. If it doesn't work, the board will have to find somebody else for August. Henry . . . you'll have to go full-time and take Malin's place as assistant editor. Then we'll need to hire a new employee. But that will be up to all of you, and to the board."

She studied the group thoughtfully.

"One more thing. I'll be starting at another publication. For all practical purposes, *S.M.P.* and *Millennium* are not competitors, but nevertheless I don't want to know any more than I already do about the content of the next two issues. All such matters should be discussed with Malin, effective immediately."

"What should we do about this Salander story?" Cortez said.

"Discuss it with Mikael. I know something about Salander, but I'm putting what I know in mothballs. I won't take it to *S.M.P.*"

Berger suddenly felt an enormous wave of relief. "That's about it," she said, and she ended the meeting by getting up and going back to her office without another word.

Millennium's staff sat in silence.

It was not until an hour later that Eriksson knocked on Berger's door.

"Hello there."

"Yes?" said Berger.

"The staff would like to have a word."

"What is it?"

"Out here."

Berger got up and went to the door. They had set a table with cake and Friday afternoon coffee.

"We think we should have a party and give you a real send-off in due course," Malm said. "But for now, coffee and cake will have to do."

Berger smiled, for the first time in a long time.

CHAPTER 3

Friday, 8.iv – Saturday, 9.iv

Zalachenko had been awake for eight hours when Inspectors Modig and Erlander came to his room at 7.00 in the evening. He had undergone a rather extensive operation in which a significant section of his jaw was realigned and fixed with titanium screws. His head was wrapped in so many bandages that you could see only his left eye and a narrow slit of mouth. A doctor had explained that the axe blow had crushed his cheekbone and damaged his forehead, peeling off a large part of the flesh on the right side of his face and tugging at his eye socket. His injuries were causing him immense pain. He had been given large doses of painkillers, yet was relatively lucid and able to talk. But the officers were warned not to tire him.

"Good evening, Herr Zalachenko," Modig said. She introduced herself and her colleague.

"My name is Karl Axel Bodin," Zalachenko said laboriously through clenched teeth. His voice was steady.

"I know exactly who you are. I've read your file from Säpo."

This, of course, was not true.

"That was a long time ago," Zalachenko said. "I'm Karl Axel Bodin now."

"How are you doing? Are you able to have a conversation?"

"I want to report a serious crime. I have been the victim of attempted murder by my daughter."

"We know. That matter will be taken up at the appropriate time," Erlander said. "But we have more urgent issues to talk about."

"What could be more urgent than attempted murder?"

"Right now we need information from you about three murders in Stockholm, at least three murders in Nykvarn, and a kidnapping."

"I don't know anything about that. Who was murdered?"

"Herr Bodin, we have good reason to believe that your associate, 35-year-old Ronald Niedermann, is guilty of these crimes," Erlander said. "Last night he also murdered a police officer from Trollhättan."

44

Modig was surprised that Erlander had acquiesced to Zalachenko's wish to be called Bodin. Zalachenko turned his head a little so that he could see Erlander. His voice softened slightly.

"That is . . . unfortunate to hear. I know nothing about Niedermann's affairs. I have not killed any policeman. I was the victim of attempted murder myself last night."

"There's a manhunt under way for Ronald Niedermann even as we speak. Do you have any idea where he might hide?"

"I am not aware of the circles he moves in. I . . ." Zalachenko hesitated a few seconds. His voice took on a confidential tone. "I must admit . . . just between us . . . that sometimes I worry about Niedermann."

Erlander bent towards him.

"What do you mean?"

"I have discovered that he can be a violent person . . . I am actually afraid of him."

"You mean you felt threatened by Niedermann?" Erlander said.

"Precisely. I'm old and handicapped. I cannot defend myself."

"Could you explain your relationship to Niedermann?"

"I'm disabled." Zalachenko gestured towards his feet. "This is the second time my daughter has tried to kill me. I hired Niedermann as an assistant a number of years ago. I thought he could protect me . . . but he has actually taken over my life. He comes and goes as he pleases . . . I have nothing more to say about it."

"What does he help you with?" Modig broke in. "Doing things that you can't do yourself?"

Zalachenko gave Modig a long look with his only visible eye.

"I understand that your daughter threw a Molotov cocktail into your car in the early '90s," Modig said. "Can you explain what prompted her to do that?"

"You would have to ask my daughter. She is mentally ill." His tone was again hostile.

"You mean that you can't think of any reason why Lisbeth Salander attacked you in 1991?"

"My daughter is mentally ill. There is substantial documentation."

Modig cocked her head to one side. Zalachenko's answers were much more aggressive and hostile when she asked the questions. She saw that Erlander had noticed the same thing. O.K. . . . . *Good cop, bad cop.* Modig raised her voice.

"You don't think that her actions could have anything to do with the fact that you had beaten her mother so badly that she suffered permanent brain damage?"

Zalachenko turned his head towards Modig.

"That is all bullshit. Her mother was a whore. It was probably one of her punters who beat her up. I just happened to be passing by."

Modig raised her eyebrows. "So you're completely innocent?"

"Of course I am."

"Zalachenko . . . let me repeat that to see if I've understood you correctly. You say that you never beat your girlfriend, Agneta Sofia Salander, Lisbeth's mother, despite the fact that the whole business is the subject of a long report, stamped TOP SECRET, written at the time by your handler at Säpo, Gunnar Björck."

"I was never convicted of anything. I have never been charged. I cannot help it if some idiot in the Security Police fantasizes in his reports. If I had been a suspect, they would have at the very least questioned me."

Modig made no answer. Zalachenko seemed to be grinning beneath his bandages.

"So I wish to press charges against my daughter. For trying to kill me."

Modig sighed. "I'm beginning to understand why she felt an uncontrollable urge to slam an axe into your head."

Erlander cleared his throat. "Excuse me, Herr Bodin . . . We should get back to any information you might have about Ronald Niedermann's activities."

Modig made a call to Inspector Bublanski from the corridor outside Zalachenko's hospital room.

"Nothing," she said.

"*Nothing*?" Bublanski said.

"He's lodging a complaint with the police against Salander – for G.B.H. and attempted murder. He says that he had nothing to do with the murders in Stockholm."

"And how does he explain the fact that Salander was buried in a trench on his property in Gosseberga?"

"He says he had a cold and was asleep most of the day. If Salander was shot in Gosseberga, it must have been something that Niedermann decided to do."

"O.K. So what do we have?"

"She was shot with a Browning, .22 calibre. Which is why she's still alive. We found the weapon. Zalachenko admits that it's his."

"I see. In other words, he knows we're going to find his prints on the gun."

"Exactly. But he says that the last time he saw the gun, it was in his desk drawer."

"Which means that the excellent Herr Niedermann took the weapon while Zalachenko was asleep and shot Salander. This is one cold bastard. Do we have any evidence to the contrary?"

Modig thought for a few seconds before she replied. "He's well versed in Swedish law and police procedure. He doesn't admit to a thing, and he has Niedermann as a scapegoat. I don't have any idea what we can prove. I asked Erlander to send his clothes to forensics and have them examined for traces of gunpowder, but he's bound to say that he was doing target practice two days ago."

Salander was aware of the smell of almonds and ethanol. It felt as if she had alcohol in her mouth and she tried to swallow, but her tongue felt numb and paralysed. She tried to open her eyes, but she could not. In the distance she heard a voice that seemed to be talking to her, but she could not understand the words. Then she heard the voice quite clearly.

"I think she's coming round."

She felt someone touch her forehead and tried to brush away the intrusive hand. At the same moment she felt intense pain in her left shoulder. She forced herself to relax.

"Can you hear me, Lisbeth?"

Go away.

"Can you open your eyes?"

Who was this bloody idiot harping on at her?

Finally she did open her eyes. At first she just saw strange lights until a figure appeared in the centre of her field of vision. She tried to focus her gaze, but the figure kept slipping away. She felt as if she had a stupendous hangover and the bed seemed to keep tilting backwards.

"Pnkllrs," she said.

"Say that again?"

"'diot," she said.

"That sounds good. Can you open your eyes again?"

She opened her eyes to narrow slits. She saw the face of a complete stranger and memorized every detail. A blond man with intense blue eyes and a tilted, angular face about a foot from hers.

"Hello. My name is Anders Jonasson. I'm a doctor. You're in a hospital. You were injured and you're waking up after an operation. Can you tell me your name?"

"Pshalandr," Salander said.

"O.K. Would you do me a favour and count to ten?"

"One two four . . . no . . . three four five six . . ."

Then she passed out.

Dr Jonasson was pleased with the response he had got. She had said her name and started to count. That meant that she still had her cognitive abilities somewhat intact and was not going to wake up a vegetable. He wrote down her wake-up time as 9.06 p.m., about sixteen hours after he had finished the operation. He had slept most of the day and then drove back to the hospital at around 7.00 in the evening. He was actually off that day, but he had some paperwork to catch up on.

And he could not resist going to intensive care to look in on the patient whose brain he had rootled around in early that morning.

"Let her sleep a while, but check her E.E.G. regularly. I'm worried there might be swelling or bleeding in the brain. She seemed to have sharp pain in her left shoulder when she tried to move her arm. If she wakes up again you can give her two mg. of morphine per hour."

He felt oddly exhilarated as he left by the main entrance of Sahlgrenska.

Anita Kaspersson, a dental nurse who lived in Alingsås, was shaking all over as she stumbled through the woods. She had severe hypothermia. She wore only a pair of wet trousers and a thin sweater. Her bare feet were bleeding. She had managed to free herself from the barn where the man had tied her up, but she could not untie the rope that bound her hands behind her back. Her fingers had no feeling in them at all.

She felt as if she were the last person on earth, abandoned by everyone.

She had no idea where she was. It was dark and she had no sense of how long she had been aimlessly walking. She was amazed to be still alive.

And then she saw a light through the trees and stopped.

For several minutes she did not dare to approach the light. She pushed through some bushes and stood in the yard of a one-storey house of grey brick. She looked about her in astonishment.

She staggered to the door and turned to kick it with her heel.

Salander opened her eyes and saw a light in the ceiling. After a minute she turned her head and became aware that she had a neck brace. She had a heavy, dull headache and acute pain in her left shoulder. She closed her eyes.

Hospital, she thought. *What am I doing here?*

She felt exhausted, could hardly get her thoughts in order. Then the memories came rushing back to her. For several seconds she was seized by panic as the fragmented images of how she had dug herself out of a trench came flooding over her. Then she clenched her teeth and concentrated on breathing.

She was alive, but she was not sure whether that was a good thing or bad.

She could not piece together all that had happened, but she summoned up a foggy mosaic of images from the woodshed and how she had swung an axe in fury and struck her father in the face. Zalachenko. Was he alive or dead?

She could not clearly remember what had happened with Niedermann. She had a memory of being surprised that he had run away and she did not know why.

Suddenly she remembered having seen *Kalle Bastard Blomkvist.* Perhaps she had dreamed the whole thing, but she remembered a kitchen – it must have been the kitchen in the Gosseberga farmhouse – and she thought she remembered seeing him coming towards her. *I must have been hallucinating.*

The events in Gosseberga seemed already like the distant past, or possibly a ridiculous dream. She concentrated on the present and opened her eyes again.

She was in a bad way. She did not need anyone to tell her that. She raised her right hand and felt her head. There were bandages. She had a brace on her neck. Then she remembered it all. *Niedermann.*

Zalachenko. The old bastard had a pistol too. A .22 calibre Browning. Which, compared to all other handguns, had to be considered a toy. That was why she was still alive.

I was shot in the head. I could stick my finger in the entry wound and touch my brain.

She was surprised to be alive. Yet she felt indifferent. If death was the black emptiness from which she had just woken up, then death was nothing to worry about. She would hardly notice the difference. With which esoteric thought she closed her eyes and fell asleep again.

She had been dozing only a few minutes when she was aware of movement and opened her eyelids to a narrow slit. She saw a nurse in a white uniform bending over her. She closed her eyes and pretended to be asleep.

"I think you're awake," the nurse said.

"Mmm," Salander said.

"Hello, my name is Marianne. Do you understand what I'm saying?"

Salander tried to nod, but her head was immobilized by the brace.

"No, don't try to move. You don't have to be afraid. You've been hurt and had surgery."

"Could I have some water?" Salander whispered.

The nurse gave her a beaker with a straw to drink water through. As she swallowed the water she saw another person appear on her left side.

"Hello, Lisbeth. Can you hear me?"

"Mmm."

"I'm Dr Helena Endrin. Do you know where you are?"

"Hospital."

"You're at the Sahlgrenska in Göteborg. You've had an operation and you're in the intensive care unit."

"Umm-hmm."

"There is no need to be afraid."

"I was shot in the head."

Endrin hesitated for a moment, then said, "That's right. So you remember what happened."

"The old bastard had a pistol."

"Ah . . . yes, well someone did."

"A .22."

50

"I see. I didn't know that."

"How badly hurt am I?"

"Your prognosis is good. You were in pretty bad shape, but we think you have a good chance of making a full recovery."

Salander weighed this information. Then she tried to fix her eyes on the doctor. Her vision was blurred.

"What happened to Zalachenko?"

"Who?"

"The old bastard. Is he alive?"

"You must mean Karl Axel Bodin."

"No, I don't. I mean Alexander Zalachenko. That's his real name."

"I don't know anything about that. But the elderly man who came in at the same time as you is critical but out of danger."

Salander's heart sank. She considered the doctor's words.

"Where is he?"

"He's down the hall. But don't worry about him for the time being. You have to concentrate on getting well."

Salander closed her eyes. She wondered whether she could manage to get out of bed, find something to use as a weapon, and finish the job. But she could scarcely keep her eyes open. She thought, *He's going to get away again*. She had missed her chance to kill Zalachenko.

"I'd like to examine you for a moment. Then you can go back to sleep," Dr Endrin said.

Blomkvist was suddenly awake and he did not know why. He did not know where he was, and then he remembered that he had booked himself a room in City Hotel. It was as dark as coal. He fumbled to turn on the bedside lamp and looked at the clock. 2.00. He had slept through fifteen hours.

He got up and went to the bathroom. He would not be able to get back to sleep. He shaved and took a long shower. Then he put on some jeans and the maroon sweatshirt that needed washing. He called the front desk to ask if he could get coffee and a sandwich at this early hour. The night porter said that was possible.

He put on his sports jacket and went downstairs. He ordered a coffee and a cheese and liver pâté sandwich. He bought the *Göteborgs-Posten*. The arrest of Lisbeth Salander was front-page news. He took his breakfast back to his room and read the paper. The reports at the time of going to press were somewhat confused, but they were on the right track. Ronald Niedermann, thirty-five, was being sought for the killing of a policeman. The police wanted to question him also in connection with the murders in Stockholm. The police had released nothing about Salander's condition, and the name Zalachenko was not mentioned. He was referred to only as a 66-year-old landowner from Gosseberga, and apparently the media had taken him for an innocent victim.

When Blomkvist had finished reading, he flipped open his mobile and saw that he had twenty unread messages. Three were messages to call Berger. Two were from his sister Annika. Fourteen were from reporters at various newspapers who wanted to talk to him. One was from Malm, who had sent him the brisk advice: *It would be best if you took the first train home.*

Blomkvist frowned. That was unusual, coming from Malm. The text was sent at 7.06 in the evening. He stifled the impulse to call and wake someone up at 3.00 in the morning. Instead he booted up his iBook and plugged the cable into the broadband jack. He found that the first train to Stockholm left at 5.20, and there was nothing new in *Aftonbladet* online.

He opened a new Word document, lit a cigarette, and sat for three minutes staring at the blank screen. Then he began to type.

```
Her name is Lisbeth Salander. Sweden has got to
know her through police reports and press releases
and the headlines in the evening papers. She is
twenty-seven years old and one metre fifty centime-
tres tall. She has been called a psychopath, a
murderer, and a lesbian Satanist. There has been
almost no limit to the fantasies that have been
circulated about her. In this issue, Millennium
will tell the story of how government officials
conspired against Salander in order to protect
a pathological murderer . . .
```

He wrote steadily for fifty minutes, primarily a recapitulation of the night on which he had found Dag Svensson and Mia Johansson and why the police had focused on Salander as the suspected killer. He quoted the newspaper headlines about lesbian Satanists and the media's apparent hope that the murders might have involved S. & M. sex.

When he checked the clock he quickly closed his iBook. He packed his bag and went down to the front desk. He paid with a credit card and took a taxi to Göteborg Central Station.

Blomkvist went straight to the dining car and ordered more coffee and sandwiches. He opened his iBook again and read through his text. He was so absorbed that he did not notice Inspector Modig until she cleared her throat and asked if she could join him. He looked up, smiled sheepishly, and closed his computer.

"On your way home?"

"You too, I see."

She nodded. "My colleague is staying another day."

"Do you know anything about how Salander is? I've been sound asleep since I last saw you."

"She had an operation soon after she was brought in and was awake in the early evening. The doctors think she'll make a full recovery. She was incredibly lucky."

Blomkvist nodded. It dawned on him that he had not been worried about her. He had assumed that she would survive. Any other outcome was unthinkable.

"Has anything else of interest happened?" he said.

Modig wondered how much she should say to a reporter, even to one who knew more of the story than she did. On the other hand, she had joined him at his table, and maybe a hundred other reporters had by now been briefed at police headquarters.

"I don't want to be quoted," she said.

"I'm simply asking out of personal interest."

She told him that a nationwide manhunt was under way for Ronald Niedermann, particularly in the Malmö area.

"And Zalachenko? Have you questioned him?"

"Yes, we questioned him."

"And?"

"I can't tell you anything about that."

"Come on, Sonja. I'll know exactly what you talked about less than an hour after I get to my office in Stockholm. And I won't write a word of what you tell me."

She hesitated for a while before she met his gaze.

"He made a formal complaint against Salander, that she tried to kill him. She risks being charged with grievous bodily harm or attempted murder."

"And in all likelihood she'll claim self-defence."

"I hope she will," Modig said.

"That doesn't sound like an official line."

"Bodin . . . Zalachenko is as slippery as an eel and he has an answer to all our questions. I'm persuaded that things are more or less as you told us yesterday, and that means that Salander has been subjected to a lifetime of injustice – since she was twelve."

"That's the story I'm going to publish," Blomkvist said.

"It won't be popular with some people."

Modig hesitated again. Blomkvist waited.

"I talked with Bublanski half an hour ago. He didn't go into any detail, but the preliminary investigation against Salander for the murder of your friends seems to have been shelved. The focus has shifted to Niedermann."

"Which means that . . ." He let the question hang in the air between them.

Modig shrugged.

"Who's going to take over the investigation of Salander?"

"I don't know. What happened in Gosseberga is primarily Göteborg's problem. I would guess that somebody in Stockholm will be assigned to compile all the material for a prosecution."

"I see. What do you think the odds are that the investigation will be transferred to Säpo?"

Modig shook her head.

Just before they reached Alingsås, Blomkvist leaned towards her. "Sonja . . . I think you understand how things stand. If the Zalachenko story gets out, there'll be a massive scandal. Säpo people conspired with a psychiatrist to lock Salander up in an asylum. The only thing they can do now is to stonewall and go on claiming that Salander is mentally ill, and that committing her in 1991 was justified."

Modig nodded.

"I'm going to do everything I can to counter any such claims. I believe that Salander is as sane as you or I. Odd, certainly, but her intellectual gifts are undeniable." He paused to let what he had said sink in. "I'm going to need somebody on the inside I can trust."

She met his gaze. "I'm not competent to judge whether or not Salander is mentally ill."

"But you are competent to say whether or not she was the victim of a miscarriage of justice."

"What are you suggesting?"

"I'm only asking you to let me know if you discover that Salander is being subjected to another miscarriage of justice."

Modig said nothing.

"I don't want details of the investigation or anything like that. I just need to know what's happening with the charges against her."

"It sounds like a good way for me to get booted off the force."

"You would be a source. I would never, ever mention your name."

He wrote an email address on a page torn from his notebook.

"This is an untraceable hotmail address. You can use it if you have anything to tell me. Don't use your official address, obviously, just set up your own temporary hotmail account."

She put the address into the inside pocket of her jacket. She did not make him any promises.

Inspector Erlander woke at 7.00 on Saturday morning to the ringing of his telephone. He heard voices from the T.V. and smelled coffee from the kitchen where his wife was already about her morning chores. He had returned to his apartment in Mölndal at 1.00 in the morning having being on duty for twenty-two hours, so he was far from wide awake when he reached to answer it.

"Rikardsson, night shift. Are you awake?"

"No," Erlander said. "Hardly. What's happened?"

"News. Anita Kaspersson has been found."

"Where?"

"Outside Seglora, south of Borås."

Erlander visualized the map in his head.

"South," he said. "He's taking the back roads. He must have driven up the 180 through Borås and swung south. Have we alerted Malmö?"

"Yes, and Helsingborg, Landskrona, and Trelleborg. And Karlskrona. I'm thinking of the ferry to the east."

Erlander rubbed the back of his neck.

"He has almost a 24-hour head start now. He could be clean out of the country. How was Kaspersson found?"

"She turned up at a house on the outskirts of Seglora."

"She what?"

"She knocked—"

"You mean she's alive?"

"I'm sorry, I'm not expressing myself clearly enough. The Kaspersson woman kicked on the door of a house at 3.10 this morning, scaring the hell out of a couple and their kids, who were all asleep. She was barefoot and suffering from severe hypothermia. Her hands were tied behind her back. She's at the hospital in Borås, reunited with her husband."

"Amazing. I think we all assumed she was dead."

"Sometimes you can be surprised. But here's the bad news: Assistant County Police Chief Spångberg has been here since 5.00 this morning. She's made it plain that she wants you up and over to Borås to interview the woman."

It was Saturday morning and Blomkvist assumed that the *Millennium* offices would be empty. He called Malm as the train was coming into Stockholm and asked him what had prompted the tone of his text message.

"Have you had breakfast?" Malm said.

"On the train."

"O.K. Come over to my place and I'll make you something more substantial."

"What's this about?"

"I'll tell you when you get here."

Blomkvist took the tunnelbana to Medborgarplatsen and walked to Allhelgonagatan. Malm's boyfriend, Arnold Magnusson, opened the door to him. No matter how hard Blomkvist tried, he could never rid himself of the feeling that he was looking at an advertisement for something. Magnusson was often onstage at the Dramaten, and was one of Sweden's most popular actors. It was always a shock to meet him in person. Blomkvist was not ordinarily impressed by celebrity, but Magnusson had such a distinctive appearance and was so familiar from his T.V. and film roles, in particular for playing the irascible but honest Inspector Frisk in a wildly popular T.V. series that aired in ninety-minute episodes. Blomkvist always expected him to behave just like Gunnar Frisk.

"Hello, Micke," Magnusson said.

"Hello," Blomkvist said.

"In the kitchen."

Malm was serving up freshly made waffles with cloudberry jam and coffee. Blomkvist's appetite was revived even before he sat down. Malm wanted to know what had happened in Gosseberga. Blomkvist gave him a succinct account. He was into his third waffle before he remembered to ask what was going on.

"We had a little problem at *Millennium* while you were away Blomkvisting in Göteborg."

Blomkvist looked at Malm intently.

"What was that?"

"Oh, nothing serious. Erika has taken the job of editor-in-chief at *Svenska Morgon-Posten*. She finished at *Millennium* yesterday."

It was several seconds before he could absorb the whole impact of the news. He sat there stunned, but did not doubt the truth of it.

"Why didn't she tell anyone before?" he said at last.

"Because she wanted to tell you first, and you've been running around being unreachable for several weeks now, and because she probably thought you had your hands full with the Salander story. She obviously wanted to tell you first, so she couldn't tell the rest of us, and time kept slipping by . . . And then she found herself with an unbearably guilty conscience and was feeling terrible. And not one of us had noticed a thing."

Blomkvist shut his eyes. "Goddamnit," he said.

"I know. Now it turns out that you're the last one in the office to find out. I wanted to have the chance to tell you myself so that you'd understand what happened and not think anyone was doing anything behind your back."

"No, I don't think that. But, Jesus . . . it's wonderful that she got the job, if she wants to work at *S.M.P.* . . . but what the hell are we going to do?"

"Malin's going to be acting editor-in-chief starting with the next issue."

"Eriksson?"

"Unless you want to be editor-in-chief . . ."

"Good God, no."

"That's what I thought. So Malin's going to be editor-in-chief."

"Have you appointed an assistant editor?"

"Henry. It's four years he's been with us. Hardly an apprentice any longer."

"Do I have a say in this?"

"No," Malm said.

Blomkvist gave a dry laugh. "Right. We'll let it stand the way you've decided. Malin is tough, but she's unsure of herself. Henry shoots from the hip a little too often. We'll have to keep an eye on both of them."

"Yes, we will."

Blomkvist sat in silence, cradling his coffee. It would be damned empty without Berger, and he wasn't sure how things would turn out at the magazine.

"I have to call Erika and—"

"No, better not."

"What do you mean?"

"She's sleeping at the office. Go and wake her up or something."

Blomkvist found Berger sound asleep on the sofa-bed in her office. She had been up until all hours emptying her desk and bookshelves of all personal belongings and sorting papers that she wanted to keep. She had filled five packing crates. He looked at her for a while from the doorway before he went in and sat down on the edge of the sofa and woke her.

"Why in heaven's name don't you go over to my place and sleep if you have to sleep on the job," he said.

"Hi, Mikael," she said.

"Christer told me."

She started to say something, but he bent down and kissed her on the cheek.

"Are you livid?"

"Insanely," he said.

"I'm sorry. I couldn't turn it down. But it feels wrong, to leave all of you in the lurch in such a bad situation."

"I'm hardly the person to criticize you for abandoning ship. I left you in the lurch in a situation that was much worse than this."

"The two have nothing to do with each other. You took a break. I'm leaving for good and I didn't tell anybody. I'm so sorry."

Blomkvist gave her a wan smile.

"When it's time, it's time." Then he added in English, "A woman's gotta do what a woman's gotta do and all that crap."

Berger smiled. Those were the words she had said to him when he moved to Hedeby. He reached out his hand and mussed her hair affectionately.

"I can understand why you'd want to quit this madhouse . . . but to be the head of Sweden's most turgid old-boy newspaper . . . that's going to take some time to sink in."

"There are quite a few girls working there nowadays."

"Rubbish. Check the masthead. It's status quo all the way. You must be a raving masochist. Shall we go and have some coffee?"

Berger sat up. "I have to know what happened in Göteborg."

"I'm writing the story now," Blomkvist said. "And there's going to be war when we publish it. We'll put it out in at the same time as the trial. I hope you're not thinking of taking the story with you to *S.M.P.* The fact is I need you to write something on the Zalachenko story before you leave here."

"Micke . . . I . . ."

"Your very last editorial. Write it whenever you like. It almost certainly won't be published before the trial, whenever that might be."

"I'm not sure that's such a good idea. What do you think it should be about?"

"Morality," Blomkvist said. "And the story of why one of our colleagues was murdered because the government didn't do its job fifteen years ago."

Berger knew exactly what kind of editorial he wanted. She had been at the helm when Svensson was murdered, after all. She suddenly felt in a much better mood.

"O.K.," she said. "My last editorial."

CHAPTER 4

Saturday, 9.iv – Sunday, 10.iv

By 1.00 on Saturday afternoon, Prosecutor Fransson in Södertälje had finished her deliberations. The burial ground in the woods in Nykvarn was a wretched mess, and the Violent Crimes Division had racked up a vast amount of overtime since Wednesday, when Paolo Roberto had fought his boxing match with Niedermann in the warehouse there. They were dealing with at least three murders with the bodies found buried on the property, along with the kidnapping and assault of Salander's friend Miriam Wu, and on top of it all, arson.

The incident in Stallarholmen was connected with the discoveries at Nykvarn, and was actually located within the Strängnäs police district in Södermanland county. Carl-Magnus Lundin of the Svavelsjö Motorcycle Club was a key player in the whole thing, but he was in hospital in Södertälje with one foot in a cast and his jaw wired shut. Accordingly, all of these crimes came under county police jurisdiction, which meant that Stockholm would have the last word.

On Friday the court hearing was held. Lundin was formally charged in connection with Nykvarn. It had eventually been established that the warehouse was owned by the Medimport Company, which in turn was owned by one Anneli Karlsson, a 52-year-old cousin of Lundin who lived in Puerto Banús, Spain. She had no criminal record.

Fransson closed the folder that held all the preliminary investigation papers. These were still in the early stages and there would need to be another hundred pages of detailed work before they were ready to go to trial. But right now she had to make decisions on several matters. She looked up at her police colleagues.

"We have enough evidence to charge Lundin with participating in the kidnapping of Miriam Wu. Paolo Roberto has identified him as the man who drove the van. I'm also going to charge him with probable involvement in arson. We'll hold back on charging him with the murders of the three individuals we dug up on the property, at least until each of them has been identified."

The officers nodded. That was what they had been expecting.

"What'll we do about Sonny Nieminen?"

Fransson leafed through to the section on Nieminen in the papers on her desk.

"This is a man with an impressive criminal history. Robbery, possession of illegal weapons, assault, G.B.H., manslaughter and drug crime. He was arrested with Lundin at Stallarholmen. I'm convinced that he's involved, but we don't have the evidence to persuade a court."

"He says he's never been to the Nykvarn warehouse and that he just happened to be out with Lundin on a motorcycle ride," said the detective responsible for Stallarholmen on behalf of the Södertälje police. "He claims he had no idea what Lundin was up to in Stallarholmen."

Fransson wondered whether she could somehow arrange to hand the entire business over to Prosecutor Ekström in Stockholm.

"Nieminen refuses to say anything about what happened," the detective went on, "but he vehemently denies being involved in any crime."

"You'd think he and Lundin were themselves the victims of a crime in Stallarholmen," Fransson said, drumming her fingertips in annoyance. "Lisbeth Salander," she added, her voice scored with scepticism. "We're talking about a girl who looks as if she's barely entered puberty and who's only one metre fifty tall. She doesn't look as though she has the tonnage to take on either Nieminen or Lundin, let alone both of them."

"Unless she was armed. A pistol would compensate for her physique."

"But that doesn't quite fit with our reconstruction of what happened."

"No. She used Mace and kicked Lundin in the balls and face with such aggression that she crushed one of his testicles and then broke his jaw. The shot in Lundin's foot must have happened after she kicked him. But I can't swallow the scenario that says she was the one who was armed."

"The lab has identified the weapon used on Lundin. It's a Polish P-83 Wanad using Makarova ammo. It was found in Gosseberga outside Göteborg and it has Salander's prints on it. We can pretty much assume that she took the pistol with her to Gosseberga."

"Sure. But the serial number shows that the pistol was stolen four years ago in the robbery of a gun shop in Örebro. The thieves were eventually caught, but they had ditched the gun. It was a local thug with a drug problem who hung out around Svavelsjö M.C. I'd much rather place the pistol with either Lundin or Nieminen."

"It could be as simple as Lundin carrying the pistol and Salander disarming him. Then a shot was fired accidentally that hit him in the foot. I mean, it can't have been her intention to kill him, since he's still alive."

"Or else she shot him in the foot out of sheer sadism. Who's to know? But how did she deal with Nieminen? He has no visible injuries."

"He does have one, or rather two, small burn marks on his chest."

"What sort of burns?"

"I'm guessing a taser."

"So Salander was supposedly armed with a taser, a Mace canister and a pistol. How much would all that stuff weigh? No, I'm quite sure that either Lundin or Nieminen was carrying the gun, and she took it from them. We're not going to be sure how Lundin came to get himself shot until one or other of the parties involved starts talking."

"Alright."

"As things now stand, Lundin has been charged for the reasons I mentioned earlier. But we don't have a damned thing on Nieminen. I'm thinking of turning him loose this afternoon."

Nieminen was in a vile mood when he left the cells at Södertälje police station. His mouth was dry so his first stop was a corner shop where he bought a Pepsi. He guzzled it down on the spot. He bought a pack of Lucky Strike and a tin of Göteborg's Rapé snuff. He flipped open his mobile and checked the battery, then dialled the number of Hans-Åke Waltari, thirty-three years old and number three in Svavelsjö M.C.'s hierarchy. It rang four times before Waltari picked up.

"Nieminen. I'm out."

"Congrats."

"Where are you?"

"Nyköping."

"What the fuck are you doing in Nyköping?"

"We decided to lay low when you and Magge were busted – until we knew the lay of the land."

"So now you know the lay of the land. Where is everybody?"

Waltari told him where the other five members of Svavelsjö M.C. were located. The news neither pleased Nieminen nor made him any calmer.

"So who the fuck is minding the store while all of you hide away like a bunch of girls?"

"That's not fair. You and Magge take off on some fucking job we know nothing about, and all of a sudden you're mixed up in a shootout with that slut the law are after, Magge gets shot and you're busted. Then they start digging up bodies at our warehouse in Nykvarn."

"So?"

"So? So we were starting to wonder if maybe you and Magge were hiding something from the rest of us."

"And what the fuck would that be? We're the ones who took the job for the sake of the club."

"Well, no-one ever told me that the warehouse was doubling up as a woodland cemetery. Who were those dead bodies?"

Nieminen had a vicious retort on the tip of his tongue, but he stopped himself. Waltari may be an idiot, but this was no time to start an argument. The important thing right now was to consolidate their forces. After stonewalling his way through five police interrogations, it was not a good idea to start boasting that he actually knew something on a mobile less than two hundred metres from a police station.

"Forget the bodies," he said. "I don't know anything about that. But Magge is in deep shit. He's going to be in the slammer for a while, and while he's gone, I'm running the club."

"O.K. What happens now?" Waltari said.

"Who's keeping an eye on the property?"

"Benny stayed at the clubhouse to hold the fort. They searched the place the day you were arrested. They didn't find anything."

"Benny Karlsson?" Nieminen yelled. "Benny K.'s hardly dry behind the ears."

"Take it easy. He's with that blond fucker you and Magge always hang out with."

Sonny froze. He glanced around and walked away from the door of the corner shop.

"*What* did you say?" he asked in a low voice.

"That blond monster you and Magge hang out with, he showed up and needed a place to hide."

"Goddamnit, Waltari! They're looking for him all over the country!"

"Yeah . . . that's why he needed somewhere to hide. What were we supposed to do? He's your and Magge's pal."

Nieminen shut his eyes for ten full seconds. Niedermann had brought Svavelsjö M.C. a lot of jobs and good money for several years. But he was absolutely not a friend. He was a dangerous bastard and a psychopath – a psychopath that the police were looking for with a vengeance. Nieminen did not trust Niedermann for one second. *The best thing would be if he was found with a bullet in his head. Then the manhunt would at least ease up a bit.*

"So what did you do with him?"

"Benny's taking care of him. He took him out to Viktor's."

Viktor Göransson was the club's treasurer and financial expert, who lived just outside Järna. He was trained in accounting and had begun his career as financial adviser to a Yugoslav who owned a string of bars, until the whole gang ended up in the slammer for fraud. He had met Lundin at Kumla prison in the early nineties. He was the only member of Svavelsjö M.C. who normally wore a jacket and tie.

"Waltari, get in your car and meet me in Södertälje. I'll be outside the train station in forty-five minutes."

"Alright. But what's the rush?"

"I have to get a handle on the situation. Do you want me to take the bus?"

Waltari sneaked a look at Nieminen sitting quiet as a mouse as they drove out to Svavelsjö. Unlike Lundin, Nieminen was never very easy to deal with. He had the face of a model and looked weak, but he had a short fuse and was a dangerous man, especially when he had been drinking. Just then he was sober, but Waltari felt uneasy about having Nieminen as their leader in the future. Lundin had somehow always managed to keep Nieminen in line. He wondered how things would unfold now with Lundin out of the way.

At the clubhouse, Benny was nowhere to be seen. Nieminen called him twice on his mobile, but got no answer.

They drove to Nieminen's place, about half a mile further down the road. The police had carried out a search, but they had evidently found nothing of value to the Nykvarn investigation. Which was why Nieminen had been released.

He took a shower and changed his clothes while Waltari waited patiently in the kitchen. Then they walked about a hundred and fifty metres into the woods behind Nieminen's property and scraped away the thin layer of soil that concealed a chest containing six handguns, including an AK5, a stack of ammunition, and around two kilos of explosives. This was Nieminen's arms cache. Two of the guns were

Polish P-83 Wanads. They came from the same batch as the weapon that Salander had taken from him at Stallarholmen.

Nieminen drove away all thought of Salander. It was an unpleasant subject. In the cell at Södertälje police station he had played the scene over and over in his head: how he and Lundin had arrived at Advokat Bjurman's summer house and found Salander apparently just leaving.

Events had been rapid and unpredictable. He had ridden over there with Lundin to burn the damned summer cabin down. On the instructions of that goddamned blond monster. And then they had stumbled upon that bitch Salander – all alone, 1.5 metres tall, thin as a stick. Nieminen wondered how much she actually weighed. And then everything had gone to hell; had exploded in a brief orgy of violence neither of them was prepared for.

Objectively, he could describe the chain of events. Salander had a canister of Mace, which she sprayed in Lundin's face. Lundin should have been ready, but he wasn't. She kicked him twice, and you don't need a lot of muscle to fracture a jaw. *She took him by surprise. That could be explained.*

But then she took him too, Sonny Nieminen, a man who well-trained men would avoid getting into a fight with. *She moved so fast. He hadn't been able to pull his gun. She had taken him out easily, as if brushing off a mosquito. It was humiliating. She had a taser. She had . . .*

He could not remember a thing when he came to. Lundin had been shot in the foot and then the police showed up. After some palaver over jurisdiction between Strängnäs and Södertälje, he fetched up in the cells in Södertälje. Plus she had stolen Magge's Harley. *She had cut the badge out of his leather jacket – the very symbol that made people step aside in the queue at the bar, that gave him a status that was beyond most people's wildest dreams. She had humiliated him.*

Nieminen was boiling over. He had kept his mouth shut through the entire series of police interrogations. He would never be able to tell anyone what had happened in Stallarholmen. Until that moment Salander had meant nothing to him. She was a little side project that Lundin was messing around with . . . again commissioned by that bloody Niedermann. Now he hated her with a fury that astonished him. Usually he was cool and analytical, but he knew that some time in the future he would have to pay her back and erase the shame. But first he had to get a grip on the chaos that Svavelsjö M.C. had landed in because of Salander and Niedermann.

Nieminen took the two remaining Polish guns, loaded them, and handed one to Waltari.

"Have we got a plan?"

"We're going to drive over and have a talk with Niedermann. He isn't one of us, and he doesn't have a criminal record. I don't know how he's going to react if they catch him, but if he talks he could send us all to the slammer. We'd be sent down so fast it'd make your head spin."

"You mean we should . . ."

Nieminen had already decided that Niedermann had to be got rid of, but he knew that it would be a bad idea to frighten off Waltari before they were in place.

"I don't know. We'll see what he has in mind. If he's planning to get out of the country as fast as hell then we could help him on his way. But as long as he risks being busted, he's a threat to us."

The lights were out at Göransson's place when Nieminen and Waltari drove up in the twilight. That was not a good sign. They sat in the car and waited.

"Maybe they're out," Waltari said.

"Right. They went to the bar with Niedermann," Nieminen said, opening the car door.

The front door was unlocked. Nieminen switched on an overhead light. They went from room to room. The house was well kept and neat, which was probably because of her, whatever-her-name-was, the woman Göransson lived with.

They found Göransson and his girlfriend in the basement, stuffed into a laundry room.

Nieminen bent down and looked at the bodies. He reached out a finger to touch the woman whose name he could not remember. She was ice-cold and stiff. That meant they had been dead maybe twenty-four hours.

Nieminen did not need the help of a pathologist to work out how they had died. Her neck had been broken when her head was turned 180 degrees. She was dressed in a T-shirt and jeans and had no other injuries that Nieminen could see.

Göransson, on the other hand, wore only his underpants. He had been beaten, had blood and bruises all over his body. His arms were bent in impossible directions, like twisted tree limbs. The battering he had been subjected to could only be defined as torture. He had been killed, as far as Nieminen could judge, by a single blow to the neck. His larynx was rammed deep into his throat.

Nieminen went up the stairs and out of the front door. Waltari followed him. Nieminen walked the fifty metres to the barn. He flipped the hasp and opened the door.

He found a dark-blue 1991 Renault.

"What kind of car does Göransson have?" Nieminen said.

"He drove a Saab."

Nieminen nodded. He fished some keys out of his jacket pocket and opened a door at the far end of the barn. One quick look around told him that they were there too late. The heavy weapons cabinet stood wide open.

Nieminen grimaced. "About 800,000 kronor," he said.

"What?"

"Svavelsjö M.C. had about 800,000 kronor stashed in this cabinet. It was our treasury."

Only three people knew where Svavelsjö M.C. kept the cash that was waiting to be invested and laundered. Göransson, Lundin, and Nieminen. *Niedermann was on the run. He needed cash. He knew that Göransson was the one who handled the money.*

Nieminen shut the door and walked slowly away from the barn. His mind was spinning as he tried to digest the catastrophe. Part of Svavelsjö M.C.'s assets were in the form of bonds that he could access, and some of their investments could be reconstructed with Lundin's help. But a large part of them had been listed only in Göransson's head, unless he had given clear instructions to Lundin. Which Nieminen doubted – Lundin had never been clever with money. Nieminen estimated that Svavelsjö M.C. had lost upwards of 60 per cent of its assets with Göransson's death. It was a devastating blow. Above all they needed the cash to take care of day-to-day expenses.

"What do we do now?" Waltari said.

"We'll go and tip off the police about what happened here."

"Tip off the *police*?"

"Yes, damn it. My prints are all over the house. I want Göransson and his bitch to be found as soon as possible, so that forensics can work out that they died while I was still locked up."

"I get it."

"Good. Go and find Benny. I want to talk to him. If he's still alive, that is. And then we'll track down Niedermann. We'll need every contact we have in the clubs all over Scandinavia to keep their eyes peeled. I want that bastard's head on a platter. He's probably riding around in Göransson's Saab. Find out the registration number."

When Salander woke up it was 2.00 on Saturday afternoon and a doctor was poking at her.

"Good morning," he said. "My name is Benny Svantesson. I'm a doctor. Are you in pain?"

"Yes," Salander said.

"I'll make sure you get some painkillers in a minute. But first I'd like to examine you."

He squeezed and poked and fingered her lacerated body. Salander was extremely aggravated by the time he had finished, but she held back; she was exhausted and decided it would be better to keep quiet than tarnish her stay at Sahlgrenska with a fight.

"How am I doing?" she said.

"You'll pull through," the doctor said and made some notes before he stood up. This was not very informative.

After he left, a nurse came in and helped Salander with a bedpan. Then she was allowed to go back to sleep.

Zalachenko, alias Karl Axel Bodin, was given a liquid lunch. Even small movements of his facial muscles caused sharp pains in his jaw and cheekbone, and chewing was out of the question. During surgery the night before, two titanium screws had been fixed into his jawbone.

But the pain was manageable. Zalachenko was used to pain. Nothing could compare with the pain he had undergone for several weeks, months even, fifteen years before when he had burned like a torch in his car. The follow-up care had been a marathon of agony.

The doctors had decided that his life was no longer at risk but that he was severely injured. In view of his age, he would stay in the intensive care unit for a few more days yet.

On Saturday he had four visitors.

At 10.00 a.m. Inspector Erlander returned. This time he had left that bloody Modig woman behind and instead was accompanied by Inspector Holmberg, who was much more agreeable. They asked pretty much the same questions about Niedermann as they had the night before. He had his story straight and did not slip up. When they started plying him with questions about his possible involvement in trafficking and other criminal activities, he again denied all knowledge of any such thing. He was living on a disability pension, and he had no idea what they were talking about. He blamed Niedermann for everything and offered to help them in any way he could to find the fugitive.

Unfortunately there was not much he could help with, practically speaking. He had no knowledge of the circles Niedermann moved in, or who he might go to for protection.

At around 11.00 he had a brief visit from a representative of the prosecutor's office, who formally advised him that he was a suspect in the grievous bodily harm or attempted murder of Lisbeth Salander. Zalachenko patiently explained that, on the contrary, he was the victim of a crime, that in point of fact it was Salander who had attempted to murder *him*. The prosecutor's office offered him legal assistance in the form of a public defence lawyer. Zalachenko said that he would mull over the matter.

Which he had no intention of doing. He already had a lawyer, and the first thing he needed to do that morning was call him and tell him to get down there as swiftly as he could. Martin Thomasson was therefore the third guest of the day at Zalachenko's sickbed. He wandered in with a carefree expression, ran a hand through his thick blond hair, adjusted his glasses, and shook hands with his client. He was a chubby and very charming man. True, he was suspected of running errands for the Yugoslav mafia, a matter which was still under investigation, but he was also known for winning his cases.

Zalachenko had been referred to Thomasson through a business associate five years earlier, when he needed to restructure certain funds connected to a small financial firm that he owned in Liechtenstein. They were not dramatic sums, but Thomasson's skill had been exceptional, and Zalachenko had avoided paying taxes on them. He then engaged Thomasson on a couple of other matters. Thomasson knew that the money came from criminal activity, which seemed not to trouble him. Ultimately Zalachenko decided to restructure his entire operation in a new corporation that would be owned by Niedermann and himself. He approached Thomasson and proposed that the lawyer come in as a third, silent partner to handle the financial side of the business. Thomasson accepted at once.

"So, Herr Bodin, none of this looks like much fun."

"I have been the victim of grievous bodily harm and attempted murder," Zalachenko said.

"I can see as much. A certain Lisbeth Salander, if I understood correctly."

Zalachenko lowered his voice: "Our partner Niedermann, as you know, has really fouled his nest this time."

"Indeed."

"The police suspect that I am involved."

"Which of course you are not. You're a victim, and it's important that we see to it at once that this is the image presented to the press. Ms Salander has already received a good deal of negative publicity . . . Let me deal with the situation."

"Thank you."

"But I have to remind you right from the start that I'm not a criminal lawyer. You're going to need a specialist. I'll arrange to hire one that you can trust."

The fourth visitor of the day arrived at 11.00 on Saturday night, and managed to get past the nurses by showing an I.D. card and stating that he had urgent business. He was shown to Zalachenko's room. The patient was still awake, and grumbling.

"My name is Jonas Sandberg," he introduced himself, holding out a hand that Zalachenko ignored.

He was in his thirties. He had reddish-brown hair and was casually dressed in jeans, a checked shirt and a leather jacket. Zalachenko scrutinized him for fifteen seconds.

"I was wondering when one of you was going to show up."

"I work for S.I.S., Swedish Internal Security," Sandberg said, and showed Zalachenko his I.D.

"I doubt that," said Zalachenko.

"I beg your pardon?"

"You may be employed by S.I.S., but I doubt that's who you're working for."

Sandberg looked around the room, then he pulled up the visitor's chair.

"I came here late so as not to attract attention. We've discussed how we can help you, and now we have to reach some sort of agreement about what's going to happen. I'm just here to have your version of the story and find out what your intentions are . . . so that we can work out a common strategy."

"What sort of strategy had you in mind?"

"Herr Zalachenko . . . I'm afraid that a process has been set in motion in which the deleterious effects are hard to foresee," Sandberg said. "We've talked it through. It's going to be difficult to explain away the grave in Gosseberga, and the fact that the girl was shot three times. But let's not lose hope altogether. The conflict between you and your daughter can explain your fear of her and why you took such drastic measures . . . but I'm afraid we're talking about your doing some time in prison."

Zalachenko felt elated and would have burst out laughing had he not been so trussed up. He managed a slight curl of his lips. Anything more would be just too painful.

"So that's our strategy?"

"Herr Zalachenko, you are aware of the concept of damage control. We have to arrive at a common strategy. We'll do everything in our power to assist you with a lawyer and so on . . . but we need your co-operation, as well as certain guarantees."

"You'll get only one guarantee from me. First, you will see to it that all this disappears." He waved his hand. "Niedermann is the scape-goat and I guarantee that no-one will ever find him."

"There's forensic evidence that—"

"*Fuck* the forensic evidence. It's a matter of how the investigation is carried out and how the facts are presented. My guarantee is this . . . if you don't wave your magic wand and make all this disappear, I'm inviting the media to a press conference. I know names, dates, events. I don't think I need to remind you who I am."

"You don't understand—"

"I understand perfectly. You're an errand boy. So go to your super-ior and tell him what I've said. He'll understand. Tell him that I have copies of . . . everything. I can take you all down."

"We have to come to an agreement."

"This conversation is over. Get out of here. And tell them that next time they should send a grown man for me to discuss things with."

Zalachenko turned his head away from his visitor. Sandberg looked at Zalachenko for a moment. Then he shrugged and got up. He was almost at the door when he heard Zalachenko's voice again.

"One more thing."

Sandberg turned.

"Salander."

"What about her?"

"She has to disappear."

"How do you mean?"

Sandberg looked so nervous for a second that Zalachenko had to smile, although the pain drilled into his jaw.

"I see that you milksops are too sensitive to kill her, and that you don't even have the resources to have it done. Who would do it . . . you? But she has to disappear. Her testimony has to be declared invalid. She has to be committed to a mental institution for life."

Salander heard footsteps in the corridor. She had never heard those footsteps before.

Her door had been open all evening and the nurses had been in to check on her every ten minutes. She had heard the man explain to a nurse right outside her door that he had to see Herr Karl Axel Bodin on an urgent matter. She had heard him offering his I.D., but no words were exchanged that gave her any clue as to who he was or what sort of I.D. he had.

The nurse had asked him to wait while she went to see whether Herr Bodin was awake. Salander concluded that his I.D., whatever it said, must have been persuasive.

She heard the nurse go down the corridor to the left. It took her 17 steps to reach the room, and the male visitor took 14 steps to cover the same distance. That gave an average of 15.5 steps. She estimated the length of a step at 60 centimetres, which multiplied by 15.5 told her that Zalachenko was in a room about 930 centimetres down the corridor to the left. O.K., approximately ten metres. She estimated that the width of her room was about five metres, which should mean that Zalachenko's room was two doors down from hers.

According to the green numerals on the digital clock on her bedside cabinet, the visit lasted precisely nine minutes.

*

72

Zalachenko lay awake for a long time after the man who called himself Jonas Sandberg had left. He assumed that it was not his real name; in his experience Swedish amateur spies had a real obsession with using false names even when it was not in the least bit necessary. In which case Sandberg, or whatever the hell his name was, was the first indication that Zalachenko's predicament had come to the attention of the Section. Considering the media attention, this would have been hard to avoid. But the visit did confirm that his predicament was a matter of anxiety to them. As well it might be.

He weighed the pros and cons, lined up the possibilities, and rejected various options. He was fully aware that everything had gone about as badly as it could have. In a well-ordered world he would be at home in Gosseberga now, Niedermann would be safely out of the country, and Salander would be buried in a hole in the ground. Despite the fact that he had a reasonable grasp of what had happened, for the life of him he could not comprehend how she had managed to dig herself out of Niedermann's trench, make her way to his farm, and damn near destroy him with two blows of an axe. She was extraordinarily resourceful.

On the other hand he understood quite well what had happened to Niedermann, and why he had run for his life instead of staying to finish Salander off. He knew that something was not quite right in Niedermann's head, that he saw visions — ghosts even. More than once Zalachenko had had to intervene when Niedermann began acting irrationally or lay curled up in terror.

This worried Zalachenko. He was convinced that, since Niedermann had not yet been captured, he must have been acting rationally during the twenty-four hours since his flight from Gosseberga. Probably he would go to Tallinn, where he would seek protection among contacts in Zalachenko's criminal empire. What worried him in the short term was that he could never predict when Niedermann might be struck by his mental paralysis. If it happened while he was trying to escape, he would make mistakes, and if he made mistakes he would end up in prison. He would never surrender voluntarily, which meant that policemen would die and Niedermann probably would as well.

This thought upset Zalachenko. He did not want Niedermann to die. Niedermann was his son. But regrettable as it was, Niedermann must not be captured alive. He had never been arrested, and Zalachenko could not predict how he would react under interrogation. He doubted that Niedermann would be able to keep quiet, as he should. So it would be a good thing if he were killed by the police. He would grieve for his son, but the alternative was worse. If Niedermann talked, Zalachenko himself would have to spend the rest of his life in prison.

But it was now forty-eight hours since Niedermann had fled, and he had not yet been caught. That was good. It was an indication that Niedermann was functioning, and a functioning Niedermann was invincible.

In the long term there was another worry. He wondered how Niedermann would get along on his own, without his father there to guide him. Over the years he had noticed that if he stopped giving instructions or gave Niedermann too much latitude to make his own decisions, he would slip into an indolent state of indecision.

Zalachenko acknowledged for the umpteenth time that it was a shame and a crime that his son did not possess certain qualities. Ronald Niedermann was without doubt a very talented person who had physical attributes to make him a formidable and feared individual. He was also an excellent and cold-blooded organizer. His problem was that he utterly lacked the instinct to lead. He always needed somebody to tell him what he was supposed to be organizing.

But for the time being all this lay outside Zalachenko's control. Right now he had to focus on himself. His situation was precarious, perhaps more precarious than ever before.

He did not think that Advokat Thomasson's visit earlier in the day had been particularly reassuring. Thomasson was and remained a corporate lawyer, and no matter how effective he was in that respect, he would not be a great support in this other business.

And then there had been the visit of Jonas Sandberg, or whatever his name was. Sandberg offered a considerably stronger lifeline. But that lifeline could also be a trap. He had to play his cards right, and he would have to take control of the situation. Control was everything.

In the end he had his own resources to fall back on. For the moment he needed medical attention, but in a couple of days, maybe a week, he would have regained his strength. If things came to a head, he might have only himself to rely on. That meant that he would have to disappear, from right under the noses of the policemen circling around him. He would need a hideout, a passport, and some cash. Thomasson could provide him with all that. But first he would have to get strong enough to make his escape.

At 1.00 a.m. the night nurse looked in. He pretended to be asleep. When she closed the door he arduously sat up and swung his legs over the edge of the bed. He sat still for while, testing his sense of balance. Then he cautiously put his left foot down on the floor. Luckily the axe blow had struck his already crippled right leg. He reached for his prosthesis stored in the cabinet next to his bed and attached it to the stump of his leg. Then he stood up, keeping his weight on his uninjured leg before trying to stand on the other. As he shifted his weight a sharp pain shot through his right leg.

He gritted his teeth and took a step. He would need crutches, and he was sure that the hospital would offer him some soon. He braced himself against the wall and limped over to the door. It took him several minutes, and he had to stop after each step to deal with the pain.

He rested on one leg as he pushed open the door a crack and peered out into the corridor. He did not see anyone, so he stuck his head out a little further. He heard faint voices to the left and turned to look. The night nurses were at their station about twenty metres down on the other side of the corridor.

He turned his head to the right and saw the exit at the other end.

Earlier in the day he had enquired about Lisbeth Salander's condition. He was, after all, her father. The nurses obviously had been instructed not to discuss other patients. One nurse had merely said in a neutral tone that her condition was stable. But she had unconsciously glanced to her left.

In one of the rooms between his own and the exit was Lisbeth Salander.

He carefully closed the door, limped back to the bed, and detached his prosthesis. He was drenched in sweat when he finally slipped under the covers.

Inspector Holmberg returned to Stockholm at lunchtime on Sunday. He was hungry and exhausted. He took the tunnelbana to City Hall, walked to police headquarters on Bergsgatan, and went up to Inspector Bublanski's office. Modig and Andersson had already arrived. Bublanski had called the meeting on Sunday because he knew that preliminary investigation leader Richard Ekström was busy elsewhere.

"Thanks for coming in," said Bublanski. "I think it's time we had

75

a discussion in peace and quiet to try to make sense of this mess. Jerker, have you got anything new?"

"Nothing I haven't already told you on the phone. Zalachenko isn't budging one millimetre. He's innocent of everything and has nothing to say. Just that—"

"Yes?"

"Sonja, you were right. He's one of the nastiest people I've ever met. It might sound stupid to say that. Policemen aren't supposed to think in those terms, but there's something really scary beneath his calculating facade."

"O.K." Bublanski cleared his throat. "What have we got? Sonja?"

She smiled weakly.

"The private investigators won this round. I can't find Zalachenko in any public register, but a Karl Axel Bodin seems to have been born in 1942 in Uddevalla. His parents were Marianne and Georg Bodin. They died in an accident in 1946. Karl Axel Bodin was brought up by an uncle living in Norway. So there is no record of him until the '70s, when he moved back to Sweden. Mikael Blomkvist's story that he's a G.R.U. agent who defected from the Soviet Union seems impossible to verify, but I'm inclined to think he's right."

"Alright. And what does that mean?"

"The obvious explanation is that he was given a false identity. It must have been done with the consent of the authorities."

"You mean the Security Police, Säpo?"

"That's what Blomkvist claims. But exactly how it was done I don't know. It presupposes that his birth certificate and a number of other documents were falsified and then slipped into our public records. I don't dare to comment on the legal ramifications of such an action. It probably depends on who made the decision. But for it to be legal, the decision would have to have been made at senior government level."

Silence descended in Bublanski's office as the four criminal inspectors considered these implications.

"O.K.," said Bublanski. "The four of us are just dumb police officers. If people in government are mixed up in this, I don't intend to interrogate them."

"Hmm," said Andersson, "this could lead to a constitutional crisis. In the United States you can cross-examine members of the government in a normal court of law. In Sweden you have to do it through a constitutional committee."

"But we could ask the boss," said Holmberg.

"Ask the boss?" said Bublanski.

"Thorbjörn Fälldin. He was Prime Minister at the time."

"O.K., we'll just cruise up to wherever he lives and ask the former Prime Minister if he faked identity documents for a defecting Russian spy. I don't think so."

"Fälldin lives in Ås, in Härnösand. I grew up a few miles from there. My father's a member of the Centre Party and knows Fälldin well. I've met him several times, both as a kid and as an adult. He's a very approachable person."

Three inspectors gave Holmberg an astonished look.

"You know Fälldin?" Bublanski said dubiously.

Holmberg nodded. Bublanski pursed his lips.

"To tell the truth," said Holmberg, "it would solve a number of issues if we could get the former Prime Minister to give us a state-ment – at least we'd know where we stand in all this. I could go up there and talk to him. If he won't say anything, so be it. But if he does, we might save ourselves a lot of time."

Bublanski weighed the suggestion. Then he shook his head. Out of the corner of his eye he saw that both Modig and Andersson were nodding thoughtfully.

"Holmberg . . . it's nice of you to offer, but I think we'll put that idea on the back burner for now. So, back to the case. Sonja."

"According to Blomkvist, Zalachenko came here in 1976. As far as I can work out, there's only one person he could have got that infor-mation from."

"Gunnar Björck," said Andersson.

"What has Björck told us?" Holmberg asked.

"Not much. He says it's all classified and that he can't discuss anything without permission from his superiors."

"And who are his superiors?"

"He won't say."

"So what's going to happen to him?"

"I arrested him for violation of the prostitution laws. We have excel-lent documentation in Dag Svensson's notes. Ekström was most upset, but since I had already filed a report, he could get himself into trouble if he closes the preliminary investigation," Andersson said.

"I see. Violation of the prostitution laws. That might result in a fine of ten times his daily income."

"Probably. But we have him in the system and can call him in again for questioning."

"But now we're getting a little too close to poaching on Säpo's preserves. That might cause a bit of turbulence."

"The problem is that none of this could have happened if Säpo weren't involved somehow. It's possible that Zalachenko really was a Russian spy who defected and was granted political asylum. It's also possible that he worked for Säpo as an expert or source or whatever title you want to give him, and that there was good reason to offer him a false identity and anonymity. But there are three problems. First, the investigation carried out in 1991 that led to Lisbeth Salander being locked away was illegal. Second, Zalachenko's activities since then have nothing whatsoever to do with national security. Zalachenko is an ordinary gangster who's probably mixed up in several murders and other criminal activities. And third, there is no doubt that Lisbeth Salander was shot and buried alive on his property in Gosseberga."

"Speaking of which, I'd really like to read the infamous report," said Holmberg.

Bublanski's face clouded over.

"Jerker . . . this is how it is: Ekström laid claim to it on Friday, and when I asked for it back he said he'd make me a copy, which he never did. Instead he called me and said that he had spoken with the Prosecutor General and there was a problem. According to the P.G., the Top Secret classification means that the report may not be disseminated or copied. The P.G. has called in all copies until the matter is investigated. Which meant that Sonja had to relinquish the copy she had too."

"So we no longer have the report?"

"No."

"Damn," said Holmberg. "The whole thing stinks."

"I know," said Bublanski. "Worst of all, it means that someone is acting against us, and acting very quickly and efficiently. The report was what finally put us on the right track."

"So we have to work out who's acting against us," said Holmberg.

"Just a moment," said Modig. "We also have Peter Teleborian. He contributed to our investigation by profiling Lisbeth Salander."

"Exactly," said Bublanski in a darker tone of voice. "And what did he say?"

"He was very concerned about her safety and wished her well. But when the discussion was over, he said that she was lethally dangerous and might well resist arrest. We based a lot of our thinking on what he told us."

"And he got Hans Faste all worked up," said Holmberg. "Have we heard anything from Faste, by the way?"

"He took some time off," Bublanski replied curtly. "The question now is how *we* should proceed."

They spent the next two hours discussing their options. The only practical decision they made was that Modig should return to Göteborg the next day to see whether Salander had anything to say. When they finally broke up, Modig and Andersson walked together down to the garage.

"I was just thinking . . ." Andersson stopped.

"Yes?"

"It's just that when we talked to Teleborian, you were the only one in the group who offered any opposition when he answered our questions."

"Yes?"

"Well . . . er . . . good instincts," he said.

Andersson was not known for handing out praise, and it was definitely the first time he had ever said anything positive or encouraging to Modig. He left her standing by her car in astonishment.

CHAPTER 5

Sunday, 10.iv

Blomkvist had spent Saturday night with Berger. They lay in bed and talked through the details of the Zalachenko story. Blomkvist trusted Berger implicitly and was never for a second inhibited by the fact that she was going to be working for a rival paper. Nor had Berger any thought of taking the story with her. It was *Millennium*'s scoop, even though she may have felt a certain frustration that she was not going to be the editor of that particular issue. It would have been a fine ending to her years at *Millennium*.

They also discussed the future structure of the magazine. Berger was determined to retain her shareholding in *Millennium* and to remain on the board, even if she had no say over the magazine's contents.

"Give me a few years at the daily and then, who knows? Maybe I'll come back to *Millennium* before I retire," she said.

And as for their own complicated relationship, why should it be any different? Except that of course they would not be meeting so often. It would be as it was in the '80s, before *Millennium* was founded and when they worked in separate offices.

"I imagine we'll have to book appointments with each other," Berger said with a faint smile.

On Sunday morning they said a hasty goodbye before Berger drove home to her husband, Greger Beckman.

After she was gone Blomkvist called the hospital in Sahlgrenska and tried to get some information about Salander's condition. Nobody would tell him anything, so finally he called Inspector Erlander, who took pity on him and vouchsafed that, given the circumstances, Salander's condition was fair and the doctors were cautiously optimistic. He asked if he would be able to visit her. Erlander told him that Salander was officially under arrest and that the prosecutor would not allow any visitors, but in any case she was in no condition to be questioned. Erlander said he would call if her condition took a turn for the worse.

When Blomkvist checked his mobile, he saw that he had forty-two messages and texts, almost all of them from journalists. There had been wild speculation in the media after it was revealed that Blomkvist was the one who had found Salander, and had probably saved her life. He was obviously closely connected with the development of events.

He deleted all the messages from reporters and called his sister, Annika, to invite himself for Sunday lunch. Then he called Dragan Armansky, C.E.O. of Milton Security, who was at his home in Lidingö.

"You certainly have a way with headlines," Armansky said.

"I tried to reach you earlier this week. I got a message that you were looking for me, but I just didn't have time—"

"We've been doing our own investigation at Milton. And I understood from Holger Palmgren that you had some information. But it seems you were far ahead of us."

Blomkvist hesitated before he said: "Can I trust you?"

"How do you mean exactly?"

"Are you on Salander's side or not? Can I believe that you want the best for her?"

"I'm her friend. Although, as you know, that's not necessarily the same thing as saying that she's my friend."

"I understand that. But what I'm asking is whether or not you're willing to put yourself in her corner and get into a pitched battle with her enemies."

"I'm on her side," he said.

"Can I share information with you and discuss things with you without the risk of your leaking it to the police or to anyone else?"

"I can't get involved in criminal activity," Armansky said.

"That's not what I asked."

"You can absolutely rely on me as long as you don't reveal that you're engaged in any sort of criminal activity."

"Good enough. We need to meet."

"I'm coming into the city this evening. Dinner?"

"I don't have time today, but I'd be grateful if we could meet tomorrow night. You and I and perhaps a few other people might need to sit down for a chat."

"You're welcome at Milton. Shall we say 6.00?"

"One more thing . . . I'm seeing my sister, the lawyer Annika Giannini, later this morning. She's considering taking on Salander as a client, but she can't work for nothing. I can pay part of her fee out of my own pocket. Would Milton Security be willing to contribute?"

"That girl is going to need a damned good criminal lawyer. Your sister might not be the best choice, if you'll forgive me for saying so. I've already talked to Milton's chief lawyer and he's looking into it. I was thinking of Peter Althin or someone like that."

"That would be a mistake. Salander needs a totally different kind of legal support. You'll see what I mean when we talk. But would you be willing, in principle, to help?"

"I'd already decided that Milton ought to hire a lawyer for her—"

"Is that a yes or a no? I know what happened to her. I know roughly what's behind it all. And I have a strategy."

Armansky laughed.

"O.K. I'll listen to what you have to say. If I like it, I'm in."

Blomkvist kissed his sister on the cheek and immediately asked: "Are you going to be representing Lisbeth Salander?"

"I'm going to have to say no. You know I'm not a criminal lawyer. Even if she's acquitted of murder, there's going to be a rack of other charges. She's going to need someone with a completely different sort of clout and experience than I have."

"You're wrong. You're a lawyer and you're a recognized authority in women's rights. In my considered view you're precisely the lawyer she needs."

"Mikael . . . I don't think you really appreciate what this involves. It's a complex criminal case, not a straightforward case of sexual harassment or of violence against a woman. If I take on her defence, it could turn out to be a disaster."

Blomkvist smiled. "You're missing the point. If she had been charged with the murders of Dag and Mia, for example, I would have gone for the Silbersky type or another of the heavy-duty criminal lawyers. But this trial is going to be about entirely different things."

"I think you'd better explain."

They talked for almost two hours over sandwiches and coffee. By the time Mikael had finished his account, Annika had been persuaded. Mikael picked up his mobile and made another call to Inspector Erlander in Göteborg.

"Hello, it's Blomkvist again."

"I don't have any news on Salander," Erlander said, plainly irritated.

"Which I assume is good news. But I actually have some news."

"What's that?"

"Well, she now has a lawyer named Annika Giannini. She's with me right now, so I'll put her on."

Blomkvist handed the mobile across the table.

"My name is Annika Giannini and I've been taken on to represent Lisbeth Salander. I need to get in touch with my client so that she can approve me as her defence lawyer. And I need the telephone number of the prosecutor."

"As far as I know," Erlander said, "a public defence has already been appointed."

"That's nice to hear. Did anyone ask Lisbeth Salander her opinion?"

"Quite frankly . . . we haven't had the opportunity to speak with her yet. We hope to be able to do so tomorrow, if she's well enough."

"Fine. Then I'll tell you here and now that until Fröken Salander says otherwise, you may regard me as her legal representative. You may not question her unless I am present. You can say hello to her and ask her whether she accepts me as her lawyer or not. But that is all. Is that understood?"

"Yes," Erlander said with an audible sigh. He was not entirely sure what the letter of the law was on this point. "Our number one objective is to discover if she has any information as to where Ronald Niedermann might be. Is it O.K. to ask her about that . . . even if you're not present?"

"That's fine . . . you may ask her questions relating to the police hunt for Niedermann. But you may not ask her any questions relating to any possible charges against her. Agreed?"

"I think so, yes."

Inspector Erlander got up from his desk and went upstairs to tell the preliminary investigation leader, Agneta Jervas, about his conversation with Giannini.

"She was obviously hired by Blomkvist. I can't believe Salander knows anything about it."

"Giannini works in women's rights. I heard her lecture once. She's sharp, but completely unsuitable for this case."

"It's up to Salander to decide."

"I might have to contest the decision in court . . . For the girl's own sake she has to have a proper defence, and not some celebrity chasing headlines. Hmm. Salander has also been declared legally incompetent. I don't know whether that affects things."

"What should we do?"

Jervas thought for a moment. "This is a complete mess. I don't know who's going to be in charge of this case or if it'll be transferred to Ekström in Stockholm. In any event she has to have a lawyer. O.K . . . ask her if she wants Giannini."

When Blomkvist reached home at 5.00 in the afternoon he turned on his iBook and took up the thread of the text he had begun writing at the hotel in Göteborg. When he had worked for seven straight hours, he had identified the most glaring holes in the story. There was still much research to be done. One question he could not answer – based on the existing documentation – was who in Säpo, apart from Gunnar Björck, had conspired to lock Salander away in the asylum. Nor had he got to the heart of the relationship between Björck and the psychiatrist Peter Teleborian.

Finally he shut down the computer and went to bed. He felt as soon as he lay down that for the first time in weeks he could relax and sleep peacefully. The story was under control. No matter how many questions remained unanswered, he already had enough material to set off a landslide of headlines.

Late as it was, he picked up the telephone to call Berger and update her. And then he remembered that she had left *Millennium*. Suddenly he found it difficult to sleep.

A man carrying a brown briefcase stepped carefully down from the 7.30 p.m. train at Stockholm Central Station. He stood for a moment in the sea of travellers, getting his bearings. He had started out from Laholm just after 8.00 in the morning. He stopped in Göteborg to have lunch with an old friend before resuming his journey to Stockholm. He had not been to Stockholm for two years. In fact he had not planned to visit the capital ever again. Even though he had lived there for large parts of his working life, he always felt a little out of place in Stockholm, a feeling that had grown stronger with every visit he made since his retirement.

He walked slowly through the station, bought the evening papers and two bananas at Pressbyrån, and paused to watch two Muslim women in veils hurry past him. He had nothing against women in veils. It was nothing to him if people wanted to dress up in costume. But he was bothered by the fact that they had to dress like that in the middle of Stockholm. In his opinion, Somalia was a much better place for that sort of attire.

He walked the three hundred metres to Frey's Hotel next to the old post office on Vasagatan. That was where he had stayed on previous visits. The hotel was centrally located and clean. And it was inexpensive, which was a factor since he was paying for the journey himself. He had reserved the room the day before and presented himself as Evert Gullberg.

When he got up to the room he went straight to the bathroom. He had reached the age when he had to use the toilet rather often. It was several years since he had slept through a whole night.

When he had finished he took off his hat, a narrow-brimmed, dark-green English felt hat, and loosened his tie. He was one metre eighty-four tall and weighed sixty-eight kilos, which meant he was thin and wiry. He wore a hound's-tooth jacket and dark-grey trousers. He opened the brown briefcase and unpacked two shirts, a second tie, and underwear, which he arranged in the chest of drawers. Then he hung his overcoat and jacket in the wardrobe behind the door.

It was too early to go to bed. It was too late to bother going for an evening walk, something he might not enjoy in any case. He sat down in the obligatory chair in the hotel room and looked around. He switched on the T.V. and turned down the volume so that he would not have to hear it. He thought about calling reception and ordering coffee, but decided it was too late. Instead he opened the mini-bar and poured a miniature of Johnny Walker into a glass, and added very little water. He opened the evening papers and read everything that had been written that day about the search for Ronald Niedermann and the case of Lisbeth Salander. After a while he took out a leather-bound notebook and made some notes.

Gullberg, formerly Senior Administrative Officer at the Security Police, was now seventy-eight years old and had been retired for thirteen years. But intelligence officers never really retire, they just slip into the shadows.

After the war, when Gullberg was nineteen years old, he had joined the navy. He did his military service first as an officer cadet and was then accepted for officer training. But instead of the usual assignment at sea that he had anticipated, he was sent to Karlskrona as a signal tracker in the navy's intelligence service. He had no difficulty with the work, which was mostly figuring out what was going on on the other side of the Baltic. But he found it dull and uninteresting. Through the service's language school, however, he did learn Russian and Polish. These linguistic skills were one of the reasons he was recruited by the Security Police in 1950, during the time when the impeccably mannered Georg Thulin was head of the third division of Säpo. When he started, the total budget of the secret police was 2.7 million kronor for a staff of ninety-six people. When Gullberg formally retired in 1992, the budget of the Security Police was in excess of 350 million kronor, and he had no idea how many employees the Firm had.

Gullberg had spent his life on his majesty's secret service, or perhaps more accurately in the secret service of the social-democratic welfare state. Which was an irony, since he had faithfully voted for the moderates in one election after another, except for 1991 when he deliberately voted against the moderates because he believed that Carl Bildt was a *realpolitik* catastrophe. He had voted instead for Ingvar Carlsson. The years of "Sweden's best government" had also confirmed his worst fears. The moderate government had come to power when the Soviet Union was collapsing, and in his opinion no government had been less prepared to meet the new political opportunities emerging in the East, or to make use of the art of espionage. On the contrary, the Bildt government had cut back the Soviet desk for financial reasons and had at the same time got themselves involved in the international mess in Bosnia and Serbia – as if Serbia could ever threaten Sweden. The result was that a fabulous opportunity to plant long-term informants in Moscow had been lost. Some day, when relations would once again worsen – which according to Gullberg was inevitable – absurd demands would be made on the Security Police and the military intelligence service; they would be expected to wave their magic wand and summon up well-placed agents out of a bottle.

*

Gullberg had begun at the Russia desk of the third division of the state police, and after two years in the job had undertaken his first tentative field work in 1952 and 1953 as an Air Force attaché with the rank of captain at the embassy in Moscow. Strangely enough, he was following in the footsteps of another well-known spy. Some years earlier that post had been occupied by the notorious Colonel Wennerström.

Back in Sweden, Gullberg had worked in Counter-Espionage, and ten years later he was one of the younger security police officers who, working under Otto Danielsson, exposed Wennerström and eventually got him a life sentence for treason at Långholmen prison.

When the Security Police was reorganized under Per Gunnar Vinge in 1964 and became the Security Division of the National Police Board, or Swedish Internal Security – S.I.S. – the major increase in personnel began. By then Gullberg had worked at the Security Police for fourteen years, and had become one of its trusted veterans.

Gullberg had never used the designation "Säpo" for Säkerhetspolisen, the Security Police. He used the term "S.I.S." in official contexts, and among colleagues he would also refer to "the Company" or "the Firm", or merely "the Division" – but never "Säpo". The reason was simple. The Firm's most important task for many years was so-called personnel control, that is, the investigation and registration of Swedish citizens who might be suspected of harbouring communist or subversive views. Within the Firm the terms communist and traitor were synonymous. The later conventional use of the term "Säpo" was actually something that the potentially subversive communist publication *Clarté* had coined as a pejorative name for the communist-hunters within the police force. For the life of him Gullberg could never imagine why his former boss P.G. Vinge had entitled his memoirs *Säpo Chief 1962–1970*.

It was the reorganization of 1964 that had shaped Gullberg's future career.

The designation S.I.S. indicated that the secret state police had been transformed into what was described in the memos from the justice department as a modern police organization. This involved recruiting new personnel and continual problems breaking them in. In this expanding organization "the Enemy" were presented with dramatically improved opportunities to place agents within the division. This meant in turn that internal security had to be intensified – the Security Police could no longer be a club of former officers, where everyone knew everyone else, and where the commonest qualification for a new recruit was that his father was or had been an officer.

In 1963 Gullberg was transferred from Counter-Espionage to personnel control, a role that took on added significance in the wake of Wennerström's exposure as a double agent. During that period the foundation was laid for the "register of political opinions", a list which towards the end of the '60s amounted to around 300,000 Swedish citizens who were held to harbour undesirable political sympathies. Checking the backgrounds of Swedish citizens was one thing, but the crucial question was: how would security control within S.I.S. itself be implemented?

The Wennerström debacle had given rise to an avalanche of dilemmas within the Security Police. If a colonel on the defence staff could work for the Russians – he was also the government's adviser on matters involving nuclear weapons and security policy – it followed that the Russians might have an equally senior agent within the Security Police. Who would guarantee that the top ranks and middle management at the Firm were not working for the Russians? Who, in short, was going to spy on the spies?

In August 1964 Gullberg was summoned to an afternoon meeting with the assistant chief of the Security Police, Hans Wilhelm Francke. The other participants at the meeting were two individuals from the top echelon of the Firm, the assistant head of Secretariat and the head of Budget. Before the day was over, Gullberg had been appointed head of a newly created division with the working title of "the Special Section". The first thing he did was to rename it "Special Analysis". That held for a few minutes until the head of Budget pointed out that S.A. was not much better than S.S. The organization's final name became "the Section for Special Analysis", the S.S.A., and in daily parlance "the Section", to differentiate it from "the Division" or "the Firm", which referred to the Security Police as a whole.

"The Section" was Francke's idea. He called it "the last line of defence". An ultra-secret unit that was given strategic positions within the Firm, but which was invisible. It was never referred to in writing, even in budget memoranda, and therefore it could not be infiltrated. Its task was to watch over national security. He had the authority to make it happen. He needed the Budget chief and the Secretariat chief to create the hidden substructure, but they were old colleagues, friends from dozens of skirmishes with the Enemy.

During the first year the Section consisted of Gullberg and three hand-picked colleagues. Over the next ten years it grew to include no more than eleven people, of whom two were administrative secretaries of the old school and the remainder were professional spy hunters. It was a structure with only two ranks. Gullberg was the chief. He would ordinarily meet each member of his team every day. Efficiency was valued more highly than background.

Formally, Gullberg was subordinate to a line of people in the hierarchy under the head of Secretariat of the Security Police, to whom he had to deliver monthly reports, but in practice he had been given a unique position with exceptional powers. He, and he alone, could decide to put Säpo's top bosses under the microscope. If he wanted to, he could even turn Per Gunnar Vinge's life inside out. (Which he also did.) He could initiate his own investigations or carry out telephone tapping without having to justify his objective or even report it to a higher level. His model was the legendary James Jesus Angleton, who had a similar position in the C.I.A., and whom he came to know personally.

The Section became a micro-organization within the Division – outside, above, and parallel to the rest of the Security Police. This also had geographical consequences. The Section had its offices at Kungsholmen, but for security reasons almost the whole team was moved out of police headquarters to an eleven-room apartment in Östermalm that had been discreetly remodelled into a fortified office. It was staffed twenty-four hours a day since the faithful old retainer and secretary Eleanor Badenbrink was installed in permanent lodgings in two of its rooms closest to the entrance. Badenbrink was an implacable colleague in whom Gullberg had implicit trust.

In the organization, Gullberg and his employees disappeared from public view – they were financed through a special fund, but they did not exist anywhere in the formal structure of the Security Police, which reported to the police commission or the justice department. Not even the head of S.I.S. knew about the most secret of the secret, whose task it was to handle the most sensitive of the sensitive.

At the age of forty Gullberg consequently found himself in a situation where he did not have to explain his actions to any living soul and could initiate investigations of anyone he chose.

It was clear to Gullberg that the Section for Special Analysis could become a politically sensitive unit and the job description was expressly vague. The written record was meagre in the extreme. In September 1964, Prime Minister Erlander signed a directive that guaranteed the setting aside of funds for the Section for Special Analysis, which was understood to be essential to the nation's security. This was one of twelve similar matters which the assistant chief of S.I.S., Hans Wilhelm Francke, brought up during an afternoon meeting. The document was stamped TOP SECRET and filed in the special protocol of S.I.S.

The signature of the Prime Minister meant that the Section was now a legally approved institution. The first year's budget amounted to 52,000 kronor. That the budget was so low was a stroke of genius, Gullberg thought. It meant that the creation of the Section appeared to be just another routine matter.

In a broader sense, the signature of the Prime Minister meant that he had sanctioned the need for a unit that would be responsible for "internal personnel control". At the same time it could be interpreted as the Prime Minister giving his approval to the establishment of a body that would also monitor particularly sensitive individuals outside S.I.S., such as the Prime Minister himself. It was this last which created potentially acute political problems.

Evert Gullberg saw that his whisky glass was empty. He was not fond of alcohol, but it had been a long day and a long journey. At this stage of life he did not think it mattered whether he decided to have one glass of whisky or two. He poured himself the miniature Glenfiddich.

The most sensitive of all issues, of course, was to be that of Olof Palme.*

Gullberg remembered every detail of Election Day 1976. For the first time in modern history, Sweden had voted for a conservative government. Most regrettably it was Thorbjörn Fälldin who became Prime Minister, not Gösta Bohman, a man infinitely better qualified. But above all, Palme was defeated, and for that Gullberg could breathe a sigh of relief.

Palme's suitability as Prime Minister had been the object of more than one lunch conversation in the corridors of S.I.S. In 1969, Vinge had been dismissed from the service after he had given voice to the view, shared by many inside the Division, that Palme might be an agent of influence for the K.G.B. Vinge's view was not even controversial in the climate prevailing inside the Firm. Unfortunately, he had openly discussed the matter with County Governor Lassinanti on a visit to Norrbotten. Lassinanti had been astonished and had informed the government chancellor, with the result that Vinge was summoned to explain himself at a one-on-one meeting.

To Gullberg's frustration, the question of Palme's possible Russian contacts was never resolved. Despite persistent attempts to establish the truth and uncover the crucial evidence – the smoking gun – the Section had never found any proof. In Gullberg's eyes this did not mean that Palme might be innocent, but rather that he was an especially cunning and intelligent spy who was not tempted to make the same mistakes that other Soviet spies had made. Palme continued to baffle them, year after year. In 1982 the Palme question arose again when he became Prime Minister for the second time. Then the assassin's shots rang out on Sveavägen and the matter became irrelevant.

1976 had been a problematic year for the Section. Within S.I.S. – among the few people who actually knew about the existence of the Section – a certain amount of criticism had surfaced. During the past ten years, sixty-five employees from within the Security Police had been dismissed from the organization on the grounds of presumed political unreliability. Most of the cases, however, were of the kind that were never going to be proven, and some very senior officers began to wonder whether the Section was not run by paranoid conspiracy theorists.

Gullberg still raged to recall the case of an officer hired by S.I.S. in 1968 whom he had personally evaluated as unsuitable. He was Inspector Bergling, a lieutenant in the Swedish army who later turned out to be a colonel in the Soviet military intelligence service, the G.R.U. On four separate occasions Gullberg tried to have Bergling removed, but each time his efforts were stymied. Things did not change until 1977, when Bergling became the object of suspicion outside the Section as well. His became the worst scandal in the history of the Swedish Security Police.

Criticism of the Section had increased during the first half of the seventies, and by mid-decade Gullberg had heard several proposals that the budget be reduced, and even suggestions that the operation was altogether unnecessary.

The criticism meant that the Section's future was questioned. That year the threat of terrorism was made a priority in S.I.S. In terms of espionage it was a sad chapter in their history, dealing as they were mainly with confused youths flirting with Arab or pro-Palestinian elements. The big question within the Security Police was to what extent personnel control would be given special authority to investigate foreign citizens residing in Sweden, or whether this would go on being the preserve of the Immigration Division.

Out of this somewhat esoteric bureaucratic debate, a need had arisen for the Section to assign a trusted colleague to the operation who could reinforce its control, espionage in fact, against members of the Immigration Division.

The job fell to a young man who had worked at S.I.S. since 1970, and whose background and political loyalty made him eminently qualified to work alongside the officers in the Section. In his free time he was a member of an organization called the Democratic Alliance, which was described by the social-democratic media as extreme right-wing. Within the Section this was no obstacle. Three others were members of the Democratic Alliance too, and the Section had in fact been instrumental in the very formation of the group. It had also contributed a small part of its funding. It was through this organization that the young man was brought to the attention of the Section and recruited.

His name was Gunnar Björck.

It was an improbable stroke of luck that when Alexander Zalachenko walked into Norrmalm police station on Election Day 1976 and requested asylum, it was a junior officer called Gunnar Björck who received him in his capacity as administrator of the Immigration Division. An agent already connected to the most secret of the secret.

Björck recognized Zalachenko's importance at once and broke off the interview to install the defector in a room at the Hotel Continental. It was Gullberg whom Björck notified when he sounded the alarm, and not his formal boss in the Immigration Division. The call came just as the voting booths had closed and all signs pointed to the fact that Palme was going to lose. Gullberg had just come home and was watching the election coverage on T.V. At first he was sceptical about the information that the excited young officer was telling him. Then he drove down to the Continental, not 250 metres from the hotel room where he found himself today, to assume control of the Zalachenko affair.

That night Gullberg's life underwent a radical change. The notion of secrecy took on a whole new dimension. He saw immediately the need to create a new structure around the defector.

He decided to include Björck in the Zalachenko unit. It was a reasonable decision, since Björck already knew of Zalachenko's existence. Better to have him on the inside than a security risk on the outside. Björck was moved from his post within the Immigration Division to a desk in the apartment in Östermalm.

In the drama that followed, Gullberg chose from the beginning to inform only one person in S.I.S., namely the head of Secretariat, who already had an overview of the activities of the Section. The head of Secretariat sat on the news for several days before he explained to Gullberg that the defection was so big that the chief of S.I.S. would have to be informed, as well as the government.

By that time the new chief of S.I.S. knew about the Section for Special Analysis, but he had only a vague idea of what the Section actually did. He had come on board recently to clean up the shambles of what was known as the Internal Bureau affair, and was already on his way to a higher position within the police hierarchy. The chief of S.I.S. had been told in a private conversation with the head of Secretariat that the Section was a secret unit appointed by the government. Its mandate put it outside regular operations, and no questions should be asked. Since this particular chief was a man who never asked questions that might yield unpleasant answers, he acquiesced. He accepted that there was something known only as S.S.A. and that he should have nothing more to do with the matter.

Gullberg was content to accept this situation. He issued instructions that required even the chief of S.I.S. not to discuss the topic in his office without taking special precautions. It was agreed that Zalachenko would be handled by the Section for Special Analysis.

The outgoing Prime Minister was certainly not to be informed. Because of the merry-go-round associated with a change of government, the incoming Prime Minister was fully occupied appointing ministers and negotiating with other conservative parties. It was not until a month after the government was formed that the chief of S.I.S., along with Gullberg, drove to Rosenbad to inform the incoming Prime Minister. Gullberg had objected to telling the government at all, but the chief of S.I.S. had stood his ground – it was constitutionally indefensible not to inform the Prime Minister. Gullberg used all his eloquence to convince the Prime Minister not to allow information about Zalachenko to pass beyond his own office – there was, he insisted, no need for the Foreign Minister, the Minister of Defence or any other member of the government to be informed.

It had upset Fälldin that an important Soviet agent had sought asylum in Sweden. The Prime Minister had begun to talk about how, for the sake of fairness, he would be obliged to take up the matter at least with the leaders of the other two parties in the coalition government. Gullberg was expecting this objection and played the strongest card he had available. He explained in a low voice that, if that happened, he would be forced to tender his resignation immediately. This was a threat that made an impression on Fälldin. It was intended to convey that the Prime Minister would bear the responsibility if the story ever got out and the Russians sent a death squad to liquidate Zalachenko. And if the person responsible for Zalachenko's safety had seen fit to resign, such a revelation would be a political disaster for the Prime Minister.

Fälldin, still relatively unsure in his role, had acquiesced. He approved a directive that was immediately entered into the secret protocol, making the Section responsible for Zalachenko's safety and debriefing. It also laid down that information about Zalachenko would not leave the Prime Minister's office. By signing this directive, Fälldin had in practice demonstrated that he had been informed, but it also prevented him from ever discussing the matter. In short, he could forget about Zalachenko. But Fälldin had required that one person in his office, a hand-picked state secretary, should also be informed. He would function as a contact person in matters relating to the defector. Gullberg allowed himself to agree to this. He did not anticipate having any problem handling a state secretary.

The chief of S.I.S. was pleased. The Zalachenko matter was now constitutionally secured, which in this case meant that the chief had covered his back. Gullberg was pleased as well. He had managed to create a quarantine, which meant that he would be able to control the flow of information. He alone controlled Zalachenko.

When he got back to Östermalm he sat at his desk and wrote down a list of the people who knew about Zalachenko: himself, Björck, the operations chief of the Section Hans von Rottinger, Assistant Chief Fredrik Clinton, the Section's secretary Eleanor Badenbrink, and two officers whose job it was to compile and analyse any intelligence information that Zalachenko might contribute. Seven individuals who over the coming years would constitute a special Section within the Section. He thought of them as the Inner Circle.

Outside the Section the information was known by the chief of S.I.S., the assistant chief, and the head of Secretariat. Besides them, the Prime Minister and a state secretary. A total of twelve. Never before had a secret of this magnitude been known to such a very small group.

Then Gullberg's expression darkened. The secret was known also to a thirteenth person. Björck had been accompanied at Zalachenko's original reception by a lawyer, Nils Erik Bjurman. To include Bjurman in the special Section would be out of the question. Bjurman was not a real security policeman – he was really no more than a trainee at S.I.S. – and he did not have the requisite experience or skills. Gullberg considered various alternatives and then chose to steer Bjurman carefully out of the picture. He used the threat of imprisonment for life, for treason, if Bjurman were to breathe so much as one syllable about Zalachenko, and at the same time he offered inducements, promises of future assignments, and finally he used flattery to bolster Bjurman's feeling of importance. He arranged for Bjurman to be hired by a well-regarded law firm, who then provided him with a steady stream of assignments to keep him busy. The only problem was that Bjurman was such a mediocre lawyer that he was hardly capable of exploiting his opportunities. He left the firm after ten years and opened his own practice, which eventually became a law office at Odenplan.

Over the following years Gullberg kept Bjurman under discreet but regular surveillance. That was Björck's job. It was not until the end of the '80s that he stopped monitoring Bjurman, at which time the Soviet Union was heading for collapse and Zalachenko had ceased to be a priority.

For the Section, Zalachenko had at first been thought of as a potential breakthrough in the Palme mystery. Palme had accordingly been one of the first subjects that Gullberg discussed with him during the long debriefing.

The hopes for a breakthrough, however, were soon dashed, since Zalachenko had never operated in Sweden and had little knowledge of the country. On the other hand, Zalachenko had heard the rumour of a "Red Jumper", a highly placed Swede – or possibly other Scandinavian politician – who worked for the K.G.B.

Gullberg drew up a list of names that were connected to Palme: Carl Lidbom, Pierre Schori, Sten Andersson, Marita Ulfskog, and a number of others. For the rest of his life, Gullberg would come back again and again to that list, but he never found an answer.

Gullberg was suddenly a big player: he was welcomed with respect in the exclusive club of selected warriors, all known to each other, where the contacts were made through personal friendship and trust, not through official channels and bureaucratic regulations. He met Angleton, and he got to drink whisky at a discreet club in London with the chief of M.I.6. He was one of the elite.

He was never going to be able to tell anyone about his triumphs, not even in posthumous memoirs. And there was the ever-present anxiety that the Enemy would notice his overseas journeys, that he might attract attention, that he might involuntarily lead the Russians to Zalachenko. In that respect Zalachenko was his worst enemy.

During the first year, the defector had lived in an anonymous apartment owned by the Section. He did not exist in any register or in any public document. Those within the Zalachenko unit thought they had plenty of time before they had to plan his future. Not until the spring of 1978 was he given a passport in the name of Karl Axel Bodin, along with a laboriously crafted personal history – a fictitious but verifiable background in Swedish records.

By that time it was already too late. Zalachenko had gone and fucked that stupid whore Agneta Sofia Salander, née Sjölander, and he had heedlessly told her his real name – Zalachenko. Gullberg began to believe that Zalachenko was not quite right in the head. He suspected that the Russian defector *wanted* to be exposed. It was as if he needed a platform. How else to explain the fact that he had been so fucking stupid.

There were whores, there were periods of excessive drinking, and there were incidents of violence and trouble with bouncers and others. On three occasions Zalachenko was arrested by the Swedish police for drunkenness and twice more in connection with fights in bars. Every time the Section had to intervene discreetly and bail him out, seeing to it that documents disappeared and records were altered. Gullberg assigned Björck to babysit the defector almost around the clock. It was not an easy job, but there was no alternative.

Everything could have gone fine. By the early '80s Zalachenko had calmed down and begun to adapt. But he never gave up the whore Salander – and worse, he had become the father of Camilla and Lisbeth Salander.

Lisbeth Salander.

Gullberg pronounced the name with displeasure.

Ever since the girls were nine or ten, he had had a bad feeling about Lisbeth. He did not need a psychiatrist to tell him that she was not normal. Björck had reported that she was vicious and aggressive towards her father and that she seemed to be not in the least afraid of him. She did not say much, but she expressed in a thousand other ways her dissatisfaction with how things stood. She was a problem in the making, but how gigantic this problem would become was something Gullberg could never have imagined in his wildest dreams. What he most feared was that the situation in the Salander family would give rise to a social welfare report that named Zalachenko. Time and again he urged the man to cut his ties and disappear from their lives. Zalachenko would give his word, and then would always break it. He had other whores. He had plenty of whores. But after a few months he was always back with the Salander woman.

That bastard Zalachenko. An intelligence agent who let his cock rule any part of his life was obviously not a good intelligence agent. It was as though the man thought himself above all normal rules. If he could have screwed the whore without beating her up every time, that would have been one thing, but Zalachenko was guilty of repeated assault against his girlfriend. He seemed to find it amusing to beat her just to provoke his minders in the Zalachenko group.

Gullberg had no doubt that Zalachenko was a sick bastard, but he was in no position to pick and choose among defecting G.R.U. agents. He had only one, a man very aware of his value to Gullberg.

The Zalachenko unit had taken on the role of clean-up patrol in that sense. It was undeniable. Zalachenko knew that he could take liberties and that they would resolve whatever problems there might be. When it came to Agneta Sofia Salander, he exploited his hold over them to the maximum.

Not that there were not warnings. When Salander was twelve, she had stabbed Zalachenko. His wounds had not been life-threatening, but he was taken to St Göran's hospital and the group had more of a mop-up job to do than ever. Gullberg then made it crystal clear to Zalachenko that he must never have any more dealings with the Salander family, and Zalachenko had given his promise. A promise he kept for more than six months before he turned up at Agneta Sofia Salander's place and beat her so savagely that she ended up in a nursing home where she would be for the rest of her life.

That the Salander girl would go so far as to make a Molotov cocktail Gullberg had not foreseen. That day had been utter chaos. All manner of investigations loomed, and the future of the Zalachenko unit – of the whole Section even – had hung by a thread. If Salander talked, Zalachenko's cover was at risk, and if that were to happen a number of operations put in place across Europe over the past fifteen years might have to be dismantled. Furthermore, there was a possibility that the Section would be subjected to official scrutiny, and that had to be prevented at all costs.

Gullberg had been consumed with worry. If the Section's archives were opened, a number of practices would be revealed that were not always consistent with the dictates of the constitution, not to mention their years of investigations of Palme and other prominent Social Democrats. Just a few years after Palme's assassination that was still a sensitive issue. Prosecution of Gullberg and several other employees of the Section would inevitably follow. Worse, as like as not, some ambitious scribbler would float the theory that the Section was behind the assassination of Palme, and that in turn would lead to even more damaging speculation and perhaps yet more insistent investigation. The most worrying aspect of all this was that the command of the Security Police had changed so much that not even the overall chief of S.I.S. now knew about the existence of the Section. All contacts with S.I.S. stopped at the desk of the new assistant chief of Secretariat, and he had been on the staff of the Section for ten years.

A mood of acute panic, even fear, overtook the unit. It was in fact Björck who had proposed the solution. Peter Teleborian, a psychiatrist, had become associated with S.I.S.'s department of Counter-Espionage in a quite different case. He had been key as a consultant in connection with Counter-Espionage's surveillance of a suspected industrial spy. At a critical stage of the investigation they needed to know how the person in question might react if subjected to a great deal of stress. Teleborian had offered concrete, definite advice. In the event, S.I.S. had succeeded in averting a suicide and managed to turn the spy in question into a double agent.

After Salander's attack on Zalachenko, Björck had surreptitiously engaged Teleborian as an outside consultant to the Section.

The solution to the problem had been very simple. Karl Axel Bodin would disappear into rehabilitative custody. Agneta Sofia Salander would necessarily disappear into an institution for long-term care. All the police reports on the case were collected up at S.I.S. and transferred by way of the assistant head of Secretariat to the Section.

Teleborian was assistant head physician at St Stefan's psychiatric clinic for children in Uppsala. All that was needed was a legal psychiatric report, which Björck and Teleborian drafted together, and then a brief and, as it turned out, uncontested decision in a district court. It was a question only of how the case was presented. The constitution had nothing to do with it. It was, after all, a matter of national security.

Besides, it was surely pretty obvious that Salander was insane. A few years in an institution would do her nothing but good. Gullberg had approved the operation.

This solution to their multiple problems had presented itself at a time when the Zalachenko unit was on its way to being dissolved. The Soviet Union had ceased to exist and Zalachenko's usefulness was definitively on the wane.

The unit had procured a generous severance package from Security Police funds. They had arranged for him to have the best rehabilitative care, and after six months they had put him on a flight to Spain. From that moment on, they had made it clear to him that Zalachenko and the Section were going their separate ways. It had been one of Gullberg's last responsibilities. One week later he had reached retirement age and handed over to his chosen successor, Fredrik Clinton. Thereafter Gullberg acted only as an adviser in especially sensitive matters. He had stayed in Stockholm for another three years and worked almost daily at the Section, but the number of his assignments decreased, and gradually he disengaged himself. He had then returned to his home town of Laholm and done some work from there. At first he had travelled frequently to Stockholm, but he made these journeys less and less often, and eventually not at all.

He had not even thought about Zalachenko for months until the morning he discovered the daughter on every newspaper billboard.

Gullberg followed the story in a state of awful confusion. It was no accident, of course, that Bjurman had been Salander's guardian; on the other hand he could not see why the old Zalachenko story should surface. Salander was obviously deranged, so it was no surprise that she had killed these people, but that Zalachenko might have any connection to the affair had not dawned on him. The daughter would sooner or later be captured and that would be the end of it. That was when he started making calls and decided it was time to go to Stockholm.

The Section was faced with its worst crisis since the day he had created it.

Zalachenko dragged himself to the toilet. Now that he had crutches, he could move around his room. On Sunday he forced himself through short, sharp training sessions. The pain in his jaw was still excruciating and he could manage only liquid food, but he could get out of his bed and begin to make himself mobile. Having lived so long with a prosthesis he was used enough to crutches. He practised moving noiselessly on them, manoeuvring back and forth around his bed. Every time his right foot touched the floor, a terrible pain shot up his leg.

He gritted his teeth. He thought about the fact that his daughter was very close by. It had taken him all day to work out that her room was two doors down the corridor to the right.

The night nurse had been gone ten minutes, everything was quiet, it was 2.00 in the morning. Zalachenko laboriously got up and fumbled for his crutches. He listened at the door, but heard nothing. He pulled open the door and went into the corridor. He heard faint music from the nurses' station. He made his way to the end of the corridor, pushed open the door, and looked into the empty landing where the lifts were. Going back down the corridor, he stopped at the door to his daughter's room and rested there on his crutches for half a minute, listening.

*

Salander opened her eyes when she heard a scraping sound. It was as though someone was dragging something along the corridor. For a moment there was only silence, and she wondered if she were imagining things. Then she heard the same sound again, moving away. Her uneasiness grew.

Zalachenko was out there somewhere.

She felt fettered to her bed. Her skin itched under the neck brace. She felt an intense desire to move, to get up. Gradually she succeeded in sitting up. That was all she could manage. She sank back on to the pillow.

She ran her hand over the neck brace and located the fastenings that held it in place. She opened them and dropped the brace to the floor. Immediately it was easier to breathe.

What she wanted more than anything was a weapon, and to have the strength to get up and finish the job once and for all.

With difficulty she propped herself up, switched on the night light and looked around the room. She could see nothing that would serve her purpose. Then her eyes fell on a nurses' table by the wall three metres from her bed. Someone had left a pencil there.

She waited until the night nurse had been and gone, which tonight she seemed to be doing about every half hour. Presumably the reduced frequency of the nurse's visits meant that the doctors had decided her condition had improved; over the weekend the nurses had checked on her at least once every fifteen minutes. For herself, she could hardly notice any difference.

When she was alone she gathered her strength, sat up, and swung her legs over the side of the bed. She had electrodes taped to her body to record her pulse and breathing, but the wires stretched in the direction of the pencil. She put her weight on her feet and stood up. Suddenly she swayed, off balance. For a second she felt as though she would faint, but she steadied herself against the bedhead and concentrated her gaze on the table in front of her. She took small, wobbly steps, reached out and grabbed the pencil.

Then she retreated slowly to the bed. She was exhausted.

After a while she managed to pull the sheet and blanket up to her chin. She studied the pencil. It was a plain wooden pencil, newly sharpened. It would make a passable weapon – for stabbing a face or an eye.

She laid it next to her hip and fell asleep.

CHAPTER 6

Monday, 11.iv

Blomkvist got up just after 9.00 and called Eriksson at *Millennium*.

"Good morning, editor-in-chief," he said.

"I'm still in shock that Erika is gone and you want me to take her place. I can't believe she's gone already. Her office is empty."

"Then it would probably be a good idea to spend the day moving in there."

"I feel extremely self-conscious."

"Don't be. Everyone agrees that you're the best choice. And if need be you can always come to me or Christer."

"Thank you for your trust in me."

"You've earned it," Blomkvist said. "Just keep working the way you always do. We'll deal with any problems as and when they crop up."

He told her he was going to be at home all day writing. Eriksson realized that he was reporting in to her the way he had with Berger.

"O.K. Is there anything you want us to do?"

"No. On the contrary . . . if you have any instructions for me, just call. I'm still on the Salander story, trying to find out what's happening there, but for everything else to do with the magazine, the ball's in your court. You make the decisions. You'll have my support if you need it."

"And what if I make a wrong decision?"

"If I see or hear anything out of the ordinary, we'll talk it through. But it would have to be something very unusual. Generally there aren't any decisions that are 100 per cent right or wrong. You'll make your decisions, and they might not be the same ones Erika would have made. If I were to make the decisions they would be different again, but your decisions are the ones that count."

"Alright."

"If you're a good leader then you'll discuss any concerns with the others. First with Henry and Christer, then with me, and we'll raise any awkward problems at the editorial meetings."

"I'll do my best."

"Good luck."

He sat down on the sofa in the living room with his iBook on his lap and worked without any breaks all day. When he was finished, he had a rough draft of two articles totalling twenty-one pages. That part of the story focused on the deaths of Svensson and Johansson – what they were working on, why they were killed, and who the killer was. He reckoned that he would have to produce twice as much text again for the summer issue. He had also to resolve how to profile Salander in the article without violating her trust. He knew things about her that she would never want published.

Gullberg had a single slice of bread and a cup of black coffee in Frey's café. Then he took a taxi to Artillerigatan in Östermalm. At 9.15 he introduced himself on the entry phone and was buzzed inside. He took the lift to the seventh floor, where he was received by Birger Wadensjöö, the new chief of the Section.

Wadensjöö had been one of the latest recruits to the Section around the time Gullberg retired. He wished that the decisive Fredrik was still there. Clinton had succeeded Gullberg and was the chief of the Section until 2002, when diabetes and coronary artery disease had forced him into retirement. Gullberg did not have a clear sense of what Wadensjöö was made of.

"Welcome, Evert," Wadensjöö said, shaking hands with his former chief. "It's good of you to take the time to come in."

"Time is more or less all I have," Gullberg said.

"You know how it goes. I wish we had the leisure to stay in touch with faithful old colleagues."

Gullberg ignored the insinuation. He turned left into his old office and sat at the round conference table by the window. He assumed it was Wadensjöö who was responsible for the Chagall and Mondrian reproductions. In his day plans of *Kronan* and *Wasa* had hung on the walls. He had always dreamed about the sea, and he was in fact a naval officer, although he had spent only a few brief months at sea during his military service. There were computers now, but otherwise the room looked almost exactly as when he had left. Wadensjöö poured coffee.

"The others are on their way," he said. "I thought we could have a few words first."

"How many in the Section are still here from my day?"

"Apart from me . . . only Otto Hallberg and Georg Nyström are still here. Hallberg is retiring this year, and Nyström is turning sixty. Otherwise it's new recruits. You've probably met some of them before."

"How many are working for the Section today?"

"We've reorganized a bit."

"And?"

"There are seven full-timers. So we've cut back. But there's a total of thirty-one employees of the Section within S.I.S. Most of them never come here. They take care of their normal jobs and do some discreet moonlighting for us should the need or opportunity arise."

"Thirty-one employees."

"Plus the seven here. You were the one who created the system, after all. We've just fine-tuned it. Today we have what's called an internal and an external organization. When we recruit somebody, they're given a leave of absence for a time to go to our school. Hallberg is in charge of training, which is six weeks for the basics. We do it out at the Naval School. Then they go back to their regular jobs in S.I.S., but now they're working for us."

"I see."

"It's an excellent system. Most of our employees have no idea of the others' existence. And here in the Section we function principally as report recipients. The same rules apply as in your day. We have to be a single-level organization."

"Have you an operations unit?"

Wadensjöö frowned. In Gullberg's day the Section had a small operations unit consisting of four people under the command of the shrewd Hans von Rottinger.

"Well, not exactly. Von Rottinger died five years ago. We have a younger talent who does some field work, but usually we use someone from the external organization if necessary. But of course things have become more complicated technically, for example when we need to arrange a telephone tap or enter an apartment. Nowadays there are alarms and other devices everywhere."

Gullberg nodded. "Budget?"

"We have about eleven million a year total. A third goes to salaries, a third to overheads, and a third to operations."

"So the budget has shrunk."

"A little. But we have fewer people, which means that the operations budget has actually increased."

"Tell me about our relationship to S.I.S."

Wadensjöö shook his head. "The chief of Secretariat and the chief of Budget belong to us. Formally, of course, the chief of Secretariat is the only one who has insight into our activities. We're so secret that we don't exist. But in practice two assistant chiefs know of our existence. They do their best to ignore anything they hear about us."

"Which means that if problems arise, the present S.I.S. leadership will have an unpleasant surprise. What about the defence leadership and the government?"

"We cut off the defence leadership some ten years ago. And governments come and go."

"So if the balloon goes up, we're on our own?"

Wadensjöö nodded. "That's the drawback with this arrangement. The advantages are obvious. But our assignments have also changed. There's a new *realpolitik* in Europe since the Soviet Union collapsed. Our work is less and less about identifying spies. It's about terrorism, and about evaluating the political suitability of individuals in sensitive positions."

"That's what it was always about."

There was a knock at the door. Gullberg looked up to see a smartly dressed man of about sixty and a younger man in jeans and a tweed jacket.

"Come in . . . Evert Gullberg, this is Jonas Sandberg. He's been working here for four years and is in charge of operations. He's the one I told you about. And Georg Nyström you know."

"Hello, Georg," Gullberg said.

They all shook hands. Then Gullberg turned to Sandberg.

"So where do you come from?"

"Most recently from Göteborg," Sandberg said lightly. "I went to see him."

"Zalachenko?"

Sandberg nodded.

"Have a seat, gentlemen," Wadensjöö said.

"Björck," Gullberg said, frowning when Wadensjöö lit a cigarillo. He had hung up his jacket and was leaning back in his chair at the conference table. Wadensjöö glanced at Gullberg and was struck by how thin the old man had become.

"He was arrested for violation of the prostitution laws last Friday," Nyström said. "The matter has gone to court, but in effect he confessed and slunk home with his tail between his legs. He lives out in Smådalarö, but he's on disability leave. The press haven't picked up on it yet."

"He was once one of the very best we had here in the Section," Gullberg said. "He played a key role in the Zalachenko affair. What's happened to him since I retired?"

"Björck is probably one of the very few internal colleagues who left the Section and went back to external operations. He was out flitting around even in your day."

"Well, I do recall that he needed a little rest and wanted to expand his horizons. He was on leave of absence from the Section for two years in the '80s when he worked as intelligence attaché. He had worked like a fiend with Zalachenko, practically around the clock from 1976 on, and I thought that he needed a break. He was gone from 1985 to 1987, when he came back here."

"You could say that he quit the Section in 1994 when he went over to the external organization. In 1996 he became assistant chief of the Immigration Division and ended up in a stressful position. His official duties took up a great deal of his time. Naturally he has stayed in contact with the Section throughout, and I can also say that we had conversations with him about once a month until recently."

"So he's ill?"

"It's nothing serious, but very painful. He has a slipped disc. He's had recurring trouble with it over the past few years. Two years ago he was on sick leave for four months. And then he was taken ill again in August last year. He was supposed to start work again at new year, but his sick leave was extended and now it's a question of waiting for an operation."

"And he spent his sick leave running around with prostitutes?" Gullberg said.

"Yes. He's not married, and his dealings with whores appear to have been going on for many years, if I've understood correctly," said Sandberg, who had been silent for almost half an hour. "I've read Dag Svensson's manuscript."

"I see. But can anyone explain to me what actually happened?"

"As far as we can tell, it was Björck who set this whole mess rolling.

How else can we explain the report from 1991 ending up in the hands of Advokat Bjurman?"

"Another man who spends his time with prostitutes?" Gullberg said.

"Not as far as we know, and he wasn't mentioned in Svensson's material. He was, however, Lisbeth Salander's guardian."

Wadensjöö sighed. "You could say it was my fault. You and Björck arrested Salander in 1991, when she was sent to the psychiatric hospital. We expected her to be away for much longer, but she became acquainted with a lawyer, Advokat Palmgren, who managed to spring her loose. She was then placed with a foster family. By that time you had retired."

"And then what happened?"

"We kept an eye on her. In the meantime her twin sister, Camilla, was placed in a foster home in Uppsala. When they were seventeen, Lisbeth started digging into her past. She was looking for Zalachenko, and she went through every public register she could find. Somehow – we're not sure how it happened – she found out that her sister knew where Zalachenko was."

"Was it true?"

Wadensjöö shrugged. "I have no idea. The sisters had not seen each other for several years when Lisbeth Salander ran Camilla to ground and tried to persuade her to tell her what she knew. It ended in a violent argument and a spectacular fight between the sisters."

"Then what?"

"We kept close track of Lisbeth during those months. We had also informed Camilla that her sister was violent and mentally ill. She was the one who got in touch with us after Lisbeth's unexpected visit, and thereafter we increased our surveillance of her."

"So the sister was your informant?"

"Camilla was mortally afraid of her sister. Lisbeth had aroused attention in other quarters as well. She had several run-ins with people from the social welfare agency, and in our estimation she still represented a threat to Zalachenko's anonymity. Then there was the incident in the tunnelbana."

"She attacked a paedophile—"

"Precisely. She was obviously prone to violence and mentally disturbed. We thought that it would be best for all concerned if she disappeared into some institution again and availed herself of the opportunities there, so to speak. Clinton and von Rottinger were the ones who took the lead. They engaged the psychiatrist Teleborian again and through a representative filed a request in the district court to get her institutionalized for a second time. Palmgren stood up for Salander, and against all odds the court decided to follow his recommendation – so long as she was placed under guardianship."

"But how did Bjurman get involved?"

"Palmgren had a stroke in the autumn of 2002. We still flag Salander for monitoring whenever she turns up in any database, and I saw to it that Bjurman became her new guardian. Bear in mind that he had no clue she was Zalachenko's daughter. The brief was simply for Bjurman to sound the alarm if she started blabbing about Zalachenko."

"Bjurman was an idiot. He should never have been allowed to have anything to do with Zalachenko, even less with his daughter." Gullberg looked at Wadensjöö. "That was a serious mistake."

"I know," Wadensjöö said. "But he seemed the right choice at the time. I never would have dreamed that—"

"Where's the sister today? Camilla Salander."

"We don't know. When she was nineteen she packed her bag and ran away from her foster family. We haven't found hide nor hair of her since."

"O.K., go on . . ."

"I have a man in the regular police who has spoken with Prosecutor Ekström," Sandberg said. "The officer running the investigation, Inspector Bublanski, thinks that Bjurman raped Salander."

Gullberg looked at Sandberg with blank astonishment.

"Raped?" he said.

"Bjurman had a tattoo across his belly which read *I am a sadistic pig, a pervert, and a rapist.*"

Sandberg put a colour photograph from the autopsy on the table. Gullberg stared at it with distaste.

"Zalachenko's daughter is supposed to have given him that?"

"It's hard to find another explanation. And she's not known for being a shrinking violet. She spectacularly kicked the shit out of two complete thugs from Svavelsjö M.C."

"Zalachenko's daughter," Gullberg repeated. He turned to Wadensjöö. "You know what? I think you ought to recruit her for the Section."

Wadensjöö looked so startled that Gullberg quickly explained that he was joking.

"O.K. Let's take it as a working hypothesis that Bjurman raped her and that she somehow took her revenge. What else?"

"The only one who could tell us exactly what happened, of course, is Bjurman, and he's dead. But the thing is, he shouldn't have had a clue that she was Zalachenko's daughter; it's not in any public records. But somehow, somewhere along the way, Bjurman discovered the connection."

"But, Goddamnit Wadensjöö! *She* knew who her father was and could have told Bjurman at any time."

"I know. We . . . that is, *I* simply wasn't thinking straight."

"That is unforgivably incompetent," Gullberg said.

"I've kicked myself a hundred times about it. But Bjurman was one of the very few people who knew of Zalachenko's existence and my thought was that it would be better if he discovered that she was Zalachenko's daughter rather than some other unknown guardian. She could have told anyone at all."

Gullberg pulled on his earlobe. "Alright . . . go on."

"It's all hypothetical," Nyström said. "But our supposition is that Bjurman assaulted Salander and that she struck back and did that . . ." He pointed at the tattoo in the autopsy photograph.

"Her father's daughter," Gullberg said. There was more than a trace of admiration in his voice.

"With the result that Bjurman made contact with Zalachenko, hoping to get rid of the daughter. As we know, Zalachenko had good reason to hate the girl. And he gave the contract to Svavelsjö M.C. and this Niedermann that he hangs out with."

"But how did Bjurman get in touch—" Gullberg fell silent. The answer was obvious.

"Björck," Wadensjöö said. "Björck gave him the contact."

"Damn," Gullberg said.

In the morning two nurses had come to change her bedlinen. They had found the pencil.

"Oops. How did this get here?" one of them said, putting the pencil in her pocket. Salander looked at her with murder in her eyes.

She was once more without a weapon, but she was too weak to protest.

Her headache was unbearable and she was given strong painkillers. Her left shoulder stabbed like a knife if she moved carelessly or tried to shift her weight. She lay on her back with the brace around her neck. It was supposed to be left on for a few more days until the wound in her head began to heal. On Sunday she had a temperature of 102. Dr Endrin could tell that there was infection in her body. Salander did not need a thermometer to work that out.

She realized that once again she was confined to an institutional bed, even though this time there was no strap holding her down. That would have been unnecessary. She could not sit up even, let alone leave the room.

At lunchtime on Monday she had a visit from Dr Jonasson.

"Hello. Do you remember me?"

She shook her head.

"I was the one who woke you after surgery. I operated on you. I just wanted to hear how you're doing and if everything is going well."

Salander looked at him, her eyes wide. It should have been obvious that everything was not going well.

"I heard you took off your neck brace last night."

She acknowledged as much with her eyes.

"We put the neck brace on for a reason – you have to keep your head still for the healing process to get started." He looked at the silent girl. "O.K.," he said at last. "I just wanted to check on you."

He was at the door when he heard her voice.

"It's Jonasson, right?"

He turned and smiled at her in surprise. "That's right. If you remember my name then you must have been more alert than I thought."

"And you were the one who operated to remove the bullet?"

"That's right."

"Please tell me how I'm doing. I can't get a sensible answer from anyone."

He went back to her bedside and looked her in the eye.

"You were lucky. You were shot in the head, but the bullet did not, I believe, injure any vital areas. The risk you are running is that you could have bleeding in your brain. That's why we want you to stay still. You have an infection in your body. The wound in your shoulder seems to be the cause. It's possible that you'll need another operation – on your shoulder – if we can't arrest the infection with antibiotics. You are going to have some painful times ahead while your body heals. But as things look now, I'm optimistic that you'll make a full recovery."

"Can this cause brain damage?"

He hesitated before nodding. "Yes, there is that possibility. But all

the signs indicate that you made it through fine. There's also a possibility that you'll develop scar tissue in your brain, and that might cause
trouble . . . for instance, you might develop epilepsy or some other
problem. But to be honest, it's all speculation. Right now, things look
good. You're healing. And if problems crop up along the way, we'll
deal with them. Is that a clear enough answer?"

She shut her eyes to say yes. "How long do I have to lie here like this?"

"You mean in the hospital? It will be at the least a couple of weeks
before we can let you go."

"No, I mean how long before I can get up and start walking and
moving around?"

"That depends on how the healing progresses. But count on two
weeks before we can start you on some sort of physical therapy."

She gave him a long look. "You wouldn't happen to have a cigarette, would you?" she said.

Dr Jonasson burst out laughing and shook his head. "Sorry. There's
no smoking allowed in the hospital. But I can see to it that you get a
nicotine patch or some gum."

She thought for a moment before she looked at him again. "How's
the old bastard doing?"

"Who? You mean—"

"The one who came in the same time as I did."

"No friend of yours, I presume. Well, he's going to survive and he's
been up walking around on crutches. He's actually in worse shape than
you are, and he has a very painful facial wound. As I understood it,
you slammed an axe into his head."

"He tried to kill me," Salander said in a low voice.

"That doesn't sound good. I have to go. Do you want me to come
back and look in on you again?"

Salander thought for a moment, then she signalled yes. When he
was gone she stared at the ceiling. *Zalachenko has been given crutches.
That was the sound I heard last night.*

Sandberg, the youngest person at the meeting, was sent out to get some
food. He came back with sushi and light beer and passed the food
around the conference table. Gullberg felt a thrill of nostalgia. This is
just the way it was in his day, when some operation went into a critical
phase and they had to work around the clock.

III

The difference, he observed, was possibly that in his day there was nobody who would have come up with the wild idea of ordering raw fish. He wished Sandberg had ordered Swedish meatballs with mashed potatoes and lingonberries. On the other hand he was not really hungry, so he pushed the sushi aside. He ate a piece of bread and drank some mineral water.

They continued the discussion over their meal. They had to decide what to do. The situation was urgent.

"I never knew Zalachenko," Wadensjöö said. "What was he like?"

"Much as he is today, I assume," Gullberg said. "Phenomenally intelligent, with a damn near photographic memory. But in my opinion he's a pig. And not quite right in the head, I should think."

"Jonas, you talked to him yesterday. What's your take on this?" Wadensjöö said.

Sandberg put down his chopsticks.

"He's got us over a barrel. I've already told you about his ultimatum. Either we make the whole thing disappear, or he cracks the Section wide open."

"How the hell do we make something disappear that's been plastered all over the media?" Nyström said.

"It's not a question of what we can or can't do. It's a question of his need to control us," Gullberg said.

"Would he, in your opinion, talk to the press?" Wadensjöö said.

Gullberg hesitated. "It's almost impossible to answer that question. Zalachenko doesn't make empty threats, and he's going to do what's best for him. In that respect he's predictable. If it benefits him to talk to the media . . . if he thought he could get an amnesty or a reduced sentence, then he'd do it. Or if he felt betrayed and wanted to get even."

"Regardless of the consequences?"

"Especially regardless of the consequences. For him the point is to be seen to be tougher than all of us."

"If Zalachenko were to talk, it's not certain that anyone would believe him. And to prove anything they'd have to get hold of our archives."

"Do you want to take the chance? Let's say Zalachenko talks. Who's going to talk next? What do we do if Björck signs an affidavit confirming his story? And Clinton, sitting at his dialysis machine . . . what would happen if he turned religious and felt bitter about everything and everyone? What if he wanted to make a confession? Believe me, if anyone starts talking, it's the end of the Section."

"So . . . what should we do?"

Silence settled over the table. It was Gullberg who took up the thread.

"There are several parts to this problem. First of all, we can agree on what the consequences would be if Zalachenko talked. The entire legal system would come crashing down on our heads. We would be demolished. My guess is that several employees of the Section would go to prison."

"Our activity is completely legal . . . we're actually working under the auspices of the government."

"Spare me the bullshit," Gullberg said. "You know as well as I do that a loosely formulated document that was written in the mid-'60s isn't worth a damn today. I don't think any one of us could even imagine what would happen if Zalachenko talked."

Silence descended once again.

"So our starting point has to be to persuade Zalachenko to keep his mouth shut," Nyström said at last.

"And to be able to persuade him to keep his mouth shut, we have to be able to offer him something substantial. The problem is that he's unpredictable. He would scorch us out of sheer malice. We have to think about how we can keep him in check."

"And what about his demand . . . ," Sandberg said, "that we make the whole thing disappear and put Salander back in an asylum?"

"Salander we can handle. It's Zalachenko who's the problem. But that leads us to the second part – damage control. Teleborian's report from 1991 has been leaked, and it's potentially as serious a threat as Zalachenko."

Nyström cleared his throat. "As soon as we realized that the report was out and in the hands of the police, I took certain measures. I went through Forelius, our lawyer in S.I.S., and he got hold of the Prosecutor General. The P.G. ordered the report confiscated from the police – it's not to be disseminated or copied."

"How much does the P.G. know?" Gullberg said.

"Not a thing. He's acting on an official request from S.I.S. It's classified material and the P.G. has no alternative."

"Who in the police has read the report?"

"There were two copies which were read by Bublanski, his colleague

113

Inspector Modig, and finally the preliminary investigation leader, Richard Ekström. We can assume that another two police officers . . . ," Nyström leafed through his notes, " . . . that Curt Andersson and Jerker Holmberg at least, are aware of the contents."

"So, four police officers and one prosecutor. What do we know about them?"

"Prosecutor Ekström, forty-two, regarded as a rising star. He's been an investigator at Justice and has handled a number of cases that got a fair bit of attention. Zealous. P.R.-savvy. Careerist."

"Social Democrat?" Gullberg said.

"Probably. But not active."

"So Bublanski is leading the investigation. I saw him in a press conference on T.V. He didn't seem comfortable in front of the cameras."

"He's older and has an exceptional record, but he also has a reputation for being crusty and obstinate. He's Jewish and quite conservative."

"And the woman . . . who's she?"

"Sonja Modig. Married, thirty-nine, two kids. Has advanced rather quickly in her career. I talked to Teleborian, who described her as emotional. She asks questions non-stop."

"Next."

"Andersson is a tough customer. He's thirty-eight and comes from the gangs unit in Söder. He landed in the spotlight when he shot dead some hooligan a couple of years ago. Acquitted of all charges, according to the report. He was the one Bublanski sent to arrest Björck."

"I see. Keep in mind that he shot someone dead. If there's any reason to cast doubt on Bublanski's group, we can always single him out as a rogue policeman. I assume we still have relevant media contacts. And the last guy?"

"Holmberg, fifty-five. Comes from Norrland and is in fact a specialist in crime scene investigation. He was offered supervisory training a few years ago but turned it down. He seems to like his job."

"Are any of them politically active?"

"No. Holmberg's father was a city councillor for the Centre Party in the '70s."

"It seems to be a modest group. We can assume they're fairly tight-knit. Could we isolate them somehow?"

"There's a fifth officer involved," Nyström said. "Hans Faste, forty-seven. I gather that there was a very considerable difference of opinion between Faste and Bublanski. So much so that Faste took sick leave."

"What do we know about him?"

"I get mixed reactions when I ask. He has an exemplary record with no real criticisms. A pro. But he's tricky to deal with. The disagreement with Bublanski seems to have been about Salander."

"In what way?"

"Faste appears to have become obsessed by one newspaper story about a lesbian Satanist gang. He really doesn't like Salander and seems to regard her existence as a personal insult. He may himself be behind half of the rumours. I was told by a former colleague that he has difficulty working with women."

"Interesting," Gullberg said slowly. "Since the newspapers have already written about a lesbian gang, it would make sense to continue promoting that story. It won't exactly bolster Salander's credibility."

"But the officers who've read Björck's report are a big problem," Sandberg said. "Is there any way we can isolate them?"

Wadensjöö lit another cigarillo. "Well, Ekström is the head of the preliminary investigation . . ."

"But Bublanski's leading it," Nyström said.

"Yes, but he can't go against an administrative decision." Wadensjöö turned to Gullberg. "You have more experience than I do, but this whole story has so many different threads and connections . . . It seems to me that it would be wise to get Bublanski and Modig away from Salander."

"That's good, Wadensjöö," Gullberg said. "And that's exactly what we're going to do. Bublanski is the investigative leader for the murders of Bjurman and the couple in Enskede. Salander is no longer a suspect. Now it's all about this German, Ronald Niedermann. Bublanski and his team have to focus on Niedermann. Salander is not their assignment any more. Then there's the investigation at Nykvarn . . . three cold-case killings. And there's a connection to Niedermann there too. That investigation is presently allocated to Södertälje, but it ought to be brought into a single investigation. That way Bublanski would have his hands full for a while. And who knows? Maybe he'll catch Niedermann. Meanwhile, Hans Faste . . . do you think he might come back on duty? He sounds like the right man to investigate the allegations against Salander."

"I see what you're thinking," Wadensjöö said. " It's all about getting Ekström to split the two cases. But that's only if we can control Ekström."

"That shouldn't be such a big problem," Gullberg said. He glanced at Nyström, who nodded.

"I can take care of Ekström," he said. "I'm guessing that he's sitting there wishing he'd never heard of Zalachenko. He turned over Björck's report as soon as S.I.S. asked him for it, and he's agreed to comply with every request that may have a bearing on national security."

"What do you have in mind?" Wadensjöö said.

"Allow me to manufacture a scenario," Nyström said. "I assume that we're going to tell him in a subtle way what he has to do to avoid an abrupt end to his career."

"The most serious problem is going to be the third part," Gullberg said. "The police didn't get hold of Björck's report by themselves . . . they got it from a journalist. And the press, as you are all aware, is a real problem here. *Millennium*."

Nyström turned a page his notebook. "Mikael Blomkvist."

Everyone around the table had heard of the Wennerström affair and knew the name.

"Svensson, the journalist who was murdered, was freelancing at *Millennium*. He was working on a story about sex trafficking. That was how he lit upon Zalachenko. It was Blomkvist who found Svensson and his girlfriend's bodies. In addition, Blomkvist knows Salander and has always believed in her innocence."

"How the hell can he know Zalachenko's daughter . . . that sounds like too big a coincidence."

"We don't think it is a coincidence," Wadensjöö said. "We believe that Salander is in some way the link between all of them, but we don't yet know how."

Gullberg drew a series of concentric circles on his notepad. At last he looked up.

"I have to think about this for a while. I'm going for a walk. We'll meet again in an hour."

Gullberg's excursion lasted nearly three hours. He had walked for only about ten minutes before he found a café that served many unfamiliar types of coffee. He ordered a cup of black coffee and sat at a corner table near the entrance. He spent a long time thinking things over, trying to dissect the various aspects of their dilemma. Occasionally he would jot down notes in a pocket diary.

After an hour and a half a plan had begun to take shape.

It was not a perfect plan, but after weighing all the options he concluded that the problem called for a drastic solution.

As luck would have it, the human resources were available. It was doable.

He got up to find a telephone booth and called Wadensjöö.

"We'll have to postpone the meeting a bit longer," he said. "There's something I have to do. Can we meet again at 2.00 p.m.?"

Gullberg went down to Stureplan and hailed a taxi. He gave the driver an address in the suburb of Bromma. When he was dropped off, he walked south one street and rang the doorbell of a small, semi-detached house. A woman in her forties opened the door.

"Good afternoon. I'm looking for Fredrik Clinton."

"Who should I say is here?"

"An old colleague."

The woman nodded and showed him into the living room, where Clinton rose slowly from the sofa. He was only sixty-eight, but he looked much older. His ill health had taken a heavy toll.

"Gullberg," Clinton said in surprise.

For a long moment they stood looking at each other. Then the two old agents embraced.

"I never thought I'd see you again," Clinton said. He pointed to the front page of the evening paper, which had a photograph of Niedermann and the headline POLICE KILLER HUNTED IN DENMARK. "I assume that's what's brought you out here."

"How are you?"

"I'm sick," Clinton said.

"I can see that."

"If I don't get a new kidney I'm not long for this world. And the likelihood of my getting one in this people's republic is pretty slim."

The woman came to the living-room doorway and asked if Gullberg would like anything.

"A cup of coffee, thank you," he said. When she was gone he turned to Clinton. "Who's that?"

"My daughter."

It was fascinating that despite the collegial atmosphere they had shared for so many years at the Section, hardly anyone socialized with each other in their free time. Gullberg knew the most minute character traits, strengths and weaknesses of all his colleagues, but he had only a vague notion of their family lives. Clinton had probably been Gullberg's closest colleague for twenty years. He knew that he had been married and had children, but he did not know the daughter's name, his late wife's name, or even where Clinton usually spent his holidays. It was as if everything outside the Section were sacred, not to be discussed.

"What can I do for you?" asked Clinton.

"Can I ask you what you think of Wadensjöö."

Clinton shook his head. "I don't want to get into it."

"That's not what I asked. You know him. He worked with you for ten years."

Clinton shook his head again. "He's the one running the Section today. What I think is no longer of any interest."

"Can he handle it?"

"He's no idiot."

"But?"

"He's an analyst. Extremely good at puzzles. Instinctual. A brilliant administrator who balanced the budget, and did it in a way we didn't think was possible."

Gullberg nodded. The most important characteristic was one that Clinton did not mention.

"Are you ready to come back to work?"

Clinton looked up. He hesitated for a long time.

"Evert . . . I spend nine hours every other day on a dialysis machine at the hospital. I can't go up stairs without gasping for breath. I simply have no energy. No energy at all."

"I need you. One last operation."

"I can't."

"Yes, you can. And you can still spend nine hours every other day on dialysis. You can take the lift instead of going up the stairs. I'll even arrange for somebody to carry you back and forth on a stretcher if necessary. It's your mind I need."

Clinton sighed. "Tell me."

"Right now we're confronted with an exceptionally complicated situation that requires operational expertise. Wadensjöö has a young kid, still wet behind the ears, called Jonas Sandberg. He's the entire operations department and I don't think Wadensjöö has the drive to do what needs to be done. He might be a genius at finessing the budget, but he's afraid to make operational decisions, and he's afraid to get the Section involved in the necessary field work."

Clinton gave him a feeble smile.

"The operation has to be carried out on two separate fronts. One part concerns Zalachenko. I have to get him to listen to reason, and I think I know how I'm going to do it. The second part has to be handled from here, in Stockholm. The problem is that there isn't anyone in the Section who can actually run it. I need you to take command. One last job. Sandberg and Nyström will do the legwork, you control the operation."

"You don't understand what you're asking."

"Yes, I do. But you're going to have to make up your mind whether to take on the assignment or not. Either we ancients step in and do our bit, or the Section will cease to exist a few weeks from now."

Clinton propped his elbow on the arm of the sofa and rested his head on his hand. He thought about it for two minutes.

"Tell me your plan," he said at last.

Gullberg and Clinton talked for a long time.

Wadensjöö stared in disbelief when Gullberg returned at 2.57 with Clinton in tow. Clinton looked like . . . a skeleton. He seemed to have difficulty breathing; he kept one hand on Gullberg's shoulder.

"What in the world . . ." Wadensjöö said.

"Let's get the meeting moving again," Gullberg said, briskly.

They settled themselves again around the table in Wadensjöö's office. Clinton sank silently on to the chair that was offered.

"You all know Fredrik Clinton," Gullberg said.

"Indeed," Wadensjöö said. "The question is, what's he doing here?"

"Clinton has decided to return to active duty. He'll be leading the Section's operations department until the present crisis is over," Gullberg raised a hand to forestall Wadensjöö's objections. "Clinton is tired. He's going to need assistance. He has to go regularly to the hospital for dialysis. Wadensjöö, assign two personal assistants to help him with all the practical matters. But let me make this quite clear . . . with regards to this affair it's Clinton who will be making the operational decisions."

He paused for a moment. No-one voiced any objections.

"I have a plan. I think we can handle this matter successfully, but we're going to have to act fast so that we don't squander the opportunity," he said. "It depends on how decisive you can be in the Section these days."

"Let's hear it." Wadensjöö said.

"First of all, we've already discussed the police. This is what we're going to do. We'll try to isolate them in a lengthy investigation, side-tracking them into the search for Niedermann. That will be Nyström's task. Whatever happens, Niedermann is of no importance. We'll arrange for Faste to be assigned to investigate Salander."

"That may not be such a bright idea," Nyström said. "Why don't I just go and have a discreet talk with Prosecutor Ekström?"

"And if he gets difficult—"

"I don't think he will. He's ambitious and on the lookout for anything that will benefit his career. I might be able to use some leverage if I need to. He would hate to be dragged into any sort of scandal."

"Good. Stage two is *Millennium* and Mikael Blomkvist. That's why Clinton has returned to duty. This will require extraordinary measures."

"I don't think I'm going to like this," Wadensjöö said.

"Probably not. But *Millennium* can't be manipulated in the same straightforward way. On the other hand, the magazine is a threat because of one thing only: Björck's 1991 police report. I presume that the report now exists in two places, possibly three. Salander found the report, but Blomkvist somehow got hold of it. Which means that there was some degree of contact between the two of them while Salander was on the run."

Clinton held up a finger and uttered his first words since he had arrived.

"It also tells us something about the character of our adversary. Blomkvist is not afraid to take risks. Remember the Wennerström affair."

Gullberg nodded. "Blomkvist gave the report to his editor-in-chief, Erika Berger, who in turn messengered it to Bublanski. So she's read it too. We have to assume that they made a copy for safekeeping. I'm guessing that Blomkvist has a copy and that there's one at the editorial offices."

"That sounds reasonable," Wadensjöö said.

"*Millennium* is a monthly, so they won't be publishing it tomorrow. We've got a little time – find out exactly how long before the next issue is published – but we have to confiscate both those copies. And here we can't go through the Prosecutor General."

"I understand."

"So we're talking about an operation, getting into Blomkvist's apartment and *Millennium*'s offices. Can you handle that, Jonas?"

Sandberg glanced at Wadensjöö.

"Evert . . . you have to understand that . . . we don't do things like that any more," Wadensjöö said. "It's a new era. We deal more with computer hacking and electronic surveillance and such like. We don't have the resources for what you'd think of as an operations unit."

Gullberg leaned forward. "Wadensjöö, you're going to have to sort out some resources pretty damn fast. Hire some people. Hire a bunch of skinheads from the Yugo mafia who can whack Blomkvist over the head if necessary. But those two copies have to be recovered. If they don't have the copies, they don't have the evidence. If you can't manage a simple job like that then you might as well sit here with your thumb up your backside until the constitutional committee comes knocking on your door."

Gullberg and Wadensjöö glared at each other for a long moment.

"I can handle it," Sandberg said suddenly.

"Are you sure?"

Sandberg nodded.

"Good. Starting now, Clinton is your boss. He's the one you take your orders from."

Sandberg nodded his agreement.

"It's going to involve a lot of surveillance," Nyström said. "I can suggest a few names. We have a man in the external organization, Mårtensson – he works as a bodyguard in S.I.S. He's fearless and shows promise. I've been considering bringing him in here. I've even thought that he could take my place one day."

"That sounds good," Gullberg said. "Clinton can decide."

"I'm afraid there might be a third copy," Nyström said.

"Where?"

"This afternoon I found out that Salander has taken on a lawyer. Her name is Annika Giannini. She's Blomkvist's sister."

Gullberg pondered this news. "You're right. Blomkvist will have given his sister a copy. He must have. In other words, we have to keep tabs on all three of them – Berger, Blomkvist and Giannini – until further notice."

"I don't think we have to worry about Berger. There was a report today that she's going to be the new editor-in-chief at *Svenska Morgon-Posten*. She's finished with *Millennium*."

"Check her out anyway. As far as *Millennium* is concerned, we're going to need telephone taps and bugs in everyone's homes, and at the offices. We have to check their email. We have to know who they meet and who they talk to. And we would very much like to know what strategy they're planning. Above all we have to get those copies of the report. A whole lot of stuff, in other words."

Wadensjöö sounded doubtful. "Evert, you're asking us to run an operation against an influential magazine and the editor-in-chief of *S.M.P.* That's just about the riskiest thing we could do."

"Understand this: you have no choice. Either you roll up your sleeves or it's time for somebody else to take over here."

The challenge hung like a cloud over the table.

"I think I can handle *Millennium*," Sandberg said at last. "But none of this solves the basic problem. What do we do with Zalachenko? If he talks, anything else we pull off is useless."

"I know. That's my part of the operation," Gullberg said. "I think I have an argument that will persuade Zalachenko to keep his mouth shut. But it's going to take some preparation. I'm leaving for Göteborg later this afternoon."

He paused and looked around the room. Then he fixed his eyes on Wadensjöö.

"Clinton will make the operational decisions while I'm gone," he said.

Not until Monday evening did Dr Endrin decide, in consultation with her colleague Dr Jonasson, that Salander's condition was stable enough for her to have visitors. First, two police inspectors were given fifteen minutes to ask her questions. She looked at the officers in sullen silence as they came into her room and pulled up chairs.

"Hello. My name is Marcus Erlander, Criminal Inspector. I work in the Violent Crimes Division here in Göteborg. This is my colleague Inspector Modig from the Stockholm police."

Salander said nothing. Her expression did not change. She recognized Modig as one of the officers in Bublanski's team. Erlander gave her a cool smile.

"I've been told that you don't generally communicate much with the authorities. Let me put it on record that you do not have to say anything at all. But I would be grateful if you would listen to what we have to say. We have a number of things to discuss with you, but we don't have time to go into them all today. There'll be opportunities later."

Salander still said nothing.

"First of all, I'd like to let you know that your friend Mikael Blomkvist has told us that a lawyer by the name of Annika Giannini is willing to represent you, and that she knows about the case. He says that he already mentioned her name to you in connection with something else. I need you to confirm that this would be your intention. I'd also like to know if you want Giannini to come here to Göteborg, the better to represent you."

Annika Giannini. Blomkvist's sister. He had mentioned her in an email. Salander had not thought about the fact that she would need a lawyer.

"I'm sorry, but I have to insist that you answer the question. A yes or no will be fine. If you say yes, the prosecutor here in Göteborg will contact Advokat Giannini. If you say no, the court will appoint a defence lawyer on your behalf. Which do you prefer?"

Salander considered the choice. She assumed that she really would need a lawyer, but having Kalle Bastard Blomkvist's sister working for her was hard to stomach. On the other hand, some unknown lawyer appointed by the court would probably be worse. She rasped out a single word:

"Giannini."

"Good. Thank you. Now I have a question for you. You don't have to say anything before your lawyer gets here, but this question does not, as far as I can see, affect you or your welfare. The police are looking for a German citizen by the name of Ronald Niedermann, wanted for the murder of a policeman."

Salander frowned. She had no clue as to what had happened after she had swung the axe at Zalachenko's head.

"As far as the Göteborg police are concerned, they are anxious to arrest him as soon as possible. My colleague here would like to question him also in connection with the three recent murders in Stockholm. You should know that you are no longer a suspect in those cases. So we are asking for your help. Do you have any idea . . . can you give us any help at all in finding this man?"

Salander flicked her eyes suspiciously from Erlander to Modig and back.

They don't know that he's my brother.

Then she considered whether she wanted Niedermann caught or not. Most of all she wanted to take him to a hole in the ground in Gosseberga and bury him. Finally she shrugged. Which she should not have done, because pain flew through her left shoulder.

"What day is it today?" she said.

"Monday."

She thought about that. "The first time I heard the name Ronald Niedermann was last Thursday. I tracked him to Gosseberga. I have no idea where he is or where he might go, but he'll try to get out of the country as soon as he can."

"Why would he flee abroad?"

Salander thought about it. "Because while Niedermann was out digging a grave for me, Zalachenko told me that things were getting too hot and that it had already been decided that Niedermann should leave the country for a while."

Salander had not exchanged this many words with a police officer since she was twelve.

"Zalachenko . . . so that's your father?"

Well, at least they had worked that one out. Probably thanks to Kalle Bastard Blomkvist.

"I have to tell you that your father has made a formal accusation to the police stating that you tried to murder him. The case is now at the prosecutor's office, and he has to decide whether to bring charges. But you have already been placed under arrest on a charge of grievous bodily harm, for having struck Zalachenko on the head with an axe."

There was a long silence. Then Modig leaned forward and said in a low voice, "I just want to say that we on the police force don't put much faith in Zalachenko's story. Do have a serious discussion with your lawyer so we can come back later and have another talk."

The detectives stood up.

"Thanks for the help with Niedermann," Erlander said.

Salander was surprised that the officers had treated her in such a correct, almost friendly manner. She thought about what the Modig woman had said. There would be some ulterior motive, she decided.

CHAPTER 7

Monday, 11.iv – Tuesday, 12.iv

At 5.45 p.m. on Monday Blomkvist closed the lid on his iBook and got up from the kitchen table in his apartment on Bellmansgatan. He put on a jacket and walked to Milton Security's offices at Slussen. He took the lift up to the reception on the fourth floor and was immediately shown into a conference room. It was 6.00 p.m. on the dot, but he was the last to arrive.

"Hello, Dragan," he said and shook hands. "Thank you for being willing to host this informal meeting."

Blomkvist looked around the room. There were four others there: his sister, Salander's former guardian Holger Palmgren, Malin Eriksson, and former Criminal Inspector Sonny Bohman, who now worked for Milton Security. At Armansky's instruction Bohman had been following the Salander investigation from the very start.

Palmgren was on his first outing in more than two years. Dr Sivarnandan of the Ersta rehabilitation home had been less than enchanted at the idea of letting him out, but Palmgren himself had insisted. He had come by special transport for the disabled, accompanied by his personal nurse, Johanna Karolina Oskarsson, whose salary was paid from a fund that had been mysteriously established to provide Palmgren with the best possible care. The nurse was sitting in an office next to the conference room. She had brought a book with her. Blomkvist closed the door behind him.

"For those of you who haven't met her before, this is Malin Eriksson, *Millennium*'s editor-in-chief. I asked her to be here because what we're going to discuss will also affect her job."

"O.K.," Armansky said. "Everyone's here. I'm all ears."

Blomkvist stood at Armansky's whiteboard and picked up a marker. He looked around.

"This is probably the craziest thing I've ever been involved with," he said. "When this is all over I'm going to found an association called 'The Knights of the Idiotic Table' and its purpose will be to arrange an annual dinner where we tell stories about Lisbeth Salander. You're all members."

He paused.

"So, this is how things really are," he said, and he began to make a list of headings on Armansky's whiteboard. He talked for a good thirty minutes. Afterwards the discussion went on for almost three hours.

Gullberg sat down next to Clinton when their meeting was over. They spoke in low voices for a few minutes before Gullberg stood up. The old comrades shook hands.

Gullberg took a taxi to Frey's, packed his briefcase and checked out. He took the late afternoon train to Göteborg. He chose first class and had the compartment to himself. When he passed Årstabron he took out a ballpoint pen and a plain paper pad. He thought for a long while and then began to write. He filled half the page before he stopped and tore the sheet off the pad.

Forged documents had never been his department or his expertise, but here the task was simplified by the fact that the letters he was writing would be signed by himself. What complicated the issue was that not a word of what he was writing was true.

By the time the train went through Nyköping he had already discarded a number of drafts, but he was starting to get a line on how the letters should be expressed. When they arrived in Göteborg he had twelve letters he was satisfied with. He made sure he had left clear fingerprints on each sheet.

At Göteborg Central Station he tracked down a photocopier and made copies of the letters. Then he bought envelopes and stamps and posted the letters in a box with a 9.00 p.m. collection.

Gullberg took a taxi to City Hotel on Lorensbergsgatan, where Clinton had already booked a room for him. It was the same hotel Blomkvist had spent the night in several days before. He went straight to his room and sat on the bed. He was completely exhausted and realized that he had eaten only two slices of bread all day. Yet he was not hungry. He undressed, stretched out in bed, and almost at once fell asleep.

Salander woke with a start when she heard the door open. She knew right away that it was not one of the night nurses. She opened her eyes to two narrow slits and saw a silhouette with crutches in the doorway. Zalachenko was watching her in the light that came from the corridor.

Without moving her head she glanced at the digital clock: 3.10 a.m.

She then glanced at the bedside table and saw the water glass. She calculated the distance. She could just reach it without having to move her body.

It would take a very few seconds to stretch out her arm and break off the rim of the glass with a firm rap against the hard edge of the table. It would take half a second to shove the broken edge into Zalachenko's throat if he leaned over her. She looked for other options, but the glass was her only reachable weapon.

She relaxed and waited.

Zalachenko stood in the doorway for two minutes without moving. Then gingerly he closed the door.

She heard the faint scraping of the crutches as he quietly retreated down the corridor.

Five minutes later she propped herself up on her right elbow, reached for the glass, and took a long drink of water. She swung her legs over the edge of the bed and pulled the electrodes off her arms and chest. With an effort she stood up and swayed unsteadily. It took her about a minute to gain control over her body. She hobbled to the door and leaned against the wall to catch her breath. She was in a cold sweat. Then she turned icy with rage.

Fuck you, Zalachenko. Let's end this right here and now.

She needed a weapon.

The next moment she heard quick heels clacking in the corridor.

Shit. The electrodes.

"What in God's name are you doing up?" the night nurse said.

"I had to . . . go . . . to the toilet," Salander said breathlessly.

"Get back into bed at once."

She took Salander's hand and helped her into the bed. Then she got a bedpan.

"When you have to go to the toilet, just ring for us. That's what this button is for."

Blomkvist woke up at 10.30 on Tuesday, showered, put on coffee, and then sat down with his iBook. After the meeting at Milton Security the previous evening, he had come home and worked until 5.00 a.m. The story was beginning at last to take shape. Zalachenko's biography was still vague – all he had was what he had blackmailed Björck to reveal, as well as the handful of details Palmgren had been able to provide. Salander's story was pretty much done. He explained step by step how she had been targeted by a gang of Cold-Warmongers at S.I.S. and locked away in a psychiatric hospital to stop her blowing the gaff on Zalachenko.

He was pleased with what he had written. There were still some holes that he would have to fill, but he knew that he had one hell of a story. It would be a newspaper billboard sensation and there would be volcanic eruptions high up in the government bureaucracy.

He smoked a cigarette while he thought.

He could see two particular gaps that needed attention. One was manageable. He had to deal with Teleborian, and he was looking forward to that assignment. When he was finished with him, the renowned children's psychiatrist would be one of the most detested men in Sweden. That was one thing.

The second thing was more complicated.

The men who conspired against Salander – he thought of them as the Zalachenko club – were inside the Security Police. He knew one, Gunnar Björck, but Björck could not possibly be the only man responsible. There had to be a group . . . a division or unit of some sort. There must be chiefs, operations managers. There had to be a budget. But he had no idea how to go about identifying these people, where even to start. He had only the vaguest notion of how Säpo was organized.

On Monday he had begun his research by sending Cortez to the second-hand bookshops on Södermalm, to buy every book which in any way dealt with the Security Police. Cortez had come to his apartment in the afternoon with six books.

Espionage in Sweden by Mikael Rosquist (Tempus, 1988); *Säpo Chief 1962–1970* by P.G. Vinge (Wahlström & Widstrand, 1988); *Secret Forces* by Jan Ottosson and Lars Magnusson (Tiden, 1991); *Power Struggle for Säpo* by Erik Magnusson (Corona, 1989); *An Assignment* by Carl Lidbom (Wahlström & Widstrand, 1990); and – somewhat surprisingly – *An Agent in Place* by Thomas Whiteside (Ballantine, 1966), which dealt with the Wennerström affair. The Wennerström affair of the '60s, not Blomkvist's own much more recent Wennerström affair.

He had spent much of Monday night and the early hours of Tuesday morning reading or at least skimming the books. When he had finished he made some observations. First, most of the books published about the Security Police were from the late '80s. An Internet search showed that there was hardly any current literature on the subject.

Second, there did not seem to be any intelligible basic overview of the activities of the Swedish secret police over the years. This may have been because many documents were stamped Top Secret and were therefore off limits, but there did not seem to be any single institution, researcher or media that had carried out a critical examination of Säpo.

He also noticed another odd thing: there was no bibliography in any one of the books Cortez had found. On the other hand, the footnotes often referred to articles in the evening newspapers, or to interviews with some old, retired Säpo hand.

The book *Secret Forces* was fascinating but largely dealt with the time before and during the Second World War. Blomkvist regarded P.G. Vinge's memoir as propaganda, written in self-defence by a severely criticized Säpo chief who was eventually fired. *An Agent in Place* contained so much inaccurate information about Sweden in the first chapter that he threw the book into the wastepaper basket. The only two books with any real ambition to portray the work of the Security Police were *Power Struggle for Säpo* and *Espionage in Sweden*. They contained data, names and organizational charts. He found Magnusson's book to be especially worthwhile reading. Even though it did not offer any answers to his immediate questions, it provided a good account of Säpo as a structure as well as its primary concerns over several decades.

The biggest surprise was Lidbom's *An Assignment*, which described the problems encountered by the former Swedish ambassador to France when he was commissioned to examine Säpo in the wake of the Palme assassination and the Ebbe Carlsson affair. Blomkvist had never before read anything by Lidbom, and he was taken aback by the sarcastic tone combined with razor-sharp observations. But even Lidbom's book brought Blomkvist no closer to an answer to his questions, even if he was beginning to get an idea of what he was up against.

He opened his mobile and called Cortez.

"Hi, Henry. Thanks for the legwork yesterday."

"What do you need now?"

"A little more legwork."

"Micke, I hate to say this, but I have a job to do. I'm editorial assistant now."

"An excellent career advancement."

"What is it you want?"

"Over the years there have been a number of public reports on Säpo. Carl Lidbom did one. There must be several others like it."

"I see."

"Order everything you can find from parliament: budgets, public reports, interpellations, and the like. And get Säpo's annual reports as far back as you can find them."

"Yes, master."

"Good man. And, Henry . . ."

"Yes?"

"I don't need them until tomorrow."

Salander spent the whole day brooding about Zalachenko. She knew that he was only two doors away, that he wandered in the corridors at night, and that he had come to her room at 3.10 this morning.

She had tracked him to Gosseberga fully intending to kill him. She had failed, with the result that Zalachenko was alive and tucked up in bed barely ten metres from where she was. And she was in hot water. She could not tell how bad the situation was, but she supposed that she would have to escape and discreetly disappear abroad herself if she did not want to risk being locked up in some nuthouse again with Teleborian as her warder.

The problem was that she could scarcely sit upright in bed. She did notice improvements. The headache was still there, but it came in waves instead of being constant. The pain in her left shoulder had subsided a bit, but it resurfaced whenever she tried to move.

She heard footsteps outside the door and saw a nurse open it to admit a woman wearing black trousers, a white blouse, and a dark jacket. She was a pretty, slender woman with dark hair and a boyish hairstyle. She radiated a cheerful confidence. She was carrying a black briefcase. Salander saw at once that she had the same eyes as Blomkvist.

"Hello, Lisbeth. I'm Annika Giannini," she said. "May I come in?"

Salander studied her without expression. All of a sudden she did not have the slightest desire to meet Blomkvist's sister and regretted that she had accepted this woman as her lawyer.

Giannini came in, shut the door behind her, and pulled up a chair. She sat there for some time, looking at her client.

The girl looked terrible. Her head was wrapped in bandages. She had purple bruises around her bloodshot eyes.

"Before we begin to discuss anything, I have to know whether you really do want me to be your lawyer. Normally I'm involved in civil cases in which I represent victims of rape or domestic violence. I'm not a criminal defence lawyer. I have, however, studied the details of your case, and I would very much like to represent you, if I may. I should also tell you that Mikael Blomkvist is my brother – I think you already know that – and that he and Dragan Armansky are paying my fee."

She paused, but when she got no response she continued.

"If you want me to be your lawyer, it's you I will be working for. Not for my brother or for Armansky. I have to tell you too that I will receive advice and support during any trial from your former guardian, Holger Palmgren. He's a tough old boy, and he dragged himself out of his sickbed to help you."

"Palmgren?"

"Yes."

"Have you seen him?"

"Yes."

"How's he doing?"

"He's absolutely furious, but strangely he doesn't seem to be at all worried about you."

Salander smiled lopsidedly. It was the first time she had smiled at Sahlgrenska hospital.

"How are you feeling?"

"Like a sack of shit."

"Well then. Do you want me to be your lawyer? Armansky and Mikael are paying my fee and—"

"No."

"What do you mean, no?"

"I'll pay your fee myself. I don't want a single öre from Armansky or Kalle Blomkvist. But I can't pay before I have access to the Internet."

"I understand. We'll deal with that problem when it arises. In any case, the state will be paying most of my salary. But do you want me to represent you?"

Salander gave a curt nod.

"Good. Then I'll get started by giving you a message from Mikael. It sounds a little cryptic, but he says you'll know what he means."

"Oh?"

"He wants you to know that he's told me most of the story, except for a few details, of which the first concerns the skills he discovered in Hedestad."

He knows that I have a photographic memory . . . and that I'm a hacker. He's kept quiet about that.

"O.K."

"The other is the D.V.D. I don't know what he's referring to, but he was adamant that it's up to you to decide whether you tell me about it or not. Do you know what he's referring to?"

The film of Bjurman raping me.

"Yes."

"That's good, then." Giannini was suddenly hesitant. "I'm a little miffed at my brother. Even though he hired me, he'll only tell me what he feels like telling me. Do you intend to hide things from me too?"

"I don't know. Could we leave that question for later?" Salander said.

"Certainly. We're going to be talking to each other quite a lot. I don't have time for a long conversation now – I have to meet Prosecutor Jervas in forty-five minutes. I just wanted to confirm that you really do want me to be your lawyer. But there's something else I need to tell you."

"Yes?"

"It's this: if I'm not present, you're not to say a single word to the police, no matter what they ask you. Even if they provoke you or accuse you of whatever . . . Can you promise me?"

"I could manage that."

Gullberg had been completely exhausted after all his efforts on Monday. He did not wake until 9.00 on Tuesday morning, four hours later than usual. He went to the bathroom to shower and brush his teeth. He stood for a long time looking at his face in the mirror before he turned off the light and went to get dressed. He chose the only clean shirt he had left in the brown briefcase and put on a brown-patterned tie.

He went down to the hotel's breakfast room, drank a cup of black coffee and ate a slice of wholemeal toast with cheese and a little marmalade on it. He drank a glass of mineral water.

Then he went to the hotel lobby and called Clinton's mobile from the public telephone.

"It's me. Status report?"

"Rather unsettled."

"Fredrik, can you handle this?"

"Yes, it's like the old days. But it's a shame von Rottinger isn't still with us. He was better at planning operations than I."

"You were equally good. You could have switched places at any time. Which indeed you quite often did."

"It's a matter of intuition. He was always a little sharper."

"Tell me, how are you all doing?"

"Sandberg is brighter than we thought. We brought in the external help in the form of Mårtensson. He's a gofer, but he's usable. We have taps on Blomkvist's landline and mobile. We'll take care of Giannini's and the *Millennium* office telephones today. We're looking at the blueprints for all the relevant offices and apartments. We'll be going in as soon as it can be done."

"First thing is to locate all the copies . . ."

"I've already done that. We've had some unbelievable luck. Giannini called Blomkvist this morning. She actually asked him how many copies there were in circulation, and it turned out that Blomkvist only has one. Berger copied the report, but she sent the copy on to Bublanski."

"Good. No time to waste."

"I know. But it has to be done in one fell swoop. If we don't lift all the copies simultaneously, it won't work."

"True."

"It's a bit complicated, since Giannini left for Göteborg this morning. I've sent a team of externals to tail her. They're flying down right now."

"Good." Gullberg could not think of anything more to say. "Thanks, Fredrik," he said at last.

"My pleasure. This is a lot more fun than sitting around waiting for a kidney."

They said goodbye. Gullberg paid his hotel bill and went out to the street. The ball was in motion. Now it was just a matter of mapping out the moves.

He started by walking to Park Avenue Hotel, where he asked to used the fax machine. He did not want to do it at the hotel where he had been staying. He faxed copies of the letters he had written the day before. Then he went out on to Avenyn to look for a taxi. He stopped at a rubbish bin and tore up the photocopies of his letters.

*

Giannini was with Prosecutor Jervas for fifteen minutes. She wanted to know what charges she was intending to bring against Salander, but she soon realized that Jervas was not yet sure of her plan.

"Right now I'll settle for charges of grievous bodily harm or attempted murder. I refer to the fact that Salander hit her father with an axe. I take it that you will plead self-defence?"

"Maybe."

"To be honest with you, Niedermann is my priority at the moment."

"I understand."

"I've been in touch with the Prosecutor General. Discussions are ongoing as to whether to combine all the charges against your client under the jurisdiction of a prosecutor in Stockholm and tie them in with what happened here."

"I assumed that the case would be handled in Stockholm," Giannini said.

"Fine. But I need an opportunity to question the girl. When can we do that?"

"I have a report from her doctor, Anders Jonasson. He says that Salander won't be in a condition to participate in an interview for several days yet. Quite apart from her injuries, she's on powerful painkillers."

"I received a similar report, and as you no doubt realize, this is frustrating. I repeat that my priority is Niedermann. Your client says that she doesn't know where he's hiding."

"She doesn't know Niedermann at all. She happened to identify him and track him down to Gosseberga, to Zalachenko's farm."

"We'll meet again as soon as your client is strong enough to be interviewed," Jervas said.

Gullberg had a bunch of flowers in his hand when he got into the lift at Sahlgrenska hospital at the same time as a short-haired woman in a dark jacket. He held the lift door open for her and let her go first to the reception desk on the ward.

"My name is Annika Giannini. I'm a lawyer and I'd like to see my client again, Lisbeth Salander."

Gullberg turned his head very slowly and looked in surprise at the woman he had followed out of the lift. He glanced down at her brief-case as the nurse checked Giannini's I.D. and consulted a list.

"Room twelve," the nurse said.

"Thank you. I know the way." She walked off down the corridor.

"May I help you?"

"Thank you, yes. I'd like to leave these flowers for Karl Axel Bodin."

"He's not allowed visitors."

"I know. I just want to leave the flowers."

"We'll take care of them."

Gullberg had brought the flowers with him mainly as an excuse. He wanted to get an idea of how the ward was laid out. He thanked the nurse and followed the sign to the staircase. On the way he passed Zalachenko's door, room fourteen according to Jonas Sandberg.

He waited in the stairwell. Through a glass pane in the door he saw the nurse take the bouquet into Zalachenko's room. When she returned to her station, Gullberg pushed open the door to room fourteen and stepped quickly inside.

"Good morning, Alexander," he said.

Zalachenko looked up in surprise at his unannounced visitor. "I thought you'd be dead by now," he said.

"Not quite yet."

"What do you want?"

"What do you think?"

Gullberg pulled up the chair and sat down.

"Probably to see me dead."

"Well, that's gratitude for you. How could you be so bloody stupid? We give you a whole new life and you finish up here."

If Zalachenko could have laughed he would have. In his opinion, the Swedish Security Police were amateurs. That applied to Gullberg and equally to Björck. Not to mention that complete idiot Bjurman.

"Once again we have to haul you out of the furnace."

The expression did not sit well with Zalachenko, once the victim of a petrol bomb attack – from that bloody daughter of his two doors down the corridor.

"Spare me the lectures. Just get me out of this mess."

"That's what I wanted to discuss with you."

Gullberg put his briefcase on to his lap, took out a notebook, and turned to a blank page. Then he gave Zalachenko a long, searching look.

"There's one thing I'm curious about . . . were you really going to betray us after all we've done for you?"

"What do you think?"

"It depends how crazy you are."

"Don't call me crazy. I'm a survivor. I do what I have to do to survive."

Gullberg shook his head. "No, Alexander, you do what you do because you're evil and rotten. You wanted a message from the Section. I'm here to deliver it. We're not going to lift a finger to help you this time."

All of a sudden Zalachenko looked uncertain. He studied Gullberg, trying to figure out if this was some puzzling bluff.

"You don't have a choice," he said.

"There's always a choice," Gullberg said.

"I'm going to—"

"You're not going to do anything at all."

Gullberg took a deep breath, unzipped the outside pocket of his case, and pulled out a 9 mm Smith & Wesson with a gold-plated butt. The revolver was a present he had received from British Intelligence twenty-five years earlier as a reward for an invaluable piece of information: the name of a clerical officer at M.I.5 who in good Philby style was working for the Russians.

Zalachenko looked astonished. Then he burst out laughing.

"And what are you going to do with that? Shoot me? You'll spend the rest of your miserable life in prison."

"I don't think so."

Zalachenko was suddenly very unsure whether Gullberg was bluffing.

"There's going to be a scandal of enormous proportions."

"Again, I don't think so. There'll be a few headlines, but in a week nobody will even remember the name Zalachenko."

Zalachenko's eyes narrowed.

"You're a filthy swine," Gullberg said then with such coldness in his voice that Zalachenko froze.

Gullberg squeezed the trigger and put the bullet right in the centre of Zalachenko's forehead just as the patient was starting to swing his prosthesis over the edge of the bed. Zalachenko was thrown back on to the pillow. His good leg kicked four, five times before he was still. Gullberg saw a red flower-shaped splatter on the wall behind the bedhead. He became aware that his ears were ringing after the shot and he rubbed his left one with his free hand.

Then he stood up and put the muzzle to Zalachenko's temple and squeezed the trigger twice. He wanted to be sure this time that the bastard really was dead.

Salander sat up with a start the instant she heard the first shot. Pain stabbed through her shoulder. When the next two shots came she tried to get her legs over the edge of the bed.

Giannini had only been there for a few minutes. She sat paralysed and tried to work out from which direction the sharp reports had come. She could tell from Salander's reaction that something deadly was in the offing.

"Lie still," she shouted. She put her hand on Salander's chest and shoved her client down on to the bed.

Then Giannini crossed the room and pulled open the door. She saw two nurses running towards another room two doors away. The first nurse stopped short on the threshold. "No, don't!" she screamed and then took a step back, colliding with the second nurse.

"He's got a gun. Run!"

Giannini watched as the two nurses took cover in the room next to Salander's.

The next moment she saw a thin, grey-haired man in a hound's-tooth jacket walk into the corridor. He had a gun in his hand. Annika recognized him as the man who come up in the lift with her.

Then their eyes met. He appeared confused. He aimed the revolver at her and took a step forward. She pulled her head back in and slammed the door shut, looking around in desperation. A nurses' table stood right next to her. She rolled it quickly over to the door and wedged the tabletop under the door handle.

She heard a movement and turned to see Salander just starting to clamber out of bed again. In a few quick steps she crossed the floor, wrapped her arms around her client and lifted her up. She tore electrodes and I.V. tubes loose as she carried her to the bathroom and set her on the toilet seat. Then she turned and locked the bathroom door. She dug her mobile out of her jacket pocket and dialled 112.

Gullberg went to Salander's room and tried the door handle. It was blocked. He could not move it even a millimetre.

For a moment he stood indecisively outside the door. He knew that the lawyer Giannini was in the room, and he wondered if a copy of Björck's report might be in her briefcase. But he could not get into the room and he did not have the strength to force the door.

That had not been part of the plan anyway. Clinton would take care of Giannini. Gullberg's only job was Zalachenko.

He looked around the corridor and saw that he was being watched by nurses, patients and visitors. He raised the pistol and fired at a picture hanging on the wall at the end of the corridor. His spectators vanished as if by magic.

He glanced one last time at the door to Salander's room. Then he walked decisively back to Zalachenko's room and closed the door. He sat in the visitor's chair and looked at the Russian defector who had been such an intimate part of his own life for so many years.

He sat still for almost ten minutes before he heard movement in the corridor and was aware that the police had arrived. By now he was not thinking of anything in particular.

Then he raised the revolver one last time, held it to his temple, and squeezed the trigger.

As the situation developed, the futility of attempting suicide in the middle of a hospital became apparent. Gullberg was transported at top speed to the hospital's trauma unit, where Dr Jonasson received him and immediately initiated a battery of measures to maintain his vital functions.

For the second time in less than a week Jonasson performed emergency surgery, extracting a full-metal-jacketed bullet from human brain tissue. After a five-hour operation, Gullberg's condition was critical. But he was still alive.

Yet Gullberg's injuries were considerably more serious than those that Salander had sustained. He hovered between life and death for several days.

Blomkvist was at the Kaffebar on Hornsgatan when he heard on the radio that a 66-year-old unnamed man, suspected of attempting to murder the fugitive Lisbeth Salander, had been shot and killed at Sahlgrenska hospital in Göteborg. He left his coffee untouched, picked up his laptop case, and hurried off towards the editorial offices on Götgatan. He had crossed Mariatorget and was just turning up St Paulsgatan when his mobile beeped. He answered on the run.

"Blomkvist."

"Hi, it's Malin."

"I heard the news. Do we know who the killer was?"

"Not yet. Henry is chasing it down."

"I'm on the way in. Be there in five minutes."

Blomkvist ran into Cortez at the entrance to the *Millennium* offices.

"Ekström's holding a press conference at 3.00," Cortez said. "I'm going to Kungsholmen now."

"What do we know?" Blomkvist shouted after him.

"Ask Malin," Cortez said, and was gone.

Blomkvist headed into Berger's . . . wrong, Eriksson's office. She was on the telephone and writing furiously on a yellow Post-it. She waved him away. Blomkvist went into the kitchenette and poured coffee with milk into two mugs marked with the logos of the K.D.U. and S.S.U. political parties. When he returned she had just finished her call. He gave her the S.S.U. mug.

"Right," she said. "Zalachenko was shot dead at 1.15." She looked at Blomkvist. "I just spoke to a nurse at Sahlgrenska. She says that the murderer was a man in his seventies, who arrived with flowers for Zalachenko minutes before the murder. He shot Zalachenko in the head several times and then shot himself. Zalachenko is dead. The murderer is just about alive and in surgery."

Blomkvist breathed more easily. Ever since he had heard the news at the Kaffebar he had had his heart in his throat and a panicky feeling that Salander might have been the killer. That really would have thrown a spanner in the works.

"Do we have the name of the assailant?"

Eriksson shook her head as the telephone rang again. She took the call, and from the conversation Blomkvist gathered that it was a stringer in Göteborg whom Eriksson had sent to Sahlgrenska. He went to his own office and sat down.

It felt as if it was the first time in weeks that he had even been to his office. There was a pile of unopened post that he shoved firmly to one side. He called his sister.

"Giannini."

"It's Mikael. Did you hear what happened at Sahlgrenska?"

"You could say so."

"Where are you?"

"At the hospital. That bastard aimed at me, too."

139

Blomkvist sat speechless for several seconds before he fully took in what his sister had said.

"What on *earth* . . . you were there?"

"Yes. It was the most horrendous thing I've ever experienced."

"Are you hurt?"

"No. But he tried to get into Lisbeth's room. I blockaded the door and locked us in the bathroom."

Blomkvist's whole world suddenly felt off balance. *His sister had almost . . .*

"How is she?" he said.

"She's not hurt. Or, I mean, she wasn't hurt in today's drama at least."

He let that sink in.

"Annika, do you know anything at all about the murderer?"

"Not a thing. He was an older man, neatly dressed. I thought he looked rather bewildered. I've never seen him before, but I came up in the lift with him a few minutes before it all happened."

"And Zalachenko is dead, no question?"

"Yes. I heard three shots, and according to what I've overheard he was shot in the head all three times. But it's been utter chaos here, with a thousand policemen, and they're evacuating a ward for acutely ill and injured patients who really ought not to be moved. When the police arrived one of them tried to question Lisbeth before they even bothered to ask what shape she's in. I had to read them the riot act."

Inspector Erlander saw Giannini through the doorway to Salander's room. The lawyer had her mobile pressed to her ear, so he waited for her to finish her call.

Two hours after the murder there was still chaos in the corridor. Zalachenko's room was sealed off. Doctors had tried resuscitation immediately after the shooting, but soon gave up. He was beyond all help. His body was sent to the pathologist, and the crime scene investigation proceeded as best it could under the circumstances.

Erlander's mobile chimed. It was Fredrik Malmberg from the investigative team.

"We've got a positive I.D. on the murderer," Malmberg said. "His name is Evert Gullberg and he's seventy-eight years old."

Seventy-eight. Quite elderly for a murderer.

"And who the hell is Evert Gullberg?"

"Retired. Lives in Laholm. Apparently he was a tax lawyer. I got a call from S.I.S. who told me that they had recently initiated a preliminary investigation against him."

"When and why?"

"I don't know when. But apparently he had a habit of sending crazy and threatening letters to people in government."

"Such as who?"

"The Minister of Justice, for one."

Erlander sighed. So, a madman. A fanatic.

"This morning Säpo got calls from several newspapers who had received letters from Gullberg. The Ministry of Justice also called, because Gullberg had made specific death threats against Karl Axel Bodin."

"I want copies of the letters."

"From Säpo?"

"Yes, damn it. Drive up to Stockholm and pick them up in person if necessary. I want them on my desk when I get back to H.Q. Which will be in about an hour."

He thought for a second and then asked one more question.

"Was it Säpo that called you?"

"That's what I told you."

"I mean . . . they called you, not vice versa?"

"Exactly."

Erlander closed his mobile.

He wondered what had got into Säpo to make them, out of the blue, feel the need to get in touch with the police – of their own accord. Ordinarily you couldn't get a word out of them.

Wadensjöö flung open the door to the room at the Section where Clinton was resting. Clinton sat up cautiously.

"Just what the bloody hell is going on?" Wadensjöö shrieked. "Gullberg has murdered Zalachenko and then shot himself in the head."

"I know," Clinton said.

"You *know*?" Wadensjöö yelled. He was bright red in the face and looked as if he was about to have a stroke. "He shot himself, for Christ's sake. He tried to commit suicide. Is he out of his mind?"

"You mean he's alive?"

"For the time being, yes, but he has massive brain damage."

Clinton sighed. "Such a shame," he said with real sorrow in his voice.

"*Shame*?" Wadensjöö burst out. "Gullberg is out of his mind. Don't you understand what—"

Clinton cut him off.

"Gullberg has cancer of the stomach, colon and bladder. He's been dying for several months, and in the best case he had only a few months left."

"Cancer?"

"He's been carrying that gun around for the past six months, determined to use it as soon as the pain became unbearable and before the disease turned him into a vegetable. But he was able to do one last favour for the Section. He went out in grand style."

Wadensjöö was almost beside himself. "You *knew*? You knew that he was thinking of killing Zalachenko?"

"Naturally. His assignment was to make sure that Zalachenko never got a chance to talk. And as you know, you couldn't threaten or reason with that man."

"But don't you understand what a scandal this could turn into? Are you just as barmy as Gullberg?"

Clinton got to his feet laboriously. He looked Wadensjöö in the eye and handed him a stack of fax copies.

"It was an operational decision. I mourn for my friend, but I'll probably be following him pretty soon. As far as a scandal goes . . . A retired tax lawyer wrote paranoid letters to newspapers, the police, and the Ministry of Justice. Here's a sample of them. Gullberg blames Zalachenko for everything from the Palme assassination to trying to poison the Swedish people with chlorine. The letters are plainly the work of a lunatic and were illegible in places, with capital letters, underlining, and exclamation marks. I especially like the way he wrote in the margin."

Wadensjöö read the letters with rising astonishment. He put a hand to his brow.

Clinton said: "Whatever happens, Zalachenko's death will have nothing to do with the Section. It was just some demented pensioner who fired the shots." He paused. "The important thing is that, starting from now, you have to get on board with the program. And don't rock the boat." He fixed his gaze on Wadensjöö. There was steel in the sick man's eyes. "What you have to understand is that the Section functions as the spear head for the total defence of the nation. We're Sweden's last line of defence. Our job is to watch over the security of our country. Everything else is unimportant."

Wadensjöö regarded Clinton with doubt in his eyes.

"We're the ones who don't exist," Clinton went on. "We're the ones nobody will ever thank. We're the ones who have to make the decisions that nobody else wants to make. Least of all the politicians." His voice quivered with contempt as he spoke those last words. "Do as I say and the Section might survive. For that to happen, we have to be decisive and resort to tough measures."

Wadensjöö felt the panic rise.

Cortez wrote feverishly, trying to get down every word that was said from the podium at the police press office at Kungsholmen. Prosecutor Ekström had begun. He explained that it had been decided that the investigation into the police killing in Gosseberga – for which Ronald Niedermann was being sought – would be placed under the jurisdiction of a prosecutor in Göteborg. The rest of the investigation concerning Niedermann would be handled by Ekström himself. Niedermann was a suspect in the murders of Dag Svensson and Mia Johansson. No mention was made of Advokat Bjurman. Ekström had also to investigate and bring charges against Lisbeth Salander, who was under suspicion for a long list of crimes.

He explained that he had decided to go public with the information in the light of events that had occurred in Göteborg that day, including the fact that Salander's father, Karl Axel Bodin, had been shot dead. The immediate reason for calling the press conference was that he wanted to deny the rumours already being circulated in the media. He had himself received a number of calls concerning these rumours.

"Based on current information, I am able to tell you that Karl Axel Bodin's daughter, who is being held for the attempted murder of her father, had nothing to do with this morning's events."

"Then who was the murderer?" a reporter from *Dagens Eko* shouted.

"The man who at 1.15 today fired the fatal shots at Karl Axel Bodin before attempting to commit suicide has now been identified. He is a 78-year-old man who has been undergoing treatment for a terminal illness and the psychiatric problems associated with it."

"Does he have any connection to Lisbeth Salander?"

"No. The man is a tragic figure who evidently acted alone, in accordance with his own paranoid delusions. The Security Police recently initiated an investigation of this man because he had written a number of apparently unstable letters to well-known politicians and the media. As recently as this morning, newspaper and government offices received letters in which he threatened to kill Karl Axel Bodin."

"Why didn't the police give Bodin protection?"

"The letters naming Bodin were sent only last night and thus arrived at the same time as the murder was being committed. There was no time to act."

"What's the killer's name?"

"We will not give out that information until his next of kin have been notified."

"What sort of background does he have?"

"As far as I understand, he previously worked as an accountant and tax lawyer. He has been retired for fifteen years. The investigation is still under way, but as you can appreciate from the letters he sent, it is a tragedy that could have been prevented if there had been more support within society."

"Did he threaten anyone else?"

"I have been advised that he did, yes, but I do not have any details to pass on to you."

"What will this mean for the case against Salander?"

"For the moment, nothing. We have Karl Axel Bodin's own testimony from the officers who interviewed him, and we have extensive forensic evidence against her."

"What about the reports that Bodin tried to murder his daughter?"

"That is under investigation, but there are strong indications that he did indeed attempt to kill her. As far as we can determine at the moment, it was a case of deep antagonism in a tragically dysfunctional family."

Cortez scratched his ear. He noticed that the other reporters were taking notes as feverishly as he was.

Gunnar Björck felt an almost unquenchable panic when he heard the news about the shooting at Sahlgrenska hospital. He had terrible pain in his back.

It took him an hour to make up his mind. Then he picked up the

144

telephone and tried to call his old protector in Laholm. There was no answer.

He listened to the news and heard a summary of what had been said at the press conference. Zalachenko had been shot by a 78-year-old tax specialist.

Good Lord, seventy-eight years old.

He tried again to call Gullberg, but again in vain.

Finally his uneasiness took the upper hand. He could not stay in the borrowed summer cabin in Smådalarö. He felt vulnerable and exposed. He needed time and space to think. He packed clothes, painkillers, and his wash bag. He did not want to use his own telephone, so he limped to the telephone booth at the grocer's to call Landsort and book himself a room in the old ships' pilot lookout. Landsort was the end of the world, and few people would look for him there. He booked the room for two weeks.

He glanced at his watch. He would have to hurry to make the last ferry. He went back to the cabin as fast as his aching back would permit. He made straight for the kitchen and checked that the coffee machine was turned off. Then he went to the hall to get his bag. He happened to look into the living room and stopped short in surprise.

At first he could not grasp what he was seeing.

In some mysterious way the ceiling lamp had been taken down and placed on the coffee table. In its place hung a rope from a hook, right above a stool that was usually in the kitchen.

Björck looked at the noose, failing to understand.

Then he heard movement behind him and felt his knees buckle.

Slowly he turned to look.

Two men stood there. They were southern European, by the look of them. He had no will to react when calmly they took him in a firm grip under both arms, lifted him off the ground, and carried him to the stool. When he tried to resist, pain shot like a knife through his back. He was almost paralysed as he felt himself being lifted on to the stool.

Sandberg was accompanied by a man who went by the nickname of Falun and who in his youth had been a professional burglar. He had, in time, retrained as a locksmith. Hans von Rottinger had first hired Falun for the Section in 1986 for an operation that involved forcing entry into the home of the leader of an anarchist group. After that, Falun had been hired from time to time until the mid-'90s, when there was less demand for this type of operation. Early that morning Clinton had revived the contact and given Falun an assignment. Falun would make 10,000 kronor tax-free for a job that would take about ten minutes. In return he had pledged not to steal anything from the apartment that was the target of the operation. The Section was not a criminal enterprise, after all.

Falun did not know exactly what interests Clinton represented, but he assumed it had something to do with the military. He had read Jan Guillou's books, and he did not ask any questions. But it felt good to be back in the saddle again after so many years of silence from his former employer.

His job was to open the door. He was expert at breaking and entering. Even so, it still took five minutes to force the lock to Blomkvist's apartment. Then Falun waited on the landing as Sandberg went in.

"I'm in," Sandberg said into a handsfree mobile.

"Good," Clinton said into his earpiece. "Take your time. Tell me what you see."

"I'm in the hall with a wardrobe and hat-rack on my right. Bathroom on the left. Otherwise there's one very large room, about fifty square metres. There's a small kitchen alcove at the far end on the right."

"Is there any desk or . . ."

"He seems to work at the kitchen table or sitting on the living-room sofa . . . wait."

Clinton waited.

"Yes. Here we are, a folder on the kitchen table. And Björck's report is in it. It looks like the original."

"Very good. Anything else of interest on the table?"

"Books. P.G. Vinge's memoirs. *Power Struggle for Säpo* by Erik Magnusson. Four or five more of the same."

"Is there a computer?"

"No."

"Any safe?"

"No . . . not that I can see."

"Take your time. Go through the apartment centimetre by centimetre. Mårtensson reports that Blomkvist is still at the office. You're wearing gloves, right?"

"Of course."

*

146

Erlander had a chat with Giannini in a brief interlude between one or other or both of them talking on their mobiles. He went into Salander's room and held out his hand to introduce himself. Then he said hello to Salander and asked her how she was feeling. Salander looked at him, expressionless. He turned to Giannini.

"I need to ask some questions."

"Alright."

"Can you tell me what happened this morning?"

Giannini related what she had seen and heard and how she had reacted up until the moment she had barricaded herself with Salander in the bathroom. Erlander glanced at Salander and then back to her lawyer.

"So you're sure that he came to the door of this room?"

"I heard him trying to push down the door handle."

"And you're perfectly sure about that? It's not difficult to imagine things when you're scared or excited."

"I definitely heard him at the door. He had seen me and pointed his pistol at me, he knew that this was the room I was in."

"Do you have any reason to believe that he had planned, beforehand that is, to shoot you too?"

"I have no way of knowing. When he took aim at me I pulled my head back in and blockaded the door."

"Which was the sensible thing to do. And it was even more sensible of you to carry your client to the bathroom. These doors are so thin that the bullets would have gone clean through them if he had fired. What I'm trying to figure out is whether he wanted to attack you personally or whether he was just reacting to the fact that you were looking at him. You were the person nearest to him in the corridor."

"Apart from the two nurses."

"Did you get the sense that he knew you or perhaps recognized you?"

"No, not really."

"Could he have recognized you from the papers? You've had a lot of publicity over several widely reported cases."

"It's possible. I can't say."

"And you'd never seen him before?"

"I'd seen him in the lift, that's the first time I set eyes on him."

"I didn't know that. Did you talk?"

"No. I got in at the same time he did. I was vaguely aware of him for just a few seconds. He had flowers in one hand and a briefcase in the other."

"Did you make eye contact?"

"No. He was looking straight ahead."

"Who got in first?"

"We got in more or less at the same time."

"Did he look confused or—"

"I couldn't say one way or the other. He got into the lift and stood perfectly still, holding the flowers."

"What happened then?"

"We got out of the lift on the same floor, and I went to visit my client."

"Did you come straight here?"

"Yes . . . no. That is, I went to the reception desk and showed my I.D. The prosecutor has forbidden my client to have visitors."

"Where was this man then?"

Giannini hesitated. "I'm not quite sure. He was behind me, I think. No, wait . . . he got out of the lift first, but stopped and held the door for me. I couldn't swear to it, but I think he went to the reception desk too. I was just quicker on my feet than he was. But the nurses would know."

Elderly, polite, and a murderer, Erlander thought.

"Yes, he did go to the reception desk," he confirmed. "He did talk to the nurse and he left the flowers at the desk, at her instruction. But you didn't see that?"

"No. I have no recollection of any of that."

Erlander had no more questions. Frustration was gnawing at him. He had had the feeling before and had trained himself to interpret it as an alarm triggered by instinct. Something was eluding him, something that was not right.

The murderer had been identified as Evert Gullberg, a former accountant and sometime business consultant and tax lawyer. A man in advanced old age. A man against whom Säpo had lately initiated a preliminary investigation because he was a nutter who wrote threatening letters to public figures.

Erlander knew from long experience that there were plenty of nutters out there, some pathologically obsessed ones who stalked celebrities and looked for love by hiding in woods near their villas. When their love was not reciprocated – as why would it be? – it could quickly turn to violent hatred. There were stalkers who travelled from Germany or Italy to follow a 21-year-old lead singer in a pop band from gig to gig, and who then got upset because she would not drop everything to start a relationship with them. There were bloody-minded individuals who harped on and on about real or imaginary injustices and who sometimes turned to threatening behaviour. There were psychopaths and conspiracy theorists, nutters who had the gift to read messages hidden from the normal world.

There were plenty of examples of these fools taking the leap from fantasy to action. Was not the assassination of Anna Lindh* the result of precisely such a crazy impulse?

But Inspector Erlander did not like the idea that a mentally ill accountant, or whatever he was, could wander into a hospital with a bunch of flowers in one hand and a pistol in the other. Or that he could, for God's sake, execute someone who was the object of a police investigation – *his* investigation. A man whose name in the public register was Karl Axel Bodin but whose real name, according to Blomkvist, was Zalachenko. A bastard defected Soviet Russian agent and professional gangster.

At the very least Zalachenko was a witness; but in the worst case he was involved up to his neck in a series of murders. Erlander had been allowed to conduct two brief interviews with Zalachenko, and at no time during either had he been swayed by the man's protestations of innocence.

His murderer had shown interest also in Salander, or at least in her lawyer. He had tried to get into her room.

And then he had attempted suicide. According to the doctors, he had probably succeeded, even if his body had not yet absorbed the message that it was time to shut down. It was highly unlikely that Evert Gullberg would ever be brought before a court.

Erlander did not like the situation, not for a moment. But he had no proof that Gullberg's shots had been anything other than what they seemed. So he had decided to play it safe. He looked at Giannini.

"I've decided that Salander should be moved to a different room. There's a room in the connecting corridor to the right of the reception area that would be better from a security point of view. It's in direct line-of-sight of the reception desk and the nurses' station. No visitors will be permitted other than you. No-one can go into her room without permission except for doctors or nurses who work here at

Sahlgrenska. And I'll see to it that a guard is stationed outside her door round the clock."

"Do you think she's in danger?"

"I know of nothing to indicate that she is. But I want to play it safe."

Salander listened attentively to the conversation between her lawyer and her adversary, a member of the police. She was impressed that Giannini had replied so precisely and lucidly, and in such detail. She was even more impressed by her lawyer's way of keeping cool under stress.

Otherwise she had had a monstrous headache ever since Giannini had dragged her out of bed and carried her into the bathroom. Instinctively she wanted as little as possible to do with the hospital staff. She did not like asking for help or showing any sign of weakness. But the headaches were so overpowering that she could not think straight. She reached out and rang for a nurse.

Giannini had planned her visit to Göteborg as a brisk, necessary prologue to long-term work. She wanted to get to know Salander, question her about her actual condition, and present a first outline of the strategy that she and Blomkvist had cobbled together to deal with the legal proceedings. She had originally intended to return to Stockholm that evening, but the dramatic events at Sahlgrenska had meant that she still had not had a real conversation with Salander. Her client was in much worse shape than she had been led to believe. She was suffering from acute headaches and a high fever, which prompted a doctor by the name of Endrin to prescribe a strong painkiller, an antibiotic, and rest. Consequently, as soon as her client had been moved to a new room and a security guard had been posted outside, Giannini was asked, quite firmly, to leave.

It was already 4.30 p.m. She hesitated. She could go back to Stockholm knowing that she might have to take the train to Göteborg again as soon as the following day. Or else she could stay overnight. But her client might be too ill to deal with a visit tomorrow as well. She had not booked a hotel room. As a lawyer who mainly represented abused women without any great financial resources, she tried to avoid padding her bill with expensive hotel charges. She called home first and then rang Lillian Josefsson, a lawyer colleague who was a member of the Women's Network and an old friend from law school.

"I'm in Göteborg," she said. "I was thinking of going home tonight, but certain things happened today that require me to stay overnight. Is it O.K. if I sleep at your place?"

"Oh, please do, that would be fun. We haven't seen each other in ages."

"I'm not interrupting anything?"

"No, of course not. But I've moved. I'm now on a side street off Linnégatan. But I do have a spare room. And we can go out to a bar later if we feel like it."

"If I have the energy," Giannini said. "What time is good?"

They agreed that Giannini should turn up at around 6.00.

Giannini took the bus to Linnégatan and spent the next hour in a Greek restaurant. She was famished, and ordered a shish kebab with salad. She sat for a long time thinking about the day's events. She was a little shaky now that the adrenaline had worn off, but she was pleased with herself. In a time of great danger she had been cool, calm and collected. She had instinctively made the right decisions. It was a pleasant feeling to know that her reactions were up to an emergency.

After a while she took her Filofax from her briefcase and opened it to the notes section. She read through it carefully. She was filled with doubt about the plan that her brother had outlined to her. It had sounded logical at the time, but it did not look so good now. Even so, she did not intend to back out.

At 6.00 she paid her bill and walked to Lillian's place on Olivedalsgatan. She punched in the door code her friend had given her. She stepped into the stairwell and was looking for a light switch when the attack came out of the blue. She was slammed up against a tiled wall next to the door. She banged her head hard, felt a rush of pain and fell to the ground.

The next moment she heard footsteps moving swiftly away and then the front door opening and closing. She struggled to her feet and put her hand to her forehead. There was blood on her palm. *What the hell?* She went out on to the street and just caught a glimpse of someone turning the corner towards Sveaplan. In shock she stood still for about a minute. Then she walked back to the door and punched in the code again.

Suddenly she realized that her briefcase was gone. She had been robbed. It took a few seconds before the horror of it sank in. *Oh no. The Zalachenko folder.* She felt the alarm spreading up from her diaphragm.

Slowly she sat down on the staircase.

Then she jumped up and dug into her jacket pocket. *The Filofax.*

Thank God. Leaving the restaurant she had stuffed it into her pocket instead of putting it back in her briefcase. It contained the draft of her strategy in the Salander case, point by detailed point.

Then she stumbled up the stairs to the fifth floor and pounded on her friend's door.

Half an hour had passed before she had recovered enough to call her brother. She had a black eye and a gash above her eyebrow that was still bleeding. Lillian had cleaned it with alcohol and put a bandage on it. No, she did not want to go to hospital. Yes, she would like a cup of tea. Only then did she begin to think rationally again. The first thing she did was to call Blomkvist.

He was still at *Millennium*, where he was searching for information about Zalachenko's murderer with Cortez and Eriksson. He listened with increasing dismay to Giannini's account of what had happened.

"No bones broken?" he said.

"Black eye. I'll be O.K. after I've had a chance to calm down."

"Did you disturb a robbery, was that it?"

"Mikael, my briefcase was stolen, with the Zalachenko report you gave me."

"Not a problem. I can make another copy—"

He broke off as he felt the hair rise on the back of his neck. *First Zalachenko. Now Annika.*

He closed his iBook, stuffed it into his shoulder bag and left the office without a word, moving fast. He jogged home to Bellmansgatan and up the stairs.

The door was locked.

As soon as he entered the apartment he saw that the folder he had left on the kitchen table was gone. He did not even bother to look for it. He knew exactly where it had been. He sank on to a chair at the kitchen table as thoughts whirled through his head.

Someone had been in his apartment. Someone who was trying to cover Zalachenko's tracks.

His own copy and his sister's copy were gone.

Bublanski still had the report.

Or did he?

Blomkvist got up and went to the telephone, but stopped with his hand on the receiver. *Someone had been in his apartment.* He looked at his telephone with the utmost suspicion and took out his mobile.

But how easy is it to eavesdrop on a mobile conversation?

He slowly put the mobile down next to his landline and looked around.

I'm dealing with pros here, obviously. People who could bug an apartment as easily as get into one without breaking a lock.

He sat down again.

He looked at his laptop case.

How hard is it to hack into my email? Salander can do it in five minutes.

He thought for a long time before he went back to the landline and called his sister. He chose his words with care.

"How are you doing?"

"I'm fine, Micke."

"Tell me what happened from the moment you arrived at Sahlgrenska until you were attacked."

It took ten minutes for Giannini to give him her account. Blomkvist did not say anything about the implications of what she told him, but asked questions until he was satisfied. He sounded like an anxious brother, but his mind was working on a completely different level as he reconstructed the key points.

She had decided to stay in Göteborg at 4.30 that afternoon. She called her friend on her mobile, got the address and door code. The robber was waiting for her inside the stairwell at 6.00 on the dot.

Her mobile was being monitored. It was the only possible explanation.

Which meant that his was being monitored too.

Foolish to think otherwise.

"And the Zalachenko report is gone," Giannini repeated.

Blomkvist hesitated. Whoever had stolen the report already knew that his copy too had been stolen. It would only be natural to mention that.

"Mine too," he said.

"What?"

He explained that he had come home to find that the blue folder on his kitchen table was gone.

"It's a disaster," he said in a gloomy voice. "That was the crucial part of the evidence."

"Micke . . . I'm so sorry."

"Me too," Blomkvist said. "*Damn it!* But it's not your fault. I should have published the report the day I got it."

"What do we do now?"

"I have no idea. This is the worst thing that could have happened. It will turn our whole plan upside down. We don't have a shred of evidence left against Björck or Teleborian."

They talked for another two minutes before Blomkvist ended the conversation.

"I want you to come back to Stockholm tomorrow," he said.

"I have to see Salander."

"Go and see her in the morning. We have to sit down and think about where we go from here."

When Blomkvist hung up he sat on the sofa staring into space. Whoever was listening to their conversation knew now that *Millennium* had lost Björck's report along with the correspondence between Björck and Dr Teleborian. They could be satisfied that Blomkvist and Giannini were in despair.

If nothing else, Blomkvist had learned from the preceding night's study of the history of the Security Police that disinformation was the basis of all espionage activity. And he had just planted disinformation that in the long run might prove invaluable.

He opened his laptop case and took out the copy made for Armansky which he had not yet managed to deliver. The only remaining copy, and he did not intend to waste it. On the contrary, he would make five more copies and put them in safe places.

Then he called Eriksson. She was about to lock up for the day.

"Where did you disappear to in such a hurry?" she said.

"Could you hang on there a few minutes please? There's something I have to discuss with you before you leave."

He had not had time to do his laundry for several weeks. All his shirts were in the basket. He packed a razor and *Power Struggle for Säpo* along with the last remaining copy of Björck's report. He went to Dressman and bought four shirts, two pairs of trousers and some underwear and took the clothes with him to the office. Eriksson waited while he took a quick shower, wondering what was going on.

"Someone broke into my apartment and stole the Zalachenko report.

154

Someone mugged Annika in Göteborg and stole her copy. I have proof that her phone is tapped, which may well mean that mine is too. Maybe yours at home and all the *Millennium* phones have been bugged. And if someone took the trouble to break into my apartment, they'd be pretty dim if they didn't bug it as well."

"I see," said Eriksson in a flat voice. She glanced at the mobile on the desk in front of her.

"Keep working as usual. Use the mobile, but don't give away any information. Tomorrow, tell Henry."

"He went home an hour ago. He left a stack of public reports on your desk. But what are you doing here?"

"I plan to sleep here tonight. If they shot Zalachenko, stole the reports, and bugged my apartment today, there's a good chance they've just got started and haven't done the office yet. People have been here all day. I don't want the office to be empty tonight."

"You think that the murder of Zalachenko . . . but the murderer was a geriatric psycho."

"Malin, I don't believe in coincidence. Somebody is covering Zalachenko's tracks. I don't care who people think that old lunatic was or how many crazy letters he wrote to government ministers. He was a hired killer of some sort. He went there to kill Zalachenko . . . and maybe Lisbeth too."

"But he committed suicide, or tried to. What hired killer would do that?"

Blomkvist thought for a moment. He met the editor-in-chief's gaze.

"Maybe someone who's seventy-eight and hasn't much to lose. He's mixed up in all this, and when we finish digging we'll prove it."

Eriksson studied Blomkvist's face. She had never before seen him so composed and unflinching. She shuddered. Blomkvist noticed her reaction.

"One more thing. We're no longer in a battle with a gang of criminals, this time it's with a government department. It's going to be tough."

Eriksson nodded.

"I didn't imagine things would go this far. Malin . . . what happened today makes very plain how dangerous this could get. If you want out, just say the word."

She wondered what Berger would have said. Then stubbornly she shook her head.

PART II

HACKER REPUBLIC

I — 22.V

An Irish law from the year 697 forbids women to be soldiers – which means that women *had* been soldiers previously. Peoples who over the centuries have recruited female soldiers include Arabs, Berbers, Kurds, Rajputs, Chinese, Filipinos, Maoris, Papuans, Australian aborigines, Micronesians and American Indians.

There is a wealth of legend about fearsome female warriors from ancient Greece. These tales speak of women who were trained in the arts of war from childhood – in the use of weapons, and how to cope with physical privation. They lived apart from the men and went to war in their own regiments. The tales tell us that they conquered men on the field of battle. Amazons occur in Greek literature in the *Iliad* of Homer, for example, in 600 B.C.

It was the Greeks who coined the term Amazon. The word literally means "without breast". It is said that in order to facilitate the drawing of a bow, the female's right breast was removed, either in early childhood or with a red-hot iron after she became an adult. Even though the Greek physicians Hippocrates and Galen are said to have agreed that this operation would enhance the ability to use weapons, it is doubtful whether such operations were actually performed. Herein lies a linguistic riddle – whether the prefix "a-" in Amazon does indeed mean "without". It has been suggested that it means the opposite – that an Amazon was a woman with especially large breasts. Nor is there a single example in any museum of a drawing, amulet or statue of a woman without her right breast, which should have been a common motif had the legend about breast amputation been based on fact.

CHAPTER 8

SUNDAY, 1.v – MONDAY, 2.v

Berger took a deep breath as the lift door opened and she walked into the editorial offices of *Svenska Morgon-Posten*. It was 10.15 in the morning. She was dressed for the office in black trousers, a red jumper and a dark jacket. It was glorious May 1 weather, and on her way through the city she noticed that the workers' groups had begun to gather. It dawned on her that she had not been part of such a parade in more than twenty years.

For a moment she stood, alone and invisible, next to the lift doors. *First day on the job.* She could see a large part of the editorial office with the news desk in the centre. She saw the glass doors of the editor-in-chief's office, which was now hers.

She was not at all sure right now that she was the person to lead the sprawling organization that comprised *S.M.P.* It was a gigantic step up from *Millennium* with a staff of five to a daily newspaper with eighty reporters and another ninety people in administration, with I.T. personnel, layout artists, photographers, advertising reps, and all else it takes to publish a newspaper. Add to that a publishing house, a production company and a management company. More than 230 people.

As she stood there she asked herself whether the whole thing was not a hideous mistake.

Then the older of the two receptionists noticed who had just come into the office. She got up and came out from behind the counter and extended her hand.

"Fru Berger, welcome to *S.M.P.*"

"Call me Erika. Hello."

"Beatrice. Welcome. Shall I show you where to find Editor-in-Chief Morander? I should say 'outgoing editor-in-chief'?"

"Thank you, I see him sitting in the glass cage over there," said Berger with a smile. "I can find my way, but thanks for the offer."

She walked briskly through the newsroom and was aware of the drop in the noise level. She felt everyone's eyes upon her. She stopped at the half-empty news desk and gave a friendly nod.

"We'll introduce ourselves properly in a while," she said, and then walked over to knock on the door of the glass cubicle.

The departing editor-in-chief, Håkan Morander, had spent twelve years in the glass cage. Just like Berger, he had been head-hunted from outside the company – so he had once taken that very same first walk to his office. He looked up at her, puzzled, and then stood up.

"Hello, Erika," he said. "I thought you were starting Monday."

"I couldn't stand sitting at home one more day. So here I am."

Morander held out his hand. "Welcome. I can't tell you how glad I am that you're taking over."

"How are you feeling?" Berger said.

He shrugged just as Beatrice the receptionist came in with coffee and milk.

"It feels as though I'm already operating at half speed. Actually I don't want to talk about it. You walk around feeling like a teenager and immortal your whole life, and suddenly there isn't much time left. But one thing is for sure – I don't mean to spend the rest of it in this glass cage."

He rubbed his chest. He had heart and artery problems, which was the reason for his going and why Berger was to start several months earlier than originally announced.

Berger turned and looked out over the landscape of the newsroom. She saw a reporter and a photographer heading for the lift, perhaps on their way to cover the May Day parade.

"Håkan . . . if I'm being a nuisance or if you're busy today, I'll come back tomorrow or the day after."

"Today's task is to write an editorial on the demonstrations. I could do it in my sleep. If the pinkos want to start a war with Denmark, then I have to explain why they're wrong. If the pinkos want to avoid a war with Denmark, I have to explain why they're wrong."

"Denmark?"

"Correct. The message on May Day has to touch on the immigrant integration question. The pinkos, of course, no matter what they say, are wrong."

He burst out laughing.

"Always so cynical?"

"Welcome to *S.M.P.*"

Erika had never had an opinion about Morander. He was an anonymous power figure among the elite of editors-in-chief. In his editorials he came across as boring and conservative. Expert in complaining about taxes, and a typical libertarian when it came to freedom of the press. But she had never met him in person.

"Do you have time to tell me about the job?"

"I'm gone at the end of June. We'll work side by side for two months. You'll discover positive things and negative things. I'm a cynic, so mostly I see the negative things."

He got up and stood next to her to look through the glass at the newsroom.

"You'll discover that – it comes with the job – you're going to have a number of adversaries out there – daily editors and veterans among the editors who have created their own little empires. They have their own club that you can't join. They'll try to stretch the boundaries, to push through their own headlines and angles. You'll have to fight hard to hold your own."

Berger nodded.

"Your night editors are Billinger and Karlsson . . . they're a whole chapter unto themselves. They hate each other and, importantly, they don't work the same shift, but they both act as if they're publishers and editors-in-chief. Then there's Anders Holm, the news editor – you'll be working with him a lot. You'll have your share of clashes with him. In point of fact, he's the one who gets *S.M.P.* out every day. Some of the reporters are prize primadonnas, and some of them should really be put out to grass."

"Have you got any good colleagues?"

Morander laughed again.

"Oh yes, but you're going to have to decide for yourself which ones you can get along with. Some of the reporters out there are seriously good."

"How about management?"

"Magnus Borgsjö is chairman of the board. He was the one who recruited you. He's charming. A bit old school and yet at the same time a bit of a reformer, but he's above all the one who makes the decisions. Some of the board members, including several from the family which owns the paper, mostly seem to sit and kill time, while others flutter around, professional board-member types."

"You don't seem to be exactly enamoured of your board."

"There's a division of labour. We put out the paper. They take care of the finances. They're not supposed to interfere with the content, but situations do crop up. To be honest, Erika, between the two of us, this is going to be tough."

"Why's that?"

"Circulation has dropped by nearly 150,000 copies since the glory days of the '60s, and there may soon come a time when *S.M.P.* is no longer profitable. We've reorganized, cut more than 180 jobs since 1980. We went over to tabloid format – which we should have done twenty years sooner. *S.M.P.* is still one of the big papers, but it wouldn't take much for us to be regarded as a second-class paper. If it hasn't already happened."

"Why did they pick me then?" Berger said.

"Because the median age of our readers is fifty-plus, and the growth in readers in their twenties is almost zero. The paper has to be rejuvenated. And the reasoning among the board was to bring in the most improbable editor-in-chief they could think of."

"A woman?"

"Not just any woman. *The* woman who crushed Wennerström's empire, who is considered the queen of investigative journalism, and who has a reputation for being the toughest. Picture it. It's irresistible. If *you* can't rejuvenate this paper, nobody can. *S.M.P.* isn't just hiring Erika Berger, we're hiring the whole mystique that goes with your name."

When Blomkvist left Café Copacabana next to the Kvarter cinema at Hornstull, it was just past 2.00 p.m. He put on his dark glasses and turned up Bergsundsstrand on his way to the tunnelbana. He noticed the grey Volvo at once, parked at the corner. He passed it without slowing down. Same registration, and the car was empty.

It was the seventh time he had seen the same car in four days. He had no idea how long the car had been in his neighbourhood. It was pure chance that he had noticed it at all. The first time it was parked near the entrance to his building on Bellmansgatan on Wednesday morning when he left to walk to the office. He happened to read the registration number, which began with KAB, and he paid attention because those were the initials of Zalachenko's holding company, Karl Axel Bodin Inc. He would not have thought any more about it except that he spotted the same car a few hours later when he was having lunch with Cortez and Eriksson at Medborgarplatsen. That time the Volvo was parked on a side street near the *Millennium* offices.

He wondered whether he was becoming paranoid, but when he visited Palmgren the same afternoon at the rehabilitation home in Ersta, the car was in the visitors' car park. That could not have been chance. Blomkvist began to keep an eye on everything around him. And when he saw the car again the next morning he was not surprised.

Not once had he seen its driver.

A call to the national vehicle register revealed that the car belonged to a Göran Mårtensson of Vittangigaten in Vällingby. An hour's research turned up the information that Mårtensson held the title of business consultant and owned a private company whose address was a P.O. box on Fleminggatan in Kungsholmen. Mårtensson's C.V. was an interesting one. In 1983, at eighteen, he had done his military service with the coast guard, and then enrolled in the army. By 1989 he had advanced to lieutenant, and then he switched to study at the police academy in Solna. Between 1991 and 1996 he worked for the Stockholm police. In 1997 he was no longer on the official roster of the external service, and in 1999 he had registered his own company.

So – Säpo.

An industrious investigative journalist could get paranoid on less than this. Blomkvist concluded that he was under surveillance, but it was being carried out so clumsily that he could hardly have helped but notice.

Or was it clumsy? The only reason he first noticed the car was the registration number, which just happened to mean something to him. But for the KAB, he would not have given the car a second glance.

On Friday KAB was conspicuous by its absence. Blomkvist could not be absolutely sure, but he thought he had been tailed by a red Audi that day. He had not managed to catch the registration number. On Friday the Volvo was back.

Exactly twenty seconds after Blomkvist left Café Copacabana, Malm raised his Nikon in the shadows of Café Rosso's awning across the street and took a series of twelve photographs of the two men who followed Blomkvist out of the café and past the Kvarter cinema.

One of the men looked to be in his late thirties or early forties and had blond hair. The other seemed a bit older, with thinning reddish-blond hair and sunglasses. Both were dressed in jeans and leather jackets.

They parted company at the grey Volvo. The older man got in, and the younger one followed Blomkvist towards Hornstull tunnelbana station.

Malm lowered the camera. Blomkvist had given him no good reason for insisting that he patrol the neighbourhood near the Copacabana on Sunday afternoon looking for a grey Volvo with a registration beginning KAB. Blomkvist told him to position himself where he could photograph whoever got into the car, probably just after 3.00. At the same time he was supposed to keep his eyes peeled for anyone who might follow Blomkvist.

It sounded like the prelude to a typical Blomkvist adventure. Malm was never quite sure whether Blomkvist was paranoid by nature or if he had paranormal gifts. Since the events in Gosseberga his colleague had certainly become withdrawn and hard to communicate with. Nothing unusual about this, though. But when Blomkvist was working on a complicated story – Malm had observed the same obsessive and secretive behaviour in the weeks before the Wennerström story broke – it became more pronounced.

On the other hand, Malm could see for himself that Blomkvist was indeed being tailed. He wondered vaguely what new nightmare was in the offing. Whatever it was, it would soak up all of *Millennium*'s time, energy and resources. Malm did not think it was a great idea for Blomkvist to set off on some wild scheme just when the magazine's editor-in-chief had deserted to the Big Daily, and now *Millennium*'s laboriously reconstructed stability was suddenly hanging once again in the balance.

But Malm had not participated in any parade – apart from Gay Pride – in at least ten years. He had nothing better to do on this May Day Sunday than humour his wayward publisher. He sauntered after the man tailing Blomkvist even though he had not been instructed to do so, but he lost sight him on Långholmsgatan.

One of the first things Blomkvist did when he realized that his mobile was bugged was to send Cortez out to buy some used handsets. Cortez bought a job lot of Ericsson T10s for a song. Blomkvist then opened some anonymous cash-card accounts on Comviq and distributed the mobiles to Eriksson, Cortez, Giannini, Malm and Armansky, also keeping one for himself. They were to be used only for conversations that absolutely must not be overheard. Day-to-day stuff they could and should do on their own mobiles. Which meant that they all had to carry two mobiles with them.

Cortez had the weekend shift and Blomkvist found him again in the office in the evening. Since the murder of Zalachenko, Blomkvist had devised a 24/7 roster, so that *Millennium*'s office was always staffed and someone slept there every night. The roster included himself, Cortez, Eriksson and Malm. Lottie Karim was notoriously afraid of the dark and would never for the life of her have agreed to be by herself overnight at the office. Nilsson was not afraid of the dark, but she worked so furiously on her projects that she was encouraged to go home when the day was done. Magnusson was getting on in years and as advertising manager had nothing to do with the editorial side. He was also about to go on holiday.

"Anything new?"

"Nothing special," Cortez said. "Today is all about May 1, naturally enough."

"I'm going to be here for a couple of hours," Blomkvist told him. "Take a break and come back around 9.00."

After Cortez left, Blomkvist got out his anonymous mobile and called Daniel Olsson, a freelance journalist in Göteborg. Over the years *Millennium* had published several of his articles and Blomkvist had great faith in his ability to gather background material.

"Hi, Daniel. Mikael Blomkvist here. Can you talk?"

"Sure."

"I need someone for a research job. You can bill us for five days, and you don't have to produce an article at the end of it. Well, you can write an article on the subject if you want and we'll publish it, but it's the research we're after."

"Fine. Tell me."

"It's sensitive. You can't discuss this with anyone except me, and you can communicate with me only via hotmail. You must not even mention that you're doing research for *Millennium*."

"This sounds fun. What are you looking for?"

"I want you to do a workplace report on Sahlgrenska hospital. We're calling the report 'E.R.', and it's to look at the differences between reality and the T.V. series. I want you to go to the hospital and observe the work in the emergency ward and the intensive care unit for a couple of days. Talk with doctors, nurses and cleaners – everybody who works there in fact. What are their working conditions like? What do they actually *do*? That sort of stuff. Photographs too, of course."

"Intensive care?" Olsson said.

"Exactly. I want you to focus on the follow-up care given to severely injured patients in corridor 11C. I want to know the whole layout of the corridor, who works there, what they look like, and what sort of background they have."

"Unless I'm mistaken, a certain Lisbeth Salander is a patient on 11C."

Olsson was not born yesterday.

"How interesting," Blomkvist said. "Find out which room she's in, who's in the neighbouring rooms, and what the routines are in that section."

"I have a feeling that this story is going to be about something altogether different," Olsson said.

"As I said . . . all I want is the research you come up with."

They exchanged hotmail addresses.

Salander was lying on her back on the floor when Nurse Marianne came in.

"Hmm," she said, thereby indicating her doubts about the wisdom of this style of conduct in the intensive care unit. But it was, she accepted, her patient's only exercise space.

Salander was sweating. She had spent thirty minutes trying to do arm lifts, stretches and sit-ups on the recommendation of her physiotherapist. She had a long list of the movements she was to perform each day to strengthen the muscles in her shoulder and hip in the wake of her operation three weeks earlier. She was breathing hard and felt wretchedly out of shape. She tired easily and her left shoulder was tight and hurt at the very least effort. But she was on the path to recovery. The headaches that had tormented her after surgery had subsided and came back only sporadically.

She realized that she was sufficiently recovered now that she could have walked out of the hospital, or at any rate hobbled out, if that had been possible, but it was not. First of all, the doctors had not yet declared her fit, and second, the door to her room was always locked and guarded by a fucking hit-man from Securitas, who sat on his chair in the corridor.

She was healthy enough to be moved to a normal rehabilitation ward, but after going back and forth about this, the police and hospital administration had agreed that Salander should remain in room eighteen for the time being. The room was easier to guard, there was round-the-clock staff close by, and the room was at the end of an L-shaped corridor. And in corridor 11C the staff were security-conscious after the killing of Zalachenko; they were familiar with her situation. Better not to move her to a new ward with new routines.

Her stay at Sahlgrenska was in any case going to come to an end in a few more weeks. As soon as the doctors discharged her, she would be transferred to Kronoberg prison in Stockholm to await trial. And the person who would decide when it was time for that was Dr Jonasson.

It was ten days after the shooting in Gosseberga before Dr Jonasson gave permission for the police to conduct their first real interview, which Giannini viewed as being to Salander's advantage. Unfortunately Dr Jonasson had made it difficult even for Giannini to have access to her client, and that was annoying.

After the tumult of Zalachenko's murder and Gullberg's attempted suicide, he had done an evaluation of Salander's condition. He took into account that Salander must be under a great deal of stress for having been suspected of three murders plus a damn-near fatal assault on her late father. Jonasson had no idea whether she was guilty or innocent, and as a doctor he was not the least bit interested in the answer to that question. He simply concluded that Salander was suffering from stress, that she had been shot three times, and that one bullet had entered her brain and almost killed her. She had a fever that would not abate, and she had severe headaches.

He had played it safe. Murder suspect or not, she was his patient, and his job was to make sure she got well. So he filled out a "no visitors" form that had no connection whatsoever to the one that was set in place by the prosecutor. He prescribed various medications and complete bedrest.

But Jonasson also realized that isolation was an inhumane way of punishing people; in fact it bordered on torture. No-one felt good when they were separated from all their friends, so he decided that Salander's lawyer should serve as a proxy friend. He had a serious talk with

Giannini and explained that she could have access to Salander for one hour a day. During this hour she could talk with her or just sit quietly and keep her company, but their conversations should not deal with Salander's problems or impending legal battles.

"Lisbeth Salander was shot in the head and was *very* seriously injured," he explained. "I think she's out of danger, but there is always a risk of bleeding or some other complication. She needs to rest and she has to have time to heal. Only when that has happened can she begin to confront her legal problems."

Giannini understood Dr Jonasson's reasoning. She had some general conversations with Salander and hinted at the outline of the strategy that she and Blomkvist had planned, but Salander was simply so drugged and exhausted that she would fall asleep while Giannini was speaking.

Armansky studied Malm's photographs of the men who had followed Blomkvist from the Copacabana. They were in sharp focus.

"No," he said. "Never seen them before."

Blomkvist nodded. They were in Armansky's office on Monday morning. Blomkvist had come into the building via the garage.

"The older one is Göran Mårtensson, who owns the Volvo. He followed me like a guilty conscience for at least a week, but it could have been longer."

"And you reckon that he's Säpo."

Blomkvist referred to Mårtensson's C.V. Armansky hesitated.

You could take it for granted that the Security Police invariably made fools of themselves. That was the natural order of things, not for Säpo alone but probably for intelligence services all over the world. The French secret police had sent frogmen to New Zealand to blow up the Greenpeace ship *Rainbow Warrior*, for God's sake. That had to be the most idiotic intelligence operation in the history of the world. With the possible exception of President Nixon's lunatic break-in at Watergate. With such cretinous leadership it was no wonder that scandals occurred. Their successes were never reported. But the media jumped all over the Security Police whenever anything improper or foolish came to light, and with all the wisdom of hindsight.

On the one hand, the media regarded Säpo as an excellent news source, and almost any political blunder gave rise to headlines: "Säpo suspects that . . ." A Säpo statement carried a lot of weight in a headline.

On the other hand, politicians of various affiliations, along with the media, were particularly diligent in condemning exposed Säpo agents if they had spied on Swedish citizens. Armansky found this entirely contradictory. He did not have anything against the existence of Säpo. Someone had to take responsibility for seeing to it that national-Bolshevist crackpots – who had read too much Bakunin or whoever the hell these neo-Nazis read – did not patch together a bomb made of fertilizer and oil and park it in a van outside Rosenbad. Säpo was necessary, and Armansky did not think a little discreet surveillance was such a bad thing, so long as its objective was to safeguard the security of the nation.

The problem, of course, was that an organization assigned to spy on citizens must remain under strict public scrutiny. There had to be a high level of constitutional oversight. But it was almost impossible for Members of Parliament to have oversight of Säpo, even when the Prime Minister appointed a special investigator who, on paper at least, was supposed to have access to everything. Armansky had Blomkvist's copy of Lidbom's book *An Assignment*, and he was reading it with gathering astonishment. If this were the United States a dozen or so senior Säpo hands would have been arrested for obstruction of justice and forced to appear before a public committee in Congress. In Sweden apparently they were untouchable.

The Salander case demonstrated that something was out of joint inside the organization. But when Blomkvist came over to give him a secure mobile, Armansky's first thought was that the man was paranoid. It was only when he heard the details and studied Malm's photographs that he reluctantly admitted that Blomkvist had good reason to be suspicious. It did not bode well, but rather indicated that the conspiracy that had tried to eliminate Salander fifteen years earlier was not a thing of the past.

There were simply too many incidents for this to be coincidence. Never mind that Zalachenko had supposedly been murdered by a nutter. It had happened at the same time that both Blomkvist and Giannini were robbed of the document that was the cornerstone in the burden of proof. That was a shattering misfortune. And then the key witness, Gunnar Björck, had gone and hanged himself.

"Are we agreed that I pass this on to my contact?" Armansky said, gathering up Blomkvist's documentation.

"And this is a person that you say you can trust?"

"An individual of the highest moral standing."

"Inside *Säpo*?" Blomkvist said with undisguised scepticism.

"We have to be of one mind. Both Holger and I have accepted your plan and are co-operating with you. But we can't clear this matter up all by ourselves. We have to find allies within the bureaucracy if this is not going to end in calamity."

"O.K." Blomkvist nodded reluctantly. "I've never had to give out information on a story before it's published."

"But in this case you already have. You've told me, your sister, and Holger."

"True enough."

"And you did it because even you recognize that this is far more than just a scoop in your magazine. For once you're not an objective reporter, but a participant in unfolding events. And as such you need help. You're not going to win on your own."

Blomkvist gave in. He had not, in any case, told the *whole* truth either to Armansky or to his sister. He still had one or two secrets that he shared only with Salander.

He shook hands with Armansky.

CHAPTER 9

Wednesday, 4.v

Three days after Berger started as acting editor-in-chief of *S.M.P.*, Editor-in-Chief Morander died at lunchtime. He had been in the glass cage all morning, while Berger and assistant editor Peter Fredriksson met the sports editors so that she could get to know her colleagues and find out how they worked. Fredriksson was forty-five years old and also relatively new to the paper. He was taciturn but pleasant, with a broad experience. Berger had already decided that she would be able to depend on Fredriksson's insights when she took command of the ship. She was spending a good part of her time evaluating the people she might be able to count on and could then make part of her new regime. Fredriksson was definitely a candidate.

When they got back to the news desk they saw Morander get up and come over to the door of the glass cage. He looked startled.

Then he leaned forward, grabbed the back of a chair and held on to it for a few seconds before he collapsed to the floor.

He was dead before the ambulance arrived.

There was a confused atmosphere in the newsroom throughout the afternoon. Chairman of the Board Borgsjö arrived at 2.00 and gathered the employees for a brief memorial to Morander. He spoke of how Morander had dedicated the past fifteen years of his life to the newspaper, and the price that the work of a newspaperman can sometimes exact. Finally he called for a minute's silence.

Berger realized that several of her new colleagues were looking at her. *The unknown quantity.*

She cleared her throat and without being invited to, without knowing what she would say, took half a step forward and spoke in a firm voice: "I knew Håkan Morander for all of three days. That's too short a time, but from even the little I managed to know of him, I can honestly say that I would have wanted very much to know him better."

She paused when she saw out of the corner of her eye that Borgsjö was staring at her. He seemed surprised that she was saying anything at all. She took another pace forward.

"Your editor-in-chief's untimely departure will create problems in the newsroom. I was supposed to take over from him in two months, and I was counting on having the time to learn from his experience."

She saw that Borgsjö had opened his mouth as if to say something himself.

"That won't happen now, and we're going to go through a period of adjustment. But Morander was editor-in-chief of a daily newspaper, and this paper will come out tomorrow too. There are now nine hours left before we go to press and four before the front page has to be resolved. May I ask . . . who among you was Morander's closest confidant?"

A brief silence followed as the staff looked at each other. Finally Berger heard a voice from the left side of the room.

"That would probably be me."

It was Gunnar Magnusson, assistant editor of the front page who had worked on the paper for thirty-five years.

"Somebody has to write an obit. I can't do it . . . that would be presumptuous of me. Could you possibly write it?"

Magnusson hesitated a moment but then said, "I'll do it."

"We'll use the whole front page and move everything else back."

Magnusson nodded.

"We need images." She glanced to her right and met the eye of the pictures editor, Lennart Torkelsson. He nodded.

"We have to get busy on this. Things might be a bit rocky at first. When I need help making a decision, I'll ask your advice and I'll depend on your skill and experience. You know how the paper is made and I have a while to go on the school bench."

She turned to Fredriksson.

"Peter, Morander put a great deal of trust in you. You will have to be something of a mentor to me for the time being, and carry a heavier load than usual. I'm asking you to be my adviser."

He nodded. What else could he do?

She returned to the subject of the front page.

"One more thing. Morander was writing his editorial this morning. Gunnar, could you get into his computer and see whether he finished it? Even if it's not quite rounded out, we'll publish it. It was his last editorial and it would be a crying shame not to print it. The paper we're making today is still Håkan Morander's paper."

Silence.

"If any of you need a little personal time, or want to take a break to think for a while, do it, please. You all know our deadlines."

Silence. She noticed that some people were nodding their approval.

"Go to work, boys and girls," she said in English in a low voice.

Holmberg threw up his hands in a helpless gesture. Bublanski and Modig looked dubious. Andersson's expression was neutral. They were scrutinizing the results of the preliminary investigation that Holmberg had completed that morning.

"Nothing?" Modig said. She sounded surprised.

"Nothing," Holmberg said, shaking his head. "The pathologist's final report arrived this morning. Nothing to indicate anything but suicide by hanging."

They looked once more at the photographs taken in the living room of the summer cabin in Smådalarö. Everything pointed to the conclusion that Gunnar Björck, assistant chief of the Immigration Division of the Security Police, had climbed on to a stool, tied a rope to the lamp hook, placed it around his neck, and then with great resolve kicked the stool across the room. The pathologist was unable to supply the exact time of death, but he had established that it occurred on the afternoon of April 12. The body had been discovered on April 19 by none other than Inspector Andersson. This happened because Bublanski had repeatedly tried to get hold of Björck. Annoyed, he finally sent Andersson to bring him in.

Sometime during that week, the lamp hook in the ceiling came away and Björck's body fell to the floor. Andersson had seen the body through a window and called in the alarm. Bublanski and the others who arrived at the summer house had treated it as a crime scene from the word go, taking it for granted that Björck had been garrotted by someone. Later that day the forensic team found the lamp hook. Holmberg had been tasked to work out how Björck had died.

"There's nothing whatsoever to suggest a crime, or that Björck was not alone at the time," Holmberg said.

"The lamp?"

"The ceiling lamp has fingerprints from the owner of the cabin – who put it up two years ago – and Björck himself. Which says that he took the lamp down."

"Where did the rope come from?"

"From the flagpole in the garden. Someone cut off about two metres of rope. There was a Mora sheath knife on the windowsill outside the back door. According to the owner of the house, it's his knife. He normally keeps in a tool drawer underneath the draining board. Björck's prints were on the handle and the blade, as well as the tool drawer."

"Hmm," Modig said.

"What sort of knots?" Andersson said.

"Granny knots. Even the noose was just a loop. It's probably the only thing that's a bit odd. Björck was a sailor, he would have known how to tie proper knots. But who knows how much attention a person contemplating suicide would pay to the knots on his own noose?"

"What about drugs?"

"According to the toxicology report, Björck had traces of a strong painkiller in his blood. That medication had been prescribed for him. He also had traces of alcohol, but the percentage was negligible. In other words, he was more or less sober."

"The pathologist wrote that there were graze wounds."

"A graze over three centimetres long on the outside of his left knee. A scratch, really. I've thought about it, but it could have come about in a dozen different ways . . . for instance, if he walked into the corner of a table or a bench, whatever."

Modig held up a photograph of Björck's distorted face. The noose had cut so deeply into his flesh that the rope itself was hidden in the skin of his neck. The face was grotesquely swollen.

"He hung there for something like twenty-four hours before the hook gave way. All the blood was either in his head – the noose having prevented it from running into his body – or in the lower extremities. When the hook came out and his body fell, his chest hit the coffee table, causing deep bruising there. But this injury happened long after the time of death."

"Hell of a way to die," said Andersson.

"I don't know. The noose was so thin that it pinched deep and stopped the blood flow. He was probably unconscious within a few seconds and dead in one or two minutes."

Bublanski closed the preliminary report with distaste. He did not like this. He absolutely did not like the fact that Zalachenko and Björck had, so far as they could tell, both died on the same day. But no amount of speculating could change the fact that the crime scene investigation offered no grain of support to the theory that a third party had helped Björck on his way.

"He was under a lot of pressure," Bublanski said. "He knew that the whole Zalachenko affair was in danger of being exposed and that he risked a prison sentence for sex-trade crimes, plus being hung out to dry in the media. I wonder which scared him more. He was sick, had been suffering chronic pain for a long time . . . I don't know. I wish he had left a letter."

"Many suicides don't."

"I know. O.K. We'll put Björck to one side for now. We have no choice."

Berger could not bring herself to sit at Morander's desk right away, or to move his belongings aside. She arranged for Magnusson to talk to Morander's family so that the widow could come herself when it was convenient, or send someone to sort out his things.

Instead she had an area cleared off the central desk in the heart of the newsroom, and there she set up her laptop and took command. It was chaotic. But three hours after she had taken the helm of *S.M.P.* in such appalling circumstances, the front page went to press. Magnusson had put together a four-column article about Morander's life and career. The page was designed around a black-bordered portrait, almost all of it above the fold, with his unfinished editorial to the left and a frieze of photographs along the bottom edge. The layout was not perfect, but it had a strong moral and emotional impact.

Just before 6.00, as Berger was going through the headlines on page two and discussing the texts with the head of revisions, Borgsjö approached and touched her shoulder. She looked up.

"Could I have a word?"

They went together to the coffee machine in the canteen.

"I just wanted to say that I'm really very pleased with the way you took control today. I think you surprised us all."

"I didn't have much choice. But I may stumble a bit before I really get going."

"We understand that."

"We?"

"I mean the staff and the board. The board especially. But after what happened today I'm more than ever persuaded that you were the ideal choice. You came here in the nick of time, and you took charge in a very difficult situation."

Berger almost blushed. But she had not done that since she was fourteen.

"Could I give you a piece of advice?"

"Of course."

"I heard that you had a disagreement about a headline with Anders Holm."

"We didn't agree on the angle in the article about the government's tax proposal. He inserted an opinion into the headline in the news section, which is supposed to be neutral. Opinions should be reserved for the editorial page. And while I'm on this topic . . . I'll be writing editorials from time to time, but as I told you I'm not active in any political party, so we have to solve the problem of who's going to be in charge of the editorial section."

"Magnusson can take over for the time being," said Borgsjö.

Erika shrugged. "It makes no difference to me who you appoint. But it should be somebody who clearly stands for the newspaper's views. That's where they should be aired . . . not in the news section."

"Quite right. What I wanted to say was that you'll probably have to give Holm some concessions. He's worked at *S.M.P.* a long time and he's been news chief for fifteen years. He knows what he's doing. He can be surly sometimes, but he's irreplaceable."

"I know. Morander told me. But when it comes to *policy* he's going to have to toe the line. I'm the one you hired to run the paper."

Borgsjö thought for a moment and said: "We're going to have to solve these problems as they come up."

Giannini was both tired and irritated on Wednesday evening as she boarded the X2000 at Göteborg Central Station. She felt as if she had been living on the X2000 for a month. She bought a coffee in the restaurant car, went to her seat, and opened the folder of notes from her last conversation with Salander. Who was also the reason why she was feeling tired and irritated.

She's hiding something. That little fool is not telling me the truth. And Micke is hiding something too. God knows what they're playing at.

She also decided that since her brother and her client had not so far communicated with each other, the conspiracy – if it was one –

had to be a tacit agreement that had developed naturally. She did not understand what it was about, but it had to be something that her brother considered important enough to conceal.

She was afraid that it was a moral issue, and that was one of his weaknesses. He was Salander's friend. She knew her brother. She knew that he was loyal to the point of foolhardiness once he had made someone a friend, even if the friend was impossible and obviously flawed. She also knew that he could accept any number of idiocies from his friends, but that there was a boundary and it could not be infringed. Where exactly this boundary was seemed to vary from one person to another, but she knew he had broken completely with people who had previously been close friends because they had done something that he regarded as beyond the pale. And he was inflexible. The break was for ever.

Giannini understood what went on in her brother's head. But she had no idea what Salander was up to. Sometimes she thought that there was nothing going on in there at all.

She had gathered that Salander could be moody and withdrawn. Until she met her in person, Giannini had supposed it must be some phase, and that it was a question of gaining her trust. But after a month of conversations – ignoring the fact that the first two weeks had been wasted time because Salander was hardly able to speak – their communication was still distinctly one-sided.

Salander seemed at times to be in a deep depression and had not the slightest interest in dealing with her situation or her future. She simply did not grasp or did not care that the only way Giannini could provide her with an effective defence would be if she had access to all the facts. There was no way in the world she was going to be able to work in the dark.

Salander was sulky and often just silent. When she did say something, she took a long time to think and she chose her words carefully. Often she did not reply at all, and sometimes she would answer a question that Giannini had asked several days earlier. During the police interviews, Salander had sat in utter silence, staring straight ahead. With rare exceptions, she had refused to say a single word to the police. The exceptions were on those occasions when Inspector Erlander had asked her what she knew about Niedermann. Then she looked up at him and answered every question in a perfectly matter-of-fact way. As soon as he changed the subject, she lost interest.

On principle, she knew, Salander never talked to the authorities. In this case, that was an advantage. Despite the fact that she kept urging her client to answer questions from the police, deep inside she was pleased with Salander's silence. The reason was simple. It was a consistent silence. It contained no lies that could entangle her, no contradictory reasoning that would look bad in court.

But she was astonished at how imperturbable Salander was. When they were alone she had asked her why she so provocatively refused to talk to the police.

"They'll twist what I say and use it against me."

"But if you don't explain yourself, you risk being convicted anyway."

"Then that's how it'll have to be. I didn't make all this mess. And if they want to convict me, it's not my problem."

Salander had in the end described to her lawyer almost everything that had happened at Stallarholmen. All except for one thing. She would not explain how Magge Lundin had ended up with a bullet in his foot. No matter how much she asked and nagged, Salander would just stare at her and smile her crooked smile.

She had also told Giannini what happened in Gosseberga. But she had not said anything about why she had run her father to ground. Did she go there expressly to murder him – as the prosecutor claimed – or was it to make him listen to reason?

When Giannini raised the subject of her former guardian, Nils Bjurman, Salander said only that she was not the one who shot him. And that particular murder was no longer one of the charges against her. And when Giannini reached the very crux of the whole chain of events, the role of Dr Teleborian in the psychiatric clinic in 1991, Salander lapsed into such inexhaustible silence that it seemed she might never utter a word again.

This is getting us nowhere, Giannini decided. *If she won't trust me, we're going to lose the case.*

Salander sat on the edge of her bed, looking out of the window. She could see the building on the other side of the car park. She had sat undisturbed and motionless for an hour, ever since Giannini had stormed out and slammed the door behind her. She had a headache again, but it was mild and it was distant. Yet she felt uncomfortable.

She was irritated with Giannini. From a practical point of view she could see why her lawyer kept going on and on about details from her past. Rationally she understood it. Giannini needed to have all the facts. But she did not have the remotest wish to talk about her feelings or her actions. Her life was her own business. It was not her fault that her father had been a pathological sadist and murderer. It was not her fault that her brother was a murderer. And thank God nobody yet knew that he was her brother, which would otherwise no doubt also be held against her in the psychiatric evaluation that sooner or later would inevitably be conducted. She was not the one who had killed Svensson and Johansson. She was not responsible for appointing a guardian who turned out to be a pig and a rapist.

And yet it was *her* life that was going to be turned inside out. She would be forced to explain herself and to beg for forgiveness because she had defended herself.

She just wanted to be left in peace. And when it came down to it, she was the one who would have to live with herself. She did not expect anyone to be her friend. Annika Bloody Giannini was most likely on her side, but it was the professional friendship of a professional person who was her lawyer. Kalle Bastard Blomkvist was out there somewhere – Giannini was for some reason reluctant to talk about her brother, and Salander never asked. She did not expect that he would be quite so interested now that the Svensson murder was solved and he had got his story.

She wondered what Armansky thought of her after all that had happened.

She wondered how Holger Palmgren viewed the situation.

According to Giannini, both of them had said they would be in her corner, but that was words. They could not do anything to solve her private problems.

She wondered what Miriam Wu felt about her.

She wondered what she thought of herself, come to that, and came to the realization that most of all she felt indifference towards her entire life.

She was interrupted when the Securitas guard put the key in the door to let in Dr Jonasson.

"Good evening, Fröken Salander. And how are you feeling today?"

"O.K.," she said.

He checked her chart and saw that she was free of her fever. She had got used to his visits, which came a couple of times a week. Of all the people who touched her and poked at her, he was the only one in whom she felt a measure of trust. She never felt that he was giving her strange looks. He visited her room, chatted a while, and examined her to check on her progress. He did not ask any questions about Niedermann or Zalachenko, or whether she was off her rocker or why the police kept her locked up. He seemed to be interested only in how her muscles were working, how the healing in her brain was progressing, and how she felt in general.

Besides, he had – literally – rooted around in her brain. Someone who rummaged around in your brain had to be treated with respect. To her surprise she found the visits of Dr Jonasson pleasant, despite the fact that he poked at her and fussed over her fever chart.

"Do you mind if I check?"

He made his usual examination, looking at her pupils, listening to her breathing, taking her pulse, her blood pressure, and checking how she swallowed.

"How am I doing?"

"You're on the road to recovery. But you have to work harder on the exercises. And you're picking at the scab on your head. You need to stop that." He paused. "May I ask a personal question?"

She looked at him. He waited until she nodded.

"That dragon tattoo . . . Why did you get it?"

"You didn't see it before?"

He smiled all of a sudden.

"I mean I've *glanced* at it, but when you were uncovered I was pretty busy stopping the bleeding and extracting bullets and so on."

"Why do you ask?"

"Out of curiosity, nothing more."

Salander thought for a while. Then she looked at him.

"I got it for reasons that I don't want to discuss."

"Forget I asked."

"Do you want to see it?"

He looked surprised. "Sure. Why not?"

She turned her back and pulled the hospital gown off her shoulder. She sat so that the light from the window fell on her back. He looked at her dragon. It was beautiful and well done, a work of art.

After a while she turned her head.

"Satisfied?"

"It's beautiful. But it must have hurt like hell."

"Yes," she said. "It hurt."

181

Jonasson left Salander's room somewhat confused. He was satisfied with the progress of her physical rehabilitation. But he could not work out this strange girl. He did not need a master's degree in psychology to know that she was not doing very well emotionally. The tone she used with him was polite, but riddled with suspicion. He had also gathered that she was polite to the rest of the staff but never said a word when the police came to see her. She was locked up inside her shell and kept her distance from those around her.

The police had locked her in her hospital room, and a prosecutor intended to charge her with attempted murder and grievous bodily harm. He was amazed that such a small, thin girl had the physical strength for this sort of violent criminality, especially when the violence was directed at full-grown men.

He had asked about her dragon tattoo, hoping to find a personal topic he could discuss with her. He was not particularly interested in why she had decorated herself in such a way, but he supposed that since she had chosen such a striking tattoo, it must have a special meaning for her. He thought simply that it might be a way to start a conversation.

His visits to her were outside his schedule, since Dr Endrin was assigned to her case. But Jonasson was head of the trauma unit, and he was proud of what had been achieved that night when Salander was brought into A. & E. He had made the right decision, electing to remove the bullet. As far as he could see she had no complications in the form of memory lapses, diminished bodily function, or other handicaps from the injury. If she continued to heal at the same pace, she would leave hospital with a scar on her scalp, but with no other visible damage. Scars on her soul were another matter.

Returning to his office he discovered a man in a dark suit leaning against the wall outside his door. He had a thick head of hair and a well-groomed beard.

"Dr Jonasson?"

"Yes?"

"My name is Peter Teleborian. I'm the head physician at St Stefan's psychiatric clinic in Uppsala."

"Yes, I recognize you."

"Good. I'd like to have a word in private with you if you have a moment."

Jonasson unlocked the door and ushered the visitor in. "How can I help you?"

"It's about one of your patients, Lisbeth Salander. I need to visit her."

"You'll have to get permission from the prosecutor. She's under arrest and all visitors are prohibited. And any applications for visits must also be referred in advance to Salander's lawyer."

"Yes, yes, I know. I thought we might be able to cut through all the red tape in this case. I'm a physician, so you could let me have the opportunity to visit her on medical grounds."

"Yes, there might be a case for that, but I can't see what your objective is."

"For several years I was Lisbeth Salander's psychiatrist when she was institutionalized at St Stefan's. I followed up with her until she turned eighteen, when the district court released her back into society, albeit under guardianship. I should perhaps mention that I opposed that action. Since then she has been allowed to drift aimlessly, and the consequences are there for all to see today."

"Indeed?"

"I feel a great responsibility towards her still, and would value the chance to gauge how much deterioration has occurred over the past ten years."

"Deterioration?"

"Compared with when she was receiving qualified care as a teenager. I thought we might be able to come to an understanding here, as one doctor to another."

"While I have it fresh in my mind, perhaps you could help me with a matter I don't quite understand . . . as one doctor to another, that is. When she was admitted to Sahlgrenska hospital I performed a comprehensive medical examination on her. A colleague sent for the forensic report on the patient. It was signed by a Dr Jesper H. Löderman."

"That's correct. I was Dr Löderman's assistant when he was in practice."

"I see. But I noticed that the report was vague in the extreme."

"Really?"

"It contains no diagnosis. It almost seems to be an academic study of a patient who refuses to speak."

Teleborian laughed. "Yes, she certainly isn't easy to deal with. As it says in the report, she consistently refused to participate in conversations with Dr Löderman. With the result that he was bound to express himself rather imprecisely. Which was entirely correct on his part."

"And yet the recommendation was that she should be institutionalized?"

"That was based on her prior history. We had experience with her pathology compiled over many years."

"That's exactly what I don't understand. When she was admitted here, we sent for a copy of her file from St Stefan's. But we still haven't received it."

"I'm sorry about that. But it's been classified Top Secret by order of the district court."

"And how are we supposed to give her the proper care here if we can't have access to her records? The medical responsibility for her right now is ours, no-one else's."

"I've taken care of her since she was twelve, and I don't think there is any other doctor in Sweden with the same insight into her clinical condition."

"Which is what . . .?"

"Lisbeth Salander suffers from a serious mental disorder. Psychiatry, as you know, is not an exact science. I would hesitate to confine myself to an exact diagnosis, but she has obvious delusions with distinct paranoid schizophrenic characteristics. Her clinical status also includes periods of manic depression and she lacks empathy."

Jonasson looked intently at Dr Teleborian for ten seconds before he said: "I won't argue a diagnosis with you, Dr Teleborian, but have you ever considered a significantly simpler diagnosis?"

"Such as?"

"For example, Asperger's syndrome. Of course I haven't done a psychiatric evaluation of her, but if I had spontaneously to hazard a guess, I would consider some form of autism. That would explain her inability to relate to social conventions."

"I'm sorry, but Asperger's patients do not generally set fire to their parents. Believe me, I've never met so clearly defined a sociopath."

"I consider her to be withdrawn, but not a paranoid sociopath."

"She is extremely manipulative," Teleborian said. "She acts the way she thinks you would expect her to act."

Jonasson frowned. Teleborian was contradicting his own reading of Salander. If there was one thing Jonasson felt sure about her, it was that she was certainly not manipulative. On the contrary, she was a person who stubbornly kept her distance from those around her and showed no emotion at all. He tried to reconcile the picture that Teleborian was painting with his own image of Salander.

"And you have seen her only for a short period when she has been forced to be passive because of her injuries. I have witnessed her violent outbursts and unreasoning hatred. I have spent years trying to help Lisbeth Salander. That's why I'm here. I propose a co-operation between Sahlgrenska hospital and St Stefan's."

"What sort of co-operation are you talking about?"

"You're responsible for her medical condition, and I'm convinced that it's the best care she could receive. But I'm extremely worried about her mental state, and I would like to be included at an early stage. I'm ready to offer all the help I can."

"I see."

"So I do need to visit her to do a first-hand evaluation of her condition."

"There, unfortunately, I cannot help you."

"I beg your pardon?"

"As I said, she's under arrest. If you want to initiate any psychiatric treatment of her, you'll have to apply to Prosecutor Jervas here in Göteborg. She's the one who makes the decisions on these things. And it would have to be done, I repeat, in co-operation with her lawyer, Annika Giannini. If it's a matter of a forensic psychiatric report, then the district court would have to issue you a warrant."

"It was just that sort of bureaucratic procedure I wanted to avoid."

"Understood, but I'm responsible for her, and if she's going to be taken to court in the near future, we need to have clear documentation of all the measures we have taken. So we're bound to observe the bureaucratic procedures."

"Alright. Then I might as well tell you that I've already received a formal commission from Prosecutor Ekström in Stockholm to do a forensic psychiatric report. It will be needed in connection with the trial."

"Then you can also obtain formal access to visit her through the appropriate channels without side-stepping regulations."

"But while we're going backwards and forwards with bureaucracy, there is a risk that her condition may continue to deteriorate. I'm only interested in her wellbeing."

"And so am I," Jonasson said. "And between us, I can tell you that I see no sign of mental illness. She has been badly treated and is under a lot of pressure. But I see no evidence whatsoever that she is schizophrenic or suffering from paranoid delusions."

When at long last he realized that it was fruitless trying to persuade Jonasson to change his mind, Teleborian got up abruptly and took his leave.

Jonasson sat for a while, staring at the chair Teleborian had been sitting in. It was not unusual for other doctors to contact him with advice or opinions on treatment. But that usually happened only with patients whose doctors were already managing their treatment. He had never before seen a psychiatrist land like a flying saucer and more or less demand to be given access to a patient, ignoring all the protocols, and a patient, at that, whom he obviously had not been treating for several years. After a while Jonasson glanced at his watch and saw that it was almost 7.00. He picked up the telephone and called Martina Karlgren, the psychologist at Sahlgrenska who had been made available to trauma patients.

"Hello. I'm assuming you've already left for the day. Am I disturbing you?"

"No problem. I'm at home, but just pottering."

"I'm curious about something. You've spoken to our notorious patient, Lisbeth Salander. Could you give me your impression of her?"

"Well, I've visited her three times and offered to talk with her. Every time she declined in a friendly but firm way."

"What's your impression of her?"

"What do you mean?"

"Martina, I know that you're not a psychiatrist, but you're an intelligent and sensible person. What general impression did you get of her nature, her state of mind?"

After a while Karlgren said: "I'm not sure how I should answer that question. I saw her twice soon after she was admitted, but she was in such wretched shape that I didn't make any real contact with her. Then I visited her about a week ago, at the request of Helena Endrin."

"Why did Helena ask you to visit her?"

"Salander is starting to recover. She mainly just lies there staring at the ceiling. Dr Endrin wanted me to look in on her."

"And what happened?"

"I introduced myself. We chatted for a couple of minutes. I asked how she was feeling and whether she felt the need to have someone to talk to. She said that she didn't. I asked if I could help her with anything. She asked me to smuggle in a pack of cigarettes."

"Was she angry, or hostile?"

"No, I wouldn't say that. She was calm, but she kept her distance. I considered her request for cigarettes more of a joke than a serious need. I asked if she wanted something to read, whether I could bring her books of any sort. At first she said no, but later she asked if I had any scientific journals that dealt with genetics and brain research."

"With *what*?"

"Genetics."

"*Genetics?*"

"Yes. I told her that there were some popular science books on the subject in our library. She wasn't interested in those. She said she'd read books on the subject before, and she named some standard works that I'd never heard of. She was more interested in pure research in the field."

"Good grief."

"I said that we probably didn't have any more advanced books in the patient library – we have more Philip Marlowe than scientific literature – but that I'd see what I could dig up."

"And did you?"

"I went upstairs and borrowed some copies of *Nature* magazine and *The New England Journal of Medicine*. She was pleased and thanked me for taking the trouble."

"But those journals contain mostly scholarly papers and pure research."

"She reads them with obvious interest."

Jonasson sat speechless for a moment.

"And how would you rate her mental state?"

"Withdrawn. She hasn't discussed anything of a personal nature with me."

"Do you have the sense that she's mentally ill? Manic depressive or paranoid?"

"No, no, not at all. If I thought that, I'd have sounded the alarm. She's strange, no doubt about it, and she has big problems and is under stress. But she's calm and matter-of-fact and seems to be able to cope with her situation. Why do you ask? Has something happened?"

"No, nothing's happened. I'm just trying to take stock of her."

CHAPTER 10

Saturday, 7.v – Thursday, 12.v

Blomkvist put his laptop case on the desk. It contained the findings of Olsson, the stringer in Göteborg. He watched the flow of people on Götgatan. That was one of the things he liked best about his office. Götgatan was full of life at all hours of the day and night, and when he sat by the window he never felt isolated, never alone.

He was under great pressure. He had kept working on the articles that were to go into the summer issue, but he had finally realized that there was so much material that not even an issue devoted entirely to the topic would be sufficient. He had ended up in the same situation as during the Wennerström affair, and he had again decided to publish all the articles as a book. He had enough text already for 150 pages, and he reckoned that the final book would run to 320 or 336 pages.

The easy part was done. He had written about the murders of Svensson and Johansson and described how he happened to be the one who came upon the scene. He had dealt with why Salander had become a suspect. He spent a chapter debunking first what the press had written about Salander, then what Prosecutor Ekström had claimed, and thereby indirectly the entire police investigation. After long deliberation he had toned down his criticism of Bublanski and his team. He did this after studying a video from Ekström's press conference, in which it was clear that Bublanski was uncomfortable in the extreme and obviously annoyed at Ekström's rapid conclusions.

After the introductory drama, he had gone back in time and described Zalachenko's arrival in Sweden, Salander's childhood, and the events that led to her being locked away in St Stefan's in Uppsala. He was careful to annihilate both Teleborian and the now dead Björck. He rehearsed the psychiatric report of 1991 and explained why Salander had become a threat to certain unknown civil servants who had taken it upon themselves to protect the Russian defector. He quoted from the correspondence between Teleborian and Björck.

He then described Zalachenko's new identity and his criminal operations. He described his assistant Niedermann, the kidnapping of Miriam Wu, and Paolo Roberto's intervention. Finally, he summed up the dénouement in Gosseberga which led to Salander being shot and buried alive, and explained how a policeman's death was a needless catastrophe because Niedermann had already been shackled.

Thereafter the story became more sluggish. Blomkvist's problem was that the account still had gaping holes in it. Björck had not acted alone. Behind this chain of events there had to be a larger group with resources and political influence. Anything else did not make sense. But he had eventually come to the conclusion that the unlawful treatment of Salander would not have been sanctioned by the government or the bosses of the Security Police. Behind this conclusion lay no exaggerated trust in government, but rather his faith in human nature. An operation of that type could never have been kept secret if it were politically motivated. Someone would have called in a favour and got someone to talk, and the press would have uncovered the Salander affair several years earlier.

He thought of the Zalachenko club as small and anonymous. He could not identify any one of them, except possibly Mårtensson, a policeman with a secret appointment who devoted himself to shadowing the publisher of *Millennium*.

It was now clear that Salander would definitely go to trial.

Ekström had brought a charge for grievous bodily harm in the case of Magge Lundin, and grievous bodily harm or attempted murder in the case of Karl Axel Bodin.

No date had yet been set, but his colleagues had learned that Ekström was planning for a trial in July, depending on the state of Salander's health. Blomkvist understood the reasoning. A trial during the peak holiday season would attract less attention than one at any other time of the year.

Blomkvist's plan was to have the book printed and ready to distribute on the first day of the trial. He and Malm had thought of a paperback edition, shrink-wrapped and sent out with the special summer issue. Various assignments had been given to Cortez and Eriksson, who were to produce articles on the history of the Security Police, the IB affair,* and the like.

He frowned as he stared out of the window.

It's not over. The conspiracy is continuing. It's the only way to explain the tapped telephones, the attack on Annika, and the double theft of the Salander report. Perhaps the murder of Zalachenko is a part of it too.

But he had no evidence.

Together with Eriksson and Malm, he had decided that Millennium Publishing would publish Svensson's text about sex trafficking, also to coincide with the trial. It was better to present the package all at once, and besides, there was no reason to delay publication. On the contrary – the book would never be able to attract the same attention at any other time. Eriksson was Blomkvist's principal assistant for the Salander book. Karim and Malm (against his will) had thus become temporary assistant editors at *Millennium*, with Nilsson as the only available reporter. One result of this increased workload was that Eriksson had had to contract several freelancers to produce articles for future issues. It was expensive, but they had no choice.

Blomkvist wrote a note on a yellow Post-it, reminding himself to discuss the rights to the book with Svensson's family. His parents lived in Örebro and they were his sole heirs. He did not really need permission to publish the book in Svensson's name, but he wanted to go and see them to get their approval. He had postponed the visit because he had had too much to do, but now it was time to take care of the matter.

Then there were a hundred other details. Some of them concerned how he should present Salander in the articles. To make the ultimate decision he needed to have a personal conversation with her to get her approval to tell the truth, or at least parts of it. And he could not have that conversation because she was under arrest and no visitors were allowed.

In that respect, his sister was no help either. Slavishly she followed the regulations and had no intention of acting as Blomkvist's go-between. Nor did Giannini tell him anything of what she and her client discussed, other than the parts that concerned the conspiracy against her – Giannini needed help with those. It was frustrating, but all very correct. Consequently Blomkvist had no clue whether Salander had revealed that her previous guardian had raped her, or that she had taken revenge by tattooing a shocking message on his stomach. As long as Giannini did not mention the matter, neither could he.

But Salander's being isolated presented one other acute problem. She was a computer expert, also a hacker, which Blomkvist knew but Giannini did not. Blomkvist had promised Salander that he would never reveal her secret, and he had kept his promise. But now he had a great need for her skills in that field.

Somehow he had to establish contact with her.

He sighed as he opened Olsson's folder again. There was a photocopy of a passport application form for one Idris Ghidi, born 1950. A man with a moustache, olive skin and black hair going grey at the temples.

He was Kurdish, a refugee from Iraq. Olsson had dug up much more on Ghidi than on any other hospital worker. Ghidi had apparently aroused media attention for a time, and appeared in several articles.

Born in the city of Mosul in northern Iraq, he graduated as an engineer and had been part of the "great economic leap forward" in the '70s. In 1984 he was a teacher at the College of Construction Technology in Mosul. He had not been known as a political activist, but he was a Kurd, and so a potential criminal in Saddam Hussein's Iraq. In 1987 Ghidi's father was arrested on suspicion of being a Kurdish militant. No elaboration was forthcoming. He was executed in January 1988. Two months later Idris Ghidi was seized by the Iraqi secret police, taken to a prison outside Mosul, and tortured there for eleven months to make him confess. What he was expected to confess, Ghidi never discovered, so the torture continued.

In March 1989, one of Ghidi's uncles paid the equivalent of 50,000 Swedish kronor, to the local leader of the Ba'ath Party, as compensation for the injury Ghidi had caused the Iraqi state. Two days later he was released into his uncle's custody. He weighed thirty-nine kilos and was unable to walk. Before his release, his left hip was smashed with a sledgehammer to discourage any mischief in the future.

He hovered between life and death for several weeks. When, slowly, he began to recover, his uncle took him to a farm well away from Mosul and there, over the summer, he regained his strength and was eventually able to walk again with crutches. He would never regain full health. The question was: what was he going to do in the future? In August he learned that his two brothers had been arrested. He would never see them again. When his uncle heard that Saddam Hussein's police were looking once more for Ghidi, he arranged, for a fee of 30,000 kronor, to get him across the border into Turkey and thence with a false passport to Europe.

Idris Ghidi landed at Arlanda airport in Sweden on 19 October, 1989. He did not know a word of Swedish, but he had been told to go to the passport police and immediately to ask for political asylum, which he did in broken English. He was sent to a refugee camp in Upplands Väsby. There he would spend almost two years, until the immigration authorities decided that Ghidi did not have sufficient grounds for a residency permit.

By this time Ghidi had learned Swedish and obtained treatment for his shattered hip. He had two operations and could now walk without crutches. During that period the Sjöbo debate* had been conducted in Sweden, refugee camps had been attacked, and Bert Karlsson had formed the New Democracy Party.

The reason why Ghidi had appeared so frequently in the press archives was that at the eleventh hour he came by a new lawyer who went directly to the press, and they published reports on his case. Other Kurds in Sweden got involved, including members of the prominent Baksi family. Protest meetings were held and petitions were sent to Minister of Immigration Birgit Friggebo, with the result that Ghidi was granted both a residency permit and a work visa in the kingdom of Sweden. In January 1992 he left Upplands Väsby a free man.

Ghidi soon discovered that being a well-educated and experienced construction engineer counted for nothing. He worked as a newspaper boy, a dish-washer, a doorman, and a taxi driver. He liked being a taxi driver except for two things. He had no local knowledge of the streets in Stockholm county, and he could not sit still for more than an hour before the pain in his hip became unbearable.

In May 1998 he moved to Göteborg after a distant relative took pity on him and offered him a steady job at an office-cleaning firm. He was given a part-time job managing a cleaning crew at Sahlgrenska hospital, with which the company had a contract. The work was routine. He swabbed floors six days a week including, as Olsson's ferreting had revealed, in corridor 11C.

Blomkvist studied the photograph of Idris Ghidi from the passport application. Then he logged on to the media archive and picked out several of the articles on which Olsson's report was based. He read attentively. He lit a cigarette. The smoking ban at *Millennium* had soon been relaxed after Berger left. Cortez now kept an ashtray on his desk.

Finally Blomkvist read what Olsson had produced about Dr Anders Jonasson.

Blomkvist did not see the grey Volvo on Monday, nor did he have the feeling that he was being watched or followed, but he walked briskly from the Academic bookshop to the side entrance of N.K. department store, and then straight through and out of the main entrance. Anybody who could keep up surveillance inside the bustling N.K. would have to be superhuman. He turned off both his mobiles and walked through the Galleria to Gustav Adolfs Torg, past the parliament building, and into Gamla Stan. Just in case anyone was still following him, he took a zigzag route through the narrow streets of the old city until he reached the right address and knocked at the door of Black/White Publishing.

It was 2.30 in the afternoon. He was there without warning, but the editor, Kurdo Baksi, was in and delighted to see him.

"Hello there," he said heartily. "Why don't you ever come and visit me any more?"

"I'm here to see you right now," Blomkvist said.

"Sure, but it's been three years since the last time."

They shook hands.

Blomkvist had known Baksi since the '80s. Actually, Blomkvist had been one of the people who gave Baksi practical help when he started the magazine *Black/White* with an issue that he produced secretly at night at the Trades Union Federation offices. Baksi had been caught in the act by Per-Erik Åström – the same man who went on to be the paedophile hunter at Save the Children – who in the '80s was the research secretary at the Trades Union Federation. He had discovered stacks of pages from *Black/White*'s first issue along with an oddly subdued Baksi in one of the copy rooms. Åström had looked at the front page and said: "God Almighty, that's not how a magazine is supposed to look." After that Åström had designed the logo that was on *Black/White*'s masthead for fifteen years before *Black/White* magazine went to its grave and became the book publishing house Black/White. At the same time Blomkvist had been suffering through an appalling period as I.T. consultant at the Trades Union Federation – his only venture into the I.T. field. Åström had enlisted him to proof-read and give *Black/White* some editorial support. Baksi and Blomkvist had been friends ever since.

Blomkvist sat on a sofa while Baksi got coffee from a machine in the hallway. They chatted for a while, the way you do when you haven't seen someone for some time, but they were constantly being interrupted by Baksi's mobile. He would have urgent-sounding conversations in Kurdish or possibly Turkish or Arabic or some other language that Blomkvist did not understand. It had always been this way on his other visits to Black/White Publishing. People called from all over the world to talk to Baksi.

"My dear Mikael, you look worried. What's on your mind?" he said at last.

"Could you turn off your telephone for a few minutes?"

Baksi turned off his telephone.

"I need a favour. A really important favour, and it has to be done immediately and cannot be mentioned outside this room."

"Tell me."

"In 1989 a refugee by the name of Idris Ghidi came to Sweden from Iraq. When he was faced with the prospect of deportation, he received help from your family until he was granted a residency permit. I don't know if it was your father or somebody else in the family who helped him."

"It was my uncle Mahmut. I know Ghidi. What's going on?"

"He's working in Göteborg. I need his help to do a simple job. I'm willing to pay him."

"What kind of job?"

"Do you trust me, Kurdo?"

"Of course. We've always been friends."

"The job I need done is very odd. I don't want to say what it entails right now, but I assure you it's in no way illegal, nor will it cause any problems for you or for Ghidi."

Baksi gave Blomkvist a searching look. "You don't want to tell me what it's about?"

"The fewer people who know, the better. But I need your help for an introduction – so that Idris will listen to me."

Baksi went to his desk and opened an address book. He looked through it for a minute before he found the number. Then he picked up the telephone. The conversation was in Kurdish. Blomkvist could see from Baksi's expression that he started out with words of greeting and small talk before he got serious and explained why he was calling. After a while he said to Blomkvist:

"When do you want to meet him?"

"Friday afternoon, if that would work. Ask if I can visit him at home."

Baksi spoke for a short while before he hung up.

"Idris lives in Angered," he said. "Do you have the address?"

Blomkvist nodded.

"He'll be home by 5.00 on Friday afternoon. You're welcome to visit him there."

"Thanks, Kurdo."

"He works at Sahlgrenska hospital as a cleaner," Baksi said.

"I know."

"I couldn't help reading in the papers that you're mixed up in this Salander story."

"That's right."

"She was shot."

"Yes."

"I heard she's at Sahlgrenska."

"That's also true."

Baksi knew that Blomkvist was busy planning some sort of mischief, which was what he was famous for doing. He had known him since the '80s. They might not have been best friends, but they never argued either, and Blomkvist had never hesitated if Baksi asked him a favour.

"Am I going to get mixed up in something I ought to know about?"

"You're not going to get involved. Your role was only to do me the kindness of introducing me to one of your acquaintances. And, I repeat, I won't ask him to do anything illegal."

This assurance was enough for Baksi. Blomkvist stood up. "I owe you one."

"We always owe each other one."

Cortez put down the telephone and drummed so loudly with his finger-tips on the edge of his desk that Nilsson glared at him. But she could see that he was lost in his own thoughts, and since she was feeling irritated in general she decided not to take it out on him.

She knew that Blomkvist was doing a lot of whispering with Cortez and Eriksson and Malm about the Salander story, while she and Karim were expected to do all the spadework for the next issue of a magazine that had not had any real leadership since Berger left. Eriksson was fine, but she lacked experience and the gravitas of Berger. And Cortez was just a young whippersnapper.

Nilsson was not unhappy that she had been passed over, nor did she want their jobs – that was the last thing she wanted. Her own job was to keep tabs on the government departments and parliament on behalf of *Millennium*. It was a job she enjoyed, and she knew it inside out. Besides, she had had it up to here with other work, like writing a column in a trade journal every week, or various volunteer tasks for Amnesty International and the like. She was not interested in being editor-in-chief of *Millennium* and working a minimum of twelve hours a day as well as sacrificing her weekends.

She did, however, feel that something had changed at *Millennium*. The magazine suddenly felt foreign. She could not put her finger on what was wrong.

As always, Blomkvist was irresponsible and kept vanishing on another of his mysterious trips, coming and going as he pleased. He was one of the owners of *Millennium*, fair enough, he could decide for himself what he wanted to do, but Jesus, a little sense of responsibility would not hurt.

Malm was the other current part-owner, and he was about as much help as he was when he was on holiday. He was talented, no question, and he could step in and take over the reins when Berger was away or busy, but usually he just followed through with what other people had already decided. He was brilliant at anything involving graphic design or presentations, but he was right out of his depth when it came to planning a magazine.

Nilsson frowned.

No, she was being unfair. What bothered her was that something had happened at the office. Blomkvist was working with Eriksson and Cortez, and the rest of them were somehow excluded. Those three had formed an inner circle and were always shutting themselves in Berger's office ... well, Eriksson's office, and then they'd all come trooping out in silence. Under Berger's leadership the magazine had always been a collective.

Blomkvist was working on the Salander story and would not share any part of it. But this was nothing new. He had not said a word about the Wennerström story either – not even Berger had known – but this time he had two confidants.

In a word, Nilsson was pissed off. She needed a holiday. She needed to get away for a while. Then she saw Cortez putting on his corduroy jacket.

"I'm going out for a while," he said. "Could you tell Malin that I'll be back in two hours?"

"What's going on?"

"I think I've got a lead on a story. A really good story. About toilets. I want to check a few things, but if this pans out we'll have a fantastic article for the June issue."

"Toilets," Nilsson muttered. "A likely story."

Berger clenched her teeth and put down the article about the forthcoming Salander trial. It was short, two columns, intended for page five under national news. She looked at the text for a minute and pursed her lips. It was 3.30 on Thursday. She had been working at S.M.P. for exactly twelve days. She picked up the telephone and called Holm, the news editor.

"Hello, it's Berger. Could you find Johannes Frisk and bring him to my office asap?"

She waited patiently until Holm sauntered into the glass cage with the reporter Frisk in tow. Berger looked at her watch.

"Twenty-two," she said.

"Twenty-two what?" said Holm.

"Twenty-two minutes. That's how long it's taken you to get up from the editorial desk, walk the fifteen metres to Frisk's desk, and drag yourself over here with him."

"You said there was no rush. I was pretty busy."

"I did not say there was no rush. I asked you to get Frisk and come to my office. I said asap, and I meant asap, not tonight or next week or whenever you feel like getting your arse out of your chair."

"But I don't think—"

"Shut the door."

She waited until Holm had closed the door behind him and studied him in silence. He was without doubt a most competent news editor. His role was to make sure that the pages of S.M.P. were filled every day with the correct text, logically organized, and appearing in the order and position they had decided on in the morning meeting. This meant that Holm was juggling a colossal number of tasks every day. And he did it without ever dropping a ball.

The problem with him was that he persistently ignored the decisions Berger made. She had done her best to find a formula for working with him. She had tried friendly reasoning and direct orders, she had encouraged him to think for himself, and generally she had done everything she could think of to make him understand how she wanted the newspaper to be shaped.

Nothing made any difference.

An article she had rejected in the afternoon would appear in the newspaper sometime after she had gone home. *We had a hole we needed to fill so I had to put in something.*

The headline that Berger had decided to use was suddenly replaced by something entirely different. It was not always a bad choice, but it would be done without her being consulted. As an act of defiance.

It was always a matter of details. An editorial meeting at 2.00 was suddenly moved to 1.30 without her being told, and most of the decisions were already made by the time she arrived. *I'm sorry . . . in the rush I forgot to let you know.*

For the life of her, Berger could not see why Holm had adopted this attitude towards her, but she knew that calm discussions and friendly reprimands did not work. Until now she had not confronted him in front of other colleagues in the newsroom. Now it was time to express herself more clearly, and this time in front of Frisk, which would ensure that the exchange was common knowledge in no time.

"The first thing I did when I started here was to tell you that I had a special interest in everything to do with Lisbeth Salander. I explained that I wanted information in advance on all proposed articles, and that I wanted to look at and approve everything that was to be published. I've reminded you about this at least half a dozen times, most recently at the editorial meeting on Friday. Which part of these instructions do you not understand?"

"All the articles that are planned or in production are on the daily memo on our intranet. They're always sent to your computer. You're always kept informed," Holm said.

"Bullshit," Berger said. "When the city edition of the paper landed in my letterbox this morning we had a three-column story about Salander and the developments in the Stallarholmen incident in our best news spot."

"That was Margareta Orring's article. She's a freelancer, she didn't turn it in until 7.00 last night."

"Margareta called me with the proposal at 11.00 yesterday morning. You approved it and gave her the assignment at 11.30. You didn't say a word about it at the two o'clock meeting."

"It's in the daily memo."

"Oh, right . . . here's what it says in the daily memo: quote, *Margareta Orring, interview with Prosecutor Martina Fransson, re: narcotics bust in Södertälje*, unquote."

"The basic story was an interview with Martina Fransson about the confiscation of anabolic steroids. A would-be Svavelsjö biker was busted for that," Holm said.

"Exactly. And not a word in the daily memo about Svavelsjö M.C., or that the interview would be focused on Magge Lundin and Stallarholmen, and therefore the investigation of Salander."

"I assume it came up during the interview—"

"Anders, I don't know why, but you're standing here lying to my face. I spoke to Margareta and she said that she clearly explained to you what her interview was going to focus on."

"I must not have realized that it would centre on Salander. Then I got an article late in the evening. What was I supposed to do, kill the whole story? Orring turned in a good piece."

"There I agree with you. It's an excellent story. But that's now your third lie in about the same number of minutes. Orring turned it in at 3.20 in the afternoon, long before I went home at 6.00."

"Berger, I don't like your tone of voice."

"Great. Then I can tell you that I like neither your tone nor your evasions nor your lies."

"It sounds as if you think I'm organizing some sort of conspiracy against you."

"You still haven't answered the question. And item two: today this piece by Johannes shows up on my desk. I can't recall having any discussion about it at the two o'clock meeting. Why has one of our reporters spent the day working on Salander without anybody telling me?"

Frisk squirmed. He was bright enough to keep his mouth shut.

"So . . . ," Holm said. "We're putting out a newspaper, and there must be hundreds of articles you don't know about. We have routines here at *S.M.P.* and we all have to adapt to them. I don't have time to give special treatment to specific articles."

"I didn't ask you to give special treatment to specific articles. I asked you for two things: first, that I be informed of everything that has a bearing on the Salander case. Second, I want to approve everything we publish on that topic. So, one more time . . . what part of my instructions did you not understand?"

Holm sighed and adopted an exasperated expression.

"O.K.," Berger said. "I'll make myself crystal clear. I am not going to argue with you about this. Just let's see if you understand this message. If it happens again I'm going to relieve you of your job as news editor. You'll hear bang-boom, and then you'll find yourself editing the family page or the comics page or something like that. I cannot have a news editor that I can't trust or work with and who devotes his precious time to undermining my decisions. Understood?"

Holm threw up his hands in a gesture that indicated he considered Berger's accusations to be absurd.

"Do you understand me? Yes or no?"

"I heard what you said."

"I asked if you understood. Yes or no?"

"Do you really think you can get away with this? This paper comes out because I and the other cogs in the machinery work our backsides off. The board is going to—"

"The board is going to do as I say. I'm here to revamp this paper. I have a carefully worded agreement that gives me the right to make far-reaching editorial changes at section editors' level. I can get rid of the dead meat and recruit new blood from outside if I choose. And Holm . . . you're starting to look like dead meat to me."

She fell silent. Holm met her gaze. He was furious.

"That's all," Berger said. "I suggest you consider very carefully what we've talked about today."

"I don't think—"

"It's up to you. That's all. Now go."

He turned on his heel and left the glass cage. She watched him disappear into the editorial sea in the direction of the canteen. Frisk stood up and made to follow.

"Not you, Johannes. You stay here and sit down."

She picked up his article and read it one more time.

"You're here on a temporary basis, I gather."

"Yes. I've been here five months – this is my last week."

"How old are you?"

"Twenty-seven."

"I apologize for putting you in the middle of a duel between me and Holm. Tell me about this story."

"I got a tip this morning and took it to Holm. He told me to follow up on it."

"I see. It's about the police investigating the possibility that Lisbeth Salander was mixed up in the sale of anabolic steroids. Does this story have any connection to yesterday's article about Södertälje, in which steroids also appeared?"

"Not that I know of, but it's possible. This thing about steroids has to do with her connection to boxers. Paolo Roberto and his pals."

"Paolo Roberto uses steroids?"

"What? No, of course not. It's more about the boxing world in general. Salander used to train at a gym in Söder. But that's the angle the police are taking. Not me. And somewhere the idea seems to have popped up that she might have been involved in selling steroids."

"So there's no actual substance to this story at all, just a rumour?"

"It's no rumour that the police are looking into the possibility. Whether they're right or wrong, I have no idea yet."

"O.K., Johannes. I want you to know that what I'm discussing with you now has nothing to do with my dealings with Holm. I think you're an excellent reporter. You write well and you have an eye for detail. In short, this is a good story. My problem is that I don't believe it."

"I can assure you that it's quite true."

"And I have to explain to you why there's a fundamental flaw in the story. Where did the tip come from?"

"From a source within the police."

"Who?"

Frisk hesitated. It was an automatic response. Like every other journalist the world over, he was unwilling to name his source. On the other hand, Berger was editor-in-chief and therefore one of the few people who could demand that information from him.

"An officer named Faste in the Violent Crimes Division."

"Did he call you or did you call him?"

"He called me."

"Why do you think he called you?"

"I interviewed him a couple of times during the hunt for Salander. He knows who I am."

"And he knows you're twenty-seven and a temp and that you're useful when he wants to plant information that the prosecutor wants put out."

"Sure, I understand all that. But I get a tip from the police investigation and go over and have a coffee with Faste and he tells me this. He is correctly quoted. What am I supposed to do?"

"I'm persuaded that you quoted him accurately. What should have happened is that you should have taken the information to Holm, who should have knocked on the door of my office and explained the situation, and together we would have decided what to do."

"I get it. But I—"

"You left the material with Holm, who's the news editor. You acted correctly. But let's analyse your article. First of all, why would Faste want to leak this information?"

Frisk shrugged.

"Does that mean that you don't know, or that you don't care?"

"I don't know."

"If I were to tell you that this story is untrue, and that Salander doesn't have a thing to do with anabolic steroids, what do you say then?"

"I can't prove otherwise."

"No indeed. But you think we should publish a story that might be a lie just because we have no proof that it's a lie."

"No, we have a journalistic responsibility. But it's a balancing act. We can't refuse to publish when we have a source who makes a specific claim."

"We can ask why the source might want this information to get out. Let me explain why I gave orders that everything to do with Salander has to cross my desk. I have special knowledge of the subject that no-one else at *S.M.P.* has. The legal department has been informed that I possess this knowledge but cannot discuss it with them. *Millennium* is going to publish a story that I am contractually bound not to reveal to *S.M.P.*, despite the fact that I work here. I obtained the information in my capacity as editor-in-chief of *Millennium*, and right now I'm caught between two loyalties. Do you see what I mean?"

"Yes."

"What I learned at *Millennium* tells me that I can say without a doubt that this story is a lie, and its purpose is to damage Salander before the trial."

"It would be hard to do her any more damage, considering all the revelations that have already come out about her."

"Revelations that are largely lies and distortions. Hans Faste is one of the key sources for the claims that Salander is a paranoid and violence-prone lesbian devoted to Satanism and S. & M. And the media as a whole bought Faste's propaganda simply because he appears to be a serious source and it's always cool to write about S. & M. And now he's trying a new angle which will put her at a disadvantage in the public consciousness, and which he wants *S.M.P.* to help disseminate. Sorry, but not on my watch."

"I understand."

"Do you? Good. Then I can sum up everything I said in two sentences. Your job description as a journalist is to question and scrutinize most critically. And never to repeat claims uncritically, no matter how highly placed the sources in the bureaucracy. Don't ever forget that. You're a terrific writer, but that talent is completely worthless if you forget your job description."

"Right."

"I intend to kill this story."

"I understand."

"This doesn't mean that I distrust you."

"Thank you."

"So that's why I'm sending you back to your desk with a proposal for a new story."

"Alright."

"The whole thing has to do with my contract with *Millennium*. I'm not allowed to reveal what I know about the Salander story. At the same time I'm editor-in-chief of a newspaper that's in danger of skidding because the newsroom doesn't have the information that I have. And we can't allow that to happen. This is a unique situation and applies only to Salander. That's why I've decided to choose a reporter and steer him in the right direction so that we won't end up with our trousers down when *Millennium* comes out."

"And you think that *Millennium* will be publishing something noteworthy about Salander?"

"I don't think so, I know so. *Millennium* is sitting on a scoop that will turn the Salander story on its head, and it's driving me crazy that I can't go public with it."

"You say you're rejecting my article because you know that it isn't true. That means there's something in the story that all the other reporters have missed."

203

"Exactly."

"I'm sorry, but it's difficult to believe that the entire Swedish media has been duped in the same way . . ."

"Salander has been the object of a media frenzy. That's when normal rules no longer apply, and any drivel can be posted on a billboard."

"So you're saying that Salander isn't exactly what she seems to be."

"Try out the idea that she's innocent of these accusations, that the picture painted of her on the billboards is nonsense, and that there are forces at work you haven't even dreamed of."

"Is that the truth?"

Berger nodded.

"So what I just handed in is part of a continuing campaign against her."

"Precisely."

Frisk scratched his head. Berger waited until he had finished thinking.

"What do you want me to do?"

"Go back to your desk and start working on another story. You don't have to stress out about it, but just before the trial begins we might be able to publish a whole feature that examines the accuracy of all the statements that have been made about Salander. Start by reading through the clippings, list everything that's been said about her, and check off the allegations one by one."

"Alright."

"Think like a reporter. Investigate who's spreading the story, why it's being spread, and ask yourself whose interests it might serve."

"But I probably won't be at *S.M.P.* when the trial starts. This is my last week."

Berger took a plastic folder from a desk drawer and laid a sheet of paper in front of him.

"I've extended your assignment by three months. You'll finish off this week with your ordinary duties and report in here on Monday."

"Thank you."

"If you want to keep working at *S.M.P.*, that is."

"Of course I do."

"You're contracted to do investigative work outside the normal editorial job. You'll report directly to me. You're going to be a special correspondent assigned to the Salander trial."

"The news editor is going to have something to say—"

"Don't worry about Holm. I've talked with the head of the legal department and fixed it so there won't be any hassle there. But you're going to be digging into the background, not news reporting. Does that sound good?"

"It sounds fantastic."

"Right then . . . that's all. I'll see you on Monday."

As she waved him out of the glass cage she saw Holm watching her from the other side of the news desk. He lowered his gaze and pretended that he had not been looking at her.

CHAPTER 11

Friday, 13.v – Saturday, 14.v

Blomkvist made sure that he was not being watched when he walked from the *Millennium* offices early on Friday morning to Salander's old apartment block on Lundagatan. He had to meet Idris Ghidi in Göteborg. The question was how to travel there without being observed or leaving a trail. He decided against the train, since he did not want to use a credit card. Normally he would borrow Berger's car, but that was no longer possible. He had thought about asking Cortez or someone else to rent a car for him, but that too would leave a trace.

Finally he lit upon the obvious solution. He withdrew cash from an A.T.M. on Götgatan. He had Salander's keys to her burgundy Honda. It had been parked outside her building since March. He adjusted the seat and saw that the petrol tank was half full. Then he backed out and headed across Liljeholmsbron towards the E4.

At 2.50 he parked on a side street off Avenyn in Göteborg. He had a late lunch at the first café he saw. At 4.10 he took the tram to Angered and got off in the centre of town. It took twenty minutes to find the address where Idris Ghidi lived. He was about ten minutes late for their meeting.

Ghidi opened the door, shook hands with Blomkvist, and invited him into a living room with spartan furnishings. He had a limp. He asked Blomkvist to take a seat at the table next to a dresser on which were a dozen framed photographs, which Blomkvist studied.

"My family," Ghidi said.

He spoke with a thick accent. Blomkvist suspected that he would not pass the language test recommended by the People's Party of Sweden.

"Are those your brothers?"

"My two brothers on the left who were murdered by Saddam in the '80s. That's my father in the middle. My two uncles were murdered by Saddam in the '90s. My mother died in 2000. My three sisters are still alive. Two are in Syria and my little sister is in Madrid."

Ghidi poured Turkish coffee.

"Kurdo Baksi sends his greetings."

"Kurdo said you wanted to hire me for a job, but not what it was. I have to tell you, right away, that I won't take the job if it's illegal. I don't dare get mixed up in anything like that."

"There is nothing illegal in what I am going to ask you to do. But it is unusual. The job itself will last for a couple of weeks. It must be done each day, but it will take only a minute of your time. For this I'm willing to pay you a thousand kronor a week. You will be paid by me, and I won't report it to the tax authorities."

"I understand. What is it I have to do?"

"One of your jobs at Sahlgrenska hospital – six days a week, if I understood correctly – is to clean corridor 11C, the intensive care unit."

Ghidi nodded.

"This is what I want you to do."

Blomkvist leaned forward and explained his plan.

Prosecutor Ekström took stock of his visitor. It was the third time he had met Superintendent Nyström. He saw a lined face framed by short grey hair. Nyström had first come to see him in the days following the murder of Karl Axel Bodin. He had offered credentials to indicate that he worked for S.I.S. They had had a long, subdued conversation.

"It's important that you understand this: in no way am I trying to influence how you might act or how you do your job. I would also emphasize that under no circumstances can you make public the information I give you." Nyström said.

"I understand."

If truth be told, Ekström did not entirely understand, but he did not want to seem very unclever by asking questions. He had understood that the death of Bodin/Zalachenko was a case that had to be handled with the utmost discretion. He had also understood that Nyström's visit was off the record, although endorsed by the highest authorities within the Security Police.

"This is most assuredly a matter of life or death," Nyström had said at their very first meeting. "As far as the Security Police are concerned, everything related to the Zalachenko case is Top Secret. I can tell you that he is a defector, a former agent of Soviet military intelligence, and a key player in the Russians' offensive against western Europe in the '70s."

"That's what Blomkvist at *Millennium* is evidently alleging."

"And in this instance Blomkvist is quite correct. He's a journalist who happened to stumble upon one of the most secret operations ever conducted by Swedish defence."

"He's going to publish the information."

"Of course. He represents the media, with all the advantages and drawbacks. We live in a democracy and naturally we cannot influence what is written in the press. The problem in this case is that Blomkvist knows only a fraction of the truth about Zalachenko, and much of what he thinks he knows is wrong."

"I see."

"What Blomkvist doesn't grasp is that if the truth about Zalachenko comes out, the Russians will swiftly identify our informants and sources in Russia. People who have risked their lives for democracy will be in danger of being killed."

"But isn't Russia a democracy now too? I mean, if this had been during the communist days—"

"That's an illusion. This is about people who spied formerly within the Soviet Union – no regime in the world would stand for that, even if it happened many years ago. And a number of these sources are still active."

No such agents existed, but Ekström could not know that. He was bound to take Nyström at his word. And he could not help feeling flattered that he was being given information – off the record, of course – that was among the most secret to be found in Sweden. He was slightly surprised that the Swedish Security Police had been able to penetrate the Russian military to the degree Nyström was describing, and he perfectly understood that this was, of course, information that absolutely could not be disseminated.

"When I was assigned to make contact with you, we did an extensive investigation of your background," Nyström said.

The seduction always involved discovering someone's weaknesses. Prosecutor Ekström's weakness was his conviction as to his own importance. He was like everyone else, he appreciated flattery. The trick was to make him feel that he had been specially chosen.

"And we have been able to satisfy ourselves that you are a man who enjoys enormous respect within the police force . . . and of course in government circles."

Ekström looked pleased. That unnamed individuals in government circles had great confidence in him implied that he could count on their gratitude if he played his cards right.

"Simply stated, my assignment is to provide you with background as necessary, and as discreetly as possible. You must understand how improbably complicated this story has become. For one thing, a preliminary investigation is under way, for which you bear the primary responsibility. No-one – not in the government or in the Security Police or anywhere else – can interfere in how you run this investigation. Your job is to ascertain the truth and bring the guilty parties to court. One of the most crucial functions in a democratic state."

Ekström nodded.

"It would be a national catastrophe if the whole truth about Zalachenko were to leak out."

"So what exactly is the purpose of your visit?"

"First, to make you aware of the sensitive nature of the situation. I don't think Sweden has been in such an exposed position since the end of the Second World War. One might say that, to a certain extent, the fate of Sweden rests in your hands."

"And who is your superior?"

"I regret it, but I cannot reveal the name of anyone working on this case. But I *can* say that my instructions come from the very highest levels."

Good Lord. He's acting on orders from the government. But he can't say without unleashing a political firestorm.

Nyström saw that Ekström had swallowed the bait.

"What I am able to do, however, is to provide you with information. I have been given the authority to use my own judgement in giving you sight of material that is, some of it, the most highly classified in this country."

"I see."

"This means that if you have questions about something, whatever it may be, then you should turn to me. You must not talk to anyone else in the Security Police, only to me. My assignment is to be your guide in this labyrinth, and if clashes between various interests threaten to arise, then we will assist each other in finding solutions."

"I understand. In that case I should say how grateful I am that you and your colleagues are willing to facilitate matters for me."

"We want the legal process to take its course even though this is a difficult situation."

"Good. I assure you that I will exercise the utmost discretion. This isn't the first time I've handled Top Secret information, after all."

"No, we are quite aware of that."

Ekström had a dozen questions that Nyström meticulously noted, and then answered as best he could. On this third visit Ekström would be given answers to several of the questions he had asked earlier. Among them, and most crucially: what was the truth surrounding Björck's report from 1991?

"That is a serious matter." Nyström adopted a concerned expression. "Since this report surfaced, we have had an analysis group working almost round the clock to discover exactly what happened. We are now close to the point where we can draw conclusions. And they are most unpleasant."

"I can well imagine. That report alleges that the Security Police and the psychiatrist Peter Teleborian co-operated to place Lisbeth Salander in psychiatric care."

"If only that were the case," Nyström said with a slight smile.

"I don't understand."

"If that was all there was to it, the matter would be simple. Then a crime would have been committed and led to a prosecution. The difficulty is that this report does not correspond with other reports that we have in our archives." Nyström took out a blue folder and opened it. "What I have here is the report that Gunnar Björck actually wrote in 1991. Here too are the original documents from the correspondence between him and Teleborian. The two versions do not agree."

"Please explain."

"The appalling thing is that Björck has hanged himself. Presumably because of the threat of revelations about his sexual deviations. Blomkvist's magazine was intending to expose him. That drove him to such depths of despair that he took his own life."

"Well . . ."

"The original report is an account of Lisbeth Salander's attempt to murder her father, Alexander Zalachenko, with a petrol bomb. The first thirty pages of the report that Blomkvist discovered agree with the original. These pages, frankly, contain nothing remarkable. It's not until page thirty-three, where Björck draws conclusions and makes recommendations, that the discrepancy arises."

"What discrepancy?"

"In the original version Björck presents five well-argued recommendations. We don't need to hide the fact that they concern playing down the Zalachenko affair in the media and so forth. Björck proposes that Zalachenko's rehabilitation – he suffered very severe burns – be carried out abroad. And things similar. He also recommends that Salander should be offered the best conceivable psychiatric care."

"I see . . ."

"The problem is that a number of sentences were altered in a very subtle way. On page thirty-four there is a paragraph in which Björck appears to suggest that Salander be branded psychotic, so that she will not be believed if anyone should start asking questions about Zalachenko."

"And this suggestion is not in the original report."

"Precisely. Gunnar Björck's own report never suggested anything of the kind. Quite apart from anything else, that would have been against the law. He warmly recommended that she be given the care she quite clearly needed. In Blomkvist's copy, this was made out to be a conspiracy."

"Could I read the original?"

"Certainly you can. I have to take the report with me when I go. And before you read it, let me direct your attention to the appendix containing the subsequent correspondence between Björck and Teleborian. It is almost entirely fabricated. Here it's not a matter of subtle alterations, but of gross falsifications."

"Falsifications?"

"I think that's the only appropriate description. The original shows that Peter Teleborian was assigned by the district court to do a forensic psychiatric examination of Lisbeth Salander. Nothing out of the ordinary there. Salander was twelve years old and had tried to kill her father – it would have been very strange if that shocking event had *not* resulted in a psychiatric report."

"That's true."

"If you had been the prosecutor, I assume that you would have insisted on both social and psychiatric investigations."

"Of course."

"Even then Teleborian was a well-respected child psychiatrist who had also worked in forensic medicine. He was given the assignment, conducted a normal investigation, and came to the conclusion that the girl was mentally ill. I don't have to use their technical terms."

"No, no . . ."

"Teleborian wrote this in a report that he sent to Björck. The report was then given to the district court, which decided that Salander should be cared for at St Stefan's. Blomkvist's version is missing the entire investigation conducted by Teleborian. In its place is an exchange between Björck and Teleborian, which has Björck instructing Teleborian to falsify a mental examination."

"And you're saying that it's an invention, a forgery?"

"No question about it."

"But who would be interested in creating such a thing?"

Nyström put down the report and frowned. "Now you're getting to the heart of the problem."

"And the answer is . . .?"

"We don't know. That's the question our analytical group is working very hard to answer."

"Could it be that Blomkvist made some of it up?"

Nyström laughed. "That was one of our first thoughts too. But we don't think so. We incline to the view that the falsification was done a long time ago, presumably more or less simultaneously with the writing of the original report. And that leads to one or two disagreeable conclusions. Whoever did the falsification was extremely well informed. In addition, whoever did it had access to the very typewriter that Björck used."

"You mean . . ."

"We don't know *where* Björck wrote the report. It could have been at his home or at his office or somewhere else altogether. We can imagine two alternatives. Either the person who did the falsification was someone in the psychiatric or forensic medicine departments, who for some reason wanted to involve Teleborian in a scandal. Or else the falsification was done for a completely different purpose by someone inside the Security Police."

"For what possible reason?"

"This happened in 1991. There could have been a Russian agent inside S.I.S. who had picked up Zalachenko's trail. Right now we're examining a large number of old personnel files."

"But if the K.G.B. had found out . . . then it should have leaked years ago."

"You're right. But don't forget that this was during the period when the Soviet Union was collapsing and the K.G.B. was dissolved. We have no idea what went wrong. Maybe it was a planned operation that was shelved. The K.G.B. were masters of forgery and disinformation."

"But why would the K.G.B. want to plant such a forgery?"

"We don't know that either. But the most obvious purpose would have been to involve the Swedish government in a scandal."

Ekström pinched his lip. "So what you're saying is that the medical assessment of Salander is correct?"

"Oh yes. Salander is, to put it in colloquial terms, stark raving mad. No doubt about that. The decision to commit her to an institution was absolutely correct."

"*Toilets?*" Eriksson sounded as if she thought Cortez was pulling her leg.

"Toilets," Cortez repeated.

"You want to run a story on toilets? In *Millennium*?"

Eriksson could not help laughing. She had observed his ill-concealed enthusiasm when he sauntered into the Friday meeting, and she recognized all the signs of a reporter who had a story in the works.

"Explain."

"It's really quite simple," Cortez said. "The biggest industry in Sweden by far is construction. It's an industry that in practice cannot be outsourced overseas, even if Skanska Construction opens an office in London and stuff like that. No matter what, the houses have to be built in Sweden."

"But that's nothing new."

"No, but what *is* new is that the construction industry is a couple of light-years ahead of all other Swedish industries when it comes to competition and efficiency. If Volvo built cars the same way, the latest model would cost about one, maybe even two million kronor. For most of industry, cutting prices is the constant challenge. For the construction industry it's the opposite. The price per square metre keeps going up. The state subsidizes the cost with taxpayers' money just so that the prices aren't prohibitive."

"Is there a story in that?"

"Wait. It's complicated. Let's say the price curve for hamburgers had been the same since the '70s – so a Big Mac would cost about 150 kronor or more. I don't want to guess what it would cost with fries and a Coke, but my salary at *Millennium* might not cover it. How many people around this table would go to McDonald's and buy a burger for 100 kronor?"

Nobody said a word.

"Understandable. But when N.C.C. bangs together some sheet-metal cubes for exclusive rental at Gåshaga on Lidingö, they ask 10–12,000 kronor a month for a three-cube apartment. How many of you are paying that much?"

"I couldn't afford it," Nilsson said.

"No, of course not. But you already live in a one-bedroom apartment by Danvikstull which your father bought for you twenty years ago, and if you were to sell it you'd probably get a million and a half for it. But what does a twenty-year-old do who wants to move out of the family home? They can't afford to. So they sublet or sub-sublet or they live at home with their mothers until they retire."

"So where do the toilets come into the picture?" Malm said.

"I'm getting to that. The question is, why are apartments so bloody expensive? Because the people commissioning the buildings don't know how to set the price. To put it simply, a developer calls up Skanska Construction and says that they want a hundred apartments and asks what it will cost. And Skanska calculates it and comes back and says it'll cost around 500 million kronor. Which means that the price per square metre will be X kronor and it would cost 10,000 a month if you wanted to move in. But unlike the McDonald's example, you don't really have a choice – you have to live somewhere. So you have to pay the going rate."

"Henry, dear . . . please get to the point."

"But that *is* the point. Why should it cost 10,000 a month to live in those crappy dumps in Hammarbyhamnen? Because the construction companies don't give a damn about keeping prices down. The customer's going to have to pay, come what may. One of the big costs is building materials. The trade in building materials goes through wholesalers who set their own prices. Since there isn't any real competition there, a bathtub retails at 5,000 kronor in Sweden. The same bathtub from the same manufacturer retails at 2,000 kronor in Germany. There is no added cost that can satisfactorily explain the price difference."

There was impatient muttering around the table.

"You can read about a lot of this in a report from the government's

Construction Cost Delegation, which was active in the late '90s. Since then not much has happened. No-one is talking to the construction companies about the unreasonable prices. The buyers cheerfully pay what they are told it costs, and in the end the price burden falls on the renters or the taxpayers."

"Henry, the toilets?"

"The little that has changed since the Construction Cost Delegation's report has happened at the local level, and primarily outside Stockholm. There are buyers who got fed up with the high construction prices. One example is Karlskrona Homes, which builds houses less expensively than anyone else by buying the materials themselves. And Svensk Handel has also got into the game. They think that the price of construction materials is absurd, so they've been trying to make it easier for companies to buy less expensive products that are equally good. And that led to a little clash at the Construction Fair in Älvsjö last year. Svensk Handel had brought in a man from Thailand who was selling toilets for 500 kronor apiece."

"And what happened?"

"His nearest competitor was a Swedish wholesale outfit called Vitavara Inc., which sells genuine Swedish toilets for 1700 kronor apiece. And shrewd municipal buyers started to scratch their heads and wonder why they were shelling out 1700 kronor when they could get a similar toilet from Thailand for 500."

"Better quality maybe," Karim said.

"No. The exact same."

"Thailand," Malm said. "That sounds like child labour and stuff like that. Which could explain the low price."

"Not so," Cortez said. "Child labour exists mostly in the textile and souvenir industries in Thailand. And the paedophile industry, of course. The United Nations keeps an eye on child labour, and I've checked out this company. They're a reputable manufacturer. It's a big, modern, respectable operation producing appliances and plumbing goods."

"Alright . . . but we're talking about low-wage countries, and that means that you risk writing an article proposing that Swedish industry should be outbid by Thai industry. Fire the Swedish workers and close the factories here, and import everything from Thailand. You won't win any points with the Trades Union Federation."

A smile spread over Cortez's face. He leaned back and looked ridiculously pleased with himself.

"No again," he said. "Guess where Vitavara Inc. makes its toilets to sell at 1700 kronor apiece?"

Silence fell over the room.

"Vietnam," Cortez said.

"You've got to be kidding," Eriksson said.

"They've been making toilets there for at least ten years. Swedish workers were already out of that race in the '90s."

"Oh, shit."

"But here comes my point. If you imported directly from the factory in Vietnam, the price would be in the order of 390 kronor. Guess how you can explain the price difference between Thailand and Vietnam?"

"Don't tell me that—"

"Oh, yes. Vitavara Inc. subcontracts the work to an outfit called Fong Soo Industries. They're on the U.N. list of companies that use child labour, at least they were in an investigation from 2001. But the majority of the workers are convicts."

Eriksson burst out laughing. "This is great. This is really great. I'm sure you're going to be a journalist when you grow up. How fast can you have the story ready?"

"Two weeks. I have a lot of international trade stuff to check out. And then we need a bad guy for the story, so I'm going to see who owns Vitavara Inc."

"Then we could run it in the June issue?"

"No problem."

Inspector Bublanski listened to Prosecutor Ekström without expression. The meeting had lasted forty minutes, and Bublanski was feeling an intense desire to reach out and grab the copy of *The Law of the Swedish Kingdom* that lay on the edge of Ekström's desk and ram it into the prosecutor's face. He wondered what would happen if he acted on his impulse. There would certainly be headlines in the evening papers and it would probably result in an assault charge. He pushed the thought away. The whole point of the socialized human being was to not give in to that sort of impulse, regardless of how belligerently an opponent might behave. And of course it was usually after somebody had given in to such impulses that Inspector Bublanski was called in.

"I take it that we're in agreement," Ekström said.

"No, we are not in agreement," Bublanski said, getting to his feet. "But you're the leader of the preliminary investigation."

He muttered to himself as he turned down the corridor to his office, summoning Andersson and Modig as he went. They were the only colleagues available to him that afternoon as Holmberg had regrettably opted to take a two-week holiday.

"My office," Bublanski said. "Bring some coffee."

After they had settled in, Bublanski looked at the notes from his meeting with Ekström.

"As the situation stands, our preliminary investigation leader has dropped all charges against Lisbeth Salander relating to the murders for which she was being sought. She is no longer part of the preliminary investigation so far as we're concerned."

"That can be considered a step forward, at any rate," Modig said.

Andersson, as usual, said nothing.

"I'm not so sure about that," Bublanski said. "Salander is still suspected of G.B.H. in connection with the events at Stallarholmen and Gosseberga. But we're no longer involved with those investigations. We have to concentrate on finding Niedermann and working on the graves in the woods at Nykvarn. On the other hand it's now clear that Ekström is going to bring charges against Salander. The case has been transferred to Stockholm, and an entirely new investigation has been set up for the purpose."

"Oh, really?" Modig said.

"And who do you think is going to investigate Salander?" Bublanski said.

"I'm fearing the worst."

"Hans Faste is back on duty, and he's going to assist Ekström."

"That's insane. Faste is grossly unsuited to investigate anything at all to do with Salander."

"I know that. But Ekström has a good argument. Faste has been out sick since . . . hmm . . . he collapsed in April, and this would be the perfect, simple case for him to focus on."

Silence.

"The long and the short of it is that we're to hand all our material on Salander over to him this afternoon."

"And this story about Gunnar Björck and Säpo and the 1991 report . . ."

". . . is going to be handled by Faste and Ekström."

"I don't like this," Modig said.

"Nor do I. But Ekström's the boss, and he has backing from higher up in the bureaucracy. In other words, our job is still to find the killer. Curt, what's the situation?"

Andersson shook his head. "Niedermann seems to have been swallowed up by the earth. I have to admit that in all my years on the force I've never seen anything like it. We haven't had any tip-offs, and we don't have a single informer who knows him or has any idea where he might be."

"That sounds fishy," Modig said. "But he's being sought for the police murder in Gosseberga, for G.B.H on another officer, for the attempted murder of Salander, and for the aggravated kidnapping and assault of the dental nurse Anita Kaspersson, as well as for the murders of Svensson and Johansson. In every instance there's good forensic evidence."

"That helps a bit, at least. How's it going with the case of Svavelsjö M.C.'s treasurer?"

"Viktor Göransson – and his girlfriend, Lena Nygren. Fingerprints and D.N.A. from Göransson's body. Niedermann must have bloodied his knuckles pretty badly during the beating."

"Anything new on Svavelsjö M.C.?"

"Nieminen has taken over as club president while Lundin remains in custody, awaiting trial for the kidnapping of Miriam Wu. There's a whisper that Nieminen has offered a big reward to anyone who could provide information as to Niedermann's whereabouts."

"Which makes it even stranger that he hasn't been found, if the entire underworld is looking for him. What about Göransson's car?"

"Since we found Kaspersson's car at Göransson's place, we're sure that Niedermann switched vehicles. But we have no trace of the car he took."

"So we have to ask ourselves, one, is Niedermann still hiding out somewhere in Sweden?; two, if so, with whom?; three, is he out of the country? What do we think?"

"We have nothing to tell us that he has left the country, but really that seems his most logical course."

"If he *has* gone, where did he ditch the car?"

Modig and Andersson shook their heads. Nine times out of ten, police work was largely uncomplicated when it came to looking for one specific individual. It was about initiating a logical sequence of inquiries. Who were his friends? Who had he been in prison with? Where does his girlfriend live? Who did he drink with? In what area was his mobile last used? Where is his vehicle? At the end of that sequence the fugitive would generally be found.

The problem with Niedermann was that he had no friends, no girlfriend, no listed mobile, and he had never been in prison.

The inquiries had concentrated on finding Göransson's car, which Niedermann was presumed to be using. They had expected the car to turn up in a matter of days, probably in some car park in Stockholm. But there was as yet no sign of it.

"If he's out of the country, where would he be?"

"He's a German citizen, so the obvious thing would be for him to head for Germany."

"He seems not to have had any contact with his old friends in Hamburg."

Andersson waved his hand. "If his plan was to go to Germany . . . Why would he drive to Stockholm? Shouldn't he have made for Malmö and the bridge to Copenhagen, or for one of the ferries?"

"I know. And Inspector Erlander in Göteborg has been focusing his search in that direction from day one. The Danish police have been informed about Göransson's car, and we know for sure that he didn't take any of the ferries."

"But he did drive to Stockholm and to Svavelsjö, and there he murdered the club's treasurer and − we may assume − went off with an unspecified sum of money. What would his *next* step be?"

"He has to get out of Sweden," Bublanski said. "The most obvious thing would be to take one of the ferries across the Baltic. But Göransson and his girlfriend were murdered late on the night of April 9. Niedermann could have taken the ferry the next morning. We got the alarm roughly sixteen hours after they died, and we've had an A.P.B. out on the car ever since."

"If he took the morning ferry, then Göransson's car would have been parked at one of the ports," Modig said.

"Perhaps we haven't found the car because Niedermann drove out of the country to the north via Haparanda? A big detour around the Gulf of Bothnia, but in sixteen hours he could have been in Finland."

"Sure, but soon after he would have had to abandon the car in Finland, and it should have been found by now."

They sat in silence. Finally Bublanski got up and stood at the window.

"Could he have found a hiding place where he's just lying low, a summer cabin or—"

"I don't think it would be a summer cabin. This time of year every cabin owner is out checking their property."

"And he wouldn't try anywhere connected to Svavelsjö M.C. They're the last people he'd want to run into."

"And the entire underworld should be excluded as well . . . Any girlfriend we don't know about?"

They could speculate, but they had no facts.

When Andersson had left for the day, Modig went back to Bublanski's office and knocked on the door jamb. He waved her in.

"Have you got a couple of minutes?" she said.

"What's up?"

"Salander. I don't like this business with Ekström and Faste and a new trial. You've read Björck's report. I've read Björck's report. Salander was unlawfully committed in 1991 and Ekström knows it. What the hell is going on?"

Bublanski took off his reading glasses and tucked them into his breast pocket. "I don't know."

"Have you got any idea at all?"

"Ekström claims that Björck's report and the correspondence with Teleborian were falsified."

"That's rubbish. If it were a fake, then Björck would have said so when we brought him in."

"Ekström says Björck refused to discuss it, on the grounds that it was Top Secret. I was given a dressing down because I jumped the gun and brought him in."

"I'm beginning to have strong reservations about Ekström."

"He's getting squeezed from all sides."

"That's no excuse."

"We don't have a monopoly on the truth, Sonja. Ekström says he's received evidence that the report is a fake – that there is no real report with that protocol number. He also says that the forgery is a good one and that the content is a clever blend of truth and fantasy."

"Which part was truth and which part was fantasy, that's what I need to know," Modig said.

"The outline story is pretty much correct. Zalachenko is Salander's father, and he was a bastard who beat her mother. The problem is the familiar one – the mother never wanted to make a complaint so it went on for several years. Björck was given the job of finding out what happened when Salander tried to kill her father. He corresponded with Teleborian – but the correspondence in the form we've seen it is apparently a forgery. Teleborian did a routine psychiatric examination of Salander and concluded that she was mentally unbalanced. A prosecutor decided not to take the case any further. She needed care, and she got it at St Stefan's."

"And if it is a forgery . . . who did it and why?"

Bublanski shrugged. As I understand it, Ekström is going to commission one more thorough evaluation of Salander."

"I can't accept that."

"It's not our case any more."

"And Faste has replaced us. Jan, I'm going to the media if these bastards piss all over Salander one more time."

"No, Sonja. You won't. First of all, we no longer have access to the report, so you have no way of backing up your claims. You're going to look like a paranoid, and then your career will be over."

"I still have the report," Modig said in a low voice. "I made a copy for Curt but I never had a chance to give it to him before the Prosecutor General collected the others."

"If you leak that report, you'll not only be fired but you'll be guilty of gross misconduct."

Modig sat in silence for a moment and looked at her superior.

"Sonja, don't do it. Promise me."

"No, Jan. I can't promise that. There's something very sick about this whole story."

"You're right, it is sick. But since we don't know who the enemy is, you're not going to do anything for the moment."

Modig tilted her head to one side. "Are you going to do anything?"

"I'm not going to discuss that with you. Trust me. It's Friday night. Take a break, go home. And . . . this discussion never took place."

Niklas Adamsson, the Securitas guard, was studying for a test in three weeks' time. It was 1.30 on Saturday afternoon when he heard the sound of rotating brushes from the low-humming floor polisher and saw that it was the dark-skinned immigrant who walked with a limp.

The man would always nod politely but never laughed if he said anything humorous. Adamsson watched as he took a bottle of cleaning fluid and sprayed the reception counter-top twice before wiping it with a rag. Then he took his mop and swabbed the corners in the reception area where the brushes of the floor polisher could not reach. The guard put his nose back into his book about the national economy and kept reading.

It took ten minutes for the cleaner to work his way over to Adamsson's spot at the end of the corridor. They nodded to each other. Adamsson stood to let the man clean the floor around his chair outside Salander's room. He had seen him almost every day since he had been posted outside the room, but he could not remember his name – some sort of foreign name – but Adamsson did not feel the need to check his I.D. For one thing, the nigger was not allowed to clean inside the prisoner's room – that was done by two cleaning women in the morning – and besides, he did not feel that the cripple was any sort of threat.

When the cleaner had finished in the corridor, he opened the door to the room next to Salander's. Adamsson glanced his way, but this was no deviation from the daily routine. This was where the cleaning supplies were kept. In the course of the next five minutes he emptied his bucket, cleaned the brushes, and replenished the cart with plastic bags for the wastepaper baskets. Finally he manoeuvred the cart into the cubbyhole.

Ghidi was aware of the guard in the corridor. It was a young blond man who was usually there two or three days a week, reading books. Part-time guard, and part-time student. He was about as aware of his surroundings as a brick.

Ghidi wondered what Adamsson would do if someone actually tried to get into the Salander woman's room.

He also wondered what Blomkvist was really after. He had read about the eccentric journalist in the newspapers, and he had made the connection to the woman in 11C, expecting that he would be asked to smuggle something in for her. But he did not have access to her room and had never even seen her. Whatever he had expected, it was not this.

He could not see anything illegal about his task. He looked through the crack in the doorway at Adamsson, who was once more reading his book. He checked that nobody else was in the corridor. He reached into the pocket of his smock and took out the Sony Ericsson Z600 mobile. Ghidi had seen in an advertisement that it cost around 3,500 kronor and had all the latest features.

He took a screwdriver from his pocket, stood on tiptoe and unscrewed the three screws in the round white cover of a vent in the wall of Salander's room. He pushed the telephone as far into the vent as he could, just as Blomkvist had asked him to. Then he screwed on the cover again.

It took him forty-five seconds. The next day it would take less. He was supposed to get down the mobile, change the batteries and put it back in the vent. He would then take the used batteries home and recharge them overnight.

That was all Ghidi had to do.

But this was not going to be of any help to Salander. On her side of the wall there was presumably a similar screwed-on cover. She would never be able to get at the mobile, unless she had a screwdriver and a ladder.

"I know that," Blomkvist had said. "But she doesn't have to reach the phone."

Ghidi was to do this every day until Blomkvist told him it was no longer necessary.

And for this job Ghidi would be paid 1000 kronor a week, straight into his pocket. And he could keep the mobile when the job was over.

He knew, of course, that Blomkvist was up to some sort of funny business, but he could not work out what it was. Putting a mobile telephone into an air vent inside a locked cleaning supplies room, turned on but not uplinked, was so crazy that Ghidi could not imagine what use it could be. If Blomkvist wanted a way of communicating with the patient, he would be better off bribing one of the nurses to smuggle the telephone in to her.

On the other hand, he had no objection to doing Blomkvist this favour – a favour worth 1000 kronor a week. He was better off not asking any questions.

Jonasson slowed his pace when he saw a man with a briefcase leaning on the wrought-iron gates outside his housing association apartment on Hagagatan. He looked somehow familiar.

"Dr Jonasson?" he said.

"Yes?"

"Apologies for bothering you on the street outside your home. It's just that I didn't want to track you down at work, and I do need to talk to you."

"What's this about, and who are you?"

"My name is Blomkvist, Mikael Blomkvist. I'm a journalist and I work at *Millennium* magazine. It's about Lisbeth Salander."

"Oh, now I recognize you. You were the one who called the paramedics. Was it you who put duct tape on her wounds?"

"Yes."

"That was a smart thing to have done. But I don't discuss my patients with journalists. You'll have to speak to the P.R. department at Sahlgrenska, like everyone else."

"You misunderstand me. I don't want information and I'm here in a completely private capacity. You don't have to say a word or give me any information. Quite the opposite: I want to give you some information."

Jonasson frowned.

"Please hear me out," Blomkvist said. "I don't go around accosting surgeons on the street, but what I have to tell you is very important. Can I buy you a cup of coffee?"

"Tell me what it's about."

"It's about Lisbeth Salander's future and wellbeing. I'm a friend."

Jonasson thought that if it had been anyone other than Blomkvist he would have refused. But Blomkvist was a man in the public eye, and Jonasson could not imagine that this would be some sort of tomfoolery.

"I won't under any circumstances be interviewed, and I won't discuss my patient."

"Perfectly understood," Blomkvist said.

Jonasson accompanied Blomkvist to a café nearby.

"So what's this all about?" he said when they had got their coffee.

"First of all, I'm not going to quote you or mention you even in anything I write. And as far as I'm concerned this conversation never took place. Which said, I am here to ask you a favour. But I have to explain why, so that you can decide whether you can or you can't."

"I don't like the sound of this."

"All I ask is that you hear me out. It's your job to take care of

Lisbeth's physical and mental health. As her friend, it's *my* job to do the same. I can't poke around in her skull and extract bullets, but I have another skill that is as crucial to her welfare."

"Which is?"

"I'm an investigative journalist, and I've found out the truth about what happened to her."

"O.K."

"I can tell you in general terms what it's about and you can come to your own conclusions."

"Alright."

"I should also say that Annika Giannini, Lisbeth's lawyer – you've met her I think – is my sister, and I'm the one paying her to defend Salander."

"I see."

"I can't, obviously, ask Annika to do this favour. She doesn't discuss Lisbeth with me. She has to keep her conversations with Lisbeth confidential. I assume you've read about Lisbeth in the newspapers."

Jonasson nodded.

"She's been described as a psychotic, and a mentally ill lesbian mass murderer. All that is nonsense. Lisbeth Salander is not psychotic. She may be as sane as you and me. And her sexual preferences are nobody's business."

"If I've understood the matter correctly, there's been some reassessment of the case. Now it's this German who's being sought in connection with the murders."

"To my certain knowledge, Niedermann is a murderer who has no grain of conscience. But Lisbeth has enemies. Big and nasty enemies. Some of these are in the Security Police."

Jonasson looked at Blomkvist in astonishment.

"When Lisbeth was twelve, she was put in a children's psychiatric clinic in Uppsala. Why? Because she had stirred up a secret that Säpo was trying at any price to keep a lid on. Her father, Alexander Zalachenko – otherwise known as Karl Axel Bodin, who was murdered in your hospital – was a Soviet defector, a spy, a relic from the Cold War. He also beat up Lisbeth's mother year after year. When Lisbeth was twelve, she hit back and threw a Molotov cocktail at him as he sat in his car. That was why she was locked up."

"I don't understand. If she tried to kill her father, then surely there was good reason to take her in for psychiatric treatment."

225

"My story – which I am going to publish – is that Säpo knew about Zalachenko the wife beater, they knew what had provoked Lisbeth to do what she did, but they chose to protect Zalachenko because he was a source of valuable information. So they faked a diagnosis to make sure that Lisbeth was committed."

Jonasson looked so sceptical that Blomkvist had to laugh.

"I can document every detail. And I'm going to write a full account in time for Lisbeth's trial. Believe me – it's going to cause uproar. You might bear in mind that the beating that provoked Lisbeth's attack put her mother in hospital for the rest of her life."

"O.K. Go on."

"I'm going to expose two doctors who were errand boys for Säpo, and who helped bury Lisbeth in the asylum. I'm going to hang them out to dry. One of these is a well-known and respected person. But, as I said, I have all the documentation."

"If a doctor were mixed up in something like this, it's a blot on the entire profession."

"I don't believe in collective guilt. It concerns only those directly involved. The same is true of Säpo. I don't doubt that there are excellent people working in Säpo. This is about a small group of conspirators. When Lisbeth was eighteen they tried to institutionalize her again. This time they failed, and she was instead put under guardianship. In the trial, whenever it is, they're once again going to try to throw as much shit at her as they can. I – or rather, my sister Annika – will fight to see that she is acquitted, and that her still-extant declaration of incompetence is revoked."

"I see."

"But she needs ammunition. So that's the background for this tactic. I should probably also mention that there are some individuals in the police force who are actually on Lisbeth's side in all this. But not the prosecutor who brought the charges against her. In short, Lisbeth needs help before the trial."

"But I'm not a lawyer."

"No. But you're Lisbeth's doctor and you have access to her."

Jonasson's eyes narrowed.

"What I'm thinking of asking you is unethical, and it might also be illegal."

"Indeed?"

"But morally it's the right thing to do. Her constitutional rights are being violated by the very people who ought to be protecting her. Let me give you an example. Lisbeth is not allowed to have visitors, and she can't read newspapers or communicate with the outside world. The prosecutor has also pushed through a prohibition of disclosure for her lawyer. Annika has obeyed the rules. However, the prosecutor himself is the primary source of leaks to the reporters who keep writing all the shit about Lisbeth."

"Is that really so?"

"This story, for example." Blomkvist held up a week-old evening newspaper. "A source within the investigation claims that Lisbeth is *non compos mentis*, which prompted the newspaper to speculate about her mental state."

"I read the article. It's nonsense."

"So you don't think she's crazy."

"I won't comment on that. But I do know that no psychiatric evaluations have been done. Accordingly, the article is nonsense."

"I can show you chapter and verse to prove that the person who leaked this information is a police officer called Hans Faste. He works for Prosecutor Ekström."

"Oh."

"Ekström is going to seek to have the trial take place behind closed doors, so that no outsider will have knowledge of or be able to weigh the evidence against Lisbeth. But what is worse . . . Because the prosecutor has isolated Lisbeth, she won't be able to do the research she needs to do to prepare her defence."

"But isn't that supposed to be done by her lawyer?"

"As you must have gathered by now, Lisbeth is an extraordinary person. She has secrets I happen to know about, but I can't reveal them to my sister. But Lisbeth should be able to choose whether she wants to make use of them in her trial."

"I see."

"And in order to do that, she needs this."

Blomkvist laid Salander's Palm Tungsten T3 hand-held computer and a battery charger on the table between them.

"This is the most important weapon Lisbeth has in her arsenal – she has to have it."

Jonasson looked suspiciously at the Palm.

"Why not give it to her lawyer?"

"Because Lisbeth is the only one who knows how to get at the evidence."

Jonasson sat for a while, still not touching the computer.

"Let me tell you one or two things about Dr Peter Teleborian," Blomkvist said, taking a folder from his briefcase.

It was just after 8.00 on Saturday evening when Armansky left his office and walked to the synagogue of the Söder congregation on St Paulsgatan. He knocked on the door, introduced himself, and was admitted by the rabbi himself.

"I have an appointment to meet someone I know here," Armansky said.

"One flight up. I'll show you the way."

The rabbi offered him a kippa for his head, which Armansky hesitantly put on. He had been brought up in a Muslim family and he felt foolish wearing it.

Bublanski was also wearing a kippa.

"Hello, Dragan. Thanks for coming. I've borrowed a room from the rabbi so we can speak undisturbed."

Armansky sat down opposite Bublanski.

"I presume you have good reason for such secrecy."

"I'm not going to spin this out: I know that you're a friend of Salander's."

Armansky nodded.

"I need to know what you and Blomkvist have cooked up to help her."

"Why would we be cooking something up?"

"Because Prosecutor Ekström has asked me a dozen times how much you at Milton Security actually knew about the Salander investigation. It's not a casual question – he's concerned that you're going to spring something that could result in repercussions . . . in the media."

"I see."

"And if Ekström is worried, it's because he knows or suspects that you've got something brewing. Or at least he's talked to someone who has suspicions."

"Someone?"

"Dragan, let's not play games. You know Salander was the victim of an injustice in the early '90s, and I'm afraid she's going to get the same medicine when the trial begins."

"You're a police officer in a democracy. If you have information to that effect you should take action."

Bublanski nodded. "I'm thinking of doing just that. The question is, how?"

"Tell me what you want to know."

"I want to know what you and Blomkvist are up to. I assume you're not just sitting there twiddling your thumbs."

"It's complicated. How do I know I can trust you?"

"There's a report from 1991 that Blomkvist discovered . . ."

"I know about it."

"I no longer have access to the report."

"Nor do I. The copies that Blomkvist and his sister – now Salander's lawyer – had in their possession have both disappeared."

"Disappeared?"

"Blomkvist's copy was taken during a break-in at his apartment, and Giannini's was stolen when she was mugged, punched to the ground in Göteborg. All this happened on the day Zalachenko was murdered."

Bublanski said nothing for a long while.

"Why haven't we heard anything about this?"

"Blomkvist put it like this: there's only one right time to publish a story, and an endless number of wrong times."

"But you two . . . he'll publish it?"

Armansky gave a curt nod.

"A nasty attack in Göteborg and a break-in here in Stockholm. On the same day," Bublanski said. "That means that our adversary is well organized."

"I should probably also mention that we know Giannini's telephone is tapped."

"A whole bunch of crimes."

"The question is, whose?"

"That's what I'm wondering. Most likely it's Säpo – they would have an interest in suppressing Björck's report. But Dragan . . . we're talking about the Swedish Security Police, a government agency. I can't believe this would be something sanctioned by Säpo. I don't even believe Säpo has the expertise to do anything like this."

"I'm having trouble digesting it myself. Not to mention that someone else saunters into Sahlgrenska and blows Zalachenko's head off. And at the same time, Gunnar Björck, author of the report, hangs himself."

"So you think there's a single hand behind all this? I know Inspector Erlander, who did the investigation in Göteborg. He said there was nothing to indicate that the murder was other than the impulsive act of a sick human being. And we did a thorough investigation of Björck's place. Everything points towards a suicide."

"Gullberg, seventy-eight years old, suffering from cancer, recently treated for depression. Our operations chief Johan Fräklund has been looking into his background."

"And?"

"He did his military service in Karlskrona in the '40s, studied law and eventually became a tax adviser. Had an office here in Stockholm for thirty years: low profile, private clients ... whoever they might have been. Retired in 1991. Moved back to his home town of Laholm in 1994. Unremarkable, except—"

"Except what?"

"Except for one or two surprising details. Fräklund cannot find a single reference to Gullberg anywhere. He's never referred to in any newspaper or trade journal, and there's no-one who can tell us who his clients were. It's as if he never actually existed in the professional world."

"What are you saying?"

"Säpo is the obvious link. Zalachenko was a Soviet defector. Who else but Säpo would have taken charge of him? Then the question of a co-ordinated strategy to get Salander locked away in an institution. Now we have burglaries, muggings and telephone tapping. Personally I don't think Säpo is behind this. Blomkvist calls them 'the Zalachenko club', a small group of dormant Cold-Warmongers who hide out in some dark corridor at Säpo."

"So what should we do?" Bublanski said.

CHAPTER 12

Sunday, 15.v – Monday, 16.v

Superintendent Torsten Edklinth, Director of Constitutional Protection at the Security Police, slowly twirled his glass of red wine and listened attentively to the C.E.O. of Milton Security, who had called out of the blue and insisted on his coming to Sunday dinner at his place on Lidingö. Armansky's wife Ritva had made a delicious casserole. They had eaten well and talked politely about nothing in particular. Edklinth was wondering what was on Armansky's mind. After dinner Ritva repaired to the sofa to watch T.V. and left them at the table. Armansky had begun to tell him the story of Lisbeth Salander.

Edklinth and Armansky had known each other for twelve years, ever since a woman Member of Parliament had received death threats. She had reported the matter to the head of her party, and parliament's security detail had been informed. In due course the matter came to the attention of the Security Police. At that time, Personal Protection had the smallest budget of any unit in the Security Police, but the Member of Parliament was given protection during the course of her official appearances. She was left to her own devices at the end of the working day, the very time when she was obviously more vulnerable. She began to have doubts about the ability of the Security Police to protect her.

She arrived home late one evening to discover that someone had broken in, daubed sexually explicit epithets on her living-room walls, and masturbated in her bed. She immediately hired Milton Security to take over her personal protection. She did not advise Säpo of this decision. The next morning, when she was due to appear at a school in Täby, there was a confrontation between the government security forces and her Milton bodyguards.

At that time Edklinth was acting deputy chief of Personal Protection. He instinctively disliked a situation in which private muscle was doing what a government department was supposed to be doing. He did recognize that the Member of Parliament had reason enough for complaint. Instead of exacerbating the issue, he invited Milton Security's C.E.O. to lunch. They agreed that the situation might be more serious than Säpo had at first assumed, and Edklinth realized that Armansky's people not only had the skills for the job, but they were as well trained and probably better equipped too. They solved the immediate problem by giving Armansky's people responsibility for bodyguard services, while the Security Police took care of the criminal investigation and paid the bill.

The two men discovered that they liked each other a good deal, and they enjoyed working together on a number of assignments in subsequent years. Edklinth had great respect for Armansky, and when he was pressingly invited to dinner and a private conversation, he was willing to listen.

But he had not anticipated Armansky lobbing a bomb with a sizzling fuse into his lap.

"You're telling me that the Security Police is involved in flagrant criminal activity."

"No," Armansky said. "You misunderstand me. I'm saying that *some* people within the Security Police are involved in such activity. I don't believe that this activity is sanctioned by the leadership of S.I.S., or that it has government approval."

Edklinth studied Malm's photographs of a man getting into a car with a registration number that began with the letters KAB.

"Dragan . . . this isn't a practical joke?"

"I wish it were."

The next morning Edklinth was in his office at police headquarters. He was meticulously cleaning his glasses. He was a grey-haired man with big ears and a powerful face, but for the moment his expression was more puzzled than powerful. He had spent most of the night worrying about how he was going to deal with the information Armansky had given him.

They were not pleasant thoughts. The Security Police was an institution in Sweden that all parties (well, almost all) agreed had an indispensable value. This led each of them to distrust the group and at the same time concoct imaginative conspiracy theories about it. The scandals had undoubtedly been many, especially in the leftist-radical '70s when a number of constitutional blunders had certainly occurred. But after five governmental – and roundly criticized – Säpo investigations, a new generation of civil servants had come through. They represented a younger school of activists recruited from the financial, weapons and fraud units of the state police. They were officers used to investigating real crimes, and not chasing political mirages. The Security Police had been modernized and the Constitutional Protection Unit in particular had taken on a new, conspicuous role. Its task, as set out in the government's instruction, was to uncover and prevent threats to the internal security of the nation. i.e. *unlawful activity that uses violence, threat or coercion for the purpose of altering our form of government, inducing decision making political entities or authorities to take decisions in a certain direction, or preventing individual citizens from exercising their constitutionally protected rights and liberties.*

In short, to defend Swedish democracy against real or presumed anti-democratic threats. They were chiefly concerned with the anarchists and the neo-Nazis: the anarchists because they persisted in practising civil disobedience; the neo-Nazis because they were Nazis and so by definition the enemies of democracy.

After completing his law degree, Edklinth had worked as a prosecutor and then twenty-one years ago joined the Security Police. He had at first worked in the field in the Personal Protection Unit, and then within the Constitutional Protection Unit as an analyst and administrator. Eventually he became director of the agency, the head of the police forces responsible for the defence of Swedish democracy. He considered himself a democrat. The constitution had been established by the parliament, and it was his job to see to it that it stayed intact.

Swedish democracy is based on a single premise: the Right to Free Speech (R.F.S.). This guarantees the inalienable right to say aloud, think and believe anything whatsoever. This right embraces all Swedish citizens, from the crazy neo-Nazi living in the woods to the rock-throwing anarchist – and everyone in between.

Every other basic right, such as the Formation of Government and the Right to Freedom of Organization, are simply practical extensions of the Right to Free Speech. On this law democracy stands or falls.

All democracy has its limits, and the limits to the R.F.S. are set by the Freedom of the Press regulation (F.P.). This defines four restrictions on democracy. It is forbidden to publish child pornography and the depiction of certain violent sexual acts, regardless of how artistic the originator believes the depiction to be. It is forbidden to incite or exhort someone to crime. It is forbidden to defame or slander another person. It is forbidden to engage in the persecution of an ethnic group.

Press freedom has also been enshrined by parliament and is based on the socially and democratically acceptable restrictions of society, that is, the social contract that makes up the framework of a civilized society. The core of the legislation has it that no person has the right to harass or humiliate another person.

Since R.F.S. and F.P. are laws, some sort of authority is needed to guarantee the observance of these laws. In Sweden this function is divided between two institutions.

The first is the office of the Prosecutor General, assigned to prosecute crimes against F.P. This did not please Torsten Edklinth. In his view, the Prosecutor General was too lenient with cases concerning what were, in his view, direct crimes against the Swedish constitution. The Prosecutor General usually replied that the principle of democracy was so important that it was only in an extreme emergency that he should step in and bring a charge. This attitude, however, had come under question more and more in recent years, particularly after Robert Hårdh, the general secretary of the Swedish Helsinki Committee, had submitted a report which examined the Prosecutor General's want of initiative over a number of years. The report claimed that it was almost impossible to charge and convict anyone under the law of persecution against an ethnic group.

The second institution was the Security Police division for Constitutional Protection, and Superintendent Edklinth took on this responsibility with the utmost seriousness. He thought that it was the most important post a Swedish policeman could hold, and he would not exchange his appointment for any other position in the entire Swedish legal system or police force. He was the only policeman in Sweden whose official job description was to function as a political police officer. It was a delicate task requiring great wisdom and judicial restraint, since experience from far too many countries has shown that a political police department could easily transform itself into the principal threat to democracy.

The media and the public assumed for the most part that the main function of the Constitutional Protection Unit was to keep track of Nazis and militant vegans. These types of group did attract interest from the Constitutional Protection Unit, but a great many institutions and phenomena also fell within the bailiwick of the division. If the king, for example, or the commander-in-chief of the armed forces, took it into their hearts that parliamentary government had outlived its role and that parliament should be replaced by a dictatorship, the king or the commander-in-chief would very swiftly come under observation by the Constitutional Protection Unit. Or, to give a second example, if a group of police officers decided to stretch the laws so that an individual's constitutionally guaranteed rights were infringed, then it was the Constitutional Protection Unit's duty to react. In such serious instances the investigation was also assumed to come under the authority of the Prosecutor General.

The problem, of course, was that the Constitutional Protection Unit had only an analytical and investigative function, and no operations arm. That was why it was generally either the regular police or other divisions within the Security Police who stepped in when Nazis were to be arrested.

In Edklinth's opinion, this state of affairs was deeply unsatisfactory. Almost every democratic country maintains an independent constitutional court in some form, with a mandate to see to it that authorities do not ride roughshod over the democratic process. In Sweden the task is that of the Prosecutor General or the Parliamentary Ombudsman, who, however, can only pursue recommendations forwarded to them by other departments. If Sweden had a constitutional court, then Salander's lawyer could instantly charge the Swedish government with violation of her constitutional rights. The court could then order all the documents on the table and summon anyone it pleased, including the Prime Minister, to testify until the matter was resolved. As the situation now stood, the most her lawyer could do was to file a report with the Parliamentary Ombudsman, who did not have the authority to walk into the Security Police and start demanding documents and other evidence.

Over the years Edklinth had been an impassioned advocate of the establishment of a constitutional court. He could then more easily have acted upon the information he had been given by Armansky: by initiating a police report and handing the documentation to the court. With that an inexorable process would have been set in motion.

As things stood, Edklinth lacked the legal authority to initiate a preliminary investigation.

He took a pinch of snuff.

If Armansky's information was correct, Security Police officers in senior positions had looked the other way when a series of savage assaults were committed against a Swedish woman. Then her daughter was locked up in a mental hospital on the basis of a fabricated diagnosis. Finally, they had given *carte blanche* to a former Soviet intelligence officer to commit crimes involving weapons, narcotics and sex trafficking. Edklinth grimaced. He did not even want to begin to estimate how many counts of illegal activity must have taken place. Not to mention the burglary at Blomkvist's apartment, the attack on Salander's lawyer – which Edklinth could not bring himself to accept was a part of the same pattern – and possible involvement in the murder of Zalachenko.

It was a mess, and Edklinth did not welcome the necessity to get mixed up in it. Unfortunately, from the moment Armansky invited him to dinner, he had become involved.

How now to handle the situation? Technically, that answer was simple. If Armansky's account was true, Lisbeth Salander had at the very least been deprived of the opportunity *to exercise her constitutionally protected rights and liberties*. From a constitutional standpoint, this was the first can of worms. *Decision-making political bodies had been induced to take decisions in a certain direction.* This too touched on the core of the responsibility delegated to the Constitutional Protection Unit. Edklinth, a policeman, had knowledge of a crime and thus he had the obligation to submit a report to a prosecutor. In real life, the answer was not so simple. It was, on the contrary and to put it mildly, decidedly unsimple.

Inspector Monica Figuerola, in spite of her unusual name, was born in Dalarna to a family that had lived in Sweden at least since the time of Gustavus Vasa in the sixteenth century. She was a woman who people usually paid attention to, and for several reasons. She was thirty-six, blue eyed, and one metre eighty-four tall. She had short, light-blonde, naturally curly hair. She was attractive and dressed in a way that she knew made her more so. And she was exceptionally fit.

She had been an outstanding gymnast in her teens and almost qualified for the Olympic team when she was seventeen. She had given up classic gymnastics, but she still worked out obsessively at the gym five nights a week. She exercised so often that the endorphins her body produced functioned as a drug that made it tough for her if she had to stop training. She ran, lifted weights, played tennis, did karate. She had cut back on bodybuilding, that extreme variant of bodily glorification, some years ago. In those days she was spending two hours a day pumping iron. Even so, she trained so hard and her body was so muscular that malicious colleagues still called her Herr Figuerola. When she wore a sleeveless T-shirt or a summer dress, no-one could fail to notice her biceps and powerful shoulders.

Her intelligence, too, intimidated many of her male colleagues. She had left school with top marks, studied to become a police officer at twenty, and then served for nine years in Uppsala police and studied law in her spare time. For fun, she said, she had also studied for a degree in political science.

When she left patrol duty to become a criminal inspector, it was a great loss to Uppsala street safety. She worked first in the Violent Crime Division and then in the unit that specialized in financial crime. In 2000 she applied to the Security Police in Uppsala, and by 2001 she had moved to Stockholm. She first worked in Counter-Espionage, but was almost immediately hand-picked by Edklinth for the Constitutional Protection Unit. He happened to know Figuerola's father and had followed her career over the years.

When at long last Edklinth concluded that he had to act on Armansky's information, he called Figuerola into his office. She had been at Constitutional Protection for less than three years, which meant that she was still more of a real police officer than a fully fledged desk warrior.

She was dressed that day in tight blue jeans, turquoise sandals with a low heel, and a navy blue jacket.

"What are you working on at the moment, Monica?"

"We're following up on the robbery of the grocer's in Sunne."

The Security Police did not normally spend time investigating robberies of groceries, and Figuerola was the head of a department of five officers working on political crimes. They relied heavily on computers connected to the incident reporting network of the regular police. Nearly every report submitted in any police district in Sweden passed through the computers in Figuerola's department. The software scanned every report and reacted to 310 keywords, *nigger*, for example, or *skinhead, swastika, immigrant, anarchist, Hitler salute, Nazi, National Democrat, traitor, Jew-lover, or nigger-lover.* If such a keyword cropped up, the report would be printed out and scrutinized.

The Constitutional Protection Unit publishes an annual report, *Threats to National Security*, which supplies the only reliable statistics on political crime. These statistics are based on reports filed with local police authorities. In the case of the robbery of the shop in Sunne, the computer had reacted to three keywords – *immigrant, shoulder patch*, and *nigger*. Two masked men had robbed at gunpoint a shop owned by an immigrant. They had taken 2,780 kronor and a carton of cigarettes. One of the robbers had a mid-length jacket with a Swedish flag shoulder patch. The other had screamed "fucking nigger" several times at the manager and forced him to lie on the floor.

This was enough for Figuerola's team to initiate the preliminary investigation and to set about enquiring whether the robbers had a connection to the neo-Nazi gang in Värmland, and whether the robbery could be defined as a racist crime. If so, the incident might be included in that year's statistical compilation, which would then itself be incorporated within the European statistics put together by the E.U.'s office in Vienna.

"I've a difficult assignment for you," Edklinth said. "It's a job that could land you in big trouble. Your career might be ruined."

"I'm all ears."

"But if things go well, it could be a major step forward in your career. I'm thinking of moving you to the Constitutional Protection operations unit."

"Forgive me for mentioning this, but Constitutional Protection doesn't have an operations unit."

"Yes, it does," Edklinth said. "I established it this morning. At present it consists of you."

"I see," said Figuerola hesitantly.

"The task of Constitutional Protection is to defend the constitution against what we call 'internal threats', most often those on the extreme left or the extreme right. But what do we do if a threat to the constitution comes from within our own organization?"

For the next half hour he told her what Armansky had told him the night before.

"Who is the source of these claims?" Figuerola said when the story was ended.

"Focus on the information, not the source."

"What I'm wondering is whether you consider the source to be reliable."

"I consider the source to be totally reliable. I've know this person for many years."

"It all sounds a bit . . . I don't know. Improbable?"

"Doesn't it? One might think it's the stuff of a spy novel."

"How do you expect me to go about tackling it?"

"Starting now, you're released from all other duties. Your task, your *only* task, is to investigate the truth of this story. You have to either verify or dismiss the claims one by one. You report directly and only to me."

"I see what you mean when you say I might land in it up to my neck."

"But if the story is true . . . if even a fraction of it is true, then we have a constitutional crisis on our hands."

"Where do you want me to begin?"

"Start with the simple things. Start by reading the Björck report. Then identify the people who are allegedly tailing this guy Blomkvist. According to my source, the car belongs to Göran Mårtensson, a police officer living on Vittangigaten in Vällingby. Then identify the other person in the pictures taken by Blomkvist's photographer. The younger blond man here."

Figuerola was making notes.

"Then look into Gullberg's background. I had never heard his name before, but my source believes there to be a connection between him and the Security Police."

"So somebody here at S.I.S. put out a contract on a long-ago spy using a 78-year-old man. It beggars belief."

"Nevertheless, you check it out. And your entire investigation has to be carried out without a single person other than me knowing anything at all about it. Before you take one single positive action I want to be informed. I don't want to see any rings on the water or hear of a single ruffled feather."

"This is one hell of an investigation. How am I going to do all this alone?"

"You won't have to. You have only to do the first check. You come back and say that you've checked and didn't find anything, then everything is fine. You come back having found that *anything* is as my source describes it, then we'll decide what to do."

*

Figuerola spent her lunch hour pumping iron in the police gym. Lunch consisted of black coffee and a meatball sandwich with beetroot salad, which she took back to her office. She closed her door, cleared her desk, and started reading the Björck report while she ate her sandwich.

She also read the appendix with the correspondence between Björck and Dr Teleborian. She made a note of every name and every incident in the report that had to be verified. After two hours she got up and went to the coffee machine and got a refill. When she left her office she locked the door, part of the routine at S.I.S.

The first thing she did was to check the protocol number. She called the registrar and was informed that no report with that protocol number existed. Her second check was to consult a media archive. That yielded better results. The evening papers and a morning paper had reported a person being badly injured in a car fire on Lundagatan on the date in question in 1991. The victim of the incident was a middle-aged man, but no name was given. One evening paper reported that, according to a witness, the fire had been started deliberately by a young girl.

Gunnar Björck, the author of the report, was a real person. He was a senior official in the immigration unit, lately on sick leave and now, very recently, deceased – a suicide.

The personnel department had no information about what Björck had been working on in 1991. The file was stamped Top Secret, even for other employees at S.I.S. Which was also routine.

It was a straightforward matter to establish that Salander had lived with her mother and twin sister on Lundagatan in 1991 and spent the following two years at St Stefan's children's psychiatric clinic. In these sections at least, the record corresponded with the report's contents.

Peter Teleborian, now a well-known psychiatrist often seen on T.V., had worked at St Stefan's in 1991 and was today its senior physician.

Figuerola then called the assistant head of the personnel department.

"We're working on an analysis here in C.P. that requires evaluating a person's credibility and general mental health. I need to consult a psychiatrist or some other professional who's approved to handle classified information. Dr Peter Teleborian was mentioned to me, and I was wondering whether I could hire him."

It took some while before she got an answer.

"Dr Teleborian has been an external consultant for S.I.S. in a couple of instances. He has security clearance and you can discuss classified information with him in general terms. But before you approach him you have to follow the bureaucratic procedure. Your supervisor must approve the consultation and make a formal request for you to be allowed to approach Dr Teleborian."

Her heart sank. She had verified something that could be known only to a very restricted group of people. Teleborian had indeed had dealings with S.I.S.

She put down the report and focused her attention on other aspects of the information that Edklinth had given her. She studied the photographs of the two men who had allegedly followed the journalist Blomkvist from Café Copacabana on May 1.

She consulted the vehicle register and found that Göran Mårtensson was the owner of a grey Volvo with the registration number legible in the photographs. Then she got confirmation from the S.I.S. personnel department that he was employed there. Her heart sank again.

Mårtensson worked in Personal Protection. He was a bodyguard. He was one of the officers responsible on formal occasions for the safety of the Prime Minister. For the past few weeks he had been loaned to Counter-Espionage. His leave of absence had begun on April 10, a couple of days after Zalachenko and Salander had landed in Sahlgrenska hospital. But that sort of temporary reassignment was not unusual – covering a shortage of personnel here or there in an emergency situation.

Then Figuerola called the assistant chief of Counter-Espionage, a man she knew and had worked for during her short time in that department. Was Göran Mårtensson working on anything important, or could he be borrowed for an investigation in Constitutional Protection?

The assistant chief of Counter-Espionage was puzzled. Inspector Figuerola must have been misinformed. Mårtensson had not been reassigned to Counter-Espionage. Sorry.

Figuerola stared at her receiver for two minutes. In Personal Protection they believed that Mårtensson had been loaned out to Counter-Espionage. Counter-Espionage said that they definitely had *not* borrowed him. Transfers of that kind had to be approved by the chief of Secretariat. She reached for the telephone to call him, but stopped short. If Personal Protection had loaned out Mårtensson, then the chief of Secretariat must have approved the decision. But Mårtensson was not at Counter-Espionage, which the chief of Secretariat must be aware of. And if Mårtensson was loaned out to some department that was tailing journalists, then the chief of Secretariat would have to know about that too.

Edklinth had told her: no rings in the water. To raise the matter with the chief of Secretariat might be to chuck a very large stone into a pond.

Berger sat at her desk in the glass cage. It was 10.30 on Monday morning. She badly needed the cup of coffee she had just got from the machine in the canteen. The first hours of her workday had been taken up entirely with meetings, starting with one lasting fifteen minutes in which Assistant Editor Fredriksson presented the guidelines for the day's work. She was increasingly dependent on Fredriksson's judgement in the light of her loss of confidence in Anders Holm.

The second was an hour-long meeting with the chairman Magnus Borgsjö, *S.M.P.*'s C.F.O. Christer Sellberg, and Ulf Flodin, the budget chief. The discussion was about the slump in advertising and the downturn in single-copy sales. The budget chief and the C.F.O. were both determined on action to cut the newspaper's overheads.

"We made it through the first quarter of this year thanks to a marginal rise in advertising sales and the fact that two senior, highly paid employees retired at the beginning of the year. Those positions have not been filled," Flodin said. "We'll probably close out the present quarter with a small deficit. But the free papers, *Metro* and *Stockholm City*, are cutting into our ad. revenue in Stockholm. My prognosis is that the third quarter will produce a significant loss."

"So how do we counter that?" Borgsjö said.

"The only option is cutbacks. We haven't laid anyone off since 2002. But before the end of the year we will have to eliminate ten positions."

"Which positions?" Berger said.

"We need to work on the 'cheese plane' principle, shave a job here and a job there. The sports desk has six and a half jobs at the moment. We should cut that to five full-timers."

"As I understand it, the sports desk is on its knees already. What you're proposing means that we'll have to cut back on sports coverage."

Flodin shrugged. "I'll gladly listen to other suggestions."

"I don't have any better suggestions, but the principle is this: if we cut personnel, then we have to produce a smaller newspaper, and if we make a smaller newspaper, the number of readers will drop and the number of advertisers too."

"The eternal vicious circle," Sellberg said.

"I was hired to turn this downward trend around," said Berger. "I see my job as taking an aggressive approach to change the newspaper and make it more attractive to readers. I can't do that if I have to cut staff." She turned to Borgsjö. "How long can the paper continue to bleed? How big a deficit can we take before we hit the limit?"

Borgsjö pursed his lips. "Since the early '90s S.M.P. has eaten into a great many old consolidated assets. We have a stock portfolio that has dropped in value by about 30 per cent compared to ten years ago. A large portion of these funds were used for investments in I.T. We've also had enormous expenses."

"I gather that S.M.P. has developed its own text editing system, the A.X.T. What did that cost?"

"About five million kronor to develop."

"Why did S.M.P. go to the trouble of developing its own software? There are inexpensive commercial programs already on the market."

"Well, Erika . . . that may be true. Our former I.T. chief talked us into it. He persuaded us that it would be less expensive in the long run, and that S.M.P. would also be able to license the program to other newspapers."

"And did any of them buy it?"

"Yes, as a matter of fact, a local paper in Norway bought it."

"Meanwhile," Berger said in a dry voice, "we're sitting here with P.C.s that are five or six years old . . ."

"It's simply out of the question that we invest in new computers in the coming year," Flodin said.

The discussion had gone back and forth. Berger was aware that her objections were being systematically stonewalled by Flodin and Sellberg. For them costcutting was what counted, which was understandable enough from the point of view of a budget chief and a C.F.O., but unacceptable for a newly appointed editor-in-chief. What irritated her most was that they kept brushing off her arguments with patronizing smiles, making her feel like a teenager being quizzed on her homework. Without actually uttering a single inappropriate word, they displayed towards her an attitude that was so antediluvian it was almost comical. *You shouldn't worry your pretty head over complex matters, little girl.*

Borgsjö was not much help. He was biding his time and letting the other participants at the meeting say their piece, but she did not sense the same condescension from him.

She sighed and plugged in her laptop. She had nineteen new messages. Four were spam. Someone wanted to sell her Viagra, cybersex with "The Sexiest Lolitas on the Net" for only $4.00 per minute, "Animal Sex, the Juiciest Horse Fuck in the Universe", and a subscription to *fashion.nu*. The tide of this crap never receded, no matter how many times she tried to block it. Another seven messages were those so-called "Nigeria letters" from the widow of the former head of a bank in Abu Dhabi offering her ludicrous sums of money if she would only assist with a small sum of start-up money, and other such drivel.

There was the morning memo, the lunchtime memo, three emails from Fredriksson updating her on developments in the day's lead story, one from her accountant who wanted a meeting to check on the implications of her move from *Millennium* to *S.M.P.*, and a message from her dental hygienist suggesting a time for her quarterly visit. She put the appointment in her calendar and realized at once that she would have to change it because she had a major editorial conference planned for that day.

Finally she opened the last one, sent from <centraled@smpost.se> with the subject line [Attn: Editor-in-Chief]. Slowly she put down her coffee cup.

YOU WHORE! YOU THINK YOU'RE SOMETHING YOU FUCKING CUNT. DON'T THINK YOU CAN COME HERE AND THROW YOUR WEIGHT AROUND. YOU'RE GOING TO GET FUCKED IN THE CUNT WITH A SCREWDRIVER, WHORE! THE SOONER YOU DISAPPEAR THE BETTER.

Berger looked up and searched for the news editor, Holm. He was not at his desk, nor could she see him in the newsroom. She checked the sender and then picked up the telephone and called Peter Fleming, the I.T. manager.

"Good morning, Peter. Who uses the address <centraled@smpost.se>?"

"That isn't a valid address at *S.M.P.*"

"I just got an email from that address."

"It's a fake. Does the message contain a virus?"

"I wouldn't know. At least, the antivirus program didn't react."

"O.K. That address doesn't exist. But it's very simple to fake an apparently legitimate address. There are sites on the Net that you can use to send anonymous mail."

"Is it possible to trace an email like that?"

"Almost impossible, even if the person in question is so stupid that he sends it from his home computer. You might be able to trace the I.P. number to a server, but if he uses an account that he set up at hotmail, for instance, the trail will fizzle out."

Berger thanked him. She thought for a moment. It was not the first time she had received a threatening email or a message from a crackpot. This one was obviously referring to her new job as editor-in-chief. She wondered whether it was some lunatic who had read about her in connection with Morander's death, or whether the sender was in the building.

Figuerola thought long and hard as to what she should do about Gullberg. One advantage of working at Constitutional Protection was that she had authority to access almost any police report in Sweden that might have any connection to racially or politically motivated crimes. Zalachenko was technically an immigrant, and her job included tracking violence against persons born abroad to decide whether or not the crime was racially motivated. Accordingly she had the right to involve herself in the investigation of Zalachenko's murder, to determine whether Gullberg, the known killer, had a connection to any racist organization, or whether he was overheard making racist remarks at the time of the murder. She requisitioned the report. She found the letters that had been sent to the Minister of Justice and discovered that alongside the diatribe and the insulting personal attacks were also the words *nigger-lover* and *traitor*.

By then it was 5.00 p.m. Figuerola locked all the material in her safe, shut down her computer, washed up her coffee mug, and clocked out. She walked briskly to a gym at St Eriksplan and spent the next hour doing some easy strength training.

When she was finished she went home to her one-bedroom apartment on Pontonjärgatan, showered, and ate a late but nutritious dinner. She considered calling Daniel Mogren, who lived three blocks down the same street. Mogren was a carpenter and bodybuilder and had been her training partner off and on for three years. In recent months they had also had sex as friends.

Sex was almost as satisfying as a rigorous workout at the gym, but at a mature thirty-plus or, rather, forty-minus, Figuerola had begun to think that maybe she ought to start looking for a steady partner and a more permanent living arrangement. Maybe even children. But not with Mogren.

She decided that she did not feel like seeing anyone that evening. Instead she went to bed with a history of the ancient world.

CHAPTER 13

Tuesday, 17.v

Figuerola woke at 6.10 on Tuesday morning, took a long run along Norr Mälarstrand, showered, and clocked in at police headquarters at 8.10. She prepared a memorandum on the conclusions she had arrived at the day before.

At 9.00 Edklinth arrived. She gave him twenty minutes to deal with his post, then knocked on his door. She waited while he read her four pages. At last he looked up.

"The chief of Secretariat," he said.

"He must have approved loaning out Mårtensson. So he must know that Mårtensson is not at Counter-Espionage, even though according to Personal Protection that's where he is."

Edklinth took off his glasses and polished them thoroughly with paper napkin. He had met Chief of Secretariat Albert Shenke at meetings and internal conferences on countless occasions, but he could not claim to know the man well. Shenke was rather short, with thin reddish-blond hair, and by now rather stout. He was about fifty-five and had worked at S.I.S. for at least twenty-five years, possibly longer. He had been chief of Secretariat for a decade, and was assistant chief before that. Edklinth thought him taciturn, and a man who could act ruthlessly when necessary. He had no idea what he did in his free time, but he had a memory of having once seen him in the garage of the police building in casual clothes, with a golf bag slung over his shoulder. He had also run into him once at the Opera.

"There was one thing that struck me," Figuerola said

"What's that?"

"Evert Gullberg. He did his military service in the '40s and became an accountant or some such, and then in the '50s he vanished into thin air."

"And?"

"When we were discussing this yesterday, we were talking about him as if he were some sort of a hired killer."

"It sounds far-fetched, I know, but—"

"It struck me that there is so little background on him that it seems almost like a smokescreen. Both IB and S.I.S. established cover companies outside the building in the '50s and '60s."

"I was wondering when you'd think of that," Edklinth said.

"I'd like permission to go through the personnel files from the '50s," Figuerola said.

"No," Edklinth said, shaking his head. "We can't go into the archives without authorization from the chief of Secretariat, and we don't want to attract attention until we have more to go on."

"So what next?"

"Mårtensson," Edklinth said. "Find out what he's working on."

Salander was studying the vent window in her room when she heard the key turn in the door. In came Jonasson. It was past 10.00 on Tuesday night. He had interrupted her planning how to break out of Sahlgrenska hospital.

She had measured the window and discovered that her head would fit through it and that she would not have much problem squeezing the rest of her body through. It was three storeys to the ground, but a combination of torn sheets and a ten-foot extension cord from a floor lamp would dispose of that problem.

She had plotted her escape step by step. The problem was what she would wear. She had knickers, a hospital nightshirt and a pair of plastic flip-flops that she had managed to borrow. She had 200 kronor in cash from Annika Giannini to pay for sweets from the hospital snack shop. That should be enough for a cheap pair of jeans and a T-shirt at the Salvation Army store, if she could find one in Göteborg. She would have to spend what was left of the money on a call to Plague. Then everything would work out. She planned on landing in Gibraltar a few days after she escaped, and from there she would create a new identity somewhere in the world.

Jonasson sat in the visitor's chair. She sat on the edge of her bed.

"Hello, Lisbeth. I'm sorry I've not come to see you the past few days, but I've been up to my eyes in A. & E. and I've also been made a mentor for a couple of interns."

She had not expected Jonasson to make special visits to see her.

He picked up her chart and studied her temperature graph and the record of medications. Her temperature was steady, between 37 and 37.2 degrees, and for the past week she had not taken any headache tablets.

"Dr Endrin is your doctor. Do you get along with her?"

"She's alright," Salander said without enthusiasm.

"Is it O.K. if I do an examination?"

She nodded. He took a pen torch out of his pocket and bent over to shine it into her eyes, to see how her pupils contracted and expanded. He asked her to open her mouth and examined her throat. Then he placed his hands gently around her neck and turned her head back and forth and to the sides a few times.

"You don't have any pain in your neck?" he said.

She shook her head.

"How's the headache?"

"I feel it now and then, but it passes."

"The healing process is still going on. The headache will eventually go away altogether."

Her hair was still so short that he hardly needed to push aside the tufts to feel the scar above her ear. It was healing, but there was still a small scab.

"You've been scratching the wound. You shouldn't do that."

She nodded. He took her left elbow and raised the arm.

"Can you lift it by yourself?"

She lifted her arm.

"Do you have any pain or discomfort in the shoulder?"

She shook her head.

"Does it feel tight?"

"A little."

"I think you have to do a bit more physio on your shoulder muscles."

"It's hard when you're locked up like this."

He smiled at her. "That won't last. Are you doing the exercises the therapist recommended?"

She nodded.

He pressed his stethoscope against his wrist for a moment to warm it. Then he sat on the edge of the bed and untied the strings of her nightshirt, listened to her heart and took her pulse. He asked her to lean forward and placed the stethoscope on her back to listen to her lungs.

"Cough."

She coughed.

"O.K., you can do up your nightshirt and get into bed. From a medical standpoint, you're just about recovered."

She expected him to get up and say he would come back in a few days, but he stayed, sitting on the bed. He seemed to be thinking about something. Salander waited patiently.

"Do you know why I became a doctor?" he said.

She shook her head.

"I come from a working-class family. I always thought I wanted to be a doctor. I'd actually thought about becoming a psychiatrist when I was a teenager. I was terribly intellectual."

Salander looked at him with sudden alertness as soon as he mentioned the word "psychiatrist".

"But I wasn't sure that I could handle the studies. So when I finished school I studied to be a welder and I even worked as one for several years. I thought it was a good idea to have something to fall back on if the medical studies didn't work out. And being a welder wasn't so different from being a doctor. It's all about patching up things. And now I'm working here at Sahlgrenska and patching up people like you."

She wondered if he were pulling her leg.

"Lisbeth . . . I'm wondering . . ."

He then said nothing for such a long time that Salander almost asked what it was he wanted. But she waited for him to speak.

"Would you be angry with me if I asked you a personal question? I want to ask you as a private individual, not as a doctor. I won't make any record of your answer and I won't discuss it with anyone else. And you don't have to answer if you don't want to."

"What is it?"

"Since you were shut up at St Stefan's when you were twelve, you've refused to respond when any psychiatrist has tried to talk to you. Why is that?"

Salander's eyes darkened, but they were utterly expressionless as she looked at Jonasson. She sat in silence for two minutes.

"Why?" she said at last.

"To be honest, I'm not really sure. I think I'm trying to understand something."

Her lips curled a little. "I don't talk to crazy-doctors because they never listen to what I have to say."

Jonasson laughed. "O.K. Tell me . . . what do you think of Peter Teleborian?"

Jonasson threw out the name so unexpectedly that Salander almost jumped. Her eyes narrowed.

"What the hell is this, 'Twenty Questions'? What are you after?" Her voice sounded like sandpaper.

Jonasson leaned forward, almost too close.

"Because a . . . what did you call it . . . a crazy-doctor by the name of Peter Teleborian, who's somewhat renowned in my profession, has been to see me twice in the past few days, trying to convince me to let him examine you."

Salander felt an icy chill run down her spine.

"The district court is going to appoint him to do a forensic psychiatric assessment of you."

"And?"

"I don't like the man. I've told him he can't see you. Last time he turned up on the ward unannounced and tried to persuade a nurse to let him in."

Salander pressed her lips tight.

"His behaviour was a bit odd and a little too eager. So I want to know what you think of him."

This time it was Jonasson's turn to wait patiently for Salander's reply.

"Teleborian is a beast," she said at last.

"Is it something personal between the two of you?"

"You could say that."

"I've also had a conversation with an official who wants me to let Teleborian see you."

"And?"

"I asked what sort of medical expertise he thought he had to assess your condition and then I told him to go to hell. More diplomatically than that, of course. And one last question. Why are you talking to *me*?"

"You asked me a question, didn't you?"

"Yes, but I'm a doctor and I've studied psychiatry. So why are you talking to me? Should I take it to mean that you have a certain amount of trust in me?"

She did not reply.

"Then I'll choose to interpret it that way. I want you to know this: you are my patient. That means that I work for you and not for anyone else."

She gave him a suspicious look. He looked back at her for a moment. Then he spoke in a lighter tone of voice.

"From a medical standpoint, as I said, you're more or less healthy. You don't need any more weeks of rehab. But unfortunately you're a bit too healthy."

"Why 'unfortunately'?"

He gave her a cheerful smile. "You're getting better too fast."

"What do you mean?"

"It means that I have no legitimate reason to keep you isolated here. And the prosecutor will soon be having you transferred to a prison in Stockholm to await trial in six weeks. I'm guessing that such a request will arrive next week. And that means that Teleborian will be given the chance to observe you."

She sat utterly still. Jonasson seemed distracted and bent over to arrange her pillow. He spoke as if thinking out loud.

"You don't have much of a headache or any fever, so Dr Endrin is probably going to discharge you." He stood up suddenly. "Thanks for talking to me. I'll come back and see you before you're transferred."

He was already at the door when she spoke.

"Dr Jonasson?"

He turned towards her.

"Thank you."

He nodded curtly once before he went out and locked the door.

Salander stared for a long time at the locked door. And then she lay back and stared up at the ceiling.

That was when she felt that there was something hard beneath her head. She lifted the pillow and saw to her surprise a small cloth bag that had definitely not been there before. She opened it and stared in amazement at a Palm Tungsten T3 hand-held computer and battery charger. Then she looked more closely at the computer and saw the little scratch on the top left corner. Her heart skipped a beat. *It's my Palm. But how* . . . In amazement she glanced over at the locked door. Jonasson was a catalogue of surprises. In great excitement she turned on the computer at once and discovered that it was password-protected.

She stared in frustration at the blinking screen. It seemed to be challenging her. *How the hell did they think I would* . . . Then she looked

252

in the cloth bag and found at the bottom a scrap of folded paper. She unfolded it and read a line written in an elegant script:

You're the hacker, work it out! / Kalle B.

Salander laughed aloud for the first time in weeks. *Touché.* She thought for a few seconds. Then she picked up the stylus and wrote the number combination 9277, which corresponded to the letters W-A-S-P on the keyboard. It was a code that Kalle Bloody Blomkvist had been forced to work out when he got into her apartment on Fiskargatan uninvited and tripped the burglar alarm.

It did not work.

She tried 52553, which corresponded to the letters K-A-L-L-E.

That did not work either. Since Blomkvist presumably intended that she should use the computer, he must have chosen a simple password. He had used the signature Kalle, which normally he hated. She free-associated. She thought for a moment. It must be some insult. Then she typed in 74774, which corresponded to the word P-I-P-P-I – Pippi Bloody Longstocking.

The computer started up.

There was a smiley face on the screen with a cartoon speech balloon:

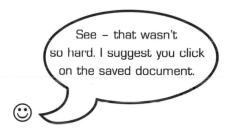

See – that wasn't so hard. I suggest you click on the saved document.

She found the document [Hi Sally] at the top of the list. She clicked on it and read:

```
First of all, this is only between you and me.
Your lawyer, my sister Annika, has no idea that
you have access to this computer. It has to stay
that way.

I don't know how much you understand of what
is happening outside your locked room, but
```

strangely enough (despite your personality), you have a number of loyal idiots working on your behalf. I have already established an elite body called *The Knights of the Idiotic Table*. We will be holding an annual dinner at which we'll have fun talking crap about you. (No, you're not invited.)

So, to the point. Annika is doing her best to prepare for your trial. One problem of course is that she's working for you and is bound and fettered by one of those damned confidentiality oaths. So she can't tell me what the two of you discuss, which in this case is a bit of a handicap. Luckily she does accept information.

We have to talk, you and I.

Don't use my email.

I may be paranoid, but I have reason to suspect that I'm not the only one reading it. If you want to deliver something, go to Yahoo group [Idiotic_Table]. I.D. Pippi and the password is p9i2p7p7i. / Mikael

----

Salander read his letter twice, staring in bewilderment at the Palm. After a period of computer celibacy, she was suffering from massive cyber-abstinence. And she wondered which big toe Blomkvist had been thinking with when he smuggled her a computer but forgot that she needed a mobile to connect to the Net.

She was still thinking when she heard footsteps in the corridor. She turned the computer off at once and shoved it under her pillow. As she heard the key in the door she realized that the cloth bag and charger were still in view on the bedside table. She reached out and slid the bag under the covers and pressed the coil of cord into her crotch. She lay passively looking up at the ceiling when the night nurse came in, said a polite hello, and asked how she was doing and whether she needed anything.

Salander told her that she was doing fine and that she wanted a pack of cigarettes. This request was turned down in a firm but friendly tone. She was given a pack of nicotine gum. As the nurse was closing the door Salander glimpsed the guard on his chair out in the corridor. She waited until she heard the nurse's steps receding before she once again picked up her Palm.

She turned it on and searched for connectivity.

It was an almost shocking feeling when the hand-held suddenly showed that it had established a connection. *Contact with the Net. Inconceivable.*

She jumped out of bed so fast that she felt a pain in her injured hip. She looked around the room. *How?* She walked all the way round, examining every nook and cranny. *No, there was no mobile in the room.* And yet she had connectivity. Then a crooked grin spread across her face. The connection was radio-controlled and locked into a mobile via Bluetooth, which had a range of ten to twelve metres. Her eyes lit upon an air vent just below the ceiling.

Kalle Bloody Blomkvist had somehow planted a mobile just outside her room. That could be the only explanation.

But why not smuggle in the mobile too? Ah, of course. The batteries.

Her Palm had to be recharged only once every three days. A mobile that was connected, if she surfed it hard, would burn out its batteries in much less time. Blomkvist — or more likely somebody he had hired and who was *out there* – would have to change the batteries at regular intervals.

But he had sent in the charger for her Palm. *He isn't so stupid after all.*

Salander began by deciding where to keep the hand-held. She had to find a hiding place. There were plug sockets by the door and in the panel behind the bed, which provided electricity for her bedside lamp and digital clock. There was a recess where a radio had been removed. She smiled. Both the battery charger and the Palm could fit in there. She could use the socket inside the bedside table to charge up the Palm during the day.

*

Salander was happy. Her heart was pounding hard when she started up the hand-held for the first time in two months and ventured on to the Internet.

Surfing on a Palm hand-held with a tiny screen and a stylus was not the same thing as surfing on a PowerBook with a 17″ screen. *But she was connected*. From her bed at Sahlgrenska she could now reach the entire world.

She started by going on to a website that advertised rather uninteresting pictures by an unknown and not especially skilled amateur photographer called Gil Bates in Jobsville, Pennsylvania. Salander had once checked it out and confirmed that the town of Jobsville did not exist. Nevertheless, Bates had taken more than 200 photographs of the community and created a gallery of small thumbnails. She scrolled down to image 167 and clicked to enlarge it. It showed the church in Jobsville. She put her cursor on the spire of the church tower and clicked. She instantly got a pop-up dialog box that asked for her I.D. and password. She took out her stylus and wrote the word *Remarkable* on the screen as her I.D. and *A(89)Cx#magnolia* as the password.

She got a dialog box with the text [ERROR – you have the wrong password] and a button that said [OK – Try again]. Lisbeth knew that if she clicked on [OK – Try again] and tried a different password, she would get the same dialog box again – for years and years, for as long as she kept trying. Instead she clicked on the [O] in [ERROR].

The screen went blank. Then an animated door opened and a Lara Croft-like figure stepped out. A speech bubble materialized with the text [WHO GOES THERE?].

She clicked on the bubble and wrote *Wasp*. She got the instant reply [PROVE IT – OR ELSE . . .] as the animated Lara Croft unlocked the safety catch on her gun. Salander knew it was no empty threat. If she wrote the wrong password three times in a row the site would shut down and the name *Wasp* would be struck from the membership list. Carefully she wrote the password *MonkeyBusiness*.

The screen changed again and now had a blue background with the text:

[Welcome to Hacker Republic, citizen Wasp. It has been 56 days since your last visit. There are 11 citizens online. Do you want to [a] Browse the Forum [b] Send a Message [c] Search the Archive [d] Talk [e] Get Laid?]

She clicked on [[d] Talk] and then went to the menu selection [Who's online?] and got a list with the names Andy, Bambi, Dakota, Jabba, BuckRogers, Mandrake, Pred, Slip, SisterJen, SixOfOne, and Trinity.

<Hi gang.> Wasp wrote.
<Wasp. That really U?> SixOfOne wrote. <Look who's back.>
<Where you been keeping yourself?> Trinity wrote.
<Plague said you were in some trouble.> Dakota wrote.

Salander was not sure, but she suspected that Dakota was a woman. The other citizens online, including the one who called himself SisterJen, were guys. Hacker Republic had a total (the last time she was connected) of sixty-two citizens, of whom four were female.
<Hi Trinity> Wasp wrote. <Hi everybody.>
<Why are you saying hi to Trin? Is there something on G and is there something wrong with the rest of us?> Dakota wrote.
<We've been dating> Trinity wrote. <Wasp only hangs out with intelligent people.>
He got abuse from five directions at once.
Of the sixty-two citizens, Wasp had met two face to face. Plague, who for some strange reason was not online, was one. Trinity was the other. He was English and lived in London. Two years earlier she had met him for a few hours when he helped her and Blomkvist in the hunt for Harriet Vanger by doing an illegal tapping of a landline in St Albans. Salander fumbled with the clumsy stylus and wished she had a keyboard.
<Still there?> Mandrake wrote.
She punched letters. <Sorry. Only have a Palm. Slow going.>
<What happened to your computer?> Pred wrote.
<My computer is O.K. It's me that's the problem.>
<Tell big brother.> Slip wrote.
<I'm under arrest by the government.>
<What? Why?> Three chatters at once.
Salander summed up her situation in five lines, which were greeted by a worried muttering.
<How are you doing?> Trinity wrote.
<I have a hole in my head.>

<I can't tell the difference> Bambi wrote.

<Wasp has always had air in her head> SisterJen wrote, and that was followed by a spate of disparaging remarks about Wasp's mental abilities. Salander smiled. The conversation resumed with a contribution from Dakota.

<Wait. This is an attack against a citizen of Hacker Republic. How are we going to respond?>

<Nuclear attack on Stockholm?> SixOfOne wrote.

<No, that would be overdoing it a bit> Wasp wrote.

<A little tiny bomb?>

<Go jump in the lake, SixOO.>

<We could shut down Stockholm> Mandrake wrote.

<A virus to shut down the government?>

The citizens of Hacker Republic did not generally spread computer viruses. On the contrary – they were hackers and consequently implacable adversaries of those idiots who created viruses whose sole purpose was to sabotage the Net and crash computers. The citizens were information junkies and wanted a functioning Internet that they could hack.

But their proposal to shut down the Swedish government was not an idle threat. Hacker Republic comprised a very exclusive club of the best of the best, an elite force that any defence organization in the world would have paid enormous sums to use for cyber-military purposes, if the citizens could be persuaded to feel any kind of loyalty to any state. Which was not very likely.

But they were every one of them computer wizards, and they were well versed in the art of contriving viruses. Nor did they need much convincing to carry out particular campaigns if the situation warranted. Some years earlier a citizen of Hacker Republic, who in their private life was a software developer in California, had been cheated out of a patent by a hot dot.com company that had the nerve to take the citizen to court. This caused the activists in Hacker Republic to devote a startling amount of energy for six months to hacking and destroying every computer owned by that company. All the company's secrets and emails – along with some fake documents that might lead people to think that its C.E.O. was involved in tax fraud – were gleefully posted on the Net, along with information about the C.E.O.'s now not-so-secret mistress and pictures from a party in Hollywood in which he could be seen snorting cocaine.

The company went under in six months, and several years later some members of the "people's militia" in Hacker Republic, who did not easily forget an enemy, were still haunting the former C.E.O.

If fifty of the world's foremost hackers decided to launch a coordinated attack against an entire country, the country might survive, but not without having serious problems. The costs would certainly run into the billions if Salander gave it the thumbs-up. She thought for a moment.

<Not right now. But if things don't go the way I need them to I might ask for help.>

<Just say the word> Dakota wrote.

<It's been a long time since we messed with a government> Mandrake wrote.

<I've got a suggestion for reversing the tax-payment system. A program that could be custom-tailored for a small country like Norway> Bambi wrote.

<Great, but Stockholm is in Sweden> Trinity wrote.

<Same difference. Here's what you could do ...>

Salander leaned back against the pillow and followed the conversation with a smile. She wondered why she, who had such difficulty talking about herself with people of flesh and blood, could blithely reveal her most intimate secrets to a bunch of completely unknown freaks on the Internet. The fact was that if Salander could claim to have any sort of family or group affiliation, then it was with these lunatics. None of them actually had a hope of helping her with the problems she had with the Swedish state. But she knew that, if the need arose, they would devote both time and cunning to performing effective demonstrations of their powers. Through this network she could also find herself hide-outs abroad. It had been Plague's contacts on the Net who had provided her with a Norwegian passport in the name of Irene Nesser.

Salander had no idea who the citizens of Hacker Republic were, and she had only a vague notion of what they did when they were not on the Net – the citizens were uniformly vague about their identities. SixOfOne had once claimed that he was a black, male American of Catholic origin living in Toronto. He could just as easily be white, female and Lutheran, and living in Skövde.

The one she knew best was Plague – he had introduced her to the family, and nobody became a member of this exclusive club without

259

very strong recommendations. And for anyone to become a member they had also to be known personally to one other citizen.

On the Net, Plague was an intelligent and socially gifted citizen. In real life he was a severely overweight and socially challenged thirty-year-old living on disability benefit in Sundbyberg. He bathed too seldom and his apartment smelled like a monkey house. Salander visited him only once in a blue moon. She was content to confine her dealings with him to the Net.

As the chat continued, Wasp downloaded mail that had been sent to her private mailbox at Hacker Republic. One was from another member, Poison, and contained an improved version of her program Asphyxia 1.3, which was available in the Republic's archive for its citizens. Asphyxia was a program that could control other people's computers via the Internet. Poison said that he had used it successfully, and that his updated version included the latest versions of Unix, Apple and Windows. She emailed him a brief reply and thanked him for the upgrade.

During the next hour, as evening approached in the United States, another half-dozen citizens had come online and welcomed back Wasp before joining the debate. When Salander logged off, the others were discussing to what extent the Swedish Prime Minister's computer could be made to send civil but crazy emails to other heads of state. A working group had been formed to explore the matter. Salander logged off by writing a brief message:

`<Keep talking but don't do anything unless I O.K. it. I'll come back when I can uplink again.>`

Everyone sent her hugs and kisses and admonished her to keep the hole in her head warm.

Only when Salander had logged out of Hacker Republic did she go into Yahoo and log on to the private newsgroup [Idiotic_Table]. She discovered that the group had two members – herself and Blomkvist. The mailbox had one message, sent on May 15. It was entitled [Read this first].

> Hi Sally. The situation is as follows:
> The police haven't found your apartment and don't
> have access to the D.V.D. of Bjurman's rape. The
> disk is very strong evidence. I don't want to

turn it over to Annika without your approval. I
have the keys to your apartment and a passport
in name of Nesser.

But the police do have the rucksack you had in
Gosseberga. I don't know if it contains anything
compromising.

Salander thought for a moment. Don't think so. A half-empty thermos
of coffee, some apples, a change of clothes. No problem.

You're going to be charged with G.B.H. against
or the attempted murder of Zalachenko, and G.B.H
against Carl-Magnus Lundin at Stallarholmen —
i.e., because you shot him in the foot and broke
his jaw when you kicked him. But a source in
the police whom I trust tells me that the evidence
in each case is woolly. The following is important:
(1) Before Zalachenko was shot he denied everything and claimed that it could only have been
Niedermann who shot and buried you. He laid a
charge against you for attempting to murder him.
The prosecutor is going to go on about this being
the second time you have tried to kill him.

(2) Neither Lundin or Sonny Nieminen has said a
word about what happened at Stallarholmen. Lundin
has been arrested for kidnapping Miriam. Nieminen
has been released.

Salander had already discussed all of this with Giannini. That was
nothing new. She *had* told Giannini everything that had happened in
Gosseberga, but she had refrained from telling her anything about
Bjurman.

What I think you haven't understood are the rules of the game.

It's like this. Säpo got saddled with Zalachenko in the middle of the Cold War. For fifteen years he was protected, no matter what havoc he wrought. Careers were built on Zalachenko. On any number of occasions they cleaned up behind his rampages. This is all criminal activity: Swedish authorities helping to cover up crime against individual citizens.

If this gets out, there'll be a scandal that will affect both the conservative and social democratic parties. Above all, people in high places within Säpo will be exposed as accomplices in criminal and immoral activities. Even though by now the statute of limitations has run out on the specific instances of crime, there'll still be a scandal. It involves big beasts who are either retired now or close to retirement.

They will do everything they can to reduce the damage to themselves and their group, and that means you'll once again be a pawn in their game. But this time it's not a matter of them sacrificing a pawn — it'll be a matter of them actively needing to limit the damage to themselves personally. So you'll have to be locked up again.

This is how it will work. They know that they can't keep the lid on the Zalachenko secret for long. I've got the story, and they know that sooner or later I'm going to publish it. It doesn't matter so much, of course, now that he's dead. What matters to them is their own survival. The following points are therefore high on their agenda:

(1) They have to convince the district court (the public, in effect) that the decision to lock you up in St Stefan's in 1991 was a legitimate one, that you really were mentally ill.

(2) They have to separate the "Salander affair" from the "Zalachenko affair". They'll try to create a situation where they can say that "certainly Zalachenko was a fiend, but that had nothing to do with the decision to lock up his daughter. She was locked up because she was deranged — any claims to the contrary are the sick fantasies of bitter journalists. No, we did not assist Zalachenko in any crime — that's the delusion of a mentally ill teenage girl."

(3) The problem is that if you're acquitted, it would mean that the district court finds you not only not guilty, but also not a nutcase. And that would have to mean that locking you up in 1991 was illegal. So they have, at all costs, to condemn you again to the locked psychiatric ward. If the court determines that you are mentally ill, the media's interest in continuing to dig around in the "Salander affair" will die away. That is how the media work.

Are you with me?

All of this she had already worked out for herself. The problem was that she did not know what she should do.

Lisbeth — seriously — this battle is going to be decided in the mass media and not in the courtroom. Unfortunately the trial is going to be held behind closed doors "to protect your privacy".

The day that Zalachenko was shot there was a robbery at my apartment. There were no signs on my door of a break-in, and nothing was touched or moved — except for one thing. The folder from Bjurman's summer cabin with Björck's report was taken. At the same time my sister was mugged and her copy of the report was also stolen. That folder is your most important evidence.

I have let it be known that our Zalachenko documents are gone, disappeared. In fact I had a third copy that I was going to give to Armansky. I made several copies of that one and have tucked them away in safe places.

Our opponents — who include several high-powered figures and certain psychiatrists — are of course also preparing for the trial together with Prosecutor Ekström. I have a source who provides me with some info. on what's going on, but I suspect that you might have a better chance of finding out the relevant information. This is urgent.

The prosecutor is going to try to get you locked up in the psychiatric ward. Assisting him he has your old friend Peter Teleborian.

Annika won't be able to go out and do a media campaign in the same way that the prosecution can (and does), leaking information as they see fit. Her hands are tied.

But I'm not lumbered with that sort of restriction. I write whatever I want — and I also have an entire magazine at my disposal.

Two important details are still needed:

(1) First of all, I want to have something that shows that Prosecutor Ekström is today working with Teleborian in some inappropriate manner, and that the objective once more is to confine you to a nuthouse. I want to be able to go on any talk show on T.V. and present documentation that annihilates the prosecution's game.

(2) To wage a media war I must be able to appear in public to discuss things that you may consider your private business. Hiding behind the arras in this situation is a wildly overrated tactic in view of all that has been written about you since Easter. I have to be able to construct a completely new media image of you, even if that, in your opinion, means invading your privacy — preferably with your approval. Do you understand what I mean?

She opened the archive in [Idiotic_Table]. It contained twenty-six documents.

Figuerola got up at 5.00 on Wednesday morning and went for an unusually short run before she showered and dressed in black jeans, a white top, and a lightweight grey linen jacket. She made coffee and poured it into a thermos and then made sandwiches. She also strapped on a shoulder holster and took her Sig Sauer from the gun cabinet. Just after 6.00 she drove her white Saab 9-5 to Vittangigatan in Vällingby.

Mårtensson's apartment was on the top floor of a three-storey building in the suburbs. The day before, she had assembled everything that could be found out about him in the public archives. He was unmarried, but that did not mean that he might not be living with someone. He had no black marks in police records, no great fortune, and did not seem to lead a fast life. He very seldom called in sick.

The one conspicuous thing about him was that he had licences for no fewer than sixteen weapons. Three of them were hunting rifles, the others were handguns of various types. As long as he had a licence, of course, there was no crime, but Figuerola harboured a deep scepticism about anyone who collected weapons on such a scale.

The Volvo with the registration beginning KAB was in the car park about thirty metres from where Figuerola herself parked. She poured black coffee into a paper cup and ate a lettuce and cheese baguette. Then she peeled an orange and sucked each segment to extinction.

At morning rounds, Salander was out of sorts and had a bad headache. She asked for a Tylenol, which she was immediately given.

After an hour the headache had grown worse. She rang for the nurse and asked for another Tylenol. That did not help either. By lunchtime she had such a headache that the nurse called Dr Endrin, who examined her patient briskly and prescribed a powerful painkiller.

Salander held the tablets under her tongue and spat them out as soon as she was alone.

At 2.00 in the afternoon she threw up. This recurred at around 3.00.

At 4.00 Jonasson came up to the ward just as Dr Endrin was about to go home. They conferred briefly.

"She feels sick and she has a strong headache. I gave her Dexofen. I don't understand what's going on with her. She's been doing so well lately. It might be some sort of flu . . ."

"Does she have a fever?" asked Jonasson.

"No. She had 37.2 an hour ago."

"I'm going to keep an eye on her overnight."

"I'll be going on holiday for three weeks," Endrin said. "Either you or Svantesson will have to take over her case. But Svantesson hasn't had much to do with her . . ."

"I'll arrange to be her primary care doctor while you're on holiday."

"Good. If there's a crisis and you need help, do call."

They paid a short visit to Salander's sickbed. She was lying with the sheet pulled up to the tip of her nose, and she looked miserable. Jonasson put his hand on her forehead and felt that it was damp.

"I think we'll have to do a quick examination."

He thanked Dr Endrin, and she left.

At 5.00 Jonasson discovered that Salander had developed a temperature of 37.8, which was noted on her chart. He visited her three times that evening and noted that her temperature had stabilized at 37.8 – too high, certainly, but not so high as to present a real problem. At 8.00 he ordered a cranial X-ray.

When the X-rays came through he studied them intently. He could not see anything remarkable, but he did observe that there was a barely visible darker area immediately adjacent to the bullet hole. He wrote a carefully worded and noncommittal comment on her chart: *Radiological examination gives a basis for definitive conclusions but the condition of the patient has deteriorated steadily during the day. It cannot be ruled out that there is a minor bleed that is not visible on the images. The patient should be confined to bedrest and kept under strict observation until further notice.*

Berger had received twenty-three emails by the time she arrived at *S.M.P.* at 6.30 on Wednesday morning.

One of them had the address <editorial-sr@swedishradio.com>. The text was short. A single word.

She raised her index finger to delete the message. At the last moment she changed her mind. She went back to her inbox and opened the message that had arrived two days before. The sender was <centraled@smpost.se>. So ... two emails with the word "whore" and a phoney sender from the world of mass media. She created a new folder called [MediaFool] and saved both messages. Then she got busy on the morning memo.

Mårtensson left home at 7.40 that morning. He got into his Volvo and drove towards the city but turned off to go across Stora Essingen and Gröndal into Södermalm. He drove down Hornsgatan and across to Bellmansgatan via Brännkyrkagatan. He turned left on to Tavastgatan at the Bishop's Arms pub and parked at the corner.

Just as Figuerola reached the Bishop's Arms, a van pulled out and left a parking space on Bellmansgatan at the corner with Tavastgatan. From her ideal location at the top of the hill she had an unobstructed view. She could just see the back window of Mårtensson's Volvo. Straight ahead of her, on the steep slope down towards Pryssgränd, was Bellmansgatan 1. She was looking at the building from the side, so she could not see the front door itself, but as soon as anyone came out on to the street, she would see them. She had no doubt that this particular address was the reason for Mårtensson's being there. It was Blomkvist's front door.

Figuerola could see that the area surrounding Bellmansgatan 1 would be a nightmare to keep under surveillance. The only spot from which the entrance door to the building could be observed directly was from the promenade and footbridge on upper Bellmansgatan near the Maria lift and the Laurinska building. There was nowhere there to park a car, and the watcher would stand exposed on the footbridge like a swallow perched on an old telephone wire in the country. The cross-roads of Bellmansgatan and Tavastgatan, where Figuerola had parked, was basically the only place where she could sit in her car and have a view of the whole. She had been incredibly lucky. Yet it was not a particularly good place because any alert observer would see her in her car. But she did not want to leave the car and start walking around the area. She was too easily noticeable. In her role as undercover officer her looks worked against her.

Blomkvist emerged at 9.10. Figuerola noted the time. She saw him look up at the footbridge on upper Bellmansgatan. He started up the hill straight towards her.

She opened her handbag and unfolded a map of Stockholm which she placed on the passenger seat. Then she opened a notebook and took a pen from her jacket pocket. She pulled out her mobile and pretended to be talking, keeping her head bent so that the hand holding her telephone hid part of her face.

She saw Blomkvist glance down Tavastgatan. He knew he was being watched and he must have seen Mårtensson's Volvo, but he kept walking without showing any interest in the car. *Acts calm and cool. Somebody should have opened the car door and scared the shit out of him.*

The next moment he passed Figuerola's car. She was obviously trying to find an address on the map while she talked on the telephone, but she could sense Blomkvist looking at her as he passed. *Suspicious of everything around him.* She saw him in the wing mirror on the passenger side as he went on down towards Hornsgatan. She had seen him on T.V. a couple of times, but this was the first time she had seen him in person. He was wearing blue jeans, a T-shirt and a grey jacket. He carried a shoulder bag and he walked with a long, loose stride. A nice-looking man.

Mårtensson appeared at the corner by the Bishop's Arms and watched Blomkvist go. He had a large sports bag over his shoulder and was just finishing a call on his mobile. Figuerola expected him to follow his quarry, but to her surprise he crossed the street right in front of her car and turned down the hill towards Blomkvist's building. A second later a man in blue overalls passed her car and caught up with Mårtensson. *Hello, where did you spring from?*

They stopped outside the door to Blomkvist's building. Mårtensson punched in the code and they disappeared into the stairwell. *They're checking the apartment. Amateur night. What the hell does he think he's doing?*

Then Figuerola raised her eyes to the rear-view mirror and gave a start when she saw Blomkvist again. He was standing about ten metres behind her, close enough that he could keep an eye on Mårtensson and his buddy by looking over the crest of the steep hill down towards Bellmansgatan 1. She watched his face. He was not looking at her. But he had seen Mårtensson go in through the front door of his building. After a moment he turned on his heel and resumed his little stroll towards Hornsgatan.

Figuerola sat motionless for thirty seconds. *He knows he's being watched. He's keeping track of what goes on around him. But why doesn't he react? A normal person would react, and pretty strongly at that . . . He must have something up his sleeve.*

Blomkvist hung up and rested his gaze on the notebook on his desk. The national vehicle register had just informed him that the car he had seen at the top of Bellmansgatan with the blonde woman inside was owned by Monica Figuerola, born in 1969, and living on Pontonjärgatan in Kungsholmen. Since it was a woman in the car, Blomkvist assumed it was Figuerola herself.

She had been talking on her mobile and looking at a map that was unfolded on the passenger seat. Blomkvist had no reason to believe that she had anything to do with the Zalachenko club, but he made a note of every deviation from the norm in his working day, and especially around his neighbourhood.

He called Karim in.

"Who is this woman, Lottie? Dig up her passport picture, where she works . . . and anything else you can find."

Sellberg looked rather startled. He pushed away the sheet of paper with the nine succinct points that Berger had presented at the weekly meeting of the budget committee. Flodin looked similarly concerned. Chairman Borgsjö appeared neutral, as always.

"This is impossible," Sellberg said with a polite smile.

"Why so?" Berger said.

"The board will never go along with this. It defies all rhyme or reason."

"Shall we take it from the top?" Berger said. "I was hired to make *S.M.P.* profitable again. To do that I have to have something to work with, don't you think?"

"Well, yes, but—"

"I can't wave a magic wand and conjure up the contents of a daily newspaper by sitting in my glass cage and just wishing for things."

"You don't quite understand the hard economic facts."

"That's quite possible. But I understand making newspapers. And the reality is that over the past fifteen years, *S.M.P.*'s personnel has been reduced by 118. Half were graphic artists and so on, replaced by new technology . . . but the number of reporters contributing to copy was reduced by 48 during that period."

"Those were necessary cuts. If the staff hadn't been cut, the paper would have folded long since. At least Morander understood the necessity of the reductions."

"Well, let's wait and see what's necessary and what isn't. In three years, nineteen reporter jobs have disappeared. In addition, we now have a situation in which nine positions at *S.M.P.* are vacant and are being to some extent covered by temps. The sports desk is dangerously understaffed. There should be nine employees there, and for more than a year two positions have remained unfilled."

"It's a question of saving money we're not going to have. It's that simple."

"The culture section has three unfilled positions. The business section has one. The legal desk does not even in practice exist . . . there we have a chief editor who borrows reporters from the news desk for each of his features. And so on. *S.M.P.* hasn't done any serious coverage of the civil service and government agencies for at least eight years. We depend for that on freelancers and the material from the T.T. wire service. And as you know, T.T. shut down its civil service desk some years ago. In other words, there isn't a single news desk in Sweden covering the civil service and the government agencies."

"The newspaper business is in a vulnerable position—"

"The reality is that *S.M.P.* should either be shut down immediately, or the board should find a way to take an aggressive stance. Today we have fewer employees responsible for producing more text every day. The articles they turn out are terrible, superficial, and they lack credibility. That's why *S.M.P.* is losing its readers."

"You don't understand the situation—"

"I'm tired of hearing that I don't understand the situation. I'm not some temp. who's just here for the bus fare."

"But your proposal is off the wall."

"Why is that?"

"You're proposing that the newspaper should not be profitable."

"Listen, Sellberg, this year you will be paying out a huge amount of money in dividends to the paper's twenty-three shareholders. Add to this the unforgivably absurd bonuses that will cost *S.M.P.* almost ten million kronor for nine individuals who sit on *S.M.P.*'s board.

You've awarded yourself a bonus of 400,000 kronor for administering cutbacks. Of course it's a long way from being a bonus as huge as the ones that some of the directors of Skandia grabbed. But in my eyes you're not worth a bonus of so much as one single öre. Bonuses should be paid to people who do something to strengthen S.M.P. The plain truth is that your cutbacks have weakened S.M.P. and deepened the crisis we now find ourselves in."

"That is grossly unfair. The board approved every measure I proposed."

"The board approved your measures, of course they did, because you guaranteed a dividend each year. That's what has to stop, and now."

"So you're suggesting in all seriousness that the board should decide to abolish dividends and bonuses. What makes you think the shareholders would agree to that?"

"I'm proposing a zero-profit operating budget this year. That would mean savings of almost 21 million kronor and the chance to beef up S.M.P.'s staff and finances. I'm also proposing wage cuts for management. I'm being paid a monthly salary of 88,000 kronor, which is utter insanity for a newspaper that can't add a job to its sports desk."

"So you want to cut your own salary? Is this some sort of wage-communism you're advocating?"

"Don't bullshit me. You make 112,000 kronor a month, if you add in your annual bonus. *That's* off the wall. If the newspaper were stable and bringing in a tremendous profit, then pay out as much as you want in bonuses. But this is no time for you to be increasing your own bonus. I propose cutting all management salaries by half."

"What you don't understand is that our shareholders bought stock in the paper because they want to make money. That's called capitalism. If you arrange that they're going to lose money, then they won't want to be shareholders any longer."

"I'm not suggesting that they should lose money, though it might come to that. Ownership implies responsibility. As you yourself have pointed out, capitalism is what matters here. S.M.P.'s owners want to make a profit. But it's the market decides whether you make a profit or take a loss. By your reasoning, you want the rules of capitalism to apply solely to the *employees* of S.M.P., while you and the shareholders will be exempt."

Sellberg rolled his eyes and sighed. He cast an entreating glance at

Borgsjö, but the chairman of the board was intently studying Berger's nine-point program.

Figuerola waited for forty-nine minutes before Mårtensson and his companion in overalls came out of Bellmansgatan 1. As they started up the hill towards her, she very steadily raised her Nikon with its 300-mm telephoto lens and took two pictures. She put the camera in the space under her seat and was just about to fiddle with her map when she happened to glance towards the Maria lift. Her eyes opened wide. At the end of upper Bellmansgatan, right next to the gate to the Maria lift, stood a dark-haired woman with a digital camera filming Mårtensson and his companion. *What the hell? Is there some sort of spy convention on Bellmansgatan today?*

The two men parted at the top of the hill without exchanging a word. Mårtensson went back to his car on Tavastgatan. He pulled away from the curb and disappeared from view.

Figuerola looked into her rear-view mirror, where she could still see the back of the man in the blue overalls. She then saw that the woman with the camera had stopped filming and was heading past the Laurinska building in her direction.

Heads or tails? She already knew who Mårtensson was and what he was up to. The man in the blue overalls and the woman with the camera were unknown entities. But if she left her car, she risked being seen by the woman.

She sat still. In her rear-view mirror she saw the man in the blue overalls turn into Brännkyrkagatan. She waited until the woman reached the crossing in front of her, but instead of following the man in the overalls, the woman turned 180 degrees and went down the steep hill towards Bellmansgatan 1. Figuerola reckoned that she was in her mid-thirties. She had short dark hair and was dressed in dark jeans and a black jacket. As soon as she was a little way down the hill, Figuerola pushed open her car door and ran towards Brännkyrkagatan. She could not see the blue overalls. The next second a Toyota van pulled away from the kerb. Figuerola saw the man in half-profile and memorized the registration number. But if she got the registration wrong she would be able to trace him anyway. The sides of the van advertised *Lars Faulsson Lock and Key Service* – with a telephone number.

273

There was no need to follow the van. She walked calmly back to the top of the hill just in time to see the woman disappear through the entrance door of Blomkvist's building.

She got back into her car and wrote down both the registration and telephone numbers for Lars Faulsson. There was a lot of mysterious traffic around Blomkvist's address that morning. She looked up towards the roof of Bellmansgatan 1. She knew that Blomkvist's apartment was on the top floor, but on the blueprints from the city construction office she knew that it was on the other side of the building, with dormer windows looking out on Gamla Stan and the waters of Riddarfjärden. An exclusive address in a fine old cultural quarter. She wondered whether he was an ostentatious *nouveau riche*.

Ten minutes later the woman with the camera came out of the building again. Instead of going back up the hill to Tavastgatan, she continued down the hill and turned right at the corner of Pryssgränd. *Hmm*. If she had a car parked down on Pryssgränd, Figuerola was out of luck. But if she was walking, there was only one way out of the dead end – up to Brännkyrkagatan via Pustegränd and towards Slussen.

Figuerola decided to leave her car behind and turned left in the direction of Slussen on Brännkyrkagatan. She had almost reached Pustegränd when the woman appeared, coming up towards her. *Bingo*. She followed her past the Hilton on Södermalmstorg and past the Stadsmuseum at Slussen. The woman walked quickly and purpose-fully without once looking round. Figuerola gave her a lead of about thirty metres. When she went into Slussen tunnelbana Figuerola picked up her pace, but stopped when she saw the woman head for the Pressbyrån kiosk instead of through the turnstiles.

She watched the woman as she stood in the queue at the kiosk. She was about one metre seventy and looked to be in pretty good shape. She was wearing running shoes. Seeing her with both feet planted firmly as she stood by the window of the kiosk, Figuerola suddenly had the feeling that she was a policewoman. She bought a tin of Catch Dry snuff and went back out on to Södermalmstorg and turned right across Katarinavägen.

Figuerola followed her. She was almost certain the woman had not seen her. The woman turned the corner at McDonald's and Figuerola hurried after her, but when she got to the corner, the woman had vanished without a trace. Figuerola stopped short in consternation.

Shit. She walked slowly past the entrances to the buildings. Then she caught sight of a brass plate that read *Milton Security*.

Figuerola walked back to Bellmansgatan.

She drove to Götgatan where the offices of *Millennium* were and spent the next half hour walking around the streets in the area. She did not see Mårtensson's car. At lunchtime she returned to police headquarters in Kungsholmen and spent two hours thinking as she pumped iron in the gym.

"We've got a problem," Cortez said.

Eriksson and Blomkvist looked up from the typescript of the book about the Zalachenko case. It was 1.30 in the afternoon.

"Take a seat," Eriksson said.

"It's about Vitavara Inc., the company that makes the 1700 kronor toilets in Vietnam."

"Alright. What's the problem?" Blomkvist said.

"Vitavara Inc. is a wholly owned subsidiary of Svea Construction Inc."

"I see. That's a very large firm."

"Yes, it is. The chairman of the board is Magnus Borgsjö, a professional board member. He's also the chairman of the board of *Svenska Morgon-Posten* and owns about 10 per cent of it."

Blomkvist gave Cortez a sharp look. "Are you sure?"

"Yep. Berger's boss is a bloody crook, a man who exploits child labour in Vietnam."

Assistant Editor Fredriksson looked to be in a bad mood as he knocked on the door of Berger's glass cage at 2.00 in the afternoon.

"What is it?"

"Well, this is a little embarrassing, but somebody in the newsroom got an email from you."

"From me? So? What does it say?

He handed her some printouts of emails addressed to Eva Carlsson, a 26-year-old temp on the culture pages. According to the headers the sender was <erika.berger@smpost.se>:

Darling Eva. I want to caress you and kiss your
breasts. I'm hot with excitement and can't control
myself. I beg you to reciprocate my feelings.
Could we meet? Erika

And then two emails on the following days:

Dearest, darling Eva. I beg you not to reject
me. I'm crazy with desire. I want to have you
naked. I have to have you. I'm going to make
you so happy. You'll never regret it. I'm going
to kiss every inch of your naked skin, your
lovely breasts, and your delicious grotto. Erika

Eva. Why don't you reply? Don't be afraid of me.
Don't push me away. You're no innocent. You know
what it's all about. I want to have sex with
you and I'm going to reward you handsomely. If
you're nice to me then I'll be nice to you.
You've asked for an extension of your temporary
job. I have the power to extend it and even make
it a full-time position. Let's meet tonight at
9.00 by my car in the garage. Your Erika

"Alright," Berger said. "And now she's wondering if it was me that
wrote to her, is that it?"

"Not exactly . . . I mean . . . geez."

"Peter, please speak up."

"She sort of halfway believed the first email although she was quite
surprised by it. But then she realized that this isn't exactly your style
and then . . ."

"Then?"

"Well, she thinks it's embarrassing and doesn't quite know what to do. Part of it is probably that she's very impressed by you and likes you a lot . . . as a boss, I mean. So she came to me and asked for my advice."

"And what did you tell her?"

"I said that someone had faked your address and is obviously harassing her. Or possibly both of you. And I said I'd talk to you about it."

"Thank you. Could you please ask her to come to my office in ten minutes?"

In the meantime Berger composed her own email.

```
It has come to my attention that an employee of
S.M.P. has received a number of emails that appear
to come from me. The emails contain vulgar sexual
innuendos. I have also received similar emails
from a sender who purports to be "centraled" at
S.M.P. No such address exists.

I have consulted the head of the I.T. depart-
ment, who informs me that it is very easy to
fake a sender's address. I don't understand how
it's done, but there are sites on the Internet
where such things can be arranged. I have to
draw the conclusion that some sick individual is
doing this.

I want to know if any other colleagues have
received strange emails. If so, I would like
them to inform Fredriksson of this immediately.
If these very unpleasant pranks continue we will
have to consider reporting them to the police.

Erika Berger, Editor-in-Chief
```

She printed a copy of the email and then pressed send so that the message went out to all employees in the company. At that moment, Eva Carlsson knocked on the door.

"Hello, have a seat," Berger said. "Peter told me that you got an email from me."

"Well, I didn't really think it came from you."

"Thirty seconds ago you did get an email from me. I wrote it all by myself and sent it to everyone in the company."

She handed Carlsson the printout.

"O.K. I get it," the girl said.

"I'm really sorry that somebody decided to target you for this ugly campaign."

"You don't have to apologize for the actions of some idiot."

"I just want to make sure that you don't have one lingering grain of a suspicion that I had anything to do with these emails."

"I never believed you sent them."

"Thanks," Berger said with a smile.

Figuerola spent the afternoon gathering information. She started by ordering passport photographs of Faulsson. Then she ran a check in the criminal records and got a hit at once.

Lars Faulsson, forty-seven years old and known by the nickname Falun, had begun his criminal career stealing cars at seventeen. In the '70s and '80s he was twice arrested and charged with breaking and entering, burglary and receiving stolen goods. The first time he was given a light prison sentence; the second time he got three years. At that time he was regarded as "up and coming" in criminal circles and had been questioned as a suspect in three other burglaries, one of which was a relatively complicated and widely reported safe-cracking heist at a department store in Västerås. When he got out of prison in 1984 he kept his nose clean – or at least he did not pull any jobs that got him arrested and convicted again. But he had retrained himself to be a locksmith (of all professions), and in 1987 he started his own company, the Lock and Key Service, with an address near Norrtull in Stockholm.

Identifying the woman who had filmed Mårtensson and Faulsson proved to be easier than she had anticipated. She simply called Milton Security and explained that she was looking for a female employee she had met a while ago and whose name she had forgotten. She could give a good description of the woman. The switchboard told her that it sounded like Susanne Linder, and put her through. When Linder answered the telephone, Figuerola apologized and said she must have dialled the wrong number.

The public register listed eighteen Susanne Linders in Stockholm county, three of them around thirty-five years old. One lived in Norrtälje, one in Stockholm, and one in Nacka. She requisitioned their passport photographs and identified at once the woman she had followed from Bellmansgatan as the Susanne Linder who lived in Nacka.

She set out her day's work in a memo and went in to see Edklinth.

Blomkvist closed Cortez's research folder and pushed it away with distaste. Malm put down the printout of his article, which he had read four times. Cortez sat on the sofa in Eriksson's office looking guilty.

"Coffee," Eriksson said, getting up. She came back with four mugs and the coffee pot.

"This is a great sleazy story," Blomkvist said. "First-class research. Documentation to the hilt. Perfect dramaturgy with a bad guy who swindles Swedish tenants through the system – which is legal – but who is so greedy and so bloody stupid that he outsources to this company in Vietnam."

"Very well written too," Malm said. "The day after we publish this, Borgsjö is going to be *persona non grata*. T.V. is going to pick this up. He's going to be right up there with the directors of Skandia. A genuine scoop for *Millennium*. Well done, Henry."

"But this thing with Erika is a real fly in the ointment," Blomkvist said.

"Why should that be a problem?" Eriksson said. "Erika isn't the villain. We have to be free to examine any chairman of the board, even if he happens to be her boss."

"It's a hell of a dilemma," Blomkvist said.

"Erika hasn't altogether left here," Malm said. "She owns 30 per cent of *Millennium* and sits on our board. In fact, she's chairman of the board until we can elect Harriet Vanger at the next board meeting, and that won't be until August. Plus Erika is working at *S.M.P.*, where she also sits on the board, and you're about to expose her chairman."

Glum silence.

"So what the hell are we going to do?" Cortez said. "Do we kill the article?"

Blomkvist looked Cortez straight in the eye. "No, Henry. We're not going to kill the article. That's not the way we do things at *Millennium*.

But this is going to take some legwork. We can't just dump it on Erika's desk as a newspaper billboard."

Malm waved a finger in the air. "We're really putting Erika on the spot. She'll have to choose between selling her share of *Millennium* and leaving our board . . . or in the worst case, she could get fired by *S.M.P.* Either way she would have a fearful conflict of interest. Honestly, Henry . . . I agree with Mikael that we should publish the story, but we may have to postpone it for a month."

"Because we're facing a conflict of loyalties too," Blomkvist said.

"Should I call her?"

"No, Christer," Blomkvist said. "I'll call her and arrange to meet. Say for tonight."

Figuerola gave a summary of the circus that had sprung up around Blomkvist's building on Bellmansgatan. Edklinth felt the floor sway slightly beneath his chair.

"An employee of S.I.S. goes into Blomkvist's building with an ex-safebreaker, now retrained as a locksmith."

"Correct."

"What do you think they did in the stairwell?"

"I don't know. But they were in there for forty-nine minutes. My guess is that Faulsson opened the door and Mårtensson spent the time in Blomkvist's apartment."

"And what did they do there?"

"It couldn't have been to plant bugs, because that takes only a minute or so. Mårtensson must have been looking through Blomkvist's papers or whatever else he keeps at his place."

"But Blomkvist has already been warned . . . they stole Björck's report from there."

"Quite right. He knows he's being watched, and he's watching the ones who are watching him. He's calculating."

"Calculating what?"

"I mean, he has a plan. He's gathering information and is going to expose Mårtensson. That's the only reasonable explanation."

"And then this Linder woman?"

"Susanne Linder, former police officer."

"Police officer?"

"She graduated from the police academy and worked for six years on the Södermalm crime team. She resigned abruptly. There's nothing in her file that says why. She was out of a job for several months before she was hired by Milton Security."

"Armansky," Edklinth said thoughtfully. "How long was she in the building?"

"Nine minutes."

"Doing what?"

"I'm guessing – since she was filming Mårtensson and Faulsson on the street – that she's documenting their activities. That means that Milton Security is working with Blomkvist and has placed surveillance cameras in his apartment or in the stairwell. She probably went in to collect the film."

Edklinth sighed. The Zalachenko story was beginning to get tremendously complicated.

"Thank you. You go home. I have to think about this."

Figuerola went to the gym at St Eriksplan.

Blomkvist used his second mobile when he punched in Berger's number at *S.M.P.* He interrupted a discussion she was having with her editors about what angle to give an article on international terrorism.

"Oh, hello, it's you . . . wait a second."

Berger put her hand over the mouthpiece.

"I think we're done," she said, and gave them one last instruction. When she was alone she said: "Hello, Mikael. Sorry not to have been in touch. I'm just so swamped here. There are a thousand things I've got to learn. How's the Salander stuff going?"

"Good. But that's not why I called. I have to see you. Tonight."

"I wish I could, but I have to be here until 8.00. And I'm dead tired. I've been at it since dawn. What's it about?"

"I'll tell you when I see you. But it's not good."

"I'll come to your place at 8.30."

"No. Not at mine. It's a long story, but my apartment is unsuitable for the time being. Let's meet at Samir's Cauldron for a beer."

"I'm driving."

"Then we'll have a light beer."

*

Berger was slightly annoyed when she walked into Samir's Cauldron. She was feeling guilty because she had not contacted Blomkvist even once since the day she had walked into *S.M.P.*

Blomkvist waved from a corner table. She stopped in the doorway. For a second he seemed a stranger. *Who's that over there? God, I'm so tired.* Then he stood and kissed her on the cheek, and she realized to her dismay that she had not even thought about him for several weeks and that she missed him terribly. It was as though her time at *S.M.P.* had been a dream and she might suddenly wake up on the sofa at *Millennium*. It felt unreal.

"Hello, Mikael."

"Hello, editor-in-chief. Have you eaten?"

"It's 8.30. I don't have your disgusting eating habits."

Samir came over with the menu and, she realised she was hungry. She ordered a beer and a small plate of calamari with Greek potatoes. Blomkvist ordered couscous and a beer.

"How are you?" she said.

"These are interesting times we're living in. I'm swamped too."

"And Salander?"

"She's part of what makes it so interesting."

"Micke, I'm not going to steal your story."

"I'm not trying to evade your question. The truth is that right now everything is a little confused. I'd love to tell you the whole thing, but it would take half the night. How do you like being editor-in-chief?"

"It's not exactly *Millennium*. I fall asleep like a blown-out candle as soon as I get home, and when I wake up, I see spreadsheets before my eyes. I've missed you. Can't we go back to your place and sleep? I don't have the energy for sex, but I'd love to curl up and sleep next to you."

"I'm sorry, Ricky. The apartment isn't a good place right now."

"Why not? Has something happened?"

"Well, some spooks have bugged the place and they listen, presumably, to every word I say. I've had cameras installed to record what happens when I'm not home. I don't think we should let the state archives have footage of your naked self."

"Are you kidding?"

"No. But that wasn't why I had to see you tonight."

"What is it? Tell me."

"Well, I'll be very direct. We've come across a story that will sink your chairman. It's about using child labour and exploiting political prisoners in Vietnam. We're looking at a conflict of interest."

Berger put down her fork and stared at him. She saw at once that he was not being funny.

"This is how things stand," he said. "Borgsjö is chairman and majority shareholder of a company called Svea Construction, which in turn is sole owner of a subsidiary called Vitavara Inc. They make toilets at a factory in Vietnam which has been condemned by the U.N. for using child labour."

"Run that by me again."

Blomkvist told her the details of the story that Cortez had compiled. He opened his laptop bag and took out a copy of the documentation. Berger read slowly through the article. Finally she looked up and met Blomkvist's eyes. She felt unreasoning panic mixed with disbelief.

"Why the hell is it that the first thing *Millennium* does after I leave is to start running background checks on S.M.P.'s board members?"

"That's not what happened, Ricky." He explained how the story had developed.

"And how long have you known about this?"

"Since today, since this afternoon. I feel deeply uncomfortable about how this has unfolded."

"And what are you going to do?"

"I don't know. We have to publish. We can't make an exception just because it deals with your boss. But not one of us wants to hurt you." He threw up his hands. "We are all extremely unhappy about the situation. Henry especially."

"I'm still a member of *Millennium*'s board. I'm a part-owner . . . it's going to be viewed as—"

"I know exactly how it's going to be viewed. You're going to land in a shitload of trouble at S.M.P."

Berger felt weariness settling over her. She clenched her teeth and stifled an impulse to ask Blomkvist to sit on the story.

"God *damn* it," she said. "And there's no doubt in your mind . . ."

Blomkvist shook his head. "I spent the whole afternoon going over Henry's documentation. We have Borgsjö ready for the slaughter."

"So what are you planning, and when?"

"What would you have done if we'd uncovered this story two months ago?"

Berger looked intently at her friend, who had also been her lover over the past twenty years. Then she lowered her eyes.

"You know what I would have done."

"This is a disastrous coincidence. None of it is directed at you. I'm terribly, terribly sorry. That's why I insisted on seeing you at once. We have to decide what to do."

"We?"

"Listen . . . the story was slated to run in the July issue. I've killed that idea. The earliest it could come out is August, and it can be postponed for longer if you need more time."

"I understand." Her voice took on a bitter tone.

"I suggest we don't decide anything now. Take the documentation and go home and think it over. Don't do anything until we can agree a strategy. We've got time."

"A common strategy?"

"You either have to resign from *Millennium*'s board before we publish, or resign from *S.M.P.* You can't wear both hats."

She nodded. "I'm so linked to *Millennium* that no-one will believe I didn't have a finger in this, whether I resign or not."

"There is an alternative. You could take the story to *S.M.P.* and confront Borgsjö and demand his resignation. I'm quite sure Henry would agree to that. But don't do anything until we all agree."

"So I start by getting the person who recruited me fired."

"I'm sorry."

"He isn't a bad person."

"I believe you. But he's greedy."

Berger got up. "I'm going home."

"Ricky, I—"

She interrupted him. "I'm just dead tired. Thanks for warning me. I'll let you know."

She left without kissing him, and he had to pay the bill.

Berger had parked two hundred metres from the restaurant and was halfway to her car when she felt such strong heart palpitations that she had to stop and lean against a wall. She felt sick.

She stood for a long time breathing in the mild May air. She had been working fifteen hours a day since May 1. That was almost three weeks. How would she feel after three years? Was that how Morander

284

had felt before he dropped dead in the newsroom?

After ten minutes she went back to Samir's Cauldron and ran into Blomkvist as he was coming out of the door. He stopped in surprise.

"Erika . . ."

"Mikael, don't say a word. We've been friends so long – nothing can destroy that. You're my best friend, and this feels exactly like the time you disappeared to Hedestad two years ago, only vice versa. I feel stressed out and unhappy."

He put his arms around her. She felt tears in her eyes.

"Three weeks at *S.M.P.* have already done me in," she said.

"Now now. It takes more than that to do in Erika Berger."

"Your apartment is compromised. And I'm too tired to drive home. I'd fall asleep at the wheel and die in a crash. I've decided. I'm going to walk to the Scandic Crown and book a room. Come with me."

"It's called the Hilton now."

"Same difference."

They walked the short distance without talking. Blomkvist had his arm around her shoulders. Berger glanced at him and saw that he was just as tired as she was.

They went straight to the front desk, took a double room, and paid with Berger's credit card. When they got to the room they undressed, showered, and crawled into bed. Berger's muscles ached as though she had just run the Stockholm marathon. They cuddled for a while and then both fell asleep in seconds.

Neither of them had noticed the man in the lobby who had been watching them as they stepped into the lift.

CHAPTER 15

Thursday, 19.v – Sunday, 22.v

Salander spent most of Wednesday night and early Thursday morning reading Blomkvist's articles and the chapters of the *Millennium* book that were more or less finished. Since Prosecutor Ekström had tentatively referred to a trial in July, Blomkvist had set June 20 as his deadline for going to press. That meant that Blomkvist had about a month to finish writing and patching up all the holes in his text.

She could not imagine how he could finish in time, but that was his problem, not hers. Her problem was how to respond to his questions.

She took her Palm and logged on to the Yahoo group [Idiotic_Table] to check whether he had put up anything new in the past twenty-four hours. He had not. She opened the document that he had called [Central questions]. She knew the text by heart already, but she read through it again anyway.

He outlined the strategy that Giannini had already explained to her. When her lawyer spoke to her she had listened with only half an ear, almost as though it had nothing to do with her. But Blomkvist, knowing things about her that Giannini did not, could present a more forceful strategy. She skipped down to the fourth paragraph.

```
The only person who can decide your future is
you. It doesn't matter how hard Annika works for
you, or how much Armansky and Palmgren and I,
and others, try to support you. I'm not going
to try to convince you one way or the other.
You've got to decide for yourself. You could
turn the trial to your advantage or let them
convict you. But if you want to win, you're going
to have to fight.

-----------
```

She disconnected and looked up at the ceiling. Blomkvist was asking her for permission to tell the truth in his book. He was not going to mention the fact of Bjurman raping her, and he had already written that section. He had filled in the gaps by saying that Bjurman had made a deal with Zalachenko which collapsed when Bjurman lost control. Therefore Niedermann was obliged to kill him. Blomkvist did not speculate about Bjurman's motives.

Kalle Bloody Blomkvist was complicating life for her.

At 2.00 in the morning she opened the word processing program on her Palm. She clicked on New Document, took out the stylus and began to tap on the letters on the digital keypad.

```
My name is Lisbeth Salander. I was born on 30
April 1978. My mother was Agneta Sofia Salander.
She was seventeen when I was born. My father was
a psychopath, a killer and wife beater whose name
was Alexander Zalachenko. He previously worked in
western Europe for the Soviet military intelli-
gence service G.R.U.
```

It was a slow process, writing with the stylus on the keypad. She thought through each sentence before she tapped it in. She did not make a single revision to the text she had written. She worked until 4.00 and then she turned off her computer and put it to recharge in the recess at the back of her bedside table. By that time she had produced a document corresponding to two single-spaced A4 pages.

Twice since midnight the duty nurse had put her head around the door, but Salander could hear her a long way off and even before she turned the key the computer was hidden and the patient asleep.

Berger woke at 7.00. She felt far from rested, but she had slept uninterrupted for eight hours. She glanced at Blomkvist, still sleeping soundly beside her.

She turned on her mobile to check for messages. Greger Beckman, her husband, had called eleven times. *Shit. I forgot to call.* She dialled the number and explained where she was and why she had not come home. He was angry.

"Erika, don't do that again. It has nothing to do with Mikael, but I've been worried sick all night. I was terrified that something had happened. You know you have to call and tell me if you're not coming home. You mustn't ever forget something like that."

Beckman was completely O.K. with the fact that Blomkvist was his wife's lover. Their affair was carried on with his assent. But every time she had decided to sleep at Blomkvist's, she had called her husband to tell him.

"I'm sorry," she said. "I just collapsed in exhaustion last night."

He grunted.

"Try not to be furious with me, Greger. I can't handle it right now. You can give me hell tonight."

He grunted some more and promised to scold her when she got home. "O.K. How's Mikael doing?"

"He's dead to the world." She burst out laughing. "Believe it or not, we were fast asleep moments after we got here. That's never happened."

"This is serious, Erika. I think you ought to see a doctor."

When she hung up she called the office and left a message for Fredriksson. Something had come up and she would be in a little later than usual. She asked him to cancel a meeting she had arranged with the culture editor.

She found her shoulder bag, ferreted out a toothbrush and went to the bathroom. Then she got back into the bed and woke Blomkvist.

"Hurry up – go and wash and brush your teeth."

"What . . . huh?" He sat up and looked around in bewilderment. She had to remind him that he was at the Slussen Hilton. He nodded.

"So. To the bathroom with you."

"Why the hurry?"

"Because as soon as you come back I need you to make love to me." She glanced at her watch. "I've got a meeting at 11.00 that I can't postpone. I have to look presentable, and it'll take me at least half an hour to put on my face. And I'll have to buy a new shift dress or something on the way to work. That gives us only two hours to make up for a whole lot of lost time."

Blomkvist headed for the bathroom.

*

Holmberg parked his father's Ford in the drive of former Prime Minister Thorbjörn Fälldin's house in Ås just outside Ramvik in Härnösand county. He got out of the car and looked around. At the age of seventy-nine, Fälldin could hardly still be an active farmer, and Holmberg wondered who did the sowing and harvesting. He knew he was being watched from the kitchen window. That was the custom in the village. He himself had grown up in Hälledal outside Ramvik, very close to Sandöbron, which was one of the most beautiful places in the world. At any rate Holmberg thought so.

He knocked at the front door.

The former leader of the Centre Party looked old, but he seemed alert still, and vigorous.

"Hello, Thorbjörn. My name is Jerker Holmberg. We've met before but it's been a few years. My father is Gustav Holmberg, a delegate for the Centre in the '70s and '80s."

"Yes, I recognize you, Jerker. Hello. You're a policeman down in Stockholm now, aren't you? It must be ten or fifteen years since I last saw you."

"I think it's probably longer than that. May I come in?"

Holmberg sat at the kitchen table while Fälldin poured them some coffee.

"I hope all's well with your father. But that's not why you came, is it?"

"No, Dad's doing fine. He's out repairing the roof of the cabin."

"How old is he now?"

"He turned seventy-one two months ago."

"Is that so?" Fälldin said, joining Holmberg at the kitchen table. "So what's this visit all about then?"

Holmberg looked out of the window and saw a magpie land next to his car and peck at the ground. Then he turned to Fälldin.

"I am sorry for coming to see you without warning, but I have a big problem. It's possible that when this conversation is over, I'll be fired from my job. I'm here on a work issue, but my boss, Criminal Inspector Jan Bublanski of the Violent Crimes Division in Stockholm, doesn't know I'm here."

"That sounds serious."

"Just to say that I'd be on very thin ice if my superiors found out about this visit."

"I understand."

"On the other hand I'm afraid that if I don't do something, there's a risk that a woman's rights will be shockingly violated, and to make matters worse, it'll be the second time it's happened."

"You'd better tell me the whole story."

"It's about a man named Alexander Zalachenko. He was an agent for the Soviets' G.R.U. and defected to Sweden on Election Day in 1976. He was given asylum and began to work for Säpo. I have reason to believe that you know his story."

Fälldin regarded Holmberg attentively.

"It's a long story," Holmberg said, and he began to tell Fälldin about the preliminary investigation in which he had been involved for the past few months.

Erika Berger finally rolled over on to her stomach and rested her head on her fists. She broke out in a big smile.

"Mikael, have you ever wondered if the two of us aren't completely nuts?"

"What do you mean?"

"It's true for me, at least. I'm smitten by an insatiable desire for you. I feel like a crazy teenager."

"Oh yes?"

"And then I want to go home and go to bed with my husband."

Blomkvist laughed. "I know a good therapist."

She poked him in the stomach. "Mikael, it's starting to feel like this thing with *S.M.P.* was a seriously big mistake."

"Nonsense. It's a huge opportunity for you. If anyone can inject life into that dying body, it's you."

"Maybe so. But that's just the problem. *S.M.P.* feels like a dying body. And then you dropped that bombshell about Borgsjö."

"You've got to let things settle down."

"I know. But the thing with Borgsjö is going to be a real problem. I don't have the faintest idea how to handle it."

"Nor do I. But we'll think of something."

She lay quiet for a moment.

"I miss you."

"I miss you too."

"How much would it take for you to come to *S.M.P.* and be the news editor?"

"I wouldn't do it for anything. Isn't what's-his-name, Holm, the news editor?"

"Yes. But he's an idiot."

"You got him in one."

"Do you know him?"

"I certainly do. I worked for him for three months as a temp in the mid-'80s. He's a prick who plays people off against each other. Besides . . ."

"Besides what?"

"It's nothing."

"Tell me."

"Some girl, Ulla something, who was also a temp, claimed that he sexually harassed her. I don't know how much was true, but the union did nothing about it and her contract wasn't extended."

Berger looked at the clock and sighed. She got up from the bed and made for the shower. Blomkvist did not move when she came out, dried herself, and dressed.

"I think I'll doze for a while," he said.

She kissed his cheek and waved as she left.

Figuerola parked seven cars behind Mårtensson's Volvo on Luntma-kargatan, close to the corner of Olof Palmes Gata. She watched as Mårtensson walked to the machine to pay his parking fee. He then walked on to Sveavägen.

Figuerola decided not to pay for a ticket. She would lose him if she went to the machine and back, so she followed him. He turned left on to Kungsgatan, and went into Kungstornet. She waited three minutes before she followed him into the café. He was on the ground floor talking to a blond man who looked to be in very good shape. *A policeman* she thought. She recognized him as the other man Malm had photographed outside the Copacabana on May Day.

She bought herself a coffee and sat at the opposite end of the café and opened her *Dagens Nyheter*. Mårtensson and his companion were talking in low voices. She took out her mobile and pretended to make a call, although neither of the men were paying her any attention. She took a photograph with the mobile that she knew would be only 72 dpi – low quality, but it could be used as evidence that the meeting had taken place.

After about fifteen minutes the blond man stood up and left the café. Figuerola cursed. Why had she not stayed outside? She would have recognized him when he came out. She wanted to leap up and follow him. But Mårtensson was still there, calmly nursing his coffee. She did not want to draw attention to herself by leaving so soon after his unidentified companion.

And then Mårtensson went to the toilet. As soon as he closed the door Figuerola was on her feet and back out on Kungsgatan. She looked up and down the block, but the blond man was gone.

She took a chance and hurried to the corner of Sveavägen. She could not see him anywhere, so she went down to the tunnelbana concourse, but it was hopeless.

She turned back towards Kungstornet, feeling stressed. Mårtensson had left too.

Berger swore when she got back to where she had parked her B.M.W. the night before.

The car was still there, but during the night some bastard had punctured all four tyres. Infernal bastard piss rats, she fumed.

She called the vehicle recovery service, told them that she did not have time to wait, and put the key in the exhaust pipe. Then she went down to Hornsgaten and hailed a taxi.

Lisbeth Salander logged on to Hacker Republice and saw that Plague was online. She pinged him.

<Hi Wasp. How's Sahlgrenska?>
<Restful. I need your help.>
<Shoot.>
<I never thought I'd have to ask this.>
<It must be serious.>
<Göran Mårtensson, living in Vällingby. I need access to his computer.>
<O.K.>
<Everything on it has to be copied to Blomkvist at Millennium.>
<I'll deal with it.>
<Big Brother is bugging Blomkvist's phone and probably

his email. You'll have to send the material to a hotmail address.>

<O.K.>

<If I can't be reached for any reason, Blomkvist is going to need your help. He has to be able to contact you.>

<Oh?>

<He's a bit square, but you can trust him.>

<Hmm.>

<How much do you want?>

Plague went quiet for a few seconds. <Does this have something to do with your situation?>

<Yes.>

<Then I'll do it for nothing.>

<Thanks. But I always pay my debts. I'm going to need your help all the way to the trial. I'll send you 30 thousand.>

<Can you afford it?>

<I can.>

<Then O.K.>

<I think we're going to need Trinity too. Can you persuade him to come to Sweden?>

<To do what?>

<What he's best at. I'll pay him a standard fee + expenses.>

<OK. What is this job?>

She explained what she needed to have done.

On Friday morning Jonasson was faced with an obviously irritated Inspector Faste on the other side of his desk.

"I don't understand this," Faste said. "I thought Salander had recovered. I came to Göteborg for two reasons: to interview her and to get her ready to be transferred to a cell in Stockholm, where she belongs."

"I'm sorry for your wasted journey," Jonasson said. "I'd be glad to discharge her because we certainly don't have any beds to spare here. But—"

"Could she be faking?"

Jonasson smiled politely. "I really don't think so. You see, Lisbeth

Salander was shot in the head. I removed a bullet from her brain, and it was 50/50 whether she would survive. She did survive and her prognosis has been exceedingly satisfactory . . . so much so that my colleagues and I were getting ready to discharge her. Then yesterday she had a setback. She complained of severe headaches and developed a fever that has been fluctuating up and down. Last night she had a temperature of 38 and vomited on two occasions. During the night the fever subsided; she was almost back down to normal and I thought the episode had passed. But when I examined her this morning her temperature had gone up to almost 39. That is serious."

"So what's wrong with her?"

"I don't know, but the fact that her temperature is fluctuating indicates that it's not flu or any other viral infection. Exactly what's causing it I can't say, but it could be something as simple as an allergy to her medication or to something else she's come into contact with."

He clicked on an image on his computer and turned the screen towards Faste.

"I had a cranial X-ray done. There's a darker area here, as you can see right next to her gunshot wound. I can't determine what it is. It could be scar tissue as a product of the healing process, but it could also be a minor haemorrhage. And until we've found out what's wrong, I can't release her, no matter how urgent it may be from a police point of view."

Faste knew better than to argue with a doctor, since they were the closest things to God's representatives here on earth. Policemen possibly excepted.

"What is going to happen now?"

"I've ordered complete bedrest and put her physiotherapy on hold – she needs therapeutic exercise because of the wounds in her shoulder and hip."

"Understood. I'll have to call Prosecutor Ekström in Stockholm. This will come as a bit of a surprise. What can I tell him?"

"Two days ago I was ready to approve a discharge, possibly for the end of this week. As the situation is now, it will take longer. You'll have to prepare him for the fact that probably I won't be in a position to make a decision in the coming week, and that it might be two weeks before you can move her to Stockholm. It depends on her rate of recovery."

"The trial has been set for July."

"Barring the unforeseen, she should be on her feet well before then."

Bublanski cast a sceptical glance at the muscular woman on other side of the table. They were drinking coffee in the pavement area of a café on Norr Mälarstrand. It was Friday, May 20, and the warmth of summer was in the air. Inspector Monica Figuerola, her I.D. said, S.I.S. She had caught up with him just as he was leaving for home; she had suggested a conversation over a cup of coffee, just that.

At first he had been almost hostile, but she had very straightforwardly conceded that she had no authority to interview him and that naturally he was perfectly free to tell her nothing at all if he did not want to. He asked her what her business was, and she told him that she had been assigned by her boss to form an unofficial picture of what was true and what not true in the so-called Zalachenko case, also in some quarters known as the Salander case. She vouchsafed that it was not absolutely certain whether she had the right to question him. It was entirely up to him to decide whether he would talk to her or not.

"What would you like to know?" Bublanski said at last.

"Tell me what you know about Salander, Mikael Blomkvist, Gunnar Björck, and Zalachenko. How do the pieces fit together?"

They talked for more than two hours.

Edklinth thought long and hard about how to proceed. After five days of investigations, Figuerola had given him a number of indisputable indications that something was rotten within S.I.S. He recognized the need to move very carefully until he had enough information. He found himself, furthermore, on the horns of a constitutional dilemma: he did not have the authority to conduct secret investigations, and most assuredly not against his colleagues.

Accordingly he had to contrive some cause that would legitimize what he was doing. If the worst came to the worst, he could always fall back on the fact that it was a policeman's duty to investigate a crime – but the breach was now so sensitive from a constitutional standpoint that he would surely be fired if he took a single wrong step. So he spent the whole of Friday brooding alone in his office.

Finally he concluded that Armansky was right, no matter how improbable it might seem. There really was a conspiracy inside S.I.S., and a number of individuals were acting outside of, or parallel to, regular operations. Because this had been going on for many years – at least since 1976, when Zalachenko arrived in Sweden – it had to be organized and sanctioned from the top. Exactly how high up the conspiracy went he had no idea.

He wrote three names on a pad:

Göran Mårtensson, Personal Protection. Criminal Inspector.
Gunnar Björck, assistant chief of Immigration Division.
  Deceased (Suicide?).
Albert Shenke, chief of Secretariat, S.I.S.

Figuerola was of the view that the chief of Secretariat at least must have been calling the shots when Mårtensson in Personal Protection was supposedly moved to Counter-Espionage, although he had not in fact been working there. He was too busy monitoring the movements of the journalist Mikael Blomkvist, and that did not have anything at all to do with the operations of Counter-Espionage.

Some other names from outside S.I.S. had to be added to the list:

Peter Teleborian, psychiatrist
Lars Faulsson, locksmith

Teleborian had been hired by S.I.S. as a psychiatric consultant on specific cases in the late '80s and early '90s – on three occasions, to be exact, and Edklinth had examined the reports in the archive. The first had been extraordinary – Counter-Espionage had identified a Russian informer inside the Swedish telecom industry, and the spy's background indicated that he might be inclined to suicide in the event that his actions were exposed. Teleborian had done a strikingly good analysis, which helped them turn the informer so that he could become a double agent. His other two reports had involved less significant evaluations: one was of an employee inside S.I.S. who had an alcohol problem, and the second was an analysis of the bizarre sexual behaviour of an African diplomat.

Neither Teleborian nor Faulsson – especially not Faulsson – had any position inside S.I.S. And yet through their assignments they were connected to . . . *to what?*

The conspiracy was intimately linked to the late Alexander Zalachenko, the defected G.R.U. agent who had apparently turned up in Sweden on Election Day in 1976. A man no-one had ever heard of before. *How was that possible?*

Edklinth tried to imagine what reasonably would have happened if he had been sitting at the chief's desk at S.I.S. in 1976 when Zalachenko defected. What would he have done? Absolute secrecy. It would have been essential. The defection could only be known to a small group without risking that the information might leak back to the Russians and . . . How small a group?

An operations department?

An unknown operations department?

If the affair had been appropriately handled, Zalachenko's case should have ended up in Counter-Espionage. Ideally he should have come under the auspices of the military intelligence service, but they had neither the resources nor the expertise to run this sort of operational activity. So, S.I.S. it was.

But Counter-Espionage had not ever had him. Björck was the key; he had been one of the people who handled Zalachenko. And yet Björck had never had anything to do with Counter-Espionage. Björck was a mystery. Officially he had held a post in the Immigration Division since the '70s, but in reality he had scarcely been seen in the department before the '90s, when suddenly he became assistant director.

And yet Björck was the primary source of Blomkvist's information. How had Blomkvist been able to persuade Björck to reveal such explosive material? And to a journalist at that.

Prostitutes. Björck messed around with teenage prostitutes and *Millennium* were going to expose him. Blomkvist must have blackmailed Björck.

Then Salander came into the picture.

The deceased lawyer Nils Bjurman had worked in the Immigration Division at the same time as the deceased Björck. They were the ones who had taken care of Zalachenko. But what did they do with him?

Somebody must have made the decision. With a defector of such provenance the order must have come from the highest level.

From the government. It must have been backed by the government. Anything else would be unthinkable.

Surely?

Edklinth felt cold shivers of apprehension. This was all conceivable in practice. A defector of Zalachenko's status would have to be handled with the utmost secrecy. He would have decided as much himself. That was what Fälldin's administration must have decided too. It made sense.

But what happened in 1991 did not make sense. Björck had hired Teleborian effectively to lock Salander up in a psychiatric hospital for children on the – false – pretext that she was mentally deranged. That was a crime. That was such a monstrous crime that Edklinth felt yet more apprehensive.

Somebody must have made that decision. It simply could not have been the government. Ingvar Carlsson had been Prime Minister at the time, and then Carl Bildt.* But no politician would dare to be involved in such a decision, which contradicted all law and justice and which would result in a disastrous scandal if it were ever discovered.

If the government was involved, then Sweden was not one iota better than any dictatorship in the entire world.

It was impossible.

And what about the events of April 12? Zalachenko was conveniently murdered at Sahlgrenska hospital by a mentally ill fanatic at the same time as a burglary was committed at Blomkvist's apartment and Advokat Giannini was mugged. In both latter instances, copies of Björck's strange report dating from 1991 were stolen. Armansky had contributed this information, but it was completely off the record. No police report was ever filed.

And at the same time, Björck hangs himself – a person with whom Edklinth wished he could have had a serious talk.

Edklinth did not believe in coincidence on such a grand scale. Inspector Bublanski did not believe in such coincidence either. And Blomkvist did not believe it. Edklinth took up his felt pen once more:

Evert Gullberg, seventy-eight years old. Tax specialist. ???

Who the hell was Evert Gullberg?

He considered calling up the chief of S.I.S., but he restrained himself for the simple reason that he did not know how far up in the organization the conspiracy reached. He did not know whom he could trust.

For a moment he considered turning to the regular police. Jan Bublanski was the leader of the investigation concerning Ronald Niedermann, and obviously he would be interested in any related information. But from a purely political standpoint, it was out of the question.

He felt a great weight on his shoulders.

There was only one option left that was constitutionally correct, and which might provide some protection if he ended up in political hot water. He would have to turn to the *chief* to secure political support for what he was working on.

It was just before 4.00 on Friday afternoon. He picked up the telephone and called the Minister of Justice, whom he had known for many years and had dealings with at numerous departmental meetings. He got him on the line within five minutes.

"Hello, Torsten. It's been a long time. What's the problem?"

"To tell you the truth . . . I think I'm calling to check how much credibility I have with you."

"Credibility? That's a peculiar question. As far as I'm concerned you have *absolute* credibility. What makes you ask such a dramatic question?"

"It's prompted by a dramatic and extraordinary request. I need to have a meeting with you and the Prime Minister, and it's urgent."

"Whoa!"

"If you'll forgive me, I'd rather explain when we can talk in private. Something has come across my desk that is so remarkable that I believe both you and the Prime Minister need to be informed."

"Does it have anything to do with terrorists and threat assessments—"

"No. It's more serious than that. I'm putting my reputation and career on the line by calling you with this request."

"I see. That's why you asked about your credibility. How soon do you need the meeting with the P.M.?"

"This evening if possible."

"Now you've got me worried."

"Unhappily, there's good reason for you to be worried."

"How long will the meeting take?"

"It'll probably take an hour."

"Let me call you back."

The Minister of Justice called back ten minutes later and said that the Prime Minister would meet with Edklinth at his residence at 9.30 that evening. Edklinth's palms were sweating when he put down the telephone. *By tomorrow morning my career could be over.*

He called Figuerola.

"Hello, Monica. At 9.00 tonight you have to report for duty. You'd better dress nicely."

"I always dress nicely," Figuerola said.

The Prime Minister gave the Director of Constitutional Protection a long, wary look. Edklinth had a sense that cogs were whirring at high speed behind the P.M.'s glasses.

The P.M. shifted his gaze to Figuerola, who had not said a word during the presentation. He saw an unusually tall and muscular woman looking back at him with a polite, expectant expression. Then he turned to the Minister of Justice, who had paled in the course of the presentation.

After a while the P.M. took a deep breath, removed his glasses, and stared for a moment into the distance.

"I think we need a little more coffee," he said.

"Yes, please," Figuerola said.

Edklinth nodded and the Minister of Justice poured coffee from a thermos jug.

"I'll sum up so that I am absolutely certain that I understood you correctly," the Prime Minister said. "You suspect that there's a conspiracy within the Security Police that is acting outside its constitutional mandate, and that over the years this conspiracy has committed what could be categorized as serious criminal acts."

"Yes."

"And you're coming to me because you don't trust the leadership of the Security Police?"

"No, not exactly," Edklinth said. "I decided to turn directly to you because this sort of activity is unconstitutional. But I don't know the objective of the conspiracy, or whether I have possibly misinterpreted something. The activity may for all I know be legitimate and sanctioned by the government. Then I risk proceeding on faulty or misunderstood information, thereby compromising some secret operation."

The Prime Minister looked at the Minister of Justice. Both understood that Edklinth was covering his back.

"I've never heard of anything like this. Do you know anything about it?"

"Absolutely not," the Minister of Justice said. "There's nothing in any report that I've seen from the Security Police that could have a bearing on this matter."

"Blomkvist thinks there's a faction within Säpo. He refers to it as the Zalachenko club," Edklinth said.

"I'd never even heard that Sweden had taken in and protected a Russian defector of such importance," the P.M. said. "He defected during the Fälldin administration, you say?"

"I don't believe Fälldin would have covered up something like this," the Minister of Justice said. "A defection like this would have been given the highest priority, and would have been passed over to the next administration."

Edklinth cleared his throat. "Fälldin's conservative government was succeeded by Olof Palme's. It's no secret that some of my predecessors at S.I.S. had a certain opinion of Palme—"

"You're suggesting that somebody forgot to inform the social democratic government?"

Edklinth nodded. "Let's remember that Fälldin was in power for two separate mandates. Each time the coalition government collapsed. First he handed over to Ola Ullsten, who had a minority government in 1979. The government collapsed again when the moderates jumped ship, and Fälldin governed together with the People's Party. I'm guessing that the government secretariat was in turmoil during those transition periods. It's also possible that knowledge of Zalachenko was confined to so small a circle that Prime Minister Fälldin had no real oversight, so he never had anything to hand over to Palme."

"In that case, who's responsible?" the P.M. said.

All except Figuerola shook their heads.

"I assume that this is bound to leak to the media," the P.M. said.

"Blomkvist and *Millennium* are going to publish it. In other words, we're caught between the proverbial rock and hard place." Edklinth was careful to use the word "we".

The P.M. nodded. He realized the gravity of the situation. "Then I'll have to start by thanking you for coming to me with this matter as soon as you did. I don't usually agree to this sort of unscheduled meeting, but the minister here said that you were a prudent person, and that something serious must have happened if you wanted to see me outside all normal channels."

Edklinth exhaled a little. Whatever happened, the wrath of the Prime Minister was not going to come down on him.

"Now we just have to decide how we're going to handle it. Do you have any suggestions?"

"Perhaps," Edklinth said tentatively.

He was silent for so long that Figuerola cleared her throat. "May I say something?"

"Please do," the P.M. said.

"If it's true that the government doesn't know about this operation, then it's illegal. The person responsible in such a case is the criminal civil servant – or civil servants – who overstepped his authority. If we can verify all the claims Blomkvist is making, it means that a group of officers within S.I.S. have been devoting themselves to criminal activity for a long time. The problem would then unfold in two parts."

"How do you mean?"

"First we have to ask the question: how could this have been possible? Who is responsible? How did such a conspiracy develop within the framework of an established police organization? I myself work for S.I.S., and I'm proud of it. How can this have gone on for so long? How could this activity have been both concealed and financed?"

"Go on," the P.M. said.

"Whole books will probably be written about this first part. It's clear that there must have been financing, at least several million kronor annually I'd say. I looked over the budget of the Security Police and found nothing resembling an allocation for the Zalachenko club. But, as you know, there are a number of hidden funds controlled by the chief of Secretariat and chief of Budget that I have no access to."

The Prime Minister nodded grimly. Why did Säpo always have to be such a nightmare to administer?

"The second part is: who is involved? And very specifically, which individuals should be arrested? From my standpoint, all these questions depend on the decision you make in the next few minutes," she said to the P.M.

Edklinth was holding his breath. If he could have kicked Figuerola in the shin he would have done so. She had cut through all the rhetoric and intimated that the Prime Minister himself was responsible. He had considered coming to the same conclusion, but not before a long and diplomatic circumlocution.

"What decision do you think I should make?"

"I believe we have common interests. I've worked at Constitutional Protection for three years. I consider this office of central importance

302

to Swedish democracy. The Security Police has worked satisfactorily within the framework of the constitution in recent years. Naturally I don't want the scandal to affect S.I.S. For us it's important to bear in mind that this is a case of criminal activity perpetrated by a small number of individuals."

"Activity of this kind is most definitely not sanctioned by the government," the Minister of Justice said.

Figuerola nodded and thought for a few seconds. "It is, in my view, essential that the scandal should not implicate the government – which is what would happen if the government tried to cover up the story."

"The government does not cover up criminal activity," the Minister of Justice said.

"No, but let's assume, hypothetically, that the government might want to do so. There would be a scandal of enormous proportions."

"Go on," the P.M. said.

"The situation is complicated by the fact that we in Constitutional Protection are being forced to conduct an operation which is itself against regulations in order to investigate this matter. So we want everything to be legitimate and in keeping with the constitution."

"As do we all," the P.M. said.

"In that case I suggest that you – in your capacity as Prime Minister – instruct Constitutional Protection to investigate this mess with the utmost urgency," Figuerola said. "Give us a written order and the authority we need."

"I'm not sure that what you propose is legal," the Minister of Justice said.

"It *is* legal. The government has the power to adopt a wide range of measures in the event that breaches of the constitution are threatened. If a group from the military or police starts pursuing an independent foreign policy, a *de facto* coup has taken place in Sweden."

"Foreign policy?" the Minister of Justice said.

The P.M. nodded all of a sudden.

"Zalachenko was a defector from a foreign power," Figuerola said. "The information he contributed was supplied, according to Blomkvist, to foreign intelligence services. If the government was not informed, a coup has taken place."

"I follow your reasoning," the P.M. said. "Now let me say my piece."

303

He got up and walked once around the table before stopping in front of Edklinth.

"You have a very talented colleague. She has hit the nail on the head."

Edklinth swallowed and nodded. The P.M. turned to the Minister of Justice.

"Get on to the Undersecretary of State and the head of the legal department. By tomorrow morning I want a document drawn up granting the Constitutional Protection Unit extraordinary authority to act in this matter. Their assignment is to determine the truth behind the assertions we have discussed, to gather documentation about its extent, and to identify the individuals responsible or in any way involved. The document must not state that you are conducting a preliminary investigation – I may be wrong, but I think only the Prosecutor General could appoint a preliminary investigation leader in this situation. But I can give you the authority to conduct a one-man investigation. What you are doing is therefore an official public report. Do you understand?"

"Yes. But I should point out that I myself am a former prosecutor."

"We'll have to ask the head of the legal department to take a look at this and determine exactly what is formally correct. In any case, you alone are responsible for your investigation. You will choose the assistants you require. If you find evidence of criminal activity, you must turn this information over to the P.G., who will decide on the charges."

"I'll have to look up exactly what applies, but I think you'll have to inform the speaker of parliament and the constitutional committee . . . This is going to leak out fast," the Minister of Justice said.

"In other words, we have to work faster," the P.M. said.

Figuerola raised a hand.

"What is it?" the P.M. said.

"There are two problems remaining. First, will *Millennium*'s publication clash with our investigation, and second, Lisbeth Salander's trial will be starting in a couple of weeks."

"Can we find out when *Millennium*'s going to publish?"

"We could ask," Edklinth said. "The last thing we want to do is to interfere with the press."

"With regard to this girl Salander . . ." the Minister of Justice began, and then he paused for a moment. "It would be terrible if she really has been subjected to the injustices that *Millennium* claims. Could it really be possible?"

"I'm afraid it is," Edklinth said.

"In that case we have to see to it that she is given redress for these wrongs, and above all that she is not subjected to new injustices," the P.M. said.

"And how would that work?" asked the Minister of Justice. "The government cannot interfere in an ongoing prosecution case. That would be against the law."

"Could we talk to the prosecutor?"

"No," Edklinth said. "As Prime Minister you may not influence the judicial process in any way."

"In other words, Salander will have to take her chances in court," the Minister of Justice said. "Only if she loses the trial and appeals to the government can the government step in and pardon her or require the P.G. to investigate whether there are grounds for a new trial. But this applies only if she's sentenced to prison. If she's sentenced to a secure psychiatric facility, the government cannot do a thing. Then it's a medical matter, and the Prime Minister has no jurisdiction to determine whether or not she is sane."

At 10.00 on Friday night, Salander heard the key turn in the door. She instantly switched off her Palm and slipped it under the mattress. When she looked up she saw Jonasson closing the door.

"Good evening, Fröken Salander," he said. "And how are you doing this evening?"

"I have a splitting headache and I feel feverish."

"That doesn't sound so good."

Salander looked to be not particularly bothered by either the fever or the headache. Jonasson spent ten minutes examining her. He noticed that over the course of the evening her fever had again risen dramatically.

"It's a shame that you should be having this setback when you've been recovering so well over the past few weeks. Unfortunately I won't now be able to discharge you for at least two more weeks."

"Two weeks should be sufficient."

*

The distance by land from London to Stockholm is roughly 1900 kilometres, or 1180 miles. In theory that would be about twenty hours' driving. In fact it had taken almost twenty hours to reach the northern border of Germany with Denmark. The sky was filled with leaden thunderclouds, and when the man known as Trinity found himself on Sunday in the middle of the Öresundsbron, there was a downpour. He slowed and turned on his windscreen wipers.

Trinity thought it was sheer hell driving in Europe, since everyone on the Continent insisted on driving on the wrong side of the road. He had packed his van on Friday morning and taken the ferry from Dover to Calais, then crossed Belgium by way of Liege. He crossed the German border at Aachen and then took the Autobahn north towards Hamburg and on to Denmark.

His companion, Bob the Dog, was asleep in the back. They had taken it in turns to drive, and apart from a couple of hour-long stops along the way, they had maintained a steady ninety kilometres an hour. The van was eighteen years old and was not able to go much faster anyway.

There were easier ways of getting from London to Stockholm, but it was not likely that he would be able to take thirty kilos of electronic gear on a normal flight. They had crossed six national borders but they had not been stopped once, either by customs or by passport control. Trinity was an ardent fan of the E.U., whose regulations simplified his visits to the Continent.

Trinity was born in Bradford, but he had lived in north London since childhood. He had had a miserable formal education, and then attended a vocational school and earned a certificate as a trained telecommunications technician. For three years after his nineteenth birthday he had worked as an engineer for British Telecom. Once he had understood how the telephone network functioned and realized how hopelessly antiquated it was, he switched to being a private security consultant, installing alarm systems and managing burglary protection. For special clients he would also offer his video surveillance and telephone tapping services.

Now thirty-two years old, he had a theoretical knowledge of electronics and computer science that allowed him to knock spots off any professor in the field. He had lived with computers since he was ten, and he hacked his first computer when he was thirteen.

It had whetted his appetite, and when he was sixteen he had advanced to the extent that he could compete with the best in the world. There was a period in which he spent every waking minute in front of his computer screen, writing his own programs and planting insidious tendrils on the Internet. He infiltrated the B.B.C., the Ministry of Defence and Scotland Yard. He even managed – for a short time – to take command of a nuclear submarine on patrol in the North Sea. It was as well that Trinity belonged to the inquisitive rather than the malicious type of computer marauder. His fascination was extinguished the moment he had cracked a computer, gained access, and appropriated its secrets.

He was one of the founders of Hacker Republic. And Wasp was one of its citizens.

It was 7.30 on Sunday evening as he and Bob the Dog were approaching Stockholm. When they passed Ikea at Kungens Kurva in Skärholmen, Trinity flipped open his mobile and dialled a number he had memorized.

"Plague," Trinity said.

"Where are you guys?"

"You said to call when we passed Ikea."

Plague gave him directions to the youth hostel on Långholmen where he had booked a room for his colleagues from England. Since Plague hardly ever left his apartment, they agreed to meet at his place at 10.00 the next morning.

Plague decided to make an exceptional effort and washed the dishes, generally cleaned up, and opened the windows in anticipation of his guests' arrival.

PART III

DISK CRASH

27.v – 6.vi

The historian Diodorus from Sicily, 100 B.C. (who is regarded as an unreliable source by other historians), describes the Amazons of Libya, which at that time was a name used for all of north Africa west of Egypt. This Amazon reign was a gynaecocracy, that is, only women were allowed to hold high office, including in the military. According to legend, the realm was ruled by a Queen Myrina, who with thirty thousand female soldiers and three thousand female cavalry swept through Egypt and Syria and all the way to the Aegean, defeating a number of male armies along the way. After Queen Myrina finally fell in battle, her army scattered.

But the army did leave its imprint on the region. The women of Anatolia took to the sword to crush an invasion from the Caucasus, after the male soldiers were all slaughtered in a far-reaching genocide. These women trained in the use of all types of weapons, including bow and arrow, spear, battle-axe, and lance. They copied their bronze breastplates and armour from the Greeks.

They rejected marriage as subjugation. So that they might have children they were granted a leave of absence, during which they copulated with randomly selected males from nearby towns.

Only a woman who had killed a man in battle was allowed to give up her virginity.

CHAPTER 16

Friday, 27.v – Tuesday, 31.v

Blomkvist left the *Millennium* offices at 10.30 on Friday night. He took the stairs down to the ground floor, but instead of going out on to the street he turned left and went through the basement, across the inner courtyard, and through the building behind theirs on to Hökens Gata. He ran into a group of youths on their way from Mosebacke, but saw no-one who seemed to be paying him any attention. Anyone watching the building would think that he was spending the night at *Millennium*, as he often did. He had established that pattern as early as April. Actually it was Malm who had the night shift.

He spent fifteen minutes walking down the alleys and boulevards around Mosebacke before he headed for Fiskargatan 9. He opened the entrance door using the code and took the stairs to the top-floor apartment, where he used Salander's keys to get in. He turned off the alarm. He always felt a bit bemused when he went into the apartment: twenty-one rooms, of which only three were furnished.

He began by making coffee and sandwiches before he went into Salander's office and booted up her PowerBook.

From the moment in mid-April when Björck's report was stolen and Blomkvist realized that he was under surveillance, he had established his own headquarters at Salander's apartment. He had transferred the most crucial documentation to her desk. He spent several nights a week at the apartment, slept in her bed, and worked on her computer. She had wiped her hard drive clean before she left for Gosseberga and the confrontation with Zalachenko. Blomkvist supposed that she had not planned to come back. He had used her system disks to restore her computer to a functioning state.

Since April he had not even plugged in the broadband cable to his own machine. He logged on to her broadband connection, started up the I.C.Q. chat program, and pinged up the address she had created for him through the Yahoo group [Idiotic_Table].

`<Hi Sally.>`

<Talk to me.>

<I've been working on the two chapters we discussed earlier this week. New version is on Yahoo. How's it going with you?>

<Finished with 17 pages. Uploading now.>

Ping.

<O.K. Got 'em. Let me read, then we'll talk later.>

<I've got more.>

<More what?>

<I created another Yahoo group called The_Knights.>

Blomkvist smiled.

< The Knights of the Idiotic Table.>

<Password yacaraca12.>

<Four members. You, me, Plague and Trinity.>

<Your mysterious night-time buddies.>

<Protection.>

<O.K.>

<Plague has copied info from Prosecutor Ekström's computer. We hacked it in April. If I lose the Palm he'll keep you informed.>

<Good. Thanks.>

Blomkvist logged in to I.C.Q. and went into the newly created Yahoo group [The_Knights]. All he found was a link from Plague to an anonymous U.R.L. which consisted solely of numbers. He copied the address into Explorer, hit the return key, and came to a website somewhere on the Internet that contained the sixteen gigabytes of Ekström's hard drive.

Plague had obviously made it simple for himself by copying over Ekström's entire hard drive, and Blomkvist spent more than an hour sorting through its contents. He ignored the system files, software and endless files containing preliminary investigations that seemed to stretch back several years. He downloaded four folders. Three of them were called [PrelimInv/Salander], [Slush/Salander], and [PrelimInv/-Niedermann]. The fourth was a copy of Ekström's email folder made at 2.00 p.m. the previous day.

"Thanks, Plague," Blomkvist said to himself.

He spent three hours reading through Ekström's preliminary investigation and strategy for the trial. Not surprisingly, much of it dealt with Salander's mental state. Ekström wanted an extensive psychiatric examination and had sent a lot of messages with the object of getting her transferred to Kronoberg prison as a matter of urgency.

Blomkvist could tell that Ekström's search for Niedermann was making no headway. Bublanski was the leader of that investigation. He had succeeding in gathering some forensic evidence linking Niedermann to the murders of Svensson and Johansson, as well as to the murder of Bjurman. Blomkvist's own three long interviews in April had set them on the trail of this evidence. If Niedermann were ever apprehended, Blomkvist would have to be a witness for the prosecution. At long last D.N.A. from sweat droplets and two hairs from Bjurman's apartment were matched to items from Niedermann's room in Gosseberga. The same D.N.A. was found in abundant quantities on the remains of Svavelsjö M.C.'s Göransson.

On the other hand, Ekström had remarkably little on the record about Zalachenko.

Blomkvist lit a cigarette and stood by the window looking out towards Djurgården.

Ekström was leading two separate preliminary investigations. Criminal Inspector Faste was the investigative leader in all matters dealing with Salander. Bublanski was working only on Niedermann.

When the name Zalachenko turned up in the preliminary investigation, the logical thing for Ekström to do would have been to contact the general director of the Security Police to determine who Zalachenko actually was. Blomkvist could find no such enquiry in Ekström's email, journal or notes. But among the notes Blomkvist found several cryptic sentences.

The Salander investigation is fake. Björck's original doesn't match Blomkvist's version. Classify TOP SECRET.

Then a series of notes claiming that Salander was paranoid and a schizophrenic.

Correct to lock up Salander 1991.

He found what linked the investigations in the Salander slush, that is, the supplementary information that the prosecutor considered irrelevant to the preliminary investigation, and which would therefore not be presented at the trial or make up part of the chain of evidence against her. This included almost everything that had to do with Zalachenko's background.

The investigation was totally inadequate.

Blomkvist wondered to what extent this was a coincidence and to what extent it was contrived. Where was the boundary? And was Ekström aware that there was a boundary?

Could it be that someone was deliberately supplying Ekström with believable but misleading information?

Finally Blomkvist logged into hotmail and spent ten minutes checking the half-dozen anonymous email accounts he had created. Each day he had checked the address he had given to Criminal Inspector Modig. He had no great hope that she would contact him, so he was mildly surprised when he opened the inbox and found an email from <ressallskap9april@hotmail.com>. The message consisted of a single line:

Café Madeleine, upper level, 11.00 a.m. Saturday.

Plague pinged Salander at midnight and interrupted her in the middle of a sentence she was writing about her time with Holger Palmgren as her guardian. She cast an irritated glance at the display.
<What do you want?>
<Hi Wasp, nice to hear from you too.>
<Yeah yeah. What is it?>
<Teleborian.>
She sat up in bed and looked eagerly at the screen of her Palm.
<Tell me.>
<Trinity fixed it in record time.>
<How?>
<The crazy-doctor won't stay in one place. He travels between Uppsala and Stockholm all the time and we can't do a hostile takeover.>
<I know. How?>
<He plays tennis twice a week. About two hours. Left his computer in the car in a garage.>
<Aha.>
<Trinity easily disabled the car alarm to get the computer. Took him 30 minutes to copy everything via Firewire and install Asphyxia.>
<Where?>
Plague gave her the U.R.L. of the server where he kept Teleborian's hard drive.
<To quote Trinity ... This is one nasty shit.>

316

<?>
<Check his hard drive.>

Salander disconnected from Plague and accessed the server he had directed her to. She spent nearly three hours scrutinizing folder after folder on Teleborian's computer.

She found correspondence between Teleborian and a person with a hotmail address who sent encrypted mail. Since she had access to Teleborian's P.G.P. key, she easily decoded the correspondence. His name was Jonas, no last name. Jonas and Teleborian had an unhealthy interest in seeing that Salander did not thrive.

Yes . . . we can prove that there is a conspiracy.

But what really interested Salander were the forty-seven folders containing close to nine thousand photographs of explicit child pornography. She clicked on image after image of children aged about fifteen or younger. A number of pictures were of infants. The majority were of girls. Many of them were sadistic.

She found links to at least a dozen people abroad who traded child porn with each other.

Salander bit her lip, but her face was otherwise expressionless.

She remembered the nights when, as a twelve-year-old, she had been strapped down in a stimulus-free room at St Stefan's. Teleborian had come into the room again and again to look at her in the glow of the nightlight.

She knew. He had never touched her, but she had always known.

She should have dealt with Teleborian years ago. But she had repressed the memory of him. She had chosen to ignore his existence.

After a while she pinged Blomkvist on I.C.Q.

Blomkvist spent the night at Salander's apartment on Fiskargatan. He did not shut down the computer until 6.30 a.m. and fell asleep with photographs of gross child pornography whirling through his mind. He woke at 10.15 and rolled out of Salander's bed, showered, and called a taxi to pick him up outside Södra theatre. He got out at Birger Jarlsgatan at 10.55 and walked to Café Madeleine.

Modig was waiting for him with a cup of black coffee in front of her.

"Hi," Blomkvist said.

"I'm taking a big risk here," she said without greeting.

"Nobody will hear of our meeting from me."

She seemed stressed.

"One of my colleagues recently went to see former Prime Minister Fälldin. He went there off his own bat, and his job is on the line now too."

"I understand."

"I need a guarantee of anonymity for both of us."

"I don't even know which colleague you're talking about."

"I'll tell you later. I want you to promise to give him protection as a source."

"You have my word."

She looked at her watch.

"Are you in a hurry?"

"Yes. I have to meet my husband and kids at the Sturegalleria in ten minutes. He thinks I'm still at work."

"And Bublanski knows nothing about this?"

"No."

"Right. You and your colleague are sources and you have complete source protection. Both of you. As long as you live."

"My colleague is Jerker Holmberg. You met him down in Göteborg. His father is a Centre Party member, and Jerker has known Prime Minister Fälldin since he was a child. He seems to be pleasant enough. So Jerker went to see him and asked about Zalachenko."

Blomkvist's heart began to pound.

"Jerker asked what he knew about the defection, but Fälldin didn't reply. When Holmberg told him that we suspect that Salander was locked up by the people who were protecting Zalachenko, well, that really upset him."

"Did he say how much he knew?"

"Fälldin told him that the chief of Säpo at the time and a colleague came to visit him very soon after he became Prime Minister. They told a fantastic story about a Russian defector who had come to Sweden, told him that it was the most sensitive military secret Sweden possessed ... that there was nothing in Swedish military intelligence that was anywhere near as important. Fälldin said that he hadn't known how he should handle it, that there was no-one with much experience in government, the Social Democrats having been in power for more than forty years. He was advised that he alone had to make the decisions, and that if he discussed it with his government colleagues then Säpo would wash their hands of it. He remembered the whole thing as having been very unpleasant."

"What *did* he do?"

"He realized that he had no choice but to do what the gentlemen from Säpo were proposing. He issued a directive putting Säpo in sole charge of the defector. He undertook never to discuss the matter with anyone. Fälldin was never told Zalachenko's name."

"Extraordinary."

"After that he heard almost nothing more during his two terms in office. But he had done something extremely shrewd. He had insisted that an Undersecretary of State be let in on the secret, in case there was a need for a go-between for the government secretariat and those who were protecting Zalachenko."

"Did he remember who it was?"

"It was Bertil K. Janeryd, now Swedish ambassador in the Hague. When it was explained to Fälldin how serious this preliminary investigation was, he sat down and wrote to Janeryd."

Modig pushed an envelope across the table.

Dear Bertil,

The secret we both protected during my administration is now the subject of some very serious questions. The person referred to in the matter is now deceased and can no longer come to harm. On the other hand, other people can.

It is of the utmost importance that answers are provided to certain questions that must be answered.

The person who bears this letter is working unofficially and has my trust. I urge you to listen to his story and answer his questions.

Use your famous good judgement.

T.F.

"This letter is referring to Holmberg?"

"No. Jerker asked Fälldin not to put a name. He said that he couldn't know who would be going to the Hague."

"You mean . . ."

"Jerker and I have discussed it. We're already out on ice so thin that we'll need paddles rather than ice picks. We have no authority to travel to Holland to interview the ambassador. But you could do it."

Blomkvist folded the letter and was putting it into his jacket pocket when Modig grabbed his hand. Her grip was hard.

"Information for information," she said. "We want to hear everything Janeryd tells you."

Blomkvist nodded. Modig stood up.

"Hang on. You said that Fälldin was visited by two people from Säpo. One was the chief of Säpo. Who was the other?"

"Fälldin met him only on that one occasion and couldn't remember his name. No notes were taken at the meeting. He remembered him as thin with a narrow moustache. But he did recall that the man was introduced as the boss of the Section for Special Analysis, or something like that. Fälldin later looked at an organizational chart of Säpo and couldn't find that department."

The Zalachenko club, Blomkvist thought.

Modig seemed to be weighing her words.

"At risk of ending up shot," she said at last, "there is one record that neither Fälldin nor his visitors thought of."

"What was that?"

"Fälldin's visitors' logbook at Rosenbad. Jerker requisitioned it. It's a public document."

"And?"

Modig hesitated once again. "The book states only that the Prime Minister met with the chief of Säpo along with a colleague to discuss general questions."

"Was there a name?"

"Yes. E. Gullberg."

Blomkvist could feel the blood rush to his head.

"Evert Gullberg," he said.

Blomkvist called from Café Madeleine on his anonymous mobile to book a flight to Amsterdam. The plane would take off from Arlanda at 2.50. He walked to Dressman on Kungsgatan and bought a shirt and a change of underwear, and then he went to a pharmacy to buy a toothbrush and other toiletries. He checked carefully to see that he was not being followed and hurried to catch the Arlanda Express.

The plane landed at Schiphol airport at 4.50, and by 6.30 he was checking into a small hotel about fifteen minutes' walk from the Hague's Centraal Station.

He spent two hours trying to locate the Swedish ambassador and made contact by telephone at around 9.00. He used all his powers of persuasion and explained that he was there on a matter of great urgency. The ambassador finally relented and agreed to meet him at 10.00 on Sunday morning.

Then Blomkvist went out and had a light dinner at a restaurant near his hotel. He was asleep by 11.00.

Ambassador Janeryd was in no mood for small talk when he offered Blomkvist coffee at his residence on Lange Voorhout.

"Well . . . what is it that's so urgent?"

"Alexander Zalachenko. The Russian defector who came to Sweden in 1976," Blomkvist said, handing him the letter from Fälldin.

Janeryd looked surprised. He read the letter and laid it on the table beside him.

Blomkvist explained the background and why Fälldin had written to him.

"I . . . I can't discuss this matter," Janeryd said at last.

"I think you can."

"No, I could only speak of it with the constitutional committee."

"There's a great probability that you will have to do just that. But this letter tells you to use your own good judgement."

"Fälldin is an honest man."

"I don't doubt that. And I'm not looking to damage either you or Fälldin. Nor do I ask you to tell me a single military secret that Zalachenko may have revealed."

"I don't know any secrets. I didn't even know that his name was Zalachenko. I only knew him by his cover name. He was known as Ruben. But it's absurd that you should think I would discuss it with a journalist."

"Let me give you one very good reason why you should," Blomkvist said and sat up straight in his chair. "This whole story is going to be published very soon. And when that happens, the media will either tear you to pieces or describe you as an honest civil servant who made the best of an impossible situation. You were the one Fälldin assigned

321

to be the go-between with those who were protecting Zalachenko. I already know that."

Janeryd was silent for almost a minute.

"Listen, I never had any information, not the remotest idea of the background you've described. I was rather young . . . I didn't know how I should deal with these people. I met them about twice a year during the time I worked for the government. I was told that Ruben . . . your Zalachenko, was alive and healthy, that he was co-operating, and that the information he provided was invaluable. I was never privy to the details. I had no 'need to know'."

Blomkvist waited.

"The defector had operated in other countries and knew nothing about Sweden, so he was never a major factor for security policy. I informed the Prime Minister on a couple of occasions, but there was never very much to report."

"I see."

"They always said that he was being handled in the customary way and that the information he provided was being processed through the appropriate channels. What could I say? If I asked what it meant, they smiled and said that it was outside my security clearance level. I felt like an idiot."

"You never considered the fact that there might be something wrong with the arrangement?"

"No. There was nothing wrong with the arrangement. I took it for granted that Säpo knew what they were doing and had the appropriate routines and experience. But I can't talk about this."

Janeryd had by this time been talking about it for several minutes.

"O.K. . . . but all this is beside the point. Only one thing is important right now."

"What?"

"The names of the individuals you had your meetings with."

Janeryd gave Blomkvist a puzzled look.

"The people who were looking after Zalachenko went far beyond their jurisdiction. They've committed serious criminal acts and they'll be the object of a preliminary investigation. That's why Fälldin sent me to see you. He doesn't know who they are. You were the one who met them."

Janeryd blinked and pressed his lips together.

"One was Evert Gullberg . . . he was the top man."

Janeryd nodded.

"How many times did you meet him?"

"He was at every meeting except one. There were about ten meetings during the time Fälldin was Prime Minister."

"Where did you meet?"

"In the lobby of some hotel. Usually the Sheraton. Once at the Amaranth on Kungsholmen and sometimes at the Continental pub."

"And who else was at the meetings?"

"It was a long time ago . . . I don't remember."

"Try."

"There was a . . . Clinton. Like the American president."

"First name?"

"Fredrik. I saw him four or five times."

"Others?"

"Hans von Rottinger. I knew him through my mother."

"Your mother?"

"Yes, my mother knew the von Rottinger family. Hans von Rottinger was always a pleasant chap. Before he turned up out of the blue at a meeting with Gullberg, I had no idea that he worked for Säpo."

"He didn't," Blomkvist said.

Janeryd turned pale.

"He worked for something called the Section for Special Analysis," Blomkvist said. "What were you told about that group?"

"Nothing. I mean, just that they were the ones who took care of the defector."

"Right. But isn't it strange that they don't appear anywhere in Säpo's organizational chart?"

"That's ridiculous."

"It is, isn't it? So how did they set up the meetings? Did they call you, or did you call them?"

"Neither. The time and place for each meeting was set at the preceding one."

"What happened if you needed to get in contact with them? For instance, to change the time of a meeting or something like that?"

"I had a number to call."

"What was the number?"

"I couldn't possibly remember."

"Who answered if you called the number?"

"I don't know. I never used it."

"Next question. Who did you hand everything over to?"

"How do you mean?"

"When Fälldin's term came to an end. Who took your place?"

"I don't know."

"Did you write a report?"

"No. Everything was classified. I couldn't even take notes."

"And you never briefed your successor?"

"No."

"So what happened?"

"Well . . . Fälldin left office, and Ola Ullsten came in. I was told that we would have to wait until after the next election. Then Fälldin was re-elected and our meetings were resumed. Then came the election in 1985. The Social Democrats won, and I assume that Palme appointed somebody to take over from me. I transferred to the foreign ministry and became a diplomat. I was posted to Egypt, and then to India."

Blomkvist went on asking questions for another few minutes, but he was sure that he already had everything Janeryd could tell him. Three names.

Fredrik Clinton.

Hans von Rottinger.

And Evert Gullberg – the man who had shot Zalachenko.

The Zalachenko club.

He thanked Janeryd for the meeting and walked the short distance along Lange Voorhout to Hotel des Indes, from where he took a taxi to Centraal. It was not until he was in the taxi that he reached into his jacket pocket and stopped the tape recorder.

Berger looked up and scanned the half-empty newsroom beyond the glass cage. Holm was off that day. She saw no-one who showed any interest in her, either openly or covertly. Nor did she have reason to think that anyone on the editorial staff wished her ill.

The email had arrived a minute before. The sender was <editorial-@aftonbladet.com>. Why Aftonbladet? The address was another fake.

Today's message contained no text. There was only a jpeg that she opened in Photoshop.

The image was pornographic: a naked woman with exceptionally large breasts, a dog collar around her neck. She was on all fours and being mounted from the rear.

The woman's face had been replaced with Berger's. It was not a skilled collage, but probably that was not the point. The picture was from her old byline at *Millennium* and could be downloaded off the Net.

At the bottom of the picture was one word, written with the spray function in Photoshop.

Whore.

This was the ninth anonymous message she had received containing the word "whore", sent apparently by someone at a well-known media outlet in Sweden. She had a cyber-stalker on her hands.

The telephone tapping was a more difficult task than the computer monitoring. Trinity had no trouble locating the cable to Prosecutor Ekström's home telephone. The problem was that Ekström seldom or never used it for work-related calls. Trinity did not even consider trying to bug Ekström's work telephone at police H.Q. on Kungsholmen. That would have required extensive access to the Swedish cable network, which he did not have.

But Trinity and Bob the Dog devoted the best part of a week to identifying and separating out Ekström's mobile from the background noise of about 200,000 other mobile telephones within a kilometre of police headquarters.

They used a technique called Random Frequency Tracking System. The technique was not uncommon. It had been developed by the U.S. National Security Agency, and was built into an unknown number of satellites that performed pinpoint monitoring of capitals around the world as well as flashpoints of special interest.

The N.S.A. had enormous resources and used a vast network in order to capture a large number of mobile conversations in a certain region simultaneously. Each individual call was separated and processed digitally by computers programmed to react to certain words, such as *terrorist* or *Kalashnikov*. If such a word occurred, the computer automatically sent an alarm, which meant that some operator would go in manually and listen to the conversation to decide whether it was of interest or not.

It was a more complex problem to identify a specific mobile telephone. Each mobile has its own unique signature – a fingerprint – in the form of the telephone number. With exceptionally sensitive equipment the N.S.A. could focus on a specific area to separate out and monitor mobile calls. The technique was simple but not 100 per cent effective. Outgoing calls were particularly hard to identify. Incoming calls were simpler because they were preceded by the fingerprint that would enable the telephone in question to receive the signal.

The difference between Trinity and the N.S.A. attempting to eavesdrop could be measured in economic terms. The N.S.A. had an annual budget of several billion U.S. dollars, close to twelve thousand full-time agents, and access to cutting-edge technology in I.T. and telecommunications. Trinity had a van with thirty kilos of electronic equipment, much of which was home-made stuff that Bob the Dog had set up. Through its global satellite monitoring the N.S.A. could home in highly sensitive antennae on a specific building anywhere in the world. Trinity had an antenna constructed by Bob the Dog which had an effective range of about five hundred metres.

The relatively limited technology to which Trinity had access meant that he had to park his van on Bergsgatan or one of the nearby streets and laboriously calibrate the equipment until he had identified the fingerprint that represented Ekström's mobile number. Since he did not know Swedish, he had to relay the conversations via another mobile back home to Plague, who did the actual eavesdropping.

For five days Plague, who was looking more and more hollow-eyed, listened in vain to a vast number of calls to and from police headquarters and the surrounding buildings. He had heard fragments of ongoing investigations, uncovered planned lovers' trysts, and taped hours and hours of conversations of no interest whatsoever. Late on the evening of the fifth day, Trinity sent a signal which a digital display instantly identified as Ekström's mobile number. Plague locked the parabolic antenna on to the exact frequency.

The technology of R.F.T.S. worked primarily on incoming calls to Ekström. Trinity's parabolic antenna captured the search for Ekström's mobile number as it was sent through the ether.

Because Trinity could record the calls from Ekström, he also got voiceprints that Plague could process.

Plague ran Ekström's digitized voice through a program called V.P.R.S., Voiceprint Recognition System. He specified a dozen commonly occurring words, such as "O.K." or "Salander". When he had five separate examples of a word, he charted it with respect to the time it took to speak the word, what tone of voice and frequency range it had, whether the end of the word went up or down, and a dozen other markers. The result was a graph. In this way Plague could also monitor outgoing calls from Ekström. His parabolic antenna would be permanently listening out for a call containing Ekström's characteristic graph curve for one of a dozen commonly occurring words. The technology was not perfect, but roughly half of all the calls that Ekström made on his mobile from anywhere near police headquarters were monitored and recorded.

The system had an obvious weakness. As soon as Ekström left police headquarters, it was no longer possible to monitor his mobile, unless Trinity knew where he was and could park his van in the immediate vicinity.

With the authorization from the highest level, Edklinth had been able to set up a legitimate operations department. He picked four colleagues, purposely selecting younger talent who had experience on the regular police force and were only recently recruited to S.I.S. Two had a background in the Fraud Division, one had been with the financial police, and one was from the Violent Crimes Division. They were summoned to Edklinth's office and told of their assignment as well as the need for absolute secrecy. He made plain that the investigation was being carried out at the express order of the Prime Minister. Inspector Figuerola was named as their chief, and she directed the investigation with a force that matched her physical appearance.

But the investigation proceeded slowly. This was largely due to the fact that no-one was quite sure who or what should be investigated. On more than one occasion Edklinth and Figuerola considered bringing Mårtensson in for questioning. But they decided to wait. Arresting him would reveal the existence of the investigation.

Finally, on Tuesday, eleven days after the meeting with the Prime Minister, Figuerola came to Edklinth's office.

"I think we've got something."

"Sit down."

"Evert Gullberg. One of our investigators had a talk with Marcus Erlander, who's leading the investigation into Zalachenko's murder. According to Erlander, S.I.S. contacted the Göteborg police just two hours after the murder and gave them information about Gullberg's threatening letters."

"That was fast."

"A little too fast. S.I.S. faxed nine letters that Gullberg had supposedly written. There's just one problem."

"What's that?"

"Two of the letters were sent to the justice department – to the Minister of Justice and to the Deputy Minister."

"I know that."

"Yes, but the letter to the Deputy Minister wasn't logged in at the department until the following day. It arrived with a later delivery."

Edklinth stared at Figuerola. He felt very much afraid that his suspicions were going to turn out to be justified. Figuerola went implacably on.

"So we have S.I.S. sending a fax of a threatening letter that hadn't yet reached its addressee."

"Good Lord," Edklinth said.

"It was someone in Personal Protection who faxed them through."

"Who?"

"I don't think he's involved in the case. The letters landed on his desk in the morning, and shortly after the murder he was told to get in touch with the Göteborg police."

"Who gave him the instruction?"

"The chief of Secretariat's assistant."

"Good God, Monica. Do you know what this means? It means that S.I.S. was involved in Zalachenko's murder."

"Not necessarily. But it definitely does mean that some individuals within S.I.S. had knowledge of the murder before it was committed. The only question is: who?"

"The chief of Secretariat . . ."

"Yes. But I'm beginning to suspect that this Zalachenko club is out of house."

"How do you mean?"

"Mårtensson. He was moved from Personal Protection and is working on his own. We've had him under surveillance round the clock for the past week. He hasn't had contact with anyone within S.I.S. as far as we can tell. He gets calls on a mobile that we cannot monitor. We don't know what number it is, but it's not his normal mobile number. He did meet with the fair-haired man, but we haven't been able to identify him."

Edklinth frowned. At the same instant Anders Berglund knocked on the door. He was one of the new team, the officer who had worked with the financial police.

"I think I've found Evert Gullberg," Berglund said.

"Come in," Edklinth said.

Berglund put a dog-eared, black-and-white photograph on the desk. Edklinth and Figuerola looked at the picture, which showed a man that both of them immediately recognized. He was being led through a doorway by two broad-shouldered plain-clothes police officers. The legendary double agent Colonel Stig Wennerström.*

"This print comes from Åhlens & Åkerlunds Publishers and was used in *Se* magazine in the spring of 1964. The photograph was taken in the course of the trial. Behind Wennerström you can see three people. On the right, Detective Superintendent Otto Danielsson, the policeman who arrested him."

"Yes . . ."

"Look at the man on the left behind Danielsson."

They saw a tall man with a narrow moustache who was wearing a hat. He reminded Edklinth vaguely of the writer Dashiell Hammett.

"Compare his face with this passport photograph of Gullberg, taken when he was sixty-six."

Edklinth frowned. "I wouldn't be able to swear it's the same person—"

"But it is," Berglund said. "Turn the print over."

On the reverse was a stamp saying that the picture belonged to Åhlens & Åkerlunds Publishers and that the photographer's name was Julius Estholm. The text was written in pencil. *Stig Wennerström flanked by two police officers on his way into Stockholm district court. In the background O. Danielsson, E. Gullberg and H.W. Francke.*

"Evert Gullberg," Figuerola said. "He was S.I.S."

"No," Berglund said. "Technically speaking, he wasn't. At least not when this picture was taken."

"Oh?"

"S.I.S. wasn't established until four months later. In this photograph he was still with the Secret State Police."

"Who's H.W. Francke?" Figuerola said.

"Hans Wilhelm Francke," Edklinth said. "Died in the early '90s, but was assistant chief of the Secret State Police in the late '50s and early

329

'60s. He was a bit of a legend, just like Otto Danielsson. I actually met him a couple of times."

"Is that so?" Figuerola said.

"He left S.I.S. in the late '60s. Francke and P.G. Vinge never saw eye to eye, and he was more or less forced to resign at the age of fifty or fifty-five. Then he opened his own shop."

"His own *shop*?"

"He became a consultant in security for industry. He had an office on Stureplan, but he also gave lectures from time to time at S.I.S. training sessions. That's where I met him."

"What did Vinge and Francke quarrel about?"

"They were just very different. Francke was a bit of a cowboy who saw K.G.B. agents everywhere, and Vinge was a bureaucrat of the old school. Vinge was fired shortly thereafter. A bit ironic, that, because he thought Palme was working for the K.G.B."

Figuerola looked at the photograph of Gullberg and Francke standing side by side.

"I think it's time we had another talk with Justice," Edklinth told her.

"*Millennium* came out today," Figuerola said.

Edklinth shot her a glance.

"Not a word about the Zalachenko affair," she said.

"So we've got a month before the next issue. Good to know. But we have to deal with Blomkvist. In the midst of all this mess he's like a hand grenade with the pin pulled."

CHAPTER 17

Wednesday, 1.vi

Blomkvist had no warning that someone was in the stairwell when he reached the landing outside his top-floor apartment at Bellmansgatan 1. It was 7.00 in the evening. He stopped short when he saw a woman with short, blonde curly hair sitting on the top step. He recognized her straightaway as Monica Figuerola of S.I.S. from the passport photograph Karim had located.

"Hello, Blomkvist," she said cheerfully, closing the book she had been reading. Blomkvist looked at the book and saw that it was in English, on the idea of God in the ancient world. He studied his unexpected visitor as she stood up. She was wearing a short-sleeved summer dress and had laid a brick-red leather jacket over the top stair.

"We need to talk to you," she said.

She was tall, taller than he was, and that impression was magnified by the fact that she was standing two steps above him. He looked at her arms and then at her legs and saw that she was much more muscular than he was.

"You spend a couple of hours a week at the gym," he said.

She smiled and took out her I.D.

"My name is—"

"Monica Figuerola, born in 1969, living on Pontonjärgatan on Kungsholmen. You came from Borlänge and you've worked with the Uppsala police. For three years you've been working in S.I.S., Constitutional Protection. You're an exercise fanatic and you were once a top-class athlete, almost made it on to the Swedish Olympic team. What do you want with me?"

She was surprised, but she quickly regained her composure.

"Fair enough," she said in a low voice. "You know who I am – so you don't have to be afraid of me."

"I don't?"

"There are some people who need to have a talk with you in peace and quiet. Since your apartment and mobile seem to be bugged and we have reason to be discreet, I've been sent to invite you."

"And why would I go anywhere with somebody who works for Säpo?"

She thought for a moment. "Well . . . you could just accept a friendly personal invitation, or if you prefer, I could handcuff you and take you with me." She smiled sweetly. "Look, Blomkvist. I understand that you don't have many reasons to trust anyone who comes from S.I.S. But it's like this: not everyone who works there is your enemy, and my superiors really want to talk to you. So, which do you prefer? Handcuffed or voluntary?"

"I've been handcuffed by the police once already this year. And that was enough. Where are we going?"

She had parked around the corner down on Pryssgränd. When they were settled in her new Saab 9-5, she flipped open her mobile and pressed a speed-dial number.

"We'll be there in fifteen minutes."

She told Blomkvist to fasten his seat belt and drove over Slussen to Östermalm and parked on a side street off Artillerigatan. She sat still for a moment and looked at him.

"This is a friendly invitation, Blomkvist. You're not risking anything."

Blomkvist said nothing. He was reserving judgement until he knew what this was all about. She punched in the code on the street door. They took the lift to the fifth floor, to an apartment with the name Martinsson on the door.

"We've borrowed the place for tonight's meeting," she said, opening the door. "To your right, into the living room."

The first person Blomkvist saw was Torsten Edklinth, which was no surprise since Säpo was deeply involved in what had happened, and Edklinth was Figuerola's boss. The fact that the Director of Constitutional Protection had gone to the trouble of bringing him in said that somebody was nervous.

Then he saw a figure by the window. The Minister of Justice. That *was* a surprise.

Then he heard a sound to his right and saw the Prime Minister get up from an armchair. This he had not for a moment expected.

"Good evening, Herr Blomkvist," the P.M. said. "Excuse us for summoning you to this meeting at such short notice, but we've discussed the situation and agreed that we need to talk to you. May I offer you some coffee, or something else to drink?"

Blomkvist looked around. He saw a dining-room table of dark wood that was cluttered with glasses, coffee cups and the remnants of sandwiches. They must have been there for a couple of hours already.

"Ramlösa," he said.

Figuerola poured him a mineral water. They sat down on the sofas as she stayed in the background.

"He recognized me and knew my name, where I live, where I work, and the fact that I'm a workout fanatic," Figuerola said to no-one in particular.

The Prime Minister glanced quickly at Edklinth and then at Blomkvist. Blomkvist realized at once that he was in a position of some strength. The Prime Minister needed something from him and presumably had no idea how much Blomkvist knew or did not know.

"How did you know who Inspector Figuerola was?" Edklinth said.

Blomkvist looked at the Director of Constitutional Protection. He could not be sure why the Prime Minister had set up a meeting with him in a borrowed apartment in Östermalm, but he suddenly felt inspired. There were not many ways it could have come about. It was Armansky who had set this in train by giving information to someone he trusted. Which must have been Edklinth, or someone close to him. Blomkvist took a chance.

"A mutual friend spoke with you," he said to Edklinth. "You sent Figuerola to find out what was going on, and she discovered that some Säpo activists are running illegal telephone taps and breaking into my apartment and stealing things. This means that you have confirmed the existence of what I call the Zalachenko club. It made you so nervous that you knew you had to take the matter further, but you sat in your office for a while and didn't know in which direction to go. So you went to the justice minister, and he in turn went to the Prime Minister. And now here we all are. What is it that you want from me?"

Blomkvist spoke with a confidence that suggested that he had a source right at the heart of the affair and had followed every step Edklinth had taken. He knew that his guesswork was on the mark when Edklinth's eyes widened.

"The Zalachenko club spies on me, I spy on them," Blomkvist went on. "And you spy on the Zalachenko club. This situation makes the Prime Minister both angry and uneasy. He knows that at the end of this conversation a scandal awaits that the government might not survive."

Figuerola understood that Blomkvist was bluffing, and she knew how he had been able to surprise her by knowing her name and shoe size.

He saw me in my car on Bellmansgatan. He took the registration number and looked me up. But the rest is guesswork.

She did not say a word.

The Prime Minister certainly looked uneasy now.

"Is that what awaits us?" he said. "A scandal to bring down the government?"

"The survival of the government isn't my concern," Blomkvist said. "My role is to expose shit like the Zalachenko club."

The Prime Minister said: "And my job is to run the country in accordance with the constitution."

"Which means that my problem is definitely the government's problem. But not vice versa."

"Could we stop going round in circles? Why do you think I arranged this meeting?"

"To find out what I know and what I intend to do with it."

"Partly right. But more precisely, we've landed in a constitutional crisis. Let me first say that the government has absolutely no hand in this matter. We have been caught napping, without a doubt. I've never heard mention of this . . . what you call the Zalachenko club. The minister here has never heard a word about this matter either. Torsten Edklinth, an official high up in S.I.S. who has worked in Säpo for many years, has never heard of it."

"It's still not my problem."

"I appreciate that. What I'd like to know is when you mean to publish your article, and exactly what it is you intend to publish. And this has nothing to do with damage control."

"Does it not?"

"Herr Blomkvist, the worst possible thing I could do in this situation would be to try to influence the shape or content of your story. Instead, I am going to propose a co-operation."

"Please explain."

"Since we have now had confirmation that a conspiracy exists within an exceptionally sensitive part of the administration, I have ordered an investigation." The P.M. turned to the Minister of Justice. "Please explain what the government has directed."

"It's very simple," said the Minister of Justice. "Torsten Edklinth has been given the task of finding out whether we can confirm this. He is to gather information that can be turned over to the Prosecutor General, who in turn must decide whether charges should be brought.

It is a very clear instruction. And this evening Edklinth has been reporting on how the investigation is proceeding. We've had a long discussion about the constitutional implications – obviously we want it to be handled properly."

"Naturally," Blomkvist said in a tone that indicated he had scant trust in the Prime Minister's assurances.

"The investigation has already reached a sensitive stage. We have not yet identified exactly who is involved. That will take time. And that's why we sent Inspector Figuerola to invite you to this meeting."

"It wasn't exactly an invitation."

The Prime Minister frowned and glanced at Figuerola.

"It's not important," Blomkvist said. "Her behaviour was exemplary. Please come to the point."

"We want to know your publication date. This investigation is being conducted in great secrecy. If you publish before Edklinth has completed it, it could be ruined."

"And when would you like me to publish? After the next election, I suppose?"

"You decide that for yourself. It's not something I can influence. Just tell us, so that we know exactly what our deadline is."

"I see. You spoke about co-operation . . ."

The P.M. said: "Yes, but first let me say that under normal circum stances I would not have dreamed of asking a journalist to come to such a meeting."

"Presumably in normal circumstances you would be doing everything you could to keep journalists away from a meeting like this."

"Quite so. But I've understood that you're driven by several factors. You have a reputation for not pulling your punches when there's corruption involved. In this case there are no differences of opinion to divide us."

"Aren't there?"

"No, not in the least. Or rather . . . the differences that exist might be of a legal nature, but we share an objective. If this Zalachenko club exists, it is not merely a criminal conspiracy – it is a threat to national security. These activities must be stopped, and those responsible must be held accountable. On that point we would be in agreement, correct?"

Blomkvist nodded.

"I've understood that you know more about this story than anyone else. We suggest that you share your knowledge. If this were a regular

335

police investigation of an ordinary crime, the leader of the preliminary investigation could decide to summon you for an interview. But, as you can appreciate, this is an extreme state of affairs."

Blomkvist weighed the situation for a moment.

"And what do I get in return – if I do co-operate?"

"Nothing. I'm not going to haggle with you. If you want to publish tomorrow morning, then do so. I won't get involved in any horse-trading that might be constitutionally dubious. I'm asking you to co-operate in the interests of the country."

"In this case 'nothing' could be quite a lot," Blomkvist said. "For one thing . . . I'm very, very angry. I'm furious at the state and the government and Säpo and all these fucking bastards who for no reason at all locked up a twelve-year-old girl in a mental hospital until she could be declared incompetent."

"Lisbeth Salander has become a government matter," the P.M. said, and smiled. "Mikael, I am personally very upset over what happened to her. Please believe me when I say that those responsible will be called to account. But before we can do that, we have to know who they are."

"My priority is that Salander should be acquitted and declared competent."

"I can't help you with that. I'm not above the law, and I can't direct what prosecutors and the courts decide. She has to be acquitted by a court."

"O.K.," Blomkvist said. "You want my co-operation. Then give me some insight into Edklinth's investigation, and I'll tell you when and what I plan to publish."

"I can't give you that insight. That would be placing myself in the same relation to you as the Minister of Justice's predecessor once stood to the journalist Ebbe Carlsson."*

"I'm not Ebbe Carlsson," Blomkvist said calmly.

"I know that. On the other hand, Edklinth can decide for himself what he can share with you within the framework of his assignment."

"Hmm," Blomkvist said. "I want to know who Evert Gullberg was."

Silence fell over the group.

"Gullberg was presumably for many years the chief of that division within S.I.S. which you call the Zalachenko club," Edklinth said.

The Prime Minister gave him a sharp look.

"I think he knows that already," Edklinth said by way of apology.

"That's correct," Blomkvist said. "He started at Säpo in the '50s.

336

In the '60s he became chief of some outfit called the Section for Special Analysis. He was the one in charge of the Zalachenko affair."

The P.M. shook his head. "You know more than you ought to. I would very much like to discover how you came by all this information. But I'm not going to ask."

"There are holes in my story," Blomkvist said. "I need to fill them. Give me information and I won't try to compromise you."

"As Prime Minister I'm not in a position to deliver any such information. And Edklinth is on a very thin ice if he does so."

"Don't pull the wool over my eyes. I know what you want and you know what I want. If you give me information, then you'll be my sources – with all the enduring anonymity that implies. Don't misunderstand me . . . I'll tell the truth as I see it in what I publish. If you are involved, I will expose you and do everything I can to ensure that you are never re-elected. But as yet I have no reason to believe that is the case."

The Prime Minister glanced at Edklinth. After a moment he nodded. Blomkvist took it as a sign that the Prime Minister had just broken the law – if only of the more academic specie – by giving his consent to the sharing of classified information with a journalist.

"This can all be solved quite simply," Edklinth said. "I have my own investigative team and I decide for myself which colleagues to recruit for the investigation. You can't be employed by the investigation because that would mean you would be obliged to sign an oath of confidentiality. But I can hire you as an external consultant."

Berger's life had been filled with meetings and work around the clock the minute she had stepped into Morander's shoes.

It was not until Wednesday night, almost two weeks after Blomkvist had given her Cortez's research papers on Borgsjö, that she had time to address the issue. As she opened the folder she realized that her procrastination had also to do with the fact that she did not really want to face up to the problem. She already knew that however she dealt with it, calamity would be inevitable.

She arrived home in Saltsjöbaden at 7.00, unusually early, and it was only when she had to turn off the alarm in the hall that she remembered her husband was not at home. She had given him an especially long kiss that morning because he was flying to Paris to deliver some lectures and would not be back until the weekend. She had no idea where he was giving the lectures, or what they were about.

She went upstairs, ran the bath, and undressed. She took Cortez's folder with her and spent the next half hour reading through the whole story. She could not help but smile. The boy was going to be a formidable reporter. He was twenty-six years old and had been at *Millennium* for four years, right out of journalism school. She felt a certain pride. The story had *Millennium*'s stamp on it from beginning to end, every *t* was crossed, every *i* dotted.

But she also felt tremendously depressed. Borgsjö was a good man, and she liked him. He was soft-spoken, sharp-witted and charming, and he seemed unconcerned with prestige. Besides, he was her employer. *How in God's name could he have been so bloody stupid?*

She wondered whether there might be an alternative explanation or some mitigating circumstances, but she already knew it would be impossible to explain this away.

She put the folder on the windowsill and stretched out in the bath to ponder the situation.

Millennium was going to publish the story, no question. If she had still been there, she would not have hesitated. That *Millennium* had leaked the story to her in advance was nothing but a courtesy – they wanted to reduce the damage to her personally. If the situation had been reversed – if *S.M.P.* had made some damaging discovery about *Millennium*'s chairman of the board (who happened to be herself) – they would not have hesitated either.

Publication would be a serious blow to Borgsjö. The damaging thing was not that his company, Vitavara Inc., had imported goods from a company on the United Nations blacklist of companies using child labour – and in this case slave labour too, in the form of convicts, and undoubtedly some of these convicts were political prisoners. The really damaging thing was that Borgsjö knew about all this and still went on ordering toilets from Fong Soo Industries. It was a mark of the sort of greed that did not go down well with the Swedish people in the wake of the revelations about other criminal capitalists such as Skandia's former president.

Borgsjö would naturally claim that he did not know about the conditions at Fong Soo, but Cortez had solid evidence. If Borgsjö took that tack he would be exposed as a liar. In June 1997 Borgsjö had gone to Vietnam to sign the first contracts. He had spent ten days there on that occasion and been round the company's factories. If he claimed not to have known that many of the workers there were only twelve or thirteen years old, he would look like an idiot.

Cortez had demonstrated that in 1999, the U.N. commission on child labour had added Fong Soo Industries to its list of companies that exploit child labour, and that this had then been the subject of magazine articles. Two organizations against child labour, one of them the globally recognized International Joint Effort Against Child Labour in London, had written letters to companies that had placed orders with Fong Soo. Seven letters had been sent to Vitavara Inc., and two of those were addressed to Borgsjö personally. The organization in London had been very willing to supply the evidence. And Vitavara Inc. had not replied to any of the letters.

Worse still, Borgsjö went to Vietnam twice more, in 2001 and 2004, to renew the contracts. This was the *coup de grâce*. It would be impossible for Borgsjö to claim ignorance.

The inevitable media storm could lead only to one thing. If Borgsjö was smart, he would apologize and resign from his positions on various boards. If he decided to fight, he would be steadily annihilated.

Berger did not care if Borgsjö was or was not chairman of the board of Vitavara Inc. What mattered to her was that he was the board chairman of *S.M.P.* At a time when the newspaper was on the edge and a campaign of rejuvenation was under way, *S.M.P.* could not afford to keep him as chairman.

Berger's decision was made.

She would go to Borgsjö, show him the document, and thereby hope to persuade him to resign before the story was published.

If he dug in his heels, she would call an emergency board meeting, explain the situation, and force the board to dismiss Borgsjö. And if they did not, she would have to resign, effective immediately.

She had been thinking for so long that the bathwater was now cold. She showered and towelled herself and went to the bedroom to put on a dressing gown. Then she picked up her mobile and called Blomkvist. No answer. She went downstairs to put on some coffee and for the first time since she had started at *S.M.P.*, she looked to see whether there was a film on T.V. that she could watch to relax.

As she walked into the living room, she felt a sharp pain in her foot. She looked down and saw blood. She took another step and pain shot through her entire foot, and she had to hop over to an antique chair to sit down. She lifted her foot and saw to her dismay that a shard of glass had pierced her heel. At first she felt faint. Then she steeled herself and took hold of the shard and pulled it out. The pain was appalling, and blood gushed from the wound.

She pulled open a drawer in the hall where she kept scarves, gloves and hats. She found a scarf and wrapped it around her foot and tied it tight. That was not going to be enough, so she reinforced it with another improvised bandage. The bleeding had apparently subsided.

She looked at the bloodied piece of glass in amazement. *How did this get here?* Then she discovered more glass on the hall floor. *Jesus Christ . . .* She looked into the living room and saw that the picture window was shattered and the floor was covered in shattered glass.

She went back to the front door and put on the outdoor shoes she had kicked off as she came home. That is, she put on one shoe and stuck the toes of her injured foot into the other, and hopped into the living room to take stock of the damage.

Then she found the brick in the middle of the living-room floor.

She limped over to the balcony door and went out to the garden. Someone had sprayed in metre-high letters on the back wall:

WHORE

It was just after 9.00 in the evening when Figuerola held the car door open for Blomkvist. She went around the car and got into the driver's seat.

"Should I drive you home or do you want to be dropped off somewhere?"

Blomkvist stared straight ahead. "I haven't got my bearings yet, to be honest. I've never had a confrontation with a prime minister before."

Figuerola laughed. "You played your cards very well," she said. "I would never have guessed you were such a good poker player."

"I meant every word."

"Of course, but what *I* meant was that you pretended to know a lot more than you actually do. I realized that when I worked out how you identified me."

Blomkvist turned and looked at her profile.

"You wrote down my car registration when I was parked on the hill outside your building. You made it sound as if you knew what was being discussed at the Prime Minister's secretariat."

"Why didn't you say anything?" Blomkvist said.

She gave him a quick look and turned on to Grev Turegatan. "The rules of the game. I shouldn't have picked that spot, but there wasn't anywhere else to park. You keep a sharp eye on your surroundings, don't you?"

"You were sitting with a map spread out on the front seat, talking on the telephone. I took down your registration and ran a routine check. I check out every car that catches my attention. I usually draw a blank. In your case I discovered that you worked for Säpo."

"I was following Mårtensson."

"Aha. So simple."

"Then I discovered that you were tailing him using Susanne Linder at Milton Security."

"Armansky's detailed her to keep an eye on what goes on around my apartment."

"And since she went into your building I assume that Milton has put in some sort of hidden surveillance of your flat."

"That's right. We have an excellent film of how they break in and go through my papers. Mårtensson carries a portable photocopier with him. Have you identified Mårtensson's sidekick?"

"He's unimportant. A locksmith with a criminal record who's probably being paid to open your door."

"Name?"

"Protected source?"

"Naturally."

"Lars Faulsson. Forty-seven. Alias Falun. Convicted of safe-cracking in the '80s and some other minor stuff. Has a shop at Norrtull."

"Thanks."

"But let's save the secrets till we meet again tomorrow."

The meeting had ended with an agreement that Blomkvist would come to Constitutional Protection the next day to set in train an exchange of information. Blomkvist was thinking. They were just passing Sergels Torg in the city centre.

"You know what? I'm incredibly hungry. I had a late lunch and was going to make a pasta when I got home, but I was waylaid by you. Have you eaten?"

"A while ago."

"Take us to a restaurant where we can get some decent food."

"All food is decent."

He looked at her. "I thought you were a health-food fanatic."

"No, I'm a workout fanatic. If you work out you can eat whatever you want. Within reason."

She braked at the Klaraberg viaduct and considered the options. Instead of turning down towards Södermalm she kept going straight to Kungsholmen.

"I don't know what the restaurants are like in Söder, but I know an excellent Bosnian place at Fridhemsplan. Their *burek* is fantastic."

"Sounds good," Blomkvist said.

Salander tapped her way, letter by letter, through her report. She had worked an average of five hours each day. She was careful to express herself precisely. She left out all the details that could be used against her.

That she was locked up had turned out to be a blessing. She always had plenty of warning to put away her Palm when she heard the rattling of a key ring or a key being put in the lock.

I was about to lock up Bjurman's cabin outside
Stallarholmen when Carl-Magnus Lundin and Sonny
Nieminen arrived on motorbikes. Since they had
been searching for me in vain for a while on
behalf of Zalachenko and Niedermann, they were
surprised to see me there. Magge Lundin got off
his motorbike and declared, quote, *I think the
dyke needs some cock*, unquote. Both he and Nieminen
acted so threateningly that I had no choice but
to resort to my right of self-defence. I left
the scene on Lundin's motorbike which I then
abandoned at the shopping centre in Älvsjö.

There was no reason to volunteer the information that Lundin had called her a whore or that she had bent down and picked up Nieminen's P-83 Wanad and punished Lundin by shooting him in the foot. The

342

police could probably work that out for themselves, but it was up to them to prove it. She did not mean to make their job any easier by confessing to something that would lead to a prison sentence.

The text had grown to thirty-three pages and she was nearing the end. In some sections she was particularly reticent about details and went to a lot of trouble not to supply any evidence that could back up in any way the many claims she was making. She went so far as to obscure some obvious evidence and instead moved on to the next link in the chain of events.

She scrolled back and read through the text of a section where she told how Advokat Bjurman had violently and sadistically raped her. That was the part she had spent the most time on, and one of the few she had rewritten several times before she was satisfied. The section took up nineteen lines in her account. She reported in a matter-of-fact manner how he had hit her, thrown her on to her stomach on the bed, taped her mouth and handcuffed her. She then related how he had repeatedly committed acts of sexual violence against her, including anal penetration. She went on to report how at one point during the rape he had wound a piece of clothing – her own T-shirt – around her neck and strangled her for such a long time that she temporarily lost consciousness. Then there were several lines of text where she identified the implements he had used during the rape, which included a short whip, an anal plug, a rough dildo, and clamps which he attached to her nipples.

She frowned and studied the text. At last she raised the stylus and tapped out a few more lines of text.

```
On one occasion when I still had my mouth taped
shut, Bjurman commented on the fact that I had
several tattoos and piercings, including a ring
in my left nipple. He asked if I liked being
pierced and then left the room. He came back
with a needle which he pushed through my right
nipple.
```

- - - - - - - - - - -

The matter-of-fact tone gave the text such a surreal touch that it sounded like an absurd fantasy.

The story simply did not sound credible.

343

That was her intention.

At that moment she heard the rattle of the guard's key ring. She turned off the Palm at once and put it in the recess in the back of the bedside table. It was Giannini. She frowned. It was 9.00 in the evening and Giannini did not usually appear this late.

"Hello, Lisbeth."

"Hello."

"How are you feeling?"

"I'm not finished yet."

Giannini sighed. "Lisbeth, they've set the trial date for July 13."

"That's O.K."

"No, it's not O.K. Time is running out, and you're not telling me anything. I'm beginning to think that I made a colossal mistake taking on the job. If we're going to have the slightest chance, you have to trust me. We have to work together."

Salander studied her for a long moment. Finally she leaned her head back and looked up at the ceiling.

"I know what we're supposed to be doing. I understand Mikael's plan. And he's right."

"I'm not so sure about that."

"But I am."

"The police want to interrogate you again. A detective named Hans Faste from Stockholm."

"Let him interrogate me. I won't say a word."

"You have to hand in a statement."

Salander gave Giannini a sharp look. "I repeat: we won't say a word to the police. When we get to that courtroom the prosecutor won't have a single syllable from any interrogation to fall back on. All they'll have is the statement that I'm composing now, and large parts of it will seem preposterous. And they're going to get it a few days before the trial."

"So when are you actually going to sit down with a pen and paper and write this statement?"

"You'll have it in a few days. But it can't go to the prosecutor until just before the trial."

Giannini looked sceptical. Salander suddenly gave her a cautious smile. "You talk about trust. Can I trust you?"

"Of course you can."

"O.K., could you smuggle me in a hand-held computer so that I can keep in touch with people online?"

"No, of course not. If it were discovered I'd be charged with a crime and lose my licence to practise."

"But if someone else got one in . . . would you report it to the police?"

Giannini raised her eyebrows. "If I didn't know about it . . ."

"But if you did know about it, what would you do?"

"I'd shut my eyes. How about that?"

"This hypothetical computer is soon going to send you a hypothetical email. When you've read it I want you to come again."

"Lisbeth—"

"Wait. It's like this. The prosecutor is dealing with a marked deck. I'm at a disadvantage no matter what I do, and the purpose of the trial is to get me committed to a secure psychiatric ward."

"I know."

"If I'm going to survive, I have to fight dirty."

Finally Giannini nodded.

"When you came to see me the first time," Salander said, "you had a message from Blomkvist. He said that he'd told you almost everything, with a few exceptions. One of those exceptions had to do with the skills he discovered I had when we were in Hedestad."

"That's correct."

"He was referring to the fact that I'm extremely good with computers. So good that I can read and copy what's on Ekström's machine."

Giannini went pale.

"You can't be involved in this. And you can't use any of that material at the trial," Salander said.

"Hardly. You're right about that."

"So you know nothing about it."

"O.K."

"But someone else – your brother, let's say – could publish selected excerpts from it. You'll have to think about this possibility when you plan your strategy."

"I understand."

"Annika, this trial is going to turn on who uses the toughest methods."

"I know."

"I'm happy to have you as my lawyer. I trust you and I need your help."

"Hmm."

"But if you get difficult about the fact that I'm going to use unethical methods, then we'll lose the trial."

"Right."

"And if that were the case, I need to know now. I'd have to get myself a new lawyer."

"Lisbeth, I can't break the law."

"You don't have to break any law. But you do have to shut your eyes to the fact that I am. Can you manage that?"

Salander waited patiently for almost a minute before Annika nodded.

"Good. Let me tell you the main points that I'm going to put in my statement."

Figuerola had been right. The *burek* was fantastic. Blomkvist studied her carefully as she came back from the ladies'. She moved as gracefully as a ballerina, but she had a body like . . . hmm. Blomkvist could not help being fascinated. He repressed an impulse to reach out and feel her leg muscles.

"How long have you been working out?" he said.

"Since I was a teenager."

"And how many hours a week do you do it?"

"Two hours a day. Sometimes three."

"Why? I mean, I understand why people work out, but . . ."

"You think it's excessive."

"I'm not sure exactly what I think."

She smiled and did not seem at all irritated by his questions.

"Maybe you're just bothered by seeing a girl with muscles. Do you think it's a turn-off, or unfeminine?"

"No, not at all. It suits you somehow. You're very sexy."

She laughed.

"I'm cutting back on the training now. Ten years ago I was doing rock-hard bodybuilding. It was cool. But now I have to be careful that the muscles don't turn to fat. I don't want to get flabby. So I lift weights once a week and spend the rest of the time doing some cross-training, or running, playing badminton, or swimming, that sort of thing. It's exercise more than hard training."

"I see."

"The reason I work out is that it feels great. That's a normal phenomenon among people who do extreme training. The body produces a pain-suppressing chemical and you become addicted to it. If you don't run every day, you get withdrawal symptoms after a while.

You feel an enormous sense of wellbeing when you give something your all. It's almost as powerful as good sex."

Blomkvist laughed.

"You should start working out yourself," she said. "You're getting a little thick in the waist."

"I know," he said. "A constant guilty conscience. Sometimes I start running regularly and lose a couple of kilos. Then I get involved in something and don't get time to do it again for a month or two."

"You've been pretty busy these last few months. I've been reading a lot about you. You beat the police by several lengths when you tracked down Zalachenko and identified Niedermann."

"Lisbeth Salander was faster."

"How did you find out Niedermann was in Gosseberga?"

Blomkvist shrugged. "Routine research. I wasn't the one who found him. It was our assistant editor, well, now our editor-in-chief Malin Eriksson who managed to dig him up through the corporate records. He was on the board of Zalachenko's company, K.A.B Import."

"That simple . . ."

"And why did you become a Säpo activist?" he said.

"Believe it or not, I'm something as old-fashioned as a democrat. I mean, the police are necessary, and a democracy needs a political safeguard. That's why I'm proud to be working at Constitutional Protection."

"Is it really something to be proud of?" said Blomkvist.

"You don't like the Security Police."

"I don't like institutions that are beyond normal parliamentary scrutiny. It's an invitation to abuse of power, no matter how noble the intentions. Why are you so interested in the religion of antiquity?"

Figuerola looked at Blomkvist.

"You were reading a book about it on my staircase," he said.

"The subject fascinates me."

"I see."

"I'm interested in a lot of things. I've studied law and political science while I've worked for the police. Before that I studied both philosophy and the history of ideas."

"Do you have any weaknesses?"

"I don't read fiction, I never go to the cinema, and I watch only the news on T.V. How about you? Why did you become a journalist?"

"Because there are institutions like Säpo that lack parliamentary oversight and which have to be exposed from time to time. I don't really know. I suppose my answer to that is the same one you gave me: I believe in a constitutional democracy and sometimes it has to be protected."

"The way you did with Hans-Erik Wennerström?"

"Something like that."

"You're not married. Are you and Erika Berger together?"

"Erika Berger's married."

"So all the rumours about you two are nonsense. Do you have a girlfriend?"

"No-one steady."

"So the rumours might be true after all."

Blomkvist smiled.

Eriksson worked at her kitchen table at home in Årsta until the small hours. She sat bent over spreadsheets of *Millennium*'s budget and was so engrossed that Anton, her boyfriend, eventually gave up trying to have a conversation with her. He washed the dishes, made a late snack, and put on some coffee. Then he left her in peace and sat down to watch a repeat of *C.S.I.*

Malin had never before had to cope with anything more complex than a household budget, but she had worked alongside Berger balancing the monthly books, and she understood the principles. Now she was suddenly editor-in-chief, and with that role came responsibility for the budget. Sometime after midnight she decided that, whatever happened, she was going to have to get an accountant to help her. Ingela Oscarsson, who did the bookkeeping one day a week, had no responsibility for the budget and was not at all helpful when it came to making decisions about how much a freelancer should be paid or whether they could afford to buy a new laser printer that was not already included in the sum earmarked for capital investments or I.T. upgrades. In practice it was a ridiculous situation – *Millennium* was making a profit, but that was because Berger had always managed to balance an extremely tight budget. Instead of investing in something as fundamental as a new colour laser printer for 45,000 kronor, they would have to settle for a black-and-white printer for 8,000 instead.

For a moment she envied Berger. At *S.M.P.* she had a budget in which such a cost would be considered pin money.

Millennium's financial situation had been healthy at the last annual general meeting, but the surplus in the budget was primarily made up of the profits from Blomkvist's book about the Wennerström affair. The revenue that had been set aside for investment was shrinking alarmingly fast. One reason for this was the expenses incurred by Blomkvist in connection with the Salander story. *Millennium* did not have the resources to keep any employee on an open-ended budget with all sorts of expenses in the form of rental cars, hotel rooms, taxis, purchase of research material, new mobile telephones and the like.

Eriksson signed an invoice from Daniel Olsson in Göteborg. She sighed. Blomkvist had approved a sum of 14,000 kronor for a week's research on a story that was not now going to be published. Payment to an Idris Ghidi went into the budget under fees to sources who could not be named, which meant that the accountant would remonstrate about the lack of an invoice or receipt and insist that the matter have the board's approval. *Millennium* had paid a fee to Advokat Giannini which was supposed to come out of the general fund, but she had also invoiced *Millennium* for train tickets and other costs.

She put down her pen and looked at the totals. Blomkvist had blown 150,000 kronor on the Salander story, way beyond their budget. Things could not go on this way.

She was going to have to have a talk with him.

Berger spent the evening not on her sofa watching T.V., but in A. & E. at Nacka hospital. The shard of glass had penetrated so deeply that the bleeding would not stop. It turned out that one piece had broken off and was still in her heel, and would have to be removed. She was given a local anaesthetic and afterwards the wound was sewn up with three stitches.

Berger cursed the whole time she was at the hospital, and she kept trying to call her husband or Blomkvist. Neither chose to answer the telephone. By 10.00 she had her foot wrapped in a thick bandage. She was given crutches and took a taxi home.

She spent a while limping around the living room, sweeping up the floor. She called Emergency Glass to order a new window. She was in luck. It had been a quiet evening and they arrived within twenty minutes. But the living-room window was so big that they did not have the glass in stock. The glazier offered to board up the window with plywood for the time being, and she accepted gratefully.

As the plywood was being put up, she called the duty officer at Nacka Integrated Protection, and asked why the hell their expensive burglar alarm had not gone off when someone threw a brick through her biggest window.

Someone from N.I.P. came out to look at the damage. It turned out that whoever had installed the alarm several years before had neglected to connect the leads from the windows in the living room.

Berger was furious.

The man from N.I.P. said they would fix it first thing in the morning. Berger told him not to bother. Instead she called the duty officer at Milton Security and explained her situation. She said that she wanted to have a complete alarm package installed the next morning. *I know I have to sign a contract, but tell Armansky that Erika Berger called and make damn sure someone comes round in the morning.*

Then, finally, she called the police. She was told that there was no car available to come and take her statement. She was advised to contact her local station in the morning. *Thank you. Fuck off.*

Then she sat and fumed for a long time until her adrenaline level dropped and it began to sink in that she was going to have to sleep alone in a house without an alarm while somebody was running around the neighbourhood calling her a whore and smashing her windows.

She wondered whether she ought to go into the city to spend the night at a hotel, but Berger was not the kind of person who liked to be threatened. And she liked giving in to threats even less.

But she did take some elementary safety precautions.

Blomkvist had told her once how Salander had put paid to the serial killer Martin Vanger with a golf club. So she went to the garage and spent several minutes looking for her golf bag, which she had hardly even thought about for fifteen years. She chose an iron that she thought had a certain heft to it and laid it within easy reach of her bed. She left a putter in the hall and an 8-iron in the kitchen. She took a hammer from the tool box in the basement and put that in the master bathroom too.

She put the canister of Mace from her shoulder bag on her bedside table. Finally she found a rubber doorstop and wedged it under the bedroom door. And then she almost hoped that the moron who had called her a whore and destroyed her window would be stupid enough to come back that night.

By the time she felt sufficiently entrenched it was 1.00. She had to be at *S.M.P.* at 8.00. She checked her diary and saw that she had four meetings, the first at 10.00. Her foot was aching badly. She undressed and crept into bed.

Then, inevitably, she lay awake and worried.

Whore.

She had received nine emails, all of which had contained the word "whore", and they all seemed to come from sources in the media. The first had come from her own newsroom, but the source was a fake.

She got out of bed and took out the new Dell laptop that she had been given when she had started at *S.M.P.*

The first email – which was also the most crude and intimidating with its suggestion that she would be fucked with a screwdriver had come on May 16, a couple of weeks ago.

Email number two had arrived two days later, on May 18.

Then a week went by before the emails started coming again, now at intervals of about twenty-four hours. Then the attack on her home. Again, *whore.*

During that time Carlsson on the culture pages had received an ugly email purportedly sent by Berger. And if Carlsson had received an email like that, it was entirely possible that the emailer had been busy elsewhere too – that other people had got mail apparently from her that she did not know about.

It was an unpleasant thought.

The most disturbing was the attack on her house.

Someone had taken the trouble to find out where she lived, drive out here, and throw a brick through the window. It was obviously premeditated – the attacker had brought his can of spray paint. The next moment she froze when she realized that she could add another attack to the list. All four of her tyres had been slashed when she spent the night with Blomkvist at the Slussen Hilton.

The conclusion was just as unpleasant as it was obvious. She was being stalked.

Someone, for some unknown reason, had decided to harass her.

The fact that her home had been subject to an attack was understandable – it was where it was and impossible to disguise. But if her car had been damaged on some random street in Södermalm, her stalker must have been somewhere nearby when she parked it. They must have been following her.

CHAPTER 18

Thursday, 2.vi

Berger's mobile was ringing. It was 9.05.

"Good morning, Fru Berger. Dragan Armansky. I understand you called last night."

Berger explained what had happened and asked whether Milton Security could take over the contract from Nacka Integrated Protection.

"We can certainly install an alarm that will work," Armansky said. "The problem is that the closest car we have at night is in Nacka centre. Response time would be about thirty minutes. If we took the job I'd have to subcontract out your house. We have an agreement with a local security company, Adam Security in Fisksätra, which has a response time of ten minutes if all goes as it should."

"That would be an improvement on N.I.P., which doesn't bother to turn up at all."

"It's a family-owned business, a father, two sons, and a couple of cousins. Greeks, good people. I've known the father for many years. They handle coverage about 320 days a year. They tell us in advance the days they aren't available because of holidays or something else, and then our car in Nacka takes over."

"That works for me."

"I'll be sending a man out this morning. His name is David Rosin, and in fact he's already on his way. He's going to do a security assessment. He needs your keys if you're not going to be home, and he needs your authorization to do a thorough examination of your house, from top to bottom. He's going to take pictures of the entire property and the immediate surroundings."

"Alright."

"Rosin has a lot of experience, and we'll make you a proposal. We'll have a complete security plan ready in a few days which will include a personal attack alarm, fire security, evacuation and break-in protection."

"O.K."

"If anything should happen, we also want you to know what to do in the ten minutes before the car arrives from Fisksätra."

"Sounds good."

"We'll install the alarm this afternoon. Then we'll have to sign a contract."

Only after she had finished her conversation with Armansky did Berger realize that she had overslept. She picked up her mobile to call Fredriksson and explained that she had hurt herself. He would have to cancel the 10.00.

"What's happened?" he said.

"I cut my foot," Berger said. "I'll hobble in as soon as I've pulled myself together."

She used the toilet in the master bathroom and then pulled on some black trousers and borrowed one of Greger's slippers for her injured foot. She chose a black blouse and put on a jacket. Before she removed the doorstop from the bedroom door, she armed herself with the canister of Mace.

She made her way cautiously through the house and switched on the coffeemaker. She had her breakfast at the kitchen table, listening out for sounds in the vicinity. She had just poured a second cup of coffee when there was a firm knock on the front door. It was David Rosin from Milton Security.

Figuerola walked to Bergsgatan and summoned her four colleagues for an early morning conference.

"We've got a deadline now," she said. "Our work has to be done by July 13, the day the Salander trial begins. We have just under six weeks. Let's agree on what's most important right now. Who wants to go first?"

Berglund cleared his throat. "The blond man with Mårtensson. Who is he?"

"We have photographs, but no idea how to find him. We can't put out an A.P.B."

"What about Gullberg, then? There must be a story to track down there. We have him in the Secret State Police from the early '50s to 1964, when S.I.S. was founded. Then he vanishes."

Figuerola nodded.

"Should we conclude that the Zalachenko club was an association formed in 1964? That would be some time before Zalachenko even came to Sweden."

"There must have been some other purpose . . . a secret organization within the organization."

"That was after Stig Wennerström. Everyone was paranoid."

"A sort of secret spy police?"

"There are in fact parallels overseas. In the States a special group of internal spy chasers was created within the C.I.A. in the '60s. It was led by a James Jesus Angleton, and it very nearly sabotaged the entire C.I.A. Angleton's gang were as fanatical as they were paranoid – they suspected everyone in the C.I.A. of being a Russian agent. As a result the agency's effectiveness in large areas was paralysed."

"But that's all speculation . . ."

"Where are the old personnel files kept?"

"Gullberg isn't in them. I've checked."

"But what about a budget? An operation like this has to be financed."

The discussion went on until lunchtime, when Figuerola excused herself and went to the gym for some peace, to think things over.

Berger did not arrive in the newsroom until lunchtime. Her foot was hurting so badly that she could not put any weight on it. She hobbled over to her glass cage and sank into her chair with relief. Fredriksson looked up from his desk and she waved him in.

"What happened?" he said.

"I trod on a piece of glass and a shard lodged in my heel."

"That . . . wasn't so good."

"No. It wasn't good. Peter, has anyone received any more weird emails?"

"Not that I've heard."

"O.K. Keep your ears open. I want to know if anything odd happens around *S.M.P.*"

"What sort of odd?"

"I'm afraid some idiot is sending really vile emails and he seems to have targeted me. So I want to know if you hear of anything going on."

"The type of email Eva Carlsson got?"

"Right, but anything strange at all. I've had a whole string of crazy emails accusing me of being all kinds of things – and suggesting various perverse things that ought to be done to me."

Fredriksson's expression darkened. "How long has this been going on?"

"A couple of weeks. Keep your eyes peeled . . . So tell me, what's going to be in the paper tomorrow?"

"Well . . ."

"Well, *what*?"

"Holm and the head of the legal section are on the warpath."

"Why is that?"

"Because of Frisk. You extended his contract and gave him a feature assignment. And he won't tell anybody what it's about."

"He is forbidden to talk about it. My orders."

"That's what he says. Which means that Holm and the legal editor are up in arms."

"I can see that they might be. Set up a meeting with legal at 3.00. I'll explain the situation."

"Holm is not best pleased—"

"I'm not best pleased with Holm, so we're all square."

"He's so upset that he's complained to the board."

Berger looked up. *Damn it. I'm going to have to face up to the Borgsjö problem.*

"Borgsjö is coming in this afternoon and wants a meeting with you. I suspect it's Holm's doing."

"O.K. What time?"

"2.00," said Fredriksson, and he went back to his desk to write the midday memo.

Jonasson visited Salander during her lunch. She pushed away a plate of the health authority's vegetable stew. As always, he did a brief examination of her, but she noticed that he was no longer putting much effort into it.

"You've recovered nicely," he said.

"Hmm. You'll have to do something about the food at this place."

"What about it?"

"Couldn't you get me a pizza?"

"Sorry. Way beyond the budget."

"I was afraid of that."

"Lisbeth, we're going to have a discussion about the state of your health tomorrow—"

"Understood. And I've recovered nicely."

"You're now well enough to be moved to Kronoberg prison. I might be able to postpone the move for another week, but my colleagues are going to start wondering."

"You don't need to do that."

"Are you sure?"

She nodded. "I'm ready. And it had to happen sooner or later."

"I'll give the go-ahead tomorrow, then," Jonasson said. "You'll probably be transferred pretty soon."

She nodded.

"It might be as early as this weekend. The hospital administration doesn't want you here."

"Who could blame them."

"Er . . . that device of yours—"

"I'll leave it in the recess behind the table here." She pointed.

"Good idea."

They sat in silence for a moment before Jonasson stood up.

"I have to check on my other patients."

"Thanks for everything. I owe you one."

"Just doing my job."

"No. You've done a great deal more. I won't forget it."

Blomkvist entered police headquarters on Kungsholmen through the entrance on Polhemsgatan. Figuerola accompanied him up to the offices of the Constitutional Protection Unit. They exchanged only silent glances in the lift.

"Do you think it's such a good idea for me to be hanging around at police H.Q.?" Blomkvist said. "Someone might see us together and start to wonder."

"This will be our only meeting here. From now on we'll meet in an office we've rented at Fridhemsplan. We get access tomorrow. But this will be O.K. Constitutional Protection is a small and more or less self-sufficient unit, and nobody else at S.I.S. cares about it. And we're on a different floor from the rest of Säpo."

He greeted Edklinth without shaking hands and said hello to two colleagues who were apparently part of his team. They introduced themselves only as Stefan and Anders. He smiled to himself.

"Where do we start?" he said.

"We could start by having some coffee . . . Monica?" Edklinth said.

"Thanks, that would be nice," Figuerola said.

Edklinth had probably meant for her to serve the coffee. Blomkvist noticed that the chief of the Constitutional Protection Unit hesitated for only a second before he got up and brought the thermos over to the conference table, where place settings were already laid out. Blomkvist saw that Edklinth was also smiling to himself, which he took to be a good sign. Then Edklinth turned serious.

"I honestly don't know how I should be managing this. It must be the first time a journalist has sat in on a meeting of the Security Police. The issues we'll be discussing now are in very many respects confidential and highly classified."

"I'm not interested in military secrets. I'm only interested in the Zalachenko club."

"But we have to strike a balance. First of all, the names of today's participants must not be mentioned in your articles."

"Agreed."

Edklinth gave Blomkvist a look of surprise.

"Second, you may not speak with anyone but myself and Monica Figuerola. We're the ones who will decide what we can tell you."

"If you have a long list of requirements, you should have mentioned them yesterday."

"Yesterday I hadn't yet thought through the matter."

"Then I have something to tell you too. This is probably the first and only time in my professional career that I will reveal the contents of an unpublished story to a police officer. So, to quote you . . . I honestly don't know how I should be managing this."

A brief silence settled over the table.

"Maybe we—"

"What if we—"

Edklinth and Figuerola had started talking at the same time before falling silent.

"My target is the Zalachenko club," Blomkvist said. "You want to bring charges against the Zalachenko club. Let's stick to that."

Edklinth nodded.

"So, what have you got?" Blomkvist said.

Edklinth explained what Figuerola and her team had unearthed. He showed Blomkvist the photograph of Evert Gullberg with Colonel Wennerström.

357

"Good. I'll have a copy of that."

"It's in Åhlen's archive," Figuerola said.

"It's on the table in front of me. With text on the back," Blomkvist said.

"Give him a copy," Edklinth said.

"That means that Zalachenko was murdered by the Section."

"Murder, coupled with the suicide of a man who was dying of cancer. Gullberg's still alive, but the doctors don't give him more than a few weeks. After his suicide attempt he sustained such severe brain damage that he is to all intents and purposes a vegetable."

"And he was the person with primary responsibility for Zalachenko when he defected."

"How do you know that?"

"Gullberg met Prime Minister Fälldin six weeks after Zalachenko's defection."

"Can you prove that?"

"I can. The visitors' log of the government Secretariat. Gullberg arrived together with the then chief of S.I.S."

"And the chief has since died."

"But Fälldin is alive and willing to talk about the matter."

"Have you—"

"No, I haven't. But someone else has. I can't give you the name. Source protection."

Blomkvist explained how Fälldin had reacted to the information about Zalachenko and how he had travelled to the Hague to interview Janeryd.

"So the Zalachenko club is somewhere in this building," Blomkvist said, pointing at the photograph.

"Partly. We think it's an organization inside the organization. What you call the Zalachenko club cannot exist without the support of key people in this building. But we think that the so-called Section for Special Analysis set up shop somewhere outside."

"So that's how it works? A person can be employed by Säpo, have his salary paid by Säpo, and then in fact report to another employer?"

"Something like that."

"So who in the building is working for the Zalachenko club?"

"We don't know yet. But we have several suspects."

"Mårtensson," Blomkvist suggested.

Edklinth nodded.

"Mårtensson works for Säpo, and when he's needed by the Zala-chenko club he's released from his regular job," Figuerola said.

"How does that work in practice?"

"That's a very good question," Edklinth said with a faint smile. "Wouldn't you like to come and work for us?"

"Not on your life," Blomkvist said.

"I jest, of course. But it's a good question. We have a suspect, but we're unable to verify our suspicions just yet."

"Let's see . . . it must be someone with administrative authority."

"We suspect Chief of Secretariat Albert Shenke," Figuerola said.

"And here we are at our first stumbling block," Edklinth said. "We've given you a name, but we have no proof. So how do you intend to proceed?"

"I can't publish a name without proof. If Shenke is innocent he would sue *Millennium* for libel."

"Good. Then we are agreed. This co-operative effort has to be based on mutual trust. Your turn. What have you got?"

"Three names," Blomkvist said. "The first two were members of the Zalachenko club in the '80s."

Edklinth and Figuerola were instantly alert.

"Hans von Rottinger and Fredrik Clinton. Von Rottinger is dead. Clinton is retired. But both of them were part of the circle closest to Zalachenko."

"And the third name?" Edklinth said.

"Teleborian has a link to a person I know only as Jonas. We don't know his last name, but we do know that he was with the Zalachenko club in 2005 . . . We've actually speculated a bit that he might be the man with Mårtensson in the pictures from Café Copacabana."

"And in what context did the name Jonas crop up?"

Salander hacked Teleborian's computer, and we can follow the corre-spondence that shows how Teleborian is conspiring with Jonas in the same way he conspired with Björck in 1991.

"He gives Teleborian instructions. And now we come to another stumbling block," Blomkvist said to Edklinth with a smile. "I can prove my assertions, but I can't give you the documentation without revealing a source. You'll have to accept what I'm saying."

Edklinth looked thoughtful.

"Maybe one of Teleborian's colleagues in Uppsala. O.K. Let's start with Clinton and von Rottinger. Tell us what you know."

Borgsjö received Berger in his office next to the boardroom. He looked concerned.

"I heard that you hurt yourself," he said, pointing to her foot.

"It'll pass," Berger said, leaning her crutches against his desk as she sat down in the visitor's chair.

"Well . . . that's good. Erika, you've been here a month and I want us to have a chance to catch up. How do you feel it's going?"

I have to discuss Vitavara with him. But how? When?

"I've begun to get a handle on the situation. There are two sides to it. On the one hand, S.M.P. has financial problems and the budget is strangling the newspaper. On the other, S.M.P. has a huge amount of dead meat in the newsroom."

"Aren't there any positive aspects?"

"Of course there are. A whole bunch of experienced professionals who know how to do their jobs. The problem is the ones who won't let them do their jobs."

"Holm has spoken to me . . ."

"I know."

Borgsjö looked puzzled. "He has a number of opinions about you. Almost all of them are negative."

"That's O.K. I have a number of opinions about him too."

"Negative too? It's no good if the two of you can't work together—"

"I have no problem working with him. But he does have a problem with me." Berger sighed. "He's driving me nuts. He's very experienced and doubtless one of the most competent news chiefs I've come across. At the same time he's a bastard of exceptional proportions. He enjoys indulging in intrigue and playing people against each other. I've worked in the media for twenty-five years and I have never met a person like him in a management position."

"He has to be tough to handle the job. He's under pressure from every direction."

"Tough . . . by all means. But that doesn't mean he has to behave like an idiot. Unfortunately Holm is a walking disaster, and he's one of the chief reasons why it's almost impossible to get the staff to work as a team. He takes divide-and-rule as his job description."

"Harsh words."

"I'll give him one month to sort out his attitude. If he hasn't managed it by then, I'm going to remove him as news editor."

"You can't do that. It's not your job to take apart the operational organization."

Berger studied the chairman of the board.

"Forgive me for pointing this out, but that was exactly why you hired me. We also have a contract which explicitly gives me free rein to make the editorial changes I deem necessary. My task here is to rejuvenate the newspaper, and I can do that only by changing the organization and the work routines."

"Holm has devoted his life to *S.M.P.*"

"Right. And he's fifty eight with six years to go before retirement. I can't afford to keep him on as a dead weight all that time. Don't misunderstand me, Magnus. From the moment I sat down in that glass cage, my life's goal has been to raise *S.M.P.*'s quality as well as its circulation figures. Holm has a choice: either he can do things my way, or he can do something else. I'm going to bulldoze anyone who is obstructive or who tries to damage *S.M.P.* in some other way."

Damn . . . I've got to bring up the Vitavara thing. Borgsjö is going to be fired.

Suddenly Borgsjö smiled. "By God, I think you're pretty tough too."

"Yes, I am, and in this case it's regrettable since it shouldn't be necessary. My job is to produce a good newspaper, and I can do that only if I have a management that functions and colleagues who enjoy their work."

After the meeting with Borgsjö, Berger limped back to the glass cage. She felt depressed. She had been with Borgsjö for forty-five minutes without mentioning one syllable about Vitavara. She had not, in other words, been particularly straight or honest with him.

When she sat at her computer she found a message from <MikBlom@millennium.nu>. She knew perfectly well that no such address existed at Millennium. She opened the email:

```
YOU THINK THAT BORGSJÖ CAN SAVE YOU, YOU LITTLE
WHORE.  HOW DOES YOUR FOOT FEEL?
```

She raised her eyes involuntarily and looked out across the news-room. Her gaze fell on Holm. He looked back at her. Then he smiled.

It can only be someone at S.M.P.

The meeting at the Constitutional Protection Unit lasted until after 5.00, and they agreed to have another meeting the following week. Blomkvist could contact Figuerola if he needed to be in touch with S.I.S. before then. He packed away his laptop and stood up.

"How do I get out of here?" he asked.

"You certainly can't go running around on your own," Edklinth said.

"I'll show him out," Figuerola said. "Give me a couple of minutes, I just have to pick up a few things from my office." They walked together through Kronoberg park towards Fridhemsplan.

"So what happens now?" Blomkvist said.

"We stay in touch," Figuerola said.

"I'm beginning to like my contact with Säpo."

"Do you feel like having dinner later?"

"Bosnian again?"

"No, I can't afford to eat out every night. I was thinking of some-thing simple at my place."

She stopped and smiled at him.

"Do you know what I'd like to do now?" she said.

"No."

"I'd like to take you home and undress you."

"This could get a bit awkward."

"I know. But I hadn't thought of telling my boss."

"We don't know how this story's going to turn out. We could end up on opposite sides of the barricades."

"I'll take my chances. Now, are you going to come quietly or do I have to handcuff you?"

The consultant from Milton Security was waiting for Berger when she got home at around 7.00. Her foot was throbbing painfully, and she limped into the kitchen and sank on to the nearest chair. He had made coffee and he poured her some.

"Thanks. Is making coffee part of Milton's service agreement?"

He gave her a polite smile. David Rosin was a short, plump man in his fifties with a reddish goatee. "Thanks for letting me borrow your kitchen today."

"It's the least I could do. What's the situation?"

"Our technicians were here and installed a proper alarm. I'll show you how it works in a minute. I've also gone over every inch of your house from the basement to the attic and studied the area around it. I'll review your situation with my colleagues at Milton, and in a few days we'll present an assessment that we'll go over with you. But before that there are one or two things we ought to discuss."

"Go ahead."

"First of all, we have to take care of a few formalities. We'll work out the final contract later – it depends what services we agree on – but this is an agreement saying that you've commissioned Milton Security to install the alarm we put in today. It's a standard document saying that we at Milton require certain things of you and that we commit to certain things, client confidentiality and so forth."

"You require things of me?"

"Yes. An alarm is an alarm and is completely pointless if some nutcase is standing in your living room with an automatic weapon. For the security to work, we want you and your husband to be aware of certain things and to take certain routine measures. I'll go over the details with you."

"O.K."

"I'm jumping ahead and anticipating the final assessment, but this is how I view the general situation. You and your husband live in a detached house. You have a beach at the back of the house and a few large houses in the immediate vicinity. Your neighbours do not have an unobstructed view of your house. It's relatively isolated."

"That's correct."

"Therefore an intruder would have a good chance of approaching your house without being observed."

"The neighbours on the right are away for long periods, and on the left is an elderly couple who go to bed quite early."

"Precisely. In addition, the houses are positioned with their gables facing each other. There are few windows, and so on. Once an intruder comes on to your property – and it takes only five seconds to turn off the road and arrive at the rear of the house – then the view is completely blocked. The rear is screened by your hedge, the garage, and that large freestanding building."

"That's my husband's studio."

"He's an artist, I take it?"

"That's right. Then what?"

"Whoever smashed your window and sprayed your outside wall was able to do so undisturbed. There might have been some risk that the sound of the breaking window would be heard and someone might have reacted . . . but your house sits at an angle and the sound was deflected by the facade."

"I see."

"The second thing is that you have a large property here with a living area of approximately 250 square metres, not counting the attic and basement. That's eleven rooms on two floors."

"The house is a monster. It's my husband's old family home."

"There are also a number of different ways to get into the house. Via the front door, the balcony at the back, the porch on the upper floor, and the garage. There are also windows on the ground floor and six basement windows that were left without alarms by our predecessors. Finally, I could break in by using the fire escape at the back of the house and entering through the roof hatch leading to the attic. The trapdoor is secured by nothing more than a latch."

"It sounds as if there are revolving doors into the place. What do we have to do?"

"The alarm we installed today is temporary. We'll come back next week and do the proper installation with alarms on every window on the ground floor and in the basement. That's your protection against intruders in the event that you and your husband are away."

"That's good."

"But the present situation has arisen because you have been subject to a direct threat from a specific individual. That's much more serious. We don't know who this person is, what his motives are, or how far he's willing to go, but we can make a few assumptions. If it were just a matter of anonymous hate mail we would make a decreased threat assessment, but in this case a person has actually taken the trouble to drive to your house – and it's pretty far to Saltsjöbaden – to carry out an attack. That is worrisome."

"I agree with you there."

"I talked with Dragan today, and we're of the same mind: until we know more about the person making the threat, we have to play it safe."

"Which means—"

"First of all, the alarm we installed today contains two components. On the one hand it's an ordinary burglar alarm which is on when you're not at home, but it's also a sensor for the ground floor that you'll have to turn on when you're upstairs at night."

"Hmm."

"It's an inconvenience because you have to turn off the alarm every time you come downstairs."

"I've got you."

"Second, we changed your bedroom door today."

"You changed the whole door?"

"Yes. We installed a steel safety door. Don't worry . . . it's painted white and looks just like a normal bedroom door. The difference is that it locks automatically when you close it. To open the door from the inside you just have to press down the handle as on any normal door. But to open the door from the outside, you have to enter a three-digit code on a plate on the door handle."

"And you've done all this today . . ."

"If you're threatened in your home then you have a safe room into which you can barricade yourself. The walls are sturdy and it would take quite a while to break down that door even if your assailant had tools at hand."

"That's a comfort."

"Third, we're going to install surveillance cameras, so that you'll be able to see what's going on in the garden and on the ground floor when you're in the bedroom. That will be done later this week, at the same time as we install the movement detectors outside the house."

"It sounds like the bedroom won't be such a romantic place in the future."

"It's a small monitor. We can put it inside a wardrobe or a cabinet so that it isn't in full view."

"Thank you."

"Later in the week I'll change the doors in your study and in a downstairs room too. If anything happens you should quickly seek shelter and lock the door while you wait for assistance."

"Alright."

"If you trip the burglar alarm by mistake, then you'll have to call Milton's alarm centre immediately to cancel the emergency vehicle. To cancel it you'll have to give a password that will be registered with us.

If you forget the password, the emergency vehicle will come out anyway and you'll be charged a fee."

"Understood."

"Fourth, there are now attack alarms in four places inside the house. Here in the kitchen, in the hall, in your study upstairs, and in your bedroom. The attack alarm consists of two buttons that you press simultaneously and hold down for three seconds. You can do it with one hand, but you can't do it by mistake. If the attack alarm is sounded, three things will happen. First, Milton will send cars out here. The closest car will come from Adam Security in Fisksätra. Two strong men will be here in ten to twelve minutes. Second, a car from Milton will come down from Nacka. For that the response time is at best twenty minutes but more likely twenty-five. Third, the police will be alerted automatically. In other words, several cars will arrive at the scene within a short time, a matter of minutes."

"O.K."

"An attack alarm can't be cancelled the same way you would cancel the burglar alarm. You can't call and say that it was a mistake. Even if you meet us in the driveway and say it was a mistake, the police will enter the house. We want to be sure that nobody's holding a gun to your husband's head or anything like that. So you use the attack alarm, obviously, only when there is real danger."

"I understand."

"It doesn't have to be a physical attack. It could be if someone is trying to break in or turns up in the garden or something like that. If you feel threatened in any way, you should set off the alarm, but use your good judgement."

"I promise."

"I notice that you have golf clubs planted here and there around the house."

"Yes. I slept here alone last night."

"I myself would have checked into a hotel. I have no problem with you taking safety precautions on your own. But you ought to know that you could easily kill an intruder with a golf club."

"Hmm."

"And if you did that, you would most probably be charged with manslaughter. If you admitted that you put golf clubs around the place with the intent of arming yourself, it could also be classified as murder."

"If someone attacks me then the chances are that I do intend to bash in that person's skull."

"I understand you. But the point of hiring Milton Security is so that you have an alternative to doing that. You should be able to call for help, and above all you shouldn't end up in a situation where you have to bash in someone's skull."

"I'm only too happy to hear it."

"And, by the way, what would you do with the golf clubs if an intruder had a gun? The key to good security is all about staying one step ahead of anyone who means you harm."

"Tell me how I'm supposed to do that if I have a stalker after me?"

"You see to it that he never has a chance to get close to you. Now, we won't be finished with the installations here for a couple of days, and then we'll also have to have a talk with your husband. He'll have to be as safety-conscious as you are."

"He will be."

"Until then I'd rather you didn't stay here."

"I can't move anywhere else. My husband will be home in a couple of days. But both he and I travel fairly often, and one or other of us has to be here alone from time to time."

"I understand. But I'm only talking about a couple of days until we have all the installations ready. Isn't there a friend you could stay with?"

Berger thought for a moment about Blomkvist's apartment but remembered that just now it was not such a good idea.

"Thanks, but I'd rather stay here."

"I was afraid of that. In that case, I'd like you to have company here for the rest of the week."

"Well . . ."

"Do you have a friend who could come and stay with you?"

"Sure. But not at 7.30 in the evening if there's a nutcase on the prowl outside."

Rosin thought for a moment. "Do you have anything against a Milton employee staying here? I could call and find out if my colleague Susanne Linder is free tonight. She certainly wouldn't mind earning a few hundred kronor on the side."

"What would it cost exactly?"

"You'd have to negotiate that with her. It would be outside all our formal agreements. But I really don't want you to stay here alone."

"I'm not afraid of the dark."

"I didn't think you were or you wouldn't have slept here last night. Susanne Linder is also a former policewoman. And it's only temporary. If we had to arrange for bodyguard protection that would be a different matter – and it would be rather expensive."

Rosin's seriousness was having an effect. It dawned on her that here he was calmly talking of the possibility of there being a threat to her life. Was he exaggerating? Should she dismiss his professional caution? In that case, why had she telephoned Milton Security in the first place and asked them to install an alarm?

"O.K. Call her. I'll get the spare room ready."

It was not until after 10.00 p.m. that Figuerola and Blomkvist wrapped sheets around themselves and went to her kitchen to make a cold pasta salad with tuna and bacon from the leftovers in her fridge. They drank water with their dinner.

Figuerola giggled.

"What's so funny?"

"I'm thinking that Edklinth would be a little bit disturbed if he saw us right now. I don't believe he intended for me to go to bed with you when he told me to keep a close eye on you."

"You started it. I had the choice of being handcuffed or coming quietly," Blomkvist said.

"True, but you weren't very hard to convince."

"Maybe you aren't aware of this – though I doubt that – but you give off the most incredible sexual vibrations. Who on earth do you think can resist that?"

"You're very kind, but I'm not that sexy. And I don't have sex quite that often either."

"You amaze me."

"I don't, and I don't end up in bed with that many men. I was going out with a guy this spring. But it ended."

"Why was that?"

"He was sweet, but it turned into a wearisome sort of arm-wrestling contest. I was stronger than he was and he couldn't bear it. Are you the kind of man who'll want to arm-wrestle me?"

"You mean, am I someone who has a problem with the fact that you're fitter and physically stronger than I am? No, I'm not."

"Thanks for being honest. I've noticed that quite a few men get

368

interested, but then they start challenging me and looking for ways to dominate me. Especially if they discover I'm a policewoman."

"I'm not going to compete with you. I'm better than you are at what I do. And you're better than I am at what you do."

"I can live with that attitude."

"Why did you pick me up?"

"I give in to impulses. And you were one of them!"

"But you're an officer in Säpo, of all places, and we're in the middle of an investigation in which I'm involved . . ."

"You mean it was unprofessional of me. You're right. I shouldn't have done it. And I'd have a serious problem if it became known. Edklinth would go through the roof."

"I won't tell him."

"Very chivalrous."

They were silent for a moment.

"I don't know what this is going to turn into. You're a man who gets more than his fair share of action, as I gather. Is that accurate?"

"Yes, unfortunately. And I may not be looking for a steady girl-friend."

"Fair warning. I'm probably not looking for a steady boyfriend either. Can we keep it on a friendly level?"

"I think that would be best. Monica, I'm not going to tell anybody that we got together. But if we aren't careful I could end up in one hell of a conflict with your colleagues."

"I don't think so. Edklinth is as straight as a die. And we share the same objective, you and my people."

"We'll see how it goes."

"You had a thing with Lisbeth Salander too."

Blomkvist looked at her. "Listen . . . I'm not an open book for everyone to read. My relationship with Lisbeth is none of anyone's business."

"She's Zalachenko's daughter."

"Yes, and she has to live with that. But she isn't Zalachenko. There's the world of difference."

"I didn't mean it that way. I was wondering about your involvement in this story."

"Lisbeth is my friend. That should be enough of an explanation."

*

Linder from Milton Security was dressed in jeans, a black leather jacket and running shoes. She arrived in Saltsjöbaden at 9.00 in the evening and Rosin showed her around the house. She had brought a green military bag containing her laptop, a spring baton, a Mace canister, handcuffs and a toothbrush, which she unpacked in Berger's spare room.

Berger made coffee.

"Thanks for the coffee. You're probably thinking of me as a guest you have to entertain. The fact is, I'm not a guest at all. I'm a necessary evil that's suddenly appeared in your life, albeit just for a couple of days. I was in the police for six years and I've worked at Milton for four. I'm a trained bodyguard."

"I see."

"There's a threat against you and I'm here to be a gatekeeper so that you can sleep in peace or work or read a book or do whatever you feel like doing. If you need to talk, I'm happy to listen. Otherwise, I brought my own book."

"Understood."

"What I mean is that you should go on with your life and not feel as though you need to entertain me. Then I'd just be in the way. The best thing would be for you to think of me as a temporary work colleague."

"Well, I'm certainly not used to this kind of situation. I've had threats before, when I was editor-in-chief at *Millennium*, but then it was to do with my work. Right now it's some seriously unpleasant individual—"

"Who's got a hang-up about you in particular."

"Something along those lines."

"If we have to arrange full bodyguard protection, it'll cost a lot of money. And for it to be worth the cost, there has to be a very clear and specific threat. This is just an extra job for me. I'll ask you for 500 kronor a night to sleep here the rest of the week. It's cheap and far below what I would charge if I took the job for Milton. Is that O.K. with you?"

"It's completely O.K."

"If anything happens, I want you to lock yourself in your bedroom and let me handle the situation. Your job is to press the attack alarm. That's all. I don't want you underfoot if there's any trouble."

*

Berger went to bed at 11.00. She heard the click of the lock as she closed her bedroom door. Deep in thought, she undressed and climbed into bed.

She had been told not to feel obliged to entertain her "guest", but she had spent two hours with Linder at the kitchen table. She discovered that they got along famously. They had discussed the psychology that causes certain men to stalk women. Linder told her that she did not hold with psychological mumbo-jumbo. She thought the most important thing was simply to stop the bastards, and she enjoyed her job at Milton Security a great deal, since her assignments were largely to act as a counter-force to raging lunatics.

"So why did you resign from the police force?" Berger said.

"A better question would be why did I become a police officer in the first place."

"Why *did* you become a police officer?"

"Because when I was seventeen a close friend of mine was mugged and raped in a car by three utter bastards. I became a police officer because I thought, rather idealistically, that the police existed to prevent crimes like that."

"Well—"

"I couldn't prevent shit. As a policewoman I invariably arrived on the scene *after* a crime had been committed. I couldn't cope with the arrogant lingo on the squad. And I soon found out that some crimes are never even investigated. You're a typical example. Did you try to call the police about what happened?"

"Yes."

"And did they bother to come out here?"

"Not really. I was told to file a report at the local station."

"So now you know. I work for Armansky, and I come into the picture *before* a crime is committed."

"Mostly to do with women who are threatened?"

"I work with all kinds of things. Security assessments, bodyguard protection, surveillance and so on. But the work is often to do with people who have been threatened. I get on considerably better at Milton than on the force, although there's a drawback."

"What's that?"

"We are only there for clients who can pay."

As she lay in bed Berger thought about what Linder had said. Not everyone can afford security. She herself had accepted Rosin's proposal for several new doors, engineers, back-up alarm systems and everything else without blinking. The cost of all that work would be almost 50,000 kronor. But she could afford it.

She pondered for a moment her suspicion that the person threatening her had something to do with *S.M.P.* Whoever it was had known that she had hurt her foot. She thought of Holm. She did not like him, which added to her mistrust of him, but the news that she had been injured had spread fast from the second she appeared in the newsroom on crutches.

And she had the Borgsjö problem.

She suddenly sat up in bed and frowned, looking around the bedroom. She wondered where she had put Cortez's file on Borgsjö and Vitavara Inc.

She got up, put on her dressing gown and leaned on a crutch. She went to her study and turned on the light. No, she had not been in her study since . . . since she had read through the file in the bath the night before. She had put it on the windowsill.

She looked in the bathroom. It was not on the windowsill.

She stood there for a while, worrying.

She had no memory of seeing the folder that morning. She had not moved it anywhere else.

She turned ice-cold and spent the next five minutes searching the bathroom and going through the stacks of papers and newspapers in the kitchen and bedroom. In the end she had to admit that the folder was gone.

Between the time when she had stepped on the shard of glass and Rosin's arrival that morning, somebody had gone into her bathroom and taken *Millennium*'s material about Vitavara Inc.

Then it occurred to her that she had other secrets in the house. She limped back to the bedroom and opened the bottom drawer of the chest by her bed. Her heart sank like a stone. Everyone has secrets. She kept hers in the chest of drawers in her bedroom. Berger did not regularly write a diary, but there were periods when she had. There were also old love letters which she had kept from her teenage years.

There was an envelope with photographs that had been cool at the time, but . . . When Berger was twenty-five she had been involved in Club Xtreme, which arranged private dating parties for people who were into leather. There were photographs from various parties, and if she had been sober at the time, she would have recognized that she looked completely demented.

And – most disastrous of all – there was a video taken on holiday in the early '90s when she and Greger had been guests of the glass artist Torkel Bollinger at his villa on the Costa del Sol. During the holiday Berger had discovered that her husband had a definite bisexual tendency, and they had both ended up in bed with Torkel. It had been a pretty wonderful holiday. Video cameras were still a relatively new phenomenon. The movie they had playfully made was definitely not for general release.

The drawer was empty.

How could I have been so bloody stupid?

On the bottom of the drawer someone had spray-painted the familiar five-letter word.

CHAPTER 19

Friday, 3.vi – Saturday 4.vi

Salander finished her autobiography at 4.00 on Friday morning and sent a copy to Blomkvist via the Yahoo group [Idiotic_Table]. Then she lay quite still in bed and stared at the ceiling.

She knew that on Walpurgis Night she had had her twenty-seventh birthday, but she had not even reflected on the fact at the time. She was imprisoned. She had experienced the same thing at St Stefan's. If things did not go right for her there was a risk that she would spend many more birthdays in some form of confinement.

She was not going to accept a situation like that.

The last time she had been locked up she was scarcely into her teens. She was grown-up now, and had more knowledge and skills. She wondered how long it would take for her to escape and settle down safely in some other country to create a new identity and a new life for herself.

She got up from the bed and went to the bathroom where she looked in the mirror. She was no longer limping. She ran her fingers over her hip where the wound had healed to a scar. She twisted her arms and stretched her left shoulder back and forth. It was tight, but she was more or less healed. She tapped herself on the head. She supposed that her brain had not been too greatly damaged after being perforated by a bullet with a full-metal jacket.

She had been extraordinarily lucky.

Until she had access to a computer, she had spent her time trying to work out how to escape from this locked room at Sahlgrenska.

Then Dr Jonasson and Blomkvist had upset her plans by smuggling in her Palm. She had read Blomkvist's articles and brooded over what he had to say. She had done a risk assessment and pondered his plan, weighing her chances. She had decided that for once she was going to do as he advised. She would test the system. Blomkvist had convinced her that she had nothing to lose, and he was offering her a chance to escape in a very different way. If the plan failed, she would simply have to plan her escape from St Stefan's or whichever other nuthouse.

What actually convinced her to decide to play the game Blomkvist's way was her desire for revenge.

She forgave nothing.

Zalachenko, Björck and Bjurman were dead.

Teleborian, on the other hand, was alive.

So too was her brother, the so-called Ronald Niedermann, even though in reality he was not her problem. Certainly, he had helped in the attempt to murder and bury her, but he seemed peripheral. *If I run into him sometime, we'll see, but until such time he's the police's problem.*

Yet Blomkvist was right: behind the conspiracy there had to be others not known to her who had contributed to the shaping of her life. She had to put names and social security numbers to these people.

So she had decided to go along with Blomkvist's plan. That was why she had written the plain, unvarnished truth about her life in a cracklingly terse autobiography of forty pages. She had been quite precise. Everything she had written was true. She had accepted Blomkvist's reasoning that she had already been so savaged in the Swedish media by such grotesque libels that a little sheer nonsense could not possibly further damage her reputation.

The autobiography was a fiction in the sense that she had not, of course, told the *whole* truth. She had no intention of doing that.

She went back to bed and pulled the covers over her.

She felt a niggling irritation that she could not identify. She reached for a notebook, given to her by Giannini and hardly used. She turned to the first page, where she had written:

$$(x^3 + y^3 = z^3)$$

She had spent several weeks in the Caribbean last winter working herself into a frenzy over Fermat's theorem. When she came back to Sweden, before she got mixed up in the hunt for Zalachenko, she had kept on playing with the equations. What was maddening was that she had the feeling she had seen a solution . . . *that she had discovered a solution.*

But she could not remember what it was.

Not being able to remember something was a phenomenon unknown to Salander. She had tested herself by going on the Net and picking out random H.T.M.L. codes that she glanced at, memorized, and reproduced exactly.

She had not lost her photographic memory, which she had always considered a curse.

Everything was running as usual in her head.

Save for the fact that she thought she recalled seeing a solution to Fermat's theorem, but she could not remember how, when, or where.

The worst thing was that she did not have the least interest in it. Fermat's theorem no longer fascinated her. That was ominous. That was just the way she usually functioned. She would be fascinated by a problem, but as soon as she had solved it, she lost interest.

That was how she felt about Fermat. He was no longer a demon riding on her shoulder, demanding her attention and vexing her intellect. It was an ordinary formula, some squiggles on a piece of paper, and she felt no desire at all to engage with it.

This bothered her. She put down the notebook.

She should get some sleep.

Instead she took out her Palm again and went on the Net. She thought for a moment and then went into Armansky's hard drive, which she had not done since she got the hand-held. Armansky was working with Blomkvist, but she had not had any particular need to read what he was up to.

Absentmindedly she read his email.

She found the assessment Rosin had carried out of Berger's house. She could scarcely believe what she was reading.

Erika Berger has a stalker.

She found a message from Susanne Linder, who had evidently stayed at Berger's house the night before and who had emailed a report late that night. She looked at the time of the message. It had been sent just before 3.00 in the morning and reported Berger's discovery that diaries, letters and photographs, along with a video of a personal nature, had been stolen from a chest of drawers in her bedroom.

```
After discussing the matter with Fru Berger, we
determined that the theft must have occurred
during the time she was at Nacka hospital. That
left a period of c. 2.5 hours when the house
was empty, and the defective alarm from N.I.P.
was not switched on. At all other times either
Berger or David were in the house until the theft
was discovered.
```

Conclusion: Berger's stalker remained in her area
and was able to observe that she was picked up
by a taxi, also possibly that she was injured.
The stalker then took the opportunity to get into
the house.

Salander updated her download of Armansky's hard drive and then switched off the Palm, lost in thought. She had mixed feelings.

She had no reason to love Berger. She remembered still the humiliation she had felt when she saw her walk off down Hornsgatan with Blomkvist the day before New Year's Eve a year and a half ago.

It had been the stupidest moment of her life and she would never again allow herself those sorts of feelings.

She remembered the terrible hatred she had felt, and her desire to run after them and hurt Berger.

Embarrassing.

She was cured.

But she had no reason to sympathize with Berger.

She wondered what the video "of a personal nature" contained. She had her own film of a personal nature which showed how Advokat Bastard Bjurman had raped her. And it was now in Blomkvist's keeping. She wondered how she would have reacted if someone had broken into her place and stolen the D.V.D. Which Blomkvist by definition had actually done, even though his motives were not to harm her.

Hmm. An awkward situation.

Berger had not been able to sleep on Thursday night. She hobbled restlessly back and forth while Linder kept a watchful eye on her. Her anxiety lay like a heavy fog over the house.

At 2.30 Linder managed to talk Berger into getting into bed to rest, even if she did not sleep. She heaved a sigh of relief when Berger closed her bedroom door. She opened her laptop and summarized the situation in an email to Armansky. She had scarcely sent the message before she heard that Berger was up and moving about again.

At 7.30 she made Berger call *S.M.P.* and take the day off sick. Berger had reluctantly agreed and then fallen asleep on the living-room sofa in front of the boarded-up picture window. Linder spread a blanket over her. Then she made some coffee and called Armansky, explaining her presence at the house and that she had been called in by Rosin.

"Stay there with Berger," Armansky told her, "and get a couple of hours' sleep yourself."

"I don't know how we're going to bill this—"

"We'll work that out later."

Berger slept until 2.30. She woke up to find Linder sleeping in a recliner on the other side of the living room.

Figuerola slept late on Friday morning; she did not have time for her morning run. She blamed Blomkvist for this state of affairs as she showered and then rousted him out of bed.

Blomkvist drove to *Millennium*, where everyone was surprised to see him up so early. He mumbled something, made some coffee, and called Eriksson and Cortez into his office. They spent three hours going over the articles for the themed issue and keeping track of the book's progress.

"Dag's book went to the printer yesterday," Eriksson said. "We're going down the perfect-bound trade paperback route."

"The special issue is going to be called *The Lisbeth Salander Story*," Cortez said. "They're bound to move the date of the trial, but at the moment it's set for Wednesday, July 13. The magazine will be printed by then, but we haven't fixed on a distribution date yet. You can decide nearer the time."

"Good. That leaves the Zalachenko book, which right now is a nightmare. I'm calling it *The Section*. The first half is basically what's in the magazine. It begins with the murders of Dag and Mia, and then follows the hunt for Salander first, then Zalachenko, and then Niedermann. The second half will be everything that we know about the Section."

"Mikael, even if the printer breaks every record for us, we're going to have to send them the camera-ready copy by the end of this month – at the latest," Eriksson said. "Christer will need a couple of days for the layout, the typesetter, say, a week. So we have about two weeks left for the text. I don't know how we're going to make it."

"We won't have time to dig up the whole story," Blomkvist conceded. "But I don't think we could manage that even if we had a whole year. What we're going to do in this book is to state what happened. If we don't have a source for something, then I'll say so. If we're flying kites, we'll make that clear. So, we're going to write about what happened, what we can document, and what we believe to have happened."

"That's pretty vague," Cortez said.

Blomkvist shook his head. "If I say that a Säpo agent broke into my apartment and I can document it – and him – with a video, then it's documented. If I say that he did it on behalf of the Section, then that's speculation, but in the light of all the facts we're setting out, it's a reasonable speculation. Does that make sense?"

"It does."

"I won't have time to write all the missing pieces myself. I have a list of articles here that you, Henry, will have to cobble together. It corresponds to about fifty pages of book text. Malin, you're back-up for Henry, just as when we were editing Dag's book. All three of our names will be on the cover and title page. Is that alright with you two?"

"That's fine," Eriksson said. "But we have other urgent problems."

"Such as?"

"While you were concentrating on the Zalachenko story, we had a hell of a lot of work to do here—"

"You're saying I wasn't available?"

Eriksson nodded.

"You're right. I'm sorry."

"No need to apologize. We all know that when you're in the throes of a story, nothing else matters. But that won't work for the rest of us, and it definitely doesn't work for me. Erika had me to lean on. I have Henry, and he's an ace, but he's putting in an equal amount of time on your story. Even if we count you in, we're still two people short in editorial."

"Two?"

"And I'm not Erika. She had a routine that I can't compete with. I'm still learning this job. Monika is working her backside off. And so is Lottie. Nobody has a moment to stop and think."

"This is all temporary. As soon as the trial begins—"

"No, Mikael. It won't be over then. When the trial begins, it'll be sheer hell. Remember what it was like during the Wennerström affair. We won't see you for three months while you hop from one T.V. interview sofa to another."

Blomkvist sighed. "What do you suggest?"

"If we're going to run *Millennium* effectively during the autumn, we're going to need new blood. Two people at least, maybe three. We just don't have the editorial capacity for what we're trying to do, and . . ."

"And?"

"And I'm not sure that I'm ready to do it."

"I hear you, Malin."

"I mean it. I'm a damn good assistant editor – it's a piece of cake with Erika as your boss. We said that we were going to try this over the summer . . . well, we've tried it. I'm not a good editor-in-chief."

"Stuff and nonsense," Cortez said.

Eriksson shook her head.

"I hear what you're saying," Blomkvist said, "But remember that it's been an extreme situation."

Eriksson smiled at him sadly. "You could take this as a complaint from the staff," she said.

The operations unit of Constitutional Protection spent Friday trying to get a handle on the information they had received from Blomkvist. Two of their team had moved into a temporary office at Fridhemsplan, where all the documentation was being assembled. It was inconvenient because the police intranet was at headquarters, which meant that they had to walk back and forth between the two buildings several times a day. Even if it was only a ten-minute walk, it was tiresome. By lunchtime they already had extensive documentation of the fact that both Fredrik Clinton and Hans von Rottinger had been associated with the Security Police in the '60s and early '70s.

Von Rottinger came originally from the military intelligence service and worked for several years in the office that coordinated military defence with the Security Police. Clinton's background was in the air force and he began working for the Personal Protection Unit of the Security Police in 1967.

They had both left S.I.S.: Clinton in 1971 and von Rottinger in 1973. Clinton had gone into business as a management consultant, and von Rottinger had entered the civil service to do investigations for the Swedish Atomic Energy Agency. He was based in London.

It was late afternoon by the time Figuerola was able to convey to Edklinth with some certainty the discovery that Clinton's and von Rottinger's careers after they left S.I.S. were falsifications. Clinton's career was hard to follow. Being a consultant for industry can mean almost anything at all, and a person in that role is under no obligation to report his activities to the government. From his tax returns it was clear that he made good money, but his clients were for the most part corporations with head offices in Switzerland or Liechtenstein, so it was not easy to prove that his work was a fabrication.

Von Rottinger, on the other hand, had never set foot in the office in London where he supposedly worked. In 1973 the office building where he had claimed to be working was in fact torn down and replaced by an extension to King's Cross Station. No doubt someone made a blunder when the cover story was devised. In the course of the day Figuerola's team had interviewed a number of people now retired from the Swedish Atomic Energy Agency. Not one of them had heard of Hans von Rottinger.

"Now we know," Edklinth said. "We just have to discover what it was they really were doing."

Figuerola said: "What do we do about Blomkvist?"

"In what sense?"

"We promised to give him feedback if we uncovered anything about Clinton and von Rottinger."

Edklinth thought about it. "He's going to be digging up that stuff himself if he keeps at it for a while. It's better that we stay on good terms with him. You can give him what you've found. But use your judgement."

Figuerola promised that she would. They spent a few minutes making arrangements for the weekend. Two of Figuerola's team were going to keep working. She would be taking the weekend off.

Then she clocked out and went to the gym at St Eriksplan, where she spent two hours driving herself hard to catch up on lost training time. She was home by 7.00. She showered, made a simple dinner, and turned on the T.V. to listen to the news. But then she got restless and put on her running kit. She paused at the front door to think. *Bloody Blomkvist*. She flipped open her mobile and called his Ericsson.

"We found out a certain amount about von Rottinger and Clinton."

"Tell me."

"I will if you come over."

"Sounds like blackmail," Blomkvist said.

"I've just changed into jogging things to work off a little of my surplus energy," Figuerola said. "Should I go now or should I wait for you?"

"Would it be O.K. if I came after 9.00?"

"That'll be fine."

At 8.00 on Friday evening Salander had a visit from Dr Jonasson. He sat in the visitor's chair and leaned back.

"Are you going to examine me?" Salander said.

"No. Not tonight."

"O.K."

"We studied all your notes today and we've informed the prosecutor that we're prepared to discharge you."

"I understand."

"They want to take you over to the prison in Göteborg tonight."

"So soon?"

He nodded. "Stockholm is making noises. I said I had a number of final tests to run on you tomorrow and that I couldn't discharge you until Sunday."

"Why's that?"

"Don't know. I was just annoyed they were being so pushy."

Salander actually smiled. Given a few years she would probably be able to make a good anarchist out of Dr Anders Jonasson. In any case he had a penchant for civil disobedience on a private level.

"Fredrik Clinton," Blomkvist said, staring at the ceiling above Figuerola's bed.

"If you light that cigarette I'll stub it out in your navel," Figuerola said.

Blomkvist looked in surprise at the cigarette he had extracted from his jacket.

"Sorry," he said. "Could I borrow your balcony?"

"As long as you brush your teeth afterwards."

He tied a sheet around his waist. She followed him to the kitchen and filled a large glass with cold water. Then she leaned against the door frame by the balcony.

"Clinton first?"

"If he's still alive, he's the link to the past."

"He's dying, he needs a new kidney and spends a lot of his time in dialysis or some other treatment."

"But he's alive. We should contact him and put the question to him directly. Maybe he'll talk."

"No," Figuerola said. "First of all, this is a preliminary investigation and the police are handling it. In that sense, there is no 'we' about it. Second, you're receiving this information in accordance with your agreement with Edklinth, but you've given your word not to take any initiatives that could interfere with the investigation."

Blomkvist smiled at her. "Ouch," he said. "The Security Police are pulling on my leash." He stubbed out his cigarette.

"Mikael, this is not a joke."

Berger drove to the office on Saturday morning still feeling queasy. She had thought that she was beginning to get to grips with the actual process of producing a newspaper and had planned to reward herself with a weekend off – the first since she started at S.M.P. – but the discovery that her most personal and intimate possessions had been stolen, and the Borgsjö report too, made it impossible for her to relax.

During a sleepless night spent mostly in the kitchen with Linder, Berger had expected the "Poison Pen" to strike, disseminating pictures of her that would be deplorably damaging. What an excellent tool the Internet was for freaks. *Good grief . . . a video of me shagging my husband and another man – I'm going to end up on half the websites in the world.*

Panic and terror had dogged her through the night.

It took all of Linder's powers of persuasion to send her to bed.

At 8.00 she got up and drove to S.M.P. She could not stay away. If a storm was brewing, then she wanted to face it first before anyone else got wind of it.

But in the half-staffed Saturday newsroom everything was normal. People greeted her as she limped past the central desk. Holm was off today. Fredriksson was the acting news editor.

"Morning. I thought you were taking today off," he said.

"Me too. But I wasn't feeling well yesterday and I've got things I have to do. Anything happening?"

"No, it's pretty slow today. The hottest thing we've got is that the timber industry in Dalarna is reporting a boom, and there was a robbery in Norrköping in which one person was injured."

"Right. I'll be in the cage for a while."

She sat down, leaned her crutches against the bookshelves, and logged on. First she checked her email. She had several messages, but nothing from Poison Pen. She frowned. It had been two days now since the break-in, and he had not yet acted on what had to be a treasure trove of opportunities. *Why not? Maybe he's going to change tactics. Blackmail? Maybe he just wants to keep me guessing.*

She had nothing specific to work on, so she clicked on the strategy document she was writing for *S.M.P.* She stared at the screen for fifteen minutes without seeing the words.

She tried to call Greger, but with no success. She did not even know if his mobile worked in other countries. Of course she could have tracked him down with a bit of effort, but she felt lazy to the core. Wrong, she felt helpless and paralysed.

She tried to call Blomkvist to tell him that the Borgsjö folder had been stolen, but he did not answer.

By 10.00 she had accomplished nothing and decided to go home. She was just reaching out to shut down her computer when her I.C.Q. account pinged. She looked in astonishment at the icon bar. She knew what I.C.Q. was but she seldom chatted, and she had not used the program since starting at *S.M.P.*

She clicked hesitantly on Answer.

`<Hi Erika.>`

`<Hi. Who's this?>`

`<Private. Are you alone?>`

A trick? Poison Pen?

`<Who are you?>`

`<We met at Kalle Blomkvist's place when he came home from Sandhamn.>`

Berger stared at the screen. It took her a few seconds to make the connection. *Lisbeth Salander. Impossible.*

`<Are you there?>`

`<Yes.>`

`<No names. You know who I am?>`

`<How do I know this isn't a bluff?>`

`<I know how Mikael got that scar on his neck.>`

Berger swallowed. Only four people in the world knew how he had come by that scar. Salander was one of them.

`<But how can you be chatting with me?>`

`<I'm pretty good with computers.>`

Salander is a devil with computers. But how the hell is she managing to communicate from Sahlgrenska, where she's been isolated since April?

```
<I believe it.>
<Can I trust you?>
<How do you mean?>
<This conversation must not be leaked.>
```
She doesn't want the police to know she has access to the Net. Of course not. Which is why she's chatting with the editor-in-chief of one of the biggest newspapers in Sweden.

```
<No problem. What do you want?>
<To pay my debt.>
<What do you mean?>
<Millennium backed me up.>
<We were just doing our job.>
<No other publication did.>
<You're not guilty of what you were accused of.>
<You have a stalker.>
```
Berger's heart beat furiously.

```
<What do you know?>
<Stolen video. Break-in.>
<Correct. Can you help?>
```
Berger could not believe she was asking this question. It was absurd. Salander was in rehabilitation at Sahlgrenska and was up to her neck in her own problems. She was the most unlikely person Berger could turn to with any hope of getting help.

```
<Dunno. Let me try.>
<How?>
<Question. You think the creep is at S.M.P.?>
<I can't prove it.>
<Why do you think so?>
```
Berger thought for while before she replied.

```
<Just a hunch. It started when I began working at
S.M.P. Other people here have received crude messages
from the Poison Pen that looked as though they came
from me.>
<The Poison Pen?>
<My name for the creep.>
<O.K. Why did you become the object of Poison Pen's
attention?>
<No idea.>
```

\<Is there anything to suggest that it's personal?\>
\<How do you mean?\>
\<How many employees at S.M.P.?\>
\< 230 + or − including the publishing company.\>
\<How many do you know personally?\>
\<Can't say. I've met several journalists and other colleagues over the years.\>
\<Anyone you argued with before you went to S.M.P.?\>
\<Nobody that I can think of.\>
\<Anyone who might want to get revenge?\>
\<Revenge? What for?\>
\<Revenge is a powerful motive.\>

Berger stared at the screen as she tried to work out what Salander was getting at.

\<Still there?\>
\<Yes. Why do you ask about revenge?\>
\<I read Rosin's list of all the incidents you connect to Poison Pen.\>

Why am I not surprised?

\<And???\>
\<Doesn't feel like a stalker.\>
\<Why not?\>
\<Stalkers are driven by sexual obsession. This looks like somebody imitating a stalker. Screwdriver in your cunt ... hello? Pure parody.\>
\<You think?\>
\<I've seen real stalkers. They're considerably more perverted, coarse and grotesque. They express love and hate at the same time. This just doesn't feel right.\>
\<You don't think it's perverted enough?\>
\<No. Mail to Eva Karlsson all wrong. Somebody who wants to get even.\>
\<Wasn't thinking along those lines.\>
\<Not a stalker. Personal against you.\>
\<O.K. What do you suggest?\>
\<Can you trust me?\>
\<Maybe.\>
\<I need access to S.M.P.'s intranet.\>

<Whoa, hold everything.>

<Now. I'm going to be moved soon and lose the Net.>

Berger hesitated for ten seconds. Open up *S.M.P.* to ... what? A complete loony? Salander might be innocent of murder, but she was definitely not normal.

But what did she have to lose?

<How?>

<I have to load a program into your computer.>

<We have firewalls.>

<You have to help. Start the Internet.>

<Already logged on.>

<Explorer?>

<Yes.>

<I'll type an address. Copy and paste it into Explorer.>

<Done.>

<Now you see a list of programs. Click on Asphyxia Server and download it.>

Berger followed the instruction.

<Done.>

<Start Asphyxia. Click on Install and choose Explorer.>

It took three minutes.

<Done. O.K. Now you have to reboot your computer. We'll lose contact for a minute.>

<Got you.>

<When we reboot I'm going to copy your hard disk to a server on the Net.>

<O.K.>

<Restart. Talk to you soon.>

Berger stared in fascination at the screen as her computer slowly rebooted. She wondered whether she was mad. Then her I.C.Q. pinged.

<Hi again.>

<Hi.>

<It'll be faster if you do it. Start up the Internet and copy in the address I email you.>

<Done.>

<Now you see a question. Click on Start.>

<Done.>

<Now you're asked to name the hard disk. Call it
S.M.P.-2.>
<Done.>
<Go and get a coffee. This is going to take a
while.>

Figuerola woke at 8.00 on Saturday morning, about two hours later than usual. She sat up in bed and looked at the man beside her. He was snoring. *Well, nobody's perfect.*

She wondered where this affair with Blomkvist was going to lead. He was obviously not the faithful type, so no point in looking forward to a long-term relationship. She knew that much from his biography. Anyway, she was not so sure she wanted a stable relationship herself – with a partner and a mortgage and kids. After a dozen failed relationships since her teens, she was tending towards the theory that stability was overrated. Her longest had been with a colleague in Uppsala – they had shared an apartment for two years.

But she was not someone who went in for one-night stands, although she did think that sex was an underrated therapy for just about all ailments. And sex with Blomkvist, out of shape as he was, was just fine. More than just fine, actually. Plus, he was a good person. He made her want more.

A summer romance? A love affair? Was she in love?

She went to the bathroom and washed her face and brushed her teeth. Then she put on her shorts and a thin jacket and quietly left the apartment. She stretched and went on a 45-minute run out past Rålambshov hospital and around Fredhäll and back via Smedsudden. She was home by 9.00 and discovered Blomkvist still asleep. She bent down and bit him on the ear. He opened his eyes in bewilderment.

"Good morning, darling. I need somebody to scrub my back."

He looked at her and mumbled something.

"What did you say?"

"You don't need to take a shower. You're soaked to the skin already."

"I've been running. You should come along."

"If I tried to go at your pace, I'd have a heart attack on Norr Mälarstrand."

"Nonsense. Come on, time to get up."

He scrubbed her back and soaped her shoulders. And her hips. And her stomach. And her breasts. And after a while she had completely lost interest in her shower and pulled him back to bed.

They had their coffee at the pavement café beside Norr Mälarstrand.

"You could turn out to be a bad habit," she said. "And we've only known each other a few days."

"I find you incredibly attractive. But you know that already."

"Why do you think that is?"

"Sorry, can't answer that question. I've never understood why I'm attracted to one woman and totally uninterested in another."

She smiled thoughtfully. "I have today off," she said.

"But not me. I have a mountain of work before the trial begins, and I've spent the last three evenings with you instead of getting on with it."

"What a shame."

He stood up and gave her a kiss on the cheek. She took hold of his shirtsleeve.

"Blomkvist, I'd like to spend some more time with you."

"Same here. But it's going to be a little up and down until we put this story to bed."

He walked away down Hantverkargatan.

Berger got some coffee and watched the screen. For fifty-three minutes absolutely nothing happened except that her screen saver started up from time to time. Then her I.C.Q. pinged again.

```
<Ready. You have a whole bunch of shit on your
hard drive, including a couple of viruses.>
<Sorry. What's the next step?>
<Who's the admin for S.M.P.'s intranet?>
<Don't know. Probably Peter Fleming, our I.T.
manager.>
<Right.>
<What should I do?>
<Nothing. Go home.>
<Just like that?>
<I'll be in touch.>
<Should I leave the computer on?>
```

But Salander was gone from her I.C.Q. Berger stared at the screen in frustration. Finally she turned off the computer and went out to find a café where she could sit and think.

CHAPTER 20

Saturday, 4.vi

Blomkvist spent twenty-five minutes on the tunnelbana changing lines and going in different directions. He finally got off a bus at Slussen, jumped on the Katarina lift up to Mosebacke and took a circuitous route to Fiskargatan 9. He had bought bread, milk and cheese at the mini supermarket next to the County Council building and he put the groceries straight into the fridge. Then he turned on Salander's computer.

After a moment's thought he also turned on his Ericsson T10. He ignored his normal mobile because he did not want to talk to anyone who was not involved in the Zalachenko story. He saw that he had missed six calls in the past twenty-four hours: three from Cortez, two from Eriksson, and one from Berger.

First he called Cortez who was in a café in Vasastad and had a few details to discuss, nothing urgent.

Eriksson had only called, she told him, to keep in touch.

Then he called Berger, who was engaged.

He opened the Yahoo group [Idiotic_Table] and found the final version of Salander's autobiographical statement. He smiled, printed out the document and began to read it at once.

Salander switched on her Palm Tungsten T3. She had spent an hour infiltrating and charting the intranet at *S.M.P.* with the help of Berger's account. She had not tackled the Peter Fleming account because she did not need to have full administrator rights. What she was interested in was access to *S.M.P.*'s personnel files. And Berger's account had complete access to those.

She fervently wished that Blomkvist had been kind enough to smuggle in her PowerBook with a real keyboard and a 17″ screen instead of only the hand-held. She downloaded a list of everyone who worked at *S.M.P.* and began to check them off. There were 223 employees, 82 of whom were women.

She began by crossing off all the women. She did not exclude women on the grounds of their being incapable of such folly, but statistics showed that the absolute majority of people who harassed women were men. That left 141 individuals.

Statistics also argued that the majority of poison pen artists were either teenagers or middle-aged. Since S.M.P. did not have any teenagers on its staff, she drew an age curve and deleted everyone over fifty-five and under twenty-five. That left 103.

She thought for a moment. She did not have much time. Maybe not even twenty-four hours. She made a snap decision. At a stroke she eliminated all employees in distribution, advertising, the picture department, maintenance and I.T. She focused on a group of journalists and editorial staff, forty-eight men between the ages of twenty-six and fifty-four.

Then she heard the rattle of a set of keys. She turned off the Palm and put it under the covers between her thighs. This would be her last Saturday lunch at Sahlgrenska. She took stock of the cabbage stew with resignation. After lunch she would not, she knew, be able to work undisturbed for a while. She put the Palm in the recess behind the bedside table and waited while two Eritrean women vacuumed the room and changed her bedlinen.

One of the women was named Sara. She had regularly smuggled in a few Marlboro Lights for Salander during the past month. She had also given her a lighter, now hidden behind the bedside table. Salander gratefully accepted two cigarettes, which she planned to smoke by the vent window during the night.

Not until 2.00 p.m. was everything quiet again in her room. She took out the Palm and connected to the Net. She had intended to go straight back to S.M.P.'s administration, but she had also to deal with her own problems. She made her daily sweep, starting with the Yahoo group [Idiotic_Table]. She saw that Blomkvist had not uploaded anything new for three days and wondered what he was working on. *The son-of-a-bitch is probably out screwing around with some bimbo with big boobs.*

She then proceeded to the Yahoo group [The_Knights] and checked whether Plague had added anything. He had not.

Then she checked the hard drives of Ekström (some routine correspondence about the trial) and Teleborian.

Every time she accessed Teleborian's hard drive she felt as if her body temperature dropped a few degrees.

She found that he had already written her forensic psychiatric report, even though he was obviously not supposed to write it until after he had been given the opportunity to examine her. He had brushed up his prose, but there was nothing much new. She downloaded the report and sent it off to [Idiotic_Table]. She checked Teleborian's emails from the past twenty-four hours, clicking through one after another. She almost missed the terse message:

```
Saturday, 3.00 at the Ring in Central Station.
Jonas
```

Shit. Jonas. He was mentioned in a lot of correspondence with Teleborian. Used a hotmail account. Not identified.

Salander glanced at the digital clock on her bedside table. 2.28. She immediately pinged Blomkvist's I.C.Q. No response.

Blomkvist printed out the 220 pages of the manuscript that were finished. Then he shut off the computer and sat down at Salander's kitchen table with an editing pencil.

He was pleased with the text. But there was still a gigantic gaping hole. How could he find the remainder of the Section? Eriksson might be right: it might be impossible. He was running out of time.

Salander swore in frustration and pinged Plague. He did not answer either. She looked again at the clock. 2.30.

She sat on the edge of the bed and tried Cortez next and then Eriksson. *Saturday. Everybody's off work.* 2.32.

Then she tried to reach Berger. No luck. *I told her to go home. Shit.* 2.33.

She should be able to send a text message to Blomkvist's mobile . . . but it was tapped. She tugged her lip.

Finally in desperation she rang for the nurse.

It was 2.35 when she heard the key in the lock and Nurse Agneta looked in on her.

"Hello. Are you O.K.?"

"Is Dr Jonasson on duty?"

"Aren't you feeling well?"

"I feel fine. But I need to have a few words with him. If possible."

"I saw him a little while ago. What's it about?"

"I just have to talk to him."

Nurse Agneta frowned. Lisbeth Salander had seldom rung for a nurse if she did not have a severe headache or some other equally serious problem. She never pestered them for anything and had never before asked to speak to a specific doctor. But Nurse Agneta had noticed that Dr Jonasson had spent time with the patient who was under arrest and otherwise seemed withdrawn from the world. It was possible that he had established some sort of rapport.

"I'll find out if he has time," Nurse Agneta said gently, and closed the door. And then locked it. It was 2.36, and then the clock clicked over to 2.37.

Salander got up from the edge of the bed and went to the window. She kept an eye on the clock. 2.39. 2.40.

At 2.44 she heard steps in the corridor and the rattle of the Securitas guard's key ring. Jonasson gave her an inquisitive glance and stopped in his tracks when he saw her desperate look.

"Has something happened?"

"Something is happening *right now*. Have you got a mobile on you?"

"A what?"

"A mobile. I have to make a call."

Jonasson looked over his shoulder at the door.

"Anders – I need a mobile. *Now!*"

When he heard the desperation in her voice he dug into his inside pocket and handed her his Motorola. Salander grabbed it from him. She could not call Blomkvist because he had not given her the number of his Ericsson T10. It had never come up, and he had never supposed that she would be able to call him from her isolation. She hesitated a tenth of a second and punched in Berger's number. It rang three times before Berger answered.

Berger was in her B.M.W. half a mile from home in Saltsjöbaden when her mobile rang.

"Berger."

"Salander. No time to explain. Have you got the number of Mikael's second mobile? The one that's not tapped."

"Yes."

Salander had already surprised her once today.

"Call him. Now! Teleborian is meeting Jonas at the Ring in Central Station at 3.00."

"What's—"

"Just hurry. Teleborian. Jonas. The Ring in Central Station. 3.00. He has fifteen minutes."

Salander flipped the mobile shut so that Berger would not be tempted to waste precious seconds with unnecessary questions.

Berger pulled over to the curb. She reached for the address book in her bag and found the number Blomkvist had given her the night they met at Samir's Cauldron.

Blomkvist heard his mobile beeping. He got up from the kitchen table, went to Salander's office and picked up the telephone from the desk.

"Yes?"

"Erika."

"Hi."

"Teleborian is meeting Jonas at the Ring in Central Station at 3.00. You've only got a few minutes."

"What? What? What?"

"Teleborian—"

"I heard you. How do you know about that?"

"Stop arguing and make it snappy."

Mikael glanced at the clock. 2.47. "Thanks. Bye."

He grabbed his laptop case and took the stairs instead of waiting for the lift. As he ran he called Cortez on his T10.

"Cortez."

"Where are you now?"

"At the Academy bookshop."

"Teleborian is meeting Jonas at the Ring in Central Station at 3.00. I'm on my way, but you're closer."

"Oh, boy. I'm on my way."

Blomkvist jogged down to Götgatan and sped up towards Slussen. When he reached Slussplan he was badly out of breath. Maybe Figuerola had a point. He was not going to make it. He looked about for a taxi.

*

Salander handed back the mobile to Dr Jonasson.

"Thanks," she said.

"Teleborian?" Jonasson could not help overhearing the name.

She met his gaze. "Teleborian is a really, really bad bastard. You have no idea."

"No, but I could see that something happened just now that got you more agitated than I've seen you in all the time you've been in my care. I hope you know what you're doing."

Salander gave Jonasson a lopsided smile.

"You should have the answer to that question quite soon," she said.

Cortez left the Academy bookshop running like a madman. He crossed Sveavägen on the viaduct at Mäster Samuelsgatan and went straight down to Klara Norra, where he turned up the Klaraberg viaduct and across Vasagatan. He flew across Klarabergsgatan between a bus and two cars, one of whose drivers punched his windscreen in fury, and through the doors of Central Station as the station clock ticked over to 3.00 sharp.

He took the escalator three steps at a time down to the main ticket hall, and jogged past the Pocket bookshop before slowing down so as not to attract attention. He scanned every face of every person standing or walking near the Ring.

He did not see Teleborian or the man Malm had photographed outside Café Copacabana, whom they believed to be Jonas. He looked back at the clock. 3.01. He was gasping as if he had just run a marathon.

He took a chance and hurried across the hall and out through the doors on to Vasagatan. He stopped and looked about him, checking one face after another, as far as his eyes could see. No Teleborian. No Jonas.

He turned back into the station. 3.03. The Ring area was almost deserted.

Then he looked up and got a split second's glimpse of Teleborian's dishevelled profile and goatee as he came out of Pressbyrån on the other side of the ticket hall. A second later the man from Malm's photograph materialized at Teleborian's side. *Jonas.* They crossed the concourse and went out on to Vasagatan by the north door.

Cortez exhaled in relief. He wiped the sweat from his brow with the back of his hand and set off in pursuit of the two men.

Blomkvist's taxi got to Central Station at 3.07. He walked rapidly into the ticket hall, but he could see neither Teleborian nor anyone looking like they might be Jonas. Nor Cortez for that matter.

He was about to call Cortez when the T10 rang in his hand.

"I've got them. They're sitting in the Tre Remmare pub on Vasagatan by the stairs down to the Akalla line."

"Thanks, Henry. Where are you?"

"I'm at the bar. Having my afternoon beer. I earned it."

"Very good. They know what I look like, so I'll stay out of it. I don't suppose you have any chance of hearing what they're saying."

"Not a hope. I can only see Jonas' back and that bloody psycho-analyst mumbles when he speaks, so I can't even see his lips move."

"I get it."

"But we may have a problem."

"What's that?"

"Jonas has put his wallet and mobile on the table. And he put his car keys on top of the wallet."

"O.K. I'll handle it."

Figuerola's mobile played out the theme tune from *Once Upon a Time in the West*. She put down her book about God in antiquity. It did not seem as though she would ever be able to finish it

"Hi. It's Mikael. What are you up to?"

"I'm sitting at home sorting through my collection of photographs of old lovers. I was ignominiously ditched earlier today."

"Do you have your car nearby?"

"The last time I checked it was in the parking space outside."

"Good. Do you feel like an afternoon on the town?"

"Not particularly. What's going on?"

"A psychiatrist called Teleborian is having a beer with an under-cover agent – code name Jonas – down on Vasagatan. And since I'm co-operating with your Stasi-style bureaucracy, I thought you might be amused to tag along."

Figuerola was on her feet and reaching for her car keys.

"This is not your little joke, is it?"

"Hardly. And Jonas has his car keys on the table in front of him."

"I'm on my way."

Eriksson did not answer the telephone, but Blomkvist got lucky and caught Karim, who had been at Åhlens department store buying a birthday present for her husband. He asked her to please – on overtime – hurry over to the pub as back-up for Cortez. Then he called Cortez.

"Here's the plan. I'll have a car in place in five minutes. It'll be on Järnvägsgatan, down the street from the pub. Lottie is going to join you in a few minutes as back-up."

"Good."

"When they leave the pub, you tail Jonas. Keep me posted by mobile. As soon as you see him approach a car, we have to know. Lottie will follow Teleborian. If we don't get there in time, make a note of his registration number."

"O.K."

Figuerola parked beside the Nordic Light Hotel next to the Arlanda Express platforms. Blomkvist opened the driver's door a minute later.

"Which pub are they in?"

Blomkvist told her.

"I have to call for support."

"I'd rather you didn't. We've got them covered. Too many cooks might wreck the whole dish."

Figuerola gave him a sceptical look. "And how did you know that this meeting was going to take place?"

"I have to protect my source. Sorry."

"Do you have your own bloody intelligence service at *Millennium*?" she burst out.

Blomkvist looked pleased. It was cool to outdo Säpo in their own field of expertise.

In fact he did not have the slightest idea how Berger came to call him out of the blue to tell him of the meeting. She had not had access to ongoing editorial work at *Millennium* since early April. She knew about Teleborian, to be sure, but Jonas had not come into the picture until May. As far as he knew, Berger had not even known of his existence, let alone that he was the focus of intense speculation both at Säpo and *Millennium*.

He needed to talk to Berger.

Salander pressed her lips together and looked at the screen of her handheld. After using Jonasson's mobile, she had pushed all thoughts of the Section to one side and concentrated on Berger's problem. She had next, after careful consideration, eliminated all the men in the twenty-six to fifty-four age group who were married. She was working with a broad brush, of that she was perfectly aware. The selection was scarcely based on any statistical, sociological or scientific rationale. Poison Pen might easily be a married man with five children and a dog. He might also be a man who worked in maintenance. "He" could even be a woman.

She simply needed to prune the number of names on the list, and her group was now down from forty-eight to eighteen since her latest cut. The list was made up largely of the better-known reporters, managers or middle managers aged thirty-five or older. If she did not find anything of interest in that group, she could always widen the net again.

At 4.00 she logged on to Hacker Republic and uploaded the list to Plague. He pinged her a few minutes later.

<18 names. What is this?>

<A little project on the side. Consider it a training exercise.>

<O.K. ...I guess.>

<One of the guys on the list is a tosser. Find him.>

<What are the parameters?>

<Have to work fast. Tomorrow they're pulling the plug on me. Need to find him before then.>

She outlined the Poison Pen situation.

<Is there any profit in this?>

<Yes. I won't come out to the Swamp and set your place on fire.>

<Would you really?>

<I pay you every time I ask you to do something for me. This isn't for me. View it as a tax write-off.>

<You're beginning to exhibit signs of a social conscience.>

<Oh yeah?>

She sent him the access codes for *S.M.P.*'s newsroom and then logged off from I.C.Q.

It was 4.20 before Cortez called.

"They're showing signs of leaving."

"We're ready."

Silence.

"They're going their separate ways outside the pub. Jonas heading north. Teleborian to the south. Lottie's going after him."

Blomkvist raised a finger and pointed as Jonas flashed past them on Vasagatan. Figuerola nodded and started the engine. Seconds later Blomkvist could also see Cortez.

"He's crossing Vasagatan, heading towards Kungsgatan," Cortez said into his mobile.

"Keep your distance so he doesn't spot you."

"Quite a few people out."

Silence.

"He's turning north on Kungsgatan."

"North on Kungsgatan," Blomkvist said.

Figuerola changed gear and turned up Vasagatan. They were stopped by a red light.

"Where is he now?" Blomkvist said as they turned on to Kungsgatan.

"Opposite P.U.B. department store. He's walking fast. Whoops, he's turned up Drottninggatan heading north."

"Drottninggatan heading north," Blomkvist said.

"Right," Figuerola said, making an illegal turn on to Klara Norra and heading towards Olof Palmes Gata. She turned and braked outside the S.I.F. building. Jonas crossed Olof Palmes Gata and turned up towards Sveavägen. Cortez stayed on the other side of the street.

"He turned east—"

"We can see you both."

"He's turning down Holländargatan. *Hello* . . . Car. Red Audi."

"Car," Blomkvist said, writing down the registration number Cortez read off to him.

"Which way is he facing?" Figuerola said.

399

"Facing south," Cortez reported. "He's pulling out in front of you on Olof Palmes Gata . . . *now*."

Monica was already on her way and passing Drottninggatan. She signalled and headed off a couple of pedestrians who tried to sneak across even though their light was red.

"Thanks, Henry. We'll take him from here."

The red Audi turned south on Sveavägen. As Figuerola followed she flipped open her mobile with her left hand and punched in a number.

"Could I get an owner of a red Audi?" she said, rattling off the number.

"Jonas Sandberg, born 1971. What did you say? Helsingörsgatan, Kista. Thanks."

Blomkvist wrote down the information.

They followed the red Audi via Hamngatan to Strandvägen and then straight up to Artillerigatan. Jonas parked a block away from the Armémuseum. He walked across the street and through the front door of an 1890s building.

"Interesting," Figuerola said, turning to Blomkvist.

Jonas Sandberg had entered a building that was only a block away from the apartment the Prime Minister had borrowed for their private meeting.

"Nicely done," Figuerola said.

Just then Karim called and told them that Teleborian had gone up on to Klarabergsgatan via the escalators in Central Station and from there to police headquarters on Kungsholmen.

"Police headquarters at 5.00 on a Saturday afternoon?"

Figuerola and Blomkvist exchanged a sceptical look. Monica pondered this turn of events for a few seconds. Then she picked up her mobile and called Criminal Inspector Jan Bublanski.

"Hello, it's Monica from S.I.S. We met on Norr Mälarstrand a while back."

"What do you want?" Bublanski said.

"Have you got anybody on duty this weekend?"

"Modig," Bublanski said.

"I need a favour. Do you know if she's at headquarters?"

"I doubt it. It's beautiful weather and Saturday afternoon."

"Could you possibly reach her or anyone else on the investigative team who might be able to take a look in Prosecutor Ekström's corridor . . . to see if there's a meeting going on in his office at the moment."

"What sort of meeting?"

"I can't explain just yet. I just need to know if he has a meeting with anybody right now. And if so, who."

"You want me to spy on a prosecutor who happens to be my superior?"

Figuerola raised her eyebrows. Then she shrugged. "Yes, I do."

"I'll do what I can," he said and hung up.

Sonja Modig was closer to police headquarters than Bublanski had thought. She was having coffee with her husband on the balcony of a friend's place in Vasastaden. Their children were away with her parents who had taken them on a week's holiday, and they planned to do something as old-fashioned as have a bite to eat and go to the movies.

Bublanski explained why he was calling.

"And what sort of excuse would I have to barge in on Ekström?" Modig asked.

"I promised to give him an update on Niedermann yesterday, but in fact I forgot to deliver it to his office before I left. It's on my desk."

"O.K.," said Modig. She looked at her husband and her friend. "I have to go in to H.Q. I'll take the car and with a little luck I'll be back in an hour."

Her husband sighed. Her friend sighed.

"I'm on call this weekend," Modig said in apology.

She parked on Bergsgatan, took the lift up to Bublanski's office, and picked up the three A4 pages that comprised the meagre results of their search for Niedermann. Not much to hang on the Christmas tree, she thought.

She took the stairs up to the next floor and stopped at the door to the corridor. Headquarters was almost deserted on this summer afternoon. She was not exactly sneaking around. She was just walking very quietly. She stopped outside Ekström's closed door. She heard voices and all of a sudden her courage deserted her. She felt a fool. In any normal situation she would have knocked on the door, pushed it open and exclaimed, "Hello! So you're still here?" and then sailed right in. Now it seemed all wrong.

She looked around.

Why had Bublanski called her? What was this meeting about?

She glanced across the corridor. Opposite Ekström's office was a conference room big enough for ten people. She had sat through a number of presentations there herself. She went into the room and closed the door. The blinds were down, and the glass partition to the corridor was covered by curtains. It was dark. She pulled up a chair and sat down, then opened the curtains a crack so that she would have a view of the corridor.

She felt uneasy. If anyone opened the door she would have quite a problem explaining what she was doing there. She took out her mobile and looked at the time display. Just before 6.00. She changed the ring to silent and leaned back in her chair, watching the door of Ekström's office.

At 7.00 Plague pinged Salander.

<O.K. I'm the admin for S.M.P.>

<Where?>

He sent over a U.R.L.

<We won't be able to make it in 24 hours. Even if we have email addresses for all 18, it's going to take days to hack their home P.C.s. Most probably aren't even online on a Saturday night.>

<Concentrate on their home P.C.s and I'll take care of the ones at S.M.P.>

<I thought of that. Your Palm is a bit limited. Anything you want me to focus on?>

<No. Just try them.>

<O.K.>

<Plague?>

<Yeah.>

<If we don't find anything by tomorrow I want you to keep at it.>

<O.K.>

<In which case I'll pay you.>

<Forget about it. This is just fun.>

She logged out and went to the U.R.L. where Plague had uploaded all the administrator rights for S.M.P. She started by checking whether Fleming was online and at work. He was not. So she borrowed his identity and went into S.M.P.'s mail server. That way she could look

402

at all the activity in the email system, even messages that had long since been deleted from individual accounts.

She started with Ernst Teodor Billing, one of the night editors at *S.M.P.*, forty-three years old. She opened his mail and began to click back in time. She spent about two seconds on each message, just long enough to get an idea of who sent it and what it was about. After a few minutes she had worked out what was routine mail in the form of daily memos, schedules and other uninteresting stuff. She started to scroll past these.

She went through three months' worth of messages one by one. Then she skipped month to month and read only the subject lines, opening the message only if it was something that caught her attention. She learned that Billing was going out with a woman named Sofia and that he used an unpleasant tone with her. She saw that this was nothing unusual, since Billing took an unpleasant tone with most of the people to whom he wrote messages – reporters, layout artists and others. Even so, she thought it odd that a man would consistently address his girl-friend with the words *fucking fatty*, *fucking airhead* or *fucking cunt*.

After an hour of searching, she shut down Billing and crossed him off the list. She moved on to Lars Örjan Wollberg, a veteran reporter at fifty-one who was on the legal desk.

Edklinth walked into police headquarters at 7.30 on Saturday evening. Figuerola and Blomkvist were waiting for him. They were sitting at the same conference table at which Blomkvist had sat the day before.

Edklinth reminded himself that he was on very thin ice and that a host of regulations had been violated when he gave Blomkvist access to the corridor. Figuerola most definitely had no right to invite him here on her own authority. Even the spouses of his colleagues were not permitted in the corridors of S.I.S., but were asked instead to wait on the landings if they were meeting their partner. And to cap it all, Blomkvist was a journalist. From now on Blomkvist would be allowed only into the temporary office at Fridhemsplan.

But outsiders *were* allowed into the corridors by special invitation. Foreign guests, researchers, academics, freelance consultants . . . he put Blomkvist into the category of freelance consultant. All this nonsense about security classification was little more than words anyway. Some-one decides that a certain person should be given a particular level of clearance. And Edklinth had decided that if criticism were raised, he would say that he personally had given Blomkvist clearance.

If something went wrong, that is. He sat down and looked at Figuerola.

"How did you find out about the meeting?"

"Blomkvist called me at around 4.00," she said with a satisfied smile.

Edklinth turned to Blomkvist. "And how did you find out about the meeting?"

"Tipped off by a source."

"Am I to conclude that you're running some sort of surveillance on Teleborian?"

Figuerola shook her head. "That was my first thought too," she said in a cheerful voice, as if Blomkvist were not in the room. "But it doesn't add up. Even if somebody were following Teleborian for Blomkvist, that person could not have known in advance that he was on his way to meet Jonas Sandberg."

"So . . . what else? Illegal tapping or something?" Edklinth said.

"I can assure you," Blomkvist said to remind them that he was there in the room, "that I'm not conducting illegal eavesdropping on anyone. Be realistic. Illegal tapping is the domain of government authorities."

Edklinth frowned. "So you aren't going to tell us how you heard about the meeting?"

"I've already told you that I won't. I was tipped off by a source. The source is protected. Why don't we concentrate on what we've discovered?"

"I don't like loose ends," Edklinth said. "But O.K. What have you found out?"

"His name is Jonas Sandberg," Figuerola said. "Trained as a navy frogman and then attended the police academy in the early '90s. Worked first in Uppsala and then in Södertälje."

"You're from Uppsala."

"Yes, but we missed each other by about a year. He was recruited by S.I.S. Counter-Espionage in 1998. Reassigned to a secret post abroad in 2000. According to our documents, he's at the embassy in Madrid. I checked with the embassy. They have no record of a Jonas Sandberg on their staff."

"Just like Mårtensson. Officially moved to a place where he doesn't exist."

"The chief of Secretariat is the only person who could make this sort of arrangement."

"And in normal circumstances everything would be dismissed as muddled red tape. We've noticed it only because we're specifically looking for it. And if anyone starts asking awkward questions, they'll say it's confidential or that it has something to do with terrorism."

"There's quite a bit of budget work to check up on."

"The chief of Budget?"

"Maybe."

"Anything else?"

"Sandberg lives in Sollentuna. He's not married, but he has a child with a teacher in Södertälje. No black marks on his record. Licence for two handguns. Conscientious and a teetotaller. The only thing that doesn't quite fit is that he seems to be an evangelical and was a member of the Word of Life in the '90s."

"Where did you find that out?"

"I had a word with my old chief in Uppsala. He remembers Sandberg quite well."

"A Christian frogman with two weapons and offspring in Södertälje. More?"

"We only I.D.'d him about three hours ago. This is pretty fast work, you have to admit."

"Fair enough. What do we know about the building on Artillerigatan?"

"Not a lot yet. Stefan went to chase someone up from the city building office. We have blueprints of the building. A housing association block since the 1890s. Six floors with a total of twenty-two apartments, plus eight apartments in a small building in the courtyard. I looked up the tenants, but didn't find anything that stood out. Two of the people living in the building have police records."

"Who are they?"

"Lindström on the second floor, sixty-three. Convicted of insurance fraud in the '70s. Wittfelt on the fourth floor, forty-seven. Twice convicted for beating his ex-wife. Otherwise what sounds like a cross-section of middle-class Sweden. There's one apartment that raises a question mark though."

"What?"

"It's on the top floor. Eleven rooms and apparently a bit of a snazzy joint. It's owned by a company called Bellona Inc."

"And what's their stated business?"

"God only knows. They do marketing analyses and have annual sales of around thirty million kronor. All the owners live abroad."

"Aha."

"Aha what?"

"Nothing. Just 'aha'. Do some more checks on Bellona."

At that moment the officer Blomkvist knew only as Stefan entered the room.

"Hi, chief," he greeted Edklinth. "This is really cool. I checked out the story behind the Bellona apartment."

"And?" Figuerola said.

"Bellona Inc. was founded in the '70s. They bought the apartment from the estate of the former owner, a woman by the name of Kristina Cederholm, born in 1917, married to Hans Wilhelm Francke, the loose cannon who quarrelled with P.G. Vinge at the time S.I.S. was founded."

"Good," Edklinth said. "Very good. Monica, we want surveillance on that apartment around the clock. Find out what telephones they have. I want to know who goes in and who comes out, and what vehicles drop anyone off at that address. The usual."

Edklinth turned to Blomkvist. He looked as if he wanted to say something, but he restrained himself. Blomkvist looked at him expectantly.

"Are you satisfied with the information flow?" Edklinth said at last.

"Very satisfied. Are you satisfied with *Millennium*'s contribution?"

Edklinth nodded reluctantly. "You do know that I could get into very deep water for this."

"Not because of me. I regard the information that I receive here as source-protected. I'll report the facts, but I won't mention how or where I got them. Before I go to press I'm going to do a formal interview with you. If you don't want to give me an answer to something, you just say 'No comment'. Or else you could expound on what you think about the Section for Special Analysis. It's up to you."

"Indeed," Edklinth nodded.

Blomkvist was happy. Within a few hours the Section had taken on tangible form. A real breakthrough.

To Modig's great frustration the meeting in Ekström's office was lasting a long time. Mercifully someone had left a full bottle of mineral water on the conference table. She had twice texted her husband to tell him that she was still held up, promising to make it up to him as soon as she could get home. She was starting to get restless and felt like an intruder.

The meeting did not end until 7.30. She was taken completely by surprise when the door opened and Faste came out. And then Dr Teleborian. Behind them came an older, grey-haired man Modig had never seen before. Finally Prosecutor Ekström, putting on a jacket as he switched off the lights and locked the door to his office.

Modig held up her mobile to the gap in the curtains and took two low-res photographs of the group outside Ekström's door. Seconds later they had set off down the corridor.

She held her breath until they were some distance from the conference room in which she was trapped. She was in a cold sweat by the time she heard the door to the stairwell close. She stood up, weak at the knees.

Bublanski called Figuerola just after 8.00.

"You wanted to know if Ekström had a meeting."

"Correct," Figuerola said.

"It just ended. Ekström met with Dr Peter Teleborian and my former colleague Criminal Inspector Faste, and an older gentleman we didn't recognize."

"Just a moment," Figuerola said. She put her hand over the mouthpiece and turned to the others. "Teleborian went straight to Ekström."

"Hello, are you still there?"

"Sorry. Do we have a description of the third man?"

"Even better. I'm sending you a picture."

"A picture? I'm in your debt."

"It would help if you'd tell me what's going on."

"I'll get back to you."

They sat in silence around the conference table for a moment.

"So," Edklinth said at last. "Teleborian meets with the Section and then goes directly to see Prosecutor Ekström. I'd give a lot of money to find out what they talked about."

"Or you could just ask me," Blomkvist said.

Edklinth and Figuerola looked at him.

"They met to finalize their strategy for nailing Salander at her trial."

Figuerola gave him a look. Then she nodded slowly.

"That's a guess," Edklinth said. "Unless you happen to have paranormal abilities."

"It's no guess," said Mikael. "They met to discuss the forensic psychiatric report on Salander. Teleborian has just finished writing it."

"Nonsense. Salander hasn't even been examined."

Blomkvist shrugged and opened his laptop case. "That hasn't stopped Teleborian in the past. Here's the latest version. It's dated, as you can see, the week the trial is scheduled to begin."

Edklinth and Figuerola read through at the text before them. At last they exchanged glances and then looked at Blomkvist.

"And where the devil did you get hold of this?" Edklinth said.

"That's from a source I have to protect," said Blomkvist.

"Blomkvist . . . we have to be able to trust each other. You're withholding information. Have you got any more surprises up your sleeve?"

"Yes. I do have secrets, of course. Just as I'm persuaded that you haven't given me *carte blanche* to look at everything you have here at Säpo."

"It's not the same thing."

"It's precisely the same thing. This arrangement involves cooperation. You said it yourself: we have to trust each other. I'm not holding back anything that could be useful to your investigation of the Section or throw light on the various crimes that have been committed. I've already handed over evidence that Teleborian committed crimes with Björck in 1991, and I told you that he would be hired to do the same thing again now. And this is the document that proves me right."

"But you're still withholding key material."

"Naturally, and you can either suspend our co-operation or you can live with that."

Figuerola held up a diplomatic finger. "Excuse me, but does this mean that Ekström is working for the Section?"

Blomkvist frowned. "That I don't know. My sense is that he's more a useful fool being used by the Section. He's ambitious, but I think he's honest, if a little stupid. One source did tell me that he swallowed most of what Teleborian fed him about Salander at a presentation of reports when the hunt for her was still on."

"So you don't think it takes much to manipulate him?"

"Exactly. And Criminal Inspector Faste is an unadulterated idiot who believes that Salander is a lesbian Satanist."

Berger was at home. She felt paralysed and unable to concentrate on any real work. All the time she expected someone to call and tell her that pictures of her were posted on some website.

She caught herself thinking over and over about Salander, although she realized that her hopes of getting help from her were most likely in vain. Salander was locked up at Sahlgrenska. She was not allowed visitors and could not even read the newspapers. But she was an oddly resourceful young woman. Despite her isolation she had managed to contact Berger on I.C.Q. and then by telephone. And two years ago she had single-handedly destroyed Wennerström's financial empire and saved *Millennium*.

At 8.00 Linder arrived and knocked on the door. Berger jumped as though someone had fired a shot in her living room.

"Hello, Erika. You're sitting here in the dark looking glum."

Berger nodded and turned on a light. "Hi. I'll put on some coffee—"

"No. Let me do it. Anything new?"

You can say that again. Lisbeth Salander got in touch with me and took control of my computer. And then she called to say that Teleborian and somebody called Jonas were meeting at Central Station this afternoon.

"No. Nothing new," she said. "But I have something I'd like to try on you."

"Try it."

"What do you think the chances are that this isn't a stalker but somebody I know who wants to fuck with me?"

"What's the difference?"

"To me a stalker is someone I don't know who's become fixated on me. The alternative is a person who wants to take some sort of revenge and sabotage my life for personal reasons."

"Interesting thought. Why did this come up?"

"I was . . . discussing the situation with someone today. I can't give you her name, but she suggested that threats from a real stalker would be different. She said a stalker would never have written the email to the girl on the culture desk. It seems completely beside the point."

409

Linder said: "There is something to that. You know, I never read the emails. Could I see them?"

Berger set up her laptop on the kitchen table.

Figuerola escorted Blomkvist out of police headquarters at 10.00 p.m. They stopped at the same place in Kronoberg park as the day before.

"Here we are again. Are you going to disappear to work or do you want to come to my place and come to bed with me?"

"Well . . ."

"You don't have to feel pressured, Mikael. If you have to work, then do it."

"Listen, Figuerola, you're worryingly habit-forming."

"And you don't want to be dependent on anything. Is that what you're saying?"

"No. That's not what I'm saying. But there's someone I have to talk to tonight and it'll take a while. You'll be asleep before I'm done."

She shrugged.

"See you."

He kissed her cheek and headed for the bus stop on Fridhemsplan.

"Blomkvist," she called.

"What?"

"I'm free tomorrow morning as well. Come and have breakfast if you can make it."

CHAPTER 21

Saturday, 4.vi – Monday, 6.vi

Salander picked up a number of ominous vibrations as she browsed the emails of the news editor, Holm. He was fifty-eight and thus fell outside the group, but Salander had included him anyway because he and Berger had been at each other's throats. He was a schemer who wrote messages to various people telling them how someone had done a rotten job.

It was obvious to Salander that Holm did not like Berger, and he certainly wasted a lot of space talking about how the bitch had said this or done that. He used the Net exclusively for work-related sites. If he had other interests, he must google them in his own time on some other machine.

She kept him as a candidate for the title of Poison Pen, but he was not a favourite. Salander spent some time thinking about why she did not believe he was the one, and arrived at the conclusion that he was so damned arrogant he did not have to go to the trouble of using anonymous email. If he wanted to call Berger a whore, he would do it openly. And he did not seem the type to go sneaking into Berger's home in the middle of the night.

At 10.00 in the evening she took a break and went into [Idiotic_Table]. She saw that Blomkvist had not come back yet. She felt slightly peeved and wondered what he was up to, and whether he had made it in time to Teleborian's meeting.

Then she went back into S.M.P.'s server.

She moved to the next name on the list, assistant sports editor Claes Lundin, twenty-nine. She had just opened his email when she stopped and bit her lip. She closed it again and went instead to Berger's.

She scrolled back in time. There was relatively little in her inbox, since her email account had been opened only on May 2. The very first message was a midday memo from Peter Fredriksson. In the course of Berger's first day several people had emailed her to welcome her to S.M.P.

Salander carefully read each message in Berger's inbox. She could see how even from day one there had been a hostile undertone in her correspondence with Holm. They seemed unable to agree on anything, and Salander saw that Holm was already trying to exasperate Berger by sending several emails about complete trivialities.

She skipped over ads, spam and news memos. She focused on any kind of personal correspondence. She read budget calculations, advertising and marketing projections, an exchange with C.F.O. Sellberg that went on for a week and was virtually a brawl over staff layoffs. Berger had received irritated messages from the head of the legal department about some temp. by the name of Johannes Frisk. She had apparently detailed him to work on some story and this had not been appreciated. Apart from the first welcome emails, it seemed as if no-one at management level could see anything positive in any of Berger's arguments or proposals.

After a while Salander scrolled back to the beginning and did a statistical calculation in her head. Of all the upper-level managers at S.M.P., only four did not engage in sniping. They were the chairman of the board Magnus Borgsjö, assistant editor Fredriksson, front-page editor Magnusson, and culture editor Sebastian Strandlund.

Had they never heard of women at S.M.P.? All the heads of department were men.

Of these, the one that Berger had least to do with was Strandlund. She had exchanged only two emails with the culture editor. The friendliest and most engaging messages came from front-page editor Gunnar Magnusson. Borgsjö's were terse and to the point.

Why the hell had this group of boys hired Berger at all, if all they did was tear her limb from limb?

The colleague Berger seemed to have the most to do with was Fredriksson. His role was to act as a kind of shadow, to sit in on her meetings as an observer. He prepared memos, briefed Berger on various articles and issues, and got the jobs moving.

He emailed Berger a dozen times a day.

Salander sorted all of Fredriksson's emails to Berger and read them through. In a number of instances he had objected to some decision Berger had made and presented counter-proposals. Berger seemed to have confidence in him since she would then often change her decision or accept his argument. He was never hostile. But there was not a hint of any personal relationship to her.

Salander closed Berger's email and thought for a moment. She opened Fredriksson's account.

Plague had been fooling around with the home computers of various employees of *S.M.P.* all evening without much success. He had managed to get into Holm's machine because it had an open line to his desk at work; any time of the day or night he could go in and access whatever he was working on. Holm's P.C. was one of the most boring Plague had ever hacked. He had no luck with the other eighteen names on Salander's list. One reason was that none of the people he tried to hack was online on a Saturday night. He was beginning to tire of this impossible task when Salander pinged him at 10.30.

```
<What's up?>
<Peter Fredriksson.>
<O.K.>
<Forget the others. Focus on him.>
<Why?>
<Just a hunch.>
<This is going to take a while.>
<There's a shortcut. Fredriksson is assistant editor
and uses a program called Integrator to keep track
of what's happening on his work computer from home.>
<I don't know anything about Integrator.>
<A little program that was released a couple of
years ago. It's obsolete now. Integrator has a bug.
It's in the archive at Hacker Rep. In theory you
could reverse the program and get into his home
computer from S.M.P.>
```

Plague sighed. This girl who had once been his student now had a better handle on things than he did.

```
<O.K. I'll try.>
<If you find anything and I'm not online, give it
to Kalle Blomkvist.>
```


Blomkvist was back at Salander's apartment on Mosebacke just before midnight. He was tired. He took a shower and put on some coffee, and then he booted up Salander's computer and pinged her I.C.Q.

```
<It's about time.>
<Sorry.>
<Where've you been the past few days?>
<Having sex with a secret agent. And chasing Jonas.>
<Did you make it to the meeting?>
<Yep. You tipped off Erika?>
<Only way to reach you.>
<Smart.>
<I'm being moved to prison tomorrow.>
<I know.>
<Plague's going to help out on the Net.>
<Good.>
<So all that's left is the finale.>
<Sally . . . we're going to do what we have to.>
<I know. You're predictable.>
<As always, my little charmer.>
<Is there anything else that I need to know?>
<No.>
<In that case I have a lot of work to finish up
online.>
<Good luck.>
```

Linder woke with a start when her earpiece beeped. Someone had just tripped the motion detector she had placed in the hall on the ground floor. She propped herself up on her elbow. It was 5.23 on Sunday morning. She slipped silently out of bed and pulled on her jeans, a T-shirt and trainers. She stuffed the Mace in her back pocket and picked up her spring-loaded baton.

She passed the door to Berger's bedroom without a sound, noticing that it was closed and therefore locked.

She stopped at the top of the stairs and listened. She heard a faint clinking sound and movement from the ground floor. Slowly she went down the stairs and paused in the hall to listen again.

A chair scraped in the kitchen. She held the baton in a firm grip and crept to the kitchen door. She saw a bald, unshaven man sitting at the kitchen table with a glass of orange juice, reading *S.M.P.* He sensed her presence and looked up.

"And who the hell are you?"

Linder relaxed and leaned against the door jamb. "Greger Beckman, I presume. Hello. I'm Susanne Linder."

"I see. Are you going to hit me over the head or would you like a glass of juice?"

"Yes, please," Linder said, putting down her baton. "Juice, that is."

Beckman reached for a glass from the draining board and poured some for her.

"I work for Milton Security," Linder said. "I think it's probably best if your wife explains what I'm doing here."

Beckman stood up. "Has something happened to Erika?"

"Your wife is fine. But there's been some trouble. We tried to get hold of you in Paris."

"Paris? Why Paris? I've been in Helsinki, for God's sake."

"Alright. I'm sorry, but your wife thought you were in Paris."

"That's next month," said Beckman on his way out of the door.

"The bedroom is locked. You need a code to open the door," Linder said.

"I beg your pardon . . . what code?"

She told him the three numbers he had to punch in to open the bedroom door. He ran up the stairs.

At 10.00 on Sunday morning Jonasson came into Salander's room.

"Hello, Lisbeth."

"Hello."

"Just thought I'd warn you: the police are coming at lunchtime."

"Fine."

"You don't seem worried."

"I'm not."

"I have a present for you."

"A present? What for?"

"You've been one of my most interesting patients in a long time."

"You don't say," Salander said sceptically.

"I heard that you're fascinated by D.N.A. and genetics."

"Who's been gossiping? That psychologist lady, I bet."

Jonasson nodded. "If you get bored in prison . . . this is the latest thing on D.N.A. research."

He handed her a brick of a book entitled *Spirals – Mysteries of DNA*, by Professor Yoshito Takamura of Tokyo University. Salander opened it and studied the table of contents.

"Beautiful," she said.

"Someday I'd be interested to hear how it is that you can read academic texts that even I can't understand."

As soon as Jonasson had left the room, she took out her Palm. Last chance. From *S.M.P.*'s personnel department Salander had learned that Fredriksson had worked at the paper for six years. During that time he had been off sick for two extended periods: two months in 2003 and three months in 2004. From the personnel files she concluded that the reason in both instances was burnout. Berger's predecessor Morander had on one occasion questioned whether Fredriksson should indeed stay on as assistant editor.

Yak, yak, yak. Nothing concrete to go on.

At 11.45 Plague pinged her.

<What?>

<Are you still at Sahlgrenska?>

<What do you think.>

<It's him.>

<Are you sure?>

<He accessed his work computer from home half an hour ago. I took the opportunity to go in. He has pictures of Berger scanned on to his hard drive at home.>

<Thanks.>

<She looks pretty tasty.>

<Plague, please.>

<I know. What do you want me to do?>

<Did he post the pictures on the Net?>

<Not that I can see.>

<Can you mine his computer?>

<Already done. If he tries to email or upload any-thing bigger than 20 KBs, his hard disk will crash.>

<Cool.>

<I'm going to bed. Take care of yourself.>

<As always.>

Salander logged off from I.C.Q. She glanced at the clock and real-ized that it would soon be lunchtime. She rapidly composed a message that she addressed to the Yahoo group [Idiotic_Table]:

    Mikael. Important. Call Berger right away and tell
    her Fredriksson is Poison Pen.

The instant she sent the message she heard movement in the corridor. She polished the screen of her Palm Tungsten T3 and then switched it off and placed it in the recess behind the bedside table.

"Hello, Lisbeth." It was Giannini in the doorway.

"Hello."

"The police are coming for you in a while. I've brought you some clothes. I hope they're the right size."

Salander looked distrustfully at the selection of neat, dark-coloured linen trousers and pastel-coloured blouses.

Two uniformed Göteborg policewomen came to get her. Giannini was to go with them to the prison.

As they walked from her room down the corridor, Salander noticed that several of the staff were watching her with curiosity. She gave them a friendly nod, and some of them waved back. As if by chance, Jonasson was standing by the reception desk. They looked at each other and nodded. Even before they had turned the corner Salander noticed that he was heading for her room.

During the entire procedure of transporting her to the prison, Salander did not say a word to the police.

Blomkvist had closed his iBook at 7.00 on Sunday morning. He sat for a moment at Salander's desk listless, staring into space.

Then he went to her bedroom and looked at her gigantic, king-size bed. After a while he went back to her office and flipped open his mobile to call Figuerola.

"Hi. It's Mikael."

"Hello there. Are you already up?"

"I've just finished working and I'm on my way to bed. I just wanted to call and say hello."

"Men who just want to call and say hello generally have ulterior motives."

He laughed.

"Blomkvist . . . you could come here and sleep if you like."

"I'd be wretched company."

"I'll get used to it."

He took a taxi to Pontonjärgatan.

Berger spent Sunday in bed with her husband. They lay there talking and dozing. In the afternoon they got dressed and went for a walk down to the steamship dock.

"S.M.P. was a mistake," Berger said when they got home.

"Don't say that. Right now it's tough, but you knew it would be. Things will calm down after you've been there a while."

"It's not the job. I can handle that. It's the atmosphere."

"I see."

"I don't like it there, but on the other hand I can't walk out after a few weeks."

She sat at the kitchen table and stared morosely into space. Beckman had never seen his wife so stymied.

Inspector Faste met Salander for the first time at 11.30 on Sunday morning when a woman police officer brought her into Erlander's office at Göteborg police headquarters.

"You were difficult enough to catch," Faste said.

Salander gave him a long look, satisfied herself that he was an idiot, and decided that she would not waste too many seconds concerning herself with his existence.

"Inspector Gunilla Wäring will accompany you to Stockholm," Erlander said.

"Alright," Faste said. "Then we'll leave at once. There are quite a few people who want to have a serious talk with you, Salander."

Erlander said goodbye to her. She ignored him.

They had decided for simplicity's sake to do the prisoner transfer to Stockholm by car. Wäring drove. At the start of the journey Hans Faste sat in the front passenger seat with his head turned towards the back as he tried to have some exchange with Salander. By the time they reached Alingsås his neck was aching and he gave up.

Salander looked at the countryside. In her mind Faste did not exist.

Teleborian was right. She's fucking retarded, Faste thought. *We'll see about changing that attitude when we get to Stockholm.*

Every so often he glanced at Salander and tried to form an opinion of the woman he had been desperate to track down for such a long time. Even he had some doubts when he saw the skinny girl. He wondered how much she could weigh. He reminded himself that she was a lesbian and consequently not a real woman.

But it was possible that the bit about Satanism was an exaggeration. She did not look the type.

The irony was that he would have preferred to arrest her for the three murders that she was originally suspected of, but reality had caught up with his investigation. Even a skinny girl can handle a weapon. Instead she had been taken in for assaulting the top leadership of Svavelsjö M.C., and she was guilty of that crime, no question. There was forensic evidence related to the incident which she no doubt intended to refute.

Figuerola woke Blomkvist at 1.00 in the afternoon. She had been sitting on her balcony and had finished reading her book about the idea of God in antiquity, listening all the while to Blomkvist's snores from the bedroom. It had been peaceful. When she went in to look at him it came to her, acutely, that she was more attracted to him than she had been to any other man in years.

It was a pleasant yet unsettling feeling. There he was, but he was not a stable element in her life.

They went down to Norr Mälarstrand for a coffee. Then she took him home and to bed for the rest of the afternoon. He left her at 7.00. She felt a vague sense of loss a moment after he kissed her cheek and was gone.

At 8.00 on Sunday evening Linder knocked on Berger's door. She would not be sleeping there now that Beckman was home, and this visit was not connected with her job. But during the time she had spent at Berger's house they had both grown to enjoy the long conversations they had in the kitchen. She had discovered a great liking for Berger. She recognized in her a desperate woman who succeeded in concealing her true nature. She went to work apparently calm, but in reality she was a bundle of nerves.

Linder suspected that her anxiety was due not solely to Poison Pen. But Berger's life and problems were none of her business. It was a friendly visit. She had come out here just to see Berger and to be sure that everything was alright. The couple were in the kitchen in a solemn mood. It seemed as though they had spent their Sunday working their way through one or two serious issues.

Beckman put on some coffee. Linder had been there only a few minutes when Berger's mobile rang.

Berger had answered every call that day with a feeling of impending doom.

"Berger," she said.

"Hello, Ricky."

Blomkvist. Shit. I haven't told him the Borgsjö file has disappeared.

"Hi, Micke."

"Salander was moved to the prison in Göteborg this evening, to wait for transport to Stockholm tomorrow."

"O.K."

"She sent you a . . . well, a message."

"Oh?"

"It's pretty cryptic."

"What did she say?"

"She says: 'Poison Pen is Peter Fredriksson.'"

Erika sat for ten seconds in silence while thoughts rushed through her head. *Impossible. Peter isn't like that. Salander has to be wrong.*

"Was that all?"

"That's the whole message. Do you know what it's about?"

"Yes."

"Ricky . . . what are you and that girl up to? She rang you to tip me off about Teleborian and—"

"Thanks, Micke. We'll talk later."

She turned off her mobile and looked at Linder with an expression of absolute astonishment.

"Tell me," Linder said.

Linder was in two minds. Berger had been told that her assistant editor was the one sending the vicious emails. She talked non-stop. Then

Linder had asked her *how* she knew Fredriksson was her stalker. Then Berger was silent. Linder noticed her eyes and saw that something had changed in her attitude. She was all of a sudden totally confused.

"I can't tell you . . ."

"What do you mean you can't tell me?"

"Susanne, I just know that Fredriksson is responsible. But I can't tell you how I got that information. What can I do?"

"If I'm going to help you, you have to tell me."

"I . . . I can't. You don't understand."

Berger got up and stood at the kitchen window with her back to Linder. Finally she turned.

"I'm going to his house."

"You'll do nothing of the sort. You're not going anywhere, least of all to the home of somebody who obviously hates you."

Berger looked torn.

"Sit down. Tell me what happened. It was Blomkvist calling you, right?"

Berger nodded.

"I . . . today I asked a hacker to go through the home computers of the staff."

"Aha. So you've probably by extension committed a serious computer crime. And you don't want to tell me who your hacker is?"

"I promised I would never tell anyone . . . Other people are involved. Something that Mikael is working on."

"Does Blomkvist know about the emails and the break-in here?"

"No, he was just passing on a message."

Linder cocked her head to one side, and all of a sudden a chain of associations formed in her mind.

Erika Berger. Mikael Blomkvist. Millennium. *Rogue policemen who broke in and bugged Blomkvist's apartment. Linder watching the watchers. Blomkvist working like a madman on a story about Lisbeth Salander.*

The fact that Salander was a wizard at computers was widely known at Milton Security. No-one knew how she had come by her skills, and Linder had never heard any rumours that Salander might be a hacker. But Armansky had once said something about Salander delivering quite incredible reports when she was doing personal investigations. A hacker . . .

But Salander is under guard on a ward in Göteborg.

It was absurd.

"Is it Salander we're talking about?" Linder said.

Berger looked as though she had touched a live wire.

"I can't discuss where the information came from. Not one word."

Linder laughed aloud.

It was Salander. Berger's confirmation of it could not have been clearer. She was completely off balance.

Yet it's impossible.

Under guard as she was, Salander had nevertheless taken on the job of finding out who Poison Pen was. Sheer madness.

Linder thought hard.

She could not understand the whole Salander story. She had met her maybe five times during the years she had worked at Milton Security and had never had so much as a single conversation with her. She regarded Salander as a sullen and asocial individual with a skin like a rhino. She had heard that Armansky himself had taken Salander on and since she respected Armansky she assumed that he had good reason for his endless patience towards the sullen girl.

Poison Pen is Peter Fredriksson.

Could she be right? What was the proof?

Linder then spent a long time questioning Erika on everything she knew about Fredriksson, what his role was at *S.M.P.*, and how their relationship had been. The answers did not help her at all.

Berger had displayed a frustrating indecision. She had wavered between a determination to drive out to Fredriksson's place and confront him, and an unwillingness to believe that it could really be true. Finally Linder convinced her that she could not storm into Fredriksson's apartment and launch into an accusation – if he was innocent, she would make an utter fool of herself.

So Linder had promised to look into the matter. It was a promise she regretted as soon as she made it, because she did not have the faintest idea how she was going to proceed.

She parked her Fiat Strada as close to Fredriksson's apartment building in Fisksätra as she could. She locked the car and looked about her. She was not sure what she was going to do, but she supposed she would have to knock on his door and somehow get him to answer a number of questions. She was acutely aware that this was a job that lay well outside her remit at Milton, and she knew Armansky would be furious if he found out what she was doing.

It was not a good plan, and in any case it fell apart before she had managed to put it into practice. She had reached the courtyard and was approaching Fredriksson's apartment when the door opened. Linder recognized him at once from the photograph in his personnel file which she had studied on Berger's computer. She kept walking and they passed each other. He disappeared in the direction of the garage. It was just before 11.00 and Fredriksson was on his way somewhere. Linder turned and ran back to her car.

Blomkvist sat for a long time looking at his mobile after Berger hung up. He wondered what was going on. In frustration he looked at Salander's computer. By now she had been moved to the prison in Göteborg, and he had no chance of asking her anything.

He opened his Ericsson T10 and called Idris Ghidi in Angered.

"Hello. Mikael Blomkvist."

"Hello," Ghidi said.

"Just to tell you that you can stop that job you were doing for me."

Ghidi had already worked out that Blomkvist would call since Salander had been taken from the hospital.

"I understand," he said.

"You can keep the mobile as we agreed. I'll send you the final payment this week."

"Thanks."

"I'm the one who should thank you for your help."

Blomkvist opened his iBook. The events of the past twenty-four hours meant that a significant part of the manuscript had to be revised and that in all probability a whole new section would have to be added.

He sighed and got to work.

At 11.15 Fredriksson parked three streets away from Berger's house. Linder had already guessed where he was going and had stopped trying to keep him in sight. She drove past his car fully two minutes after he parked. The car was empty. She went on a short distance past Berger's house and stopped well out of sight. Her palms were sweating.

She opened her tin of Catch Dry snuff and tucked a teenage-sized portion inside her upper lip.

Then she opened her car door and looked around. As soon as she could tell that Fredriksson was on his way to Saltsjöbaden, she knew that Salander's information must be correct. And obviously he had not come all this way for fun. Trouble was brewing. Which was fine by her, so long as she could catch him red-handed.

She took her telescopic baton from the side pocket of her car door and weighed it in her hand for a moment. She pressed the lock in the handle and out shot a heavy, spring-loaded steel cable. She clenched her teeth.

That was why she had left the Södermalm force.

She had had one mad outbreak of rage when for the third time in as many days the squad car had driven to an address in Hägersten after the same woman had called the police and screamed for help because her husband had abused her. And just as on the first two occasions, the situation had resolved itself before they arrived.

They had detained the husband on the staircase while the woman was questioned. *No, she did not want to file a police report. No, it was all a mistake. No, he was fine . . . it was actually all her fault. She had provoked him . . .*

And the whole time the bastard had stood there grinning, looking Linder straight in the eye.

She could not explain why she did it. But suddenly something had snapped in her, and she took out her baton and slammed it across his face. The first blow had lacked power. She had only given him a fat lip and forced him on to his knees. In the next ten seconds – until her colleagues grabbed her and half dragged, half carried her out of the halfway – she had let the blows rain down on his back, kidneys, hips and shoulders.

Charges were never filed. She had resigned the same evening and went home and cried for a week. Then she pulled herself together and went to see Dragan Armansky. She explained what she had done and why she had left the force. She was looking for a job. Armansky had been sceptical and said he would need some time to think it over. She had given up hope by the time he called six weeks later and told her he was ready to take her on trial.

Linder frowned and stuck the baton into her belt at the small of her back. She checked that she had the Mace canister in her right-hand pocket and that the laces of her trainers were securely tied. She walked back to Berger's house and slipped into the garden.

She knew that the outside motion detector had not yet been installed, and she moved soundlessly across the lawn, along the hedge at the border of the property. She could not see him. She went around the house and stood still. Then she spotted him as a shadow in the darkness near Beckman's studio.

He can't know how stupid it is for him to come back here.

He was squatting down, trying to see through a gap in a curtain in the room next to the living room. Then he moved up on to the veranda and looked through the cracks in the drawn blinds at the big picture window.

Linder suddenly smiled.

She crossed the lawn to the corner of the house while he still had his back to her. She crouched behind some currant bushes by the gable end and waited. She could see him through the branches. From his position Fredriksson would be able to look down the hall and into part of the kitchen. Apparently he had found something interesting to look at, and it was ten minutes before he moved again. This time he came closer to Linder.

As he rounded the corner and passed her, she stood up and spoke in a low voice:

"Hello there, Fredriksson."

He stopped short and spun towards her.

She saw his eyes glistening in the dark. She could not see his expression, but she could hear that he was holding his breath and she could sense his shock.

"We can do this the easy way or we can do it the hard way," she said. "We're going to walk to your car and—"

He turned and made to run away.

Linder raised her baton and directed a devastatingly painful blow to his left kneecap.

He fell with a moan.

She raised the baton a second time, but then caught herself. She thought she could feel Armansky's eyes on the back of her neck.

She bent down, flipped him over on to his stomach and put her knee in the small of his back. She took hold of his right hand and twisted it round on to his back and handcuffed him. He was frail and he put up no resistance.

*

Berger turned off the lamp in the living room and limped upstairs. She no longer needed the crutches, but the sole of her foot still hurt when she put any weight on it. Beckman turned off the light in the kitchen and followed his wife upstairs. He had never before seen her so unhappy. Nothing he said could soothe her or alleviate the anxiety she was feeling.

She got undressed, crept into bed and turned her back to him.

"It's not your fault, Greger," she said when she heard him get in beside her.

"You're not well," he said. "I want you to stay at home for a few days."

He put an arm around her shoulders. She did not to push him away, but she was completely passive. He bent over, kissed her cautiously on the neck, and held her.

"There's nothing you can say or do to make the situation any better. I know I need to take a break. I feel as though I've climbed on to an express train and discovered that I'm on the wrong track."

"We could go sailing for a few days. Get away from it all."

"No. I can't get away from it all."

She turned to him. "The worst thing I could do now would be to run away. I have to sort things out first. Then we can go."

"O.K," Beckman said. "I'm not being much help."

She smiled wanly. "No, you're not. But thanks for being here. I love you insanely – you know that."

He mumbled something inaudible.

"I simply can't believe it's Fredriksson," Berger said. "I've never felt the least bit of hostility from him."

Linder was just wondering whether she should ring Berger's doorbell when she saw the lights go off on the ground floor. She looked down at Fredriksson. He had not said a word. He was quite still. She thought for a long time before she made up her mind.

She bent down and grabbed the handcuffs, pulled him to his feet, and leaned him against the wall.

"Can you stand by yourself?" she said.

He did not answer.

"Right, we'll make this easy. You struggle in any way and you'll get the same treatment on your right leg. You struggle even more and I'll break your arms. Do you understand?"

She could hear him breathing heavily. Fear?

426

She pushed him along in front of her out on to the street all the way to his car. He was limping badly so she held him up. Just as they reached the car they met a man out walking his dog. The man stopped and looked at Fredriksson in his handcuffs.

"This is a police matter," Linder said in a firm voice. "You go home." The man turned and walked away in the direction he had come.

She put Fredriksson in the back seat and drove him home to Fisksätra. It was 12.30 and they saw no-one as they walked into his building. Linder fished out his keys and followed him up the stairs to his apartment on the fourth floor.

"You can't go into my apartment," said Fredriksson.

It was the first thing he had said since she cuffed him. She opened the apartment door and shoved him inside.

"You have no right. You have to have a search warrant—"

"I'm not a police officer," she said in a low voice.

He stared at her suspiciously.

She took hold of his shirt and dragged him into the living room, pushing him down on to a sofa. He had a neatly kept two-bedroom apartment. Bedroom to the left of the living room, kitchen across the hall, a small office off the living room.

She looked in the office and heaved a sigh of relief. *The smoking gun.* Straightaway she saw photographs from Berger's album spread out on a desk next to a computer. He had pinned up thirty or so pictures on the wall behind the computer. She regarded the exhibition with raised eyebrows. Berger was a fine-looking woman. And her sex life was more active than Linder's own.

She heard Fredriksson moving and went back to the living room, rapped him once across his lower back and then dragged him into the office and sat him down on the floor.

"You stay there," she said.

She went into the kitchen and found a paper carrier bag from Konsum. She took down one picture after another and then found the stripped album and Berger's diaries.

"Where's the video?" she said.

Fredriksson did not answer. Linder went into the living room and turned on the T.V. There was a tape in the V.C.R., but it took a while before she found the video channel on the remote so she could check it. She popped out the video and looked around to ensure he had not made any copies.

She found Berger's teenage love letters and the Borgsjö folder. Then she turned her attentions to Fredriksson's computer. She saw that he had a Microtek scanner hooked up to his P.C., and when she lifted the lid she found a photograph of Berger at a Club Xtreme party, New Year's Eve 1986 according to a banner on the wall.

She booted up the computer and discovered that it was password-protected.

"What's your password," she asked.

Fredriksson sat obstinately silent and refused to answer.

Linder suddenly felt utterly calm. She knew that technically she had committed one crime after another this evening, including unlawful restraint and even aggravated kidnapping. She did not care. On the contrary, she felt almost exhilarated.

After a while she shrugged and dug in her pocket for her Swiss Army knife. She unplugged all the cables from the computer, turned it round and used the screwdriver to open the back. It took her fifteen minutes to take it apart and remove the hard drive.

She had taken everything, but for safety's sake she did a thorough search of the desk drawers, the stacks of paper and the shelves. Suddenly her gaze fell on an old school yearbook lying on the windowsill. She saw that it was from Djurholm Gymnasium 1978. Did Berger not come from Djurholm's upper class? She opened the yearbook and began to look through that year's school leavers.

She found Erika Berger, eighteen years old, with student cap and a sunny smile with dimples. She wore a thin, white cotton dress and held a bouquet of flowers in her hand. She looked the epitome of an innocent teenager with top grades.

Linder almost missed the connection, but there it was on the next page. She would never have recognized him but for the caption. Peter Fredriksson. He was in a different class from Berger. Linder studied the photograph of a thin boy in a student cap who looked into the camera with a serious expression.

Her eyes met Fredriksson's.

"Even then she was a whore."

"Fascinating," Linder said.

"She fucked every guy in the school."

"I doubt that."

"She was a fucking—"

"Don't say it. So what happened? Couldn't you get into her knickers?"

428

"She treated me as though I didn't exist. She laughed at me. And when she started at *S.M.P.* she didn't even recognize me."

"Right," said Linder wearily. "I'm sure you had a terrible childhood. How about we have a serious talk?"

"What do you want?"

"I'm not a police officer," Linder said. "I'm someone who takes care of people like you."

She paused and let his imagination do the work.

"I want to know if you put photographs of her anywhere on the Internet."

He shook his head.

"Are you quite sure about that?"

He nodded.

"Berger will have to decide for herself whether she wants to make a formal complaint against you for harassment, threats, and breaking and entering, or whether she wants to settle things amicably."

He said nothing.

"If she decides to ignore you – and I think that's about what you're worth – then I'll be keeping an eye on you."

She held up her baton.

"If you ever go near her house again, or send her email or otherwise molest her, I'll be back. I'll beat you so hard so that even your own mother won't recognize you. Do I make myself clear?"

Still he said nothing.

"So you have the opportunity to influence how this story ends. Are you interested?"

He nodded slowly.

"In that case, I'm going to recommend to Fru Berger that she lets you off, but don't think about coming into work again. As of right now you're fired."

He nodded.

"You will disappear from her life and move out of Stockholm. I don't give a shit what you do with your life or where you end up. Find a job in Göteborg or Malmö. Go on sick leave again. Do whatever you like. But leave Berger in peace. Are we agreed?"

Fredriksson began to sob.

"I didn't mean any harm," he said. "I just wanted—"

"You just wanted to make her life a living hell and you certainly succeeded. Do I or do I not have your word?"

He nodded.

She bent over, turned him on to his stomach and unlocked the hand-cuffs. She took the Konsum bag containing Berger's life and left him there on the floor.

It was 2.30 a.m. on Monday when Linder left Fredriksson's building. She considered letting the matter rest until the next day, but then it occurred to her that if she had been the one involved, she would have wanted to know straightaway. Besides, her car was still parked out in Saltsjöbaden. She called a taxi.

Beckman opened the door even before she managed to ring the bell. He was wearing jeans and did not look as if he had just got out of bed.

"Is Erika awake?" Linder asked.

He nodded.

"Has something else happened?" he said.

She smiled at him.

"Come in. We're just talking in the kitchen."

They went in.

"Hello, Erika," Linder said. "You need to learn to get some sleep once in a while."

"What's happened?"

Linder held out the Konsum bag.

"Fredriksson promises to leave you alone from now on. God knows if we can trust him, but if he keeps his word it'll be less painful than hassling with a police report and a trial. It's up to you."

"So it *was* him?"

Linder nodded. Beckman poured a coffee, but she did not want one. She had drunk much too much coffee over the past few days. She sat down and told them what had happened outside their house that night.

Berger sat in silence for a moment. Then she went upstairs, and came back with her copy of the school yearbook. She looked at Fredriksson's face for a long time.

"I do remember him," she said at last. "But I had no idea it was the same Peter Fredriksson. I wouldn't even have remembered his name if it weren't written here."

"What happened?" Linder asked.

"Nothing. Absolutely nothing. He was a quiet and totally uninteresting

430

boy in another class. I think we might have had some subjects together. French, if I remember correctly."

"He said that you treated him as though he didn't exist."

"I probably did. He wasn't somebody I knew and he wasn't in our group."

"I know how cliques work. Did you bully him or anything like that?"

"No . . . no, for God's sake. I hated bullying. We had campaigns against bullying in the school, and I was president of the student council. I don't remember that he ever spoke to me."

"O.K," Linder said. "But he obviously had a grudge against you. He was off sick for two long periods, suffering from stress and overwork. Maybe there were other reasons for his being off sick that we don't know about."

She got up and put on her leather jacket.

"I've got his hard drive. Technically it's stolen goods so I shouldn't leave it with you. You don't have to worry – I'll destroy it as soon as I get home."

"Wait, Susanne. How can I ever thank you?"

"Well, you can back me up when Armansky's wrath hits me like a bolt of lightning."

Berger gave her a concerned look.

"Will you get into trouble for this?"

"I don't know. I really don't know."

"Can we pay you for—"

"No. But Armansky may bill you for tonight. I hope he does, because that would mean he approves of what I did and probably won't decide to fire me."

"I'll make sure he sends us a bill."

Berger stood up and gave Linder a long hug.

"Thanks, Susanne. If you ever need a friend, you've got one in me. If there's anything I can do for you . . ."

"Thanks. Don't leave those pictures lying around. And while we're on the subject, Milton could install a much better safe for you."

Berger smiled as Beckman walked Linder back to her car.

CHAPTER 22

Monday, 6.vi

Berger woke up at 6.00 on Monday morning. She had not slept for more than an hour, but she felt strangely rested. She supposed that it was a physical reaction of some sort. For the first time in several months she put on her jogging things and went for a furious and excruciatingly painful sprint down to the steamboat wharf. But after a hundred metres or so her heel hurt so much that she had to slow down and go on at a more leisurely pace, relishing the pain in her foot with each step she took.

She felt reborn. It was as though the Grim Reaper had passed by her door and at the last moment changed his mind and moved on to the next house. She could still not take in how fortunate she was that Fredriksson had had her pictures in his possession for four days and done nothing with them. The scanning he had done indicated that he had something planned, but he had simply not got around to what-ever it was.

She decided to give Susanne Linder a very expensive Christmas present this year. She would think of something really special.

She left her husband asleep and at 7.30 drove to *S.M.P.*'s office at Norrtull. She parked in the garage, took the lift to the newsroom, and settled down in the glass cage. Before she did anything else, she called someone from maintenance.

"Peter Fredriksson has left the paper. He won't be back," she said. "Please bring as many boxes as you need to empty his desk of personal items and have them delivered to his apartment this morning."

She looked over towards the news desk. Holm had just arrived. He met her gaze and nodded to her.

She nodded back.

Holm was a bloody-minded bastard, but after their altercation a few weeks earlier he had stopped trying to cause trouble. If he continued to show the same positive attitude, he might possibly survive as news editor. Possibly.

She should, she felt, be able to turn things around.

At 8.45 she saw Borgsjö come out of the lift and disappear up the internal staircase to his office on the floor above. *I have to talk to him today.*

She got some coffee and spent a while on the morning memo. It looked like it was going to be a slow news day. The only item of interest was an agency report, to the effect that Lisbeth Salander had been moved to the prison in Stockholm the day before. She O.K.'d the story and forwarded it to Holm.

At 8.59 Borgsjö called.

"Berger, come up to my office right away." He hung up.

He was white in the face when Berger found him at his desk. He stood up and slammed a thick wad of papers on to his desk.

"What the hell is this?" he roared.

Berger's heart sank like a stone. She only had to glance at the cover to see what Borgsjö had found in the morning post.

Fredriksson hadn't managed to do anything with her photographs. But he had posted Cortez's article and research to Borgsjö.

Calmly she sat down opposite him.

"That's an article written by a reporter called Henry Cortez. *Millennium* had planned to run it in last week's issue."

Borgsjö looked desperate.

"How the hell do you *dare*? I brought you into S.M.P. and the first thing you do is to start digging up dirt. What kind of a media whore are you?"

Berger's eyes narrowed. She turned ice-cold. She had had enough of the word "whore".

"Do you really think anyone is going to care about this? Do you think you can trap me with this crap? And why the hell did you send it to me anonymously?"

"That's not what happened, Magnus."

"Then tell me what did happen."

"The person who sent that article to you anonymously was Fredriksson. He was fired from S.M.P. yesterday."

"What the hell are you talking about?"

"It's a long story. But I've had a copy of the article for more than two weeks, trying to work out a way of raising the subject with you."

"You're behind this article?"

"No, I am not. Cortez researched and wrote the article entirely off his own bat. I didn't know anything about it."

433

"You expect me to believe that?"

"As soon as my old colleagues at *Millennium* saw how you were implicated in the story, Blomkvist stopped its publication. He called me and gave me a copy, out of concern for my position. It was then stolen from me, and now it's ended up with you. *Millennium* wanted me to have a chance to talk with you before they printed it. Which they mean to do in the August issue."

"I've never met a more unscrupulous media whore in my whole life. It defies belief."

"Now that you've read the story, perhaps you have also considered the research behind it. Cortez has a cast-iron story. You know that."

"What the hell is that supposed to mean?"

"If you're still here when *Millennium* goes to press, that will hurt *S.M.P.* I've worried myself sick and tried to find a way out . . . but there isn't one."

"What do you mean?"

"You'll have to go."

"Don't be absurd. I haven't done anything illegal."

"Magnus, don't you understand the impact of this exposé? I don't want to have to call a board meeting. It would be too embarrassing."

"You're not going to call anything at all. You're finished at *S.M.P.*"

"Wrong. Only the board can sack me. Presumably you're allowed to call them in for an extraordinary meeting. I would suggest you do that for this afternoon."

Borgsjö came round the desk and stood so close to Berger that she could feel his breath.

"Berger, you have one chance to survive this. You have to go to your damned colleagues at *Millennium* and get them to kill this story. If you do a good job I might even forget what you've done."

Berger sighed.

"Magnus, you aren't understanding how serious this is. I have no influence whatsoever on what *Millennium* is going to publish. This story is going to come out no matter what I say. The only thing I care about is how it affects *S.M.P.* That's why you have to resign."

Borgsjö put his hands on the back of her chair.

"Berger, your cronies at *Millennium* might change their minds if they knew that you would be fired the instant they leak this bullshit."

He straightened up.

434

"I'll be at a meeting in Norrköping today." He looked at her, furious and arrogant. "At Svea Construction."

"I see."

"When I'm back tomorrow you will report to me that this matter has been taken care of. Understood?"

He put on his jacket. Berger watched him with her eyes half closed.

"Maybe then you'll survive at *S.M.P.* Now get out of my office."

She went back to the glass cage and sat quite still in her chair for twenty minutes. Then she picked up the telephone and asked Holm to come to her office. This time he was there within a minute.

"Sit down."

Holm raised an eyebrow and sat down.

"What did I do wrong this time?" he said sarcastically.

"Anders, this is my last day at *S.M.P.* I'm resigning here and now. I'm calling in the deputy chairman and as many of the board as I can find for a meeting over lunch."

He stared at her with undisguised shock.

"I'm going to recommend that you be made acting editor-in-chief."

"What?"

"Are you O.K. with that?"

Holm leaned back in his chair and looked at her.

"I've never wanted to be editor-in-chief," he said.

"I know that. But you're tough enough to do the job. And you'll walk over corpses to be able to publish a good story. I just wish you had more common sense."

"So what happened?"

"I have a different style to you. You and I have always argued about what angle to take, and we'll never agree."

"No," he said. "We never will. But it's possible that my style is old-fashioned."

"I don't know if old-fashioned is the right word. You're a very good newspaperman, but you behave like a bastard. That's totally unnecessary. But what we were most at odds about was that you claimed that as news editor you couldn't allow personal considerations to affect how the news was assessed."

Berger suddenly gave Holm a sly smile. She opened her bag and took out her original text of the Borgsjö story.

"Let's test your sense of news assessment. I have a story here that came to us from a reporter at *Millennium*. This morning I'm thinking that we should run this article as today's top story." She tossed the folder into Holm's lap. "You're the news editor. I'd be interested to hear whether you share my assessment."

Holm opened the folder and began to read. Even the introduction made his eyes widen. He sat up straight in his chair and stared at Berger. Then he lowered his eyes and read through the article to the end. He studied the source material for ten more minutes before he slowly put the folder aside.

"This is going to cause one hell of an uproar."

"I know. That's why I'm leaving. *Millennium* was planning to run the story in their July issue, but Mikael Blomkvist stopped publication. He gave me the article so that I could talk with Borgsjö before they run it."

"And?"

"Borgsjö ordered me to suppress it."

"I see. So you're planning to run it in *S.M.P.* out of spite?"

"Not out of spite, no. There's no other way. If *S.M.P.* runs the story, we have a chance of getting out of this mess with our honour intact. Borgsjö has no choice but to go. But it also means that I can't stay here any longer."

Holm sat in silence for two minutes.

"Damn it, Berger . . . I didn't think you were that tough. I never thought I'd ever say this, but if you're that thick-skinned, I'm actually sorry you're leaving."

"You could stop publication, but if both you and I O.K. it . . . Do you think you'll run the story?"

"Too right we'll run it. It would leak anyway."

"Exactly."

Holm got up and stood uncertainly by her desk.

"Get to work," said Berger.

After Holm left her office she waited five minutes before she picked up the telephone and rang Eriksson.

"Hello, Malin. Is Henry there?"

"Yes, he's at his desk."

"Could you call him into your office and put on the speakerphone? We have to have a conference."

Cortez was there within fifteen seconds.

"What's up?"

"Henry, I did something immoral today."

"Oh, you did?"

"I gave your story about Vitavara to the news editor here at *S.M.P.*"

"You *what*?"

"I told him to run the story in *S.M.P.* tomorrow. Your byline. And you'll be paid, of course. In fact, you can name your price."

"Erika . . . what the hell is going on?"

She gave him a brisk summary of what had happened during the last weeks, and how Fredriksson had almost destroyed her.

"Jesus Christ," Cortez said.

"I know that this is your story, Henry. But equally I have no choice. Can you agree to this?"

Cortez was silent for a long while.

"Thanks for asking." he said. "It's O.K. to run the story with my byline. If it's O.K. with Malin, I should say."

"It's O.K. with me," Eriksson said.

"Thank you both," Berger said. "Can you tell Mikael? I don't suppose he's in yet."

"I'll talk to Mikael," Eriksson said. "But Erika, does this mean that you're out of work from today?"

Berger laughed. "I've decided to take the rest of the year off. Believe me, a few weeks at *S.M.P.* was enough."

"I don't think you ought to start thinking in terms of a holiday yet," Eriksson said.

"Why not?"

"Could you come here this afternoon?"

"What for?"

"I need help. If you want to come back to being editor-in-chief here, you could start tomorrow morning."

"Malin, you're the editor-in-chief. Anything else is out of the question."

"Then you could start as assistant editor," Eriksson laughed.

"Are you serious?"

"Oh, Erika, I miss you so much that I'm ready to die. One reason I took the job here was so that I'd have a chance to work with you. And now you're somewhere else."

Berger said nothing for a minute. She had not even thought about the possibility of making a comeback at *Millennium*.

"Do you think I'd really be welcome?" she said hesitantly.

"What do you think? I reckon we'd begin with a huge celebration which I would arrange myself. And you'd be back just in time for us to publish you-know-what."

Berger checked the clock on her desk. 10.55. In a couple of hours her whole world had been turned upside down. She realized what a longing she had to walk up the stairs at *Millennium* again.

"I have a few things to take care of here over the next few hours. Is it O.K. if I pop in at around 4.00?"

Linder looked Armansky directly in the eye as she told him exactly what had happened during the night. The only thing she left out was her sudden intuition that the hacking of Fredriksson's computer had something to do with Salander. She kept that to herself for two reasons. First, she thought it sounded too implausible. Second, she knew that Armansky was somehow up to his neck in the Salander affair along with Blomkvist.

Armansky listened intently. When Linder finished her account, he said: "Beckman called about an hour ago."

"Oh?"

"He and Berger are coming in later this week to sign a contract. He wants to thank us for what Milton has done and above all for what *you* have done."

"I see. It's nice to have a satisfied client."

"He also wants to order a safe for the house. We'll install it and finish up the alarm package before this weekend."

"That's good."

"He says he wants us to invoice him for your work over the weekend. That'll make it quite a sizable bill we'll be sending them." Armansky sighed. "Susanne, you do know that Fredriksson could go to the police and get you into very deep water on a number of counts."

She nodded.

"Mind you, he'd end up in prison so fast it would make his head spin, but he might think it was worth it."

"I doubt he has the balls to go to the police."

"You may be right, but what you did far exceeded instructions."

"I know."

"So how do you think I should react?"

438

"Only you can decide that."

"How did you think I *would* to react?"

"What I think has nothing to do with it. You could always sack me."

"Hardly. I can't afford to lose a professional of your calibre."

"Thanks."

"But if you do anything like this again, I'm going to get very angry."

Linder nodded.

"What did you do with the hard drive?"

"It's destroyed. I put it in a vice this morning and crushed it."

"Then we can forget about all this."

Berger spent the rest of the morning calling the board members of *S.M.P.* She reached the deputy chairman at his summer house near Vaxholm and persuaded him to drive to the city as quickly as he could. A rather makeshift board assembled over lunch. Berger began by explaining how the Cortez folder had come to her, and what consequences it had already had.

When she finished it was proposed, as she had anticipated, that they try to find another solution. Berger told them that *S.M.P.* was going to run the story the next day. She also told them that this would be her last day of work and that her decision was final.

She got the board to approve two decisions and enter them in the minutes. Magnus Borgsjö would be asked to vacate his position as chairman, effective immediately, and Anders Holm would be appointed acting editor-in-chief. Then she excused herself and left the board members to discuss the situation among themselves.

At 2.00 she went down to the personnel department and had a contract drawn up. Then she went to speak to Sebastian Strandlund, the culture editor, and the reporter Eva Karlsson.

"As far as I can tell, you consider Eva to be a talented reporter."

"That's true," said Strandlund.

"And in your budget requests over the past two years you've asked that your staff be increased by at least two."

"Correct."

"Eva, in view of the email to which you were subjected, there might be ugly rumours if I were to hire you full-time. But are you still interested?"

"Of course."

"In that case my last act here at *S.M.P.* will be to sign this employment contract."

"Your last act?"

"It's a long story. I'm leaving today. Could you two be so kind as to keep quiet about it for an hour or so?"

"What . . ."

"There'll be a memo coming around soon."

Berger signed the contract and pushed it across the desk towards Karlsson.

"Good luck," she said, smiling.

"The older man who participated in the meeting with Ekström on Saturday is Georg Nyström, a police superintendent," Figuerola said as she put the surveillance photographs from Modig's mobile on Edklinth's desk.

"Superintendent," Edklinth muttered.

"Stefan identified him last night. He went to the apartment on Artillerigatan."

"What do we know about him?"

"He comes from the regular police and has worked for S.I.S. since 1983. Since 1996 he's been serving as an investigator with his own area of responsibility. He does internal checks and examines cases that S.I.S. has completed."

"O.K."

"Since Saturday morning six persons of interest have been to the building. Besides Sandberg and Nyström, Clinton is definitely operating from there. This morning he was taken by ambulance to have dialysis."

"Who are the other three?"

"A man named Otto Hallberg. He was in S.I.S. in the '80s but he's actually connected to the Defence General Staff. He works for the navy and the military intelligence service."

"I see. Why am I not surprised?"

Figuerola laid down one more photograph. "This man we haven't identified yet. He went to lunch with Hallberg. We'll have to see if we can get a better picture when he goes home tonight. But the most interesting one is this man." She laid another photograph on the desk.

"I recognize him," Edklinth said.

"His name is Wadensjöö."

"Precisely. He worked on the terrorist detail around fifteen years ago. A desk man. He was one of the candidates for the post of top boss here at the Firm. I don't know what became of him."

"He resigned in 1991. Guess who he had lunch with an hour or so ago."

She put her last photograph on the desk.

"Chief of Secretariat Shenke and Chief of Budget Gustav Atterbom. I want to have surveillance on these gentlemen around the clock. I want to know exactly who they meet."

"That's not practical," Edklinth said. "I have only four men available."

Edklinth pinched his lower lip as he thought. Then he looked up at Figuerola.

"We need more people," he said. "Do you think you could reach Inspector Bublanski discreetly and ask him if he might like to have dinner with me today? Around 7.00, say?"

Edklinth then reached for his telephone and dialled a number from memory.

"Hello, Armansky. It's Edklinth. Might I reciprocate for that wonderful dinner? No, I insist. Shall we say 7.00?"

Salander had spent the night in Kronoberg prison in a two-by-four-metre cell. The furnishings were pretty basic, but she had fallen asleep within minutes of the key being turned in the lock. Early on Monday morning she was up and obediently doing the stretching exercises prescribed for her by the physio at Sahlgrenska. Breakfast was then brought to her, and she sat on her cot and stared into space.

At 9.30 she was led to an interrogation cell at the end of the corridor. The guard was a short, bald, old man with a round face and horn-rimmed glasses. He was polite and cheerful.

Giannini greeted her affectionately. Salander ignored Faste. She was meeting Prosecutor Ekström for the first time, and she spent the next half hour sitting on a chair staring stonily at a spot on the wall just above Ekström's head. She said nothing and she did not move a muscle.

At 10.00 Ekström broke off the fruitless interrogation. He was annoyed not to be able to get the slightest response out of her. For the first time he felt uncertain as he observed the thin, doll-like young woman. How was it possible that she could have beaten up those two thugs Lundin and Nieminen in Stallarholmen? Would the court really believe that story, even if he did have convincing evidence?

Salander was brought a simple lunch at noon and spent the next hour solving equations in her head. She focused on an area of spherical astronomy from a book she had read two years earlier.

At 2.30 she was led back to the interrogation cell. This time her guard was a young woman. Salander sat on a chair in the empty cell and pondered a particularly intricate equation.

After ten minutes the door opened.

"Hello, Lisbeth." A friendly tone. It was Teleborian.

He smiled at her, and she froze. The components of the equation she had constructed in the air before her came tumbling to the ground. She could hear the numbers and mathematical symbols bouncing and clattering as if they had physical form.

Teleborian stood still for a minute and looked at her before he sat down on the other side of the table. She continued to stare at the same spot on the wall.

After a while she met his eyes.

"I'm sorry that you've ended up in this situation," Teleborian said. "I'm going to try to help you in every way I can. I hope we can establish some level of mutual trust."

Salander examined every inch of him. The dishevelled hair. The beard. The little gap between his front teeth. The thin lips. The brand-new brown jacket. The shirt open at the neck. She listened to his smooth and treacherously friendly voice.

"I also hope that I can be of more help to you than the last time we met."

He placed a small notebook and pen on the table. Salander lowered her eyes and looked at the pen. It was a pointed, silver-coloured tube.

Risk assessment.

She suppressed an impulse to reach out and grab the pen.

Her eyes sought the little finger of his left hand. She saw a faint white mark where fifteen years earlier she had sunk in her teeth and locked her jaws so hard that she almost bit his finger off. It had taken three guards to hold her down and prise open her jaws.

I was a scared little girl barely into my teens then. Now I'm a grown woman. I can kill you whenever I want.

Again she fixed her eyes on the spot on the wall, and gathered up the scattered numbers and symbols and began to reassemble the equation.

Teleborian studied Salander with a neutral expression. He had not become an internationally respected psychiatrist for nothing. He had a gift for reading emotions and moods. He could sense a cold shadow passing through the room, and interpreted this as a sign that the patient felt fear and shame beneath her imperturbable exterior. He assumed that she was reacting to his presence, and was pleased that her attitude towards him had not changed over the years. *She's going to hang herself in the district court.*

Berger's final act at *S.M.P.* was to write a memo to the staff. To begin with her mood was angry, and she filled two pages explaining why she was resigning, including her opinion of various colleagues. Then she deleted the whole text and started again in a calmer tone.

She did not refer to Fredriksson. If she had done, all interest would have focused on him, and her real reasons would be drowned out by the sensation a case of sexual harassment would inevitably cause.

She gave two reasons. The principal one was that she had met implacable resistance from management to her proposal that managers and owners should reduce their salaries and bonuses. Which meant that she would have had to start her tenure at *S.M.P.* with damaging cutbacks in staff. This was not only a breach of the promise she had been given when she accepted the job, but it would undercut her every attempt to bring about long-term change in order to strengthen the newspaper.

The second reason she gave was the revelation about Borgsjo. She wrote that she had been instructed to cover up the story, and this flew in the face of all she believed to be her job. It meant that she had no choice but to resign her position as editor. She concluded by saying that *S.M.P.*'s dire situation was not a personnel problem, but a management problem.

She read through the memo, corrected the typos, and emailed it to all the paper's employees. She sent a copy to *Pressens Tidning*, a media journal, and also to the trade magazine *Journalisten*. Then she packed away her laptop and went to see Holm at his desk.

"Goodbye," she said.

"Goodbye, Berger. It was hellish working with you."

They smiled at each other.

"One last thing," she said.

"Tell me?"

"Frisk has been working on a story I commissioned."

"Right, and nobody has any idea what it's about."

"Give him some support. He's come a long way, and I'll be staying in touch with him. Let him finish the job. I guarantee you'll be pleased with the result."

He looked wary. Then he nodded.

They did not shake hands. She left her card key on his desk and took the lift down to the garage. She parked her B.M.W. near the *Millennium* offices at a little after 4.00.

PART 4

REBOOTING SYSTEM

1.vii – 7.x

Despite the rich variety of Amazon legends from ancient Greece, South America, Africa and elsewhere, there is only one historically documented example of female warriors. This is the women's army that existed among the Fon of Dahomey in West Africa, now Benin.

These female warriors have never been mentioned in the published military histories; no romanticized films have been made about them, and today they exist as no more than footnotes to history. Only one scholarly work has been written about these women, *Amazons of Black Sparta* by Stanley B. Alpern (C. Hurst & Co., London, 1998), and yet they made up a force that was the equal of every contemporary body of male elite soldiers from among the colonial powers.

It is not clear exactly when Fon's female army was founded, but some sources date it to the 1600s. It was originally a royal guard, but it developed into a military collective of six thousand soldiers with a semi-divine status. They were not merely window-dressing. For almost two hundred years they constituted the vanguard of the Fon against European colonizers. They were feared by the French forces, who lost several battles against them. This army of women was not defeated until 1892, when France sent troops with artillery, the Foreign Legion, a marine infantry regiment and cavalry.

It is not known how many of these female warriors fell in battle. For many years survivors continued to wage guerrilla warfare, and veterans of the army were interviewed and photographed as late as the 1940s.

CHAPTER 23

Friday, 1.vii – Sunday, 10.vii

Two weeks before the trial of Lisbeth Salander began, Malm finished the layout of the 352-page book tersely entitled *The Section*. The cover was blue with yellow type. Malm had positioned seven postage-stamp-sized black-and-white images of Swedish Prime Ministers along the bottom. Over the top of them hovered a photograph of Zalachenko. He had used Zalachenko's passport photograph as an illustration, increasing the contrast so that only the darkest areas stood out like a shadow across the whole cover. It was not a particularly sophisticated design, but it was effective. Blomkvist, Cortez and Eriksson were named as the authors.

It was 5.00 in the morning and he had been working all night. He felt slightly sick and had badly wanted to go home and sleep. Eriksson had sat up with him doing final corrections page by page as Malm O.K.'d them and printed them out. By now she was asleep on the sofa.

Malm put the entire text plus illustrations into a folder. He started up the Toast program and burned two C.D.s. One he put in the safe. The other was collected by a sleepy Blomkvist just before 7.00.

"Go and get some rest," Blomkvist said.

"I'm on my way."

They left Eriksson asleep and turned on the door alarm. Cortez would be in at 8.00 to take over.

Blomkvist walked to Lundagatan, where he again borrowed Salander's abandoned Honda without permission. He drove to Hallvigs Reklam, the printers near the railway tracks in Morgongåva, west of Uppsala. This was a job he would not entrust to the post.

He drove slowly, refusing to acknowledge the stress he felt, and then waited until the printers had checked that they could read the C.D. He made sure that the book would indeed be ready to distribute on the first day of the trial. The problem was not the printing but the binding, which could take time. But Jan Köbin, Hallvigs' manager, promised to deliver at least five hundred copies of the first printing of ten thousand by that day. The book would be a trade paperback.

Finally, Blomkvist made sure that everyone understood the need for the greatest secrecy, although this reminder was probably unnecessary. Two years earlier Hallvigs had printed Blomkvist's book about Hans-Erik Wennerström under very similar circumstances. They knew that books from this peculiar publisher Millennium always promised something extra.

Blomkvist drove back to Stockholm in no particular hurry. He parked outside Bellmansgatan 1 and went to his apartment to pack a change of clothes and a wash bag. He drove on to Stavsnäs wharf in Värmdö, where he parked the Honda and took the ferry out to Sandhamn.

It was the first time since Christmas that he had been to the cabin. He unfastened the window shutters to let in the air and drank a Ramlösa. As always when a job was finished and at the printer, and nothing could be changed, he felt empty.

He spent an hour sweeping and dusting, scouring the shower tray, switching on the fridge, checking the water pipes and changing the bedclothes up in the sleeping loft. He went to the grocery and bought everything he would need for the weekend. Then he started up the coffeemaker and sat outside on the veranda, smoking a cigarette and not thinking about anything in particular.

Just before 5.00 he went down to the steamboat wharf and met Figuerola.

"I thought you said you couldn't take time off," he said, kissing her on the cheek.

"That's what I thought too. But I told Edklinth I've been working every waking minute for the past few weeks and I'm starting to burn out. I said I needed two days off to recharge my batteries."

"In Sandhamn?"

"I didn't tell him where I was going," she said with a smile.

Figuerola ferreted around in Blomkvist's 25-square-metre cabin. She subjected the kitchen area, the bathroom and the loft to a critical inspection before she nodded in approval. She washed and changed into a thin summer dress while Blomkvist cooked lamb chops in red wine sauce and set the table on the veranda. They ate in silence as they watched the parade of sailing boats on their way to or from the marina. They shared the rest of the bottle of wine.

"It's a wonderful cabin. Is this where you bring all your girlfriends?" Figuerola said.

"Just the important ones."

"Has Erika Berger been here?"

"Many times."

"And Salander?"

"She stayed here for a few weeks when I was writing the book about Wennerström. And we spent Christmas here two years ago."

"So both Berger and Salander are important in your life?"

"Erika is my best friend. We've been friends for twenty-five years. Lisbeth is a whole different story. She's certainly unique, and she the most antisocial person I've ever known. You could say that she made a big impression on me when we first met. I like her. She's a friend."

"You don't feel sorry for her?"

"No. She has herself to blame for a lot of the crap that's happened to her. But I do feel enormous sympathy and solidarity with her."

"But you aren't in love either with her or with Berger?"

He shrugged. Figuerola watched an Amigo 23 coming in late with its navigation lights glowing as it chugged past a motorboat on the way to the marina.

"If love is liking someone an awful lot, then I suppose I'm in love with several people," Blomkvist said.

"And now with me?"

Blomkvist nodded. Figuerola frowned and looked at him.

"Does it bother you?"

"That you've brought other women here? No. But it does bother me that I don't really know what's happening between us. And I don't think I can have a relationship with a man who screws around whenever he feels like it . . ."

"I'm not going to apologize for the way I've led my life."

"And I guess that in some way I'm falling for you because you are who you are. It's easy to sleep with you because there's no bullshit and you make me feel safe. But this all started because I gave in to a crazy impulse. It doesn't happen very often, and I hadn't planned it. And now we've got to the stage where I've become just another one of the girls you invite out here."

They sat in silence for a moment.

"You didn't have to come."

"Yes, I did. Oh, Mikael . . ."

"I know."

"I'm unhappy. I don't want to fall in love with you. It'll hurt far too much when it's over."

"Listen, I've had this cabin for twenty-five years, since my father died and my mother moved back to Norrland. We shared out the property so that my sister got our apartment and I got the cabin. Apart from some casual acquaintances in the early years, there are five women who have been here before you: Erika, Lisbeth and my ex-wife, who I was together with in the '80s, a woman I was in a serious relationship with in the late '90s, and someone I met two years ago, whom I still see occasionally. It's sort of special circumstances . . ."

"I bet it is."

"I keep this cabin so that I can get away from the city and have some quiet time. I'm mostly here on my own. I read books, I write, and I relax and sit on the wharf and look at the boats. It's not a secret love nest."

He stood up to get the bottle of wine he had put in the shade.

"I won't make any promises. My marriage broke up because Erika and I couldn't keep away from each other," he said, and then he added in English, "Been there, done that, got the T-shirt."

He filled their glasses.

"But you're the most interesting person I've met in a long time. It's as if our relationship took off at full speed from a standing start. I think I fell for you the moment you picked me up outside my apartment. The few times I've slept at my place since then, I've woken up in the middle of the night needing you. I don't know if I want a steady relationship, but I'm terrified of losing you." He looked at her. "So what do you think we should do?"

"Let's think about things," Figuerola said. "I'm badly attracted to you too."

"This is starting to get serious," Blomkvist said.

She suddenly felt a great sadness. They did not say much for a long time. When it got dark they cleared the table, went inside and closed the door.

On the Friday before the week of the trial, Blomkvist stopped at the Pressbyrån news-stand at Slussen and read the billboards for the morning papers. *Svenska Morgon-Posten*'s C.E.O. and chairman of the board

452

Magnus Borgsjö had capitulated and tendered his resignation. Blomkvist bought the papers and walked to Java on Hornsgatan to have a late breakfast. Borgsjö cited family reasons as the explanation for his unexpected resignation. He would not comment on claims that Berger had also resigned after he ordered her to cover up a story about his involvement in the wholesale enterprise Vitavara Inc. But in a sidebar it was reported that the chair of Svenskt Näringsliv, the confederation of Swedish enterprise, had decided to set up an ethics committee to investigate the dealings of Swedish companies with businesses in South East Asia known to exploit child labour.

Blomkvist burst out laughing, and then he folded the morning papers and flipped open his Ericsson to call the woman who presented *She* on T.V.4, who was in the middle of a lunchtime sandwich.

"Hello, darling," Blomkvist said. "I'm assuming you'd still like dinner sometime."

"Hi, Mikael," she laughed. "Sorry, but you couldn't be further from my type."

"Still, how about coming out with me this evening to discuss a job?"

"What have you got going?"

"Erika Berger made a deal with you two years ago about the Wennerström affair. I want to make a similar deal that will work just as well."

"I'm all ears."

"I can't tell you about it until we've agreed on the terms. I've got a story in the works. We're going to publish a book and a themed issue of the magazine, and it's going to be huge. I'm offering you an exclusive look at all the material, provided you don't leak anything before we publish. This time the publication is extra complicated because it has to happen on a specific day."

"How big is the story?"

"Bigger than Wennerström," Blomkvist said. "Are you interested?"

"Are you serious? Where shall we meet?"

"How about Samir's Cauldron? Erika's going to sit in on the meeting."

"What's going with on her? Is she back at *Millennium* now that she's been thrown out of *S.M.P.*?"

"She didn't get thrown out. She resigned because of differences of opinion with Magnus Borgsjö."

"He seems to be a real creep."

"You're not wrong there," Blomkvist said.

Clinton was listening to Verdi through his earphones. Music was pretty much the only thing left in life that could take him away from dialysis machines and the growing pain in the small of his back. He did not hum to the music. He closed his eyes and followed the notes with his right hand, which hovered and seemed to have a life of its own alongside his disintegrating body.

That is how it goes. We are born. We live. We grow old. We die. He had played his part. All that remained was the disintegration.

He felt strangely satisfied with life.

He was playing for his friend Evert Gullberg.

It was Saturday, July 9. Only four days until the trial, and the Section could set about putting this whole wretched story behind them. He had had the message that morning. Gullberg had been tougher than almost anyone he had known. When you fire a 9 mm full-metal-jacketed bullet into your own temple you expect to die. Yet it was three months before Gullberg's body gave up at last. That was probably due as much to chance as to the stubbornness with which the doctors had waged the battle for Gullberg's life. And it was the cancer, not the bullet, that had finally determined his end.

Gullberg's death had been painful, and that saddened Clinton. Although incapable of communicating with the outside world, he had at times been in a semi-conscious state, smiling when the hospital staff stroked his cheek or grunting when he seemed to be in pain. Sometimes he had tried to form words and even sentences, but nobody was able to understand anything he said.

He had no family, and none of his friends came to his sickbed. His last contact with life was an Eritrean night nurse by the name of Sara Kitama, who kept watch at his bedside and held his hand as he died.

Clinton realized that he would soon be following his former comrade-in-arms. No doubt about that. The likelihood of his surviving a transplant operation decreased each day. His liver and intestinal functions appeared to have declined at each examination.

He hoped to live past Christmas.

Yet he was contented. He felt an almost spiritual, giddy satisfaction that his final days had involved such a sudden and surprising return to service.

It was a boon he could not have anticipated.

454

The last notes of Verdi faded away just somebody opened the door to the small room in which he was resting at the Section's headquarters on Artillerigatan.

Clinton opened his eyes. It was Wadensjöö.

He had come to the conclusion that Wadensjöö was a dead weight. He was entirely unsuitable as director of the most important vanguard of Swedish national defence. He could not conceive how he and von Rottinger could ever have made such a fundamental miscalculation as to imagine that Wadensjöö was the appropriate successor.

Wadensjöö was a warrior who needed a fair wind. In a crisis he was feeble and incapable of making a decision. A timid encumbrance lacking steel in his backbone who would most likely have remained in paralysis, incapable of action, and let the Section go under.

It was this simple. Some had it. Others would always falter when it came to the crunch.

"You wanted a word?"

"Sit down," Clinton said.

Wadensjöö sat.

"I'm at a stage in my life when I can no longer waste time. I'll get straight to the point. When all this is over, I want you to resign from the management of the Section."

"You do?"

Clinton tempered his tone.

"You're a good man, Wadensjöö. But unfortunately you're completely unsuited to shouldering the responsibility after Gullberg. You should not have been given that responsibility. Von Rottinger and I were at fault when we failed to deal properly with the succession after I got sick."

"You've never liked me."

"You're wrong about that. You were an excellent administrator when von Rottinger and I were in charge of the Section. We would have been helpless without you, and I have great admiration for your patriotism. It's your inability to make decisions that lets you down."

Wadensjöö smiled bitterly. "After this, I don't know if I even want to stay in the Section."

"Now that Gullberg and von Rottinger are gone, I've had to make the crucial decisions myself," Clinton said. "And you've obstructed every decision I've made during the past few months."

"And I maintain that the decisions you've made are absurd. It's going to end in disaster."

455

"That's possible. But your indecision would have guaranteed our collapse. Now at least we have a chance, and it seems to be working. *Millennium* don't know which way to turn. They may suspect that we're somewhere out here, but they lack documentation and they have no way of finding it – or us. And we know at least as much as they do."

Wadensjöö looked out of the window and across the rooftops.

"The only thing we still have to do is to get rid of Zalachenko's daughter," Clinton said. "If anyone starts burrowing about in her past and listening to what she has to say, there's no knowing what might happen. But the trial starts in a few days and then it'll be over. This time we have to bury her so deep that she'll never come back to haunt us."

Wadensjöö shook his head.

"I don't understand your attitude," Clinton said.

"I can see that. You're sixty-eight years old. You're dying. Your decisions are not rational, and yet you seem to have bewitched Nyström and Sandberg. They obey you as if you were God the Father."

"I am God the Father in everything that has to do with the Section. We're working according to a plan. Our decision to act has given the Section a chance. And it is with the utmost conviction that I say that the Section will never find itself in such an exposed position again. When all this is over, we're going to put in hand a complete overhaul of our activities."

"I see."

"Nyström will be the new director. He's really too old, but he's the only choice we have, and he's promised to stay on for six years at least. Sandberg is too young and – as a direct result of your management policies – too inexperienced. He should have been fully trained by now."

"Clinton, don't you see what you've done? You've murdered a man. Björck worked for the Section for thirty-five years, and you ordered his death. Do you not understand—"

"You know quite well that it was necessary. He betrayed us, and he would never have withstood the pressure when the police closed in."

Wadensjöö stood up.

"I'm not finished."

"Then we'll have to take it up later. I have a job to do while you lie here fantasizing that you're the Almighty."

"If you're so morally indignant, why don't you go to Bublanski and confess your crimes?"

"Believe me, I've considered it. But whatever you may think, I'm doing everything in my power to protect the Section."

He opened the door and met Nyström and Sandberg on their way in.

"Hello, Fredrik," Nyström said. "We have to talk."

"Wadensjöö was just leaving."

Nyström waited until the door had closed. "Fredrik, I'm seriously worried."

"What's going on?"

"Sandberg and I have been thinking. Things are happening that we don't understand. This morning Salander's lawyer lodged her autobiographical statement with the prosecutor."

"*What?*"

Inspector Faste scrutinized Advokat Giannini as Ekström poured coffee from a thermos jug. The document Ekström had been handed when he arrived at work that morning had taken both of them by surprise. He and Faste had read the forty pages of Salander's story and discussed the extraordinary document at length. Finally he felt compelled to ask Giannini to come in for an informal chat.

They were sitting at the small conference table in Ekström's office.

"Thank you for agreeing to come in," Ekström said. "I have read this . . . hmm, account that arrived this morning, and there are a few matters I'd like to clarify."

"I'll do what I can to help" Giannini said.

"I don't know exactly where to start. Let me say from the outset that both Inspector Faste and I are profoundly astonished."

"Indeed?"

"I'm trying to understand what your objective is."

"How do you mean?"

"This autobiography, or whatever you want to call it . . . What's the point of it?"

"The point is perfectly clear. My client wants to set down her version of what has happened to her."

Ekström gave a good-natured laugh. He stroked his goatee, an oft-repeated gesture that was beginning to irritate Giannini.

"Yes, but your client has had several months to explain herself. She hasn't said a word in all her interviews with Faste."

"As far as I know there is no law that forces my client to talk simply when it suits Inspector Faste."

"No, but I mean . . . Salander's trial will begin in four days' time, and at the eleventh hour she comes up with this. To tell the truth, I feel a responsibility here which is beyond my duties as prosecutor."

"You do?"

"I do not in the very least wish to sound offensive. That is not my intention. But we have a procedure for trials in this country. You, Fru Giannini, are a lawyer specialising in women's rights, and you have never before represented a client in a criminal case. I did not charge Lisbeth Salander because she is a woman, but on a charge of grievous bodily harm. Even you, I believe, must have realized that she suffers from a serious mental illness and needs the protection and assistance of the state."

"You're afraid that I won't be able to provide Lisbeth Salander with an adequate defence," Giannini said in a friendly tone.

"I do not wish to be judgemental," Ekström said, "and I don't question your competence. I'm simply making the point that you lack experience."

"I do understand, and I completely agree with you. I am woefully inexperienced when it comes to criminal cases."

"And yet you have all along refused the help that has been offered by lawyers with considerably more experience—"

"At the express wish of my client. Lisbeth Salander wants me to be her lawyer, and accordingly I will be representing her in court." She gave him a polite smile.

"Very well, but I do wonder whether in all seriousness you intend to offer the content of this statement to the court."

"Of course. It's her story."

Ekström and Faste glanced at one another. Faste raised his eyebrows. He could not see what Ekström was fussing about. If Giannini did not understand that she was on her way to sinking her client, then that certainly was not the prosecutor's fault. All they needed to do was to say thank you, accept the document, and put the issue aside.

As far as he was concerned, Salander was off her rocker. He had employed all his skills to persuade her to tell them, at the very least, where she lived. But in interview after interview that damn girl had just sat there, silent as a stone, staring at the wall behind him. She had refused the cigarettes he offered, and had never so much as accepted a coffee or a cold drink. Nor had she registered the least reaction when he pleaded with her, or when he raised his voice in moments of extreme annoyance. Faste had never conducted a more frustrating set of interviews.

"Fru Giannini," Ekström said at last, "I believe that your client ought to be spared this trial. She is not well. I have a psychiatric report from a highly qualified doctor to fall back on. She should be given the psychiatric care that for so many years she has badly needed."

"I take it that you will be presenting this recommendation to the district court."

"That's exactly what I'll be doing. It's not my business to tell you how to conduct her defence. But if this is the line you seriously intend to take, then the situation is, quite frankly, absurd. This statement contains wild and unsubstantiated accusations against a number of people . . . in particular against her guardian, Advokat Bjurman, and Dr Peter Teleborian. I hope you do not in all seriousness believe that the court will accept an account that casts suspicion on Dr Teleborian without offering a single shred of evidence. This document is going to be the final nail in your client's coffin, if you'll pardon the metaphor."

"I hear what you're saying."

"In the course of the trial you may claim that she is not ill and request a supplementary psychiatric assessment, and then the matter can be submitted to the medical board. But to be honest her statement leaves me in very little doubt that every other forensic psychiatrist will come to the same conclusion as Dr Teleborian. Its very existence confirms all documentary evidence that she is a paranoid schizophrenic."

Giannini smiled politely. "There is an alternative view," she said.

"What's that?"

"That her account is in every detail true and that the court will elect to believe it."

Ekström looked bewildered by the notion. Then he smiled and stroked his goatee.

Clinton was sitting at the little side table by the window in his office. He listened attentively to Nyström and Sandberg. His face was furrowed, but his peppercorn eyes were focused and alert.

"We've been monitoring the telephone and email traffic of

459

Millennium's key employees since April," Clinton said. "We've confirmed that Blomkvist and Eriksson and this Cortez fellow are pretty downcast on the whole. We've read the outline version of the next issue. It seems that even Blomkvist has reversed his position and is now of the view that Salander is mentally unstable after all. There is a socially linked defence for her – he's claiming that society let her down, and that as a result it's somehow not her fault that she tried to murder her father. But that's hardly an argument. There isn't one word about the break-in at his apartment or the fact that his sister was attacked in Göteborg, and there's no mention of the missing reports. He knows he can't prove anything."

"That is precisely the problem," Sandberg said. "Blomkvist must know that someone has their eye on him. But he seems to be completely ignoring his suspicions. Forgive me, but that isn't *Millennium*'s style. Besides, Erika Berger is back in editorial and yet this whole issue is so bland and devoid of substance that it seems like a joke."

"What are you saying? That it's a decoy?"

Sandberg nodded. "The summer issue should have come out in the last week of June. According to one of Malin Eriksson's emails, it's being printed by a company in Södertälje, but when I rang them this morning, they told me they hadn't even got the C.R.C. All they'd had was a request for a quote about a month ago."

"Where have they printed before?" Clinton said.

"At a place called Hallvigs in Morgongåva. I called to ask how far they had got with the printing – I said I was calling from *Millennium*. The manager wouldn't tell me a thing. I thought I'd drive up there this evening and take a look."

"Makes sense. Georg?"

"I've reviewed all the telephone traffic from the past week," Nyström said. "It's bizarre, but the *Millennium* staff never discuss anything to do with the trial or Zalachenko."

"Nothing at all?"

"No. They mention it only when they're talking with someone outside *Millennium*. Listen to this, for instance. Blomkvist gets a call from a reporter at *Aftonbladet* asking whether he has any comment to make on the upcoming trial."

He put a tape recorder on the table.

"Sorry, but I have no comment."

"You've been involved with the story from the start. You were the one who found Salander down in Gosseberga. And you haven't published a single word since. When do you intend to publish?"

"When the time is right. Provided I have anything to say."

"Do you?"

"Well, you can buy a copy of Millennium *and see for yourself."*

He turned off the recorder.

"We didn't think about this before, but I went back and listened to bits at random. It's been like this the entire time. He hardly discusses the Zalachenko business except in the most general terms. He doesn't even discuss it with his sister, and she's Salander's lawyer."

"Maybe he really doesn't have anything to say."

"He consistently refuses to speculate about anything. He seems to live at the offices round the clock; he's hardly ever at his apartment. If he's working night and day, then he ought to have come up with something more substantial than whatever's going to be in the next issue of *Millennium*."

"And we still haven't been able to tap the phones at their offices?"

"No," Sandberg said. "There's been somebody there twenty-four hours a day – and that's significant – ever since we went into Blomkvist's apartment the first time. The office lights are always on, and if it's not Blomkvist it's Cortez or Eriksson, or that faggot . . . er, Christer Malm."

Clinton stroked his chin and thought for a moment.

"Conclusions?"

Nyström said: "If I didn't know better, I'd think they were putting on an act for us."

Clinton felt a cold shiver run down the back of his neck. "Why hasn't this occurred to us before?"

"We've been listening to what they've been saying, not to what they haven't been saying. We've been gratified when we've heard their confusion or noticed it in an email. Blomkvist knows damn well that someone stole copies of the 1991 Salander report from him and his sister. But what the hell is he doing about it?"

"And they didn't report her mugging to the police?"

Nyström shook his head. "Giannini was present at the interviews with Salander. She's polite, but she never says anything of any weight. And Salander herself never says anything at all."

"But that will work in our favour. The more she keeps her mouth shut, the better. What does Ekström say?"

"I saw him a couple of hours ago. He'd just been given Salander's statement." He pointed to the pages in Clinton's lap.

"Ekström is confused. It's fortunate that Salander is no good at expressing herself in writing. To an outsider this would look like a totally insane conspiracy theory with added pornographic elements. But she still shoots very close to the mark. She describes exactly how she came to be locked up at St Stefan's, and she claims that Zalachenko worked for Säpo and so on. She says she thinks everything is connected with a little club inside Säpo, pointing to the existence of something corresponding to the Section. All in all it's fairly accurate. But as I said, it's not plausible. Ekström is in a dither because this also seems to be the line of defence Giannini is going to use at the trial."

"Shit," Clinton said. He bowed his head and thought intently for several minutes. Finally he looked up.

"Jonas, drive up to Morgongåva this evening and find out if anything is going on. If they're printing *Millennium*, I want a copy."

"I'll take Falun with me."

"Good. Georg, I want you to see Ekström this afternoon and take his pulse. Everything has gone smoothly until now, but I can't ignore what you two are telling me."

Clinton sat in silence for a moment more.

"The best thing would be if there wasn't any trial . . ." he said at last.

He raised his eyes and looked at Nyström. Nyström nodded. Sandberg nodded.

"Nyström, can you investigate our options?"

Sandberg and the locksmith known as Falun parked a short distance from the railway tracks and walked through Morgongåva. It was 8.30 in the evening. It was too light and too early to do anything, but they wanted to reconnoitre and get a look at the place.

"If the building is alarmed, I'm not doing it," Falun said. "It would be better to have a look through the window. If there's anything lying around, you can just chuck a rock through, jump in, grab what you need and run like hell."

"That'll work," Sandberg said.

"If you only need one copy of the magazine, we can check the dustbins round the back. There must be overruns and test printings and things like that."

Hallvigs Reklam printing factory was in a low, brick building. They approached from the south on the other side of the street. Sandberg was about to cross when Falun took hold of his elbow.

"Keep going straight," he said.

"What?"

"Keep going straight, as if we're out for an evening stroll."

They passed Hallvigs and made a tour of the neighbourhood.

"What was all that about?" Sandberg said.

"You've got to keep your eyes peeled. The place isn't just alarmed. There was a car parked alongside the building."

"You mean somebody's there?"

"It was a car from Milton Security. The factory is under surveillance, for Christ's sake."

"Milton Security?" Clinton felt the shock hit him in the gut.

"If it hadn't been for Falun, I would have walked right into their arms," Sandberg said.

"There's something fishy going on," Nyström said. "There is no rationale for a small out of town printer to hire Milton Security for 24-hour surveillance."

Clinton's lips were pressed tight. It was after 11.00 and he needed to rest.

"And that means *Millennium* really *is* up to something," Sandberg said.

"I can see that," Clinton said. "O.K. Let's analyse the situation. What's the worst-case scenario? What *could* they know?" He gave Nyström an urgent look.

"It has to be the Salander report," he said. "They beefed up their security after we lifted the copies. They must have guessed that they're under surveillance. The worst case is that they still have a copy of the report."

"But Blomkvist was at his wits' end when it went missing."

"I know. But we may have been duped. We can't shut our eyes to that possibility."

"We'll work on that assumption," Clinton said. "Sandberg?"

"We do know what Salander's defence will be. She's going to tell the truth as she sees it. I've read this autobiography of hers. In fact it plays right into our hands. It's full of such outrageous accusations of rape and violation of her civil rights that it will come across as the ravings of a paranoid personality."

Nyström said: "Besides, she can't prove a single one of her claims. Ekström will use the account against her. He'll annihilate her credibility."

"O.K. Teleborian's new report is excellent. There is, of course, the possibility that Giannini will call in her own expert who'll say that Salander isn't crazy, and the whole thing will end up before the medical board. But again – unless Salander changes tactics, she's going to refuse to talk to them too, and then they'll conclude that Teleborian is right. She's her own worst enemy."

"The best thing would still be if there was no trial," Clinton said.

Nyström shook his head. "That's virtually impossible. She's in Kronoberg prison and she has no contact with other prisoners. She gets an hour's exercise each day in the little area on the roof, but we can't get to her up there. And we have no contacts among the prison staff."

"There may still be time."

"If we'd wanted to dispose of her, we should have done it when she was at Sahlgrenska. The likelihood that a hit man would do time is almost 100 per cent. And where would we find a gun who'd agree to that? And at such short notice it would be impossible to arrange a suicide or an accident."

"I was afraid of that. And unexpected deaths have a tendency to invite questions. O.K., we'll have to see how the trial goes. In reality, nothing has changed. We've always anticipated that they would make some sort of counter-move, and it seems to be this so-called autobiography."

"The problem is *Millennium*," Sandberg said.

"*Millennium* and Milton Security," Clinton said pensively. "Salander has worked for Armansky, and Blomkvist once had a thing with her. Should we assume that they've joined forces?"

"It doesn't seem unreasonable that Milton Security is watching the factory where *Millennium* is being printed. And it can't be a coincidence."

"When are they going to publish? Sandberg, you said that they're almost two weeks behind schedule. If we assume that Milton is keeping an eye on the printer's to make sure that nobody gets hold of a copy, that means either that they're publishing something that they don't want to leak, or that the magazine has already been printed."

"To coincide with the opening of the trial," Sandberg said. "That's the only reasonable explanation."

Clinton nodded. "O.K. What's going to be in the magazine?"

They thought for a while, until Nyström broke the silence.

"In the worst case they have a copy of the 1991 report, as we said."

Clinton and Sandberg had reached the same conclusion.

"But what can they do with it?" Sandberg said. "The report implicates Björck and Teleborian. Björck is dead. They can press hard with Teleborian, but he'll claim that he was doing a routine forensic psychiatric examination. It'll be their word against his."

"And what can we do if they publish the report?" Nyström said.

"I think we're holding the trump card," Clinton said. "If there's a ruckus over the report, the focus will be on Säpo, not the Section. And when reporters start asking questions, Säpo will just pull it out of the archive . . ."

"And it won't be the same report," Sandberg said.

"Shenke has put the modified version in the archive, that is, the version Ekström was given to read. It was assigned a case number. So we could swiftly present a lot of disinformation to the media . . . We have the original, which Bjurman got hold of, and *Millennium* only has a copy. We could even spread information to suggest that it was Blomkvist himself who falsified the original."

"Good. What else could *Millennium* know?"

"They can't know anything about the Section. That wouldn't be possible. They'll have to focus on Säpo, and that would mean Blomkvist being cast as a conspiracy theorist."

"By now he's rather well known," Clinton said slowly. "Since the resolution of the Wennerström affair he's been taken pretty seriously."

"Could we somehow reduce his credibility?" Sandberg said.

Nyström and Clinton exchanged glances. Clinton looked at Nyström.

"Do you think you could put your hands on . . . let's say, fifty grams of cocaine?"

"Maybe from the Yugos."

"Give it a try. And get a move-on. The trial starts in three days."

"I don't get it," Sandberg said.

"It's a trick as old as the profession. But still extremely effective."

"Morgongåva?" Edklinth said with a frown. He was sitting in his dressing gown on the sofa at home, reading through Salander's autobiography for the third time, when Figuerola called. Since it was after midnight, he assumed that something was up.

"Morgongåva," Figuerola repeated. "Sandberg and Lars Faulsson were there at 8.30 this evening. They were tailed by Inspector Andersson from Bublanski's gang, and we had a radio transmitter planted in Sandberg's car. They parked near the old railway station, walked around for a while, and then returned to the car and drove back to Stockholm."

"I see. Did they meet anyone, or—"

"No. That was the strange thing. They just got out of the car and walked around a little, then drove straight back to Stockholm, so Andersson told me."

"I see. And why are you calling me at 12.30 at night to tell me this?"

"It took a little while to work it out. They walked past Hallvigs printers. I talked to Blomkvist about it. That's where *Millennium*'s being printed."

"Oh shit," Edklinth said. He saw the implications immediately.

"Since Falun was along, I have to suppose that they were intending to pay the printer's a late-night visit, but they abandoned the expedition," Figuerola said.

"Why?"

"Because Blomkvist asked Armansky to keep an eye on the factory until the magazine was distributed. They probably saw the car from Milton Security. I thought you'd want to know straightaway."

"You're right. It means that they've begun to smell a rat."

"Alarm bells must have gone off in their heads when they saw the car. Sandberg dropped Faulsson off in town and then went back to Artillerigatan. We know that Clinton is there. Nyström arrived at about the same time. The question is, what are they going to do?"

"The trial starts on Wednesday . . . Can you reach Blomkvist and urge him to double up on security at *Millennium*? Just in case."

"They already have good security. And they blew smoke rings round their tapped telephones – like old pros. Blomkvist is so paranoid already that he's using diversionary tactics we could learn from."

"I'm happy to hear it, but call him anyway."

Figuerola closed her mobile and put it on the bedside table. She looked up and studied Blomkvist as he lay naked with his head against the foot of the bed.

"I'm to call you and tell you to beef up security at *Millennium*," she said.

"Thanks for the suggestion," he said wryly.

"I'm serious. If they start to smell a rat, there's a danger that they'll go and do something without thinking. They might break in."

"Henry's sleeping there tonight. And we have a burglar alarm that goes straight to Milton Security, three minutes away."

He lay in silence with his eyes shut.

"Paranoid," he muttered.

CHAPTER 24

Monday, 11.vii

It was 6.00 on Monday morning when Linder from Milton Security called Blomkvist on his T10.

"Don't you people ever rest?" Blomkvist said, drunk with sleep.

He glanced at Figuerola. She was up already and had changed into jogging shorts, but had not yet put on her T-shirt.

"Sure. But the night duty officer woke me. The silent alarm we installed at your apartment went off at 3.00."

"Did it?"

"I drove down to see what was going on. This is a bit tricky. Could you come to Milton this morning? As soon as possible, that is."

"This is serious," Armansky said.

It was just after 8.00 when Armansky, Blomkvist and Linder were gathered in front of a T.V. monitor in a conference room at Milton Security. Armansky had also called in Johan Fräklund, a retired criminal inspector in the Solna police, now chief of Milton's operations unit, and the former inspector Sonny Bohman, who had been involved in the Salander affair from the start. They were pondering the surveillance video that Linder had just shown them.

"What we see here is Säpo officer Jonas Sandberg opening the door to Mikael's apartment at 3.17. He has his own keys. You will recall that Faulsson the locksmith made copies of the spare set when he and Göran Mårtensson broke in several weeks ago."

Armansky nodded sternly.

"Sandberg is in the apartment for approximately eight minutes. During that time he does the following things. First, he takes a small plastic bag from the kitchen, which he fills. Then he unscrews the back plate of a loudspeaker which you have in the living room, Mikael. That's where he places the bag. The fact that he takes a bag from your kitchen is significant."

"It's a Konsum bag," Blomkvist said. "I save them to put cheese and stuff in."

"I do the same. What matters, of course, is that the bag has your fingerprints on it. Then he takes a copy of *S.M.P.* from the recycling bin in the hall. He tears off a page to wrap up an object which he puts on the top shelf of your wardrobe. Same thing there: the paper has your fingerprints on it."

"I get you," Blomkvist said.

"I drive to your apartment at around 5.00," Linder said. "I find the following items: in your loudspeaker there are now approximately 180 grams of cocaine. I've taken a sample which I have here."

She put a small evidence bag on the conference table.

"What's in the wardrobe?" Blomkvist said.

"About 120,000 kronor in cash."

Armansky motioned to Linder to turn off the T.V. He turned to Fräklund.

"So Mikael Blomkvist is involved in cocaine dealing," Fräklund said good-naturedly. "Apparently they've started to get a little worried about what Blomkvist is working on."

"This is a counter-move," Blomkvist said.

"A counter-move to what?"

"They ran into Milton's security patrol in Morgongåva last night."

He told them what he had heard from Figuerola about Sandberg's expedition to the printing factory.

"That busy little rascal," Bohman said.

"But why now?"

"They must be nervous about what *Millennium* might publish when the trial starts," Fräklund said. "If Blomkvist is arrested for dealing cocaine, his credibility will drop dramatically."

Linder nodded. Blomkvist looked sceptical.

"How are we going to handle this?" Armansky said.

"We should do nothing," Fräklund said. "We hold all the cards. We have crystal-clear evidence of Sandberg planting the stuff in your apartment. Let them spring the trap. We can prove your innocence in a second, and besides, this will be further proof of the Section's criminal activities. I would so love to be prosecutor when those guys are brought to trial."

"I don't know," Blomkvist said slowly. "The trial starts the day after tomorrow. The magazine is on the stands on Friday, day three of the trial. If they plan to frame me for dealing cocaine, I'll never have the time to explain how it happened before the magazine comes out. I risk sitting in prison and missing the beginning of the trial."

"So, all the more reason for you to stay out of sight this week," Armansky said.

"Well . . . I have to work with T.V.4 and I've got a number of other things to do. It would be enormously inconvenient—"

"Why right now?" Linder said suddenly.

"How do you mean?" Armansky said.

"They've had three months to smear Blomkvist. Why do it right now? Whatever happens they're not going to be able to prevent publication."

They all sat in silence for a moment.

"It might be because they don't have a clue what you're going to publish, Mikael," Armansky said. "They have to suppose that you have something in the offing . . . but they might think all you have is Björck's report. They have no reason to know that you're planning on rolling up the whole Section. If it's only about Björck's report, then it's certainly enough to blacken your reputation. Any revelations you might come up with would be drowned out when you're arrested and charged. Big scandal. The famous Mikael Blomkvist arrested on a drugs charge. Six to eight years in prison."

"Could I have two copies of the video?" Blomkvist said.

"What are you going to do with them?"

"Lodge one copy with Edklinth. And in three hours I'm going to be at T.V.4. I think it would be prudent to have this ready to run on T.V. if or when all hell breaks loose."

Figuerola turned off the D.V.D. player and put the remote on the table. They were meeting in the temporary office on Fridhemsplan.

"Cocaine," Edklinth said. "They're playing a very dirty game here."

Figuerola looked thoughtful. She glanced at Blomkvist.

"I thought it best to keep all of you up to date," he said with a shrug.

"I don't like this," Figuerola said. "It implies a recklessness. Someone hasn't really thought this through. They must realize that you wouldn't go quietly and let yourself be thrown into Kumla bunker under arrest on a drugs charge."

"I agree," Blomkvist said.

"Even if you were convicted, there's still a strong likelihood that people would believe what you have to say. And your colleagues at *Millennium* wouldn't keep quiet either."

"Furthermore, this is costing them a great deal," Edklinth said. "They have a budget that allows them to distribute 120,000 kronor here and there without blinking, plus whatever the cocaine costs them."

"I know, but the plan is actually not bad," Blomkvist said. "They're counting on Salander landing back in the asylum while I disappear in a cloud of suspicion. They're also assuming that any attention would be focused on Säpo – not on the Section."

"But how are they going to convince the drug squad to search your apartment? I mean, an anonymous tip will hardly be enough for someone to kick in the door of a star journalist. And if this is going to work, suspicion would have to be cast on you within forty-eight hours."

"Well, we don't really know anything about their schedule," Blomkvist said.

He felt exhausted and longed for all this to be over. He got up.

"Where are you off to?" Figuerola said. "I'd like to know where you're going to be for the next few days."

"I have a meeting with T.V.4 at lunchtime. And at 6.00 I'm going to catch up with Erika Berger over a lamb stew at Samir's. We're going to fine-tune the press release. The rest of the afternoon and evening I'll be at *Millennium*, I imagine."

Figuerola's eyes narrowed slightly at the mention of Berger.

"I need you to stay in touch during the day. I'd prefer it if you stayed in close contact until the trial starts."

"Maybe I could move in with you for a few days," Blomkvist said with a playful smile.

Figuerola's face darkened. She cast a hasty glance at Edklinth.

"Monica's right," Edklinth said. "I think it would be best if you stay more or less out of sight for the time being."

"You take care of your end," Blomkvist said, "and I'll take care of mine."

The presenter of *She* on T.V.4 could hardly conceal her excitement over the video material that Blomkvist had delivered. Blomkvist was amused at her undisguised glee. For a week they had worked like dogs to put together coherent material about the Section that they could use on T.V. Her producer and the news editor at T.V.4 were in no doubt as to what a scoop the story would be. It was being produced in the utmost secrecy, with only a very few people involved. They had agreed to Blomkvist's insistence that the story be the lead on the evening of the third day of the trial. They had decided to do an hour-long news special.

Blomkvist had given her a quantity of still photographs to work with, but on television nothing compares to the moving image. She was simply delighted when he showed her the video – in razor-sharp definition – of an identifiable police officer planting cocaine in his apartment.

"This is great T.V.," she said. "Camera shot: *Here is Säpo planting cocaine in the reporter's apartment.*"

"Not Säpo . . . *the Section*," Blomkvist corrected her. "Don't make the mistake of muddling the two."

"Sandberg works for Säpo, for God's sake," she said.

"Sure, but in practice he should be regarded as an infiltrator. Keep the boundary line very clear."

"Understood. It's the Section that's the story here. Not Säpo. Mikael, can you explain to me how it is that you keep getting mixed up in these sensational stories? And you're right. This is going to be bigger than the Wennerström affair."

"Sheer talent, I guess. Ironically enough this story also begins with a Wennerström. The spy scandal of the '60s, that is."

Berger called at 4.00. She was in a meeting with the newspaper publishers' association sharing her views on the planned cutbacks at S.M.P., which had given rise to a major conflict in the industry after she had resigned. She would not be able to make it to their dinner before 6.30.

Sandberg helped Clinton move from the wheelchair to the daybed in the room that was his command centre in the Section's headquarters on Artillerigatan. Clinton had just returned from a whole morning spent in dialysis. He felt ancient, infinitely weary. He had hardly slept the past few days and wished that all this would soon come to an end. He had managed to make himself comfortable, sitting up in the bed, when Nyström appeared.

Clinton concentrated his energy. "Is it ready?"

"I've just come from a meeting with the Nikolich brothers," Nyström said. "It's going to cost 50,000."

"We can afford it," Clinton said.

Christ, if only I were young again.

He turned his head and studied Nyström and Sandberg in turn.

"No qualms of conscience?" he said.

They shook their heads.

"When?" Clinton said.

"Within twenty-four hours," Nyström said. "It's difficult to pin down where Blomkvist is staying, but if the worst comes to the worst they'll do it outside *Millennium*'s offices."

"We have a possible opportunity tonight, two hours from now," said Sandberg.

"Oh, really?"

"Erika Berger called him a while ago. They're going to have dinner at Samir's Cauldron. It's a restaurant near Bellmansgatan."

"Berger . . ." Clinton said hesitantly.

"I hope for God's sake that she doesn't—" Nyström said.

"That wouldn't be the end of the world," Sandberg said.

Clinton and Nyström both stared at him.

"We're agreed that Blomkvist is our greatest threat, and that he's going to publish something damaging in the next issue of *Millennium*. We can't prevent publication, so we have to destroy his credibility. If he's killed in what appears to be a typical underworld hit and the police then find drugs and cash in his apartment, the investigators will draw certain conclusions. They won't initially be looking for conspiracies involving the Security Police."

"Go on," Clinton said.

"Erika Berger is actually Blomkvist's lover," Sandberg said with some force. "She's unfaithful to her husband. If she too were to be a victim, that would lead to further speculation."

Clinton and Nyström exchanged glances. Sandberg had a natural talent when it came to creating smokescreens. He learned fast. But Clinton and Nyström felt a surge of anxiety. Sandberg was too cavalier about life-and-death decisions. That was not good. Extreme measures were not to be employed just because an opportunity had presented itself. Murder was no easy solution; it should be resorted to only when there was no alternative.

Clinton shook his head.

Collateral damage, he thought. He suddenly felt disgust for the whole operation.

After a lifetime in service to the nation, here we sit like primitive mercenaries. Zalachenko was necessary. Björck was . . . regrettable, but Gullberg was right: Björck would have caved in. Blomkvist is . . . possibly necessary. But Erika Berger could only be an innocent bystander.

He looked steadily at Sandberg. He hoped that the young man would not develop into a psychopath.

"How much do the Nikolich brothers know?"

"Nothing. About us, that is. I'm the only one they've met. I used another identity and they can't trace me. They think the killing has to do with trafficking."

"What happens to them after the hit?"

"They leave Sweden at once," Nyström said. "Just like after Björck. If the murder investigation yields no results, they can very cautiously return after a few weeks."

"And the method?"

"Sicilian style. They walk up to Blomkvist, empty a magazine into him, and walk away."

"Weapon?"

"They have an automatic. I don't know what type."

"I do hope they won't spray the whole restaurant—"

"No danger of that. They're cold-blooded, they know what they have to do. But if Berger is sitting at the same table—"

Collateral damage.

"Look here," Clinton said. "It's important that Wadensjöö doesn't get wind of this. Especially not if Berger becomes a victim. He's stressed to breaking point as it is. I'm afraid we're going to have to put him out to pasture when this is over."

Nyström nodded.

"Which means that when we get word that Blomkvist has been shot, we're going to have to put on a good show. We'll call a crisis meeting and act thunderstruck by the development. We can speculate who might be behind the murder, but we'll say nothing about the drugs until the police find the evidence."

Blomkvist took leave of the presenter of *She* just before 5.00. They had spent the afternoon filling in the gaps in the material. Then

474

Blomkvist had gone to make-up and subjected himself to a long interview on film.

One question had been put to him which he struggled to answer in a coherent way, and they had to film that section several times.

How is it possible that civil servants in the Swedish government will go so far as to commit murder?

Blomkvist had brooded over the question long before *She*'s presenter had asked it. The Section must have considered Zalachenko an unacceptable threat, but it was still not a satisfactory answer. The reply he eventually gave was not satisfactory either:

> *"The only reasonable explanation I can give is that over the years the Section developed into a cult in the true sense of the word. They became like Knutby, or the pastor Jim Jones or something like that. They write their own laws, within which concepts like right and wrong have ceased to be relevant. And through these laws they imagine themselves isolated from normal society."*
>
> *"It sounds like some sort of mental illness, don't you think?"*
>
> *"That wouldn't be an inaccurate description."*

Blomkvist took the tunnelbana to Slussen. It was too early to go to Samir's Cauldron. He stood on Södermalmstorg for a while. He was worried still, yet all of a sudden life felt right again. It was not until Berger came back to *Millennium* that he realized how terribly he had missed her. Besides, her retaking of the helm had not led to any internal strife; Eriksson had reverted happily to the position of assistant editor, indeed was almost ecstatic – as she put it – that life would now return to normal.

Berger's coming back had also meant that everyone discovered how incredibly understaffed they had been during the past three months. Berger had had to resume her duties at *Millennium* at a run, and she and Eriksson managed to tackle together some of the organizational issues that had been piling up.

Blomkvist decided to buy the evening papers and have coffee at Java on Hornsgatan to kill time before he was to meet Berger.

*

Prosecutor Ragnhild Gustavsson of the National Prosecutors' Office set her reading glasses on the conference table and studied the group. She had a lined but apple-cheeked face and short, greying hair. She had been a prosecutor for twenty-five years and had worked at the N.P.O. since the early '90s. She was fifty-eight

Only three weeks had passed since she had been without warning summoned to the N.P.O. to meet Superintendent Edklinth, Director of Constitutional Protection. That day she had been busily finishing up one or two routine matters so she could begin her six-week leave at her cabin on the island of Husarö with a clear conscience. Instead she had been assigned to lead the investigation of a group of civil servants who went by the name of "the Section". Her holiday plans had quickly to be shelved. She had been advised that this would be her priority for the foreseeable future, and she had been given a more or less free hand to shape her operational team and take the necessary decisions.

"This may prove one of the most sensational criminal investigations this country has witnessed," the Prosecutor General had told her.

She was beginning to think he was right.

She had listened with increasing amazement to Edklinth's summary of the situation and the investigation he had undertaken at the instruction of the Prime Minister. The investigation was not yet complete, but he believed that his team had come far enough to be able to present the case to a prosecutor.

First of all Gustavsson had reviewed all the material that Edklinth had delivered. When the sheer scope of the criminal activity began to emerge, she realized that every decision she made would some day be pored over by historians and their readers. Since then she had spent every waking minute trying to get to grips with the numerous crimes. The case was unique in Swedish law, and since it involved charting criminal activity that had gone on for at least thirty years, she recognized the need for a very particular kind of operational team. She was reminded of the Italian government's anti-Mafia investigators who had been forced in the '70s and '80s to work almost underground in order to survive. She knew why Edklinth himself had been bound to work in secret. He did not know whom he could trust.

Her first action was to call in three colleagues from the N.P.O. She selected people she had known for many years. Then she hired a renowned historian who had worked on the Crime Prevention Council to help with an analysis of the growth of Security Police responsibilities and powers over the decades. She formally appointed Inspector Figuerola head of the investigation.

At this point the investigation of the Section had taken on a constitutionally valid form. It could now be viewed like any other police investigation, even though its operation would be conducted in absolute secrecy.

Over the past two weeks Prosecutor Gustavsson had summoned a large number of individuals to official but extremely discreet interviews. As well as with Edklinth and Figuerola, interviews had been conducted with Criminal Inspectors Bublanski, Modig, Andersson and Holmberg. She had called in Mikael Blomkvist, Malin Eriksson, Henry Cortez, Christer Malm, Advokat Giannini, Dragan Armansky and Susanne Linder, and she had herself gone to visit Lisbeth Salander's former guardian, Holger Palmgren. Apart from the members of *Millennium*'s staff who on principle did not answer questions that might reveal the identity of their sources, all had readily provided detailed answers, and in some cases supporting documentation as well.

Prosecutor Gustavsson had not been at all pleased to have been presented with a timetable that had been determined by *Millennium*. It meant that she would have to order the arrest of a number of individuals on a specific date. She knew that ideally she would have had several months of preparation before the investigation reached its present stage, but she had no choice. Blomkvist had been adamant. *Millennium* was not subject to any governmental ordinances or regulations, and he intended to publish the story on day three of Salander's trial. Gustavsson was thus compelled to adjust her own schedule to strike at the same time, so that those individuals who were under suspicion would not be given a chance to disappear along with the evidence. Blomkvist received a surprising degree of support from Edklinth and Figuerola, and the prosecutor came to see that Blomkvist's plan had certain clear advantages. As prosecutor she would get just the kind of fully focused media back-up she needed to push forward the prosecution. In addition, the whole process would move ahead so quickly that this complex investigation would not have time to leak into the corridors of the bureaucracy and thus risk being unearthed by the Section.

"Blomkvist's first priority is to achieve justice for Salander. Nailing the Section is merely a by-product," Figuerola said.

The trial of Lisbeth Salander was to commence on Wednesday, in two days' time. The meeting on Monday involved doing a review of the latest material available to them and dividing up the work assignments.

Thirteen people participated in the meeting. From N.P.O., Ragnhild Gustavsson had brought her two closest colleagues. From Constitutional Protection, Inspector Monica Figuerola had come with Bladh and Berglund. Edklinth, as Director of Constitutional Protection, was sitting in as an observer.

But Gustavsson had decided that a matter of this importance could not credibly be restricted to S.I.S. She had therefore called in Inspector Bublanski and his team, consisting of Modig, Holmberg and Andersson from the regular police force. They had, after all, been working on the Salander case since Easter and were familiar with all the details. Gustavsson had also called in Prosecutor Jervas and Inspector Erlander from the Göteborg police. The investigation of the Section had a direct connection to the investigation of the murder of Alexander Zalachenko.

When Figuerola mentioned that former Prime Minister Thorbjörn Fälldin might have to take the stand as a witness, Holmberg and Modig were scarcely able to conceal their discomfort.

For five hours they examined one individual after another who had been identified as an activist in the Section. After that they established the various crimes that could be linked to the apartment on Artillerigatan. A further nine people had been identified as being connected to the Section, although they never visited Artillerigatan. They worked primarily at S.I.S. on Kungsholmen, but had met with some of the Section's activists.

"It is still impossible to say how widespread the conspiracy is. We do not know under what circumstances these people meet with Wadensjöö or with anyone else. They could be informers, or they may have been given the impression that they're working for internal affairs or something similar. So there is some uncertainty about the degree of their involvement, and that can be resolved only after we've had a chance to interview them. Furthermore, these are merely those individuals we have observed during the weeks the surveillance has been in effect; there could be more that we do not yet know about."

"But the chief of Secretariat and the chief of Budget—"

"We have to assume that they're working for the Section."

It was 6.00 on Monday when Gustavsson gave everyone an hour's break for dinner, after which they would reconvene.

It was just as everyone had stood up and begun to move about that

Jesper Thoms, Figuerola's colleague from C.P.'s operations unit, drew her aside to report on what had developed during the last few hours of surveillance.

"Clinton has been in dialysis for most of the day and got back to Artillerigatan at 3.00. The only one who did anything of interest was Nyström, although we aren't quite sure what it was he did."

"Tell me," said Figuerola.

"At 1.30 he drove to Central Station and met up with two men. They walked across to the Sheraton and had coffee in the bar. The meeting lasted for about twenty minutes, after which Nyström returned to Artillerigatan."

"O.K. So who were they?"

"They're new faces. Two men in their mid-thirties who seem to be of eastern European origin. Unfortunately our observer lost them when they went into the tunnelbana."

"I see," Figuerola said wearily.

"Here are the pictures," Thoms said. He handed her a series of surveillance photographs.

She glanced at the enlargements of two faces she had never set eyes on before.

"Thanks," she said, laying out the photographs on the conference table. She picked up her handbag to go and find something to eat.

Andersson, who was standing nearby, bent to look more closely at the pictures.

"Oh shit," he said. "Are the Nikolich brothers involved in this?"

Figuerola stopped in her tracks. "Who did you say?"

"These two are seriously rotten apples," Andersson said. "Tomi and Miro Nikolich."

"Have you had dealings with them?"

"Sure. Two brothers from Huddinge. Serbs. We had them under observation several times when they were in their twenties and I was in the gangs unit. Miro is the dangerous one. He's been wanted for about a year for G.B.H. I thought they'd both gone back to Serbia to become politicians or something."

"Politicians?"

"Right. They went down to Yugoslavia in the early '90s and helped carry out ethnic cleansing. They worked for a Mafia leader, Arkan, who was running some sort of private fascist militia. They got a reputation for being shooters."

"Shooters?"

"Hit men. They've been flitting back and forth between Belgrade and Stockholm. Their uncle has a restaurant in Norrmalm, and they've apparently worked there once in a while. We've had reports that they were mixed up in at least two of the killings in what was known as the 'cigarette war', but we never got close to charging them with anything."

Figuerola gazed mutely at the photographs. Then suddenly she turned pale as a ghost. She stared at Edklinth.

"Blomkvist," she cried with panic in her voice. "They're not just planning to involve him in a scandal, they're planning to murder him. Then the police will find the cocaine during the investigation and draw their own conclusions."

Edklinth stared back at her.

"He's supposed to be meeting Erika Berger at Samir's Cauldron," Figuerola said. She grabbed Andersson by the shoulder. "Are you armed?"

"Yes . . ."

"Come with me."

Figuerola rushed out of the conference room. Her office was three doors down. She ran in and took her service weapon from the desk drawer. Against all regulations she left the door to her office unlocked and wide open as she raced off towards the lifts. Andersson hesitated for a second.

"Go," Bublanski told him. "Sonja, you go with them too."

Blomkvist got to Samir's Cauldron at 6.20. Berger had just arrived and found a table near the bar, not far from the entrance. He kissed her on the cheek. They both ordered lamb stew and strong beers from the waiter.

"How was the *She* woman?" Berger said.

"Cool, as usual."

Berger laughed. "If you don't watch out you're going to become obsessed by her. Imagine, a woman who can resist the famous Blomkvist charm."

"There are in fact several women who haven't fallen for me over the years," Blomkvist said. "How has your day been?"

"Wasted. But I accepted an invitation to be on a panel to debate the whole *S.M.P.* business at the Publicists' Club. That will be my final contribution."

"Great."

"It's just such a relief to be back at *Millennium*."

"You have no idea how good it is that you're back. I'm still elated."

"It's fun to be at work again."

"Mmm."

"I'm happy."

"And I have to go to the gents'," Blomkvist said, getting up.

He almost collided with a man who had just walked in. Blomkvist noticed that he looked vaguely eastern European and was staring at him. Then he saw the sub-machine gun.

As they passed Riddarholmen, Edklinth called to tell them that neither Blomkvist nor Berger were answering their mobiles. They had presumably turned them off for dinner.

Figuerola swore and passed Södermalmstorg at a speed of close to eighty kilometres an hour. She kept her horn pressed down and made a sharp turn on to Hornsgatan. Andersson had to brace himself against the door. He had taken out his gun and checked the magazine. Modig did the same in the back seat.

"We have to call for back-up," Andersson said. "You don't play games with the Nikolich boys."

Figuerola ground her teeth.

"This is what we'll do," she said. "Sonja and I will go straight into the restaurant and hope they're sitting inside. Curt, you know what these guys look like, so you stay outside and keep watch."

"Right."

"If all goes well, we'll take Blomkvist and Berger straight out to the car and drive them down to Kungsholmen. If we suspect anything's wrong, we stay inside the restaurant and call for back-up."

"O.K.," Modig said.

Figuerola was nearly at the restaurant when the police radio crackled beneath the dashboard.

All units. Shots fired on Tavastgatan on Södermalm. Samir's Cauldron restaurant.

Figuerola felt a sudden lurch in her chest.

Berger saw Blomkvist bump into a man as he was heading past the entrance towards the gents'. She frowned without really knowing why.

She saw the other man stare at Blomkvist with a surprised expression. She wondered if it was somebody he knew.

Then she saw the man take a step back and drop a bag to the floor. At first she did not know what she was seeing. She sat paralysed as he raised some kind of gun and aimed it at Blomkvist

Blomkvist reacted without stopping to think. He flung out his left hand, grabbed the barrel of the gun, and twisted it up towards the ceiling. For a microsecond the muzzle passed in front of his face.

The burst of fire from the sub-machine gun was deafening in the small room. Mortar and glass from the overhead lights rained down on Blomkvist as Miro Nikolich squeezed off eleven shots. For a moment Blomkvist looked directly into the eyes of his attacker.

Then Nikolich took a step back and yanked the gun towards him. Blomkvist was unprepared and lost his grip on the barrel. He knew at once that he was in mortal danger. Instinctively he threw himself at the attacker instead of crouching down or trying to take cover. Later he realized that if he had ducked or backed away, he would have been shot on the spot. He got a new grip on the barrel of the sub-machine gun and used his entire weight to drive the man against the wall. He heard another six or seven shots go off and tore desperately at the gun to direct the muzzle at the floor.

Berger instinctively took cover when the second series of shots was fired. She stumbled and fell, hitting her head on a chair. As she lay on the floor she looked up and saw that three holes had appeared in the wall just behind where she had been sitting.

In shock she turned her head and saw Blomkvist struggling with the man by the door. He had fallen to his knees and was gripping the gun with both hands, trying to wrench it loose. She saw the attacker struggling to get free. He kept smashing his fist over and over into Blomkvist's face and temple.

Figuerola braked hard opposite Samir's Cauldron, flung open the car door and ran across the road towards the restaurant. She had her Sig Sauer in her hand with the safety off when she noticed the car parked right outside the restaurant.

She saw one of the Nikolich brothers behind the wheel and pointed her weapon at his face behind the driver's door

"Police. Hands up," she screamed.

Tomi Nikolich held up his hands.

"Get out of the car and lie face down on the pavement," she roared, fury in her voice. She turned and glanced at Andersson and Modig beside her. "The restaurant," she said.

Modig was thinking of her children. It was against all police protocol to gallop into a building with her weapon drawn without first having back-up in place and without knowing the exact situation.

Then she heard the sound of more shots from inside.

Blomkvist had his middle finger between the trigger and the trigger guard as Miro Nikolich tried to keep shooting. He heard glass shattering behind him. He felt a searing pain as the attacker squeezed the trigger again and again, crushing his finger. As long as his finger was in place the gun could not be fired. But as Nikolich's fist pummelled again and again on the side of his head, it suddenly occurred to him that he was too old for this sort of thing.

Have to end it, he thought.

That was his first rational thought since he had become aware of the man with the sub-machine gun.

He clenched his teeth and shoved his finger further into the space behind the trigger.

Then he braced himself, rammed his shoulder into the attacker's body and forced himself back on to his feet. He let go of the gun with his right hand and raised elbow up to protect his face from the pummelling. Nikolich switched to hitting him in the armpit and ribs. For a second they stood eye to eye again.

The next moment Blomkvist felt the attacker being pulled away from him. He felt one last devastating pain in his finger and became aware of Andersson's huge form. The police officer literally picked up Nikolich with a firm grip on his neck and slammed his head into the wall by the door. Nikolich collapsed to the ground.

"Get down! This is the police. Stay very still," he heard Modig yell.

He turned his head and saw her standing with her legs apart and her gun held in both hands as she surveyed the chaos. At last she raised her gun to point it at the ceiling and looked at Blomkvist.

"Are you hurt?" she said.

In a daze Blomkvist looked back at her. He was bleeding from his eyebrows and nose.

"I think I broke a finger," he said, sitting down on the floor.

Figuerola received back-up from the Södermalm armed response team less than a minute after she forced Tomi Nikolich on to the pavement at gunpoint. She showed her I.D. and left the officers to take charge of the prisoner. Then she ran inside. She stopped in the entrance to take stock of the situation.

Blomkvist and Berger were sitting side by side. His face was bloodied and he seemed to be in shock. She sighed in relief. He was alive. Then she frowned as Berger put her arm around his shoulders. At least her face was bruised.

Modig was squatting down next to them, examining Blomkvist's hand. Andersson was handcuffing Nikolich, who looked as though he had been hit by a truck. She saw a Swedish Army model M/45 sub-machine gun on the floor.

Figuerola looked up and saw shocked restaurant staff and terror-stricken patrons, along with shattered china, overturned chairs and tables, and debris from the rounds that had been fired. She smelled cordite. But she was not aware of anyone dead or wounded in the restaurant. Officers from the armed response team began to squeeze into the room with their weapons drawn. She reached out and touched Andersson's shoulder. He stood up.

"You said that Miro Nikolich was on our wanted list?"

"Correct. G.B.H. About a year ago. A street fight down in Hallunda."

"O.K. Here's what we'll do," Figuerola said. "I'll take off as fast as I can with Blomkvist and Berger. You stay here. The story is that you and Modig came here to have dinner and you recognized Nikolich from your time in the gangs unit. When you tried to arrest him he pulled a weapon and started shooting. So you sorted him out."

Andersson looked completely astonished. "That's not going to hold up. There are witnesses."

"The witnesses will say that somebody was fighting and shots were fired. It only has to hold up until tomorrow's evening papers. The story is that the Nikolich brothers were apprehended by sheer chance because you recognized them."

Andersson surveyed the shambles all around him.

Figuerola pushed her way through the knot of police officers out on the street and put Blomkvist and Berger in the back seat of her car. She turned to the armed response team leader and spoke in a low voice with him for half a minute. She gestured towards the car in which Blomkvist and Berger were now sitting. The leader looked puzzled but at last he nodded. She drove to Zinkensdamm, parked, and turned around to her passengers.

"How badly are you hurt?"

"I took a few punches. I've still got all my teeth, but my middle finger's hurt."

"I'll take you to A. & E. at St Göran's."

"What happened?" Berger said. "And who are you?"

"I'm sorry," Blomkvist said. "Erika, this is Inspector Monica Figuerola. She works for Säpo. Monica, this is Erika Berger."

"I worked that out all by myself," Figuerola said in a neutral tone. She did not spare Berger a glance.

"Monica and I met during the investigation. She's my contact at S.I.S."

"I understand," Berger said, and she began to shake as suddenly the shock set in.

Figuerola stared hard at Berger.

"What went wrong?" Blomkvist said.

"We misinterpreted the reason for the cocaine," Figuerola said. "We thought they were setting a trap for you, to create a scandal. Now we know they wanted to kill you. They were going to let the police find the cocaine when they went through your apartment."

"What cocaine?" Berger said.

Blomkvist closed his eyes for a moment.

"Take me to St Göran's," he said.

"Arrested?" Clinton barked. He felt a butterfly-light pressure around his heart.

"We think it's alright," Nyström said. "It seems to have been sheer bad luck."

"Bad luck?"

"Miro Nikolich was wanted on some old assault story. A policeman from the gangs unit happened to recognize him when he went into Samir's Cauldron and wanted to arrest him. Nikolich panicked and tried to shoot his way out."

"And Blomkvist?"

"He wasn't involved. We don't even know if he was in the restaurant at the time."

"This cannot be fucking true," Clinton said. "What do the Nikolich brothers know?"

"About us? Nothing. They think Björck and Blomkvist were both hits that had to do with trafficking."

"But they know that Blomkvist was the target?"

"Sure, but they're hardly going to start blabbing about being hired to do a hit. They'll keep their mouths shut all the way to district court. They'll do time for possession of illegal weapons and, as like as not, for resisting arrest."

"Those damned fuck-ups," Clinton said.

"Well, they seriously screwed up. We've had to let Blomkvist give us the slip for the moment, but no harm was actually done."

It was 11.00 by the time Linder and two hefty bodyguards from Milton Security's personal protection unit collected Blomkvist and Berger from Kungsholmen.

"You really do get around," Linder said.

"Sorry," Berger said gloomily.

Berger had been in a state of shock as they drove to St Göran's. It had dawned on her all of a sudden that both she and Blomkvist had very nearly been killed.

Blomkvist had spent an hour in A. & E. having his head X-rayed and his face bandaged. His left middle finger was put in a splint. The end joint of his finger was badly bruised and he would lose the fingernail. Ironically the main injury was caused when Andersson came to his rescue and pulled Nikolich off him. Blomkvist's middle finger had been caught in the trigger guard of the M/45 and had snapped straight across. It hurt a lot but was hardly life-threatening.

For Blomkvist the shock did not set in until two hours later, when he had arrived at Constitutional Protection at S.I.S. and reported to

Inspector Bublanski and Prosecutor Gustavsson. He began to shiver and felt so tired that he almost fell asleep between questions. At that point a certain amount of palavering ensued.

"We don't know what they're planning and we have no idea whether Mikael was the only intended victim," Figuerola said. "Or whether Erika here was supposed to die too. We don't know if they will try again or if anyone else at *Millennium* is being targeted. And why not kill Salander? After all, she's the truly serious threat to the Section."

"I've already rung my colleagues at *Millennium* while Mikael was being patched up," Berger said. "Everyone's going to lie extremely low until the magazine comes out. The office will be left unstaffed."

Edklinth's immediate reaction had been to order bodyguard protection for Blomkvist and Berger. But on reflection he and Figuerola decided that it would not be the smartest move to contact S.I.S.'s Personal Protection unit. Berger solved the problem by declining police protection. She called Armansky to explain what had happened, which was why, later that night, Linder was called in for duty.

Blomkvist and Berger were lodged on the top floor of a safe house just beyond Drottningholm on the road to Ekerö. It was a large '30s villa overlooking Lake Mälaren. It had an impressive garden, outbuildings and extensive grounds. The estate was owned by Milton Security, but Martina Sjögren lived there. She was the widow of their colleague of many years, Hans Sjögren, who had died in an accident on assignment fifteen years earlier. After the funeral, Armansky had talked with Fru Sjögren and then hired her as housekeeper and general caretaker of the property. She lived rent-free in a wing of the ground floor and kept the top floor ready for those occasions, a few times each year, when Milton Security at short notice needed to hide away individuals who for real or imagined reasons feared for their safety.

Figuerola went with them. She sank on to a chair in the kitchen and allowed Fru Sjögren to serve her coffee, while Berger and Blomkvist installed themselves upstairs and Linder checked the alarm and electronic surveillance equipment around the property.

"There are toothbrushes and so on in the chest of drawers outside the bathroom," Sjögren called up the stairs.

Linder and Milton's bodyguards installed themselves in rooms on the ground floor.

"I've been on the go ever since I was woken at 4.00," Linder said. "You can put together a watch rota, but let me sleep till at least 5.00."

"You can sleep all night. We'll take care of this," one of the bodyguards said.

"Thanks," Linder said, and she went straight to bed.

Figuerola listened absent-mindedly as the bodyguards switched on the motion detector in the courtyard and drew straws to see who would take the first watch. The one who lost made himself a sandwich and went into the T.V. room next to the kitchen. Figuerola studied the flowery coffee cups. She too had been on the go since early morning and was feeling fairly exhausted. She was just thinking about driving home when Berger came downstairs and poured herself a cup of coffee. She sat down opposite Figuerola.

"Mikael went out like a light as soon as his head hit the pillow."

"Reaction to the adrenaline," Figuerola said.

"What happens now?"

"You'll have to lie low for a few days. Within a week this will all be over, whichever way it ends. How are you feeling?"

"So-so. A bit shaky still. It's not every day something like this happens. I just called my husband to explain why I wouldn't be coming home."

"Hmm."

"I'm married to—"

"I know who you're married to."

Silence. Figuerola rubbed her eyes and yawned.

"I have to go home and get some sleep," she said.

"Oh, for God's sake, stop talking rubbish and go and lie down with Mikael," Berger said.

Figuerola looked at her.

"Is it that obvious?" she said.

Berger nodded.

"Did Mikael say anything—"

"Not a word. He's generally rather discreet when it comes to his lady friends. But sometimes he's an open book. And you're clearly hostile every time you even look at me. The pair of you obviously have something to hide."

"It's my boss," Figuerola said.

"Where does he come into it?"

"He'd fly off the handle if he knew that Mikael and I were—"

"I can quite see that."

Silence.

"I don't know what's going on between you two, but I'm not your rival," Berger said.

"You're not?"

"Mikael and I sleep together now and then. But I'm not married to him."

"I heard that you two had a special relationship. He told me about you when we were out at Sandhamn."

"So you've been to Sandhamn? Then it *is* serious."

"Don't make fun of me."

"Monica, I hope that you and Mikael   I'll try to stay out of your way."

"And if you can't?"

Berger shrugged. "His ex-wife flipped out big time when Mikael was unfaithful with me. She threw him out. It was my fault. As long as Mikael is single and available, I would have no compunction. But I promised myself that if he was ever serious about someone, then I'd keep my distance."

"I don't know if I dare count on him."

"Mikael is special. Are you in love with him?"

"I think so."

"Alright, then. Just don't tell him too soon. Now go to bed."

Figuerola thought about it for a moment. Then she went upstairs, undressed and crawled into bed next to Blomkvist. He mumbled something and put his arm around her waist.

Berger sat alone in the kitchen for a long time. She felt deeply unhappy.

CHAPTER 25

Wednesday, 13.vii – Thursday, 14.vii

Blomkvist had always wondered why the loudspeakers in the district court were so faint, discreet almost. He could hardly make out the words of the announcement that the trial vs Lisbeth Salander would begin in courtroom 5 at 10.00. But he had arrived in plenty of time and positioned himself to wait right by the entrance to the courtroom. He was one of the first to be let in. He chose a seat in the public gallery on the left-hand side of the room, where he would have the best view of the defence table. The seats filled up fast. Media interest had steadily increased in the weeks leading up to the trial, and over the past week Prosecutor Ekström had been interviewed daily.

Lisbeth Salander was charged with assault and grievous bodily harm in the case of Carl-Magnus Lundin; with unlawful threats, attempted murder and grievous bodily harm in the case of Karl Axel Bodin, alias Alexander Zalachenko, now deceased; with two counts of breaking and entering – the first at the summer cabin of the deceased lawyer Nils Erik Bjurman in Stallarholmen, the second at Bjurman's home on Odenplan; with the theft of a vehicle – a Harley-Davidson owned by one Sonny Nieminen of Svavelsjö M.C.; with three counts of possession of illegal weapons – a canister of Mace, a taser and a Polish P-83 Wanad, all found in Gosseberga; with the theft of or withholding of evidence – the formulation was imprecise but it referred to the documentation she had found in Bjurman's summer cabin; and with a number of further misdemeanours. In all, sixteen charges had been filed against Lisbeth Salander.

Ekström had been busy.

He had also leaked information indicating that Salander's mental state was cause for alarm. He cited first the forensic psychiatric report by Dr Jesper H. Löderman that had been compiled at the time of her eighteenth birthday, and second, a report which, in accordance with a decision by the district court at a preliminary hearing, had been written by Dr Peter Teleborian. Since the mentally ill girl had, true to form, refused categorically to speak to psychiatrists, the analysis was made on the basis of "observations" carried out while she was detained at Kronoberg prison in Stockholm during the month before her trial. Teleborian, who had many years of experience with the patient, had determined that Salander was suffering from a serious mental disturbance and employed words such as psychopathy, pathological narcissism, paranoid schizophrenia, and similar.

The press had also reported that seven police interviews had been conducted with Salander. At each of these interviews the defendant had declined even to say good morning to those who were leading the interrogation. The first few interviews had been conducted by the Göteborg police, the remainder had taken place at police headquarters in Stockholm. The tape recordings of the interview protocol revealed that the police had used every means of persuasion and repeated questioning, but had not received the favour of a single reply.

She had not even bothered to clear her throat.

Occasionally Advokat Giannini's voice could be heard on the tapes, at such points as she realized that her client evidently was not going to answer any questions. The charges against Salander were accordingly based exclusively on forensic evidence and on whatever facts the police investigation had been able to determine.

Salander's silence had at times placed her defence lawyer in an awkward position, since she was compelled to be almost as silent as her client. What Giannini and Salander discussed in private was confidential.

Ekström made no secret of the fact that his primary objective was secure psychiatric care for the defendant; of secondary interest to him was a substantial prison sentence. The normal process was the reverse, but he believed that in her case there were such transparent mental disturbances and such an unequivocal forensic psychiatric assessment that he was left with no alternative. It was highly unusual for a court to decide against a forensic psychiatric assessment.

He also believed that Salander's declaration of incompetence should be rescinded. In an interview he had explained with a concerned expression that in Sweden there were a number of sociopaths with such grave mental disturbances that they presented a danger to themselves as well as to others, and modern medicine could offer no alternative to keeping these individuals safely locked up. He cited the case of a violent girl, Anette, who in the '70s had been a frequent focus of attention in the media, and who thirty years on was still in a secure psychiatric institution. Every endeavour to ease the restrictions had resulted in her launching reckless and violent attacks on relatives and carers, or in attempts to injure herself. Ekström was of the view that Salander suffered from a similar form of psychopathic disturbance.

Media interest had also increased for the simple reason that Salander's defence lawyer, Advokat Giannini, had made not a single statement to the press. She had refused all requests to be interviewed so that the media were, as they many times put it, "unable to have an opportunity to present the views of the other side of the case". Journalists were therefore in a difficult situation: the prosecution kept on shovelling out information while the defence, uncharacteristically, gave not the slightest hint of Salander's reaction to the charges against her, nor of what strategy the defence might employ.

This state of affairs was commented on by the legal expert engaged to follow the trial in one of the evening newspapers. The expert had stated in his column that Advokat Giannini was a respected women's rights lawyer, but that she had absolutely no experience in criminal law outside this case. He concluded that she was unsuitable for the purpose of defending Salander. From his sister Blomkvist had also learned that several distinguished lawyers had offered their services. Giannini had, on behalf of her client, courteously turned down every such proposal.

As he waited for the trial to begin, Blomkvist glanced around at the other spectators. He caught sight of Armansky sitting near the exit and their eyes met for a moment.

Ekström had a large stack of papers on his table. He greeted several journalists.

Giannini sat at her table opposite Ekström. She had her head down and was sorting through her papers. Blomkvist thought that his sister looked a bit tense. Stage fright, he supposed.

Then the judge, assessor and lay assessors entered the courtroom. Judge Jörgen Iversen was a white-haired, 57-year-old man with a gaunt face and a spring in his step. Blomkvist had researched Iversen's background and found that he was an exacting judge of long experience who had presided over many high-profile cases.

Finally Salander was brought into the courtroom.

Even though Blomkvist was used to Salander's penchant for shocking clothing, he was amazed that his sister had allowed her to turn up to the courtroom in a black leather miniskirt with frayed seams and a black top – with the legend *I am annoyed* – which barely covered her many tattoos. She had ten piercings in her ears and rings through her lower lip and left eyebrow. Her head was covered in three months' worth of uneven stubble after her surgery. She wore grey lipstick and heavily darkened eyebrows, and had applied more black mascara than Blomkvist had ever seen her wear. In the days when he and Salander had spent time together, she had shown almost no interest in make-up.

She looked a bit vulgar, to put it mildly. It was almost a Goth look. She reminded him of a vampire in some pop-art movie from the '60s. Blomkvist was aware of some of the reporters in the press gallery catching their breath in astonishment or smiling broadly. They were at last getting a look at the scandal-ridden young woman they had written so much about, and she was certainly living up to all their expectations.

Then he realized that Salander was in costume. Usually her style was sloppy and rather tasteless. Blomkvist had assumed that she was not really interested in fashion, but that she tried instead to accentuate her own individuality. Salander always seemed to mark her private space as hostile territory, and he had thought of the rivets in her leather jacket as a defence mechanism, like the quills of a hedgehog. To everyone around her it was as good a signal as any: *Don't try to touch me – it will hurt.*

But here in the district court she had exaggerated her style to the point of parody.

It was no accident, it was part of Giannini's strategy.

If Salander had come in with her hair smoothed down and wearing a twin-set and pearls and sensible shoes, she would have came across as a con artist trying to sell a story to the court. It was a question of credibility. She had come as herself and no-one else. Way over the top – for clarity. She was not pretending to be someone she was not. Her message to the court was that she had no reason to be ashamed or to put on a show. If the court had a problem with her appearance, it was no concern of hers. The state had accused her of a multitude of things, and the prosecutor had dragged her into court. With her very appearance she had already indicated that she intended to brush aside the prosecutor's accusations as nonsense.

493

She moved with confidence and sat down next to her lawyer. She surveyed the spectators. There was no curiosity in her gaze. She seemed instead defiantly to be observing and registering those who had already convicted her in the press.

It was the first time Blomkvist had seen her since she lay like a bloody rag doll on the bench in that kitchen in Gosseberga, and a year and a half or more since he had last seen her under normal circumstances. If the term "normal circumstances" could ever be used in connection with Salander. For a matter of seconds their eyes met. Hers lingered on him, but she betrayed no sign of recognition. Yet she did seem to study the bruises that covered Blomkvist's cheek and temple and the surgical tape over his right eyebrow. Blomkvist thought he discerned the merest hint of a smile in her eyes but could not be sure he had not imagined it. Then Judge Iversen pounded his gavel and called the court to order.

The spectators were allowed to be present in the courtroom for all of thirty minutes. They listened to Ekström's introductory presentation of the case.

Every reporter except Blomkvist was busily taking notes even though by now all of them knew the charges Ekström intended to bring. Blomkvist had already written his story.

Ekström's introductory remarks went on for twenty-two minutes. Then it was Giannini's turn. Her presentation took thirty seconds. Her voice was firm.

"The defence rejects all the charges brought against her except one. My client admits to possession of an illegal weapon, that is, one spray canister of Mace. To all other counts, my client pleads not guilty of criminal intent. We will show that the prosecutor's assertions are flawed and that my client has been subjected to grievous encroachment of her civil rights. I will demand that my client be acquitted of all charges, that her declaration of incompetence be revoked, and that she be released."

There was a murmuring from the press gallery. Advokat Giannini's strategy had at last been revealed. It was obviously not what the reporters had been expecting. Most had speculated that Giannini would in some way exploit her client's mental illness to her advantage. Blomkvist smiled.

"I see," Judge Iversen said, making a swift note. He looked at Giannini. "Are you finished?"

"That is my presentation."

"Does the prosecutor have anything to add?" Judge Iversen said.

It was at this point that Ekström requested a private meeting in the judge's chambers. There he argued that the case hinged upon one vulnerable individual's mental state and welfare, and that it also involved matters which, if explored before the public in court, could be detrimental to national security.

"I assume that you are referring to what may be termed the Zalachenko affair," Judge Iversen said.

"That is correct. Alexander Zalachenko came to Sweden as a political refugee and sought asylum from a terrible dictatorship. There are elements in the handling of his situation, personal connections and the like, that are still classified, even though Herr Zalachenko is now deceased. I therefore request that the deliberations be held behind closed doors and that a rule of confidentiality be applied to those sections of the deliberations that are particularly sensitive."

"I believe I understand your point," Judge Iversen said, knitting his brows.

"In addition, a large part of the deliberations will deal with the defendant's guardianship. This touches on matters which in all normal cases become classified almost automatically, and it is out of respect for the defendant that I am requesting a closed court."

"How does Advokat Giannini respond to the prosecutor's request?"

"For our part it makes no difference."

Judge Iversen consulted his assessor and then announced, to the annoyance of the reporters present, that he had accepted the prosecutor's request. So Blomkvist left the courtroom.

Armansky waited for Blomkvist at the bottom of the stairs in the courthouse. It was sweltering in the July heat and Blomkvist could feel sweat in his armpits. His two bodyguards joined him as he emerged from the courthouse. Both nodded to Armansky and then they busied themselves studying the surroundings.

"It feels strange to be walking around with bodyguards," Blomkvist said. "What's all this going to cost?"

"It's on the firm. I have a personal interest in keeping you alive. But, since you ask, we've spent roughly 250,000 kronor on *pro bono* work in the past few months."

"Coffee?" Blomkvist said, pointing to the Italian café on Bergsgatan.

Blomkvist ordered a *latte* and Armansky a double espresso with a teaspoon of milk. They sat in the shade on the pavement outside. The bodyguards sat at the next table drinking Cokes.

"Closed court," Armansky said.

"That was expected. And it's O.K., since it means that we can control the news flow better."

"You're right, it doesn't matter to us, but my opinion of Prosecutor Ekström is sinking fast," Armansky said.

They drank their coffee and contemplated the courthouse in which Salander's future would be decided.

"Custer's last stand," Blomkvist said.

"She's well prepared," Armansky said. "And I must say I'm impressed with your sister. When she began planning her strategy I thought it made no sense, but the more I think about it, the more effective it seems."

"This trial won't be decided in there," Blomkvist said. He had been repeating these words like a mantra for several months.

"You're going to be called as a witness," Armansky said.

"I know. I'm ready. But it won't happen before the day after tomorrow. At least that's what we're counting on."

Ekström had left his reading glasses at home and had to push his glasses up on to his forehead and squint to be able to read the last-minute handwritten additions to his text. He stroked his blond goatee before once more he readjusted his glasses and surveyed the room.

Salander sat with her back ramrod straight and gave the prosecutor an unfathomable look. Her face and eyes were impassive and she did not appear to be wholly present. It was time for the prosecutor to begin questioning her.

"I would like to remind Fröken Salander that she is speaking under oath," Ekström said at last.

Salander did not move a muscle. Prosecutor Ekström seemed to be anticipating some sort of response and waited for a few seconds. He looked at her expectantly.

"You are speaking under oath," he said.

Salander tilted her head very slightly. Giannini was busy reading something in the preliminary investigation protocol and seemed unconcerned by whatever Prosecutor Ekström was saying. Ekström shuffled his papers. After an uncomfortable silence he cleared his throat.

"Very well then," Ekström said. "Let us proceed directly to the events at the late Advokat Bjurman's summer cabin outside Stallarholmen on April 6 of this year, which was the starting point of my presentation of the case this morning. We shall attempt to bring clarity to how it happened that you drove down to Stallarholmen and shot Carl-Magnus Lundin."

Ekström gave Salander a challenging look. Still she did not move a muscle. The prosecutor suddenly seemed resigned. He threw up his hands and looked pleadingly at the judge. Judge Iversen seemed wary. He glanced at Giannini who was still engrossed in some papers, apparently unaware of her surroundings.

Judge Iversen cleared his throat. He looked at Salander. "Are we to interpret your silence to mean that you don't want to answer any questions?" he asked.

Salander turned her head and met Judge Iversen's eyes.

"I will gladly answer questions," she said.

Judge Iversen nodded.

"Then perhaps you can answer the question," Ekström put in.

Salander looked at Ekström and said nothing.

"Could you please answer the question?" Judge Iversen urged her.

Salander looked back at the judge and raised her eyebrows. Her voice was clear and distinct.

"Which question? Until now that man there" – she nodded towards Ekström – "has made a number of unverified statements. I haven't yet heard a question."

Giannini looked up. She propped her elbow on the table and leaned her chin on her hand with an interested expression.

Ekström lost his train of thought for few seconds.

"Could you please repeat the question?" Judge Iversen said.

"I asked whether . . . you drove down to Advokat Bjurman's summer cabin in Stallarholmen with the intention of shooting Carl-Magnus Lundin."

"No. You said that you were going to try to bring clarity to how it happened that I drove down to Stallarholmen and shot Carl-Magnus

497

Lundin. That was not a question. It was a general assertion in which you anticipated my answer. I'm not responsible for the assertions you are making."

"Don't quibble. Answer the question."

"No."

Silence.

"No what?"

"No is my answer to the question."

Prosecutor Ekström sighed. This was going to be a long day. Salander watched him expectantly.

"It might be best to take this from the beginning," he said. "Were you at the late Advokat Bjurman's summer cabin in Stallarholmen on the afternoon of April 6 this year?"

"Yes."

"How did you get there?"

"I went by shuttle train to Södertälje and took the Strängnäs bus."

"What was your reason for going to Stallarholmen? Had you arranged a meeting there with Carl-Magnus Lundin and his friend Sonny Nieminen?"

"No."

"How was it that they showed up there?"

"You'll have to ask them that."

"I'm asking you."

Salander did not reply.

Judge Iversen cleared his throat. "I presume that Fröken Salander is not answering because – purely semantically – you have once again made an assertion," the judge said helpfully.

Giannini suddenly sniggered just loud enough to be heard. She pulled herself together at once and studied her papers again. Ekström gave her an irritated glance.

"Why do you think Lundin and Nieminen went to Bjurman's summer cabin?"

"I don't know. I suspect that they went there to commit arson. Lundin had a litre of petrol in a plastic bottle in the saddlebag of his Harley-Davidson."

Ekström pursed his lips. "Why did you go to Advokat Bjurman's summer cabin?"

"I was looking for information."

"What sort of information?"

"The information that I suspect Lundin and Nieminen were there to destroy, and which could contribute to clarifying who murdered the bastard."

"Is it your opinion that Advokat Bjurman was a bastard? Is that correctly construed?"

"Yes."

"And why do you think that?"

"He was a sadistic pig, a pervert, and a rapist – and therefore a bastard."

She was quoting the text that had been tattooed on the late Advokat Bjurman's stomach and thus indirectly admitting that she was responsible for it. This affray, however, was not included in the charges against Salander. Bjurman had never filed a report of assault, and it would be impossible now to prove whether he had allowed himself to be tattooed or whether it had been done against his will.

"In other words, you are alleging that your guardian forced himself on you. Can you tell the court when these assaults are supposed to have taken place?"

"They took place on Tuesday, February 18, 2003 and again on Friday, March 7 of the same year."

"You have refused to answer every question asked by the police in their attempts to interview you. Why?"

"I had nothing to say to them."

"I have read the so called 'autobiography' that your lawyer delivered without warning a few days ago. I must say it is a strange document, and we'll come back to it in more detail later. But in it you claim that Advokat Bjurman allegedly forced you to perform oral sex on the first occasion, and on the second subjected you to an entire night of repeated and consummated rape and severe torture."

Lisbeth did not reply.

"Is that correct?"

"Yes."

"Did you report the rapes to the police?"

"No."

"Why not?"

"The police never listened before when I tried to tell them something. So there seemed no point in reporting anything to them then."

"Did you discuss these assaults with any of your acquaintances? A girlfriend?"

"No."

"Why not?"

"Because it's none of their business."

"Did you try to contact a lawyer?"

"No."

"Did you go to a doctor to be treated for the injuries you claim to have sustained?"

"No."

"And you didn't go to any women's crisis centre either."

"Now you're making an assertion again."

"Excuse me. Did you go to any women's crisis centre?"

"No."

Ekström turned to the judge. "I want to make the court aware that the defendant has stated that she was subjected to sexual assaults on two occasions, the second of which should be considered exceptionally severe. The person she claims committed these rapes was her guardian, the late Advokat Nils Bjurman. The following facts should be taken into account at this juncture . . ." Ekström pointed at the text in front of him. "In the investigation carried out by the Violent Crimes Division, there was nothing in Advokat Bjurman's past to support the credibility of Lisbeth Salander's account. Bjurman was never convicted of any crime. He has never been reported to the police or been the subject of an investigation. He had previously been a guardian or trustee to several other young people, none of whom have claimed that they were subjected to any sort of attack. On the contrary, they assert that Bjurman invariably behaved correctly and kindly towards them."

Ekström turned a page.

"It is also my duty to remind the court that Lisbeth Salander has been diagnosed as a paranoid schizophrenic. This is a young woman with a documented violent tendency, who since her early teens has had serious problems in her interactions with society. She spent several years in a children's psychiatric institution and has been under guardianship since the age of eighteen. However regrettable this may be, there are reasons for it. Lisbeth Salander is a danger to herself and to those around her. It is my conviction that she does not need a prison sentence. She needs psychiatric care."

He paused for effect.

"Discussing a young person's mental state is an innately disagreeable task. So much is an invasion of privacy, and her mental state becomes the subject of interpretation. In this case, however, we have Lisbeth Salander's own confused world view on which to base our decision. It becomes manifestly clear in what she has termed her 'autobiography'. Nowhere is her want of a foothold in reality as evident as it is here. In this instance we need no witnesses or interpretations to invariably contradict one another. We have her own words. We can judge for ourselves the credibility of her assertions."

His gaze fell on Salander. Their eyes met. She smiled. She looked malicious. Ekström frowned.

"Does Advokat Giannini have anything to say?" Judge Iversen said.

"No," Giannini said. "Other than that Prosecutor Ekström's conclusions are nonsensical."

The afternoon session began with the cross-questioning of witnesses. The first was Ulrika von Liebenstaahl from the guardianship agency. Ekström had called her to the stand to establish whether complaints had ever been lodged against Advokat Bjurman. This was strongly denied by von Liebenstaahl. Such assertions were defamatory.

"There exists a rigorous supervision of guardianship cases. Advokat Bjurman had been active on behalf of the guardianship agency for almost twenty years before he was so shockingly murdered."

She gave Salander a withering look, despite the fact that Salander was not accused of murder; it had already been established that Bjurman was murdered by Ronald Niedermann.

"In all these years there has not been a single complaint against Advokat Bjurman. He was a conscientious person who evidenced a deep commitment to his wards."

"So you don't think it's plausible that he would have subjected Lisbeth Salander to aggravated sexual assault?"

"I think that statement is ridiculous. We have monthly reports from Advokat Bjurman, and I personally met him on several occasions to go over the assignment."

"Advokat Giannini has presented a request that Lisbeth Salander's guardianship be rescinded, effective immediately."

"No-one is happier than we who work at the agency when a guardianship can be rescinded. Unfortunately we have a responsibility, which means that we have to follow the appropriate regulations. For the agency's part, we are required in accordance with normal protocol to see to it that Lisbeth Salander is declared fit by a psychiatric expert before there can be any talk of changes to her legal status."

"I understand."

"This means that she has to submit to a psychiatric examination. Which, as everyone knows, she has refused to do."

The questioning of Ulrika von Liebenstaahl lasted for about forty minutes, during which time Bjurman's monthly reports were examined.

Giannini asked only one question before Ulrika von Liebenstaahl was dismissed.

"Were you in Advokat Bjurman's bedroom on the night of 7 to 8 March, 2003?"

"Of course not."

"In other words, you haven't the faintest idea whether my client's statement is true or not?"

"The accusation against Advokat Bjurman is preposterous."

"That is your *opinion*. Can you give him an alibi or in any other way document that he did not assault my client?"

"That's impossible, naturally. But the probability—"

"Thank you. That will be all," Giannini said.

Blomkvist met his sister at Milton's offices near Slussen at around 7.00 to go through the day's proceedings.

"It was pretty much as expected," Giannini said. "Ekström has bought Salander's autobiography."

"Good. How's she holding up?"

Giannini laughed.

"She's holding up very well, coming across as a complete psychopath. She's merely being herself."

"Wonderful."

"Today has mostly been about what happened at the cabin in Stallarholmen. Tomorrow it'll be about Gosseberga, interrogations of people from forensics and so forth. Ekström is going to try to prove that Salander went down there intending to murder her father."

"Well . . ."

"But we may have a technical problem. This afternoon Ekström called Ulrika von Liebenstaahl from the guardianship agency. She started going on about how I had no right to represent Lisbeth."

"Why so?"

"She says that Lisbeth is under guardianship and therefore isn't entitled to choose her own lawyer. So, technically, I may not be her lawyer if the guardianship agency hasn't rubber-stamped it."

"And?"

"Judge Iversen is to decide tomorrow morning. I had a brief word with him after today's proceedings. I *think* he'll decide that I can continue to represent her. My point was that the agency has had three whole months to raise the objection – to show up with that kind of objection after proceedings have started is an unwarranted provocation."

"Teleborian will testify on Friday, I gather. You *have* to be the one who cross-examines him."

On Thursday Prosecutor Ekström explained to the court that after studying maps and photographs and listening to extensive technical conclusions about what had taken place in Gosseberga, he had determined that the evidence indicated that Salander had gone to her father's farmhouse at Gosseberga with the intention of killing him. The strongest link in the chain of evidence was that she had taken a weapon with her, a Polish P-83 Wanad.

The fact that Alexander Zalachenko (according to Salander's account) or possibly the police murderer Ronald Niedermann (according to testimony that Zalachenko had given before he was murdered at Sahlgrenska) had in turn attempted to kill Salander and bury her in a trench in woods nearby could in no way be held in mitigation of the fact that she had tracked down her father to Gosseberga with the express intention of killing him. Moreover, she had all but succeeded in that objective when she struck him in the face with an axe. Ekström demanded that Salander be convicted of attempted murder or premeditation with the intent to kill and, in that case, grievous bodily harm.

Salander's own account stated that she had gone to Gosseberga to confront her father, to persuade him to confess to the murders of Dag Svensson and Mia Johansson. This statement was of dramatic significance in the matter of establishing intent.

When Ekström had finished questioning the witness Melker Hansson from the technical unit of the Göteborg police, Advokat Giannini had asked some succinct questions.

"Herr Hansson, is there anything at all in your investigation or in all the technical documentation that you have compiled which could in any way establish that Lisbeth Salander is lying about her intent regarding the visit to Gosseberga? Can you prove that she went there with the intention of murdering her father?"

Hansson thought for a moment.

"No," he said at last.

"Do you have anything to say about her intent?"

"No."

"Prosecutor Ekström's conclusion, eloquent and extensive as it is, is therefore speculation?"

"I believe so."

"Is there anything in the forensic evidence that contradicts Lisbeth Salander's statement that she took with her the Polish weapon, a P-83 Wanad, by chance simply because it was in her bag, and she didn't know what she should do with the weapon having taken it the day before from Sonny Nieminen in Stallarholmen?"

"No."

"Thank you," Giannini said and sat down. Those were her only words throughout Hansson's testimony, which had lasted one hour.

Wadensjöö left the Section's apartment on Artillerigatan at 6.00 on Thursday evening with a feeling that he was hedged about by ominous clouds of turmoil, of imminent ruin. For several weeks he had known that his title as director, that is, the chief of the Section for Special Analysis, was but a meaningless label. His opinions, protests and entreaties carried no weight. Clinton had taken over all decision-making. If the Section had been an open and public institution, this would not have been a problem – he would merely have gone to his superior and lodged his protests.

As things stood now, there was no-one he could protest to. He was alone and subject to the mercy or disfavour of a man whom he regarded as insane. And the worst of it was that Clinton's authority was absolute. Snot-nosed kids like Sandberg and faithful retainers like Nyström . . . they all seemed to jump into line at once and obey the fatally ill lunatic's every whim.

No question that Clinton was a soft-spoken authority who was not working for his own gain. He would even acknowledge that Clinton was working in the best interests of the Section, or at least in what he regarded as its best interests. The whole organization seemed to be in free fall, indulging in a collective fantasy in which experienced colleagues refused to admit that every movement they made, every decision that was taken and implemented, only led them one step closer to the abyss.

Wadensjöö felt a pressure in his chest as he turned on to Linnégatan, where he had found a parking spot earlier that day. He disabled the alarm and was about to open the car door when he heard a movement behind him. He turned around, squinting against the sun. It was a few seconds before he recognized the stately man on the pavement before him.

"Good evening, Herr Wadensjöö," Edklinth said. "I haven't been out in the field in ten years, but today I felt that my presence might be appropriate."

Wadensjöö looked in confusion at the two plain-clothes policemen flanking Edklinth. Bublanski he knew, but not the other man.

Suddenly he guessed what was going to happen.

"It is my unenviable duty to inform you that the Prosecutor General has decided that you are to be arrested for such a long string of crimes that it will surely take weeks to compile a comprehensive catalogue of them."

"What's going on here?" Wadensjöö said indignantly.

"What is going on at this moment is that you are being arrested, suspected of being an accessory to murder. You are also suspected of extortion, bribery, illegal telephone tapping, several counts of criminal forgery, criminal embezzlement of funds, participation in breaking and entering, misuse of authority, espionage and a long list of other lesser but that's not to say insignificant offences. The two of us are going to Kungsholmen to have a very serious talk in peace and quiet."

"I haven't committed murder," Wadensjöö said breathlessly.

"That will have to be established by the investigation."

"It was Clinton. It was always Clinton," Wadensjöö said.

Edklinth nodded in satisfaction.

Every police officer knows that there are two classic ways to conduct the interrogation of a suspect. The bad cop and the good cop. The bad cop threatens, swears, slams his fist on the table and generally

CHAPTER 26

Friday, 15.vii

Teleborian's appearance inspired confidence as he sat in the witness box in the courtroom on Friday morning. He was questioned by Prosecutor Ekström for some ninety minutes and he replied with calm authority to every question. The expression on his face was sometimes concerned and sometimes amused.

"To sum up . . ." Ekström said, leafing through his sheaf of papers. "It is your judgement as a psychiatrist of long standing that Lisbeth Salander suffers from paranoid schizophrenia?"

"I have said that it is unusually difficult to make a precise evaluation of her condition. The patient is, as you know, almost autistic in her relation to doctors and other figures of authority. My assessment is that she suffers from a serious mental disorder, but that at the present time I cannot give an exact diagnosis. Nor can I determine what stage of the psychosis she is in without more extensive study."

"At any rate, you don't consider her to be sane."

"Indeed her entire history presents most compelling proof that she is not sane."

"You have been allowed to read what Lisbeth Salander has termed her 'autobiography', which she has presented to the district court. What are your comments on this?"

Teleborian threw up his hands and shrugged.

"How would you judge the credibility of her account?"

"There is no credibility. It is a series of assertions about various individuals, one story more fantastical than the other. Taken as a whole, her written explanation confirms our suspicions that she suffers from paranoid schizophrenia."

"Could you give an instance?"

"The most obvious is of course the description of the alleged rape by her guardian Advokat Bjurman."

"Could you expand on that?"

"The description is extremely detailed. It is a classic example of the

508

sort of grotesque fantasy that children are capable of. There are plenty of parallel examples from familial incest cases in which the child gives an account which falls through due to its utter improbability, and for which there is no forensic evidence. These are erotic fantasies which even children of a very young age can have . . . Almost as if they were watching a horror film on television."

"But Lisbeth Salander is not a child, she is a grown woman," Ekström said.

"That is correct. Although it remains to be seen exactly what her mental level may be. But basically you are correct. She is a grown woman, and presumably she believes in the account she has presented."

"So you're saying it is all lies."

"No. If she believes what she says, then it is not a lie. It's a story which shows that she cannot distinguish fantasy from reality."

"So she was not raped by Advokat Bjurman?"

"No. There is no likelihood of that at all. She needs expert care."

"You yourself appear in Lisbeth Salander's account—"

"Yes, and that is rather intriguing. But once again, it's a figment of her imagination. If we are to believe the poor girl, then I'm something approximate to a paedophile . . ." He smiled and continued. "But this is all just another expression of what I was speaking of before. In Salander's autobiography we are told that she was abused by being placed in restraints for long spells at St Stefan's. And that I came to her room at night . . . This is a classic manifestation of her inability to interpret reality, or rather, she is giving reality her own interpretation."

"Thank you. I leave it to the defence, if Fru Giannini has any questions."

Since Giannini had not had any questions or objections on the first two days of the trial, those in the courtroom expected that she would once again ask some obligatory questions and then bring the questioning to an end. *This really is an embarrassingly deficient effort by the defence*, Ekström thought.

"Yes, I do," Giannini said. "I do in fact have a number of questions, and they may take some time. It's 11.30 now. May I propose that we break for lunch, and that I be allowed to carry out my cross-examination of the witness after lunch without interval?"

Judge Iversen agreed that the court should adjourn for lunch.

*

Andersson was accompanied by two uniformed officers when he placed his huge hand on Superintendent Nyström's shoulder outside the Mäster Anders restaurant on Hantverkargatan at noon precisely. Nyström looked up in amazement at the man who was shoving his police I.D. right under his nose.

"Hello. You're under arrest, suspected of being an accessory to murder and attempted murder. The charges will be explained to you by the Prosecutor General at a hearing this afternoon. I suggest that you come along peacefully," he said.

Nyström did not seem to comprehend the language Andersson was speaking in, but he could see that he was a man you went along with without protest.

Inspector Bublanski was accompanied by Modig and seven uniformed officers when Stefan Bladh of the Constitutional Protection Unit admitted them at noon precisely into the locked section that comprised the domain of the Security Police at Kungsholmen. They walked through the corridors behind Bladh until he stopped and pointed at an office door. The chief of Secretariat's assistant looked up and was utterly perplexed when Bublanski held up his I.D.

"Kindly remain where you are. This is a police action."

He strode to the inner door. Chief of Secretariat Albert was on the telephone.

"What is this interruption?" Shenke said.

"I am Criminal Inspector Jan Bublanski. You are under arrest for violation of the Swedish constitution. There is a long list of specific points in the charge, all of which will be explained to you this afternoon."

"This is outrageous," Shenke said.

"It most certainly is," Bublanski said.

He had Shenke's office sealed and then placed two officers on guard outside the door, with instructions to let no-one cross the threshold. They had permission to use their batons and even draw their service weapons if anyone tried to enter the sealed office by force.

They continued their procession down the corridor until Bladh pointed to another door, and the procedure was repeated with chief of Budget, Gustav Atterbom.

*

Inspector Holmberg had the Södermalm armed response team as back-up when at exactly noon he knocked on the door of an office rented temporarily on the fourth floor just across the street from *Millennium*'s offices on Götgatan.

Since no-one opened the door, Holmberg ordered the Södermalm police to force the lock, but the door was opened a crack before the crowbar was used.

"Police," Holmberg said. "Come out with your hands up."

"I'm a policeman myself," Inspector Mårtensson said.

"I know. And you have licences for a great many guns."

"Yes, well . . . I'm an officer on assignment."

"I think not," Holmberg said.

He accepted the assistance of his colleagues in propping Mårtensson against the wall so he could confiscate his service weapon.

"You are under arrest for illegal telephone tapping, gross dereliction of duty, repeated break-ins at Mikael Blomkvist's apartment on Bellmansgatan, and additional counts. Handcuff him."

Holmberg took a swift look around the room and saw that there was enough electronic equipment to furnish a recording studio. He detailed an officer to guard the premises, but told him to sit still on a chair so he would not leave any fingerprints.

As Mårtensson was being led through the front door of the building, Cortez took a series of twenty-two photographs with his Nikon. He was, of course, no professional photographer, and the quality left something to be desired. But the best images were sold the next day to an evening newspaper for an obscene sum of money.

Figuerola was the only police officer participating in the day's raids who encountered an unexpected incident. She had back-up from the Norrmalm team and three colleagues from S.I.S. when at noon she walked through the front door of the building on Artillerigatan and went up the stairs to the top-floor apartment, registered in the name of Bellona Inc.

The operation had been planned at short notice. As soon as the group was assembled outside the door of the apartment, she gave the go-ahead. Two burly officers from the Norrmalm team raised a forty-kilo steel battering ram and opened the door with two well-aimed blows. The team, equipped with bulletproof vests and assault rifles, took control of the apartment within ten seconds of the door being forced.

According to surveillance carried out at dawn that morning, five individuals identified as members of the Section had arrived at the apartment that morning. All five were apprehended and put in handcuffs.

Figuerola was wearing a protective vest. She went through the apartment, which had been the headquarters of the Section since the '60s, and flung open one door after another. She was going to need an archaeologist to sort through the reams and reams of paper that filled the rooms.

A few seconds after she entered the apartment, she opened the door to a small room towards the back and discovered that it was used for overnight stays. She found herself eye to eye with Jonas Sandberg. He had been a question mark during that morning's assignment of tasks, as the surveillance officer detailed to watch him had lost track of him the evening before. His car had been parked on Kungsholmen and he had not been home to his apartment during the night. This morning they had not expected to locate and apprehend him.

They man the place at night for security reasons. Of course. And Sandberg sleeps over after the night shift.

Sandberg had on only his underpants and seemed to be dazed with sleep. He reached for his service weapon on the bedside table, but Figuerola bent over and swept the weapon away from him on to the floor.

"Jonas Sandberg . . . you are under arrest as a suspect and accessory to the murders of Gunnar Björck and Alexander Zalachenko, and as an accomplice in the attempted murders of Mikael Blomkvist and Erika Berger. Now get your trousers on."

Sandberg threw a punch at Figuerola. She blocked it instinctively.

"You must be joking," she said. She took hold of his arm and twisted his wrist so hard that he was forced backwards to the floor. She flipped him over on to his stomach and put her knee in the small of his back. She handcuffed him herself. It was the first time she had used handcuffs on an assignment since she began at S.I.S.

She handed Sandberg over to one of the back-up team and continued her passage through the apartment until she opened the last door at the very back. According to the blueprints, this was a small cubbyhole looking out on to the courtyard. She stopped in the doorway and looked at the most emaciated figure she had ever seen. She did not for one second doubt that here was a person who was mortally ill.

"Fredrik Clinton, you are under arrest as an accomplice to murder, attempted murder, and for a long list of further crimes," she said. "Stay where you are in bed. We've called an ambulance to take you to Kungsholmen."

Malm was stationed immediately outside the building on Artillerigatan. Unlike Cortez, he knew how to handle his digital Nikon. He used a short telephoto lens and the pictures he took were of excellent quality.

They showed the members of the Section, one by one, being led out through the front door and down to the police cars. And finally the ambulance that arrived to pick up Clinton. His eyes were fixed on the lens as the shutter clicked. Clinton looked nervous and confused.

The photograph later won the Picture of the Year award.

CHAPTER 27

Friday, 15.vii

Judge Iversen banged his gavel at 12.30 and decreed that district court proceedings were thereby resumed. He noticed that a third person had appeared at Advokat Giannini's table. It was Holger Palmgren in a wheelchair.

"Hello, Holger," Judge Iversen said. "I haven't seen you in a courtroom in quite a while."

"Good day to you, Judge Iversen. Some cases are so complicated that these younger lawyers need a little assistance."

"I thought you had retired."

"I've been ill. But Advokat Giannini engaged me as assistant counsel in this case."

"I see."

Giannini cleared her throat.

"It is germane to the case that Advokat Palmgren was until his illness Lisbeth Salander's guardian."

"I have no intention of commenting on that matter," Judge Iversen said.

He nodded to Giannini to begin and she stood up. She had always disliked the Swedish tradition of carrying on court proceedings informally while sitting around a table, almost as though the occasion were a dinner party. She felt better when she could speak standing up.

"I think we should begin with the concluding comments from this morning. Dr Teleborian, what leads you so consistently to dismiss as untrue everything that Lisbeth Salander says?"

"Because her statements so obviously *are* untrue," replied Teleborian.

He was relaxed. Giannini turned to the judge.

"Judge Iverson, Dr Teleborian claims that Lisbeth Salander tells lies and that she fantasizes. The defence will now demonstrate that every word in her autobiography is true. We will present copious documentation, both visual and written, as well as the testimony of witnesses. We have now reached the point in this trial when the prosecutor has presented

514

the principal elements of his case . . . We have listened and we now know the exact nature of the accusations against Lisbeth Salander."

Giannini's mouth was suddenly dry and she felt her hands shake. She took a deep breath and sipped her mineral water. Then she placed her hands in a firm grip on the back of the chair so that they would not betray her nervousness.

"From the prosecutor's presentation we may conclude that he has a great many opinions but a woeful shortage of evidence. He *believes* that Lisbeth Salander shot Carl-Magnus Lundin in Stallarholmen. He *claims* that she went to Gosseberga to kill her father. He *assumes* that my client is a paranoid schizophrenic and mentally ill in every sense. And he *bases* this assumption on information from a single source, to wit, Dr Peter Teleborian."

She paused to catch her breath and forced herself to speak slowly.

"As it now stands, the case presented by the prosecutor rests on the testimony of Dr Teleborian. If he is right, then my client would be best served by receiving the expert psychiatric care that both he and the prosecutor are seeking."

Pause.

"But if Dr Teleborian is wrong, this prosecution case must be seen in a different light. Furthermore, if he is lying, then my client is now, here in this courtroom, being subjected to a violation of her civil rights, a violation that has gone on for many years."

She turned to face Ekström.

"What we shall do this afternoon is to show that your witness is a false witness, and that you as prosecutor have been deceived into accepting these false testimonies."

Teleborian flashed a smile. He held out his hands and nodded to Giannini, as if applauding her presentation. Giannini now turned to the judge.

"Your honour. I will show that Dr Teleborian's so-called forensic psychiatric investigation is nothing but a deception from start to finish. I will show that he is lying about Lisbeth Salander. I will show that my client has in the past been subjected to a gross violation of her rights. And I will show that she is just as sane and intelligent as anyone in this room."

"Excuse me, but—" Ekström began.

"Just a moment." She raised a finger. "I have for two days allowed you to talk uninterrupted. Now it's my turn."

She turned back to Judge Iversen.

"I would not make so serious an accusation before the court if I did not have ample evidence to support it."

"By all means, continue," the judge said. "But I don't want to hear any long-winded conspiracy theories. Bear in mind that you can be charged with slander for statements that are made before a court."

"Thank you. I will bear that in mind."

She turned to Teleborian. He still seemed entertained by the situation.

"The defence has repeatedly asked to be allowed to examine Lisbeth Salander's medical records from the time when she, in her early teens, was committed to your care at St Stefan's. Why have we not been shown those records?"

"Because a district court decreed that they were classified. That decision was made out of solicitude for Lisbeth Salander, but if a higher court were to rescind that decision, I would naturally hand them over."

"Thank you. For how many nights during the two years that Lisbeth Salander spent at St Stefan's was she kept in restraints?"

"I couldn't recall that offhand."

"She herself claims that it was 380 out of the total of 786 days and nights she spent at St Stefan's."

"I can't possibly answer as to the exact number of days, but that is a fantastic exaggeration. Where do those figures come from?"

"From her autobiography."

"And you believe that today she is able to remember accurately each night she was kept in restraints? That's preposterous."

"Is it? How many nights do you recall?"

"Lisbeth Salander was an extremely aggressive and violence-prone patient, and undoubtedly she was placed in a stimulus-free room on a number of occasions. Perhaps I should explain the purpose of a stimulus-free room—"

"Thank you, that won't be necessary. According to theory, it is a room in which a patient is denied any sensory input that might provoke agitation. For how many days and nights did thirteen-year-old Lisbeth Salander lie strapped down in such a room?"

"It would be . . . I would estimate perhaps on thirty occasions during the time she was at the hospital."

"Thirty. Now that's only a fraction of the 380 that she claims."

"Undeniably."

"Not even 10 per cent of her figure."

"Yes . . ."

"Would her medical records perhaps give us more accurate information?"

"It's possible."

"Excellent," Giannini said, taking out a large sheaf of paper from her briefcase. "Then I ask to be allowed to hand over to the court a copy of Lisbeth Salander's medical records from St Stefan's. I have counted the number of notes about the restraining straps and find that the figure is 381, one more than my client claims."

Teleborian's eyes widened.

"Stop . . . this is classified information. Where did you get that from?"

"I got it from a reporter at *Millennium* magazine. It can hardly be classified if it's lying around a newspaper's offices. Perhaps I should add that extracts from these medical records were published today in *Millennium*. I believe, therefore, that even this district court should have the opportunity to look at the records themselves."

"This is illegal—"

"No, it isn't. Lisbeth Salander has given her permission for the extracts to be published. My client has nothing to hide."

"Your client has been declared incompetent and has no right to make any such decision for herself."

"We'll come back to her declaration of incompetence. But first we need to examine what happened to her at St Stefan's."

Judge Iversen frowned as he accepted the papers that Giannini handed to him.

"I haven't made a copy for the prosecutor. On the other hand, he received a copy of this privacy-invading document more than a month ago."

"How did that happen?" the judge said.

"Prosecutor Ekström got a copy of these classified records from Teleborian at a meeting which took place in his office at 5.00 p.m. on Saturday, June 4 this year."

"Is that correct?" Judge Iversen said.

Ekström's first impulse was to deny it. Then he realized that Giannini might somehow have evidence.

"I requested permission to read parts of the records if I signed a confidentiality agreement," Ekström said. "I had to make sure that Salander had the history she was alleged to have."

517

"Thank you," Giannini said. "This means that we now have confirmation that Dr Teleborian not only tells lies but also broke the law by disseminating records that he himself claims are classified."

"Duly noted," said the judge.

Judge Iversen was suddenly very alert. In a most unorthodox way, Giannini had launched a serious attack on a witness, and she already made mincemeat of an important part of his testimony. *And she claims that she can document everything she says.* Judge Iversen adjusted his glasses.

"Dr Teleborian, based on these records which you yourself wrote . . . could you now tell me how many days Lisbeth Salander was kept in restraints?"

"I have no recollection that it could have been so extensive, but if that's what the records say, then I have to believe it."

"A total of 381 days and nights. Does that not strike you as excessive?"

"It is unusually long . . . yes."

"How would you perceive it if you were thirteen years old and someone strapped you to a steel-framed bed for more than a year? Would it feel like torture?"

"You have to understand that the patient was dangerous to herself as well as to others—"

"O.K. Let's look at *dangerous to herself.* Has Lisbeth Salander ever injured herself?"

"There were such misgivings—"

"I'll repeat the question: has Lisbeth Salander ever injured herself? Yes or no?"

"As psychiatrists we must teach ourselves to interpret the overall picture. With regard to Lisbeth Salander, you can see on her body, for example, a multitude of tattoos and piercings, which are also a form of self-destructive behaviour and a way of damaging one's own body. We can interpret that as a manifestation of self-hate."

Giannini turned to Salander.

"Are your tattoos a manifestation of self-hate?" she said.

"No," Salander said.

Giannini turned back to Teleborian. "So you believe that I am also dangerous to myself because I wear earrings and actually have a tattoo in a private place?"

Palmgren sniggered, but he managed to transform the snigger into a clearing of his throat.

"No, not at all . . . tattoos can also be part of a social ritual."

"Are you saying that Lisbeth Salander is not part of this social ritual?"

"You can see for yourself that her tattoos are grotesque and extend over large parts of her body. That is no normal measure of fetishism or body decoration."

"What percentage?"

"Excuse me?"

"At what percentage of tattooed body surface does it stop being fetishism and become a mental illness?"

"You're distorting my words."

"Am I? How is it that, in your opinion, it is part of a wholly acceptable social ritual when it applies to me or to other young people, but it becomes dangerous when it's a matter of evaluating my client's mental state?"

"As a psychiatrist I have to look at the whole picture. The tattoos are merely an indicator. As I have already said, it is one of many indicators which need to be taken into account when I evaluate her condition."

Giannini was silent for a few seconds as she fixed Teleborian with her gaze. She now spoke very slowly.

"But Dr Teleborian, you began strapping down my client when she was twelve years old, going on thirteen. At that time she did not have a single tattoo, did she?"

Teleborian hesitated and Giannini went on.

"I presume that you did not strap her down because you predicted that she would begin tattooing herself sometime in the future."

"Of course not. Her tattoos had nothing to do with her condition in 1991."

"With that we are back to my original question. Did Lisbeth Salander ever injure herself in a way that would justify keeping her bound to a bed for a whole year? For example, did she cut herself with a knife or a razor blade or anything like that?"

Teleborian looked unsure for a second.

"No . . . I used the tattoos as an *example* of self-destructive behaviour."

"And we have just agreed that tattoos are a legitimate part of a social ritual. I asked why you restrained her for a year and you replied that it was because she was a danger to herself."

"We had reason to believe that she was a danger to herself."

"*Reason to believe*. So you're saying that you restrained her because you guessed something?"

"We carried out assessments."

"I have now been asking the same question for about five minutes. You claim that my client's self-destructive behaviour was one reason why she was strapped down for a total of more than a year out of the two years she was in your care. Can you please finally give me some examples of the self-destructive behaviour she evidenced at the age of twelve?"

"The girl was extremely undernourished, for example. This was partially due to the fact that she refused food. We suspected anorexia."

"I see. Was she anorexic? As you can see, my client is even today uncommonly thin and fine-boned."

"Well, it's difficult to answer that question. I would have to observe her eating habits for quite a long time."

"You did observe her eating habits – for two years. And now you're suggesting that you confused anorexia with the fact that my client is small and thin. You say that she refused food."

"We were compelled to force-feed her on several occasions."

"And why was that?"

"Because she refused to eat, of course."

Giannini turned to her client.

"Lisbeth, is it true that you refused to eat at St Stefan's?"

"Yes."

"And why was that?"

"Because that bastard was mixing psychoactive drugs into my food."

"I see. So Dr Teleborian wanted to give you medicine. Why didn't you want to take it?"

"I didn't like the medicine I was being given. It made me sluggish. I couldn't think and I was sedated for most of the time I was awake. And the bastard refused to tell me what the drugs contained."

"So you refused to take the medicine?"

"Yes. Then he began putting the crap in my food instead. So I stopped eating. Every time something had been put in my food, I stopped eating for five days."

"So you had to go hungry."

"Not always. Several of the attendants smuggled sandwiches in to me on various occasions. One in particular gave me food late at night. That happened quite often."

"So you think that the nursing staff at St Stefan's saw that you were hungry and gave you food so that you would not have to starve?"

"That was during the period when I was battling with this bastard over psychoactive drugs."

"Tell us what happened."

"He tried to drug me. I refused to take his medicine. He started putting it in my food. I refused to eat. He started force-feeding me. I began vomiting up the food."

"So there was a completely rational reason why you refused the food."

"Yes."

"It was not because you didn't want food?"

"No. I was often hungry."

"And since you left St Stefan's . . . do you eat regularly?"

"I eat when I'm hungry."

"Would it be correct to say that a conflict arose between you and Dr Teleborian?"

"You could say that."

"You were sent to St Stefan's because you had thrown petrol at your father and set him on fire."

"Yes."

"Why did you do that?"

"Because he abused my mother."

"Did you ever explain that to anyone?"

"Yes."

"And who was that?"

"I told the police who interviewed me, the social workers, the children's care workers, the doctors, a pastor, and that bastard."

"By 'that bastard' you are referring to . . .?"

"That man." She pointed at Dr Teleborian.

"Why do you call him a bastard?"

"When I first arrived at St Stefan's I tried to explain to him what had happened."

"And what did Dr Teleborian say?"

"He didn't want to listen to me. He claimed that I was fantasizing. And as punishment I was to be strapped down until I stopped fantasizing. And then he tried to force-feed me psychoactive drugs."

"This is nonsense," Teleborian said.

"Is that why you won't speak to him?"

521

"I haven't said a word to the bastard since the night I turned thirteen. I was strapped to the bed. It was my birthday present to myself."

Giannini turned to Teleborian. "This sounds as if the reason my client refused to eat was that she did want the psychoactive drugs you were forcing upon her."

"It's possible that she views it that way."

"And how do you view it?"

"I had a patient who was abnormally difficult. I maintain that her behaviour showed that she was a danger to herself, but this might be a question of interpretation. However, she was violent and exhibited psychotic behaviour. There is no doubt that she was dangerous to others. She came to St Stefan's after she tried to murder her father."

"We'll get to that later. For 381 of those days you kept her in restraints. Could it have been that you used strapping as a way to punish my client when she didn't do as you said?"

"That is utter nonsense."

"Is it? I notice that according to the records the majority of the strapping occurred during the first year . . . 320 of 381 instances. Why was the strapping discontinued?"

"I suppose the patient changed her behaviour and became less agitated."

"Is it not true that your measures were considered unnecessarily brutal by other members of staff?"

"How do you mean?"

"Is it not true that the staff lodged complaints against the force-feeding of Lisbeth Salander, among other things?"

"Inevitably people will arrive at differing evaluations. This is nothing unusual. But it became a burden to force-feed her because she resisted so violently—"

"Because she refused to take psychoactive drugs which made her listless and passive. She had no problem eating when she was not being drugged. Wouldn't that have been a more reasonable method of treatment than resorting to forcible measures?"

"If you don't mind my saying so, Fru Giannini, I am actually a physician. I suspect that my medical expertise is rather more extensive than yours. It is my job to determine what medical treatments should be employed."

"It's true, I'm not a physician, *Doctor* Teleborian. However, I am not entirely lacking in expertise. Besides my qualifications as lawyer I was also trained as a psychologist at Stockholm University. This is necessary background training in my profession."

You could have heard a pin drop in the courtroom. Both Ekström and Teleborian stared in astonishment at Giannini. She continued inexorably.

"Is it not correct that your methods of treating my client eventually resulted in serious disagreements between you and your superior, Dr Johannes Caldin, head physician at the time?"

"No, that is not correct."

"Dr Caldin passed away several years ago and cannot give testimony. But here in the court we have someone who met Dr Caldin on several occasions. Namely my assistant counsel, Holger Palmgren."

She turned to him.

"Can you tell us how that came about?"

Palmgren cleared his throat. He still suffered from the after-effects of his stroke and had to concentrate to pronounce the words.

"I was appointed as trustee for Lisbeth Salander after her mother was so severely beaten by Lisbeth's father that she was disabled and could no longer take care of her daughter. She suffered permanent brain damage and repeated brain haemorrhages."

"You're speaking of Alexander Zalachenko, I presume." Ekström was leaning forward attentively.

"That's correct," Palmgren said.

Ekström said: "I would ask you to remember that we are now into a subject which is highly classified."

"It's hardly a secret that Alexander Zalachenko persistently abused Lisbeth's mother," Giannini said.

Teleborian raised his hand.

"The matter is probably not quite as self-evident as Fru Giannini is presenting it."

"What do you mean by that?" Giannini said.

"There is no doubt that Lisbeth Salander witnessed a family tragedy . . . that something triggered a serious beating in 1991. But there is no documentation to suggest that this was a situation that went on for many years, as Fru Giannini claims. It could have been an isolated incident or a quarrel that got out of hand. If truth be told, there is not even any documentation to point towards Herr Zalachenko as Lisbeth's mother's aggressor. We have been informed that she was a prostitute, so there could have been a number of other possible perpetrators."

Giannini looked in astonishment at Teleborian. She seemed to be speechless for a moment. Then her eyes bored into him.

"Could you expand on that?" she said.

"What I mean is that in practice we have only Lisbeth Salander's assertions to go on."

"And?"

"First of all, there were two sisters, twins in fact. Camilla Salander has never made any such claims, indeed she has denied that such a thing occurred. And if there was abuse to the extent your client maintains, then it would naturally have been noted in social welfare reports and so forth."

"Is there an interview with Camilla Salander that we might examine?"

"Interview?"

"Do you have any documentation to show that Camilla Salander was even asked about what occurred at their home?"

Salander squirmed in her seat at the mention of her sister. She glanced at Giannini.

"I presume that the social welfare agency filed a report—"

"You have just stated that Camilla Salander never made any assertions that Alexander Zalachenko abused their mother, that on the contrary she denied it. That was a categorical statement. Where did you get that information?"

Teleborian sat in silence for several seconds. Giannini could see that his eyes changed when he realized that he had made a mistake. He could anticipate what it was that she wanted to introduce, but there was no way to avoid the question.

"I seem to remember that it appeared in the police report," he said at last.

"You seem to remember . . . I myself have searched high and low for police reports about the incident on Lundagatan during which Alexander Zalachenko was severely burned. The only ones available are the brief reports written by the officers at the scene."

"That's possible—"

"So I would very much like to know how it is that you were able to read a police report that is not available to the defence."

"I can't answer that," Teleborian said. "I was shown the report in 1991 when I wrote a forensic psychiatric report on your client after the attempted murder of her father."

"Was Prosecutor Ekström shown this report?"

Ekström squirmed. He stroked his goatee. By now he knew that he had underestimated Advokat Giannini. However, he had no reason to lie.

"Yes, I've seen it."

"Why wasn't the defence given access to this material?"

"I didn't consider it of interest to the trial."

"Could you please tell me how you were allowed to see this report? When I asked the police, I was told only that no such report exists."

"The report was written by the Security Police. It's classified."

"So Säpo wrote a report on a case involving grievous bodily harm on a woman and decided to make the report classified."

"It's because of the perpetrator . . . Alexander Zalachenko. He was a political refugee."

"Who wrote the report?"

Silence.

"I don't hear anything. What name was on the title page?"

"It was written by Gunnar Björck from the Immigration Division of S.I.S."

"Thank you. Is that the same Gunnar Björck who my client claims worked with *Doctor* Teleborian to fabricate the forensic psychiatric report about her in 1991?"

"I assume it is."

Giannini turned her attention back to Teleborian.

"In 1991 you committed Lisbeth Salander to the secure ward of St Stefan's children's psychiatric clinic—"

"That's not correct."

"Is it not?"

"No. Lisbeth Salander was *sentenced* to the secure psychiatric ward. This was the outcome of an entirely routine legal action in a district court. We're talking about a seriously disturbed minor. That was not my own decision—"

"In 1991 a district court decided to lock up Lisbeth Salander in a children's psychiatric clinic. Why did the district court make that decision?"

"The district court made a careful assessment of your client's actions and mental condition – she had tried to murder her father with a petrol bomb, after all. This is not an activity that a normal teenager would engage in, whether they are tattooed or not." Teleborian gave her a polite smile.

"And what did the district court base their judgement on? If I've understood correctly, they had only one forensic medical assessment to go on. It was written by yourself and a policeman by the name of Gunnar Björck."

"This is about Fröken Salander's conspiracy theories, Fru Giannini. Here I would have to—"

"Excuse me, but I haven't asked a question yet," Giannini said and turned once again to Palmgren. "Holger, we were talking about your meeting Dr Teleborian's superior, Dr Caldin."

"Yes. In my capacity as trustee for Lisbeth Salander. At that stage I had met her only very briefly. Like everyone else, I got the impression that she had a serious mental illness. But since it was my job, I undertook to research her general state of health."

"And what did Dr Caldin say?"

"She was Dr Teleborian's patient, and Dr Caldin had not paid her any particular attention except in routine assessments and the like. It wasn't until she had been there for more than a year that I began to discuss how she could be rehabilitated back into society. I suggested a foster family. I don't know exactly what went on internally at St Stefan's, but after about a year Dr Caldin began to take an interest in her."

"How did that manifest itself?"

"I discovered that he had arrived at an opinion that differed from Dr Teleborian's," Palmgren said. "He told me once that he had decided to change the type of care she was receiving. I did not understand until later that he was referring to the strap restraints. Dr Caldin had decided that she should not be restrained. He didn't think there was any reason for it."

"So he went against Dr Teleborian's directives?"

Ekström interrupted. "Objection. That's hearsay."

"No," Palmgren said. "Not entirely. I asked for a report on how Lisbeth Salander was supposed to re-enter society. Dr Caldin wrote that report. I still have it today."

He handed a document to Giannini.

"Can you tell us what it says?"

"It's a letter from Dr Caldin to me dated October 1992, which is when Lisbeth had been at St Stefan's for twenty months. Here Dr Caldin expressly writes that, I quote, *My decision for the patient not to be restrained or force-fed has also produced the noticeable effect that she is now calm. There is no need for psychoactive drugs. However, the patient is extremely withdrawn and uncommunicative and needs continued supportive therapies.* End quote."

"So he *expressly writes* that it was *his* decision," Giannini said.

"That is correct. It was also Dr Caldin himself who decided that Lisbeth should be able to re-enter society by being placed with a foster family."

Salander nodded. She remembered Dr Caldin the same way she remembered every detail of her stay at St Stefan's. She had refused to talk to Dr Caldin . . . He was a "crazy-doctor", another man in a white coat who wanted to rootle around in her emotions. But he had been friendly and good-natured. She had sat in his office and listened to him when he explained things to her.

He had seemed hurt when she did not want to speak to him. Finally she had looked him in the eye and explained her decision: *I will never ever talk to you or any other crazy-doctor. None of you listen to what I have to say. You can keep me locked up here until I die. That won't change a thing. I won't talk to any of you.* He had looked at her with surprise and hurt in his eyes. Then he had nodded as if he understood.

"Dr Teleborian," Giannini said, "we have established that you had Lisbeth Salander committed to a children's psychiatric clinic. You were the one who furnished the district court with the report, and this report constituted the only basis for the decisions that were made. Is this correct?"

"That is essentially correct. But I think—"

"You'll have plenty of time to explain what you think. When Lisbeth Salander was about to turn eighteen, you once again interfered in her life and tried to have her locked up in a clinic."

"This time I wasn't the one who wrote the forensic medical report—"

"No, it was written by Dr Jesper H. Löderman. And he just happened to be a doctoral candidate at that time. You were his supervisor. So it was your assessments that caused the report to be approved."

"There's nothing unethical or incorrect in these reports. They were done according to the proper regulations of my profession."

"Now Lisbeth Salander is twenty-seven years old, and for the third time we are in a situation in which you are trying to convince a district court that she is mentally ill and must be committed to a secure psychiatric ward."

Teleborian took a deep breath. Giannini was well prepared. She had surprised him with a number of tricky questions and she had succeeded in distorting his replies. She had not fallen for his charms, and she completely ignored his authority. He was used to having people nod in agreement when he spoke.

How much does she know?

He glanced at Prosecutor Ekström but realized that he could expect no help from that quarter. He had to ride out the storm alone.

He reminded himself that, in spite of everything, he *was* an authority.

It doesn't matter what she says. It's my assessment that counts.

Giannini picked up his forensic psychiatric report.

"Let's take a closer look at your latest report. You expend a great deal of energy analysing Lisbeth Salander's emotional life. A large part deals with your interpretation of her personality, her behaviour and her sexual habits."

"In this report I have attempted to give a complete picture."

"Good. And based on this complete picture you came to the conclusion that Lisbeth suffers from paranoid schizophrenia."

"I prefer not to restrict myself to a precise diagnosis."

"But you have not reached this conclusion through conversations with my client, have you?"

"You know very well that your client resolutely refuses to answer questions that I or any other person in authority might put to her. This behaviour is in itself particularly telling. One can conclude that the patient's paranoid traits have progressed to such an extent that she is literally incapable of having a simple conversation with anyone in authority. She believes that everyone is out to harm her and feels so threatened that she shuts herself inside an impenetrable shell and goes mute."

"I notice that you're expressing yourself very carefully. You say, for example, that one *can* conclude . . ."

"Yes, that's right. I *am* expressing myself carefully. Psychiatry is not an exact science, and I must be careful with my conclusions. At the same time it is not true that we psychiatrists sit around making assumptions that have no basis in fact."

"What you are being very precise about is protecting yourself. The literal fact is that you have not exchanged one single word with my client since the night of her thirteenth birthday because she has refused to talk to you."

"Not only to me. She appears unable to have a conversation with any psychiatrist."

"This means that, as you write here, your conclusions are based on *experience* and on *observations* of my client."

"That's right."

"What can you learn by studying a girl who sits on a chair with her arms crossed and refuses to talk to you?"

Teleborian sighed as though he thought it was irksome to have to explain the obvious. He smiled.

"From a patient who sits and says nothing, you can learn only that this is a patient who is good at sitting and saying nothing. Even this is disturbed behaviour, but that's not what I'm basing my conclusions upon."

"Later this afternoon I will call upon another psychiatrist. His name is Svante Brandén and he's senior physician at the Institute of Forensic Medicine and a specialist in forensic psychiatry. Do you know him?"

Teleborian felt confident again. He had expected Giannini to call upon another psychiatrist to question his own conclusions. It was a situation for which he was ready, and in which he would be able to dismiss every objection without difficulty. Indeed, it would be easier to handle an academic colleague in a friendly debate than someone like Advokat Giannini who had no inhibitions and was bent on distorting his words. He smiled.

"He is a highly respected and skilled forensic psychiatrist. But you must understand, Fru Giannini, that producing a report of this type is an academic and scientific process. You yourself may disagree with my conclusions, and another psychiatrist may interpret an action or an event in a different way. You may have dissimilar points of view, or perhaps it would be a question purely of how well one doctor or another knows the patient. He might arrive at a very different conclusion about Lisbeth Salander. That is not at all unusual in psychiatry."

"That's not why I'm calling him. He has not met or examined Lisbeth

Salander, and he will not be making any evaluations about her mental condition."

"Oh, is that so?"

"I have asked him to read your report and all the documentation you have produced on Lisbeth Salander and to look at her medical records from St Stefan's. I have asked him to make an assessment, not about the state of my client's health, but about whether, from a purely scientific point of view, there is adequate foundation for your conclusions in the material you recorded."

Teleborian shrugged.

"With all due respect, I think I have a better understanding of Lisbeth Salander than any other psychiatrist in the country. I have followed her development since she was twelve, and regrettably my conclusions were always confirmed by her actions."

"Very well," Giannini said. "Then we'll take a look at your conclusions. In your statement you write that her treatment was interrupted when she was placed with a foster family at the age of fifteen."

"That's correct. It was a serious mistake. If we had been allowed to complete the treatment we might not be here in this courtroom today."

"You mean that if you had had the opportunity to keep her in restraints for another year she might have become more tractable?"

"That is unworthy."

"I do beg your pardon. You cite extensively the report that your doctoral candidate Jesper Löderman put together when she was about to turn eighteen. You write that, quote, *Lisbeth Salander's self-destructive and antisocial behaviour is confirmed by drug abuse and the promiscuity which she has exhibited since she was discharged from St Stefan's*, unquote. What did you mean by this statement?"

Teleborian sat in silence for several seconds.

"Well . . . now I'll have to go back a bit. After Lisbeth Salander was discharged from St Stefan's she developed, as I had predicted, problems with alcohol and drug abuse. She was repeatedly arrested by the police. A social welfare report also determined that she had had profligate sexual relations with older men and that she was very probably involved in prostitution."

"Let's analyse this. You say that she abused alcohol. How often was she intoxicated?"

"I'm sorry?"

"Was she drunk every day from when she was released until she turned eighteen? Was she drunk once a week?"

"Naturally I can't answer that."

"But you have just stated that she had problems with alcohol abuse."

"She was a minor and arrested repeatedly by the police for drunkenness."

"That's the second time you have said that she was arrested repeatedly. How often did this occur? Was it once a week or once every other week?"

"No, it's not a matter of so many individual occasions . . ."

"Lisbeth Salander was arrested on two occasions for drunkenness, once when she was sixteen, once when she was seventeen. On one of those occasions she was so blind drunk that she was taken to hospital. These are the *repeatedly* you refer to. Was she intoxicated on more than these occasions?"

"I don't know, but one might fear that her behaviour was—"

"Excuse me, did I hear you correctly? You *do not know* whether she was intoxicated on more than two occasions during her teenage years, but you *fear* that this was the case. And yet you write reports maintaining that Lisbeth Salander was engaged in repeated alcohol and drug abuse?"

"That is the social service's information, not mine. It has to do with Lisbeth Salander's whole lifestyle. Not surprisingly her prognosis was dismal after her treatment was interrupted, and her life became a round of alcohol abuse, police intervention, and uncontrolled promiscuity."

"You say 'uncontrolled promiscuity'."

"Yes. That's a term which indicates that she had no control over her own life. She had sexual relations with older men."

"That's not against the law."

"No, but it's abnormal behaviour for a sixteen-year-old girl. The question might be asked as to whether she participated in such encounters of her own free will or whether she was in a situation of uncontrollable compulsion."

"But you said that she was very probably a prostitute."

"That may have been a natural consequence of the fact that she lacked education, was incapable of completing school or continuing to higher education, and therefore could not get a job. It's possible that she viewed older men as father figures and that financial

531

remuneration for sexual favours was simply a convenient spin-off. In which case I perceive it as neurotic behaviour."

"So you think that a sixteen-year-old girl who has sex is neurotic?"

"You're twisting my words."

"But you do not know whether she ever took money for sexual favours."

"She was never arrested for prostitution."

"And she could hardly be arrested for it since prostitution is not a crime in our country."

"Well, yes, that's right. In her case this has to do with compulsive neurotic behaviour."

"And you did not hesitate to conclude that Lisbeth Salander is mentally ill based on these unverifiable assumptions? When I was sixteen years old, I drank myself silly on half a bottle of vodka which I stole from my father. Do you think that makes me mentally ill?"

"No, of course not."

"If I may be so bold, is it not a fact that when you were seventeen you went to a party and got so drunk that you all went out on the town and smashed the windows around the square in Uppsala? You were arrested by the police, detained until you were sober, and then let off with a fine."

Teleborian looked shocked.

"Is that not a fact, Dr Teleborian?"

"Well, yes. People do so many stupid things when they're seventeen. But—"

"But that doesn't lead you – or anyone else – to believe that you have a serious mental illness?"

Teleborian was angry. That infernal lawyer kept twisting his words and homing in on details. She refused to see the larger picture. And his own childish escapade . . . *How the hell had she got hold of that information?*

He cleared his throat and spoke in a raised voice.

"The reports from social services were unequivocal. They confirmed that Lisbeth Salander had a lifestyle that revolved around alcohol, drugs and promiscuity. Social services also said that she was a prostitute."

"No, social services never said that she was a prostitute."

"She was arrested at—"

"No. She was not arrested," Giannini said. "She was searched in Tantolunden at the age of seventeen when she was in the company of a much older man. That same year she was arrested for drunkenness. Also in the company of a much older man. Social services *feared* that she *might* be engaged in prostitution. But no *evidence* was ever presented."

"She had very loose sexual relations with a large number of individuals, both male and female."

"In your own report, you dwell on my client's sexual habits. You claim that her relationship with her friend Miriam Wu *confirms the misgivings about a sexual psychopathy*. Why does it *confirm* any such thing?"

Teleborian made no answer.

"I sincerely hope that you are not thinking of claiming that homosexuality is a mental illness," Giannini said. "That might even be an illegal statement."

"No, of course not. I'm alluding to the elements of sexual sadism in the relationship."

"You think that she's a sadist?"

"I—"

"We have Miriam Wu's statement here. There was, it says, no violence in their relationship."

"They engaged in S. & M. sex and—"

"Now I'm beginning to think you've been reading too many evening newspapers. Lisbeth Salander and her friend Miriam Wu engaged in sexual games on some occasions which involved Miriam Wu tying up my client and giving her sexual satisfaction. That is neither especially unusual nor is it against the law. Is that why you want to lock up my client?"

Teleborian waved a hand in a dismissive gesture.

"When I was sixteen and still at school I was intoxicated on a good many occasions. I have tried drugs. I have smoked marijuana, and I even tried cocaine on one occasion about twenty years ago. I had my first sexual experience with a schoolfriend when I was fifteen, and I had a relationship with a boy who tied my hands to the bedstead when I was twenty. When I was twenty-two I had a relationship with a man who was forty-seven that lasted several months. Am I, in your view, mentally ill?"

"Fru Giannini, you joke about this, but your sexual experiences are irrelevant in this case."

"Why is that? When I read your so-called psychiatric assessment of Lisbeth Salander, I find point after point which, taken out of context, would apply to myself. Why am I healthy and sound while Lisbeth Salander is considered a dangerous sadist?"

"These are not the details that are relevant. You didn't twice try to murder your father—"

"Dr Teleborian, the reality is that it's none of your business who Lisbeth Salander wants to have sex with. It's none of your business which gender her partner is or how they conduct their sexual relations. And yet in her case you pluck out details from her life and use them as the basis for saying that she is sick."

"Lisbeth Salander's whole life – from the time she was in junior school – is a document of unprovoked and violent outbursts of anger against teachers and other pupils."

"Just a moment." Giannini's voice was suddenly like an ice scraper on a car window. "Look at my client."

Everyone looked at Salander.

"My client grew up in abominable family circumstances. Over a period of years her father persistently abused her mother."

"That's—"

"Let me finish. Lisbeth Salander's mother was mortally afraid of Alexander Zalachenko. She did not dare to protest. She did not dare to go to a doctor. She did not dare to go to a women's crisis centre. She was ground down and eventually beaten so badly that she suffered irreversible brain damage. The person who had to take responsibility, the only person who tried to take responsibility for the family long before she reached her teens even, was Lisbeth Salander. She had to shoulder that burden all by herself, since Zalachenko the *spy* was more important to the state and its social services than Lisbeth's mother."

"I cannot—"

"The result, excuse me, was a situation in which society abandoned Lisbeth's mother and her two children. Are you surprised that Lisbeth had problems at school? Look at her. She's small and skinny. She has always been the smallest girl in her class. She was introverted and eccentric and she had no friends. Do you know how children tend to treat fellow pupils who are *different*?"

Teleborian sighed.

Giannini continued. "I can go back to her school records and examine one situation after another in which Lisbeth turned violent. They were always preceded by some kind of provocation. I can easily recognize the signs of bullying. Let me tell you something."

"What?"

"I admire Lisbeth Salander. She's tougher than I am. If I had been strapped down for a year when I was thirteen, I would probably have broken down altogether. She fought back with the only weapon she had available – her contempt for you."

Her nervousness was long gone. She felt that she was in control.

"In your testimony this morning you spoke a great deal about fantasies. You stated, for instance, that Lisbeth's Salander's account of her rape by Advokat Bjurman is a fantasy."

"That's correct."

"On what do you base your conclusion?"

"On my experience of the way she usually fantasizes."

"On your experience of the way she usually fantasizes? How do you decide when she is fantasizing? When she says that she was strapped to a bed for 380 days and nights, then in your opinion it's a fantasy, despite the fact that your very own records tell us that this was indeed the case."

"This is something entirely different. There is not a shred of evidence that Bjurman committed rape against Lisbeth Salander. I mean, needles through her nipples and such gross violence that she unquestionably should have been taken by ambulance to hospital? It's obvious that this could not have taken place."

Giannini turned to Judge Iversen. "I asked to have a projector available today . . ."

"It's in place," the judge said.

"Could we close the curtains, please?"

Giannini opened her PowerBook and plugged in the cables to the projector. She turned to her client.

"Lisbeth. We're going to look at the film. Are you ready for this?"

"I've lived through it," Salander said dryly.

"And I have your approval to show it here?"

Salander nodded. She fixed her eyes on Teleborian.

"Can you tell us when the film was made?"

"On 7 March, 2003."

"Who shot the film?"

"I did. I used a hidden camera, standard equipment at Milton Security."

"Just one moment," Prosecutor Ekström shouted. "This is beginning to resemble a circus act."

"What is it we are about to see?" Judge Iversen said with a sharp edge to his voice.

"Dr Teleborian claims that Lisbeth Salander's account of her rape by Advokat Bjurman is a fantasy. I am going to show you evidence to the contrary. The film is ninety minutes long, but I will only show a few short excerpts. I warn you that it contains some very unpleasant scenes."

"Is this some sort of trick?" Ekström said.

"There's a good way to find out," said Giannini and started the D.V.D. in her laptop.

"Haven't you even learned to tell the time?" Advokat Bjurman greets her gruffly. The camera enters his apartment.

After nine minutes Judge Iversen banged his gavel. Advokat Bjurman was being shown violently shoving a dildo into Lisbeth Salander's anus. Giannini had turned up the volume. Salander's half-stifled screams through the duct tape that covered her mouth were heard throughout the courtroom.

"Turn off the film," Judge Iversen said in a very loud and commanding voice.

Giannini pressed stop and the ceiling lights were turned back on. Judge Iversen was red in the face. Prosecutor Ekström sat as if turned to stone. Teleborian was as pale as a corpse.

"Advokat Giannini . . . How long is this film, did you say?"

"Ninety minutes. The rape itself went on in stages for about five or six hours, but my client only has a vague sense of the violence inflicted upon her in the last few hours." Giannini turned to Teleborian. "There is a scene, however, in which Bjurman pushes a needle through my client's nipple, something that *Doctor* Teleborian maintains is an expression of Lisbeth Salander's wild imagination. It takes place in minute seventy-two, and I'm offering to show the episode here and now."

"Thank you, that won't be necessary," the judge said. "Fröken Salander . . ."

For a second he lost his train of thought and did not know how to proceed.

"Fröken Salander, why did you record this film?"

"Bjurman had already subjected me to one rape and was demanding more. The first time he made me suck him off, the old creep. I thought it was going to be a repeat. I thought I'd be able to get such good evidence of what he did that I could then blackmail him into staying away from me. I misjudged him."

"But why did you go not to the police when you have such . . . irrefutable evidence?"

"I don't talk to policemen," Salander said flatly.

Palmgren stood up from his wheelchair. He supported himself by leaning on the edge of the table. His voice was very clear.

"Our client on principle does not speak to the police or to other persons of authority, and least of all to psychiatrists. The reason is simple. From the time she was a child she tried time and again to talk to police and social workers to explain that her mother was being abused by Alexander Zalachenko. The result in every instance was that she was punished because government civil servants had decided that Zalachenko was more important than she was."

He cleared his throat and continued.

"And when she eventually concluded that nobody was listening to her, her only means of protecting her mother was to fight Zalachenko with violence. And then this bastard who calls himself a doctor" – he pointed at Teleborian – "wrote a fabricated psychiatric diagnosis which described her as mentally ill, and it gave him the opportunity to keep her in restraints at St Stefan's for 380 days. What a bastard."

Palmgren sat down. Judge Iversen was surprised by this outburst. He turned to Salander.

"Would you perhaps like to take a break . . ."

"Why?" Salander said.

"Alright, then we'll continue. Advokat Giannini, the recording will be examined, and I will require a technical opinion to verify its authenticity. But I cannot tolerate seeing any more of these appalling scenes at present. Let's proceed."

"Gladly. I too find them appalling," said Giannini. "My client has been subjected to multiple instances of physical and mental abuse and legal misconduct. And the person most to blame for this is Dr Peter Teleborian. He betrayed his oath as a physician and he betrayed his patient. Together with a member of an illegal group within the Security

Police, Gunnar Björck, he patched together a forensic psychiatric assessment for the purpose of locking up an inconvenient witness. I believe that this case must be unique in Swedish jurisprudence."

"These are outrageous accusations," Teleborian said. "I have done my best to help Lisbeth Salander. She tried to murder her father. It's perfectly obvious that there's something wrong with her—"

Giannini interrupted him.

"I would now like to bring to the attention of the court Dr Teleborian's second forensic psychiatric assessment of my client, presented at this trial today. I maintain that it is a lie, just as the report from 1991 was a lie."

"Well, this is simply—" Teleborian spluttered.

"Judge Iversen, could you please ask the witness to stop interrupting me?"

"Herr Teleborian . . ."

"I will be quiet. But these are outrageous accusations. It's not surprising that I'm upset—"

"Herr Teleborian, please be quiet until a question is directed at you. Do go on, Advokat Giannini."

"This is the forensic psychiatric assessment that Dr Teleborian has presented to the court. It is based on what he has termed 'observations' of my client which were supposed to have taken place after she was moved to Kronoberg prison on June 5. The examination was supposed to have been concluded on July 5."

"Yes, so I have understood," Judge Iversen said.

"Dr Teleborian, is it the case that you did not have the opportunity to examine or observe my client before June 6? Before that she was at Sahlgrenska hospital in Göteborg, where she was being kept in isolation, as we know."

"Yes."

"You made attempts on two separate occasions to gain access to my client at Sahlgrenska. Both times you were denied admittance."

Giannini opened her briefcase and took out a document. She walked around her table and handed it to Judge Iversen.

"I see," the judge said. "This appears to be a copy of Dr Teleborian's report. What is your point?"

"I would like to call upon two witnesses. They are waiting outside the courtroom now."

"Who are these witnesses?"

538

"They are Mikael Blomkvist from *Millennium* magazine, and Superintendent Torsten Edklinth, Director of the Constitutional Protection Unit of the Security Police."

"And they are outside?"

"Yes."

"Show them in," Judge Iversen said.

"This is highly irregular," Prosecutor Ekström said.

Ekström had watched in extreme discomfort as Giannini shredded his key witness. The film had been devastating evidence. The judge ignored Ekström and gestured to the bailiff to open the door to admit Blomkvist and Edklinth.

"I would first like to call upon Mikael Blomkvist."

"Then I would ask that Herr Teleborian stand down for a while," Judge Iverson said.

"Are you finished with me?" Teleborian said.

"No, not by any means," Giannini said.

Blomkvist replaced Teleborian in the witness box. Judge Iversen swiftly dealt with the formalities, and Blomkvist took the oath.

"Mikael," Giannini said, and then she smiled. "I would find it difficult, if your honour will forgive me, to call my brother Herr Blomkvist, so I will settle for his first name."

She went to Judge Iversen's bench and asked for the forensic psychiatric report which she had just handed to him. She then gave it to Blomkvist.

"Have you seen this document before?"

"Yes, I have. I have three versions in my possession. The first I acquired on May 12, the second on May 19, and the third – this one – on June 3."

"Can you tell us how you acquired the copies?"

"I received them in my capacity as a journalist from a source I do not intend to name."

Salander stared at Teleborian. He was once more deathly pale.

"What did you do with the report?"

"I gave it to Torsten Edklinth at Constitutional Protection."

"Thank you, Mikael. Now I'd like to call Torsten Edklinth," Giannini said, taking back the report. She handed it to Judge Iversen and the procedure with the oath was repeated.

539

"Superintendent Edklinth, is it correct that you received a forensic psychiatric report on Lisbeth Salander from Mikael Blomkvist?"

"Yes, it is."

"When did you receive it?"

"It was logged in at S.I.S. on June 4."

"And this is the same report I have just handed to Judge Iversen?"

"If my signature is on the back, then it's the same one."

The judge turned over the document and saw Edklinth's signature there.

"Superintendent Edklinth, could you explain how you happened to have a forensic psychiatric report in your possession which claims have analysed a patient who was still in isolation at Sahlgrenska?"

"Yes, I can. Herr Teleborian's report is a sham. It was put together with the help of a person by the name of Jonas Sandberg, just as he produced a similar document in 1991 with Gunnar Björck."

"That's a lie," Teleborian said in a weak voice.

"Is it a lie?" Giannini said.

"No, not at all," Edklinth said. "I should perhaps mention that Jonas Sandberg is one of a dozen or so individuals who were arrested today by order of the Prosecutor General. Sandberg is being held as an accomplice to the murder of Gunnar Björck. He is part of a criminal unit operating within the Security Police which has been protecting Alexander Zalachenko since the '70s. This same group of officers was responsible for the decision to lock up Lisbeth Salander in 1991. We have incontrovertible evidence, as well as a confession from the unit's director."

The courtroom was hushed, transfixed.

"Would Herr Teleborian like to comment on what has just been said?" Judge Iversen said.

Teleborian shook his head.

"In that case it is my duty tell you that you risk being charged with perjury and possibly other counts in addition," Judge Iversen said.

"If you'll excuse me, your honour," Blomkvist said.

"Yes?"

"Herr Teleborian has bigger problems than this. Outside the courtroom are two police officers who would like to bring him for questioning."

"I see," the judge said. "Is it a matter which concerns this court?"

"I believe it is, your honour."

Judge Iversen gestured to the bailiff, who admitted Inspector Modig and a woman Prosecutor Ekström did not immediately recognize. Her name was Lisa Collsjö, criminal inspector for the Special Investigations Division, the unit within the National Police Board responsible for investigating cases of child pornography and sexual assault on children.

"And what is your business here?" Judge Iversen said.

"We are here to arrest Peter Teleborian with your permission, and without wishing to disturb the court's proceedings."

Judge Iversen looked at Advokat Giannini.

"I'm not quite finished with him . . . but the court may have heard enough of Herr Teleborian."

"You have my permission," Judge Iversen said to the police officers.

Collsjö walked across to the witness box. "Peter Teleborian, you are under arrest for violation of the law on child pornography."

Teleborian sat still, hardly breathing. Giannini saw that all light seemed to have been extinguished in his eyes.

"Specifically, for possession of approximately eight thousand pornographic photographs of children found on your computer."

She bent down to pick up his laptop case, which he had brought with him.

"This is confiscated as evidence," she said.

As he was being led from the courtroom, Salander's blazing eyes bored into Teleborian's back.

CHAPTER 28

Friday, 15.vii – Saturday, 16.vii

Judge Iversen tapped his pen on the edge of his table to quell the murmuring that had arisen in the wake of Teleborian's departure. He seemed unsure how to proceed. Then he turned to Prosecutor Ekström.

"Do you have any comment to make to the court on what has been seen and heard in the past hour?"

Ekström stood up and looked at Judge Iversen and then at Edklinth before he turned his head and met Salander's unwavering gaze. He understood that the battle was lost. He glanced over at Blomkvist and realized with sudden terror that he too risked being exposed to *Millennium*'s investigators . . . Which could ruin his career.

He was at a loss to comprehend how this had happened. He had come to the trial convinced that he knew everything about the case.

He had understood the delicate balance sought by national security after his many candid talks with Superintendent Nyström. It had been explained to him that the Salander report from 1991 had been fabricated. He had received the inside information he needed. He had asked questions – hundreds of questions – and received answers to all of them. A deception in the national interest. And now Nyström had been arrested, according to Edklinth. He had believed in Teleborian, who had, after all, seemed so . . . so competent. So convincing.

Good Lord. What sort of a mess have I landed in?

And then, *How the hell am I going to get out of it?*

He stroked his goatee. He cleared his throat. Slowly he removed his glasses.

"I regret to say that it seems I have been misinformed on a number of essential points in this investigation."

He wondered if he could shift the blame on to the police investigators. Then he had a vision of Inspector Bublanski. Bublanski would never back him up. If Ekström made one wrong move, Bublanski would call a press conference and sink him.

Ekström met Salander's gaze. She was sitting there patiently, and in her eyes he read both curiosity and vengeance.

No compromises.

He could still get her convicted of grievous bodily harm in Stallarholmen. And he could probably get her convicted for the attempted murder of her father in Gosseberga. That would mean changing his strategy immediately; he would drop everything that had anything to do with Teleborian. All claims that she was a psychopath had to go, but that meant that her story would be strengthened all the way back to 1991. The whole declaration of incompetence was bogus, and with that . . .

Plus she had that blasted film . . .

Then it struck him.

Good God. She's a victim, pure and simple.

"Judge Iverson . . . I believe I can no longer rely on the documents I have here in my hand."

"I suppose not," Judge Iversen said.

"I'm going to have to ask for a recess, or that the trial be suspended until I am able to make certain adjustments to my case."

"Advokat Giannini?" the judge said.

"I request that my client be at once acquitted on all counts and be released immediately. I also request that the district court take a definite position on the question of Fröken Salander's declaration of incompetence. Moreover, I believe that she should adequately be compensated for the violations of her rights that have occurred."

Lisbeth Salander turned towards Judge Iversen.

No compromises.

Judge Iversen looked at Salander's autobiography. He then looked over at Prosecutor Ekström.

"I too believe we would be wise to investigate exactly what has happened that brings us to this sorry pass. I fear that you are probably not the right person to conduct that investigation. In all my years as a jurist and judge, I have never been party to anything even approaching the legal dilemma in this case. I confess that I am at a loss for words. I have never even heard of a case in which the prosecutor's chief witness is arrested during a court in session, or of a quite convincing argument turning out to be an utter fabrication. I honestly do not see what is left of the prosecutor's case."

Palmgren cleared his throat.

"Yes?" Iversen said.

"As a representative for the defence, I can only share your feelings. Sometimes one must step back and allow common sense to guide the formal procedures. I'd like to state that you, in your capacity as judge, have seen only the first stage of a scandal that is going to rock the whole establishment. Today ten police officers from within Säpo have been arrested. They will be charged with murder and a list of crimes so long that it will take quite some time to draw up the report."

"I presume that I must decide on a suspension of this trial."

"If you'll excuse me for saying so, I think that would be an unfortunate decision."

"I'm listening."

"Lisbeth Salander is innocent. Her 'fantastical' autobiography, as Herr Ekström so contemptuously dismissed it, is in fact true. And it can all be proven. She has suffered an outrageous violation of her rights. As a court we could now stick with formal procedure and continue with the trial until finally we arrive at an acquittal, but there is an obvious alternative: to let a new investigation take over everything concerning Lisbeth Salander. An investigation is already underway to sort out an integral part of this mess."

"I see what you mean."

"As the judge of this case you have a choice. The wise thing to do would be to reject the prosecutor's entire preliminary investigation and request that he does his homework."

Judge Iversen looked long and hard at Ekström.

"The *just* thing to do would be to acquit our client at once. She deserves in addition an apology, but the redress will take time and will depend upon the rest of the investigation."

"I understand the points you're making, Advokat Palmgren. But before I can declare your client innocent I will have to have the whole story clear in my mind. That will probably take a while . . ."

He hesitated and looked at Giannini.

"If I decide that the court will adjourn until Monday and accommodate your wishes insofar as I see no reason to keep your client in custody any longer – which would mean that you could expect that, no matter what else happens, she will not be given a prison sentence – can you guarantee that she will appear for continued proceedings when summoned?"

"Of course," Palmgren said quickly.

"No," Salander said in a sharp voice.

Everyone's eyes turned to the person who was at the heart of the entire drama.

"What do you mean by that?" Judge Iversen said.

"The moment you release me I'm going to leave the country. I do not intend to spend one more minute of my time on this trial."

"You would refuse to appear?"

"That is correct. If you want me to answer more questions, then you'll have to keep me in prison. The moment you release me, this story is settled as far as I'm concerned. And that does not include being available for an indefinite time to you, to Ekström, or to any police officers."

Judge Iversen sighed. Palmgren looked bewildered.

"I agree with my client," Giannini said. "It is the government and the authorities who have committed crimes against Lisbeth Salander, not the other way around. At the very least she deserves to be able to walk out of that door with an acquittal and the chance to put this whole story behind her."

No compromises.

Judge Iversen glanced at his watch.

"It is 3.00. That means that you're going to force me to keep your client in custody."

"If that's your decision, then we accept it. As Fröken Salander's representative I request that she be acquitted of the charges brought by Prosecutor Ekström. I request that you release my client without restrictions, and without delay. And I request that her previous declaration of incompetence be rescinded and that her civil rights be immediately restored."

"The matter of the declaration of incompetence is a significantly longer process. I would have to get statements from psychiatric experts after she has been examined. I cannot simply make a snap decision about that."

"No," Giannini said. "We do not accept that."

"Why not?"

"Lisbeth Salander must have the same civil rights as any other citizen of Sweden. *She* has been the victim of a crime. She was *falsely* declared incompetent. We have heard evidence of that falsification. The decision to place her under guardianship therefore lacks a legal basis and must be unconditionally rescinded. There is no reason whatsoever for my client to submit to a psychiatric examination. No-one else has to

545

prove that they are not mentally ill if they are the victim of a crime."

Judge Iversen considered the matter for a moment. "Advokat Giannini, I realize that this is an exceptional situation. I'm calling a recess of fifteen minutes so that we can stretch our legs and gather our thoughts. I have no wish that your client be kept in custody tonight if she is innocent, but that means that this trial will have to continue today until we are done."

"That sounds good to me," said Giannini.

Blomkvist hugged his sister. "How did it go?"

"Mikael, I was brilliant against Teleborian. I annihilated him."

"I told you you'd be unbeatable. When it comes down to it, this story is not primarily about spies and secret government agencies; it's about violence against women, and the men who enable it. From what little I heard and saw, you were phenomenal. She's going to be acquitted."

"You're right. There's no longer any doubt"

Judge Iversen banged his gavel.

"Could you please sum up the facts from beginning to end, so that I can get a clear picture of what actually happened?"

"Let's begin," Giannini said, "with the astounding story of a group within the Security Police who call themselves 'the Section', and who got hold of a Soviet defector in the mid-'70s. The story is published today in *Millennium* magazine. I imagine it will be the lead story on all the news broadcasts this evening . . ."

At 6.00 that evening Judge Iversen decided to release Salander and to revoke her declaration of incompetence.

But the decision was made on one condition: Judge Iversen demanded that Salander submit to an interview in which she would formally testify to her knowledge of the Zalachenko affair. At first she refused. This refusal brought about a moment's wrangling until Judge Iversen raised his voice. He leaned forward and fixed his gaze on Salander.

"Fröken Salander, if I rescind your declaration of incompetence, that will mean that you have exactly the same rights as all other citizens. It also means that you have the same obligations. It is therefore your duty to manage your finances, pay taxes, obey the law, and assist the police in investigations of serious crimes. So I am summoning you to be questioned like any other citizen who has information that might be vital to an investigation."

The force of this logic seemed to sink in. She pouted and looked cross, but she stopped arguing.

"When the police have interviewed you, the leader of the preliminary investigation – in this case the Prosecutor General – will decide whether you will be summoned as a witness in any future legal proceedings. Like any other Swedish citizen, you can refuse to obey such a summons. How you act is none of my concern, but you do not have *carte blanche*. If you refuse to appear, then like any other adult you may be charged with obstruction of justice or perjury. There are no exceptions."

Salander's expression darkened yet more.

"So, what is your decision?" Judge Iversen said.

After thinking it over for a minute, Salander gave a curt nod.

O.K. A little compromise.

During her summary of the Zalachenko affair that evening, Giannini launched a savage attack on Prosecutor Ekström. Eventually Ekström admitted that the course of events had proceeded more or less as Giannini had described them. He had been helped during the preliminary investigation by Superintendent Nyström, and had received his information from Dr Teleborian. In Ekström's case there was no conspiracy. He had gone along with the Section in good faith in his capacity as leader of the preliminary investigation. When the whole extent of the conspiracy finally dawned on him, he decided to withdraw all charges against Salander, and that decision meant that a raft of bureaucratic formalities could be set aside. Judge Iversen looked relieved.

Palmgren was exhausted after his day in court, the first in many years. He needed to go back to the Ersta rehabilitation home and go to bed. He was driven there by a uniformed guard from Milton Security. As he was leaving, he put a hand on Salander's shoulder. They looked at each other, saying nothing. After a moment she nodded.

Giannini called Blomkvist at 7.00 to tell him that Salander had been acquitted of all charges, but that she was going to have to stay at police headquarters for what might be another couple of hours for her interview.

The news came as the entire staff of *Millennium* were gathered at the office. The telephones had been ringing incessantly since the first copies of the magazine had been distributed by messenger that lunchtime to other newsrooms across the city. In the early evening T.V.4 had broadcast its first special program on Zalachenko and the Section. The media were having a field day.

Blomkvist walked into the main office, stuck his fingers in his mouth and gave a loud whistle.

"Great news. Salander has been acquitted on all counts."

Spontaneous applause broke out. Then everyone went back to talking on their telephones as if nothing had happened.

Blomkvist looked up at the television that had been turned on in the editorial office. The news on T.V.4 was just starting. The trailer was a brief clip of the film showing Sandberg planting cocaine in his apartment on Bellmansgatan.

> *"Here we can clearly see a Säpo officer planting what we later learn is cocaine at the apartment of Mikael Blomkvist, journalist at* Millennium *magazine."*

Then the anchorman came on the screen.

> *"Twelve officers of the Security Police were today arrested on a range of criminal charges, including murder. Welcome to this extended news broadcast."*

Blomkvist turned off the sound when *She* came on, and he saw himself sitting in a studio armchair. He already knew what he had said. He looked over at the desk where Svensson had sat. All his research documents on the sex-trafficking industry were gone, and the desk was once more home to stacks of newspapers and piles of unsorted paper that nobody had time to deal with.

For Blomkvist, it was at that desk that the Zalachenko affair had begun. He wished that Svensson had been able to see the conclusion of it. A pile of copies of his just-published book was on the table next to Blomkvist's own about the Section.

You would have loved this moment, Dag.

He heard the telephone in his office ringing, but he could not face picking it up. He pulled the door shut and went into Berger's office and sank into a comfortable chair by the window. Berger was on the telephone. He looked about. She had been back a month, but had not yet got around to putting up the paintings and photographs that she had taken away when she left in April. The bookshelves were still bare.

"How does it feel?" she said when she hung up.

"I think I'm happy," he said.

She laughed. "*The Section* is going to be a sensation. Every newsroom is going crazy for it. Do you feel like appearing on *Aktuellt* at 9.00 for an interview?"

"I think not."

"I suspected as much."

"We're going to be talking about this for several months. There's no rush."

She nodded.

"What are you doing later this evening?" Berger said.

"I don't know." He bit his lip. "Erika . . . I . . ."

"Figuerola," Berger said with a smile.

He nodded.

"So it's serious?"

"I don't know."

"She's terribly in love with you."

"I think I'm in love with her too," he said.

"I promise I'll keep my distance until, you know . . . well, maybe," she said.

At 8.00 Armansky and Linder appeared at *Millennium*'s offices. They thought the occasion called for champagne, so they had brought over a crate from the state liquor store. Berger hugged Linder and introduced her to everyone. Armansky took a seat in Blomkvist's office.

They drank their champagne. Neither of them said anything for quite a while. It was Armansky who broke the silence.

"You know what, Blomkvist? The first time we met, on that job in Hedestad, I didn't much care for you."

"You don't say."

"You came over to sign a contract when you hired Lisbeth as a researcher."

"I remember."

"I think I was jealous of you. You'd known her only for a couple of hours, yet she was laughing with you. For some years I'd tried to be Lisbeth's friend, but I have never once made her smile."

"Well . . . I haven't really been that successful either."

They sat in silence once again.

"Great that all this is over," Armansky said.

"Amen to that," Blomkvist said, and they raised their glasses in salute.

Inspectors Bublanski and Modig conducted the formal interview with Salander. They had both been at home with their families after a particularly taxing day but were immediately summoned to return to police headquarters.

Salander was accompanied by Giannini. She gave precise responses to all the questions that Bublanski and Modig asked, and Giannini had little occasion to comment or intervene.

Salander lied consistently on two points. In her description of what had happened in Stallarholmen, she stubbornly maintained that it was Nieminen who had accidentally shot "Magge" Lundin in the foot at the instant that she nailed him with the taser. Where had she got the taser? She had confiscated it from Lundin, she explained.

Bublanski and Modig were both sceptical, but there was no evidence and no witnesses to contradict her story. Nieminen was no doubt in a position to protest, but he refused to say anything about the incident; in fact he had no notion of what had happened in the seconds after he was stunned with the taser.

As far as Salander's journey to Gosseberga was concerned, she claimed that her only objective had been to convince her father to turn himself in to the police.

Salander looked completely guileless; it was impossible to say whether she was telling the truth or not. Giannini had no reason to arrive at an opinion on the matter.

The only person who knew for certain that Salander had gone to Gosseberga with the intention of terminating any relationship she had with her father once and for all was Blomkvist. But he had been sent out of the courtroom shortly after the proceedings were resumed. No-one knew that he and Salander had carried on long conversations online by night while she was confined to Sahlgrenska.

The media missed altogether her release from custody. If the time of it had been known, a huge contingent would have descended on police headquarters. But many of the reporters were exhausted after the chaos and excitement that had ensued when *Millennium* reached the news-stands and certain members of the Security Police were arrested by other Security Police officers.

The presenter of *She* at T.V.4 was the only journalist who knew what the story was all about. Her hour-long broadcast became a classic, and some months later she won the award for Best T.V. News Story of the Year.

Modig got Salander away from police headquarters by very simply taking her and Giannini down to the garage and driving them to Giannini's office on Kungholm's Kyrkoplan. There they switched to Giannini's car. When Modig had driven away, Giannini headed for Södermalm. As they passed the parliament building she broke the silence.

"Where to?" she said.

Salander thought for a few seconds.

"You can drop me somewhere on Lundagatan."

"Miriam isn't there."

Salander looked at her.

"She went to France quite soon after she came out of hospital. She's staying with her parents if you want to get hold of her."

"Why didn't you tell me?"

"You never asked. She said she needed some space. This morning Mikael gave me these and said you'd probably like to have them back."

She handed her a set of keys. Salander took it and said: "Thanks. Could you drop me somewhere on Folkungagatan instead?"

"You don't even want to tell me where you live?"

"Later. Right now I want to be left in peace."

"O.K."

Giannini had switched on her mobile when they left police head-quarters. It started beeping as they were passing Slussen. She looked at the display.

"It's Mikael. He's called every ten minutes for the past couple of hours."

"I don't want to talk to him."

"Tell me . . . Could I ask you a personal question?"

"Yes."

"What did Mikael do to you that you hate him so much? I mean, if it weren't for him, you'd probably be back on a secure ward tonight."

"I don't hate Mikael. He hasn't done anything to me. I just don't want to see him right now."

Giannini glanced across at her client. "I don't mean to pry, but you fell for him, didn't you?"

Salander looked out of the window and did not answer.

"My brother is completely irresponsible when it comes to relationships. He screws his way through life and doesn't seem to grasp how much it can hurt those women who think of him as more than a casual affair."

Salander met her gaze. "I don't want to discuss Mikael with you."

"Right," Giannini said. She pulled into the kerb just before the junction with Erstagatan. "Is this O.K.?"

"Yes."

They sat in silence for a moment. Salander made no move to open the door. Then Giannini turned off the engine.

"What happens now?" Salander said at last.

"What happens now is that as from today you are no longer under guardianship. You can live your life however you want. Even though we won in the district court, there's still a whole mass of red tape to get through. There will be reports on accountability within the guardianship agency and the question of compensation and things like that. And the criminal investigation will continue."

"I don't want any compensation. I want to be left in peace."

"I understand. But what you want won't play much of a role here. This process is beyond your control. I suggest that you get yourself a lawyer to represent you."

"Don't you want to go on being my lawyer?"

Giannini rubbed her eyes. After all the stress of the day she felt utterly drained. She wanted to go home and have a shower. She wanted her husband to massage her back.

"I don't know. You don't trust me. And I don't trust you. I have no desire to be drawn into a long process during which I encounter nothing but frustrating silence when I make a suggestion or want to discuss something."

Salander said nothing for a long moment. "I . . . I'm not good at relationships. But I do trust you."

It sounded almost like an apology.

"That may be. And it needn't be my problem if you're bad at relationships. But it does become my problem if I have to represent you."

Silence.

"Would you want me to go on being your lawyer?"

Salander nodded. Giannini sighed.

"I live at Fiskargatan 9. Above Mosebacke Torg. Could you drive me there?"

Giannini looked at her client and then she started the engine. She let Salander direct her to the address. They stopped short of the building.

"O.K.," Giannini said. "We'll give it a try. Here are my conditions. I agree to represent you. When I need to get hold of you I want you to answer. When I need to know what you want me to do, I want clear answers. If I call you and tell you that you have to talk to a policeman or a prosecutor or anything else that has to do with the criminal investigation, then I have already decided that it's necessary. You will have to turn up at the appointed place, on time, and not make a fuss about it. Can you live with that?"

"I can."

"And if you start playing up, I stop being your lawyer. Understood?"

Salander nodded.

"One more thing. I don't want to get involved in a big drama between you and my brother. If you have a problem with him, you'll have to work it out. But, for the record, he's not your enemy."

"I know. I'll deal with it. But I need some time."

"What do you plan to do now?"

"I don't know. You can reach me on email. I promise to reply as soon as I can, but I might not be checking it every day—"

"You won't become a slave just because you have a lawyer. O.K., that's enough for the time being. Out you get. I'm dead tired and I want to go home and sleep."

Salander opened the door and got out. She paused as she was about to close the car door. She looked as though she wanted to say something but could not find the words. For a moment she appeared to Giannini almost vulnerable.

"That's alright, Lisbeth," Giannini said. "Go and get some sleep. And stay out of trouble for a while."

Salander stood at the curb and watched Giannini drive away until her tail lights disappeared around the corner.

"Thanks," she said at last.

CHAPTER 29

Saturday, 16.vii – Friday, 7.x

Salander found her Palm Tungsten T3 on the hall table. Next to it were her car keys and the shoulder bag she had lost when Lundin attacked her outside the door to her apartment building on Lundagatan. She also found both opened and unopened post that had been collected from her P.O. Box on Hornsgatan. *Mikael Blomkvist.*

She took a slow tour through the furnished part of her apartment. She found traces of him everywhere. He had slept in her bed and worked at her desk. He had used her printer, and in the wastepaper basket she found drafts of the manuscript of *The Section* along with discarded notes.

He had bought a litre of milk, bread, cheese, caviar and a jumbo pack of Billy's Pan Pizza and put them in the fridge.

On the kitchen table she found a small white envelope with her name on it. It was a note from him. The message was brief. His mobile number. That was all.

She knew that the ball was in her court. He was not going to get in touch with her. He had finished the story, given back the keys to her apartment, and he would not call her. If she wanted something then she could call him. *Bloody pig-headed bastard.*

She put on a pot of coffee, made four open sandwiches, and went to sit in her window seat to look out towards Djurgården. She lit a cigarette and brooded.

It was all over, and yet now her life felt more claustrophobic than ever.

Miriam Wu had gone to France. *It was my fault that you almost died.* She had shuddered at the thought of having to see Mimmi, but had decided that that would be her first stop when she was released. *But she had gone to France.*

All of a sudden she was in debt to people.

Palmgren. Armansky. She ought to contact them to say thank you. Paolo Roberto. And Plague and Trinity. Even those damned police officers, Bublanski and Modig, who had so obviously been in her corner.

She did not like feeling beholden to anyone. She felt like a chess piece in a game she could not control.

Kalle Bloody Blomkvist. And maybe even *Erika Bloody Berger* with the dimples and the expensive clothes and all that self-assurance.

But it was over, Giannini had said as they left police headquarters. Right. The trial was over. It was over for Giannini. And it was over for Blomkvist. He had published his book and would end up on T.V. and probably win some bloody prize too.

But it was not over for Lisbeth Salander. This was only the first day of the rest of her life.

At 4.00 in the morning she stopped thinking. She discarded her punk outfit on the floor of her bedroom and went to the bathroom and took a shower. She cleaned off all the make-up she had worn in court, put on loose, dark linen trousers, a white top and a thin jacket. She packed an overnight bag with a change of underwear and a couple of tops and put on some simple walking shoes.

She picked up her Palm and called a taxi to collect her from Mosebacke Torg. She drove out to Arlanda Airport and arrived just before 6.00. She studied the departure board and booked a ticket to the first place that took her fancy. She used her own passport in her own name. She was surprised that nobody at the ticket desk or at the check-in counter seemed to recognize her or react to her name.

She had a seat on the morning flight to Málaga and landed in the blazing midday heat. She stood inside the terminal building for a moment, feeling uncertain. At last she went and looked at a map and thought about what she might do now that she was in Spain. A minute later she decided. She did not waste time trying to figure out bus routes or other means of transportation. She bought a pair of sunglasses at an airport shop, went out to the taxi stand and climbed into the back seat of the first taxi.

"Gibraltar. I'm paying with a credit card."

The trip took three hours via the new motorway along the coast. The taxi dropped her off at British passport control and she walked across the border and over to the Rock Hotel on Europa Road, partway up the slope of the 425-metre monolith. She asked if they had a room and was told there was a double room available. She booked it for two weeks and handed over her credit card.

She showered and sat on the balcony wrapped up in a bath towel, looking out over the Straits of Gibraltar. She could see freighters and a few yachts. She could just make out Morocco in the haze on the other side of the straits. It was peaceful.

After a while she went in and lay down and slept.

The next morning Salander woke at 5.00. She got up, showered and had a coffee in the hotel bar on the ground floor. At 7.00 she left the hotel and set out to buy mangos and apples. She took a taxi to the Peak and walked over to the apes. She was so early that few tourists had yet appeared, and she was practically alone with the animals.

She liked Gibraltar. It was her third visit to the strange rock that housed an absurdly densely populated English town on the Mediterranean. Gibraltar was a place that was not like anywhere else. The town had been isolated for decades, a colony that obstinately refused to be incorporated into Spain. The Spaniards protested the occupation, of course. (But Salander thought that the Spaniards should keep their mouths shut on that score so long as they occupied the enclave of Ceuta on Moroccan territory across the straits.) It was a place that was comically shielded from the rest of the world, consisting of a bizarre rock, about three quarters of a square mile of town and an airport that began and ended in the sea. The colony was so small that every square inch of it was used, and any expansion had to be over the sea. Even to get into the town, visitors had to walk across the landing strip at the airport.

Gibraltar gave the concept of "compact living" a whole new meaning.

Salander watched a big male ape climb up on to a wall next to the path. He glowered at her. He was a Barbary ape. She knew better than to try to stroke any of the animals.

"Hello, friend," she said. "I'm back."

The first time she visited Gibraltar she had not even heard about these apes. She had gone up to the top just to look at the view, and she was surprised when she followed some tourists and found herself in the midst of a group of apes climbing and scrambling on both sides of the pathway.

It was a peculiar feeling to be walking along a path and suddenly have two dozen apes around you. She looked at them with great wariness. They were not dangerous or aggressive, but they were certainly capable of giving you a bad bite if they got agitated or felt threatened.

She found one of the guards and showed him her bag of fruit and asked if she could give it to the apes. He said that it was O.K.

She took out a mango and put it on the wall a little way away from the male ape.

"Breakfast," she said, leaning against the wall and taking a bite of an apple.

The male ape stared at her, bared his teeth, and contentedly picked up the mango.

In the middle of the afternoon five days later, Salander fell off her stool in Harry's Bar on a side street off Main Street, two blocks from her hotel. She had been drunk almost continuously since she left the apes on the rock, and most of her drinking had been done with Harry O'Connell, who owned the bar and spoke with a phoney Irish accent, having never in his life set foot in Ireland. He had been watching her anxiously.

When she had ordered her first drink several days earlier, he had asked to see her I.D. Her name was Lisbeth, he knew, and he called her Liz. She would come in after lunch and sit on a high stool at the far end of the bar with her back leant against the wall. Then she would drink an impressive number of beers or shots of whisky.

When she drank beer she did not care about what brand or type it was; she accepted whatever he served her. When she ordered whisky she always chose Tullamore Dew, except on one occasion when she studied the bottles behind the bar and asked for Lagavulin. When the glass was brought to her, she sniffed at it, stared at it for a moment, and then took a tiny sip. She set down her glass and stared at it for a minute with an expression that seemed to indicate that she considered its contents to be a mortal enemy.

Finally she pushed the glass aside and asked Harry to give her something that could not be used to tar a boat. He poured her another Tullamore Dew and she went back to her drinking. Over the past four days she had consumed almost a whole bottle. He had not kept track of the beers. Harry was surprised that a young woman with her slender build could hold so much, but he took the view that if she wanted alcohol she was going to get it, whether in his bar or somewhere else.

She drank slowly, did not talk to any of the other customers, and did not make any trouble. Her only activity apart from the consumption of alcohol seemed to be to play with a hand-held computer which she connected to a mobile now and then. He had several times tried to start a conversation but was met with a sullen silence. She seemed to avoid company. Sometimes, when there were too many people in the bar, she had moved outside to a table on the pavement, and at other times she had gone two doors down to an Italian restaurant and had dinner. Then she would come back to Harry's and order another Tullamore Dew. She usually left the bar at around 10.00 and made her way unsteadily off, always to the north.

Today she had drunk more and at a faster rate than on the other days, and Harry had kept a watchful eye on her. When she had put away seven glasses of Tullamore Dew in a little over two hours, he decided not to give her any more. It was then that he heard the crash as she fell off the bar stool.

He put down the glass he was drying and went around the counter to pick her up. She seemed offended.

"I think you've had enough, Liz," he said.

She looked at him, bleary-eyed.

"I believe you're right," she said in a surprisingly lucid voice.

She held on to the bar with one hand as she dug some notes out of her top pocket and then wobbled off towards the door. He took her gently by the shoulder.

"Hold on a minute. Why don't you go to the toilet and throw up the last of that whisky and then sit at the bar for a while? I don't want to let you go in this condition."

She did not object when he led her to the toilet. She stuck her fingers down her throat. When she came back out to the bar he had poured her a large glass of club soda. She drank the whole glass and burped. He poured her another.

"You're going to feel like death in the morning," Harry said.

She nodded.

"It's none of my business, but if I were you I'd sober up for a couple of days."

She nodded. Then she went back to the toilet and threw up again.

She stayed at Harry's Bar for another hour until she looked sober enough to be turned loose. She left the bar on unsteady legs, walked down to the airport and followed the shoreline around the marina. She walked until after 8.00, when the ground at last stopped swaying under her feet. Then she went back to the hotel. She took the lift to her room, brushed her teeth and washed her face, changed her clothes, and went back down to the hotel bar to order a cup of black coffee and a bottle of mineral water.

She sat there, silent and unnoticed next to a pillar, studying the people in the bar. She saw a couple in their thirties engaged in quiet conversation. The woman was wearing a light-coloured summer dress, and the man was holding her hand under the table. Two tables away sat a black family, the man with the beginnings of grey at his temples, the woman wearing a lovely, colourful dress in yellow, black and red. They had two young children with them. She studied a group of businessmen in white shirts and ties, their jackets hung over the backs of their chairs. They were drinking beer. She saw a group of elderly people, without a doubt American tourists. The men wore baseball caps, polo shirts and loose-fitting trousers. She watched a man in a light-coloured linen jacket, grey shirt and dark tie come in from the street and pick up his room key at the front desk before he headed over to the bar and ordered a beer. He sat down three metres away from her. She gave him an expectant look as he took out his mobile and began to speak in German.

"Hello, is that you? . . . Is everything alright? . . . It's going fine, we're having our next meeting tomorrow afternoon . . . No, I think it'll work out . . . I'll be staying here five or six days at least, and then I go to Madrid . . . No, I won't be home before the end of next week . . . Me too. I love you . . . Sure . . . I'll call you later in the week . . . Kiss kiss."

He was a little over one metre eighty-five tall, about fifty years old maybe fifty-five, blond hair that was turning grey and was a bit on the long side, a weak chin, and too much weight around the middle. But still reasonably well preserved. He was reading the *Financial Times*. When he finished his beer and headed for the lift, Salander got up and followed him.

He pushed the button for the sixth floor. Salander stood next to him and leaned her head against the side of the lift.

"I'm drunk," she said.

He smiled down at her. "Oh, really?"

"It's been one of those weeks. Let me guess. You're a businessman of some sort, from Hanover or somewhere in northern Germany. You're married. You love your wife. And you have to stay here in

Gibraltar for another few days. I gathered that much from your telephone call in the bar."

The man looked at her, astonished.

"I'm from Sweden myself. I'm feeling an irresistible urge to have sex with somebody. I don't care if you're married and I don't want your phone number."

He looked startled.

"I'm in room 711, the floor above yours. I'm going to go up to my room, take a bath and get into bed. If you want to keep me company, knock on the door within half an hour. Otherwise I'll be asleep."

"Is this some kind of joke?" he said as the lift stopped.

"No. It's just that I can't be bothered to go out to some pick-up bar. Either you knock on my door or you don't."

Twenty-five minutes later there was a knock on the door of Salander's room. She had a bath towel around her when she opened the door.

"Come in," she said.

He stepped inside and looked around the room suspiciously.

"I'm alone here," she said.

"How old are you, actually?"

She reached for her passport on top of a chest of drawers and handed it to him.

"You look younger."

"I know," she said, taking off the bath towel and throwing it on to a chair. She went over to the bed and pulled off the bedspread.

She glanced over her shoulder and saw that he was staring at her tattoos.

"This isn't a trap. I'm a woman, I'm single, and I'll be here for a few days. I haven't had sex for months."

"Why did you choose me?"

"Because you were the only man in the bar who looked as if you were here alone."

"I'm married—"

"And I don't want to know who she is or even who you are. And I don't want to discuss sociology. I want to fuck. Take off your clothes or go back down to your room."

"Just like that?"

"Yes. Why not? You're a grown man – you know what you're supposed to do."

He thought about it for all of thirty seconds. He looked as if he was going to leave. She sat on the edge of the bed and waited. He bit his lip. Then he took off his trousers and shirt and stood hesitantly in his boxer shorts.

"Take it all off," Salander said. "I don't intend to fuck somebody in his underwear. And you have to use a condom. I know where I've been, but I don't know where you've been."

He took off his shorts and went over to her and put his hand on her shoulder. Salander closed her eyes when he bent down to kiss her. He tasted good. She let him tip her back on to the bed. He was heavy on top of her.

Jeremy Stuart MacMillan, solicitor, felt the hairs rise on the back of his neck as soon as he tried to unlock the door to his office at Buchanan House on Queensway Quay above the marina. It was already unlocked. He opened it and smelled tobacco smoke and heard a chair creak. It was just before 7.00, and his first thought was that he had surprised a burglar.

Then he smelled the coffee from the machine in the kitchenette. After a couple of seconds he stepped hesitantly over the threshold and walked down the corridor to look into his spacious and elegantly furnished office. Salander was sitting in his desk chair with her back to him and her feet on the windowsill. His P.C. was turned on. Obviously she had not had any problem cracking his password. Nor had she had any problem opening his safe. She had a folder with his most private correspondence and bookkeeping on her lap.

"Good morning, Miss Salander," he said at last.

"Ah, there you are," she said. "There's freshly brewed coffee and croissants in the kitchen."

"Thanks," he said, sighing in resignation.

He had, after all, bought the office with her money and at her request, but he had not expected her to turn up without warning. What is more, she had found and apparently read a gay porn magazine that he had kept hidden in a desk drawer.

So embarrassing.

Or maybe not.

When it came to Salander, he felt that she was the most judgemental person he had ever met. But she never once raised an eyebrow at people's weaknesses. She knew that he was officially heterosexual, but his dark secret was that he was attracted to men; since his divorce fifteen years ago he had been making his most private fantasies a reality.

It's funny, but I feel safe with her.

Since she was in Gibraltar anyway, Salander had decided to visit MacMillan, the man who handled her finances. She had not been in touch with him since just after New Year, and she wanted to know if he had been busy ruining her ever since.

But there had not been any great hurry, and it was not for him that she had gone straight to Gibraltar after her release. She did it because she felt a burning desire to get away from everything, and in that respect Gibraltar was an excellent choice. She had spent almost a week getting drunk, and then a few days having sex with the German businessman, who eventually introduced himself as Dieter. She doubted it was his real name but had not bothered to check. He spent the days sitting in meetings and the evenings having dinner with her before they went back to his or her room.

He was not at all bad in bed, Salander thought, although he was a bit out of practice and sometimes needlessly rough.

Dieter seemed genuinely astonished that on sheer impulse she had picked up an overweight German businessman who was not even looking for it. He was indeed married, and he was not in the habit of being unfaithful or seeking female company on his business trips. But when the opportunity was presented on a platter in the form of a thin, tattooed young woman, he could not resist the temptation. Or so he said.

Salander did not care much what he said. She had not been looking for anything more than recreational sex, but she was gratified that he actually made an effort to satisfy her. It was not until the fourth night, their last together, that he had a panic attack and started going on about what his wife would say. Salander thought he should keep his mouth shut and not tell his wife a thing.

But she did not tell him what she thought.

He was a grown man and could have said no to her invitation. It was not her problem if he was now attacked by feelings of guilt, or if he confessed anything to his wife. She had lain with her back to him and listened for fifteen minutes, until finally she rolled her eyes in exasperation, turned over and straddled him.

"Do you think you could take a break from the worryguts stuff and get me off again?" she said.

Jeremy MacMillan was a very different story. He held zero erotic attraction for her. He was a crook. Amusingly enough, he looked a lot like Dieter. He was forty-eight, a bit overweight, with greying, dark-blond curly hair that he combed straight back from a high forehead. He wore thin gold-rimmed glasses.

He had once been a Cambridge-educated business lawyer and stock-broker in London. He had had a promising future and was a partner in a law firm that was engaged by big corporations and wealthy yuppies interested in real estate and tax planning. He had spent the go-go '80s hanging out with *nouveau riche* celebrities. He had drunk hard and snorted coke with people that he really did not want to wake up with the next morning. He had never been charged with anything, but he did lose his wife and two kids along with his job when he mismanaged several transactions and tottered drunk into a mediation hearing.

Without thinking too much about it, he sobered up and fled London with his tail between his legs. Why he picked Gibraltar he did not know, but in 1991 he went into partnership with a local solicitor and opened a modest back-street law office which officially dealt with much less glamorous matters: estate planning, wills and such like. Unofficially, MacMillan & Marks also helped to set up P.O. Box companies and acted as gatekeepers for a number of shady figures in Europe. The firm was barely making ends meet when Salander selected Jeremy MacMillan to administer the $2.4 billion she had stolen from the collapsing empire of the Swedish financier Hans-Erik Wennerström.

MacMillan was a crook, no doubt about it, but she regarded him as *her* crook, and he had surprised himself by being impeccably honest in his dealings with her. She had first hired him for a simple task. For a modest fee he had set up a string of P.O. Box companies for her to use; she put a million dollars into each of them. She had contacted him by telephone and had been nothing more than a voice from afar. He never tried to discover where the money came from. He had done what she asked and took 5 per cent commission. A little while later she had transferred a large sum of money that he was to use to set up a corporation, Wasp Enterprises, which then acquired a substantial apartment in Stockholm. His dealings with Salander were becoming quite lucrative, even if it was still only quite modest pickings.

Two months later she had paid a visit to Gibraltar. She had called him and suggested dinner in her room at the Rock Hotel, which was, if not the biggest hotel in Gibraltar, then certainly the most famous. He was not sure what he had expected, but he could not believe that his client was this doll-like girl who looked as if she were in her early teens. He thought he was the butt of some outlandish practical joke.

He soon changed his mind. The strange young woman talked with him impersonally, without ever smiling or showing any warmth. Or coolness, for that matter. He had sat paralysed as, over the course of a few minutes, she obliterated the professional facade of sophisticated respectability that he was always so careful to maintain.

"What is it that you want?" he had asked.

"I've stolen a sum of money," she replied with great seriousness. "I need a crook who can administer it."

He had stared at her, wondering whether she was deranged, but politely he played along. She might be a possible mark for a con game that could bring in a small income. Then he had sat as if struck by lightning when she explained who she had stolen the money from, how she did it, and what the amount was. The Wennerström affair was the hottest topic of conversation in the world of international finance.

"I see."

The possibilities flew through his head.

"You're a skilled business lawyer and stockbroker. If you were an idiot you would never have got the jobs you did in the '80s. However, you behaved like an idiot and managed to get yourself fired."

He winced.

"In the future I will be your only client."

She had looked at him with the most ingenuous expression he had ever seen.

"I have two conditions. The first is that you never ever commit a crime or get mixed up in anything that could create problems for us and focus the authorities' attention on my companies and accounts. The second is that you never lie to me. Never ever. Not a single time. And not for any reason. If you lie to me, our business relationship will terminate instantly, and if you make me cross enough I will ruin you."

She poured him a glass of wine.

"There's no reason to lie to me. I already know everything worth knowing about your life. I know how much you make in a good month and a bad month. I know how much you spend. I know that you never really have enough money. I know that you owe £120,000

564

in both long-term and short-term debts, and that you always have to take risks and skim some money to make the loan payments. You wear expensive clothes and try to keep up appearances, but in reality you've gone to the dogs and haven't bought a new sports jacket in several months. But you did take an old jacket in to have the lining mended two weeks ago. You used to collect rare books but have been gradually selling them off. Last month you sold an early edition of *Oliver Twist* for £760."

She stopped talking and fixed him with her gaze. He swallowed hard.

"Last week you actually made a killing. A quite clever fraud perpetrated against that widow you represent. You ripped her off £6,000, which she'll probably never miss."

"How the hell do you know that?"

"I know that you were married, that you have two children in England who don't want to see you, and that you've taken the big leap since your divorce and now have primarily homosexual relationships. You're probably ashamed of that and avoid the gay clubs, and you avoid being seen in town with any of your male friends. You regularly cross the border into Spain to meet men."

MacMillan was shaken to the core. And he was suddenly terrified. He had no idea how she had come by all this information, but she knew enough to destroy him.

"And I'm only going to say this one time. I don't give a shit who you have sex with. It's none of my business. I want to know who you are, but I will never use what I know. I won't threaten you or blackmail you."

MacMillan was no fool. He was perfectly aware, of course, that her knowledge of all that information about him constituted a threat. She was in control. For a moment he had considered picking her up and throwing her over the edge of the terrace, but he restrained himself. He had never in his life been so scared.

"What do you want?" he managed to say.

"I want to have a partnership with you. You will bring to a close all the other business you're working on and will work exclusively for me. You will make more money from my company than you could ever dream of making any other way."

She explained what she required him to do, and how she wanted the arrangements to be made.

"I want to be invisible," she said. "And I want you to take care of my affairs. Everything has to be legitimate. Whatever money I make on my own will not have any connection to our business together."

"I understand."

"You have one week to phase out your other clients and put a stop to all your little schemes."

He also realized that he had been given an offer that would never come round again. He thought about it for sixty seconds and then accepted. He had only one question.

"How do you know that I won't swindle you?"

"Don't even think about it. You'd regret it for the rest of your miserable life."

He had no reason to cook the books. Salander had made him an offer that had the potential of such a silver lining that it would have been idiotic to risk it for bits of change on the side. As long as he was relatively discreet and did not get involved in any financial chicanery, his future would be assured.

Accordingly he had no thought of swindling Ms Salander.

So he went straight, or as straight as a burned-out lawyer could go who was administering an astronomical sum of stolen money.

Salander was simply not interested in the management of her finances. MacMillan's job was to invest her money and see to it that there were funds to cover the credit cards she used. She told him how she wanted her finances to be handled. His job was to make sure it was done.

A large part of the money had been invested in gilt-edged funds that would provide her with economic independence for the rest of her life, even if she chose to live it recklessly and dissolutely. It was from these funds that her credit card bills were paid.

The rest of the money he could play with and invest as he saw fit, provided that he did not invest in anything that might cause problems with the police in any way. She forbade him to engage in stupid petty crimes and cheap con games which – if he was unlucky – might prompt investigations which in turn could put her under scrutiny.

All that remained was to agree on how much he would make on the transactions.

"I'll pay you £500,000 as a retainer. With that you can pay off all your debts and have a good deal left over. After that you'll earn money for yourself. You will start a company with the two of us as partners. You get 20 per cent of all the profits generated. I want you to be rich enough that you won't be tempted to try it on, but not so rich that you won't make an effort."

He had started his new job on February 1 the year before. By the end of March he had paid off all his debts and stabilized his personal finances. Salander had insisted that he make cleaning up his own affairs a priority so that he would be solvent. In May he dissolved the partnership with his alcoholic colleague George Marks. He felt a twinge of conscience towards his former partner, but getting Marks mixed up in Salander's business was out of the question.

He discussed the matter with Salander when she returned to Gibraltar on another unheralded visit in early July and discovered that MacMillan was working out of his apartment instead of from the office he had previously occupied.

"My partner's an alcoholic and wouldn't be able to handle this. And he would be an enormous risk factor. At the same time, fifteen years ago he saved my life when he took me into his business."

She pondered this a while as she studied MacMillan's face.

"I see. You're a crook who's loyal. That could be a commendable quality. I suggest you set up a small account that he can play around with. See to it that he makes a couple of thousand a month so he gets by."

"Is that O.K. with you?"

She nodded and looked around his bachelor pad. He lived in a studio apartment with a kitchen nook on one of the alleys near the hospital. The only pleasant thing about the place was the view. On the other hand, it was a view that was hard to avoid in Gibraltar.

"You need an office and a nicer place to live," she said.

"I haven't had time," he said.

Then she went out and found an office for him, choosing a 130 square-metre place with a little balcony facing the sea in Buchanan House on Queensway Quay, which was definitely upmarket in Gibraltar. She hired an interior decorator to renovate and furnish it.

MacMillan recalled that while he had been busy shuffling papers, Salander had personally supervised the installation of an alarm system, computer equipment, and the safe that she had already rummaged through by the time he entered the office that morning.

"Am I in trouble?" he said.

She put down the folder with the correspondence she had been perusing.

"No, Jeremy. You're not in trouble."

"That's good," he said as he poured himself some coffee. "You have a way of popping up when I least expect it."

"I've been busy lately. I just wanted to get an update on what's been happening."

"I believe you were suspected of killing three people, you got shot in the head, and you were charged with a whole assortment of crimes. I was pretty worried for a while. I thought you were still in prison. Did you break out?"

"No. I was acquitted of all the charges and released. How much have you heard?"

He hesitated a moment. "Well, when I heard that you were in trouble, I hired a translation agency to comb the Swedish press and give me regular updates. I'm *au fait* with the details."

"If you're basing your knowledge on what you read in the papers, then you're not *au fait* at all. But I dare say you discovered a number of secrets about me."

He nodded.

"What's going to happen now?" he said.

She gave him a surprised look. "Nothing. We keep on exactly as before. Our relationship has nothing to do with my problems in Sweden. Tell me what's been happening since I've been away. Have you been doing alright?"

"I'm not drinking, if that's what you mean."

"No. Your private life doesn't concern me so long as it doesn't encroach on our business. I mean, am I richer or poorer than I was a year ago?"

He pulled out the visitor's chair and sat down. Somehow it did not matter to him that she was sitting in *his* chair.

"You turned over $2.4 billion to me. We put $200 million into personal funds for you. You gave me the rest to play with."

"And?"

"Your personal funds haven't grown by much more than the amount of interest. I could increase the profit if—"

"I'm not interested in increasing the profit."

"O.K. You've spent a negligible amount. The principal expenses have been the apartment I bought for you and the fund you started for that lawyer Palmgren. Otherwise you've just had normal expenses. The interest rate has been favourable. You're running about even."

"Good."

"The rest I invested. Last year we didn't make very much. I was a little rusty and spent the time learning the market again. We've had expenses. We didn't really start generating income until this year. Since the start of the year we've taken about 7 million. Dollars, that is."

"Of which 20 per cent goes to you."

"Of which 20 per cent goes to me."

"Are you satisfied with that?"

"I've made more than a million dollars in six months. Yes, I'm satisfied."

"You know . . . you shouldn't get too greedy. You can cut back on your hours when you're satisfied. Just make sure you spend a few hours on my affairs every so often."

"Ten million dollars," he said.

"Excuse me?"

"When I get ten million together I'll pack it in. It was good that you turned up in my life. We have a lot to discuss."

"Fire away."

He threw up his hands.

"This is so much money that it scares the shit out of me. I don't know how to handle it. I don't know the purpose of the company besides making more money. What's all the money going to be used for?"

"I don't know."

"Me neither. But money can become an end in itself. It's crazy. That's why I've decided to call it quits when I've earned ten million for myself. I don't want the responsibility any longer."

"Fair enough."

"But before I call it a day I want you to decide how this fortune is to be administered in the future. There has to be a purpose and guidelines and some kind of organization that can take over."

"Mmm."

"It's impossible to conduct business this way. I've divided up the sum into long-term fixed investments – real estate, securities and so forth. There's a complete list on the computer."

"I've read it."

"The other half I've put into speculation, but it's so much money to keep track of that I can't keep up. So I set up an investment company on Jersey. At present you have six employees in London. Two talented young brokers and some clerical staff."

"Yellow Ballroom Ltd? I was wondering what that could be."

"Our company. Here in Gibraltar I've hired a secretary and a promising young lawyer. They'll be here in half an hour, by the way."

"I know. Molly Flint, forty-one, and Brian Delaney, twenty-six."

"Do you want to meet them?"

"No. Is Brian your lover?"

"What? No." He looked shocked. "I don't mix—"

"Good."

"By the way, I'm not interested in young guys . . . inexperienced ones, I mean."

"No . . . you're more attracted to men with a tough attitude than to some snot-nosed kid. But it's still none of my business. But Jeremy . . ."

"Yes?"

"Be careful."

Salander had not planned to stay in Gibraltar for more than two weeks, just long enough, she thought, to get her bearings. But she suddenly discovered that she had no idea what she was going to do or where she should go. She stayed for three months. She checked her email once a day and replied promptly to messages from Giannini on the few occasions her lawyer got in touch. She did not tell her where she was. She did not answer any other email.

She still went to Harry's Bar, but now she came in only for a beer or two in the evenings. She spent large parts of her days at the Rock Hotel, either on her balcony or in bed. She got together with a thirty-year-old Royal Navy officer, but it was a one-night stand and all in all an uninteresting experience.

She was bored.

Early in October she had dinner with MacMillan. They had met up only a few times during her stay. It was dark and they drank a fruity white wine and discussed what they should use her billions for. And then he surprised her by asking what was upsetting her.

She studied his face for a long time and pondered the matter. Then she had, just as surprisingly, told him about her relationship with Miriam Wu, and how Mimmi had been beaten and almost killed. And she, Lisbeth, was to blame. Apart from one greeting sent by way of Giannini, Salander had not heard a word from Mimmi. And now she was in France.

MacMillan listened in silence.

"Are you in love with her?" he said at last.

Salander shook her head.

"No. I don't think I'm the type who falls in love. She was a friend. And we had good sex."

"Nobody can avoid falling in love," he said. "They might want to deny it, but friendship is probably the most common form of love."

She looked at him in astonishment.

"Will you get cross if I say something personal?"

"No."

"Go to Paris, for God's sake," he said.

She landed at Charles de Gaulle airport at 2.30 in the afternoon, took the airport bus to the Arc de Triomphe and spent two hours wandering around the nearby neighbourhoods trying to find a hotel room. She walked south towards the Seine and finally found a room at a small hotel, the Victor Hugo on rue Copernic.

She took a shower and called Miriam Wu. They met that evening at a bar near Notre Dame. Mimmi was dressed in a white shirt and jacket. She looked fabulous. Salander instantly felt shy. They kissed each other on the cheek.

"I'm sorry I haven't called, and that I didn't come to the trial," Mimmi said.

"That's O.K. The trial was behind closed doors anyway."

"I was in hospital for three weeks, and then it was chaos when I got home to Lundagatan. I couldn't sleep. I had nightmares about that bastard Niedermann. I called my mother and told her I wanted to come here, to Paris."

Salander said she understood.

"Forgive me," Mimmi said.

"Don't be such an idiot. I'm the one who's come here to ask you to forgive *me*."

"For what?"

"I wasn't thinking. It never occurred to me that I was putting you in such danger by turning over my old apartment to you. It was my fault that you were almost murdered. You'd have every right to hate me."

Mimmi looked shocked. "Lisbeth, I never even gave it a thought. It was Ronald Niedermann who tried to murder me, not you."

They sat in silence for a while.

"Alright," Salander said finally.

"Right," Mimmi said.

"I didn't follow you here because I'm in love with you," Salander said.

Mimmi nodded.

"We had great sex, but I'm not in love with you."

"Lisbeth, I think . . ."

"What I wanted to say was that I hope you . . . *damn*."

"What?"

"I don't have many friends . . ."

Mimmi nodded. "I'm going to be in Paris for a while. My studies at home were a mess so I signed up at the university here instead. I'll probably stay at least one academic year. After that I don't know. But I'm going to come back to Stockholm. I'm still paying the service charges on Lundagatan and I mean to keep the apartment. If that's O.K. with you."

"It's your apartment. Do what you want with it."

"Lisbeth, you're a very special person," Mimmi said. "I'd still like to be your friend."

They talked for two hours. Salander did not have any reason to hide her past from Miriam Wu. The Zalachenko business was familiar to everyone who had access to a Swedish newspaper, and Mimmi had followed the story with great interest. She gave Salander a detailed account of what had happened in Nykvarn the night Paolo Roberto saved her life.

Then they went back to Mimmi's student lodgings near the university.

EPILOGUE

INVENTORY OF ESTATE

Friday, 2.xii – Sunday, 18.xii

Giannini met Salander in the bar of the Södra theatre at 9.00. Salander was drinking beer and was already coming to the end of her second glass.

"Sorry I'm late," Giannini said, glancing at her watch. "I had to deal with another client."

"That's O.K.," said Lisbeth.

"What are you celebrating?"

"Nothing. I just feel like getting drunk."

Giannini looked at her sceptically and took a seat.

"Do you often feel that way?"

"I drank myself stupid after I was released, but I have no tendency to alcoholism. It just occurred to me that for the first time in my life I have a legal right to get drunk here in Sweden."

Giannini ordered a Campari.

"O.K. Do you want to drink alone," she said, "or would you like some company?"

"Preferably alone. But if you don't talk too much you can sit with me. I take it you don't feel like coming home with me and having sex."

"I beg your pardon?" Giannini said.

"No, I didn't think so. You're one of those insanely heterosexual people."

Giannini suddenly looked amused.

"That's the first time in my life that one of my clients has proposed sex."

"Are you interested?"

"No, not in the least, sorry. But thanks for the offer."

"So what was it you wanted, counsellor?"

"Two things. Either I quit as your lawyer here and now or you start answering your telephone when I call. We've already had this discussion, when you were released."

Salander looked at Giannini.

"I've been trying to get hold of you for a week. I've called, I've sent letters, I've emailed."

"I've been away."

"In fact you've been impossible to get hold of for most of the autumn. This just isn't working. I said I would represent you in all negotiations with the government. There are formalities that have to be taken care of. Papers to be signed. Questions to be answered. I have to be able to reach you, and I have no wish to be made to feel like an idiot because I don't know where the hell you are."

"I was away again for two weeks. I came home yesterday and called you as soon as I knew you were looking for me."

"That's not good enough. You have to keep me informed of where you are and get in touch at least once a week until all the issues about compensation and such are resolved."

"I don't give a shit about compensation. I just want the government to leave me alone."

"But the government isn't going to leave you alone, no matter how much you may want it to. Your acquittal has set in motion a long chain of consequences. It's not just about you. Teleborian is going to be charged for what he did to you. You're going to have to testify. Ekström is the subject of an investigation for dereliction of duty, and he may even be charged too if it turns out that he deliberately disregarded his duty at the behest of the Section."

Salander raised her eyebrows. For a moment she looked interested.

"I don't think it's going to come to an indictment. He was led up the garden path by the Section and in fact he had nothing to do with them. But as recently as last week a prosecutor initiated a preliminary investigation against the guardianship agency. It involves several reports being sent to the Parliamentary Ombudsman, as well as a report to the Ministry of Justice."

"I didn't report anyone."

"No. But it's obvious that there has been gross dereliction of duty. You're not the only person affected."

Salander shrugged. "This has nothing to do with me. But I promise to be in closer contact with you. These last two weeks have been an exception. I've been working."

Giannini did not look as though she believed her. "What are you working on?"

"Consulting."

"I see," she said. "The other thing is that the inventory of the estate is now ready."

"Inventory of what estate?"

"Your father's. The state's legal representative contacted me since nobody seemed to know how to get in touch with you. You and your sister are the sole heirs."

Salander looked at Giannini blankly. Then she caught the waitress's eye and pointed at her glass.

"I don't want any inheritance from my father. Do whatever the hell you want with it."

"Wrong. *You* can do what you want with the inheritance. My job is to see to it that you have the opportunity to do so."

"I don't want a single öre from that pig."

"Then give the money to Greenpeace or something."

"I don't give a shit about whales."

Giannini's voice suddenly softened. "Lisbeth, if you're going to be a legally responsible citizen, then you're going to have to start behaving like one. I don't give a damn what you do with your money. Just sign here that you received it, and then you can get drunk in peace."

Salander glanced at her and then looked down at the table. Annika assumed this was some kind of conciliatory gesture that perhaps corresponded to an apology in Salander's limited register of expressions.

"What kind of figures are we talking about?"

"They're not insignificant. Your father had about 300,000 kronor in shares. The property in Gosseberga would sell for around 1.5 million – there's a little woodland included. And there are three other properties."

"What sort of properties?"

"It seems that he invested a significant amount of money. There's nothing of enormous value, but he owns a small building in Udderalla with six apartments, and they bring in some income. But the property is not in good shape. He didn't bother with upkeep and the apartments have even been up before the rental board. You won't get rich, but you'd get a good price if you sold it. He also owns a summer cabin in Småland that's worth around 250,000 kronor. Plus he owns a dilapidated industrial site outside Norrtälje."

"Why in the world did he buy all this shit?"

"I have no idea. But the estate could bring in over four million kronor after taxes etc., but..."

"But what?"

"The inheritance has to be divided equally between you and your sister. The problem is that nobody knows where your sister is."

Salander looked at Giannini in silence.

"Well?"

"Well what?"

"Where is your sister?"

"I have no idea. I haven't seen her for ten years."

"Her file is classified, but I found out that she is listed as out of the country."

"I see," Salander said, showing little interest.

Giannini sighed in exasperation.

"I would suggest that we liquidate all the assets and deposit half the proceeds in the bank until your sister can be found. I can initiate the negotiations if you give me the go-ahead."

Salander shrugged. "I don't want anything to do with his money."

"I understand that. But the balance sheet still has to be sorted out. It's part of your responsibility as a citizen."

"Sell the crap, then. Put half in the bank and send the rest to whoever you like."

Giannini stared at her. She had understood that Salander had money stashed away, but she had not realized that her client was so well off that she could ignore an inheritance that might amount to a million kronor or more. What is more, she had no idea where Salander had got her money, or how much was involved. On the other hand she was keen to finalize the bureaucratic procedure.

"Lisbeth, please . . . could you read through the estate inventory and give me the green light so that we can get this matter resolved?"

Salander grumbled for a moment, but finally she acquiesced and stuffed the folder into her shoulder bag. She promised to read through it and send instructions as to what she wanted Giannini to do. Then she went back to her beer. Giannini kept her company for an hour, drinking mostly mineral water.

It was not until several days later, when Giannini telephoned to remind her about the estate inventory, that Salander took out the crumpled papers. She sat at the kitchen table, smoothed out the documents, and read through them.

The inventory covered several pages. There was a detailed list of all kinds of junk – the china in the kitchen cupboards in Gosseberga, clothing, cameras and other personal effects. Zalachenko had not left behind much of real value, and not one of the objects had the slightest sentimental value for Salander. She decided that her attitude had not changed since she met with Giannini at the theatre bar. Sell the crap and give the money away. Or something. She was positive that she did not want a single öre of her father's wealth, but she also was pretty sure that Zalachenko's real assets were hidden where no tax inspector would look for them.

Then she opened the title deeds for the property in Norrtälje.

It was an industrial site of three buildings totalling twenty thousand square metres in the vicinity of Skederid, between Norrtälje and Rimbo.

The estate assessor had apparently paid a cursory visit, and noted that it was an old brickworks that had been more or less empty and abandoned since it was shut down in the '60s, apart from a period in the '70s when it had been used to store timber. He noted that the buildings were in "extremely poor condition" and could not in all likelihood be renovated for any other activity. The term "poor condition" was also used to describe the "north building", which had in fact been destroyed by fire and collapsed. Some repairs, he wrote, had been made to the "main building".

What gave Salander a jolt was the site's history. Zalachenko had acquired the property for a song on 12 March, 1984, but the signatory on the purchase documents was Agneta Sofia Salander.

So Salander's mother had in fact been the owner of the property. Yet in 1987 her ownership had ceased. Zalachenko had bought her out for 2,000 kronor. After that the property had stood unused for fifteen years. The inventory showed that on 17 September, 2003, K.A.B. Import A.B. had hired the builders NorrBygg Inc. to do renovations which included repairs to the floor and roof, as well as improvements to the water and electrical systems. Repair work had gone on for two months, until the end of November, and then discontinued. NorrBygg had sent an invoice which had been paid.

Of all the assets in her father's estate, this was the only surprising entry. Salander was puzzled. Ownership of the industrial site made sense if her father had wanted to give the impression that K.A.B. Import was carrying on legitimate activities or owned certain assets. It also made sense that he had used her mother as a front in the purchase and had then for a pittance bought back the property.

But why in heaven's name would he spend almost 440,000 kronor to renovate a ramshackle building, which according to the assessor was still not being used for anything in 2005?

She could not understand it, but was not going to waste time wondering. She closed the folder and called Giannini.

"I've read the inventory. What I said still holds. Sell the shit and do whatever you like with the money. I want nothing from him."

"Very well. I'll see to it that half the revenue is deposited in an account for your sister, and I'll suggest some suitable recipients for the rest."

"Right," Salander said and hung up without further discussion.

She sat in her window seat, lit a cigarette, and looked out towards Saltsjön.

Salander spent the next week helping Armansky with an urgent matter. She had to help track down and identify a person suspected of being hired to kidnap a child in a custody battle resulting from a Swedish woman divorcing her Lebanese husband. Salander's job amounted to checking the email of the person who was presumed to have hired the kidnapper. Milton Security's role was discontinued when the parties reached a legal solution.

On December 18, the Sunday before Christmas, Salander woke at 6.00 and remembered that she had to buy a Christmas present for Palmgren. For a moment she wondered whether there was anyone else she should buy presents for – Giannini perhaps. She got up and took a shower in no particular hurry, and ate a breakfast of toast with cheese and marmalade and a coffee.

She had nothing special planned for the day and spent a while clearing papers and magazines from her desk. Then her gaze fell on the folder with the estate inventory. She opened it and reread the page about the title registration for the site in Norrtälje. She sighed. *O.K. I have to find out what the hell he had going on there.*

She put on warm clothes and boots. It was 8.30 when she drove her burgundy Honda out of the garage beneath Fiskargatan 9. It was icy cold but beautiful, sunshine and a pastel-blue sky. She took the road via Slussen and Klarabergsleden and wound her way on to the E18 going north, heading for Norrtälje. She was in no hurry. At 10.00 she turned into an O.K. petrol station and shop a few miles outside Skederid to ask the way to the old brickworks. No sooner had she parked than she realized that she did not even need to ask.

She was on a hillside with a good view across the valley on the other side of the road. To the left towards Norrtälje she could see a paint warehouse, some sort of builder's yard, and another yard with bulldozers. To the right, at the edge of the industrial area, about four hundred metres from the road was a dismal brick building with a crumbling chimney-stack. The factory stood like a last outpost of the industrial area, somewhat isolated beyond a road and a narrow stream. She surveyed the building thoughtfully and asked herself what on earth had possessed her to drive all the way up to Norrtälje.

She turned and glanced at the O.K. station, where a long-distance truck and trailer with the emblem of the International Road Transport Union had just pulled in. She remembered that she was on the main road from the ferry terminal at Kapellskär, through which a good deal of the freight traffic between Sweden and the Baltic countries passed.

She started the car and drove out on to the road towards the old brickworks. She parked in the middle of the yard and got out. It was below freezing outside, and she put on a black knitted cap and leather gloves.

The main building was on two floors. On the ground floor all the windows had been boarded up with plywood, and she could see that on the floor above many of them had been broken. The factory was a much bigger building than she had imagined, and it was incredibly dilapidated. She could see no evidence of repairs. There was no trace of a living soul, but she saw that someone had discarded a used condom in the yard, and that graffiti artists had attacked part of the facade.

Why had Zalachenko owned this building?

She walked around the factory and found the ramshackle north building to the rear. She saw that the doors to the main building were locked. In frustration she studied a door at one end of the building. All the other doors had padlocks attached with iron bolts and galvanized security strips, but the lock on the gable end seemed weaker and was in fact attached only with rough spikes. *Damn it, it's my building.*

She looked about and found a narrow iron pipe in a pile of rubbish. She used it to lever open the fastening of the padlock.

She entered a stairwell with a doorway on to the ground floor area. The boarded-up windows meant that it was pitch black inside, except for a few shafts of light seeping in at the edges of the boards. She stood still for several minutes until her eyes adjusted to the darkness. She saw a sea of junk, wooden pallets, old machine parts and timber in a workshop that was forty-five metres long and about twenty metres wide, supported by massive pillars. The old brick ovens seemed to have been disassembled, and in their place were big pools of water and patches of mould on the floor. There was a stale, foul smell from all the debris. She wrinkled her nose in disgust.

She turned back and went up the stairs. The top floor was dry and consisted of two similar rooms, each about twenty by twenty metres square, and at least eight metres high. There were tall, inaccessible windows close to the ceiling which provided no view but let in plenty of light. The upper floor, just like the workshop downstairs, was full of junk. There were dozens of one-metre-high packing cases stacked on top of one another. She gripped one of them but could not move it. The text on the crate read: *Machine parts 0-A77*, with an apparently corresponding text in Russian underneath. She noticed an open goods lift halfway down one wall of the first room.

A machine warehouse of some sort, but that would hardly generate income so long as the machinery stood there rusting.

She went into the inner room and discovered that this was where the repair work must have been carried out. The room was again full of rubbish, boxes and old office furniture arranged in some sort of labyrinthine order. A section of the floor was exposed where new floor planks had been laid. Salander guessed that the renovation work had been stopped abruptly. Tools, a crosscut saw and a circular saw, a nail gun, a crowbar, an iron rod and tool boxes were still there. She frowned. *Even if the work had been discontinued, the joiners should have collected up their tools*. But this question too was answered when she held a screwdriver up to the light and saw that the writing on the handle was Russian. Zalachenko had imported the tools and probably the workers as well.

She switched on the circular saw and a green light went on. There was power. She turned it off.

At the far end of the room were three doors to smaller rooms, perhaps the old offices. She tried the handle of the door on the north side of the building. Locked. She went back to the tools and got a crowbar. It took her a while to break open the door.

It was pitch black inside the room and smelled musty. She ran her hand along the wall and found a switch that lit a bare bulb in the ceiling. Salander looked around in astonishment.

The furniture in the room consisted of three beds with soiled mattresses and another three mattresses on the floor. Filthy bedlinen was strewn around. To the right was a two-ring electric hob and some pots next to a rusty water tap. In a corner stood a tin bucket and a roll of toilet paper.

Somebody had lived here. Several people.

Then she saw that there was no handle on the inside of the door. She felt an ice-cold shiver run down her back.

There was a large linen cupboard at the far end of the room. She opened it and found two suitcases. Inside the one on top were some clothes. She rummaged through them and held up a dress with a Russian label. She found a handbag and emptied the contents on the floor. From among the cosmetics and other bits and pieces she retrieved a passport belonging to a young, dark-haired woman. It was a Russian passport, and she spelled out the name as Valentina.

Salander walked slowly from the room. She had a feeling of *déjà vu*. She had done the same kind of crime scene examination in a basement in Hedeby two and a half years earlier. Women's clothes. A prison. She stood there for a long time, thinking. It bothered her that the passport and clothes had been left behind. It did not feel right.

Then she went back to the assortment of tools and rummaged about until she found a powerful torch. She checked that there was life in the batteries and went downstairs into the larger workshop. The water from the puddles on the floor seeped into her boots.

The nauseating stench of rotting matter grew stronger the further into the workshop she went, and seemed to be worst when she was in the middle of the room. She stopped next to the foundations of one of the old brick furnaces, which was filled with water almost to the brim. She shone her torch on to the coal-black surface of the water but could not make anything out. The surface was partly covered by algae that had formed a green slime. Nearby she found a long steel rod which she stuck into the pool and stirred around. The water was only about fifty centimetres deep. Almost immediately the rod bumped into something. She manipulated it this way and that for several seconds before a body rose to the surface, face first, a grinning mask of death and decomposition. Breathing through her mouth, Salander looked at the face in the beam of the torch and saw that it was a woman, possibly the woman from the passport photograph. She knew nothing about the speed of decay in cold, stagnant water, but the body seemed to have been in the pool for a long time.

There was something moving on the surface of the water. Larvae of some sort.

She let the body sink back beneath the surface and poked around more with the rod. At the edge of the pool she came across something that might have been another body. She left it there and pulled out the rod, letting it fall to the floor as she stood thinking next to the pool.

Salander went back up the stairs. She used the crowbar to break open the middle door. The room was empty.

She went to the last door and slotted the crowbar in place, but before she began to force it, the door swung open a crack. It was not locked. She nudged it open with the crowbar and looked around.

The room was about thirty metres square. It had windows at a normal height with a view of the yard in front of the brickworks. She could see the O.K. petrol station on the hill. There was a bed, a table, and a sink with dishes. Then she saw a bag lying open on the floor. There were banknotes in it. In surprise she took two steps forward before she noticed that it was warm and saw an electric heater in the middle of the room. Then she saw that the red light was on on the coffee machine.

Someone was living here. She was not alone in the building.

She spun around and ran through the inner room, out of the doors and towards the exit in the outer workshop. She stopped five steps short of the stairwell when she saw that the exit had been closed and padlocked. She was locked in. Slowly she turned and looked around, but there was no-one.

"Hello, little sister," came a cheerful voice from somewhere to her right.

She turned to see Niedermann's vast form materialize from behind some packing crates.

In his hand was a large knife.

"I was hoping I'd have a chance to see you again," Niedermann said. "Everything happened so fast the last time."

Salander looked about her.

"Don't bother," Niedermann said. "It's just you and me, and there's no way out except through the locked door behind you."

Salander turned her eyes to her half-brother.

"How's the hand?" she said.

Niedermann was smiling at her. He raised his right hand and showed her. His little finger was missing.

"It got infected. I had to chop it off."

Niedermann could not feel pain. Salander had sliced his hand open with a spade at Gosseberga only seconds before Zalachenko had shot her in the head.

"I should have aimed for your skull," Salander said in a neutral tone. "What the hell are you doing here? I thought you'd left the country months ago."

He smiled at her again.

If Niedermann had tried to answer Salander's question as to what he was doing in the dilapidated brickworks, he probably would not have been able to explain. He could not explain it to himself.

He had left Gosseberga with a feeling of liberation. He was counting on the fact that Zalachenko was dead and that he would take over the business. He knew he was an excellent organizer.

He had changed cars in Alingsås, put the terror-stricken dental nurse Anita Kaspersson in the boot, and driven towards Borås. He had no plan. He improvised as he went. He had not reflected on Kaspersson's fate. It made no difference to him whether she lived or died, and he assumed that he would be forced to do away with a bothersome witness. Somewhere on the outskirts of Borås it came to him that he could use her in a different way. He turned south and found a desolate forest outside Seglora. He tied her up in a barn and left her there. He reckoned that she would be able to work her way loose within a few hours and then lead the police south in their hunt for him. And if she did not manage to free herself, and starved or froze to death in the barn, it did not matter, it was no concern of his.

Then he drove back to Borås and from there east towards Stockholm. He had driven straight to Svavelsjö, but he avoided the clubhouse itself.

585

It was a drag that Lundin was in prison. He went instead to the home of the club's sergeant-at-arms, Hans-Åke Waltari. He said he was looking for a place to hide, which Waltari sorted out by sending him to Göransson, the club's treasurer. But he had stayed there only a few hours.

Niedermann had, theoretically, no money worries. He had left behind almost 200,000 kronor in Gosseberga, but he had access to considerably larger sums that had been deposited abroad. His problem was that he was short of actual cash. Göransson was responsible for Svavelsjö M.C.'s finances, and it had not been difficult for Niedermann to persuade him to take him to the cabinet in the barn where the cash was kept. Niedermann was in luck. He had been able to help himself to 800,000 kronor.

He seemed to remember that there had been a woman in the house too, but he had forgotten what he had done with her.

Göransson had also provided a car that the police were not yet looking for. Niedermann went north. He had a vague plan to make it on to one of the ferries at Kapellskär that would take him to Tallinn.

When he got to Kapellskär he sat in the car park for half an hour, studying the area. It was crawling with policemen.

He drove on aimlessly. He needed a place where he could lie low for a while. When he passed Norrtälje he remembered the old brickworks. He had not even thought about the place in more than a year, since the time when repairs had been under way. The brothers Harry and Atho Ranta were using the brickworks as a depot for goods moving to and from the Baltic ports, but they had both been out of the country for several weeks, ever since that journalist Svensson had started snooping around the whore trade. The brickworks would be empty.

He had driven Göransson's Saab into a shed behind the factory and gone inside. He had had to break open a door on the ground floor, and one of the first things he did was to create an emergency exit through a loose plywood board at one end of the ground floor. He later replaced the broken padlock. Then he had made himself at home in a cosy room on the upper floor.

A whole afternoon had passed before he heard the sounds coming through the walls. At first he thought these were his familiar phantoms. He sat alert and listened for almost an hour before he got up and went out to the workshop to listen more closely. At first he heard nothing, but he stood there patiently until he heard more scraping noises.

He found the key next to the sink.

Niedermann had seldom been as amazed as when he opened the door and found the two Russian whores. They were skin and bones. They seemed to have had no food for several weeks and had been living on tea and water since the last packet of rice had run out.

One of the girls was so exhausted that she could not get up from the bed. The other was in better shape. She spoke only Russian, but he knew enough of the language to understand that she was thanking God and him for saving them. She fell on her knees and threw her arms around his legs. He pushed her away, then left the room and locked the door behind him.

He had not known what to do with the whores. He heated up some soup from the cans he found in the kitchen and gave it to them while he thought. The weaker woman on the bed seemed to be getting some of her strength back. He spent the evening questioning them. It was a while before he understood that the two women were not whores at all, but students who had paid the Ranta brothers to get them into Sweden. They had been promised visas and work permits. They had come from Kapellskär in February and were taken straight to the warehouse, and there they were locked up.

Niedermann's face had darkened with anger. Those bastard Ranta brothers were collecting an income that they had not told Zalachenko about. Then they had completely forgotten about the women, or maybe had knowingly left them to their fate when they fled Sweden in such a hurry.

The question was: what was he supposed to do with them? He had no reason to harm them, and yet he could not really let them go, considering that they would probably lead the police to the brickworks. It was that simple. He could not send them back to Russia, because that would mean he would have to drive them down to Kapellskär. That seemed too difficult. The dark-haired woman, whose name was Valentina, had offered him sex if he helped them. He was not the least bit interested in having sex with the girls, but the offer had turned her into a whore too. All women were whores. It was that simple.

After three days he had tired of their incessant pleading, nagging and knocking on the wall. He could see no other way out. So he unlocked the door one last time and swiftly solved the problem. He asked Valentina to forgive him before he reached out and in one movement broke her neck between the second and third cervical vertebrae. Then he went over to the blonde girl on the bed whose name he did not know. She lay there passively, did not put up any resistance. He carried the bodies downstairs and put them in one of the flooded pits. At last he could feel some sort of peace.

Niedermann had not intended to stay long at the brickworks. He thought he would have to lie low only until the initial police manhunt had died down. He shaved his head and let his beard grow to half an inch, and that altered his appearance. He found a pair of overalls belonging to one of the workers from NorrBygg which were almost big enough to fit him. He put on a Becker's Paint baseball cap and stuffed a folding ruler into a leg pocket. At dusk he drove to the O.K. shop on the hill and bought supplies. He had all the cash he needed from Svavelsjö M.C.'s piggy bank. He looked like any workman stopping on his way home, and nobody seemed to pay him any attention. He shopped once or twice a week at the same time of day. At the O.K. shop they were always perfectly friendly to him.

From the very first day he had spent a considerable amount of time fending off the creatures that inhabited the building. They lived in the walls and came out at night. He could hear them wandering around the workshop.

He barricaded himself in his room. After several days he had had enough. He armed himself with a large knife which he had found in a kitchen drawer and went out to confront the monsters. It had to end.

All of a sudden he discovered that they were retreating. For the first time in his life he had been able to dominate his phantoms. They shrank back when he approached. He could see their deformed bodies and their tails slinking off behind the packing crates and cabinets. He howled at them. They fled.

Relieved, he went back to his warm room and sat up all night, waiting for them to return. They mounted a renewed attack at dawn and he faced them down once more. They fled.

He was teetering between panic and euphoria.

All of his life he had been haunted by these creatures in the dark, and for the very first time he felt that he was in control of the situation. He did nothing. He slept. He ate. He thought. It was peaceful.

The days turned to weeks and spring turned to summer. From his transistor radio and the evening papers he could tell that the hunt for the killer Ronald Niedermann was winding down. He read with interest the reports of the murder of Zalachenko. *What a laugh. A psycho had put an end to Zalachenko.* In July his interest was again aroused when he followed the reports of Salander's trial. He was appalled when she was acquitted and released. It did not feel right. She was free while he was forced to hide.

He bought the *Millennium* special issue at the O.K. shop and read all about Salander and Zalachenko and Niedermann. A journalist named Blomkvist had described Niedermann as a pathological murderer and a psychopath. He frowned.

Autumn came suddenly and still he had not made a move. When it got colder he bought an electric heater at the O.K. shop. He did not know what kept him from leaving the brickworks.

Occasionally some young people had driven into the yard and parked there, but no-one had disturbed him or tried to break into the building. In September a car drove up and a man in a blue windcheater had tried the doors and snooped around the property. Niedermann had watched him from the window on the upper floor. The man kept writing in his notebook. He had stayed for twenty minutes before he looked around one last time and got into his car and drove away. Niedermann breathed a sigh of relief. He had no idea who the man was or what business had brought him there, but he appeared to be doing a survey of the property. It did not occur to Niedermann that Zalachenko's death had prompted an inventory of his estate.

He thought a lot about Salander. He had never expected to see her again, but she fascinated and frightened him. He was not afraid of any living person. But his sister – his half-sister – had made a particular impression on him. No-one else had ever defeated him the way she had done. She had come back to life, even though he had buried her. She had come back and hunted him down. He dreamed about her every night. He would wake up in a cold sweat, and he recognized that she had replaced his usual phantoms.

In October he made a decision. He was not going to leave Sweden before he had found his sister and destroyed her. He did not have a plan, but at least his life now had a purpose. He did not know where she was or how he would trace her. He just sat in his room on the upper floor of the brickworks, staring out of the window, day after day, week after week.

Until one day a burgundy Honda parked outside the building and, to his complete astonishment, he saw Salander get out of the car. *God is merciful*, he thought. Salander would join the two women whose names he no longer remembered in the pool downstairs. His wait was over, and he could at last get on with his life.

Salander assessed the situation and saw that it was anything but under control. Her brain was working at high speed. *Click, click, click.* She still held the crowbar in her hand but she knew that it was a feeble weapon against a man who could not feel pain. She was locked inside an area of about a thousand square metres with a murderous robot from hell.

When Niedermann suddenly moved towards her she threw the crowbar at him. He dodged it easily. Salander moved fast. She stepped on to a pallet, swung herself up on to a packing crate and kept climbing, like a monkey, up two more crates. She stopped and looked down at Niedermann, now four metres below her. He was looking up at her and waiting.

"Come down," he said patiently. "You can't escape. The end is inevitable."

She wondered if he had a gun of some sort. Now that *would* be a problem.

He bent down and picked up a chair and threw it at her. She ducked.

Niedermann was getting annoyed. He put his foot on the pallet and started climbing up after her. She waited until he was almost at the top before she took a running start of two quick steps and jumped across an aisle to land on top of another crate. She swung down to the floor and grabbed the crowbar.

Niedermann was not actually clumsy, but he knew that he could not risk jumping from the stack of crates and perhaps breaking a bone in his foot. He had to climb down carefully and set his feet on the floor. He always had to move slowly and methodically, and he had spent a lifetime mastering his body. He had almost reached the floor when he heard footsteps behind him and turned just in time to block a blow from the crowbar with his shoulder. He lost his grip on the knife.

Salander dropped the crowbar just as she had delivered the blow. She did not have time to pick up the knife, but kicked it away from him along the pallets, dodging a backhand blow from his huge fist and retreating back up on to the packing crates on the other side of the aisle. Out of the corner of her eye she saw Niedermann reach for her. Quick as lightning she pulled up her feet. The crates stood in two rows, stacked up three high next to the centre aisle and two high along the outside. She swung down on to the two crates and braced herself, using all the strength in her legs and pushing her back against the crate next to her. It must have weighed two hundred kilos. She felt it begin to move and then tumble down towards the centre aisle.

Niedermann saw the crate coming and threw himself to one side. A corner of the crate struck him on the chest, but he seemed not to have been injured. He picked himself up. *She was resisting.* He started climbing up after her. His head was just appearing over the third crate when she kicked at him. Her boot struck him with full force in the forehead. He grunted and heaved himself up on top of the packing crates. Salander fled, leaping back to the crates on the other side of the aisle. She dropped over the edge and vanished immediately from his sight. He could hear her footsteps and caught a glimpse of her as she passed through the doorway to the inner workshop.

Salander took an appraising look around. *Click.* She knew that she did not have a chance. She could survive for as long as she could avoid Niedermann's enormous fists and keep her distance. But when she made a mistake — which would happen sooner or later — she was dead. She had to evade him. He would only have to grab hold of her once, and the fight would be over.

She needed a weapon.

A pistol. A sub-machine gun. A rocket-propelled grenade. A personnel mine.

Any bloody thing at all.

But there was nothing like that to hand.

She looked everywhere.

No weapons.

Only tools. *Click*. Her eyes fell on the circular saw, but he was hardly going to lie down on the saw bench. *Click*. *Click*. She saw an iron rod that could be used as a spear, but it was probably too heavy for her to handle effectively. *Click*. She glanced through the door and saw that Niedermann was down from the crates and no more than fifteen metres away. He was coming towards her again. She started to move away from the door. She had maybe five seconds left before Niedermann was upon her. She glanced one last time at the tools.

A weapon . . . or a hiding place.

Niedermann was in no hurry. He knew that there was no way out and that sooner or later he would catch his sister. But she was dangerous, no doubt about it. She was, after all, Zalachenko's daughter. And he did not want to be injured. It was better to let her run around and wear herself out.

He stopped in the doorway to the inner room and looked around at the jumble of tools, furniture and half-finished floorboards. She was nowhere to be seen.

"I know you're in here. And I'm going to find you."

Niedermann stood still and listened. All he could hear was his own breathing. She was hiding. He smiled. She was challenging him. Her visit had suddenly turned into a game between brother and sister.

Then he heard a clumsy rustling noise from somewhere in the centre of the room. He turned his head but at first could not tell where the sound was coming from. Then he smiled again. In the middle of the floor set slightly apart from the other debris stood a five-metre-long wooden workbench with a row of drawers and sliding cabinet doors beneath it.

He approached the workbench from the side and glanced behind it to make sure that she was not trying to fool him. Nothing there.

She was hiding inside the cabinet. So stupid.

He slid open the first door on the far left.

He instantly heard movement inside the cabinet, from the middle section. He took two quick steps and opened the middle door with a triumphant expression on his face.

Empty.

Then he heard a series of sharp cracks that sounded like pistol shots. The sound was so close that at first he could not tell where it was coming from. He turned to look. Then he felt a strange pressure against his left foot. He felt no pain, but he looked down at the floor just in time to see Salander's hand moving the nail gun over to his right foot.

She was underneath the cabinet.

He stood as if paralysed for the seconds it took her to put the mouth of the nail gun against his boot and fire another five seven-inch nails straight through his foot.

He tried to move.

It took him precious seconds to realize that his feet were nailed solidly to the newly laid plank floor. Salander's hand moved the nail gun back to his left foot. It sounded like an automatic weapon getting shots off in bursts. She managed to shoot in another four nails as reinforcement before he was able to react.

He reached down to grab her hand, but immediately lost his balance and regained it only by bracing himself against the workbench as he heard the nail gun being fired again and again, *ka-blam, ka-blam, ka-blam*. She was back to his right foot. He saw that she was firing the nails diagonally through his heel and into the floor.

Niedermann howled in sudden rage. He lunged again for Salander's hand.

From her position under the cabinet Salander saw his trouser leg slide up, a sign that he was trying to bend down. She let go of the nail gun. Niedermann saw her hand disappear quick as a lizard beneath the cabinet just before he reached her.

He reached for the nail gun, but the instant he touched it with the tips of his fingers she drew it under the cabinet.

The gap between the floor and the cabinet was about twenty centimetres. With all the strength he could muster he toppled the cabinet on to its back. Salander looked up at him with big eyes and an offended expression. She aimed the nail gun and fired it from a distance of fifty centimetres. The nail hit him in the middle of his shin.

The next instant she dropped the nail gun, rolled fast as lightning away from him and got to her feet beyond his reach. She backed up several feet and stopped.

Niedermann tried to move and again lost his balance, swaying backwards and forwards with his arms flailing. He steadied himself and bent down in rage.

This time he managed to grab hold of the nail gun. He pointed it at Salander and pulled the trigger.

Nothing happened. He looked in dismay at the nail gun and then at Salander again. She looked back at him blankly and held up the plug. In fury he threw the nail gun at her. She dodged to the side.

Then she plugged in the cord again and hauled in the nail gun.

He met Salander's expressionless eyes and was amazed. She had defeated him. *She's supernatural.* Instinctively he tried to pull one foot from the floor. *She's a monster.* He could lift his foot only a few millimetres before his boot hit the heads of the nails. They had been driven into his feet at different angles, and to free himself he would have to rip his feet to shreds. Even with his almost superhuman strength he was unable to pull himself loose. For several seconds he swayed back and forth as if he were swimming. He saw a pool of blood slowly forming between his shoes.

Salander sat down on a stool and watched for signs that he might be able to tear his feet loose. Since he could not feel pain, it was a matter of whether he was strong enough to pull the heads of the nails straight through his feet. She sat stock still and observed his struggle for ten minutes. The whole time her eyes were frozen blank

After a while she stood up and walked behind him and held the nail gun to his spine, just below the nape of his neck.

Salander was thinking hard. This man had transported, drugged, abused and sold women both retail and wholesale. He had murdered at least eight people, including a policeman in Gosseberga and a member of Svavelsjö M.C. and his wife. She had no idea how many other lives her half-brother might have on his account, if not his conscience, but thanks to him she had been hunted all over Sweden like a mad dog, suspected of three of the murders he had committed.

Her finger rested heavily on the trigger.

He had murdered the journalist Dag Svensson and his partner Mia Johansson.

With Zalachenko he had also murdered *her* and buried her in Gosseberga. And now he had resurfaced to murder her again.

You could get pretty angry with less provocation.

She saw no reason to let him live any longer. He hated her with a passion that she could not even fathom. What would happen if she turned him over to the police? A trial? A life sentence? When would he be granted parole? How soon would he escape? And now that her father was finally gone – how many years would she have to look over her shoulder, waiting for the day when her brother would suddenly turn up again? She felt the heft of the nail gun. She could end this thing once and for all.

Risk assessment.

She bit her lip.

Salander was afraid of no-one and nothing. She realized that she lacked the necessary imagination – and that was evidence enough that there was something wrong with her brain.

Niedermann hated her and she responded with an equally implacable hatred towards him. He joined the ranks of men like Magge Lundin and Martin Vanger and Zalachenko and dozens of other creeps who in her estimation had absolutely no claim to be among the living. If she could put them all on a desert island and set off an atomic bomb, then she would be satisfied.

But murder? Was it worth it? What would happen to her if she killed him? What were the odds that she would avoid discovery? What would she be ready to sacrifice for the satisfaction of firing the nail gun one last time?

She could claim self-defence . . . no, not with his feet nailed to the floorboards.

She suddenly thought of Harriet Fucking Vanger, who had also been tormented by her father and her brother. She recalled the exchange she had had with Mikael Bastard Blomkvist in which she cursed Harriet Vanger in the harshest possible terms. It was Harriet Vanger's fault that her brother Martin had been allowed to go on murdering women year after year.

"*What would you do?*" *Blomkvist had said.*

"*I'd kill the fucker,*" *she had said with a conviction that came from the depths of her cold soul.*

And now she was standing in exactly the same position in which Harriet Vanger had found herself. How many more women would Niedermann kill if she let him go? She had the legal right of a citizen and was socially responsible for her actions. How many years of her life did she want to sacrifice? How many years had Harriet Vanger been willing to sacrifice?

Suddenly the nail gun felt too heavy for her to hold against his spine, even with both hands.

She lowered the weapon and felt as though she had come back to reality. She was aware of Niedermann muttering something incoherent. He was speaking German. He was talking about a devil that had come to get him.

She knew that he was not talking to her. He seemed to see somebody at the other end of the room. She turned her head and followed his gaze. There was nothing there. She felt the hairs rise on the back of her neck.

She turned on her heel, grabbed the iron rod, and went to the outer room to find her shoulder bag. As she bent to retrieve it she caught sight of the knife. She still had her gloves on, and she picked up the weapon.

She hesitated a moment and then placed it in full view in the centre aisle between the stacks of packing crates. With the iron rod she spent three minutes prising loose the padlock so that she could get outside.

She sat in her car and thought for a long time. Finally she flipped open her mobile. It took her two minutes to locate the number for Svavelsjö M.C.'s clubhouse.

"Yeah?"

"Nieminen," she said.

"Wait."

She waited for three minutes before Sonny Nieminen came to the telephone.

"Who's this?"

"None of your bloody business," Salander said in such a low voice that he could hardly make out the words. He could not even tell whether it was a man or a woman.

"Alright, so what do you want?"

"You want a tip about Niedermann?"

"Do I?"

"Don't give me shit. Want to know where he is or not?"

"I'm listening."

Salander gave him directions to the brickworks outside Norrtälje. She said that he would be there long enough for Nieminen to find him if he hurried.

She closed her mobile, started the car and drove up to the O.K.

petrol station across the road. She parked so that she had a clear view of the brickworks.

She had to wait for more than two hours. It was just before 1.30 in the afternoon when she saw a van drive slowly past on the road below her. It stopped at the turning off the main road, stood there for five minutes, and then drove down to the brickworks. On this December day, twilight was setting in.

She opened the glove box and took out a pair of Minolta 16 × 50 binoculars and watched as the van parked. She identified Nieminen and Waltari with three men she did not recognize. *New blood. They had to rebuild their operation.*

When Nieminen and his pals had found the open door at the end of the building, she opened her mobile again. She composed a message and sent it to the police station in Norrtälje.

POLICE MURDERER R. NIEDERMANN IN OLD BRICK-WORKS BY THE O.K. STATION OUTSIDE SKEDERID. ABOUT TO BE MURDERED BY S. NIEMINEN AND MEMBERS OF SVAVELSJÖ M.C. WOMEN DEAD IN PIT ON GROUND FLOOR.

She could not see any movement from the factory.

She bided her time.

As she waited she removed the S.I.M. card from her telephone and cut it up with some nail scissors. She rolled down the window and tossed out the pieces. Then she took a new S.I.M. card from her wallet and inserted it in her mobile. She was using a Comviq cash card, which was virtually impossible to track. She called Comviq and credited 500 kronor to the new card.

Eleven minutes after her message was sent, two police vans with their sirens off but with blue lights flashing drove at speed up to the factory from the direction of Norrtälje. They parked in the yard next to Nieminen's van. A minute later two squad cars arrived. The officers conferred and then moved together towards the brickworks. Salander raised her binoculars. She saw one of the policemen radio through the registration number of Nieminen's van. The officers stood around waiting. Salander watched as another team approached at high speed two minutes later.

Finally it was all over.

The story that had begun on the day she was born had ended at the brickworks.

She was free.

When the policemen officers took out assault rifles from their vehicles, put on Kevlar vests and started to fan out around the factory site, Salander went inside the shop and bought a coffee and a sandwich wrapped in cellophane. She ate standing at a counter in the café.

It was dark by the time she got back to her car. Just as she opened the door she heard two distant reports from what she assumed were handguns on the other side of the road. She saw several black figures, presumably policemen, pressed against the wall near the entrance at one end of the building. She heard sirens as another squad car approached from the direction of Uppsala. A few cars had stopped at the side of the road below her to watch the drama.

She started the Honda, turned on to the E18, and drove home.

It was 7.00 that evening when Salander, to her great annoyance, heard the doorbell ring. She was in the bath and the water was still steaming. There was really only one person who could be at her front door.

At first she thought she would ignore it, but at the third ring she sighed, got out of the bath, and wrapped a towel around her. With her lower lip pouting, she trailed water down the hall floor. She opened the door a crack.

"Hello," Blomkvist said.

She did not answer.

"Did you hear the evening news?"

She shook her head.

"I thought you might like to know that Ronald Niedermann is dead. He was murdered today in Norrtälje by a gang from Svavelsjö M.C."

"Really?" Salander said.

"I talked to the duty officer in Norrtälje. It seems to have been some sort of internal dispute. Apparently Niedermann had been tortured and slit open with a knife. They found a bag at the factory with several hundred thousand kronor."

"Jesus."

"The Svavelsjö mob was arrested, but they put up quite a fight.

There was a shoot-out and the police had to send for a back-up team from Stockholm. The bikers surrendered at around 6.00."

"Is that so?"

"Your old friend Sonny Nieminen bit the dust. He went completely nuts and tried to shoot his way out."

"That's nice."

Blomkvist stood there in silence. They looked at each other through the crack in the door.

"Am I interrupting something?" he said.

She shrugged. "I was in the bath."

"I can see that. Do you want some company?"

She gave him an acid look.

"I didn't mean in the bath. I've brought some bagels," he said, holding up a bag. "And some espresso coffee. Since you own a Jura Impressa X7, you should at least learn how to use it."

She raised her eyebrows. She did not know whether to be disappointed or relieved.

"Just company?"

"Just company," he confirmed. "I'm a good friend who's visiting a good friend. If I'm welcome, that is."

She hesitated. For two years she had kept as far away from Mikael Blomkvist as she could. And yet he kept sticking to her life like gum on the sole of her shoe, either on the Net or in real life. On the Net it was O.K. There he was no more than electrons and words. In real life, standing on her doorstep, he was still fucking attractive. And he knew her secrets just as she knew all of his.

She looked at him for a moment and realized that she now had no feelings for him. At least not those kinds of feelings.

He had in fact been a good friend to her over the past year.

She trusted him. Maybe. It was troubling that one of the few people she trusted was a man she spent so much time avoiding.

Then she made up her mind. It was absurd to pretend that he did not exist. It no longer hurt her to see him.

She opened the door wide and let him into her life again.

NOTES

Olof Palme was the leader of the Social Democratic Party and Prime Minister of Sweden at the time of his assassination on 28 February 1986. He was an outspoken politician, popular on the left and detested by the right. Two years after his death a petty criminal and drug addict was convicted of his murder, but later acquitted on appeal. Although a number of alternative theories as to who carried out the murder have since been proposed, to this day the crime remains unsolved.

Prompted by Olof Palme's assassination, Prime Minister **Ingvar Carlsson** called an investigation into the procedures of the Swedish security police (Säpo) in the autumn of 1987. Carl Lidbom, then Swedish ambassador to France, was given the task of leading the investigation. One of his old acquaintances, the publisher **Ebbe Carlsson**, firmly believed that the Kurdish organization PKK was involved in the murder and was given resources to start a private investigation. The Ebbe Carlsson affair exploded as a major political scandal in 1988, when it was revealed that the publisher had been secretly supported by the then Minister of Justice, Anna-Greta Leijon. She was subsequently forced to resign.

Informationsbyrån (IB) was a secret intelligence agency without official status within the Swedish armed forces. Its main purpose was to gather information about communists and other individuals who were perceived to be a threat to the nation. It was thought that these findings were passed on to key politicians at cabinet level, most likely the defence minister at the time, Sven Andersson, and Prime Minister Olof Palme. The exposure of the agency's operations by journalists Jan Guillou and Peter Bratt in the magazine *Folket i Bild/Kulturfront* in 1973 became known as **the IB affair**.

Carl Bildt was Prime Minister of Sweden between 1991 and 1994 and leader of the liberal conservative Moderate Party from 1986 to 1999.

Anna Lindh was a Swedish Social Democratic politician who served as foreign minister from 1998 until her assassination in 2003. She was considered by many as one of the leading candidates to succeed Göran Persson as leader of the Social Democrats and Prime Minister of Sweden. In the final weeks of her life she was intensely involved in the pro-euro campaign preceding the Swedish referendum on the euro.

Colonel Stig Wennerström of the Swedish air force was convicted of treason in 1964. During the '50s he was suspected of leaking air defence plans to the Soviets and in 1963 was informed upon by his maid, who had been recruited by Säpo. Initially sentenced to life imprisonment, his sentence was commuted to twenty years in 1973, of which he served only ten. He died in 2006. Not to be confused with Hans-Erik Wennerström, the crooked financier who appears in *The Girl with the Dragon Tattoo* and *The Girl Who Played with Fire*.

The Sjöbo debate – In the late '80s and early '90s there was an immigration crisis in Sweden. The number of asylum seekers increased, and the resulting unemployment and backlash from local government prompted the city of Sjöbo to hold a referendum 1998, where the population voted against accepting immigrants. The subsequent political debate led to a combined immigration and integration system in the Aliens Act of 1989.

RUAIRI Mc GREGOR

| | metals | | nonmetals | | metalloids | | noble gases |

KT-433-786

							VIII
							2 He 4.00
		III	IV	V	VI	VII	
			5 B 10.81	6 C 12.01	7 N 14.01	8 O 16.00	9 F 19.00	10 Ne 20.18
			13 Al 26.98	14 Si 28.09	15 P 30.97	16 S 32.06	17 Cl 35.45	18 Ar 39.95

28 Ni 58.69	29 Cu 63.55	30 Zn 65.38	31 Ga 69.72	32 Ge 72.59	33 As 74.92	34 Se 78.96	35 Br 79.90	36 Kr 83.80
46 Pd 106.42	47 Ag 107.87	48 Cd 112.41	49 In 114.82	50 Sn 118.69	51 Sb 121.75	52 Te 127.60	53 I 126.90	54 Xe 131.29
78 Pt 195.08	79 Au 196.97	80 Hg 200.59	81 Tl 204.38	82 Pb 207.2	83 Bi 208.98	84 Po (209)	85 At (210)	86 Rn (222)

63 Eu 151.96	64 Gd 157.25	65 Tb 158.92	66 Dy 162.50	67 Ho 164.93	68 Er 167.26	69 Tm 168.93	70 Yb 173.04	71 Lu 174.97

95 Am (243)	96 Cm (247)	97 Bk (247)	98 Cf (251)	99 Es (252)	100 Fm (257)	101 Md (258)	102 No (259)	103 Lr (260)

General, Organic, and Biochemistry

Third Edition

General, Organic, and Biochemistry

Third Edition

William H. Brown
Beloit College

Elizabeth P. Rogers
University of Illinois

RUAIRI M^c GREGOR
BSc

Brooks/Cole Publishing Company
Monterey, California

Brooks/Cole Publishing Company
A Division of Wadsworth, Inc.

Printed in the United States of America
10 9 8 7 6 5 4 3 2 1

Library of Congress Cataloging-in-Publication Data
Brown, William Henry, [date]–
   General, organic, and biochemistry.
   Includes index.
   1. Chemistry.   I. Rogers, Elizabeth P.   II. Title.
QD31.2.B79   1987   540   86-18864
ISBN 0-534-06870-7

Sponsoring Editor: *Sue Ewing*
Editorial Assistant: *Lorraine McCloud*
Production Editor: *Phyllis Larimore*
Production Assistants: *Dorothy Bell and Sara Hunsaker*
Manuscript Editor: *Janet Wright*
Interior and Cover Design: *Sharon L. Kinghan*
Cover Photo: *© Manfred Kage, Peter Arnold, Inc.*
Art Coordinators: *Judith Macdonald and Sue C. Shepherd*
Interior Illustration: *John Foster*
Photo Editor and Researcher: *Judy Blamer*
Typesetting: *Syntax International, Singapore*
Cover Printing: *Phoenix Color Corporation, Long Island City, New York*
Printing and Binding: *R. R. Donnelley & Sons Co., Crawfordsville, Indiana*

Photo Credits
Page 142: Werner H. Müller, Peter Arnold, Inc.; **145:** Joel Gordon Photography; **149:** (both) © Yoav
Levy, Phototake; **157:** Lew Merrim, Monkmeyer Press Photo Service; **366B:** Chevron Corporation; **450C:**
United States Department of Agriculture; **473B:** Upjohn Corporation; **506F:** United States Army, Natick
Research and Development Center; **626B:** SEM Photomicrographs taken by Professor Marion I.
Barnhart, Wayne State University.

Preface

This text is written for students of the life sciences, particularly those planning careers in one of the many health professions. While we recognize that these students are not planning to become professional chemists, we also know that they need to understand how living systems depend on chemistry. In this survey of general, organic, and biochemistry, we have tried to reveal this relationship and provide a foundation in chemistry that's necessary for further study.

The category of life and health sciences includes a great variety of academic majors. Although all students in these majors need a knowledge of chemistry, some need to know more about certain areas than do others. An inhalation therapist, for example, needs to know more about the properties of gases than does a physical education major; a radiation technologist requires a greater background in radiochemistry than does a dietician. These diverse needs impose special requirements on a text.

First, in addition to covering basic concepts of chemistry, the text must contain a wide choice of material on which instructors can draw to tailor courses to the needs of their particular students. For this reason, we have included more material than most courses will cover. We leave the decision on topic selection to each instructor.

Second, the organization of the text must be flexible enough to allow selected topics to be presented in an order that is logical for each particular course. We have organized this text in a way that seems logical to us, but we realize that other approaches will work equally well. For this reason, we have divided chapters into many freestanding sections and subsections to give instructors as much latitude as possible in choosing and arranging the material to cover. For example, nuclear chemistry is presented at the end of Chapter 2, but the material is designed so that it might be included just as easily later in the course, or omitted. In the Instructor's Manual we suggest other points of flexibility.

Third, the presentation must be even, neither slighting one topic nor going overboard on another. To this end, we have attempted throughout to bring a high degree of pedagogical, organizational, and stylistic unity to this book.

Text Organization

The chapters of this text can be divided into four parts: general chemistry, organic chemistry, biomolecules, and metabolism.

General Chemistry: Chapters 1–9

The first part of the book presents the fundamental concepts of chemistry. Because quantitative thinking is often a major stumbling block for beginning students, we have given special attention in Chapters 1–9 to calculations and problem solving. Problem solving by unit analysis is introduced in the first chapter with a detailed algorithm that enables students to analyze a problem, identify the data, and arrange the problem in solvable form. We use the same algorithm throughout the book. Chapters 2 and 3 concentrate on atomic structure, including radioactivity and the use of radioisotopes in medicine. Chapter 4 covers compounds, their composition, and their properties, with particular emphasis on bonding and the geometry of molecules and ions. We present chemical reactions and stoichiometry in Chapter 5, the kinetic molecular theory of matter in Chapter 6, the properties of solutions and colloids in Chapter 7, and reaction rates and chemical equilibrium in Chapter 8. This part of the book concludes in Chapter 9 with a detailed discussion of acids, bases, pH, and acid-base buffers.

There are two major changes in this part of the Third Edition. First, we have curtailed the discussion of energy, and second, we have reorganized and expanded the discussion of acids and bases. We now present this material in a new, separate chapter. All other changes are intended to clarify difficult concepts.

Organic Chemistry: Chapters 10–18

The second part of the book begins in Chapter 10 with covalent bonding in organic compounds and an introduction to the concepts of structural and functional group isomerism. This chapter also introduces hybridization of atomic orbitals, and covalent bond formation by the overlap of atomic orbitals. Chapters 11–17 present the chemistry of specific functional groups: saturated hydrocarbons, unsaturated hydrocarbons, alcohols and phenols, amines, aldehydes and ketones, carboxylic acids, and finally, functional derivatives of carboxylic acids. These chapters are similarly organized to include structure, nomenclature, physical properties, and reactions. This part concludes in Chapter 18 with a discussion of chirality, a major theme that connects the study of organic chemistry and biochemistry.

Our goal in revising the organic chapters has been to tighten them as much as possible, and to make them flow smoothly and directly into the sections on biomolecules and metabolism. Further, there are two major revisions in chapter organization. We moved the chapter on amines forward to Chapter 14 so that the discussion of these molecules follows immediately the discussion of alcohols, ethers, and phenols in Chapter 13. Also, we moved the discussion of chirality to the end of the organic chemistry section where it now serves as a transition from organic molecules to biomolecules.

Biomolecules: Chapters 19–23

We introduce the major classes of biomolecules in Chapters 19–23. In Chapter 19 we discuss the chemistry of carbohydrates, and in Chapter 20, the chemistry of lipids. In Chapter 21 we present amino acids and proteins, and in Chapter 22, enzymes. The discussion of biomolecules concludes in Chapter 23 with the structure and function of nucleic acids.

Among the major revisions in this part are addition of Michaelis-Menton kinetics and a more quantitative treatment of enzyme kinetics, an expanded discussion of allosteric regulation of enzyme activity, and new material on using enzymes in the health sciences.

Metabolism: Chapters 24–27

In Chapter 24 we introduce metabolism and bioenergetics, and clearly delineate the several stages in oxidation of foodstuffs and generation of ATP. Discussion of the metabolism of carbohydrates, fatty acids, and amino acids follows in Chapters 25–27. Throughout these chapters we point out that the metabolism of these foodstuff molecules is interrelated and precisely regulated.

Features

Several features of this edition make it an especially effective teaching tool.

Example Problems with step-by-step solutions appear in each chapter and are followed by similar problems for students to solve. Students can find the answers to all in-chapter problems in the back of the book.

End-of-Chapter Problems are grouped according to chapter section. This feature ensures a balanced and representative group of problems for each section of the text.

Key Terms and Concepts are listed at the end of each chapter. The section reference following each term or concept directs the student to the place in the text where it is defined and used.

Sixteen Mini-Essays are included. Two of them, ''Alkaloids,'' and ''Biogenic Amines and Emotions,'' are new to this edition. The mini-essays have several purposes: they bridge the gap between the study of chemistry and the projected vocational areas of life science students; they demonstrate some of the creativity and excitement inherent in chemistry; and they offer a glimpse of the human involvement in research and development.

Extensive use of graphics, all of it newly designed and redrawn for this edition, enhances the visual appeal and pedagogical effectiveness of the text.

Supplements

The following supplemental materials that we have prepared are available for use with the text.

Student Study Guide   Contains complete solutions to all end-of-chapter problems. It makes use of a detailed step-by-step learning approach centered around the important concepts and terms used in the text.

Laboratory Manual   Includes 35 experiments keyed to specific chapters.

Instructor's Manual   Contains suggestions for course organization and scheduling.

Overhead Transparency Masters   More than 60 important figures and tables used in the text have been prepared as masters. Using these masters, instructors can produce overhead transparencies for use as lecture aids or in quizzes.

Acknowledgments

We would like to acknowledge the help we have received from Bruce Thrasher of Willard Grant Press on previous editions and from Sue Ewing of Brooks/Cole on this edition. And we thank the very capable staff of Brooks/Cole, coordinated by Phyllis Larimore, for leading us through the intricacies of design, copyediting, and production. Certainly we thank users of the first and second editions, and the following reviewers for their valuable contributions: William Bull, University of Tennessee at Knoxville; Allen Clark, Old Dominion University; James Golen, Southeastern Massachusetts University; Robert Klein, East Carolina University; Jon Robertus, University of Texas; Louis Perlgut, California State University–Long Beach; and James Takacs, University of Utah. Most of all we acknowledge with profound thanks the patience and understanding of our spouses, Hazel S. Brown and Robert W. Rogers, and our children, all of whom we fear were sometimes given short shrift as deadlines came and went.

William H. Brown

Elizabeth P. Rogers

Brief Contents

ix

Contents

Chapter   7   Solutions and Colloids   199

Chapter   8   Reaction Rates and Chemical Equilibrium   231

Chapter   9   Acids and Bases   247

Chapter 10   Organic Chemistry: The Compounds of Carbon   274

Chapter 11   Alkanes and Cycloalkanes   295

Chapter 12   Unsaturated Hydrocarbons   330

Chapter 25   Metabolism of Carbohydrates   719

Chapter 26   Metabolism of Fatty Acids   750

Chapter 27   Metabolism of Amino Acids   773

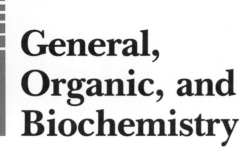

General, Organic, and Biochemistry

Third Edition

1 Matter and Its Properties

1.1 What Is Chemistry?

Chemistry is defined as the study of matter and its properties. **Matter** is defined as everything that has mass and occupies space. From these definitions, we can see the breadth of application chemistry has to our lives. It touches everything in the world. The human body is a complex chemical factory that uses chemical processes to change the food we eat and the air we breathe into bone, muscle, blood, and other tissues and also into the energy necessary for going about our daily living. When illness prevents correct functioning of any of these processes, the doctor may prescribe a therapeutic chemical compound—something that has been either isolated from nature or prepared in a chemical laboratory.

The world around us is a vast chemical laboratory. The daily news often refers to acid rain, toxic wastes, nuclear power plants, and to disasters such as derailment of trains carrying vinyl chloride or sulfuric acid or ammonia. Other chemical news may involve new drugs that cure old diseases, new insecticides and herbicides designed by chemists to help farmers increase their production, and other new products to make our lives more pleasant. The packages we bring home from the grocery list their contents, like the box that not only proclaims the supermoist yellow cake mix but also describes the chemicals therein and the nutritional content, comprising vitamins, minerals, fats, carbohydrates, and proteins. Everyday life is quite involved with things chemical.

Although the latest miracle drug may be the chemical we are most familiar with, it is wise to start our study of chemistry with something simpler. So, we shall first examine the composition of matter and the kinds of matter. With that understanding, we can then study the properties of the different kinds of matter and the changes that each kind can undergo. Each of these changes is accompanied by an energy change of special significance.

As you learn more about chemistry, you will find that you are acquiring a new vocabulary and a new way of looking at and thinking about the changes that go on around us. In this book we will try to teach you these skills in ways that make sense, for chemistry is a logical science. Its hypotheses and theories are based on observations developed through logical thinking about carefully made observations.

1

1.2 A General View of Chemistry

A. Early History and the Scientific Method

Chemistry as we know it today has its roots in the earliest human times. The ancients were proficient in the arts of metallurgy and dyeing; these are chemical processes. The philosophers of Greece and Rome discussed the structure of matter. The alchemists of the Middle Ages practiced chemistry as they searched for the philosopher's stone, which would change base matter into gold.

During the eighteenth century, when science became a popular hobby of the rich, it was common for noblemen to have laboratories in their homes. There they conducted experiments, considered the implications of their experimental findings, and formulated theories that could be tested by new experiments. These experimentalists met with one another to discuss their work and formulate theories on the nature of matter. This approach to science formed the basis for the pattern of experimentation that we call the **scientific method**.

According to the scientific method, an observer gains new knowledge and understanding of the world most easily by organizing work around the following steps (Figure 1.1):

1. Careful observations are collected about a given natural event. These observations of nature may be direct or ones that others have made.

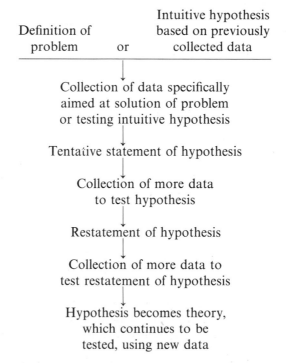

Figure 1.1 Steps of the scientific method. The steps of hypothesizing and data collecting may continue to alternate for some time before the hypotheis earns the right to be called a theory.

2. A hypothesis or a model is constructed that explains or consolidates these observations.

3. New experiments to test the hypothesis are planned and carried out.

4. The original hypothesis is modified so that it is consistent with both the new and the original observations.

A **hypothesis** that survives extensive testing becomes accepted as a **theory**. Although our present hypotheses and theories are the best we have been able to devise so far, there is no guarantee that they are final. Regardless of how many experiments have been done to test a given theory and how many data have been accumulated to support it, a single experiment that can be repeated by other scientists with contradictory results forces the modification or rejection of that theory. Some of our current theories on the nature of matter may in the future have to be modified or even rejected because of data from new experiments. It is essential to keep an open mind and be ready to accept new data and new theories.

Science is a dynamic process, moving by fits and starts. It may leap forward or may become bogged down for lack of a workable hypothesis. Science is less like a wide, smoothly flowing river than like a mountain stream, sometimes rushing ahead, at other times scarcely moving, and even wandering off into dead-end swamps. Chemistry seems to be moving forward toward a greater understanding of our world, but there is still a long way to go before this chemical world and the chemistry of life is understood.

It is important to note the differences between scientific fact and scientific hypothesis and between a scientific law and a scientific theory. A scientific fact is an observed phenomenon; the fact that wood burns on heating is an observation. A scientific hypothesis would try to explain why heat caused this change. A **scientific law** is the compilation of the observation of many scientific facts; a scientific law would be that cellulose (the principal component of wood) burns. The accompanying theory would involve the effect of the added energy (heat) on the bonds that combine carbon, hydrogen, and oxygen into cellulose.

B. Modern Chemistry

In this last part of the twentieth century, chemistry has become a discipline that intrudes on our lives from all directions. There are today hundreds of thousands of practicing chemists. In 1985, the American Chemical Society numbered about 130,000 members. And all chemists do not do the same things; chemistry has many areas.

Analytical chemistry   Analytical chemists have devised and carried out the tests that determine the amount and identity of pollutants in our air and water. They have also devised tests by which officials can identify the unsanctioned use of drugs and steroids by athletes.

Biological chemistry (biochemistry)   Biochemists are concerned with the chemistry of living things. They have discovered the composition and function of

DNA, and are the chemists concerned with the chemical basis of disease and the way your body uses food.

Organic chemistry   Organic chemistry used to be defined as the chemistry of substances derived from living matter; that definition is no longer valid. We can say only that the substances with which organic chemists work usually contain a great deal of carbon and not many metals. Polymer chemists, petroleum chemists, and rubber chemists are organic chemists.

Inorganic chemistry   Originally, inorganic chemists were concerned with minerals and ores, substances not derived from living things; but the exact line separating inorganic chemistry from organic chemistry or biological chemistry has blurred. Some inorganic chemists, for example, study the behavior of iron (an inorganic substance) in hemoglobin (an organic substance) in blood (clearly the province of a biochemist).

There are numerous other branches of chemistry: nuclear chemistry, physical chemistry, geochemistry, to name three. It is a broad and exciting field. In this book we will introduce you first to the basic concepts that all chemists use. We will then go on to show how organic and biochemistry are related to one another and to the many health-related professions.

1.3 Conservation and Classification of Matter

Matter, as we have said, is anything that has mass and occupies space. We will not study all matter but concentrate instead on simple substances and their properties.

A. The Law of Conservation of Mass

All matter obeys one very important law, the **law of conservation of mass**. This law states that *matter can be changed from one form to another, mixtures can be separated or made, and pure substances can be decomposed, while the total amount of matter remains constant.* This important law can be stated in other ways: *The total mass of the universe is, within measurable limits, constant.* Or, *whenever matter undergoes a change, the total mass of the products of the change is, within measurable limits, the same as the total mass of the reactants.*

B. Pure Substances

A **pure substance** consists of a single kind of matter. It always has the same composition and the same set of properties. Baking soda, for example, is a single kind of matter that is known chemically as sodium hydrogen carbonate. A sample of pure baking soda, regardless of its source or size, is a white solid containing 57.1% sodium, 1.2% hydrogen, 14.3% carbon, and 27.4% oxygen. The sample will dissolve in water. When heated to 270°C, the sample will decompose, giving off carbon dioxide and water vapor and leaving a residue of sodium carbonate. Baking soda is a pure substance, since it has a constant composition and a unique set of properties, some of which we have listed. These properties hold true for all samples of baking soda, and are the kinds of properties in which we are interested.

A note about the term *pure*. In chemistry, the word *pure* means one substance only—not a mixture. As the U.S. Food and Drug Administration uses the term *pure*, it means "fit for human consumption." Milk, whether whole, 2% fat, or skim, may be pure (fit for human consumption) by public health standards, but it is hardly pure in the chemical sense. Milk is a mixture of many substances, including water, butterfat, proteins, and sugars. Each of these substances has a unique set of properties and is present in different amounts in each of the different kinds of milk (Figure 1.2).

C. Mixtures

A **mixture** consists of two or more pure substances. Most of the matter around us is composed of mixtures. Seawater contains dissolved salts, river water contains suspended mud, and hard water contains salts of calcium, magnesium, and iron. Both seawater and river water also contain dissolved oxygen, without which fish and other aquatic life could not survive.

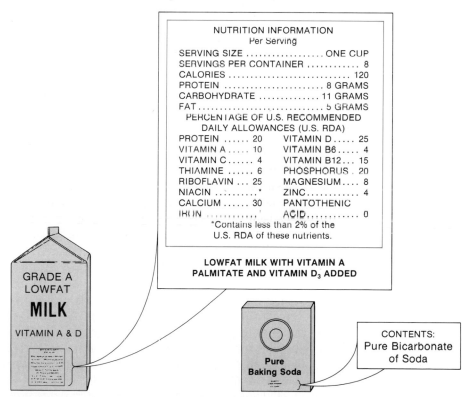

Figure 1.2 Pure substances versus mixtures. The labels on the cartons show that milk is a mixture and baking soda is a pure substance.

Unlike the composition of a pure substance, which is constant, the composition of a mixture can be changed. The properties of the mixture depend on the percentage of each pure substance in it. Of the various categories of milk just mentioned, all contain the same pure substances. Because there is a difference in the percentage of each substance present, however, a noticeable difference exists among the forms that milk takes. You are probably most aware of the difference in butterfat content between, for example, skim milk and whipping cream.

You can often tell, from the appearance of a sample, whether or not it is a mixture. If river water, say, is clouded with mud or silt particles, you know that it is a mixture. If a layer of brown haze hovers over a city, you know that the air is mixed with atmospheric pollutants. The appearance of a sample does not always provide sufficient evidence by which to judge composition, however. A sample of matter may look like a pure substance without being one. Rubbing alcohol, for instance, is a clear, colorless liquid, and so are its two components, water and isopropyl alcohol; but the components are pure substances and rubbing alcohol is a mixture.

Figure 1.3 shows the relations between different kinds of matter.

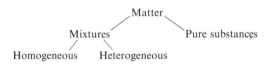

Figure 1.3 Classification of matter.

1.4 Properties of Matter

Each kind of matter has numerous properties by which it can be identified. Some of the properties by which the pure substance baking soda can be identified, we already know (Section 1.3B). Properties fall into two large categories: (1) **physical properties**, or those that can be observed without a change in the composition of the sample, and (2) **chemical properties**, those whose observation involves a change in composition.

Baking soda has the property of dissolving in water. If the water is evaporated from a solution of baking soda, the baking soda is recovered unchanged. Solubility is a physical property. The decomposition of baking soda on being heated is a chemical property. You can observe the decomposition of baking soda, but after you make this observation, you no longer have baking soda. Instead, you have carbon dioxide, water, and sodium carbonate. A physical change alters only physical properties—size, shape, and so on. A chemical change alters chemical properties, such as composition (see Figure 1.4).

One of the important physical properties of a substance is its physical state at room temperature. The three physical states of matter are **solid**, **liquid**, and **gas**. Most kinds of matter can exist in all three states. You are familiar with water as a solid (ice), a liquid, and a gas (steam). (See Figure 1.5.) You have seen wax as a solid at room temperature and a liquid when heated. You have probably seen carbon dioxide as a solid (dry ice) and been aware of it as a

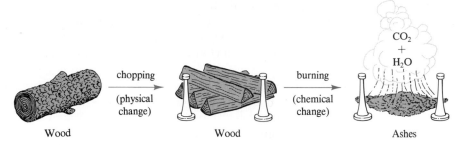

Figure 1.4 Physical and chemical properties of matter. Chopping wood physically changes its size but not its composition. Burning wood changes it chemically, turning it into other substances, among which are carbon dioxide and water.

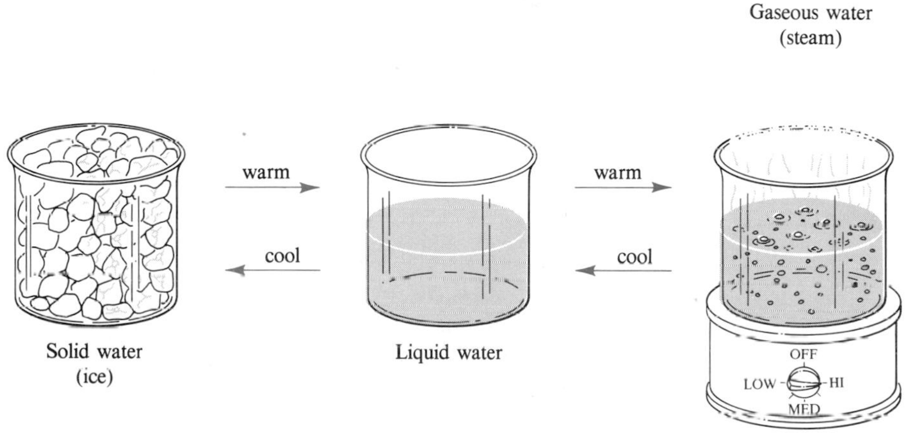

Figure 1.5 The three physical states of water: ice (solid), water (liquid), and steam (gas).

colorless gas at higher temperatures. The temperatures at which a given kind of matter changes from solid to liquid (its melting point) or from liquid to gas (its boiling point) are physical properties. The melting point of ice ($0°C$) and the boiling point of water ($100°C$) are two physical properties of the compound water.

Mixtures too can exist in three different physical states: solid, liquid, and gas. Air is a gaseous mixture of approximately 78% nitrogen, 21% oxygen, and varying percentages of several other gases. Rubbing alcohol is a liquid mixture of approximately 70% isopropyl alcohol and 30% water. Steel is a solid mixture of iron with other pure substances.

1.5 Energy

A study of the properties of matter must include a study of its energy. **Energy** is defined as the capacity to do work. It has many forms. **Potential energy** is stored energy. It may be due to composition (the composition of a battery determines the energy it can release); to position (a rock at the top of a cliff will release energy if it falls to lower ground); or to condition (a hot stone can release heat energy if it is moved to a cooler place). **Kinetic energy** is energy of motion. (A flying bullet has kinetic energy due to its motion. It has a greater capacity to do work than a bullet in a cartridge belt.) Both light and heat are other forms of energy.

One of the characteristics of energy is that one form can be converted to another. Some of the potential energy of wood is changed on burning to radiant energy (heat and light). Some is changed to kinetic energy of motion as the water and carbon dioxide formed move away from the burning log. Some remains as potential energy in the composition of the water and carbon dioxide produced by the burning. Throughout all these changes, the total amount of energy remains constant. This is because all changes must obey the **law of conservation of energy**. This law states: *Energy can be neither created nor destroyed.* An alternative statement is: *The total amount of energy in the universe remains constant.*

The law of conservation of mass and the law of conservation of energy are not separate principles but interrelated. Mass can be changed to energy and energy to mass according to the equation

$$E = c^2 m \quad \text{where} \quad E = \text{energy change; } c = \text{speed of light } (3.00 \times 10^8 \text{ m/sec};$$
$$m = \text{mass change.}$$

This relation allows the two laws to be stated as a single law, the **law of conservation of mass/energy**. The statement of this law is: Energy and mass can be interconverted, but together they are conserved. Albert Einstein (1879–1955) first stated this law. Although the mass lost during any energy-releasing change is too small to be detected by most instruments, it is because of this interconvertibility that our statement of the law of conservation of matter includes the phrase "within measurable limits." We are aware of the relationship, however, since nuclear energy is produced through such a conversion.

1.6 Scientific Measurement

We have said that chemists study the properties of matter. They can estimate these properties (hot or cold, large or small) or they can measure them. Measurement is preferred. You know much more about a metal sample if you know its weight and volume than if you merely conclude that it is heavy for its size. A system of measurement is necessary.

A. The SI System

Measurements in the scientific world, and increasingly in the nonscientific world, are standardized under the International System of Units (or SI, for Système International). The **SI units** and their relative values were adopted by an international association of scientists meeting in Paris in 1960. Table 1.1 lists the basic SI units and derived units. **Metric units** are part of this system.

Table 1.1
SI units.

Property	SI Unit	Derived and Related Units	Relation to English Unit
length	meter (m)	kilometer (km) (1000 m = 1 km) centimeter (cm) (100 cm = 1 m)	1 m = 39.37 in. 1.61 km = 1 mile 2.54 cm = 1 in.
mass	kilogram (kg)	gram (g) (1000 g = 1 kg)	1 kg = 2.204 lb. 453.6 g = 1 lb.
volume	cubic meter (m³)	liter (L) (1 L = 0.001 m³) cubic centimeter (cm³) (1000 cm³ = 1 L) milliliter (mL) (1 mL = 1 cm³)	1 liter = 1.057 qt
temperature	Kelvin (K)	Celsius (°C) (K = °C + 273.15)	Fahrenheit (°F) $°C = \dfrac{°F - 32}{1.8}$
energy	joule (J)	caloric (cal) (1 cal = 4.184 J) kilocalorie (kcal) (1000 cal = 1 kcal)	

The system still in common, nonscientific use in the United States is called the **English system**, even though England, like most other developed countries, now uses metric units. Anyone using units from both the English and the SI systems needs to be aware of a few simple relationships between the two systems. These are given in Table 1.1.

Two features of the SI system make its use easy. First, it is a base 10 system; that is, the various units of a particular dimension vary by multiples of ten. Once a base unit is defined, units larger and smaller than the base unit are indicated by prefixes added to the name of the base unit. Table 1.2 lists some of these **prefixes**, along with the abbreviation for each and the numerical factor

Table 1.2
Prefixes used in the SI system.

Prefix	Symbol	Multiply Base Unit By
mega	M	100 000, or 10^6
kilo	k	1000, or 10^3
deci	d	0.1, or 10^{-1}
centi	c	0.01, or 10^{-2}
milli	m	0.001, or 10^{-3}
micro	μ	0.000 001, or 10^{-6}
nano	n	0.000 000 001, or 10^{-9}
pico	p	0.000 000 000 001, or 10^{-12}

relating it to the base unit. (Exponential notation is discussed in Section 1.7B. A positive exponent means "raised to the power indicated." Thus 10^2 means 10×10, or 10 squared. A negative exponent means "divided by that power of ten." Thus 10^{-2} means $\frac{1}{100}$, or 0.01.)

The following examples illustrate the use of these prefixes. The solution to Example 1.1 is given. Following it is a similar problem for you to solve, to test whether you understand the method of solution. The answer to this similar problem is in the back of the book. (There are many examples in this text, all with worked-out solutions. Following each is a similar problem for you to solve. Working through these problems will ensure that you can indeed solve this type of problem.)

Example 1.1

The unit of time in the SI system is the second (sec). How many seconds are in the following?

a. one nanosecond   **b.** one kilosecond   **c.** one millisecond

☐ *Solution*

a. From Table 1.2, we learn that the prefix *nano* means 10^{-9}. Therefore one nanosecond is 10^{-9} sec.
b. The prefix *kilo* means 10^3 or 1000. Therefore one kilosecond means 1000 sec.
c. The prefix *milli* means 10^{-3}. Therefore one millisecond means 10^{-3} sec.

Problem 1.1

The hertz is an accepted unit of frequency. What is the meaning of the following?

a. one picohertz   **b.** one microhertz   **c.** one megahertz

The second feature that increases the usefulness of the SI system is the direct relationship between base units of different dimensions. The unit of volume (cubic meter) is the cube of the unit of length (meter), and the unit of mass is similarly related to the unit of volume.

The base length in the SI system is the **meter** (m). The meter, approximately 10% longer than a yard, is equivalent to 39.37 in., or 1.094 yd. The most common metric units of length in chemistry are listed in Table 1.3 and illustrated in Figure 1.6.

Table 1.3
SI units of length.

Unit of Length	Abbreviation	Relation to Base Unit
kilometer	km	1 kilometer = 1000 meters
meter	m	. . . . .
decimeter	dm	10 decimeters = 1 meter
centimeter	cm	100 centimeters = 1 meter
millimeter	mm	1000 millimeters = 1 meter
micrometer	μm	10^6 micrometers = 1 meter
nanometer	nm	10^9 nanometers = 1 meter

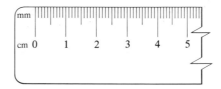

Figure 1.6 Each centimeter contains 10 millimeters (shown actual size).

The base unit of volume in the SI system is the cubic meter (m^3). Other common units of volume are the liter (L), the cubic centimeter (cm^3), and the milliliter (mL).

One liter has a volume equal to 0.001 m^3. The nearest unit of comparable volume in the English system is the quart; 1.000 L equals 1.057 qt. The SI volume units are summarized in Table 1.4 and illustrated in Figure 1.7. Note particularly that a volume of 1 cm^3 is the same as the volume of 1 mL.

Table 1.4
SI units
of volume.

Unit of Volume	Abbreviation	Relation to Liter
liter	L	. . . . .
milliliter	mL	1000 milliliters = 1 liter
cubic centimeter	cm^3, cc	1000 cubic centimeters = 1 liter
microliter	μL	10^6 microliters = 1 liter

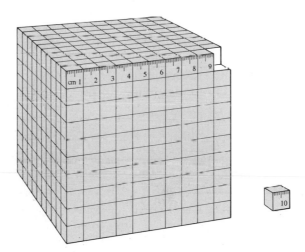

Figure 1.7 The large cube measures 10 cm on a side and has a volume of 1000 cm^3, or 1 L. The small cube next to the large one has a volume of 1 cm^3, or 1 mL.

The standard of mass in the SI system is the kilogram (kg). In a safe in Sevres, France, is a metal cylinder with a mass of exactly one kilogram. The mass of that cylinder is the same as the mass of 1000 cm^3 (1 L) of water at 4°C, thereby relating mass to volume. The most common SI units of mass are listed in Table 1.5.

Unit of Mass	Abbreviation	Relation to Base Unit
kilogram	kg	. . . . .
gram	g	1000 grams = 1 kilogram
milligram	mg	1000 milligrams = 1 gram
microgram	μg	10^6 micrograms = 1 gram

B. Mass versus Weight

In discussing SI units, we have used the term *mass* instead of the more familiar term *weight*. **Mass** measures the amount of matter in a particular sample regardless of its location; it is the same whether measured on Earth, on the moon, or anywhere in space. **Weight** is a measure of the pull of gravity on a sample and its value depends on where the sample is weighed.

Astronauts traveling in space and landing on the moon have experienced the difference between mass and weight. In the Earth's gravitational field at sea level, a particular astronaut may weigh 90 kg (198 lb). On the surface of the moon, this astronaut still has the same mass, but his weight, 15 kg (33 lb), is only one-sixth of what it is on Earth. The reason is that the moon has a much weaker gravitational field than that of the Earth. In outer space the astronaut is weightless, but his mass remains unchanged.

Weight and mass are measured on different instruments. Mass is measured on a balance (Figure 1.8). An object of unknown mass is put at one end of a straight beam and objects of known mass are added to the other end until the masses at each end exactly balance. Because both ends of the beam, at the moment of balancing, are the same distance from the center of the Earth, this measurement is independent of gravity. Weight, on the other hand, is measured on a scale. A scale determines weight by measuring the distortion of a spring. Such a measurement depends on the pull of gravity. You will weigh less at the top of a mountain than you will in the valley below because the pull of gravity

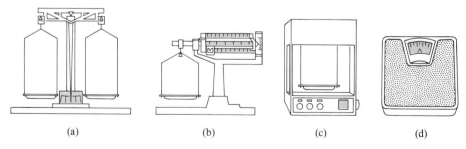

(a)   (b)   (c)   (d)

Figure 1.8 Balances of several types and a scale: (a) a classical balance with the weighing pans suspended from a straight beam; (b) a common laboratory balance, which weighs to 0.01 g and hence is called a *centigram balance*; the three beams give rise to the balance's other, less precise name *triple-beam balance*; (c) an electric balance, which weighs rapidly to 0.0001 g; (d) a common bathroom scale, which measures weight by the distortion of a spring.

decreases as you move farther from the Earth's center. Nevertheless, your mass is the same in both places.

In spite of the clear difference in meaning between the terms *mass* and *weight*, measuring the mass of an object is often called weighing, and the terms *mass* and *weight* are frequently and incorrectly interchanged. Remember that the correct way to describe the amount of matter in a sample is to state its mass.

1.7 Recording Measurements

A. Accuracy and Precision

Chemistry is an exact science. Its development has been based on careful measurements of properties of matter and on careful observations of changes in these properties. Measurements in chemistry must be both accurate and precise (Figure 1.9). An **accurate** measurement is one that is close to the actual value of the property being measured. The accuracy of a measurement depends on the calibration and the proper use of the measuring tool. If you are, for example, measuring the distance between two cities by driving between them, an accurate measurement requires that the odometer in your car read 1 km for each kilometer driven. If it reads only 0.95 km for each kilometer driven, the accuracy of your measurement will be reduced.

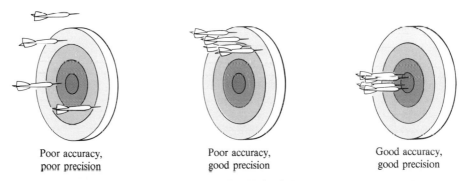

Poor accuracy, poor precision

Poor accuracy, good precision

Good accuracy, good precision

Figure 1.9 Accuracy and precision. Accurate measurements are close to the true value. Precise measurements are close to one another.

A **precise** measurement is one that can be reproduced. For example, the driving distance between Detroit and Chicago is 493 km. An accurate odometer, one that reads 1.00 km for every kilometer traveled, measures the distance between these two cities as 493 km. However, an odometer that reads 1.00 km for every 0.95 km traveled will measure the Detroit-Chicago distance as 519 km. Each time the inaccurate odometer is used on the trip, it records the same value, 519 km. This odometer reading is precise because it can be reproduced time after time. It is not accurate, however, because the odometer itself is not properly calibrated. Accuracy requires precision, but precison does not guarantee accuracy.

The importance of obtaining measurements that are both accurate and precise is rarely greater than in a medical laboratory. Patients and doctors alike want to be certain that instruments give readings that are not only precise but accurate. For this reason, instruments used in medical laboratories are calibrated each day (and often at the beginning of each shift) against samples of known values. Periodically, accrediting agencies send the laboratories' samples to be analyzed. The results obtained on these samples must be accurate within the range allowed by accrediting agencies. Precision is not enough; the determinations must also be accurate.

B. Exponential Notation

Measurements in chemistry often involve very large or very small numbers. An example of a very small number is the mass of a hydrogen atom:

Mass of hydrogen atom = 0.000 000 000 000 000 000 000 001 67 g

At the opposite extreme is the mass of the Earth:

Mass of the Earth = 5 993 000 000 000 000 000 000 000 Kg

It is hard to deal with numbers written like this; copying them without mistakes is difficult and saying them, almost impossible. To simplify writing and tabulating such numbers, we use **exponential notation**, called sometimes **scientific notation**. When exponential notation is used, the measurement is expressed as a number between 1 and 10 multiplied by a power of 10. Table 1.2, which lists the prefixes used in the SI system, shows the decimal equivalent of some powers of 10. When exponential notation is used to express a measurement greater than 1, the original number is expressed as a number between 1 and 10, multiplied by 10 to the nth power, where n is the number of places by which the decimal point was moved to the left. How this works can best be understood by studying Example 1.2.

Example 1.2

Express in exponential notation:

a. 436 207   **b.** 1 060 435

☐ *Solution*

a. Express 436 207 as a number between 1 and 10 multiplied by 10^{+n}.

$$4.362\,07 \times 10^{+n}$$

Now determine the value of n. In the change from 436 207 to $4.362\,07 \times 10^{+n}$, the decimal point was moved 5 places to the left. The value of n is then 5. Therefore,

$$436\,207 = 4.362\,07 \times 10^{5}$$

b. Express 1 060 435 as a number between 1 and 10 multiplied by 10^{+n}.

$$1.060\,435 \times 10^{+n}$$

Now determine the value of *n*. The decimal point was moved 6 places to the left in making this change. The value of *n* is 6.

$$1\,060\,435 = 1.060\,435 \times 10^6$$

Problem 1.2

a. Express the mass of the Earth in exponential notation.
b. The planet Pluto is $7\,382\,000\,000$ km from the sun at the most distant point in its orbit. Express this distance in exponential notation.

If the number to be expressed in exponential notation is less than 1, the original number is expressed as a number between 1 and 10, multiplied by 10 to the minus *n* power, where *n* equals the number of places by which the decimal point was moved to the right.

Example 1.3

Express the following numbers in exponential notation.

a. $0.006\,39$ b. $0.000\,010\,45$

Solution

a. Express $0.006\,39$ as a number between 1 and 10 multiplied by 10^{-n}.

$$6.39 \times 10^{-n}$$

Determine the value of *n*. In the change from $0.006\,39$ to 6.39, the decimal point was moved 3 places to the right. Therefore the value of *n* is 3.

$$6.39 \times 10^{-3}$$

b. Express $0.000\,010\,45$ as a number between 1 and 10 multiplied by 10^{-n}.

$$1.045 \times 10^{-n}$$

Determine the value of *n*. In the change, the decimal point was moved 5 places to the right; *n* equals 5. The number becomes

$$1.045 \times 10^{-5}$$

Problem 1.3

a. Express the mass of a proton in exponential notation.
b. The radius of a proton is $0.000\,000\,015\,4$ m. Express this number in exponential notation.

C. Uncertainty in Chemical Measurement

1. Reading and Recording Measurements

Each time we measure length, volume, mass, or any other physical quantity, some degree of uncertainty exists in the measurement. If we write a measurement as 372, for example, we understand that the uncertainty is ± 1; if we write 0.017, we understand that the uncertainty is ± 0.001.

Uncertainty in measurements is indicated by the number of significant figures used. **Significant figures** are all those measured plus one that is estimated. In Figure 1.10, we show the uncertainty in reading the volume in each container. Notice that the last recorded figure is estimated. The number of significant figures in each of the readings is:

25 mL	contains 2 significant figures
25.2 mL	contains 3 significant figures
25.28 mL	contains 4 significant figures

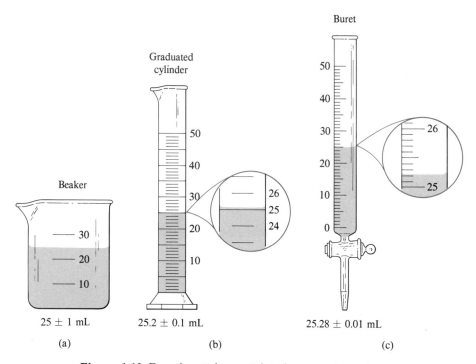

Figure 1.10 Experimental uncertainty in measuring volume.

2. Zero as a Significant Figure

A zero that only locates the decimal point is not significant; zeros that are not needed to locate the decimal point are significant for they report a measurement. If the above measurements were given in liters, they would be 0.025 L, 0.0252 L, and 0.025 28 L. The number of significant figures in each measurement is the same as before; the zeros have been added to show the location of the decimal point.

Suppose you had reported the volume of liquid in a buret as 30.50 mL, or 0.030 50 L. Are any of these zeros significant? The zeros to the left of the 3 are not significant, for their purpose is to locate the decimal point. The zero between the 3 and the 5 is significant, because it shows that the measured volume in that place is 0. The zero after the 5 is also significant. It does not locate the decimal point; it does report a measurement.

Exponential notation clarifies this point. Any zero that disappears when a number is expressed exponentially is not significant.

For example, the mass of a hydrogen atom has been given as

$$0.000\ 000\ 000\ 000\ 000\ 000\ 000\ 001\ 67\ g$$

In exponential notation, this number becomes

$$1.67 \times 10^{-24}\ g$$

Since the zeros in the number have disappeared, we know that they merely showed the location of the decimal point and the magnitude of the number; they were not significant. Similarly, the mass of the Earth expressed exponentially is

$$5.993 \times 10^{24}\ Kg$$

The zeros shown in the original expression of the measurement (Section 1.7B) have disappeared; they were not significant.

A problem arises when a zero shows both a measurement and the location of the decimal point. The problem can be solved by putting a decimal point after such zeros. Thus 250. means that the zero reflects a measurement; 250 means that the zero is there to show the magnitude of the number. Similarly, 480 000 means the same as 4.8×10^5, but 480 000. means $4.800\ 00 \times 10^5$.

3. Rounding Off

In a calculation, the number of significant figures in the numerical answer is determined by the precision of the measurements used in the calculation. It is often necessary to round off the calculated result to the proper number of significant figures. The rules of **rounding off** are:

1. If the digit following the last to be kept is less than 5, all unwanted digits are discarded. To report, for example, the quantity 36.723 mL using four significant figures, write 36.72 mL; to report it using three significant figures, write 36.7 mL.

2. If the digit following the last one to be kept is 5 or greater, the digit to be kept is increased by one. Thus, to report 36.785 mL using four significant figures, write 36.79 mL. For three significant figures, write 36.8 mL. For two significant figures, write 37 mL.

Example 1.4

Express the following numbers in exponential notation to three significant figures.

a. 506 251   **b.** 0.005 278   **c.** 50 192   **d.** 0.082 63

☐ *Solution*

a. The decimal point is moved five places to the left, giving 10^5. Three digits must be dropped to leave three significant figures. The last digit to be dropped is 2. This is less than 5; the 6 is not changed. The final number is 5.06×10^5.

b. The decimal point has been moved three places to the right, giving 10^{-3}. The zeros are not significant since they show only the location of the decimal point. The fourth digit must be dropped. It is 8, or greater than 5; therefore the remaining digit must be increased. The number becomes 5.28×10^{-3}.

c. The decimal point has been moved four places to the left, giving 10^4. The digit next to the last to be kept is 9. As it is bigger than 5, the last retained digit is increased. The number becomes 5.02×10^4.

d. The decimal point has been moved two places to the right, giving 10^{-2}. The zeros do not show a measurement, so they are dropped. As the digit to be dropped, 3, is less than 5, no change is made in the last digit retained. The number becomes 8.26×10^{-2}.

Problem 1.4

Express the numbers in exponential notation to three significant figures:

a. 109 810   **b.** 90 360   **c.** 0.000 000 610 1   **d.** 0.070 08

4. Significant Figures in Calculations

Most often, the measurements that we make are not final answers in themselves. Rather, they are used in further calculations. In such calculations, we must remember that the accuracy of a measurement cannot be improved by calculation. In calculations involving multiplication and division, the answer should contain the same number of significant figures as the measurement in the calculation that contains the fewest significant figures.

Example 1.5

A piece of steel measures 2.6 cm × 5.02 cm × 6.36 cm. What is its volume?

☐ *Solution*

The volume is the product of the three dimensions,

$$2.6 \text{ cm} \times 5.02 \text{ cm} \times 6.36 \text{ cm} = 83.011 \text{ cm}^3$$

The measurement 2.6 cm has only two significant figures. Because the operation is multiplication, the answer can have only as many significant figures as the least accurate measurement going into the calculation. The answer must be rounded off to two figures, and becomes 83 cm^3.

Problem 1.5

A car travels 456 miles in 8.5 hr. What is its average speed?

Example 1.6

A sample of straight carbon steel (the kind commonly used to make railroad-track bolts and automobile axles) has a mass of 0.795 g and contains 3.6×10^{-3} g carbon. What is the percentage of carbon in this steel alloy?

☐ *Solution*

The arithmetic solution to the problem is

$$\frac{3.6 \times 10^{-3} \text{ g}}{0.795 \text{ g}} \times 100\% = 0.452\,83\%$$

The measurements were divided. In such an operation, the answer can have only as many significant figures as the least precise measurement used. The numerator, 3.6×10^{-3}, contains two significant figures; 0.795 contains three significant figures. The answer should contain two significant figures. The answer is 0.45%.

Problem 1.6

Our bodies require tiny amounts of zinc to maintain good health. The body of a person weighing 78 kg, for example, should contain 1.61×10^{-4} g zinc. What percentage of body weight is this requirement?

In calculations involving addition or subtraction, the answer can show only as many decimal places as are common to all the measurements in the calculation. It is not the number of significant figures in each of the measurements but the location of the decimal point that guides you in determining the number of significant figures in the answer to a problem involving addition or subtraction.

Example 1.7

A 2.65 mL sample is withdrawn from a bottle containing 375 mL of alcohol. What is the volume of liquid remaining in the bottle?

☐ *Solution*

$$375 \text{ mL} - 2.65 \text{ mL} = 372.35 \text{ mL}$$

One of the numbers in the calculation, 375 mL is reported only to the units place. The units place is the smallest place common to both numbers; therefore, the answer can be reported only to the units place. Thus, the correct answer is 372 mL.

Problem 1.7

Three samples of blood are drawn from a patient. One sample has a volume of 0.51 mL, the second a volume of 0.06 mL, and the third a volume of 15.0 mL. What is the total volume of blood drawn from the patient?

5. Significant Figures and Pocket Calculators

The use of pocket electronic calculators has increased enormously the importance of understanding significant figures and of observing the rules governing their use. A calculator with an eight-digit display capability may display eight digits in the answer to a calculation, regardless of the number of digits punched in. Dividing 5.0 by 1.67 on a calculator, for example, may give the following answer:

$$\frac{5.0}{1.67} = 2.9940119$$

The correct answer, 3.0, has only two significant figures, the same as the least accurate number, 5.0, in the problem. All other digits displayed by the calculator are insignificant.

1.8 Solving Problems by Unit or Dimensional Analysis

A. Conversion Factors

Measurements made during a chemical experiment are often used to calculate another property. Frequently, it is necessary to change measurements from one unit to another: inches to feet, meters to centimeters, hours to seconds. A relationship between two units measuring the same quantity is a conversion factor. The conversion factor between feet and yards, for example, is

$$1 \text{ yd} = 3 \text{ ft}$$

A **conversion factor** relates two measurements of the same sample. The measurements may be of the same property. (In 3 ft = 1 yd, both measurements are of the same dimension, length.) Or the measurements may be of different dimensions. In saying that 3 mL of alcohol weighs 2.4 g, we are measuring two different dimensions of the same sample, mass and volume. Together, these measurements express a conversion factor for they refer to the same sample and show a relationship between its mass and volume.

Conversion factors are so-named because they offer a way of converting a measurement made in one dimension to another dimension. They do *not* change the original property—only how it is measured. Table 1.1 listed many conversion factors within the metric system and between the metric and English systems.

Conversion factors that define relationships, such as 3 ft = 1 yd or 1 L = 1000 mL, are said to be infinitely significant. This means that the number of figures in these factors does not affect the number of significant figures in the answer to the problem.

B. Solving Problems by Dimensional Analysis

Problem solving by dimensional analysis is based on the premise that in an arithmetic operation units as well as numbers can be canceled. The idea may be new to you but the method is familiar. For example, if you were asked how many inches there are in 6 ft, you would reply without hesitation that 6 ft equals 72 in. In doing this calculation, you would be using a familiar relationship or conversion factor between inches and feet, namely, 12 in. = 1 ft. There are two ways to write this as a conversion factor:

$$\frac{12 \text{ in.}}{1 \text{ ft}} \quad \text{and} \quad \frac{1 \text{ ft}}{12 \text{ in.}}$$

To convert 6 ft to inches, you use the conversion factor on the left, because it allows you to cancel the units or dimensions you do not want (feet) and arrive at an answer with the units you do want (inches):

$$6 \text{ ft} \times \frac{12 \text{ in.}}{1 \text{ ft}} = 72 \text{ in.}$$

Note that although the unit cancels, the numerical values remain.

> **Problem solving by unit analysis can be divided into the following steps:**
>
> 1. Determine what quantity is wanted and in what units.
> 2. Determine what quantity is given and in what units.
> 3. Determine what conversion factor or factors can be used to convert from the units given to the units wanted.
> 4. Determine how the quantity and units given and the appropriate conversion factors can be combined in an equation so that the unwanted units cancel and only the wanted units remain.
> 5. Perform the mathematical calculations and express the answer using the proper number of significant figures. After you have done the calculation, it is always wise to look at the equation again and estimate the answer. If your estimate is close to the calculated answer, all is probably well. If it is quite different, check your calculations. Be sure that you have performed all operations correctly and have not misplaced the decimal point.

How many centimeters are there in 1.63 m?

Example 1.8

☐ *Solution*

Wanted: Length in centimeters (? cm).
Given: 1.63 m. We can write the partial equation

$$? \text{ cm} = 1.63 \text{ m} \times \text{conversion factor}$$

Conversion factors: (We need one that relates meters to centimeters.)

$$1 \text{ m} = 100 \text{ cm (from Table 1.3)}$$

This conversion factor can be written as either

$$\frac{1 \text{ m}}{100 \text{ cm}} \quad \text{or} \quad \frac{100 \text{ cm}}{1 \text{ m}}$$

Equation: By combining this quantity and conversion factor in the following way, the unit meters cancels, and centimeters, the unit we want in the answer, remains.

$$? \text{ cm} = 1.63 \text{ m} \times \frac{100 \text{ cm}}{1 \text{ m}}$$

Arithmetic: Calculation gives 163 cm. The result must then be expressed in exponential notation to the proper number of significant figures, which gives the final answer:

$$1.63 \times 10^2 \text{ cm}$$

Many problems require two or more conversion factors for conversion from the units given to the units wanted.

Example 1.9

A typical birth weight in the United States is 6.45 lb. How many kilograms is this?

☐ *Solution*

Wanted: Weight in kilograms (? kg).
Given: 6.45 lb. Therefore, we can start the equation:

$$? \text{ kg} = 6.45 \text{ lb} \times \text{conversion factor(s)}$$

Conversion factors: We know from Table 1.1 that 1 lb = 453.6 g. Since the problem asks for the number of kilograms, and not the number of grams, we also need the conversion factor relating grams and kilograms: 1000 g = 1 kg. Thus, the conversion factors we need in solving this problem are

$$\frac{1 \text{ lb}}{453.6 \text{ g}} \quad \text{or} \quad \frac{453.6 \text{ g}}{1 \text{ lb}} \qquad \frac{1000 \text{ g}}{1 \text{ kg}} \quad \text{or} \quad \frac{1 \text{ kg}}{1000 \text{ g}}$$

Equation: The quantity given and the appropriate conversion factors are combined in an equation so that the unwanted units (pounds and grams) cancel and only the wanted unit (kilograms) remains:

$$? \text{ kg} = 6.45 \text{ lb} \times \frac{453.6 \text{ g}}{1 \text{ lb}} \times \frac{1 \text{ kg}}{1000 \text{ g}}$$

Arithmetic: The mathematical calculation gives 2.9257 kg. Expressing this result using only three significant figures (the number of significant figures in 6.45 lb), we arrive at the final answer: 2.93 kg.

Example 1.10

Blood donors typically give 1.00 pt of blood during each visit to the blood bank. Calculate the volume in liters.

☐ *Solution*

Wanted: Volume in liters (? L blood).
Given: 1.00 pt blood.

$$? \text{ L blood} = 1.00 \text{ pt} \times \text{conversion factor(s)}$$

Conversion factors:

$$1 \text{ qt} = 2 \text{ pt}; \ 1 \text{ L} = 1.057 \text{ qt}$$

Equation:

$$? \text{ L blood} = 1.00 \text{ pt} \times \frac{1 \text{ qt}}{2 \text{ pt}} \times \frac{1 \text{ L}}{1.057 \text{ qt}}$$

Answer: 0.473 L blood.

Problem 1.8

A football player runs the opening kickoff back 45 yd. If football were to convert to the metric system, how many meters would this run be?

Problem 1.9

Aspirin tablets weigh 5.00 grains. One grain is 2.29×10^{-3} ounce (oz). There are 16 oz in a pound. What is the mass in milligrams of one aspirin tablet?

Problem 1.10

The gas tank of a car holds 19.5 gal. How many liters does it hold?

You can see from these examples, that solving problems by dimensional analysis is a straightforward method by which you can organize your thinking and attack problems systematically. We shall use this method and these same five steps for all the numerical problems that follow.

1.9 Physical Properties

A. Density

Chemists determine the properties of matter, particularly those properties that can be used to identify the composition of a sample. It is possible to measure the mass and volume of a sample, as was done for several samples of iron in Table 1.6 but neither of these properties shows that all the samples are of the same kind of matter. All those samples do have the same ratio of mass to volume, however, as shown in the last column of the table. This ratio is called **density**:

$$\text{Density} = \frac{\text{mass}}{\text{volume}}$$

All samples of the same kind of matter under the same conditions have the same density. Density is a physical property by which a particular kind of matter can be characterized and identified. Table 1.7 lists the density values for some common solids, liquids, and gases under normal conditions.

Table 1.6
Volume, mass, and density of iron samples.

Sample	Volume (mL)	Mass (g)	Density (g/mL)
A	1.05	8.25	7.86
B	25.63	201.5	7.862
C	90.7	713	7.86
D	0.02471	0.1942	7.859

Table 1.7
Densities of some common solids (g/cm^3), liquids (g/mL), and gases (g/L) at 0°C and normal pressure.

Metals		Other Solids		Liquids		Gases	
aluminum	2.70	bone	1.85	chloroform	1.49	air	1.20
gold	19.32	butter	0.86	ethyl alcohol	0.791	carbon dioxide	1.83
magnesium	1.74	cork	0.24	gasoline	0.67	carbon monoxide	1.16
mercury	13.59	diamond	3.51	water (at 4°C)	1.000	hydrogen	0.08
sodium	0.97	sugar	1.59			oxygen	1.33

The density of solids and liquids is usually given in grams per milliliter. From the information in the table, some generalizations can be made. Most metals have a density that is greater than that of water. The density of liquids varies; some liquids (like gasoline) are less dense than water, while others (like chloroform) are more dense. Gases are so much less dense than solids and liquids that their densities are commonly given in units of grams per liter.

Density varies with temperature. The density of water at 4°C is 1.000 g/mL and at 80°C is 0.9718 g/mL. The density of oxygen is 1.33 g/L at 0°C and 1.10 g/L at 80°C.

Density is a conversion factor that relates mass to volume. If you know two of the three quantities (mass, volume, and density), you can calculate the third.

Example 1.11

Uranium is a heavy metal. A sample of uranium weighing 13.65 g has a volume of 0.72 mL. What is the density of uranium?

☐ *Solution*

Density = mass/volume.
Wanted: ? g/mL.
Conversion factor: 13.65 g uranium weighs 0.72 mL.

Equation: Density of uranium = ? g/mL = $\dfrac{13.65 \text{ g}}{0.72 \text{ mL}}$

$$= 18.958 \text{ g/mL}$$

Rounding off to two significant figures gives

$$\text{Density of uranium} = 19 \text{ g/mL}$$

Problem 1.11

A piece of granite having a volume of 59.3 mL weighs 156.6 g. What is the density of granite?

Example 1.12

A sample of ethyl alcohol has a mass of 2.02 g. What is the volume of this sample in metric units?

☐ *Solution*

Wanted: Volume in a metric unit. It is a small sample, so we choose milliliters (? mL).
Given: 2.02 g ethyl alcohol.

$$? \text{ mL} = 2.02 \text{ g} \times \text{conversion factor}$$

Conversion factors: From Table 1.7, we know that the density of ethyl alcohol = 0.791 g/mL. This can also be stated as 1.00 mL ethyl alcohol weighs 0.791 g.

Equation: $? \text{ mL} = 2.02 \text{ g} \times \dfrac{1.00 \text{ mL}}{0.791 \text{ g}}$

Answer: 2.55 mL.

Problem 1.12

A sample of lead has a mass of 16.5 g. What is the volume of this sample?

B. Energy Related Properties

Chemistry is concerned with the properties of matter and the energy changes that matter undergoes. We have discussed properties related to the mass and volume of a sample of matter. In this section we will talk about properties related to energy. Energy is measured in **joules** (J) or **calories** (cal). The conversion factor between the two units is

$$4.184 \text{ J} = 1 \text{ cal}$$

The terms *kilojoule* (kJ) (10^3 J) and *kilocalorie* (kcal) (10^3 cal) are also used. The large calorie (Calorie) used frequently in nutrition studies equals one kilocalorie.

The amount of heat energy associated with a particular sample depends on its temperature, mass, and composition.

1. Temperature and Temperature Scales

Temperature measures how hot or cold a sample is compared with some arbitrary standard. Temperature is measured with a thermometer and is usually reported in one of three different scales: Fahrenheit, F; Celsius, C, sometimes called Centigrade; and Kelvin, K, sometimes called absolute.

The relation among temperatures on these three scales is straightforward if you understand how a thermometer is constructed and calibrated. Two essential features of a thermometer are (1) a substance that expands as it is heated and contracts as it is cooled; and (2) some means to measure the expansion and contraction. In the thermometer with which you may be most familiar, the substance that expands and contracts is mercury. So that its expansion or contraction can be measured, the mercury is confined within a small, thin-walled glass bulb connected to a narrow capillary tube. When the temperature increases, the mercury expands and its level in the capillary tube rises. This increase in height is proportional to the increase in temperature.

A thermometer is calibrated in the following way. First, the mercury bulb of a new thermometer is immersed in a mixture of ice and water. When the height of the mercury in the column becomes constant, a mark is made. This mark is one reference point. The ice-water mixture is then heated to boiling and kept at that temperature until the height of the mercury in the column rises to a new constant level. Another mark is made on the column at this level; this mark is a second reference point. Now the manufacturer must decide whether this thermometer will measure temperature on the Celsius, Fahrenheit, or Kelvin scale. If it is to be on the **Celsius** scale, the reference point is labeled 0°C for the ice-water mixture and 100°C for boiling water. The distance between these two reference points is divided into 100 equal parts. If the thermometer is to measure temperature on the **Fahrenheit** scale, the reference point is labeled 32°F for the ice-water mixture and 212°F for boiling water. The distance between 32°F and

212°F is divided into 180 equal divisions. If the thermometer is to measure temperature on the **Kelvin** scale, the ice-water reference point is labeled 273.15 K, the boiling-water reference point is labeled 373.15 K, and the distance between these two marks is divided equally into 100 divisions. As you can see, there is no difference in the temperatures measured by any of these thermometers; the difference is in the units in which each temperature is reported. The relations among the three temperature scales are illustrated in Figure 1.11.

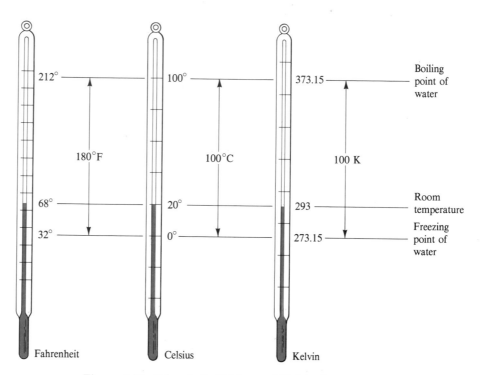

Figure 1.11 Fahrenheit, Celsius, and Kelvin thermometers.

2. Conversion between Temperature Scales

A temperature reading on any one of the three scales can be converted to a reading on any other. First, consider a conversion from degrees Celsius to degrees Fahrenheit. Figure 1.11 shows that between the temperature readings of the ice-water and boiling-water marks, there are 180 Fahrenheit degrees but only 100 Celsius degrees. This relation can be written as a conversion factor:

$$180°F = 100°C \qquad \text{or} \qquad \frac{180°F}{100°C} = \frac{9°F}{5°C} = \frac{1.8°F}{1°C}$$

In other words, a temperature increase of 9 Fahrenheit degrees is equivalent to an increase of 5 Celsius degrees. Figure 1.11 also shows that the numerical values assigned to the two ice-water reference points differ by 32 degrees; a reading of 0° on the Celsius scale corresponds to a reading of 32° on the

Fahrenheit scale. Putting these facts together in an equation gives

$$°F = \tfrac{9}{5}(°C) + 32 \quad \text{or} \quad °F = 1.8(°C) + 32$$

This equation can be rearranged to give the reverse conversion equation:

$$\tfrac{9}{5}(°C) = °F - 32 \quad \text{or} \quad °C = \frac{5(°F - 32)}{9}$$

$$= \frac{(°F - 32)}{1.8}$$

Example 1.13

a. A recommended temperature setting for household hot-water heaters is 140°F. What is this temperature on the Celsius scale?
b. The boiling point of pure ethyl alcohol is 78.5°C. What is its boiling point on the Fahrenheit scale?

☐ *Solution*

a. $°C = \dfrac{(140 - 32)}{1.8} = 60°C$

b. $°F = 1.8(78.5) + 32 = 173°F$

Problem 1.13

Perform the following temperature conversions:

a. 68°F to Celsius   **b.** 45°C to Fahrenheit

What is the relationship between the Celsius and Kelvin scales? As each scale has exactly 100 divisions, or degrees, between the ice-water temperature and the boiling-water temperature, the size of a degree on the Celsius scale is the same as that of a Kelvin degree. The difference between the scales lies in the readings at the ice-water reference points; the reading is 0° on the Celsius scale and 273.15 on the Kelvin scale. Therefore, to convert a reading from the Celsius scale to the Kelvin scale, simply add 273.15:

$$K = °C + 273.15$$

Note that the symbol K stands for "degrees Kelvin," or more properly Kelvins. It is not preceded by the degree symbol. The symbols for Fahrenheit and Celsius do require the degree symbol, for example, 212°F and 100°C, but 373 K.

Example 1.14

Perform the temperature conversions:

a. 28°C to Kelvin   **b.** 310 K to Celsius

☐ *Solution*

a. The equation for conversion is

$$K = °C + 273.15$$

Therefore the Kelvin temperature is

$$K = 28°C + 273.15 = 301 \text{ K}$$

(Note that this is addition; the last significant figure is in the units place.)

b. Use the same equation as in (a) rearranged to give °C:

$$°C = K - 273.15 \qquad \text{or} \qquad °C = 310 \text{ K} - 273.15 = 37°C$$

■

**Problem
1.14**

Perform the temperature conversions:

a. 105°C to Kelvin   **b.** 230 K to Celsius

∎

3. Melting Points and Boiling Points

Among the data used to identify a substance are the temperatures at which it changes state. The **melting point** of a substance is the temperature at which the substance changes from a solid to a liquid. If the change of state is the reverse, from liquid to solid, that same temperature is then the **freezing point**. The **boiling point** of a substance is the temperature at which under normal conditions the substance changes from a liquid to a gas. The melting points and boiling points of several substances are shown in Table 1.8.

Table 1.8
The melting point, boiling point, and physical state of several substances.

Substance	Melting Point (°C)	Boiling Point (°C)	Physical State at 20°C
propane	−190	−42	gas
chloroform	−64	62	liquid
sodium chloride (table salt)	801	1413	solid
quartz	1610	2230	solid

The last column in Table 1.8 shows the physical state of these substances at room temperature (20°C) and normal conditions. *Normal conditions* means at one atmosphere pressure. (The precise meaning of this will be described in Chapter 6.) The physical state is predictable from the melting and boiling points of a substance. A substance that boils below 20°C is a gas under normal conditions. One that melts below room temperature (about 20°C) and boils above room temperature is a liquid at room temperature. And a substance that melts above room temperature is a solid under normal conditions.

■

**Example
1.15**

The boiling point of sulfur dioxide is given as −10°C and the melting point as −72.7°C under normal conditions. What is the physical state of sulfur dioxide under normal conditions?

☐ *Solution*

Sulfur dioxide both melts and boils below 20°C. It must then be a gas under normal conditions.

**Problem
1.15**

Under normal conditions, naphthalene melts at 80.5°C and boils at 218°C. What is the physical state of naphthalene at room temperature under normal conditions?

─── ■

4. Specific Heat

When energy in the form of heat is added to a sample, the resulting temperature change depends on the sample's mass and composition. We are aware of this dependence on composition when we notice that a piece of iron left in bright summer sunshine quickly becomes too hot to touch, whereas a sample of water having the same mass left in the same sunshine the same length of time as the piece of iron becomes only pleasantly warm. The difference is due to the differ- ence in composition of the two materials and is expressed quantitatively as the **specific heat** of each. The specific heat of a substance is the amount of energy required to change the temperature of a one gram sample one degree Celsius. It uses the unit calorie per gram degree Celsius (cal/g·°C), or joule per gram degree Celcius (J/g·°C).

The specific heat of iron is 0.1082 cal/g·°C (or 0.4525 J/g·°C). The quantity 0.1082 cal is needed to raise the temperature of 1 g of iron 1°C. The specific heat of water is 1 cal/g·°C (4.184 J/g·C), and 1 cal is required to change the temperature of 1 g of water 1°C. Each kind of matter has a unique specific heat.

Specific heat is a conversion factor that relates the amount of energy added to the sample, its mass, its composition, and its temperature change.

**Example
1.16**

How much energy is required to raise the temperature of 56 g of water from 20°C to 81°C?

☐ *Solution*

Wanted: The amount of energy needed (? cal).
Given: A 56-g sample and a temperature change of 61°C. We also know that the energy depends on both the mass of the sample and the size of the tem- perature change. We start the equation:

$$? \text{ cal} = 56 \text{ g} \times 61°C \times \text{conversion factor(s)}$$

Conversion factors: The specific heat of water is

$$\frac{1.00 \text{ cal}}{1.0 \text{ g} \times 1.0°C}$$

Equation:

$$? \text{ cal} = 56 \text{ g} \times 61°C \times \frac{1.00 \text{ cal}}{1.0 \text{ g} \times 1.0°C}$$

Answer:

$$? \text{ cal} = 3.416 \times 10^3 \text{ cal} = 3.4 \times 10^3 \text{ cal}$$

Problem 1.16

How much energy is needed to change the temperature of 235 g iron from 19°C to 85°C?

The specific heat of a substance can be calculated if we know the amount of energy needed to cause a measured temperature change in a sample of known mass.

Example 1.17

A sample of aluminum weighs 56 g. To raise the temperature of this sample from 22°C to 82°C, 712 cal is needed. Calculate the specific heat of aluminum.

☐ *Solution*

Specific heat has the units calories per gram · temperature change in °C. We are given a value for each of these quantities in the problem. Substituting them in the definition for specific heat gives

$$\text{Sp ht of aluminum} = \frac{712 \text{ cal}}{56 \text{ g} \times 60°C} = 0.21 \text{ cal/g·°C}$$

Problem 1.17

To raise the temperature of 29.5 g magnesium from 22°C to 157°C, 968 cal is needed. Calculate the specific heat of magnesium.

Key Terms and Concepts

accuracy (1.7A)

boiling point (1.9B3)

calorie (1.9B)

Celsius (1.9B1)

chemical property (1.4)

conversion factor (1.8A)

density (1.9A)

energy (1.5)

English system (1.6A)

exponential notation (1.7B)

Fahrenheit (1.9B1)

freezing point (1.9B3)

gas (1.4)

hypothesis (1.2A)

joule (1.9B)

Kelvin (1.9B1)

kinetic energy (1.5)

law of conservation of energy (1.5)

law of conservation of mass (1.3A)

law of conservation of mass/energy (1.5)

liquid (1.4)

mass (1.6B)

matter (1.1)

melting point (1.9B3)

meter (1.6A)

metric units (1.6A)

mixture (1.3C)

physical property (1.4)

physical states (1.4)

potential energy (1.5)

precision (1.7A)

prefixes (1.6A)

pure substance (1.3B)

rounding off (1.7C3)

scientific law (1.2A)

scientific method (1.2A)

scientific notation (1.7B)

significant figures (1.7C1)

SI prefixes (1.6A)

SI units (1.6A)

solid (1.4)

specific heat (1.9B4)

theory (1.2A)

weight (1.6B)

Problems

Scientific measurement (Section 1.6)

1.18 Carry out these conversions to metric units.
  a. 1.0 cup to milliliters (4 cups = 1.0 qt)
  b. 1.5 acres (1.0 acre = 4840 sq yd) to square meters
  c. $\frac{1}{4}$ lb to grams
  d. 100 yd to meters

1.19 Carry out these conversions. Be certain that your answers have the correct number of significant figures.
  a. 39 cm to inches   **b.** 145 g to pounds
  c. 13.0 yd to meters   **d.** 1.6 qt to liters

1.20 Carry out these conversions, giving answers with the correct number of significant figures.
  a. 6246 m to kilometers   **b.** 1963 g to milligrams
  c. 15,960 g to kilograms   **d.** 235,616 cm to meters

1.21 Express in the indicated metric units.
  a. $\frac{1}{2}$ gal milk in liters   **b.** 4.0 min/mile in minutes per kilometer
  c. 2.3 lb in kilograms   **d.** 7 ft 6 in. in meters

Recording measurements (Section 1.7)

1.22 Report these numbers in exponential notation using three significant figures.
  a. 160,502   **b.** 0.006,059   **c.** 132.419

1.23 Calculate the following and report your answers using the correct number of significant figures.
  a. $396 + 1.05 + 16\,203.526 + 2900 =$
  b. $14.70 \times 0.0025 \times 9.2 =$
  c. $29.62 - 1.009 =$
  d. $0.00159 + 0.01956 =$

Solving problems by unit analysis (Section 1.8)

1.24 Are you exceeding the speed limit if you are driving 97 km/hr in a 55-mi/hr zone?

1.25 A person weighs 96.4 kg and is 1.90 m tall. What are this person's weight and height as measured in the English system (ft, in., lb)?

1.26 Calculate your weight and height as measured in the metric system (kg, cm).

1.27 According to the Food and Nutrition Board of the National Research Council, the recommended weight for a woman 5 ft, 4 in. tall is 122 ± 10 lb. Calculate the woman's height in centimeters and her recommended range of weight in kilograms.

1.28 Driving in Europe, you plan to buy 6.3 gal of gasoline. The pump registers in the metric system. How many liters will you buy?

Density
(Section 1.9A)

1.29 Calculate the density of the samples described.

Mass	Volume	Density
13.6 g	21.9 mL	_____
4.6 g	1.2 L	_____
155.1 g	13.2 mL	_____
5.23 g	6.9 mL	_____

1.30 Calculate the missing quantity.

Mass	Volume	Density
_____	23 mL	1.45 g/mL
5.6 g	_____	0.831 g/mL
_____	11.4 mL	5.4 g/mL
_____	0.54 L	1.3 g/mL

1.31 A liquid weighing 19.8 g has a volume of 25 mL. Identify the liquid, using the data in Table 1.7.

1.32 A given sample of gas may be pure oxygen or it may be oxygen mixed with another gas. The sample weighs 2.75 g and has a volume of 2.40 L at 0°C and normal pressure. Is the sample pure oxygen? If not, does the other gas have a density greater or less than that of oxygen?

1.33 A sample of magnesium has a volume of 7.43 mL and a density of 1.74 g/mL. What is the mass of the sample?

1.34 At 20°C, the volume of a colorless liquid is 9.43 mL and its density is 0.789 g/mL. What is the mass of the sample? Could this liquid be water?

1.35 A piece of iron weighs 6.53 g and has a density of 7.86 g/cm^3. What is the volume of the iron?

Temperature
(Section 1.9B1)

1.36 Complete the temperature chart.

°F	°C	K
55	13	286
_____	165	_____
_____	_____	450
_____	−40	_____
−25	_____	_____

1.37 Normal body temperature is 98.6°F. What is normal body temperature on the Celsius scale? on the Kelvin scale?

1.38 If body temperature rises from 98.6°F to 104.6°F, how many Celsius degrees has the temperature risen?

1.39   The boiling point of benzene is 80.1°C. At what temperature on the Fahrenheit scale does benzene boil?

Specific heat
(Section 1.9B4)

1.40   The specific heat of ethyl alcohol is 0.581 cal/g·°C. How much energy is needed to raise the temperature of 75 g of ethyl alcohol from 21°C to 37°C (body temperature)?

1.41   The specific heat of magnesium is 0.235 cal/g·°C. How much energy must be added to 7.15 g of magnesium to raise its temperature by 15°C?

1.42   The average specific heat of dry air is 0.24 cal/g·°C.
   a. If 125 cal of heat is added to 75 g of dry air at 20°C, what is the final temperature of the air?
   b. The average specific heat of water is 1.00 cal/g·°C. If 125 cal is added to 75 g of water of 20°C, what is the final temperature of the water sample?
   c. Why are the temperature variations between day and night more extreme in a desert than near an ocean?

1.43   **a.** How many joules are required to raise the temperature of 15.6 g of water from 5°C to 15°C?
   b. How many calories are required to raise the temperature of 15.6 g of ice from −15°C to −5°C? Use 2.05 J/g·°C for the specific heat of ice.

1.44   How much energy must be removed from 555 g of water to cool the sample from 25°C to 0°C?

General
problems

1.45   A person has a mass of 113 lb. What volume (in liters) of mercury has the same mass?

1.46   The Earth is 9.29×10^7 miles from the sun.
   a. What is this distance in meters?
   b. If light travels 3.0×10^8 m/sec how long does it take light to travel from the sun to the Earth?

1.47   When "burned" as a metabolic fuel, 1 g of body fat is equivalent to 7.70 kcal of energy. How much energy must an adult use to lose the equivalent of 1 lb of body fat?

1.48   Jojoba wax has a density of 0.864 g/mL. What is the volume of 10.0 lb jojoba wax? The melting point of jojoba wax is 11.2°C. What is its physical state at room temperature under normal conditions?

1.49   Pure ammonia melts at −78°C and boils at −33°C. Under normal conditions, 10.0 L ammonia has a mass of 7.710 g. What is the density of pure ammonia and its physical state under normal conditions? Is liquid household ammonia a pure substance?

1.50   The rocket fuel hydrazine melts at 1.4°C and boils at 113.5°C. The mass of 25.00 mL of hydrazine is 25.3 g. What is the density of hydrazine and its physical state at room temperature under normal conditions?

1.51   Chicago declares an ozone alert when the concentration of ozone in the air reaches 137 micrograms (μg) per cubic meter.
   a. Express this ozone concentration in micrograms per liter (μg/L) and nanograms per liter (ng/L).

b. The lung capacity per breath of an adult is about 2 qt. What is the mass of ozone taken into the lungs per breath by an adult breathing air containing 137 μg ozone per cubic meter of air?

1.52 For an adult in good health on an adequate diet, the concentration of ascorbic acid (vitamin C) in the blood is about 0.2 mg/100 mL of blood.

a. What is this concentration in grams per liter? in milligrams per milliliter?

b. The average person has about 5 L blood. Calculate the total number of milligrams of ascorbic acid in the blood of a healthy adult who has an adequate diet.

c. According to the National Research Council, the recommended daily allowance for ascorbic acid is 45 mg. How does this compare with the milligrams of ascorbic acid in the blood of a healthy adult who has an adequate diet?

Elements and Atoms

From a chemist's point of view, matter in its simplest form exists as elements. Throughout the universe, elements are found in different concentrations, different physical states, and different combinations or compounds. Elements exist as atoms. Modern atomic theory was born in 1803, when Dalton published his postulates concerning the existence and behavior of atoms. Since then many scientists, using the results of ingenious experiments, have refined and elaborated those postulates. We now have a model structure for atoms that describes their composition and explains the relationship between atoms of different elements. Closely related to atomic structure is radioactivity and the changes that atomic nuclei can undergo.

2.1 Elements, Compounds, and Mixtures

A pure substance can be either an element or a compound. **Elements** are those pure substances that cannot be decomposed by ordinary chemical means such as heating, electrolysis, or reaction. Gold, silver, and oxygen are elements. They cannot be decomposed by ordinary chemical reaction. **Compounds** are pure substances formed by the combination of elements. Compounds can be decomposed. Baking soda (Section 1.3B) is a compound; it contains the elements sodium, hydrogen, carbon, and oxygen. On being heated, it decomposes. Water is another compound. It contains the elements hydrogen and oxygen; it can be decomposed by electrolysis but not by heating.

Compounds differ from mixtures. The elements in a compound are held together by chemical bonds. The components of a mixture are not joined by any chemical bonds and can be separated one from the other because of differences in physical properties. A mixture of salt and sand can be separated because the two components differ in their solubilities in water (a physical property). If water is added to the mixture, the salt will dissolve. The sand will remain undissolved. The elements that compose a compound can never be separated by such a simple procedure. The elements of baking soda—sodium, hydrogen, carbon and oxygen—differ in their solubility in water, but baking soda does not separate into these elements when added to water.

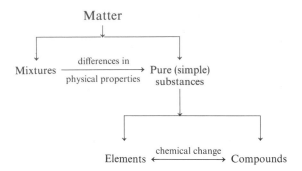

Figure 2.1 Different kinds of matter.

Figure 2.1 shows the relationships among the different kinds of matter. Notice that mixtures can be separated into their components by differences in physical properties. Compounds can be separated into their components only by chemical change.

2.2 Atoms; The Atomic Theory

By the late 1700s, it was well established that each pure substance had its own characteristic set of properties, such as density, specific heat, melting point, and boiling point. It was also established that certain quantitative relationships, such as the law of conservation of mass, governed all chemical changes. But there was still no understanding of the nature of matter itself. Was matter continuous, like a ribbon from which varying amounts could be snipped, or was it granular, like a string of beads from which only whole units or groups of units could be removed? Some scientists believed strongly in the continuity of matter, and others believed equally strongly in granular matter. Despite the conviction, both opinions were reasoned solely from speculation and philosophy.

In 1803, an English schoolmaster named John Dalton (1766–1844) proposed a theory of matter based on his work with gases. The postulates of his theory, changed only slightly from their original statement, form the basis of modern **atomic theory**. Today, we express these four postulates as follows:

1. Matter is made up of tiny particles called **atoms**. A typical atom has a mass of approximately 10^{-23} g and a radius of approximately 10^{-10} m. Atoms are made up of even smaller particles (see Section 2.5A) and some decompose by a process called radioactive disintegration.

2. There are over 100 different kinds of atoms; each kind is an element. A list of the elements is on the inside cover of this textbook. All the atoms of a particular element are alike chemically but can vary slightly in mass and other physical properties.

3. Atoms of different elements combine in small, whole-number ratios to form compounds. Hydrogen and oxygen atoms combine in the ratio 2:1 to form the compound water. Carbon and oxygen atoms combine in the ratio 1:2 to form the compound carbon dioxide. Iron and oxygen atoms combine in the ratio 2:3 to form the familiar substance rust.

4. Atoms of the same two elements may combine in different whole-number ratios to form different compounds. Whereas hydrogen and oxygen atoms combine in a ratio of 2:1 to form water, they also combine in a 1:1 ratio to form hydrogen peroxide (Figure 2.2). Carbon and oxygen atoms combine in a 1:2 ratio to form carbon dioxide; they also combine in a 1:1 ratio to form carbon monoxide.

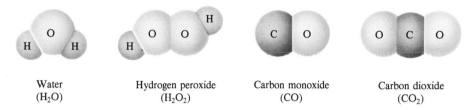

| Water (H_2O) | Hydrogen peroxide (H_2O_2) | Carbon monoxide (CO) | Carbon dioxide (CO_2) |

Figure 2.2 Atoms of the same elements combine in different ratios to form different compounds.

2.3 Elements

Approximately 110 elements are now known. Of these, 106 had been unequivocally characterized and accepted by the International Union of Pure and Applied Chemistry (IUPAC) by 1980.

A. Names and Symbols

Each element has a name. Many of these are already familiar to you; gold, silver, copper, chlorine, platinum, carbon, oxygen, and nitrogen are elements. Many of the names of the elements refer to a property of the element. The Latin name for gold is *aurum*, from the Latin word *aurora*, which means "bright dawn." The Latin name for mercury, *hydrargyrum*, means "liquid silver." Cesium was discovered in 1860 by the German chemist Robert Bunsen (the inventor of the Bunsen burner). Because this element imparts a blue color to a flame, Bunsen named it *cesium*, from the Latin word *caesius*, meaning "sky blue." Other elements are named for people. Curium is named for Marie Curie (1867–1934), pioneer in the study of radioactivity. Madame Curie, a French scientist of Polish birth, was awarded the Nobel Prize in physics in 1903 for her studies of radioactivity. She was also awarded the Nobel Prize in chemistry in 1911 for her discovery of the elements polonium (name after Poland) and radium (Latin, *radius*, "ray"). Some elements are named for places. One small town in Sweden, Ytterby, has four elements named for it: terbium, yttrium, erbium, and ytterbium. Californium is another example of an element named for its place of discovery. This element does not occur in nature. It was first produced in 1950, by a team of scientists headed by Glenn Seaborg, in the Radiation Laboratory at the University of California, Berkeley. Seaborg was the first to identify curium at the metallurgical laboratory of the University of Chicago, now Argonne National Laboratory, in 1944. Seaborg himself became a Nobel laureate in 1951 in honor of his pioneering work in the preparation of hitherto unknown elements.

Each element has a **symbol**, one or two letters that represent the element, much as your initials represent you. The symbol of an element stands for one atom of that element. For fourteen of the elements, the symbol is one letter. You are probably familiar with the names of most of these elements. They are

B	boron	W	tungsten	P	phosphorus
F	fluorine	V	vanadium	S	sulfur
I	iodine	C	carbon	U	uranium
O	oxygen	H	hydrogen	Y	yttrium
K	potassium	N	nitrogen		

For twelve of the elements, the symbol is the first letter of the name. The symbol K of potassium comes from *kalium*, the Latin word for "potash." Potassium was first isolated in 1807 from potash. Tungsten, discovered in 1783, has the symbol W, from wolframite, the mineral from which tungsten was first isolated.

Most other elements have two-letter symbols. In these two-letter symbols, the first letter is always capitalized and the second is always lowercase.

Those few elements with three-letter symbols are in the accompanying chart.

Name	Symbol	Atomic Number
unnilquadium	Unq	104
unnilpentium	Unp	105
unnilhexium	Unh	106
unnilseptium	Uns	107
unnilennium	Une	109

In these names, *unnil* stands for 100, and the rest of the name represents the Latin word for the number; *quad* means 4, *pent* means 5, and so on. This system, recently established by IUPAC, means that new elements can now be named systematically. Unfortunately, it also means we can no longer name new elements for the persons and places identified with their discovery to commemorate them, as in the past.

B. Lists of the Elements

As you study chemistry, you will often need a list of the elements. In this book there are two such lists. You will find the elements listed alphabetically by name on the inside back cover. The list includes the symbol of the element, its atomic number and its atomic weight. (The significance of atomic numbers and weights will be discussed later in this chapter.) Each element has a number called its atomic number, which is between 1 and 110. This number, like its name or symbol, is unique to the element. The second list, called the **periodic table**, arranges the elements in order of increasing atomic number in rows of varying length. (The significance of the length of the row and the relation among elements in the same row or column will be discussed in Chapter 3.) This table is on the inside front cover of this textbook.

Figure 2.3 shows the periodic table with the symbols of only some elements. These are the symbols of the elements you will most often encounter.

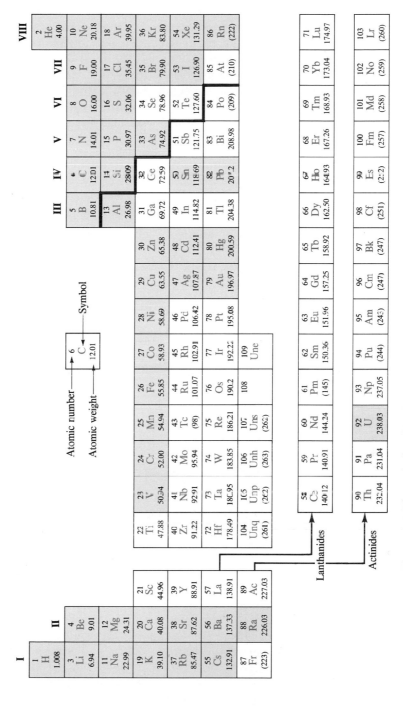

Figure 2.3 The periodic table of the elements. The symbols of the most common elements appear in the screened areas.

Metals are below and to the left of the heavy stair-step line that crosses the table diagonally from boron, B, to astatine, At. The elements above and to the right of this line are nonmetallic. The characteristic properties of a **metal** are its shine, or luster, its capacity to conduct heat and electricity, and its ductility and malleability. All but mercury are solids at 20°C. Mercury melts at −39°C and is a liquid at room temperature. Two others, gallium and cesium, have melting points close to room temperature (29.8°C and 28.4°C).

Nonmetals vary more in their properties than metals do; some even have one or more of the metallic properties listed above. Some nonmetals, like chlorine and nitrogen, are gaseous. One is a liquid (bromine); and others are solids—for example, carbon, sulfur, and phosphorus.

Example 2.1

Give the symbol of the following elements. Tell whether each is a metal or a nonmetal. If it is a metal, tell its physical state at 20°C.

a. fluorine   **b.** bismuth   **c.** potassium

☐ *Solution*

The symbol of the element is found in the alphabetical list of elements. Notice that the symbol for potassium is K, not P. Now find the elements on the periodic table. Note that both bismuth and potassium are below the diagonal line; therefore they are metals. Fluorine is a nonmetal, as it is above the line. Since mercury is the only metal liquid at 20°C, potassium and bismuth must be solids at 20°C. We can make a chart.

Name	Symbol	Character	Physical State
fluorine	F	nonmetal	no way of knowing
bismuth	Bi	metal	solid
potassium	K	metal	solid

Note that fluorine is the only element in its column of the periodic table to have a single letter for its symbol.

Problem 2.1

List the symbols of the following elements. Tell whether each is a metal or a nonmetal. If it is a metal, tell its physical state at 20°C.

a. strontium   **b.** phosphorus   **c.** chromium

C. Distribution

The known elements are not equally distributed throughout the world. Only 91 are found in the Earth's crust, oceans, and atmosphere; the others have been produced in laboratories. Traces of some but not all of these latter elements have been found on Earth or in stars. The search for them in nature continues; you may sometime read of its success. Figure 2.4 shows the most common elements and the percentage of each in the Earth's crust. The biologically important elements, those found in a normal, healthy body, are listed in Table 2.1. The

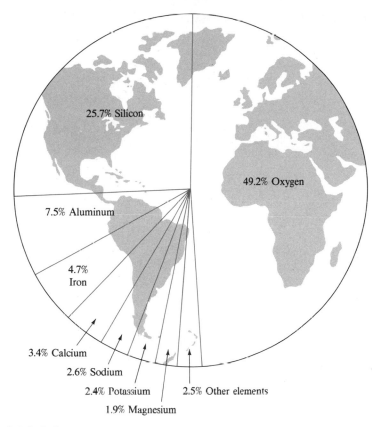

Figure 2.4 Relative percentages by mass of elements in the Earth's crust, oceans, and atmosphere.

Table 2.1
Biologically
important
elements.

Major Elements	Approximate Amount (kg) in 70-kg Man	Elements Present in Less Than 1-mg Amounts in 70-kg Man (in Alphabetical Order)
oxygen	45.5	arsenic
carbon	12.6	chromium
hydrogen	7.0	cobalt
nitrogen	2.1	copper
calcium	1.0	fluorine
phosphorus	0.70	iodine
magnesium	0.35	manganese
potassium	0.24	molybdenum
sulfur	0.18	nickel
sodium	0.10	selenium
chlorine	0.10	silicon
iron	0.003	vanadium
zinc	0.002	

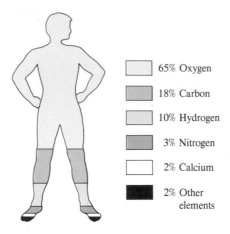

Figure 2.5 Distribution (by mass) of elements in the human body.

first four of these elements—carbon, oxygen, hydrogen, and nitrogen—make up about 96% of total body weight (see Figure 2.5). The other elements listed in Table 2.1, although present in only trace (tiny) amounts, are nonetheless necessary for good health.

2.4 How Atoms Occur in Nature

Elements occur as single atoms or as groups of chemically bonded atoms. (See Chapter 4.) Such groups are called **molecules**. Molecules may contain atoms of a single element; or they may contain atoms of different elements, in which case the molecule is of a compound. Just as an atom is the smallest unit of an element, a molecule is the least unit of a compound—the smallest unit that has the chemical identity of that compound. Let us consider how elements are found in the universe.

A. Noble Gases

Only a few elements are found as single uncombined atoms. Table 2.2 lists these elements. Under normal conditions all these elements are gases; collectively, they are known as the **noble gases**. They are also known as monatomic gases,

Table 2.2
The noble gases.

Name	Symbol
helium	He
neon	Ne
argon	Ar
krypton	Kr
xenon	Xe
radon	Rn

meaning that they exist uncombined as single atoms (*mono* means "one"). The formula of one of the noble gases is then simply its symbol. When the formula of helium is required, the symbol of helium, He, is used. The subscript 1 is understood.

B. Metals

Pure metals are treated as if they existed as single uncombined atoms even though a sample of pure metal is an aggregate of billions of atoms. Thus, when the formula of copper is required, its symbol, Cu, is used, meaning one atom of copper.

C. Nonmetals

Some nonmetals exist under normal conditions of temperature and pressure as molecules containing two, four, or eight atoms. Those found as **diatomic** (two-atom) **molecules** are listed in Table 2.3. Thus, when the formula of oxygen is needed, we use O_2; of nitrogen, N_2, and so on. For the other nonmetals, such as sulfur, which exists as S_8, and phosphorus, which is found as P_4, and others not listed in Tables 2.2 and 2.3, we can use a monatomic formula—that is, S for sulfur, P for phosphorus, and Se for selenium.

Table 2.3
Diatomic
elements.

Name	Formula	Normal State
hydrogen	H_2	colorless gas
nitrogen	N_2	colorless gas
oxygen	O_2	colorless gas
fluorine	F_2	pale yellow gas
chlorine	Cl_2	greenish yellow gas
bromine	Br_2	dark red liquid
iodine	I_2	violet black solid

Example 2.2

Tell whether each of the following elements is a metal or a nonmetal, and give its formula in the uncombined state.

a. iodine   **b.** calcium   **c.** carbon   **d.** xenon

Solution

To do this:

1. Look up the symbol of each element.
2. Find its location in the periodic table and decide whether the element is a metal or a nonmetal.
3. Look through the preceding discussion and determine into which category the element falls.

Name	Symbol	Character	Formula	Reference
iodine	I	nonmetal	I_2	Table 2.3
calcium	Ca	metal	Ca	Section 2.4B
carbon	C	nonmetal	C	Section 2.4C
xenon	Xe	nonmetal	Xe	Section 2.4A

Problem 2.2

Tell whether each of the following elements is a metal or nonmetal and give its formula in the uncombined state.

a. nitrogen   **b.** strontium   **c.** chromium   **d.** helium

D. Compounds

Although many elements can exist in the uncombined state, all except some of the noble gases are also found in compounds, combined with other elements. A compound was earlier defined (Section 2.1) as a substance that could be decomposed by ordinary chemical means. A compound can also be defined as a pure substance containing two or more elements. The composition of a compound is expressed by a **formula** containing the symbols of the elements combined in the compound. Each symbol is followed by a subscript indicating the number of atoms of the element in the simplest unit of the compound. The subscript 1 is understood and not shown. Water is a compound. It has the formula H_2O, meaning that one molecule of water contains two hydrogen atoms and one oxygen atom. The compound sodium bicarbonate has the formula $NaHCO_3$, meaning that a unit of sodium bicarbonate contains one atom of sodium, one atom of hydrogen, one atom of carbon, and three atoms of oxygen. Note that the symbols of the metals in sodium bicarbonate are written first, followed by the symbols of the nonmetals; the symbol of the nonmetal, oxygen, comes last. This order is customary.

Example 2.3

A molecule of hydrogen sulfide contains two atoms of hydrogen and one atom of sulfur. Write the formula for hydrogen sulfide.

☐ *Solution*

1. Write the symbols of each element: H   S.
2. Follow each symbol with a subscript indicating the number of atoms per molecule: H_2S.

Problem 2.3

Ethanol is composed of 2 atoms of carbon, 6 atoms of hydrogen, and 1 atom of oxygen. Write the formula for ethanol.

Example 2.4

The formula of glucose is $C_6H_{12}O_6$. What is the composition of a molecule of glucose?

☐ *Solution*   The symbols tell us which elements are contained in glucose: carbon, hydrogen, oxygen.

The subscripts tell how many atoms of each element are in each molecule of glucose: 6 atoms carbon, 12 atoms hydrogen, 6 atoms oxygen.

■
Problem 2.4   The formula of vinyl chloride is C_2H_3Cl. What is the composition of a molecule of vinyl chloride?

_____ ■

A compound has properties unlike those of the elements from which it is formed. This is apparent if we compare the properties of carbon dioxide (a colorless gas used in fire extinguishers) with the properties of carbon (a black, combustible solid) and of oxygen (a colorless gas necessary for burning). We will discuss the properties of compounds in greater detail in Chapter 4.

2.5 Composition of the Atom

An atom is very small. It has a mass between 10^{-21} and 10^{-23} g. A row of 10^7 atoms (10 million atoms) extends only 1.0 mm. Scientists have learned that atoms contain many different **subatomic particles**, such as electrons, protons, neutrons, mesons, neutrinos, quarks, and others. The atomic model used by chemists requires only knowledge of electrons, protons, and neutrons, so we limit our discussion to them.

A. Subatomic Particles

1. The Electron

An **electron** is a tiny particle with a negative charge and a mass of 9.108×10^{-28} g, a mass negligible compared with that of an atom. All neutral atoms contain electrons. The electron was discovered and its properties defined during the last quarter of the nineteenth century.

2. The Proton

The mass of a proton is 1.6726×10^{-24} g, or about 1845 times the mass of an electron. The **proton** carries a positive charge that is equal in magnitude to the charge of the electron but opposite in sign. As these charges are equal in size, we refer to them in relative terms; we say that the charge on an electron is -1 and the charge on a proton is $+1$. All atoms contain one or more protons.

3. The Neutron

The third subatomic particle of interest to us is the **neutron**. It has a mass of 1.6749×10^{-24} g, very close to that of the proton. A neutron carries no charge. Except for the lightest atoms of hydrogen, all atoms contain one or more neutrons.

Table 2.4
Properties of
proton, neutron,
and electron.

Particle	Mass (g)	Relative Mass (amu)	Relative Charge
proton	1.6726×10^{-24}	1.007	$+1$
neutron	1.6749×10^{-24}	1.008	0
electron	9.110×10^{-28}	5.45×10^{-4}	-1

The properties of these three subatomic particles are summarized in Table 2.4. The third column of this table lists the relative masses of these particles. Because the actual masses of atoms and subatomic particles are very small, we often describe them by comparison rather than in SI units. The relative mass means that if a proton is assigned a mass of 1.007, then a neutron has a mass of 1.008 and an electron a mass of 5.45×10^{-4}. When talking about relative masses, we often use the term *atomic mass unit* (amu). With this unit, a proton has a mass of 1.007 amu, a neutron a mass of 1.008 amu, and an electron a mass of 5.45×10^{-4} amu.

B. Atomic Numbers

The **atomic number** of an element equals the number of protons in one atom of the element. Atoms are electrically neutral; therefore the atomic number of an element also equals the number of electrons in its neutral atoms.

Different elements have different atomic numbers; atoms of different elements contain different numbers of protons (and electrons). Oxygen has the atomic number 8; its atoms contain 8 protons and 8 electrons. Uranium has the atomic number 92; its atoms contain 92 protons and 92 electrons.

The relationship between atomic number and protons and electrons can be stated as follows:

$$\text{Atomic number} = \text{number of protons per neutral atom}$$
$$= \text{number of electrons per neutral atom}$$

C. Mass Numbers

Each atom also has a mass number. The **mass number** of an atom equals the number of protons plus the number of neutrons it contains. In other words, the number of neutrons in any atom is its mass number minus its atomic number:

$$\text{Number of neutrons} = \text{mass number} - \text{atomic number}$$

or

$$\text{Mass number} = \text{number of protons} + \text{number of neutrons}$$

We frequently indicate the atomic number and the mass number of an atom of an element by writing the mass number as a superscript and the atomic number as a subscript, placing them both before the symbol of the element:

$$^{\text{mass number}}_{\text{atomic number}}\text{Symbol of the element}$$

For example, an atom of gold (symbol Au), atomic number 79, has a mass number of 196 and can be shown as:

$$^{196}_{79}\text{Au}$$

Example 2.5

Describe the composition of a silver atom, shown as

$$^{107}_{47}\text{Ag}$$

☐ *Solution*   The atomic number of the silver atom is given by the subscript 47; the atom therefore contains 47 protons and 47 electrons. The mass number of this atom is given by the superscript 107; the atom therefore contains 60 neutrons $(107 - 47)$.

Problem 2.5

Describe the composition of an atom of phosphorus, shown as

$$^{31}_{15}\text{P}$$

D. Isotopes

Although all atoms of a given element must have the same atomic number, they need not all have the same mass number. Some atoms of carbon (atomic number 6) have a mass number of 12, others have a mass number of 13, and still others have a mass number of 14. We refer to these different kinds of atoms as **isotopes**. Isotopes are atoms that have the same atomic number (and are therefore of the same element) but different mass numbers. The composition of atoms of the naturally occurring isotopes of carbon are shown in Table 2.5.

Table 2.5
Composition of the naturally occurring isotopes of carbon.

Isotope	Protons	Electrons	Neutrons
$^{12}_{6}\text{C}$	6	6	6
$^{13}_{6}\text{C}$	6	6	7
$^{14}_{6}\text{C}$	6	6	8

The various isotopes of an element can be designated by superscripts and subscripts to show mass number and atomic number, as in Table 2.5. They can also be identified by the name of the element with the mass number of the particular isotope. For example, instead of writing

$$^{12}_{6}\text{C}, \quad ^{13}_{6}\text{C}, \quad ^{14}_{6}\text{C},$$

we can write carbon-12, carbon-13, and carbon-14.

About 350 isotopes are found naturally on Earth and another 1500 have been produced artificially. The isotopes of a given element are by no means equally abundant. For example, 98.89% of all carbon in nature is carbon-12, 1.11% is carbon-13, and only a trace is carbon-14. Some elements occur as only

Table 2.6
Relative abundance of naturally occurring isotopes of several elements.

Isotope	Abundance (%)	Isotope	Abundance (%)
hydrogen-1	99.985	silicon-28	92.21
hydrogen-2	0.015	silicon-29	4.70
hydrogen-3	trace	silicon-30	3.09
carbon-12	98.89	phosphorus-31	100
carbon-13	1.11	chlorine-35	75.53
carbon-14	trace	chlorine-37	24.47
nitrogen-14	99.63	iron-54	5.82
nitrogen-15	0.37	iron-56	91.66
oxygen-16	99.76	iron-57	2.19
oxygen-17	0.037	iron-58	0.33
oxygen-18	0.204		
aluminum-27	100		

one isotope. Table 2.6 lists the naturally occurring isotopes of several common elements, along with their relative abundance.

Example 2.6

There are three isotopes of hydrogen: hydrogen-1 (protium); hydrogen-2 (deuterium); and hydrogen-3 (tritium). Give the symbol and atomic composition of each isotope.

□ *Solution*

$_1^1H$ 1 proton, 0 neutrons, 1 electron
$_1^2H$ 1 proton, 1 neutron, 1 electron
$_1^3H$ 1 proton, 2 neutrons, 1 electron

Problem 2.6

Naturally occurring uranium is 99.3% uranium-238 and 0.7% uranium-235. Give the composition of an atom of each of these isotopes of uranium.

2.6 Inner Structure of the Atom

So far, we have discussed electrons, protons, and neutrons and ways to determine how many of each a particular atom contains. The question now remains: Are these particles randomly distributed inside the atom like blueberries in a muffin, or does an atom have some organized inner structure? Scientists at the beginning of the twentieth century were trying to answer this question. Various theories had been proposed but none had been verified by experiment. In our discussion of the history of science we suggested that at various points in its development science has marked time until someone performs a key experiment that provides new insights. In the history of the study of atoms, a key experiment was performed in 1911 by Ernest Rutherford and his colleagues.

A. Rutherford's Experiment

In 1911, it was generally accepted that the atom contained electrons and protons and that these were probably not arranged in any set pattern. **Rutherford** wanted to establish whether there was a pattern. He hoped to gain this information by studying how the protons in an atom deflected the path of other charged particles through the atom. For his second particle, he chose alpha (α) particles. An alpha particle contains two protons and two neutrons, giving it a relative mass of 4 and a charge of $+2$. It is sufficiently close in mass and charge to the proton that it would be deflected from its path if it passed close to a proton.

In the experiment, a beam of alpha particles was directed at a piece of gold foil, so thin as to be translucent, and more important for Rutherford, only a few atoms thick. The foil was surrounded by a zinc sulfide screen that flashed each time it was struck by an alpha particle. By plotting the location of those flashes, he could determine how the path of the alpha particles through the atom was changed by the protons in the atom.

The three paths shown in Figure 2.6 (paths A, B, and C) represent those observed. Most of the alpha particles followed path A; they passed directly through the foil as if it were not there. Some were deflected slightly from their original path, as in path B; and an even smaller number bounced back from the foil as if they had hit a solid wall (path C).

You may be surprised that any alpha particles passed through the gold foil. Rutherford was not—he had expected that many would pass straight through (path A). He had also expected that because positively charged protons were present in the atom, some alpha particles would follow a slightly deflected

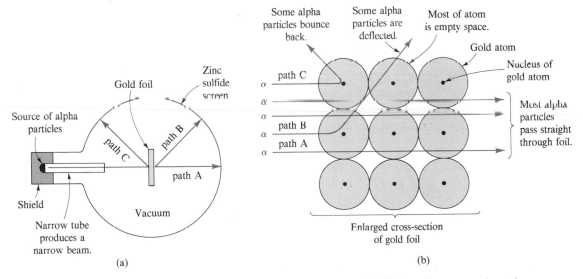

Figure 2.6 (a) Cross-section of Rutherford's apparatus. (b) Enlarged cross-section of the gold foil in the apparatus, showing the deflection of alpha particles by the nuclei of the gold atoms.

path (path *B*). That some alpha particles bounced back (path *C*) astounded Rutherford. Their action suggested that the particles had smashed into a region of dense mass and bounced back. To use Rutherford's analogy, the possibility of such a bounce was as unlikely as a cannonball bouncing off a piece of tissue paper.

B. Conclusions from Rutherford's Experiment

Careful consideration of the results and particularly of path *C* convinced Rutherford (and the scientific community) that an atom contains a very small, dense **nucleus** and a large amount of **extranuclear space**. According to Rutherford's theory, the nucleus contains all the mass of the atom and therefore all the protons and neutrons. The protons give the nucleus a positive charge. Because like charges repel each other, positively charged alpha particles passing close to the nucleus are deflected (path *B*). The nucleus, containing all the protons and neutrons, is more massive than an alpha particle. Therefore, an alpha particle striking the nucleus of a gold atom bounces back from the collision, like the alpha particles following path *C*.

Outside the nucleus, in the relatively enormous extranuclear space of the atom, are the tiny electrons. Because electrons are so small relative to the space they occupy, the extranuclear space of the atom is essentially empty. In Rutherford's experiment, alpha particles encountering this part of the atoms in the gold foil passed through the foil undeflected (path *A*).

If the nucleus contains virtually all the mass of the atom, it must be extremely dense. Its diameter is about 10^{-12} cm, about $\frac{1}{10,000}$ of that of the whole atom. By this model, if the nucleus were the size of a marble, the atom with its extranuclear electrons would be 300 m in diameter. If a marble had the same density as the nucleus of an atom, it would weigh 3.3×10^{10} kg.

The model of the atom based on Rutherford's work is, of course, no more than a model, for we cannot see these subatomic particles nor their arrangement within the atom. The model does, however, give us a way of thinking about the atom that coincides with observations about its properties. We can now determine not only what subatomic particles a particular atom contains, but also whether or not they are in its nucleus. For example, an atom of carbon-12, $^{12}_{6}C$, contains 6 protons and 6 neutrons in its nucleus and 6 electrons outside the nucleus.

Example 2.7

Iodine-131 is used in thyroid therapy. What is the composition of an atom of this iodine isotope? In which part of the atom are these particles?

☐ *Solution*

The atomic number of iodine is 53 (from the table of the elements). Therefore, an atom of iodine contains 53 protons in the nucleus and 53 electrons outside the nucleus. The mass number of this isotope is 131. Hence, in addition to 53 protons, the nucleus of an atom of iodine-131 contains $131 - 53 = 78$ neutrons.

Problem 2.7 Cobalt-60 is used in cancer therapy. What is the composition of an atom of this isotope? In which part of the atom are these particles?

We have then two distinct parts of an atom, the nucleus and the extranuclear space. The nucleus of an atom does not play any part in chemical reactions. The nucleus does participate in radioactive reactions. The chemistry of an atom depends on its electrons, how many there are and how they are arranged in the extranuclear space.

2.7 Atomic Weights

The **atomic weight** of an element measures the average mass of the naturally occurring atoms of that element. Both the periodic table and the alphabetical list of the elements show the atomic weights of the elements. Most elements have more than one naturally occurring isotope; atomic weights reflect this fact.

A collection of naturally occurring carbon atoms contains 98.89% carbon-12 atoms and 1.11% carbon-13 atoms, along with a trace percentage of carbon-14 atoms. The atomic weight of carbon (12.01) reflects the relative abundance of these three isotopes. The atomic weight of chlorine (35.45) reflects the fact that 75.53% of naturally occurring chlorine is chlorine-35 and 24.47% is chlorine-37.

For some elements, the atomic weight is given as a whole number enclosed by parentheses. These elements are unstable; their nuclei decompose radioactively. The number in parentheses is the mass number of the most stable, or best-known, isotope of that element.

Atomic weights are measured in atomic mass units. One **atomic mass unit** is one-twelfth the mass of an atom of carbon-12. By this standard, no element has an atomic weight less than unity.

2.8 The Mole

Atoms are very small, too small to be weighed or counted individually. Nevertheless, one often must know how many atoms (or molecules or electrons, and so on) a sample contains. To obtain this information, we use a counting unit called **Avogadro's number**, named after the Italian scientist Amadeo Avogadro (1776–1856).

$$\text{Avogadro's number} = 6.02 \times 10^{23}$$

Just as the number 12 is described by the term *dozen*, Avogadro's number is described by the term *mole*. A dozen eggs is 12 eggs; a mole of atoms is 6.02×10^{23} atoms. Avogadro's number can be used to count anything. You could have a mole of apples or a mole of Ping–Pong balls. You can get some idea of the magnitude of Avogadro's number when you realize that a mole of

Ping–Pong balls would cover the surface of the Earth with a layer approximately 60 miles thick.

Thus, one **mole** of a substance contains 6.02×10^{23} units of that substance. Equally important is the fact that one mole of a pure substance has a mass in grams numerically equal to the formula weight of that substance.

$$\text{Formula weight} = \frac{\text{grams}}{\text{mole}}$$

One mole of an element has a mass in grams equal to the atomic weight of the element and contains 6.02×10^{23} atoms of the element.

These definitions allow a new definition of atomic weight. The **atomic weight** of an element is the mass in grams of one mole of naturally occurring atoms of that element.

Using these relationships we can calculate the number of atoms in a given mass of an element or the mass of a given number of atoms.

Example 2.8

The atomic weight of antimony (Sb) is 121.87. How many moles of antimony are contained in 5.05 g of antimony?

☐ *Solution*

Wanted: Moles of antimony
Given: 5.05 g Sb
Conversion factor:

$$1 \text{ mol Sb} = 121.87 \text{ g Sb}$$

Equation:

$$? \text{ mol Sb} = 5.05 \text{ g Sb} \times \frac{1 \text{ mol Sb}}{121.87 \text{ g Sb}}$$

Answer: 0.0414 mol Sb

Problem 2.8

The atomic weight of carbon is 12.01. What is the mass of 1.62 mol of carbon?

Example 2.9

What mass of copper (Cu) contains 5.14×10^{22} atoms of copper?

☐ *Solution*

Wanted: Mass of copper
Given: 5.14×10^{22} atoms Cu
Conversion factors: 1 mol Cu weighs 63.54 g
                              1 mol contains 6.02×10^{23} atoms
Equation:

$$? \text{ g copper} = 5.14 \times 10^{22} \text{ atoms Cu} \times \frac{1 \text{ mol atoms}}{6.02 \times 10^{23} \text{ atoms}} \times \frac{63.54 \text{ g Cu}}{1 \text{ mol Cu}}$$

Answer: 5.43 g Cu

Problem 2.9

A sample of uranium contains 5.15×10^{20} atoms. What is the mass of the sample?

Example 2.10

Calculate the atoms of lead (Pb) in 4.26 lb lead.

☐ *Solution*

Wanted: ? atoms lead
Given: 4.26 lb Pb
Conversion factors:

> 1.00 lb = 453.6 g (Table 1.1)
> 1.00 mol Pb = 207.19 g Pb (atomic weight)
> 1.00 mol contains 6.02×10^{23} atoms (Avogadro's number)

Equation:

$$? \text{ atoms Pb} = 4.26 \text{ lb Pb} \times \frac{453.6 \text{ g}}{1.00 \text{ lb}} \times \frac{1.00 \text{ mol Pb}}{207.19 \text{ g Pb}} \times \frac{6.02 \times 10^{23} \text{ atoms}}{1.00 \text{ mol}}$$

$$= 5.61 \times 10^{24} \text{ atoms Pb}$$

Problem 2.10

Calculate the number of atoms in 9.86 lb copper.

2.9 Radioactivity

A. General Characteristics

From the discussions in the previous section, we know that the atoms of any element have two distinct parts: the nucleus that contains the protons and neutrons and the extranuclear space that contains the electrons. The electrons in the atom, particularly those farthest from the nucleus, determine the chemical properties of the element. We will discuss electrons and the chemical properties of elements in Chapter 3.

In the remainder of this chapter, we will describe properties of the nucleus and, in particular, the characteristics of radioactivity or radioactive decay of the nucleus. Nuclei of radioactive atoms decay spontaneously to form other nuclei. This process, called **radioactivity**, causes a loss of energy and often involves the release of one or more small particles. Some atoms are naturally radioactive. Others that are normally stable can be made radioactive by bombarding them with subatomic particles. Often, one isotope of an element is radioactive and others of the same element are stable.

Radioactivity is a common phenomenon. Of the 350 isotopes known to occur in nature, 67 are radioactive. Over a thousand radioactive isotopes have been produced in the laboratory. Every element has at least one natural or artificially produced radioactive isotope. Of the 3 known isotopes of hydrogen, only hydrogen-3, more commonly known as tritium, is radioactive. Oxygen, the Earth's most abundant element, has 8 known isotopes, 5 of which are radioactive (oxygen-13, -14, -15, -19, and -20). Iodine, an element widely used in nuclear medicine, has 22 known isotopes ranging in mass from 117 to 139. Of these, only iodine-127 is stable, and only this isotope is naturally occurring. Uranium has 14 known isotopes, all of which are radioactive.

B. Radioactive Emissions

Nuclei undergoing radioactive decay release various kinds of emissions. Three of these are alpha particles, beta particles, and gamma rays. All are forms of **ionizing radiation**, so called because their passage through matter leaves a trail of ions (Section 3.5C) and molecular debris.

1. Alpha Particles

An **alpha particle** is a helium atom stripped of its two electrons; that is, it contains 2 protons and 2 neutrons. Because there are no electrons to balance the positive charges of the 2 protons, an alpha particle has a charge of $+2$ and can be represented as He^{2+}. Another symbol for this particle is ^4_2He.

Alpha particles, when ejected from a decaying nucleus, interact with all matter in their path, whether it is photographic film, lead shielding, or body tissue. In their wake, the particles leave a trail of positive ions (atoms from which electrons have been removed) and free electrons. A single alpha particle, ejected at high speed from a nucleus, can create up to 100,000 ions along its path before it takes on 2 electrons to become a neutral helium atom.

In air, an alpha particle travels about 4 cm before gaining 2 electrons. Within body tissue, its average path is only a few thousandths of a centimeter. An alpha particle is unable to penetrate the outer layer of human skin. Because of this, external exposure to alpha particles is not nearly so serious as internal exposure. If a source of alpha emissions is taken internally, the alpha radiation can do massive damage to the surrounding tissue. For this reason, alpha emitters are never used in nuclear medicine. Notice in Table 2.10 that none of the radioisotopes widely used in nuclear medicine is an alpha emitter.

2. Beta Particles

A **beta particle** (β) is a high-speed electron ejected from a decaying nucleus; it carries a charge of -1. (Section 2.10A discusses how a nucleus can eject an electron even though it does not contain electrons.) A beta particle can be represented as

$$_{-1}^{0}e \qquad \text{or} \qquad _{-1}^{0}\beta$$

Like alpha particles, beta particles cause ionization by interacting with whatever matter is in their path. However, because they are far less massive than alpha particles and have only half the charge, beta particles produce less ionization and travel farther through matter before coming to rest in combination with a positive ion. A beta particle has a penetrating power of about 100 times that of an alpha particle. About 25 cm of wood, 1 cm of aluminum, or 0.5 cm of body tissue will stop a beta particle. The lower ionization levels of beta particles make them more suitable for use in radiation therapy, since the likelihood of damage to healthy tissue is greatly reduced. Beta emitters such as calcium-46, iron-59, cobalt-60, and iodine-131 are widely used in nuclear medicine.

3. Gamma Rays

The release of either alpha or beta particles from a decaying nucleus is generally accompanied by the release of nuclear energy in the form of **gamma rays** (γ):

$$_{0}^{0}\gamma$$

Gamma rays have no charge or mass and are equivalent to X-rays, except that they have higher energy. Even though gamma rays bear no charge, they can produce ionization as they pass through matter. Gamma rays penetrate matter to a very much greater extent than either alpha or beta particles. Gamma rays are easily detectable. Virtually all radioactive isotopes used in diagnostic nuclear medicine are gamma emitters. Each of the beta emitters listed in the previous paragraph is also a gamma emitter. Additional gamma emitters common in nuclear medicine include chromium-51, arsenic-74, technetium-99, and gold-198.

The characteristics of alpha particles, beta particles, and gamma rays are summarized in Table 2.7.

Table 2.7 Characteristics of radioactive emission.

Name	Symbol	Charge	Mass (amu)	Penetration of Matter
alpha particle	$_{2}^{4}\text{He}$ or $_{2}^{4}\alpha$	$+2$	4	air, 4.0 cm tissue, 0.005 cm lead, none
beta particle	$_{-1}^{0}e$ or $_{-1}^{0}\beta$	-1	5.5×10^{-4}	air, 6–300 cm tissue, 0.006–0.5 cm lead, 0.0005–0.03 cm
gamma ray	$_{0}^{0}\gamma$	0	0	air, 400 m tissue, 50 cm lead, 3 cm

2.10 Characteristics of Nuclear Reactions

A. Equations for Nuclear Reactions

Radioactivity is the decay or disintegration of the nucleus of an atom. During the process, either alpha or beta particles may be emitted. Energy, in the form of gamma rays, may also be released. All these characteristics and more can be shown by using an equation to describe the radioactive process.

A nuclear equation must be balanced with respect to mass, charge, and energy. First, the mass of the products (the sum of their mass numbers) must equal the mass of the reactants (the sum of their mass numbers). The mass lost by transformation to energy is negligible in these reactions. Second, the total charge of the reactants (the sum of their atomic numbers) must equal the total charge of the products (the sum of their atomic numbers).

Consider the equation for the decay of radium-226 to radon-222. Radium-226 is the reactant; radon-222, an alpha particle, and a gamma ray are the products. The equation is

$$\underset{\text{radium-226}}{^{226}_{88}\text{Ra}} \longrightarrow \underset{\text{radon-222}}{^{222}_{86}\text{Rn}} + \underset{\substack{\text{alpha}\\\text{particle}}}{^{4}_{2}\text{He}} + \underset{\text{energy}}{^{0}_{0}\gamma}$$

The superscripts show the mass numbers of the particles; the subscripts show their charges. (Note that these equations refer only to the nuclei of atoms.) The charge on each of these particles is its atomic number, the number of protons each contains. The equation is balanced with respect to mass, because the mass of the reactant (226) equals the sum of the masses of the products (4 + 222 + 0). The equation is balanced with respect to charge, because the atomic number of the reactant (88) equals the sum of the atomic numbers of the products (86 + 2 + 0). The energy change accompanying the reaction is accounted for by the release of gamma rays.

A similar equation can be written for nuclear decay by beta emission. Iodine-131 is a beta emitter often used in nuclear medicine. The equation for its decay is

$$^{131}_{53}\text{I} \longrightarrow {}^{131}_{54}\text{Xe} + {}^{0}_{-1}\beta + {}^{0}_{0}\gamma$$

Note that both charge and mass are balanced, and that iodine-131 emits a gamma ray at the same time it emits the beta particle. For this reason, iodine-131 is known as a beta-gamma emitter. Carbon-14, the isotope widely used in radiodating archaeological artifacts containing carbon, is also a beta emitter:

$$^{14}_{6}\text{C} \longrightarrow {}^{14}_{7}\text{N} + {}^{0}_{-1}\beta$$

In the decay of carbon-14, only a beta particle is emitted. The energy released by the reaction is not intense enough to be called a gamma ray. Carbon-14 is therefore known as a pure beta emitter. Phosphorus-32 is also a pure beta emitter.

How can nuclei give off beta particles, which are actually electrons, if there are no electrons in the nucleus? The process is not understood, but it may occur through the disintegration of a neutron to form a proton and the emitted electron:

$$\text{Neutron} \longrightarrow \text{proton} + \text{electron}$$

The electron is ejected and the proton remains in the nucleus. In beta emission, the product nucleus has an atomic number greater by 1 than that of the reactant nucleus, because the nucleus now contains one more proton. The product nucleus has approximately the same mass as the reactant nucleus, because an electron's mass is negligible relative to the mass of a proton.

Emission of a gamma ray changes the mass of the nucleus only marginally and the charge not at all. It accompanies the rearrangement of a nucleus from

Table 2.8
Changes resulting
from radiation
emission.

Radiation Emitted	Atomic Number Change	Mass Number Change
alpha particle	-2	-4
beta particle	$+1$	0
gamma ray	0	0

an unstable, more energetic nuclear configuration to a more stable, less energetic form. The identity and mass of the nucleus stay the same. The changes caused by the emission of the three types of radiation are summarized in Table 2.8.

From the atomic number and mass number of a radioactive isotope and the type of radiation emitted during its decay, it is an easy matter to predict the mass number, atomic number, and identity of the new element formed.

Example 2.11

Cobalt-60 decays by emission of a beta particle. Predict the atomic number, mass number, and name of the isotope formed.

☐ *Solution*

First, write an equation showing the radioactive decay.

$$^{60}_{27}\text{Co} \longrightarrow {}^{\text{mass number}}_{\text{atomic number}}\text{element} + {}^{0}_{-1}\beta$$

Second, determine the mass number and atomic number of the new isotope. Since mass number is unchanged in beta emission, the isotope formed must also have the mass number 60. The atomic number increases by 1 in beta emission; the isotope formed must have an atomic number of 28. We can write

$$^{60}_{27}\text{Co} \longrightarrow {}^{60}_{28}\text{element} + {}^{0}_{-1}\beta$$

Consult a table of the elements and find the element whose atomic number is 28. This is the atomic number of nickel. The complete equation for the radioactive decay of cobalt-60 is

$$^{60}_{27}\text{Co} \longrightarrow {}^{60}_{28}\text{Ni} + {}^{0}_{-1}\beta$$

Problem 2.11

Radium-226 decomposes with the loss of an alpha particle. Write the equation for this reaction and identify the element formed.

B. Half-Life

The rate of decay of a radioactive isotope (also called a radioisotope) is measured in terms of its half-life. **Half-life** is defined as the length of time required for one-half of the sample to decay. Half-lives vary from fractions of a second for some isotopes to billions of years for others. Table 2.9 lists half-lives and modes of decay for several isotopes.

Table 2.9
Half-lives of some
radioisotopes.

Isotope	Emissions	Half-Life
carbon-14	$_{-1}^{0}\beta$	5730 yr
cobalt-60	$_{-1}^{0}\beta, \, _{0}^{0}\gamma$	5.26 yr
gold-198	$_{-1}^{0}\beta, \, _{0}^{0}\gamma$	2.7 days
iodine-131	$_{-1}^{0}\beta, \, _{0}^{0}\gamma$	8.1 days
iron-59	$_{-1}^{0}\beta, \, _{0}^{0}\gamma$	45.1 days
molybdenum-99	$_{-1}^{0}\beta, \, _{0}^{0}\gamma$	67.0 hr

Iodine-131 has a half-life of 8.1 days. If you start today with a sample containing 25 mg of iodine-131, after 8.1 days that sample will contain only 12.5 mg of iodine-131. At the end of 16.2 days, the sample will contain only 6.2 mg of iodine-131. Of course, the matter in the sample does not gradually disappear; instead it changes to xenon-131, the product of the radioactive decay of iodine-131. Figure 2.7 shows the amounts of iodine-131 remaining after the passage of several half-lives, given an initial sample containing 25 mg of the isotope.

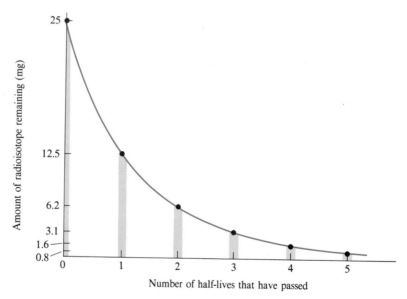

Figure 2.7 Decay of iodine-131 as a function of time.

Knowing the identity of the radioisotope, its half-life, and the type of radiation it emits, you can calculate the identity of the product and the amount formed in a given period.

Phosphorus-32 is a beta emitter with a half-life of 14.3 days.

**Example
2.12**

a. Write the equation for the radioactive disintegration of phosphorus-32.

$$_{15}^{32}\text{P} \longrightarrow \, _{-1}^{0}\beta + \, ?$$

b. A package containing 5 mg of phosphorus-32 was shipped at 5:00 A.M. on October 1, 1986, but did not arrive at its destination until 7:30 P.M. on October 29, 1986. How much phosphorus-32 did the package contain on arrival?

☐ *Solution*

a. In beta emission, the mass number remains the same and the atomic number increases by 1. The element with atomic number 16 is sulfur. Thus, the equation is

$$^{32}_{15}P \longrightarrow \, ^{\,\,0}_{-1}\beta + \, ^{32}_{16}S$$

b. How many half-lives have elapsed?

$$28 \text{ days} + 14.5 \text{ hr} = 28.6 \text{ days}$$

$$28.6 \text{ days} \times \frac{1 \text{ half-life}}{14.3 \text{ days}} = 2 \text{ half-lives}$$

Five milligrams of phosphorus-32 would decrease by half during one half-life (to 2.50 mg) and by another half in the second half-life. Therefore, only one-fourth (1.25 mg) of the original sample would be phosphorus-32; the rest would be sulfur-32.

Problem 2.12

Strontium-90, an important product of the disintegration of uranium, decays by beta emission and has a half-life of 28 yr. The equation for its decay is

$$^{90}_{38}Sr \longrightarrow \, ^{90}_{39}Y + \, ^{\,\,0}_{-1}\beta$$

Once absorbed into the bones, strontium-90 emits beta rays, damaging the bone marrow. The maximum permissible dose of strontium-90 for an adult is 6.9×10^{-9} g. If an adult received this dose at age 20, and if it were all incorporated in bone tissue, what mass of strontium-90 would be found after death at the age of 76?

2.11 Applications of Radioactivity

Radioisotopes are widely used in chemistry, biology, medicine, and many other areas of science and industry. All these uses balance the good and bad aspects of the characteristics of radioisotopes and nuclear decomposition listed here:

1. A radioisotope has exactly the same chemical properties and reactions as those of a nonradioactive isotope of the same element.
2. Radiation can be detected some distance from its source.
3. Each radioisotope has a characteristic half-life.
4. Radioactive emissions interfere with normal cell growth.

Several uses of radioisotopes illustrate ways in which they can provide information that it would be difficult or impossible to get by any other means.

A. Tracers

Because a radioisotope has chemical properties and reactions exactly the same as those of a nonradioactive isotope of the same element, a radioisotope can be substituted for a stable isotope of the same element in a molecule or compound, without changing the chemical properties of the compound. Such a compound is said to be tagged, or labeled. Since the radiation emitted by the radioisotope can be detected some distance from the radiating atom, the progress of those atoms through the body can be followed, or traced. Such labeled compounds are called **tracers**.

Radioactive tracers are used in medicine for diagnosis. For example, both chromium-51, in the form of sodium chromate, Na_2CrO_4, and iron-59, in the form of iron citrate, $FeC_6H_6O_7$, are routinely used in determining red-blood-cell volume, the rates of red-blood-cell production and destruction, and iron metabolism. Sodium chromate is used because it is soluble in blood, easily penetrates the red-blood-cell membrane, and then becomes firmly attached to hemoglobin molecules within the red blood cell. Iron can also be used, because it is a natural component of hemoglobin molecules. To estimate the survival time of red blood cells, a blood sample is taken from a patient, the red blood cells are tagged with chromium-51, and the sample is reinjected. Samples of blood are withdrawn after 24 hr and then every 3–4 days to determine the time required for the blood radioactivity to fall to half of its initial value. This time, corrected for the amount of decay of the chromium-51, represents the half-life of red blood cells. These studies show that the half-life of a red blood cell averages 29 days in a normal adult in good health. A knowledge of red-blood-cell survival time

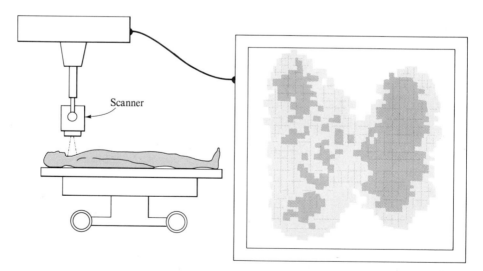

Figure 2.8 The uptake of iodine by the thyroid gland can be measured by tracing atoms of the radioisotope iodine-131. The plot at the right shows the location in the thyroid of the source of each radioactive emission detected by the counter. Note that radioactivity counts show more iodine in one lobe of the thyroid gland than in the other.

can be very valuable to the physician in diagnosing and treating cases of un-explained anemia.

Iodine-131 is the radioisotope most commonly used for studying iodine metabolism in humans. The thyroid gland has a remarkable ability to extract iodine from the bloodstream and use it to produce the thyroid hormones thyroxine, T4, and triiodothyronine, T3. These two hormones directly affect the body's metabolism. Very small amounts of iodine-131, in the form of sodium iodide, can be injected into the bloodstream and within minutes begin to con-centrate in the thyroid gland. It is possible, by monitoring the accumulation of radioactivity, to estimate the size and shape of the thyroid gland and to determine whether any part of it is functioning abnormally (Figure 2.8).

Several other radioisotopes often used in nuclear medicine are listed in Table 2.10. Notice that all have comparatively short half-lives and that all are beta-gamma or pure gamma emitters, a requirement for radioisotopes used in medicine.

Table 2.10
Radioisotopes for clinical diagnosis.

Radioisotope	Radiation Emitted	Half-Life	Object of Study
cobalt-57	$_{-1}^{0}\beta, {_0^0}\gamma$	270 days	absorption, storage, and metabolism of vitamin B-12
iodine-131	$_{-1}^{0}\beta, {_0^0}\gamma$	8.1 days	thyroid activity and iodine metabolism
iron-59	$_{-1}^{0}\beta, {_0^0}\gamma$	45.1 days	red blood cells
molybdenum-99	$_{-1}^{0}\beta, {_0^0}\gamma$	67 hr	general metabolism
phosphorus-32	$_{-1}^{0}\beta, {_0^0}\gamma$	14.3 days	liver function
strontium-87	${_0^0}\gamma$	2.8 hr	bone metabolism
technetium-99	${_0^0}\gamma$	6.0 hr	bones, liver, lungs
xenon-133	$_{-1}^{0}\beta, {_0^0}\gamma$	5.27 days	lungs, emphysema

B. Biological Effects of Radiation

While the exact manner in which radiation causes damage to tissues and cells is not fully understood, it is clear that cellular damage can occur any time alpha, beta, or other ionizing radiation (Section 2.9B) passes through the cell. The effects of ionizing radiation range from minor damage in specific molecules to the death of the cell. Ionizing radiation is especially damaging to the cell nucleus, particularly to nuclei undergoing rapid division and to nuclei of younger, less mature cells. Many types of cancer cells are especially sensitive to gamma radiation because they are growing rapidly and are less mature than cells of surrounding noncancerous tissue. This sensitivity is the reason for using radiation to destroy cancer cells. The apparatus for such treatments is designed so that the radiation can be sharply focused on the cancer cells, thus minimizing damage to nearby healthy cells (Figure 2.9).

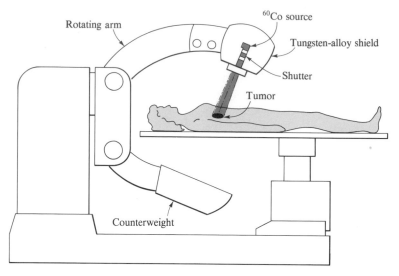

Figure 2.9 Cancer treatment with cobalt-60. The source moves along a circular track, rotating the radioactive beam around the patient, so that only the tumor receives continuous radiation.

2.12 Using Nuclear Reactions to Produce Energy

A. Fission

In Section 2.11 we listed four characteristics of radioactivity and nuclear decay that form the basis for the use of radioisotopes in the health and biological sciences. A fifth characteristic of nuclear reactions is that they release enormous amounts of energy. The first nuclear reactor to achieve controlled nuclear dis-integration was built in the early 1940s by Enrico Fermi and colleagues at the University of Chicago. Since then, much effort and expense have gone into de-veloping nuclear reactors as sources of energy. The nuclear reactions now used or under study by the nuclear power industry fall into two categories: fission and fusion. In **nuclear fission**, a large nucleus is split into two medium-sized nuclei. Only a few nuclei are known to undergo fission. Nuclear power plants currently in use depend primarily on the fission of uranium-235 and plutonium-239.

When a nucleus of U-235 undergoes fission, it splits into two smaller atoms and simultaneously releases neutrons and energy. Some of these neutrons are absorbed by other atoms of U-235. In turn, these atoms split apart, releasing more energy and more neutrons. A typical reaction is

$$^{235}_{92}\text{U} + ^{1}_{0}\text{n} \longrightarrow [^{236}_{92}\text{U}] \longrightarrow ^{139}_{56}\text{Ba} + ^{94}_{36}\text{K} + 3^{1}_{0}\text{n} + \text{energy}$$

Under proper conditions, the fission of a few nuclei of uranium-235 sets in motion a chain reaction (Figure 2.10), which can proceed with explosive violence if not controlled. In fact, this reaction is the source of energy in the atomic bomb.

In nuclear power plants, the energy released by the controlled fission of U-235 or other fissionable nuclei is collected in the reactor and used to produce steam

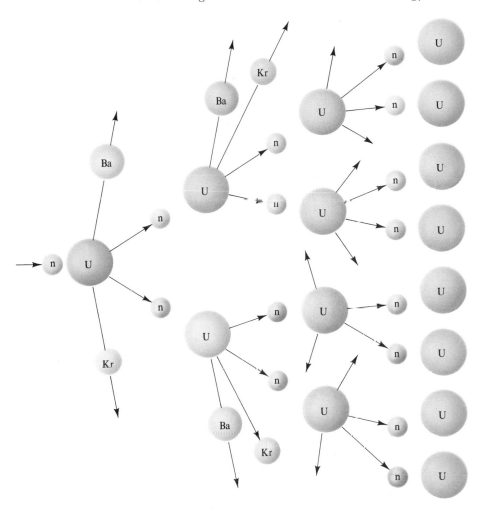

Figure 2.10 Diagram of a nuclear fission chain reaction. Each fission produces two (or more) neutrons that can react with other uranium atoms, so that the number of nuclear fissions soon reaches an enormous number.

in a heat exchanger. The steam then drives a turbine to produce electricity. Energy generation can be regulated by inserting control rods between the fuel rods in the reactor to absorb excess neutrons. Figure 2.11 shows a schematic diagram of a typical nuclear power plant.

The first nuclear power plant in this country to produce electricity for commercial use began operation in 1957 in Shippingport, Pennsylvania. A typical nuclear power plant in operation today uses about 2 kg of uranium-235 to generate 1000 megawatts (mW) of electricity. About 5000 metric tons of coal are needed to produce the same amount of electricity in a conventional power plant.

Uranium-235 (natural abundance 0.71%) is very scarce and its separation from uranium-238 (natural abundance 99.28%) is difficult. The much more abundant U-238 does not undergo fission and therefore cannot be used as a

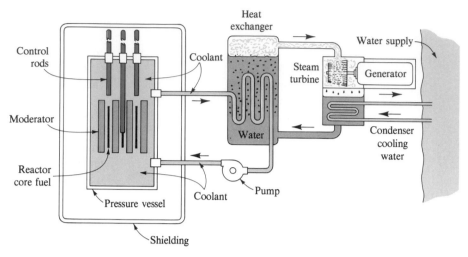

Figure 2.11 Diagram of a nuclear power plant.

fuel for nuclear reactors. However, if U-238 is bombarded with neutrons (from U-235, for example), it absorbs a neutron and is transformed into U-239. This isotope undergoes beta emission to generate neptunium-239, which in turn undergoes another beta emission, to produce plutonium-239:

$$^{238}_{92}U + ^{1}_{0}n \longrightarrow ^{239}_{92}U$$
$$^{239}_{92}U \longrightarrow ^{239}_{93}Np + ^{0}_{-1}\beta$$
$$^{239}_{93}Np \longrightarrow ^{239}_{94}Pu + ^{0}_{-1}\beta$$

Plutonium-239 also undergoes fission, with the production of more energy and more neutrons. These neutrons can then be used to breed more plutonium-239 from uranium-238. Thus, a so-called breeder reactor can produce its own supply of fissionable material. Several breeder reactors are now functioning in Europe.

Nuclear reactors using fissionable materials pose several serious dangers to the environment. First, there is always the chance that leaks, accidents, or acts of sabotage will release radioactive materials from the reactor into the environment. This has become a continuing concern, especially in this country, since the Three Mile Island nuclear-plant accident in March 1979. International concern about nuclear reactors rose in May 1986 as radioactive fallout spread across the globe within days of the disaster at the Chernobyl reactor in the Soviet Union. A second danger is that many of the products of nuclear fission are themselves radioactive. The radioactivity from spent nuclear fuel and from the products of nuclear fission will remain lethal for thousands of years, and the safe disposal of these materials is a problem that has not yet been solved. Obsolete generating plants will also present a problem to future generations, for they too will contain much radioactive material. One suggestion has been to encase such plants in concrete for 100 or more years. This may become necessary, but it is hardly a simple or permanent solution.

B. Fusion

Nuclear fusion, the other process currently under study for the generation of atomic energy, depends on putting together or fusing two nuclei to form a single nucleus. One of the most promising fusion reactions generates energy by the fusion of two deuterium atoms to form an atom of helium-3:

$$\mathrm{^2_1H + ^2_1H \longrightarrow {}^3_2He + {}^1_0n + energy}$$

Reactions such as this require enormous amounts of energy to force the two positively charged nuclei close enough together to fuse. Once the nuclei fuse, however, much more energy is released than is needed for the reaction. Nuclear fusion occurs in the core of the sun, where the temperature is approximately 40 million degrees Celsius. Unfortunately, scientists have not yet found a way to produce and control nuclear fusion on Earth. Controlled nuclear fusion produces almost no radioactive wastes and would therefore be a nonpolluting source of energy. A massive effort is going on in this country and abroad to find ways to harness this energy source. It would, however, be foolish to think that this or any other method of producing energy is going to be without problems.

Key Terms and Concepts

alpha particles (2.9B1)

atomic mass unit (amu) (2.7)

atomic number (2.5B)

atomic theory (2.2)

atomic weight (2.7, 2.8)

atoms (2.2)

Avogadro's number (2.8)

beta particle (2.9B2)

compounds (2.1)

diatomic molecule (2.4C)

electron (2.5A1)

elements (2.1)

extranuclear space (2.6B)

formula (2.4D)

gamma rays (2.9B3)

half-life (2.10B)

ionizing radiation (2.9B)

isotope (2.5D)

mass number (2.5C)

metals (2.3B1)

mole (2.8)

molecule (2.4)

neutron (2.5A3)

noble gases (2.4A)

nonmetals (2.3B)

nuclear fission (2.12A)

nuclear fusion (2.12B)

nucleus of an atom (2.6B)

periodic table (2.3B)

proton (2.5A2)

radioactivity (2.9A)

Rutherford (2.6A)

subatomic particles (2.5)

symbols (2.3A)

tracers (2.11A)

Problems

2.13 State the postulates of the atomic theory.

2.14 Nitrogen and oxygen combine to form the compounds nitrogen oxide, NO; nitrogen dioxide, NO_2; dinitrogen trioxide, N_2O_3; dinitrogen tetroxide, N_2O_4; and others. Tell how the atomic theory predicts a series of compounds like this.

2.15 Classify these pure substances as elements or compounds:
mercury   lime (calcium oxide)   table salt
hydrogen   neon   water

2.16 Give the symbol for each of these elements. Try to do this without looking at the text. Classify each as metal or nonmetal.
a. phosphorus   **b.** oxygen   **c.** cobalt   **d.** calcium

2.17 Give the names of the elements that have the following symbols. Try to do this without looking them up. Classify each as metal or nonmetal.
a. Na   **b.** S   **c.** I   **d.** Ce

2.18 From a list of the elements, choose those whose symbols do not begin with the same letter. Match these elements with the appropriate Latin or German name from the following list:
natrium   aurum   stibium
ferrum   argentum   wolfram
stannum   hydrargyrum   kalium

2.19 Look up these elements in a dictionary and determine the origin of their name. What characterizes the atomic numbers of the group?
americium   einsteinium   nobelium   neptunium
berkelium   californium   lawrencium

2.20 The elements in column VII of the periodic table are known collectively as the halogens. List the names and symbols of the halogens.

2.21 The elements in column VI of the periodic table are occasionally known as the chalcogens. List these elements by name and symbol.

2.22 List the elements with one-letter symbols. Tell whether each is metal or nonmetal, whether it is diatomic, and if possible its physical state at 20°C.

2.23 Write the formulas and names of all compounds mentioned in the discussion of atomic theory (Section 2.2).

2.24 From the composition of these compounds as given, write the formula of the compound.
sodium bromide: 1 atom of sodium, 1 atom of bromine
methane: 1 atom of carbon, 4 atoms of hydrogen
aspirin: 9 atoms of carbon, 8 atoms of hydrogen, 4 atoms of oxygen
ammonia: 1 atom of nitrogen, 3 atoms of hydrogen
urea: 2 atoms of nitrogen, 1 atom of carbon, 4 atoms of hydrogen, 1 atom of oxygen

2.25 Using the formulas given, state the atomic composition of these compounds:

sodium hydroxide, NaOH   silver nitrate, $AgNO_3$
potassium chloride, KCl   calcium carbonate, $CaCO_3$
sulfuric acid, H_2SO_4 zinc sulfide, ZnS

2.26 The following compounds may be familiar to you. For each, both its common name and its correct chemical name are given. From the formula, tell the composition of each.

dry ice	carbon dioxide	CO_2
blue vitriol	copper sulfate	$CuSO_4$
muriatic acid	hydrochloric acid	HCl
wood alcohol	methanol	CH_4O
lime	calcium oxide	CaO

The composition of the atom (Section 2.5)

2.27 Make a table showing the relative mass and charge of these particles:
a. proton   **b.** alpha particle   **c.** neutron   **d.** electron

2.28 Complete the table.

			Number of		
Element	Atomic Number	Mass Number	Electrons	Protons	Neutrons
	11	23	____	____	____
sulfur	____	34	____	____	____
barium	____	____	56		81
____	20	40	____	____	____
____	____	____	____	8	8

2.29 Write symbols showing the mass number and atomic number for the atoms described in Problem 2.28.

2.30 Describe the difference in composition between chromium-53 and manganese-53; between uranium-238 and neptunium-238.

2.31 Describe the difference in composition between antimony-121 and antimony-123; between gallium-69 and gallium-71.

2.32 Name and give the composition of atoms with the descriptions given. Are they metals or nonmetals?

	a.	**b.**	**c.**
atomic number	28	27	26
mass number	58	59	58

2.33 Name and give the atomic composition of atoms with the descriptions given.

	a.	**b.**	**c.**
atomic number	35	80	88
mass number	79	200	226

Inner structure of the atom (Section 2.6)

2.34 Describe the apparatus, the process studied, and the results of Rutherford's gold-foil experiment.

The mole
(Section 2.8)

2.35 Complete the table.

Mass of Sample	Moles of Sample	Atoms in Sample
_____	0.20 mol sodium	_____
5.0 g barium	_____	_____
_____	_____	1.0×10^{23} atoms calcium
_____	0.42 mol potassium	_____
9.3 g lithium	_____	_____

2.36 Calculate the mass of 0.15 mol of these elements:
a. carbon   **b.** helium   **c.** zinc   **d.** lead

2.37 Calculate the number of atoms in 2.5 g of these elements:
a. fluorine   **b.** sulfur   **c.** arsenic   **d.** tin

2.38 Calculate the volume occupied by 1.00 mol of the gases neon ($d = 3.733$ g/L) and radon ($d = 9.73$ g/L).

2.39 Calculate the volume of 1.00 mol of the two liquid elements:
a. bromine ($d = 3.12$ g/mL at 20°C)
b. mercury ($d = 13.55$ g/mL at 20°C)

2.40 Calculate the number of moles of element in each of the following:
a. 16.3 g nickel   **b.** 56.3 g antimony
c. 109.01 g boron   **d.** 0.00546 g platinum

Radioactivity
(Section 2.9)

2.41 Complete the equations.
$$^{103}_{46}\text{Pd} + {}^{0}_{-1}\beta \longrightarrow \underline{\hspace{1cm}}$$
$$^{210}_{84}\text{Po} \longrightarrow {}^{4}_{2}\text{He} + \underline{\hspace{1cm}}$$
$$^{9}_{4}\text{Be} + {}^{4}_{2}\text{He} \longrightarrow {}^{1}_{0}\text{n} + \underline{\hspace{1cm}}$$

2.42 What is the half-life of an isotope if 6.00 g of the isotope decays to 0.75 g in 27 days?

2.43 Lead-210 has a half-life of 22 yr. If a 1.0-g sample of lead-210 is buried in 1988, how much of it will remain as lead in 2076? Lead-210 decays with the loss of an alpha particle. Write the equation for this decay.

2.44 What happens to the atomic number and mass number of an atom if it loses (a) an alpha particle? (b) a gamma ray? (c) a beta particle? In which cases will the atom change its chemical nature?

2.45 Why is radioactivity measured in half-lives rather than in the time required for total decay?

General
problems

2.46 What volume of bromine ($d = 3.10$ g/mL) will weigh 2.95 kg?

2.47 A cube of osmium measuring 1.5 cm on a side weighs 75.9 g. What is the density of osmium?

2.48 You have a piece of iron measuring $2.0 \times 4.6 \times 3.2$ cm^3 and a piece of nickel measuring $1.8 \times 2.6 \times 2.1$ cm^3. The density of iron is 7.9 g/mL; of nickel, 8.9 g/mL. Which metal piece is heavier and by how much?

2.49 At what temperature are the Fahrenheit and Celsius temperature readings the same numerically but opposite in sign?

2.50 When gold costs $375 per ounce, what is the value of one atom of gold?

2.51 If copper is selling for $0.755 per pound, what is its cost per mole?

2.52 A normal, healthy body contains 34 parts per million (ppm) by weight of zinc (1 g Zn/10^6 g body weight). How many zinc atoms would be found in the body of a healthy person weighing 52.3 kg?

2.53 If regulations permit no more than 2 μg of vanadium per cubic meter of air occupied by humans, how many atoms of vanadium would be contained in a room 3.0 m × 2.5 m × 4.0 m that contained the maximum allowable amount of vanadium?

2.54 According to the Food and Drug Administration, fish sold for human consumption can contain no more than 5 parts per million of mercury by weight (5 g Hg/10^6 g fish). How many atoms of mercury would there be in 1 lb of fish that contained this amount of mercury?

2.55 At a busy street intersection, the lead concentration in the air may be 9 μg/m^3 of air. If 40% of the lead passing through the lungs is absorbed and a typical adult breathes 20 m^3 of air per day, how many moles of lead are absorbed during an 8-hr working day by a newspaper vendor at this corner?

Elements in the Body

Each of us is aware of the importance of diet in maintaining good health. A good diet contains vitamins and minerals as well as fats, carbohydrates, and proteins. The elements present in the largest amounts in our bodies are carbon, hydrogen, oxygen, sulfur, and nitrogen, the same elements that are found in fats, carbohydrates, and proteins. Lesser quantities of other elements, called minerals, are also essential for good health. Table I-1 lists those elements, along with the daily amounts required.

Group A of the table lists minerals needed in substantial quantities for the formation of bones, cartilage, and teeth. Group B contains the elements whose ions maintain electrochemical balance across the cell membranes. Sodium and potassium cations and chloride, sulfate, bicarbonate, and phosphate anions are small ions; hence they can migrate easily through the cell membranes to maintain charge balance on both sides of the cell membranes.

Group C elements in Table I-1 are called trace elements. These elements are necessary for good health but only in very small amounts.

Figure I-1 shows the groups of elements discussed above, arranged in the periodic table (the lanthanides and actinides are not shown). The five elements shaded in light gray are those present in the largest quantities in our bodies. The

Table I-1 Daily mineral requirements for 70-kg male aged 23–50.

	Element	Amount (mg)
Group A	calcium	800
	phosphorus	800
	magnesium	350
Group B	potassium	1875–5625
	chlorine	1700–5100
	sodium	1100–3300
Group C	zinc	15
	iron	10
	manganese	2.5
	copper	2.0
	fluorine	1.5
	iodine	0.15
	molybdenum	0.15
	chromium	0.05
	selenium vanadium cobalt nickel arsenic silicon	Minimum daily requirement not yet established.

Source: National Research Council, *Recommended Dietary Allowances*, 9th ed. (Washington, D.C.: National Academy of Sciences).

elements from Group A of Table I-1 are shaded in dark gray. The elements shaded in light color

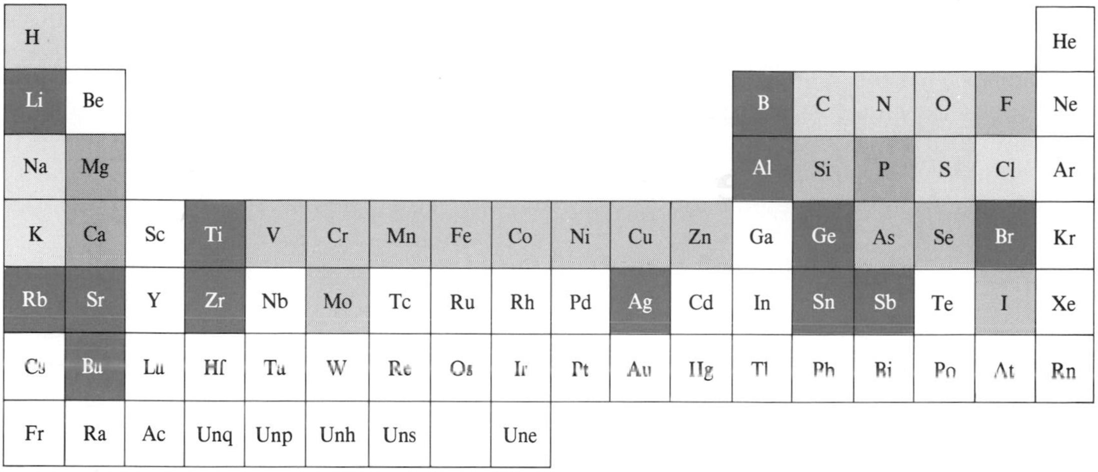

Figure I-1 Elements in the body.

are the ones in Group B. The trace elements (Group C of Table I-1) are shaded in a darker color. The elements shown in the darkest color, with white letters, are consistently found in human tissue in trace amounts. The role of all these elements has not yet been defined. It has not yet been established whether they are essential or just so prevalent in the environment that they become part of every living thing. Notice that of the elements in the first four rows of the table, all but the noble gases beryllium, scandium, and gallium are regularly found in human tissue.

The functions of the elements in body metabolism are varied. Sometimes, these elements function structurally. Many are incorporated into the structure of large molecules such as enzymes and hormones—compounds involved in metabolism. Sulfur is present in the amino acids cystine and cysteine. These amino acids are in many proteins, and in especially large concentrations in keratin, the protein in hair. Iodine is incorporated by the thyroid gland in thyroxin, the hormone important to growth and metabolism. Absence of the proper concentration of thyroxin, resulting from a dietary deficiency of iodine, causes goiter, a chronic enlargment of the thyroid gland. Iron is in the heme fraction of the hemoglobin molecule, the blood protein that carries oxygen throughout the body. Cobalt is

in vitamin B_{12}, which is important in blood formation. A deficiency of vitamin B_{12} causes severe anemia. Fluorine is found in tooth enamel that has proved resistant to decay. Throughout the United States during the last quarter century, fluorine has been added to drinking water and applied to teeth in an effort to decrease the incidence of tooth decay in the general population.

All the elements in Table I-1 act as cofactors (activators) of enzymes, the catalysts of biological reactions. The exact function of an enzyme cofactor is variable, ranging from promoting the correct spatial orientation of the reactants to forming an intermediate with one of the molecules. Whatever the association, they aid the reaction. Zinc, iron, chromium, molybdenum, and copper are particularly important as cofactors in the body. Zinc, for example, activates the enzyme that catalyzes the decomposition of carbonic acid to carbon dioxide and water. Zinc is also a cofactor for other enzymes, such as kidney phosphatase, necessary for phosphorylation reactions in the kidneys. Calcium is a cofactor in the reactions of heart muscle.

Each of the elements considered above has an optimum concentration in the body (Table I-1). Below that amount, symptoms of the element's deficiency appear; above that amount, the element is toxic. Certainly the potential toxicity of the trace element arsenic has been well established.

Selenium has recently received much publicity as a trace element required for good health. For years, only its toxic properties were recognized. It has now been established that selenium is beneficial to metabolism in several ways. As the selenate ion (SeO_4^{2-}), it activates the enzyme glutathione peroxidase; it is involved in vitamin E activity; and it is required for the efficient oxidation of the sulfhydryl (—SH) group of proteins. Selenium is found in heart muscle, and increased selenium intake is associated with lower incidence of heart disease.

Natural sources of selenium include whole-wheat grain cereals and products derived from such cereals, certain yeasts, liver, kidney, and seafoods. The amount of selenium in the diet depends on the selenium content of these natural sources, which depends, in turn, on the selenium content of the soil. This interrelationship has been explored in studies showing the antagonism of selenium to cancer. In one such study, statistics from twenty-seven countries showed that the death rate attributable to cancer is inversely proportional to the dietary intake of selenium and to the selenium content of the soils in the area. Another study tabulated the birth months of 180,000 cancer patients and found that an unexpectedly large number of the patients were born in the winter, while surprisingly few were born in the summer. This difference has been attributed to seasonal variations in the amount of selenium in the diet. In another study, statistics from seventeen countries showed the selenium content of female blood to be inversely proportional to the incidence of breast cancer.

Some elements interfere with the toxic effects of other metals. Selenium has been shown to be an antidote in cases of cadmium poisoning. Increased amounts of dietary selenium seem to protect against tumors caused by high levels of dietary zinc. Increased intake of arsenic will off-set a toxic dose of selenium. The mechanisms causing these antagonistic effects are unknown.

In the future, perhaps other elements of low atomic weight will be identified as essential. Aluminum *in vitro* activates succinic dehydrogenase but does not seem an essential cofactor *in vivo*. Is aluminum a cofactor of another enzyme? Lithium has been used in treating mental disorders, such as schizophrenia. Is a deficiency of lithium the cause of this disease? Why is boron found so frequently in mammalian tissue? Is it essential?

Which heavy elements might be identified in the future as essential, although in trace amounts? For generations, gold has been used to treat certain forms of arthritis. Gold has been found in mammalian liver tissue in concentrations of 2–3 parts per billion (ppb). In some Asian countries, mercury has been used to treat the common cold. Rubidium has been found in human tissue in concentrations of 20–40 ppm. Are these, too, essential elements? Are lead and cadmium toxic in all amounts, or are they beneficial in trace amounts? As our analytical methods become more sophisticated and our studies of biochemical processes more refined, we can look forward to answers to these questions.

Sources

Bowen, H. M. J. 1966. *Trace elements in biochemistry.* New York: Academic Press.

Mertz, W. 1981. Essential trace elements. *Science* 273:1332.

National Research Council. 1980. *Recommended Dietary Allowances.* 9th ed. Washington, D.C.: National Academy of Sciences.

Schrauzer, G. N. 1977. *Nutritional aspects of cancer: A conference report.* New York: Plenum Press.

Sevin, M. J., ed. 1960. *Metal binding in medicine.* Philadelphia: J. B. Lippincott.

Underwood, E. J. 1977. *Trace elements in human and animal nutrition.* 4th ed. New York: Academic Press.

3 Electrons and the Properties of Atoms

An atom contains protons, neutrons, and electrons. Rutherford showed in 1911 that the more massive particles, the protons and the neutrons, were inside the nucleus of the atom, and the electrons were outside. The diameter of the nucleus is only 10^{-5} that of the atom. The extranuclear space of the atom is empty except for the rapidly moving tiny electrons it contains. Research has predicted the properties of these electrons and explained how their number and individual properties are related to the properties of the elements.

3.1 An Atomic Model

The currently accepted model of the atom is based on the concept of energy levels for electrons within an atom. The requirements for our model are as follows:

1. Each electron in a particular atom has a unique energy that depends on the negatively charged electron's relation to the positively charged nucleus and to the other negatively charged electrons in the atom.
2. The energy of an electron in an atom can increase or decrease, but only by specific amounts.

A. Energy Levels

We picture an atom as a small nucleus surrounded by a much larger volume of space containing the electrons. This space is divided into regions called **principal energy levels**, numbered 1, 2, 3, 4, . . . , ∞ outward from the nucleus. Early theories on the structure of the atom called these levels **shells** and designated them by letters. Occasionally, this designation is still found. In it, the first energy level is the K shell, the second the L shell, and so on through the alphabet.

Each principal energy level can contain up to $2n^2$ electrons, where n is the number of the level. Thus, the first level can contain up to 2, or $2(1)^2$, electrons, the second up to 8, or $2(2^2)$, electrons, the third up to 18, or $2(3)^2$, and so on. Only seven energy levels are needed to contain all the electrons in the atoms of those elements now known.

The energy associated with an energy level increases as the distance of the energy level from the nucleus increases. An electron in the seventh energy level has more energy associated with it than does an electron in the first energy level. In addition, the lower the number of the principal energy level, the closer the negatively charged electron in that level is to the positively charged nucleus; it is consequently more difficult to remove this electron from the atom.

B. Sublevels and Orbitals

When an electron is in a particular energy level, it is more likely to be found in some parts of that level than in others. These parts are called **orbitals**. Orbitals of equivalent energy are grouped in **sublevels**. Each orbital can contain a maximum of two electrons. The two electrons in a particular orbital differ slightly in energy due to a property called electron spin. The theory of **electron spin** states that the two electrons in a single orbital spin in opposite directions on their axes, causing an energy difference between them. Like many models, this is an oversimplification, but for our purposes, a useful description.

Each principal energy level has one sublevel containing one orbital, an *s* orbital, which can contain one or two electrons. Electrons in this orbital are called *s* electrons and have the lowest energy of any electrons in that principal energy level. The first principal energy level contains only an *s* sublevel; therefore, it can hold a maximum of two electrons.

Each principal energy level above the first contains one *s* orbital and three *p* orbitals. A set of three *p* orbitals, called the *p* sublevel, can hold a maximum of 6 electrons. Therefore, the second level can contain a maximum of 8 electrons, that is, 2 in the *s* orbital and 6 in the three *p* orbitals.

Each principal energy level above the second contains, in addition to an *s* orbital and three *p* orbitals, five *d* orbitals, making up the *d* sublevel. The five *d* orbitals can hold up to 10 electrons. Thus, the third level can hold up to 18 electrons: 2 in the *s* orbital, 6 in the three *p* orbitals, and 10 in the five *d* orbitals.

The fourth and higher levels also contain an *f* sublevel, containing seven *f* orbitals, which can hold a maximum of 14 electrons. Thus, the fourth level can hold up to 32 electrons: 2 in the *s* orbital, 6 in the three *p* orbitals, 10 in the five *d* orbitals, and 14 in the seven *f* orbitals. The sublevels of the first four principal energy levels and the maximum number of electrons that each type of sublevel can contain are summarized in Table 3.1.

To distinguish which of the *s*, *p*, *d*, and *f* sublevels we are talking about, we use the number of the principal energy level the particular sublevel is in. For example, the *s* sublevel of the second principal energy level is designated 2*s*; the *s* sublevel of the third principal energy level is designated 3*s*; and so on. The number of electrons in a particular type of sublevel is shown by a superscript

Table 3.1
Sublevels of the
first four energy
levels.

Energy Level	Sublevel	No. Orbitals in Sublevel	Total Possible Occupying Electrons
1	s	1	2
2	s	1	2 } 8
	p	3	6
3	s	1	2
	p	3	6 } 18
	d	5	10
4	s	1	2
	p	3	6
	d	5	10 } 32
	f	7	14

after the letter of the sublevel. The notation

means that there are 5 electrons in the p sublevel of the fourth energy level.

Example 3.1

For the third energy level, list the different kinds of orbitals, how many of each there are, and the total number of electrons the energy level can contain.

☐ *Solution*

The third energy level contains the following:

1s orbital, which can contain a total of 2 electrons
3p orbitals, which can contain a total of 6 electrons
5d orbitals, which can contain a total of 10 electrons

giving for the entire energy level 18 electron spaces.

Problem 3.1

For the fourth energy level, list the different kinds of orbitals present, how many of each there are, and the total number of electron spaces in this energy level.

1. Orbital Shapes and Sizes

The **shapes** of s and p orbitals are shown in Figure 3.1. In these diagrams, the nucleus is at the origin of the axes. The s orbitals are spherically symmetrical about the nucleus. The 2s orbital is a larger sphere than the 1s orbital, the 3s orbital is larger than the 2s orbital, and so on (see Figure 3.2).

The three p orbitals (p_x, p_y, and p_z) are more or less dumbbell-shaped, with the center of the dumbbell at the nucleus. They are oriented at right angles to each other along the x, y, and z axes. Like the s orbitals, the p orbitals increase in size as the number of the principal energy level they occupy increases. A 4p orbital is larger than a 3p orbital.

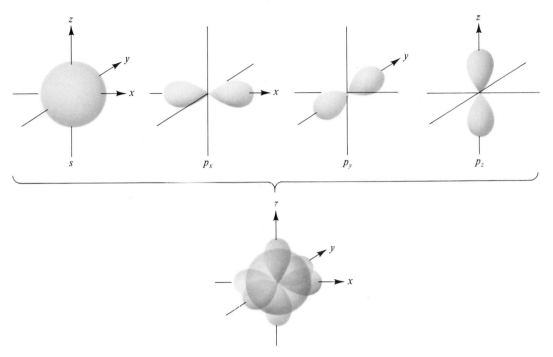

Figure 3.1 Perspective representations of the *s* and the three *p* orbitals of a single energy level. The clouds show the space within which the electron is most apt to be. The lower sketch shows how these orbitals overlap in the energy level.

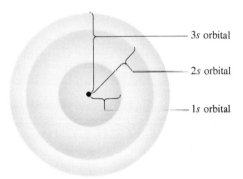

Figure 3.2 Cross-sectional view of the *s* orbitals of an atom showing relative sizes and overlap.

The shapes of *d* orbitals are shown in Figure 3.3. Notice that these shapes are more complex than those of *p* orbitals, and recall that *p* orbitals have more complex shapes than *s* orbitals have. Clearly the shape of an orbital becomes more complex as the energy associated with that orbital increases. We can predict that *f* orbitals will have even more complex shapes than those of *d* orbitals.

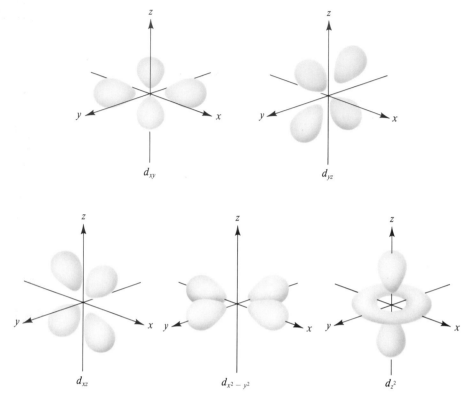

Figure 3.3 The shapes and orientations of the *d* orbitals.

One further and important word about orbital shapes. These shapes do *not* represent the path of an electron within the atom. They *do* represent the region of space in which an electron of that sublevel is most apt to be found. Thus a *p* electron is most apt to be within a dumbbell-shaped space within the atom, although we make no pretense of describing its path within that volume.

2. Orbital Energies

Within a given principal energy level, electrons in *p* orbitals are always more energetic than those in *s* orbitals, those in *d* orbitals are always more energetic than those in *p* orbitals, and electrons in *f* orbitals are always more energetic than those in *d* orbitals. Within the fourth principal energy level, for example, we have

$$\text{4s} < \text{4p} < \text{4d} < \text{4f}$$

Lowest-energy electrons   *Highest-energy electrons*

increasing energy

In addition, the energy associated with an orbital increases as the number of the principal energy level of the orbital increases. For instance, the energy associated with a 3*p* orbital is always higher than the energy associated with a 2*p* orbital, and the energy of a 4*d* orbital is always higher than the energy associated with a 3*d* orbital. The same is true of *s* orbitals:

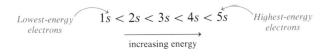

$1s < 2s < 3s < 4s < 5s$

Lowest-energy
electrons

Highest-energy
electrons

increasing energy

Figure 3.2 also shows that the orbitals are not completely separate and distinct regions of space. For example, the orbital of a 3s electron overlaps the space assigned to a 1s or a 2s orbital.

Energy levels also interweave. Figure 3.4 shows, in order of increasing energy, all the orbitals of the first four energy levels. Notice that a 3d orbital has slightly higher energy than a 4s orbital, and a 4d orbital has a little higher energy than a 5s orbital. Note especially the overlap of orbitals in the higher principal energy levels.

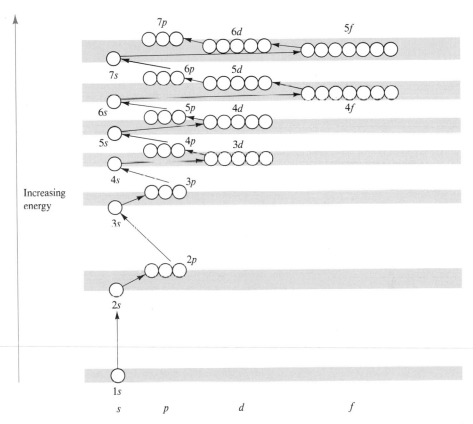

Increasing
energy

Figure 3.4 The principal energy levels of an atom and the sublevels and orbitals each contains. The arrows show the order in which the sublevels fill.

Example 3.2

Arrange the following orbitals in order of increasing energy: 4f, 1s, 3d, 4p, 5s.

Solution

Looking at Figure 3.4, we can arrange the order: 1s, 3d, 4p, 5s, 4f.

Problem 3.2 ■

Arrange the following orbitals in order of increasing energy: 3*s*, 6*s*, 4*d*, 4*f*, 5*d*. ■

3.2 Electron Configurations of Atoms

The **electron configuration** of an atom lists the number of electrons in each kind of orbital in each energy level of the ground-state atom. To obtain the electron configuration of a particular atom, start at the nucleus and add electrons one by one until the number added equals the number of protons in the nucleus. Each added electron is assigned to the available orbital of lowest energy. The first orbital filled will be the 1*s* orbital, then the 2*s* orbital, the 2*p* orbitals, the 3*s*, 3*p*, 4*s*, 3*d*, and so on. This order is difficult to remember and often hard to determine from energy-level diagrams such as Figure 3.4. Some students prefer to remember the order by using Figure 3.5. The energy levels are listed here in rows, starting with the 1*s* level. To use this figure, read along the diagonal lines in the direction of the arrows. The order is summarized under the diagram.

An atom of hydrogen (atomic number 1) has one proton and one electron. The single electron is assigned to the 1*s* sublevel, the lowest-energy sublevel in the lowest-energy level. Therefore, the electron configuration of hydrogen is written

For helium (atomic number 2), which has two electrons, the electron configuration is

$$\text{He:}\quad 1s^2$$

Two electrons completely fill the first energy level. Because the helium nucleus is different from the hydrogen nucleus, neither of the helium electrons will have exactly the same energy as the single hydrogen electron.

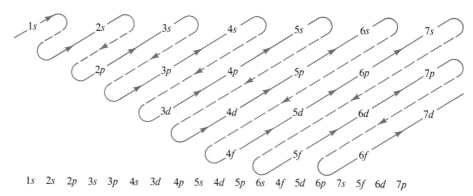

Figure 3.5 The arrow shows a second way of remembering the order in which sublevels fill.

The element lithium (atomic number 3) has three electrons. To write its electron configuration, we must first determine from Figure 3.4 that the 2s sublevel is next higher in energy after the 1s sublevel. Therefore, the electron configuration of lithium is

$$\text{Li:} \quad 1s^2 2s^1$$

Boron (atomic number 5) has five electrons. Four electrons fill both the 1s and 2s orbitals. The fifth electron is added to a 2p orbital, the sublevel next higher in energy (Figure 3.4). The electron configuration of boron is

$$\text{B:} \quad 1s^2 2s^2 2p^1$$

Table 3.2 shows the electron configurations of the elements with atomic numbers 1–18.

Table 3.2
Electron configurations of the first 18 elements.

Element	Atomic Number	Electron Configuration
hydrogen	1	$1s^1$
helium	2	$1s^2$
lithium	3	$1s^2 2s^1$
beryllium	4	$1s^2 2s^2$
boron	5	$1s^2 2s^2 2p^1$
carbon	6	$1s^2 2s^2 2p^2$
nitrogen	7	$1s^2 2s^2 2p^3$
oxygen	8	$1s^2 2s^2 2p^4$
fluorine	9	$1s^2 2s^2 2p^5$
neon	10	$1s^2 2s^2 2p^6$
sodium	11	$1s^2 2s^2 2p^6 3s^1$
magnesium	12	$1s^2 2s^2 2p^6 3s^2$
aluminum	13	$1s^2 2s^2 2p^6 3s^2 3p^1$
silicon	14	$1s^2 2s^2 2p^6 3s^2 3p^2$
phosphorus	15	$1s^2 2s^2 2p^6 3s^2 3p^3$
sulfur	16	$1s^2 2s^2 2p^6 3s^2 3p^4$
chlorine	17	$1s^2 2s^2 2p^6 3s^2 3p^5$
argon	18	$1s^2 2s^2 2p^6 3s^2 3p^6$

The electron configuration of elements with higher atomic numbers can be written by following the orbital-filling chart in Figure 3.5.

Write the electron configuration of vanadium.

Example 3.3

☐ *Solution*

The atomic number of vanadium is 23; we must therefore account for 23 electrons. The first orbitals to fill are 1s, 2s, 2p, 3s, 3p, 4s, which can hold 20 electrons.

The remaining three electrons must be in the $3d$ orbital, giving the configuration

$$V: \quad 1s^2 2s^2 2p^6 3s^2 3p^6 4s^2 3d^3$$

Problem 3.3   Write the electron configuration of arsenic (atomic number 33).

3.3 Periodic Table

In the **periodic table** (Section 2.3B), the elements are arranged in horizontal rows, in order of increasing atomic number. Each row is called a period. The periods are numbered 1 through 7 and differ in the number of elements they contain. Period 1 contains two elements, periods 2 and 3 contain eight elements apiece, periods 4 and 5 contain eighteen elements each, and there is room for thirty-two elements in both periods 6 and 7, although period 7 contains at present only twenty elements. Looking at Figure 3.6, you will notice that, in order to fit the periodic table onto a normal book page, certain elements have been placed below the table: those elements of period 6 with atomic numbers 58 through 71 and those elements of period 7 with atomic numbers 90 and above.

A. Electron Configuration and the Periodic Table

What does the arrangement of the elements within the periodic table have to do with their electron configuration? Let us compare the number of elements in each period of the table with the number of electrons added to an atom in building its electron configuration. The first energy level is filled when it contains two electrons. Similarly, the first period of the table contains only two elements, hydrogen (atomic number 1) and helium (atomic number 2). The second energy level is filled when it contains eight electrons, and the second period contains eight elements, beginning at lithium (atomic number 3) and ending with neon (atomic number 10). The third energy level can add only eight electrons before electrons enter the fourth energy level. Likewise, the third period contains eight elements: sodium (atomic number 11) through argon (atomic number 18).

The fourth energy level, like the third, can add only eight electrons before electrons are added to the fifth energy level. Between the two $4s$ and the six $4p$ electrons, ten $3d$ electrons are added. This gives eighteen electrons in all, and there are eighteen elements in the fourth period of the table. Eight of these are in the same columns used by elements in the first, second, and third periods; the remaining ten elements start new columns. The addition of electrons to the fifth energy level follows the pattern of the fourth level: eighteen electrons are added to the fifth level before electrons enter the sixth level. The fifth period has eighteen elements, placed below those in the fourth period.

In the sixth period there are thirty-two elements, eighteen in the main body of the table and fourteen, cerium (element 58) through lutetium (element 71), below the table. These thirty-two elements correspond to the addition of thirty-two electrons; they start with the addition of the $6s$ electrons and end with

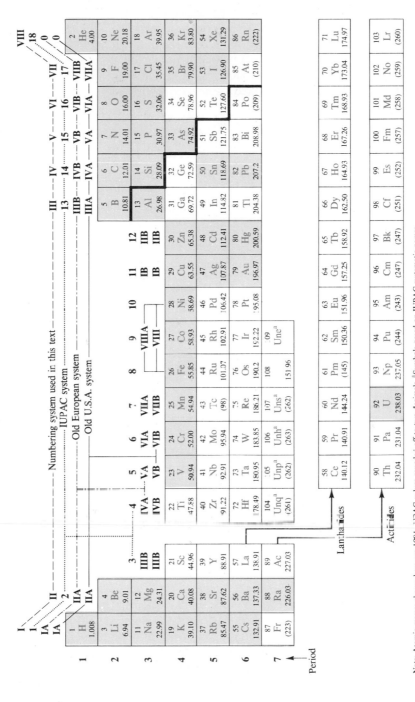

Figure 3.6 Periodic table of the elements. This figure shows the confusion that has existed in designating the columns of the periodic table. In this textbook, only the long columns are numbered (with Roman numerals). The A and B designations are not used.

Note: Atomic masses shown here are 1981 IUPAC values rounded off to two decimals. [a] Symbols based on IUPAC systematic names.

the complete filling of the $6p$ sublevel (two $6s$ electrons, fourteen $4f$ electrons, ten $5d$ electrons, and six $6p$ electrons).

The seventh period is at present incomplete although, in theory, it too should contain thirty-two elements, eighteen in the main body of the table and fourteen below. Most of the known elements in this period have been identified as the products of nuclear reactions. Those of atomic number greater than 109 have not yet been discovered.

B. Categories of Elements within the Periodic Table

A very close relationship exists between the location of an element in the table and its electron configuration. The table divides easily into three sections as shown in Figure 3.7. These sections contain, respectively, the representative elements, the transition elements, and the inner transition elements.

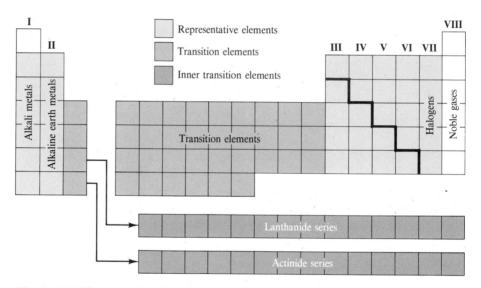

Figure 3.7 The periodic table, showing the location of the representative, transition, and inner transition elements.

1. The Representative Elements

These elements are called **representative elements** because their chemistry was believed to be representative of all elements. They are found in that part of the table that contains the long columns numbered with Roman numerals. The last added, or the differentiating electron, of these elements is an s or a p electron. If it is an s electron, the element is in column I or II; together these two columns are sometimes known as the s block. If the differentiating electron is a p electron, the element is in the p block that encompasses columns III through VIII.

The number of the column equals the sum of the s and p electrons that the element in its ground state has in its highest-occupied energy level. The period of the table that contains the element has the same number as the energy level in which those electrons are found. Sodium is a representative element. It has eleven electrons. Its electron configuration is

$$1s^2 2s^2 2p^6 3s^1$$

Sodium is in column I of the third period. In a sodium atom, the highest-energy level containing electrons is the third, and that energy level contains one electron.

Example 3.4

Relate the electron configuration of arsenic to its location in the periodic table.

☐ *Solution*

The atomic number of arsenic is 33. Its electron configuration is

$$1s^2 2s^2 2p^6 3s^2 3p^6 3d^{10} 4s^2 4p^3$$

The highest-occupied energy level is the fourth: and arsenic is in the fourth period of the table. There are five *s* and *p* electrons in the fourth energy level; arsenic is in column V.

Problem 3.4

Relate the electron configuration of chlorine to its location in the periodic table.

2. The Transition Elements

The **transition elements** are those in the short columns of the table found between column II and column III. For a transition element, the differentiating electron is a *d* electron that has been added to an energy level numbered one less than the period of the table in which the element is found. In the highest-occupied energy level, these elements have one or two *s* electrons. Many familiar metals are in this block of elements, including the coinage metals: gold, silver, copper, and platinum. Iron, the principal ingredient of steel, is here, and also those elements (chromium, nickel, manganese, and others) that are added to iron to make particular kinds of steel. These elements owe many of their chemical properties to the partially filled condition of their two outermost electron shells.

Occasionally you will find this section of the periodic table referred to as the *d* block.

3. The Inner Transition Elements

The **inner transition** elements are those in the two rows below the main body of the periodic table. For these elements, the differentiating electron is an *f* electron; this section of the table is therefore sometimes known as the *f* block. The structures of the elements in this block differ in the number of electrons in the energy level two numbers lower than the highest occupied. The elements in the top row are known as **lanthanides**, or **rare earths**; their differentiating electrons are in the 4*f* sublevel.

The elements in the bottom row are known as **actinides**; their differentiating electrons are in the $5f$ sublevel. All the actinides are radioactive. Only the first three—thorium, proactinium, and uranium—are present in appreciable concentration in the Earth's crust. Some of the others have been found in trace amounts in the Earth or in stars. All have been produced in the laboratories of nuclear science. Of the elements that would represent the filling of the $6d$ sublevel, only five (those with atomic numbers 104, 105, 106, 107, and 109) have been prepared by nuclear scientists. Thus far none of the elements that would have electrons in the $7p$ sublevel has been isolated, although efforts are being made in laboratories around the world.

C. Electron Configuration of the Noble Gases; Core Notation

We have established that the electron configuration of an element and its location in the periodic table are related. Let us more closely consider the electron configuration of the **noble gases**, those elements in column VIII of the periodic table. The electron configurations of these elements are shown in Table 3.3.

Table 3.3
Electron configurations of the noble gases.

Element	Atomic Number	Electron Configuration
He	4	$1s^2$
Ne	10	$1s^2 2s^2 2p^6$
Ar	18	$1s^2 2s^2 2p^6 3s^2 3p^6$
Kr	36	$1s^2 2s^2 2p^6 3s^2 3p^6 3d^{10} 4s^2 4p^6$
Xe	54	$1s^2 2s^2 2p^6 3s^2 3p^6 3d^{10} 4s^2 4p^6 4d^{10} 5s^2 5p^6$
Rn	86	$1s^2 2s^2 2p^6 3s^2 3p^6 3d^{10} 4s^2 4p^6 4d^{10} 4f^{14} 5s^2 5p^6 5d^{10} 6s^2 6p^6$

A careful examination of these configurations shows that none has any partially filled sublevels. In the electron configurations of other elements, although the sublevels in the lower-energy levels are filled, those in the highest-occupied levels are only partially filled. Consider the electron configuration of bromine as an example:

$$1s^2 2s^2 3p^6 3s^2 3p^6 3d^{10} 4s^2 4p^5$$

The first eighteen electrons are in the same orbitals as those of an atom of argon. If we use the symbol [Ar] to represent those eighteen electrons, we can write the electron configuration of bromine as

$$[\text{Ar}]3d^{10} 4s^2 4p^5$$

This is a useful device, since it is a quicker way of writing electron configurations. In addition, it emphasizes the configurations in the higher-energy levels that determine the chemistry of an element. This way of using the noble gases to represent certain electron configurations is known as **core notation**. The symbol of a noble gas enclosed in brackets represents the inner filled orbitals of an element. Additional electrons are shown in the standard way. Only the noble gases can be used to write electron configurations in this manner. In writing electron configurations by this method, remember that even though the inner configurations of an element may be written the same as for a noble gas, the energies of these inner electrons are slightly different.

Example 3.5

Using core notation, write the electron configuration of lead, atomic number 82.

Solution

Lead has 82 electrons. The nearest noble gas of fewer electrons is xenon, atomic number 54. Let $[Xe]$ represent the first 54 electrons of lead. Xenon is at the end of period 5 of the table. Its last electrons must be $5p$ electrons. The configuration of the next 28 electrons can be determined by picking up the arrow in Figure 3.5, starting after $5p$. Filling the sublevels in proper order, we get

$$Pb: \quad [Xe]6s^2 4f^{14} 5d^{10} 6p^2$$

Expressed in order of increasing energy level, the electron configuration of lead is

$$Pb: \quad [Xe]4f^{14} 5d^{10} 6s^2 6p^2$$

Problem 3.5

In core notation, write the electron configuration of (a) strontium; (b) arsenic.

Table 3.4 shows in core notation the electron configurations of the elements in columns I and VI of the periodic table. Notice how this method emphasizes the similarity of structure of the elements in a single column.

Table 3.4
Electron configurations of elements in columns I and VI in core notation.

I		VI	
H	$1s^1$		
Li	$[He]2s^1$	O	$[He]2s^2 2p^4$
Na	$[Ne]3s^1$	S	$[Ne]3s^2 3p^4$
K	$[Ar]4s^1$	Se	$[Ar]4s^2 3d^{10} 4p^4$
Rb	$[Kr]5s^1$	Te	$[Kr]5s^2 4d^{10} 5p^4$
Cs	$[Xe]6s^1$	Po	$[Xe]6s^2 4f^{14} 5d^{10} 6p^4$
Fr	$[Rn]7s^1$		

D. Valence Electrons

In discussing the chemical properties of an element, we often focus on electrons in the outermost energy level. These outer-shell electrons are called **valence electrons**, and the energy level they are in is called the valence shell. Valence electrons participate in chemical bonding and chemical reactions. The valence electrons of an element are shown by using a representation of the element called an **electron-dot structure**, or **Lewis structure**, named after G. N. Lewis, the twentieth-century American chemist who first pointed out the importance of outer-shell electrons. A Lewis structure shows the symbol of the element surrounded by a number of dots equal to the number of electrons in the outer energy level of the element.

In electron configurations, the s sublevel of a principal energy level n is always occupied before d electrons are added to the principal energy level numbered $n - 1$ and immediately after the d sublevel of principal level $n - 1$ is filled, the p sublevel of principal level n is filled. The next sublevel filled will be the s sublevel of the $n + 1$ principal energy level. This order of filling is illustrated in the configurations of krypton, xenon, and radon in Table 3.3, and of selenium, tellurium, and polonium in Table 3.4. The significance of these observations is that in the electron configuration of any atom, the principal energy level with the highest number that contains any electrons cannot contain more than eight (two s and six p) electrons. This also means that the valence electrons of an atom are the s and p electrons in the occupied principal energy level of highest number. Consequently no atom can have more than eight valence electrons.

In drawing the Lewis structure of an atom, we imagine a four-sided box around the symbol of the atom and consider that each side of that box corresponds to an orbital. We represent each valence electron as a dot. The first two valence electrons will be s electrons; they are represented by two dots on a single side (it doesn't matter which side) of the symbol. The valence electrons that are in the p subshell are placed, first, one on each of the remaining sides of the symbol, and then a second one added to each side. Consider, as an example, the Lewis structure of sodium. Looking back at Table 3.4, we see that the core notation for sodium is [Ne]$3s^1$. This tells us that a sodium atom has one electron in its outer shell, so its Lewis structure is Na·. The core notation for selenium is

$$[Ar]3d^{10}4s^24p^4$$

Its Lewis structure is ·S̈e:. The $3d$ electrons of selenium are not shown because they are not in the outer shell. Lewis structures for the elements in the first three periods and group II of the periodic table are shown in Table 3.5.

Table 3.5
Lewis structures for the elements of the first three periods and group II.

Period	I	II	III	IV	V	VI	VII	VIII
1	H·							He:
2	Li·	Be:	B̈:	·C̈:	·N̈:	·Ö:	:F̈:	:N̈e:
3	Na·	Mg:	Äl:	·S̈i:	·P̈:	·S̈:	:C̈l:	:Är:
4		Ca:						
5		Sr:						
6		Ba:						
7		Ra:						

■ ────────────── Give the Lewis structure of (a) gallium and (b) bromine.

Example 3.6

☐ *Solution*   **a.** Gallium is in column III. Its atoms have three electrons in the highest-energy level. The Lewis structure is Ga·.

b. Bromine is in column VII. Its atoms have seven electrons in the highest-energy level. Its Lewis structure is :Br·.

■ ────────────── Give the Lewis structure of (a) potassium and (b) arsenic.

Problem 3.6 ── ■

3.4 Historical Classification of the Elements

A. Families of Elements

A family of elements contains those elements in the same column of the periodic table. Members of such a family are much alike in both chemical and physical properties. The **alkali metals**—lithium, sodium, potassium, rubidium, cesium, and francium—form one family. These alkali metals are found in column I of the periodic table and have a single valence electron. They are all soft, silvery gray solids with a clearly metallic luster. They are all very reactive; their reactions with water are vigorous, the metal sample often catching fire during the reaction. These elements do not exist free in nature; they are found combined with other elements, often with chlorine. The most common of these compounds is sodium chloride (table salt). Sodium chloride is the substance that makes seawater salty; it is also found in huge underground deposits (salt mines).

The **alkaline earth metals** form another family and are the elements in column II of the periodic table. Their atoms have two valence electrons. These metals are harder and stronger than the alkali metals. They, too, are found in compounds with other elements. While all alkaline earth metals have similar chemical reactivity, they have a wider range of reactivity than the alkali metals do. Beryllium and magnesium are unaffected by water, calcium reacts slowly with boiling water, and barium reacts violently with cold water.

The elements of group VII with seven valence electrons are known as the **halogens**. Chemically, these elements are very similar; physically, they are less alike. The lightest halogen, fluorine, is a pale yellow gas; iodine, is a shiny, black solid. The heaviest halogen, astatine, is quite rare. The element is isolated from uranium ores, and the total amount of astatine in the Earth's crust is probably less than 1 g. All isotopes of the element are radioactive; the longest-lived isotope, astatine-210, has a half-life of 8.3 hr.

Several characteristic properties of the other halogens are shown in Table 3.6. Note how these properties change as the atomic number increases.

The elements of group VIII are the noble gases. Recall (Chapter 2) that these elements are all monatomic gases and occur in nature free and uncombined. They are all singularly unreactive, so much so that they were known earlier as

Table 3.6
Properties of
halogens.

	Symbol	Atomic Number	Lewis Structure	Atomic Weight	Radius × 10^{-8} cm	Melting Point (°C)
Fluorine	F	9	$:\!\ddot{F}\!:$	19.0	0.72	−219.6
Chlorine	Cl	17	$:\!\ddot{Cl}\!:$	35.5	0.99	−101.0
Bromine	Br	35	$:\!\ddot{Br}\!:$	79.9	1.14	−7.2
Iodine	I	53	$:\!\ddot{I}\!:$	126.9	1.33	113.7
Astatine	At	85	$:\!\ddot{At}\!:$	(210)	1.45	302

the inert gases. Only in 1960 were any of them shown to take part in chemical reactions. Even now, only krypton and xenon are known to form chemical compounds with other elements.

The elements in other columns of the table do not show striking similarities in property. These columns are crossed by the line that separates metals from nonmetals, so they have nonmetals at the top and metals at the bottom. For example, group IV is headed by the nonmetal carbon and has lead, a typical metal, as its heaviest member. Group V has the nonmetal nitrogen at the top and the metal bismuth at the bottom.

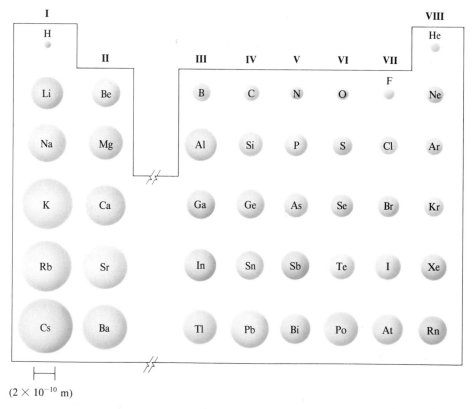

$(2 \times 10^{-10}$ m)

Figure 3.8 The relative sizes of the atoms of the representative elements.

3.5 Properties That Can Be Predicted from the Periodic Table

A. Atomic Radius

Figure 3.8 shows the relative sizes of the atoms of the representative elements. Notice that the size of the atoms increases from top to bottom in a column and decreases from left to right across a row.

This trend is related to electron configuration. As you read down column I, for example, the single valence electron is in a successively higher principal energy level, farther and farther away from the positively charged nucleus; hence, the **atomic radius** increases from the top to the bottom of the column. This same regular increase in size can be observed in each column of the periodic table.

Across a period from left to right, the atoms decrease in size. For elements within a period, electrons are being added one by one to the same principal energy level. At the same time, protons are also being added one by one to the nucleus, increasing its positive charge. This increasing positive charge pulls each electron shell closer to the nucleus, decreasing the atom's radius. Thus, atomic size is a periodic property that increases from top to bottom within a column and decreases from left to right across a period.

Example 3.7

Arrange the following elements in order of increasing atomic radius: calcium, sulfur, magnesium.

☐ *Solution*

Magnesium is above calcium in column II of the periodic table; magnesium atoms will be smaller than calcium atoms. Sulfur and magnesium are both in period 3; sulfur is farther to the right, and its atoms will be smaller. The order is sulfur, magnesium, calcium.

Problem 3.7

Arrange these elements in order of increasing atomic radius: iodine, sodium, chlorine.

B. Ionization Energy

The **ionization energy** of an element is the minimum energy required to remove an electron from a gaseous atom of that element. In the process a positive charge is left on the atom. Using sodium as an example, we write the equation for this process as

$$Na \longrightarrow Na^+ + e^-$$

Electrons are held in the atom by the attractive force of the positively charged nucleus. The farther the outermost electrons are from the nucleus, the less tightly they are held. Thus, the ionization energy within a group of elements decreases as the elements increase in atomic number. Among the naturally occurring alkali metal atoms, cesium has its single valence electron farthest from the nucleus (in the sixth energy level), and we can correctly predict that the ionization energy of cesium is the lowest of all these alkali metals. (Francium occurs in only trace amounts in the Earth; scientists have been unable to measure its ionization energy.)

Across a period, the ionization energy increases. The number of protons in the nucleus (the nuclear charge) increases, yet the valence electrons of the elements are in the same energy level. It becomes increasingly more difficult to remove an electron from the atom. The ionization energy of chlorine is much greater than that of sodium, an element in the same period.

The ionization energies of elements 1 through 36 are plotted against their atomic numbers in Figure 3.9. The peaks of the graph are the high ionization energies of the noble gases. The height of the peaks decreases as the number of the highest-occupied energy level increases. The low points of the graph are the ionization energies of the alkali metals, which have only one electron in their valence shells. These points, too, decrease slightly as the number of the highest-occupied energy level increases. The graph shows that ionization energy is periodically related to atomic number. Even within a row of the periodic table, the variations in ionization energy are closely related to electron configuration.

The ionization energy of an element measures its metallic nature. From Figure 3.9, we see that in each group the alkali metal has the lowest ionization energy. Therefore, they are the most metallic elements. As you read up the periodic table or from left to right across it, the metallic nature of the elements decreases.

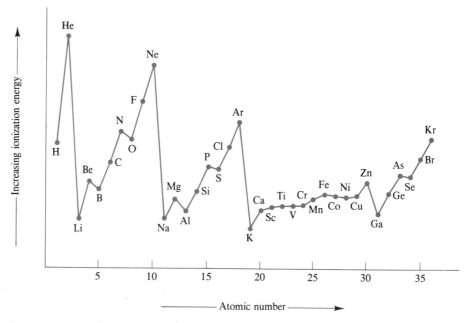

Figure 3.9 The ionization energies of elements 1 through 36 plotted versus their atomic numbers.

Nonmetals, located in the upper right-hand section of the periodic table, have high ionization energies. Except for the noble gases, fluorine has the highest ionization energy; therefore, fluorine is the least metallic or most nonmetallic element. As you read down the column or to the left of fluorine, elements become more metallic.

In summary, ionization energy increases from bottom to top on a column and from left to right across a period.

Example 3.8

a. Write the equation for the ionization of potassium.
b. Arrange the elements potassium, calcium, and fluorine in order of increasing ionization energy.

Solution

a. The equation for the loss of an electron by potassium is

$$K \longrightarrow K^+ + e^-$$

b. Since fluorine is in the top right corner of the periodic table, it has the highest ionization energy of these elements. Calcium is to the left and below fluorine; it has a smaller ionization energy. Potassium is even farther to the left and below calcium; its ionization energy is even lower. The order is potassium, calcium, fluorine.

Problem 3.8

a. Write the equation for the ionization of lithium.
b. Arrange, in order of increasing ionization energy, chlorine, cesium, and lithium.

Figure 3.10 summarizes how atomic radii, ionization energies, and metallic properties change within the periodic table

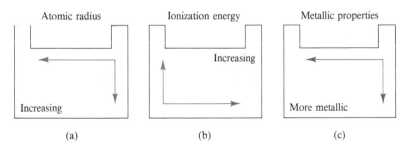

Figure 3.10 Trends of various atomic properties as related to position in the periodic table.

C. Formation of Ions

Atoms are electrically neutral. The number of positively charged protons in the nucleus of an atom equals the number of negatively charged electrons outside the nucleus. If, when an atom reacts, electrons are added or lost, the atom acquires a charge and becomes an **ion**.

1. The Octet Rule

The noble gases are very unreactive. This lack of reactivity is attributed to a stable electron configuration. Looking back to Section 3.3C, you can see that this configuration has, for all but helium, eight electrons, two s and six p, in the highest-occupied energy level. When other atoms react, they lose, gain, or share enough electrons to have a similarly stable structure, a complete outer shell. This tendency is expressed by the **octet rule**: An atom generally reacts in ways that give it an octet (or in a few cases a pair) of electrons in its outer shell.

An atom with one, two, or three valence electrons usually reacts by losing these electrons, thereby acquiring the electron configuration of the noble gas next below it in atomic number. An atom with six or seven valence electrons will usually, in reaction, add enough electrons to acquire the electron configuration of the noble gas next above it in atomic number. Other atoms may attain a complete octet by sharing electrons with a neighboring atom (Section 4.3A).

2. Positive Ions, or Cations

When a neutral atom loses an electron, it forms a positively charged ion called a **cation** (pronounced cat' i on). In general, metals lose electrons to form cations. The atom thereby attains the electron configuration of the noble gas next below it in atomic number.

An alkali metal, for example, loses one electron, to form a cation with a single positive charge. Sodium loses its single $3s$ valence electron to form the ion Na^+, which has the electron configuration of neon:

$$Na\cdot \longrightarrow Na^+ + e^-$$

An alkaline earth metal loses two electrons, to form a cation with a charge of $+2$. In forming the magnesium ion, Mg^{2+}, a magnesium atom loses its two valence electrons:

$$Mg\colon \longrightarrow Mg^{2+} + 2e^-$$

Aluminum loses its three valence electrons, to form a cation with charge $+3$:

$$\dot{Al}\colon \longrightarrow Al^{3+} + 3e^-$$

The names of these cations are the same as the metals from which they are formed, as shown in Table 3.7.

Table 3.7
Examples of cations.

Alkali Metal Cations		Alkaline Earth Metal Cations		Other Metal Cations	
Li^+	lithium ion	Mg^{2+}	magnesium ion	Al^{3+}	aluminum ion
Na^+	sodium ion	Ca^{2+}	calcium ion		
K^+	potassium ion	Sr^{2+}	strontium ion		
Rb^+	rubidium ion	Ba^{2+}	barium ion		
Cs^+	cesium ion				

Transition elements and metals to their right in the periodic table do not always follow the octet rule and frequently form more than one cation. For example, iron forms Fe^{2+} and Fe^{3+}; cobalt forms Co^{2+} and Co^{3+}. The names of these ions must indicate the charge they carry. The preferred system of nomenclature is that recommended by the International Union of Pure and Applied Chemistry (IUPAC). In this system, the name of the metal is followed by a Roman numeral showing the charge on the ion. No extra space is left between the name and the number. Thus, Fe^{2+} is iron(II) (say "iron two"), and Fe^{3+} is iron(III). In the old system, the name of the cation of lower charge ends in -*ous*. The name of the cation of higher charge ends in -*ic*. Examples of both systems of naming are given in Table 3.8.

Table 3.8
Naming cations.

Symbol	IUPAC Name	Old Name
Co^{2+}	cobalt(II)	cobaltous
Co^{3+}	cobalt(III)	cobaltic
Cu^{+}	copper(I)	cuprous
Cu^{2+}	copper(II)	cupric
Cr^{2+}	chromium(II)	chromous
Cr^{3+}	chromium(III)	chromic
Fe^{2+}	iron(II)	ferrous
Fe^{3+}	iron(III)	ferric

Often this system also uses the root of the Latin name of the element. Thus in this system, Fe^{2+} is ferrous and Fe^{3+} is ferric; Pb^{2+} is plumbous, and Pb^{4+} is plumbic. Those elements that use Latin roots are shown in Table 3.9.

Table 3.9
Some elements with non English root names (root is italicized).

Element	Root Word
copper	*cupr*um
gold	*aur*um
iron	*ferr*um
lead	*plumb*um
silver	*argent*um
tungsten	*wolf*ram

Notice that none of the cations discussed here have a charge greater than +3. When ions are formed, electrons are pulled off one by one from the atom. Thus, the first electron is removed from a neutral atom, the second electron from an ion of charge +1, the third electron from an ion of charge +2, and so on. The amount of energy necessary to remove an electron increases dramatically as the positive charge of the ion increases. The removal of a fourth electron and consequent formation of an ion of charge +4 is energetically unlikely.

3. Negative Ions, or Anions

When a neutral atom gains an electron, it forms a negatively charged ion called an **anion** (pronounced an′ i on). Typically, nonmetals form anions, gaining enough electrons to acquire the electron configuration of the noble gas of the next-higher atomic number. Elements of group VI with six valence electrons form anions by gaining two electrons, and the halogens with seven valence electrons form anions by gaining one electron. The names of these anions include the root name of the element and the ending -*ide*. Listed are several anions and their names; in each case, the root of the name is italicized.

F^-	*fluor*ide ion	I^-	*iod*ide ion
Cl^-	*chlor*ide ion	O^{2-}	*ox*ide ion
Br^-	*brom*ide ion	S^{2-}	*sulf*ide ion

4. Polyatomic Ions

The ions so far described are monatomic ions; that is, each contains only one atom. Many **polyatomic ions** are also known. These are groups of atoms that are bonded together and that carry a charge due to an excess or deficiency of electrons. The formulas and names of several common polyatomic ions follow. The symbols in the formula show which elements are present. The subscripts ("1" is understood) tell how many atoms of each element are present in the ion.

charge $+1$	NH_4^+	ammonium ion	charge -2	CO_3^{2-}	carbonate ion
				SO_4^{2-}	sulfate ion
charge -1	OH^-	hydroxide ion			
	NO_3^-	nitrate ion	charge -3	PO_4^{3-}	phosphate ion
	HCO_3^-	bicarbonate ion			

■

Example 3.9

Show how (a) magnesium and (b) sulfur follow the octet rule in forming ions.

☐ *Solution*

a. The electron configuration of magnesium is

$$1s^2 2s^2 2p^6 3s^2$$

Magnesium, with two valence electrons, loses two electrons to form the ion Mg^{2+}. The electron configuration of this ion is

$$1s^2 2s^2 2p^6$$

The equation for its formation is $Mg \longrightarrow Mg^{2+} + 2e^-$. The ion has a complete octet of electrons in its valence shell.

b. The electron configuration of sulfur is

$$1s^2 2s^2 2p^6 3s^2 3p^4$$

Sulfur has six valence electrons and therefore forms the ion S^{2-} by the addition of two electrons. This ion has the electron configuration

$$1s^2 2s^2 2p^6 3s^2 3p^6$$

The equation for its formation is $S + 2e^- \longrightarrow S^{2-}$. The outer-occupied energy level contains a complete octet.

Problem 3.9

Show how (a) potassium and (b) chlorine follow the octet rule in forming ions.

D. Nonmetals and Metals; Acids and Bases

So far, we have shown that metals usually have one, two, or three valence electrons. They have low ionization energies and are found to the bottom left in the periodic table. Nonmetals have four, five, six, or seven valence electrons; they have high ionization energies and are in the upper right corner of the periodic table. Using these distinctions to differentiate between a metal and a nonmetal requires knowledge of the electron configuration of the element. Knowledge of the difference between metals and nonmetals predates these observations.

Chemists had observed how the physical properties of metals (malleability, luster, conductivity, described in Section 2.3B) contrasted with those of non-metals. These early chemists also identified a difference in chemical property. The compounds formed when the oxide of a metal reacts with water are very much alike; and they are very different from compounds formed when the oxide of a nonmetal reacts with water.

When the **oxide** of a **metal** reacts with water, a **hydroxide** is formed.
For sodium oxide, the equation is

$$Na_2O + H_2O \longrightarrow 2NaOH$$

sodium hydroxide

For magnesium oxide,

$$MgO + H_2O \longrightarrow Mg(OH)_2$$

magnesium hydroxide

For aluminum oxide,

$$Al_2O_3 + 3H_2O \longrightarrow 2Al(OH)_3$$

aluminum hydroxide

When the **oxide** of a **nonmetal** reacts with water, an **acid** is formed.
For carbon dioxide,

$$CO_2 + H_2O \longrightarrow H_2CO_3$$

carbonic acid

For sulfur trioxide,

$$SO_3 + H_2O \longrightarrow H_2SO_4$$

sulfuric acid

For the oxide of phosphorus,

$$P_4O_{10} + 6H_2O \longrightarrow 4H_3PO_4$$

phosphoric acid

Table 3.10 lists several common hydroxides and acids.

Table 3.10
Common acids
and hydroxides.

Common Hydroxides		Common Acids	
sodium hydroxide	NaOH	hydrochloric acid	HCl
potassium hydroxide	KOH	acetic acid	$HC_2H_3O_2$
calcium hydroxide	$Ca(OH)_2$	nitric acid	HNO_3
aluminum hydroxide	$Al(OH)_3$	sulfuric acid	H_2SO_4
ammonium hydroxide	NH_4OH	carbonic acid	H_2CO_3
		phosphoric acid	H_3PO_4

Hydroxides are often referred to as **bases**, although all bases are not hydroxides. In all but ammonium hydroxide, the cation of a hydroxide is a metallic ion. A hydroxide dissolves in water to yield hydroxide ions. The solution of a hydroxide feels slippery because of the action of these ions on the skin. (You may have noticed this property in household ammonia, a dilute solution of ammonium hydroxide.) The solution of a hydroxide gives a class of compounds called **indicators** characteristic colors (see Table 3.11).

Table 3.11
Properties of acids
and hydroxides.

	Acids	Hydroxides
In aqueous solutions	release H^+	release OH^-
Indicators		
litmus	red	blue
phenolphthalein	colorless	pink
methyl orange	red	yellow
Other properties	taste sour	feel slippery

Most common acids contain a nonmetal and frequently oxygen. Acids dissolve in water to yield hydrogen ions. The solution of an acid tastes sour because of the hydrogen ions it contains. The color of an indicator in acid solutions is different from its color in solutions of hydroxides.

**Example
3.10**

Write balanced equations showing:

a. Reaction of iron with oxygen to form iron(III) oxide, Fe_2O_3, and reaction of the oxide with water to form iron(III) hydroxide, $Fe(OH)_3$.
b. Reaction of sulfur with oxygen to form sulfur dioxide, and reaction of the oxide with water to form sulfurous acid, H_2SO_3.

Solution

a. Iron is a metal; its oxide reacts with water to form a hydroxide.

$$4Fe + 3O_2 \longrightarrow 2Fe_2O_3 \qquad Fe_2O_3 + 3H_2O \longrightarrow 2Fe(OH)_3$$

b. Sulfur is a nonmetal; its oxides react with water to form acids.

$$S + O_2 \longrightarrow SO_2 \qquad SO_2 + H_2O \longrightarrow H_2SO_3$$

Problem 3.10

Write balanced equations showing (a) the reaction of calcium with oxygen to form calcium oxide, CaO, and the reaction of that oxide with water to form calcium hydroxide; (b) the reaction of chlorine with oxygen to form dichloropentoxide, Cl_2O_5, and the reaction of that oxide with water to form chloric acid, $HClO_3$.

Key Terms and Concepts

acid (3.5D)	lanthanides (3.3B3)
actinides (3.3B3)	Lewis structures (3.3D)
alkali metals (3.4A)	metallic oxides (3.5D)
alkaline earth metals (3.4A)	noble gases (3.3C)
anions (3.5C3)	nonmetallic oxides (3.5D)
atomic radius (3.5A)	octet rule (3.5C1)
bases (3.5D)	orbitals (3.1B)
cations (3.5C2)	orbital energies (3.1B2)
core notation (3.3C)	orbital shapes (3.1B1)
electron configuration (3.2)	periodic table (3.3)
electron dot (Lewis) structures (3.3D)	polyatomic ions (3.5C4)
electron spin (3.1B)	principal energy levels (3.1A)
halogens (3.4A)	rare earths (3.3B3)
hydroxide (3.5D)	representative elements (3.3B1)
indicators (3.5D)	shells (3.1A)
inner transition elements (3.3B3)	sublevels (3.1B)
ionization energy (3.5B)	transition elements (3.3B2)
ions (3.5C)	valence electrons (3.3D)

Problems

Electron configuration of atoms (Section 3.2)

3.11 Write the complete electron configuration of these elements:
a. silicon   **b.** tin   **c.** vanadium   **d.** lead

The periodic table (Section 3.3)

3.12 What characterizes the electron configuration of:
a. elements in the same column of the periodic table?
b. elements in the same period of the table?
c. the noble gases?

3.13 Classify all elements whose name begins with "C" as representative, transition, or inner transition elements.

3.14 Write the complete electron configuration of these elements. Then relate this configuration to the position of the element in the periodic table.
a. calcium   **b.** antimony   **c.** carbon   **d.** radium

3.15 Write the complete electron configuration of each of the alkaline earth metals.

3.16 For the elements in period 3 of the periodic table, (a) give the complete electron configuration, and (b) give the electron configuration using core notation.

3.17 Draw the Lewis structures of the alkali metals.

3.18 Draw the Lewis structures of atoms of these elements:
a. sulfur   **b.** chlorine   **c.** magnesium   **d.** tellurium

3.19 Draw the Lewis structure of the elements in Problem 3.16.

3.20 Draw the Lewis structure of the elements in Problem 3.11.

3.21 Draw the Lewis structure of the members of the halogen family.

Properties that can be predicted from the periodic table (Section 3.5)

3.22 **a.** How is each of the following properties related to position in the periodic table: metallic or nonmetallic nature, ionization energy, atomic radius?
b. How is each property in part (a) related to electron configuration?

3.23 Classify these elements as metals or nonmetals:
a. vanadium   **b.** palladium   **c.** selenium   **d.** sulfur

3.24 Element number 117 has not yet been discovered. We expect that when and if it is discovered, it will be in column VII of the table; explain why. Predict the following properties for this element, comparing them to those of a known element: metal or nonmetal, atomic radius, ionization energy, Lewis structure.

3.25 Which element in each of these pairs has a higher ionization energy: cesium/cerium, arsenic/bismuth, aluminum/silicon, iodine/bromine?

3.26 Which element in each of these pairs has a larger atomic radius: potassium/rubidium, nitrogen/arsenic, aluminum/sulfur, hydrogen/oxygen?

3.27 Arrange the elements within the sets in order of increasing ionization energy:
a. Be, Mg, Sr   **b.** Na, Al, S   **c.** Bi, Cs, Ba

3.28 Of the following ions known to exist, which are exceptions to the octet rule?
a. Cs^+ **b.** Ga^+ **c.** Te^{2+} **d.** Bi^{3+}

3.29 Name these ions, using both IUPAC and older systems.
a. Fe^{2+}, Fe^{3+} **b.** Cr^{2+}, Cr^{3+}
c. Cu^+, Cu^{2+} **d.** Ni^{2+}, Ni^{3+}

3.30 Write the formulas of the following cations:
a. iron(III)   **b.** silver(I)   **c.** platinum(II)   **d.** osmium(III)

3.31 Write the formula and give the name of the monatomic anion formed by:
a. iodine   **b.** oxygen   **c.** bromine   **d.** sulfur

3.32   Write the formula of the monatomic cation formed by these elements:
        a. aluminum   **b.** strontium   **c.** cesium   **d.** lithium

3.33   Complete the chart:

Name of Ion	Formula	Name of Ion	Formula
————	NH_4^+	sulfate	————
nitrate	————	————	CO_3^{2-}
————	HCO_3^-	phosphate	————

3.34   Write balanced equations showing the formation of the oxides of the elements in group II by the reaction of the element with oxygen. Write equations that show the reactions of these oxides with water.

General problems

3.35   Given the following data, calculate the density of the nucleus of an atom of sodium-23.

mass of proton = 1.0073 amu   1 amu = 1.66×10^{-24} g
mass of neutron = 1.008 amu   diam. of nucleus = 1.16×10^{-12} m
mass of electron = 5.45×10^{-4} amu   diam. of atom = 3.08×10^{-10} m
$V_{sphere} = \frac{4}{3}\pi r^3$

3.36   Plutonium is harmful to humans. It is recommended that the concentration of plutonium in the air be no greater than 3.00×10^{-11} g/m^3. How many atoms of plutonium is this per cubic meter? (At. wt. of plutonium is 244.)

3.37   The density of copper is 8.96 g/cm^3. What is the mass of a block of copper measuring 1.65 cm $\times$ 1.02 cm $\times$ 0.921 cm? How many atoms of copper are in this sample? What mass of lead contains the same number of atoms?

3.38   The addition of one part per million of fluorine to drinking water has caused a dramatic decrease in dental cavities in the population served by such water supplies. Evanston, Illinois, is one of the communities that adds fluorine to its drinking water. If you drink one glass of Evanston water (250 mL), how many atoms of fluorine do you imbibe? Assume that Evanston's drinking water and pure water have the same density.

3.39   The mass of an electron is 5.45×10^{-4} amu. In a uranium atom of mass 238 amu, what percentage of the total mass is contributed by the 92 electrons in the atom? What percentage of the mass is contributed by the 92 protons? What percentage of the mass is contributed by the neutrons in the atom?

The Past and Future of the Periodic Table

The elements in the modern periodic table are arranged in order of increasing atomic number. The configuration of rows and columns in the table is such that elements with the same outer-shell electron configuration fall in the same column. Elements in the same column are chemically very similar. Elements in the same row have their valence electrons in the same principal energy level. The periodic table as we know it is a product of the last half of this century, but its development stretches back into the mid-1800s. Its history gives some interesting insights into scientific progress.

One of the first to recognize regular similarities in the properties of groups of elements was the German chemist Johann Döbereiner (1780–1849). In 1829, Döbereiner suggested that many elements belong to three-member groups, or triads, and that within each triad similarities and trends in properties are noticeable. The halogens—chlorine, bromine, and iodine—form such a triad. They have similar chemical properties. Bromine has physical and chemical properties midway between those of chlorine and those of iodine.

John Newlands (1838–1898), a British chemist, was the first to attempt a meaningful arrangement of all the elements. In 1866, Newlands

1 H	8 F	15 Cl	22 Co, Ni	29 Br	36 Pd	42 I	50 Pt, Ir
2 Li	9 Na	16 K	23 Cu	30 Rb	37 Ag	44 Ca	51 Os
3 Be	10 Mg	17 Ca	24 Zn	31 Sr	38 Cd	45 Ba, V	52 Hg
4 B	11 Al	19 Cr	25 Y	33 Ce, La	40 U	46 Ta	53 Tl
5 C	12 Si	18 Ti	26 In	32 Zr	39 Sn	47 W	54 Pb
6 N	13 P	20 Mn	27 As	34 Di, Mo	41 Sb	48 Nb	55 Bi
7 O	14 S	21 Fe	28 Se	35 Ro, Ru	43 Te	49 Au	56 Th

Figure II-1 Newlands's table of the elements (1866). Note the following: In some cases, two elements are in the same box; some rows contain elements with dissimilar properties (chlorine and platinum, for example); and the order of elements is vertical rather than horizontal.

Series	Group I — R_2O	Group II — RO	Group III — R_2O_3	Group IV RH_4 RO_2	Group V RH_3 R_2O_5	Group VI RH_2 RO	Group VII RH R_2O_7	Group VIII — RO_4
1	H = 1							
2	Li = 7	Be = 9.1	B = 11	C = 12	N = 14	O = 16	F = 19	
3	Na = 23	Mg = 24.4	Al = 27	Si = 28	P = 31	S = 32	Cl = 35.5	Fe = 56, Ni = 58.5,
4	K = 39.1	Ca = 40	— = 44	Ti = 48.1	V = 51.2	Cr = 52.3	Mn = 55	Co 59.1, Cu 63.3.
5	(Cu) = 63.3	Zn = 65.4	— = 68	— = 72	As = 75	Se = 79	Br = 80	Rh = 103, Ru = 103.8,
6	Rb = 85.4	Sr = 87.5	Y = 89	Zr = 90.7	Nb = 94.2	Mo = 95.9	— = 100	Pd = 108, Ag = 107.9.
7	(Ag) = 107.9	Cd = 112	In = 113.7	Sn = 118	Sb = 120.3	Te = 125.2	I = 126.9	
8	Cs = 132.9	Ba = 137	La = 138.5	Ce = 141.5	Di = 145			
9	(—)	—	—	—	—	—	—	Ir = 193.1, Pt = 194.8,
10	—	—	Yb = 173.2	—	Ta = 182.8	W = 184	—	Os = 200, Au = 196.7.
11	(Au) = 196.7	Hg = 200.4	Tl = 204.1	Pb = 206.9	Bi = 208	—	—	
12	—	—	—	Tb = 233.4	—	U = 239	—	— — —

Figure II-2 Mendeleev's periodic table (1871). Note the spaces left for undiscovered elements. Columns are arranged according to the formulas of the hydrides and oxides of the elements. Note that several atomic weights are incorrect, according to present knowledge.

organized all known elements in groups of seven, in order of increasing atomic weight (Figure II-1). The first members of each group are indeed similar. Newlands was an avid musician, however, and used the term *law of octaves* in describing the ordering. The term was ridiculed by other scientists, causing a general rejection of his entire theory. One chemist even suggested that an alphabetical arrangement might be more useful. Britain's Royal Chemical Society refused to publish Newlands's paper. Much later, in 1887, after

Newlands's work had been shown to be basically correct, the Royal Chemical Society awarded him the Davy Medal, their highest honor.

A much more successful arrangement of the elements was conceived in 1869 by both Lothar Meyer (1830–1895), in Germany, and Dmitri Mendeleev (1834–1907), in Russia. Figure II-2 shows Mendeleev's periodic table as it appeared in 1871. Mendeleev's insistence that the elements be ordered by similar chemical properties led him to leave a few gaps in the table for undis-

Table II-1
Comparison of Mendeleev's predictions for the properties of the undiscovered element eka-silicon and the actual properties of the element germanium.

Properties	Predicted by Mendeleev for Eka-silicon (1871)	Actual Properties of Germanium (1886)
atomic weight	72	72.6
density	5.5 g/cm^3	5.36 g/cm^3
appearance	gray metal	gray metal
melting point	very high	960°C
specific heat	0.073 cal/g·°C	0.076 cal/g·°C
formula of oxide	EsO_2	GeO_2
density of oxide	4.7 g/cm^3	4.70 g/cm^3
formula of chloride	$EsCl_4$	$GeCl_4$
density of chloride	1.9 g/cm^3	1.88 g/cm^3
boiling point of chloride	100°C	83°C

covered elements, and he used the general trends established in the table to predict the properties of these missing elements. Table II-1 (page 97B) lists the properties Mendeleev predicted in 1871 for the element he called eka-silicon, meaning "next after silicon," (predicted atomic weight, 72) and the properties of the element germanium, atomic weight 72.6, discovered in 1886.

The remarkable agreement between Mendeleev's predictions for eka-silicon and the actual values for germanium show that his theories work. The publication of Mendeleev's table and his predictions of new elements and their properties spurred chemists to search for these new elements, using the predicted properties as a guide for isolating and identifying the elements. Each additional element discovered further confirmed the accuracy of Mendeleev's table.

In constructing the table, Mendeleev found some apparent disagreements among properties of known elements. For example, the values of the atomic weights for gold and platinum accepted at this time indicated that platinum was heavier than gold. In grouping these elements in families according to similar properties, Mendeleev observed that platinum should come before gold, which caused him to question the accepted weights for these elements. Other chemists redid their measurements, thinking to prove Mendeleev wrong; instead, they found that gold has a higher atomic weight than platinum.

By 1892, Mendeleev's periodic table was generally accepted by chemists. But in that year a new challenge to his theory arose—the discovery of an element that did not fit anywhere on the table. This was the element argon, discovered by the British physicist Baron Rayleigh (1842–1919). Baron Rayleigh's measurements of the density of nitrogen recorded a discrepancy of one part per thousand between nitrogen isolated from the atmosphere and nitrogen obtained by the decomposition of ammonia. Repetitions of the experiment failed to uncover any error, and Rayleigh became convinced that he had detected a new gas in the atmosphere. He was able to isolate this gas and determine its properties. The physical properties he observed were not unusual, but the chemical properties were singular; the new gas did not react with anything!

During the next few years, several attempts were made to account for argon within Mendeleev's periodic table. Some scientists proposed that it was really a diatomic or even a triatomic gas, since no monatomic gases were known at that time, but all attempts to break down molecules of the gas failed. Argon's atomic weight (39.9) meant it should fit between potassium and calcium in the periodic table, but that would mean a new column and several undiscovered elements. Investigation of this possibility led Rayleigh to the discovery of a second new element, also nonreactive, which he called helium. Its atomic weight of 4 compounded the problem created by argon. Most scientists had such faith in the periodic table that they hoped the new elements would prove to be compounds, since this would avoid any change in the table. Not until 1898, when Rayleigh and his coworker, Sir William Ramsay (1852–1916), announced the discovery of three more nonreactive, monatomic gases (neon, krypton, and xenon), did chemists finally accept the idea of a new family of elements.

Even so, the importance of these elements in understanding electron configuration was not appreciated for many years. They were considered to be an unsolved puzzle that confused rather than simplified the periodic table. The problem presented because the atomic weight of argon fell between the atomic weights of potassium and calcium was not cleared up until 1914, when the English physicist Henry Moseley (1887–1915) showed that arrangement of the elements by atomic number instead of atomic weight gave a truer alignment of properties within the table columns. His new ordering of the elements, based on their atomic numbers, left more spaces for undiscovered elements and led to the search for technetium, promethium, rhenium, and hafnium and their eventual discovery. Unfortunately, Moseley did not live long enough to know this; he was killed in the First World War at age 27.

Various formats for the periodic table were tried during the first half of the twentieth century, including spirals, 3-D tubes, and other shapes. The most common form at present, with the central block of transition elements, was not developed until the 1930s, when the significance of electron configurations began to be recognized. The row for the lanthanides was added during this period. The concept of the actinides row was proposed in 1944, when the American chemist Glenn Seaborg (b. 1912) developed the idea that the new elements he was trying to synthesize might have properties that were more like the properties of the lanthanides than those of the transition elements. This conjecture led him to devise new experiments that isolated the elements americium and curium. His discoveries were first announced in 1945 on a radio quiz show.

By 1986, chemists were certain of the identities of 108 elements, including 92 found in nature and 16 made in laboratories. It is difficult to study the synthetic elements, because they are highly radioactive and quickly break up into smaller atoms. The brevity of the half-lives has led to predictions that all elements heavier than 109, the so-called super heavy elements, have even shorter half-lives.

In June 1976, data published by a team of nuclear scientists suggested the existence of element 126 in a crystal sample of the mineral monazite. The data were in the form of a peak in an X-ray spectrum that corresponded to the predicted energy of a nucleus of this element, tentatively named bicentenium, in honor of the U.S. bicentennial. The find was exciting to physicists because the rock sample had been dated as being about one billion years old, suggesting a much higher stability for this element than theorists had predicted. However, additional experiments by the same researchers indicated that a peak of the exact same energy as the X-ray peak for element 126 could be generated by gamma rays emitted from an excited nucleus of praseodymium. They also found that praseodymium could be created from cerium (a principal con-

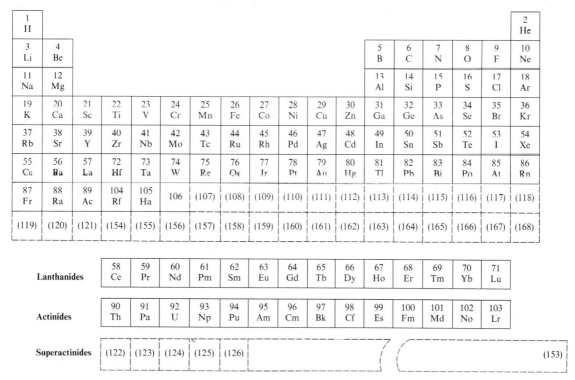

Figure II-3 Seaborg's suggested periodic table of the future.

stituent of monazite) during the proton bombardment used to generate the original X-ray spectra. Experiments performed on the same mineral samples with different identification techniques failed to reproduce the original data. Although it is not a closed question, it is now generally believed that element 126 has not yet been found in nature.

Will elements heavier than atomic weight number 109 ever be found? Although most scientists believe that no superheavy elements will be found in nature, there is no agreement on the possibility of synthesizing superheavy elements. The problem is partly one of finding a technique for fusing two nuclei into one without using so much energy that the resulting nucleus undergoes spontaneous fission. Even so, there are suggestions in the literature of methods for preparing elements with atomic numbers up to 119, along with predicted properties for these elements.

What about the future of the periodic table?

Again, without the existence of superheavy elements as evidence, there is no agreement as to how the table might continue. The energy levels in these elements become so close that no clear-cut pattern can be predicted about when one electron shell will be filled and another begin. Glenn Seaborg has suggested the theoretical periodic table shown in Figure II-3, but whether this will be the periodic table used by students taking this course 100 years from now is for the future to decide.

Sources

Robinson, A. L. 1977. Superheavy elements: Confirmation fails to materialize. *Science* 195:473.

Seaborg, G. T. 1979. The periodic table, tortuous path to manmade elements. *Chem. & Eng. News*, 16 April 1979, p. 46.

Seaborg, G. T., Loveland, W., and Morissey, D. J. 1979. Superheavy elements—A crossroads. *Science* 203:711.

Wolfenden, J. H. 1969. The noble gases and the periodic table. *J. Chem. Ed.* 46:569.

4 Compounds: Names, Formulas, and Bonding

Elements combine to form compounds. From various combinations of the hundred or so elements are formed millions of compounds. Each is unique, with a name and a formula that shows its composition. Its properties depend on its composition, the nature of the bonds between its atoms, and how those atoms are arranged in space.

4.1 Nature of Compounds

A compound is a chemical combination of elements. It has a constant composition and a unique set of properties; the compound is therefore different from other compounds and from the elements of which it is composed. Sodium, for example, is a soft silvery gray metal, toxic to humans; chlorine is a pale green gas, also toxic to humans. Yet sodium combines with chlorine to produce sodium chloride, which we know as table salt—a part of our daily diet. Water is formed by the chemical combination of the flammable gas hydrogen with oxygen. Yet how different the properties of water are from the elements of which it is composed.

The composition of a compound is represented by a formula that lists the symbols of the elements it contains; each symbol is followed by a subscript that tells how many atoms of that element are contained in the simplest unit of the compound.

Some compounds exist as molecules. Table 4.1 lists the names and formulas

Table 4.1
Some molecular compounds.

Name	Formula	Melting Point (°C)
ammonia	NH_3	−77
cane sugar	$C_{12}H_{22}O_{11}$	185
chloroform	$CHCl_3$	−63
ethyl alcohol	C_2H_6O	−117
water	H_2O	0

98

of several **molecular compounds** that may be familiar to you, and their common names and melting points. Note that these molecular compounds contain only nonmetals and that several melt below room temperature.

Other compounds are ionic. Table 4.2 shows the names and formulas of some ionic compounds that may be familiar. All these compounds are solids at room temperature. Notice that the systematic name of these compounds uses the names of the ions as given in Section 3.5 and gives first the name of the cation followed by the name of the anion.

Table 4.2
Some common ionic compounds.

Common Name	Systematic Name	Formula
bleach	sodium hypochlorite	NaOCl
chalk	calcium carbonate	$CaCO_3$
lime	calcium oxide	CaO
milk of magnesia	magnesium hydroxide	$Mg(OH)_2$

The formula of an ionic compound is neutral. The ratio of the cations and anions it contains is such that there is no excess charge. Thus, when a sodium ion, Na^+, combines with sulfate ions, SO_4^{2-}, to form sodium sulfate, it is in the ratio 2:1, so that the resulting combination, Na_2SO_4, is neutral. When an aluminum ion, Al^{3+}, combines with a chloride ion, Cl^-, to form aluminum chloride, it is in the ratio 1:3, giving the formula $AlCl_3$, which is neutral.

Example 4.1

☐ *Solution*

Write the formulas of

a. potassium sulfide   **b.** magnesium nitrate   **c.** aluminum sulfate

a. The potassium ion is K^+ (Section 3.5C2), and the sulfide ion is S^{2-} (Section 3.7C3). Their neutral combination gives two K^+ to one S^{2-}. Potassium sulfide is K_2S.

b. Magnesium ion is Mg^{2+}; nitrate ion is NO_3^- (Section 3.5C4). Their neutral combination combines one Mg^{2+} with two NO_3^-; magnesium nitrate is $Mg(NO_3)_2$.

c. Aluminum ion is Al^{3+}, sulfate ion is SO_4^{2-}. The smallest number that is divisible by both 2 and 3 is 6. If we combine two Al^{3+} with three SO_4^{2-}, the charges are balanced at 6 all. The formula of aluminum sulfate is $Al_2(SO_4)_3$.

Notice two things about these examples: (1) In both (b) and (c), the **polyatomic ion** was enclosed in parentheses because it was taken more than one time; the **monatomic ion** was not enclosed in parentheses no matter how many times it occurred. (2) If the charge on the two ions differs in magnitude as well as sign, the number of times the cation is taken equals the charge on the anion, and the number of times the anion is taken equals the charge on the cation. That is,

$$K_2S \qquad Mg(NO_3)_2 \qquad Al_2(SO_4)_3$$

$$K^+ \quad S^{2-} \qquad Mg^{2+} \quad NO_3^- \qquad Al^{3+} \quad SO_4^{2-}$$

Problem 4.1

Write the formulas of

a. copper(II) chloride **b.** barium nitrate **c.** magnesium phosphate

---

Example 4.2

Name the compounds:

a. $CrCl_3$ **b.** MgI_2 **c.** Fe_2O_3

☐ *Solution*

a. $CrCl_3$: the anion is the chloride ion, Cl^-. Note that the ending of the name has changed from *ine* (the element) to *ide* (the ion). There are three chloride ions for each chromium cation; therefore the chromium ion has a $+3$ charge and is named chromium(III). The compound is chromium(III) chloride.

b. MgI_2: the anion is iodide, I^-. Again, note the change in the ending from *ine* to *ide*. Magnesium is an alkaline earth metal and therefore its oxidation number $+2$ need not be included in its name. The compound is magnesium iodide.

c. Fe_2O_3: the anion is the oxide ion that has a -2 charge. Note the change from oxygen to oxide. There are three oxide ions, giving a total negative charge of -6. The neutral compound contains two iron cations. Together they must have a charge of $+6$. Each iron cation must then have a charge of $+3$. Therefore, the cation is iron(III), and the compound is iron(III) oxide.

Problem 4.2

Name the following compounds:

a. CuO **b.** FeS **c.** $SrCl_2$

4.2 Formula Weights

A. Calculation of Formula Weights

The **formula weight** of a compound or an ion is the sum of the atomic weights of all elements in the compound or ion, with each element's atomic weight multiplied by the number of atoms of that element appearing in the formula of the compound or ion.

Example 4.3

a. The formula of sulfuric acid is H_2SO_4. Calculate its formula weight.
b. What is the formula weight of ammonium carbonate, $(NH_4)_2CO_3$?

☐ *Solution*

In each of these examples, the mass contributed by each element in the compound is calculated by multiplying its atomic weight by the number of its atoms in the formula. The sum of these contributions is the formula weight of the compound or ion.

a. The formula weight of sulfuric acid:

	Atomic Weight		No. of Atoms in Formula		Contribution by Element (amu)
hydrogen	1.008	×	2	=	2.016
sulfur	32.06	×	1	=	32.06
oxygen	16.00	×	4	=	64.00
			Formula weight of H_2SO_4 =		98.076, or 98.08 amu

b. The formula weight of ammonium carbonate: The formula weight of ammonium carbonate is the sum of the formula weight of the carbonate ion and twice the formula weight of the ammonium ion. Calculate the formula weight of the ammonium ion.

nitrogen	14.01	×	1	=	14.01 amu
hydrogen	1.008	×	4	=	4.032 amu
			Formula weight of NH_4^+ =		18.04 amu

Calculate the formula weight of the carbonate ion.

carbon	12.01	×	1	=	12.01 amu
oxygen	16.00	×	3	=	48.00 amu
			Formula weight of CO_3^{2-} =		60.01 amu

Calculate the formula weight of ammonium carbonate.

$(NH_4^+)_2$	18.04	×	2	=	36.08 amu
CO_3^{2-}				=	60.01 amu
			Formula weight of $(NH_4)_2CO_3$ −		96.09 amu

Problem 4.3

Calculate the formula weight of

a. potassium sulfide   **b.** magnesium nitrate

B. Moles of Compounds

The **mole** is defined as 6.02×10^{23} units (Section 2.8). You have learned that one mole of a particular element has a mass in grams equal to its atomic weight. Compounds and ions can also be measured in moles. One mole of a compound has a mass in grams equal to its formula weight. In Example 4.3(a), we calculated the formula weight of sulfuric acid to be 98.08 amu. It follows that 1 mol of sulfuric acid has a mass of 98.08 g. The formula of a compound also tells how many moles of a particular element are contained in 1 mol of the compound. One mole of sulfuric acid contains:

  2 mol hydrogen atoms weighing 2×1.008 g, or 2.016 g
  1 mol sulfur atoms weighing 1×32.06 g, or 32.06 g
  4 mol oxygen atoms weighing 4×16.00 g, or 64.00 g

This relation between mass and moles of a compound is often used as a conversion factor in solving problems.

Example 4.4

An experimental procedure requires 1.76 mol of glucose, $C_6H_{12}O_6$. What mass of glucose is required?

☐ *Solution*

Use the steps developed in Section 1.8.

Wanted: ? g glucose
Given: 1.76 mol glucose. The formula weight of glucose is
  carbon: $6 \times 12.01 =$ 72.06 amu
  hydrogen: $12 \times 1.008 =$ 12.096 amu
  oxygen: $6 \times 16.00 =$ 96.00 amu
                       180.156, or 180.16 amu

Conversion factor:
  1 mol glucose = 180.16 g
Equation:

$$? \text{ g glucose} = 1.76 \text{ mol glucose} \times \frac{180.16 \text{ g glucose}}{1 \text{ mol glucose}}$$

Answer: 317 g glucose (The answer is given in three significant figures because that is the number of significant figures in 1.76 mol glucose.)

Example 4.5

How many atoms of oxygen are in 0.262 g carbon dioxide, CO_2?

☐ *Solution*

Wanted: ? atoms oxygen
Given: 0.262 g carbon dioxide
Conversion factors: The formula weight of carbon dioxide is
  carbon: $1 \times 12.01 = 12.01$ amu
  oxygen: $2 \times 16.00 = 32.00$ amu
                    44.01 amu
  1 mol CO_2 = 44.01 g
  1 mol CO_2 contains 2 mol of O atoms
  1 mol atoms is 6.02×10^{23} atoms
Equation:

$$? \text{ atoms O} = 0.262 \text{ g CO}_2 \times \frac{1 \text{ mol CO}_2}{44.01 \text{ g CO}_2}$$

$$\times \frac{2 \text{ mol O atoms}}{1 \text{ mol CO}_2} \times \frac{6.02 \times 10^{23} \text{ atoms}}{1 \text{ mol atoms}}$$

Answer: 7.17×10^{21} O atoms

Note that in Example 4.5, each factor using the mole states the chemical composition of the mole: "1 mol CO_2" and "2 mol O atoms." As problems become increasingly complex, this bookkeeping habit becomes especially important. Note also that the example deals with atoms of oxygen; it is not of concern that oxygen exists in nature as a diatomic molecule, O_2.

Example 4.6

A solution of glucose contains 9.00 g glucose per 100 mL of solution. How many moles of glucose are contained in a liter of this solution?

☐ *Solution*

Wanted: ? moles glucose per liter of solution
Given: 9.00 g glucose per 100 mL solution
Conversion factors:
   from Example 4.4, 1 mol glucose = 180.16 g glucose
   1 L = 1000 mL
Equation:

$$\frac{?\text{ moles glucose}}{1\text{ L solution}} = \frac{9.00\text{ g glucose}}{100\text{ mL}} \times \frac{1\text{ mol glucose}}{180.16\text{ g}} \times \frac{1000\text{ mL}}{1\text{ L}}$$

Answer: 0.500 mol glucose per liter of solution

Problem 4.4

Calculate the mass of 0.875 mol of carbon dioxide.

Problem 4.5

Calculate the number of hydrogen atoms in 5.32×10^{-3} g of ammonia, NH_3.

Problem 4.6

How many moles of sulfuric acid, H_2SO_4, are in 1 L of solution if 200 mL of solution contains 6.23 g of acid?

C. Percentage Composition

Percent means parts per hundred. The **percentage composition** of a compound is the number of grams of each element or group of elements in 100 g of the compound, expressed as a percentage. For example, the percentage composition of sodium chloride (NaCl) can be calculated from the atomic weights of sodium and chlorine and the formula weight of NaCl.

Formula weight of NaCl: 23.00 g + 35.45 g = 58.45 g

Percent sodium: $\dfrac{23.00\text{ g Na}}{58.45\text{ g NaCl}} \times 100\% = 39.35\%$ sodium

Percent chlorine: $\dfrac{35.45\text{ g Cl}}{58.45\text{ g NaCl}} \times 100\% = 60.65\%$ chlorine

Example 4.7

Calculate the percentage composition of carbon tetrachloride, CCl_4.

☐ *Solution*

The formula weight of carbon tetrachloride is

carbon: $12.01 \times 1 =$ 12.01 amu
chlorine: $35.45 \times 4 =$ 141.80 amu
    Formula wt of $CCl_4 =$ 153.81 amu

Percent carbon: $\dfrac{12.01 \text{ g C}}{153.8 \text{ g CCl}_4} \times 100\% = 7.809\%$ carbon

Percent chlorine: $\dfrac{141.80 \text{ g Cl}}{153.81 \text{ g CCl}_4} \times 100\% = 92.19\%$ chlorine

It is always wise to check these percentage calculations by assuring yourself that the results add up to 100%, as they do here.

Problem 4.7

Calculate the percentage composition of magnesium carbonate.

Example 4.8

Calculate the percentage of nitrogen in the fertilizer ammonium sulfate, $(NH_4)_2SO_4$.

☐ *Solution*

1. Calculate the formula weight of $(NH_4)_2SO_4$.
   The formula weight of NH_4^+ is
      N: $1 \times 14.01 = 14.01$ amu
      4H: $4 \times 1.008 =$ 4.032 amu
                  18.04 amu
   The formula weight of SO_4^{2-} is
      S: $1 \times 32.06 = 32.06$ amu
      O: $4 \times 16.00 = 64.00$ amu
                  96.06 amu
   The formula weight of $(NH_4)_2SO_4$ is
      $(NH_4)_2^+$: $2 \times 18.04 =$ 36.08 amu
      SO_4^{2-}: $1 \times 96.06 =$ 96.06 amu
                  132.14 amu

2. Calculate the percentage of nitrogen.
   Each formula unit contains 2 nitrogen atoms.
   Therefore, there are 2×14.01, or 28.02, g of nitrogen in 132.14 g ammonium sulfate.

   Percent nitrogen $= \dfrac{28.02 \text{ g N}}{132.14 \text{ g (NH}_4)_2\text{SO}_4} \times 100\% = 21.20\%$ N

Problem 4.8

Calculate the percentage of nitrogen in the fertilizer ammonium phosphate, $(NH_4)_3PO_4$.

Example 4.9

When 6.932 g silver oxide is decomposed, the silver residue weighs 5.351 g. What is the percentage composition of silver oxide?

☐ *Solution*

The percentage of silver can be calculated directly:

$$\text{Percent silver} = \frac{5.351 \text{ g silver}}{6.932 \text{ g silver oxide}} \times 100\% = 77.19\%$$

The percentage of oxygen can be calculated by subtraction:
Percent oxygen = $100\% - 77.19\% = 22.81\%$

Problem 4.9

When a red oxide of mercury is heated, oxygen is driven off, leaving a silver-colored pool of pure mercury. After a 5.00-g sample of this oxide has been heated, 4.63 g of mercury remains. Calculate the percentage of mercury in this compound.

D. Empirical Formulas

The **molecular formula** of a compound expresses a ratio among the numbers of atoms of different elements present in a molecule of the compound. This ratio is a mole ratio as well as a ratio among numbers of atoms. From the formula of a compound it is possible to calculate its percentage composition. Going in the opposite direction from the composition of a compound, one can calculate its **empirical formula**, or the simplest ratio between numbers of atoms. The molecular formula (see Section 4.2E) is a multiple of the simplest formula.

Consider the compound chloroform. The percentage composition of chloroform is 10.06% carbon, 0.85% hydrogen, and 89.09% chlorine. We know then that in 100 g chloroform there are 10.06 g carbon, 0.85 g hydrogen, and 89.09 g chlorine. This weight relation can be converted to a mole ratio by the following calculations:

carbon: $10.06 \text{ g C} \times \dfrac{1 \text{ mol C}}{12.01 \text{ g}} = 0.838 \text{ mol carbon}$

hydrogen: $0.85 \text{ g H} \times \dfrac{1 \text{ mol H}}{1.008 \text{ g}} = 0.84 \text{ mol hydrogen}$

chlorine: $89.09 \text{ g Cl} \times \dfrac{1 \text{ mol Cl}}{35.45 \text{ g}} = 2.51 \text{ mol chlorine}$

These calculations show that the mole ratio among the elements in chloroform is 0.84 mol of carbon to 0.84 mol hydrogen to 2.51 mol chlorine. This can be expressed by the formula

$$C_{0.84}H_{0.84}Cl_{2.51}$$

Formulas by definition, however, contain only whole numbers of atoms. To change this ratio to whole numbers, we can divide each subscript by the smallest

subscript, arriving at the formula

$$C_{\frac{0.84}{0.84}}H_{\frac{0.84}{0.84}}Cl_{\frac{2.51}{0.84}}$$

or $CHCl_3$, the empirical formula of chloroform.

Example 4.10

Calculate the empirical formula of a compound that contains 36.8% nitrogen and 63.2% oxygen.

☐ *Solution*

1. Assume that you have 100 g of the compound. It contains 36.8 g nitrogen and 63.2 g oxygen.
2. Convert these weights to moles.

$$\text{? moles nitrogen} = 36.8 \text{ g N} \times \frac{1 \text{ mol N}}{14.0 \text{ g N}} = 2.62 \text{ mol N}$$

$$\text{? moles oxygen} = 63.2 \text{ g O} \times \frac{1 \text{ mol O}}{16.0 \text{ g O}} = 3.95 \text{ mol O}$$

This gives the formula $N_{2.62}O_{3.95}$.
3. Simplifying gives

$$N_{\frac{2.62}{2.62}}O_{\frac{3.95}{2.62}} = NO_{1.5}$$

4. Change this ratio to whole numbers by multiplying the whole formula by 2. The answer is N_2O_3.

Problem 4.10

Calculate the empirical formula of another oxide of nitrogen that contains 63.6% nitrogen and 36.4% oxygen.

Example 4.10 presents a situation often met in calculating empirical formulas. When the result of a calculation of an empirical formula contains a subscript more than 0.1 away from a whole number, it must not be rounded off. Rather, the whole formula must be multiplied by a factor that will make that subscript a whole number. In general, when the subscript is 1.5, multiply by 2 as in Example 4.10. When the subscript is 1.3 or 1.7, multiply by 3.

We have calculated the formula of compounds from their percentage composition. Example 4.11 shows how to determine the formula of a compound when its composition is given not in percentage but in grams.

Example 4.11

Analysis of 3.23 g of a compound shows that it contains 0.728 g of phosphorus and 2.50 g chlorine. What is the empirical formula of the compound?

☐ *Solution*

1. Calculate the number of moles of each compound in 3.23 g of the compound.

$$\text{phosphorus:}\quad 0.728 \text{ g P} \times \frac{1 \text{ mol P}}{30.97 \text{ g P}} = 0.0235 \text{ mol P}$$

$$\text{chlorine:} \qquad 2.50 \text{ g Cl} \ \times \ \frac{1 \text{ mol Cl}}{35.45 \text{ g Cl}} = 0.0705 \text{ mol Cl}$$

This gives the formula $P_{0.0235}Cl_{0.0705}$.

2. Change this ratio to whole numbers by dividing through by the smallest numbers of moles:

$$P_{\frac{0.0235}{0.0235}}Cl_{\frac{0.0705}{0.0235}} = PCl_3$$

Problem 4.11

Analysis of a 1.16-g sample of a compound shows that it contains 0.51 g of iron; the rest is chlorine. What is the empirical formula of this compound?

E. Molecular versus Empirical Formulas

The molecular formula of a compound states the elements and the number of atoms of each that are found in a molecule of the compound. The molecular formula of butene, C_4H_8, for example, shows that each molecule of butene contains four atoms of carbon and eight atoms of hydrogen. The molecular formula of ethylene, C_2H_4, shows that one molecule of ethylene contains two atoms of carbon and four atoms of hydrogen. Butene and ethylene are different compounds with different molecular formulas and different properties. These two compounds do have, though, the same empirical formula, CH_2. The molecular formula of ethene, C_2H_4, is twice its empirical formula, the molecular formula of butene, C_4H_8, is four times its empirical formula. *The empirical formula of a compound is the simplest ratio between its elements; the* **molecular formula** *of a compound is a multiple of the empirical formula and states exactly how many atoms of each element are in a molecule of the compound.* The formulas we have calculated in Section 4.2D express the simplest atomic ratio between the elements in the compound and are empirical formulas.

Table 4.3 shows three groups of compounds. Within each group, the compounds have the same empirical formula and percentage composition but different molecular formulas. That they are different compounds is shown by their different boiling points.

Table 4.3
Compounds with same empirical formula but different molecular formulas.

Empirical Formula	Compound	Molecular Formula	Boiling Point (°C)
CH (92.2% C; 7.8% H)	acetylene	C_2H_2	−84
	benzene	C_6H_6	80
CH_2 (85.6% C; 14.4% H)	ethylene	C_2H_4	−103
	butene	C_4H_8	−6.3
	cyclohexane	C_6H_{12}	80.7
CH_2O (40.0% C; 6.7% H; 53.3% O)	formaldehyde	CH_2O	−21
	acetic acid	$C_2H_4O_2$	117
	glyceraldehyde	$C_3H_6O_3$	140

The molecular formula of a compound can be determined from the empirical formula if the molecular weight is known.

Example 4.12

The empirical formula of hexane is C_3H_7. Its molecular weight is 86.2 g. What is the molecular formula of hexane?

☐ *Solution*

The molecular formula of a compound is a multiple of its empirical formula. Therefore, the molecular formula weight is the same multiple of the empirical formula weight. We know the empirical formula and can calculate the empirical formula weight. We can calculate what multiple the molecular formula weight is of the empirical formula weight. The molecular formula is the same multiple of the empirical formula.

1. Calculate the formula weight of C_3H_7.

   C: $12.01 \times 3 = 36.03$ amu
   H: $1.008 \times 7 = \underline{7.07}$ amu
   43.10 amu

2. Calculate the ratio between molecular weight and empirical weight:

$$\frac{\text{Molecular weight}}{\text{Empirical weight}} = \frac{86.2 \text{ amu}}{43.1 \text{ amu}} = 2$$

3. The molecular formula is twice the empirical formula: $(C_3H_7)_2$, or C_6H_{14}.

Problem 4.12

The empirical formula of the sugar ribose is CH_2O and its molecular weight is 150 g. What is the molecular formula of ribose?

By reviewing Sections 4.3D and 4.3E, we see that two kinds of data are needed to determine the molecular formula of a compound: (1) its composition, from which we can calculate its empirical formula, and (2) its molecular weight. By comparing the molecular weight with the empirical formula weight, we can determine what multiple the molecular formula is of the empirical formula.

Example 4.13

The compound ethylene glycol is often used as an antifreeze. It contains 38.71% carbon and 9.75% hydrogen, and the rest is oxygen. The molecular weight of ethylene glycol is 62.07. What is the molecular formula of ethylene glycol?

☐ *Solution*

1. Calculate the empirical formula as in Example 4.11. Assume the amount of compound to be 100 g; this contains 38.71 g carbon and 9.75 g hydrogen, and the rest is oxygen.

   ? g oxygen = 100 g ethylene glycol − 38.71 g carbon
    − 9.75 g hydrogen = 51.54 g oxygen

2. Calculate the moles of each element present.

$$? \text{ g moles carbon} = 38.71 \text{ g C} \times \frac{1 \text{ mol C}}{12.01 \text{ g C}} = 3.22 \text{ mol C}$$

$$? \text{ moles hydrogen} = 9.75 \text{ g H} \times \frac{1 \text{ mol H}}{1.008 \text{ g H}} = 9.67 \text{ mol H}$$

$$\text{? moles oxygen} = 51.54 \text{ g O} \times \frac{1 \text{ mol O}}{16.00 \text{ g O}} = 3.22 \text{ mol O}$$

This gives the formula:

$$C_{3.22}H_{9.67}O_{3.22} \quad \text{or} \quad C_{\frac{3.22}{3.22}}H_{\frac{9.67}{3.22}}O_{\frac{3.22}{3.22}} \quad \text{or} \quad CH_3O$$

3. Calculate the ratio of molecular weight to empirical formula weight.
   The empirical formula is CH_3O.
   The empirical formula weight is

$$12.01 + 3(1.008) + 16.00 = 31.03$$

$$\frac{\text{Molecular weight}}{\text{Empirical formula}} = \frac{62.07}{31.03} = 2$$

Therefore the molecular formula is twice the empirical formula and is $C_2H_6O_2$.

Problem 4.13

A compound known as fumaric acid has a molecular weight of 116.1. It contains 41.4% carbon, 3.5% hydrogen, and the rest oxygen. What is the molecular formula of fumaric acid?

4.3 Chemical Bonds

A. Octet Rule and Valence

The chemical properties of an element depend on its electron configuration, and in particular on the number of electrons in its outer or valence shell. The chemical properties of an element depend on how it bonds with other elements to form compounds. According to the **octet rule** (Section 3.5C1), atoms bond together in such a way that each atom participating in a chemical bond acquires an electron configuration resembling that of the noble gas nearest it in the periodic table. This means that the outer shell of each bonded atom will contain eight electrons (except for hydrogen and lithium, which have two).

The number of electrons that an atom must add to or lose from its valence shell to achieve a noble gas electron configuration is called the **valence** of the element. Hydrogen has one valence electron and by bonding acquires one more electron: hydrogen has a valence of 1. Oxygen has six valence electrons and by bonding acquires two electrons; oxygen has a valence of 2. By similar reasoning, nitrogen has a valence of 3, carbon a valence of 4, and the halogens a valence of 1.

B. Forming a Chemical Bond

The atoms of a compound are held together by **chemical bonds** formed by the interaction of electrons from each atom. The simplest chemical bond is that formed between two hydrogen atoms. Each hydrogen atom has one electron. As two atoms approach one another, the nucleus of one attracts the electron of the other. Eventually the two orbitals overlap, becoming a single orbital containing two electrons (see Figure 4.1). This orbital encompasses space around both nuclei. Although the electrons may be in any part of this orbital, they are most likely, we can predict, to be in the space between the nuclei, shielding one nucleus from the other and being attracted by both. In the resulting molecule, both atoms have two electrons and a filled outer shell. These shared electrons form a bond between the two atoms; this chemical bond is a **covalent bond**, a pair of electrons shared between two atoms. When this bond forms, energy is released. This release of energy shows that the molecule of hydrogen is more stable than the separate atoms. We shall see later that covalent bonds between other atoms may contain four or six electrons.

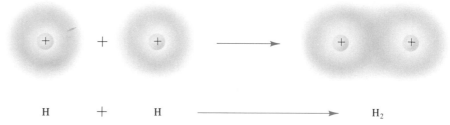

H   +   H   ⟶ H_2

Figure 4.1 Two hydrogen atoms, each with one electron, combine to form a hydrogen molecule. In the molecule, the two electrons are shared between the atoms and give each atom a filled valence shell.

C. Covalent, Polar Covalent, and Ionic Bonds

Since the hydrogen molecule contains two identical atoms, it can be assumed that the bonding electrons in this covalent bond are shared equally by these atoms. Most chemical bonds are not between like atoms but form between atoms of different elements. These bonds are slightly different from the bond in a hydrogen molecule. Consider the bond between hydrogen and chlorine. Both of these atoms also require one more electron to fill their outer shells. As the atoms come together, their orbitals likewise overlap, and the two atoms share a pair of electrons. The hydrogen-chlorine bond differs from the hydrogen-hydrogen bond because the electrons are not shared equally between hydrogen and chlorine—they are more strongly attracted to the chlorine. They are more apt to be found close to the chlorine than to the hydrogen. Because of this, the chlorine atom assumes a slightly negative character and the hydrogen atom a slightly positive character. We say that the bond is **polar covalent**, meaning that the bond consists of electrons shared between two atoms but not shared equally. We can also say that the bond is a **dipole**, or has a dipole moment, meaning that the bond has a positive end (the hydrogen) and a negative end (the chlorine).

An **ionic bond** is the extreme case of a polar covalent bond. In an ionic bond, the bonding atoms differ so markedly in their attraction for electrons that one or more than one electron is transferred from one atom to the other. The sodium-chlorine bond is an example of this. The chlorine atom attracts electrons so much more strongly than the sodium atom that the 3s electron of sodium is assumed to be completely transferred from sodium to chlorine.

There are, then, three types of bonds: (1) a covalent bond, in which the electrons are shared equally; (2) a polar covalent bond, in which the electrons are shared unequally; and (3) an ionic bond, in which electrons are transferred from one atom to the other. These are illustrated in Figure 4.2.

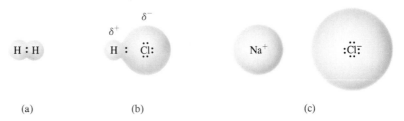

(a)   (b)   (c)

Figure 4.2 Electrons in (a) nonpolar covalent, (b) polar covalent, and (c) ionic bonds. In (a) the electrons are shared equally. In (b) the electrons are held closer to the more electronegative chlorine atom. In (c) one electron has been transferred from sodium to chlorine.

D. Electronegativity as a Predictor of Bond Type

It is possible to predict which of these three types of bonds will form between two elements. The farther apart (left to right) the two elements are in the periodic table, the more ionic and the less covalent the bond between them. Thus, metals react with nonmetals to form ions joined by predominantly ionic bonds. Bonds with the highest degree of ionic character are formed by the reaction of alkali metals or alkaline earth metals with the halogens, particularly with fluorine or chlorine. Nonmetals react together to form covalent bonds. If the bond is between two different nonmetals, it will be polar covalent. If the two nonmetals are neighbors in the table, the bond will be less polar than if the nonmetals are separated. For example, carbon and nitrogen are in neighboring columns, and carbon and fluorine are in columns IV and VII, respectively. A carbon-nitrogen bond will be less polar than a carbon-fluorine bond. Lastly, if the two atoms are of the same element, as in a hydrogen molecule or a chlorine molecule, the bond will be completely nonpolar.

The concepts in the previous paragraph have been quantified by the concept of electronegativity. The **electronegativity** of an element measures its attraction for the electrons of a chemical bond. One scale of electronegativity was developed by the American chemist Linus Pauling (b. 1901). On this scale, fluorine, the most electronegative element, has an electronegativity of 4.0. Carbon has an electronegativity of 2.5; hydrogen, 2.1; and sodium, 0.9. Figure 4.3 shows the electronegativities of the elements with which we deal most often.

Notice that the electronegativity of most metals is close to 1.0 and that the electronegativity of a nonmetal, although dependent on its location in the table, is always greater than 1.0. In general, electronegativity increases up a column and from left to right across a period.

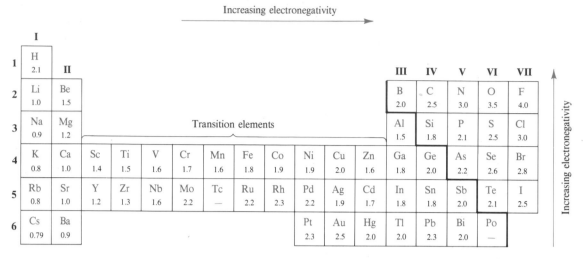

Figure 4.3 Electronegativities of some elements (Pauling scale).

Notice also that the noble gases in column VIII do not appear in this table. Electronegativity measures the relative attraction of atoms for electrons in chemical bonds. The noble gases react differently from the halogens and other nonmetals; we are not concerned with them in this discussion of electronegativity.

When two atoms combine, the nature of the bond between them is determined by the difference between their electronegativities (ΔEN). If the atoms forming the bond differ in electronegativity by more than 1.7 units, the bond will be at least 50% ionic, and we treat the bond as wholly ionic. If the values differ by less than 0.4 unit, we consider the bond essentially nonpolar. If the difference is between those two values, the bond should be considered polar covalent. It must be remembered that electronegativities have been calculated from fairly imprecise data for particular bonding situations. The concept is useful in predicting the nature of a bond and for comparing bond types, but what is obtained is only an approximation. It is also important to remember that there is not a sharp distinction between ionic, polar covalent, and nonpolar bonds. Rather, they form a continuum. Even the most ionic bond (between cesium and fluorine) has some covalent character, and only bonds between atoms of the same element have no ionic character. An even slightly polar covalent bond has some **ionic character**.

In these bonds, the atom with the higher electronegativity will be the negative end of the bond and, in extreme situations, become the negative ion. Table 4.4 summarizes these data.

Table 4.4
Predicting bond type from electronegativity data.

Range of ΔEN Values	Character of Bond	Example	ΔEN	Positive Atom
> 1.7	ionic	NaCl	2.1	sodium
1.7 − 0.4	polar covalent	C—Cl	0.5	carbon
< 0.4	nonpolar covalent	H—H	0.0	neither
		C—H	0.4	neither

Example 4.14

Predict the nature of the bonds between the following pairs of atoms—as predominantly nonpolar covalent, polar covalent, or ionic. For each polar covalent bond, show by using δ^+ or δ^- (the lowercase Greek letter δ, or *delta*, with a + or −) which atom bears a partial positive charge and which a partial negative charge.

a. S—O   **b.** C—O   **c.** Al—F

☐ *Solution*

a. The electronegativity of oxygen is 3.5 and of sulfur, 2.5. The difference is 1.0 unit; we predict the S—O bond to be polar covalent. The oxygen is partially negative and the sulfur is partially positive.

$$\overset{\delta^+}{\text{S}}-\overset{\delta^-}{\text{O}}$$

b. The electronegativity difference between oxygen and carbon is 1.0 unit (3.5 − 2.5). Therefore, we predict the C—O bond to be polar covalent. Since oxygen is the more electronegative, it carries the negative charge.

$$\overset{\delta^+}{\text{C}}-\overset{\delta^-}{\text{O}}$$

c. The electronegativity difference between fluorine and aluminum is 2.5 units (4.0 − 1.5). Therefore, we predict the Al—F bond to be ionic. The aluminum forms a cation; the fluorine, an anion.

Problem 4.14

Is the bond between carbon and nitrogen in a C—N bond nonpolar covalent, polar covalent, or ionic? In this pair of atoms, which bears the partial positive charge and which bears the partial negative charge? ∎

E. Single, Double, and Triple Bonds

A covalent bond represents the sharing of electrons between two atoms. **Single covalent bonds** result from sharing a single pair of electrons. Usually, as in the hydrogen molecule, each atom forming the bond contributes to it one electron. Sometimes, as in the reaction of ammonia with a hydrogen ion to form the ammonium ion, both electrons come from the same atom:

$$\text{H}\!:\!\ddot{\text{N}}\!:\!\text{H} + \text{H}^+ \longrightarrow \left[\, \text{H}\!:\!\ddot{\text{N}}\!:\!\text{H} \,\right]^+$$
$$\overset{..}{\phantom{\text{H}:}}\overset{\text{H}}{} \qquad\qquad \overset{\text{H}}{}$$

It is common practice to use a dash to represent a shared pair of electrons. Using this practice, the above equation becomes

$$\text{H}-\ddot{\text{N}}-\text{H} + \text{H}^+ \longrightarrow \left[\, \text{H}-\overset{\text{H}}{\underset{\text{H}}{\text{N}}}-\text{H} \,\right]^+$$

In addition to single bonds, there are double bonds and triple bonds. **A double bond** represents the sharing of four electrons by two atoms. The bond between carbon and oxygen is often a double bond, as in formaldehyde:

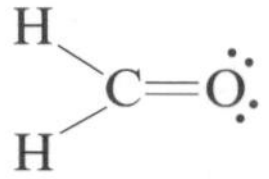

$$\begin{array}{c} H \\ \\ H \end{array}\!\!\!\!\!\!\! C\!=\!\ddot{O}:$$

Of this double bond, two electrons have come from carbon and two from oxygen. The single carbon-hydrogen bonds are nonpolar ($\Delta EN = 0.4$); the double carbon-oxygen bond is polar covalent ($\Delta EN = 1.0$). Notice that the oxygen has two pairs of unshared electrons. Such an unshared pair is sometimes known as a *lone pair*. We shall see that the negative end of a polar bond often holds unshared electrons.

A **triple bond** is formed when two atoms share six electrons (three pairs). The nitrogen molecule contains a triple bond. Its structure is

$$:N\!\!\equiv\!\!N:$$

Each nitrogen donates three electrons to the bond and retains a lone pair.

4.4 Covalent Structures; Lewis Dot Structures

Many properties of molecular compounds and polyatomic ions can be predicted from the arrangement of atoms and electrons in the compound or ion. The most convenient way to show this arrangement is by a **Lewis structure**. The structures shown in Table 4.5 are Lewis structures. To draw these structures, the following guidelines are used:

1. The atomic skeleton of the structure must be established. To do this, determine the **central atom**. This atom is the most electropositive (least electronegative) atom and the one with the highest valence. In some structures there are two or more similar atoms, all roughly equal in electropositivity and valence; these form the backbone of the molecule.

Table 4.5
Lewis structures of several small molecules. The number of valence electrons is given in parentheses.

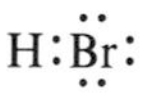

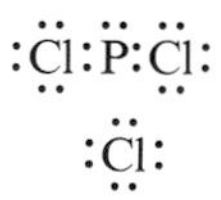

$H\!:\!\ddot{Br}\!:$

HBr (8)
hydrogen bromide

$\begin{array}{c} :\ddot{Cl}: \\ H\!:\!\ddot{C}\!:\!\ddot{Cl}: \\ :\ddot{Cl}: \end{array}$

CHCl₃ (26)
chloroform

$\begin{array}{c} :\ddot{Cl}\!:\!\ddot{P}\!:\!\ddot{Cl}: \\ :\ddot{Cl}: \end{array}$

PCl₃ (26)
phosphorus trichloride

$H\!:\!C\!:\!:\!:\!N\!:$

HCN (10)
hydrogen cyanide

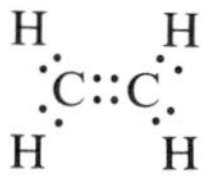

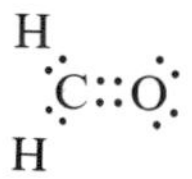

$\begin{array}{cc} H & H \\ \ddot{C}\!:\!:\!\ddot{C} \\ H & H \end{array}$

C₂H₄ (12)
ethylene

$H\!:\!C\!:\!:\!:\!C\!:\!H$

C₂H₂ (10)
acetylene

$\begin{array}{c} H \\ \ddot{C}\!:\!:\!\ddot{O}: \\ H \end{array}$

CH₂O (12)
formaldehyde

2. Arrange the other atoms symmetrically around the central atom or atoms. Hydrogen and the halogens, both having valences of 1, must be at the edge of the structure.

3. Determine the number of valence electrons in the molecule. This is the sum of the valence electrons in the individual atoms. For ions, add one electron for each unit of negative charge on the ion, or subtract one electron for each unit of positive charge on the ion.

4. Arrange the electrons in pairs around the atoms so that each atom in the molecule or ion has a complete outer shell of electrons. Each hydrogen atom must be surrounded by two electrons. Most other atoms must be surrounded by eight valence electrons, although some, like sulfur and phosphorus in the third row of the periodic table, can have ten or twelve valence electrons.

5. Show a pair of electrons involved in a covalent bond (bonding electrons) as a dash; show an unshared pair of electrons (nonbonding electrons) as a pair of dots. (In Table 4.5, all electrons are shown as dots to emphasize the filled shells. In the future, we will follow this rule.)

6. Two atoms may be bonded together with single, double, or triple bonds. In a single bond they share one pair of electrons; in a double bond they share two pairs of electrons; and in a triple bond they share three pairs of electrons.

A. Lewis Structures of Molecules

Shown in Table 4.5 are the names, molecular formulas, and Lewis structures for several small molecules. After the name of each is shown the number of valence electrons it contains. Notice that in these neutral molecules, each hydrogen atom is surrounded by two valence electrons and each atom of carbon, nitrogen, and chlorine is surrounded by eight valence electrons. Furthermore, each carbon atom has four bonds, each nitrogen atom has three bonds and one unshared pair of electrons, and each oxygen atom has two bonds and two unshared pair of electrons. Each chlorine has one bond and three unshared pair of electrons. Notice also that the most electropositive atom is central in each molecule and that hydrogen is always at the edge of the structure.

■──────

Example 4.15

☐ *Solution*

Draw Lewis structures for these molecules showing all valence electrons.

a. H_2O_2 **b.** CO_2 **c.** CH_3OH

a. Since oxygen is more electronegative than hydrogen and the two oxygens are alike, they must be bonded together to form the backbone of the molecule. The most symmetric structure has one hydrogen bonded to each oxygen in the skeletal arrangement

$$H—O—O—H$$

The Lewis structure for hydrogen perioxide, H_2O_2, must show 14 valence electrons, of which 12 are from the two oxygen atoms and 2 from the two hydrogen atoms:

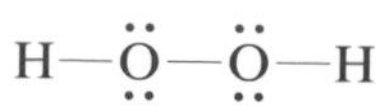

$$H-\overset{..}{\underset{..}{O}}-\overset{..}{\underset{..}{O}}-H$$

With three shared pairs of electrons and four unshared pairs of electrons, this structure has the correct number of valence electrons. Each hydrogen has 2 valence electrons and an electron configuration like that of a helium atom. Each oxygen has 8 valence electrons and an electron configuration like that of a neon atom.

b. Carbon is the most electropositive atom and therefore central. A symmetric structure has both oxygens bonded to the central carbon, giving the skeleton

$$O-C-O$$

There are 16 valence electrons to show. Sixteen electrons in single bonds will not give each atom a complete outer shell. Therefore, the molecule must have either two carbon-oxygen double bonds or one carbon-oxygen single bond and one carbon-oxygen triple bond. Symmetry suggests that both oxygens are bonded in the same way to the central carbon and therefore favors the two carbon-oxygen double bonds. This gives the Lewis structure

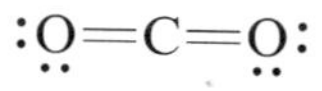

$$:\overset{..}{O}=C=\overset{..}{O}:$$

With four shared pairs and four unshared pairs of electrons, this structure has the required 16 electrons. Furthermore, each atom of carbon and oxygen has a complete octet. Notice that in this Lewis structure, carbon has four bonds and oxygen has two bonds and two unshared pairs of electrons.

c. The formula CH_3OH implies three hydrogens bonded to the carbon and one hydrogen bonded to oxygen. Carbon is the central atom, giving the skeletal arrangement

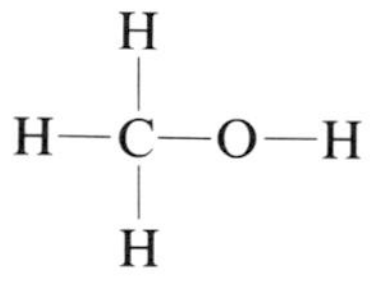

$$\begin{array}{c} H \\ | \\ H-C-O-H \\ | \\ H \end{array}$$

The structure must show 14 valence electrons: 4 from the single carbon atom, 4 from the four hydrogen atoms, and 6 from the oxygen atom. Distributing the electrons, we get

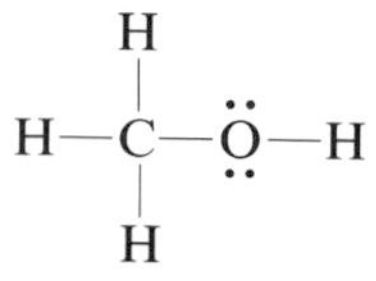

$$\begin{array}{c} H \\ | \\ H-C-\overset{..}{\underset{..}{O}}-H \\ | \\ H \end{array}$$

This structure shows five single bonds and two unshared pairs of electrons. It has the correct number of valence electrons. In addition, each hydrogen has 2 valence electrons, and carbon and oxygen each have 8 valence electrons. Notice that oxygen has two covalent bonds and two unshared pairs of electrons.

Problem 4.15

Draw Lewis structures, showing all valence electrons, for these molecules:

a. CH_3Cl **b.** CO   **c.** CS_2

B. Lewis Structures of Ions; Formal Charges

To draw a **Lewis structure of an ion**, follow the same steps you have just used for molecules. First, calculate the number of valence electrons contributed by the individual atoms in the ion. Then add one additional electron for each negative charge on the ion and subtract one electron for each positive charge on the ion.

In considering the properties of these covalently bonded ions and molecules, it is often useful to know which atom bears the positive or the negative charge. This so-called **formal charge** can be easily calculated from the Lewis structure.

To determine formal positive or formal negative charges, first assign to each particular atom all its unshared (nonbonding) electrons and half of all its shared (bonding) electrons. Second, subtract this number from the number of valence electrons in the neutral, unbonded atom. The difference is the formal charge.

Example 4.16

☐ *Solution*

Draw Lewis structures for the following ions. Show which atom in the ion bears the formal charge.

a. H_3O^+ **b.** NH_4^+ **c.** HCO_3^-

a. The hydronium ion, H_3O^+, contains 8 valence electrons: 6 from oxygen and 3 from the three hydrogens, less one for the single positive charge. Each hydrogen in H_3O^+ is assigned 1 valence electron, just as with an isolated hydrogen atom. Therefore, each hydrogen has $1 - 1 = 0$ formal charge. Oxygen is assigned 5 valence electrons, one fewer than in an isolated oxygen atom. Thus, the oxygen has a formal charge of +1.

$$H\!-\!\overset{\displaystyle ..}{O}{}^{+}\!\!\leftarrow\!\!H \qquad \textit{Assigned 5 valence electrons;}$$
$$\underset{\displaystyle H}{|} \qquad\qquad\quad \textit{formal charge of +1}$$

b. There are 8 valence electrons in the ammonium ion. Nitrogen is assigned 4 valence electrons, one fewer than in an isolated nitrogen atom, so the nitrogen has a formal charge of +1.

$$\overset{\displaystyle H}{\underset{\displaystyle H}{\overset{\displaystyle |}{\underset{\displaystyle |}{H\!-\!N^{+}\!\!\leftarrow\!\!H}}}} \qquad \textit{Assigned 4 valence electrons;}$$
$$\textit{formal charge of +1}$$

c. The bicarbonate ion contains 24 valence electrons: 18 from the three oxygens, 4 from carbon, 1 from hydrogen, plus an additional electron for the single negative charge. Because carbon is assigned 4 valence electrons, the same number in an isolated carbon atom, it has a formal charge of 0. Two of the oxygens are assigned 6 valence electrons each and also have a formal charge of 0. The third oxygen is assigned 7 valence electrons, one more than a neutral, unbonded oxygen atom, so it has a formal charge of -1.

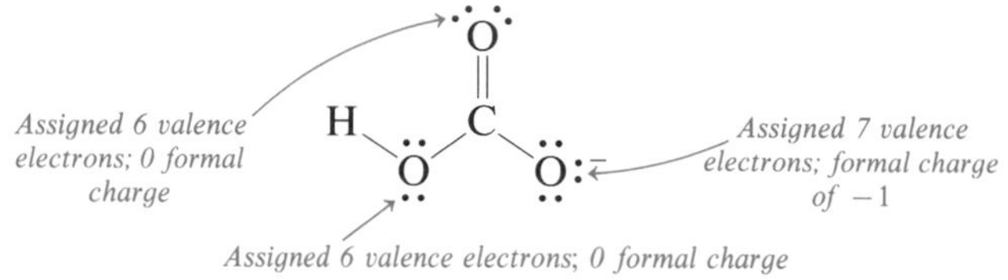

Problem 4.16

Draw Lewis structures for these ions and show which atom in the ion bears the formal charge.

a. CO_3^{2-} **b.** OH^- **c.** NO_3^-

C. Resonance

As chemists began to work with the Lewis structures, it became more and more obvious that for many molecules and ions, no single Lewis structure provided a truly accurate representation. For example, a Lewis structure for the carbonate ion, CO_3^{2-}, shows carbon bonded to three oxygen atoms by a combination of one double bond and two single bonds. Three possible Lewis structures for CO_3^{2-} are shown in Figure 4.4. Each implies that one carbon-oxygen bond is different from the other two. This is not the case, however; rather, it has been shown that all three bonds are identical.

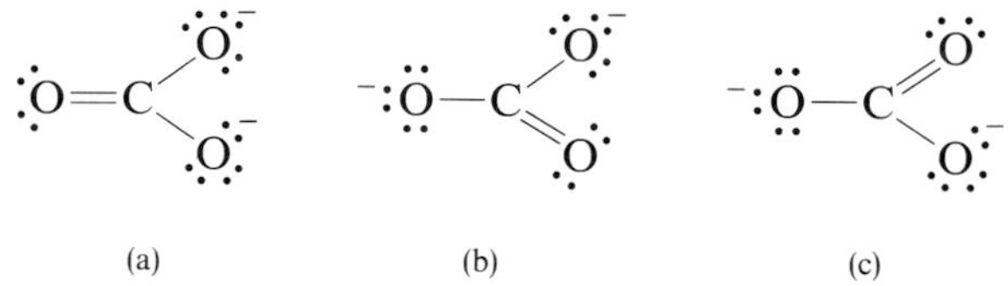

(a)   (b)   (c)

Figure 4.4 Possible Lewis structures of the carbonate ion.

To describe molecules and ions, like the carbonate ion, for which no single Lewis structure is adequate, Linus Pauling developed the theory of **resonance** in the 1930s. According to this theory, many molecules and ions are best described by writing two or more Lewis structures and considering the real molecule or ion as a hybrid of these structures. The individual Lewis structures are called contributing structures. We show that the real structure is a hybrid of the various contributing structures by connecting them with the double-headed arrows, as in Figure 4.5(a), (b), and (c).

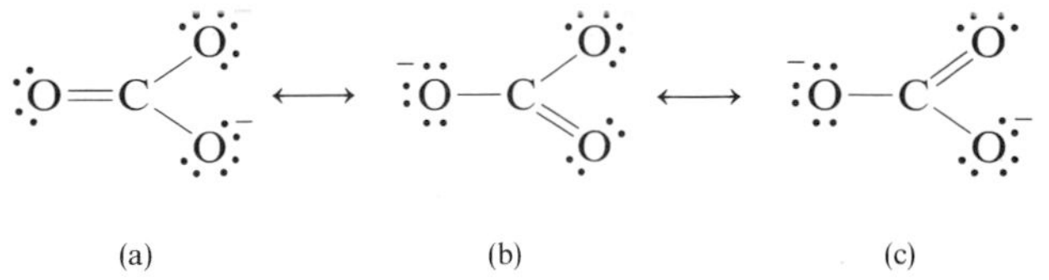

(a)   (b)   (c)

Figure 4.5 Resonance in the carbonate ion.

It is important to remember that the carbonate ion or any compound we describe in this way has one, and only one, real structure. The problem is that our systems of representation do not adequately describe the real structures of molecules and ions. The resonance method is a particularly useful way of describing the structure of these compounds, for it retains the use of Lewis structures with electron-pair bonds. Although we fully realize that the carbonate ion is not accurately represented by the contributing structures in Figure 4.5, we shall continue to represent this ion with one of these structures for convenience, understanding that what is intended is the resonance hybrid.

Example 4.17

Show that sulfur trioxide can be represented by a resonance hybrid of three contributing structures.

☐ *Solution*

The possible Lewis structures of sulfur trioxide are

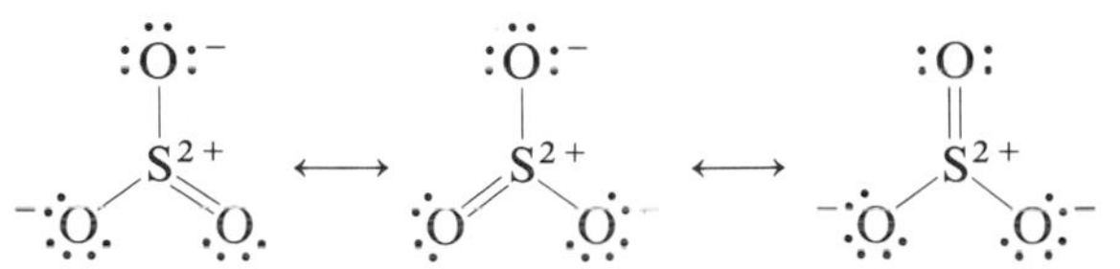

All are equivalent; therefore the molecule exhibits resonance and is a hybrid of these structures.

Problem 4.17

Show that ozone, O_3, is a resonance hybrid.

4.5 Bond Angles and the Shapes of Molecules

In Section 4.4, we used a shared pair of electrons as the fundamental unit of the covalent bond. We then drew Lewis structures for several small molecules and ions containing various combinations of single, double, and triple bonds. In this section, we shall learn how to predict the geometry of these and other covalent molecules and ions using the **valence shell electron-pair repulsion (VSEPR) model**. The VSEPR model can be explained in the following way. We know that an atom has an outer shell of valence electrons. These valence electrons may be involved in the formation of single, double, or triple bonds, or they may be unshared. Each set of electrons in a bond creates a negatively charged region of space. We have already learned that like charges repel each other. The VSEPR model states that the various regions containing electrons (or electron clouds) around an atom, since each is negatively charged, repel each other and spread out so that each is as far from the others as possible, thus forming **bond angles**.

A. Linear Molecules

It is obvious that if a molecule contains only two atoms, those two atoms form a straight line. Some three-atom molecules also have straight-line geometry, for example,

$$\ddot{\text{O}}{=}\text{C}{=}\ddot{\text{O}}\text{:} \qquad \text{H}{-}\text{C}{\equiv}\text{N:} \qquad \text{H}{-}\text{C}{\equiv}\text{C}{-}\text{H}$$

carbon dioxide   hydrogen cyanide   acetylene

Notice that in the Lewis structure of these molecules, the central atom or atoms bond with only two other atoms and have no unshared electrons. Only two electron clouds emerge from the central atom. For these to be as far away from each other as possible, they would be on opposite sides of the central atom, forming an angle of 180° with each other. An angle of 180° gives a straight line. The VSEPR theory says, then, that the geometry around an atom that has only two bonds and no unshared electrons is a straight line. Figure 4.6 shows the **linear** nature of these molecules.

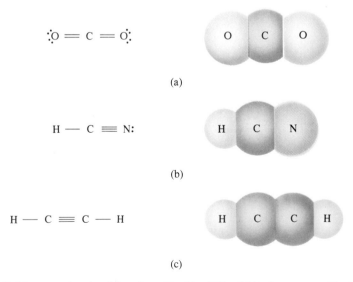

Figure 4.6 Linear molecules: (a) carbon dioxide, CO_2; (b) hydrogen cyanide, HCN; and (c) acetylene, C_2H_2.

B. Structures with Three Regions of High Electron Density around the Central Atom

Look at the following Lewis structures:

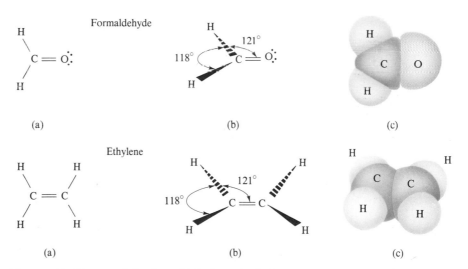

sulfur dioxide   formaldehyde   ethylene

In these molecules, each central atom has three electron clouds coming from it. In sulfur dioxide, the sulfur atom is bonded to two oxygen atoms and has one unshared pair of electrons. In formaldehyde and ethylene, each carbon has two single bonds to hydrogen, a double bond to another atom, and no unshared pair. The sulfur in sulfur dioxide and the carbon in ethylene and formaldehyde are each surrounded by three clouds of high electron density. For these clouds to be as far as possible from one another, they will form a plane containing the central atom and will radiate from the central atom at angles of 120° with each other. The structure will be "triangular," the central atom will be in the center of the triangle, and the ends of the electron clouds will be at the corners of the triangle. If you experiment with a marshmallow as the central atom and three toothpicks as electron clouds, you will prove for yourself that with this structure the toothpicks are farthest apart. Figure 4.7 illustrates these structures. Note that in the figure the angles are not exactly 120° but remarkably close to that predicted value.

Figure 4.7 Shapes of the formaldehyde and ethylene molecules: (a) Lewis structures; (b) trigonal planar arrangement of the three regions of high electron density around the carbon atom; and (c) space-filling models. In these figures, ▬ represents a bond projecting in front of the plane of the paper, and ⸽⸽⸽⸽⸽⸽ represents a bond projecting behind the plane of the paper.

Although the electron clouds of these molecules give a "trigonal planar" shape around each carbon, one describes the "geometry" of a molecule only on the basis of the relationships between its atoms. A formaldehyde molecule is trigonal planar because there is an atom at the end of each electron cloud. The ethylene molecule has trigonal planar geometry about each of its carbon atoms; the molecule is planar, its shape resembling two triangles joined point to point. The unshared pair of electrons in sulfur dioxide determines the geometry of the molecule, but the molecule is not trigonal planar; rather, it is a bent line. We say that the molecule is bent.

We conclude that a central atom surrounded by three clouds of high electron density will have **trigonal planar** geometry if it is bonded to three atoms. Its geometry will be **bent** if it is bonded to two atoms and has also an unshared pair of electrons.

C. Structures with Four Regions of High Electron Density around the Central Atom

Here are the Lewis structures of three molecules whose central atom is surrounded by four clouds of high electron density:

methane   ammonia   water

Notice that these molecules are alike in that the central atom is surrounded by four pairs of electrons, but they are different in the number of unshared electron pairs on that central atom. Remember, too, that although we have drawn them in a plane, the molecules are three-dimensional, and atoms may be in front of or behind the plane of the paper. What geometry does the VSEPR theory predict for these molecules?

Let us predict the shape of methane, CH_4. The Lewis structure of methane shows a central atom surrounded by four separate regions of high electron density. Each region consists of a pair of electrons forming a bond from the carbon to a hydrogen atom. According to the VSEPR model, these regions of high electron density spread out from the central carbon atom in such a way that they are as far from each other as possible.

You can predict the resulting shape using a Styrofoam ball or a marshmallow and four toothpicks. Poke the toothpicks into the ball, making sure that the free ends of the toothpicks are as far from one another as possible. If you have done this correctly, the angle between any two toothpicks will be 109.5°. If you now cover this model with four triangular pieces of paper, you will have built a four-sided figure called a regular tetrahedron. Figure 4.8 shows (a) the Lewis structure for methane, (b) the tetrahedral arrangement of the four regions of

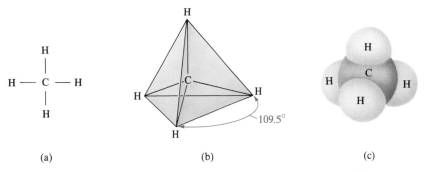

(a)   (b)   (c)

Figure 4.8 Shape of the methane molecule, CH_4: (a) its Lewis structure; (b) its tetrahedral shape; and (c) a space-filling model.

high electron density around the central carbon atom, and (c) a so-called space-filling model of methane.

According to the VSEPR model, the H—C—H bond angle in methane should be 109.5°. This angle has been measured experimentally and found to be 109.5°. Thus, the bond angle predicted by the VSEPR model is identical to the angle observed.

We say that methane has **tetrahedral** geometry. The carbon atom is at the center of a tetrahedron. Each hydrogen is at one of the corners of the tetrahedron.

We can predict the shape of the ammonia molecule in exactly the same way. The Lewis structure of NH_3 (Figure 4.9) shows a central nitrogen atom surrounded by four separate regions of high electron density. Three of these regions contain single pairs of electrons forming covalent bonds with hydrogen atoms; the fourth region contains an unshared pair of electrons. According to the VSEPR model, the four regions of high electron density around the nitrogen are arranged in a tetrahedral manner (Figure 4.9), so we predict that each H—N—H bond angle should be 109.5°. The observed bond angle is 107.3°. This small difference between the predicted angle and the observed angle can be explained by proposing that the unshared pair of electrons on nitrogen repels the adjacent bonding pairs more strongly than the bonding pairs repel each other.

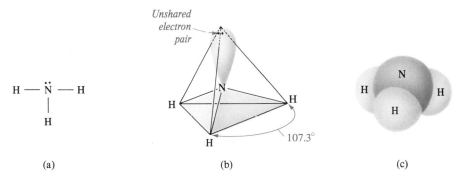

(a)   (b)   (c)

Figure 4.9 Shape of an ammonia molecule, NH_3: (a) its Lewis structure; (b) its geometry; and (c) a space-filling model. Notice how the unshared electrons create its shape.

Ammonia is not a tetrahedral molecule, however. The atoms of ammonia form a pyramid, with nitrogen at the peak and the hydrogen atoms at the corners of a triangular base. Just as the unshared pair of electrons in sulfur dioxide contribute to the geometry of the molecule but were not included in the description of the geometry, so the unshared pair of electrons in ammonia give it a tetrahedral shape although its geometry is based only on the arrangement of atoms, which is **pyramidal**.

Figure 4.10 shows the Lewis structure of the water molecule. In H_2O, a central oxygen atom is surrounded by four separate regions of high electron density. Two of these regions contain pairs of electrons used to form covalent bonds with hydrogen; the other two regions contain unshared electron pairs. The four regions of high electron density in water are arranged in a tetrahedral manner around oxygen. Using the VSEPR model, we predict an H—O—H bond angle of 109.5°. Experimental measurements show that the actual bond angle is 104.5°. The difference between the predicted and observed bond angles can be explained by proposing, as we did for NH_3, that unshared pairs of electrons repel adjacent bonding pairs more strongly than the bonding pairs repel each other. Note that the variation from 109.5° is greatest in H_2O, which has two unshared pairs of electrons; it is smaller in NH_3, which has one unshared pair; and there is no variation in CH_4.

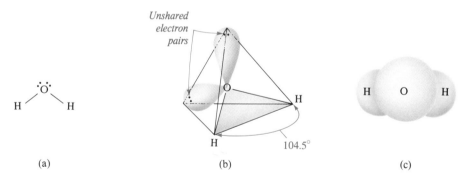

(a)   (b)   (c)

Figure 4.10 Shape of a water molecule, H_2O: (a) its Lewis structure; (b) its geometry; and (c) a space-filling model. Notice how the unshared pairs of electrons affect the tetrahedral geometry.

To describe the geometry of the water molecule, we remember that the geometry of a molecule describes only the geometric relationships between its atoms. The three atoms of a water molecule are in a "bent" line like the sulfur dioxide atoms. We say that the water molecule is bent.

A general prediction emerges from our discussions of the shapes of methane, ammonia, and water: Any time there are four separate regions of high electron density around a central atom, we can accurately predict a tetrahedral distribution of electron density and bond angles of approximately 109.5°.

Further, we can predict the geometry of the molecules. A molecule whose central atom is bonded to four other atoms is tetrahedral. One in which the central atom has one unshared pair and bonds to three other atoms is pyramidal, and one in which the central atom has two unshared pairs of electrons and is also bonded to two other atoms is bent. Table 4.6 summarizes this.

Table 4.6
Molecular shapes and bond angles.

Number of Regions of High Electron Density around Central Atom	Arrangement of Regions of High Electron Density in Space	Predicted Bond Angles	Example	Geometry of Molecule
4	tetrahedral	109.5°	CH_4 methane	tetrahedral
			NH_3 ammonia	pyramidal
			H_2O water	bent
3	trigonal planar	120°	H_2CO formaldehyde	trigonal planar
			H_2CCH_2 ethylene	planar
			SO_2 sulfur dioxide	bent
2	linear	180°	CO_2 carbon dioxide	linear
			HCCH acetylene	linear

Example 4.18

□ *Solution*

Predict all bond angles in these molecules.

a. CH_3Cl **b.** CH_3CN **c.** CH_3COOH

a. The Lewis structure of methyl chloride is

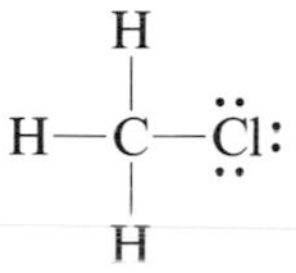

$$
\begin{array}{c}
\text{H} \\
| \\
\text{H}-\text{C}-\ddot{\text{C}}\text{l:} \\
| \\
\text{H}
\end{array}
$$

In the Lewis structure of CH_3Cl, carbon is surrounded by four regions of high electron density, each of which forms a single bond. Using the VSEPR model, we predict a tetrahedral distribution of electron pairs around carbon, H—C—H and H—C—Cl bond angles of 109.5°, and a tetrahedral shape for the molecule. Note the use of ⅲⅲⅲⅲ to represent a bond going behind the plane of the paper and ▬ to represent a bond coming forward from the plane of the paper.

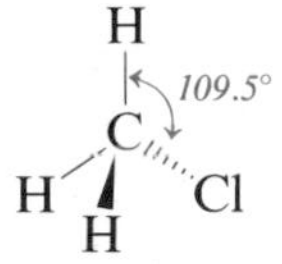

$$
\begin{array}{c}
\text{H} \\
\overset{\displaystyle 109.5°}{\underset{\text{H}}{\text{C}}} \\
\text{H} \quad \text{Cl}
\end{array}
$$

b. The Lewis structure of acetonitrile, CH_3CN, is

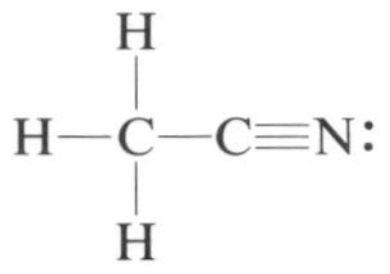

$$H - \underset{\underset{H}{|}}{\overset{\overset{H}{|}}{C}} - C \equiv N:$$

The HC_3—group is tetrahedral. The carbon of the —CN group is in the middle of a straight line stretching from the carbon of the methyl group through the nitrogen:

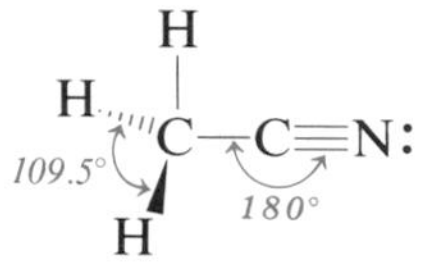

$$\underset{\underset{H}{\nearrow}}{\overset{\overset{H}{|}}{\underset{109.5°}{\overset{H_{\text{'''}}}{C}}}} - C \underset{180°}{\equiv} N:$$

c. The Lewis structure of acetic acid is

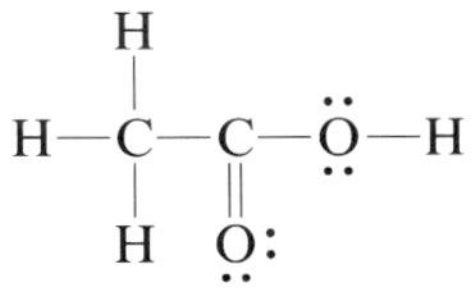

$$H - \underset{\underset{H}{|}}{\overset{\overset{H}{|}}{C}} - \underset{\underset{O:}{\|}}{C} - \overset{\cdot\cdot}{\underset{\cdot\cdot}{O}} - H$$

Both the carbon bonded to three hydrogens and the oxygen bonded to carbon and hydrogen are centers of tetrahedral structures. The central carbon will have 120° bond angles:

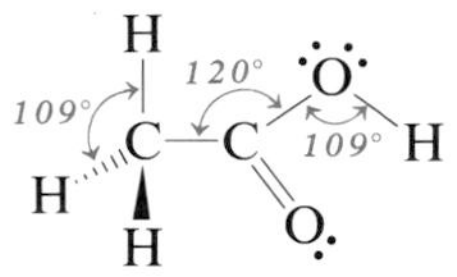

$$\underset{H}{\overset{H}{\underset{109°}{\overset{120°}{C - C}}}} \underset{109°}{\overset{\cdot\cdot\overset{\cdot\cdot}{O}\cdot\cdot}{O:}} H$$

The geometry around the first carbon is tetrahedral, around the second carbon atom is trigonal planar, and around the oxygen is bent.

Problem 4.18

Predict the bond angles and the resulting geometry of these molecules and ions:

a. CH_3CHO **b.** CO_3^{2-} **c.** CH_2Cl_2 **d.** NH_4^+

4.6 The Polarity of Molecules

We have seen that a chemical bond may be nonpolar, polar covalent, or ionic. The **polarity** of a diatomic molecule is the same as the polarity of the one bond it contains. For molecules containing more than two atoms, however, it is nec-

δ^-

δ^+

Figure 4.11
Model of an
ammonia
molecule.

essary to consider both the polarity of its bonds and the way these bonds are arranged in space. Figure 4.11 shows a three-dimensional model of an ammonia molecule of the same shape we predicted for ammonia in Section 4.5. Recall (Figure 4.3) that the difference in electronegativity between nitrogen and hydrogen is 0.9 EN unit and that the hydrogen, since it is less electronegative, will be the positive end of the bond. The base of the pyramid formed by ammonia is then more positive than the apex of the pyramid, which is nitrogen. No matter how you turn the ammonia molecule, it will always have a positive and a negative end. It is then a polar molecule.

Figure 4.12 shows a three-dimensional model of water, another polar molecule. The oxygen-hydrogen bonds are polar (Table 4.4) and point toward the corners of a tetrahedron (see Section 4.5). Water has a positive end (the hydrogens) and a negative end (the oxygen); water is a polar molecule.

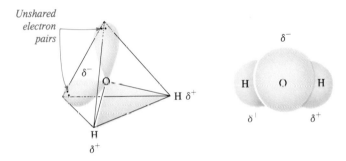

Figure 4.12 Model of a water molecule.

Figure 4.13 shows another molecule that contains polar bonds, carbon dioxide. When we draw the Lewis structure of carbon dioxide [Figure 4.13(a)], however, we see that there are only two electron clouds coming from the central carbon atom. We know from Section 4.5 that a molecule with that structure will have the geometry of a straight line. Figure 4.13(b) shows a model of carbon dioxide based on that information. Looking at the model, we see that although the carbon-oxygen bonds are polar, with the oxygen the negative end of the bond, they point toward opposite ends of a straight line; they counteract each other, and the molecule is **nonpolar**.

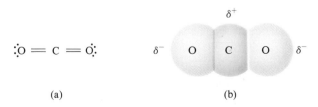

(a)   (b)

Figure 4.13 Model of a carbon dioxide molecule.

Example 4.19

Predict whether these molecules are polar or nonpolar.

a. CH_2O **b.** CCl_4 **c.** CH_3OH

☐ *Solution*

a. The Lewis structure of this molecule is

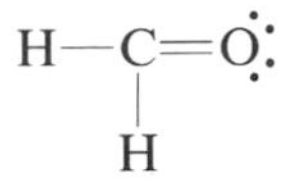

$$H—C{=}\overset{..}{\underset{|}{O}}{:}$$
$$H$$

The VSEPR theory says that it will be trigonal planar—the oxygen at one corner of the triangle, the hydrogens on the other corners, and the carbon atom at the center. The carbon-oxygen bond will be polar (see Table 4.4) and the carbon-hydrogen bonds, nonpolar. The oxygen corner will be more negative than the hydrogen corners. The molecule will have a positive and a negative end and will be polar.

b. The Lewis structure of carbon tetrachloride is

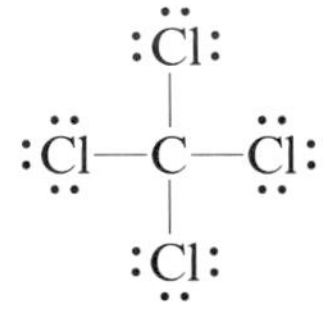

$$\overset{..}{\underset{..}{Cl}}{:}$$
$$:\overset{..}{\underset{..}{Cl}}—C—\overset{..}{\underset{..}{Cl}}:$$
$$:\overset{..}{\underset{..}{Cl}}:$$

The VSEPR theory says that the molecule will form a tetrahedron, with carbon in the center of the tetrahedron and a chlorine atom at each corner. The carbon-chlorine bonds will be polar; but as the negative ends (chlorine) will be on the outside and evenly spaced around the central carbon, the molecule will have no positive and no negative end and will therefore be nonpolar.

c. The Lewis structure of methyl alcohol is

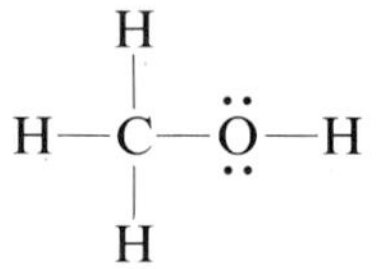

$$H$$
$$H—\underset{|}{\overset{|}{C}}—\overset{..}{\underset{..}{O}}—H$$
$$H$$

The molecule will be tetrahedral, with hydrogens on three corners and an oxygen bonded to a hydrogen on the fourth corner. The carbon-oxygen bond will be polar with the oxygen the negative end. This corner of the tetrahedron will be more negative than the others. The molecule will have a positive and a negative end and therefore will be polar.

Problem 4.19

Predict the polarity of

a. CH_3NH_2 **b.** CH_3CH_3 **c.** CH_3CHO

4.7 Interactions between Molecules; Electrolytes and Nonelectrolytes

A. Interaction between Polar Molecules

Polar molecules interact with one another. This interaction is governed by the fact that like charges repel and opposite charges attract. Figure 4.14 shows a collection of polar molecules aligned so that the partially positive end of one molecule is near the partially negative end of another.

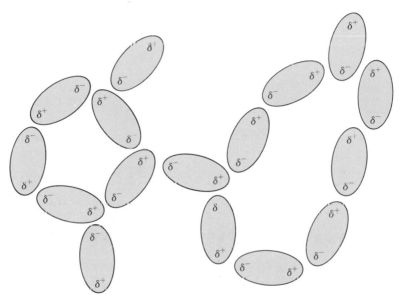

Figure 4.14 Polar molecules, when free to move around in the liquid state, will align themselves as in this diagram, with the positive end nearest the negative end of another molecule.

Polar molecules aligned by charge need not all be of the same compound. We've seen (Figure 4.10) that water is a polar compound. When another polar compound such as ammonia (Figure 4.9) is added to water, it dissolves because of the interaction between the two types of molecules. Figure 4.15 shows the interactions between these molecules.

B. Water Solutions of Ionic Compounds

An ionic bond is the extreme of a polar bond. The electrons are not shared but have been transferred from the less electronegative atom to the more electronegative atom. When an **ionic compound** dissolves in water, the solution contains ions, rather than neutral particles. For example, when sodium chloride, $NaCl$, dissolves in water, the solution contains sodium ions, Na^+, and chloride ions, Cl^-, rather than neutral units of $NaCl$. A solution of sodium nitrate, $NaNO_3$, contains sodium ions and nitrate ions, NO_3^-; there are no nitrogen

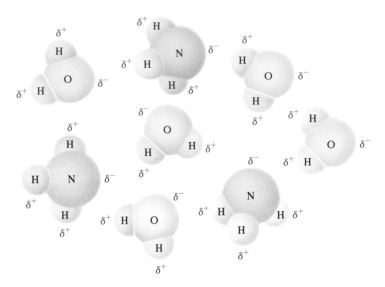

Figure 4.15 When ammonia, a polar molecule, is dissolved in water, which is another polar molecule, the two kinds of molecules orient themselves negative end to positive end, as in this diagram.

ions nor oxygen ions. A solution of ammonium sulfate, $(NH_4)_2SO_4$, contains ammonium ions, NH_4^+, and sulfate ions, SO_4^{2-}. A polyatomic ion does not break up into separate atoms in solution.

This dissolution of ions takes place because of interactions like those between ammonia and water. As shown in Figure 4.16, each ion of the solid crystal be-

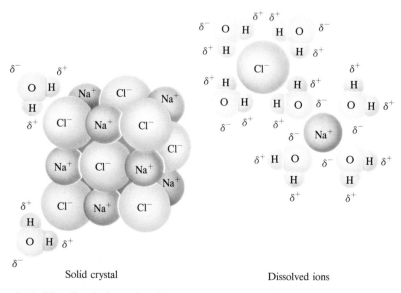

Solid crystal   Dissolved ions

Figure 4.16 The dissolution of sodium chloride in water. Notice how the polar water molecules are oriented in one way around the positive sodium ions and in another way around the oppositely charged chloride ions.

comes surrounded by water molecules; the negative ends of the water molecules approach closest to the positive cations, and the positive ends of the water molecules surround the negative anions. The water molecules pull these ions, one by one, away from the rest of the crystal. Those ionic compounds that are virtually insoluble in water have such strong interactions between their ions that the pull of the polar water molecules is not strong enough to pull the ions apart.

Frequently, when a very polar covalent molecule such as hydrogen chloride dissolves in water, there is sufficient interaction between the two molecules to cause one of them to break up into ions. With hydrogen chloride, the reaction equation is

$$HCl + H_2O \longrightarrow H_3O^+ + Cl^-$$

To some extent the same process occurs when ammonia is dissolved in water. The equation for that reaction is

$$NH_3 + H_2O \longrightarrow NH_4^+ + OH^-$$

C. Electrolytes and Nonelectrolytes; Weak Electrolytes

The presence of ions in a solution of an ionic compound can be demonstrated with an apparatus like that shown in Figure 4.17. The apparatus consists of two electrodes, one connected to a power source, the other to a light bulb, which is in turn connected to the other pole of the power source. If the two electrodes touch, an electric current flows through the completed circuit and the bulb lights [Figure 4.17(b)]. If the two electrodes are separated and then immersed in water, no current flows [Figure 4.17(c)]. Pure water does not carry an electric current.

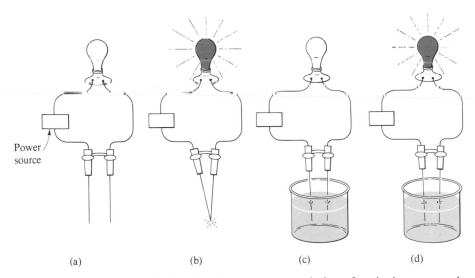

| (a) | (b) | (c) | (d) |

Figure 4.17 Conduction of electricity by an aqueous solution of an ionic compound: (a) electrodes apart, circuit broken; (b) electrodes touching, circuit complete; (c) electrodes in pure water, circuit broken; (d) electrodes in an ionic solution, circuit complete.

However, if the pure water is replaced by an aqueous (water) solution of an ionic compound, the bulb lights, indicating a flow of electricity through the solution [Figure 4.17(d)]. The electric current is carried through the solution by the dissolved ions.

Compounds whose aqueous solutions conduct electricity are called **electrolytes**. This group of compounds includes hydroxides, salts (metal/nonmetal and metal/polyatomic ion compounds), and some acids (nitric, sulfuric, hydrochloric). Compounds that dissolve in water without forming a solution that carries an electric current are called **nonelectrolytes**. These compounds dissolve as molecules. Most compounds containing only nonmetals are nonelectrolytes. If a compound containing only nonmetals ionizes, its molecules will usually contain hydrogen bonded to a very electronegative atom like oxygen (as in acetic acid) or chlorine (as in hydrochloric acid).

Compounds that react somewhat but not completely with water to form ions are said to be partially ionized. Their solutions are poor conductors of electricity. They are called **weak electrolytes**. Acetic acid is a weak electrolyte. In the apparatus in Figure 4.17, a solution of acetic acid causes the bulb to glow, but only faintly, showing that not many ions are in solution.

D. Other Differences between Ionic and Covalent Compounds

Ionic compounds are usually solid at room temperature. They have high melting points. They dissolve only in very polar solvents like water. Some are only sparingly soluble in water.

Covalent compounds are found in all three states (solid, liquid, and gas) at room temperature. Those of low molecular weight and those that are polar may dissolve in water, but a covalent compound is more apt to be soluble in a nonpolar solvent (carbon tetrachloride) or a slightly polar one (ethyl alcohol).

Example 4.20

Predict whether water solutions of the following will conduct an electric current.

a. potassium chloride, KCl
b. methyl chloride, CH_3Cl
c. ethane, C_2H_6

☐ *Solution*

a. Potassium chloride is an ionic compound. It dissolves in water, forming ions that conduct an electric current.
b. Methyl chloride contains only nonmetals. It does *not* contain hydrogen bonded to a very electronegative atom. The difference in electronegativity between carbon and chlorine is 0.5; therefore the molecule is essentially nonpolar. It is not expected to ionize, and its aqueous solution (if formed) is not expected to carry an electric current.
c. Ethane is a nonpolar molecule. (It is like methane; see Figure 4.8.) Its water solution does not conduct a current.

**Problem
4.20**

Predict whether water solutions of the following will conduct an electric current:

a. hydrogen bromide, HBr
b. calcium nitrate, $Ca(NO_3)_2$
c. ethyl bromide, C_2H_5Br

Key Terms and Concepts

bent molecule (4.5B)

bond angles (4.5)

central atom (4.4)

chemical bond (4.3B)

covalent bond (4.3B)

dipole (4.3C)

double bond (4.3E)

electrolyte (4.7C)

electronegativity (4.3D)

empirical formula (4.2E)

formal charge (4.4B)

formula weight (4.2A)

ionic bond (4.3C)

ionic character (4.3D)

ionic compound (4.7B)

Lewis structure of an
  ion (4.4B)

Lewis structure of a
  molecule (4.4A)

linear molecule (4.5A)

mole (4.2B)

molecular compounds (4.1)

molecular formula (4.2D, 4.2E)

monatomic ions (4.1)

nonelectrolyte (4.7C)

nonpolar bond (4.6)

nonpolar molecule (4.6)

octet rule (4.3A)

percentage composition (4.2C)

polar covalent bond (4.3C)

polarity (4.6)

polyatomic ions (4.1)

pyramidal molecule (4.5C)

resonance (4.4C)

single covalent bond (4.3E)

tetrahedral molecule (4.5C)

trigonal planar
  molecule (4.5B)

triple bond (4.3E)

valence (4.3A)

Valence Shell Electron Pair
  Repulsion model (VSEPR) (4.5)

weak electrolyte (4.7C)

Problems

*The nature
of compounds
(Section 4.1)*

4.21 State which elements and how many atoms of each are in a formula unit
of:
a. naphthalene, $C_{10}H_8$
b. potassium sulfate, K_2SO_4
c. lysergic acid diethylamide (LSD), $C_{20}H_{24}N_3O$

4.22 Write the formula of the compound whose formula unit contains:
a. 4 atoms phosphorus, 10 atoms oxygen

      b. 1 atom calcium, 2 atoms carbon, 4 atoms oxygen
      c. 1 atom bromine, 6 atoms carbon, 5 atoms hydrogen

4.23 Complete the following chart as exemplified for Na^+.

	SO_4^{2-}	HCO_3^-	SO_3^{2-}	Br^-	PO_4^{3-}
Na^+	Na_2SO_4	$NaHCO_3$	Na_2SO_3	$NaBr$	Na_3PO_4
NH_4^+	——	——	——	——	——
Fe^{2+}	——	——	——	——	——
Mg^{2+}	——	——	——	——	——

4.24 Give formulas for the following:
      a. silver(I) nitrate   **b.** ammonium nitrate
      c. magnesium sulfate   **d.** calcium bromide

4.25 Write the formula for each of these compounds:
      a. copper(II) chloride   **b.** iron(III) nitrate
      c. ammonium sulfate   **d.** cesium chloride

Formula weights (Section 4.2)

4.26 Calculate the formula weight of:
      a. nitric acid, HNO_3
      b. methane, CH_4
      c. sulfur dioxide, SO_2
      d. sodium phosphate, Na_3PO_4

4.27 Calculate the formula weight of:
      a. citric acid, $C_6H_8O_7$
      b. ascorbic acid, $C_6H_8O_6$ (vitamin C)
      c. cholesterol, $C_{27}H_{46}O$
      d. glucose, $C_6H_{12}O_6$

4.28 Calculate the percentage of carbon in the compounds in Problem 4.27.

4.29 What is the percentage composition of:
      a. octane, C_8H_{18}
      b. sodium bicarbonate, $NaHCO_3$
      c. magnesium chloride, $MgCl_2$

4.30 Calculate the moles present in each of the samples:
      a. 6.85 g sodium iodide, NaI
      b. 437.1 g sulfur dioxide, SO_2
      c. 0.442 g nitrogen dioxide, NO_2
      d. 7.41 g lithium oxide, Li_2O

4.31 Calculate the moles of sodium present in these samples:
      a. 0.155 g sodium chloride, $NaCl$
      b. 0.155 g sodium sulfate, Na_2SO_4
      c. 0.155 g sodium phosphate, Na_3PO_4
      d. 0.155 g sodium bicarbonate, $NaHCO_3$

4.32 Calculate the percentage of sodium in the compounds in Problem 4.31.

4.33 A compound contains 53.4% carbon, 11.1% hydrogen, and 35.5% oxygen by weight. Its formula weight is 90.1. What is the empirical formula? Its molecular formula?

4.34 A sulfide of arsenic contains 60.9% by weight of arsenic and 39.1% sulfur. What is the empirical formula of this compound?

4.35 A compound has the empirical formula C_4H_6. Its formula weight is 162. What is its molecular formula?

4.36 Which compounds in these groups have the same percentage composition?
  a. C_2H_4, C_6H_{12}, C_5H_8, $C_{16}H_{22}$
  b. N_2O_4, NO_2, N_2O_5
  c. $C_2H_4O_2$, $C_6H_8O_6$, $C_3H_6O_3$

4.37 A compound contains 85.6% carbon and 14.4% hydrogen. Its formula weight is 84.18. What is the molecular formula of this compound?

4.38 A compound having a molecular weight of 174.2 contains 41.4% carbon, 8.1% hydrogen, 18.4% oxygen, and the rest nitrogen. What is the molecular formula of this compound?

4.39 When 3.10 g of a compound containing only carbon, hydrogen, and oxygen is burned, 4.4 g carbon dioxide and 2.7 g water are obtained. In another experiment, it was determined that 0.204 mol of the compound weighed 12.7 g. What is the molecular formula of this compound?

The chemical bond (Section 4.3)

4.40 Chlorine bonds with each of the elements of period 3. Using electronegativity values, predict which of these bonds would be ionic, which polar covalent, and which nonpolar covalent?

4.41 In each of the following polar bonds, indicate which atom has a partial negative charge (δ^-) and which atom has a partial positive charge (δ^+): BrF, NI, PBr.

4.42 Predict the bond type in each of the following:
  a. HI   b. LiF   c. Br_2 d. H_2S

4.43 What is the difference between a single, a double, and a triple bond?

Lewis structures (Section 4.4)

4.44 Phosphorus forms the compound phosphine, PH_3. Draw the Lewis structure of this compound. The compound reacts with hydrogen ion to form the phosphonium ion, PH_4^+. Draw the Lewis structure of the phosphonium ion.

4.45 Draw Lewis structures of these molecules:
  a. silicon tetrachloride, $SiCl_4$
  b. sulfur dichloride, SCl_2
  c. arsine, AsH_3
  d. iodoform, CHI_3

4.46 Draw Lewis structures of these molecules:
  a. C_2H_5OH b. $CH_3CH_2CCl_3$
  c. CH_2=$CHCH_3$ d. $C_2H_5NH_2$

4.47 Draw Lewis structures of these ions:
  a. $CH_3NH_3^+$ b. OH^- c. CN^- d. NH_2^-

4.48 Draw the Lewis structure of sulfur trioxide, SO_3, and show that this molecule exhibits resonance.

4.49 Predict the geometry of each molecule in Problem 4.45.

4.50 Predict the bond angles for each compound in Problem 4.46.

4.51 Draw the Lewis structure and predict the bond angles and geometry of:
a. methyl acetylene, $CH_3C{\equiv}CH$ **b.** carbon disulfide, CS_2

4.52 Draw the Lewis structure of acetaldehyde, CH_3CHO. Predict the geometry around each carbon atom.

Polarity
(Section 7.4)

4.53 Ethyl alcohol, C_2H_5OH, and methyl ether, CH_3OCH_3, have the same empirical formula but one is more polar than the other. Draw the Lewis structures of these molecules. Predict the geometry around each carbon atom and predict which compound is more polar.

4.54 Why is ammonia polar but the ammonium ion, NH_4^+, nonpolar?

4.55 Silicon and chlorine have different electronegativities. Why, then, is silicon tetrachloride not a polar molecule?

Electrolytes
(Section 4.7)

4.56 Predict which of these molecules are electrolytes:
a. LiF   **b.** CO   **c.** CaI_2 **d.** N_2O

4.57 Sulfur dioxide is a polar molecule. Sketch how the molecules of sulfur dioxide would line up in liquid sulfur dioxide.

General
problems

4.58 The molecular weight of saccharin is 183.2 g. How many molecules of saccharin are contained in a sample weighing 0.916 g?

4.59 Calculate the empirical formula of a compound that contains 32.8% chromium and chlorine for the rest. Name this ionic compound.

4.60 Lutetium (atomic number 71) costs $26.00 a pound. What is the cost of 0.275 mol of this element?

4.61 In some states, pollution control boards regulate the amount of nitrogen that can be applied to the fields. If a farmer can apply 200 lb nitrogen every year to each acre of a crop, how many moles of ammonia can be applied to a 40-acre field for each crop grown in a single year?

4.62 What is the empirical formula of a compound that contains 39.7% potassium, 27.8% manganese, and oxygen as the remainder? Is this compound ionic or covalent? Soluble or insoluble in water?

4.63 For the element selenium, give the electron configuration. Draw its Lewis structure. Predict the formula of its compound with hydrogen. Selenium forms a chloride that contains 35.8% selenium. What is the formula of this compound?

5 Chemical Reactions and Stoichiometry

Many people consider a chemist to be a person dressed in a white coat standing in front of a laboratory bench crowded with mysteriously shaped glass containers. The contents of these containers bubble, change color, and emit strange vapors. One feels certain that the bubbling and fuming substances are about to combine and form a new miracle drug or fiber.

In spite of this picture, our study of chemistry has included little thus far about what happens when chemicals are combined and react to form new substances. In this chapter we will consider chemical reactions and so lay the groundwork for discussions in later chapters of how the food we eat and the air we breathe become flesh and bone and provide the energy we need to survive.

5.1 Chemical Changes

The observable properties of matter can be classified as physical or chemical. Physical properties are those properties whose observation does not involve a change in the composition of the sample. The water we pour from a tall pitcher into a flat bowl does not change composition. Water can be frozen to a solid or vaporized to steam; yet it remains water, with the formula H_2O. Through all these changes, the composition of the water is unchanged. Another **physical change**, the crushing of limestone, is illustrated in Figure 5.1. Even though the limestone is crushed to smaller particles, the composition of the limestone does not change.

The observation of a **chemical property** involves a change in the composition of the sample and a chemical reaction. When an electric current is passed through water containing a few drops of sulfuric acid, the water decomposes to hydrogen and oxygen. Water molecules are no longer present; instead, we have two new substances, hydrogen and oxygen. A **chemical change** is also illustrated in Figure 5.1. When heated, limestone, known chemically as calcium carbonate, is converted to two different substances, lime (calcium oxide) and carbon dioxide, that have very different properties from those of limestone.

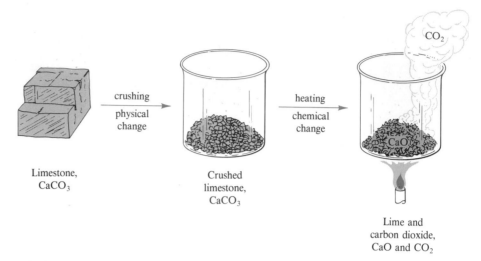

Figure 5.1 The crushing of limestone causes a physical change; it does not alter the chemical composition of the limestone. The heating of limestone causes a chemical change; the limestone decomposes into two other substances, lime and carbon dioxide.

5.2 Chemical Equations

A. Characteristics

Arithmetical equations describe mathematical operations; for example, $2 + 3 = 5$. **Chemical equations** can be used to describe both physical and chemical changes in atoms, molecules, and ions. The following chemical equation describes the vaporization of water, a physical change:

$$H_2O(l) \longrightarrow H_2O(g)$$

The letters in parentheses show the physical state of the substances in the equation; (l) means that the substance is a liquid, (g) means that it is a gas. If the substance in an equation is a solid, its formula is followed by (s); if it is in aqueous (water) solution, its formula is followed by (aq).

The equations in Section 2.10A presented nuclear changes. The radioactive decay of radium is described by the equation

$$^{226}_{88}\text{Ra} \longrightarrow {}^{222}_{86}\text{Rn} + {}^{4}_{2}\text{He} + {}^{0}_{0}\gamma$$

In Section 3.5C, equations were used to illustrate the formation of ions. The formation of the Mg^{2+} ion is shown by the equation

$$Mg \longrightarrow Mg^{2+} + 2e^-$$

Equations also describe chemical reactions. For example, the burning of propane can be described by the equation

$$C_3H_8(g) + 5O_2(g) \longrightarrow 3CO_2(g) + 4H_2O(l) \qquad \Delta H = -530.6 \text{ kcal}$$
$$(-2220 \text{ kJ})$$

Those substances whose formulas precede the arrow are called **reactants**; the arrow means "yield". And those substances whose formulas follow the arrow

Table 5.1
Parts of an
equation.

Reactants	Substances that combine in the reaction; formulas must be correct.
Products	Substances formed by the reaction; formulas must be correct.
Arrows	
$\rightarrow$	Found between reactants and products, means "reacts to form." A slash through the arrow means the equation is not balanced.
$\uparrow$	Placed after the formula of a product that is a gas.
$\downarrow$	Placed after the formula of a product that is an insoluble solid, a precipitate.
Physical State	Indicates the physical state of the substance whose formula it follows.
(g)	Indicates that the substance is a gas.
(l)	Indicates that the substance is a liquid.
(s)	Indicates that the substance is a solid.
(aq)	Indicates that the substance is in aqueous (water) solution.
$\Delta H°$	Enthalpy (heat energy) change accompanying the reaction. Energy is released if $\Delta H < 0$; is absorbed if $\Delta H > 0$.
Coefficients	Numbers placed in front of the formulas to balance the equation.
Conditions	Words or symbols over the arrow, indicating conditions used to make the reaction occur.
Δ	Heat is added.
$h\nu$	Light is added.
elec	Electrical energy is added.

are the **products** of the reaction. The numbers preceding each molecular formula are called **coefficients** and show the numerical ratio among the kinds of molecules taking part in the reaction. The ΔH term following the equation gives the **enthalpy change**, the energy change that accompanies the reaction. We read this equation as follows:

One molecule of gaseous propane reacts with five molecules of gaseous oxygen to yield three molecules of gaseous carbon dioxide and four molecules of liquid water. For each mole of propane reacting, 530.6 kilocalories, or 2220 kilojoules, of energy is released

In the SI system, the joule is the preferred unit of energy. For many people, however, the calorie (1 cal = 4.184 J) is still the unit of choice. In this chapter we will give energy values in both units.

The equation for the burning of propane is a complete equation. When the discussion centers on the reactants and products of a reaction rather than on the associated energy change, the physical states and the energy change are often omitted. Table 5.1 lists the parts of an equation.

B. Writing Chemical Equations

A correctly written equation obeys certain rules.

Rule 1: The formulas of all reactants and products must be correct.

Correct formulas must be used because the wrong formulas represent different substances and completely change the meaning of the equation. For example, the equation

$$2H_2O_2 \longrightarrow 2H_2O + O_2$$

describes the decomposition of hydrogen peroxide. This is a different reaction from the electrolysis of water, described by the equation

$$2H_2O \longrightarrow 2H_2 + O_2$$

When an uncombined element occurs in an equation, the guidelines set down in Section 2.4 should be used to determine its formula.

Rule 2: An equation must be balanced by mass.

An equation is balanced by mass when the number of atoms of each element in the reactants equals the number of atoms of that element in the products. For example, the equation shown above for the electrolysis of water has four atoms of hydrogen in the two reacting molecules of water and four atoms of hydrogen in the two molecules of hydrogen gas produced; therefore hydrogen is balanced. The equation has two atoms of oxygen in the two reacting molecules of water and two atoms of oxygen in the single molecule of oxygen produced; therefore oxygen is also balanced.

$$2H_2O \longrightarrow\!\!\!\!/\ \ 2H_2 + O_2$$

Four H on the left = four H on the right
Two O on the left = two O on the right

When the atoms are balanced, the mass is balanced, and the equation obeys the law of conservation of mass.

You can write and balance equations in three steps:

1. Write correct formulas of the reactants. Put an arrow after them. After the arrow, write the correct formulas of the products.

2. Count the number of atoms of each element on each side of the equation. Remember that all elements present must be on both sides of the equation.

3. Change the coefficients as necessary so that the number of atoms of each element on the reactant side of the equation is the same as on the product side. Only the coefficients may be changed in balancing an equation; the subscripts in a formula are constant and must never be changed.

Example 5.1

The brilliant white light in some fireworks displays is produced by burning magnesium in air. The magnesium reacts with oxygen of the air, to form magnesium oxide, MgO. Write the balanced chemical equation for this reaction.

☐ *Solution*

1. Write the correct formulas for all reactants, followed by an arrow; then write the correct formulas of the products. Magnesium is a metal so the symbol Mg is used. Oxygen is one of the diatomic nonmetals, so we use the formula O_2. The formula of the product is given, MgO. So we write

$$Mg + O_2 \longrightarrow\!\!\!\!/\ \ MgO$$

The line through the arrow indicates that the equation may not yet be balanced.

2. Count the atoms on each side:

	Reactants	Products
Magnesium	1	1
Oxygen	2	1

3. Change the coefficients in the equation so that the atoms of each element are balanced. This can be done by placing the coefficient 2 in front of Mg and MgO. The balanced equation for the combustion of magnesium is

$$2Mg + O_2 \longrightarrow 2MgO$$

Example 5.2

The rusting of iron is actually the chemical reaction of iron with oxygen to form iron(III) oxide, Fe_2O_3. Write a balanced chemical equation for this reaction.

☐ *Solution*

1. Write the formulas:

$$Fe + O_2 \nrightarrow Fe_2O_3$$

2. Count the atoms

	Reactants	Products
Iron	1	2
Oxygen	2	3

3. Balance the equation. Oxygen is the troublesome element in this equation, since the number of oxygen atoms must be divisible by both 2 and 3. The lowest possible number is 6, giving

$$Fe + 3O_2 \nrightarrow 2Fe_2O_3$$

The equation can be balanced with 4 iron atoms.

$$4Fe + 3O_2 \longrightarrow 2Fe_2O_3$$

Problem 5.1

Sodium reacts with chlorine to form table salt, NaCl. Write a balanced chemical equation for this reaction.

Problem 5.2

Octane, C_8H_{18}, a component of gasoline, burns in air to form carbon dioxide and water. Write the balanced chemical equation for this reaction.

5.3 Classification of Chemical Reactions

One common way of classifying chemical reactions separates them into four categories: combination, decomposition, displacement, and double replacement. Several examples of each type follow, partly so that you will understand the scope of each category and partly so that you can gain experience in interpreting and balancing equations.

A. Combination Reactions

In a **combination reaction**, two substances combine to form a single compound. Examples are the reaction of solid magnesium with gaseous oxygen to form magnesium oxide, a solid:

$$2Mg(s) + O_2(g) \longrightarrow 2MgO(s)$$

and the reaction of hydrogen gas with chlorine gas to form gaseous hydrogen chloride:

$$H_2(g) + Cl_2(g) \longrightarrow 2HCl(g)$$

Figure 5.2 illustrates an example of a combination reaction.

Other combination reactions have compounds as reactants. The reaction of carbon dioxide with calcium oxide to form calcium carbonate is an example of such a reaction:

$$CaO(s) + CO_2(g) \longrightarrow CaCO_3(s)$$

Figure 5.2 Magnesium combining with oxygen in fireworks.

Example 5.3   Write balanced equations for the following combination reactions:

a. When solid phosphorus, P_4, is burned in chlorine gas, phosphorus trichloride, a solid, is formed.

b. When gaseous dinitrogen pentoxide, N_2O_5, is bubbled through a solution of water, nitric acid, HNO_3, is formed.

Solution

a. Write the reactants, an arrow, the products, with the physical state of the reactants and products shown after their formulas, and the condition of the reaction over the arrow.

$$P_4(s) + Cl_2(g) \xrightarrow{\Delta} PCl_3(s)$$

Four atoms of phosphorus will give four molecules of phosphorus trichloride. These will require twelve atoms (six molecules) of chlorine. Putting in these coefficients gives the balanced equation,

$$P_4(s) + 6Cl_2(g) \xrightarrow{\Delta} 4PCl_3(s)$$

b. Write the reactants, an arrow, the products.

$$N_2O_5(g) + H_2O(l) \xrightarrow{\quad} HNO_3(aq)$$

Include the physical states and conditions of reaction as given in its statement. Start with nitrogen (it is always wise to leave hydrogen and oxygen to the last); two atoms of nitrogen in one molecule of N_2O_5 will form two molecules of nitric acid. Because each molecule of nitric acid contains one hydrogen atom, two molecules require two atoms of hydrogen, or one molecule of water. This in turn gives six atoms of oxygen in the reactants, the same number of atoms required by two molecules of nitric acid. The equation is then balanced:

$$N_2O_5(g) + H_2O(l) \longrightarrow 2HNO_3(aq)$$

Problem 5.3

Write balanced equations for the following combination reactions:

a. When solid carbon burns in a limited supply of oxygen gas, the gas carbon monoxide, CO, is formed. This gas is deadly to humans because it combines with hemoglobin in the blood, making it impossible for the blood to transport oxygen. Write the equation for the formation of carbon monoxide.

b. Lithium oxide, Li_2O, dissolves in water to form a solution of lithium hydroxide.

B. Decomposition

In **decomposition**, a compound is broken down into its component elements or into other compounds. Although some compounds decompose spontaneously, usually light or heat is needed to initiate the decomposition. The antiseptic hydrogen peroxide is sold in 30% solutions, and in brown bottles because it decomposes in light (Figure 5.3). The equation for this decomposition is

$$2H_2O_2(aq) \xrightarrow{hv} 2H_2O(l) + O_2(g)$$

Oxygen can be prepared by heating solid potassium chlorate in the presence of manganese dioxide:

$$2KClO_3(s) \xrightarrow{MnO_2} 2KCl(s) + 3O_2(g)$$

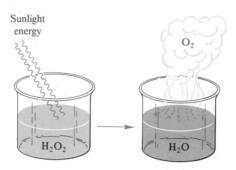

Figure 5.3 Light hastens the decomposition of hydrogen peroxide. The dark glass in which hydrogen peroxide is usually stored keeps out the light, thus protecting the hydrogen peroxide from decomposition.

When slaked lime, $Ca(OH)_2(s)$, is heated, quicklime, CaO, and water vapor are produced:

$$Ca(OH)_2(s) \xrightarrow{\Delta} CaO(s) + H_2O(g)$$

Example 5.4

Write the balanced equations for the following decomposition reactions.

a. Solid ammonium carbonate, $(NH_4)_2CO_3$, decomposes at room temperature to ammonia, carbon dioxide, and water. (Because of the ease of decomposition and the penetrating odor of ammonia, ammonium carbonate can be used as smelling salts.)

b. On heating, lead(II) nitrate crystals decompose to yield solid lead(II) oxide, and the gases oxygen and nitrogen dioxide.

☐ *Solution*

a. The unbalanced equation for the decomposition of ammonium carbonate is

$$(NH_4)_2CO_3(s) \not\longrightarrow NH_3(g) + CO_2(g) + H_2O(l)$$

Inspection of this equation indicates that 2 nitrogen atoms, therefore 2 ammonia molecules, are needed on the right. With this change, all other atoms are balanced:

$$(NH_4)_2CO_3(s) \xrightarrow{\Delta} 2NH_3(g) + CO_2(g) + H_2O(l)$$

b. Writing the formulas for the reactant and the products in the form of an equation gives

$$Pb(NO_3)_2(s) \xrightarrow{\Delta} PbO(s) + O_2(g) + NO_2(g)$$

Balance the elements in the order Pb, N, O. This leaves oxygen to the last—in general, a good practice. The lead is balanced as it stands, one atom on each side. Two nitrogen atoms are on the left, and therefore we need two NO_2 as product. The oxygen is unbalanced—six atoms in the reactants, five in the products. Try two $Pb(NO_3)_2$. This will give two PbO, four NO_2, and two more atoms of oxygen, to give one O_2. Now the equation is balanced.

$$2Pb(NO_3)_2(s) \xrightarrow{\Delta} 2PbO(s) + O_2(g) + 4NO_2(g)$$

Problem 5.4

Write balanced equations for these decomposition reactions:

a. Solid silver(I) oxide decomposes when heated to yield silver and gaseous oxygen.

b. In the chemical test for arsenic, the gas arsine, AsH_3, is prepared. When the arsine is decomposed by heating, arsenic is deposited as a mirrorlike coating on the surface of the glass container, and hydrogen comes off as a gas. Write the balanced equation for the decomposition of arsine.

C. Displacement

In **displacement** reactions, an uncombined element reacts with a compound, replacing an element in the compound. For example, bromine is found in seawater as sodium bromide. When chlorine is bubbled through seawater, bromine is released and a solution of sodium chloride is formed:

$$2NaBr(aq) + Cl_2(g) \longrightarrow 2NaCl(aq) + Br_2(l)$$

When an iron nail is dropped into a solution of copper(II) sulfate, iron(II) sulfate is formed in solution and metallic copper is deposited:

$$CuSO_4(aq) + Fe(s) \longrightarrow FeSO_4(aq) + Cu(s)$$

Figure 5.4 shows the displacement of silver by copper when copper is placed in a solution of silver nitrate.

Figure 5.4 A displacement reaction. In the first beaker a copper wire has just been placed in a solution of silver nitrate. Crystals of silver are beginning to appear on the wire. In the second beaker the reaction is almost complete; a great deal of silver has been deposited. The copper has displaced silver. The equation for this reaction is
$$2AgNO_3 + Cu \rightarrow Cu(NO_3)_2 + 2Ag.$$

Example 5.5

Write balanced equations for these displacement reactions.

a. When a piece of aluminum is dropped into hydrochloric acid, hydrogen is released as a gas and a solution of aluminum chloride is formed.

b. When chlorine is bubbled through a solution of sodium iodide, crystals of iodine appear in a solution of sodium chloride.

Solution   **a.** The unbalanced equation is

$$Al(s) + HCl(aq) \not\longrightarrow AlCl_3(aq) + H_2(g)$$

Aluminum is balanced. To balance the chlorine, we need three HCl on the reactant side. This will give $1\frac{1}{2}$ molecules of hydrogen.

$$Al(s) + 3HCl(aq) \not\longrightarrow AlCl_3(aq) + 1\tfrac{1}{2}H_2(g)$$

We need whole molecules of hydrogen. To get that and not unbalance the other elements, we can multiply everything by 2, and get

$$2Al(s) + 6HCl(aq) \longrightarrow 2AlCl_3(aq) + 3H_2(g)$$

b. The unbalanced equation is

$$Cl_2(g) + NaI(aq) \not\longrightarrow NaCl(aq) + I_2(s)$$

To balance the chlorine, we must form two NaCl. This requires two sodium or two NaI. This gives two iodine, which is what we need. The balanced equation then is

$$Cl_2(g) + 2NaI(aq) \longrightarrow 2NaCl(aq) + I_2(s)$$

Problem 5.5

Write the balanced equations for these displacement reactions.

a. When a piece of zinc is dropped into sulfuric acid, bubbles of hydrogen appear. Zinc(II) sulfate, $ZnSO_4$, is also formed in the solution.

b. If a cloth bag containing mercury is suspended in a solution of silver(I) nitrate, silver crystals form on the surface of the bag. The second product, mercury(I) nitrate, is found in the surrounding solution.

D. Double Replacement

In **double replacement**, two ionic compounds react to form two different compounds. These reactions fall into a pattern that can be expressed as

$$AB + CD \longrightarrow CB + AD$$

in which A and C are cations, B and D are anions. These reactions are often called exchanging-partner reactions, for in them, the cations A and C exchange the anions with which they are associated.

Double replacement reactions fall into two categories: (1) those in which an acid reacts with a base to form a salt and water—known as neutralization reactions; and (2) those in which one of the products is insoluble—these are usually precipitation reactions. Occasionally the insoluble product is a gas.

1. Reaction of an Acid with a Base: Neutralization Reaction

In **neutralization** reactions, an acid reacts with a base to form a salt and water. Recall (Section 3.5D) that an acid is a compound that liberates hydrogen ions in solution, and a base (we shall center here on the subgroup of bases that are hydroxides) is a compound that liberates hydroxide ions in solution. A salt is defined as an ionic compound in which the cation is not hydrogen and the anion is not hydroxide. These reactions are called neutralization reactions because the base neutralizes the acid. Some examples are:

a. The reaction of sodium hydroxide with hydrochloric acid to form sodium chloride and water:

$$NaOH(aq) + HCl(aq) \longrightarrow NaCl(aq) + H_2O(l)$$

Note that the salt formed, sodium chloride, combines the cation of the base, Na^+, with the anion of the acid, Cl^-. The formula of the salt is the neutral combination of these ions, here a 1:1 combination in sodium chloride, NaCl.

b. The reaction of magnesium hydroxide with phosphoric acid to form magnesium phosphate and water:

$$3Mg(OH)_2(aq) + 2H_3PO_4(aq) \longrightarrow Mg_3(PO_4)_2(aq) + 6H_2O(l)$$

Here again, the salt formed, magnesium phosphate, $Mg_3(PO_4)_2$, is a neutral combination of the cation of the base, Mg^{2+}, with the anion of the acid, PO_4^{3-}.

Example 5.6

Write the balanced equations for these neutralization reactions:

a. The complete neutralization of sulfuric acid with calcium hydroxide.
b. The complete neutralization of magnesium hydroxide with hydrochloric acid.

Solution

a. The cations are Ca^{2+} and H^+; the anions are SO_4^{2-} and OH^-. The products will show Ca^{2+} with SO_4^{2} instead of with OH^-, and H^+ with OH^- (HOH is the same as H_2O). Writing these facts in the form of an equation, we get

$$Ca(OH)_2(aq) + H_2SO_4(aq) \longrightarrow CaSO_4(aq) + H_2O(l)$$

To balance the equation, note that there are two H^+ and two OH^-. They combine to give two H_2O and the balanced equation:

$$Ca(OH)_2(aq) + H_2SO_4(aq) \longrightarrow CaSO_4(aq) + 2H_2O(l)$$

b. The formulas of the reactants are $Mg(OH)_2$ and HCl. The products will show Mg^{2+} with Cl^- instead of OH^-, and H^+ with OH^- instead of Cl^-. Writing this as an equation, we get

$$Mg(OH)_2(aq) + HCl(aq) \longrightarrow MgCl_2(aq) + H_2O$$

We need two chloride ions to combine with the Mg^{2+}; this requires two HCl. This leaves two H^+; the two OH^- from $Mg(OH)_2$ combine with the two H^+ from two HCl to form two H_2O:

$$Mg(OH)_2(aq) + 2HCl(aq) \longrightarrow MgCl_2(aq) + 2H_2O$$

Problem 5.6

Write the balanced equations for the following acid-base reactions.

a. The complete reaction of aluminum hydroxide and acetic acid.
b. The complete reaction of potassium hydroxide and sulfuric acid.

2. Double Replacement Reactions That Form Insoluble Ionic Products

The second group of replacement reactions results in the formation of **insoluble ionic compounds**. Ionic compounds differ enormously in solubility in water. Table 5.2 lists some **rules** by which the **solubility** of these compounds can be predicted. A compound is soluble if 0.1 g of the compound dissolves in 100 g water at 20°C.

Table 5.2
Solubility rules for ionic compounds.

NH_4^+	All common salts of ammonium ion are soluble.
Na^+ K^+	All common salts of sodium and potassium are soluble.
NO_3^-	All nitrates are soluble.
$C_2H_3O_2^-$	All acetates are soluble except iron(III) acetate, $Fe(C_2H_3O_2)_3$.
Cl^- Br^- I^-	All chlorides, bromides, and iodides are soluble except those of silver(I), mercury(I), and lead(II). $PbCl_2$ and $PbBr_2$ are slightly soluble in hot water.
SO_4^{2-}	All sulfates are soluble except $CaSO_4$, $BaSO_4$, $PbSO_4$, and Ag_2SO_4.
PO_4^{3-} CO_3^{2-}	Only alkali metal and NH_4^+ carbonates and phosphates are soluble.
S^{2-}	Only alkali metal and NH_4^+ sulfides are soluble.
OH^-	Only alkali metal and NH_4^+ hydroxides are soluble. Ca^{2+}, Ba^{2+}, and Sr^{2+} hydroxides are slightly soluble.

Example 5.7

Write the formulas of these salts and predict whether each is soluble in water.

a. lead(II) nitrate   **b.** iron(II) chloride
c. ammonium sulfide   **d.** barium sulfate

☐ *Solution*

Salt	Formula	Solubility	Reason
a. lead(II) nitrate	$Pb(NO_3)_2$	soluble	It is a nitrate.
b. iron(II) chloride	$FeCl_2$	soluble	It is a chloride but not one of the listed exceptions.
c. ammonium sulfide	$(NH_4)_2S$	soluble	It is an ammonium salt.
d. barium sulfate	$BaSO_4$	insoluble	It is listed as an insoluble sulfate.

Problem 5.7

Write formulas for the following salts and predict whether each is soluble in water.

a. barium acetate   **b.** silver(I) sulfide
c. ammonium phosphate   **d.** calcium carbonate

In a double replacement reaction of the second type, solutions of two ionic compounds are combined. If two of the ions in the resulting mixture can combine to form an insoluble compound, a reaction occurs. If no insoluble product is produced, no reaction occurs. For example, if a solution of barium iodide is added to a solution of ammonium nitrate, no reaction takes place, because the predicted products, barium nitrate and ammonium iodide, are both soluble:

$$BaI_2(aq) + 2NH_4NO_3(aq) \longrightarrow Ba(NO_3)_2(aq) + 2NH_4I(aq)$$

A double replacement reaction would occur if a solution of barium iodide were added to a solution of silver nitrate, because one of the products, silver iodide, is insoluble.

$$BaI_2(aq) + 2AgNO_3(aq) \longrightarrow Ba(NO_3)_2(aq) + 2AgI(s)$$

Figure 5.5 shows the formation of a precipitate. In the equations for these reactions, the insoluble product, or **precipitate**, is indicated by (s) or a downward-pointing arrow after its formula, whereas the soluble components of the reaction are shown as (aq).

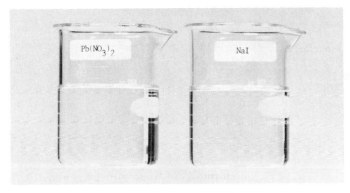

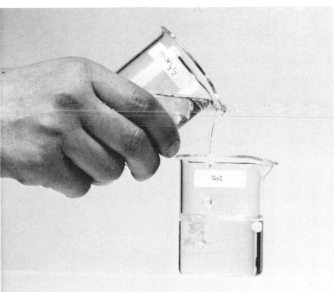

Figure 5.5 Formation of a precipitate.

Example 5.8

Write the balanced equation for the following reactions. Indicate with a downward-pointing arrow any precipitate formed; name the precipitate.

a. Solutions of lead(II) nitrate and sodium iodide react, to form a yellow precipitate.

b. The reaction between a solution of copper(II) nitrate and one of potassium sulfide yields a heavy, black precipitate.

☐ *Solution*

a. The formulas for the reactants are $Pb(NO_3)_2$ and NaI. The formulas of the products of a reaction between these two compounds would have an interchange of anions, yielding PbI_2 and $NaNO_3$. Arranging these in an unbalanced equation gives

$$Pb(NO_3)_2(aq) + NaI(aq) \nrightarrow PbI_2 + NaNO_3$$

Balancing this equation requires two iodide ions, therefore two sodium iodide. Two sodium nitrate are formed:

$$Pb(NO_3)_2(aq) + 2NaI(aq) \longrightarrow PbI_2\downarrow + 2NaNO_3(aq)$$

Because all sodium salts are soluble, the precipitate must be lead(II) iodide; an arrow is put after that formula.

b. The formulas of the reactants are $Cu(NO_3)_2$ and K_2S. The formulas of the products are CuS and KNO_3. From Table 5.2, we know that potassium nitrate is soluble, so the precipitate must be CuS, copper(II) sulfide. The unbalanced equation is

$$Cu(NO_3)_2(aq) + K_2S(aq) \nrightarrow CuS\downarrow + KNO_3(aq)$$

Balancing this equation requires two potassium nitrate. The balanced equation is

$$Cu(NO_3)_2(aq) + K_2S(aq) \longrightarrow CuS\downarrow + 2KNO_3(aq)$$

Problem 5.8

Write balanced equations for the following reactions and indicate any precipitate by a downward-pointing arrow. Name the products.

a. When chromium(III) chloride is added to a solution of sodium hydroxide, a green precipitate forms.

b. When sulfuric acid is added to a solution of barium chloride, a white precipitate forms.

5.4 A Second Way to Classify Reactions: Oxidation-Reduction

Another way of classifying reactions separates them into only two groups: (1) those that cause a decrease in the number of ions in solution, and (2) those that involve a transfer of electrons.

Those that cause a decrease in the number of ions in solution are usually double replacement reactions (Section 5.3D). In a neutralization reaction, hydrogen ion combines with hydroxide ion to form the covalent compound water, and thus the number of ions in solution is decreased. In a precipitation reaction, the insoluble product removes ions from the solution.

Those reactions that involve a transfer of electrons include combination, displacement, and decomposition reactions. These reactions are also **oxidation-reduction**, or **redox**, reactions. The reaction of sodium with chlorine is a redox reaction:

$$2Na + Cl_2 \longrightarrow 2NaCl$$

During the reaction, each sodium loses an electron, to form a sodium ion:

$$Na \longrightarrow Na^{+} + e^{-}$$

Each chlorine atom gains an electron, to form a chloride ion:

$$2e^{-} + :\overset{..}{Cl}:\overset{..}{Cl}: \longrightarrow 2:\overset{..}{Cl}:^{-}$$

The element that loses electrons is said to be **oxidized**. In the reaction of sodium with chlorine, sodium is oxidized. The element that gains electrons is said to be **reduced**. In this reaction, chlorine is reduced.

Displacement reactions are usually oxidation-reduction reactions. A typical displacement reaction is that of copper with silver nitrate solution:

$$Cu(s) + 2AgNO_3(aq) \longrightarrow 2Ag(s) + Cu(NO_3)_2(aq)$$

In this reaction, the copper loses electrons (is oxidized),

$$Cu \longrightarrow Cu^{2+} + 2e^{-}$$

and the silver ion gains electrons (is reduced),

$$Ag^{+} + e^{-} \longrightarrow Ag$$

Oxidation cannot take place without reduction. If an element in a reaction loses electrons, an element that gains electrons must also be present.

A. Identifying Oxidation-Reduction Reactions

In an oxidation-reduction reaction, elements change oxidation numbers.

1. Oxidation Numbers

The **oxidation number** of an element represents the positive or negative character of an atom of that element in a particular bonding situation. Oxidation numbers are assigned according to the following rules:

1. The oxidation number of an uncombined element is 0. In the equation

$$Zn + 2HCl \longrightarrow H_2 + ZnCl_2$$

the oxidation number of zinc as the uncombined atom is 0. The oxidation number of hydrogen in H_2 is 0.

2. The oxidation number of a monatomic ion is the charge on that ion. In $ZnCl_2$, the oxidation number of chlorine as Cl^{-} is -1, and of zinc as Zn^{2+}

is +2. In Ag_2S, the oxidation number of silver as Ag^+ is +1, and of sulfur as S^{2-} is −2.

3. Hydrogen in a compound usually has the oxidation number +1.
4. Oxygen in a compound usually has the oxidation number −2. Peroxides are an exception to this rule. In hydrogen peroxide, H_2O_2 for example, the oxidation number of oxygen is −1.
5. The sum of the oxidation numbers of the atoms in a compound is 0. For example, in the compound $ZnCl_2$, the oxidation number of zinc ion is +2 and of each chloride ion is −1. The sum of these oxidation numbers (+2 for zinc and −2 for the two chloride ions) is 0.
6. A polyatomic ion has a charge that is the sum of the oxidation numbers of the atoms in the ion. We can use this rule to calculate the oxidation number of nitrogen in the nitrate ion, NO_3^-, by setting up the following equation:

Oxidation number of nitrogen + 3 (oxidation number of oxygen) = charge on ion

Oxidation number of nitrogen +   3(−2)   = −1

Rearranging gives

Oxidation number of nitrogen = −1 − 3(−2) = −1 + 6 = +5

Example 5.9

Assign an oxidation number to each atom in these compounds and polyatomic ions:

a. CO_2 **b.** SO_4^{2-} **c.** NH_4^+

☐ *Solution*

a. CO_2: oxygen = −2 (Rule 4), carbon = +4 (Rule 5)
b. SO_4^{2-}: oxygen = −2 (Rule 4), sulfur = +6 (Rule 6)
c. NH_4^+: hydrogen = +1 (Rule 3), nitrogen = −3 (Rule 6)

Problem 5.9

Assign an oxidation number to each atom in these compounds:

a. Fe_2O_3 **b.** $NaMnO_4$ **c.** NO_2

2. The Use of Oxidation Numbers

By assigning oxidation numbers to all the elements in the reactants and the products of a reaction, we can determine whether the reaction results in a change in oxidation number. If a change does occur, the reaction is an oxidation-reduction reaction. Consider, for example, the reaction between magnesium and oxygen:

$$2Mg + O_2 \longrightarrow 2MgO$$
$$\quad 0 \qquad 0 \qquad +2, -2$$

Under each element in each substance in the equation is written its oxidation number. The oxidation number of magnesium increases from 0 to +2; magnesium is oxidized. The oxidation number of oxygen decreases from 0 to -2; oxygen is reduced. We conclude that the reaction of magnesium with oxygen is an oxidation-reduction reaction.

A reaction that is not an oxidation-reduction will cause no changes in oxidation numbers. Consider the reaction of sodium hydroxide with hydrochloric acid:

$$NaOH + HCl \longrightarrow NaCl + H_2O$$

$$+1, -2, +1 \qquad +1, -1 \qquad\qquad +1, -1 \qquad +1, -2$$

Under the equation are written the oxidation numbers of the elements. Because none has changed, we know that this neutralization reaction is not oxidation reduction.

Example 5.10

For the following reactions, answer these questions:

1. Is it an oxidation-reduction reaction?
2. If so, which element is oxidized and which element is reduced?
   a. Bromine can be prepared by bubbling chlorine gas through a solution of sodium bromide. The equation for this reaction is

$$2NaBr(aq) + Cl_2(g) \longrightarrow 2NaCl(aq) + Br_2(l)$$

   b. If you blow into limewater, the solution becomes milky. In chemical terms, if carbon dioxide is bubbled through a solution of calcium hydroxide in water, a milky-white precipitate of calcium carbonate forms:

$$CO_2(g) + Ca(OH)_2(aq) \longrightarrow CaCO_3(s) + H_2O(l)$$

☐ *Solution*

a. Write the oxidation number under each element in the equation.

$$2NaBr + Cl_2 \longrightarrow 2NaCl + Br_2$$

$$+1, -1 \qquad 0 \qquad\quad +1, -1 \qquad 0$$

1. Do any elements change oxidation number? Yes, both chlorine and bromine. Therefore, this is an oxidation-reduction reaction.
2. The oxidation number of chlorine changes from 0 to -1; chlorine is reduced. The oxidation number of bromine changes from -1 to 0; bromine is oxidized.

b. $$CO_2 + Ca(OH)_2 \longrightarrow CaCO_3 + H_2O$$

$$+4, -2 \qquad +2, -2, +1 \qquad\quad +2, +4, -2 \qquad +1, -2$$

1. Under each element is written its oxidation number. None of these numbers changed during the reaction; the reaction is not an oxidation-reduction.

Problem 5.10

Determine for each of the following whether it is an oxidation-reduction reaction. If it is, identify the element oxidized and the element reduced.

a. $NH_3(g) + HCl(g) \longrightarrow NH_4Cl(s)$
b. $Zn(s) + 2HCl(aq) \longrightarrow ZnCl_2(aq) + H_2(g)$

In an oxidation-reduction, the substance that gains electrons is the **oxidizing agent**. The substance that loses electrons is the **reducing agent**. In the reaction of magnesium with oxygen,

$$2Mg(s) \qquad + \qquad O_2(g) \qquad \longrightarrow \qquad 2MgO(s)$$
$$0 \qquad\qquad\qquad 0 \qquad\qquad\qquad +2, -2$$

Mg loses electrons. O_2 gains electrons.
Mg is oxidized to Mg^{2+}. O_2 is reduced to $2O^{2-}$.
Mg is the reducing agent. O_2 is the oxidizing agent.

Example 5.11

In the reaction of sodium with chlorine to form sodium chloride, which substance is the oxidizing agent? Which the reducing agent?

☐ *Solution*

Write the equation for the reaction and assign oxidation numbers.

$$2Na(s) + Cl_2(g) \longrightarrow 2NaCl(s)$$
$$0 \qquad\quad 0 \qquad\qquad +1, -1$$

Because chlorine changes oxidation number from 0 to -1, it is reduced; it is the oxidizing agent. Because sodium changes oxidation number from 0 to $+1$, it is oxidized; it is the reducing agent.

Problem 5.11

When a piece of copper is put in a solution of mercury(II) nitrate, droplets of mercury appear on the copper coil and the solution becomes blue because copper(II) nitrate is present. Show that this is an oxidation-reduction and identify the oxidizing and reducing agents.

The characteristics of oxidation and reduction are summarized in Table 5.3.

Table 5.3
Characteristics of redox reactions.

Substance Oxidized	Substance Reduced
Loses electrons.	Gains electrons.
Attains a more positive oxidation number.	Attains a more negative oxidation number.
Is the reducing agent.	Is the oxidizing agent.

B. Balancing Oxidation-Reduction Equations Using Half-Reactions

Although oxidation and reduction proceed simultaneously and an oxidation-reduction reaction can be shown in a single equation, the separate processes of oxidation and reduction are often shown as separate equations known as **half-reactions**. We have encountered several examples of half-reactions in Section 5.4 during the introduction to oxidation, but the term itself has not been used previously. The half-reactions for the oxidation of sodium and magnesium are

$$Na \longrightarrow Na^+ + e^-$$
$$Mg \longrightarrow Mg^{2+} + 2e^-$$

In an oxidation half-reaction, electrons are found as products. We have also encountered the reduction half-reactions for chlorine and oxygen:

$$Cl_2 + 2e^- \longrightarrow 2Cl^-$$
$$O_2 + 4e^- \longrightarrow 2O^{2-}$$

In a reduction half-reaction, electrons are reactants.

An oxidation-reduction reaction results from the combination of an oxidation half-reaction with a reduction half-reaction. The reaction of iron with copper(II) ion combines the two half-reactions:

Oxidation

$$Fe(s) \longrightarrow Fe^{2+}(aq) + 2e^-$$

Reduction

$$Cu^{2+}(aq) + 2e^- \longrightarrow Cu(s)$$

The equations have labels (*oxidation* and *reduction*). Note that electrons are a product (have been lost) in the oxidation half-equation and are a reactant (have been gained) in the reduction half-equation.

By adding an oxidation half-reaction and a reduction half reaction, the ionic equation for an oxidation-reduction reaction is obtained. This equation will be balanced if the numbers of electrons in the two half-reactions are equal. Both half-reactions shown above involve two electrons. Adding them together gives the balanced ionic equation for the overall reaction:

$$Fe(s) + Cu^{2+}(aq) + 2e^- \longrightarrow Fe^{2+}(aq) + 2e^- + Cu(s)$$

If the number of electrons in each of the two half-equations is not the same, each equation must be multiplied by an appropriate factor so that the number of electrons lost by the substance oxidized equals the number of electrons gained by the substance reduced. An example is the reaction of aluminum with hydrogen ion. The unbalanced equation for this reaction is

$$Al(s) + H^+(aq) \longrightarrow\!\!\!/ \ Al^{3+}(aq) + H_2(g)$$

The half-equations for this reaction are

Oxidation

$$Al(s) \longrightarrow Al^{3+}(aq) + 3e^-$$

Reduction

$$2H^+(aq) + 2e^- \longrightarrow H_2(g)$$

In these equations, there are three electrons lost in the oxidation half-equation and only two gained in the reduction half-equation. Before they can be added to give the net ionic equation for the overall reaction, the oxidation half-equation must be multiplied by 2 and the reduction half-equation multiplied by 3. Doing this, we get

Oxidation

$$2Al(s) \longrightarrow 2Al^{3+}(aq) + 6e^-$$

Reduction

$$6H^+(aq) + 6e^- \longrightarrow 3H_2(g)$$

which can be added to give the balanced equation

$$2Al(s) + 6H^+(aq) + \cancel{6e^-} \longrightarrow 2Al^{3+}(aq) + \cancel{6e^-} + 3H_2(g)$$

Example 5.12

☐ *Solution*

Write the equation for the reaction of zinc with hydrochloric acid. Isolate the half-reactions involved. Show that the balanced ionic equation can be obtained from these half-reactions.

The equation is

$$Zn + 2HCl \longrightarrow H_2 + ZnCl_2$$

Zinc's oxidation number changes from 0 to $+2$; it is oxidized.

$$Zn \longrightarrow Zn^{2+} + 2e^-$$

Hydrogen's oxidation number changes from $+1$ to 0; it is reduced. Because the product hydrogen is a diatomic gas, we must use two hydrogen ions as reactants:

$$2H^+ + 2e^- \longrightarrow H_2$$

Both half-reactions use two electrons; therefore they can be added as they stand, to give

$$Zn + 2H^+ + \cancel{2e^-} \longrightarrow H_2 + Zn^{2+} + \cancel{2e^-}$$

Problem 5.12

Write the equation for the reaction of bromine with sodium iodide to form sodium bromide and free iodine. Isolate the half-reactions involved. Show that the balanced equation can be obtained by adding these half-reactions.

Figure 5.6 Combustion as illustrated by burning gasoline storage tanks. The combustion of gasoline or other petroleum products is usually accompanied by yellow flames and dense black smoke.

C. Combustion Reactions

Combustion reactions are a special type of oxidation reaction. We correctly associate combustion reactions with burning. In the usual combustion reaction, the elements in the reacting compound combine with oxygen to form oxides, as in the combustion of propane to form carbon dioxide and water:

$$C_3H_8(g) + 5O_2(g) \longrightarrow 3CO_2(g) + 4H_2O(l)$$

Figure 5.6 shows the combustion of gasoline.

The above reactions take place when an adequate supply of oxygen is present. When the supply of oxygen is not adequate, carbon monoxide is formed:

$$2C_3H_8(g) + 7O_2(g) \longrightarrow 6CO(g) + 8H_2O(l)$$

Write balanced equations for the complete combustion in oxygen of:

Example 5.13

a. butane, C_4H_{10} **b.** ethyl alcohol, C_2H_5OH

☐ *Solution*   **a.** Butane contains only carbon and hydrogen, and the combustion is complete, so the products are carbon dioxide and water. The unbalanced equation is

$$C_4H_{10} + O_2 \nrightarrow CO_2 + H_2O$$

Four atoms of carbon on the left give four molecules of carbon dioxide on the right. Ten atoms of hydrogen on the left give five molecules of water on the right. These require thirteen atoms of oxygen ($6\frac{1}{2}$ molecules) on the left.

$$C_4H_{10} + 6\tfrac{1}{2}O_2 \longrightarrow 4CO_2 + 5H_2O$$

To write the equation using only whole numbers of molecules, we must multiply through by 2, and we get

$$2C_4H_{10} + 13O_2 \longrightarrow 8CO_2 + 10H_2O$$

b. Ethyl alcohol contains carbon, hydrogen, and oxygen. The products of complete combustion are carbon dioxide and water:

$$C_2H_5OH + O_2 \nrightarrow CO_2 + H_2O$$

Initial balancing gives two atoms of carbon on the left, two molecules of carbon dioxide on the right; six atoms of hydrogen on the left, three molecules of water on the right; seven atoms of oxygen on the right, three and a half molecules of oxygen on the left:

$$C_2H_5OH + 3\tfrac{1}{2}O_2 \longrightarrow 2CO_2 + 3H_2O$$

We multiply by 2 to clear fractions and get the balanced equation

$$2C_2H_5OH + 7O_2 \longrightarrow 4CO_2 + 6H_2O$$

■
Problem 5.13

Write balanced equations for the combustion of the following compounds:

a. heptane, C_7H_{16};   **b.** propyl alcohol, C_3H_7OH. ■

5.5 Mass Relationships in an Equation

A. Simple Problems

A balanced equation is a quantitative statement of a reaction. It relates amounts of reactants to amounts of products. Let us see what this statement means for a particular reaction.

Pentane, C_5H_{12}, burns in oxygen, to form carbon dioxide and water. The balanced equation for the combustion of pentane is

$$C_5H_{12} + 8O_2 \longrightarrow 5CO_2 + 6H_2O$$

In qualitative terms, this equation shows that pentane reacts with oxygen to form carbon dioxide and water. In quantitative terms, the equation states that

1 molecule of pentane reacts with 8 molecules of oxygen to form 5 molecules of carbon dioxide and 6 molecules of water. If we had 15 molecules of pentane, we should need 8 × 15, or 120, molecules of oxygen for complete reaction; 5 × 15 molecules of carbon dioxide and 6 × 15 molecules of water would be formed. We could start with any number (n) molecules of pentane and form $5n$ molecules of carbon dioxide and $6n$ molecules of water.

If 6.02×10^{23} molecules (1 mol) of pentane is burned, $8 \times (6.02 \times 10^{23})$ molecules (8 mol) of oxygen are needed. The reaction would form $5 \times (6.02 \times 10^{23})$ molecules (5 mol) of carbon dioxide and $6 \times (6.02 \times 10^{23})$ molecules (6 mol) of water. These quantitative relationships are summarized in Table 5.4.

Table 5.4
Quantitative relationships in an equation.

72 g	+	256 g	$\longrightarrow$	220 g	+	108 g
C_5H_{12}	+	$8O_2$	$\longrightarrow$	$5CO_2$	+	$6H_2O$
1 molecule	+	8 molecules	$\longrightarrow$	5 molecules	+	6 molecules
1 mol	+	8 mol	$\longrightarrow$	5 mol	+	6 mol

Thus, any balanced equation gives a ratio between moles of reactants and moles of products. If the number of moles of one component used or produced in a reaction is given, the number of moles or grams of any other component used or produced can be calculated. Such calculations are called **stoichiometry**.

A stoichiometric problem, although it can be stated in many ways, always contains the following parts:

1. The reaction involved.
2. A stated amount of one component of the reaction.
3. A question asking "how much" of another substance is needed or formed in the reaction.

The quantitative problems in previous chapters were solved by answering a series of questions:

1. What is wanted?
2. What is given?
3. What conversion factors are needed to go from "given" to "wanted"?
4. How should the arithmetic equation be set up so that the units of the "given" are converted to the units of the "wanted"?

Stoichiometric problems can be solved by answering the same set of questions. The only difference is that some of the conversion factors are derived from the balanced chemical equation for the reaction involved. The steps to follow in solving a stoichiometric problem are:

1. Write the balanced equation for the reaction.
2. Decide which substance is wanted and in what units.
3. Decide which substance is given, and in what units and what amount.
4. Determine the conversion factors required to convert:
   a. the amount of given substance into moles.
   b. moles of the given substance into moles of the wanted substance.
   c. moles of wanted substance into the units asked for in the problem.

5. Combine the amount of given substance and its units along with the appropriate conversion factors into an equation in such a way that only the wanted substance in the proper units remains.

Example 5.14

How many grams of carbon dioxide are formed when 61.5 g of pentane are burned in oxygen?

☐ *Solution*

Equation:

$$C_5H_{12} + 8O_2 \longrightarrow 5CO_2 + 6H_2O$$

Wanted: ? g CO_2
Given: 61.5 g C_5H_{12}
Conversion factors: For C_5H_{12}: to go from mass to moles, 72.2 g C_5H_{12} = 1 mol C_5H_{12}. For CO_2: to go from C_5H_{12} to CO_2, 1 mol C_5H_{12} yields 5 mol CO_2; to go from moles CO_2 to mass, 1 mol CO_2 = 44.0 g CO_2.
Arithmetic equation:

$$? \text{ g } CO_2 = 61.5 \text{ g } C_5H_{12} \times \frac{1 \text{ mol } C_5H_{12}}{72.2 \text{ g } C_5H_{12}} \times \frac{5 \text{ mol } CO_2}{1 \text{ mol } C_5H_{12}} \times \frac{44.0 \text{ g } CO_2}{1 \text{ mol } CO_2}$$

Answer: 187 g CO_2

Several points should be emphasized. First, to prevent confusion and errors, always show the name and units of each item in the equation. Second, do no arithmetic until the whole equation is written out. Third, be sure all units in the final equation cancel except for those required in the answer.

Problem 5.14

Hydrogen burns in oxygen to form water. What mass of oxygen is necessary for the complete combustion of 1.74 g of hydrogen?

Example 5.15

What mass of iron(III) oxide (rust) is formed when 6.23 g of iron reacts completely with oxygen of the air to form this product?

☐ *Solution*

Equation: The name iron(III) oxide shows that the iron is present in the product as Fe^{3+}, the oxide ion is O^{2-}. Iron (III) oxide is then Fe_2O_3. The balanced equation for the reaction is

$$4Fe + 3O_2 \longrightarrow 2Fe_2O_3$$

Wanted: ? g iron(III) oxide
Given: 6.23 g iron
Conversion factors: For Fe: to go from mass to moles, 55.85 g Fe = 1 mol Fe. For Fe_2O_3: to go from Fe to Fe_2O_3, 4 mol Fe yields 2 mol Fe_2O_3; to go from moles to mass, 1 mol Fe_2O_3 = 2(55.85) + 3(16.0) = 159.7 g Fe_2O_3.

Arithmetic equation:

$$? \text{ g Fe}_2\text{O}_3 = 6.23 \text{ g Fe} \times \frac{1 \text{ mol Fe}}{55.85 \text{ g Fe}} \times \frac{2 \text{ mol Fe}_2\text{O}_3}{4 \text{ mol Fe}} \times \frac{159.7 \text{ g Fe}_2\text{O}_3}{1 \text{ mol Fe}_2\text{O}_3}$$

$$= 8.91 \text{ g Fe}_2\text{O}_3$$

Problem 5.15

Bromine is prepared by the reaction of chlorine with sodium bromide. How many grams of chlorine are necessary for the preparation of 2.12 g of bromine?

Example 5.16

How many molecules of hydrogen will be formed by the reaction of 2.65×10^{-3} g of zinc with hydrochloric acid?

☐ *Solution*

Equation:

$$\text{Zn} + 2\text{HCl} \longrightarrow \text{ZnCl}_2 + \text{H}_2$$

Wanted: ? molecules H_2
Given: 2.65×10^{-3} g Zn
Conversion factors: For Zn: to go from mass to moles, 65.4 g Zn = 1 mol Zn. For H_2: to go from moles Zn to moles H_2, 1 mol Zn yields 1 mol H_2; to go from mass to number of molecules, 1 mol H_2 contains 6.02×10^{23} molecules H_2.
Arithmetic equation:

$$? \text{ molecules H}_2 = 2.65 \times 10^{-3} \text{ g Zn} \times \frac{1 \text{ mol Zn}}{65.4 \text{ g Zn}} \times \frac{1 \text{ mol H}_2}{1 \text{ mol Zn}}$$

$$\times \frac{6.02 \times 10^{23} \text{ molecules H}_2}{1 \text{ mol H}_2}$$

Answer: 2.44×10^{19} molecules H_2

Problem 5.16

How many molecules of oxygen are required for the complete combustion of 1.67 g methane, CH_4?

B. Percent Yield

In Examples 5.14, 5.15, and 5.16, we have calculated the **theoretical yield** of the reaction—that is, the amount of product that would be obtained if the reaction proceeded completely and only as stated in the equation. Very often, in fact in most cases, the yield of a reaction does not equal theoretical yield but is something less than that. The reasons for such discrepancies are varied. The reactant may have been impure; some of the product may have been lost; or small amounts of substances other than those shown in the equation may have been formed. In these cases, only some of the theoretical yield is obtained. The **percent yield** is calculated by comparing this actual yield to the theoretical yield.

The percent yield of a reaction depends on results obtained in the laboratory. Since the amount of reactants used is known, the theoretical yield can be calculated. The amount of obtained product can be measured. The ratio between the two gives the percent yield.

$$\frac{\text{Actual yield}}{\text{Theoretical yield}} \times 100\% = \text{percent yield}$$

To consider an example of this process, suppose that in Example 5.14 only 165 g carbon dioxide were obtained. The theoretical yield, the one calculated, is 187 g carbon dioxide. The percent yield of the reaction would be

$$\frac{165 \text{ g}}{187 \text{ g}} \times 100\% = 88.2\% \text{ yield}$$

Example 5.17 illustrates how to calculate percent yield.

■

Example 5.17

The reaction of ethane with chlorine yields ethyl chloride and hydrogen chloride:

$$C_2H_6 + Cl_2 \longrightarrow C_2H_5Cl + HCl$$

ethane   ethyl
                     chloride

When 5.6 g of ethane is reacted with chlorine, 8.2 g of ethyl chloride is obtained. Calculate the percent yield of ethyl chloride.

☐ *Solution*

Because this is a percent yield problem, the first step is to calculate the theoretical yield. This can be done using the steps outlined in Section 5.5A.

Equation: $C_2H_6 + Cl_2 \longrightarrow C_2H_5Cl + HCl$
Wanted: ? g C_2H_5Cl for a 100% yield
Given: 5.6 g C_2H_6
Conversion factors: For ethane: to go from mass to moles, 30.1 g C_2H_6 = 1 mol C_2H_6. For ethyl chloride: to go from C_2H_6 to C_2H_5Cl, 1 mol C_2H_6 yields 1 mol C_2H_5Cl; to go from moles to mass, 1 mol C_2H_5Cl = 64.5 g C_2H_5Cl.
Arithmetic equation:

$$? \text{ g } C_2H_5Cl = 5.6 \text{ g } C_2H_6 \times \frac{1 \text{ mol } C_2H_6}{30.1 \text{ g } C_2H_6} \times \frac{1 \text{ mol } C_2H_5Cl}{1 \text{ mol } C_2H_6} \times \frac{64.5 \text{ g } C_2H_5Cl}{1 \text{ mol } C_2H_5Cl}$$

$$= 12 \text{ g } C_2H_5Cl$$

The theoretical yield is 12 g C_2H_5Cl. The actual yield is 8.2 g ethyl chloride.

Answer: Percent yield = $\dfrac{8.2 \text{ g } C_2H_5Cl}{12 \text{ g } C_2H_5Cl} \times 100\% = 68\%$

Problem 5.17

When 1.6 g of oxygen reacts with an excess of nitrogen, 1.3 g of nitrogen oxide is formed. Calculate the percent yield of nitrogen oxide. The balanced equation is

$$N_2 + O_2 \longrightarrow 2NO$$

5.6 Energy Changes Accompanying Chemical Reactions

All changes, whether chemical or physical, are accompanied by a change in energy. Each reacting molecule possesses a certain amount of energy due to the nature of its chemical bonds. So does each product molecule. As the bonds of the reacting molecules break and the new bonds of the products are formed, energy is released or absorbed depending on whether the reactants have higher or lower energy than the products.

There are several ways of measuring energy changes. The two kinds of energy change of most interest to us are: (1) The change in free energy, ΔG. Free energy is the energy available to do useful work (discussed in Chapter 24). (2) The change in **enthalpy**, ΔH. The change in enthalpy is the heat energy absorbed or released by the reaction and measured at constant pressure. Because most chemical reactions, especially those in living organisms, take place under the constant pressure of the atmosphere, the energy released or absorbed by such reactions is the change in enthalpy, ΔH, which can be shown as

$$\Delta H_{\text{reaction}} = H_{\text{products}} - H_{\text{reactants}}$$

A superscript is used in reporting values of ΔH, to show the temperature at which the measurements were made. For example, the symbol $\Delta H^{0°C}$ shows that the change in enthalpy is for a reaction carried out at 0°C. If no temperature is shown, the enthalpy change was measured at 25°C. If we were to follow precisely the SI system of measurement, we should report the energy change in joules or kilojoules, but because the calorie and kilocalorie are still widely used, we shall use both calories and joules (or kilocalories and kilojoules) in discussing these energy changes.

The value of ΔH given with an equation refers to that particular equation. When this enthalpy change was measured, the physical states of the components were those stated in the equation. If the physical states are different, the enthalpy change will be different. This is illustrated by the next two equations for the formation of water. In the first, gaseous water is formed; in the second, liquid water is formed. The difference between their enthalpy changes reflects the difference in energy content between a gas and a liquid. (See Chapter 6 for more discussion of this point.)

$$H_2(g) + \tfrac{1}{2}O_2(g) \longrightarrow H_2O(g) \qquad \Delta H = -57.6 \text{ kcal}$$
$$(-241 \text{ kJ})$$

$$H_2(g) + \tfrac{1}{2}O_2(g) \longrightarrow H_2O(l) \qquad \Delta H = -68.4 \text{ kcal}$$
$$(-286 \text{ kJ})$$

The enthalpy change given for a reaction also depends on the coefficients used in the equation for the reaction. Thus if the equation for the formation of water is written

$$2H_2(g) + O_2(g) \longrightarrow 2H_2O(g) \qquad \Delta H = -115 \text{ kcal}$$
$$(-482 \text{ kJ})$$

the enthalpy change is twice what it is in the previous equation for the formation of gaseous water, in which the coefficient of water is 1. This last problem can be resolved by doing as we did in several equations where we have reported the enthalpy change per mole of one component of the reaction, thus removing any ambiguity in interpretation.

A. Endothermic and Exothermic Reactions

A reaction that absorbs energy is an **endothermic reaction**; its enthalpy change is positive. A reaction that releases energy is an **exothermic reaction**; its enthalpy change is negative. If the enthalpy of the products of a reaction is greater than the enthalpy of the reactants, the change is endothermic. Energy is absorbed from the surroundings. The following reactions are endothermic.

1. Formation of hydrogen iodide (Equation a):

$$\tfrac{1}{2}H_2(g) + \tfrac{1}{2}I_2(s) \longrightarrow HI(g) \qquad \Delta H = +6.19 \text{ kcal/mol HI}$$
$$(+25.9 \text{ kJ/mol HI})$$

2. Decomposition of water (Equation b):

$$H_2O(l) \longrightarrow H_2(g) + \tfrac{1}{2}O_2(g) \qquad \Delta H = +68.4 \text{ kcal/mol H}_2O$$
$$(+285.8 \text{ kJ/mol H}_2O)$$

If the enthalpy of the products is less than that of the reactants, the change in enthalpy is negative. Energy is released to the surroundings; the reaction is exothermic. The following reactions are exothermic.

1. Combustion of methane (Equation c):

$$CH_4(g) + 2O_2(g) \longrightarrow CO_2(g) + 2H_2O(l) \qquad \Delta H = -213 \text{ kcal/mol CH}_4$$
$$(-891 \text{ kJ/mol CH}_4)$$

2. Formation of water (Equation d):

$$H_2(g) + \tfrac{1}{2}O_2(g) \longrightarrow H_2O(l) \qquad \Delta H = -68.4 \text{ kcal/mol H}_2O$$
$$(-285.8 \text{ kJ/mol H}_2O)$$

3. Combustion of sucrose (Equation e):

$$C_{12}H_{22}O_{11}(s) + 12O_2(g) \longrightarrow 12CO_2(g) + 11H_2O(l)$$
$$\Delta H = -1.335 \times 10^3 \text{ kcal/mol sucrose}$$
$$(-5.64 \times 10^3 \text{ kJ/mol sucrose})$$

Notice that the decomposition of water (Equation b) is endothermic and requires the input of 285.8 kJ of energy per mole of water decomposed. The formation of one mole of water from hydrogen and oxygen (Equation d) is exothermic and releases 285.8 kJ of energy. The amount of energy is the same, but the sign of the energy is different.

Another example of the relationship between energy change and direction of a reaction that is much more important to us is the formation and decomposition of glucose. Glucose, $C_6H_{12}O_6$, is formed from carbon dioxide and water in the cells of green plants in the process called **photosynthesis**. Photosynthesis is an endothermic reaction. The source of the energy for the formation of glucose is light (radiant energy), usually from the sun:

$$6CO_2(g) + 6H_2O(l) \xrightarrow{\text{photosynthesis}} C_6H_{12}O_6(aq) + 6O_2(g)$$
$$\Delta H = +670 \text{ kcal/mol glucose}$$
$$(+2.80 \times 10^3 \text{ kJ/mol glucose})$$

In the reverse of this reaction, the glucose formed is metabolized (broken down) in plant and animal cells, to form carbon dioxide, water, and energy:

$$C_6H_{12}O_6(aq) + 6O_2(g) \xrightarrow{\text{metabolism}} 6CO_2(g) + 6H_2O(l)$$
$$\Delta H = -670 \text{ kcal/mol glucose}$$
$$(-2.80 \times 10^3 \text{ kJ/mol glucose})$$

Thus, green plants have the remarkable ability to trap the energy of sunlight and use that energy to produce glucose from carbon dioxide and water. The energy is stored in the glucose. Animal and plant cells have the equally remarkable ability to metabolize glucose and use the energy released to maintain body temperature or do work such as contracting muscles and thinking, which depend on biological processes.

Example 5.18

For each of the following: (1) Decide whether the reaction is exothermic or endothermic. (2) Write the equation for the reverse reaction and state the accompanying enthalpy change.

a. $N_2(g) + O_2(g) \longrightarrow 2NO(g)$ $\Delta H = +43.3 \text{ kcal}$
$(+181 \text{ kJ})$

b. $2NO_2(g) \longrightarrow N_2O_4(g)$ $\Delta H = -13.9 \text{ kcal}$
(-58.1 kJ)

c. $PCl_3(g) + Cl_2(g) \longrightarrow PCl_5(g)$ $\Delta H = -22.1 \text{ kcal}$
(-92.5 kJ)

Solution

a. The enthalpy is positive; the reaction is endothermic. The reverse reaction is

$$2NO(g) \longrightarrow N_2(g) + O_2(g) \qquad \Delta H = -43.3 \text{ kcal}$$
$$(-181 \text{ kJ})$$

b. The enthalpy change is negative; the reaction is exothermic. The reverse reaction is

$$N_2O_4(g) \longrightarrow 2NO_2(g) \qquad \Delta H = +13.9 \text{ kcal}$$
$$(+58.1 \text{ kJ})$$

c. The enthalpy change is negative; the reaction is exothermic. The reverse reaction is

$$PCl_5(g) \longrightarrow PCl_3(g) + Cl_2(g) \qquad \Delta H = +22.1 \text{ kcal}$$
$$(+92.5 \text{ kJ})$$

Problem 5.18

For each of the following: (1) State whether the reaction is exothermic or endothermic. (2) Write the equation for the reverse reaction and state its enthalpy change.

a. $N_2(g) + 3H_2(g) \longrightarrow 2NH_3(g) \qquad \Delta H = -11.0 \text{ kcal} (-46.0 \text{ kJ})$
b. $2H_2O(g) + 2Cl_2(g) \longrightarrow 4HCl(g) + O_2(g) \qquad \Delta H = +27.8 \text{ kcal}$
$$(+115 \text{ kJ})$$
c. $C_2H_5OH(l) + 3O_2(g) \longrightarrow 2CO_2(g) + 3H_2O(l) \qquad \Delta H = -327 \text{ kcal}$
$$(-1.37 \times 10^3 \text{ kJ})$$

B. The Stoichiometry of Energy Changes

The energy change associated with a reaction is a stoichiometric quantity and can be treated arithmetically, as mass changes were in Section 5.5.

Example 5.19

Calculate the enthalpy change for the combustion of 35.5 g gaseous propane, C_3H_8.

$$C_3H_8(g) + 5O_2(g) \longrightarrow 3CO_2(g) + 4H_2O(l) \qquad \Delta H = -531 \text{ kcal}$$
$$(-2.22 \times 10^3 \text{ kJ})$$

☐ *Solution*

Wanted: ? energy released (kcal)
Given: 35.5 g C_3H_8
Conversion factors: For propane, C_3H_8; to go from mass to moles, 44.1 g $C_3H_8 = 1$ mol C_3H_8. On combustion, 1 mol propane releases 531 kcal energy.
Arithmetic equation:

$$? \text{ kcal} = 35.5 \text{ g } C_3H_8 \times \frac{1 \text{ mol } C_3H_8}{44.1 \text{ g } C_3H_8} \times \frac{-531 \text{ kcal}}{1 \text{ mol } C_3H_8}$$

$$= -427 \text{ kcal}$$
$$(-1.79 \times 10^3 \text{ kJ})$$

Problem 5.19

Calculate the enthalpy change when 45.6 g liquid water is formed by the reaction of gaseous hydrogen with gaseous oxygen according to the equation

$$H_2(g) + \tfrac{1}{2}O_2(g) \longrightarrow H_2O(l) \qquad \Delta H = -68.4 \text{ kcal}$$
$$(-287 \text{ kJ})$$

Example 5.20

Calculate the enthalpy change when 15.0 g glucose is metabolized at 25°C to gaseous carbon dioxide and liquid water. The equation for the reaction is given in Section 5.6A.

Solution   *Equation:*

$$C_6H_{12}O_6(s) + 6O_2(g) \longrightarrow 6CO_2(g) + 6H_2O(l)$$
$$\Delta H = -670 \text{ kcal/mol glucose}$$

Wanted: ? kcal
Given: 15.0 g glucose
Conversion factor: For glucose: to go from mass to moles, 180 g glucose =
    1 mol glucose. The metabolism of 1 mol glucose releases 670 kcal energy.
Arithmetic equation:

$$? \text{ kcal} = 15.0 \text{ g glucose} \times \frac{1 \text{ mol glucose}}{180 \text{ g glucose}} \times \frac{-670 \text{ kcal}}{1 \text{ mol glucose}}$$

$$= -55.8 \text{ kcal}$$

Problem 5.20

Calculate the enthalpy change when 16.5 g methane is burned to gaseous carbon dioxide and liquid water at 25°C.

Key Terms and Concepts

chemical change (5.1)
chemical equation (5.2A)
chemical property (5.1)
coefficients (5.2A)
combination reactions (5.3A)
combustion (5.4C)
decomposition (5.3B)
displacement (5.3C)
double replacement (5.3D)
endothermic reaction (5.6A)
enthalpy (5.6)
enthalpy change (5.2A
    and 5.6)
exothermic reaction (5.6A)
half-reactions (5.4B)
insoluble ionic compounds (5.3D2)
neutralization (5.3D1)

oxidation (5.4)
oxidation number (5.4A1)
oxidation-reduction (5.4)
oxidizing agent (5.4A2)
percent yield (5.5B)
photosynthesis (5.6A)
physical change (5.1)
precipitate (5.3D2)
products (5.2A)
reactants (5.2A)
redox (5.4)
reducing agent (5.4A2)
reduction (5.4)
solubility (5.3D2)
solubility rules (Table 5.2)
stoichiometry (5.5A)
theoretical yield (5.5B)

Problems

Chemical equations (Section 5.2)

5.21   Explain each term in the equations.
    a. $C(s) + O_2(g) \longrightarrow CO_2(g)$ $\Delta H = -93.9 \text{ kcal}$
                                                    $(-3.93 \times 10^2 \text{ kJ})$

b. $2H_2O(g) + 2Cl_2(g) \longrightarrow 4HCl(g) + O_2(g)$ $\Delta H = 27.8$ kcal
(116 kJ)

c. $N_2(g) + O_2(g) \longrightarrow 2NO(g)$ $\Delta H = 43.3$ kcal
(181 kJ)

Kinds of chemical changes (Section 5.3)

5.22 Write balanced equations for these combustion reactions.
a. $K + O_2 \not\longrightarrow K_2O$ **b.** $Se + O_2 \not\longrightarrow SeO_2$
c. $Cr + O_2 \not\longrightarrow Cr_2O_3$

5.23 Write balanced equations for these combination reactions.
a. $Cu + S \not\longrightarrow Cu_2S$ **b.** $Al + N_2 \not\longrightarrow Al_2N_3$
c. $N_2 + I_2 \not\longrightarrow NI_3$

5.24 Write balanced equations for these displacement reactions.
a. $Fe + Cu(NO_3)_2 \not\longrightarrow Fe(NO_3)_2 + Cu$
b. $Mg + HCl \not\longrightarrow MgCl_2 + H_2$
c. $Li + H_2O \not\longrightarrow LiOH + H_2$

5.25 Write balanced equations for these displacement reactions.
a. $Hg + AgNO_3 \longrightarrow Hg(NO_3)_2 + Ag$
b. $Cl_2 + KI \not\longrightarrow KCl + I_2$
c. $Ca + H_2O \not\longrightarrow Ca(OH)_2 + H_2$

5.26 An important industrial chemical process is the electrolysis of a water solution of sodium chloride to give chlorine gas. Sodium hydroxide is also a product. Write a balanced equation for this important process.

5.27 Write complete and balanced equations for these reactions. Name the products.
a. $HCl + Mg(OH)_2 \longrightarrow$
b. $Cu(OH)_2 + H_2SO_4 \longrightarrow$
c. $H_3PO_4 + Al(OH)_3 \longrightarrow$

5.28 Write balanced equations for these reactions. All form precipitates. Identify and name the precipitate.
a. $Ba(NO_3)_2 + K_2SO_4 \longrightarrow$
b. $ZnCl_2 + H_2S \longrightarrow$
c. $Pb(NO_3)_2 + KI \longrightarrow$

Oxidation- reduction (Section 5.4)

5.29 Identify these changes as oxidation or reduction.
a. CrO_4^{2-} to Cr^{3+} **b.** MnO_4^- to Mn^{2+} **c.** SO_4^{2-} to SO_2

5.30 What characterizes an oxidation-reduction reaction?

5.31 Write balanced equations for these reactions and identify those that are oxidation-reduction.
a. $Ca(OH)_2 + HCl \not\longrightarrow CaCl_2 + H_2O$
b. $SO_3 + BaO \not\longrightarrow BaSO_4$
c. $AgNO_3 + Fe \not\longrightarrow Fe(NO_3)_2 + Ag$

5.32 In the oxidation-reduction reactions in Problem 5.31, what is oxidized and what is reduced? What changes in oxidation number have occurred?

5.33 Write a balanced equation for the combustion of each of the following to form carbon dioxide and water.
a. hexane, C_6H_{14} **b.** 1-propanol, C_3H_7OH **c.** fructose, $C_6H_{12}O_6$

Mass relationships in an equation (Section 5.5)

5.34 Chlorine dioxide is used for bleaching paper. It is prepared by the reaction

$$2NaClO_2 + Cl_2 \longrightarrow 2ClO_2 + 2NaCl.$$

a. Name the oxidizing and reducing agents in this reaction.
b. Calculate the weight of chlorine dioxide that would be prepared from 5.50 kg of sodium chlorite, $NaClO_2$.

5.35 Write the balanced equation for the reaction of chlorine with sodium to form sodium chloride. Calculate the weight of sodium that will react completely with 5.00 g chlorine.

5.36 Glucose, $C_6H_{12}O_6$, burns to form carbon dioxide and water.
a. Write the balanced equation for this reaction.
b. Calculate the moles of glucose that would be needed to form 1.55 mol carbon dioxide.
c. Calculate the mass of water formed by the reaction in (b).

5.37 Pure aluminum is prepared by electrolysis of aluminum oxide according to the balanced equation

$$2Al_2O_3 \xrightarrow{\text{elec}} 4Al + 3O_2$$

What mass of aluminum would be prepared from 6.06 g of aluminum oxide?

5.38 **a.** Write the balanced equation for the reaction of sodium hydroxide with sulfuric acid to form sodium sulfate.
b. Calculate how many moles of sulfuric acid would be neutralized by 8.00 g of sodium hydroxide.

5.39 **a.** Write the balanced equation for the complete combustion of octane, C_8H_{18}, with oxygen to form carbon dioxide and water.
b. Calculate the mass of water formed by the complete combustion of 1.8 L of octane (density = 0.703 g/mL).

5.40 When silver carbonate is heated, it decomposes to silver, oxygen, and carbon dioxide according to the unbalanced equation

$$Ag_2CO_3 \not\longrightarrow Ag + O_2 + CO_2$$

a. Balance the equation.
b. Calculate the weight of silver that would be isolated by heating 0.565 g silver carbonate.

Energy calculations (Section 5.6)

5.41 For the following reactions, calculate what the energy change is when 5.0 g of the underlined reactant is used. Express your answer in kilocalories. State whether the energy is absorbed or released.

$$H_2(g) + \underline{CO_2(g)} \longrightarrow CO(g) + H_2O(l) \qquad \Delta H = -0.69\ \text{kcal}\ (-2.89\ \text{kJ})$$

$$\underline{C_{12}H_{22}O_{11}}(s) + 12O_2(g) \longrightarrow 12CO_2(g) + 11H_2O(l) \qquad \Delta H = (-1348\ \text{kcal})\ (-5641\ \text{kJ})$$

5.42 **a.** Calculate the energy required for the formation of 0.5 mol glucose from carbon dioxide and water. (The equation is shown in Section 5.6A.) Express your answer in kilocalories.

b. Calculate the energy change when 0.50 mol glucose is metabolized to carbon dioxide and water. Express your answer in kilocalories.

5.43   Calculate the energy released by the metabolism of 6.5 g ethyl alcohol according to the equation

$$C_2H_5OH(l) + 3O_2(g) \longrightarrow 2CO_2(g) + 3H_2O(l) \qquad \Delta H = -327 \text{ kcal}$$
$$(-1.37 \times 10^3 \text{ kJ})$$

5.44   A plant requires 4178.8 kcal for the formation of 1.00 kg starch from carbon dioxide and water. Calculate the energy needed for the formation of 6.32 g starch. Express your answer in both kilocalories and kilojoules. Is this reaction endothermic or exothermic?

General problems

5.45   What mass of lead(II) iodide can be prepared by adding an excess of sodium iodide solution to 167 mL of a solution that contains 5.00 g lead(II) nitrate in each liter of solution?

5.46   Given the following data, show by calculation whether ethanol (ethyl alcohol, an ingredient of gasohol) or octane (an ingredient of regular gasoline) yields more energy per liter.

Substance	Formula	Density	Heat of Combustion
ethanol	C_2H_5OH	0.7025 g/mL	-327 kcal/mol $(-1.37 \times 10^3$ kJ/mol)
octane	C_8H_{18}	0.7893 g/mL	-1303 kcal/mol $(-5.48 \times 10^3$ kJ/mol)

6

The States of Matter

Although atoms and molecules are too small to be seen by the naked eye, chemists have learned a great deal about their properties by experimental observations. Chemists have also learned much about collections of molecules as they exist in the three states of matter: gases, liquids, and solids. In this chapter, we will consider the properties of matter in the three states.

6.1 Characteristics of the Solid, Liquid, and Gaseous States

The physical properties of a particular substance determine its state at room temperature (20°C). If both its normal melting point and its normal boiling point are below room temperature, the substance is a gas under normal conditions. The normal melting point of oxygen is −218°C; its normal boiling point is −189°C. Oxygen is a gas at room temperature. If the melting point of a substance is below room temperature and its boiling point is above room temperature, the substance is a liquid at room temperature. Benzene melts at 6°C and boils at 80°C; it is a liquid at room temperature. If both the melting point and the boiling point are above room temperature, the substance is a solid. Sodium chloride melts at 801°C and boils at 1413°C. Sodium chloride is a solid under normal conditions. Figure 6.1 illustrates the relation between physical state and normal melting and boiling points.

A. Shape and Volume

A solid has a fixed shape and volume, which do not change with the shape of its container. Consider a rock and how its size and shape stay the same, regardless of where you put it. A liquid has a constant volume, but its shape conforms to the shape of its container. Consider a sample of milk. Its volume stays the same, whether you put it in a saucer for the cat to drink or in a glass for yourself. Its shape changes to match the shape of the saucer or glass. A gas changes both

| | Room temperature (20°C) | | | | |
| | Low temperature | | | High temperature | |
	Melting point	Boiling point		Melting point	Boiling point
Solids					
sodium chloride				801°C	1413°C
naphthalene				81°C	218°C
Liquids					
water	0°C				100°C
benzene	6°C				80°C
Gases					
oxygen	−218°C	−183°C			
methane	−182°C	−164°C			

Figure 6.1 Physical state as related to normal melting and boiling points. Notice that the solids melt and boil above room temperature, the liquids melt below room temperature and boil above room temperature, and the gases melt and boil below room temperature.

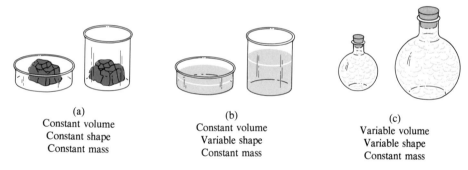

(a)
Constant volume
Constant shape
Constant mass

(b)
Constant volume
Variable shape
Constant mass

(c)
Variable volume
Variable shape
Constant mass

Figure 6.2 Constancy of volume, shape, and mass in the three states of matter: (a) solid; (b) liquid; (c) gas.

its shape and volume to conform to the shape and volume of a container. Consider a sample of air. It will fill a balloon, a tire, or a rubber raft. Its shape and volume conform to the shape and volume of the container you put it in. Figure 6.2 illustrates these points.

B. Density

The density of solids and liquids is measured in grams per milliliter and changes very little as the temperature of the sample changes. Gases have much lower densities, so much lower that gas densities are measured in grams per liter instead of grams per milliliter. The density of a gas varies considerably as the temperature of the gas changes. Table 1.7 illustrated the differences among densities in the different states.

C. Compressibility

The volume of a solid or a liquid does not change very much with pressure. You cannot change the volume of a brick by squeezing it, nor can you squeeze one liter of liquid into a 0.5-L bottle. The volume of a gas does change a great deal with pressure; you can squeeze a 1.0-L gas sample into a 0.5-L space.

D. Intermolecular Structure

The constant shape and volume of a solid suggest that its particles (atoms, ions, molecules) are held together by fairly rigid bonds. The variable shape but constant volume of a liquid suggests that there is some bonding between its particles but these bonds are not rigid and are probably less strong than bonds in a solid. That a gas has neither constant shape nor constant volume suggests that there are no bonds and only very slight attractive forces between the particles of a gas.

The variety in compressibility suggests other hypotheses. If solids and liquids cannot be compressed, the particles of which they are composed must be very close together. The high compressibility of a gas implies that the particles of a gas are very far apart with a great deal of space between them. This last hypothesis is supported by the difference between densities of solids and liquids and the densities of gases. There is always much more mass in 1 mL of a solid or liquid than in 1 mL of gas (see Table 1.7).

6.2 Kinetic Energy

Any consideration of the properties of a collection of particles, such as molecules, requires knowledge of their energy. Kinetic energy is the energy of motion. The **kinetic energy (KE)** of an object is determined by the equation

$$KE = \tfrac{1}{2}mv^2$$

where KE is kinetic energy, m is mass, and v is velocity. The equation states that the kinetic energy of an object depends on both its mass and its velocity.

A. Distribution of Kinetic Energy

In a collection of molecules, each molecule has a kinetic energy that can be calculated by the above equation. Even if the molecules in a sample have the same mass, they differ in velocity, so that in a collection of molecules there is a wide range of kinetic energies, from very low to very high. Each molecule may change its kinetic energy often but the overall distribution remains the same. Figure 6.3 shows a typical distribution of kinetic energies in a collection of molecules.

B. Kinetic Energy and Temperature

The average kinetic energy of a collection of molecules is proportional to its temperature. At absolute zero ($-273°C$), the molecules have a minimum kinetic energy. As the temperature of the sample increases, so does its average kinetic energy. As the temperature rises, the distribution of kinetic energy among the molecules in the sample also changes. Figure 6.4 shows the distribution of kinetic energy in a sample at two different temperatures. Curve *A* is at the lower temperature, curve *B* at the higher temperature.

6.3 The Kinetic Molecular Theory

The **kinetic molecular theory** describes the properties of molecules in terms of motion (kinetic energy) and of temperature. The theory is most often applied to gases but can be used to explain molecular behavior in all states of matter. As applied to gases, the kinetic molecular theory has the following postulates:

1. Gases are composed of very tiny particles (molecules). The actual volume of these molecules is so small as to be negligible compared with the total volume of the gas sample. A gas sample is, then, mostly empty space. This explains the compressibility of gases.

2. No attractive forces exist between the molecules of a gas. This explains why, over any period, the molecules of a gas do not clump.

3. The molecules of a gas are in constant, rapid, random motion. This explains why a gas spreads so rapidly through space—for example, why the smell of hot coffee can spread from the kitchen throughout the house.

4. Gas molecules, during their motion, constantly collide with each other and with the walls of the container. The collisions with the walls provide the pressure exerted by a gas. None of these collisions is accompanied by any loss of energy; instead they are what is known as **elastic collisions**. A new tennis ball collides more elastically than a "dead" tennis ball.

5. The average kinetic energy of the molecules in a gas sample is proportional to the temperature (Kelvin) of the gas and independent of its composition. In other words, at the same temperature, all gases have the same average kinetic energy. It also follows from this postulate that at zero Kelvin, all molecular motion has ceased.

These postulates and the experimental evidence for them are summarized in Table 6.1.

Clearly, the actual properties of individual gases vary somewhat from these postulates, for their molecules do have a real volume and some attraction does exist between molecules. However, our study will ignore these variations and concentrate on an "ideal" gas, one that does not vary from this model.

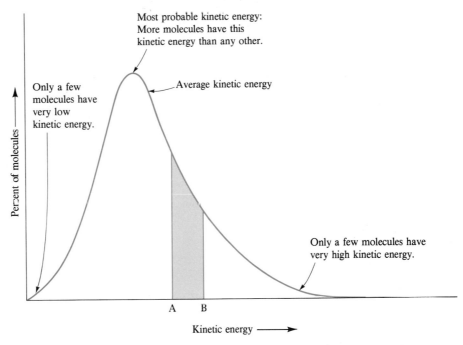

Figure 6.3 Distribution of kinetic energy in a collection of molecules.

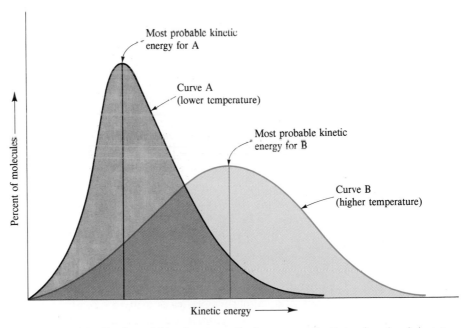

Figure 6.4 Distribution of kinetic energy in the same collection of molecules at two different temperatures.

Table 6.1
The kinetic
molecular theory.

Postulate	Evidence
1. Gases are tiny molecules surrounded by large empty space.	The compressibility of gases.
2. No attractive forces exist between molecules.	Gases do not clump.
3. Molecules move in constant, rapid, straight-line motion.	Gases mix rapidly.
4. Molecules collide elastically with the walls of their container and with each other.	Gases exert pressure that does not diminish over time.
5. The average kinetic energy of molecules is proportional to the Kelvin temperature of the sample.	Charles' law (Section 6.5B)

6.4 Measuring Gas Samples

A gas sample obeys several laws that relate its volume to its pressure, temperature, and mass. These properties can be measured. Mass and volume are familiar concepts and can be measured with familiar apparatus. Temperature can be measured on any scale: Celsius, Fahrenheit, or Kelvin. If the temperature is to be used in a calculation, however, the Kelvin scale must be used. **Standard temperature** for gases, the temperature at which the properties of different gases are compared, is 273 K.

Pressure is defined as force per unit area and is measured in units that have dimensions of force per unit area. For example, the air pressure in tires is measured in pounds per square inch (psi). The pressure of the atmosphere is frequently measured with a mercury barometer. The basic features of a mercury barometer are shown in Figure 6.5.

A barometer is made by filling a glass tube, which is at least 760 mm long and closed at one end, with mercury, then carefully inverting it in a pool of mercury. The level of the mercury in the column will fall slightly and then become steady.

The height of the column of mercury measures the pressure of the atmosphere. To understand why this is so, consider the pressure on the surface of the mercury pool at the base of the column. Above this surface rises the "sea" of air (the atmosphere) that surrounds the Earth. On each square centimeter of the surface, we can visualize a 20-km column of air pressing down. On the surface under the mercury column, the mercury is pressing down. The two pressures must be equal. If they were not, mercury would be flowing into or out of the column and the height of the column would not be steady. The atmosphere must be exerting a pressure equal to that exerted by the mercury column. The total area under the atmosphere or under the column of mercury is not important because the pressure is force per unit area under either the column or the atmosphere.

When this experiment is performed in dry air at sea level and at 0°C, the column of mercury is 760 mm high; therefore, we say that the atmosphere is exerting a pressure equal to that of 760 mm of mercury (mm Hg). This amount of pressure has been defined as one **atmosphere** (1 atm) of pressure and designated **standard pressure**.

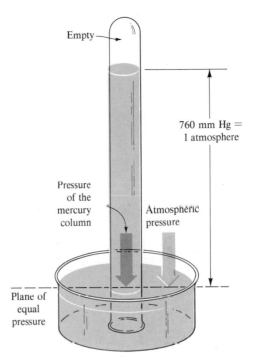

760 mm Hg =
1 atmosphere

Pressure
of the
mercury
column

Atmospheric
pressure

Empty

Plane of
equal
pressure

Figure 6.5 A mercury barometer. The height of mercury in the column is proportional to the pressure of the atmosphere.

Pressure can be measured in other units. The relation between these units and one atmosphere is:

$$1 \text{ atm} = 1.01325 \times 10^5 \text{ pascals (the \textbf{pascal} is the SI unit)}$$
$$= 76 \text{ cm, or } 760 \text{ mm, mercury}$$
$$= 760 \text{ torr (1 \textbf{torr} = the pressure exerted by 1 mm Hg)}$$
$$= 29.92 \text{ in. mercury (used to report atmospheric pressure in weather reports)}$$

Each of these relations can be used as a conversion factor, as shown in the following problems.

Example 6.1

a. How many atmospheres of pressure does a column of mercury 654 mm high exert?

b. What is this pressure in pascals?

☐ *Solution*

a. *Wanted:* pressure in atmospheres
Given: a column of mercury 654 mm high
Conversion factor: 1 atm = 760 mm Hg
Equation:

$$? \text{ atm} = 654 \text{ mm Hg} \times \frac{1 \text{ atm}}{760 \text{ mm Hg}}$$

Answer: 0.861 atm

b. *Wanted:* pressure in pascals
Given: a pressure of 0.861 atm
Conversion factor: 1 atm = 1.01325 × 10⁵ Pa
Equation:

$$? \text{ Pa} = 0.861 \text{ atm} \times \frac{1.01325 \times 10^5 \text{ Pa}}{1 \text{ atm}}$$

Answer: 8.72 × 10⁴ Pa

Problem 6.1

What pressure in pascals is equal to a pressure of 1.65 atm? Of 369 torr?

In dry air at sea level, the average air pressure is one atmosphere. Atmospheric pressure decreases as altitude increases because the sea of air above becomes less dense. Our bodies become adjusted to the normal pressure of the altitude at which we live. Minor problems of adjustment can occur when we move from sea level to the mountains, and vice versa. Serious problems develop at higher altitudes. Commercial jet aircraft must be pressurized, because passengers could not survive the low pressure at the altitude at which they fly. Travelers in space must wear pressurized suits.

Barometers measure the pressure of the atmosphere. **Manometers** measure the pressure of isolated gas samples. Some manometers measure pressure with a column of mercury, like a mercury barometer. This type of manometer has a U-shaped tube partially filled with mercury (Figure 6.6). One end of the tube is open to a chamber holding a gas sample and the other end is open to the atmosphere. If the mercury level on the side of the tube open to the gas sample is lower than the level on the side open to the atmosphere, the pressure of the gas is greater than that of the atmosphere by an amount equal to the difference in height between the two mercury columns. If the mercury level on the side of the gas sample is higher than on the side open to the atmosphere, the pressure

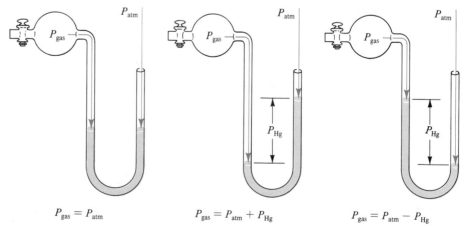

Figure 6.6 A manometer. The height difference between the mercury levels in the two sides of the tube measures the pressure difference between the gas sample and the atmosphere.

of the gas is less than atmospheric pressure by the difference in height of the two columns.

6.5 The Gas Laws

A. Boyle's Law

Boyle's law states: If the temperature of a gas sample is kept constant, the volume of the sample varies inversely as the pressure varies. This means that if the pressure increases, the volume decreases. If the pressure decreases, the volume increases. This law can be expressed as an equation that relates the initial volume V_1 and pressure P_1 to the final volume V_2 and pressure P_2.

At constant temperature,

$$\frac{V_1}{V_2} = \frac{P_2}{P_1}$$

Rearranging this equation gives

$$V_1 P_1 = P_2 V_2 \quad \text{or} \quad V_2 = V_1 \times \frac{P_1}{P_2}$$

Boyle's law is illustrated in Figure 6.7, which shows a sample of gas enclosed in a container with a movable piston. The container is kept at constant temperature. When the piston is stationary, the pressure it exerts on the gas sample

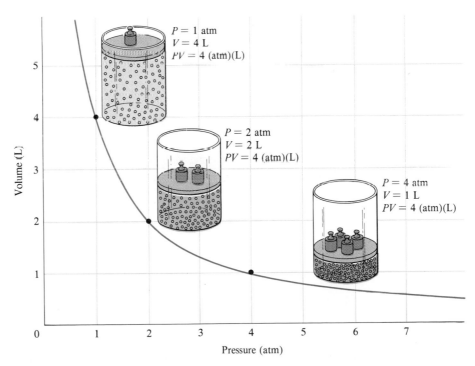

Figure 6.7 Boyle's law: At constant temperature, the volume of a gas sample is inversely proportional to the pressure. The curve is a graph based on the data listed in the figure.

equals the pressure the gas exerts on it. When the pressure on the piston is doubled, the piston moves downward until the pressure exerted by the gas equals the pressure exerted by the piston. At this point the volume of the gas is halved. If the pressure on the piston is again doubled, the volume of gas decreases to one-fourth its original volume. At the molecular level, the pressure of a gas depends on the number of collisions its molecules have with the walls of the container. If the pressure on the piston is doubled, the volume of the gas decreases by one-half. The gas molecules, now confined in half the original volume, collide with the walls of the container twice as often, and their pressure once again equals the pressure of the piston.

How does Boyle's law relate to the kinetic molecular theory? The first postulate of the theory states that a gas sample consists of relatively enormous empty space filled with molecules of negligible volume. Changing the pressure on the sample changes only the volume of that empty space—not the volume of the molecules.

Example 6.2

A sample of gas has a volume of 6.20 L at 20°C and 0.980 atm pressure. What is its volume at the same temperature and at a pressure of 1.11 atm?

☐ *Solution*

1. Tabulate the data.

	Initial Conditions	**Final Conditions**
Volume	$V_1 = 6.20$ L	$V_2 = ?$
Pressure	$P_1 = 0.980$ atm	$P_2 = 1.11$ atm

2. Check the pressure units. If they are different, use a conversion factor to make them the same. (Pressure conversion factors are found in Section 6.4).
3. Substitute in the Boyle's law equation:

$$V_2 = V_1 \times \frac{P_1}{P_2} = 6.20 \text{ L} \times \frac{0.980 \text{ atm}}{1.11 \text{ atm}} = 5.47 \text{ L}$$

4. Check that your answer is reasonable. Since the pressure has increased, the volume should decrease. The calculated final volume is less than the initial volume, as predicted.

Problem 6.2

A sample of gas has a volume of 253 mL at 0.50 atm. What is its volume at the same temperature and at a pressure of 1.0 atm?

B. Charles' Law

Charles' law states: If the pressure of a gas sample is kept constant, the volume of the sample varies directly as the Kelvin temperature. (See Figure 6.8.) As the temperature increases, so does the volume; if the temperature decreases, the volume decreases. This can be expressed by an equation relating the initial

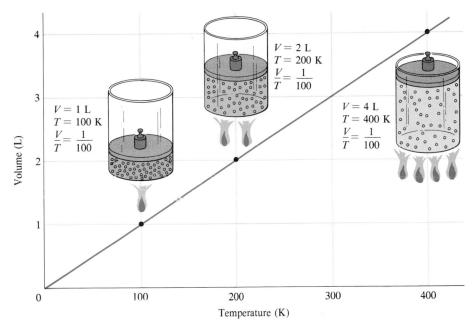

Figure 6.8 Charles' law: At constant pressure, the volume of a gas sample is directly proportional to the Kelvin temperature.

volume V_1 and temperature T_1 (measured in K) to the final volume V_2 and temperature T_2 (measured in K). At constant pressure,

$$\frac{V_1}{V_2} = \frac{T_1}{T_2}$$

Rearranging this equation gives

$$V_2 = V_1 \times \frac{T_1}{T_2} \quad \text{or} \quad \frac{V_2}{T_2} = \frac{V_1}{T_1}$$

How does Charles' law relate to the postulates of the kinetic molecular theory? The theory states that the molecules in a gas sample are in constant rapid random motion. This motion is what allows the tiny molecules to occupy effectively the relatively large volume filled by the entire gas sample.

What is meant by "effectively occupy"? Consider a basketball game. Thirteen persons are on the court during a game (ten players and three officials). Standing still, they occupy only a small fraction of the floor. During play they are in constant rapid motion, effectively occupying the entire court. You could not cross the floor without danger of collision. The behavior of the molecules in a gas sample is similar. Although the actual volume of the molecules is only a tiny fraction of the volume of the sample, the constant motion of the molecules allows them to fill effectively that space. If the temperature increases, so does the kinetic energy of the molecules. As they are all of the same mass, an increased kinetic energy must mean an increased velocity. This increased velocity allows them to occupy, or fill, an increased volume like the basketball players in fast action. Similarly, with decreased temperature, the molecules move less rapidly and fill a smaller space.

The next example shows how Charles' law can be used in calculations.

Example 6.3

The volume of a gas sample is 746 mL at 20°C. What is its volume at body temperature (37°C)? Assume that the pressure remains constant.

☐ *Solution*

1. Tabulate the data.

	Initial Conditions	**Final Conditions**
Volume	$V_1 = 746$ mL	$V_2 = ?$
Temperature	$T_1 = 20°C$	$T_2 = 37°C$

2. Check that the units match. Charles' law requires that the temperature be measured in Kelvin to give the correct numerical ratio. Therefore, change the given temperature to Kelvin:

$$T_1 = 20 + 273 = 293 \text{ K} \qquad T_2 = 37 + 273 = 310 \text{ K}$$

3. Calculate the new volume:

$$V_2 = 746 \text{ mL} \times \frac{310 \text{ K}}{293 \text{ K}} = 789 \text{ mL}$$

4. Checking that the answer is reasonable, we see that this volume is larger than the original volume, as predicted from the increase in temperature.

Problem 6.3

A balloon has a volume of 1.56 L at 25°C. If the balloon is cooled to −10°C, what will be its new volume? Assume that the pressure remains constant.

C. The Combined Gas Law

Frequently, a gas sample is subjected to changes in both temperature and pressure. In such cases, the Boyle's law and Charles' law equations can be combined in a single equation, representing the **combined gas law**:

$$V_2 = V_1 \times \frac{T_2}{T_1} \times \frac{P_1}{P_2}$$

Here, V_1, P_1, and T_1 are the initial conditions and V_2, P_2, and T_2 are the final conditions. This equation can be rearranged to another common form:

$$\frac{P_1 V_1}{T_1} = \frac{P_2 V_2}{T_2}$$

Example 6.4

A gas sample occupies a volume of 2.5 L at 10°C and 0.95 atm. What is its volume at 25°C and 0.75 atm?

Solution

Initial Conditions	Final Conditions
$V_1 = 2.5$ L	$V_2 = ?$
$P_1 = 0.95$ atm	$P_2 = 0.75$ atm
$T_1 = 10°C = 283$ K	$T_2 = 25°C = 298$ K

Check that P_1 and P_2 are measured in the same units and that both temperatures have been changed to Kelvin. Substitute in the equation:

$$\frac{0.95 \text{ atm} \times 2.5 \text{ L}}{283 \text{ K}} = \frac{0.75 \text{ atm} \times V_2}{298 \text{ K}}$$

Solving this equation, we get

$$V_2 = 3.3 \text{ L}$$

This is a reasonable answer. Both the pressure change (lower) and the temperature change (higher) would cause an increased volume.

Problem 6.4

A sample of gas occupies a volume of 5.7 L at 37°C and 9.76×10^4 Pa. What is its volume at standard temperature and pressure?

D. Avogadro's Hypothesis and Molar Volume

Avogadro's hypothesis states: At the same temperature and pressure, equal volumes of gases contain equal numbers of molecules. (See Figure 6.9.) This means that if one liter of nitrogen at a particular temperature and pressure contains 1.0×10^{22} molecules, then one liter of any other gas at the same temperature and pressure also contains 1.0×10^{22} molecules.

One corollary of Avogadro's hypothesis is the concept of molar volume. The **molar volume** (the volume occupied by one mole) of a gas under 1.0 atm pressure

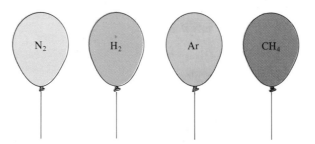

Figure 6.9 Avogadro's hypothesis: At the same temperature and pressure, equal volumes of different gases contain the same number of molecules. Each balloon holds 1.0 L of gas at 20°C and 1 atm pressure. Each contains 0.045 mol, or 2.69×10^{22} molecules, of gas.

and at 0°C (standard conditions) is 22.4 L. Molar volume can be used to calculate **gas density** under standard conditions. The equation for this is

$$\text{At STP, density of gas} = \frac{\text{mole weight in grams}}{22.4 \text{ L}}$$

Example 6.5

Calculate the density of nitrogen under standard conditions (STP).

□ *Solution*

The mole weight of nitrogen is 2 × 14.0, or 28.0 g. The molar volume is 22.4 L. Substituting in the equation, we get

$$\text{Density of nitrogen} = \frac{28.0 \text{ g}}{22.4 \text{ L}} = 1.25 \text{ g/L} \quad \text{at STP}$$

Problem 6.5

Calculate the density of helium under standard conditions.

E. Ideal Gas Equation

The various equations relating to pressure, volume, temperature, and number of moles of a gas sample can be combined in one statement: The volume V occupied by a gas is directly proportional to its Kelvin temperature T and the number of moles n it contains, and is inversely proportional to its pressure P. In mathematical form, this becomes

$$V = \frac{nRT}{P}$$

where V = volume,
   n = moles of sample,
   P = pressure,
   T = temperature in K,
   R = a proportionality constant known as the **gas constant**.

This equation is known as the **ideal gas equation** and is seen most often in the form

$$PV = nRT$$

We can determine the value of the gas constant R by substituting in the equation the known values for 1 mole of gas at standard conditions:

$$R = \frac{PV}{nT} = \frac{1 \text{ atm} \times 22.4 \text{ L}}{1 \text{ mol} \times 273 \text{ K}} = 0.0821 \frac{\text{L} \cdot \text{atm}}{\text{mol} \cdot \text{K}}$$

Table 6.2 shows what the value of the gas constant R is when the units are different from those shown here.

Table 6.2
Several values of
the gas constant R.

Value	Units
0.08206	L·atm/mol·K
8.314×10^3	L·Pa/mol·K
62.4	L·torr/mol·K
8.314	m^3·Pa/mol·K

Example 6.6

What volume is occupied by 5.50 g of carbon dioxide at 25°C and 742 torr?

☐ *Solution*

1. Identify the variables in the equation and convert units to match those of the gas constant.

$$P = 742 \text{ torr} \times \frac{1 \text{ atm}}{760 \text{ torr}} = 0.976 \text{ atm}$$

$$V = ? \text{ L}$$

$$n = 5.50 \text{ g CO}_2 \times \frac{1 \text{ mol CO}_2}{44.0 \text{ g CO}_2} = 0.125 \text{ mol}$$

$$T = 25°C + 273 = 298 \text{ K}$$

2. Substituting these values in the ideal gas equation gives

$$V = \frac{nRT}{P}$$

$$= 0.125 \text{ mol} \times \frac{0.0821 \text{ L·atm}}{\text{mol·K}} \times 298 \text{ K} \times \frac{1}{0.976 \text{ atm}}$$

$$= 3.13 \text{ L}$$

Notice how nicely the units cancel when you use the ideal gas equation. However, you have now solved enough problems to know that if the units hadn't cancelled, the arithmetic equation must have been set up incorrectly.

Problem 6.6

What mass of oxygen occupies 1.23 L at 37°C and 0.752 atm?

F. Mixtures of Gases, Partial Pressures

Since the composition of a gas does not affect the application of the gas laws to its behavior, a mixture of gases must follow those laws in the same way that a single gas does. Even so, the composition of a gas sample and its total pressure are related. This relation is known as Dalton's law of partial pressures. This is the same Dalton who proposed the atomic theory (Section 2.2). The **law of partial pressures** states that each gas in a mixture of gases exerts a pressure, known as its **partial pressure**, equal to the pressure the gas would exert if it were the only gas present; and the total pressure of the mixture is the sum of the partial pressures of all the gases present. This law is based on that postulate of the kinetic molecular theory (Section 6.3) that states that a gas sample is mostly empty space. The gas molecules are so far apart from one another that each acts independently. A mathematical expression of this statement is

$$P_T = P_1 + P_2 + P_3 + \cdots$$

where P_T equals the total pressure of the mixture and P_1, P_2, and P_3 are the partial pressures of the gases present in the mixture.

Suppose we have 1 L of oxygen at 1.0 atm pressure in one container, 1 L of nitrogen at 0.5 atm pressure in a second container, and 1 L of hydrogen at 3.0 atm pressure in a third container (Figure 6.10). If we combine the samples in a single 1-L container, the total pressure is 4.5 atm (1.0 atm + 0.5 atm + 3.0 atm). The partial pressure of oxygen, P_{O_2}, is 1.0 atm (the pressure it alone exerted in its container). Similarly, the partial pressure of nitrogen, P_{N_2}, is 0.5 atm, and of hydrogen, P_{H_2}, 3.0 atm.

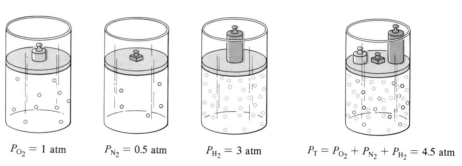

$P_{O_2} = 1$ atm $P_{N_2} = 0.5$ atm $P_{H_2} = 3$ atm $P_T = P_{O_2} + P_{N_2} + P_{H_2} = 4.5$ atm

Figure 6.10 The total pressure of a mixture of gases equals the sum of the individual gas pressures.

A corollary of this law is that in a mixture of gases, the percentage each is of the total volume is the same as the percentage each partial pressure is of the total pressure. From the total pressure of a mixture of gases and its percentage composition, we can calculate the partial pressure of the individual gases.

Example 6.7   The three main components of dry air and the percentage of each are 78.08% nitrogen, 20.95% oxygen, and 0.93% argon. Calculate the partial pressure of each gas in a sample of dry air at 760 torr. Calculate also the total pressure exerted by the three gases combined.

☐ *Solution*   **1.** Equation:

$$P_T = P_{N_2} + P_{O_2} + P_{Ar}$$

2. Calculate the partial pressure of each gas:

$$P_{N_2} = \frac{78.08}{100} \times 760 \text{ torr} = 593.4 \text{ torr}$$

$$P_{O_2} = \frac{20.95}{100} \times 760 \text{ torr} = 159.2 \text{ torr}$$

$$P_{Ar} = \frac{0.93}{100} \times 760 \text{ torr} = 7.1 \text{ torr}$$

3. Total pressure $P_T = 159.2 + 593.4 + 7.1 = 759.7$ torr. The difference between the total pressure of the three gases and the total pressure of the air sample is due to the partial pressure of other gases present in dry air, such as carbon dioxide.

Problem 6.7

Air in the trachea contains 19.4% oxygen, 0.4% carbon dioxide, 6.2% water vapor, and 74.0% nitrogen. If the pressure in the trachea is assumed to be 1.0 atm, what are the partial pressures of these gases in this part of the body?

6.6 Attractive Forces between Particles

We have assumed that all gases are ideal and behave in accordance with the postulates of the kinetic molecular theory and the ideal gas equation. Under standard conditions of temperature and pressure, and also at higher temperatures and lower pressures, the behavior of most **real gases**, such as oxygen, nitrogen, and carbon dioxide, is that predicted by the gas laws and the kinetic molecular theory. For this reason, we study ideal gases. However, as the temperature of a gas is decreased, the kinetic energy of the molecules decreases, their movement becomes more sluggish, and the attractive forces that exist between real molecules are important in determining the behavior of the sample. Likewise, if the pressure is increased and the volume decreased until the volume of the space between the molecules equals the volume of the molecules themselves, the molecules can no longer act as the wholly independent particles postulated by the kinetic molecular theory.

The **intermolecular** attractive **forces** that then come into play between molecules are **dipole-dipole interactions** (Figure 4.14) and dispersion forces. **Dispersion forces**, also called **London** or **Van der Waals forces**, are weak forces of attraction that exist between all molecules and that are the only forces acting between nonpolar molecules.

Under standard conditions of temperature and pressure, gas molecules move freely without intermolecular attraction, as illustrated in Figure 6.11(a). In Figure 6.11(b), the molecules are moving more slowly and are closer together, and they interact. The dipole in one molecule, regardless of whether it is real or temporary, interacts with the dipole of its neighbor. The lower the temperature and the closer the molecules (the result of high pressure), the more effective these dipole-dipole interactions are in preventing the free movement of molecules required by the kinetic molecular theory. The ideality of a gas is measured by how closely it follows the gas laws as the temperature is lowered. Gases of low molecular weight and no dipole, for example, hydrogen and helium, are the most ideal. We expect the behavior of real gases to deviate more and more from the ideal as the polarity and the molecular weight of the molecules increase.

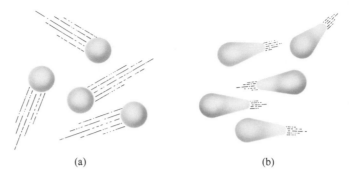

(a)   (b)

Figure 16.11 (a) Gas molecules moving freely at STP, no interaction. (b) Interaction because of temporary dipoles occurs when the gas is at low temperature or high pressure.

6.7 Physical Properties of Liquids

A liquid is a collection of molecules held together by attractive forces strong enough to keep the molecules in a single unit but not strong enough to hold them in a rigid structure. The physical properties of liquids result from this arrangement.

A. Vapor Pressure

In Section 6.2 we discussed the kinetic energy in a collection of molecules and showed in Figure 6.3 how the kinetic energies of the molecules were distributed. Figure 6.12 is similar in shape to Figure 6.3 and shows the distribution of kinetic energies in a liquid.

Let us assume that a molecule having more energy than point A in Figure 6.12 has enough energy to overcome the attraction of its neighboring molecules. If it is on the surface of the liquid, it can escape from the body of the liquid and

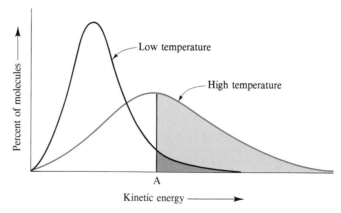

Figure 6.12 Distribution of kinetic energies among the molecules of a liquid at two different temperatures.

become a gaseous molecule. The number of molecules that have at least this much energy is represented by the area under the curve to the right of A. When these molecules escape the liquid, we say that they have evaporated, and the process is called **evaporation**. We could show this process by the equation

$$\text{Liquid} + \text{energy} \longrightarrow \text{gas}$$

If these gaseous molecules are confined in the space above the liquid, that is, if the liquid sample is in a closed container, some of these gaseous molecules in their random gaseous motion strike the surface of the liquid and are recaptured by it. This recapturing is called **condensation**.

When the rate of condensation equals the rate of evaporation, we have what is known as a dynamic equilibrium. When a system is in a state of **dynamic equilibrium**, two opposing processes are going on at the same rate. In this equilibrium, the opposing processes are evaporation and condensation, and

$$\text{Rate of evaporation} = \text{rate of condensation}$$

For this equilibrium to be established, the **closed system** (the closed flask containing both liquid and vapor) must be at constant pressure. Such molecules as have escaped are in the atmosphere over the liquid, and like all gases, exert a pressure. The partial pressure (see Section 6.5F) that they exert is the **vapor pressure** of the liquid.

Note that this equilibrium can take place only in a closed container. The vapor must accumulate enough to allow a normal distribution of energies before the rate of condensation will equal the rate of vaporization. In an open container, the vapor can escape and equilibrium will not be reached. We recognize this when we store liquids in closed containers (see Figure 6.13). Even ethyl ether,

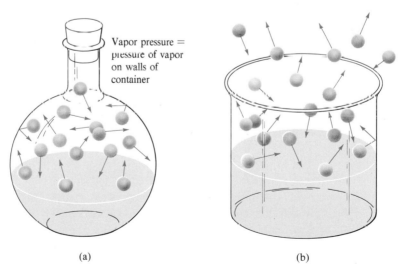

Vapor pressure = pressure of vapor on walls of container

(a)

(b)

Figure 6.13 (a) Equilibrium between vapor and liquid in a closed container. (b) Non-equilibrium (evaporation) in an open container; equilibrium cannot be established because the vapor does not collect.

in spite of its low boiling point (bp 34.5°C), can be stored at room temperature in a tightly closed container. Figure 6.13 shows the two processes: evaporation from an open container and equilibrium in a closed container.

Vapor pressure increases with temperature. At higher temperatures, more molecules have enough energy to escape the body of the liquid. Figure 6.14 illustrates how the vapor pressure of a liquid changes with temperature. In that figure, the vapor pressure of water (bp 100°C) and of carbon tetrachloride (bp 78°C) are plotted against temperature, °C. Notice how rapidly the vapor pressure increases. Notice too that for each, the vapor pressure equals 760 torr at the boiling point. This, then, defines the **normal boiling point** of a liquid—the temperature at which the vapor pressure of a liquid equals one atmosphere.

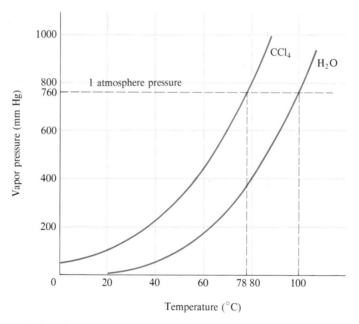

Figure 6.14 A plot of vapor pressure versus temperature for carbon tetrachloride, CCl_4, and water, H_2O. Notice that the vapor pressure of these two liquids equals 760 torr (1 atm) at their normal boiling points (78°C for CCl_4 and 100°C for H_2O).

A liquid boils whenever its vapor pressure equals the gaseous pressure in the space over the liquid. At high altitudes, such as on a mountain, liquids boil at lower temperatures than normal because the atmospheric pressure is lower. Foods take longer to cook because the water boils at a lower temperature. Conversely, in a pressure cooker, the vapor is confined and builds up a pressure greater than that of the atmosphere. The boiling point of water in a pressure cooker is above 100°C because of this greater pressure. This means that the water can be hotter than 100°C and still remain a liquid. Foods cook in a shorter time because they are cooking in water that is at a higher temperature.

These considerations also explain the behavior of topical anesthetics. These substances are low-boiling liquids. When sprayed on the skin, the molecules from the anesthetic absorb heat from the body, gaining enough kinetic energy to vaporize. They remove heat from the treated areas, and the temperature of the skin drops to a point at which the skin becomes numb.

B. Specific Heat of Liquids

At the molecular level, the temperature of a liquid is proportional to the average kinetic energy of the molecules within the liquid, and any change in temperature corresponds to a change in the average kinetic energy of the molecules.

The **specific heat** of a liquid is the amount of energy necessary to change the temperature of a one gram sample by one degree Celsius (review Section 1.9B4). The amount of energy necessary to cause this change differs among liquids. This means that each liquid has a unique specific heat. Given data that contain the mass of the sample, its temperature change ΔT, and the energy added, we can calculate the specific heat of the sample:

$$\text{Specific heat} = \frac{\text{energy change}}{\text{mass of sample} \cdot \Delta T}$$

Example 6.8

Calculate the specific heat of ethyl alcohol if 96.1 cal is required to change the temperature of a 9.63-g sample from 21°C to 38°C.

☐ *Solution*

Wanted: specific heat (cal/g·°C) of ethyl alcohol
Given:
9.63 g alcohol
96.1 cal
temperature change from 21°C to 38°C, $\Delta T = 17°C$
Equation:

$$\text{specific heat} = \frac{96.1 \text{ cal}}{(9.63 \text{ g})(17°C)}$$

Answer: 0.587 cal/g·°C

Problem 6.8

What is the specific heat of octane, C_8H_{18}, if 504 kcal is needed to change the temperature of a 16.32-g sample of octane from 25°C to 83°C?

C. Molar Heat of Vaporization

When energy is added to a liquid, its temperature rises to the boiling point at a rate that depends on the specific heat of a liquid. Energy added to a liquid at its boiling point does not change the temperature. Instead, this added energy counteracts the intermolecular forces in the liquid and the molecules vaporize, becoming gaseous. The amount of energy needed to vaporize 1 mol of a liquid at its boiling point is its **molar heat of vaporization (ΔH_{vap})**.

Table 6.3 shows the molecular weight, boiling point, specific heat, and molecular heat of vaporization for several liquids. Notice that the increase in polarity of the liquids is not related to molecular weight.

Table 6.3
Physical properties of liquids. The liquids are listed in order of increasing polarity.

Name	Molecular Weight	bp (°C)	ΔH_{vap} (kcal/mol)	Specific Heat (cal/g°C)
carbon disulfide, CS_2	76.1	46	6.79	0.239
chloroform, $CHCl_3$	119.4	61.7	7.50	0.231
ethyl alcohol, C_2H_6O	46.1	78.5	9.66	0.586
water, H_2O	18.0	100	9.73	1.000

The molar heat of vaporization of a liquid can be calculated from experimental data, as Example 6.9 shows.

Example 6.9

1.78 kcal is required to vaporize 13.6 g benzene at its boiling point. Calculate the molar heat of vaporization of benzene.

☐ *Solution*

Wanted: molar heat of vaporization, in kilocalories per mole

$\Delta H_{vap} = ?$ kcal/mol

Given: 1.78 kcal is required to vaporize 13.6 g benzene
Conversion factor: 1 mol benzene = 78.1 g benzene
Equation:

$$? \text{ cal/mol} = \frac{1.78 \text{ kcal}}{13.6 \text{ g benzene}} \times \frac{78.1 \text{ g benzene}}{1 \text{ mol benzene}}$$

Answer: 10.2 kcal/mol

Problem 6.9

Calculate the molar heat of vaporization at $-1°C$ of butane, C_4H_{10}, if it requires 2.43×10^3 cal to vaporize 26.5 g butane at its boiling point, $-1°C$.

Example 6.10

The molar heat of vaporization of octane, C_8H_{18}, is 9.22×10^3 cal/mol. Calculate the energy in calories necessary to vaporize 83.7 g octane at its boiling point, 126°C.

☐ *Solution*

Wanted: ? calories
Given: 83.7 g octane
Conversion factors:
   1 mol octane = 114.2 g
   ΔH_{vap} (octane) = 9.22×10^3 cal/mol

Equation:

$$? \text{ calories} = 83.7 \text{ g octane} \times \frac{1 \text{ mol octane}}{114.2 \text{ g}} \times \frac{9.22 \times 10^3 \text{ cal}}{\text{mol octane}}$$

$$= 6.76 \times 10^3 \text{ cal}$$

**Problem
6.10**

Calculate the heat required to vaporize 95 g of water at 100°C.

6.8 Solids

In Section 6.1 we discussed the characteristics of solids. The properties of solids suggest that the particles (ions, molecules, or atoms) in a solid occupy fixed positions, from which they cannot easily move. This orderly arrangement is called the crystal structure, or crystal lattice, of the solid. Strong attractive forces between the particles keep them in this arrangement. Even so, as suggested in Figure 6.15, each particle in a solid has some kinetic energy, or motion (unless the solid is at absolute zero, at which temperature all motion ceases). The ions, atoms, or molecules of which the solid is composed vibrate, rotate, and even move about within their assigned space in the crystal structure.

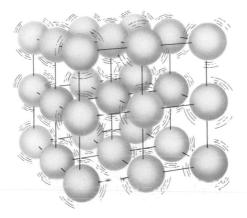

Figure 6.15 The crystal structure of a solid, showing the movement of the component ions, atoms, or molecules within their assigned spaces.

Particles in a solid, like the particles in gas and liquid samples, have a distribution of kinetic energies that depends on the temperature of the sample. At every temperature, some particles have enough energy to overcome the forces that hold them in place and escape from the solid as a vapor. Hence each solid, like each liquid, has a vapor pressure that increases as the temperature increases. The process by which atoms or molecules go directly from the solid state to the gaseous state is called **sublimation**. Solids that sublime have unusually high vapor pressures.

Dry ice (solid carbon dioxide) is a familiar example of a solid that sublimes. Its name reflects this property, for it cools without leaving a puddle of water. Water ice sublimes. If you live in a cold, dry climate, you may have noticed that ice disappears at temperatures below 0°C. (Actually it sublimes to a colorless gas.)

As a solid is heated, its change in temperature depends on its **specific heat**. Solving specific heat problems is the same whether for a liquid (Section 6.7B) or a solid (Section 1.9B).

A solid melts (changes to a liquid) when the average kinetic energy of its particles is high enough to overcome the attractive forces between them. The **melting point** of a solid is the temperature at which the liquid and solid states are in equilibrium at a pressure of one atmosphere. We show this equilibrium in an equation by writing solid as a reactant and liquid as a product connecting them by a double (equilibrium) arrow:

$$\text{Solid} \underset{\text{freezing}}{\overset{\text{melting}}{\rightleftarrows}} \text{liquid}$$

During melting, both solid and liquid are present until all the solid is converted to a liquid. Conversely, during freezing, solid and liquid are also present until all the liquid is converted to a solid. These processes are indicated by writing *melting* over the forward equilibrium arrow and *freezing* under the reverse equilibrium arrow. Because freezing is the reverse of melting, the freezing point of a substance is the same as its melting point.

The **molar heat of fusion** (ΔH_{fus}) of a substance is the amount of heat that must be supplied to convert one mole of that substance from a solid to a liquid at its melting point. Calculations involving heats of fusion are similar to those involving heats of vaporization.

Example 6.11

☐ *Solution*

The molar heat of fusion of carbon tetrachloride, CCl_4, is 0.783 kcal/mol. How much energy must be supplied to 34 g of solid carbon tetrachloride at its melting point (-23°C) to change the sample to a liquid?

Wanted: ? cal
Given: 34 g carbon tetrachloride
Conversion factors:

$$\Delta H_{fus} = \frac{7.83 \times 10^2 \text{ cal}}{\text{mol}}$$

$$1 \text{ mol } CCl_4 = 153.8 \text{ g } CCl_4$$

Equation:

$$? \text{ kcal} = 34 \text{ g} \times \frac{1 \text{ mol}}{153.8 \text{ g}} \times \frac{7.83 \times 10^2 \text{ cal}}{\text{mol}}$$

Answer: 1.73×10^2 cal

Problem 6.11

How many calories are required to melt 15 g of ice at 0°C? The molar heat of fusion of water at 0°C is 1.44×10^3 cal/mol.

Key Terms and Concepts

atmosphere (6.4)

Avogadro's hypothesis (6.5D)

barometer (6.4)

Boyle's law (6.3A)

Charles' law (6.5B)

closed system (6.7A)

combined gas law (6.5C)

condensation (6.7A)

dipole-dipole interaction (6.6)

dispersion forces (London, Van der Waals) (6.6)

dynamic equilibrium (6.7A)

elastic collisions (6.3)

evaporation (6.7A)

gas constant (6.5E)

gas density (6.5D)

ideal gas (6.5E)

ideal gas equation (6.5E)

intermolecular forces (6.6)

kinetic energy (6.2)

kinetic molecular theory (6.3)

law of partial pressures (6.5F)

manometer (6.4)

melting point (6.8)

molar heat of fusion (6.8)

molar heat of vaporization (6.7C)

molar volume (6.5D)

normal boiling point (6.7A)

partial pressure (6.5F)

pascal (6.4)

pressure (6.4)

real gases (6.6)

specific heat (6.7B and 6.8)

standard temperature and pressure (6.4)

sublimation (6.8)

torr (6.4)

vapor pressure (6.7A)

Problems

Characteristics (Section 6.1)

6.12 Why is it difficult to compress a liquid or a solid?

Kinetic molecular theory (Section 6.3)

6.13 Why, in describing the properties of gases, must we speak of the "average" kinetic energy instead of just kinetic energy?

6.14 Use the kinetic molecular theory to explain:
a. Why a foul-smelling substance is added to natural gas to aid in detecting leaks.
b. Why a baked potato sometimes explodes in the oven.
c. Hot-air ballooning.

6.15 State the postulates of the kinetic molecular theory of gases. Explain how they predict Charles' and Boyle's laws.

Measuring gas samples (Section 6.4)

6.16 A column of water 10 cm high with a cross section of 0.5 cm² exerts a pressure that is twice that of a column 5 cm high with 1.0-cm² cross section. Explain why the two pressures differ.

6.17 In Section 6.4 we described how a barometer is made. What would happen to the height of the mercury column in Figure 6.5 if the closed end of the glass tube were cut off? Why?

6.18 Convert 1.65 atm to torr and to pascals.

6.19 What is the pressure in atmospheres on a scuba diver at a depth of 50 ft? (Remember, 33 feet of water = 1 atm.)

The gas laws (Section 6.5)

6.20 A sample of gas has a volume of 1.0 L at 1.0 atm. The temperature is kept constant and the pressure is raised first to 2.0 atm, then to 4.0 atm, 8.0 atm, and finally 16.0 atm. Calculate the volume of the sample at each pressure. If the pressure continues to increase, will the volume ever reach zero?

6.21 What is the final pressure if 2.63 L of gas at 25°C and 1.00 atm pressure is allowed to expand to 8.45 L at the same temperature?

6.22 Why do aerosol cans carry the warning "Do not incinerate"?

6.23 Calculate the density of ethane, C_2H_6, at STP.

6.24 What is the density of hydrogen at standard conditions? At 25°C and 0.925 atm?

6.25 Does the density of a gas increase, or does it decrease, as the pressure increases at constant temperature? As the temperature increases at constant pressure?

6.26 Complete the table.

V_1	T_1	P_1	V_2	T_2	P_2
546 L	43°C	6.5 atm	———	65°C	1.9 atm
43 mL	−56°C	865 torr	———	43°C	1.5 atm
4.2 L	234 K	0.87 atm	3.2 L	29°C	———
1.3 L	25°C	1.89×10^4 Pa	———	0°C	1.0 atm

6.27 Complete the table.

V_1	T_1	P_1	V_2	T_2	P_2
6.35 L	10°C	0.75 atm	———	0°C	1 atm
75.6 L	0°C	1 atm	———	35°C	735 torr
1.06 L	75°C	0.55 atm	0.76 L	0°C	———

6.28 A balloon filled with a 1.2-L sample of air at 25°C and 0.98 atm pressure is submerged in liquid nitrogen at −196°C. Calculate the final volume of the air in the balloon.

6.29 **a.** 1.65 L of a gas is collected at 25°C and 450 mm pressure. What will be its volume at 40°C and 550 mm pressure?
b. How many moles of gas are contained in the sample?

6.30 The density of liquid octane, C_8H_{18}, is 0.7025 g/mL. If 1.00 mL of liquid octane is vaporized at 100°C and 725 torr, what volume does the vapor occupy?

6.31 Calculate the molecular weight of a gas if 3.03 g of the gas occupies 660 mL at 735 mm IIg and 27°C.

6.32 Calculate the volume 1.1 g oxygen occupies at 2.0 atm and 5.0°C.

6.33 If a 156-g block of dry ice, $CO_2(s)$, is sublimed at 25°C and 740 torr, what volume does the gas occupy?

6.34 Calculate the specific heat of gaseous dichlorodifluoromethane if it requires 247 J to change the temperature of 36.6 g of dichlorodifluoromethane from 0°C to 25°C.

Physical properties of liquids (Section 6.7)

6.35 Calculate the final temperature of 48.5 g water at 15°C to which 1.57 kcal of heat is added.

6.36 The heat of vaporization of dichlorodifluoromethane is 19.7 kJ/mol. Calculate the energy necessary to vaporize 39.2 g of this compound. (Its formula weight is 120.9.)

6.37 Calculate what energy is necessary to vaporize 13.9 g chloromethane (formula weight = 50.5) if the molar heat of vaporization is 1.24 kcal/mol.

6.38 The specific heat of mercury is 0.0332 cal/g·°C. Calculate the energy necessary to raise the temperature of 1 mol of mercury 36°C.

Physical properties of solids (Section 6.8)

6.39 How many calories are needed to melt 25 g of ice at 0°C and to raise its temperature to 85°C?

6.40 Compare the number of calories absorbed when 100 g of ice at 0°C is changed to water at 37°C with the number absorbed when 100 g of water is warmed from 0°C to 37°C.

6.41 Temperature is a measure of kinetic energy. At the melting point of a substance:
a. Is there a change in its kinetic energy? Explain.
b. Is there a change in temperature? Explain.

6.42 The specific heat of aluminum is 0.215 cal/g·°C. Calculate the energy necessary to change the temperature of 56 g aluminum from 36°C to 79°C.

6.43 What is the final temperature if 5783 J of energy is added to 54 g ice at 0°C?

6.44 The heat of fusion of methanol, CH_3OH, is given as 24 cal/g and the heat of vaporization as 167 cal/g. Calculate the molar heat of fusion and the molar heat of vaporization in joules per mole for methanol.

6.45 Using the data in Table 6.3, calculate the energy needed to vaporize 6.3 g chloroform at its boiling point.

6.46 How much energy is released when 10 g of steam at 100°C is condensed and cooled to body temperature (37°C)? How much energy is released when 10 g of water at 100°C is cooled to 37°C? Why are steam burns more painful than hot-water burns?

General problems

6.47   A sample of gas collected at 38°C and 740 torr weighs 0.0630 g and occupies 26.2 mL. What is its volume at STP? What is its molecular weight?

6.48   An average pair of lungs has a volume of 6.5 L. If the air they contain is 21% oxygen, how many molecules of oxygen do they contain at 1 atm and 37°C?

6.49   What volume of air (21% oxygen) measured at 25°C and 0.975 atm is required to completely burn 3.42 g aluminum?

6.50   A sample containing aluminum is treated with an excess of hydrochloric acid. 0.765 L hydrogen is produced at 20°C and 0.987 atm. What mass of aluminum is in the sample?

6.51   How many grams of sodium chloride must be decomposed to yield 65 L chlorine measured at 32°C and 723 torr?

Skiing, Diving, and the Gas Laws

We live on the surface of the earth under a blanket of air that extends miles above us. This blanket of air is approximately one-fifth (21%) oxygen; the rest is nitrogen, with small amounts of other gases, mostly carbon dioxide, argon, and water vapor. At sea level, air exerts a pressure of 1 atm, the same pressure exerted by a column of water 10.3 m (33.9 ft) high. The pressure of the oxygen alone is 0.21 atm. For those of us who live close to sea level, our bodies have become adjusted to this oxygen concentration. In normal quiet breathing, we inhale approximately 0.5 L of air per breath, containing approximately 0.02 mol of oxygen. Under these conditions, the hemoglobin in our blood is 97% saturated with oxygen, and the pressure of oxygen in arterial blood is 0.13 atm. For the hemoglobin to become 100% saturated, we must breathe about twice as much air, so that the pressure of oxygen in arterial blood becomes approximately 0.26 atm. However, when the hemoglobin is 97% saturated, enough oxygen is transported to our cells for metabolism to proceed normally.

Although the percentage composition of air remains constant at all altitudes, air density decreases with increasing altitude. This decreasing density causes a decreasing atmospheric pressure and a consequent decrease in the partial pressure of oxygen. At 1500 m (5000 ft), atmospheric pressure is 0.83 atm and the partial pressure of oxygen is 0.17 atm. At four times that height (6000 m, or 20,000 ft), atmospheric pressure is only one-third of 0.83 atm or 0.26 atm, and the partial pressure of oxygen is 0.051 atm. What effect would these changes have on some-

one flying in from sea level for a few days of skiing or mountain climbing at such an altitude?

Suppose you flew in to 3600 m (12,000 ft). At this altitude, the mountains are really spectacular; both skiing and climbing are more challenging than on the lower slopes. The partial pressure of oxygen at this altitude, however, is only 0.14 atm, or two-thirds the partial pressure of oxygen at sea level. Each breath you take delivers to your lungs only two-thirds the amount of oxygen they are accustomed to receiving. To get the amount of oxygen your body needs, you breathe more deeply and more rapidly to use the reserve capacity, approximately 5 L, of your lungs. What then happens to your body?

By breathing more deeply and more often, you exhale more carbon dioxide than normal. This decreases the acidity of the blood, causing alkalosis. The respiratory center of the brain reacts to alkalosis by sending a message to the lungs to stop getting rid of so much carbon dioxide—in other words, to stop breathing so fast. You then breath more slowly, and even less oxygen reaches the lungs.

Because there is less oxygen in the lungs, the blood leaving the lungs is less than normally saturated with the gas and has less to deliver to the tissues. The heart pumps harder because the blood must circulate more rapidly to supply the normal amount of oxygen to the tissues; arterial blood pressure increases, and the capillaries dilate. In an additional effort to get more oxygen to the lungs, you start to breathe through your mouth. The air delivered to the lungs by this route is drier and colder than what comes through the longer nasal passages. The epithelial (passage-lining) tissues quickly become dry and crusted. This situation is aggravated by the normally low moisture content of mountain air.

The severity and duration of these symptoms vary from individual to individual and are unrelated to sex or previous high-altitude experience. They are most severe when the change in altitude is rapid. Considerable data on these effects have been collected at the base camps of Mount Everest, in the Himalayas. Climbers flying in to base camps at 2800 m are more apt to have difficulty adjusting to these changes than those who hike in from lower altitudes. The difficulties are frequently more severe in young climbers than in the older ones. This may be related to the rate of ascent; young climbers try to cover more ground in less time than older ones. In the most severe form, these problems cause what is known as high-altitude sickness. The symptoms of this illness are a headache, unrelieved by aspirin; nausea; insomnia; dizziness; shortness of breath, which does not diminish when resting; and severe and unexplained lassitude. Severe cases of high-altitude sickness are sufficently like a heart attack to indicate the need for prompt removal to a lower altitude. The need is not trivial in cases where cerebral edema (swelling) occurs.

Mountaineers climbing at high altitudes without supplementary oxygen supplies give vivid pictures of the severe lassitude of high-altitude sickness. Good readers are unable to comprehend even simple sentences at an 8200-m altitude. Temporary insanity and amnesia have been observed. In one account, after months of planning and weeks of effort, a climber found himself at 8500 m, about 300 m from the summit of Mount Everest, and was too weak to continue. He remembers no particular sense of frustration or disappointment at being unable to go on to the summit. Starting down alone after a brief rest, he became engulfed in a blinding blizzard, which he found neither unpleasant nor exciting, but mildly interesting.

Does all this indicate that you should never ski or climb in the mountains if you live at sea level? Not at all. If the change in altitude is made slowly, allowing the body to adjust gradually to the decreasing oxygen pressure, difficulties can be minimized. If this is not possible, you can prepare for the change by doing exercises that increase lung capacity. After arriving at a high altitude, you can anticipate the problems and try not to do too much too soon. Knowing the problems caused by the decreased oxygen supply will help you to minimize their effects. The symptoms disappear as the body adjusts.

The problems discussed so far have been related to low partial pressures of oxygen. Diving, particularly scuba diving, subjects the body to greater than normal pressures, as each 10 m of water exerts a pressure of 1 atm on the body. Thus, at a depth of 10 m, a diver is under 2 atm pressure, one from the atmosphere and one from the water. At 20 m depth, he is under 3 atm pressure, and at 30.5 m (100 ft), the total pressure is 4.1 atm. The increased pressure can cause many problems.

What are the effects of these pressure changes? When our bodies are subjected to greater-than-normal air pressures, three kinds of effects are experienced: those due to overall changes in pressure, those due to changes in partial pressures of oxygen and nitrogen, and those due to the increased solubility of gases in liquids at high pressures. Many spaces in the body contain gases rather than liquids. The lungs are the most obvious; other air spaces are the stomach and the intestines, the sinuses, and the ear canals. Tiny air pockets may even be present under tooth fillings. As a diver descends, increasing pressure acts on all these volumes as well as on the outside of the body, and it becomes difficult to keep the internal pressure equalized using the narrow passages that interconnect these spaces. We meet this problem when going up (or down) in an express elevator. The swallowing we do instinctively in an elevator equalizes the effect of changing pressure on the gases in our body cavities. A descending diver may experience a squeeze in the ear canals, particularly if they are blocked because of allergies or a head cold. If the diver shuts off the air passages by holding the breath, a squeeze on the lungs is a likely result. A tooth filling may become excruciatingly painful. Normal breathing during descent prevents this.

The decrease in pressure coming up from a dive reverses this process. On the average, the total lung volume is 5.5 L. When one ascends to the surface from a depth of 10 m, the air in the lungs doubles in volume. It is obviously essential to exhale this excess 5.5 L during ascent from a dive, to keep the lungs from bursting.

We have already seen that too little oxygen, a situation encountered at high altitudes, is inimical to life. Too much oxygen is also toxic. The toxicity becomes severe at oxygen pressures of 2 atm. This oxygen pressure would be experienced in breathing pure oxygen at a depth of 10 m or breathing compressed air at a depth of 90 m. The symptoms of oxygen poisoning are twitching, nausea, difficulties in vision and hearing, anxiety, confusion, and fatigue. They combine to make the diver less aware of any personal actions and their consequences. The onset of these symptoms varies from one individual to another. Luckily, the symptoms disappear when the oxygen pressure decreases to the normal partial pressure of oxygen (0.21 atm).

Nitrogen is also a narcotic at high pressures. The phrase "rapture of the deep" refers to an overdose of nitrogen. The symptoms of nitrogen narcosis begin at a depth of 31 m. Here the partial pressure of nitrogen has increased from 0.79 atm at the surface to 3.2 atm. Below this depth, the symptoms become more intense. The symptoms vary from one diver to another, and so does the precise depth at which they are noticeable. Euphoria and a general inability to perform or to recognize the need to perform simple motor tasks are the most obvious symptoms. Dizziness, inability to communicate, and a false sense of well-being may also be present. The effect at 100 ft is like the effect of one dry martini; this relation is nicknamed Martini's law. Divers subject to nitrogen intoxication have been known to be wholly irresponsible for themselves and their companions. Decreasing the nitrogen

pressure by ascending is the best treatment for this condition.

The dangers associated with the increased solubility of gases at increased pressures are encountered in ascending after a dive. Everyone is familiar with the appearance of bubbles in a carbonated beverage when the cap is removed. The sudden decrease in pressure allows the dissolved carbon dioxide to come out of solution throughout the liquid. A sudden ascent from a dive has the same effect on the gases that have dissolved in the blood in ever increasing amounts as the depth of the dive and the consequent pressure on the diver have increased. The amount of dissolved gas also depends on the duration of the dive. The diver must ascend slowly so that the gases are released in the lungs rather than as bubbles in the bloodstream. Oxygen, continually burned by the body, does not cause any problems during ascent. Nitrogen, on the other hand, makes up about 80% of the dissolved gases and is the chief cause of decompression problems. A bubble in the bloodstream stops the passage of blood; it acts as an embolism, or clot, and can be fatal. Once the bubbles occur, their size and location determine their effect on the diver.

The most frequent sign of decompression sickness is pain, which is usually localized in joints, muscles, tendons, or ligaments. The term *bends* is derived from the temporary deformities caused by the stricken diver's inability to straighten his or her joints. The diver is literally "bent out of shape." This condition is treated in recompression chambers. The affected diver is subjected again to the same high pressure encountered in a deep dive, and the pressure is then decreased slowly to sea-level pressure. This slow decrease of pressure permits the dissolved gases to be transferred from the blood to the lungs in the normal way. The practice of breathing a mixture of helium and oxygen is one way of lessening the dangers of the bends, for helium is much less soluble in the blood than nitrogen is. The only sure way of avoiding the bends is a slow ascent; scuba diving manuals recommend no more than 60 ft/min. After a dive of 100 ft, the ascent should take 4.5 min, with a 3-min stop at 10 ft to allow for complete equilibration between the blood and the lungs.

Women divers should be aware that fetuses are much more sensitive than adults to the increased pressures encountered in diving. The following data come from a study done with pregnant ewes, animals chosen because the dynamics of fetal and maternal blood flow in ewes are very similar to those in women. On a dive to 30 m, humans can accept no more than 25 min at this depth without needing decompression stops during the ascent. Ewes in the final trimester of pregnancy were subjected to dives of that depth and duration. In all cases, examination of the fetuses after these dives showed many bubbles in the fetal bloodstream, probably enough to kill the fetus unless it received decompression treatment. Fetuses developed bubbles in nearly all dives deeper than 10 m. Since sheep are more resistant to decompression sickness than humans, there is little doubt that scuba diving when pregnant carries with it potential danger to the fetus, particularly in deep dives.

Respiratory therapy involves treatment of medical conditions where too little oxygen is available to the blood. Diseases involving the lungs and the diaphragm or circulatory difficulties often require such treatment. The therapist, working under a doctor's supervision, determines what partial pressures of oxygen should be administered to the patient to increase the amount of oxygen carried in the blood. Such treatment must be carefully monitored, for excessive oxygen pressure is just as dangerous as insufficient pressure. For example, oxygen is often administered to newborn babies, particularly to those born prematurely or those who have been subjected to a particularly traumatic birth. But these babies, when exposed to high oxygen concentrations, are subject to retrolental fibroplasia, a disease that results in irreversible blindness. Hence, great care must be taken to ascertain that the baby gets enough oxygen but not too much.

Source

Chem. and Eng. News, 6 November 1978, p. 52.

The Importance of Water

Water is so much a part of our daily life that we rarely consider how unusual its properties are or how important it is to our survival. In our bodies, water provides a medium for chemical reactions. Water transports nutrients to the cells through the various circulating systems of the body and carries away the waste products. It acts to regulate the temperature of the body. Outside the body, water provides a means for cooking, laundry, and bathing. In the larger view, the enormous bodies of water on our planet regulate its temperature. Water transportation is one of the oldest methods of transportation and still one of the cheapest. A large supply of water is essential to agriculture, to manufacturing, and to other activities too numerous to list.

What are the properties of water that make it so important to life? Recall that the water molecule is tiny, containing only three atoms—two hydrogens and one oxygen. Because it is such a small molecule, water can pass through the membranes of the body by osmosis, thereby maintaining fluid balance in the cells and tissues. Water is a polar molecule, with the two hydrogen-oxygen bonds forming an angle of 105° and giving the molecule a slightly positive end and a slightly negative end. Because of this polarity, water can dissolve the many polar organic and biochemical molecules involved in metabolism. In addition, because water is not a very reactive molecule, it can serve as an inert medium for the various metabolic reactions.

Water, besides being useful as a solvent in the body, has a unique set of physical properties that allow it to regulate the temperature of our bodies. These properties are related to the intermolecular structure of water. The hydrogen atoms of the water molecule, although covalently bonded to the oxygen atom of the molecule they are part of, are attracted to the electronegative oxygen atoms of other water molecules, forming hydrogen bonds between molecules. These intermolecular bonds give water the characteristics of a loosely bonded but enormous molecule. The physical properties of water reflect this structure. The boiling point is considerably higher than would be expected; compounds of similar molecular weight, such as methane, are gases at room temperature. The specific heat (1 cal/g · °C) and the heat of vaporization (540 cal/g at 40°C) are similarly higher than would be expected for a molecule of molecular weight 18. These last two properties are the ones that help regulate our body temperature.

Heat is generated in the body by reactions in the cells. Blood flowing through the body absorbs this heat. The blood then flows through tiny capillaries near the surface of the skin or lungs. As it does so, heat is transferred from the blood to the layer of moisture normally on these surfaces. This moisture evaporates into the air, taking with it the calories it has absorbed. When the body is overheated, the blood flows more rapidly and the capillaries dilate. The flushed complexion associated with exertion or fever is due to an increased amount of blood in the capillaries just below the surface of the skin. When the body is overheated, exhaled breath becomes moister and more water molecules move through the cell walls of the blood vessels to the surface of the skin as perspiration. Each gram of perspiration that evaporates and each gram of water in the exhaled breath represent the loss of about 540 cal from the body. By increasing or decreasing the amount of perspiration and the moisture content of the exhaled breath, the body regulates its temperature.

Following this line of reasoning, you would expect a person with a fever to sweat profusely in order to reduce the temperature of the body. Why, then, does a person with a fever usually have dry skin? The reason is that the regulatory mechanism is not working efficiently and the feverish person is losing water from the skin faster than it can be replenished. The fluid intake and fluid balance of a person with a high fever should therefore be a matter of concern. In connection with this, note how the treatment of patients with high fevers has changed over the years. Earlier, patients were wrapped in heavy blankets; now they are covered lightly, if at all. The more easily heat can be released to the surroundings, the better. Frequently, the patient is placed on a water bed through which cold water is circulated. Sponge baths may be given. These are all ways of reducing the temperature of the body based on the principles of specific heat and heat vaporization.

You yourself may have observed how the rate of evaporation from the skin affects body temperature. In the absence of moving air, the moisture layer on your skin tends to reach equilibrium with the water vapor in the air around it. If a breeze is constantly changing that air, there is no possibility for equilibrium, and evaporation continues. This effect is particularly noticeable when you come out of a swimming pool on a windy day. The moving air, regardless of its temperature, blows away the moisture-saturated layer of air surrounding your skin. More evaporation takes place, and you may be cold enough to shiver.

The discomfort associated with a hot, humid, windless day is also related to this evaporation process. Humidity measures the amount of water vapor in the air. At 100% humidity, the air is saturated with water vapor. At high humidity, water cannot evaporate from the skin because the air above the skin cannot absorb any more vapor. We are miserably uncomfortable. Why do we instinctively wish for a breeze? Because the moving air will remove the water-saturated air surrounding the skin and allow evaporation.

The home use of humidifiers during winter months involves the same process. If the air is dry, evaporation from the skin takes place rapidly and we feel cold. By putting moisture into the air, we lower the rate of evaporation and feel comfortable at a lower temperature.

The importance of water in our lives is even greater than suggested by the examples already presented. The average person uses about one ton of water per year for basic needs. Industries require enormous amounts of water for cooling (as in power plants) and removal of wastes (as in paper factories). The demands of agriculture for more and more water are always with us (witness the constant battle for the water of the Colorado River basin). Growing one bushel of corn requires between 10 and 20 tons of water; producing one pound of steer beef requires between 15 and 20 tons of water. All this water is part of the water cycle, which provides for the recycling of all the water on earth. Water evaporates into the atmosphere from the oceans and other bodies of water and falls as rain or snow. One-quarter of the rain falls over land and makes its way through lakes, rivers, and underground water supplies back to the ocean, for subsequent reevaporation. As the water moves toward the ocean, we divert it for our uses.

Much of the water used by industry and almost all of that used by agriculture requires no treatment. The water for public water supplies usually does require treatment. The treatment for a particular water supply depends on what has happened to the water since it precipitated from the atmosphere, including any opportunities it has had to dissolve other substances. Because of its contact with different rocks and soils, the water will probably contain some dissolved minerals, such as calcium, magnesium, and iron, and also bicarbonate and sulfate ions. Because it has been in contact with air, it will contain some dissolved gases: carbon dioxide, oxygen, and nitrogen. Because of vegetation, aquatic life, or previous use as a water supply, it may contain waste chemicals and bacteria, and also decaying vegetable and animal matter.

Providing a safe, adequate water supply to cities and towns becomes more and more difficult as these areas continue to grow. The problem becomes particularly acute as towns grow in areas that are far from a natural supply of fresh water (as in the desert) or take the water for their supply from a river into which upstream municipalities have dumped their wastes (as in New Orleans, at the mouth of the Mississippi River).

Earlier, we talked about the usefulness of water as a solvent and as a temperature regulator. These properties depend on the polarity of the water molecule and its high specific heat. Hydrogen bonds are important in causing the high specific heat of water, and they are even more important in determining the density of water in the liquid and solid states. In the liquid state, the hydrogen bonds are randomly oriented. As freezing takes place, they become arranged in a regular crystal lattice, and the molecules cannot be squashed together as they are in the liquid. Hence, the volume of the sample increases on becoming a solid. The density of liquid water at 4°C is 1.000 g/mL, and at 0°C it is 0.9998 g/mL. The density of solid water (ice) at 0°C is less, 0.9168 g/mL. Although this difference is important to humans, it is even more important to

fish. When a lake freezes, the lighter ice rises to the surface. Thus, a lake freezes from the top down. The denser liquid water sinks to the bottom of the lake, providing a winter habitat for fish and other aquatic life. The surface layer of ice provides an insulating layer above. Lakes rarely freeze all the way to the bottom. In the spring, as the air temperature rises, the ice melts to form a liquid more dense than the ice. This liquid moves to the bottom of the lake, forcing the warmer and lighter water to the top. The currents thus produced mix not only the water but also those nutrients previously concentrated on the bottom that are essential to aquatic life. If ice were more dense than liquid water, this mixing would not occur in large bodies of water. Ice would remain on the bottom all summer, insulated from the warm air by the upper layers of liquid water. It is hard to imagine the consequences of such a reversal, but there is little doubt that they would extend farther than just making the swimming hole a little colder.

Highway engineers and plumbers will also tell you that the expansion of water caused by freezing is not all good. Water freezing in pipes causes them to burst. Water freezing in tiny cracks in street pavements expands, breaking up the pavement and leading to the potholes that plague the highway engineers and drivers in northern climates.

7 Solutions and Colloids

Our discussions thus far have concentrated on the properties of pure substances: elements, compounds formed by the combination of elements, and the reactions of these pure substances. In actual experience, we do not often encounter pure substances. More often, the matter we see and use is a mixture. In this chapter we will discuss two particular kinds of mixtures: solutions and colloids.

7.1 Solutions, Colloids, and Suspensions

Consider the following mixtures, all of which contain water: tap water, milk, and a mixture of sand and water (Figure 7.1). Tap water is a **solution**. A solution is a mixture that is clear and uniform throughout: one substance (or more) has been dissolved in another. Tap water contains some dissolved substances: sometimes calcium and magnesium ions, which make it hard; fluoride ion added to

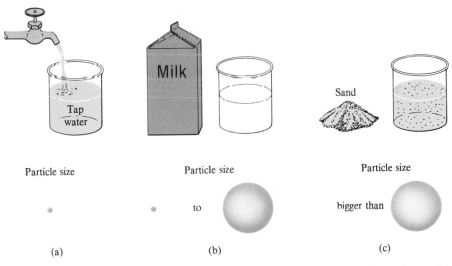

Figure 7.1 Examples of (a) a solution, (b) a colloid, and (c) a suspension, along with the relative sizes of the particles in each.

prevent tooth decay; and probably chlorine molecules added to destroy bacteria and make the water safe for consumption. Milk is a **colloid**. A colloid is uniform throughout and sometimes clear. Milk is a mixture of fats, water, and many other things. The third mixture, sand and water, is a heterogeneous **suspension**. In spite of vigorous stirring, the grains of sand settle to the bottom of the container. It is a mixture that is not uniform throughout and in which it is easy to see the two **phases**, or components.

A. Components of Solutions and Colloids

There are two components in either a solution or a colloid. A solution consists of the **solute**, or the substance dissolved, and the **solvent**, the substance the solute is dissolved in. In a colloid, one substance, the **dispersed phase**, is uniformly distributed throughout the **dispersing medium**. In mud, for example, the dispersed phase is soil and the dispersing medium is water. In fog, the dispersed phase is water and the dispersing medium is air.

You are familiar with solutions in which the solute is a gas (carbonated beverages), a liquid (rubbing alcohol), or a solid (sugar solutions). The solvent need not be a liquid; it may be a gas or a solid. Similarly, in colloids the dispersed phase may be a solid (smoke), a liquid (mayonnaise), or a gas (whipped cream). The dispersing medium can also be either solid, liquid, or gas. Many physiological fluids are colloidal dispersions of large molecules (for example, proteins) in water.

B. Differences among Solutions, Colloids, and Suspensions

The most fundamental difference among solutions, colloids, and suspensions is the **size of the particles** that are mixed with the solvent. In solutions, the dissolved particles are ions or small molecules whose diameter is usually less than 10^{-7} cm (see Figure 7.1). The suspended particles of a colloid range in diameter from about 10^{-7} cm to about 10^{-4} cm; they are large molecules or clusters of smaller molecules. The grains of sand that settle out of a suspension usually have diameters greater than 10^{-4} cm.

The particles in solutions and in colloids are small enough to be kept in constant motion by the buffeting of the solvent molecules that surround them. This constant motion keeps both solutions and colloids uniform throughout. The sand particles in the mixture are too big to be bounced around by the relatively small water molecules and also big enough to be affected by the pull of gravity. Hence, they settle to the bottom.

Colloidally suspended particles and dissolved particles are sufficiently different in size to differ in their appearance in visible light. The dissolved particles of a solution are too small to reflect visible light. Particles suspended in a colloid are larger and do reflect light. This difference gives rise to two unique properties of colloids that can be used to differentiate a solution and a colloid. The first one, the **Tyndall effect**, is illustrated in Figure 7.2. Here a flashlight beam is shining through a solution and a colloid. The path of light is invisible

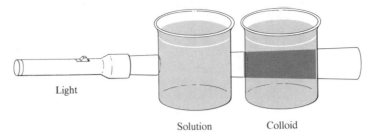

Light   Solution   Colloid

Figure 7.2 The Tyndall effect. The path of light is invisible in the solution but visible in the colloid.

through the solution, but clearly visible through the colloid as the light is reflected by the tiny, colloidally suspended particles. When you see the beam of a searchlight sweeping the sky on a foggy night, you are observing the Tyndall effect, for fog is a colloid formed by the suspension of very tiny water drops in air. The Tyndall effect can be observed even in colloids so clear as to look like solutions to the naked eye.

You have also probably seen **Brownian movement**, the second property unique to colloids. When sunlight streams into a slightly dusty, slightly darkened room, dancing specks of light are noticeable in the sunlight. These are reflections of light from colloidally dispersed dust particles. The particles are in constant motion, which gives the dancing effect. Brownian movement is characteristic of colloidally suspended particles. The constant, irregular movement of the dust particles as they reflect the light is much like that postulated for gas molecules.

Most suspensions of solids in liquids can be separated by **filtration** (Figure 7.3). The mixture of sand and water can be separated into its two components using this method, by pouring it through a filter paper or a cotton plug. A solution or colloid cannot be separated by filtration. The dissolved particles of a solution and the suspended particles of a colloid are small enough to go through the filter. The difference in property is illustrated by the difference between jam and jelly. If you have ever watched anyone make jelly, you have observed this difference. Fruit jelly is a colloidal suspension of pectin (a large molecule) in a water solution of sugar and fruit juices. Fruit jams contain solid bits of fruit pulp and seeds as well as sugar and fruit juices. When you make jam, the solids are not removed. When you make jelly, the mixture is strained through a fine cloth to remove the solids. The colloidal jelly passes through the cloth.

7.2 Solubility

The **solubility** of a substance is the amount of that substance that dissolves in a given amount of solvent. *Solubility* is a quantitative term. Solubilities vary enormously but the terms *soluble* and *insoluble* are relative. A substance is said to be **soluble** if more than 0.1 g of that substance dissolves in 100 mL of solvent. If less than 0.1 g dissolves in 100 mL of solvent, the substance is said to be **insoluble**, or more exactly, **sparingly soluble**. The terms *miscible* and *immiscible*

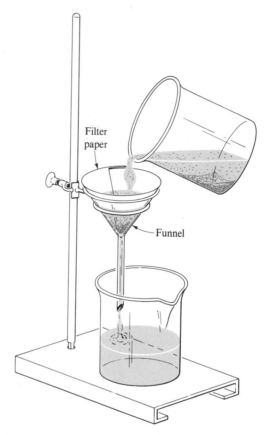

Figure 7.3 Filtration. Pouring a suspension through a filter allows the solid suspended material to be collected in the filter.

may be encountered when considering the solubility of one liquid in another. **Miscible** means soluble without limits; for example, alcohol is miscible with water. **Immiscible** and *insoluble* mean the same; oil is immiscible with water, as in oil and vinegar salad dressing (see Figure 7.4).

A. Determining Solubility

How is the solubility of a substance determined? A known amount of the solvent, for example 100 mL, is put in a container. Then the substance whose solubility is to be determined is added until, even after vigorous and prolonged stirring, some of that substance does not dissolve. Such a solution is said to be **saturated**, since it contains as much solute as possible at that temperature. In this saturated solution, the amount of solute is the solubility of that substance at that temperature in that solvent. Doing this experiment with water as the solvent and sodium chloride as the solute, we find that 35.7 g of the salt dissolves in 100 mL of water at 20°C. The solubility of sodium chloride is, then, 35.7 g/100 mL water. Sodium chloride is a moderately soluble salt. The solu-

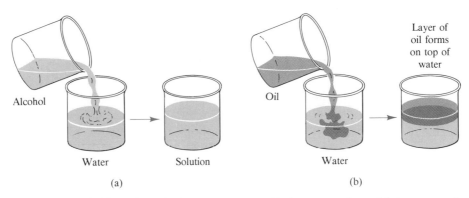

Figure 7.4 Soluble and insoluble. Alcohol is soluble in water, when added to water, it forms a clear solution. Oil is insoluble in water; when oil is added to water, the two liquids form separate layers.

bility of sodium nitrate is 92.1 g/100 mL water; sodium nitrate is a very soluble salt. At the opposite end of the scale is barium sulfate, which has a solubility of 2.3×10^{-4} g/100 mL water. Barium sulfate is an "insoluble" salt.

B. Equilibria in Saturated Solutions

A saturated solution is one in which the dissolved solute is in **equilibrium** with the undissolved solute. In the container in Figure 7.5 is a saturated solution of sucrose (cane sugar) and at the bottom of the container is some undissolved sucrose. If we could see the individual molecules of sucrose in this solution, we would see that some molecules of sucrose are dissolving and leaving the solid sucrose at the bottom of the container. The same number of molecules are coming out of solution (Figure 7.5), to become part of the undissolved sucrose. Solution and precipitation are occurring at the same rate, thereby satisfying the

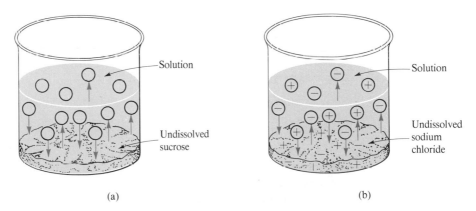

Figure 7.5 Equilibrium in solutions: (a) the equilibrium in a sucrose solution between dissolved and undissolved molecules; (b) the equilibrium in an ionic solution between dissolved ions and undissolved sodium chloride.

requirement for a **dynamic equilibrium**. This requirement was set forth in Section 6.7A, where we discussed the equilibrium between liquid and vapor. We can express the equilibrium in the sucrose solution with the equation

$$\text{sucrose(s)} \rightleftharpoons \text{sucrose(aq)}$$

In this solution, two things are true: (1) the two processes, dissolving and precipitating, are going on at the same time, and (2) the number of molecules in the solution remains constant.

A **saturated solution** of an ionic compound is quite different from a saturated solution of a covalent compound like sucrose. The ionic compound dissolves and exists as ions; the covalent compound dissolves and exists as molecules. An equilibrium in a saturated solution of sodium chloride is shown by the equation

$$\text{NaCl(s)} \rightleftharpoons \text{Na}^+\text{(aq)} + \text{Cl}^-\text{(aq)}$$

and diagrammed in Figure 7.5. Ions, not molecules, are in equilibrium with the solid.

An **unsaturated solution** contains less solute than a saturated solution does. There is no equilibrium present. Any additional solute added to an unsaturated solution dissolves. When additional solute is added to a saturated solution, the amount of dissolved solute does not increase, since the limit of solubility has already been reached. Adding more solute to a saturated solution simply increases the amount of undissolved solute.

It is important to remember that solubility changes with temperature. (We will discuss this factor further in Section 7.2C2). A solution that is saturated at one temperature may be unsaturated at a different temperature.

This is perhaps an appropriate spot for a few comments on preparing solutions. Dissolving requires interaction between the molecules (or ions) of the solute and the molecules of the solvent. Therefore, a finely divided solute will dissolve more rapidly than one that is in large chunks. As stirring changes the particular solvent molecules that are in contact with undissolved solute, constant stirring increases the rate of dissolution. Because solubility of solids and liquids generally increases with temperature, solids and liquids are often dissolved in warm solutes.

C. Factors Affecting Solubility

Many factors affect the solubility of one substance in another.

1. Nature of Intermolecular or Interionic Forces in Both Solute and Solvent

When one substance dissolves in another, the **intermolecular** or **interionic** attractive **forces** in both must be overcome. The dissolving solute must be able to break up the aggregation of molecules in the solvent, and the molecules of the solvent must have sufficient attraction for the solute particles to remove them one by one from their neighbors in the undissolved solute. If the solute is ionic, only a very polar solvent like water provides enough interaction to effect solution (see Figure 4.16).

In those ionic compounds like barium sulfate that are called insoluble, the interaction between the ions is greater than can be overcome by interaction with the polar water molecules. If the solute particles are polar molecules, they will dissolve in polar solvents such as alcohols. If the solute is nonpolar, it may dissolve only in nonpolar solvents—not because polar solvent molecules are unable to overcome the weak dispersion forces between the solute molecules, but because these dispersion forces are too weak to overcome the dipole-dipole interaction between the solvent molecules.

As a general rule, like dissolves like. Ionic and polar compounds are most apt to be soluble in **polar solvents**, like water or liquid ammonia. Nonpolar compounds are most apt to be soluble in **nonpolar solvents**, such as carbon tetrachloride, or hydrocarbon solvents, like gasoline.

The solubility of gases in water depends greatly on the polarity of the gas molecules. Those gases whose molecules are polar are much more soluble in water than nonpolar gases are. Ammonia, a strongly polar molecule, is very soluble in water (89.9 g/100 g H_2O); so is hydrogen chloride (82.3 g/100 g H_2O). Helium and nitrogen are nonpolar molecules. Helium is only slightly soluble (1.8×10^{-4} g/100 g H_2O); so is nitrogen (2.9×10^{-3} g/100 g H_2O).

Table 7.1 shows specific examples of different kinds of compounds and their relative solubilities—in water, a polar solvent; in alcohol, a less polar solvent; and in benzene, a nonpolar solvent.

Table 7.1
Solubility and interparticle bonds.

		Solvents		
Bonds	**Example**	**Water**	**Alcohol**	**Benzene**
ionic	sodium chloride	very soluble	slightly soluble	insoluble
polar covalent	sucrose (sugar)	very soluble	soluble	insoluble
nonpolar covalent	naphthalene	insoluble	soluble	very soluble

2. *Temperature*

Table 7.2 shows the solubility of several substances in water at 20°C and 100°C. Notice that the solubility of solids and liquids usually increases as the temperature increases, but the solubility of gases decreases with increasing temperature. This property of gases causes our concern for the fish population

Table 7.2
Solubility and temperature.

Compound	Type of Bonding	Solubility (g/100 mL water) at 25°C	at 100°C
sodium chloride	ionic	35.7	39.1
barium sulfate	ionic	2.3×10^{-4}	4.1×10^{-4}
sucrose	polar covalent	179	487
ammonia	polar covalent	89.9	7.4
hydrogen chloride	polar covalent	82.3	56.1
oxygen	nonpolar covalent	4.5×10^{-3}	3.3×10^{-3}

of lakes, oceans, and rivers threatened with thermal (heat) pollution. Fish require dissolved oxygen to survive. If the temperature of the water increases, the concentration of dissolved oxygen decreases, and the survival of the fish becomes questionable.

3. Pressure

The pressure on the surface of a solution has very little effect on the solubility of solids and liquids. It does have an enormous effect on the solubility of gases. As the partial pressure (see Section 6.5F) of a gas in the atmosphere above the surface of a solution increases, the solubility of that gas increases. A carbonated beverage is bottled and capped under a high partial pressure of carbon dioxide, so that much carbon dioxide dissolves. When the bottle is uncapped, the partial pressure of carbon dioxide above the liquid drops to the partial pressure in the atmosphere, the solubility of carbon dioxide decreases, and the gas, CO_2, comes out of the solution as fine bubbles.

The term *hyperbaric* means greater than normal atmospheric pressure. In **hyperbaric** medicine, patients are subjected to a pressure greater than atmospheric. This increases the amount of oxygen dissolved in the blood. Treatment in hyperbaric, or high-pressure, chambers is particularly valuable for patients who are suffering from severe anemia, hemoglobin abnormalities, or carbon monoxide exposure, or who are undergoing skin grafts, for it increases the amount of oxygen transported by the blood to the tissues.

For more information about the relationship of the gas laws to everyday living, see Mini-Essay III, "Skiing, Diving, and the Gas Laws."

7.3 Expressing Concentrations of Solutions

A complete description of a solution states what the solute is, and how much solute is dissolved in a given amount of solvent or solution. The quantitative relation between solute and solvent is the **concentration** of the solution. This concentration may be expressed using several different methods.

A. Concentration by Weight

The concentration of a solution may be given as the weight of solute in a given amount of solution, as in the following statements. The northern part of the Pacific Ocean contains 35.9 g of salt in each 1000 g of seawater. The North Atlantic Ocean has a higher salt concentration, 37.9 g salt/1000 g seawater.

B. Concentration by Percent

The concentration of a solution is often expressed as a **percent** by mass or percent by volume of solute in solution. Percent by mass is calculated from the mass of solute in a given weight of solution. A 5%-by-mass aqueous solution of sodium chloride contains 5 g sodium chloride and 95 g water in each 100 g solution.

$$\text{Percent by mass} = \frac{\text{mass of solute}}{\text{mass of solution}} \times 100\%$$

Example 7.1

☐ *Solution*

How many grams of glucose and of water are in 500 g of a 5.3%-by-mass glucose solution?

5.3% of the solution is glucose:

$$\frac{5.3 \text{ g glucose}}{100 \text{ g solution}} \times 500\text{g solution} = 26.5 \text{ g glucose}$$

The remainder of the 500 g is water:

$$500 \text{ g} - 26.5 \text{ g} = 473.5 \text{ g water}$$

Problem 7.1

What mass of sodium chloride is needed to prepare 315 g of a 0.9%-by-mass solution of sodium chloride in water?

If both solute and solvent are liquids, the concentration may be expressed as percent by volume. Both ethyl alcohol and water are liquids; the concentration of alcohol-water solutions is often given as percent by volume. For example, a 95% solution of ethyl alcohol contains 95 mL ethyl alcohol in each 100 mL solution.

$$\text{Percent by volume} = \frac{\text{volume of solute}}{\text{volume of solution}} \times 100\%$$

Example 7.2

☐ *Solution*

Rubbing alcohol is an aqueous solution containing 70% isopropyl alcohol by volume. How would you prepare 250 mL rubbing alcohol from pure isopropyl alcohol?

70% of the volume is isopropyl alcohol:

$$\frac{70 \text{ mL isopropyl alcohol}}{100 \text{ mL solution}} \times 250 \text{ mL solution} = 175 \text{ mL isopropyl alcohol}$$

To prepare the solution, then, add enough water to 175 mL isopropyl alcohol to form 250 mL solution.

Problem 7.2

Using pure ethyl alcohol and water, how would you prepare 1.0 L of a 40%-by-volume ethyl alcohol solution?

Because the density of liquids changes slightly as the temperature changes, a concentration given in percent by weight is more accurate over a range of temperatures than a concentration given in percentage by volume. Sometimes a combination of weight and volume is used to express the concentration—the weight of solute dissolved in each 100 mL solution. By this method, a 5% (wt/vol) solution of sodium chloride contains 5 g sodium chloride in each 100 mL solution.

C. Concentration in Parts per Million (ppm) and Parts per Billion (ppb)

The terms **parts per million** (ppm) and **parts per billion** (ppb) are encountered more and more frequently as we learn the effects of substances present in trace amounts in water and air, and as we develop instruments sensitive enough to detect substances present in such low concentrations. In discussing mass, *parts per million* means concentration in grams per 10^6 grams, or micrograms per gram. In discussing volume, *parts per million* may mean milliliters per cubic meter, or the mixed designation of milligrams per cubic meter. There is general movement toward the use of micrograms per liter (ppb) when discussing water contaminants, micrograms per cubic meter (ppb) for air, and micrograms per kilogram (ppb) for soil concentrations.

D. Concentration in Terms of Moles

The concentration of a solution may be stated as **molarity** (M), the number of moles of solute in a liter of solution:

$$\text{Molarity (M)} = \frac{\text{moles solute}}{\text{volume (L) solution}}$$

A 6M (say "six molar") solution of hydrochloric acid contains 6 moles (mol) of hydrochloric acid in one liter of solution. A 0.1M solution of sodium iodide contains 0.1 mole sodium iodide in one liter of solution.

The molarity of a solution gives a ratio between moles of solute and volume of solution. It can be used as a conversion factor between these two units in calculations involving solutions. Remember that as a conversion factor it can be used in two ways:

1. ____ mol/volume (L), which states the number of moles in one liter of solution. It would be used this way in calculating the number of moles in a given volume of solution.
2. Volume (L)/____ mol, which states that one liter contains ____ moles. It would be used this way to calculate the volume of a solution that contains a given quantity of solute.

Example 7.3

How many moles of hydrochloric acid are in 200 mL of 0.15M HCl?

☐ *Solution*

Wanted: ? moles HCl
Given: 200 mL of 0.15M HCl
Conversion factors:
0.15M HCl contains 0.15 mol HCl in 1 L solution, or the conversion factor

$$\frac{0.15 \text{ mol HCl}}{1\text{L of 0.15M HCl}}$$

Equation:

$$? \text{ moles HCl} = 200 \text{ mL of } 0.15\text{M HCl} \times \frac{1 \text{ L}}{1000 \text{ mL}} \times \frac{0.15 \text{ mol HCl}}{1 \text{ L of } 0.15\text{M HCl}}$$

Note that each time the volume of a solution is stated, the concentration of the solution is given. It may look confusing but without this marking it is easy to forget which solution you are referring to.
Answer: 0.030 mol HCl

Problem 7.3

How many moles of glucose are in 450 mL of 0.125 M glucose?

Example 7.4

What mass of sodium hydroxide, NaOH, is needed to prepare 100 mL of 0.125M sodium hydroxide?

☐ *Solution*

Wanted: ? g NaOH
Given: 100 mL of 0.125M NaOH
Conversion factors:
   1 L of 0.125M NaOH contains 0.125 mol NaOH, or

$$\frac{0.125 \text{ mol NaOH}}{1 \text{ L solution}}$$

   1 mol NaOH weighs 40.0 g (23.0 + 16.0 + 1.0)
Equation:

$$? \text{ g NaOH} = 100 \text{ mL of } 0.125\text{M NaOH} \times \frac{1 \text{ L}}{1000 \text{ mL}} \times \frac{0.125 \text{ mol NaOH}}{1 \text{ L solution}}$$

$$\times \frac{40.0 \text{ g NaOH}}{1 \text{ mol NaOH}}$$

Answer: 0.500 g NaOH

Problem 7.4

What mass of sodium chloride is needed to prepare 1.50 L of 0.125M NaCl?

Example 7.5

What volume of 3.25M sulfuric acid is needed to prepare 0.500 L of 0.130M H_2SO_4?

☐ *Solution*

We are to prepare 0.500 L of 0.130M H_2SO_4 by adding an amount of water to an amount of 3.25M H_2SO_4. The moles of sulfuric acid in the final (more dilute) solution will be the same as the moles of sulfuric acid in the portion taken of the more concentrated solution. We can calculate the moles of sulfuric acid in the final dilute solution:

$$? \text{ mol } H_2SO_4 \text{ in } 0.500 \text{ L of } 0.130\text{M } H_2SO_4$$

$$= 0.500 \text{ L of } 0.130\text{M } H_2SO_4 \times \frac{0.130 \text{ mol } H_2SO_4}{1 \text{ L solution}}$$

$$= 0.065 \text{ mol } H_2SO_4$$

We can calculate the volume of 3.25M H_2SO_4 that would contain 0.065 mol H_2SO_4.

$$? \text{ L of 3.25M } H_2SO_4 \text{ contains 0.065 mol } H_2SO_4$$

$$= 0.065 \text{ mol } H_2SO_4 \times \frac{1.0 \text{ L of 3.25M } H_2SO_4}{3.25 \text{ mol } H_2SO_4}$$

$$= 0.020 \text{ L of 3.25M } H_2SO_4$$

To prepare the solution, we add 0.020 L of 3.25M H_2SO_4 to an amount of water somewhat less than 480 mL and then add enough more water to raise the volume to exactly 0.500 L. Why do we first add acid to water and then add more water? First, when acid dissolves in water, much heat is generated. If the acid is added to a large volume of water, the heat is dissipated through the solution and does no harm. If the water is added to acid, the heat is generated in the small interface between the acid and the water and may cause an explosion. Secondly, having mixed the acid and water, we then add more water. When two liquids are combined, the final volume is frequently not the arithmetic sum of the added volumes. Therefore, we make up initially a smaller volume than that required and then dilute the solution up to the asked-for volume.

Problem 7.5

What volume of 6.0M HCl is needed to prepare 275 mL of 0.255M HCl?

The term *millimole* is often used in calculation. One **millimole** is 10^{-3} mole. With millimoles, molarity can be defined as

$$\text{Molarity (M)} = \frac{\text{moles}}{\text{liter}} = \frac{\text{millimoles}}{\text{milliliter}}$$

If a problem uses millimoles, the preferred volume unit is milliliters. If a problem uses moles, the preferred volume unit is liters.

Example 7.6

What volume of 6.39M sodium chloride contains 51.2 millimoles sodium chloride?

☐ *Solution*

Wanted: ? mL of 6.39M NaCl
Given: 51.2 millimoles NaCl
Conversion factors:
    1 L of 6.39M NaCl contains 6.39 mol NaCl
    1 mL of 6.39M NaCl contains 6.39 millimoles NaCl
Equation:

$$? \text{ mL of 6.39M NaCl} = 51.2 \text{ millimoles NaCl} \times \frac{1 \text{ mL of 6.39M NaCl}}{6.39 \text{ millimoles NaCl}}$$

Answer: 8.01 mL of 6.39M NaCl

■
Problem 7.6

What volume of 0.195M HCl contains 50.0 millimoles HCl?

■

■
Example 7.7

How can 75.0 mL of 0.096M sulfuric acid be prepared from 18M acid?

☐ *Solution*

This problem is similar to Example 7.5. We are to prepare 75.0 mL of 0.96M sulfuric acid by diluting 18M sulfuric acid with water. We can calculate the millimoles of sulfuric acid in the final solution.

$$? \text{ millimoles } H_2SO_4 = 75 \text{ mL} \times \frac{0.96 \text{ millimole}}{1 \text{ mL of 0.96M } H_2SO_4}$$

$$= 72 \text{ millimoles } H_2SO_4$$

We can calculate the volume of 18M H_2SO_4 that will contain 72 millimoles H_2SO_4.

$$? \text{ mL of 18M } H_2SO_4 = 72 \text{ millimoles} \times \frac{1 \text{ mL of 18M } H_2SO_4}{18 \text{ millimol}}$$

$$= 4.0 \text{ mL of 18M } H_2SO_4$$

The solution is prepared by adding 4.0 mL of 18M H_2SO_4 to about 50 mL of water and then diluting that solution up to exactly 75 mL.

■
Problem 7.7

What volume of 15M acetic acid must be used to prepare 48 mL of 0.245M acetic acid?

■

E. Osmolality

Osmolality measures the moles of particles per kilogram of solvent. The basic postulate of osmolality is that the identity of the particles is not significant. Rather, the number of particles of any type that are present in the solution is significant. Thus for a 2.0 osmolal solution, 1.0 kg solvent may contain two moles of a molecular solute like glucose or one mole of a 1:1 ionic compound like sodium chloride, or a combination of one mole of glucose and 0.5 mol sodium chloride (together these solutes would yield two moles of solute particles).

The osmolality of body fluids is closely related to health. (For a discussion of the clinical importance of osmolality see Mini-Essay V, immediately following this chapter.)

Table 7.3 lists several common ways of expressing concentrations.

Table 7.3
Common units of
concentration.

	Solute	Solvent	Solution	Comments
Percent by weight	? g	+ ? g $\longrightarrow$	100 g	accurate; independent of temperature
Percent by volume	? L	+ ? L $\longrightarrow$	100 L	used when solute is liquid; concentration varies slightly with temperature
Percent, weight/volume	? g	$\longrightarrow$	100 mL	used in technical labs
Molarity (M)	moles	____	1 L	used in chemical calculations
Millimole/liter	10^{-3} mol	____	1 L	used in medical labs to express concentrations of
Millimole/milliliter	10^{-3} mol	____	10^{-3} L	biological fluids
Parts per million (ppm)	mg	____	kg	used in environmental
Parts per billion (ppb)	μg	____	kg	studies
Osmolality (O)	mole of particles	____	kg	used for biological fluids

7.4 Calculations Involving Concentrations

Our earlier stoichiometry calculations involved pure substances (Chapter 5). We determined the amount of a solid or liquid reactant by weighing the sample. Now, by using the concentration of a solution as a conversion factor, we can extend stoichiometric calculations to include solutions.

Example 7.8

What weight of barium sulfate is precipitated by adding an excess of sulfuric acid to 55.6 mL of 0.54M barium chloride?

☐ *Solution*

Equation: $BaCl_2(aq) + H_2SO_4(aq) \longrightarrow BaSO_4\downarrow + 2HCl(aq)$
Given: 55.6 mL of 0.54M $BaCl_2$
Conversion factors:
  0.54 mol $BaCl_2$ in 1 L of 0.54M $BaCl_2$
  0.54 millimole $BaCl_2$ in 1 mL of 0.54M $BaCl_2$
  1 mol $BaCl_2$ forms 1 mol $BaSO_4$
  1 mol $BaSO_4$ weighs 233.4 g
Calculation:

$$? \text{ g } BaSO_4 = 55.6 \text{ mL of 0.54M } BaCl_2 \times \frac{0.54 \text{ millimole } BaCl_2}{1 \text{ mL of 0.54M } BaCl_2}$$

$$\times \frac{1 \text{ millimole } BaSO_4}{1 \text{ millimole } BaCl_2} \times \frac{10^{-3} \text{ mol } BaSO_4}{1 \text{ millimole } BaSO_4} \times \frac{233.4 \text{ g } BaSO_4}{1 \text{ mol } BaSO_4}$$

Answer: 7.0 g $BaSO_4$

Problem 7.8

What mass of magnesium will react completely with 125 mL of 1.25M HCl?

In Example 7.9, two solutions are used. The concentration and volume of the first are known. Only the concentration of the second is known; its volume can be calculated.

Example 7.9

What volume of 0.154M sodium hydroxide will completely react with 25.0 mL of 0.0952M hydrochloric acid?

☐ *Solution*

Equation: $NaOH(aq) + HCl(aq) \longrightarrow NaCl(aq) + H_2O(l)$
Wanted: ? mL of 0.154M NaOH
Given: 25.0 mL of 0.0952M HCl
Conversion factors:
   1 mL of 0.0952M HCl contains 0.0952 millimole of hydrochloric acid
   1 mol NaOH reacts with 1 mol HCl
   1 mL of 0.154M NaOH contains 0.154 millimole NaOH
Calculation:

$$? \text{ mL (0.154M) NaOH} = 25.0 \text{ mL (0.0952M) HCl} \times \frac{0.0952 \text{ millimole HCl}}{1 \text{ mL of 0.0952M HCl}}$$

$$\times \frac{1 \text{ millimole NaOH}}{1 \text{ millimole HCl}} \times \frac{1 \text{ mL of 0.154M NaOH}}{0.154 \text{ millimole NaOH}}$$

Answer: 15.5 mL of 0.154M NaOH

Problem 7.9

Calculate the molarity of a solution of hydrochloric acid, given that 15.0 mL of this solution reacts exactly with 26.2 mL of 0.126M potassium hydroxide.

7.5 Titration

Laboratories, whether medical or industrial, are frequently asked to determine the exact concentration of a particular substance in a solution. For example: What is the concentration of acetic acid in a sample of vinegar? What are the concentrations of iron, calcium, and magnesium ions in a hard-water sample? Such determinations can be made using a technique known as titration.

In **titration**, a known volume of a solution of unknown concentration is reacted with, or titrated by, a known volume of a solution of known concentration. If the titration volumes and the mole ratio in which the solutes react are known, the concentration of the second solution can be calculated. The method is like that used in Examples 7.8 and 7.9. The solution of unknown concentration may contain an acid (such as stomach acid), a base (such as ammonia), an ion (such as iodide ion), or any other substance whose concentration must be determined.

Analytical titrations have several requirements:

1. The equation for the reaction must be known, so that a stoichiometric ratio can be obtained for use in calculations.
2. The reaction must be fast and complete.
3. When the reactants have combined exactly, there must be a clear-cut change in some measurable property of the reaction mixture. The occurrence of this change is called the **endpoint** of the reaction.
4. Accurate measurement of the amount of each reactant must be assured, whether that reactant is initially in solution or is a solid to be dissolved.

Let us apply these requirements to a particular titration, that of a solution of sulfuric acid of known concentration with a sodium hydroxide solution of unknown concentration. The balanced equation for this acid-base reaction is

$$2NaOH(aq) + H_2SO_4(aq) \longrightarrow Na_2SO_4(aq) + 2H_2O(l)$$

Sodium hydroxide ionizes in water to form sodium ions and hydroxide ions; sulfuric acid ionizes to form hydrogen ions and sulfate ions. The reaction between hydroxide ions and hydrogen ions is rapid and complete; thus, the second requirement for an analytical titration is met.

What clear-cut change in property will occur when the reaction is complete? Suppose the sodium hydroxide solution is slowly added to the acid solution. As each hydroxide ion is added, it reacts with a hydrogen ion to form a water molecule. As long as there are unreacted hydrogen ions in solution, the solution is acidic. When the number of hydroxide ions added exactly equals the original number of hydrogen ions, the solution becomes neutral. As soon as any extra hydroxide ions are added, the solution becomes basic. How will the experimenter know when the solution becomes basic? We recall those organic compounds called **indicators**, which have one color in acidic solutions and another in basic solutions (Section 3.5D). If such an indicator is present in an acid-base titration, it changes color when the solution changes from acidic to basic. Phenolphthalein is an acid-base indicator that is colorless in acid solutions and pink in basic solutions. If phenolphthalein is added to the original sample of sulfuric acid, the solution will be colorless and remain so, as long as there is an excess of hydrogen ions. After enough sodium hydroxide solution has been added to react with all the hydrogen ions, the next drop of base will provide a slight excess of hydroxide ion, and the solution will turn pink. Thus, we will have a visible and clear-cut indication of the endpoint. Table 7.4 lists several indicators that could be used in acid-base titration.

Table 7.4
Common acid-base indicators.

Indicator	Color in Acid	Color in Base
phenolphthalein	colorless	pink
methyl orange	red	yellow
bromothymol	yellow	blue

The requirement that the volumes of solutions used must be measured is met by using **volumetric glassware**, in particular, **burets**, to measure the volumes of the solutions. Figure 7.6 shows a typical titration.

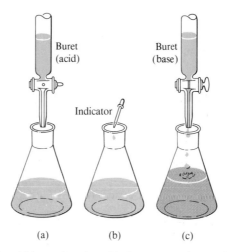

Figure 7.6 A typical acid-base titration. (a) An exact volume of a solution of known concentration of acid is measured into a flask. (b) A few drops of phenolphthalein indicator are added. (c) The solution containing sodium hydroxide in an unknown concentration is added until a faint pink color is visible for a few seconds.

Data and calculations for a typical acid-base titration are shown in the box below. Notice that three trials were run; this is a standard procedure for checking the precision of titration.

Data from the titration of 0.108M sulfuric acid with a solution of sodium hydroxide of unknown concentration.

Equation: $2NaOH + H_2SO_4 \longrightarrow Na_2SO_4 + 2H_2O$
Data:
   Molarity of H_2SO_4: 0.108M = 0.108 millimole/mL

	Trial I	Trial II	Trial III
Volume of 0.108M H_2SO_4	25.0 mL	25.0 mL	25.0 mL
Volume of NaOH solution (unknown concentration)			
Buret readings: Finish	34.12 mL	39.61 mL	35.84 mL
Start	0.64 mL	6.15 mL	2.34 mL
Volume of NaOH to reach endpoint:	33.48 mL	33.46 mL	33.50 mL

Average volume used: 33.48 mL

Calculation:

$$? \text{ M NaOH} = 25.0 \text{ mL } H_2SO_4 \times \frac{0.108 \text{ millimole } H_2SO_4}{1 \text{ mL of } 0.108M \ H_2SO_4}$$

$$\times \frac{2 \text{ millimoles NaOH}}{1 \text{ millimole } H_2SO_4} \times \frac{1}{33.48 \text{ mL NaOH}}$$

Answer: 0.161M NaOH

Titration reactions are not always acid-base reactions. They may be oxidation-reduction reactions, precipitation reactions, or combination reactions. The endpoint may be determined by a change in color of an added indicator or by a change in color of the solution when the reaction is complete. In other titrations, the endpoint may be marked by a change in electrical conductivity of the reaction mixture, by a change in turbidity, or by various other means.

Example 7.10

Three 25.00-mL samples of a sulfuric acid solution of unknown concentration were titrated to a phenolphthalein endpoint with 0.129M potassium hydroxide solution. The buret readings for each of the trials were:

	Trial I	Trial II	Trial III
Final reading	34.32 mL	33.35 mL	35.15 mL
Initial reading	1.13 mL	0.20 mL	2.07 mL

Calculate the molarity of the sulfuric acid solution.

☐ *Solution*

The solution to this problem should be set up in the form of the box on page 215.

Equation: $2KOH + H_2SO_4 \longrightarrow K_2SO_4 + 2H_2O$
Data:
  Molarity of KOH: 0.129M (0.129 millimole KOH/mL solution)

	Trial I	Trial II	Trial III
Volume of H_2SO_4 used	25.00 mL	25.00 mL	25.00 mL
Volume of KOH used	33.19 mL	33.15 mL	33.08 mL

(These data are obtained by subtracting the buret readings given in the body of the problem.)
Average volume of 0.129M KOH used: 33.14 mL
Calculation:

$$? M\ H_2SO_4 = \frac{?\ \text{millimoles}\ H_2SO_4}{mL}$$

$$= 33.14\ \text{mL of } 0.129M\ KOH \times \frac{0.129\ \text{millimole KOH}}{1\ \text{mL } 0.129M\ KOH}$$

$$\times \frac{1\ \text{millimole } H_2SO_4}{2\ \text{millimole KOH}} \times \frac{1}{25.0\ \text{mL } H_2SO_4}$$

The first three factors in the equation give the millimoles of H_2SO_4 used. Dividing by the volume of acid used gives the molarity (mol/L). The 1 in the last factor is a dimensionless number.
Answer: 0.0855M H_2SO_4

Problem 7.10

Calculate the concentration of an acetic acid solution using the following data. 25.0-mL samples of acid were titrated to a phenolphthalein endpoint with 0.121M KOH. The buret readings were recorded:

	Trial I	Trial II	Trial III
Final reading	21.31 mL	40.94 mL	30.72 mL
Initial reading	1.35 mL	21.21 mL	10.93 mL

7.6 Physical Properties of Solutions

A solution has different physical properties from those of the pure solvent. Many differences in physical properties are predictable if the solute in the pure state is **nonvolatile**— that is, if it has a very low vapor pressure. Sugar, sodium chloride, and potassium nitrate are examples of nonvolatile solutes. **Colligative properties** are those physical properties of solutions of nonvolatile solutes that depend only on the number of particles present in a given amount of solution, and not on the nature of those particles. We consider four colligative properties: vapor-pressure lowering, boiling-point elevation, freezing-point depression, and osmotic pressure.

A. Vapor-Pressure Lowering

At any given temperature, the vapor pressure of a solution containing a non-volatile solute is lower than that of the pure solvent (see Section 6.7A for a discussion of vapor pressure). The solid line in Figure 7.7 is a plot of the vapor pressure of pure water against temperature. The break in the curve at 0°C is

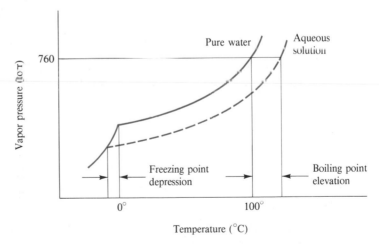

Figure 7.7 The vapor pressure of pure water is shown as a solid line; the vapor pressure of an aqueous solution is shown as a dashed line. Note the differences between the solution and the pure substance in melting point and boiling point.

the intersection of the vapor pressure of the solid with the vapor pressure of the liquid. The dashed line in Figure 7.7 is a plot of the vapor pressure of an aqueous solution of sugar against temperature. Notice that the vapor pressure of the solution is always lower than the vapor pressure of the pure solvent. What causes this difference?

The surface of a pure solvent [Figure 7.8(a)] is populated only by solvent molecules. Some of these are escaping from the surface and others are returning to the liquid state (see Section 6.7A). The surface of a solution is populated with two kinds of molecules; some are solvent molecules, and others are solute molecules. Only the solvent molecules are volatile. They alone escape to build up the vapor pressure of the solution. As a consequence, a solution has a lower vapor pressure than that of its solvent at the same temperature. [See Figure 7.8(b).]

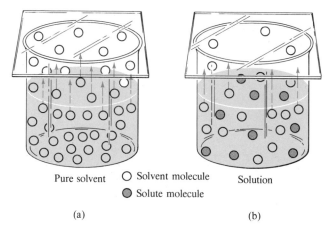

Pure solvent   ○ Solvent molecule   Solution
                ● Solute molecule

(a)   (b)

Figure 7.8 Vapor-pressure lowering: (a) the vapor pressure of a pure liquid; (b) the vapor pressure of a solution. The number of solvent molecules on the surface of the liquid has been decreased by the presence of the solute molecules. Fewer solvent molecules can vaporize, and the vapor pressure is lower.

B. Boiling-Point Elevation

The **boiling point** of a substance is the temperature at which the vapor pressure of the substance equals atmospheric pressure. A solution containing a nonvolatile solute, having a lower vapor pressure than the pure solvent, must be at a higher temperature before its vapor pressure equals atmospheric pressure and it boils. Thus, the boiling point of a solution containing a nonvolatile solute is higher than that of the pure solvent (see Figure 7.7).

C. Freezing-Point Depression

Recall that **freezing point** and melting point are two terms that describe the same temperature, the temperature at which the vapor pressure of the solid equals the vapor pressure of the liquid and the solid and the liquid are in equilibrium. Remember, too, that vapor pressure decreases as temperature decreases. A solution has a lower vapor pressure than that of the solvent, so the vapor pressure of a solution will equal the vapor pressure of the solid at a lower temperature than in the case of the pure solvent. Thus, the freezing point will be lower for a solution than for the pure solvent (see Figure 7.7). Just as it is the solvent that vaporizes when a solution boils, it is the solvent, not the solution, that becomes solid when a solution freezes. When a salt solution freezes, the ice is pure water (solid); the remaining solution contains all the salt.

Application of this principle leads us to add antifreeze (a nonvolatile solute) to the water in the radiators in our cars. We thus lower the freezing point of the solvent (water), and the solution remains a liquid, even at subfreezing temperatures.

D. Osmosis and Osmotic Pressure

Osmosis and osmotic pressure depend on the ability of small molecules to pass through a **semipermeable membrane**, such as a thin piece of rubber, a cell membrane, or a thin piece of plastic wrap. Think of the membrane as a sieve with very tiny holes. Solvent particles are small and can very easily pass through these holes; solute particles are larger and cannot (Figure 7.9). When a semipermeable membrane separates a solution from pure solvent, solvent molecules move back and forth through the membrane, but not in equal numbers. More move from the pure solvent into the solution than from the solution into the solvent.

The movement of solvent molecules will continue to be uneven until the number of solvent particles is the same on both sides of the membrane. The

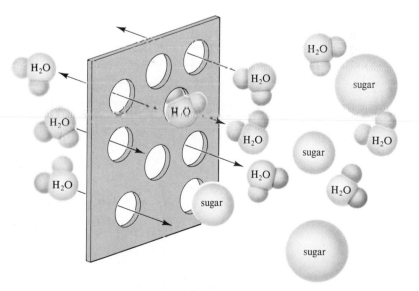

Figure 7.9 A semipermeable membrane allows small solvent molecules to pass through but prevents the passage of larger particles, like those of a nonvolatile solute.

process is called **osmosis**. When the numbers are equal, both solution and pure solvent are exerting pressure on the membrane. The excess pressure exerted by the solution is its **osmotic pressure**. Figure 7.10 illustrates these points.

In Figure 7.10(a), different amounts of pure solvent (water) are separated by a semipermeable membrane. Water molecules from both sides move through the membrane until the pressure of solvent on both sides of the membrane is equal. This equality is indicated by the equal heights of the columns [Figure 7.10(b)].

In Figure 7.10(c), solute molecules have been added on one side of the membrane, creating a solution. Now there are fewer solvent molecules next to this side of the membrane than there are on the side of the pure solvent. To overcome this difference, solvent molecules move more rapidly from the solvent side than from the solution side, tending to equate these numbers. (Notice the bigger arrow meaning migration from the solvent side.) In Figure 7.10(d), the

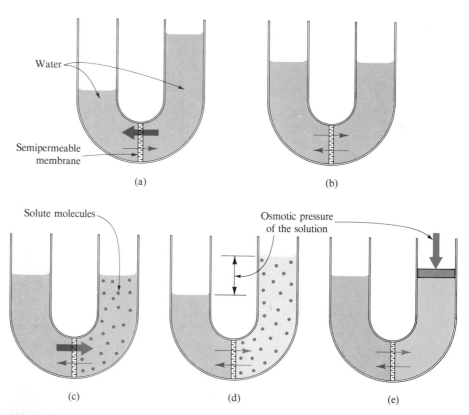

Figure 7.10 Osmosis and osmotic pressure. (a) Differing amounts of pure solvent on either side of a semipermeable membrane will, (b) through osmosis, become equally divided on either side of the membrane. However, (c) if solute molecules are added to one side, some of the solvent will migrate into the solution side, (d) causing a difference in osmotic pressure. (e) The difference in pressure can be counteracted by increased surface pressure on the solution side.

height of the solution is greater than the height of the solvent, but now the rate at which the solvent molecules pass through the membrane is the same from both sides. The difference in height of the columns is proportional to the osmotic pressure of the original solution.

Osmotic pressure is also being measured in Figure 7.10(e). Here, pressure is being applied to the surface of the solution. The osmotic pressure of the solution is the pressure of solvent molecules from the more dilute (or pure solvent) side into the solution.

Osmosis and osmotic pressure are very important to living organisms. Blood is an aqueous solution containing many solutes and has an osmotic pressure of 7.7 atm measured against pure water. When red blood cells are put in pure water, water molecules move into the cells through the cell membrane to equate the osmotic pressure in the blood cell with that of the pure water outside. So much water may pass into the cell that the cell membrane ruptures because it cannot stretch to contain the additional water; this rupturing is called **hemolysis** [Figure 7.11(a)].

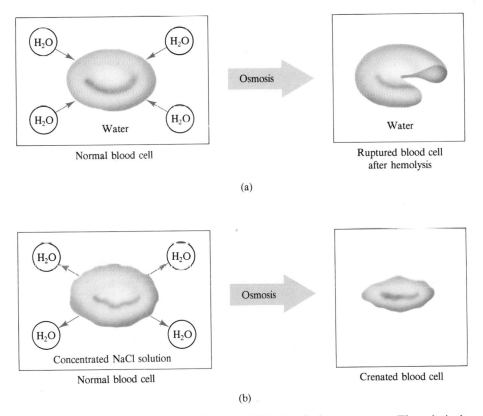

(a)

(b)

Figure 7.11 (a) Hemolysis (rupturing) of red blood cells in pure water. The relatively high osmotic pressure within the cell causes water molecules to move into the cell by osmosis, eventually causing the cell to rupture. (b) Crenation of red blood cells in a concentrated salt solution. The higher osmotic pressure outside the cell causes water to move out of the cell, resulting in crenation.

By a similar mechanism, blood cells put in a concentrated salt solution shrink as water molecules move out of the cell into the salt solution. The water molecules move out of the cell because the concentration of water is lower outside the cell than inside, hence, the osmotic pressure is higher outside the cell. This shrinking process is called **crenation** [Figure 7.11(b)].

To prevent the occurence of either of these destructive processes in the body, fluids fed intravenously must have the same osmotic pressure as blood itself. Solutions having the same osmotic pressure are called **isotonic**. An isotonic glucose solution contains 5.3 g glucose per 100 g solution; an isotonic saline solution contains 0.9 g sodium chloride per 100 g solution. Both solutions have an osmotic pressure of 7.7 atm.

E. Differences between Colligative Properties of Solutions of Ionic and of Molecular Compounds

For any solution, the amount by which the vapor pressure is lowered, the freezing point depressed, or the boiling point elevated relative to the properties of the pure solvent depends on the number of solute particles in solution, not on the nature of those particles. Similarly, osmotic pressure of a solution depends only on the number of solute particles, not on their nature. Table 7.5 shows the melting point (freezing point), boiling point, and osmotic pressure of several glucose solutions. The number of moles of glucose (therefore, the number of glucose molecules in a given amount of water) differs among these solutions. The greater the number of molecules of solute, the greater the difference between the properties of the pure solvent and of the solution.

Table 7.5 Colligative properties. Physical properties of solutions containing ionic solutes and of solutions containing molecular solutes.

Solution	Grams of Solute 1000 g Water	mp (°C)	bp (°C)	Osmotic Pressure at 25°C (atm)
water	0	0	100	0
glucose solutions	18 (0.1 mol)	−0.19	100.05	2.4
	36 (0.2 mol)	−0.36	100.10	4.8
	180 (1.0 mol)	−1.8	100.52	24
	360 (2.0 mol)	−3.6	101.04	73
NaCl solution	6 (0.1 mol)	−0.33	100.08	4.1
Na_2SO_4 solution	14 (0.1 mol)	−0.43	100.17	5.4

A solution with an ionic solute has different colligative properties from those of a solution with a molecular solute. One mole of sugar, a molecular compound, dissolves to yield one mole of particles; however, one mole of sodium chloride, an ionic compound, dissolves to yield two moles of particles, one of sodium ions and one of chloride ions. One mole of sodium sulfate, Na_2SO_4, dissolves to yield three moles of particles—two of sodium ions and one of sulfate ions. Because the number of particles is what determines the colligative properties of a solution, one mole of sodium chloride dissolved in a given amount of water causes approximately twice the change in colligative properties that one mole of glucose dissolved in the same volume of water causes. One mole of sodium sulfate dissolved in the same amount of water causes approximately three times the change. Several colligative properties of solutions of glucose, sodium chloride, and sodium sulfate are shown in Table 7.5.

7.7 Colloids

A. Properties of Colloids

A colloid is a uniform suspension of very small particles of one substance in another. Milk and mayonnaise are colloids. The suspended substance is insoluble in the second substance, as the butterfat in milk and the oil in mayonnaise are both insoluble in water. If the particles were smaller, they would dissolve to form a solution. If they were larger, they would separate out. The properties of a colloid depend on the small diameter (roughly 10^{-7} to 10^{-4} cm) of each particle and the enormous surface area represented by a large collection of small particles. To see how the total surface area depends on the particle size, picture a cube, 1 cm on each side. Its surface area is 6 cm^2; its ratio of surface area to volume is 6 cm^2:1 cm^3. If the same cube is divided into 8 equal cubes, 0.5 cm on each side, the total surface area increases to 12 cm^2 but the volume remains the same. The ratio of surface area to volume is now 12 cm^2:1 cm^3. Further dividing these cubes increases the ratio. If the original cube of volume 1 cm^3 is divided into 10^{21} cubes, each 10^{-7} cm on a side (the approximate size of a colloidal particle), the total surface area becomes 6×10^3 cm^2, or 1.5 acre. Although the colloidal particles are spherical rather than cubic, the ratio of surface area to volume is still enormous (approximately 6000:1). Colloidal particles are kept in constant motion by the buffeting and bumping of other molecules present. As the colloidal particles move around, they rub against one another and develop static electricity on their surface, much as you acquire static electricity in winter by scuffing across a carpet. The great stability of colloids, the fact that they do not easily separate into two separate phases, is due to these charges. Neutralizing these charges by adding a solution of ions can destroy the colloid. The Mississippi River picks up a lot of finely divided soil and mud as it flows south through the prairie. By the time the river reaches New Orleans, this mud is colloidally dispersed in the river. When the river empties into the ocean, this colloid is dumped into the solution of sodium and chloride ions we call salt water. The electrical charges on the surface of the tiny mud particles that kept them suspended are neutralized. The colloid separates and the mud settles out, forming the river delta.

The same phenomenon occurs when smoke (a colloidal suspension of solids in air) is released through a chimney equipped with a precipitator, shown in Figure 7.12. The precipitator consists of metal plates or wires carrying an electrical charge. As the smoke passes between these plates, the static electrical charges on the colloidal smoke particles are neutralized, the dirt falls to the bottom of the chimney, and no smoke is released to pollute the atmosphere.

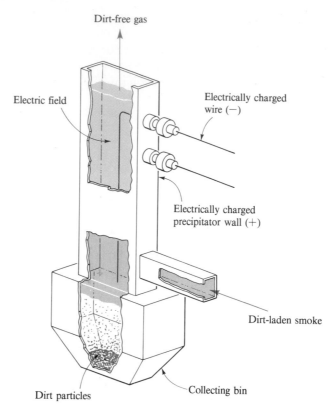

Figure 7.12 A schematic diagram of an electrostatic precipitator. The electrical charges on the wire and wall of the precipitator neutralize the charges on the particles in the smoke, causing them to settle out.

Electrostatic filters used in homes by people with severe pollen allergies work on the same principle.

B. Purification

A colloid is not always a single pure substance suspended in another pure substance. The dispersing medium may also contain dissolved ions or molecules. These ions and small molecules can be removed by a process called **dialysis**. Figure 7.13 diagrams the essential features of dialysis. The colloid is put in a thin plastic bag and the bag is suspended in a large water bath in which the water is being constantly changed. The plastic of the bag resembles the membrane shown in Figure 7.9 but is slightly more permeable. Small ions and molecules, as well as solvent molecules, can migrate through the bag walls, but not the larger colloidal particles. While the bag is suspended in the water bath, this migration takes place. The solvent molecules move in both directions, and the small ions and molecules move mostly outward from the bag into the bath tending toward equal concentration on both sides of the plastic wall. Needless to say, equilibrium is never reached, since the solvent in the bath is constantly being changed.

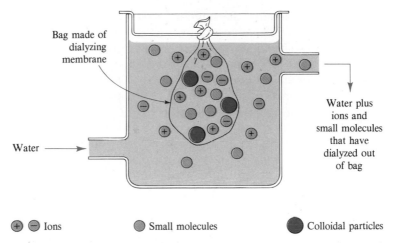

Bag made of
dialyzing
membrane

Water

Water plus
ions and
small molecules
that have
dialyzed out
of bag

⊕ ⊖ Ions   ● Small molecules   ● Colloidal particles

Figure 7.13 Dialysis. The colloid is placed in a bag made of a semipermeable membrane and lowered into a water tank. Through osmosis, the ions and small molecules migrate out into the water tank and are removed. The colloidal particles are too large to pass through the membrane. Eventually, the colloid is purified.

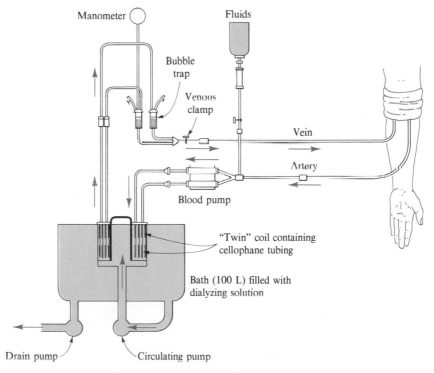

Manometer

Fluids

Bubble
trap

Venous
clamp

Vein

Artery

Blood pump

"Twin" coil containing
cellophane tubing

Bath (100 L) filled with
dialyzing solution

Drain pump   Circulating pump

Figure 7.14 Dialysis in a kidney machine.

Eventually, the solution in the bag around the colloid particles becomes infinitely dilute and the colloid is said to be purified.

The kidney machine is an application of dialysis to human needs. The machine is used to purify the blood of people whose kidneys have been removed or are not functioning properly. The blood is diverted through a long tube made of a dialyzing membrane. The tube is immersed in a container filled with a solution isotonic with blood in essential ions (sodium, potassium, and so on). This solution is continually changed. As the blood passes through the tube, unwanted electrolytes and small molecules migrate out through the membrane. The blood is returned to the body in a purified condition. The process is the same as that performed much more efficiently by healthy kidneys. Figure 7.14 shows a schematic diagram of a kidney machine.

Key Terms and Concepts

boiling point (7.6B)

Brownian movement (7.1B)

buret (7.5)

colligative properties (7.6)

colloid (7.1)

concentration (7.3)

crenation (7.6D)

dialysis (7.7B)

dispersed phase (7.1A)

dispersing medium (7.1A)

dynamic equilibrium (7.2B)

endpoint (7.5)

equilibrium (7.2B)

filtration (7.1B)

freezing point (7.6C)

hemolysis (7.6D)

hyperbaric (7.2C3)

immiscible (7.2)

indicator (7.5)

insoluble (7.2)

interionic forces (7.2C1)

intermolecular forces (7.2C1)

isotonic (7.6D)

millimole (7.3D)

miscible (7.2)

molarity (7.3D)

nonpolar solvents (7.2C1)

nonvolatile solute (7.6)

osmolality (7.3E)

osmosis (7.6D)

osmotic pressure (7.6D)

particle size (7.1B)

parts per billion (7.3C)

parts per million (7.3C)

percent concentration of
   solutions (7.3B)

phases (7.1)

polar solvents (7.2C1)

saturated (7.2A)

saturated solution (7.2B)

semipermeable membrane (7.6D)

solubility (7.2)

soluble (7.2)

solute (7.1A)

solution (7.1)

solvent (7.1A)

sparingly soluble (7.2)

suspension (7.1)

titration (7.5)

Tyndall effect (7.1B)

unsaturated solution (7.2B)

vapor-pressure lowering (7.6A)

volumetric glassware (7.5)

Problems

*Character-
istics of
solutions
(Sections 7.1
and 7.2)*

7.11 Give examples of each.
   a. A gas dissolved in a liquid.
   b. A solid dissolved in a liquid.
   c. A liquid dissolved in a liquid.

7.12 Identify the solute and solvent in these solutions.
   a. aqueous potassium nitrate
   b. iodine in carbon tetrachloride
   c. chlorine water
   d. potassium hydroxide in ethyl alcohol

7.13 Which of the following compounds should be quite soluble in water?
   a. potassium chloride, KCl
   b. benzene, C_6H_6
   c. formaldehyde, HCHO

7.14 For each of the following, predict its relative solubility in water and in gasoline, a nonpolar solvent. (Remember the solubility rules in Chapter 5.)
   a. barium sulfate
   b. lithium nitrate
   c. octane, C_8H_{18}
   d. bromine
   e. carbon tetrafluoride, CF_4

7.15 Describe an equilibrium present in each of the following:
   a. a saturated solution of potassium nitrate containing some undissolved potassium nitrate
   b. a solution from which barium sulfate has been precipitated
   c. an aqueous suspension of aspirin (a covalent molecule)

*Expressing
concentrations
of solutions
(Section 7.3)*

7.16 Carry out these conversions:
   a. 0.90%-by-weight sodium chloride to molarity
   b. 5.0 g $NaHCO_3$ in 1 L solution to molarity
   c. 12M HCl to g HCl/L solution

7.17 Describe how to prepare:
   a. 5.0 L of 0.15M sulfuric acid from 18M H_2SO_4
   b. 400 mL of 0.10M KOH from solid potassium hydroxide
   c. 450 mL of 3% (wt/vol) glucose from solid glucose

7.18 What is the weight of the solute in:
   a. 1.5 L of 0.10M $AgNO_3$
   b. 0.500 L of 3.0M H_2SO_4
   c. 25.00 mL of 0.155M NaOH

7.19 What volume of each of these solutions contains 0.10 mol solute?
   a. 0.15M barium chloride
   b. 0.25M copper(II) sulfate
   c. 5.0M ammonium nitrate

7.20 What are the differences between a saturated solution and a one-molar (1M) solution?

7.21   The solubility of sodium bicarbonate is 6.9 g/100 g water at 25°C. What weight of sodium bicarbonate dissolves in 250 g water at that temperature? What is the molarity of this solution?

7.22   A solution contains 2.6 g glucose in 150 mL solution. Calculate the percent concentration (wt/vol) and the molarity of this solution.

7.23   An aqueous solution contains one part per million by weight of fluoride ion (g/g). How would you prepare 10 L of this solution using sodium fluoride? What is the molarity of this solution?

7.24   A solution of vitamin C, ascorbic acid (MW 176.1), contains 1.0 g per 200 mL. What is the molarity of this solution?

7.25   Beer is 12% ethyl alcohol by volume.
    a. Calculate the volume of alcohol in one liter of beer.
    b. Calculate the mass of alcohol in one liter of beer (density of alcohol = 0.789 g/mL).
    c. Calculate the molarity of ethyl alcohol in beer. (The molecular formula of ethyl alcohol is C_2H_6O.)

7.26   Phenol, C_6H_6O, is a mild antiseptic used in several nonprescription mouthwashes. In two of these, the concentration of phenol is 1.4% (wt/vol). Calculate the molarity of phenol in these solutions.

7.27   A commercial liquid noncaloric sweetener contains 1.62% (wt/vol) of the calcium salt of saccharin. The molecular formula of this calcium salt is $Ca(C_8H_4NSO_3)_2$. Calculate the molarity of this solution.

7.28   Calculate the millimoles of sodium ion in 11.65 mL of 0.150M sodium carbonate.

7.29   Calculate the volume of 0.256M hydrochloric acid that would contain 36.5 millimoles of acid.

7.30   What volume of 15M HNO_3 is needed to prepare 1.65 L of 6.0M HNO_3?

7.31   What volume of 0.351M sodium hydroxide can be prepared from 35.0 mL of 4.15M NaOH?

7.32   What is the molarity of the final solution if 58.3 mL of 12M HCl is diluted to 11.5 L?

Calculations involving concentrations (Section 7.4)

7.33   What is the concentration of hydrochloric acid solution if 25.0 mL of it reacts exactly with 33.5 mL of 0.103M silver nitrate?

7.34   What is the concentration of a solution of sulfuric acid if 15.0 mL of this solution reacts completely with 26.2 mL of 0.125M potassium hydroxide solution?

7.35   Calculate the molarity of a sodium hydroxide solution, given that 23.90 mL of this solution reacts completely with 25.0 mL of 0.215M hydrochloric acid.

Titration (Section 7.5)

7.36   What are the requirements of a titration?

7.37   Using the following data, calculate the molarity of the hydrochloric acid solution.

Molarity of NaOH = 0.132M
Volume of hydrochloric acid samples: 25.0 mL
Buret reading for sodium hydroxide:

	Trial I	Trial II	Trial III
Final reading	26.14 mL	34.56 mL	44.25 mL
Initial reading	1.98 mL	10.36 mL	20.13 mL

7.38 Given the following data, calculate the concentration of the sulfuric acid solution.

Volume of acid samples: 10.0 mL
Concentration of KOH: 0.987M
Buret readings for KOH:

	Trial I	Trial II	Trial III
Final reading	35.62 mL	27.89 mL	23.76 mL
Initial reading	13.87 mL	6.01 mL	1.87 mL

Colligative properties (Section 7.6)

7.39 What is a colligative property? Explain why the vapor pressure of a pure liquid is greater than the vapor pressure of a solution in which that liquid is the solvent.

7.40 Which of the following will have the highest boiling point: 0.1M glucose, 1.0M glucose, or 10.0M glucose? Why?

7.41 The following solutions are all 0.1M. Which will have the highest boiling point?
  a. sodium chloride **b.** potassium sulfate **c.** ethyl alcohol

7.42 Which of the following 0.20M solutions will have the lowest freezing point? Explain your choice.
  a. sodium sulfate **b.** sucrose (covalent)
  c. aluminum phosphate

Solutions, colloids, and suspensions (Sections 7.1 and 7.7) General Problems

7.43 How does a colloid differ from a solution?

7.44 Give several examples of colloids. Tell what two phases are in each.

7.45 What is osmosis? Explain how osmosis works to send sap up within a tree.

7.46 What is dialysis? How does it differ from osmosis?

7.47 A solution is prepared by dissolving 16.0 g sodium hydroxide in 750 mL water. If 25 mL of this solution reacts with 40.9 mL of a solution of hydrochloric acid, what is the molarity of the hydrochloric acid solution?

7.48 What volume of carbon dioxide measured at 25°C and 0.752 atm is obtained by the reaction of 45.0 g calcium carbonate with 165 mL of 0.215M hydrochloric acid?

7.49   What mass of silver is obtained when 5.0 g copper is added to 125 mL of 0.555M silver nitrate?

7.50   75 g of pure sodium chloride is added to 125 mL water at 25°C. Is the resulting solution saturated or unsaturated? The mixture is filtered and added to 1.5 L of 0.125M silver nitrate. What weight of silver nitrate is precipitated?

7.51   What mass of sodium hydroxide is needed to prepare a solution in which the hydroxide ion concentration is 0.205M?

The Osmolality of Body Fluids

In a healthy person, the kidneys have several functions: to purge body fluids of toxic substances; to keep the body's volume of extracellular fluid constant; and to keep the body's concentration of solutes, such as sodium and bicarbonate ions, creatinine, and glucose, within a healthful range. Disorders of kidney function are among the most common in clinical medicine. Evaluation of kidney function in, for example, postsurgical patients, newborns, and patients in a comatose state must be accomplished rapidly on small samples, with minimal trauma for the patients. This can be accomplished by urinalysis or by analysis of extracellular fluid.

Traditionally, the intitial evaluation of kidney function has been based on the specific gravity of urine. However, specific gravity depends on the total mass of the material dissolved in a unit volume. Specific gravity does not really tell the concentration of the urine, due to the large differences in mass among typical solutes. The mass of a mole of sodium ions (23 g) is very different from the mass of a mole of glucose molecules (180 g) or of albumin (68,500 g). Because of these problems, tests on body fluids that measure the fluids' osmolality, not their specific gravity, are often preferred.

Osmolality measures the total number of particles in a kilogram of solvent. Osmolality depends only on the number of particles present, not their mass. Osmolality (O) is expressed as osmoles (moles of particles) per kilogram of solvent (Os/kg), or as milliosmoles per kilogram of solvent (mOs/kg). The difference between the freezing point of a solution and of the pure solvent in the solution is used to determine osmolality. Freezing-point lowering is one of the colligative properties of solutions. In aqueous solution, one mole of particles, regardless of mass or charge, lowers the freezing point from $0.00°C$ to $-1.86°C$. Apparatus has been developed, an osmometer, which can measure, in a few seconds and to $0.001°C$, the freezing point of a 0.02-mL sample. An osmometer is calibrated using sodium chloride solutions of known osmolality (mol ions/kg water) and reads directly in mOs/kg water.

In a healthy person, the osmolality of serum (ECF) is $280-300$ mOs/kg fluid water. Of this, about 140 mOs/kg is contributed by sodium ions and by molecules such as glucose and urea. Solutions that are isotonic with body fluids, such as 5% dextrose solutions or normal saline solution, are prepared to have the same osmolality as body fluids. One speaks of the tonicity of fluids: a hypertonic solution has a higher osmolality than normal body fluids do; a hypotonic solution has lower-than-normal osmolality. Normal tonicity is maintained by close regulation of renal excretion of water, which in turn depends on circulating levels of the posterior pituitary hormone vasopressin (antidiuretic hormone). A $1-2\%$ change in plasma osmolality will suppress or stimulate thirst and vasopressin secretion. This control permits enormous variation in fluid intake ($0.5-25$ L/day) without alteration in plasma. If disturbances exist in kidney function or vasopressin secretion, the urinary diluting and concentrating mechanisms fail and abnormalities of body tonicity appear.

Serum osmolality alone can indicate problems. Hyperosmolality (>295 mOs/kg) is most often due to alcohol ingestion. Hyperosmolality may also be due to diabetes insipidus and other causes of increased sodium ions in the serum. The serum of mildly comatose patients has an osmolality greater than 365 mOs/kg. Plasma hypo-osmolality indicates wholly different conditions, such as stroke, concussion, and adrenal disease.

The blood levels of sodium, glucose, and blood urea nitrogen (BUN) can be used to predict serum osmolality, using the equation

$$O_{calc'd} = Na(186) + \frac{BUN}{2.8} + \frac{glucose}{18}$$

In healthy persons, the measured osmolality is approximately the same as the calculated value. If the measured osmolality is considerably higher than what has been calculated, severe liver failure, poisoning, or severe dehydration should be suspected. Marked elevations have also been observed in patients in traumatic shock. If the difference decreases, prognosis for recovery is good; if it continues, prognosis is ominous. The elevated osmolality in such cases is caused by the continued presence in the plasma of abnormal metabolites that are not detectable by routine laboratory tests. Failure to remove these metabolites has proved fatal to human beings and animals.

Urine osmolality by itself is not useful for diagnosis unless water intake has been controlled, for the concentration of the solute depends on total volume of solution. However, urine osmolality combined with water restriction is a remarkably sensitive test of renal function. After a 14-hr fluid fast, normal urine osmolality should be greater than 800 mOs/kg. A range of 600–800 mOs/kg implies minimal kidney impairment; 400–600 mOs/kg, moderate impairment; and less than 400, severe impairment. This impairment may exist even though other tests are normal. The ratio of urine osmolality to serum osmolality also gives useful information. When kidneys are functioning normally, they concentrate the solutes. In such cases, the urine osmolality should be greater than serum osmolality, usually by a factor of 3 or more. In acute renal failure, the urine osmolality approaches serum osmolality. In untreated diabetes insipidus, urine osmolality is less than serum osmolality.

This mini-essay has touched only briefly on the usefulness of osmolality data in clinical evaluation of patients. It is remarkable that so much can be learned from a few freezing points measured quickly in the lab or at the patient's bedside. Osmolality is indeed a powerful tool.

Sources

Andreoli, T. E., Grantham, J. J., and Rector, F. C., Jr. 1977. *Disturbances in Body Fluid Osmolality.* Bethesda, Md.: American Physiological Society.

Duarte, C. G. 1980. *Renal Function Tests.* Boston: Little, Brown.

Wallach, J. 1978. *Interpretation of Diagnostic Tests.* 3d ed. Boston: Little, Brown.

8 Reaction Rates and Chemical Equilibrium

Thus far we have written equations for reactions, calculated the amounts of reactants needed to form a given amount of product, and measured the enthalpy change. We have observed that some reactions are exothermic, releasing heat energy as they occur, and others are endothermic, requiring the input of heat energy. We have up to this point assumed that a reaction occurs as soon as the reactants are mixed. Some reactions do begin immediately and are completed rapidly. Reactions between ions, such as neutralization or precipitation, do take place as soon as the reactants are combined. Other reactions require added energy to get started. We know that gasoline burns. In addition, we know that gasoline may be stored for years in contact with oxygen of the air without a resulting fire. Combustion does not take place until energy, such as a spark, is added. Some reactions occur easily in one direction at some temperatures, and equally easily in the opposite direction at other temperatures. Whereas ice begins melting immediately at room temperature, water begins freezing immediately at temperatures below 0°C. Obviously, we need to extend our study of reactions to explain these various phenomena.

8.1 Requirements for a Reaction

What is happening at the molecular level when a reaction takes place? Bonds between the atoms in the reacting molecules break, and new bonds form to combine the atoms in a different way. For this to happen, the reacting molecules must collide. This means that together they must have enough kinetic energy (energy of motion) to overcome the repulsion between the clouds of electrons that surround the molecules. As the two reacting molecules collide, they must be oriented so that those atoms that will be bonded together in the product are next to each other. Without this **orientation**, the molecules will retreat from the collision without reacting (Figure 8.1). A collision that takes place with enough energy and with the correct molecular orientation is called an effective collision. Needless to say, all collisions are not effective.

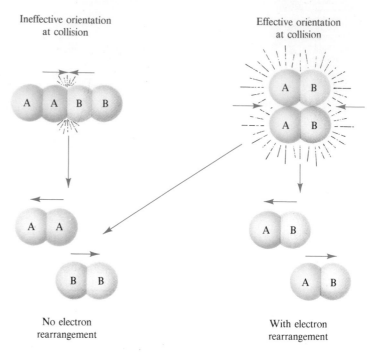

Figure 8.1 For a reaction between molecules to occur, the molecules must be correctly oriented when they collide.

8.2 The Course of a Reaction

Figure 8.2 plots the energy changes that take place as a reaction takes place. The initial average energy of the reactants is indicated at the left side of each graph. If molecules are to collide effectively, they must have more than the average energy. They must have enough to overcome the repulsive forces between molecules. This added amount of energy, the **activation energy**, is the difference between the initial energy and the energy at the peak of each graph. Molecules having that energy can collide, and if they are correctly oriented at collision, their bonds may break and the new bonds of the products will form. As the new bonds form, energy is released, leaving the product molecules with the average energy shown at the end of the graph at the right.

If the energy released is less than the activation energy, so that there is a net absorption of energy, the reaction is endothermic. A graph of an endothermic reaction is shown in Figure 8.2(a). If the energy released is greater than the activation energy, so that there is a net release of energy, the reaction is exothermic. A graph of an exothermic reaction is shown in Figure 8.2(b). Remember that of all the molecules present, only some will collide, and of those collisions, only some are effective and result in reactions.

This picture of a reaction is analogous to riding a bicycle over a mountain pass. The activation energy of the reaction is comparable with the energy needed to pedal to the top of the pass. The energy released by the rearrangement of

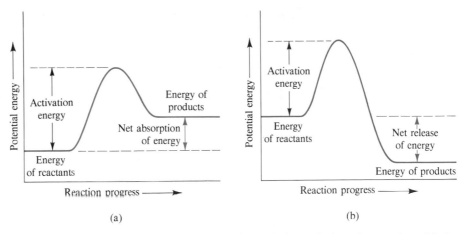

Figure 8.2 Energy changes during a reaction. (a) An endothermic reaction. (b) An exothermic reaction.

bonds is comparable with energy gained in coasting down from the top of the pass to the floor of the next valley. If this second valley is higher than the one you started from, the energy gained in coasting down is less than the energy expended in pedaling up. This corresponds to an endothermic reaction, where there is a net absorption of energy. If the second valley is lower than the one you started from, you gain more energy coasting down than was used pedaling up. This corresponds to an exothermic reaction, which results in a net release of energy.

8.3 The Rate of a Reaction

The **rate of a reaction** measures how fast the concentrations of the reactants decrease or how fast the concentrations of the products increase. The rate of a reaction is different from its **spontaneity**. In descriptions of chemical reactions, spontaneity has no connotation of speed; it refers only to whether the reaction will occur as the equation is written and at the specified temperature. The reaction of hydrogen with oxygen is a spontaneous reaction at 298 K:

$$H_2(g) + \tfrac{1}{2}O_2(g) \longrightarrow H_2O(g)$$

But a mixture of the two gases can be kept for years at room temperature (298 K) with only imperceptible amounts of water being formed. Only when more energy is added does reaction take place with a measurable rate.

A. Changing the Rate of a Reaction

A reaction forms products more rapidly if the conditions under which the reaction occurs are changed so that more molecules have enough energy to reach the peak of either of the graphs in Figure 8.2. There are three ways to increase the size of this set of molecules.

1. Increase the Concentration of Reactant Molecules

The more molecules present in the reaction vessel, the more likely a collision. We can increase the number of molecules by increasing the concentration of the reactants. If the reactants are both gases, increasing the pressure decreases the volume and brings the molecules closer together, increasing the likelihood of collision.

2. Increase the Number of Molecules with Enough Energy to React by Increasing the Temperature of the Reaction

The rate of a reaction increases if the number of molecules with enough energy to provide the activation energy of the reaction increases.

Figure 8.3 shows the distribution of energies in a collection of molecules at two different temperatures. (Notice that this is the same distribution we considered in Chapter 6; see Figure 6.4.) In Figure 8.3, molecules with an energy greater than point *A* are energetic enough to provide the activation energy necessary for collision. The shaded area under each graph represents the number of molecules at that temperature that have an energy greater than point *A*. The shaded area is much larger under the higher temperature curve. Therefore, at the higher temperature, there are more collisions and the reaction proceeds faster. At lower temperatures, these results are reversed and the reaction is slower.

We store food in a refrigerator because of the **effect of temperature** on reaction rates. The rates of the reactions that lead to food spoilage are decreased considerably by cooling the food from room temperature to the temperature in a refrigerator. The rates of these reactions are decreased even further by storing food in a freezer. Recent developments in low-temperature surgery have resulted from the application of this principle. When the patient is cooled, metabolic reactions are slowed and surgery can be performed more deliberately, with less trauma to the patient.

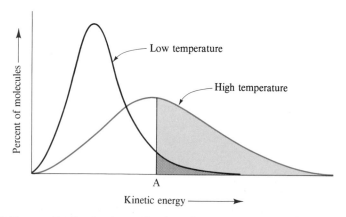

Figure 8.3 Energy distribution in a collection of molecules at two different temperatures.

3. Lower the Activation Energy Required for Reaction

A certain amount of energy, the activation energy, is necessary for reaction. If the activation energy could be lowered (in our cycling analogy, if the pass were not quite so far above the first valley), more molecules could react. In Figure 8.4, the color line represents a lower activation energy. How can the activation energy of a reaction be lowered? Just as another pass between the valleys might be lower than what was originally used, another pathway for the reaction may have a lower activation energy.

A catalyst can provide such an alternative pathway. A **catalyst** is a substance that, when added to a reaction mixture, increases the rate of the overall reaction, yet is recovered unchanged after the reaction is complete. Suppose a substance, C, is added to a reaction mixture. If the product forms faster in the presence of C than in its absence and C is recovered unchanged, then C is a catalyst for the reaction. The color line in Figure 8.4 shows the energy changes for the same reaction indicated by the black line, except that a catalyst is present. There is still an activation energy, but it is less than in the uncatalyzed reaction.

There are many examples of catalysts. Since the mid-1970s, many automobile exhaust systems have been manufactured with catalysts for the reaction

$$2CO(g) + O_2(g) \longrightarrow 2CO_2(g)$$

When no catalyst is present, this reaction requires a very high temperature and does not occur significantly at normal exhaust temperatures. The well-being of the public requires that cars do not spew out large amounts of carbon monoxide. Introducing a catalyst in the exhaust system of the car makes possible the oxidation of carbon monoxide to carbon dioxide at lower-exhaust temperatures, with considerable improvement in air quality.

The **enzymes** that trigger biological processes are catalysts. Enzymes have enormous power to change the rates of chemical reactions. In fact, most of the

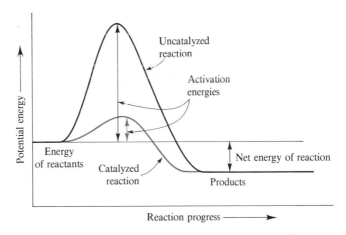

Figure 8.4 Effect of a catalyst on activation energy. The black line represents energy changes in an uncatalyzed reaction. The color line shows the energy changes for the same reaction in the presence of a catalyst.

reactions that occur so readily in the living cell would, in the absence of enzymes, occur too slowly to support life. For example, the enzyme carbonic anhydrase catalyzes the reaction of carbon dioxide and water to form carbonic acid:

$$CO_2 + H_2O \overset{\text{carbonic anhydrase}}{\rightleftharpoons} H_2CO_3$$

Carbonic anhydrase increases the rate of this reaction to almost 10^7 times the rate of the uncatalyzed reaction. Red blood cells are especially rich in this enzyme. They can thus absorb carbon dioxide as it is produced in the body and transport it back to the lungs, where it is released as one of the waste products of the body.

Catalysts, whether inorganic, like those in automotive emission control systems, or organic, like the enzymes of living systems, are so remarkably effective because they provide alternative pathways for reactions, pathways that have lower energies of activation.

4. Other Factors Affecting the Rate of Reaction

a. Surface area The rate of a reaction that is to take place between reactants in two different physical states is increased if there is an increase in the surface area of the reactant in the more condensed state. Such a reaction is that of a gas or a liquid with a solid or of a gas with a liquid. Consider the reaction between oxygen of the air with cellulose, a reaction we call burning. Cellulose is the main component of wood and of flour. A match will ignite twigs but will not ignite a large log. Further, if the cellulose is ground to a fine powder (enormous surface area) as in flour, a spark provides enough energy to start a very rapid reaction, that is, an explosion. This is the reason for the very strict regulations preventing static electricity in flour mills.

Similarly, the reaction between a gas and a liquid will be more rapid if the liquid is spread in small drops as a spray through which the gas passes than if the gas is passed over the surface of a large body of the liquid.

b. Light Some reactions, classified as **photochemical reactions**, are very sensitive to light. A mixture of the reactants in such a reaction will be stable in the dark indefinitely. When the mixture is exposed to light of the correct wavelength, the reaction occurs, often explosively.

The reaction of hydrogen with chlorine is one such reaction:

$$H_2(g) + Cl_2(g) \xrightarrow{\text{dark}} \text{no reaction}$$

$$H_2(g) + Cl_2(g) \xrightarrow{\text{light}} 2HCl(g)$$

The decomposition of nitrogen dioxide into nitrogen monoxide and atomic oxygen is another photochemical reaction. Small amounts of nitrogen dioxide are found in exhaust gases from gasoline engines. Its decomposition on bright sunny days triggers the series of reactions that causes smog.

Example 8.1

The decomposition of hydrogen peroxide is exothermic. The reaction is catalyzed by iodide ion. The equation for the reaction is

$$2H_2O_2(l) \xrightarrow{\text{I}} 2H_2O(l) + O_2(g)$$

Sketch a possible graph for this reaction twice, first without a catalyst and then with a catalyst. On both graphs show the energy of the reactants and products and the enthalpy of the reaction.

☐ *Solution*

a. The uncatalyzed reaction: Because the reaction is exothermic, the energy of the products will be lower than the energy of the reactants. The shape of the graph will be like that in Figure 8.5(a).

b. The catalyzed reaction: Because this is the same reaction as in (a), the energy of the reactants and the energy of the products are the same as in Figure 8.5(b). Because the reaction is catalyzed, the activation energy will be lower in this graph.

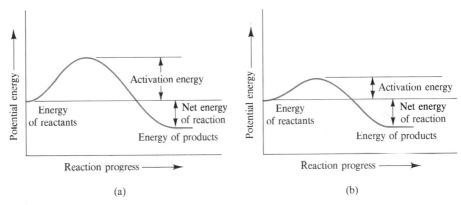

(a)   (b)

Figure 8.5 Possible energy plot for decomposition of H_2O_2 (Example 8.1): (a) uncatalyzed reaction; (b) catalyzed reaction.

Problem 8.1

Formation of ammonia from nitrogen and hydrogen is an exothermic reaction. It can be catalyzed with heavy metal oxides. Graph this reaction (a) uncatalyzed and (b) catalyzed. On both graphs show the energy of the reactants, the energy of the products, the energy of activation, and the enthalpy of the reaction.

8.4 Chemical Equilibrium

A. Definition of Chemical Equilibrium

Many chemical reactions are reversible; that is, the products of the reaction can combine to re-form the reactants. An example of a reversible reaction is that of hydrogen with iodine to form hydrogen iodide:

$$H_2(g) + I_2(g) \rightleftharpoons 2HI(g)$$

We can study this reversible reaction by placing hydrogen and iodine in a reaction vessel and then measuring the concentrations of H_2, I_2, and HI at

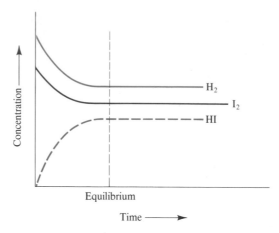

Figure 8.6 Concentration changes during the reversible reaction as it proceeds toward equilibrium.

various times after the reactants are mixed. Figure 8.6 is a plot of the concentrations of reactants and product of this reaction against time. The concentration of HI increases very rapidly at first, then more slowly, and finally, after the time indicated by the vertical line marked "Equilibrium," remains constant. Similarly, the concentrations of H_2 and I_2 are high at the start of the reaction but decrease rapidly at first, and then more slowly. Finally, they too become constant at the equilibrium line.

If this reaction were not reversible, the concentrations of hydrogen and iodine would have continued to decrease and the concentration of hydrogen iodide to increase. This does not happen. Instead, as soon as any molecules of hydrogen iodide are formed, some decompose to hydrogen and iodide. Two reactions are taking place simultaneously: the formation of hydrogen iodide and its decomposition. When the concentrations of all these components become constant (at the line marked equilibrium in Figure 8.6), the rate of the forward reaction ($H_2 + I_2 \longrightarrow 2HI$) must equal the rate of the reverse reaction ($2HI \longrightarrow H_2 + I_2$). A state of **dynamic chemical equilibrium** has then been reached, in which two opposing reactions are proceeding at equal rates, with no net changes in concentration.

We have met this criterion for equilibrium before. In the equilibrium between a liquid and its vapor, the rate of vaporization equals the rate of condensation. In the equilibrium of a saturated solution with undissolved solute, the rate of dissolution equals the rate of precipitation. In all these, the situation is not static; two opposing changes are occurring at equal rates.

B. Characteristics of Chemical Equilibrium

1. Equal Rates

At equilibrium, the rate of the forward reaction equals the rate of the reverse reaction.

2. *Constant Concentrations*

At equilibrium, the concentrations of the substances participating in the equilibrium are constant. Although individual reactant molecules may be reacting to form product molecules and individual product molecules may be reacting to re-form the reactants, the concentrations of the reactants and the products remain constant.

C. The Equilibrium Constant

When a reaction is at equilibrium, there is a mathematical relationship between the concentrations of the components of the equilibrium that is known as the **equilibrium constant (K_{eq})**. For the reaction

$$H_2 + I_2 \rightleftharpoons 2HI$$

the equilibrium constant is

$$K_{eq} = \frac{[HI]^2}{[H_2][I_2]}$$

where [ ] means concentration in moles per liter. For the general equation

$$aA + bB \rightleftharpoons cC + dD$$

the equilibrium constant is

$$K_{eq} = \frac{[C]^c[D]^d}{[A]^a[B]^b}$$

In each of these expressions, the concentrations of the products of the reaction, each raised to a power equal to the coefficient of that product in the balanced equation for the reaction, are multiplied in the numerator. The concentrations of the reactants in the equation, each raised to a power equal to the coefficient of that reactant in the balanced equation, are multiplied in the denominator.

Example 8.2

☐ *Solution*

Write the equilibrium constant for the reaction

$$N_2(g) + 3H_2(g) \rightleftharpoons 2NH_3(g)$$

1. The numerator of the constant contains the product NH_3 enclosed in brackets to represent concentration and raised to the second power, because 2 is the coefficient in the equation:

$$[NH_3]^2$$

2. The denominator includes the reactants of the equation, N_2 and H_2, each enclosed in brackets. The nitrogen term is at the first power; the hydrogen term is raised to the third power:

$$[N_2][H_2]^3$$

3. The complete expression for the equilibrium constant is

$$K_{eq} = \frac{[NH_3]^2}{[N_2][H_2]^3}$$

Problem 8.2

Write the equilibrium constant for the reaction

$$2NO(g) + O_2(g) \rightleftharpoons 2NO_2(g)$$

The value of an equilibrium constant does not depend on how equilibrium was reached. Table 8.1 presents data on the hydrogen–iodine–hydrogen iodide equilibrium. It shows several different sets of initial concentrations and the accompanying concentrations at equilibrium. The value of the equilibrium constant is given for each experiment. Notice that the value of the equilibrium constant is the same, regardless of whether the initial material was hydrogen and iodine or hydrogen iodide and whether the components were present in equal or different concentrations.

The value of the equilibrium constant does depend on how the equation for the equilibrium is written. For example, the equilibrium constants given in Table 8.1 were calculated from the expression

$$K_{eq} = \frac{[HI]^2}{[H_2][I_2]} = 45.9$$

which is the equilibrium constant for the equation

$$H_2(g) + I_2(g) \rightleftharpoons 2HI(g)$$

If the equation for the H_2–I_2–HI equilibrium is written

$$2HI(g) \rightleftharpoons H_2(g) + I_2(g)$$

then the equilibrium constant becomes

$$K_{eq} = \frac{[H_2][I_2]}{[HI]^2} = 2.18 \times 10^{-2}$$

The two equilibrium constants are related to each other:

$$2.18 \times 10^{-2} = 1/45.9$$

The value of an equilibrium constant does change with a change in temperature. The equilibrium constant for the $H_2 + I_2 \rightleftharpoons 2HI$ reaction is 45.9 only

Table 8.1
Hydrogen iodide equilibrium constant.

Original Concentration (mol/L)			Final Concentration (mol/L)			Equilibrium Constant $\frac{[HI]^2}{[H_2][I_2]}$
[H_2]	[I_2]	[HI]	[H_2]	[I_2]	[HI]	
1.0	1.0	0	0.228	0.228	1.544	45.9
0	0	2.0	0.228	0.228	1.544	45.9
1.0	2.0	3.0	0.316	1.316	4.368	45.9

at 490°C. At 445°C, it is 64. At other temperatures, the equilibrium constant for this equation has other values—increasing as the temperature decreases, decreasing as the temperature increases.

The equilibrium constant is a very useful concept for it allows the prediction and calculation of the concentrations of the various species present in a reaction mixture at equilibrium. This is important in determining the acidity of a solution, the solubility of a sparingly soluble salt, how far a reaction goes toward completion, and other similar data.

8.5 Shifting Equilibria; Le Chatelier's Principle

A system in equilibrium is a special situation, where everything is in balance. However, things rarely stay in balance; changes occur that shift the balance and the equilibrium involved. Recall the equilibrium that exists between a liquid and its vapor in a closed container:

$$Liquid \rightleftharpoons vapor$$

At a given temperature, the vapor has a particular pressure. If the temperature is increased, it has a higher pressure. Increasing the temperature causes the equilibrium to shift to the right toward a higher concentration of vapor, but if the system is maintained at that higher temperature, equilibrium will once more be established.

It is possible to predict how a particular stress or change in conditions will affect an equilibrium. Such predictions are based on a principle first stated by a French chemist named Le Chatelier (1850–1936). In 1888, Le Chatelier proposed the following:

When stress or change in conditions is applied to a system in equilibrium, the system shifts to absorb the effect of that stress.

It is important in considering this principle to realize that equilibrium is *not* present while the change is taking place. The sequence is: the system is in equilibrium, the stress is applied, the system changes to absorb the stress, and finally equilibrium is again present.

A. Effect of Concentration Changes on Equilibria

Of the various stresses that chemical equilibria are subjected to, **concentration changes** are most important to us physiologically, because biological reactions usually take place at constant temperature and pressure. Under normal conditions, our bodies are not subjected to more than slight changes in temperature and pressure, but they are subject to changes in concentration. Consider how a change in concentration of one of the reactants or products affects the hydrogen–iodine–hydrogen iodide equilibrium. Two reactions are proceeding simultaneously. The forward reaction

$$H_2 + I_2 \rightleftharpoons 2HI$$

is the combination of hydrogen and iodine, and the reverse reaction is the decomposition of hydrogen iodide. Le Chatelier's principle tells us that increasing the concentration of one of the components of an equilibrium mixture favors the reaction that consumes that component. Decreasing the concentration of a component favors the reaction that produces that component.

Suppose you have a flask containing hydrogen, iodine, and hydrogen iodide, all at equilibrium concentrations at 490°C. If we inject some iodine into the flask, the forward reaction, which consumes iodine, will be favored. That reaction will proceed more rapidly than the reverse reaction until the imbalance is corrected and the ratio of concentrations again matches the equilibrium constant. The new concentrations of iodine and of hydrogen iodide will be greater than the original concentrations of these substances, and the concentration of hydrogen will be less.

In summary, if the concentration of one of the components of an equilibrium is changed, the concentrations of the other components of the equilibrium will change to compensate for that change. Or according to Le Chatelier's principle: When a stress (such as a change in concentration) is applied to a system at equilibrium, the system shifts (all the concentrations change) to relieve that stress.

Example 8.3

Consider the equilibrium

$$PCl_3(g) + Cl_2(g) \rightleftharpoons PCl_5(g) \qquad \Delta H = -22.1 \text{ kcal}$$

Express the equilibrium constant for this reaction. Predict how the equilibrium position will be affected by (a) an increase in concentration of PCl_3, and (b) a decrease in concentration of Cl_2.

☐ *Solution*

The equilibrium constant for the reaction is

$$K_{eq} = \frac{[PCl_5]}{[PCl_3][Cl_2]}$$

a. The reaction that consumes phosphorus trichloride is the forward reaction. Increasing the rate of this reaction decreases the concentration of chlorine and increases the concentration of phosphorus pentachloride. The equilibrium will shift right.

b. The reaction that produces chlorine is the one toward the left (the reverse reaction). If the concentration of chlorine is reduced, the rate of this reaction increases. The equilibrium shifts to produce chlorine and phosphorus trichloride. When equilibrium is reestablished, there is less phosphorus pentachloride and more phosphorus trichloride present. Or, decreasing the concentration of chlorine decreases the rate of the forward reaction. Therefore, when equilibrium is reestablished, there is more phosphorus trichloride and less phosphorus pentachloride.

Problem 8.3

Consider the equilibrium

$$H_2(g) + CO_2(g) \rightleftharpoons H_2O(g) + CO(g) \qquad \Delta H = 9.8 \text{ kcal}$$

a. Write the equilibrium constant for this reaction.
b. Predict how the equilibrium position will be affected by an increase in the concentration of carbon dioxide, and by a decrease in the concentration of hydrogen.

B. Effect of Temperature Changes on Equilibria

A change in temperature is a stress on a system in equilibrium. It changes the rate of both reactions and also changes the value of the equilibrium constant.

In each equilibrium, two reactions proceed simultaneously, one forward and one reverse. One of these is endothermic ($\Delta H > 0$), and one is exothermic ($\Delta H < 0$). When the equilibrium is shown as an equation, the enthalpy term refers only to the forward reaction. For example, in the hydrogen iodide equilibrium, the forward reaction is exothermic. This is shown as

$$H_2(g) + I_2(g) \rightleftharpoons 2HI(g) \qquad \Delta H = -12.2 \text{ kcal}$$

When the temperature of an equilibrium mixture is increased, the rate of both reactions increases (see Section 8.3) but the rate of the endothermic reaction (the reaction that absorbs the added energy) is increased more. For the hydrogen iodide equilibrium, an increase in temperature favors the endothermic reverse reaction. When the system returns to equilibrium, the hydrogen iodide concentration will be smaller and the concentrations of hydrogen and iodine larger. The equilibrium constant will be changed:

$$\text{At } 445°C \quad K_{eq} = \frac{[HI]^2}{[H_2][I_2]} = 64$$

$$\text{At } 490°C \quad K_{eq} = \frac{[HI]^2}{[H_2][I_2]} = 45.9$$

Example 8.4

Explain how an increase in temperature will affect the equilibrium

$$PCl_3(g) + Cl_2(g) \rightleftharpoons PCl_5(g) \qquad \Delta H = -22.1 \text{ kcal}$$

☐ *Solution*

In this equilibrium, the forward reaction (to form phosphorus pentachloride) is exothermic; the reverse reaction (to consume phosphorus pentachloride) is endothermic. An increase in temperature favors the endothermic reaction and the equilibrium will shift to the left to absorb the added energy. This increase in temperature also increases the rate of both reactions. The overall result will be a shift to the left.

Problem 8.4

Explain how an increase in temperature will affect the equilibrium

$$H_2(g) + CO_2(g) \rightleftharpoons H_2O(g) + CO(g) \qquad \Delta H = -9.8 \text{ kcal}$$

C. Effect of Catalysts on Equilibria

A catalyst changes the rate of a reaction by providing an alternate pathway with lower energy of activation. The lower-energy pathway is available to both the forward and the reverse reactions of the equilibrium. The addition of a catalyst to a system in equilibrium does not favor one reaction over the other. Instead, it increases equally the rates of both the forward and the reverse reactions. The rate at which equilibrium is reached is increased, but the relative concentrations of reactants and products at equilibrium, and hence the equilibrium constant, are unchanged.

Example 8.5

Given the equilibrium

$$PBr_3(g) + Br_2(g) \rightleftharpoons PBr_5(g) \qquad \Delta H = -36.1 \text{ kcal}$$

a. Write the equilibrium constant for this reaction.
b. How will the equilibrium shift if the temperature is increased?
c. How will the equilibrium shift if more bromine is added to the reaction mixture? What will happen to the concentration of phosphorus tribromide, PBr_3?
d. How will the addition of a catalyst affect this equilibrium?
e. Is the value of K_{eq} increased, decreased, or unchanged by the change in conditions in parts (b), (c), and (d)?

☐ *Solution*   a.
$$K_{eq} = \frac{[PBr_5]}{[PBr_3][Br_2]}$$

b. The forward reaction is exothermic; the reverse reaction is endothermic. Increasing the temperature will increase the rate of both reactions, with a greater increase in the rate of the reverse reaction, thus changing the equilibrium constant. The concentration of phosphorus pentabromide will decrease; that of bromine and phosphorus tribromide will increase.
c. If more bromine is added to the reaction mixture, the rate of the forward reaction, the one that consumes the added bromine, will be increased. There will be more phosphorus pentabromide and less phosphorus tribromide.
d. The addition of a catalyst will change neither any concentration nor the value of K_{eq}. The rate of both equations will increase.
e. The equilibrium constant K_{eq} will not be changed by the changes in conditions of parts (c) and (d). It will be decreased by the temperature increase in (b). The reverse reaction is endothermic and favored by the increase in temperature. The reverse reaction uses up phosphorus tribromide; thus the numerator of the equilibrium constant is decreased, the denominator increased, and the value of K_{eq} decreases.

Problem 8.5

Given the equilibrium

$$2H_2O(g) \rightleftharpoons 2H_2(g) + O_2(g) \qquad \Delta H = 57.6 \text{ kcal/mol } H_2O$$

a. Write the equilibrium constant for this reaction.

b. In what way will the addition of more O_2 affect this equilibrium?
c. In what way will an increase in temperature affect this equilibrium?
d. What effect will the addition of a catalyst have on the equilibrium?
e. Which of the three changes in parts (b), (c), and (d) affect the value of K_{eq}?

Key Terms and Concepts

activation energy (8.2)

catalyst (8.3A3)

chemical equilibrium (8.4A)

concentration changes (8.5A)

dynamic chemical
  equilibrium (8.4A)

effect of temperature
  (8.3A2)

enzyme (8.3A3)

equilibrium constant (K_{eq}) (8.4C)

Le Chatelier's principle (8.5)

molecular orientation (8.1)

photochemical reaction (8.3A4)

rate of a reaction (8.3)

spontaneity (8.3)

Problems

The course of a reaction (Section 8.2)

8.6 For the reaction

$$\tfrac{1}{2}H_2(g) + \tfrac{1}{2}Cl(g) \rightleftharpoons HCl(g) \qquad \Delta H = -22.0 \text{ kcal}$$

a. Show how the molecules must be oriented at collision for the reaction to occur.
b. Plot the course of the reaction.

8.7 Plot the possible course of a reaction against energy for:
a. an exothermic reaction
b. an endothermic reaction
c. an exothermic reaction in the presence of a catalyst

8.8 Label the activation energy and the enthalpy in each part of Problem 8.7

Rate of a reaction (Section 8.3)

8.9 Explain why increasing the concentration of the reactants may increase the rate of a reaction.

8.10 Describe how a catalyst can change the rate of a reaction.

8.11 Draw a curve showing the normal distribution of energy in a collection of molecules. Draw another curve showing how this distribution of energy changes as the temperature is increased. Why does the rate of a reaction increase with increased temperature?

8.12 What role do enzymes play in biological reactions?

8.13 Consider this reaction and tell what changes would increase the rate of the reaction.

$$4NH_3(g) + 5O_2(g) \rightleftharpoons 4NO(g) + 6H_2O(g) \qquad \Delta H = -384 \text{ kcal}$$

*Chemical
equilibrium
(Section 8.4)*

8.14 **a.** What is the equilibrium constant for the hypothetical reaction $AB \rightleftharpoons A + B$ if the concentrations at equilibrium are $[AB] = 2$, $[A] = 2$, $[B] = 2$?

b. After a stress has been absorbed by this reaction, $[A] = 8$ and $[AB] = 16$. What is the new concentration of B?

8.15 For the reaction

$$2Sb(s) + 3Cl_2(g) \rightleftharpoons 2SbCl_3(g) \qquad \Delta H = -75.3 \text{ kcal/mol } SbCl_3$$

a. Draw a graph showing the progress of the forward reaction.
b. Draw a graph showing the progress of the reverse reaction.
c. Write the equilibrium constant expression.

*Shifting an
equilibrium
(Section 8.5)*

8.16 The Haber process for the industrial preparation of ammonia uses the reaction

$$N_2(g) + 3H_2(g) \rightleftharpoons 2NH_3(g) \qquad \Delta H = -22 \text{ kcal/mol } NH_3$$

a. Write the equilibrium constant for this reaction.
b. How will increased concentration of nitrogen change the concentration of ammonia?
c. How will adding a catalyst change the equilibrium?
d. How will increased temperature change the concentration of ammonia?

8.17 One of the components of smog is the brown gas nitrogen dioxide, NO_2. It participates in the equilibrium

$$2NO_2 \rightleftharpoons N_2O_4 \qquad \Delta H = -14.7 \text{ kcal}$$

Dinitrogen tetroxide, N_2O_4, is colorless. Is smog apt to be darker in winter or in summer?

8.18 Consider the equilibrium

$$2H_2O(g) + 2Cl_2(g) \rightleftharpoons 4HCl(g) + O_2(g) \qquad \Delta H = -28.7 \text{ kcal}$$

What will happen to the concentration of chlorine if:
a. the temperature is raised?
b. the concentration of HCl is increased?
c. the concentration of oxygen is decreased?
d. a catalyst is added to the system?

9

Acids and Bases

An understanding of the properties of acids and bases is essential preparation for learning the reactions of organic and biochemical molecules described in the remaining chapters of this text. Some of these properties have already been discussed. The differences between acids and bases were first introduced in Chapter 3. The reaction of an acid with a base was described in Chapter 5 and titration covered in Chapter 7. In this chapter we will review that material and, in addition, describe the nomenclature of acids, the Brønsted-Lowry acid-base definitions, and the equilibria present in the solution of a weak acid.

9.1 Definitions of Acids and Bases

A. Arrhenius Definitions

In Chapter 3 we defined an acid as a substance that releases hydrogen ions in aqueous solutions and a base as a substance that releases hydroxide ions in aqueous solution. Because this behavior depends on dissociation into ions and because the theory of ionization was first proposed by the Swedish chemist Svante Arrhenius (1859–1927), these definitions are frequently referred to as **Arrhenius definitions.**

B. Brønsted-Lowry Definitions

The Arrhenius definitions of acids and bases describe the characteristics of aqueous solutions of acids and bases. In 1923, T. M. Lowry in England and J. M. Brønsted in Denmark proposed a system that defines acids and bases in terms of how they react.

According to the **Brønsted-Lowry definitions,**

an *acid* is a proton (H^+) donor
a *base* is a proton (H^+) acceptor

Because a hydrogen ion consists of a nucleus containing a single proton, the terms *hydrogen ion* and *proton* are synonymous. These definitions somewhat change the nature of the substances that are acids or bases. The category of acids includes the Arrhenius acids as well as ions such as ammonium ion, NH_4^+, and bicarbonate ion, HCO_3^-. Among Brønsted-Lowry bases are the hydroxide ion, OH^-, the anion of any acid, and ammonia, NH_3. Many substances such as water, bicarbonate ion, and ammonia can act as either an acid or a base.

In this system, an acid reacts by donating a proton to a base. In doing so, the acid becomes its **conjugate base**. The original base becomes its **conjugate acid**. The general equation for a Brønsted-Lowry acid-base reaction is

$$HA + B^- \longrightarrow A^- + HB$$

$$\underset{acid_1}{} \quad \underset{base_2}{} \qquad \underset{\substack{conjugate \\ base_1}}{} \quad \underset{\substack{conjugate \\ acid_2}}{}$$

Note in the equation that the acid and its conjugate base both have the subscript 1 and the base and its conjugate acid have the subscript 2.

Example 9.1

a. Show how water acts as a Brønsted-Lowry acid when reacting with ammonia. Name the conjugate base of water and the conjugate acid of ammonia.
b. Show how water acts as a Brønsted-Lowry base in reacting with acetic acid. Name the conjugate acid of water and the conjugate base of acetic acid.

☐ *Solution*

a. The equation for this reaction is

$$H_2O + NH_3 \longrightarrow OH^- + NH_4^+$$

The conjugate base of water is the hydroxide ion. The conjugate acid of ammonia is the ammonium ion.
b. The equation for this reaction is

$$H_2O + HC_2H_3O_2 \longrightarrow H_3O^+ + C_2H_3O_2^-$$

The conjugate acid of water is the **hydronium ion**, H_3O^+. The conjugate base of acetic acid is the acetate ion.

Problem 9.1

a. Show how the bisulfide ion acts as a Brønsted-Lowry acid in reacting with the hydroxide ion. Name the conjugate base of the bisulfide ion and the conjugate acid of the hydroxide ion.
b. Show how the bisulfide ion acts as a Brønsted-Lowry base in reacting with hydrochloric acid. Name the conjugate acid of the bisulfide ion and the conjugate base of hydrochloric acid.

9.2 Nomenclature of Acids

The name of a metallic hydroxide combines the name of the metallic ion with the term *hydroxide*. Naming an acid is not so simple. Table 9.1 lists by name several common acids and the names of their anions.

Table 9.1
Some common
acids.

Acid	Molecular Formula	Anion Formed in Solution	Anion Name
hydrochloric acid	HCl	Cl^-	chloride
sulfuric acid	H_2SO_4	HSO_4^-	hydrogen sulfate (bisulfate)
	HSO_4^-	SO_4^{2-}	sulfate
sulfurous acid	H_2SO_3	HSO_3^-	hydrogen sulfite (bisulfite)
	HSO_3^-	SO_3^{2-}	sulfite
nitric acid	HNO_3	NO_3^-	nitrate
nitrous acid	HNO_2	NO_2^-	nitrite
phosphoric acid	H_3PO_4	$H_2PO_4^-$	dihydrogen phosphate
	$H_2PO_4^-$	HPO_4^{2-}	monohydrogen phosphate
	HPO_4^{2-}	PO_4^{3-}	phosphate
carbonic acid	H_2CO_3	HCO_3^-	hydrogen carbonate (bicarbonate)
	HCO_3^-	CO_3^{2-}	carbonate
acetic acid	$HC_2H_3O_2$	$C_2H_3O_2^-$	acetate
formic acid	$HCOOH$	$HCOO^-$	formate

An acid containing only hydrogen and a nonmetal is named hydro———ic acid; for example, HCl(aq) is hydrochloric acid, and H_2S (aq) is hydrosulfuric acid. Among the acids containing different numbers of oxygen atoms with the same nonmetal, the most common is named ———ic. Thus, H_2SO_4 is sulfuric acid, and HNO_3 is nitric acid. These names and formulas must be memorized.

The acid containing one fewer oxygen than the most common is named ———ous acid. Thus, H_2SO_3 is sulfurous acid, and HNO_2 is nitrous acid.

Occasionally one encounters an acid containing two fewer oxygen atoms than the most common. These are named hypo———ous acids. Thus, HClO is hypochlorous acid.

Acids containing carbon are named by a wholly different system. The system need not be learned now, but the formulas and names of a few of these acids should be memorized—namely, acetic acid, $HC_2H_3O_2$; carbonic acid, H_2CO_3; and formic acid, HCOOH.

Example 9.2

□ *Solution*

Give the formula and name of the acids that have the anions NO_2^-, F^-, $HCOO^-$. Name the anions.

NO_2^- is the anion of HNO_2. This formula contains one fewer oxygen than nitric acid. HNO_2 is then named nitrous acid and the anion is nitrite. F^- is the anion of HF, an acid containing no oxygen atoms. The acid is then named hydrofluoric acid, and the anion is fluoride. $HCOO^-$ is the anion of formic acid, and the anion is formate.

Problem 9.2   Give the formula and name of the acids that have the anions CO_3^{2-}, I^-, ClO_3^-. Name the anion.

9.3 Reactions of Acids

A. Neutralization

Neutralization is the reaction of an acid with a base. When Arrhenius acids and bases are used, the products of the reaction are a salt and water. The reaction of hydrochloric acid with sodium hydroxide is an example of a neutralization reaction:

$$HCl(aq) + NaOH(aq) \longrightarrow NaCl(aq) + H_2O(l)$$

hydrochloric   sodium   sodium   water
acid   hydroxide   chloride

In the Brønsted-Lowry system, an acid reacts with a base to form the conjugate base of the original acid and the conjugate acid of the original base as shown in the next equation.

$$HCl + CO_3^{2-} \longrightarrow HCO_3^- + Cl^-$$

acid$_1$ base$_2$ conjugate   conjugate
                  acid$_2$ base$_1$

B. With Metals

Acids react with some metals in displacement reactions (Section 5.3C) to form hydrogen gas and a salt, as in the reaction of zinc with sulfuric acid:

$$Zn(s) + H_2SO_4(aq) \longrightarrow ZnSO_4(aq) + H_2(g)$$

This is an oxidation-reduction reaction in which zinc is oxidized and hydrogen reduced.

Example 9.3   Write equations showing the reaction in water of hydrochloric acid with

a. sodium acetate   **b.** ammonia   **c.** magnesium

☐ *Solution*   **a.** $HCl(aq) + NaC_2H_3O_2(aq) \longrightarrow HC_2H_3O_2(aq) + NaCl(aq)$
b. $HCl(aq) + NH_3(aq) \longrightarrow NH_4^+(aq) + Cl^-(aq)$
c. $2HCl(aq) + Mg(s) \longrightarrow MgCl_2(aq) + H_2(g)$

Problem 9.3   Write equations showing the reaction in water of sulfuric acid with

a. potassium hydroxide   **b.** bicarbonate ion   **c.** zinc

9.4 Ionization

A. Weak and Strong Acids

Acids differ enormously in the extent to which they dissociate in aqueous solution into ions. Some acids, such as hydrochloric and nitric acids, are strong electrolytes, completely dissociated into ions in aqueous solution. These are known as **strong acids**.

Other acids, such as acetic acid and nitrous acid, are only partially dissociated in aqueous solution. These are weak electrolytes and are known as **weak acids**. The solution of a strong acid contains no acid molecules; the solution of a weak acid contains both molecules and ions (see Figure 9.1).

The ions of a weak acid tend to recombine to re-form molecules of the acid. We can show this in the ionization equation with a double arrow, meaning that the reaction is **reversible**, that it goes both ways. Some molecules are dissociating into ions; some ions are recombining to form molecules. Acetic acid is a weak acid; we show its ionization with a double arrow, meaning that a solution of acetic acid contains both molecules and ions.

$$HC_2H_3O_2 \rightleftarrows H^+ + C_2H_3O_2^-$$

It is customary in using a double arrow, to show a longer or heavier arrow in the direction of the predominant reaction. Thus in the ionization of a weak acid, where there are fewer ions than molecules, the longer arrow points toward the molecules.

Because the ions of a strong acid show no tendency to recombine, we show its ionization with a single arrow meaning that only the ions of the acid are present in its aqueous solutions. For the strong acid, nitric acid, the ionization would be shown as

$$HNO_3 \longrightarrow H^+ + NO_3^-$$

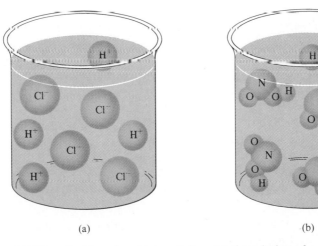

(a)   (b)

Figure 9.1 Strong and weak acids in solution: (a) the solution of a strong acid contains only ions; (b) the solution of a weak acid contains both molecules and ions.

In the Brønsted-Lowry system, a strong acid is one that easily donates its proton. The conjugate base of a strong Brønsted-Lowry acid is a **weak base**, one that has little affinity for a proton. Thus for hydrochloric acid,

$$H_2O + HCl \longrightarrow Cl^- + H_3O^+$$

weak   strong   weak conjugate   strong conjugate
base$_1$ acid$_2$ base$_2$ acid$_1$

A weak acid donates a proton reluctantly. Its conjugate base (or anion) is a relatively strong base, one with considerable attraction for a proton. Thus for acetic acid,

$$H_2O + HC_2H_3O_2 \rightleftharpoons C_2H_3O_2^- + H_3O^+$$

base$_2$ weak acid$_1$ strong conjugate   conjugate
                                        base$_1$ acid$_2$

B. Polyprotic Acids

Molecules of some acids, such as sulfuric, H_2SO_4, and phosphoric, H_3PO_4, have more than one ionizable hydrogen. These acids are **polyprotic acids**. The ionization of these acids occurs in steps, the molecule losing one proton at a time. The ionization of sulfuric acid (a diprotic acid) is shown in the following equations:

$$H_2SO_4 \longrightarrow H^+ + HSO_4^-$$
$$HSO_4^- \rightleftharpoons H^+ + SO_4^{2-}$$

Notice that although the first ionization is that of a strong acid, the second is that of weak acid.

The ionization of phosphoric acid, a triprotic acid, is shown in the following equations:

$$H_3PO_4 \rightleftharpoons H^+ + H_2PO_4^-$$
$$H_2PO_4^- \rightleftharpoons H^+ + HPO_4^{2-}$$
$$HPO_4^{2-} \rightleftharpoons H^+ + PO_4^{3-}$$

As in the ionization of sulfuric acid, and indeed that of all polyprotic acids, the first ionization is much more complete than the subsequent ionizations.

Example 9.4

Show by equation the ionization in aqueous solution of (a) chloric acid, $HClO_3$, a strong acid; (b) formic acid, $HCOOH$, a weak acid; and (c) oxalic acid, $H_2C_2O_4$, a weak polyprotic acid. For oxalic acid, both ionizations are incomplete. Predict which anion is the stronger base.

☐ *Solution*

a. A strong acid has only ions in solution, and the ionization equation calls for a single arrow:

$$HClO_3 \longrightarrow H^+ + ClO_3^-$$

b. A weak acid has both molecules and ions in solution; a double arrow is used in the ionization equation, the longer arrow pointing toward the molecules:

$$HCOOH \rightleftharpoons H^+ + HCOO^-$$

c. A diprotic acid ionizes stepwise; the first anion is a weaker base than the second, for the first ionization is more complete than the second:

$$H_2C_2O_4 \rightleftharpoons H^+ + HC_2O_4^-$$
$$HC_2O_4^- \rightleftharpoons H^+ + C_2O_4^{2-}$$

Problem 9.4

Show by equation the ionization of

a. the strong acid, $HBrO_3$ **b.** the weak acid, HNO_2
c. the polyprotic and weak acid, H_2SO_3

9.5 Equilibrium in Solutions of Weak Acids

Equilibrium exists when two opposing reactions occur at the same rate. The ionization of a weak acid is an equilibrium between molecules and ions. We have implied the existence of this equilibrium with the double arrow in the ionization equations for weak acids. In a solution of acetic acid, a weak acid, the two reactions are dissociation of molecules into ions and recombination of ions into molecules. This is shown by the equation we have already used:

$$HC_2H_3O_2 \rightleftharpoons H^+ + C_2H_3O_2^-$$

and the opposing reaction rates are

$$Rate_{dissociation} = rate_{recombination\ of\ ions}$$

In Chapter 8, we introduced the **equilibrium constant**, symbol K_{eq}. For an ionization equilibrium, this constant is called the **ionization constant**. If the ionization is that of a weak acid, the constant is known as the **acid dissociation constant**, with the symbol K_a. A weak acid with the formula HA would show in solution the equilibrium

$$HA \rightleftharpoons H^+ + A^-$$

Its acid dissociation constant is

$$K_a = \frac{[H^+][A^-]}{[HA]}$$

By convention, these ionization equilibria are always written with ions as products. Thus in an ionization constant, the concentrations of the ions are always in the numerator, and the concentration of the un-ionized molecules in the denominator.

Therefore, for acetic acid with the ionization equilibrium

$$HC_2H_3O_2 \rightleftharpoons H^+ + C_2H_3O_2^-$$

the equilibrium constant is

$$K_a = \frac{[H^+][C_2H_3O_2^-]}{[HC_2H_3O_2]}$$

Since a weak acid is only slightly ionized and its solution contains mostly molecules, and many fewer ions, the concentration values of the un-ionized molecules in the denominator of the equilibrium constant are much larger than the values of the ions in the numerator. Consequently, values of the ionization constants for weak acids are always much less than 1. Table 9.2 lists several weak acids, the equations for their ionization, and the formula and the value of their acid dissociation constants. In looking at this table, you should note several points.

1. **The acid dissociation constants of polyprotic acids:** Polyprotic acids ionize stepwise, and each anion is less ionized than its conjugate acid (Section 9.4B). For each of the ionizations, there is an equilibrium equation and an acid dissociation constant that becomes smaller with each ionization. For acids with more than one ionizable hydrogen, the first dissociation constant is always the largest; the value for each successive dissociation constant decreases. This progression goes along with our prediction (Section 9.4B) that in each successive ionization, the anion formed is a stronger base (weaker acid).

Table 9.2 Some common weak acids.

Weak Acid	Equilibrium	Acid Dissociation Constant	K_a
acetic acid	$HC_2H_3O_2 \rightleftharpoons H^+ + C_2H_3O_2^-$	$\dfrac{[H^+][C_2H_3O_2^-]}{[HC_2H_3O_2]}$	1.8×10^{-5}
formic acid	$HCO_2H \rightleftharpoons H^+ + HCO_2^-$	$\dfrac{[H^+][HCO_2^-]}{[HCO_2H]}$	1.8×10^{-4}
nitrous acid	$HNO_2 \rightleftharpoons H^+ + NO_2^-$	$\dfrac{[H^+][NO_2^-]}{[HNO_2]}$	4.6×10^{-4}
hydrocyanic acid	$HCN \rightleftharpoons H^+ + CN^-$	$\dfrac{[H^+][CN^-]}{[HCN]}$	4.9×10^{-10}
carbonic acid	$CO_2 + H_2O \rightleftharpoons H^+ + HCO_3^-$	$\dfrac{[H^+][HCO_3^-]}{[CO_2]}$	4.3×10^{-7}
	$HCO_3^- \rightleftharpoons H^+ + CO_3^{2-}$	$\dfrac{[H^+][CO_3^{2-}]}{[HCO_3^-]}$	5.6×10^{-11}
phosphoric acid	$H_3PO_4 \rightleftharpoons H^+ + H_2PO_4^-$	$\dfrac{[H^+][H_2PO_4^-]}{[H_3PO_4]}$	7.5×10^{-3}
	$H_2PO_4^- \rightleftharpoons H^+ + HPO_4^{2-}$	$\dfrac{[H^+][HPO_4^{2-}]}{[H_2PO_4^-]}$	6.2×10^{-8}
	$HPO_4^{2-} \rightleftharpoons H^+ + PO_4^{3-}$	$\dfrac{[H^+][PO_4^{3-}]}{[HPO_4^{2-}]}$	2.2×10^{-13}
ammonium ion	$NH_4^+ \rightleftharpoons H^+ + NH_3$	$\dfrac{[H^+][NH_3]}{[NH_4^+]}$	5.5×10^{-10}

2. Carbonic acid, H_2CO_3, is a solution of carbon dioxide in water. Molecules of carbonic acid are not stable. The mixture of carbon dioxide and water ionizes stepwise:

$$CO_2 + H_2O \rightleftharpoons H^+ + HCO_3^-$$
$$HCO_3^- \rightleftharpoons CO_3^{2-} + H^+$$

3. Ammonium ion acts as a weak acid, ionizing to ammonia and a hydrogen ion:

$$NH_4^+ \rightleftharpoons H^+ + NH_3$$

Example 9.5

Ascorbic acid, vitamin C, is a weak electrolyte. Its molecular formula is $C_6H_8O_6$. In aqueous solution, ascorbic acid ionizes to H^+ and ascorbate ion, $C_6H_7O_6^-$. (a) Write an equation for the equilibrium established in this ionization. (b) Write an expression for the K_a of ascorbic acid.

☐ *Solution*

a. The equation shows the loss of one hydrogen as an ion; the rest of the molecule is the ascorbate anion:

$$\underset{\text{ascorbic acid}}{C_6H_8O_6} \rightleftharpoons H^+ + \underset{\text{ascorbate ion}}{C_6H_7O_6^-}$$

b. The acid dissociation constant has the concentrations of the ions in the numerator and the concentration of the un-ionized acid molecule in the denominator:

$$K_a = \frac{[H^+][C_6H_7O_6^-]}{[C_6H_8O_6]}$$

Problem 9.5

Citric acid, $C_6H_8O_7$, is found in the juice of lemons and other citrus fruits. It is a weak electrolyte and ionizes in aqueous solution, to form H^+ and citrate ion, $C_6H_7O_7^-$.

a. Write the equilibrium equation for this ionization.
b. Write the expression for the acid dissociation constant of citric acid.

9.6 Hydrogen Ion Concentration in Acid Solutions

A. Hydrogen Ion Concentration in Solutions of Strong Acids

Strong acids with one ionizable hydrogen are completely ionized in aqueous solution; therefore, the hydrogen ion concentration of these solutions equals the molar concentration of the acid.

Example 9.6

What is the hydrogen ion concentration in 1.0M HCl?

☐ *Solution*

Hydrochloric acid is a strong acid, completely ionized in water:

$$HCl(aq) \longrightarrow H^+(aq) + Cl^-(aq)$$

Therefore, in a solution prepared by adding 1.0 mol of HCl to enough water to make one liter of solution, the concentration of H^+ is 1.0M, of Cl^- is 1.0M, and of undissociated acid is 0.

Problem 9.6

What is the hydrogen ion concentration of 0.1M HNO_3?

B. Hydrogen Ion Concentration in Solutions of Weak Acids

The hydrogen ion concentration of an aqueous solution of a weak acid depends on the value of its acid dissociation constant and is always less than the concentration of the weak acid. The hydrogen ion concentration can be calculated using the value of K_a and the molar concentration of the weak acid.

Acetic acid is a weak acid that ionizes according to the equation

$$HC_2H_3O_2 \rightleftharpoons H^+ + C_2H_3O_2^-$$

Its acid dissociation constant is

$$K_a = \frac{[H^+][C_2H_3O_2^-]}{[HC_2H_3O_2]} = 1.8 \times 10^{-5}$$

The hydrogen ion concentration of a 1.0M acetic acid solution can be calculated as follows. The solution contains 1.0 mol of acetic acid in 1.0 L of solution. Because acetic acid is a weak acid, only a small fraction of the molecules ionize; most remain as un-ionized acetic acid molecules. Let x stand for the number of moles of acetic acid that ionize. If x moles ionize, then $1.0 - x$ moles remain un-ionized. For x moles of acetic acid that ionize, x moles of H^+ and x moles of $C_2H_3O_2^-$ are formed. The resulting concentrations of acetic acid, hydrogen ion, and acetate ion at equilibrium are

$$HC_2H_3O_2 \rightleftharpoons H^+ + C_2H_3O_2^-$$
$$1.0 - x \qquad x \qquad x$$

Substituting these values in the formula for the acid dissociation constant gives

$$K_a = \frac{[H^+][C_2H_3O_2^-]}{[HC_2H_3O_2]} = \frac{(x)(x)}{1.0 - x} = 1.8 \times 10^{-5}$$

The tiny value of the acid dissociation constant suggests that the amount of acid dissociated is very small (less than 0.01M). Using the rules for the use of significant figures in addition and subtraction (Section 1.7C), we know that the quantity $(1.0 - 0.01)$ expressed to two significant figures is 1.0. If x has a value less than 0.01, it is appropriate to ignore x in the expression $1.0 - x$, changing the K_a equation to

$$K_a = \frac{x^2}{1.0} = 1.8 \times 10^{-5}$$

Solving this equation gives

$$x^2 = 1.8 \times 10^{-5} = 18 \times 10^{-6}$$
$$x = 4.2 \times 10^{-3} = [H^+] = [C_2H_3O_2^-]$$

Table 9.3 summarizes the concentrations of hydrogen ions, of acetate ions, and of acetic acid molecules in a 1.0M solution of acetic acid.

Table 9.3
Concentrations of species in 1.0M acetic acid solution.

Species Present	In Calculation	Calculated Value
acetic acid molecules	$1.0 - x$	1.0M
hydrogen ions	x	4.2×10^{-3}M
acetate ions	x	4.2×10^{-3}M

The hydrogen ion concentration in 1.0M acetic acid solution is, then, 4.2×10^{-3}M, or 0.0042M. Notice that 4.2×10^{-3} is not significant when subtracted from 1.0, so our simplification of the original equation was justified. If the acid is very dilute, for example 10^{-3}M, or if it is one with a large acid dissociation constant, such as 10^{-2}, this simplification would not be valid.

These calculations emphasize the difference between strong and weak acids. The hydrogen ion concentration of a 1.0M solution of a strong acid is 1.0M (see Example 9.6). The hydrogen ion concentration of a 1.0M solution of a weak acid can be calculated from the acid dissociation constant of the weak acid and is much less than 1.0M.

Example 9.7

Calculate the hydrogen ion concentration in 0.10M ascorbic acid, $C_6H_8O_6$. The acid dissociation constant K_a for ascorbic acid is 8.0×10^{-5}.

☐ *Solution*

In 0.10M $C_6H_8O_6$, the equilibrium equation is

$$C_6H_8O_6 \rightleftharpoons H^+ + C_6H_7O_6^-$$
$$0.10 - x \qquad x \qquad x$$

The K_a for this equilibrium is

$$K_a = \frac{[H^+][C_6H_7O_6^-]}{[C_6H_8O_6]} = 8.0 \times 10^{-5}$$

Let $[H^+] = x$. Then $[C_6H_7O_6^-]$ also equals x, and

$$[C_6H_8O_6] = 0.10 - x$$

Substituting these values in the formula for the dissociation constant gives

$$\frac{(x)(x)}{0.10 - x} = 8.0 \times 10^{-5}$$

Assuming, as before, that $[H^+]$ is so much less than 0.10 as to be insignificant, the equation becomes

$$\frac{x^2}{0.10} = 8.0 \times 10^{-5}$$

Solving for x, we get

$$x^2 = 8.0 \times 10^{-6}$$
$$x = 2.8 \times 10^{-3}$$

Then in 0.10M $C_6H_8O_6$, $[H^+] = 2.8 \times 10^{-3}M$.

Problem 9.7

Calculate the hydrogen ion concentration of 0.1M formic acid. (See Table 9.2 for the molecular formula of formic acid and the value of its acid dissociation constant.)

C. Changing the Hydrogen Ion Concentration in the Solution of a Weak Acid; The Common Ion Effect

We know that the solution of a weak acid contains the equilibrium

$$HA \rightleftharpoons H^+ + A^-$$

and that as long as the equilibrium exists, everything is in balance, so

$$K_a = \frac{[H^+][A^-]}{[HA]}$$

If something is added to the solution so one of the concentrations changes, the system goes out of equilibrium. Then either more molecules dissociate or more ions combine until the concentrations are again a set that fits the equilibrium constant expression. When this set is established, an equilibrium is again present, the opposing rates are equal, and the concentrations become constant.

It is possible to calculate the new equilibrium concentrations after a change in one concentration. Suppose we have one liter of a solution containing one-tenth mole of acetic acid and one-tenth mole of sodium acetate. The acetic acid is present as an equilibrium mixture of acetic acid molecules, hydrogen ions, and acetate ions. The sodium acetate is present only as ions because salts are completely ionized in solution (Chapter 4). The acetate ions from both the acid and the sodium acetate participate in the acetic acid equilibrium:

$$HC_2H_3O_2 \rightleftharpoons H^+ + C_2H_3O_2^- \qquad K_a = 1.8 \times 10^{-5}$$

The sodium ions present in solution do not participate in the equilibrium, they do not appear in the equation for the equilibrium, and they have no part in determining the concentrations of those substances whose formulas do appear in the equilibrium expression. To calculate the hydrogen ion concentration in this solution, we start off as we did in previous problems where only the weak acid was present. If x equals the concentration of ionized acetic acid molecules, the concentrations at equilibrium are

$0.1 - x$ = concentration of un-ionized acetic acid molecules

x = concentration of hydrogen molecules

$0.1 + x$ = concentration of acetate ions (the concentration of sodium acetate in the solution plus acetate ions from the ionization of acetic acid)

In the equilibrium equation, the concentrations are

$$HC_2H_3O_2 \rightleftharpoons H^+ + C_2H_3O_2^-$$
$$0.1 - x \qquad x \qquad 0.1 + x$$

As before, in the case of a solution containing only acetic acid, we predict that the concentrations of ionized acetic acid and therefore of hydrogen ions are very small and not significant when added to or subtracted from 0.1. By this assumption, $0.1 + x$ is approximately equal to 0.1, and $0.1 - x$ is also approximately equal to 0.1. Thus, the concentrations can be expressed as

$$[HC_2H_3O_2] \qquad [H^+] \qquad [C_2H_3O_2^-]$$
$$0.1 \qquad\qquad x \qquad\qquad 0.1$$

Substituting these values in the formula for the acid dissociation constant for acetic acid and solving give

$$K_a = \frac{[H^+][C_2H_3O_2^-]}{[HC_2H_3O_2]} = \frac{(x)(0.1)}{(0.1)} = 1.8 \times 10^{-5}$$

$$x = 1.8 \times 10^{-5}$$

$$[H^+] = 1.8 \times 10^{-5}M$$

The addition of sodium acetate has decreased the hydrogen ion concentration from $4.2 \times 10^{-3}M$ in 0.1M acetic acid solution to $1.8 \times 10^{-5}M$ in a 0.1M acetic acid solution that is also 0.1M in acetate ion. This is a tremendous decrease. Adding other concentrations of the acid or of its anion will change the hydrogen ion concentration to other values.

These calculations have shown that an ionic equilibrium such as the ionization of a weak acid can be shifted by adding another ionic substance (such as a salt) that contains one of the ions present in the equilibrium. This effect is known as the **common-ion effect**, for it is caused by the addition of an ion common to both substances.

Example 9.8

Calculate the hydrogen ion concentration of a solution that is 1.0M in acetic acid and 0.2M in sodium acetate.

☐ *Solution*   If we let x equal the moles of acetic acid that ionize, the concentrations at equilibrium will be

$$x = \text{hydrogen ion concentration}$$
$$1.0 - x = \text{acetic acid concentration}$$
$$0.2 + x = \text{acetate ion concentration}$$

We can drop x from the concentration of acetic acid and acetic ions because, as shown before, x is not significant when added to or subtracted from a number as large as 1.0 or 0.2. The equilibrium concentrations become

$$HC_2H_3O_2 \rightleftharpoons H^+ + C_2H_3O_2^-$$
$$1.0 \qquad\qquad x \qquad 0.2$$

Substituting these values in the formula for the acid dissociation constant gives

$$K_a = \frac{[H^+][C_2H_3O_2^-]}{[HC_2H_3O_2]} = \frac{(x)(0.2)}{(1.0)} = 1.8 \times 10^{-5}$$

or

$$0.2x = 1.8 \times 10^{-5}$$
$$x = 9.0 \times 10^{-5}$$

A solution that is 1.0M in acetic acid and 0.2M in sodium acetate has a hydrogen ion concentration of 9.0×10^{-5}M.

■
Problem 9.8   Calculate the hydrogen ion concentration in 1 L of solution that is 0.1M in formic acid and 0.1M in sodium formate.

9.7 pH

The **pH** of a solution describes its acidity and is the *negative log of its hydrogen ion concentration*. The hydrogen ion concentration in solutions of weak acids and in many other fluids is generally much less than 1. When this concentration is expressed exponentially, it contains a negative exponent. Many people find numbers with negative exponents confusing and answer with some hesitation such questions as, Is 1.8×10^{-4} larger or smaller than 3.6×10^{-5}? (To answer the question, state both numbers with the same exponent of 10. This changes 3.6×10^{-5} to 0.36×10^{-4}, a value that is clearly smaller than 1.8×10^{-4}.) To avoid confusion when dealing with negative exponents, as in dissociation constants and ion concentrations, these numbers are frequently given as negative logarithms. The letter p has been chosen to mean "negative logarithm of." Thus, pH means the negative log (logarithm) of the hydrogen ion concentration and **pOH** means the negative log of the hydroxide ion concentration.

$$pH = -\log[H^+] \qquad pOH = -\log[OH^-]$$

A. Calculating pH

To calculate the pH of a solution, one must state the hydrogen ion concentration in exponential form. For a solution with a hydrogen ion concentration of 0.003M, restate that concentration as 3.0×10^{-3}M. Next, determine the log of that number. The log of the product of the two numbers is the sum of their logs:

$$\log(3.0 \times 10^{-3}) = \log(3) + \log(10^{-3})$$

The log of the first term can be found in Table 9.4 or from your hand calculator; the log of the exponential term is its exponent.

$$\log(3.0 \times 10^{-3}) = 0.477 + (-3) = -2.52$$

The pH is the negative log of the hydrogen ion concentration. If $[H^+] = 3.0 \times 10^{-3}$, then pH = 2.52.

Table 9.4
Logarithms of
small whole
numbers.

log 1.0 = 0.000	log 6.0 = 0.778
log 2.0 = 0.301	log 7.0 = 0.845
log 3.0 = 0.477	log 8.0 = 0.903
log 4.0 = 0.602	log 9.0 = 0.954
log 5.0 = 0.699	log 10.0 = 1.000

Example 9.9

a. Calculate the pH of a solution with a hydrogen ion concentration of 0.00040M.
b. Calculate the hydrogen ion concentration of a solution of pH 8.52.

☐ *Solution*

a. State $[H^+]$ in exponential form:

$$[H^+] = 0.00040M = 4.0 \times 10^{-4}M$$

Determine the log of $[H^+]$, using Table 9.4 or your calculator:

$$pH = -\log(4.0 \times 10^{-4}) = -(\log 4.0 + \log 10^{-4})$$
$$= -(0.602) + (-4) = \quad 0.602 + 4 = 3.40$$

b. This calculation is performed by reversing the steps in part (a):

$$pH = -\log[H^+] = 8.52 = 9 - 0.48$$
$$\log[H^+] = -9 + 0.48$$
$$[H^+] = (\text{antilog } 0.48) \times 10^{-9}$$
$$= 3.0 \times 10^{-9}$$

Problem 9.9

a. Calculate the pH of a solution with a hydrogen ion concentration of 5.0×10^{-4}M.
b. What is the hydrogen ion concentration of a solution of pH 3.16?

B. Interpreting pH Values

When the hydrogen ion concentration is stated in exponential notation, the smaller the exponent, the greater the acidity of the solution. Consequently, with pH values, the lower the pH, the more acidic the solution.

In 0.1M HCl   **In 0.0001M HCl**

$[H^+] = 1 \times 10^{-1}$ $[H^+] = 1 \times 10^{-4}$

$pH = 1$ $pH = 4$

Figure 9.2 shows the pH of several familiar fluids. Many of these values are the midpoint of a range. Human blood plasma normally varies only between pH 7.35 and pH 7.45. Human gastric fluid is much more acidic; its normal range is from pH 1.0 to pH 3.0.

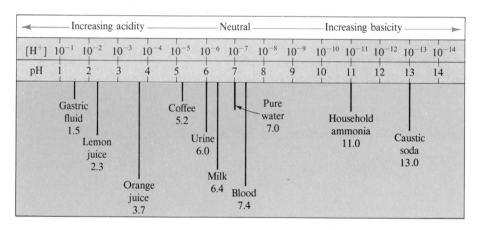

Figure 9.2 pH and hydrogen ion concentration.

9.8 pK_a

The **pK_a** of an acid is the negative log of its acid dissociation constant. Just as pH can be used to describe the hydrogen ion concentration of a solution, pK_a can be used to describe the dissociation constant of a weak acid. The higher the pK_a of an acid, the weaker the acid.

Table 9.5 lists the same weak acids that were listed in Table 9.2 and the pK_a of each. Notice that the acids with larger ionization constants have smaller pK_a's. For example, formic acid ($K_a = 1.8 \times 10^{-4}$) is a stronger acid than acetic acid ($K_a = 1.8 \times 10^{-5}$). The pK_a of formic acid is 3.74, a smaller number than 4.74, the pK_a of acetic acid. Notice, too, that for the polyprotic acids, the pK_a increases with each ionization. For example, the pK_a for the first ionization of

Weak Acid	K_a	pK_a
acetic acid	1.8×10^{-5}	4.74
formic acid	1.8×10^{-4}	3.74
nitrous acid	4.6×10^{-4}	3.34
hydrocyanic acid	4.9×10^{-10}	9.31
carbonic acid	4.3×10^{-7}	6.37
	5.6×10^{-11}	10.25
phosphoric acid	7.5×10^{-3}	2.12
	6.2×10^{-8}	7.21
	2.2×10^{-13}	12.67
ammonium ion	5.5×10^{-10}	9.26

Table 9.5
The pK_a of some weak acids.

phosphoric acid

$$H_3PO_4 \rightleftharpoons H^+ + H_2PO_4^- \qquad pK_a = 2.12$$

is much smaller than that of the second ionization,

$$H_2PO_4^- \rightleftharpoons H^+ + HPO_4^{2-} \qquad pK_a = 7.21$$

Phosphoric acid is a much stronger acid than the dihydrogen phosphate ion.

9.9 Henderson-Hasselbalch Equation

The acid dissociation constant of a weak acid, HA, is

$$K_a = \frac{[H^+][A^-]}{[HA]}$$

This can be stated in terms of pH and pK_a as

$$pK_a = pH - \log \frac{[A^-]}{[HA]}$$

This rearranges to form

$$pH = pK_a + \log \frac{[A^-]}{[HA]}$$

This last equation is known as the **Henderson-Hasselbalch equation**. Example 9.10 shows how it is used.

Example 9.10

What is the pH of 0.5M formic acid that contains 1.0 mol sodium formate per liter?

$$pK_a \text{ (formic acid)} = 3.74$$

☐ *Solution*   The concentrations are

$$[HCO_2H] = 0.5M \qquad [HCO_2^-] = 1.0M$$

Substituting in the equation $pH = pK_a + \log\dfrac{[A^-]}{[HA]}$, we get

$$pH = 3.74 + \log\frac{1.0}{0.5} = 3.74 + \log 2$$

$$= 3.74 + 0.30 \qquad \text{(from Table 9.4)}$$

$$= 4.04$$

■

Problem 9.10

Using the Henderson-Hasselbalch equation, calculate the pH of 0.2M acetic acid solution that contains 0.4 mol of sodium acetate in each liter of solution.

━━━ ∎

9.10 Water as a Weak Acid

To a very small but important extent, water is a weak acid that ionizes to yield hydrogen and hydroxide ions. This is an equilibrium reaction with the equation

$$H_2O \rightleftharpoons H^+ + OH^-$$

Like all other weak acids, it has an acid dissociation constant:

$$K_a = \frac{[H^+][OH^-]}{[H_2O]}$$

In any aqueous solution, the concentration of water is so high (55.5 mol water in 1000 mL of water) and the number of ionized water molecules is so low (1.0×10^{-7} mol in 1000 mL water), that the concentration of the water molecules is a constant. The ionization constant of water, K_w, includes the constant factor $[H_2O]$:

$$K_w = K_a[H_2O] = 1.0 \times 10^{-14} \qquad pK_w = 14$$

In pure water, the hydrogen ion concentration $[H^+]$ equals the hydroxide ion concentration $[OH^-]$. We can calculate what these concentrations are, given that the equation for the ionization of water is

$$H_2O \rightleftharpoons H^+ + OH^-$$

Let x equal the hydrogen ion concentration $[H^+]$. Then x also equals the hydroxide ion concentration, $[OH^-]$. Substituting in the equation $[H^+][OH^-] = 1.0 \times 10^{-14}$, we get

$$x^2 = 1.0 \times 10^{-14}$$
$$x = 1.0 \times 10^{-7}$$

or

$$[H^+] = [OH^-] = 1.0 \times 10^{-7} M$$

The pH of pure water is then 7.

A **neutral solution** is one that is neither acidic or basic. The hydrogen ion concentration equals the hydroxide ion concentration, and both equal $1.0 \times 10^{-7} M$. In a neutral solution, pH = pOH = 7.

An **acidic solution** is one in which the hydrogen ion concentration is greater than the hydroxide ion concentration; in other words, the hydrogen ion concentration is greater than 1.0×10^{-7}, and the hydroxide ion concentration is less than 1.0×10^{-7}. In terms of pH, an acidic solution has a pH less than 7.

What is the hydroxide ion concentration in an acid solution? To answer this question, we need to recognize that the following relationships exist whenever water is present:

$$[H^+][OH^-] = 1.0 \times 10^{-14} \quad \text{and} \quad pH + pOH = 14$$

If we know the hydrogen ion concentration, we can use the first relation to calculate the hydroxide ion concentration. Suppose we know that the hydrogen ion concentration is 0.1 M. Substituting in and rearranging the first relation gives

$$[OH^-] = \frac{1.0 \times 10^{-14}}{0.10} = 1.0 \times 10^{-13} M$$

Suppose we know that the pH of an acidic solution is 1.0. We can use the second relationship to calculate the pOH:

$$1.0 + pOH = 14 \quad pOH = 13$$

An *alkaline or a basic solution* is one in which the hydrogen ion concentration is less than $1.0 \times 10^{-7} M$. In terms of pH, an alkaline solution is one in which pH is greater than 7.0. Table 9.6 shows the relationship between pH and pOH over a scale from 0 to 14.

Table 9.6 The relationship between pH and pOH.

	Increasingly Acidic ⟵						Neutral ⟶						Increasingly Alkaline (Basic)
pH	0	1	2	3	4	5	6	7	8	9	10	11	12	13	14
pOH	14	13	12	11	10	9	8	7	6	5	4	3	2	1	0

Example 9.11

Calculate the hydroxide ion concentration, the pH, and the pOH of 0.01 M nitric acid, HNO_3.

☐ *Solution*

Nitric acid is a strong acid and is therefore completely ionized in solution. Thus, $[H^+]$ is 0.01 M and pH = 2. The hydroxide ion concentration can be calculated using the K_w constant:

$$K_w = [H^+][OH^-] = 1.0 \times 10^{-14}$$

Substituting and rearranging gives

$$0.01 \times [OH^-] = 1.0 \times 10^{-14}$$

$$[OH^-] = \frac{1.0 \times 10^{-14}}{0.01} = 1.0 \times 10^{-12}M$$

Since pH + pOH = 14, then pOH = 12.

Problem 9.11

Calculate the hydrogen ion concentration of a solution having a hydroxide ion concentration of $1.0 \times 10^{-4}M$. What is the pH of this solution?

9.11 Application of Le Chatelier's Principle; Buffers

In Chapter 8 we discussed how equilibria respond to the stress of changing concentrations. An interesting and important example of how equilibria respond to concentration changes comes in the study of buffers. A **buffer** is a chemical system that resists change in hydrogen ion concentration (pH). Buffers are important because many chemical reactions, particularly those in biological systems, proceed best at a particular pH. If the reaction takes place in a solution that is buffered to that pH, the most satisfactory results will be obtained.

A buffer system contains a weak acid and its conjugate base, both in such concentrations as will give the solution a particular pH. For example, if a buffer of pH 4.74 is needed, a solution that is 0.1M in both acetic acid and acetate ion would be suitable (see Section 9.6C for the calculations that assign this pH to this solution). This buffer of pH 4.74 contains the following equilibrium:

$$HC_2H_3O_2 \rightleftarrows H^+ + C_2H_3O_2^-$$
$$\text{0.1M} \qquad\qquad 1.8 \times 10^{-5}M \qquad \text{0.1M}$$

Notice that the concentrations of both the acid and its conjugate base are much larger than that of the hydrogen ion. From our study of equilibria, we know that if an acid (H^+) is added to this solution, the equilibrium shifts to the left, since that reaction consumes the added hydrogen ions. If on the other hand, hydroxide ion or some other strong base is added to the solution, that base will react with the hydrogen ions present and more acid will ionize to replenish the supply and keep the system in equilibrium. In the buffer we describe, if these added amounts are small, the concentrations of the acetic acid molecules and of acetate ions are sufficiently high that the pH of the solution will remain essentially constant. The calculations in the following example illustrate this point.

Example 9.12

Calculate the following:

a. The pH of a buffer solution, one liter of which contains 0.10 mol acetic acid and 0.10 mol acetate ion. The pK_a of acetic acid is 4.74.

b. The pH of 1.0 L of the buffer solution in part (a) after the addition of 0.010 mol of hydrochloric acid to the solution.

c. The pH of 1.0 L of the buffer solution in part (a) after 0.010 mol of hydroxide ion has been added.

Adding small a
not appreciably
of using a buffere
with the same pH

A solution conta
pH of 4.74. Calcu
of 0.01 mol of hy

Because HCl is a
for Cl⁻ to combi
tration of hydrog
crease this concer

Thus, the additio
strong acid causes

Calculate the final
HCl.

The following c
ticular reaction.

1. *pH.* Buffering
to the pKₐ of the

2. *Concentratio*
tion of both the
buffer can be mad
acetate in a lite
$[HC_2H_3O_2]$ + [N
centration of 0.2M
of acetic acid and
should be greater
the reaction being

3. *Capacity.* Th
hydrogen or hydr
change in pH. Cap
has a pH that equ
is 4.74; therefore, a
a buffer within a pH
is one with equal c
the pH of the solu
of acetic acid and
it is most effective
common buffers ar

□ *Solution*   The equilibrium involved is

$$HC_2H_3O_2 \rightleftharpoons H^+ + C_2H_3O_2^-$$

The original concentrations are

$$[HC_2H_3O_2] = 0.10M$$
$$[C_2H_3O_2^-] = 0.10M$$

a. We can calculate the pH of this solution using the K_a for acetic acid:

$$K_a = \frac{[H^+][C_2H_3O_2^-]}{[HC_2H_3O_2]} = 1.8 \times 10^{-5}$$

Rearranging this equation, we get

$$[H^+] = \frac{K_a[HC_2H_3O_2]}{[C_2H_3O_2^-]}$$

Solving gives

$$[H^+] = \frac{(1.8 \times 10^{-5})(0.10M)}{0.10M} = 1.8 \times 10^{-5}M$$

$$pH = 4.74$$

b. Before the addition of HCl, 1.0 L of the solution contains 0.10 mol each of acetic ion and acetic acid:

$$[C_2H_3O_2^-] = 0.10M$$
$$[HC_2H_3O_2] = 0.10M$$

The 0.010 mol of hydrochloric acid added to the solution is completely ionized and therefore adds 0.01 mol of H^+ to the solution. The added hydrogen ions combined with acetate ions to form more un-ionized molecules of acetic acid. Therefore, the concentration of acetate ion decreases and the concentration of acetic acid in the solution increases:

$$[C_2H_3O_2^-] = 0.10 - 0.010 = 0.09M$$
$$[HC_2H_3O_2] = 0.10 + 0.010 = 0.11M$$

In this solution:

$$[H^+] = \frac{(1.8 \times 10^{-5})(HC_2H_3O_2)}{[C_2H_3O_2^-]}$$

$$[H^+] = \frac{(1.8 \times 10^{-5})(0.11)}{0.090} = 2.2 \times 10^{-5}M$$

$$pH = 5.00 - 0.34 = 4.66$$

This is a change of 0.08 pH unit.

Example 9.13

□ *Solution*

Problem 9.13

c. Before a
acid and 0.10
acetic acid to
of acetate ion
same amount

For this solu

This is a char

One liter of b
formate.

a. Calculate t
b. Calculate t
c. Calculate t

Figure 9.3 s
the same solut
a change of o
0.18M to 0.02
within this rar

■

**Problem
9.12**

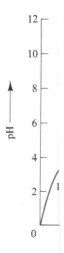

Figu

pH

12
10
8
6
4
2
0

Table 9.7 Some common buffers and the pH at which each is most effective.

Name of Acid	Acid Formula	K_a	Anion	pH of Buffer When Anion/Acid = 1
phosphoric	H_3PO_4	7.5×10^{-3}	$H_2PO_4^-$	2.12
formic	HCO_2H	1.8×10^{-4}	HCO_2^-	3.74
acetic	$HC_2H_3O_2$	1.8×10^{-5}	$C_2H_3O_2^-$	4.74
carbonic	$CO_2 + H_2O$	4.3×10^{-7}	HCO_3^-	6.37
dihydrogen phosphate	$H_2PO_4^-$	6.2×10^{-8}	HPO_4^{2-}	7.21
bicarbonate	HCO_3^-	5.6×10^{-11}	CO_3^{2-}	10.25
monohydrogen phosphate	HPO_4^{2-}	2.2×10^{-13}	PO_4^{3-}	12.67

9.12 Acid-Base Balance in Blood Plasma

In a healthy person, the pH of blood remains at the remarkably constant level of 7.35–7.45. The principal buffer of blood plasma is bicarbonate. Carbonic acid is a diprotic acid. Since about 99% of the carbonic acid in blood is in the form of dissolved carbon dioxide, it is correct to refer to the acid form as CO_2. In terms of buffering action in blood plasma, the first dissociation constant is most important. The first dissociation of carbonic acid can be written

$$CO_2 + H_2O \rightleftharpoons HCO_3^- + H^+$$

The solubility of CO_2 is greater in plasma than in water. In blood, the pK_a for this reaction is 6.1. By using the Henderson-Hasselbalch equation, we can calculate the ratio of the acid form, CO_2, to salt form, HCO_3^-, at pH 7.4.

$$pH = pK_a' + \log \frac{[HCO_3^-]}{[CO_2]}$$

$$7.4 = 6.1 + \log \frac{[HCO_3^-]}{[CO_2]}$$

Solving this equation shows that in blood plasma at pH 7.4,

$$\frac{[HCO_3^-]}{[CO_2]} = \frac{20}{1}$$

Thus, in blood plasma at pH 7.4, the ratio of bicarbonate to carbonic acid is 20 to 1. The normal concentration of bicarbonate in plasma is about 0.025 mol/L and of carbonic acid is about 0.0012 mol/L. Therefore, the concentration of this buffer system is approximately 0.026 mol/L, consisting mainly of bicarbonate.

Recall from Section 9.11 that a weak acid and its salt are most effective as an acid-base buffer in the concentration range from 10% salt/90% acid to 90% salt/10% acid, that is, in the region pH = $pK_a \pm 1$. The pK_a of carbonic acid is 1.3 units smaller than the pH of blood. At pH 7.4, this buffer is approximately 95% bicarbonate and 5% carbonic acid, CO_2. We would predict that this buffer system, being at the outer limit of the useful range, would not be effective, yet it is. Its effectiveness is enhanced by the respiratory system, which provides a means for making very rapid adjustments in the concentration of carbon dioxide in blood. In addition, the kidneys provide a means for making slower, long-term adjustments in the concentration of bicarbonate. Through the cooperative interaction of these two systems, the bicarbonate to carbon dioxide ratio can be kept very close to 20:1.

From the clinical standpoint, respiratory acidosis, respiratory alkalosis, metabolic acidosis, and metabolic alkalosis are the four major disturbances in acid-base balance. **Acidosis** is brought about by any abnormal condition that leads to the accumulation of excess acid in the body or excessive loss of alkali. In acidosis, the pH of blood falls below 7.30. Two apparently unrelated activities, starvation and unusually strenuous physical activity, can cause **alkalosis**; loss of acid or accumulation in the body of excess alkali. In alkalosis, the pH of blood rises above 7.50. Alkalosis may also occur after vomiting or forced breathing.

Any chronic respiratory difficulty or depression of breathing rate can increase the carbon dioxide concentration in blood plasma, causing acidosis:

$$pH = pK_a + \log \frac{[HCO_3^-]}{[CO_2]}$$

This increases in chronic respiratory difficulty or depression of breathing; as a consequence, pH decreases.

Because of this increase, the ratio of HCO_3 to CO_2 decreases to something less than 20:1, and the pH decreases. The blood becomes more acidic. Even holding your breath to get rid of the hiccups can temporarily decrease the pH of blood to 7.30 or below.

Hyperventilation, or prolonged rapid, deep breathing, causes a "blowoff," or decrease in the concentration, of dissolved CO_2:

$$pH = pK_a + \log \frac{[HCO_3^-]}{[CO_2]}$$

When this decreases, pH increases.

Because the concentration of CO_2 decreases, the ratio of HCO_3 to CO_2 increases to greater than 20:1 and the pH of blood increases. Even mild hyperventilation can increase blood pH to as high as 7.51.

Whenever respiratory alkalosis or respiratory acidosis occurs, the kidneys act to bring conditions back to normal. They try to increase or decrease the concentration of HCO_3^- in an effort to restore the 20:1 ratio of bicarbonate to carbonic acid in normal blood. In respiratory acidosis, the kidneys compensate by increasing the reabsorption of bicarbonate. As long as the concentration of carbon dioxide is elevated, the kidneys will stabilize the bicarbonate at an elevated level.

In respiratory alkalosis, the kidneys will increase the concentration of H^+, thereby allowing the reaction of H^+ and HCO_3^- to form more carbonic acid. Instead of excreting hydrogen ions in an acidic urine, the kidneys will excrete other cations, mainly Na^+ and K^+, and the urine will become less acidic or even slightly alkaline.

Metabolic acidosis may result from various causes, including increased biosynthesis of acids such as the *ketone bodies* (see Section 25.4) and decreased excretion of hydrogen ion due to kidney failure. Metabolic alkalosis may result from impaired nitrogen metabolism or any other factor that leads to an increase in the production of bases.

Key Terms and Concepts

acid dissociation constant (9.5)

acidic solution (9.10)

acidosis (9.12)

alkalosis (9.12)

Arrhenius definitions (9.1A)

Brønsted-Lowry definitions (9.1B)

buffer (9.11)

common-ion effect (9.6C)

conjugate acid (9.1B)

conjugate base (9.1B)

equilibrium constant (9.5)

Henderson-Hasselbalch
  equation (9.9)

hydronium ion (9.1B)

ionization constant (9.5)

K_a (9.5)

K_w (9.10)

neutral solution (9.10)

nomenclature of acids (9.2)

pH (9.7)

pK_a (9.8)

pK_w (9.10)

pOH (9.7)

polyprotic acids (9.4B)

reversible reactions (9.4A)

strong acids (9.4A)

weak acids (9.4A)

weak bases (9.4A)

Problems

Acid and base definitions (Section 9.1)

9.14 Name the following and classify each as an acid or base in the Arrhenius system.
a. $Ca(OH)_2$ **b.** $HClO$ **c.** NH_3 **d.** H_2CO_3

9.15 The following are weak acids. For each, give its name and the formula and name of its conjugate base in the Brønsted-Lowry system.
a. HPO_4^{2-} **b.** HNO_2 **c.** HS^- **d.** HCO_3^-

9.16 Each of the following can act as either a Brønsted-Lowry acid or base. Show this by appropriate equations.
a. HSO_4^- **b.** $H_2PO_4^-$

Nomenclature (Section 9.2)

9.17 Given that $HBrO_3$ is bromic acid, name the following:
a. $KBrO_3$ **b.** $HBrO(aq)$ **c.** $LiBr$ **d.** $Ca(BrO_3)_2$

9.18 Name the following:
a. $NaHSO_3$ **b.** Li_2S **c.** $H_2SO_3(aq)$ **d.** $KHSO_4$

Reactions (Section 9.3)

9.19 Write complete equations for these reactions. Name the products.
a. $H_2SO_4 + LiOH$ **b.** $HNO_2 + Ca(OH)_2$
c. $HC_2H_3O_2 + NH_3$ **d.** $HCl + Zn$

Ionization (Section 9.4)

9.20 Write equations for the equilibria present in aqueous solutions of these weak acids. Name the acids and their conjugate bases.
a. $HClO$ **b.** HNO_2
c. H_2SO_3 (2 equations)   **d.** HIO_2

[H⁺] in solutions of weak acids (Section 9.6)

9.21 Calculate the hydrogen ion concentration and pH in 0.1M HNO_2.

9.22 Calculate the hydrogen ion concentration and the pH in 3.5M formic acid.

9.23 Using the data in Table 9.2, calculate the $[H^+]$ in 1.0M HCN. Calculate the pH of one liter of this solution to which 0.1 mol solid sodium cyanide has been added.

9.24 Using the data in Table 9.2 for the ionization of NH_4^+ as a weak acid, calculate the pH of a solution of 0.10M NH_4Cl.

pH (Section 9.7)

9.25 Calculate the pH of these solutions:
a. 1×10^{-3}M HCl **b.** 0.10M $Ca(OH)_2$

9.26 Calculate the pH of one liter of a solution containing
a. 0.5M acetic acid and 1.0M potassium acetate
b. 0.5M formic acid and 0.5M sodium formate
c. 0.1M nitrous acid and 0.25M sodium nitrite

9.27 Vinegar is 5% solution (wt/vol) of acetic acid in water.
a. Calculate the molarity of the acetic acid.
b. Calculate the hydrogen ion concentration and pH of this solution.
c. What volume of 0.10M sodium hydroxide is necessary to react completely with 100 mL vinegar?

9.28 Calculate the $[H^+]$ and the pH of one liter of 0.1M acetic acid to which 31.6 g calcium acetate has been added.

General problems

9.29 **a.** Write the equilibrium constant K_b for the reaction

$$NH_3 + H_2O \rightleftharpoons NH_4^+ + OH^-$$

b. Write the equilibrium constant K_a for the reaction

$$NH_4^+ \rightleftharpoons NH_3 + H^+$$

c. Show for these reactions that $K_b \times K_a = K_w$

9.30 The ionization constant for butyric acid is 1.5×10^{-5}. Calculate the pH of a solution that is 0.01M in butyric acid and 0.02M in sodium butyrate.

9.31 At body temperature, $pK_w = 13.6$. Calculate $[H^+]$, $[OH^-]$, pH, and pOH for pure water at body temperature.

9.32 Calculate the $[H^+]$ and the pH of a 0.1M solution of nitrous acid that is also 0.1M in nitrite ion (K_a, $HNO_2 = 4.6 \times 10^{-4}$).

9.33 Calculate the $[H^+]$ and the pH of a solution of acrylic acid whose $K_a = 5.6 \times 10^{-5}$.

10 Organic Chemistry: The Compounds of Carbon

Organic chemistry is the study of the compounds of carbon. While the term *organic* reminds us that many compounds of carbon are of either plant or animal origin, by no means is that the limit of organic chemistry. Certainly, organic chemistry is the study of the naturally occurring medicines such as penicillin, cortisone, and streptomycin; but it also includes the study of novocaine, the sulfa drugs, aspirin, and other man-made medicines. Organic chemistry is the study of natural textile fibers such as cotton, silk, and wool. It is also the study of man-made textile fibers such as nylon, Dacron, Orlon, and rayon. Organic chemistry is the study of Saran, Teflon, Styrofoam, polyethylene, and other man-made polymers used to manufacture the films and molded plastics with which we are so familiar today. The list could go on and on.

Perhaps the most remarkable feature of organic chemistry is that it comprises the chemistry of carbon and only a few other elements: chiefly hydrogen, nitrogen, and oxygen. Let us begin with a review of how atoms of these elements combine to form molecules.

10.1 The Covalence of Carbon, Hydrogen, Oxygen, and Nitrogen

Recall from Section 4.4 that in discussing covalent bonding in compounds of hydrogen, carbon, nitrogen, and oxygen, we can focus our attention on electrons in the outermost, or valence, shell of each atom because it is these electrons that participate in covalent bonding and chemical reactions. Lewis structures for H, C, N, and O are shown in Table 10.1.

Table 10.1
Lewis structures for hydrogen, carbon, nitrogen, and oxygen.

H·	·C̈:	·N̈:	:Ö:

The single valence electron of hydrogen belongs to the first principal energy level; this shell is completely filled with two electrons. Thus, hydrogen can form only one covalent bond with another element; hydrogen has a valence of 1.

Carbon, with four valence electrons, needs four additional electrons to complete its octet; carbon as a valence of 4. The valence of carbon can be satisfied by appropriate combinations of single, double, or triple bonds, as illustrated by methane, ethane, ethene, and ethyne:

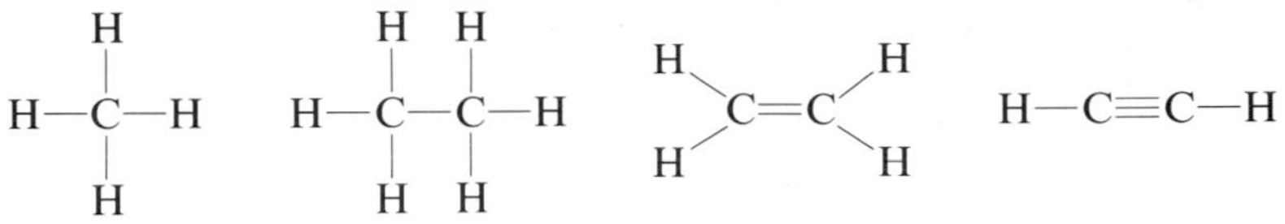

methane   ethane   ethene
(ethylene)   ethyne
(acetylene)

Nitrogen, with five valence electrons, needs three additional electrons to complete its octet; nitrogen has a valence of 3. This valence can be satisfied by appropriate combinations of single, double, or triple bonds, as illustrated by ammonia, nitrous acid, hydrogen cyanide, and nitrogen:

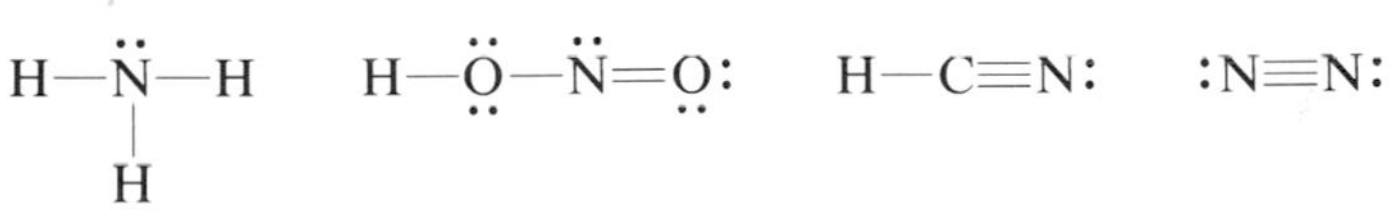

ammonia   nitrous
acid   hydrogen
cyanide   nitrogen
molecule

Oxygen, with six valence electrons, needs two additional electrons to complete its octet; oxygen has a valence of 2. This valence can be satisfied either by two single bonds, as in water and methanol, or by one double bond, as in methanal (formaldehyde) and acetic acid.

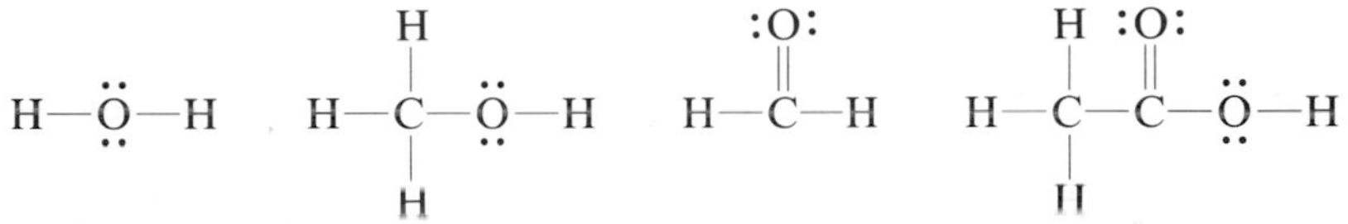

water   methanol   methanal
(formaldehyde)   acetic acid

After examining these molecules and those used in Chapter 4 to illustrate covalent bonding and using the valence-shell electron-pair repulsion model to predict bond angles, we can make the following generalizations. For stable, uncharged molecules containing atoms of carbon, nitrogen, and oxygen:

1. Carbon forms four covalent bonds. Bond angles on carbon are approximately 109.5° for four attached groups, 120° for three attached groups, and 180° for two attached groups.
2. Nitrogen forms three covalent bonds and has one unshared pair of electrons. Bond angles on nitrogen are approximately 109.5° for three attached groups

and one unshared pair of electrons; they are 120° for two attached groups and one unshared pair of electrons.

3. Oxygen forms two covalent bonds and has two unshared pairs of electrons. Bond angles on oxygen are approximately 109.5° for two attached groups.

These generalizations are summarized in Table 10.2.

Table 10.2
Summary of predicted bond angles for neutral covalent compounds of carbon, nitrogen, and oxygen according to the valence-shell electron-pair repulsion (VSEPR) model.

Regions of Electron Density		Predicted Bond Angles	Examples
Number	**Arrangement in Space**		
4	tetrahedral	109.5°	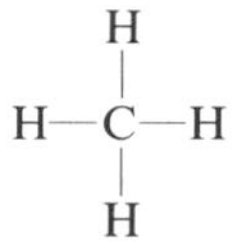 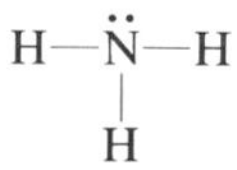 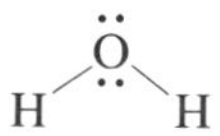 H—C—H (with H above and below); H—N—H (with H below); H O H
3	trigonal planar	120°	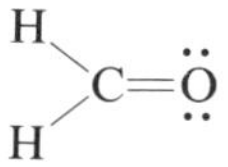 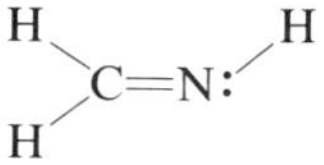 C=O (with two H); C=N: (with H's)
2	linear	180°	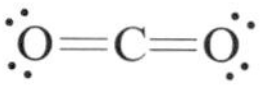  O=C=O; H—C≡N:

10.2 Functional Groups

Carbon combines with other atoms (C, H, N, O, S, halogens, and so on) to form characteristic structural units called **functional groups**. Functional groups are important for three reasons. First, they are the units by which we divide organic molecules into classes. Second, they are sites of chemical reaction; a particular functional group, in whatever compound it is found, undergoes the same types of chemical reactions. Third, functional groups are a basis for naming organic compounds.

A. Alcohols and Ethers

The characteristic structural feature of an **alcohol** is an atom of oxygen bonded to one carbon atom and one hydrogen atom. We say that an alcohol contains an —OH, or **hydroxyl group**. The characteristic structural feature of an **ether** is an atom of oxygen bonded to two carbon atoms.

$$H-\overset{\overset{\displaystyle H}{|}}{C}-\overset{..}{\underset{..}{O}}-H \qquad H-\overset{\overset{\displaystyle H}{|}}{\underset{\underset{\displaystyle H}{|}}{C}}-\overset{..}{\underset{..}{O}}-\overset{\overset{\displaystyle H}{|}}{\underset{\underset{\displaystyle H}{|}}{C}}-H$$

Characteristic structural feature:	an alcohol $C-\overset{..}{\underset{..}{O}}-H$	an ether $C-\overset{..}{\underset{..}{O}}-C$

We can write formulas for this alcohol and ether in a more abbreviated form by using what are called **condensed structural formulas**. In a condensed structural formula, CH_3—indicates a carbon with three attached hydrogens, CH_2— indicates a carbon with two attached hydrogens, and $-\overset{|}{C}H-$ indicates a carbon with one attached hydrogen. Following are Lewis structures and condensed structural formulas for the alcohol and ether of the molecular formula C_2H_6O.

Lewis Structures

$$H-\overset{\overset{\displaystyle H}{|}}{\underset{\underset{\displaystyle H}{|}}{C}}-\overset{\overset{\displaystyle H}{|}}{\underset{\underset{\displaystyle H}{|}}{C}}-\overset{..}{\underset{..}{O}}-H \qquad H-\overset{\overset{\displaystyle H}{|}}{\underset{\underset{\displaystyle H}{|}}{C}}-\overset{..}{\underset{..}{O}}-\overset{\overset{\displaystyle H}{|}}{\underset{\underset{\displaystyle H}{|}}{C}}-H$$

Condensed Structural Formulas

$$CH_3CH_2OH \qquad CH_3OCH_3$$

Example 10.1

There are two alcohols of molecular formula C_3H_8O. Draw Lewis structures and condensed structural formulas for each.

☐ *Solution*

The characteristic structural feature of an alcohol is an atom of oxygen bonded to one carbon and one hydrogen atom:

$$C-\overset{..}{\underset{..}{O}}-H$$

The molecular formula contains three carbon atoms. These can be bonded together in a chain with the —OH (hydroxyl) group attached to the end carbon of the chain or attached to the middle carbon of the chain:

$$C-C-C-\overset{..}{\underset{..}{O}}-H \qquad C-\overset{|}{\underset{\underset{\displaystyle H}{|}}{\underset{\displaystyle :O:}{C}}}-C$$

Finally, add seven hydrogens to satisfy the tetravelence of carbon and give the correct molecular formula:

Lewis Structures

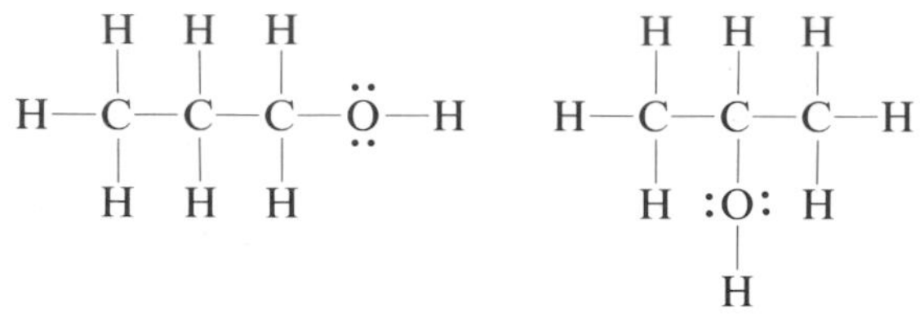

Condensed Structural Formulas

$$CH_3CH_2CH_2OH \qquad CH_3CHCH_3$$
$$\qquad\qquad\qquad\qquad\quad |$$
$$\qquad\qquad\qquad\qquad\ OH$$

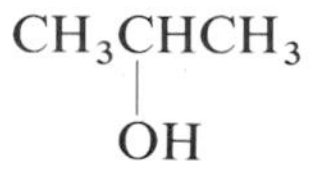

Problem 10.1

There is one ether of molecular formula C_3H_8O. Draw a Lewis structure and a condensed structural formula for this compound.

B. Aldehydes and Ketones

Both aldehydes and ketones contain a **carbonyl group**, **C═O**, the most important functional group in organic chemistry. The characteristic structural feature of an **aldehyde** is a carbonyl group bonded to a hydrogen atom. Formaldehyde is the only aldehyde that contains two hydrogen atoms bonded to a carbonyl group. All other aldehydes have one carbon and one hydrogen bonded to a carbonyl group. The characteristic structural feature of a **ketone** is a carbonyl group bonded to two carbon atoms.

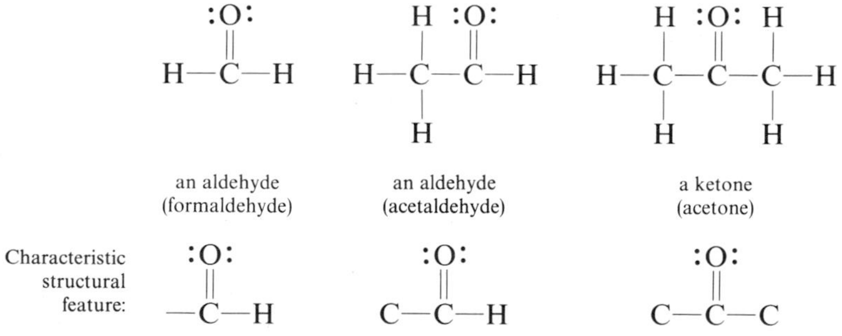

an aldehyde
(formaldehyde)

an aldehyde
(acetaldehyde)

a ketone
(acetone)

Characteristic structural feature:

Example 10.2

Draw Lewis structures and condensed structural formulas for the two aldehydes of molecular formula C_4H_8O.

☐ *Solution*

First draw the characteristic structural feature of the aldehyde group and then add the remaining carbons. These may be attached in two different ways.

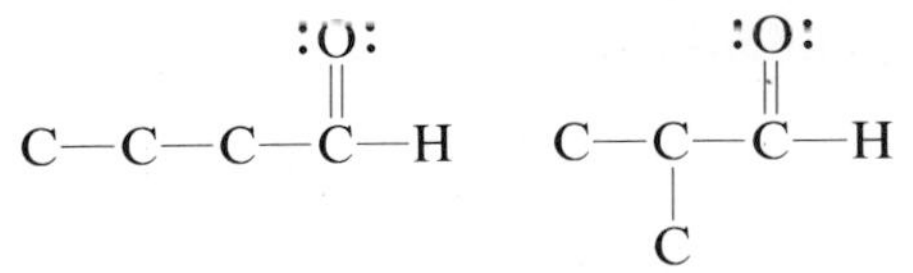

$$
\begin{array}{c}
\quad\;\; :\!O\!: \\
\quad\;\; \| \\
C-C-C-\overset{}{C}-H \qquad
\begin{array}{c}
:\!O\!: \\
\| \\
C-C-\overset{\underset{\displaystyle |}{\displaystyle C}}{C}-H
\end{array}
\end{array}
$$

Finally add seven hydrogens to complete the tetravalence of carbon and give the correct molecular formula. The aldehyde group may be written as above, or alternatively, it may be written —CHO.

Lewis Structures

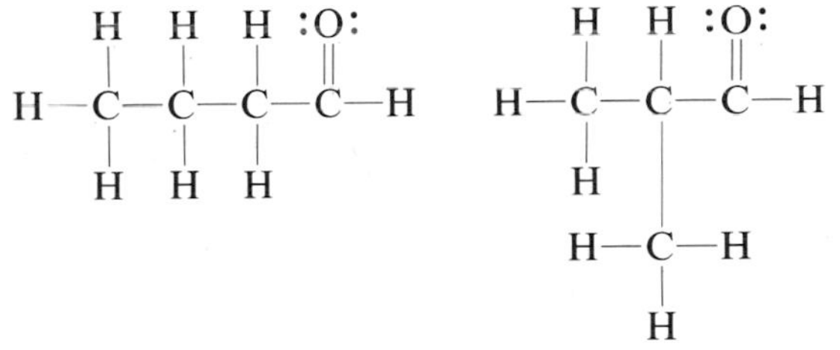

$$
\begin{array}{c}
H\;\; H\;\; H\; :\!O\!: \\
|\quad |\quad |\quad \| \\
H-C-C-C-C-H \\
|\quad |\quad | \\
H\;\; H\;\; H
\end{array}
\qquad
\begin{array}{c}
H\;\; H\; :\!O\!: \\
|\quad |\quad \| \\
H-C-C-C-H \\
|\quad | \\
H\quad H-C-H \\
\qquad\;\; | \\
\qquad\;\; H
\end{array}
$$

Condensed Structural Formulas

$$
\begin{array}{c}
O \\
\| \\
CH_3CH_2CH_2CH
\end{array}
\qquad
\begin{array}{c}
O \\
\| \\
CH_3CHCH \\
| \\
CH_3
\end{array}
$$

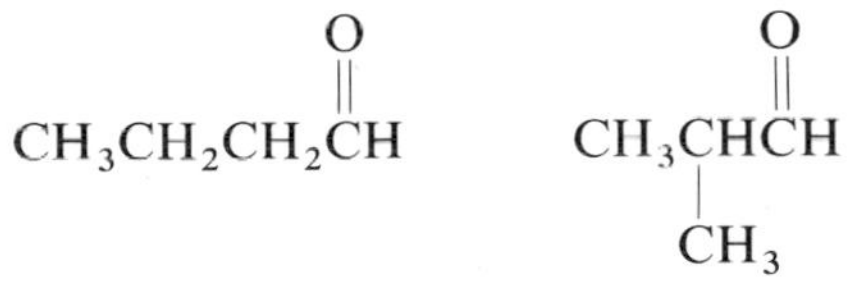

or   or

$$CH_3CH_2CH_2CHO \qquad (CH_3)_2CHCHO$$

**Problem
10.2**

Draw Lewis structures and condensed structural formulas for the three ketones of molecular formula $C_5H_{10}O$.

C. Carboxylic Acids

The characteristic structural feature of a **carboxylic acid** is a carboxyl (carbonyl + hydroxyl) group. The **carboxyl group** may be written in any of the following ways, all of which are equivalent.

A Carboxyl Group

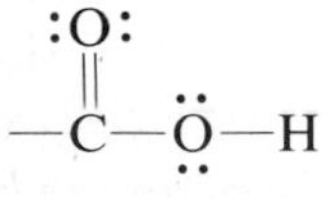

$$
\begin{array}{c}
:\!O\!: \\
\| \\
-C-\overset{..}{\underset{..}{O}}-H
\end{array}
\qquad \text{or} \qquad -COOH \qquad \text{or} \qquad -CO_2H
$$

A Carboxylic Acid

$$
\begin{array}{c}
\text{H} \quad :\!\overset{\displaystyle ..}{\text{O}}: \\
| \quad \quad \| \\
\text{H}-\text{C}-\text{C}-\overset{..}{\underset{..}{\text{O}}}-\text{H} \\
| \\
\text{H}
\end{array}
\quad \text{or} \quad \text{CH}_3\text{COOH} \quad \text{or} \quad \text{CH}_3\text{CO}_2\text{H}
$$

Example 10.3

Draw a Lewis structure and condensed structural formula for the single carboxylic acid of molecular formula $C_3H_6O_2$.

☐ *Solution*

Lewis Structure

$$
\begin{array}{c}
\text{H} \quad \text{H} \quad :\!\overset{\displaystyle ..}{\text{O}}: \\
| \quad \; | \quad \; \| \\
\text{H}-\text{C}-\text{C}-\text{C}-\overset{..}{\underset{..}{\text{O}}}-\text{H} \\
| \quad \; | \\
\text{H} \quad \text{H}
\end{array}
$$

Condensed Structural Formula

$$
\begin{array}{c}
\text{O} \\
\| \\
\text{CH}_3\text{CH}_2\text{COH}
\end{array}
\quad \text{or} \quad \text{CH}_3\text{CH}_2\text{COOH} \quad \text{or} \quad \text{CH}_3\text{CH}_2\text{CO}_2\text{H}
$$

Problem 10.3

Draw Lewis structures and condensed structural formulas for the two carboxylic acids of molecular formula $C_4H_8O_2$.

10.3 Structural Isomerism

For most molecular formulas it is possible to draw more than one structural formula. For example, the following compounds have the same molecular formula, C_2H_6O, but different structural formulas and different functional groups; the first is an alcohol, the second an ether.

$$
\begin{array}{c}
\text{H} \quad \text{H} \\
| \quad \; | \\
\text{H}-\text{C}-\text{C}-\text{O}-\text{H} \\
| \quad \; | \\
\text{H} \quad \text{H}
\end{array}
\qquad
\begin{array}{c}
\text{H} \quad \quad \text{H} \\
| \quad \quad \; | \\
\text{H}-\text{C}-\text{O}-\text{C}-\text{H} \\
| \quad \quad \; | \\
\text{H} \quad \quad \text{H}
\end{array}
$$

an alcohol   an ether

Similarly, the following compounds have the same molecular formula, C_3H_6O, and the same functional group (a carbonyl group). The first is an aldehyde, however, and the second is a ketone.

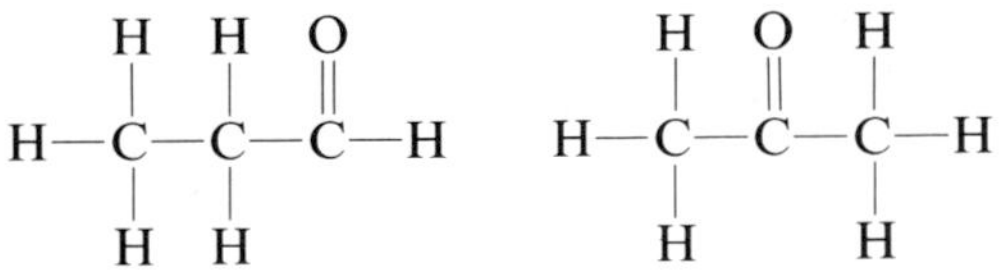

an aldehyde   a ketone

The following alcohols have the same molecular formula but different structural formulas:

$$CH_3-CH_2-CH_2-OH \qquad CH_3-CH-CH_3$$
$$\qquad\qquad\qquad\qquad\qquad\qquad | $$
$$\qquad\qquad\qquad\qquad\qquad\quad OH$$

Compounds that have the same molecular formula but different structural formulas (different orders of attachment of atoms) are called **structural isomers**. To determine whether two or more compounds are structural isomers, first write the molecular formula of each compound and then compare them. All those that have the same molecular formula but different orders of attachment of atoms are structural isomers.

Example 10.4

Divide the following into groups of structural isomers.

a. $CH_3-CH_2-\overset{\displaystyle O}{\overset{\displaystyle \|}{C}}-OH$

b. $CH_3 \quad O \quad CH_2-\overset{\displaystyle O}{\overset{\displaystyle \|}{C}}-H$

c. $CH_2=CH-CH_2-O-CH_3$

d. $CH_3-\underset{\underset{\displaystyle CH_3}{|}}{CH}-\overset{\displaystyle O}{\overset{\displaystyle \|}{C}}-H$

e. $CH_3-\overset{\displaystyle O}{\overset{\displaystyle \|}{C}}-CH_2-CH_2-CH_2-OH$

f. $CH_3-\overset{\displaystyle O}{\overset{\displaystyle \|}{C}}-CH_2-OH$

Solution

Compounds (a), (b), and (f) have the same molecular formula, $C_3H_6O_2$, but different structural formulas and are structural isomers. Compounds (c) and (d) have the same molecular formula, C_4H_8O, but different structural formulas and are also structural isomers. There are no structural isomers in this problem for compound (e).

Problem 10.4

Divide the following into groups of structural isomers.

a. $CH_2=CH-O-CH=CH_2$

b. $HC\equiv C-\overset{\displaystyle O}{\overset{\displaystyle \|}{C}}-CH_3$

c. $CH_3-CH_2-O-C\equiv CH$ d. $CH_3-CH=CH-\overset{\overset{\displaystyle O}{\|}}{C}-H$

10.4 Need for Another Model of Covalent Bonding

As much as the Lewis and valence-shell electron-pair repulsion models (Section 4.4) have helped us understand covalent bonding and the geometry of organic molecules, they leave many important questions unanswered. The most important is the relation between molecular structure and chemical reactivity. For example, a carbon-carbon single bond is different in chemical reactivity from a carbon-carbon double bond. Most carbon-carbon single bonds are unreactive, but carbon-carbon double bonds react with a great variety of reactants. The Lewis model of bonding gives us no way to account for these differences. Therefore let us turn to a new model of bonding, namely, formation of covalent bonds by the overlap of atomic orbitals.

10.5 Covalent Bond Formation by the Overlap of Atomic Orbitals

According to modern bonding theory, formation of a covalent bond between two atoms amounts to bringing them together in such a way that an atomic orbital of one atom overlaps an atomic orbital of the other. In forming the covalent bond in H_2, for example, two hydrogen atoms approach each other so their 1s atomic orbitals overlap (Figure 10.1). The new orbital formed by the overlap of two atomic orbitals encompasses both hydrogen nuclei and is called a **molecular orbital**. Like an atomic orbital, a molecular orbital can accommodate two electrons. In the covalent bond illustrated in Figure 10.1, the orbital overlap, and therefore the electron density in the resulting molecular orbital, are concentrated about the axis joining the two nuclei. A covalent bond in which orbital overlap of the bond is concentrated along the axis joining the two nuclei is called a **sigma (σ) bond**.

Carbon, nitrogen, and oxygen form covalent bonds using atomic orbitals of the second principal energy level. The second principal energy level consists of four atomic orbitals: a single 2s orbital and three 2p orbitals (Section 3.1B).

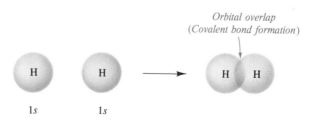

Figure 10.1 Formation of a covalent bond by overlap of two 1s atomic orbitals.

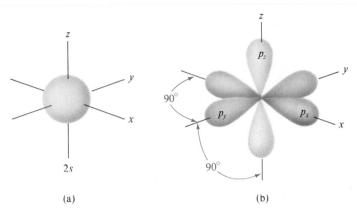

Figure 10.2 Atomic orbitals of the second principal energy level. (a) Shape of the $2s$ orbital; (b) orientations in space of the three $2p$ orbitals relative to each other.

The $2p$ orbitals are designated $2p_x$, $2p_y$, and $2p_z$ and are oriented along the x axis, y axis, and z axis respectively. Figure 10.2 shows these atomic orbitals.

The three $2p$ orbitals are at $90°$ angles to each other (Figure 10.2), and if atoms of carbon, nitrogen, or oxygen used these orbitals to form covalent bonds, bond angles around each would be approximately $90°$. Bond angles of $90°$ are not observed in organic compounds, however (Section 4.5). What we find instead are bond angles of approximately $109.5°$, $120°$, or $180°$. To account for these observed bond angles, Linus Pauling proposed that atomic orbitals may combine to form new orbitals, which then interact to form bonds with the angles we do observe. The combination of atomic orbitals is called **hybridization**, and the new atomic orbitals formed are called hybrid atomic orbitals, or more simply, hybrid orbitals.

A. sp^3 Hybrid Orbitals

Combination of one $2s$ orbital and three $2p$ orbitals produces four equivalent orbitals called **sp^3 hybrid orbitals** (Figure 10.3). The four sp^3 hybrid orbitals are directed toward the corners of a regular tetrahedron, and sp^3 hybridization produces bond angles of approximately $109.5°$.

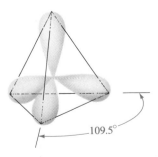

Figure 10.3 sp^3 hybrid orbitals.

In Section 4.5, we described the covalent bonding in CH_4, NH_3, and H_2O by the Lewis model. Now let us consider the bonding in these molecules in terms of the overlap of atomic orbitals. To bond to four other atoms, carbon uses sp^3 hybrid orbitals. Carbon has four valence electrons, and one electron is placed in each sp^3 orbital. Each partially filled sp^3 orbital then overlaps a partially filled $1s$ orbital of hydrogen to form a sigma bond, and hydrogen atoms occupy the corners of a regular tetrahedron (Figure 10.4). In bonding with three other atoms, the five valence electrons of nitrogen are distributed so that one sp^3 is

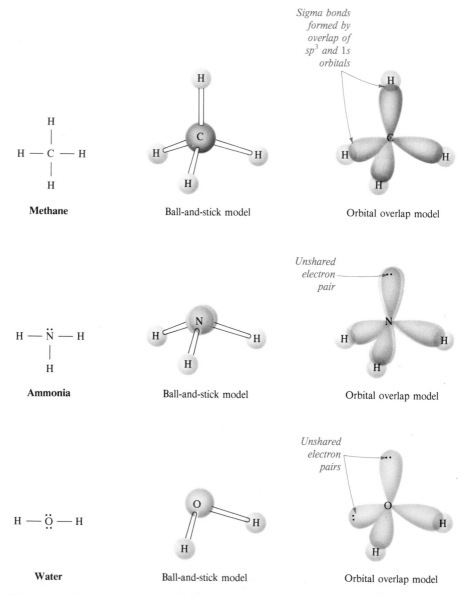

Figure 10.4 Lewis structures, ball-and-stick models, and orbital overlap diagrams for molecules of methane, CH_4, ammonia, NH_3, and water, H_2O.

filled with a pair of electrons and the other three sp^3 orbitals have one electron each. Overlap of these partially filled sp^3 orbitals by $1s$ orbitals of hydrogen gives the NH_3 molecule (Figure 10.4). In bonding with two other atoms, the six valence electrons of oxygen are distributed so that two sp^3 orbitals are filled and the remaining two have one electron each. Each partially filled sp^3 orbital overlaps a $1s$ orbital of hydrogen, and hydrogen atoms occupy two corners of a regular tetrahedron. The remaining two corners of the tetrahedron are occupied by unshared pairs of electrons (Figure 10.4).

B. sp^2 Hybrid Orbitals

Combination of one $2s$ orbital and two $2p$ orbitals produces three equivalent orbitals called sp^2 hybrid orbitals. The three sp^2 hybrid orbitals lie in a plane and are directed toward the corners of an equilateral triangle; the angle between sp^2 orbitals is 120° [Figure 10.5(a)]. Figure 10.5(b) shows three equivalent sp^2 hybrid orbitals along with the remaining unhybridized $2p$ orbital.

The sp^2 hybrid orbitals are used by second-row elements to form double bonds. Consider ethylene, C_2H_4 [see the Lewis structure in Figure 10.6(a)]. A sigma bond between carbons is formed by overlap of sp^2 orbitals along a common axis [Figure 10.6(b)]. Each carbon also forms sigma bonds to two

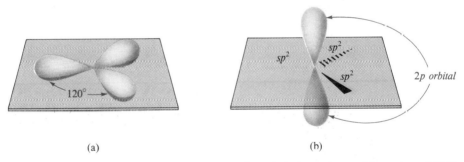

(a)   (b)

Figure 10.5 sp^2 hybrid orbitals. (a) Three sp^2 orbitals in a plane with angles of 120° between them; (b) the unhybridized $2p$ orbital is perpendicular to the plane created by the three sp^2 hybrid orbitals.

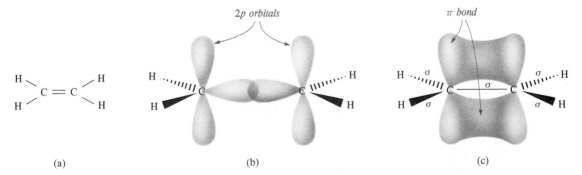

(a)   (b)   (c)

Figure 10.6 Covalent bond formation in ethylene. (a) Lewis structure; (b) a sigma bond between carbon atoms is formed by overlap of sp^2 orbitals (the unhybridized $2p$ orbitals are shown uncombined); (c) the overlap of parallel $2p$ orbitals forms a pi bond.

hydrogens. The remaining $2p$ orbitals on adjacent carbon atoms lie parallel to each other and overlap to form a bond in which electron density is concentrated above and below the axis of the two nuclei. A bond formed by the overlap of parallel p orbitals is called a **pi (π) bond**. Because of the lesser degree of overlap of orbitals forming pi bonds compared with those forming sigma bonds, pi bonds are generally weaker than sigma bonds.

All double bonds can be described in the same manner as we have described a carbon-carbon double bond. In formaldehyde, which is the simplest organic molecule containing a carbon-oxygen double bond, carbon forms sigma bonds to two hydrogens by overlap of sp^2 orbitals of carbon and $1s$ orbitals of hydrogen. Carbon and oxygen are joined by a sigma bond formed by overlap of sp^2 orbitals. Figure 10.7 shows the Lewis structure of formaldehyde, the sigma bond framework, and overlap of parallel $2p$ orbitals to form a pi bond. Similarly, a carbon-nitrogen double bond is a combination of one sigma bond and one pi bond.

C. *sp* Hybrid Orbitals

Combination of one $2s$ orbital and one $2p$ orbital produces two equivalent **sp hybrid orbitals** that lie at an angle of $180°$ with the nucleus. The unhybridized $2p$ orbitals lie in planes perpendicular to each other and perpendicular to the

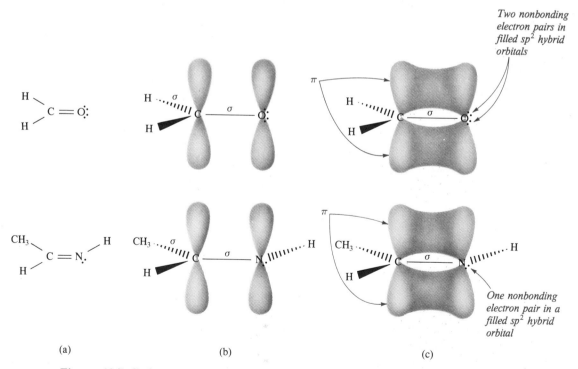

(a)   (b)   (c)

Figure 10.7 Carbon-oxygen and carbon-nitrogen double bonds. (a) Lewis structures of formaldehyde, $CH_2{=}O$, and methylene imine, $CH_2{=}NH$; (b) the sigma bond framework and nonoverlapping $2p$ orbitals; (c) overlap of parallel $2p$ orbitals to form a pi bond.

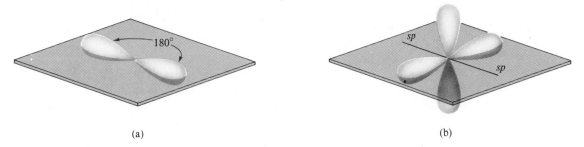

Figure 10.8 *sp* hybrid orbitals. (a) Two *sp* hybrid orbitals; (b) the two remaining
2*p* orbitals are perpendicular to each other and to the linear *sp* orbitals.

plane of the *sp* hybrid orbitals. In Figure 10.8, *sp* hybrid orbitals are shown
on the *x* axis and unhybridized 2*p* orbitals on the *y* axis and the *z* axis.

Figure 10.9 shows Lewis structures and orbital overlap pictures for acetylene
and hydrogen cyanide. A carbon-carbon triple bond consists of one sigma bond
formed by overlap of *sp* hybrid orbitals and two pi bonds. One pi bond is
formed by overlap of 2*p*$_y$ orbitals and the second by overlap of 2*p*$_z$ orbitals.
Similarly, a carbon-nitrogen triple bond also consists of one sigma bond and
two pi bonds.

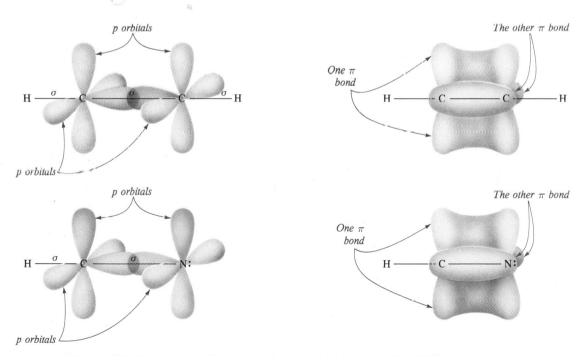

Figure 10.9 Covalent bonding in acetylene and hydrogen cyanide. (a) The sigma bond
framework, shown along with nonoverlapping 2*p* orbitals; (b) formation of two pi bonds
by the overlap of two sets of 2*p* orbitals.

If you compare the predictions of bond angles in the small molecules we have studied in this chapter, you will see that the valence-shell electron-pair repulsion model (Section 4.5) and the orbital overlap model give equally good predictions. The orbital overlap model, however, gives us a more useful understanding of double and triple bonds. A double bond is not a combination of two identical bonds. Rather, it consists of one sigma bond and one pi bond. The distribution of the bonding electrons in a pi bond is quite different from distribution in a sigma bond. Similarly, a triple bond is not a combination of three identical bonds. Rather, it consists of one sigma bond and two pi bonds. The relations among the number of groups bonded to carbon, orbital hybridization, and types of bonds involved are summarized in Table 10.3.

Table 10.3
Covalent bonding of carbon.

Groups Bonded to Carbon	Orbital Hybridization	Types of Bonds Involved	Example
4	sp^3	four sigma bonds	H—C—C—H (ethane, with H above and below each C)
3	sp^2	three sigma bonds and one pi bond	C=C (ethylene) and C=Ö (formaldehyde)
2	sp	two sigma bonds and two pi bonds	H—C≡C—H Ö=C=Ö

We will use the orbital overlap picture of covalent bonding in later chapters to help us understand why compounds containing double and triple bonds have different chemical properties from compounds containing only single bonds.

■

Example 10.5

Describe the bonding in these molecules in terms of the atomic orbitals involved, and predict all bond angles.

a. H—C—Ö—H   (with H above and below the C)

b. H—C—C—Ö—H   (with H above and below the first C, and :O: double-bonded above the second C)

□ Solution

The problem here is how to show clearly and concisely on a structural formula (1) the hybridization of each atom, (2) the atomic orbitals involved in each covalent bond, and (3) all bond angles. One way to do this is in three separate diagrams, as follows. Labels on the first diagram point to atoms and show the hybridization of each atom. Labels on the second diagram point to bonds and show the type of bond, either sigma or pi. Labels on the third diagram point to atoms and show predicted bond angles about each atom.

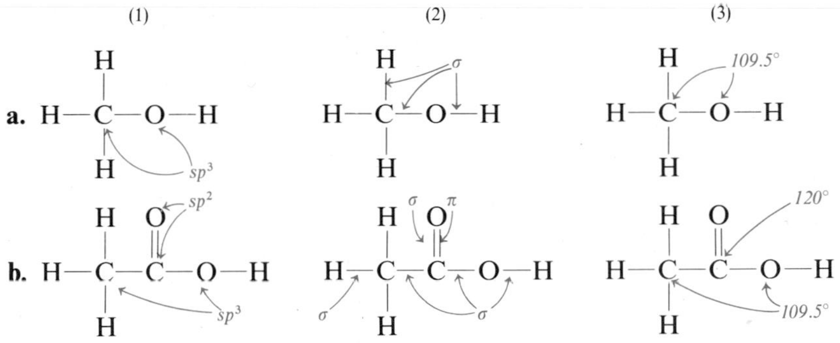

(1)   (2)   (3)

a. H—C—O—H   H—C—O—H   H—C—O—H

b. H—C—C—O—H   H—C—C—O—H   H—C—C—O—H

Problem 10.5 Describe the bonding in the following molecules in terms of atomic orbitals involved and predict all bond angles.

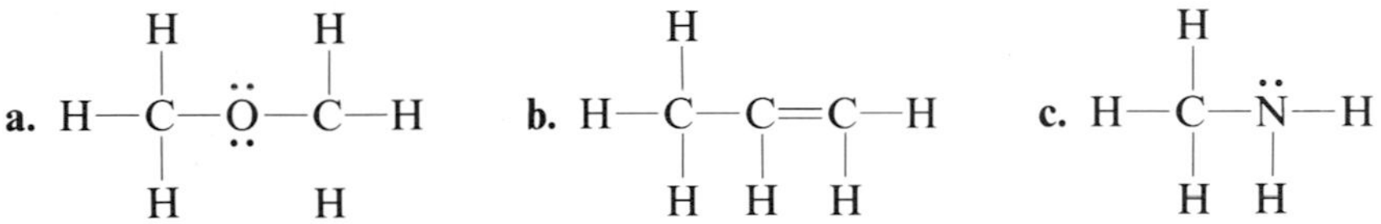

a. H—C—Ö—C—H   b. H—C—C=C—H   c. H—C—N—H

Key Terms and Concepts

alcohol (10.2A) sp^2 hybrid orbital (10.5B)
aldehyde (10.2B) sp^3 hybrid orbital (10.5A)
carbonyl group (10.2B)   hybridization (10.5)
carboxyl group (10.2C)   hydroxyl group (10.2A)
carboxylic acid (10.2C)   ketone (10.2B)
condensed structural formula (10.2A)   molecular orbital (10.5)
ether (10.2A)   pi bond (10.5B)
functional group (10.2)   sigma bond (10.5)
sp hybrid orbital (10.5C)   structural isomerism (10.3)

Problems

Lewis structures of covalent molecules and ions (Sections 4.3, 4.4, and 10.1)

10.6 What is the relationship between the Lewis structures of H, C, N, O, and F and the valence of these elements?

10.7 Write Lewis structures for the following atoms and state how many electrons each must gain, lose, or share to achieve the same electron configuration as that of the noble gas nearest it in the periodic table.
    a. carbon   **b.** nitrogen   **c.** sulfur
    d. oxygen   **e.** hydrogen   **f.** chlorine
    g. phosphorus   **h.** bromine   **i.** iodine

10.8   Write Lewis structures for these molecules. Be certain to show all valence electrons. In some parts of this problem where the order of attachment of atoms may not be obvious to you, the name of the functional group present in the molecule is given to help you arrive at the correct order of attachment of atoms.

a. H_2O_2	**b.** N_2H_4	**c.** CH_3OH
d. CH_3SH	**e.** CH_3NH_2	**f.** CH_3Cl
g. CH_3OCH_3	**h.** C_2H_6	**i.** C_2H_4
j. C_2H_2	**k.** CO_2	**l.** H_2CO_3
m. CH_2O	**n.** CH_3CHO (an aldehyde)	**o.** CH_3COCH_3 (a ketone)
p. HCO_2H (a carboxylic acid)	**q.** CH_3CO_2H (a carboxylic acid)	

10.9   Write Lewis structures for the following ions. Be certain to show all valence electrons and all formal charges.

a. CH_3O^-	**b.** H_3O^+	**c.** $CH_3NH_3^+$
d. Cl^-	**e.** HCO_3^-	**f.** CO_3^{2-}
g. $CH_3CO_2^-$	**h.** HCO_2^-	

10.10   Following are Lewis structures for several ions. All valence electrons on each atom are shown. Assign formal charges to each structure as appropriate.

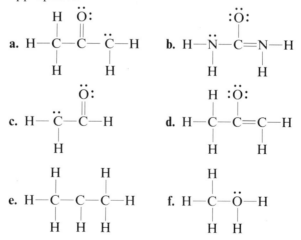

10.11   Following the rule that each atom of carbon, oxygen, nitrogen, and the halogens reacts to achieve a complete outer shell of eight valence electrons, add unshared pairs of electrons as necessary to complete the valence shells of these molecules and ions. Then assign formal charges as appropriate.

H H
d. 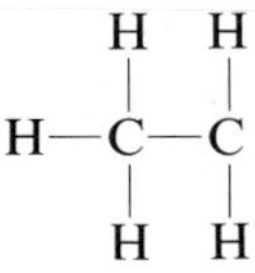 H—C—C
H H

H O
e. 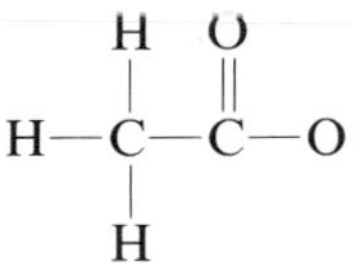 H—C—C—O
H

H H O
f. 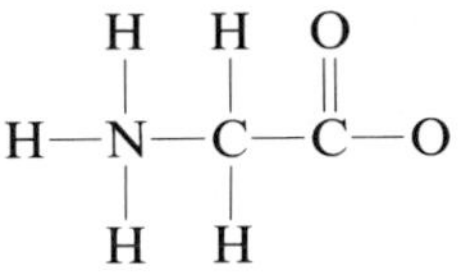 H—N—C—C—O
H H

Ionic and
covalent
bonds
(Section 4.5)

10.12 Following are compounds containing both ionic and covalent bonds. Draw Lewis structures for each. Show covalent bonds by dashes and ionic bonds by positive and negative charges on the appropriate atoms.
  a. NaOH   **b.** NH$_4$Cl   **c.** NaHCO$_3$
  d. Na$_2$CO$_3$ **e.** HCO$_2$Na   **f.** CH$_3$CO$_2$Na

Partial ionic
character of
covalent
bonds
(Section 4.7)

10.13 Arrange the single covalent bonds within each set in order of increasing partial ionic character.
  a. C—H, O—H, N—H   **b.** C—H, C—O, C—N
  c. C—H, C—Cl, C—I   **d.** C—S, C—O, C—F

10.14 For each polar covalent bond in these molecules, label the partially positive atom with δ^+ and the partially negative atom with δ^-.

a.  H—N—H
        H

H O
b. 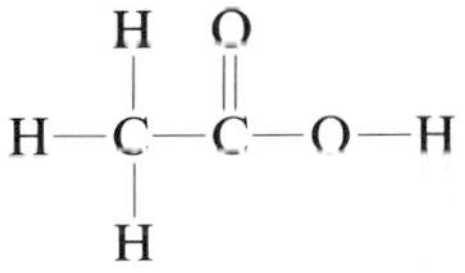 H—C—C—O—H
        H

H
c. H—C—S—H
        H

H O H
d. 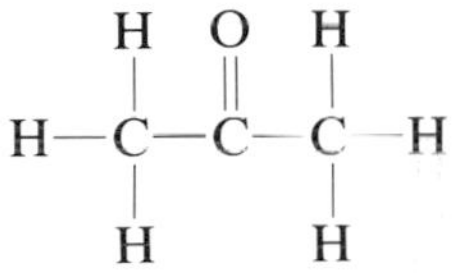 H—C—C—C—H
        H   H

H H
e. 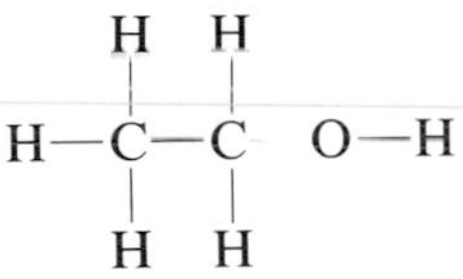 H—C—C O—H
        H H

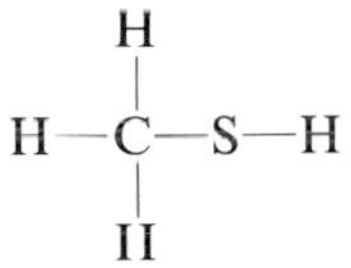

H H
f. 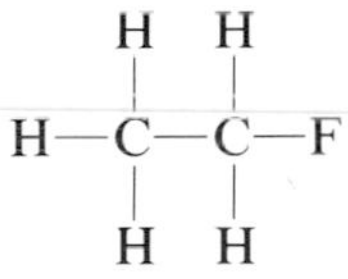 H—C—C—F
        H H

H   H
g. 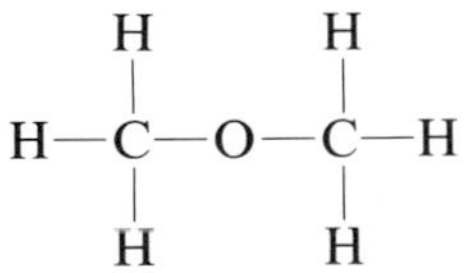 H—C—O—C—H
        H   H

Cl   H
h.   C=C
H   H

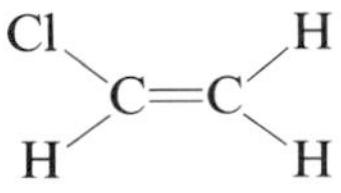

10.15 An organometallic compound is one containing a carbon-metal bond. Following are two organometallics, both of which are probably familiar to you because of particular hazards they pose to human health and the environment. For each, state whether the carbon-metal bond is pure covalent, polar covalent, or ionic. (*Hint:* Review the section on electro-negativity and its relation to chemical bonding.)

$$CH_2-CH_3$$
$$|$$
a. 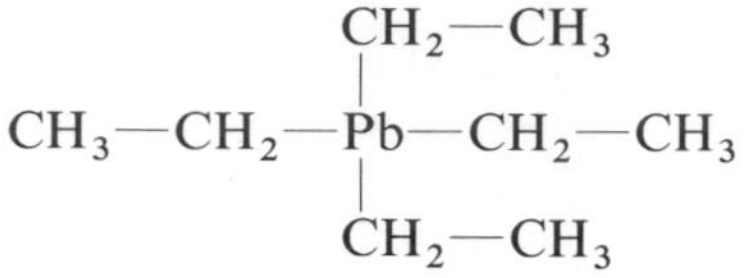 $CH_3-CH_2-Pb-CH_2-CH_3$ **b.** $CH_3-Hg-CH_3$
$$|$$
$$CH_2-CH_3$$

tetraethyl lead
(the octane-improving
additive in leaded
gasoline)

dimethyl mercury
(anaerobic bacteria in ocean
and lake sediments can convert
mercuric ion, Hg(II), to dimethyl
mercury, a substance very toxic
to higher organisms)

Bond angles and shapes of molecules (Sections 4.6 and 10.1)

10.16 Explain how the valence-shell electron-pair repulsion model is used to predict bond angles.

10.17 Following are Lewis structures for several molecules. Use the valence-shell electron-pair repulsion model to predict bond angles about each circled atom.

a. 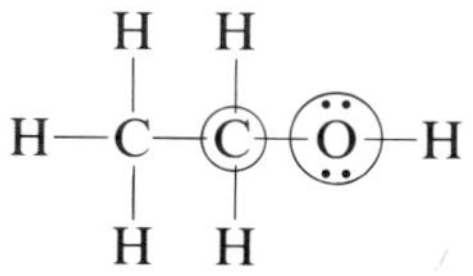 H—C—C—O—H

b. H—C—C—H

c. H—C=C—Cl:

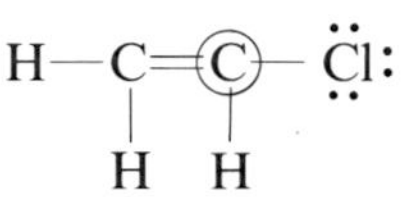

d. 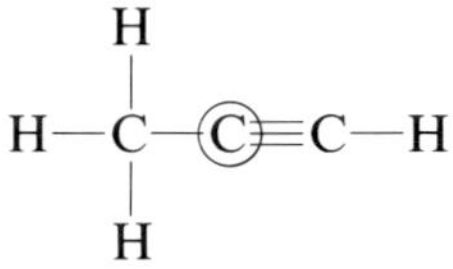 H—C—C≡C—H

e. 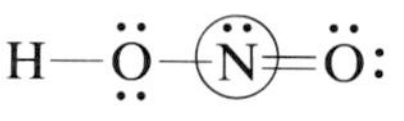 H—O—N=O:

f. 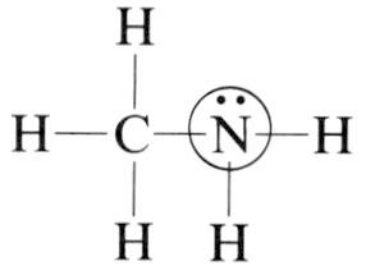 H—C—N—H

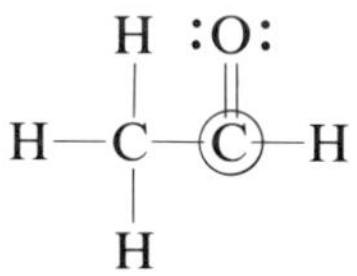

g. H—C—O—C—H

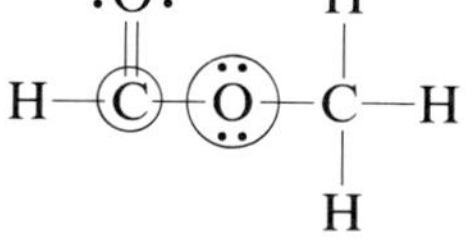

h. H—O—C—O—H

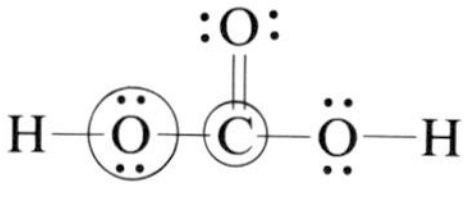

i. 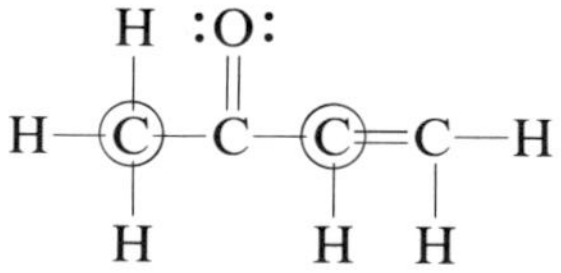 H—C—C—C=C—H

Functional groups (Section 10.2)

10.18 Draw Lewis structures for the following functional groups. Be certain to show all valence electrons on each.
    a. carbonyl group   **b.** carboxyl group   **c.** hydroxyl group

10.19 Draw condensed structural formulas for all compounds of molecular formula C_4H_8O that contain the following functional groups:
   a. a ketone (there is only one)
   b. an aldehyde (there are two)
   c. a carbon-carbon double bond and an ether (there are four)
   d. a carbon-carbon double bond and an alcohol (there are eight)

10.20 Draw structural formulas for:
   a. the eight alcohols of molecular formula $C_5H_{12}O$
   b. the six ethers of molecular formula $C_5H_{12}O$
   c. the eight aldehydes of molecular formula $C_6H_{12}O$
   d. the six ketones of molecular formula $C_6H_{12}O$
   e. the eight carboxylic acids of molecular formula $C_6H_{12}O_2$

Structural
isomerism
(Section 10.3)

10.21 Which of the following are true about structural isomers?
   a. They have the same molecular formula.
   b. They have the same molecular weight.
   c. They have the same order of attachment of atoms.
   d. They have the same physical properties.

10.22 Are the following pairs of molecules structural isomers or are they identical?

a. CH_3—CH—CH_3
           |
           O
           |
     CH_3—CH—CH_3

and CH_3—CH—O—CH—CH_3 (with CH_3 and CH_3 above)

b. CH_2=CH—CH_2—CH_3 and CH_3—CH=CH—CH_3

c. CH_3—O—C—H (with O double bond)   and CH_3—C—O—H (with O double bond)

d. HO—CH_2 CH OH (with CH_3 above)   and CH_3 CH—OH (with CH_2—OH above)

e. H—C—CH_2—CH—CH_3 (with O double bond, CH_3 below)   and CH_3 \ CH—CH_2—C—H / CH_3 (with O double bond)

f. CH_3—CH—CH_2—CH_3 and
           |
     CH_2—CH—CH_3
           |
     CH_3

CH_3—CH—CH_2—CH_2—CH—CH_3
           | |
     CH_3 CH_3

Covalent bond formation by the overlap of atomic orbitals (Section 10.5)

10.23 Following are Lewis structures for several molecules. State the orbital hybridization of each circled atom.

a.

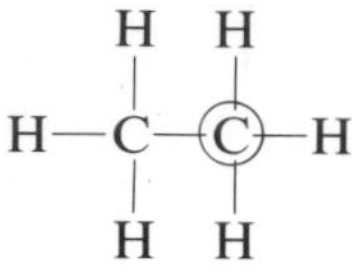

```
    H  H
    |  |
H—C—(C)—H
    |  |
    H  H
```

b.

```
  H           H
   \         /
    (C)=C
   /         \
  H           H
```

c.

```
    H           H
    |           |
H—O—(O)—C—H
    |           |
    H           H
```

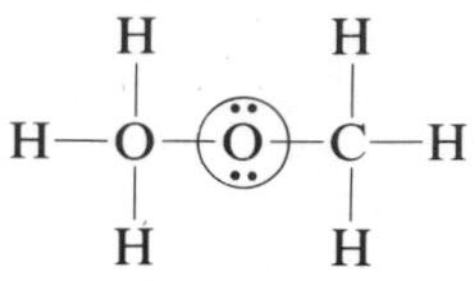

d.

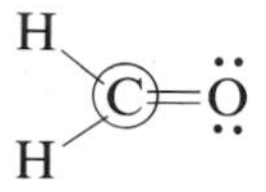

```
  H
   \
    (C)=Ö
   /
  H
```

e.

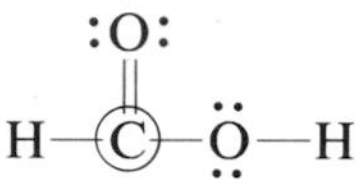

```
      :O:
       ‖
H—(C)—Ö—H
```

f.

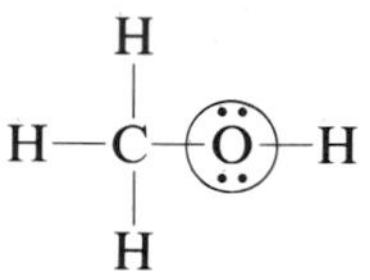

```
    H
    |
H—C—(O)—H
    |
    H
```

g.

```
    H
    |
H—C—(N)—H
    |  |
    H  H
```

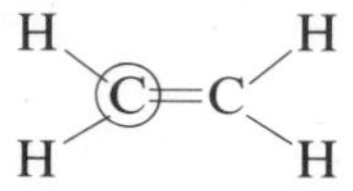

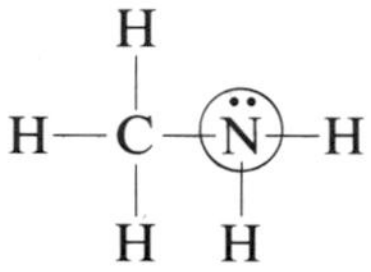

10.24 Following are Lewis structures for several molecules. Describe each circled bond in terms of the overlap of atomic orbitals.

a.

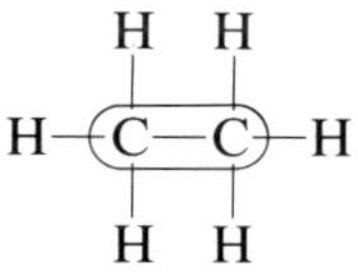

```
    H  H
    |  |
H—(C—C)—H
    |  |
    H  H
```

b.

```
  H           H
   \         /
    (C=C)
   /         \
  H           H
```

c.

```
    H           H
    |           |
H—C—(O—C)—H
    |           |
    H           H
```

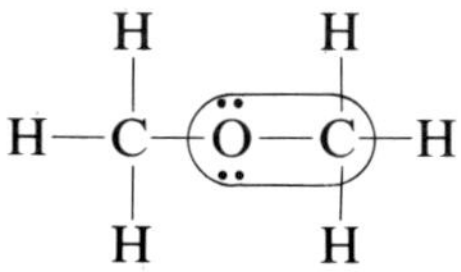

d.

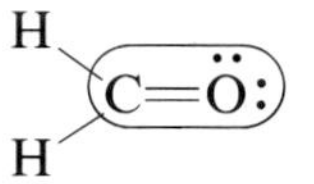

```
  H
   \
    (C=Ö:)
   /
  H
```

e.

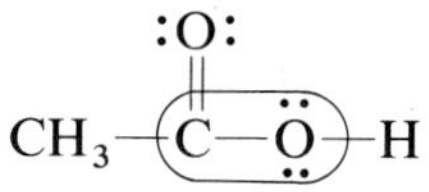

```
        :O:
         ‖
CH₃—(C—O)—H
```

f.

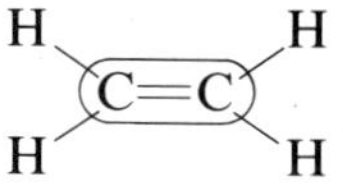

```
H—(C—O)—H
    |
    H
```

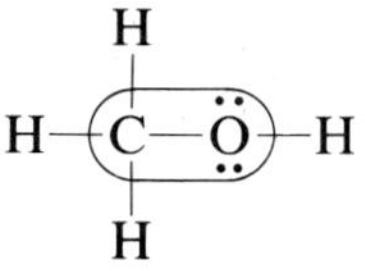

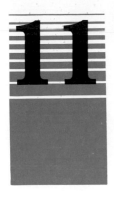

Alkanes
and Cycloalkanes

Compounds containing only carbon and hydrogen are called **hydrocarbons**. If the hydrocarbon contains only single bonds, it is called a **saturated hydrocarbon**, or **alkane**. If a hydrocarbon contains one or more double or triple bonds, it is called an **unsaturated hydrocarbon**. In this chapter we shall discuss saturated hydrocarbons, the simplest class of organic compounds.

11.1 Structure of Alkanes

Methane, CH_4, and ethane, C_2H_6, are the first members of the alkane family. Shown in Figure 11.1 are Lewis structures and ball-and-stick models for these molecules. The shape of methane is tetrahedral, and all H—C—H bond angles are 109.5° (Section 4.5C). Each of the carbon atoms in ethane is also tetrahedral, and all bond angles are approximately 109.5°. The next members of the series are propane; C_3H_8, butane, C_4H_{10}; and pentane, C_5H_{12}.

Lewis Structures

Condensed Structural Formulas

$$CH_3CH_2CH_3 \qquad CH_3CH_2CH_2CH_3 \qquad CH_3CH_2CH_2CH_2CH_3$$

propane   butane   pentane

Condensed structural formulas for these and higher alkanes can be written in an even more abbreviated form. For example, the structural formula of pentane contains three —CH_2— (**methylene**) groups in the middle of the chain. They can be grouped together and the structural formula written $CH_3(CH_2)_3CH_3$. Names, molecular formulas, and condensed structural formulas of the first twenty alkanes are given in Table 11.1.

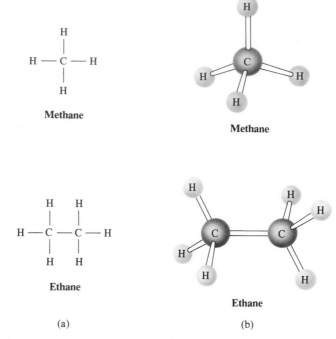

Methane

Methane

Ethane

Ethane

(a)   (b)

Figure 11.1 Methane and ethane. (a) Lewis structures; (b) ball-and-stick models.

Table 11.1 Names, molecular formulas, and condensed structural formulas for the first twenty alkanes.

Name	Molecular Formula	Condensed Structural Formula	Name	Molecular Formula	Condensed Structural Formula
methane	CH_4	CH_4	undecane	$C_{11}H_{24}$	$CH_3(CH_2)_9CH_3$
ethane	C_2H_6	CH_3CH_3	dodecane	$C_{12}H_{26}$	$CH_3(CH_2)_{10}CH_3$
propane	C_3H_8	$CH_3CH_2CH_3$	tridecane	$C_{13}H_{28}$	$CH_3(CH_2)_{11}CH_3$
butane	C_4H_{10}	$CH_3(CH_2)_2CH_3$	tetradecane	$C_{14}H_{30}$	$CH_3(CH_2)_{12}CH_3$
pentane	C_5H_{12}	$CH_3(CH_2)_3CH_3$	pentadecane	$C_{15}H_{32}$	$CH_3(CH_2)_{13}CH_3$
hexane	C_6H_{14}	$CH_3(CH_2)_4CH_3$	hexadecane	$C_{16}H_{34}$	$CH_3(CH_2)_{14}CH_3$
heptane	C_7H_{16}	$CH_3(CH_2)_5CH_3$	heptadecane	$C_{17}H_{36}$	$CH_3(CH_2)_{15}CH_3$
octane	C_8H_{18}	$CH_3(CH_2)_6CH_3$	octadecane	$C_{18}H_{38}$	$CH_3(CH_2)_{16}CH_3$
nonane	C_9H_{20}	$CH_3(CH_2)_7CH_3$	nonadecane	$C_{19}H_{40}$	$CH_3(CH_2)_{17}CH_3$
decane	$C_{10}H_{22}$	$CH_3(CH_2)_8CH_3$	eicosane	$C_{20}H_{42}$	$CH_3(CH_2)_{18}CH_3$

11.2 Structural Isomerism in Alkanes

Two or more compounds that have the same molecular formula but different orders of attachment of atoms are called **structural isomers** (Section 10.3). For the molecular formulas CH_4, C_2H_6, and C_3H_8, there is only one possible order of attachment of atoms, and therefore methane, ethane, and propane have no structural isomers. For the molecular formula C_4H_{10}, two orders of attachment of atoms are possible. In one, the four carbon atoms are attached in a chain; in the other, they are attached three in a chain with the fourth carbon as a branch on the three-carbon chain. These isomeric alkanes are named butane and 2-methylpropane:

$$CH_3-CH_2-CH_2-CH_3 \qquad CH_3-\underset{\underset{\displaystyle CH_3}{|}}{CH}-CH_3$$

butane
bp −0.5°C

2-methylpropane
bp −11.2°C

Butane and 2-methylpropane are structural isomers; they have the same molecular formula but different orders of attachment of their atoms. Structural isomers are different compounds and have different physical and chemical properties. Notice that the boiling points of butane and 2-methylpropane differ by over 10°C.

There are three structural isomers of molecular formula C_5H_{12}, five structural isomers of C_6H_{14}, eighteen of C_8H_{18}, and seventy-five of $C_{10}H_{22}$. It should be obvious that for even a small number of carbon and hydrogen atoms, a very large number of structural isomers is possible. In fact, the potential for structural and functional group individuality from just the basic building blocks of carbon, hydrogen, nitrogen, and oxygen is practically limitless.

Example 11.1

Identify these pairs as formulas of identical compounds or as formulas of structural isomers.

a. $CH_3-CH_2-CH_2-CH_2-CH_2-CH_3$ and

$CH_3-CH_2-CH_2$
$\qquad\qquad\quad |$
$\qquad\qquad\ CH_2-CH_2-CH_3$

b. $CH_3-CH_2-\underset{\underset{\displaystyle CH_3}{|}}{CH}-CH_2-CH_2-CH_3$ and

$CH_3-CH_2-CH_2-\underset{\underset{\displaystyle \underset{\underset{\displaystyle CH_3}{|}}{CH_2}}{|}}{CH}-CH_3$

c. $CH_3-\underset{\underset{\displaystyle CH_3}{|}}{CH}-CH_2-\underset{\underset{\displaystyle CH_3}{|}}{\overset{\overset{\displaystyle CH_3}{|}}{CH}}$ and $CH_3-CH_2-\underset{\underset{\displaystyle CH_3}{|}}{CH}-\overset{\overset{\displaystyle CH_3}{|}}{CH}-CH_3$

Solution

To determine whether these formulas are identical or represent structural isomers, find the longest chain of carbon atoms and number it from the end nearest the first branch. Note that in finding the longest chain, it makes no difference whether the chain is drawn straight or bent. As structural formulas are drawn in this problem, there is no attempt to show three-dimensional shapes. After you have found the longest carbon chain and numbered it from the correct end, compare the lengths of each chain and the size and locations of any branches.

a. $\overset{1}{C}H_3-\overset{2}{C}H_2-\overset{3}{C}H_2-\overset{4}{C}H_2-\overset{5}{C}H_2-\overset{6}{C}H_3$ and

$\overset{1}{C}H_3-\overset{2}{C}H_2-\overset{3}{C}H_2$

$\qquad\qquad\quad\underset{4}{C}H_2-\underset{5}{C}H_2-\underset{6}{C}H_3$

Each formula has an unbranched chain of six carbons; they are identical and represent the same compound.

b. $\overset{1}{C}H_3-\overset{2}{C}H_2-\overset{3}{C}H-\overset{4}{C}H_2-\overset{5}{C}H_2-\overset{6}{C}H_3$ and

$\qquad\qquad\qquad\;\; CH_3$

$\overset{6}{C}H_3-\overset{5}{C}H_2-\overset{4}{C}H_2-\overset{3}{C}H-CH_3$

$\qquad\qquad\qquad\quad\;\; \overset{2}{C}H_2$

$\qquad\qquad\qquad\quad\;\; \overset{1}{C}H_3$

Each has a chain of six carbons with a CH_3- group on the third carbon atom of the chain; they are identical and represent the same compound.

$\qquad\qquad\qquad\qquad\overset{5}{C}H_3 \qquad\qquad\qquad\qquad\quad \overset{1}{C}H_3$

c. $\overset{1}{C}H_3-\overset{2}{C}H-\overset{3}{C}H_2-\overset{4}{C}H$ and $\overset{5}{C}H_3-\overset{4}{C}H_2-\overset{3}{C}H-\overset{2}{C}H-CH_3$

$\qquad\quad\;\; CH_3 \qquad\;\; CH_3 \qquad\qquad\qquad\qquad\; CH_3$

Each has chains of five carbons with two CH_3- branches. While the branches are identical, they are at different locations on the chains. Therefore, these formulas represent structural isomers.

Problem 11.1

Identify the pairs as identical or as formulas of structural isomers.

$\qquad\qquad\;\; CH_3$

$\qquad\qquad\;\; CH_2$

a. $CH_3-CH-CH-CH_3$ and $CH_3-CH_2-CH-CH_2-CH-CH_3$

$\qquad\qquad\qquad\; CH_2-CH_3$

with CH_3 and CH_3 above the second CH and last CH.

$\qquad\qquad\; CH_3 \qquad\qquad\qquad\qquad\; CH_3 \;\; CH_3$

b. $CH_3-CH-CH-CH_3$ and $CH_3-CH-CH-CH_2-CH_3$

$\qquad\qquad\qquad CH_2-CH_3$

Draw structural formulas for the five structural isomers of molecular formula C_6H_{14}.

Example 11.2

☐ *Solution*

In solving problems of this type, you should devise a strategy and then follow it. One strategy for this example is the following. First, draw the structural isomer with all six carbons in an unbranched chain. Then, draw all structural isomers with five carbons in a chain and one carbon as a branch on the chain. Finally, draw all structural isomers with four carbons in a chain and two carbons as branches.

Six Carbons in an Unbranched Chain

$$\overset{1}{C}H_3 - \overset{2}{C}H_2 - \overset{3}{C}H_2 - \overset{4}{C}H_2 - \overset{5}{C}H_2 - \overset{6}{C}H_3$$

Five Carbons in a Chain; One Carbon as a Branch

$$\overset{1}{C}H_3 - \overset{2}{C}H - \overset{3}{C}H_2 - \overset{4}{C}H_2 - \overset{5}{C}H_3 \qquad \overset{1}{C}H_3 - \overset{2}{C}H_2 - \overset{3}{C}H - \overset{4}{C}H_2 - \overset{5}{C}H_3$$
$$\qquad\quad | \qquad\qquad\qquad\qquad\qquad\qquad\qquad | $$
$$\qquad\quad CH_3 \qquad\qquad\qquad\qquad\qquad\qquad\quad CH_3$$

Four Carbons in a Chain; Two Carbons as Branches

$$\qquad\quad CH_3 \qquad\qquad\qquad\qquad\qquad\quad CH_3$$
$$\qquad\quad | \qquad\qquad\qquad\qquad\qquad\qquad | $$
$$CH_3 - C - CH_2 - CH_3 \qquad CH_3 - CH - CH - CH_3$$
$$\qquad\quad | \qquad\qquad\qquad\qquad\qquad\qquad\quad | $$
$$\qquad\quad CH_3 \qquad\qquad\qquad\qquad\qquad\qquad CH_3$$

Problem 11.2

Draw structural formulas for the three structural isomers of molecular formula C_5H_{12}.

11.3 Nomenclature of Alkanes

A. The IUPAC System

Ideally every organic compound should have a name that clearly describes its structure and from which a structural formula can be drawn. For this purpose, chemists throughout the world have accepted a set of rules established by the International Union of Pure and Applied Chemistry (IUPAC). This system is known as the **IUPAC system**, or alternatively, the Geneva system, because the first meetings of the IUPAC were held in Geneva, Switzerland. The IUPAC names of alkanes with an unbranched chain of carbon atoms consist of two parts: (1) a prefix that indicates the number of carbon atoms in the chain; and (2) the ending *-ane*, to show that the compound is an alkane. Prefixes used to

Table 11.2
Prefixes used in the IUPAC system to indicate one to twenty carbon atoms in a chain.

Prefix	Number of Carbon Atoms	Prefix	Number of Carbon Atoms
meth	1	undec	11
eth	2	dodec	12
prop	3	tridec	13
but	4	tetradec	14
pent	5	pentadec	15
hex	6	hexadec	16
hept	7	heptadec	17
oct	8	octadec	18
non	9	nonadec	19
dec	10	eicos	20

show the presence of from one to twenty carbon atoms are given in Table 11.2. The first four prefixes listed in Table 11.2 were chosen by the International Union of Pure and Applied Chemistry because they were well established in the language of organic chemistry. In fact, they were well established even before there were hints of the structural theory underlying the discipline. For example, the prefix *but-* appears in the name butyric acid, a compound of four carbon atoms present in butter fat (Latin *butyrum*, butter). Roots to show five or more carbons are derived from Greek or Latin roots. Names, molecular formulas, and condensed structural formulas for the first twenty alkanes are given in Table 11.1.

The IUPAC names of substituted alkanes consist of a parent name, which indicates the longest chain of carbon atoms in the compound, and substituent names, which indicate the groups attached to the parent chain.

$$CH_3-CH_2-CH_2-\underset{\underset{CH_3}{|}}{CH}-CH_2-CH_2-CH_2-\overset{Parent}{CH_3}$$

Substituent

A substituent group derived from an alkane is called an **alkyl group**. The symbol R— is commonly used to show the presence of an alkyl group. Alkyl groups are named by dropping the *-ane* from the name of the parent alkane and adding the suffix *-yl*. For example, the alkyl substituent CH_3CH_2- is named ethyl.

$$H-\underset{\underset{H}{|}}{\overset{\overset{H}{|}}{C}}-\underset{\underset{H}{|}}{\overset{\overset{H}{|}}{C}}-H \qquad H-\underset{\underset{H}{|}}{\overset{\overset{H}{|}}{C}}-\underset{\underset{H}{|}}{\overset{\overset{H}{|}}{C}}-$$

ethane
(parent hydrocarbon)

ethyl group
(an alkyl group)

Names and structural formulas for eleven of the most common alkyl groups are given in Table 11.3.

Table 11.3 Common alkyl groups.

IUPAC Name	Condensed Structural Formula	IUPAC Name	Condensed Structural Formula
methyl	$-CH_3$	*tert*-butyl	$\begin{array}{l} \;\;CH_3 \\ \;\;\;\,| \\ -C-CH_3 \\ \;\;\;\,| \\ \;\;CH_3 \end{array}$
ethyl	$-CH_2-CH_3$		
propyl	$-CH_2-CH_2-CH_3$		
isopropyl	$\begin{array}{l} -CH-CH_3 \\ \;\;\;\,| \\ \;\;CH_3 \end{array}$	pentyl	$-CH_2-CH_2-CH_2-CH_2-CH_3$
butyl	$-CH_2-CH_2-CH_2-CH_3$	isopentyl	$\begin{array}{l} -CH_2-CH_2-CH-CH_3 \\ \qquad\qquad\quad\;\;| \\ \qquad\qquad\quad CH_3 \end{array}$
isobutyl	$\begin{array}{l} -CH_2-CH-CH_3 \\ \qquad\quad\;\;| \\ \qquad\quad CH_3 \end{array}$		
sec-butyl	$\begin{array}{l} -CH-CH_2-CH_3 \\ \;\;\;\,| \\ \;\;CH_3 \end{array}$	neopentyl	$\begin{array}{l} \qquad\quad CH_3 \\ \qquad\quad\;\;| \\ -CH_2-C-CH_3 \\ \qquad\quad\;\;| \\ \qquad\quad CH_3 \end{array}$

Following are the rules of the IUPAC system for naming alkanes.

1. The general name of a saturated hydrocarbon is *alkane.*
2. For branched-chain hydrocarbons, the hydrocarbon derived from the longest chain of carbon atoms is taken as the parent chain and the IUPAC name is derived from that of the parent chain.
3. Groups attached to the parent chain are called substituents. Each substituent is given a name and a number. The number shows the carbon atom of the parent chain to which the substituent is attached.
4. If the same substituent occurs more than once, the number of each carbon of the parent chain on which the substituent occurs is given. In addition, the number of times the substituent group occurs is indicated by a prefix *di-*, *tri-*, *tetra-*, *penta-*, *hexa-*, and so on.
5. If there is one substituent, number the parent chain from the end that gives it the lower number. If there are two or more substituents, number the parent chain from the end that gives the lower number to the substituent encountered first.
6. If there are two or more different substituents, list them in alphabetical order.

Example 11.3

Give IUPAC names for these compounds.

a. $\begin{array}{l} CH_3-CH-CH_2-CH_3 \\ \qquad\quad\;\;| \\ \qquad\quad CH_3 \end{array}$

b. $\begin{array}{l} CH_3-CH-CH_2-CH-CH_2-CH_3 \\ \qquad\quad\;\;| \qquad\qquad\;\;\;| \\ \qquad\quad CH_3 \qquad\quad CH_2-CH_3 \end{array}$

$$\overset{\displaystyle CH_3}{\underset{\displaystyle CH_3}{\text{c. } CH_3-CH_2-CH_2-\overset{\displaystyle |}{\underset{\displaystyle |}{C}}-CH_3}}$$

☐ *Solution*

a. There are four carbon atoms in the longest chain, and therefore the name of the parent chain is butane (Rule 2). The butane chain must be numbered so that the single methyl group is on carbon 2 of the chain (Rule 5). The correct name of this alkane is 2-methylbutane.

$$\overset{1}{C}H_3-\overset{2}{\underset{\underset{\displaystyle CH_3}{\displaystyle |}}{C}}H-\overset{3}{C}H_2-\overset{4}{C}H_3$$

2-methylbutane

b. The longest chain contains six carbons, and therefore the parent chain is a hexane (Rule 2). There are two alkyl substituents: a methyl group and an ethyl group. The hexane chain must be numbered so that the substituent encountered first (the methyl group) is on carbon 2 of the chain (Rule 5). The ethyl and methyl substituents are listed in alphabetical order (Rule 6) to give the name 4-ethyl-2-methylhexane.

$$\overset{1}{C}H_3-\overset{2}{\underset{\underset{\displaystyle CH_3}{\displaystyle |}}{C}}H-\overset{3}{C}H_2-\overset{4}{\underset{\underset{\displaystyle CH_2-CH_3}{\displaystyle |}}{C}}H-\overset{5}{C}H_2-\overset{6}{C}H_3$$

4-ethyl-2-methylhexane

c. The longest chain contains five carbon atoms and therefore the parent chain is a pentane (Rule 2). The pentane chain must be numbered so that the substituents are on carbon 2 of the chain (Rule 5). There are two substituents and each must have a name and a number (Rule 4). Because the substituents are identical, they are grouped together using the prefix *di-* (Rule 4). The IUPAC name is 2,2-dimethylpentane.

$$\overset{5}{C}H_3-\overset{4}{C}H_2-\overset{3}{C}H_2-\overset{2}{\underset{\underset{\displaystyle CH_3}{\displaystyle |}}{\overset{\overset{\displaystyle \overset{1}{C}H_3}{\displaystyle |}}{C}}}-CH_3$$

2,2-dimethylpentane

■ **Problem 11.3**

Name these alkanes by the IUPAC system.

$$\text{a. } CH_3-\overset{\overset{\displaystyle CH_3}{\displaystyle |}}{C}H-CH_2-CH_2-\overset{\overset{\displaystyle CH_3}{\displaystyle |}}{C}H-\underset{\underset{\underset{\displaystyle CH_2-CH_3}{\displaystyle |}}{\displaystyle CH_2}}{\overset{\displaystyle |}{C}}H-CH_3$$

$$CH_2-CH_2-CH_3$$

b. $CH_3-CH_2-CH_2-\overset{\displaystyle |}{\underset{\displaystyle |}{C}}-CH_2-CH_2-CH_3$

$$\overset{\displaystyle |}{CH}-CH_3$$

$$\overset{\displaystyle |}{CH_3}$$

B. Common Names

In spite of the precision of the IUPAC system, routine communication in organic chemistry still relies on a combination of trivial, semisystematic, and systematic names. The reasons for this are rooted in both convenience and historical development.

In the older, semisystematic nomenclature, the total number of carbon atoms in an alkane, regardless of their arrangement, determines the name. The first three alkanes are methane, ethane, and propane. All alkanes of formula C_4H_{10} are called butanes, all alkanes of formula C_5H_{12} are called pentanes, and those of formula C_6H_{14} are called hexanes. For alkanes beyond propane, **normal**, or **n-** is used to indicate that all carbons are joined in a continuous chain, and **iso-** is used to indicate that one end of an otherwise continuous chain terminates in a $(CH_3)_2CH-$ group. The first compounds of molecular formula C_5H_{12} to be discovered and named were pentane and its isomer isopentane. Subsequently, another compound of molecular formula C_5H_{12} was discovered, and because it was a "new" pentane (at least it was new to those who first discovered it), this isomer was named neopentane. Following are examples of common names.

$$CH_3-CH_2-CH_2-CH_3$$
n-butane

$$CH_3-\overset{\displaystyle CH_3}{\overset{\displaystyle |}{CH}}-CH_3$$
isobutane

$$CH_3-CH_2-CH_2-CH_2-CH_3$$
n-pentane

$$CH_3-\overset{\displaystyle CH_3}{\overset{\displaystyle |}{CH}}-CH_2 \quad CH_3$$
isopentane

$$CH_3-\overset{\displaystyle CH_3}{\underset{\displaystyle CH_3}{\overset{\displaystyle |}{\underset{\displaystyle |}{C}}}}-CH_3$$
neopentane

$$CH_3-CH_2-CH_2-CH_2-CH_2-CH_3$$
n-hexane

$$CH_3-\overset{\displaystyle CH_3}{\overset{\displaystyle |}{CH}}-CH_2-CH_2-CH_3$$
isohexane

$$CH_3-\overset{\displaystyle CH_3}{\underset{\displaystyle CH_3}{\overset{\displaystyle |}{\underset{\displaystyle |}{C}}}}-CH_2-CH_3$$
neohexane

This system of common names has no good way of handling other branching patterns, and for more complex alkanes it is necessary to use the more flexible, IUPAC system of nomenclature.

We will concentrate on IUPAC names. However, we will also use common names, especially when the common name is used almost exclusively in the everyday discussions of chemists. Where both IUPAC and common names are given in this textbook, we will always give the IUPAC name first, followed by the common name in parentheses. In this way, you should have no doubt about which name is which.

11.4 Cycloalkanes

So far we have considered only chains (branched and unbranched) of carbon atoms. A molecule that contains carbon atoms joined to form a ring is called a cyclic hydrocarbon. Further, when all carbons of the ring are saturated, the molecule is called a **cycloalkane**.

Cycloalkanes of ring size from three to over thirty are found in nature; and in principle, there is no limit to ring size. Five-membered rings (cyclopentanes) and six-membered rings (cyclohexanes) are especially abundant in nature and therefore have received special attention.

Figure 11.2 shows structural formulas of cyclopropane, cyclobutane, cyclopentane, and cyclohexane. For convenience, organic chemists usually do not write out structural formulas for cycloalkanes showing all carbons and hydrogens. Rather, the rings are represented by regular polygons with the same number of sides. For example, cyclopropane is represented by a triangle and cyclohexane by a hexagon.

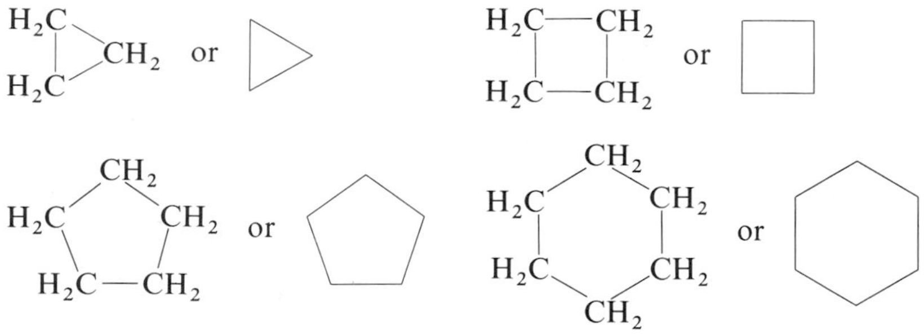

Figure 11.2 Examples of cycloalkanes.

To name cycloalkanes, prefix the name of the corresponding open-chain hydrocarbon with *cyclo-* and name each substituent on the ring. If there is only a single substituent on the cycloalkane ring, there is no need to give it a number. If there are two or more substituents, each substituent must be given a number to indicate its location on the ring.

**Example
11.4**

Name these cycloalkanes.

a. [structure: cyclopentane ring with CH₂—CH—CH₃ substituent, and CH₃ below CH]

b. [structure: cyclohexane ring with CH₃ and CH₂—CH₃ substituents]

□ *Solution*

a. The ring contains five atoms and is a cyclopentane. Because only one sub-stituent, an isobutyl group, is on the ring, there is no need to number the atoms of the ring. The IUPAC name is isobutylcyclopentane.

b. The ring is a cyclohexane. Number the atoms of the ring, beginning with the substituent of lowest alphabetical order, in this case, *ethyl*. The IUPAC name of this cycloalkane is 1-ethyl-2-methylcyclohexane.

**Problem
11.4**

Name these cycloalkanes.

a. [structure: cyclopropane ring with CH₂CH₃ and CH₃ substituents]

b. [structure: cyclopentane ring with CH₃ CH₃ on a carbon, attached to C(CH₃)—CH₃ with CH₃ below]

The use of carbon bonds to close a ring means that cycloalkanes contain two fewer hydrogen atoms than an alkane of the same number of carbon atoms. Compare, for example, the molecular formulas of cyclopropane C_3H_6, and propane, C_3H_8, or of cyclohexane, C_6H_{12}, and hexane, C_6H_{14}. The general formula of a cycloalkane is C_nH_{2n}.

11.5 The IUPAC System—A General System of Nomenclature

The naming of alkanes and cycloalkanes (Sections 11.3 and 11.4) illustrated the application of the IUPAC system of nomenclature to two specific classes of organic compounds. Now, let us describe the general approach of the IUPAC system. The name assigned to any compound with a chain of carbon atoms consists of three parts: a prefix, an infix, and a suffix. Each part provides specific information about the structural formula of the compound.

1. The prefix tells the number of carbon atoms in the parent chain. Examples are:

Prefix	Number of Carbon Atoms
but-	4
pent-	5
hex-	6

2. The infix tells the nature of the carbon-carbon bonds in the parent chain. Examples are:

Infix	Nature of Carbon-Carbon Bonds
-an-	all single bonds
-en-	one or more double bonds
-yn-	one or more triple bonds

3. The suffix tells the class of compound to which the substance belongs. Examples are:

Suffix	Class of Compound
-e	hydrocarbon
-ol	alcohol
-al	aldehyde
-one	ketone
-oic acid	carboxylic acid

Example 11.5

Following are IUPAC names and structural formulas for several compounds. Divide each name into a prefix, an infix, and a suffix and specify the information about the structural formula that is contained in each.

a. CH_2=CH—CH_3 **b.** CH_3—CH_2—OH

　　　propene   ethanol

c. CH_3—CH_2—$\overset{\overset{O}{\|}}{C}$—$CH_3$ **d.** CH_3—CH_2—CH_2—CH_2—$\overset{\overset{O}{\|}}{C}$—$OH$

　　　butanone   pentanoic acid

e.

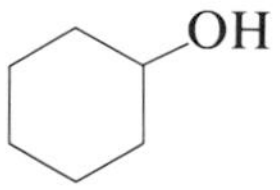

　　cyclohexanol

☐ *Solution*

a.

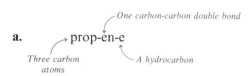

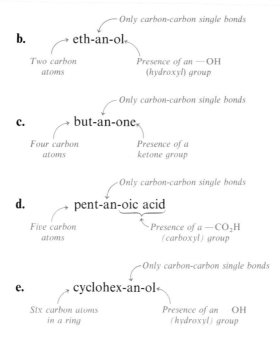

Only carbon-carbon single bonds

b.   eth-an-ol

Two carbon atoms   *Presence of an —OH (hydroxyl) group*

Only carbon-carbon single bonds

c.   but-an-one

Four carbon atoms   *Presence of a ketone group*

Only carbon-carbon single bonds

d.   pent-an-oic acid

Five carbon atoms   *Presence of a —CO₂H (carboxyl) group*

Only carbon-carbon single bonds

e.   cyclohex-an-ol

Six carbon atoms in a ring   *Presence of an OH (hydroxyl) group*

Problem 11.5

Combine the proper prefix, infix, and suffix and write IUPAC names for the following.

a. $CH_2{=}CH_2$ **b.** $CH_3{-}C{\equiv}CH$

c. $CH_3{-}CH_2{-}CH_2{-}\overset{\displaystyle O}{\overset{\|}{C}}{-}OH$ **d.** $CH_3{-}CH_2{-}CH_2{-}\overset{\displaystyle O}{\overset{\|}{C}}{-}H$

e. 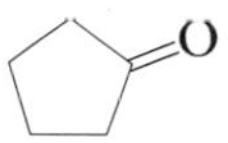 ⬠=O   **f.**  ⬡

11.6 Conformation of Alkanes and Cycloalkanes

A. Alkanes

Structural formulas are useful to show the order of attachment of atoms. However, they do not show actual three-dimensional shapes. As chemists try to understand more about how structure and the chemical and physical properties of molecules are related, it becomes increasingly important to understand more about the three-dimensional shapes of molecules.

Alkanes of two or more carbons can be twisted into a number of different three-dimensional arrangements by rotation about a carbon-carbon bond or bonds. The different three-dimensional arrangements of atoms that result by rotation about single bonds are called **conformations**. Figure 11.3(a) shows a ball-and-stick model of a staggered conformation of ethane. In a **staggered conformation**, all C—H bonds on adjacent carbons are as far apart as possible. Figure 11.3(b) is a Newman projection of this conformation of ethane. In the **Newman projection** shown, the molecule is viewed along the axis of the C—C bond. The three hydrogens nearer your eye are shown on lines extending from the center of the circle at angles of 120°. The three hydrogens of the carbon farther from your eye are shown on lines extending from the circumference of the circle. Remember that bond angles about each carbon are 109.5° and not 120°, as this Newman projection might suggest.

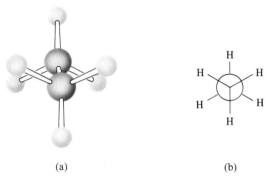

(a)   (b)

Figure 11.3 A staggered conformation of ethane. (a) Ball-and-stick model; (b) a Newman projection.

Figures 11.4(a) and 11.4(b) show ball-and-stick models for an eclipsed conformation of ethane viewed from two different perspectives. In an **eclipsed conformation**, C—H bonds on adjacent conformations are as close together as possible. An ethane molecule can be twisted into an infinite number of conformations between the staggered and eclipsed conformations. Yet any given ethane molecule spends most of its time in the staggered conformation, because in this conformation, C—H bonds on one carbon are as far apart as possible

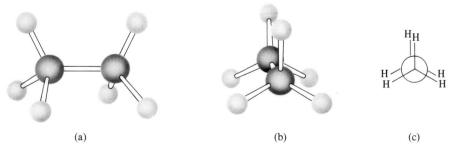

(a)   (b)   (c)

Figure 11.4 An eclipsed conformation of ethane. (a, b) Ball-and-stick models; (c) a Newman projection.

from C—H bonds on the adjacent carbon. For this reason, the staggered conformation is the most stable or preferred conformation.

Example 11.6

Draw Newman projections for two staggered conformations of butane. Consider only conformations along the bond between carbons 2 and 3 of the butane chain. Which of these is the more stable? Which is the less stable?

☐ *Solution*

The condensed structural formula of butane is

$$\overset{1}{C}H_3 - \overset{2}{C}H_2 - \overset{3}{C}H_2 - \overset{4}{C}H_3$$

First view the molecule along the bond between carbons 2 and 3. Then to see the possible conformations asked for, hold carbon 2 in place and rotate carbon 3 about the single bond between the two carbons. Staggered conformation (a) is the more stable because in it the two —CH$_3$ groups are as far apart as possible; staggered conformation (b) is less stable because the two —CH$_3$ groups are closer together.

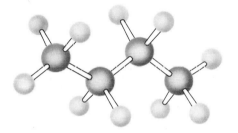

Ball-and-stick model of a staggered conformation of butane

Newman projections of two staggered conformations of butane

Problem 11.6

Draw two eclipsed conformations for butane. Consider only conformations along the bond between carbons 2 and 3. Which of these is the more stable eclipsed conformation? Which is the less stable eclipsed conformation?

B. Cycloalkanes

Figure 11.5 shows the shapes of cyclopropane, cyclobutane, and cyclopentane. For all practical purposes, these molecules are planar.

Cyclohexane and all larger rings exist in nonplanar, or puckered, conformations. Shown in Figure 11.6(b) is a ball-and-stick model of the most stable puckered conformation of cyclohexane. This conformation is called a **chair** because of its resemblance to a beach chair with a back rest, a seat, and a leg

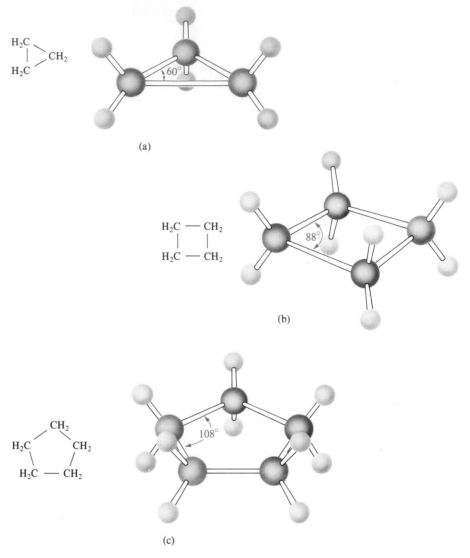

(a)

(b)

(c)

Figure 11.5 Ball-and-stick models of (a) cyclopropane, (b) cyclobutane, and (c) cyclopentane

rest. All C—C—C bond angles in a chair conformation are approximately 109.5°.

Hydrogens in a chair conformation are in two different geometrical positions (Figure 11.6c). Six, called equatorial hydrogens, project straight out from the ring and are roughly parallel to the plane of the ring. The other six, called axial hydrogens, are perpendicular to the plane of the ring.

If a hydrogen of cyclohexane is replaced by a methyl group or other substituent, the group can occupy either an axial or an equatorial position.

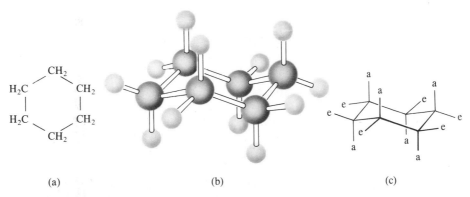

11.7 Configurational Isomerism in Cycloalkanes

All cycloalkanes with different substituents on two or more carbons of the ring show a type of isomerism called **configurational isomerism**. Configurational isomers have the same molecular formula, the same order of attachment of atoms, and an arrangement of atoms that cannot be interchanged by rotation about sigma bonds under ordinary conditions. By way of comparison, conformations such as those of ethane, propane, and butane can be interconverted easily by rotation about single bonds. The term **cis-trans isomerism**, or its alternative, **geometric isomerism**, is applied to the type of configurational isomerism that depends on the arrangement of substituent groups, either in a cyclic structure (as we shall see in this chapter), or on a double bond (Chapter 12).

Configurational isomerism in cyclic structures can be illustrated by models of 1,2-dimethylcyclopentane. In the following drawings, the cyclopentane ring is shown as a planar pentagon viewed through the plane of the ring. Carbon-carbon bonds of the ring projecting forward are shown as heavy lines. When the ring is viewed from this perspective, substituents attached to the ring project above and below its plane. In one configurational isomer of 1,2-dimethylcyclopentane, the methyl groups are on the same side of the ring; in the other, they are on opposite sides of the ring. The prefix *cis-* (Latin, on the same side) is used to indicate that the substituents are on the same side of the ring; the prefix *trans-* (Latin, across) is used to indicate that they are on opposite sides of the ring. In each isomer, the configuration of the methyl groups is fixed, and

Figure 11.6 Chair conformation of cyclohexane. (a) Condensed structural formula, (b) ball-and-stick model, and (c) three-dimensional drawing with axial and equatorial positions labeled by "a" and "e," respectively.

no amount of twisting about carbon-carbon bonds can convert the cis isomer to the trans isomer or vice versa.

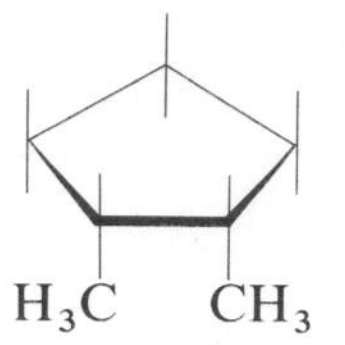

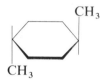

cis-1,2-dimethylcyclopentane 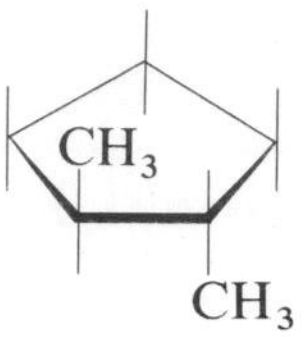   *trans*-1,2-dimethylcyclopentane

Cyclopropane, cyclobutane, and cyclopentane are accurately represented by planar drawings. Cyclohexanes and all larger rings are nonplanar, however, and therefore drawing them is more difficult. Cyclohexane, for example, is best represented as a nonplanar chair conformation. Fortunately, for the purpose of deciding how many cis-trans isomers are possible for a given substituted cyclo-alkane, it is adequate to draw the ring as a planar polygon, as is done below for cyclohexane. There are two cis-trans isomers for 1,4-dimethylcyclohexane.

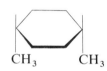

trans-1,4-dimethylcyclohexane   *cis*-1,4-dimethylcyclohexane

Example 11.7

Following are several cycloalkanes of molecular formula C_6H_{12}. State which show cis-trans isomerism, and for each that does, draw the cis and trans isomers.

a.   **b.** 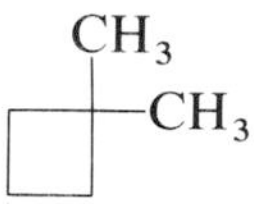   **c.**

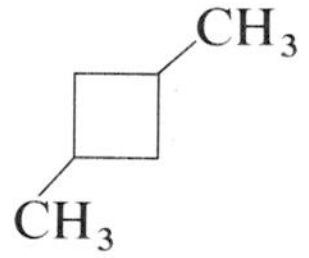

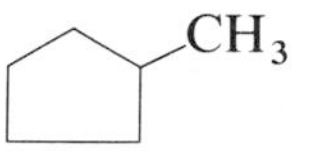

☐ *Solution*

a. Because methylcyclopentane has only one substituent on the ring, it does not show cis-trans isomerism.

b. 1,1-dimethylcyclobutane does not show cis-trans isomerism. There is only one possible arrangement for the two methyl groups on the ring; they must be trans to each other.

c. 1,3-dimethylcyclobutane shows cis-trans isomerism.

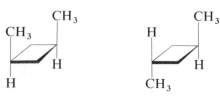

cis-1,3-dimethylcyclobutane   *trans*-1,3-dimethylcyclobutane

Problem 11.7

Following are several cycloalkanes of molecular formula C_7H_{14}. State which show cis-trans isomerism and for each that does, draw the cis and trans isomers.

a.   b.   c.   d.

11.8 Physical Properties of Alkanes and Cycloalkanes

You are already familiar with the physical properties of some alkanes and cycloalkanes from your everyday experiences. The low-molecular-weight alkanes, such as methane (marsh gas), ethane, propane, and butane, are gases at room temperature and atmospheric pressure. Higher-molecular-weight alkanes, such as those in gasoline and kerosene, are liquids. Very high-molecular-weight alkanes, such as those found in paraffin wax, are solids. Melting points, boiling points, and densities of the first ten alkanes are listed in Table 11.4.

Table 11.4
Physical properties of some alkanes.

Name	Condensed Structural Formula	mp (°C)	bp (°C)	Density of Liquid (g/mL at 0°C)
methane	CH_4	-182	-164	(a gas)
ethane	CH_3CH_3	-183	-88	(a gas)
propane	$CH_3CH_2CH_3$	-190	-42	(a gas)
butane	$CH_3(CH_2)_2CH_3$	-138	0	(a gas)
pentane	$CH_3(CH_2)_3CH_3$	-130	36	0.626
hexane	$CH_3(CH_2)_4CH_3$	-95	69	0.659
heptane	$CH_3(CH_2)_5CH_3$	-90	98	0.684
octane	$CH_3(CH_2)_6CH_3$	-57	126	0.703
nonane	$CH_3(CH_2)_7CH_3$	-51	151	0.718
decane	$CH_3(CH_2)_8CH_3$	-30	174	0.730

Methane, the lowest-molecular-weight alkane, is a gas at room temperature and atmospheric pressure. It can be converted to a liquid if cooled to $-164°C$ and to a solid if cooled to $-182°C$. That methane (or any other compound, for that matter) can exist as a liquid or a solid depends on the existence of **intermolecular forces** of attraction between particles of each pure compound. Although the forces of attraction between particles are all electrostatic, they vary widely in relative strength. The main types of intermolecular forces we deal with in this book are listed in Table 11.5. Note that both ion-ion and ion-dipole forces involve ions rather than molecules, and in this regard, the term

Table 11.5
Summary
of types of
intermolecular
forces.

Type of Interaction	Where Found	Example	Relative Strength
ion-ion	ionic solids (Section 4.4)	$Na^+\cdots\cdots Cl^-$	strongest type of interaction
ion-dipole	solutions of ionic solids (Section 4.7)	$Na^+\cdots\cdots\overset{\delta-}{O}\begin{smallmatrix}H\\ \\H\end{smallmatrix}$	
dipole-dipole	hydrogen bonding (Sections 4.7 and 6.2)	$\overset{H}{\underset{H}{}}O{-}\overset{\delta+}{H}\cdots\cdots\overset{\delta-}{O}\begin{smallmatrix}H\\ \\H\end{smallmatrix}$	
dispersion	nonpolar molecules (Section 6.6)	$CH_4\cdots\cdots CH_4$	weakest type of interaction

intermolecular is not strictly accurate for these forces. Nonetheless, they are grouped with dipole-dipole interactions and dispersion forces for purposes of comparison.

Let us use these concepts of the nature of intermolecular forces to examine the relation between the physical properties of alkanes and their molecular structure. Alkanes are nonpolar compounds and the only forces of attraction between them are dispersion forces. Because interactions between molecules of alkanes are so weak, the alkanes have lower boiling points than almost any other type of compound of the same molecular weight. As the number of atoms and molecular weight of an alkane increase, the strength of dispersion forces per molecule also increases. Therefore, the boiling points of alkanes increase as molecular weight increases (compare Table 11.4).

Melting points of alkanes also increase with increasing molecular weight. However, the increase is not as regular as that observed for boiling points. The average density of the alkanes listed in Table 11.4 is about 0.7 g/mL; the density of higher-molecular-weight alkanes is about 0.8 g/mL. All liquid alkanes are less dense than water (1.0 g/mL).

An observation you have certainly heard is "oil and water do not mix." For example, gasoline and crude oil do not dissolve in water. We refer to these and other water-insoluble compounds as hydrophobic (water-hating). Alkanes do dissolve in nonpolar liquids such as carbon tetrachloride, CCl_4, carbon disulfide, CS_2, and of course other hydrocarbons.

Alkanes that are structural isomers are different compounds and have different physical and chemical properties. Table 11.6 lists the boiling points, melting points, and densities of the five structural isomers of molecular formula C_6H_{14}. The boiling point of each of the branched-chain isomers of C_6H_{14} is lower than that of hexane itself, and the more branching there is, the lower the boiling point. These differences in boiling point are related to molecular shape in the following way. The only forces of attraction between alkane molecules are dispersion forces. As branching increases, the shape of an alkane molecule becomes more compact and its surface area decreases. As surface area decreases, contact between adjacent molecules decreases, the strength of dispersion forces

Table 11.6
Physical properties of the isomeric alkanes of molecular formula C_6H_{14}.

Name	bp (°C)	mp (°C)	Density (g/mL)
hexane	68.7	−95	0.659
2-methylpentane	60.3	−154	0.653
3-methylpentane	63.3	−118	0.664
2,3-dimethylbutane	58.0	−129	0.661
2,2-dimethylbutane	49.7	−98	0.649

decreases, and boiling points also decrease. For any group of alkane structural isomers, it is usually observed that the least branched isomer has the highest boiling point and the most branched isomer has the lowest boiling point. Figure 11.7 shows structural formulas and ball-and-stick models of hexane (a

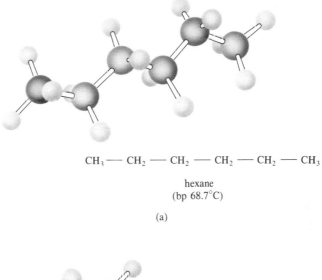

$$CH_3 — CH_2 — CH_2 — CH_2 — CH_2 — CH_3$$

hexane
(bp 68.7°C)

(a)

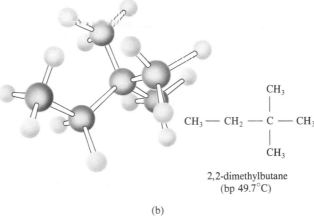

$$CH_3 — CH_2 — \underset{\underset{CH_3}{|}}{\overset{\overset{CH_3}{|}}{C}} — CH_3$$

2,2-dimethylbutane
(bp 49.7°C)

(b)

Figure 11.7 (a) Ball-and-stick models of hexane (fully staggered conformation), and (b) 2,2-dimethylbutane.

fully staggered conformation) and its most highly branched structural isomer, 2,2-dimethylbutane.

Example 11.8

Arrange the following in order of increasing boiling point.

a. $CH_3CH_2CH_2CH_3$ $\quad$ $CH_3CH_2CH_2CH_2CH_2CH_3$ $\quad$ $CH_3(CH_2)_8CH_3$

b. $CH_3(CH_2)_6CH_3$ $\qquad$ $\underset{\displaystyle CH_3}{\overset{\displaystyle CH_3\ \ CH_3}{CH_3CCH_2CHCH_3}}$ $\qquad$ $\underset{\displaystyle CH_3}{CH_3CH(CH_2)_4CH_3}$

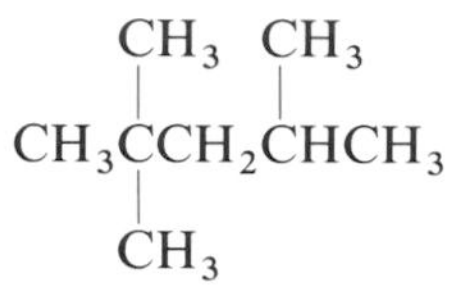

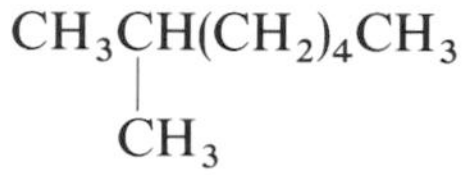

Solution

a. All are unbranched alkanes. As the number of carbon atoms in the chain increases, dispersion forces between molecules increase and boiling points increase. Predict that decane has the highest boiling point and that butane has the lowest.

$$CH_3CH_2CH_2CH_3 \qquad CH_3CH_2CH_2CH_2CH_2CH_3 \qquad CH_3(CH_2)_8CH_3$$

butane (bp −0.5°C) $\qquad$ hexane (bp 69°C) $\qquad$ decane (bp 174°C)

b. These three alkanes have the same molecular formula, C_8H_{18}, and are structural isomers of each other. Their relative boiling points depend on the degree of branching. Predict that 2,2,4-trimethylpentane, the most highly branched isomer, has the lowest boiling point, and octane, the unbranched isomer, the highest boiling point.

$$\underset{\displaystyle CH_3}{\overset{\displaystyle CH_3\ \ CH_3}{CH_3CCH_2CHCH_3}} \qquad \overset{\displaystyle CH_3}{CH_3CHCH_2CH_2CH_2CH_2CH_3} \qquad CH_3(CH_3)_6CH_3$$

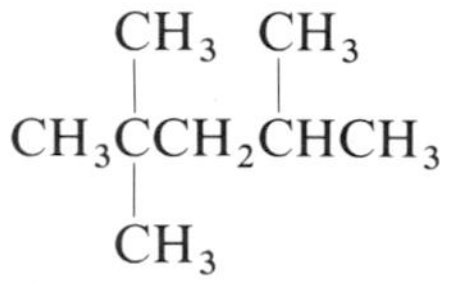

2,2,4-trimethylpentane (bp 99°C) $\qquad$ 2-methylheptane (bp 118°C) $\qquad$ octane (bp 126°C)

Problem 11.8

Arrange the following in order of increasing boiling point.

a. 2-methylbutane, 2,2-dimethylpropane, pentane
b. 3,3-dimethylheptane, 2,2,4-trimethylpentane, nonane

11.9 Reactions of Alkanes

Alkanes and cycloalkanes are unreactive to most reagents, a behavior consistent with the facts that they are nonpolar compounds and composed entirely of strong sigma bonds. However, they do react under certain conditions with oxygen and with halogens.

A. Oxidation

By far the most economically important reaction of alkanes is their **oxidation (combustion)** by O_2 to form carbon dioxide and water. Oxidation of saturated hydrocarbons is the basis for their use as energy sources for heat (natural gas, LPG, and fuel oil) and power (gasoline, diesel fuel, and aviation fuel). Following are balanced equations for complete oxidation of methane, the major component of natural gas, and 2,2,4-trimethylpentane, a component of gasoline. Also given is the heat of combustion, ΔH^0, for oxidation of one mole of each compound at 25°C, to give gaseous carbon dioxide and liquid water.

$$CH_4 + 2O_2 \longrightarrow CO_2 + 2H_2O \qquad \Delta H^0 = -212 \text{ kcal/mol}$$

methane

$$\underset{\begin{array}{c}|\\CH_3\end{array}}{\overset{\begin{array}{cc}CH_3 & CH_3\\| & |\end{array}}{CH_3CCH_2CHCH_3}} + \frac{25}{2}O_2 \longrightarrow 8CO_2 + 9H_2O \qquad \Delta H^0 = -1304 \text{ kcal/mol}$$

2,2,4-trimethylpentane
(isooctane)

B. Halogenation

If a mixture of methane and chlorine gas is kept in the dark at room temperature, no detectable change occurs. If, however, the mixture is heated or exposed to visible or ultraviolet light, a reaction begins almost at once with the evolution of heat. The products are chloromethane (methyl chloride) and hydrogen chloride. What occurs is a substitution reaction, in this case substitution of a hydrogen atom in methane by a chlorine atom and the production of an equivalent amount of hydrogen chloride.

$$\underset{\text{methane}}{\overset{\begin{array}{c}H\\|\end{array}}{H-\underset{\underset{H}{|}}{\overset{\overset{H}{|}}{C}}-H}} + Cl-Cl \xrightarrow[\text{heat}]{\text{light or}} H \quad \underset{\text{chloromethane}}{\overset{\begin{array}{c}H\\|\end{array}}{\underset{\underset{H}{|}}{\overset{\overset{H}{|}}{C}}-Cl}} + H-Cl$$

chloromethane
(methyl chloride)

Substitution is defined as a reaction in which an atom or group of atoms in a compound is replaced by another atom or group of atoms.

The IUPAC names for haloalkanes are derived according to the rules we have already used for naming alkanes. The parent chain is numbered from the direction that gives the substituent encountered first (whether it is halogen or an alkyl group) the lowest number. Halogen substituents are indicated by the prefixes *fluoro-*, *chloro-*, *bromo-*, and *iodo-*. In common names, the carbon chain is named followed by the word for the name of the halide, as in *methyl chloride*.

If chloromethane is allowed to react with more chlorine, further chlorination produces a mixture of dichloromethane (methylene chloride), trichloromethane (chloroform), and tetrachloromethane (carbon tetrachloride):

$$CH_3Cl + Cl_2 \longrightarrow \quad CH_2Cl_2 \quad + \quad HCl$$

dichloromethane
(methylene chloride)

$$CH_2Cl_2 + Cl_2 \longrightarrow \quad CHCl_3 \quad + \quad HCl$$

trichloromethane
(chloroform)

$$CHCl_3 + Cl_2 \longrightarrow \quad CCl_4 \quad + \quad HCl$$

tetrachloromethane
(carbon tetrachloride)

Reaction of ethane with chlorine gives chloroethane (ethyl chloride); reaction with bromine gives bromoethane (ethyl bromide).

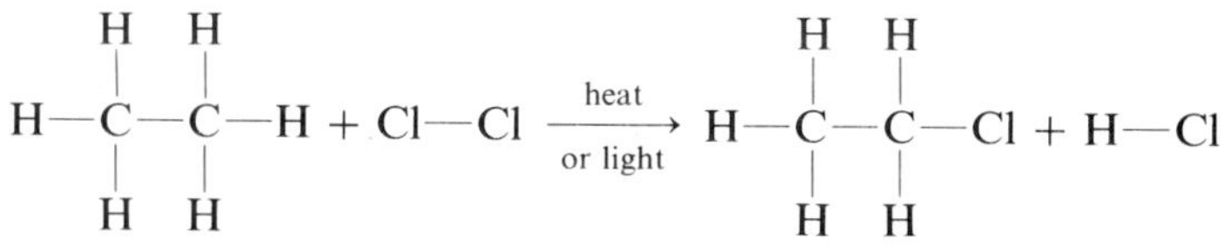

ethane   chloroethane
(ethyl chloride)

Reaction of propane with bromine gives two isomeric bromopropanes:

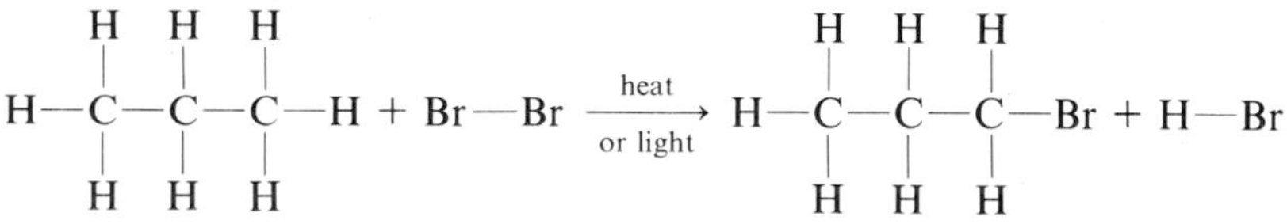

propane   1-bromopropane
(n-propyl bromide)

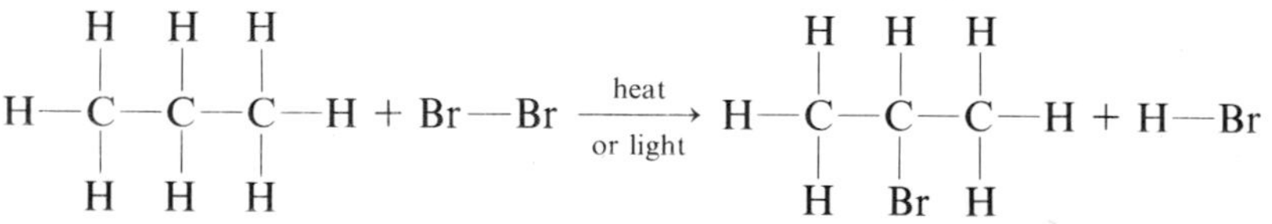

propane   2-bromopropane
(isopropyl bromide)

These are different reactions and are written separately. However, it is more common to show all products formed in one equation. The single equation below means that reaction of one mole of propane with one mole of bromine produces one mole of HBr and one mole of C_3H_7Br. Of the C_3H_7Br, approximately 8% is 1-bromopropane and the remaining 92% is 2-bromopropane.

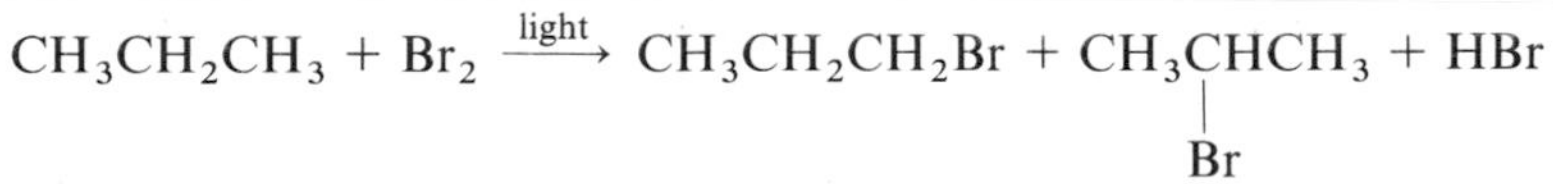

$$CH_3CH_2CH_3 + Br_2 \xrightarrow{\text{light}} CH_3CH_2CH_2Br + CH_3CHCH_3 + HBr$$

with Br on the second carbon of the CH_3CHCH_3 group

propane	1-bromopropane (8%)	2-bromopropane (92%)

Example 11.9

Draw structural formulas for all monohalogenation products formed in the following reactions. Give each product an IUPAC name and where possible, also a common name.

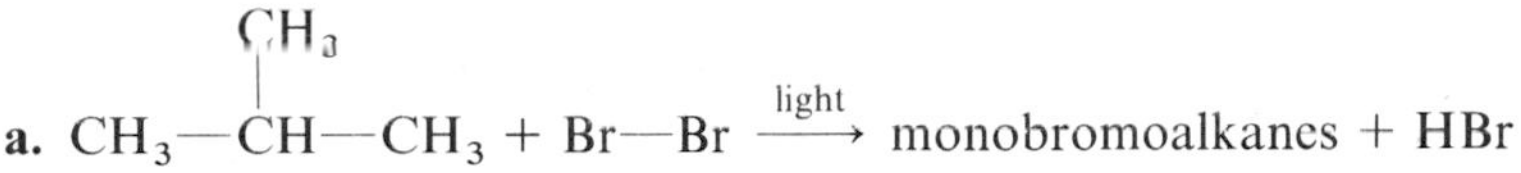

a. $CH_3—\overset{\overset{\displaystyle CH_3}{\displaystyle |}}{CH}—CH_3 + Br—Br \xrightarrow{\text{light}}$ monobromoalkanes + HBr

2-methylpropane
(isobutane)

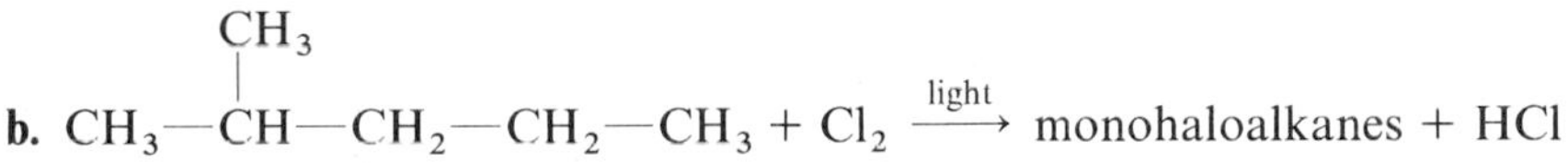

b. $CH_3—\overset{\overset{\displaystyle CH_3}{\displaystyle |}}{CH}—CH_2—CH_2—CH_3 + Cl_2 \xrightarrow{\text{light}}$ monohaloalkanes + HCl

2-methylpentane
(isohexane)

Solution

a. As we did when drawing all possible structural isomers of a given molecular formula, it is best to devise a system and then follow it. The most direct way is to start at one end of the carbon chain and substitute —Br for —H. Then do the same thing on each carbon until you come to the other end of the chain. There are only two monobromination products from 2-methylpropane. The IUPAC names are given first and then common names in parentheses.

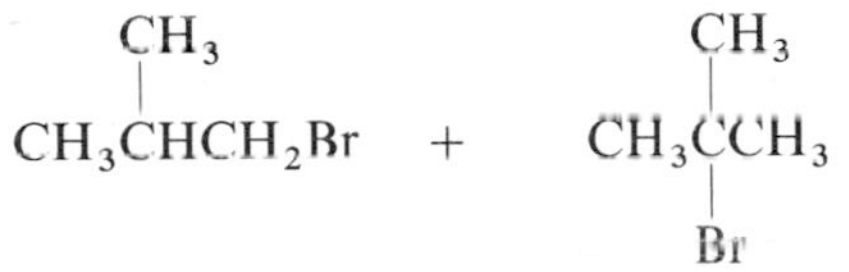

$$CH_3CHCH_2Br \quad + \quad CH_3CCH_3$$

with CH_3 groups above both structures, and Br below the second structure

1-bromo-2-methylpropane
(isobutyl bromide)

2-bromo-2-methylpropane
(*tert*-butyl bromide)

b. There are five monohaloalkanes possible from 2-methylpentane. The IUPAC names for each are given. No convenient common names exist for these compounds.

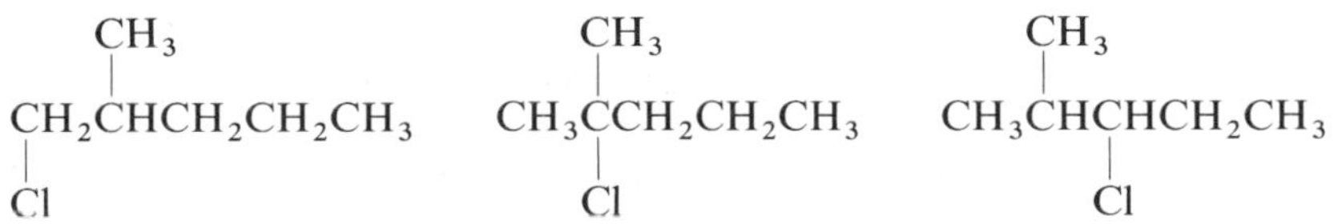

$$CH_2CHCH_2CH_2CH_3 \qquad CH_3CCH_2CH_2CH_3 \qquad CH_3CHCHCH_2CH_3$$

with CH_3 groups above each, and Cl below each respective position

1-chloro-2-methylpentane   2-chloro-2-methylpentane   3-chloro-2-methylpentane

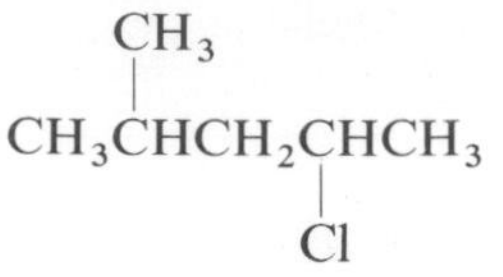

$$\underset{\substack{| \\ \text{Cl}}}{\overset{\substack{\text{CH}_3 \\ |}}{\text{CH}_3\text{CHCH}_2\text{CHCH}_3}} \qquad \underset{\substack{| \\ \text{Cl}}}{\overset{\substack{\text{CH}_3 \\ |}}{\text{CH}_3\text{CHCH}_2\text{CH}_2\text{CH}_2}}$$

2-chloro-4-methylpentane 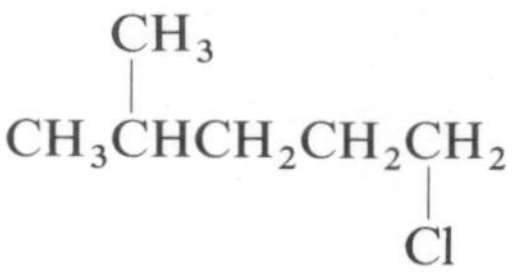   1-chloro-4-methylpentane

Problem 11.9

Draw structural formulas for all monohalogenation products of the following reactions. Give each product an IUPAC name and where possible, a common name.

a. 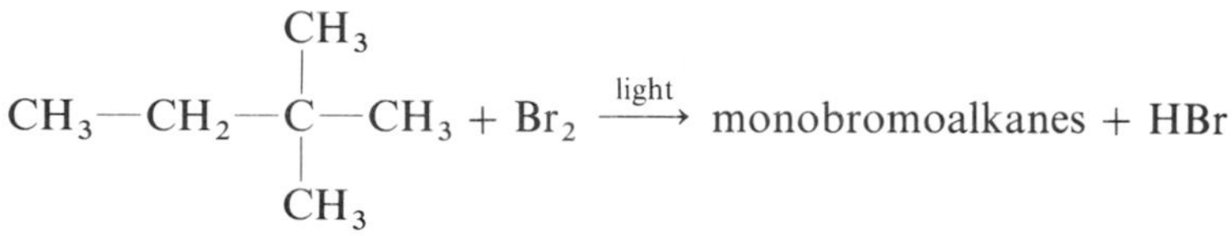 $\text{CH}_3-\text{CH}_2-\overset{\substack{\text{CH}_3 \\ |}}{\underset{\substack{| \\ \text{CH}_3}}{\text{C}}}-\text{CH}_3 + \text{Br}_2 \xrightarrow{\text{light}}$ monobromoalkanes + HBr

b.  ⬠ $+ \text{Cl}_2 \xrightarrow{\text{light}}$ monochlorocyclopentanes + HBr

Many halogenated hydrocarbons, because of their physical and chemical properties, have found wide commercial use as solvents, refrigerants, dry-cleaning agents, local and inhalation anesthetics, and insecticides. Of the halo-alkanes, the one most widely used as a solvent today is dichloromethane (methylene chloride).

Chloroethane (ethyl chloride) is used as a fast-acting topical anesthetic. This chloroalkane owes its anesthetic property more to its physical properties than to its chemical properties. Chloroethane boils at 12°C and, unless under pressure, is a gas at room temperature. When sprayed on the skin, it evaporates and cools the skin surface and underlying nerve endings. Skin and underlying nerve endings become anesthetized when skin temperature drops to about 15°C. Halothane is a widely used inhalation anesthetic.

$$\text{F}-\overset{\substack{\text{F} \\ |}}{\underset{\substack{| \\ \text{F}}}{\text{C}}}-\overset{\substack{\text{H} \\ |}}{\underset{\substack{| \\ \text{Cl}}}{\text{C}}}-\text{Br}$$

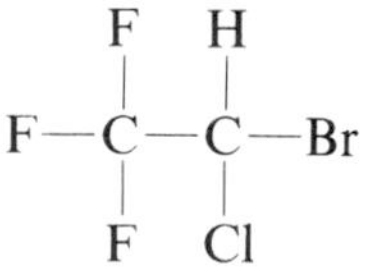

2-bromo-2-chloro-1,1,1-trifluoroethane
(Halothane)

Of all the fluoroalkanes, those manufactured under the trade name Freon are the most widely used. **Freons** were developed in a search for new refrigerants, compounds that would be nontoxic, nonflammable, odorless, and noncorrosive. In 1930, General Motors Corp. announced the discovery of just such a compound, dichlorodifluoromethane, which was marketed under the trade name Freon-12. Freons are a class of compounds manufactured by reacting a chlorinated hydrocarbon with hydrofluoric acid in the presence of an antimony pentafluoride or pentachloride catalyst:

$$CCl_4 + HF \xrightarrow{\text{SbF}_5} CCl_3F + HCl$$
Freon-11

$$CCl_3F + HF \xrightarrow{\text{SbF}_5} CCl_2F_2 + HCl$$
Freon-12

By 1974, U.S. production of Freons had grown to more than 1.1 billion pounds annually, almost one half of world production. Worldwide production of these compounds is now at an all-time high, reflecting their use in refrigeration and air-conditioning systems, in aerosols (outside of the United States), and as solvents.

Concern about the environmental effect of Freons arose in 1974 when Drs. Sherwood Rowland and Marion Molina proposed that when Freons are used in aerosols, they escape through the lower atmosphere to the stratosphere. There they absorb ultraviolet radiation from the sun, decompose, and set up a chemical reaction that may also lead to destruction of the stratospheric ozone layer that shields the earth from excess ultraviolet radiation. An increase in ultraviolet radiation reaching the earth may lead to destruction of certain crops and agricultural species, and to increased skin cancer in sensitive individuals. Controversy continues over the potential for ozone depletion and its effect on the environment. In the meantime, both government and the chemical industry in the United States have taken steps to limit sharply the use of Freons.

11.10 Sources of Alkanes

A. Natural Gas

The two main sources of alkanes throughout the world are natural gas and petroleum. **Natural gas** consists of approximately 80% methane, 10% ethane, and a mixture of other relatively low-boiling alkanes—chiefly propane, butane, and 2-methylpropane (isobutane).

B. Petroleum

Petroleum is a liquid mixture of literally thousands of compounds, most of them hydrocarbons, formed from the decomposition of marine plants and animals. Petroleum and petroleum-derived products fuel automobiles, aircraft, and trains. They provide most of the greases and lubricants required for the machinery of our highly industrialized society. Furthermore, petroleum, along with natural gas, provides close to 90% of the organic raw materials for the manufacture of synthetic fibers, plastics, detergents, drugs, dyes, and a multitude of other products.

The task of the petroleum refinery industry is to produce usable products, with a minimum of waste, from the thousands of different hydrocarbons in this liquid mixture. The various physical and chemical processes for this purpose fall into two broad categories: separation processes, which separate the complex mixture into various fractions, and conversion processes, which alter the molecular structure of the hydrocarbon components themselves.

The fundamental separation in refining petroleum is distillation. Practically all crude oil that enters a refinery goes to distillation units, where it is heated to temperatures as high as 370°C to 425°C and separated into fractions. Each fraction contains a mixture of hydrocarbons that boils within a particular range. Following are the common names associated with several of these fractions along with the principal uses of each.

1. Gases boiling below 20°C are taken off at the top of the distillation column. This fraction is a mixture of low-molecular-weight hydrocarbons, predominantly propane, butane, and 2-methylpropane, substances that can be liquefied under pressure at room temperature. The liquefied mixture, known as **liquefied petroleum gas** (**LPG**), can be stored and shipped in metal tanks and is a convenient source of gaseous fuel for home heating and cooking.

2. Naphthas, bp 20–200°C, are a mixture of C_4 to C_{10} alkanes and cycloalkanes. Naphthas also contain some aromatic hydrocarbons such as benzene, toluene, and xylene (Section 12.9). The light naphtha fraction, bp 20–150°C, is the source of what is known as straight-run gasoline and averages approximately 25% of crude petroleum. In a sense, naphthas are the most valuable distillation fractions because they are useful not only as fuel but also as sources of raw materials for the organic chemical industry.

3. Kerosene, bp 175–275°C, is a mixture of C_9 to C_{15} hydrocarbons.

4. Gas oil, bp 200–400°C, is a mixture of C_{15} to C_{25} hydrocarbons. Diesel fuel is obtained from this fraction.

5. Lubrication oil and heavy fuel oil distill from the column at temperatures over 350°C.

6. Asphalt is the name given to the black, tarry residue remaining after removal of the other volatile fractions.

Gasoline is a complex mixture of C_4 to C_{10} hydrocarbons. The quality of gasoline as a fuel for internal combustion engines is expressed by **octane number**, or antiknock index. When an engine is running normally, the air-fuel mixture is ignited by a spark plug and burns smoothly as the flame moves outward from the plug, building up pressure that forces the piston down during the compression stroke. Engine knocking occurs when a portion of the air-fuel mixture explodes prematurely (usually as a result of heat developed during compression), and independently of ignition by the spark plug. The basic procedure for measuring the antiknock quality of a gasoline was established in 1929. Two compounds were selected as reference fuels. One of these, 2,2,4-trimethylpentane (isooctane), has very good antiknock properties and was assigned an octane number of 100. The other, heptane, has very poor antiknock properties and was assigned an octane number of 0. The octane rating of a particular gasoline is that percentage of isooctane in a mixture of isooctane and heptane that has equivalent knock properties. For example, 2-methylhexane has the same knock properties as a mixture of 42% isooctane and 58% heptane; therefore, the octane rating of 2-methylhexane is 42. Octane itself has an octane rating of -20, which means that it produces even more engine knocking than heptane.

The antiknock properties of tetraethyl lead, $(CH_3CH_2)_4Pb$, and related compounds were discovered by Thomas Midgley in the 1930s. Gasoline so treated is known as ethyl, or **leaded gasoline**. Addition of 3 g of tetraethyl lead to one gallon of gasoline raises the octane rating by 15 to 20 units. At one time, regular gasoline contained 2.4 to 3.2 g of tetraethyl lead per gallon and premium gasoline contained up to 4.2 g per gallon.

The use of leaded gasoline in the United States reached a peak in 1970, when approximately 99% of all gasoline contained lead additives. In that year, almost 280,000 tons of lead was consumed in the manufacture of tetraethyl lead. This tremendous quantity of lead was emitted directly into the atmosphere, much of it as very small particles, or aerosols. Because lead is toxic, there has been great concern over the long-term effects of spewing this waste into the environment. One result of this concern has been legislation designed to restrict the use of lead additives. There are also serious research efforts to discover substances that will increase octane ratings but not simultaneously pollute our air with dangerous byproducts. One of the most promising additives is *tert*-butyl methyl ether (Chapter 13).

A second way of increasing the octane rating of hydrocarbons derived from petroleum is catalytic cracking. Catalytic cracking accomplishes two things. First, hydrocarbons of high molecular weight are broken or cracked into hydrocarbons of smaller molecular weight, thus increasing the yield of gasoline from crude oil. Second, carbon skeletons of the hydrocarbons themselves are rearranged and made more highly branched. Branched-chain hydrocarbons have higher octane numbers than linear hydrocarbons (compare, for example, the octane ratings of octane and its structural isomer 2,2,4-trimethylpentane). The first commercial catalytic cracking plant was built in 1937 by Sun Oil. By 1976, the United States produced over 150 million gallons of feedstock a day.

Catalytic re-forming supplements catalytic cracking as a means of converting low-octane components to higher octane fuels. Catalytic re-forming, for example, converts hexane to cyclohexane and then to benzene, a high-octane unsaturated hydrocarbon:

$$CH_3CH_2CH_2CH_2CH_2CH_3 \xrightarrow[-H_2]{catalyst} \bigcirc \xrightarrow[-3H_2]{catalyst} \bigcirc$$

hexane · · · · · · · cyclohexane · · · · · · · benzene

The first catalytic re-forming process came into use in 1940 and used a silica-molybdena catalyst in the presence of hydrogen gas. In 1949, Universal Oil Products introduced a platinum catalyst. This process, called Platforming, is extremely effective and remains the dominant catalytic re-forming process in use today. The petroleum industry now uses catalytic re-forming to treat more than

120 million gallons of feedstock per day, or close to 25% of the crude oil that enters refineries.

Key Terms and Concepts

alkane (introduction)

alkyl group (11.3A)

chair conformation (11.6B)

cis-trans isomerism in cycloalkanes (11.7)

combustion of alkanes (11.9A)

configurational isomerism (11.7)

conformation (11.6A)

cycloalkane (11.4)

eclipsed conformation (11.6A)

Freons (11.9B)

gasoline (11.10B)

geometric isomerism (11.7)

halogenation of alkanes (11.9B)

hydrocarbons (introduction)

intermolecular forces (11.8)

iso- (11.3B)

IUPAC system of nomenclature (11.3A and 11.5)

leaded gasoline (11.10B)

liquefied petroleum gas, LPG (11.10B)

methylene group (11.1)

n- (11.3B)

naphthas (11.10B)

natural gas (11.10A)

Newman projection (11.6A)

normal (11.3B)

octane number (11.10B)

oxidation of alkanes (11.9A)

petroleum (11.10B)

saturated hydrocarbon (introduction)

staggered conformation (11.6A)

structural isomers (11.2)

unsaturated hydrocarbon (introduction)

Key Reactions

1. Oxidation/combustion of alkanes with oxygen to give carbon dioxide and water (Section 11.9A).

2. Halogenation of alkanes with bromine or chlorine to give bromo- or chloro-alkanes (Section 11.9B).

Problems

Structural isomerism in alkanes and cycloalkanes (Section 11.2)

11.10   Are the following molecules pairs of structural isomers or are they identical?

a. 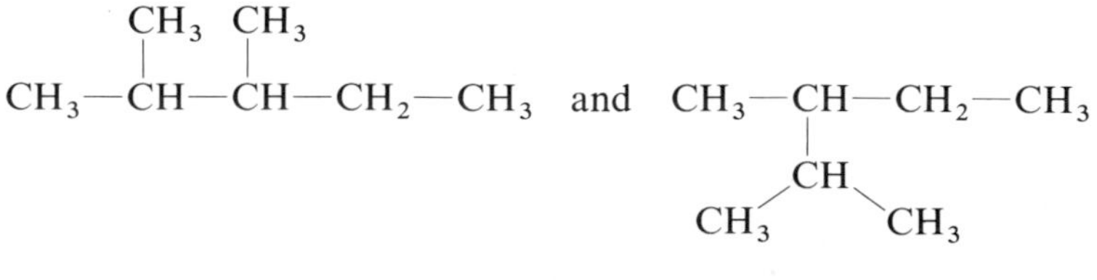 $CH_3-CH-CH-CH_2-CH_3$ and $CH_3-CH-CH_2-CH_3$

with CH_3 and CH_3 substituents on the first structure, and a CH branch with two CH_3 groups on the second structure.

$$\text{CH}_3$$

b. 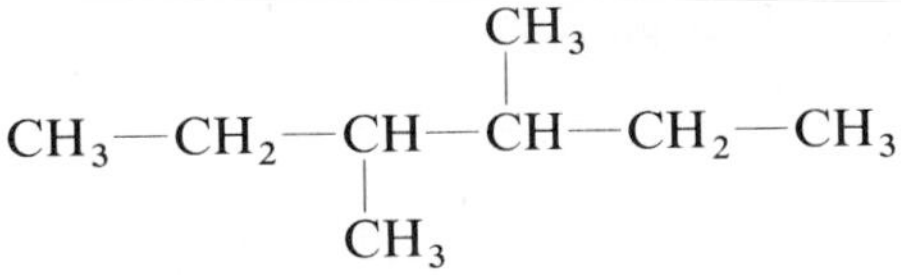 $\text{CH}_3-\text{CH}_2-\text{CH}-\overset{|}{\text{CH}}-\text{CH}_2-\text{CH}_3$ and
$\qquad\qquad\qquad\overset{|}{\text{CH}_3}$

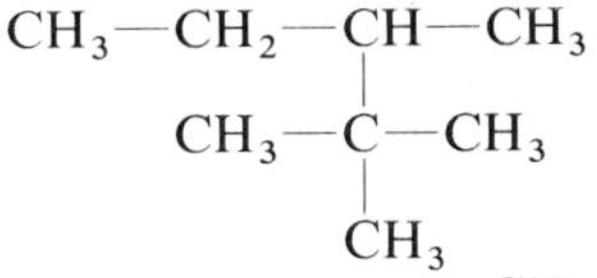

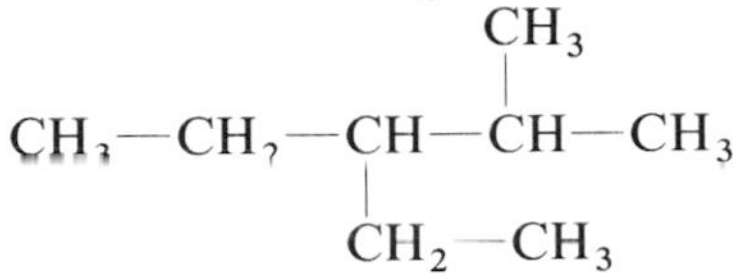

$\text{CH}_3-\text{CH}_2-\text{CH}-\text{CH}_3$
$\qquad\qquad\text{CH}_3-\overset{|}{\text{C}}-\text{CH}_3$
$\qquad\qquad\qquad\overset{|}{\text{CH}_3}$

$\qquad\qquad\qquad\qquad\text{CH}_3$

c. $\text{CH}_3-\text{CH}_2-\text{CH}-\overset{|}{\text{CH}}-\text{CH}_3$ and
$\qquad\qquad\qquad\overset{|}{\text{CH}_2}-\text{CH}_3$

$\text{CH}_3\diagdown\qquad\qquad\diagup\text{CH}_2-\text{CH}_3$
$\qquad\quad\text{CH}-\text{CH}$
$\text{CH}_3\diagup\qquad\qquad\diagdown\text{CH}_2-\text{CH}_3$

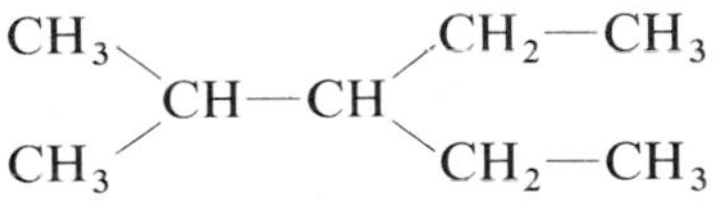

11.11 Which of the following are identical compounds and which are structural isomers?

a. 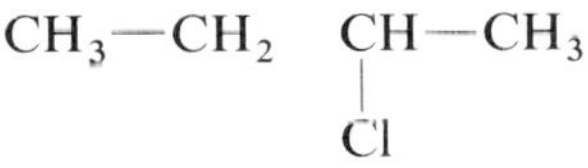 $\text{CH}_3-\text{CH}_2\quad\text{CH}-\text{CH}_3$
$\qquad\qquad\qquad\overset{|}{\text{Cl}}$

b. 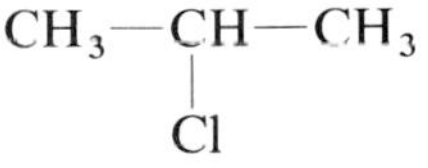 $\text{CH}_3-\text{CH}-\text{CH}_3$
$\qquad\qquad\overset{|}{\text{Cl}}$

c. 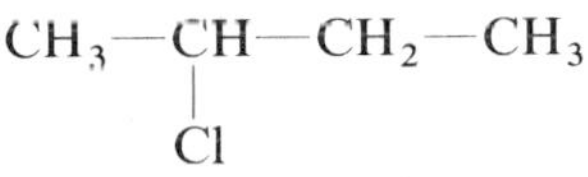 $\text{CH}_3-\text{CH}-\text{CH}_2-\text{CH}_3$
$\qquad\qquad\overset{|}{\text{Cl}}$

d. 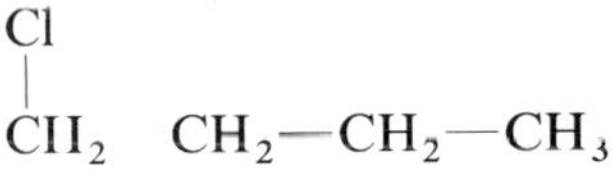 $\overset{\displaystyle\text{Cl}}{\overset{|}{\text{CH}_2}}\quad\text{CH}_2-\text{CH}_2-\text{CH}_3$

e. 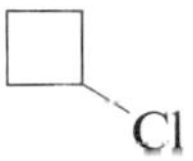 $\square$
$\qquad\diagdown\text{Cl}$

f. 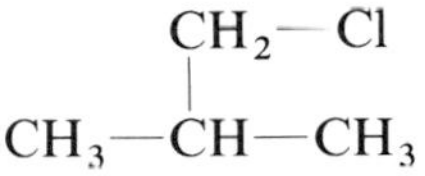 $\text{CH}_3-\overset{\displaystyle\text{CH}_2-\text{Cl}}{\overset{|}{\text{CH}}}-\text{CH}_3$

g. $\text{CH}_3-\text{CH}_2-\text{CH}_2-\text{CH}_2-\text{Cl}$

h. 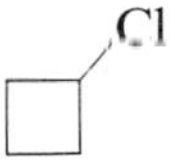 $\square\diagup\text{Cl}$

i. 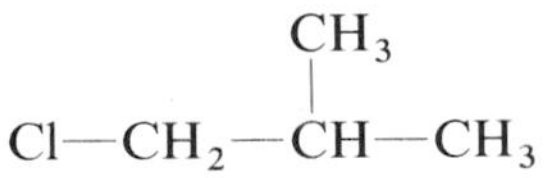 $\text{Cl}-\text{CH}_2-\overset{\displaystyle\text{CH}_3}{\overset{|}{\text{CH}}}-\text{CH}_3$

j. 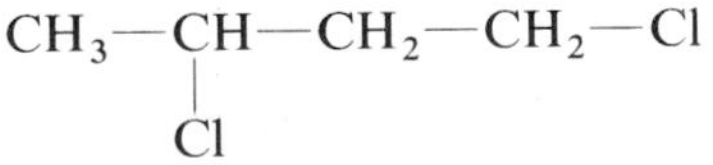 $\text{CH}_3-\text{CH}-\text{CH}_2-\text{CH}_2-\text{Cl}$
$\qquad\qquad\overset{|}{\text{Cl}}$

k. 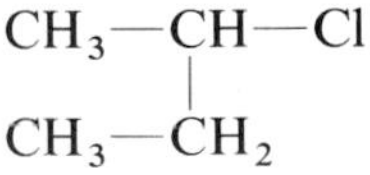 $\text{CH}_3-\text{CH}-\text{Cl}$
$\qquad\quad\overset{|}{\text{CH}_3}-\text{CH}_2$

l. 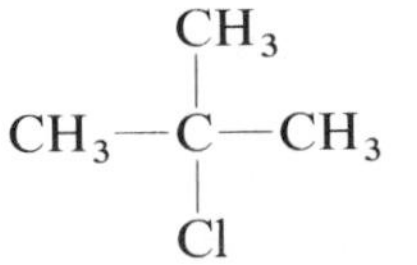 $\text{CH}_3-\overset{\displaystyle\text{CH}_3}{\underset{\displaystyle\text{Cl}}{\overset{|}{\underset{|}{\text{C}}}}}-\text{CH}_3$

Names and structural formulas of alkanes and cycloalkanes (Section 11.3)

11.12 Name these alkyl groups.

a. CH_3—

b. CH_3CH_2—

c. $CH_3\overset{\overset{\displaystyle CH_3}{|}}{C}HCH_2$—

d. $CH_3CH_2CH_2$—

e. $CH_3\overset{\overset{\displaystyle CH_3}{|}}{C}H$—

f. $\overset{\displaystyle CH_2}{\underset{\displaystyle CH_2}{|}}{>}CH$—

g. $CH_3\overset{\overset{\displaystyle CH_3}{|}}{\underset{\underset{\displaystyle CH_3}{|}}{C}}$—

h. $CH_3CH_2CH_2CH_2$—

i. ⬡—

11.13 Write IUPAC names for these structural formulas.

a. $CH_3\overset{\overset{\displaystyle }{}}{C}HCH_2CH_2CH_3$
   $\quad\;\; \overset{|}{CH_3}$

b. $CH_3\overset{}{C}HCH_2CH_2\overset{}{C}HCH_3$
   $\quad\;\; \overset{|}{CH_3}\qquad\;\; \overset{|}{CH_3}$

c. $CH_3CH_2\overset{}{C}HCH_2\overset{}{C}HCH_3$
   $\qquad\quad \overset{|}{CH_3}\quad\; \overset{|}{CH_2CH_3}$

d. $CH_3(CH_2)_4\overset{}{C}HCH_2CH_3$
   $\qquad\qquad\; \overset{|}{CH_2CH_3}$

e. $CH_3CH_2\overset{}{C}HCH_2CH_2CH_2CH_3$
   $\qquad\quad\; \overset{|}{CH_3CHCH_3}$

f. $CH_3CH_2CH_2\overset{}{C}HCH_3$
   $\qquad\qquad\quad\; \overset{|}{CH_2CH(CH_3)_2}$

g. $CH_3(CH_2)_8CH_3$

h. $(CH_3)_2CHCH_2CH_2C(CH_3)_3$

i. ◁$\overset{CH_3}{\underset{CH_3}{}}$

j. ⬠$CH_2\overset{}{C}HCH_3$ with $\overset{|}{CH_3}$

k. ⬡ with CH_2CH_3, CH_3, CH_3

l. ⬠ with Br, Br

11.14 Write structural formulas for these compounds.
a. 2,2,4-trimethylhexane
b. 1,1,2-trichlorobutane
c. 2,2-dimethylpropane
d. 3-ethyl-2,4,5-trimethyloctane
e. 2-bromo-2,4,6-trimethyloctane
f. 5-butyl-2,2-dimethylnonane
g. 4-isopropyloctane
h. 3,3-dimethylpentane
i. 1,1,1-trichloroethane
j. *trans*-1,3-dimethylcyclopentane
k. *cis*-1,2-diethylcyclobutane
l. 1,1-dichlorocycloheptane

11.15 Name and draw structural formulas for all isomeric alkanes of molecular formula C_6H_{14}.

11.16 Name and draw structural formulas for all isomeric alkanes of molecular formula C_7H_{16}.

11.17 Explain why each of the following is an incorrect IUPAC name. Write a correct IUPAC name for the intended compound.

a. 1,3-dimethylbutane
c. 2,2-diethylbutane
e. 4,4-dimethylhexane
g. 2,2-diethylheptane
i. 2,2-dimethylcyclopropane
k. 4-isopentylheptane

b. 4-methylpentane
d. 2-ethyl-3-methylpentane
f. 2-propylpentane
h. 5-butyloctane
j. 2-*sec*-butyloctane
l. 1,3-dimethyl-6-ethylcyclohexane

The IUPAC system of nomenclature (Section 11.5)

11.18   For each of these IUPAC names, draw the corresponding structural formula.

a. 3-pentanone
d. ethanoic acid
g. propanal
j. cyclopentene
m. cyclopropanol
p. ethanal

b. 2,2-dimethyl-3-pentanone
e. hexanoic acid
h. 1-propanol
k. cyclopentanol
n. ethene
q. decanoic acid

c. 2-butanone
f. propanoic acid
i. 2-propanol
l. cyclopentanone
o. ethanol
r. propanone

Conformations (Section 11.6)

11.19   Given 1-bromo-2-chloroethane, draw structural formulas for:
a. a conformation in which Br— and Cl— are eclipsed by each other.
b. a conformation in which Br— and Cl— are eclipsed by hydrogens.
c. two different staggered conformations.

Cis-trans isomerism in cycloalkanes (Section 11.7)

11.20   There are four cis-trans isomers of 2-isopropyl-5-methylcyclohexanol.

2-isopropyl-5-methylcyclohexanol

a. In the cis-trans isomer found in nature and named *menthol*, the isopropyl group is trans to the hydroxyl group and the methyl group is cis to the hydroxyl group. Using a planar hexagon representation for the cyclohexane ring, draw a structural formula for menthol.

b. Also using a planar hexagon representation for the cyclohexane ring, draw structural formulas for the other three cis-trans isomers of 2-isopropyl-5-methylcyclohexanol.

11.21   The substance 1,2,3,4,5,6-hexachlorocyclohexane shows cis-trans isomerism. A crude mixture of the isomers is sold as the insecticide benzene hexachloride (BHC), under the trade names Lindane and Gammexane. The insecticidal properties of the mixture arise from one isomer known as the gamma isomer, which is *cis*-1,2,4,5-*trans*-3,6-hexachlorocyclohexane.

a. Draw a structural formula for 1,2,3,4,5,6-hexachlorocyclohexane, disregarding for the moment the existence of cis-trans isomerism. What is the molecular formula of this compound?

b. Using a planar hexagon representation for the cyclohexane ring, draw a structural formula for the gamma isomer.

Physical
properties
(Section 11.8)

11.22 In Problem 11.16, you drew structural formulas for all isomeric alkanes of molecular formula C_7H_{16}. Predict which of these isomers has the lowest boiling point, and which the highest.

11.23 What unbranched alkane has about the same boiling point as water? (Refer to Table 11.4 on the physical properties of alkanes.) Calculate the molecular weight of this alkane and compare it with the molecular weight of water.

Reactions of
alkanes
(Section 11.9)

11.24 What is the major component of natural gas? Of bottled gas, or LPG?

11.25 Complete and balance these combustion reactions. Assume that each hydrocarbon is converted completely to carbon dioxide and water.
a. propane + O_2 $\longrightarrow$ **b.** octane + O_2 $\longrightarrow$
c. cyclohexane + O_2 $\longrightarrow$ **d.** 3-methylpentane + O_2 $\longrightarrow$

11.26 Following are heats of combustion per mole for methane, propane, and 2,2,4-trimethylpentane. On a gram-for-gram basis, which hydrocarbon is the best source of heat energy?

Hydrocarbon	Major Component of	ΔH^0 (kcal/mol)
CH_4	natural gas	-212
$CH_3CH_2CH_3$	LPG	-531
$\begin{array}{c} \quad CH_3 \ \ CH_3 \\ \quad \ | \quad \ \ | \\ CH_3CCH_2CHCH_3 \\ \quad \ | \\ \quad CH_3 \end{array}$	gasoline	-1304

11.27 Name and draw structural formulas for all possible monohalgenation products that might be formed in these reactions.

a. ⬡ + Cl_2 $\xrightarrow{\text{light}}$

b. $CH_3-CH_2-CH_2-\overset{\overset{\displaystyle CH_3}{|}}{CH}-CH_3 + Cl_2 \xrightarrow{\text{light}}$

c. $CH_3-\overset{\overset{\displaystyle CH_3}{|}}{CH}-\underset{\underset{\displaystyle CH_3}{|}}{CH}-CH_3 + Br_2 \xrightarrow{\text{light}}$

d. $\begin{array}{c} CH_2 \\ | \quad \diagdown \\ \quad \quad CH_2 \\ | \quad \diagup \\ CH_2 \end{array} + Br_2 \xrightarrow{\text{light}}$

11.28 There are three isomeric alkanes of molecular formula C_5H_{12}. When isomer A is reacted with chlorine gas at 300°C, the result is a mixture of four monochlorination products. Under the same conditions with isomer B, a mixture of three monochlorination products results, and with isomer C, only one monochlorination product is formed. From this information, assign structural formulas to isomers A, B, and C.

11.29 Consult a handbook of chemistry or other reference work, to find out the densites of dichloromethane (methylene chloride), trichloromethane (chloroform), and tetrachloromethane (carbon tetrachloride). Which are more dense than water? Which are less dense?

Unsaturated Hydrocarbons

Unsaturated hydrocarbons are hydrocarbons that contain one or more carbon-carbon double or triple bonds. There are three classes of unsaturated hydrocarbons: alkenes, alkynes, and aromatic hydrocarbons. **Alkenes** contain one or more carbon-carbon double bonds, and alkynes contain one or more carbon-carbon triple bonds. The structural formulas of ethene, the simplest alkene, and ethyne, the simplest alkyne, are

$$\underset{\substack{\text{ethene}\\ \text{(an alkene)}}}{\overset{\displaystyle H\diagdown \underset{H}{\overset{}{C}}=\underset{H}{\overset{}{C}}\diagup H}{}} \qquad \underset{\substack{\text{ethyne}\\ \text{(an alkyne)}}}{H-C\equiv C-H}$$

Because alkenes and alkynes have fewer hydrogen atoms than alkanes with the same number of carbons atoms, they are commonly referred to as unsaturated hydrocarbons; they are unsaturated with respect to hydrogen atoms. Alkynes are not widely distributed in the biological world, and therefore, we will not study them further.

The third class of unsaturated hydrocarbons are the **aromatic hydrocarbons**. The Lewis structure of benzene, the simplest aromatic hydrocarbon, is

benzene
(an aromatic hydrocarbon)

Benzene and other aromatic hydrocarbons have chemical properties quite different from those of alkenes and alkynes. However, the structural feature that relates alkenes, alkynes, and aromatic hydrocarbons is the presence of one or more pi bonds. This chapter is a study of carbon-carbon pi bonds.

12.1 Structure and Bonding in Alkenes

We have examined the formation of carbon-carbon double bonds in terms of the overlap of atomic orbitals (Section 10.5B). To bond with three other atoms, carbon uses sp^2 hybrid orbitals formed by combination of one $2s$ orbital and two $2p$ orbitals. The three sp^2 orbitals lie in a plane at angles of 120° to each other. The remaining $2p$ orbital of carbon is not hybridized and lies perpendicular to the plane created by the three sp^2 orbitals. A carbon-carbon double bond consists of one sigma bond formed by the overlap of sp^2 hybrid orbitals of adjacent carbon atoms and one pi bond formed by the overlap of unhybridized $2p$ orbitals (Figure 12.1).

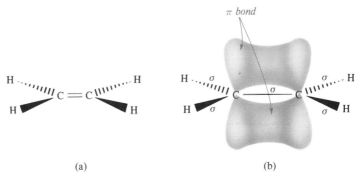

(a)   (b)

Figure 12.1 Covalent bonding in ethene. (a) Lewis structure; (b) orbital overlap model, showing sigma and pi bonds.

Using the orbital overlap model of a carbon-carbon double bond, we would predict a value of 120° for the H—C—C bond angles in ethene. The observed angle is 121.7°, a value close to that predicted. In substituted alkenes, deviations from the predicted angle of 120° may be larger. The C—C=C bond angle in propene, for example, is 124.7°.

12.2 Nomenclature of Alkenes

A. IUPAC Names

The IUPAC names of alkenes are formed by changing the -*an*- infix of the parent alkane to -*en*- (Section 11.5). Hence, CH_2—CH_2 is named ethene, and CH_3—CH=CH_2 is named propene.

$$CH_2{=}CH_2 \qquad CH_3{-}CH{=}CH_2$$

ethene   propene

Ethene and propene can contain a double bond in only one position. In higher alkenes where there are isomers that differ in location of the double bond, a numbering system must be used. According to the IUPAC system, the longest carbon chain that contains the double bond is numbered to give the carbon atoms of the double bond the lowest possible numbers. The location of the double bond is indicated by the number of the first carbon of the double bond. Branched or substituted alkenes are named like alkanes. Carbon atoms are numbered, substituent groups are located and named, the double bond is located, and the main chain is named.

$$\overset{6}{CH_3}{-}\overset{5}{CH_2}{-}\overset{4}{CH_2}{-}\overset{3}{CH}{=}\overset{2}{CH}{-}\overset{1}{CH_3} \qquad \overset{6}{CH_3}{-}\overset{5}{CH_2}{-}\overset{4}{CH}{-}\overset{3}{CH}{=}\overset{2}{CH}{-}\overset{1}{CH_3}$$

$$\underset{\textstyle CH_3}{\vert}$$

2-hexene   4-methyl-2-hexene

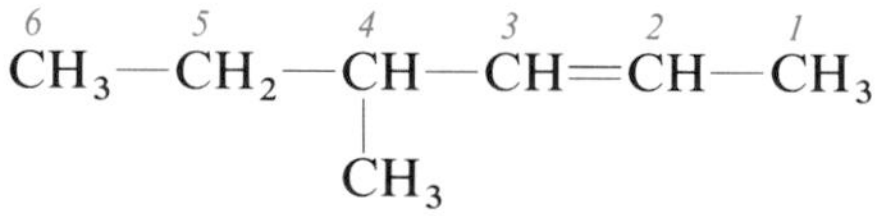

In the following alkene, there is a chain of five carbon atoms. However, because the longest chain that contains the double bond has only four carbons, the parent compound is butane and the IUPAC name of this alkene is 2-ethyl-3-methyl-1-butene.

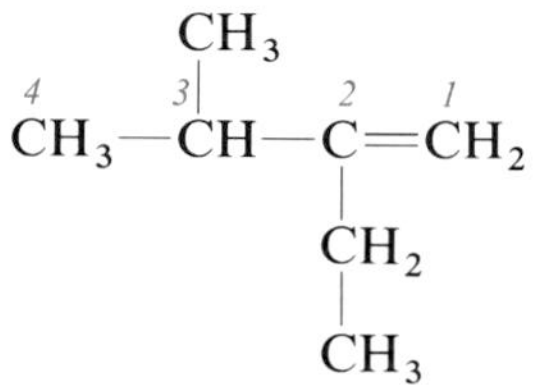

$$\overset{\textstyle CH_3}{\underset{\textstyle \vert}{}}$$
$$\overset{4}{CH_3}{-}\overset{3}{CH}{-}\overset{2}{C}{=}\overset{1}{CH_2}$$
$$\underset{\textstyle CH_2}{\vert}$$
$$\underset{\textstyle CH_3}{\vert}$$

2-ethyl-3-methyl-1-butene

When cycloalkenes are named, the carbon atoms of the ring multiple bond are numbered 1 and 2 in the direction that gives the substituent encountered first the smallest number. If there are two or more different substituents, they are listed in alphabetical order.

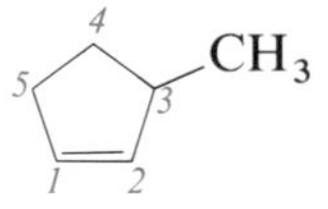

3-methylcyclopentene 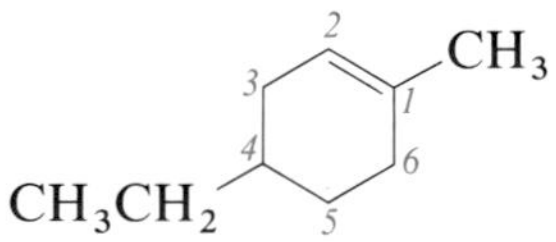   4-ethyl-1-methylcyclohexene

Alkenes that contain more than one double bond are called alkadienes, alkatrienes, or more simply dienes, trienes, and so on.

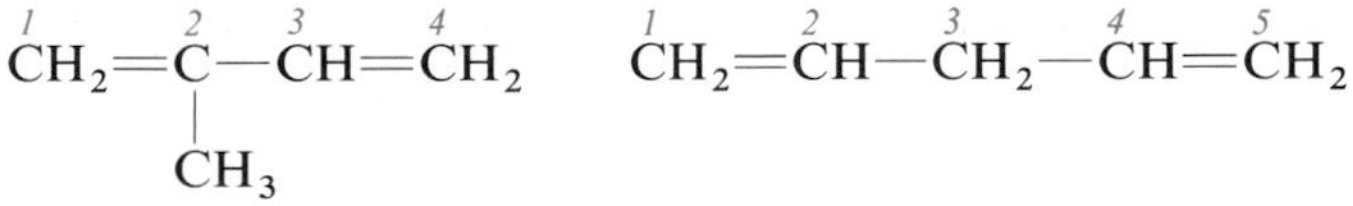

$$\overset{1}{C}H_2=\overset{2}{C}-\overset{3}{C}H=\overset{4}{C}H_2 \qquad \overset{1}{C}H_2=\overset{2}{C}H-\overset{3}{C}H_2-\overset{4}{C}H=\overset{5}{C}H_2$$
$$\underset{CH_3}{|}$$

2-methyl-1,3-butadiene   1,4-pentadiene
(isoprene)

B. Common Names

Many alkenes, particularly those of low molecular weight, are known almost exclusively by their common names.

$$CH_2=CH_2 \qquad CH_3-CH=CH_2 \qquad \underset{|}{CH_3}-C=CH_2 \qquad CH_2=CH-CH=CH_2$$

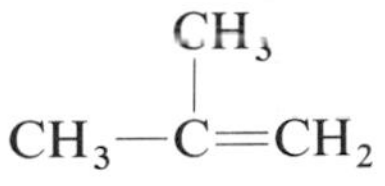

IUPAC name:	ethene	propene	2-methylpropene	1,3-butadiene
Common name:	ethylene	propylene	isobutylene	butadiene

Further, the common names **methylene**, **vinyl**, and **allyl** are often used to show the presence of alkenyl groups, as shown in Table 12.1.

Table 12.1 Names for common alkenyl groups.

Alkenyl Group	Group Name	Examples
$CH_2=$	methylene	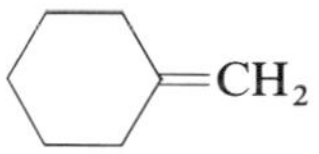 $=CH_2$ methylene cyclohexane
$CH_2=CH-$	vinyl	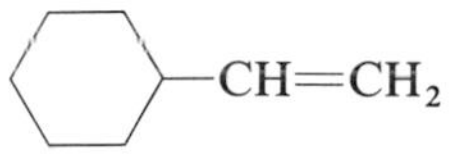 $CH_2=CH-Cl$ vinyl chloride $-CH=CH_2$ vinyl cyclohexane
$CH_2=CH-CH_2-$	allyl	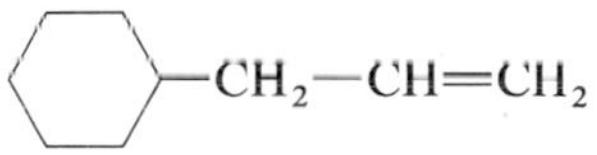 $CH_2=CH-CH_2-Cl$ allyl chloride $-CH_2-CH=CH_2$ allyl cyclohexane

The name methylene is also used to show the presence of a $-CH_2-$ group, as illustrated in the following examples:

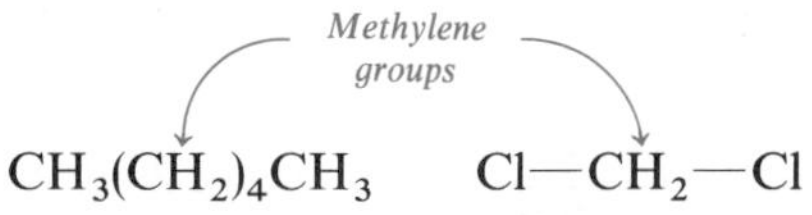

Methylene groups

$$CH_3(CH_2)_4CH_3 \qquad Cl-CH_2-Cl$$

hexane   dichloromethane
(methylene chloride)

Draw structural formulas for all alkenes of molecular formula C_5H_{10}. Give each an IUPAC name.

Example 12.1

☐ *Solution*

Approach this type of problem systematically. First draw the carbon skeletons possible for molecules of five carbon atoms. There are three such skeletons.

a. C—C—C—C—C   **b.** $\underset{\displaystyle \text{C}}{\text{C—C—C—C}}$ **c.** $\underset{\displaystyle \text{C}}{\overset{\displaystyle \text{C}}{\text{C—C—C}}}$

Because skeleton (c) cannot contain a carbon-carbon double bond (the central carbon atom already has four bonds to it), we need consider only skeletons (a) and (b) when drawing structural isomers for alkenes of molecular formula C_5H_{10}. Next, locate the double bond between carbon atoms along the chain. For carbon skeleton (a), there are two possible locations for the double bond, and for carbon skeleton (b), three possible locations.

For (a):   C=C—C—C—C   and   C—C=C—C—C

For (b): $\underset{\displaystyle \text{C}}{\text{C=C—C—C}}$ and $\underset{\displaystyle \text{C}}{\text{C—C=C—C}}$ and $\underset{\displaystyle \text{C}}{\text{C—C—C=C}}$

Finally, add hydrogens to complete the tetravalence of carbon and give the correct molecular formula. To derive IUPAC names for these alkenes, number the carbon chain from the direction that gives the carbons of the double bond the lowest numbers and then name and give a number to each substituent. Common names are given below for several of these alkenes. Note, however, that none is given for 2-pentene. You might be tempted to call it ethylmethylethylene, but that name is ambiguous. It does not tell you whether the ethyl and methyl groups are on the same carbon (as in 2-methyl-1-butene) or on adjacent carbons (as in 2-pentene) of the double bond.

$\overset{1}{C}H_2{=}\overset{2}{C}H{-}\overset{3}{C}H_2{-}\overset{4}{C}H_2{-}\overset{5}{C}H_3$ $\overset{1}{C}H_3{-}\overset{2}{C}H{=}\overset{3}{C}H{-}\overset{4}{C}H_2{-}\overset{5}{C}H_3$

1-pentene   2-pentene
(*n*-propylethylene)

$\overset{1}{C}H_2{=}\underset{\displaystyle CH_3}{\overset{2}{C}}{-}\overset{3}{C}H_2{-}\overset{4}{C}H_3$ $\overset{1}{C}H_3{-}\underset{\displaystyle CH_3}{\overset{2}{C}}{=}\overset{3}{C}H{-}\overset{4}{C}H_3$ $\overset{4}{C}H_3{-}\underset{\displaystyle CH_3}{\overset{3}{C}H}{-}\overset{2}{C}H{=}\overset{1}{C}H_2$

2-methyl-1-butene   2-methyl-2-butene   3-methyl-1-butene
                (trimethylethylene)   (isopropylethylene)

Problem 12.1

Draw structural formulas for all alkenes of molecular formula C_6H_{12} that have the following carbon skeletons. Give each alkene an IUPAC name and where possible a common name.

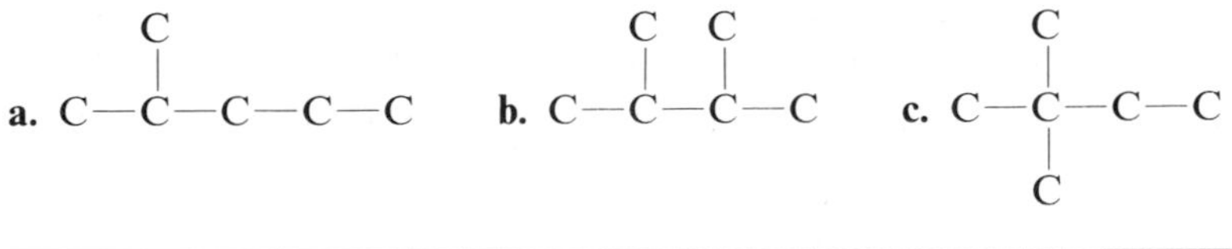

a. $C-\overset{\displaystyle C}{\underset{\displaystyle |}{C}}-C-C-C$ **b.** $C-\overset{\displaystyle C}{\underset{\displaystyle |}{C}}-\overset{\displaystyle C}{\underset{\displaystyle |}{C}}-C$ **c.** $C-\overset{\displaystyle C}{\underset{\displaystyle \underset{\displaystyle C}{|}}{\underset{\displaystyle |}{C}}}-C-C$

12.3   Cis-Trans Isomerism in Alkenes

A. The Existence of Cis-Trans Isomers

Configurational isomers have the same molecular formula, the same order of attachment of atoms, and an arrangement of atoms that is fixed in space because of restricted rotation about one or more bonds within the molecule. **Cis-trans isomerism** is one type of configurational isomerism. In cycloalkanes, cis-trans isomerism depends on the arrangement of substituent groups on a ring (Section 11.7); in alkenes, cis-trans isomerism depends on the arrangement of groups on a double bond. The structural feature that makes possible the existence of cis-trans isomerism in alkenes is restricted rotation about the two carbons of a double bond (Figure 12.2).

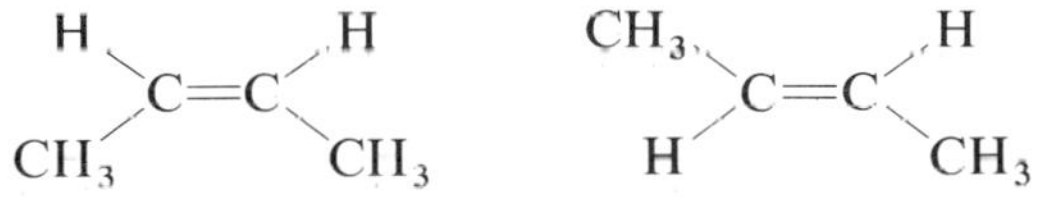

cis-2-butene
(mp −139°C;
bp 4°C)

trans-2-butene
(mp −106°C;
bp 1°C)

Figure 12.2 The cis and trans isomers of 2-butene.

Ethene, propene, 1-butene, and 2-methylpropene have only one possible arrangement of groups about the double bond. In 2-butene there are two possible arrangements. In one arrangement, the two methyl groups are on the same side of the double bond; this isomer is called *cis*-2-butene. In the other arrangement, the two methyl groups are on opposite sides of the double bond; this isomer is called *trans*-2-butene. Shown in Figure 12.2 are Lewis structures for these configurational isomers. Cis and trans isomers are different compounds and have different physical and chemical properties. The cis and trans isomers of 2-butene differ in melting points by 33°C and in boiling points by 3°C.

Example 12.2

Which of the following alkenes show cis-trans isomerism? For each that does, draw structural formulas for both isomers.

a. $CH_2=CH-CH_2-CH_2-CH_3$ **b.** $CH_3-CH=CH-CH_2-CH_3$

c. 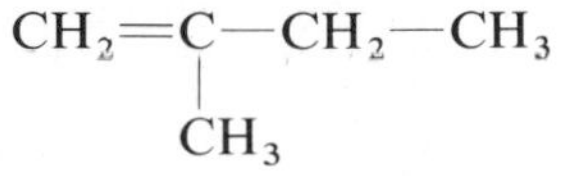 $CH_2=\overset{\displaystyle }{\underset{\displaystyle \underset{\displaystyle CH_3}{|}}{C}}-CH_2-CH_3$

Solution

a. 1-Pentene. Begin by drawing a carbon-carbon double bond to show the surrounding bond angles of 120°:

$$\text{>C=C<}$$

Next, complete the structural formula, showing all four groups attached to the double bond:

$$\begin{array}{c} H \quad\quad H \\ \text{C=C} \\ H \quad\quad CH_2CH_2CH_3 \end{array}$$

To determine whether this molecule shows cis-trans isomerism, exchange positions of the —H and —CH$_2$CH$_2$CH$_3$ groups and compare the two structural formulas to see whether they are identical or whether they represent cis and trans isomers.

$$\begin{array}{cc} \begin{array}{c} H \quad\quad H \\ \text{C=C} \\ H \quad\quad CH_2CH_2CH_3 \end{array} & \begin{array}{c} H \quad\quad CH_2CH_2CH_3 \\ \text{C=C} \\ H \quad\quad H \end{array} \end{array}$$

In this case, they are identical. To see this, imagine that you pick up either one and turn it over as you would turn your hand from palm down to palm up. If you do this correctly, you will see that one structural formula fits exactly on top of the other; that is, it is superimposable on the other. These structural formulas are identical, and 1-pentene does not show cis-trans isomerism.

b. 2-Pentene. Draw structural formulas for possible cis-trans isomers as you did in part (a).

$$\begin{array}{cc} \begin{array}{c} CH_3 \quad\quad H \\ \text{C=C} \\ H \quad\quad CH_2CH_3 \end{array} & \begin{array}{c} CH_3 \quad\quad CH_2CH_3 \\ \text{C=C} \\ H \quad\quad H \end{array} \end{array}$$

trans-2-pentene   *cis*-2-pentene

The four groups attached to the double bond in the structural formula on the left have a different orientation from that in the structural formula on the right. Therefore, the drawings represent cis-trans isomers.

c. 2-Methyl-1-butene. The structural formulas below are superimposable, and therefore this alkene does not show cis-trans isomerism.

$$\begin{array}{cc} \begin{array}{c} H \quad\quad CH_3 \\ \text{C=C} \\ H \quad\quad CH_2CH_3 \end{array} & \begin{array}{c} H \quad\quad CH_2CH_3 \\ \text{C=C} \\ H \quad\quad CH_3 \end{array} \end{array}$$

From this example and the preceding discussion, you should realize that an alkene shows cis-trans isomerism only if each of the carbon atoms of the double bond has two different groups attached to it. In 2-pentene, the different groups on the first carbon of the double bond are —H and —CH$_3$; on the second carbon of the double bond, they are —H and —CH$_2$CH$_3$. In 2-butene, the different groups on each carbon of the double bond are —H and —CH$_3$.

**Problem
12.2**

Which of the following alkenes show cis-trans isomerism? For each that does, draw structural formulas for the isomers.

a. 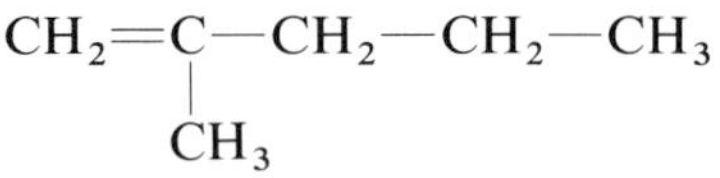 CH_2=C—CH_2—CH_2—CH_3
    |
    CH_3

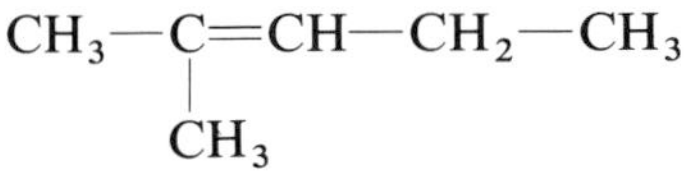

b. CH_3—C=CH—CH_2—CH_3
    |
    CH_3

c. CH_3—CH—CH=CH—CH_3
    |
    CH_3

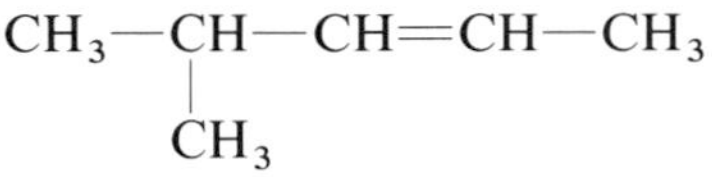

d. 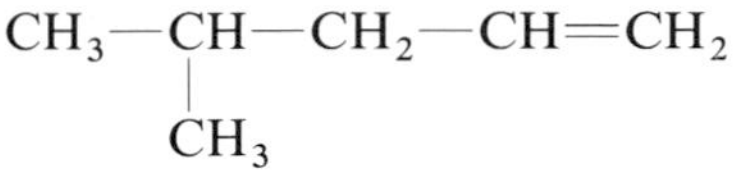 CH_3—CH—CH_2—CH=CH_2
    |
    CH_3

B. Designating Configuration of Alkenes

The most common method for specifying configuration in alkenes uses the prefixes *cis* and *trans*. There is no doubt whatsoever which configurational isomers are intended by the names *cis*-2-butene and *trans*-3-hexene.

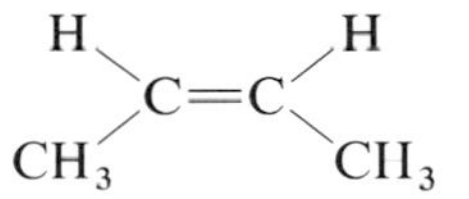

cis-2-butene 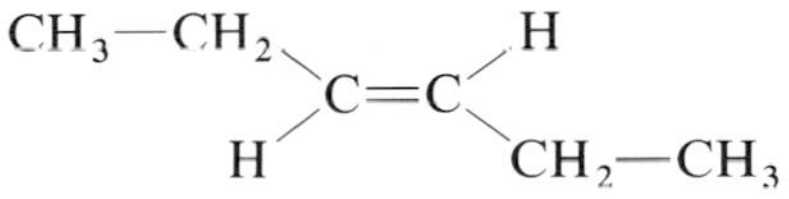   *trans*-3-hexene

For alkenes with more complex structural formulas, it is the orientation of the main carbon chain that determines cis and trans. Following is a structural formula for one configurational isomer of 3,4-dimethyl-2-pentene

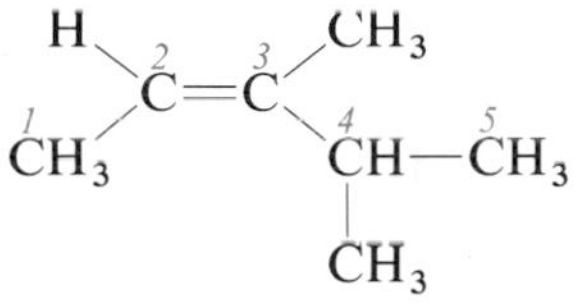

3,4-dimethyl-2-pentene

Should it be named cis because the carbon atoms of the parent chain (atoms 1-2-3-4-5) are on the same side of the double bond, or should it be named trans because the two methyl groups are on opposite sides? According to IUPAC rules, it should be named cis because of the cis orientation of the main carbon chain about the double bond.

C. Configurational Isomerism in Cycloalkenes

Configurational isomerism is possible about the carbon-carbon double bond in cycloalkenes only when the ring is large enough to accommodate a trans double bond. In cyclohexene and cycloheptene, ring formation is possible only if the carbon atoms attached directly to the double bond (carbons 3 and 6 of the cyclohexene ring, carbons 3 and 7 of the cycloheptene ring) are cis to each other (Figure 12.3). A trans configuration is not possible in these and smaller cycloalkenes.

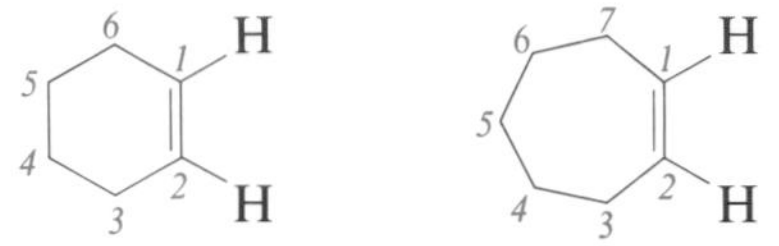

to form cyclohexene,
carbon atoms 3 and 6
must be cis to each
other

to form cycloheptene,
carbons atoms 3 and 7
must be cis to each
other

Figure 12.3 Configurational isomerism is not possible in cyclohexene and cycloheptene.

Only in cyclooctene and higher cycloalkenes is the number of carbon atoms involved in ring formation large enough so there is a possibility for configurational isomerism.

D. Configurational Isomerism in Dienes, Trienes, and Polyenes

Thus far we have considered cis-trans isomerism in compounds containing only one carbon-carbon double bond. Next let us consider compounds with two or more carbon-carbon double bonds. In 1,3-heptadiene, carbon 1 has two identical groups and there is no possibility for configurational isomerism about the first double bond. Each carbon of the double bond between carbons 3 and 4 has two different groups attached to it, and configurational isomerism is possible about this double bond.

$$\overset{1}{C}H_2=\overset{2}{C}H-\overset{3}{C}H=\overset{4}{C}H-\overset{5}{C}H_2-\overset{6}{C}H_2-\overset{7}{C}H_3$$

Each carbon atom of this double bond has two different groups attached to it

1,3-heptadiene

An example of a biologically important molecule for which there are numerous cis-trans isomers is vitamin A. There is no possibility for cis-trans isomerism about the cyclohexene double bond, because the ring contains only six atoms. There are four carbon-carbon double bonds in the chain of atoms attached to the substituted cyclohexene ring, and each has the potential for cis-trans isomerism. There are $2 \times 2 \times 2 \times 2$, or 16, possible cis-trans isomers for vitamin A.

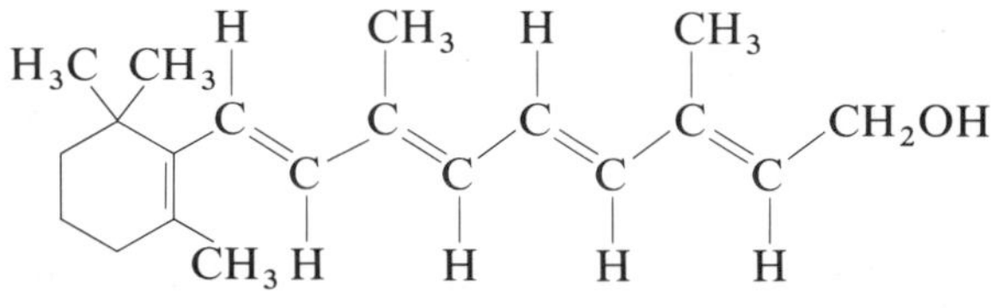

vitamin A

12.4 Reactions of Alkenes—An Overview

In contrast to alkanes, alkenes react with a variety of compounds. One characteristic reaction of alkenes takes place at the carbon-carbon double bond in such a way that the pi bond is broken and in its place are formed sigma bonds to two new atoms or groups of atoms. Such reactions are called addition reactions.

$$\underset{\diagup}{\overset{\diagdown}{C}}=\underset{\diagdown}{\overset{\diagup}{C}} + A-B \longrightarrow -\underset{\underset{A}{|}}{C}-\underset{\underset{B}{|}}{C}-$$

In addition reactions, one sigma bond (A—B) and one pi bond are broken and two new sigma bonds (C—A and C—B) are formed. Consequently, addition reactions to double bonds are almost always energetically favorable because there is net conversion of one pi bond to a sigma bond.

Each addition reaction is given a special name that describes the particular type of addition. Table 12.2 gives examples of four addition reactions.

Table 12.2
Four alkene addition reactions and the descriptive name or names associated with each.

Addition Reaction		Descriptive Name
$\diagdown C = C \diagup$ + H—H $\xrightarrow{\text{addition of hydrogen}}$ $-\underset{\underset{H}{|}}{C}-\underset{\underset{H}{|}}{C}-$		hydrogenation; reduction
$\diagdown C = C \diagup$ + Br—Br $\xrightarrow{\text{addition of bromine}}$ $-\underset{\underset{Br}{|}}{C}-\underset{\underset{Br}{|}}{C}-$		bromination; halogenation
$\diagdown C = C \diagup$ + H—Br $\xrightarrow{\text{addition of hydrobromic acid}}$ $-\underset{\underset{H}{|}}{C}-\underset{\underset{Br}{|}}{C}-$		hydrobromination; hydrohalogenation
$\diagdown C = C \diagup$ + H—OH $\xrightarrow{\text{addition of water}}$ $-\underset{\underset{H}{|}}{C}-\underset{\underset{OH}{|}}{C}-$		hydration

A second characteristic reaction of alkenes is conversion to alkanes by addition of two hydrogen atoms. A balanced half-reaction for the conversion of an alkene to an alkane shows that this transformation is a two electron reduction. (For the use of half-reactions in oxidation-reduction reactions, review Section 5.4B.)

Balanced Half-Reaction

$$\text{C}=\text{C} + 2\text{H}^+ + 2\text{e}^- \longrightarrow -\overset{|}{\underset{\text{H}}{\text{C}}}-\overset{|}{\underset{\text{H}}{\text{C}}}-$$

an alkene   an alkane

A third characteristic reaction of alkenes is oxidation. **Oxidation** almost invariably involves addition of oxygen, in some reactions without cleavage of the carbon skeleton, and in other reactions with cleavage, as illustrated by the following balanced half-reactions. The first is a two-electron oxidation and does not break the carbon skeleton. The second is a four-electron oxidation and does involve cleavage of the carbon-carbon double bond.

$$\text{C}=\text{C} + 2\text{H}_2\text{O} \xrightarrow{\text{oxidation}} -\overset{|}{\underset{\text{HO}}{\text{C}}}-\overset{|}{\underset{\text{OH}}{\text{C}}}- + 2\text{H}^+ + 2\text{e}^-$$

$$\text{C}=\text{C} + 2\text{H}_2\text{O} \xrightarrow{\text{oxidation}} \text{C}=\text{O} + \text{O}=\text{C} + 4\text{H}^+ + 4\text{e}^-$$

We will now study these characteristic alkene reactions in considerable detail, including what is known about how each occurs, or in the terminology of organic chemists, what is known about the mechanism of each reaction.

12.5 Addition to Alkenes

A. Addition of Bromine and Chlorine: Halogenation

Bromine, Br_2, and chlorine, Cl_2, add readily to alkenes to form single covalent carbon-halogen bonds (C—Br or C—Cl) on adjacent carbons. Fluorine also adds to alkenes, but because its addition is fast and not easily controlled, adding fluorine to alkenes is not a general laboratory procedure. Iodine is so unreactive that it does not add to alkenes. Halogenation with bromine or chlorine is generally carried out either with the pure reagents or by mixing them in CCl_4 or some other inert solvent.

$$\text{CH}_3-\text{CH}_2-\text{CH}=\text{CH}_2 + \text{Cl}-\text{Cl} \longrightarrow \text{CH}_3-\text{CH}_2-\overset{|}{\underset{\text{Cl}}{\text{CH}}}-\overset{|}{\underset{\text{Cl}}{\text{CH}}}_2$$

1-butene   1,2-dichlorobutane

$$\text{CH}_3-\text{CH}=\text{CH}-\text{CH}_3 + \text{Br}-\text{Br} \longrightarrow \text{CH}_3-\overset{|}{\underset{\text{Br}}{\text{CH}}}-\overset{|}{\underset{\text{Br}}{\text{CH}}}-\text{CH}_3$$

2-butene   2,3-dibromobutane

$$\text{cyclohexene} + Br\!-\!Br \longrightarrow \text{1,2-dibromocyclohexane}$$

cyclohexene   1,2-dibromocyclohexane

Alkenes are different from alkanes in reacting with Br_2 and Cl_2. Recall (Section 11.9B) that chlorine and bromine do not react with alkanes unless the halogen-alkane mixture is exposed to ultraviolet or visible light, or heated to temperatures of 250–400°C. The reaction that then occurs is substitution of halogen for hydrogen and formation of an equivalent amount of HCl or HBr. Halogenation of most alkanes invariably gives a complex mixture of products. In contrast, chlorine and bromine react with alkenes at room temperature by addition of halogen atoms to the two carbon atoms of the double bond, with the formation of two new carbon-halogen bonds.

Example 12.3

Name and draw structural formulas for the products of the following halogenation reactions:

a. $CH_3\overset{\displaystyle CH_3}{\underset{}{C}}\!\!=\!\!CHCH_3 + Br_2 \longrightarrow$

b. $\bigcirc + Cl_2 \longrightarrow$

Solution

a. $CH_3\!-\!\overset{\displaystyle CH_3}{\underset{\displaystyle Br}{C}}\!-\!\overset{}{\underset{\displaystyle Br}{CH}}\!-\!CH_3$

   2,3-dibromo-2-methylbutane

b. (structure with Cl and Cl)

   1,2-dichlorocyclohexane

Problem 12.3

Name and draw structural formulas for the alkene that reacts with bromine, to give

a. $CH_3\overset{}{\underset{\displaystyle Br}{CH}}\overset{}{\underset{\displaystyle Br}{CH}}CH_2$

b. (cyclopentane with CH₃, Br, Br)

Reaction with bromine is a particularly useful qualitative test for the presence of an alkene. A solution of bromine in carbon tetrachloride is red, whereas alkenes and dibromoalkanes are usually colorless. If a few drops of bromine in carbon tetrachloride is added to an alkene, the red color of the test solution is discharged.

B. Addition of Hydrogen Halides: Hydrohalogenation

Dry HF, HCl, HBr, and HI add to alkenes to give haloalkanes. These additions may be carried out either with the pure reagents or in the presence of a polar solvent such as acetic acid. Addition of HCl to ethene gives chloroethane (ethyl chloride):

$$CH_2{=}CH_2 + H{-}Cl \longrightarrow CH_2{-}CH_2$$
$$\qquad\qquad\qquad\qquad\qquad | \quad\ |$$
$$\qquad\qquad\qquad\qquad\qquad H \quad Cl$$

ethene

chloroethane
(ethyl chloride)

Addition of HCl to propene gives two products, 2-chloropropane (isopropyl chloride) and 1-chloropropane (*n*-propyl chloride) depending on which part of the reagent goes to which carbon of the double bond:

$$CH_3{-}CH{=}CH_2 + H{-}Cl \longrightarrow CH_3{-}CH{-}CH_2 + CH_3{-}CH{-}CH_2$$
$$\qquad\qquad\qquad\qquad\qquad\qquad\qquad\qquad | \quad\ | \qquad\qquad | \quad\ |$$
$$\qquad\qquad\qquad\qquad\qquad\qquad\qquad\qquad Cl \quad H \qquad\quad H \quad Cl$$

propene

2-chloropropane
(major product)

1-chloropropane

Of the two possible products, only 2-chloropropane is formed. This selective pattern of addition was noted by Vladimir Markovnikov, who made the generalization that in additions of H—X to alkenes, hydrogen adds to the carbon of the double bond that has the greater number of hydrogens already attached to it. It is important to remember that while **Markovnikov's rule** provides a way to predict the major product of an alkene addition reaction, it does not explain why one product predominates over other possible products.

Example 12.4

Name and draw structural formulas for the products of these alkene addition reactions. Use Markovnikov's rule to predict which is the major product.

$$\qquad\qquad CH_3$$
$$\qquad\qquad\ |$$
a. $CH_3{-}C{=}CH_2 + HI \longrightarrow$

b. (cyclopentene with CH_3 substituent) + HCl $\longrightarrow$

☐ *Solution*

a. HI adds to 2-methylpropene (isobutylene) to form two possible products:

$$\qquad\qquad CH_3 \qquad\qquad\qquad\qquad\qquad CH_3 \qquad\qquad\qquad CH_3$$
$$\qquad\qquad\ | \qquad\qquad\qquad\qquad\qquad\quad | \qquad\qquad\qquad\ |$$
$$CH_3{-}C{=}CH_2 + HI \longrightarrow CH_3{-}C{-}CH_2 + CH_3{-}C{-}CH_2$$
$$\qquad\qquad\qquad\qquad\qquad\qquad\qquad\qquad | \quad\ | \qquad\qquad | \quad\ |$$
$$\qquad\qquad\qquad\qquad\qquad\qquad\qquad\qquad I \quad H \qquad\quad H \quad I$$

2-methylpropene
(isobutylene)

2-iodo-2-methyl-
propane
(*t*-butyl iodide)
(major product)

1-iodo-2-methyl-
propane
(isobutyl iodide)
(minor product)

In forming 2-iodo-2-methylpropane (*tert*-butyl iodide), hydrogen adds to the carbon of the double bond bearing two hydrogens; in forming 1-iodo-2-methylpropane (isobutyl iodide), hydrogen adds to the carbon of the double bond bearing no hydrogens. Markovnikov's rule predicts that 2-iodo-2-methylpropane is the major product.

b. Addition of H—Cl to 1-methylcyclopentene forms two products:

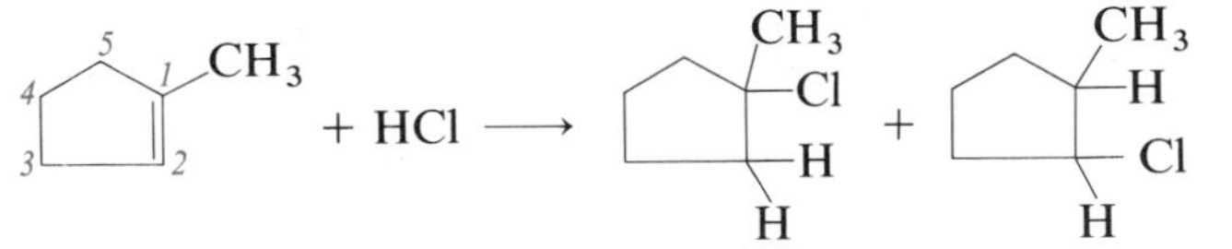

1-methylcyclo-pentene	1-chloro-1-methyl-cyclopentane (major product)	1-chloro-2-methyl-cyclopentane (minor product)

Carbon 1 of this cycloalkene contains no hydrogen atoms and carbon 2 contains one hydrogen. Using Markovnikov's rule, predict that hydrogen adds to carbon 2 and that 1-chloro-1-methylcyclopentane is the major product.

Problem 12.4

Name and draw structural formulas for the two possible products of the following alkene addition reactions. Use Markovnikov's rule to predict which is the major product.

$$
\textbf{a. } CH_3-CH=\underset{\underset{CH_3}{|}}{C}-CH_3 + HI \longrightarrow
\qquad \textbf{b. } \text{(cyclohexane ring)} {=}CH_2 + HI \quad \rangle
$$

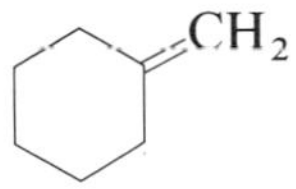

C. Addition of Water: Hydration

In the presence of an acid catalyst, most commonly concentrated sulfuric acid, water adds to alkenes to give alcohols. Addition of water to an alkene is called **hydration**. In simple alkenes, —H adds to the carbon of the double bond with the greater number of hydrogens and —OH adds to the carbon with the fewer hydrogens. Thus, H—OH adds to alkenes in accordance with Markovnikov's rule.

$$
CH_3-CH=CH_2 + H-OH \xrightarrow{H^+} CH_3-\underset{\underset{HO}{|}}{CH}-\underset{\underset{H}{|}}{CH_2}
$$

propene	2-propanol

$$
CH_3-\underset{\overset{|}{CH_3}}{C}=CH_2 + H-OH \xrightarrow{H^+} CH_3-\underset{\underset{HO}{\overset{\overset{CH_3}{|}}{|}}}{C}-\underset{\underset{H}{|}}{CH_2}
$$

2-methylpropene	2-methyl-2-propanol

Example 12.5

Draw structural formulas for the major products of these hydration reactions:

$$
\textbf{a. } CH_3-CH_2-CH=CH_2 + H_2O \xrightarrow{H^+}
\qquad \textbf{b. } \text{(cyclohexene ring)}-CH_3 + H_2O \xrightarrow{H^+}
$$

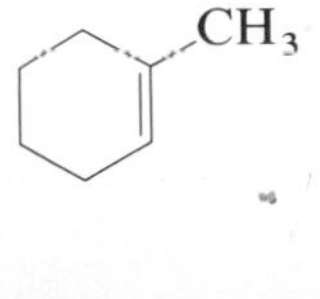

☐ *Solution*   **a.** 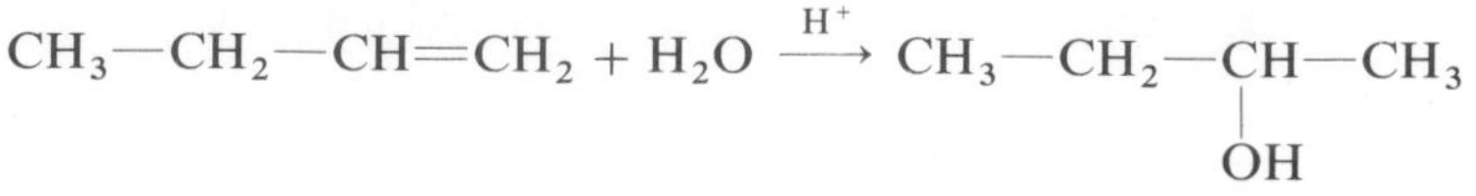 CH₃—CH₂—CH=CH₂ + H₂O $\xrightarrow{\text{H}^+}$ CH₃—CH₂—CH—CH₃
$$\underset{\text{OH}}{|}$$

2-butanol

b. 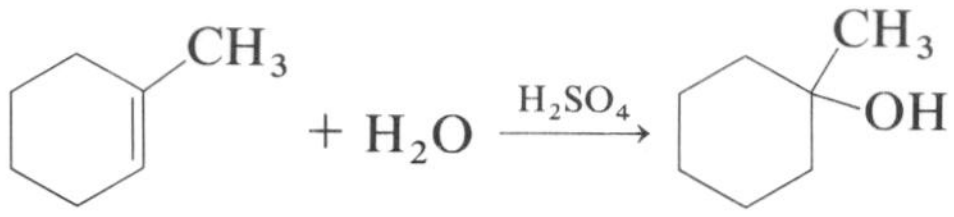 [cyclohexene with CH₃] + H₂O $\xrightarrow{\text{H}_2\text{SO}_4}$ [cyclohexane with CH₃ and OH]

1-methylcyclo-
hexanol

■
Problem 12.5

Draw structural formulas for the major products of these hydration reactions:

a. 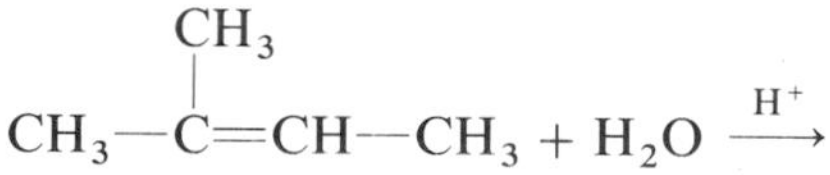 CH₃—$\overset{\overset{\text{CH}_3}{|}}{\text{C}}$=CH—CH₃ + H₂O $\xrightarrow{\text{H}^+}$

b. 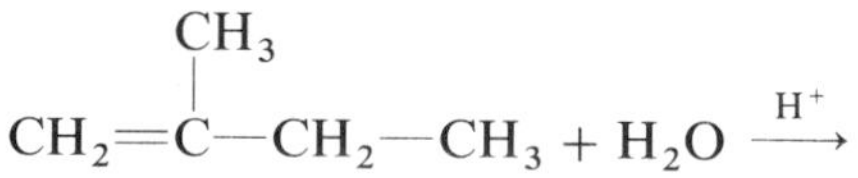 CH₂=$\overset{\overset{\text{CH}_3}{|}}{\text{C}}$—CH₂—CH₃ + H₂O $\xrightarrow{\text{H}^+}$ ■

D. Mechanism of Addition to Alkenes

It became apparent to chemists studying the addition of HX, Br₂, and Cl₂ to alkenes that initial attack on a carbon-carbon double bond is by an electrophile. An **electrophile** is any molecule or ion that can accept a pair of electrons and in the process form a new covalent bond. Following are Lewis structures for two electrophiles:

H⁺   :B̈r⁺

hydrogen   bromonium
ion   ion

The susceptibility of a double bond to attack by electrophiles is consistent with our electronic formulation; this pictures the double bond as composed of one sigma bond, in which electron density is located on the bond axis, and one pi bond, in which electron density is located in two lobes, one above and the other below the plane created by the sigma bond framework.

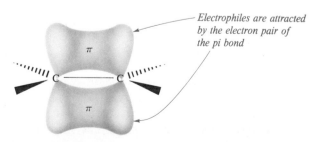

Electrophiles are attracted by the electron pair of the pi bond

1. Use of Curved Arrows in Organic Reaction Mechanisms

To show the flow of electrons in the making and breaking of bonds during a chemical reaction, chemists have adopted a symbol called a **curved arrow**. A curved arrow is used to show the flow of electron pairs *from where to where*. *From where* is shown by the tail of the arrow and may be (1) from an atom to an adjacent bond or (2) from a bond to an adjacent atom. *To where* is shown by the head of the arrow. Further, curved arrows are always read in a specific way, namely from left to right. When a curved arrow or curved arrows are shown on the left side of an equation, then the result of that flow of electrons is always shown in the structure or structures on the right, as illustrated by the flow of electrons during reaction of hydroxide ion with a proton to form a water molecule. In this illustration, the curved arrow shows that a pair of unshared electrons in the valence shell of oxygen is used to form a new covalent bond with hydrogen:

$$H—\overset{..}{\underset{..}{O}}:\curvearrowright\!\!+H^+ \longrightarrow H—\overset{..}{\underset{..}{O}}—H$$

In a sense, the curved arrow is nothing more than a bookkeeping device for keeping track of electron pairs. Do not be misled by its simplicity. Being able to follow the flow of electrons is fundamental to understanding the reactions of organic molecules and ions. Therefore, it is extremely important that you learn how to use this symbol properly.

2. Formation of Carbocation Intermediates

Addition of H—X to an alkene can be accounted for by a two-step mechanism. Addition begins by interaction of HX with the electron pair of the pi bond and formation of a new C—H bond, as illustrated by the reaction of HBr and 2-butene. The curved arrows on the left side of the equation show a combination of two bond-breaking steps and one bond-making step. First, the pi bond of the alkene is broken and the electron pair used instead to make a bond with the hydrogen atom of HBr. Second, the sigma bond in HBr is broken and the electron pair is given entirely to bromine, forming a bromide ion.

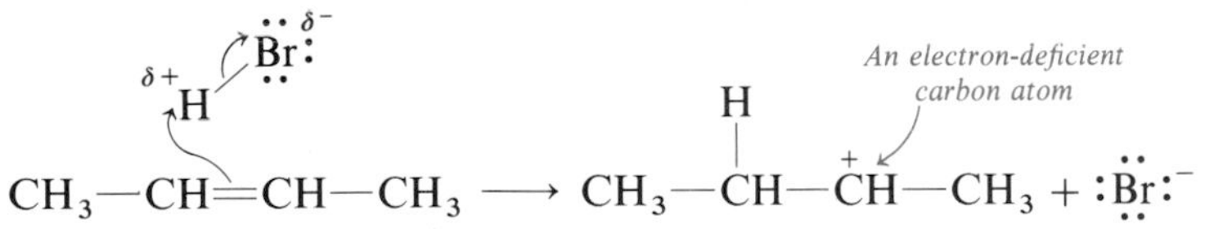

$$CH_3—CH{=}CH—CH_3 \longrightarrow CH_3—CH—\overset{+}{CH}—CH_3 + :\overset{..}{\underset{..}{Br}}:^-$$

An electron-deficient carbon atom

This step leaves one carbon atom with only six electrons in its valence shell. A carbon with six electrons in its valence shell bears a positive charge and is called a **carbocation** (carbon-containing cation). Carbocations are also called carbonium ions by analogy with the ammonium, NH_4^+, and hydronium, H_3O^+, ions. We will use the term *carbocation* throughout the text. You should, however, be aware of the term *carbonium ion*, since it is still used.

Because a carbocation contains an electron-deficient, positively charged carbon atom, it is an unstable intermediate. In reaction of H—X with an alkene, the carbocation intermediate reacts rapidly with halide ion to form a new C—X bond. The curved arrow on the left side of the equation shows that a pair of electrons on bromide ion is used to make a new C—Br bond:

$$CH_3-\overset{\underset{\displaystyle H}{|}}{CH}-\overset{+}{CH}-CH_3 + :\overset{..}{\underset{..}{Br}}:^- \longrightarrow CH_3-\overset{\underset{\displaystyle H}{|}}{CH}-\overset{\underset{\displaystyle H}{|}}{\overset{\overset{\displaystyle :\overset{..}{Br}:}{|}}{CH}}-CH_3$$

3. Relative Ease of Formation of Carbocations: An Explanation for Markovnikov's Rule

Carbocations are classified as primary (1°), secondary (2°), or tertiary (3°), depending on the number of alkyl groups bonded to the carbon bearing the positive charge. There is much experimental evidence that a tertiary carbocation is formed more easily than a secondary carbocation, which is in turn formed more easily than a primary carbocation.

$H-\overset{+}{C}\overset{H}{\underset{H}{\big<}}$	$CH_3-\overset{+}{C}\overset{H}{\underset{H}{\big<}}$	$CH_3-\overset{+}{C}\overset{CH_3}{\underset{H}{\big<}}$	$CH_3-\overset{+}{C}\overset{CH_3}{\underset{CH_3}{\big<}}$
methyl carbocation (methyl)	ethyl carbocation (1°)	isopropyl carbocation (2°)	*tert*-butyl carbocation (3°)

Example 12.6

Label these carbocations primary, secondary, or tertiary, and arrange them in order of increasing ease of formation:

a. $CH_3-\overset{+}{CH}-\overset{\overset{\displaystyle CH_3}{|}}{\underset{\underset{\displaystyle CH_3}{|}}{C}}-CH_3$ b. $CH_3-\overset{\overset{\displaystyle CH_3}{|}}{\underset{\underset{\displaystyle CH_3}{|}}{\overset{+}{C}}}-CH-CH_3$

c. $CH_3-\overset{\overset{\displaystyle CH_3}{|}}{\underset{\underset{\displaystyle CH_3}{|}}{C}}-CH_2-CH_2^+$

Solution

(a) is a secondary carbocation, (b) is tertiary and (c) is primary. In order of increasing ease of formation they are c, a, b.

Problem 12.6

Label these carbocations primary, secondary, or tertiary and arrange them in order of increasing ease of formation:

a. ⬡⁺—CH₃   b. ⬡—CH₃   c. ⬡—CH₂⁺

To account for the fact that HX adds to alkenes to give a major product and a minor product and for the observations generalized in Markovnikov's rule, the carbocation mechanism proposes that reaction of H—X and an alkene can give two different carbocation intermediates depending on how H^+ adds to the double bond. This is illustrated for the reaction of HBr with propene:

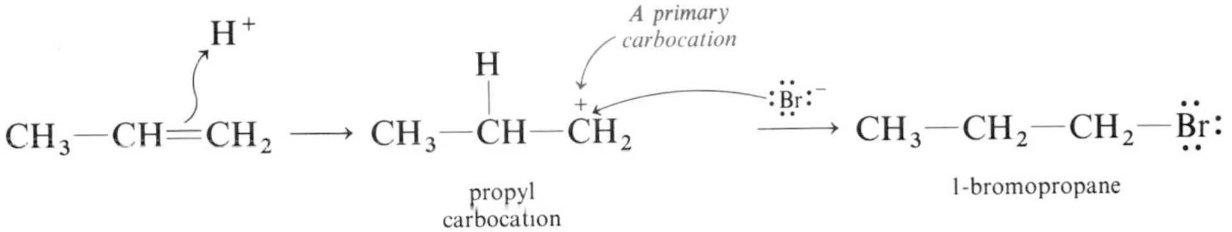

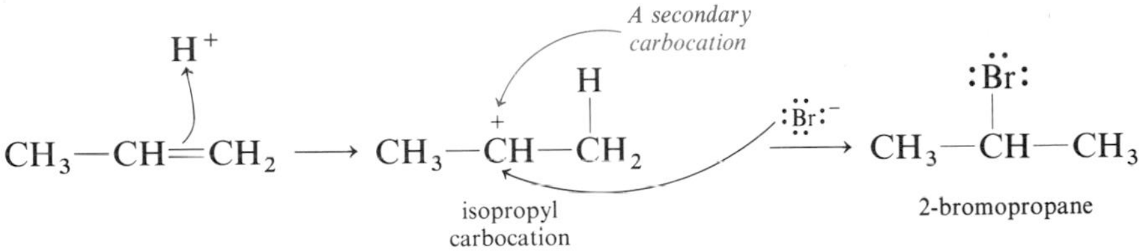

The isopropyl carbocation is a secondary carbocation and formed more easily than the propyl carbocation (a primary carbocation). Therefore, the major product of reaction of propene with HBr is 2-bromopropane, formed by reaction of the isopropyl carbocation with bromide ion.

Similarly, in the reaction of HBr with 2-methylpropene (isobutylene), adding H^+ to the carbon-carbon double bond gives either an isobutyl carbocation (a primary carbocation) or a *tert*-butyl carbocation (a tertiary carbocation).

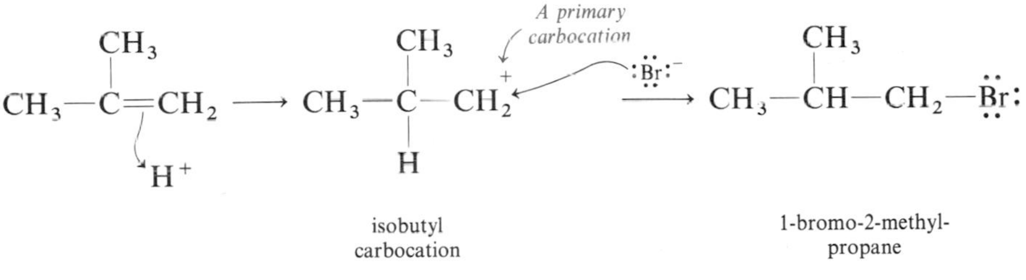

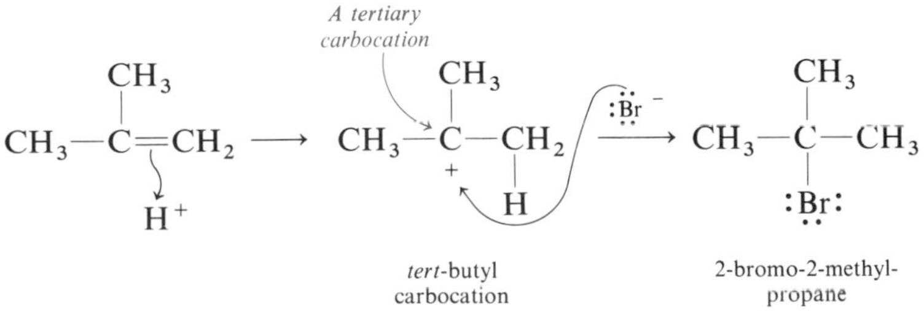

The *tert*-butyl carbocation (a tertiary carbocation) is formed more easily than the isobutyl carbocation (a primary carbocation). Therefore, the major product formed in the reaction of 2-methylpropene with HBr is 2-bromo-2-methylpropane (*tert*-butyl bromide)—formed by the reaction of the *tert*-butyl carbocation with bromide ion.

The mechanism for acid-catalyzed hydration of alkenes is similar to what we have already proposed for addition of HCl and HBr to alkenes and is illustrated by conversion of propene to 2-propanol. In step 1, a proton (an electrophile) reacts with the electron pair of the pi bond to form a carbocation (also an electrophile). In the reaction of propene with H^+, the secondary isopropyl carbocation forms more easily than the alternative primary propyl carbocation, and only the isopropyl carbocation is shown in the following mechanism. This intermediate then completes its valence shell in step 2 by forming a new covalent bond with an unshared pair of electrons of the oxygen atom of H_2O. Finally, loss of a proton in step 3 causes formation of an alcohol and regeneration of a proton.

Step 1

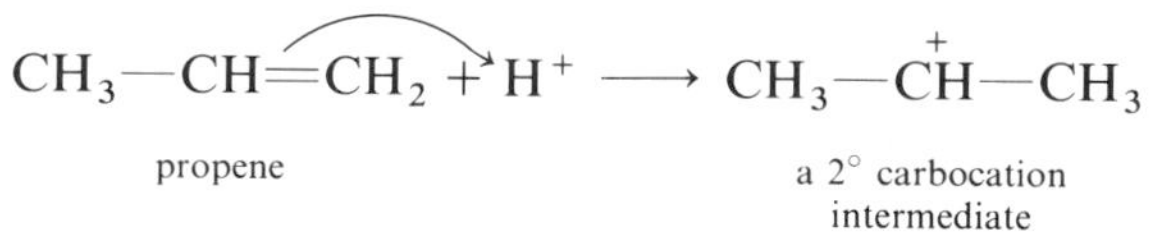

$$CH_3-CH{=}CH_2 + H^+ \longrightarrow CH_3-\overset{+}{C}H-CH_3$$

propene   a 2° carbocation
                                              intermediate

Step 2

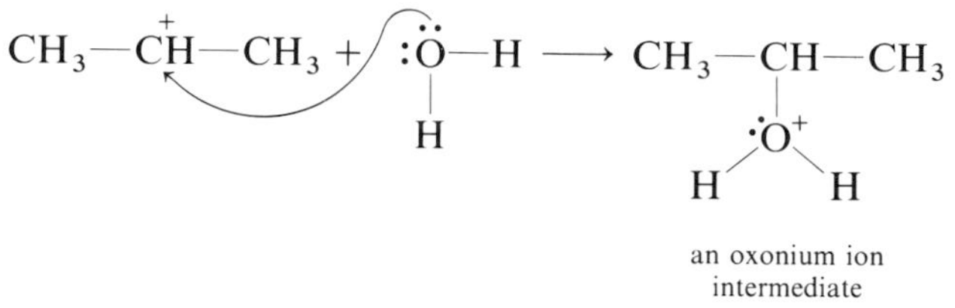

$$CH_3-\overset{+}{C}H-CH_3 + \overset{\cdot\cdot}{:}\overset{\cdot\cdot}{O}-H \longrightarrow CH_3-CH-CH_3$$

an oxonium ion
intermediate

Step 3

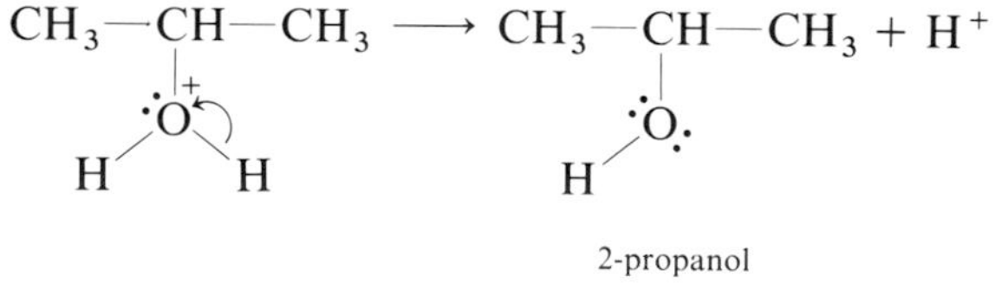

$$CH_3-CH-CH_3 \longrightarrow CH_3-CH-CH_3 + H^+$$

2-propanol

12.6 Reduction of Alkenes

Virtually all alkenes, no matter what the nature of the substituents on the double bond, react quantitatively with molecular hydrogen, H_2, in the presence of a metal catalyst. The reaction is one of addition of hydrogen to the double bond, and in the process, the alkene is converted to an alkane:

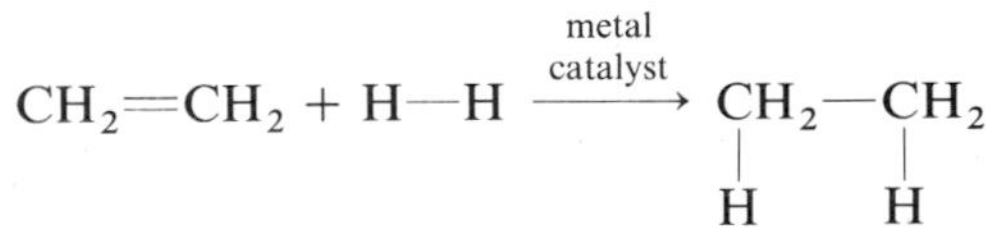

$$CH_2{=}CH_2 + H{-}H \xrightarrow{\text{metal}\atop\text{catalyst}} CH_2{-}CH_2$$

ethylene   ethane

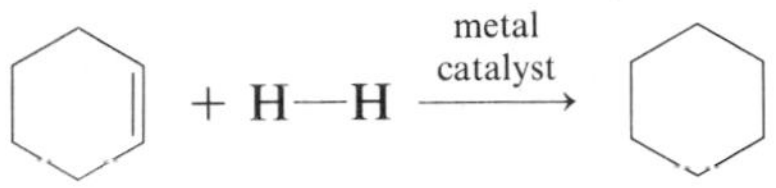

$$\text{cyclohexene} + H{-}H \xrightarrow{\text{metal}\atop\text{catalyst}} \text{cyclohexane}$$

cyclohexene   cyclohexane

A balanced half-reaction for the conversion of an alkene to an alkane shows that this transformation is a two-electron reduction:

Balanced Half-Reaction

$$\overset{\diagdown}{\underset{\diagup}{C}}{=}\overset{\diagup}{\underset{\diagdown}{C}} + 2H^+ + 2e^- \longrightarrow \overset{|}{\underset{|}{C}}{-}\overset{|}{\underset{|}{C}}{-}$$

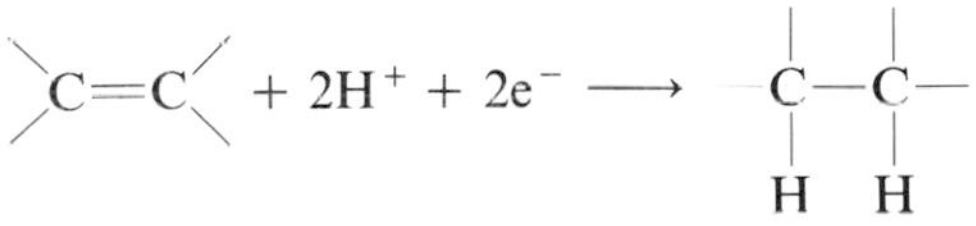

Because conversion of an alkene to an alkane involves reduction by hydrogen in the presence of a catalyst, the process is called catalytic reduction, or alternatively, catalytic hydrogenation.

The most common pattern in **catalytic reduction of an alkene** is cis addition of the two hydrogen atoms. For example, catalytic reduction of 1,2-dimethylcyclopentene gives the cis isomer in preference to the trans isomer:

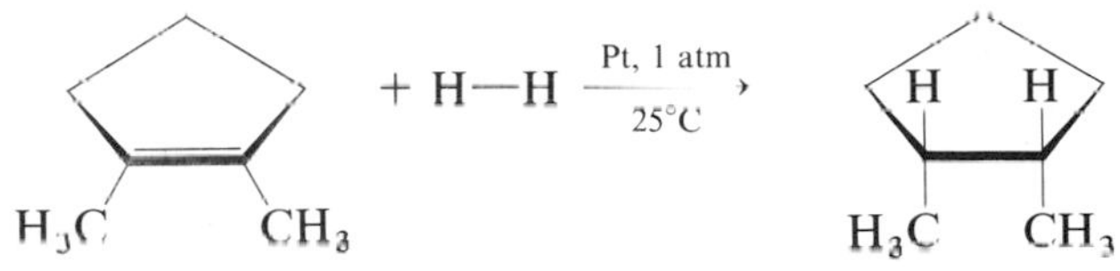

$$+ H{-}H \xrightarrow[25°C]{\text{Pt, 1 atm}}$$

1,2-dimethylcyclopentene   cis-1,2-dimethylcyclopentane

Reduction of an alkene to an alkane is immeasurably slow when no catalyst is present. It occurs rapidly, however, in the presence of transition metal catalysts such as platinum, palladium, and nickel. Separate experiments have shown that transition metals near the center of the periodic table adsorb large quantities of hydrogen onto their surfaces. During adsorption of H_2, the covalent bond between hydrogen atoms is weakened and hydrogen-metal bonds are formed. The exact nature of these bonds is not well understood. Similarly, alkenes are also adsorbed on metal surfaces and their pi bonds partially broken, with simultaneous formation of carbon-metal bonds. If both hydrogen and alkene are positioned properly on the metal surface, hydrogen atoms become attached to carbon atoms and the reduced alkane is desorbed (Figure 12.4).

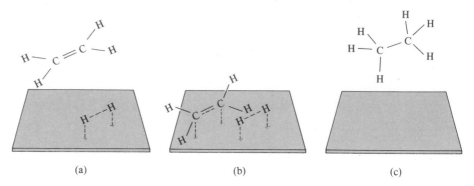

Figure 12.4 Addition of hydrogen to ethene, involving a metal cataylst.

12.7 Oxidation of Alkenes

A. Formation of Glycols

Reaction of an alkene with $KMnO_4$ in dilute alkaline solution oxidizes the alkene to a **glycol**, a compound with hydroxyl groups on adjacent carbons. In this two-electron oxidation (as we demonstrated by a balanced-half reaction in Section 12.4), permanganate is reduced to manganese dioxide, MnO_2, which precipitates as a brown solid:

$$3CH_3-CH{=}CH_2 + 2KMnO_4 + 4H_2O \longrightarrow 3CH_3-\underset{\underset{\displaystyle HO}{|}}{CH}-\underset{\underset{\displaystyle OH}{|}}{CH_2} + 2MnO_2 + 2KOH$$

| propene | potassium permanganate | 1,2-propanediol (a glycol) | manganese dioxide |

To form glycols in high yield, it is necessary to control reaction conditions very carefully. Most important, the reaction medium must be kept basic, generally between pH 11 and 12.

Reaction with permanganate is the basis for a qualitative test for alkenes. An aqueous solution of potassium permanganate is deep purple. When permanganate solution reacts with an alkene, the purple color of permanganate disappears and a brown precipitate of MnO_2 appears. Disappearance of the purple color coupled with appearance of a brown precipitate is evidence for the presence of an alkene. This test is not completely specific for alkenes, however, since several other functional groups also reduce permanganate to manganese dioxide.

B. Cleavage of Carbon-Carbon Double Bonds by Potassium Permanganate and Potassium Dichromate

Both potassium permanganate and potassium dichromate can be used to cleave a carbon-carbon double bond and form two C=O bonds in its place. Oxidation is carried out at elevated temperature in the presence of sulfuric acid. If a carbon of a double bond has one attached hydrogen, it is oxidized to a carboxylic acid; if it has no attached hydrogens, it is oxidized to a ketone.

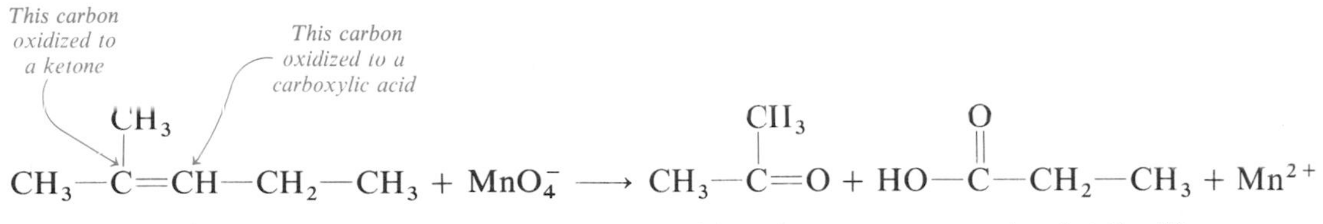

This carbon oxidized to a ketone

This carbon oxidized to a carboxylic acid

$$CH_3-\underset{\underset{CH_3}{|}}{C}=CH-CH_2-CH_3 + MnO_4^- \longrightarrow CH_3-\underset{\underset{CH_3}{|}}{C}=O + HO-\underset{\underset{O}{\|}}{C}-CH_2-CH_3 + Mn^{2+}$$

2-methyl-2-pentene   (a ketone)   (a carboxylic acid)

$$\bigcirc + Cr_2O_7^{2-} \longrightarrow HO-\underset{\underset{O}{\|}}{C}-CH_2-CH_2-CH_2-CH_2-\underset{\underset{O}{\|}}{C}-OH + Cr^{3+}$$

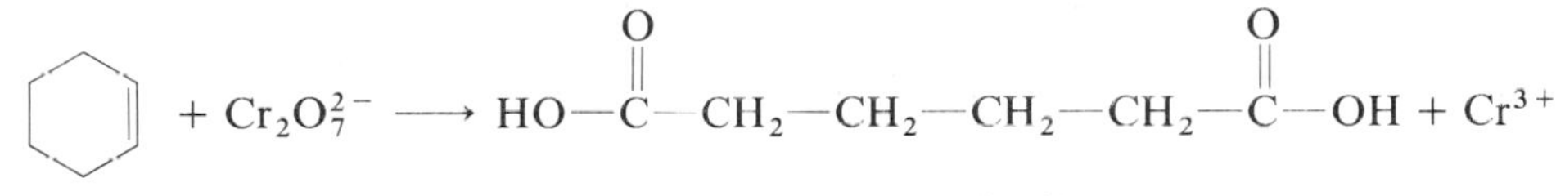

cyclohexene   (a dicarboxylic acid)

Example 12.7

Draw structural formulas for the products formed when the following alkenes are oxidized by potassium dichromate. Name the new functional group formed in each oxidation.

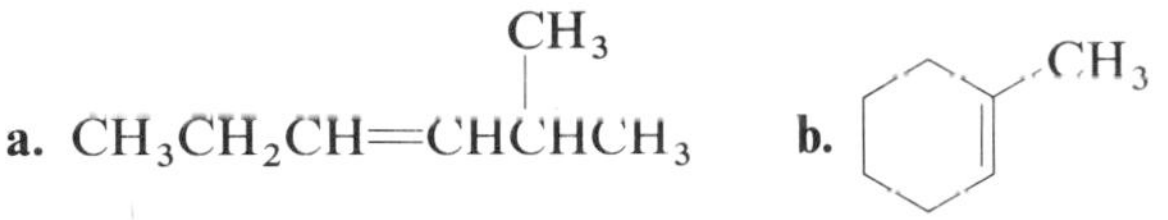

a. $CH_3CH_2CH=CHCHCH_3$ with CH_3 substituent

b. cyclohexene with CH_3 substituent

Solution

a. $CH_3CH_2\underset{\underset{O}{\|}}{C}OH + HO\underset{\underset{O}{\|}}{C}\underset{\underset{OCH_3}{|}}{C}HCH_3$

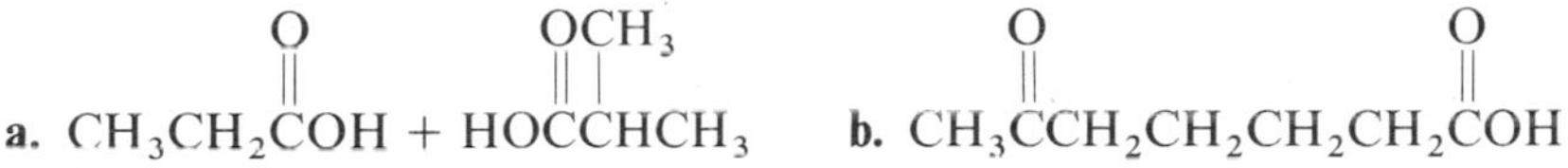

a carboxylic acid   a carboxylic acid

b. $CH_3\underset{\underset{O}{\|}}{C}CH_2CH_2CH_2CH_2\underset{\underset{O}{\|}}{C}OH$

a ketone   a carboxylic acid

Problem 12.7

Draw a structural formula for the alkene of the given molecular formula whose oxidation by potassium permanganate yields the products shown.

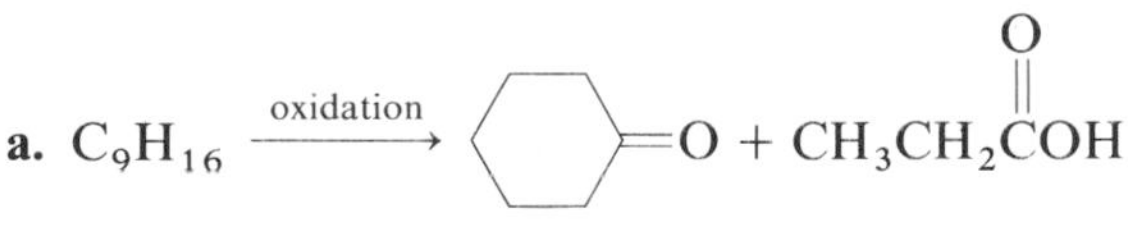

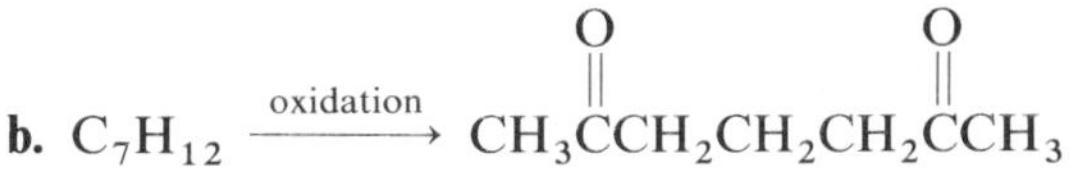

a. $C_9H_{16} \xrightarrow{\text{oxidation}} \bigcirc=O + CH_3CH_2\underset{\underset{O}{\|}}{C}OH$

b. $C_7H_{12} \xrightarrow{\text{oxidation}} CH_3\underset{\underset{O}{\|}}{C}CH_2CH_2CH_2\underset{\underset{O}{\|}}{C}CH_3$

12.8 Polymerization of Alkenes

From the perspective of the chemical industry, the single most important reaction of alkenes is **polymerization**, the building together of many small units known as **monomers** (Greek, *mono + meros*, single parts) into very large, high-molecular-weight **polymers** (Greek, *poly + meros*, many parts). In *addition polymerization* monomer units are joined together without loss of atoms. An example of addition polymerization is the formation of polyethylene from ethylene. The following equation shows three molecules of ethylene. Curved arrows are used to show how the pi bond in each molecule is broken and the pair of electrons used to form a new sigma bond to an adjacent molecule.

$$CH_2{=}CH_2 + CH_2{=}CH_2 + CH_2{=}CH_2 \xrightarrow{\text{catalyst}}$$

ethylene
(monomer)

Monomer units

$$-CH_2-CH_2-CH_2-CH_2-CH_2-CH_2-$$

polyethylene
(polymer)

For a more complete picture of addition polymerization, you must also imagine other molecules to both left and right of the three ethylene units shown. In practice, hundreds of monomer units polymerize, and molecular weights of polyethylene molecules produced range from 50,000 to over 1,500,000.

Polymerization reactions are usually written in the following way, where n is a very large number, typically several thousand:

$$nCH_2{=}CH_2 \xrightarrow{\text{catalyst}} -(CH_2-CH_2)_n-$$

Repeating monomer unit

Propylene can also be polymerized, to give polypropylene, with methyl groups repeating regularly on every other carbon atom of the polymer chain:

$$nCH_3-CH{=}CH_2 \xrightarrow{\text{catalyst}} \overset{\displaystyle CH_3}{\underset{\displaystyle}{-(CH-CH_2)_n-}}$$

propylene   polypropylene

Table 12.3 lists several important polymers derived from ethylene and substituted ethylenes, along with their common names and most important uses.

The tetrafluoroethylene polymers were discovered accidentally in 1938 by Du Pont chemists. One morning a cylinder of tetrafluoroethylene appeared to be empty (no gas escaped when the valve was open) and yet the weight of the

Table 12.3
Polymers
derived from
substituted
ethylenes.

Monomer Formula	Common Name	Polymer Names and Common Uses
$CH_2{=}CH_2$	ethylene	polyethylene, Polythene unbreakable containers and packaging materials
$CH_2{=}CHCH_3$	propylene	polypropylene, Herculon fibers for carpeting and clothing
$CH_2{=}CHCl$	vinyl chloride	polyvinyl chloride, PVC tubing
$CH_2{-}CCl_2$	1,1-dichloro-ethylene	Saran food wrapping
$CH_2{=}CHCN$	acrylonitrile	polyacrylonitrile, Orlon acrylics and acrylates
$CF_2{=}CF_2$	tetrafluoro-ethylene	polytetrafluoroethylene, Teflon nonstick coatings
$CH_2{=}CHC_6H_5$	styrene	polystyrene, Styrofoam insulating materials
$CH_2{=}CCO_2CH_3$ $\quad\mid$ $\quad CH_3$	methyl methacrylate	polymethyl methacrylate, Lucite, Plexiglas, glass substitutes
$CH_2{=}CHCO_2CH_3$	methyl acrylate	polymethyl acrylate, acrylates, latex paints
$CH_2{=}CHOCOCH_3$	vinyl acetate	polyvinyl acetate adhesives

cylinder indicated it was full. The cylinder was opened and inside was found a waxy solid, the forerunner of Teflon.

$$n CF_2{=}CF_2 \xrightarrow{\text{polymerization}} {-}(CF_2{-}CF_2)_n{-}$$

tetrafluoro-
ethylene

polytetrafluoro-
ethylene
(Teflon)

Polytetrafluoroethylene proved to have unusual properties: extraordinary chemical inertness, outstanding heat resistance, a very high melting point, and unusual frictional properties. In 1948, Du Pont built the first commercial Teflon plant, and the product was used to make gaskets, bearings for automobiles, nonstick equipment for candy manufacturers and commercial bakers, and numerous other items. Teflon became a household word in 1961, with the introduction of nonstick frying-pans in the U.S. market.

The years since the 1930s have seen extensive research and development in polymer chemistry and physics; and an almost explosive growth in plastics, coatings, and rubber technology has created a worldwide multibillion dollar industry. A few basic characteristics account for this phenomenal growth. First, the raw materials for plastics are derived mainly from petroleum and natural gas. With the development of efficient refining technology, the raw materials for the synthesis of polymers have become generally cheap and plentiful. Second, within broad limits, scientists have learned how to tailor polymers to the requirements of the end use. Third, many plastics can be fabricated more cheaply than competing materials. For example, plastics technology created the water-based (latex) paints, which have revolutionized the coatings industry; plastic films and foams have done the same for the packaging industry. The list could go on and on as we think of the manufactured items that surround us in our daily lives.

12.9 Aromatic Hydrocarbons

Benzene is a colorless liquid with a boiling point of 80°C. Michael Faraday first isolated it in 1825 from the oily liquid that collected in the illuminating gas lines of London. Its molecular formula, C_6H_6, suggested a high degree of unsaturation. Remember that a saturated alkane of six carbons has the molecular formula C_6H_{14}, and a saturated cycloalkane, the molecular formula C_6H_{12}. Considering this high degree of unsaturation, you might expect benzene to undergo many of the same reactions as alkenes. Surprisingly, benzene does not undergo characteristic alkene reactions. For example, it does not react with bromine, chlorine, hydrogen chloride, hydrogen bromide, or other reagents that usually add to carbon-carbon double bonds. It is not oxidized by potassium permanganate or potassium dichromate under conditions in which alkenes are oxidized to ketones and carboxylic acids. When benzene does react, it typically does so by substitution, in which a hydrogen atom is replaced by another atom or group of atoms. For example, benzene reacts with bromine in the presence of iron(III) bromide to form bromobenzene and hydrogen bromide:

$$C_6H_6 \ + \ Br_2 \ \xrightarrow{\text{FeBr}_3} \ C_6H_5Br \ + \ HBr$$

benzene   bromobenzene

The terms *aromatic* and *aromatic compound* have been used to classify benzene and its derivatives because many of them have distinctive odors. It has become clear, however, that a classification for these compounds should be based not on aroma but on structure and chemical reactivity. The term *aromatic* is still used today but rather than refer to aroma, it refers to the unusual chemical properties of these compounds. They do not undergo typical alkene addition and oxidation-reduction reactions; when they do react, they do so by substitution.

A. The Structure of Benzene

The six carbon atoms of benzene form a regular hexagon, with bond angles of 120°. One hydrogen atom is bonded to each carbon. Two Lewis structures, Ia and Ib, can be drawn for this arrangement of atoms. They differ only in the arrangement of double bonds within the ring.

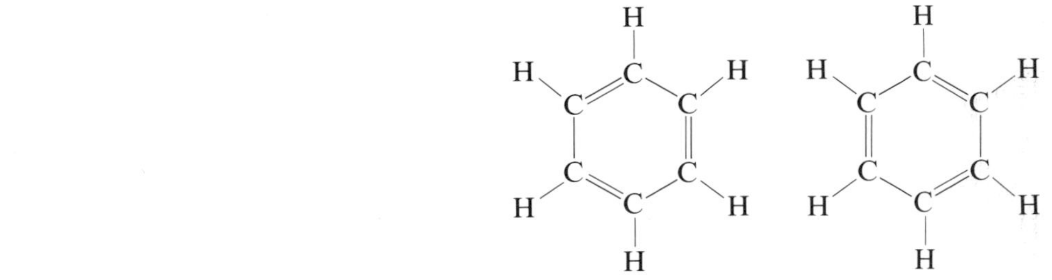

Ia   Ib

Lewis structures Ia and Ib do account for the fact that benzene is a cyclic, unsaturated hydrocarbon. They do not, however, explain why benzene does not undergo typical alkene addition reactions, oxidations, or reductions. If benzene contains three double bonds then, chemists asked, why doesn't it show reactions typical of alkenes? Why, for example, doesn't benzene add three moles of bromine to form 1,2,3,4,5,6-hexabromocyclohexane?

The first adequate description of the structure and unusual chemical properties of benzene was provided by the resonance theory proposed by Linus Pauling. Recall from Section 4.4C that when a molecule can be represented as two or more contributing structures that differ only in position of valence electrons, the actual molecule is best represented as a resonance hybrid. The two principal contributing structures for the benzene resonance hybrid are

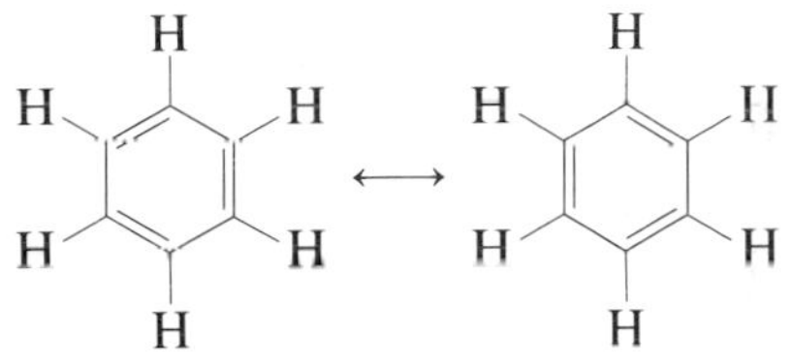

One of the consequences of resonance is a marked increase in stability of the hybrid compared with any one of the contributing structures. Resonance stabilization is particularly large and important in benzene and other aromatic hydrocarbons. Because of their stability, benzene and other aromatic hydrocarbons do not undergo typical alkene reactions.

B. Nomenclature of Aromatic Hydrocarbons

In the IUPAC system, monosubstituted alkylbenzenes are named as derivatives of benzene; for example, ethylbenzene. The IUPAC system also retains certain common names for several of the simpler monosubstituted benzenes. Examples are toluene (rather than methylbenzene), cumene (rather than isopropylbenzene), and styrene (rather than vinylbenzene).

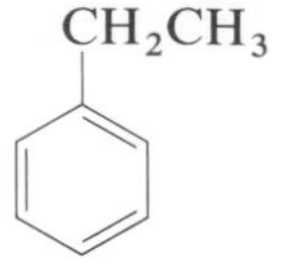

| ethylbenzene | toluene (methylbenzene) | cumene (isopropylbenzene) | styrene (vinylbenzene) |

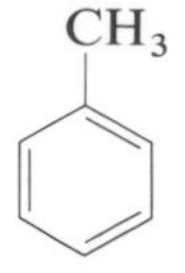

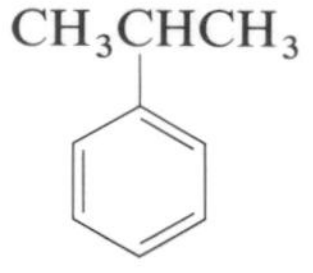

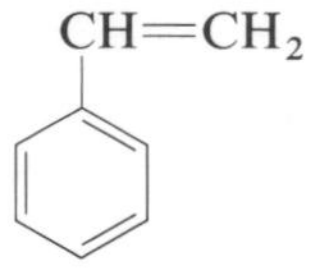

When there are two substituents on a benzene ring, three structural isomers are possible. The substituents may be located by numbering the atoms of the ring. Alternatively, the relative location of two substituents may be indicated by the prefixes *ortho*, *meta*, or *para*.

1,2-   is equivalent to   ortho
1,3-   is equivalent to   meta
1,4-   is equivalent to   para

These equivalent ways to locate two substituents are illustrated below by the three isomeric bromotoluenes.

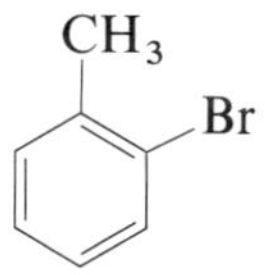

| 2-bromotoluene (*o*-bromotoluene) | 3-bromotoluene (*m*-bromotoluene) | 4-bromotoluene (*p*-bromotoluene) |

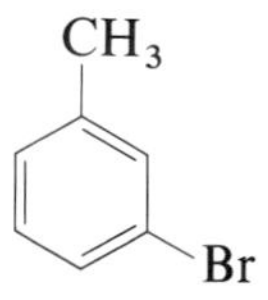

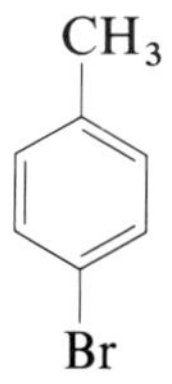

The IUPAC system retains the common name *xylene* for the three dimethyl-benzenes.

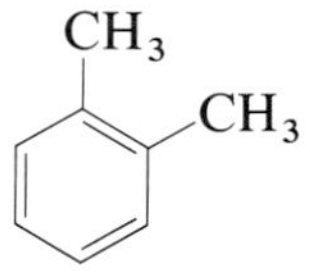

| *o*-xylene | *m*-xylene | *p*-xylene |

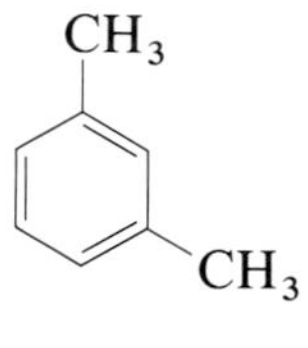

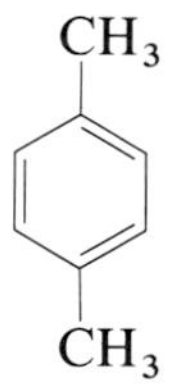

With three or more substituents, a numbering system must be used.

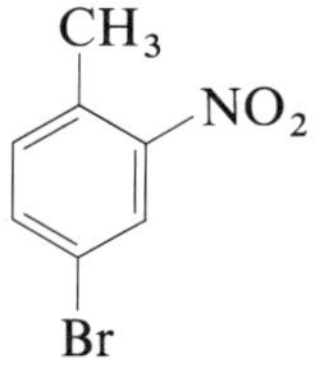

| 4-bromo-2-nitrotoluene | 2,4,6-trinitrotoluene (TNT) |

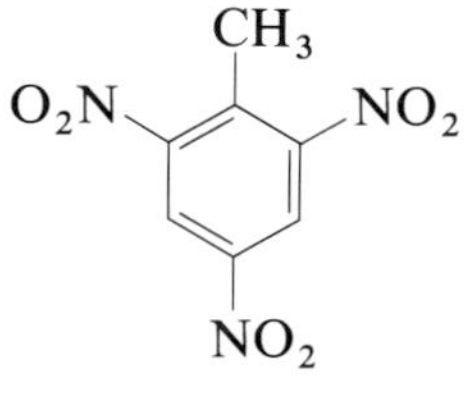

In more complex molecules, the benzene ring is often named as a substituent on a parent chain. In this case, the group C_6H_5— is called a phenyl group.

phenyl group    1-phenyl-2-butene 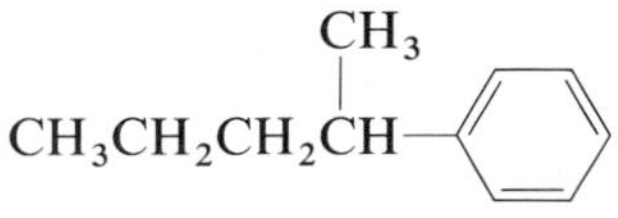   2-phenylpentane

Closely related to benzene are numerous aromatic hydrocarbons having two or more six-membered rings joined together.

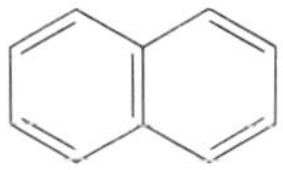

naphthalene   anthracene   phenanthrene
(mp 80°C)   (mp 217°C)   (mp 99°C)

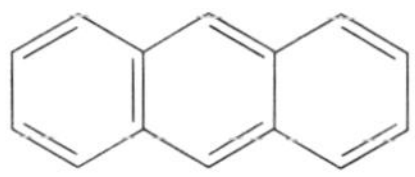

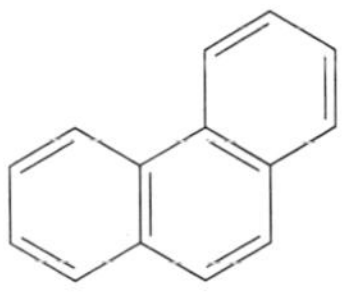

C. Reactions of Aromatic Hydrocarbons

By far the most characteristic reaction of aromatic compounds is substitution at a ring carbon. Some groups that can be introduced directly on the ring are the halogens (except fluorine); the nitro group, NO_2; the sulfonic acid group, SO_3H; and an alkyl, R. The reaction of benzene under appropriate conditions is represented for each of these substitution reactions.

Chlorination

$$C_6H_6 + Cl_2 \xrightarrow{FeCl_3} C_6H_5Cl + HCl$$

chlorobenzene

Bromination

$$C_6H_6 + Br_2 \xrightarrow{FeBr_3} C_6H_5Br + HBr$$

bromobenzene

Nitration

$$C_6H_6 + HNO_3 \xrightarrow{H_2SO_4} C_6H_5NO_2 + H_2O$$

nitrobenzene

Sulfonation

$$C_6H_6 + H_2SO_4 \xrightarrow{SO_3} C_6H_5SO_3H + H_2O$$

benzenesulfonic
acid

Alkylation

$$C_6H_6 + CH_3CH_2Cl \xrightarrow{AlCl_3} C_6H_5CH_2CH_3 + HCl$$

ethylbenzene

Key Terms and Concepts

alkene (introduction)

alkyl group (12.2B)

aromatic hydrocarbon
(introduction and 12.9)

bonding in alkenes (12.1A)

carbocation (12.5D2)

catalytic reduction of alkenes (12.6)

cis-trans isomerism in alkenes (12.3A)

curved arrows, use of (12.5D1)

electrophile (12.5D)

glycol (12.7A)

halogenation of alkenes (12.5A)

hydration of alkenes (12.5C)

hydrohalogenation of alkenes (12.5B)

Markovnikov's rule (12.5B)

methylene group (12.2B)

monomer (12.8)

nomenclature of alkenes
(12.2A and 12.2B)

oxidation of alkenes (12.7)

polymer (12.8)

polymerization of alkenes (12.8)

reduction of alkenes (12.6)

unsaturated hydrocarbon
(introduction)

vinyl group (12.2B)

Key Reactions of Alkenes

1. Addition of Br_2 and Cl_2: halogenation (Section 12.5A).
2. Addition of HCl, HBr, and HI: hydrohalogenation (Section 12.5B).
3. Addition of H_2O: hydration (Section 12.5C).
4. Addition of H_2: reduction (Section 12.6).
5. Oxidation to glycols by $KMnO_4$ (Section 12.7A).
6. Oxidation to ketones/carboxylic acids by $KMnO_4$ or $K_2Cr_2O_7$ (Section 12.7B).
7. Addition polymerization (Section 12.8).

Problems

*Structure
of alkenes
(Section 12.1)*

12.8   Predict all bond angles about each circled carbon atom. To make these predictions, use the valence-shell electron-pair repulsion model. (Review Section 4.5.)

a.

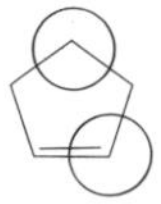

b. $CH_3 - \text{Ⓒ} H = CH - CH_2 - \text{Ⓒ} H_3$

c. 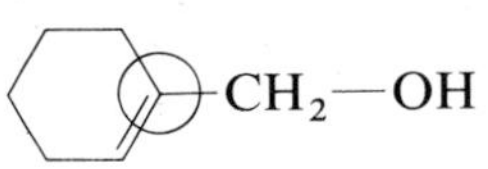 (hexene ring)—CH_2—OH d. 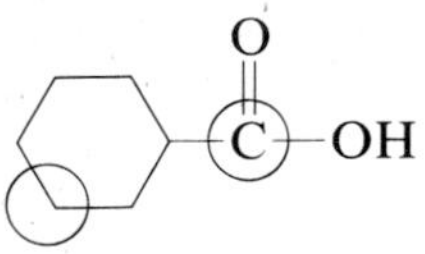 (cyclohexane ring)—$\overset{\overset{\displaystyle O}{\|}}{C}$—$OH$

e. 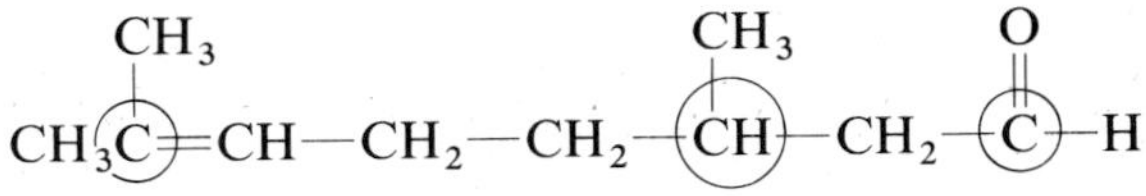 $CH_3\overset{\overset{\displaystyle CH_3}{|}}{C}$=$CH$—$CH_2$—$CH_2$—$\overset{\overset{\displaystyle CH_3}{|}}{CH}$—$CH_2$—$\overset{\overset{\displaystyle O}{\|}}{C}$—$H$

12.9   For each circled carbon atom in Problem 12.8, identify which atomic orbitals are used to form each sigma bond and which to form each pi bond.

Nomenclature   **12.10**   Name these compounds:
of alkenes
(Section 12.2)

a. 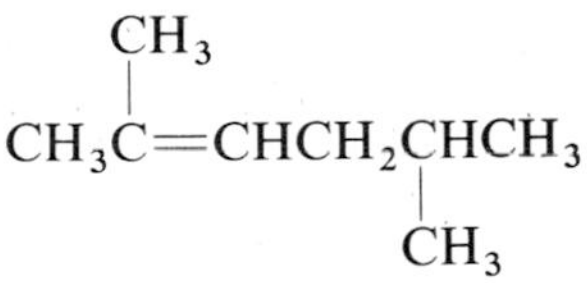 $CH_3\overset{\overset{\displaystyle CH_3}{|}}{C}$=$CHCH_2\overset{\underset{\displaystyle CH_3}{|}}{C}HCH_3$

b. CH_2=$\overset{\overset{\displaystyle CH_3}{|}}{C}CH_2CH_3$

c. CH_2=$\overset{\overset{\displaystyle CH_3}{|}}{C}CH$=$CH_2$

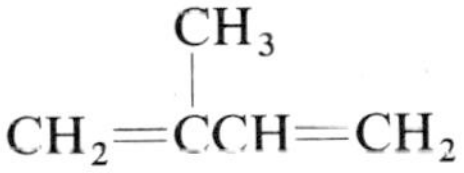

d. $ClCH$=$CHCl$

e. 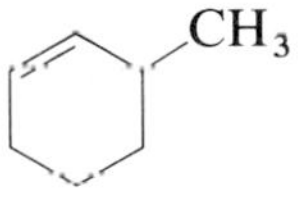 (cyclohexene ring with CH_3)

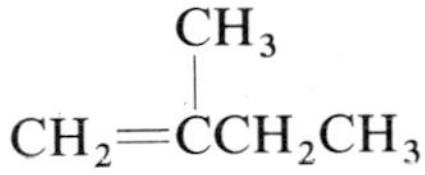

f. 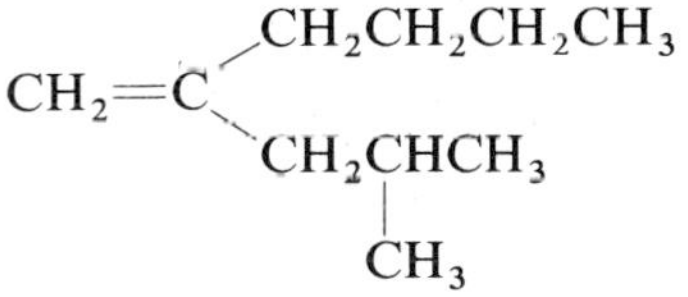 CH_2=$C\overset{\displaystyle \diagup CH_2CH_2CH_2CH_3}{\diagdown CH_2\overset{\underset{\displaystyle CH_3}{|}}{C}HCH_3}$

g. 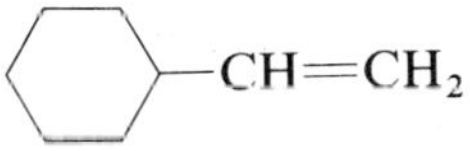 (cyclohexene ring)—CH=CH_2

h. 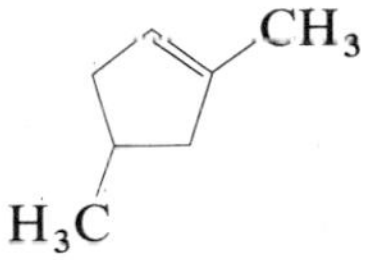 (cyclopentene ring with CH_3 and H_3C)

i. $(CH_3)_2CHCH$=$C(CH_3)_2$

j. $(CH_3)_3CCH_2CH$=CH_2

k. CH_2=$CHCH$=CH_2

l. CH_2=$CHCl$

m. 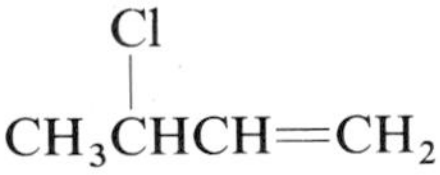 $CH_3\overset{\overset{\displaystyle Cl}{|}}{C}HCH$=$CH_2$

n. 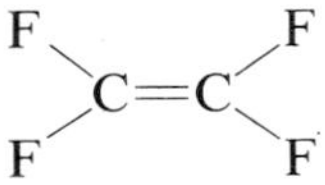 $\overset{\displaystyle F}{\underset{\displaystyle F}{}}C$=$C\overset{\displaystyle F}{\underset{\displaystyle F}{}}$

o. 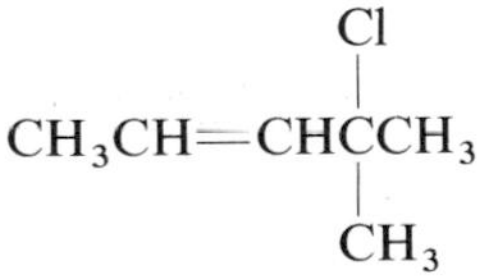 CH_3CH=$CH\overset{\overset{\displaystyle Cl}{|}}{\underset{\underset{\displaystyle CH_3}{|}}{C}}CH_3$

p. $ClCH_2CH$=$CHCH_2Cl$

12.11   Draw structural formulas for these compounds.
    a. 2-methyl-3-hexene
    b. 2-methyl-2-hexene

c. 3,3-dimethyl-1-butene
d. 3-ethyl-3-methyl-1-pentene
e. 2,3-dimethyl-2-butene
f. 1-pentene
g. 2-pentene
h. 1-chloropropene
i. 2-chloropropene
j. 3-chloro-3-methylcyclohexene
k. 1-isopropyl-4-methylcyclohexene
l. 1-phenylcyclohexene
m. 3-hexene
n. 5-isopropyl-3-octene
o. 3-phenyl-1-butene
p. tetrachloroethylene

Cis-trans isomerism in alkenes (Section 12.3)

12.12 Which of the molecules in Problem 12.11 show cis-trans isomerism? For each that does, draw both cis and trans isomers.

12.13 Which of these molecules show cis-trans isomerism?

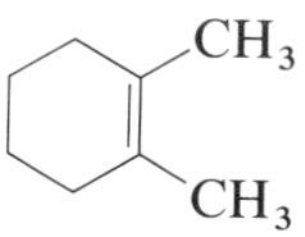

d. ClCH=CHCl   **e.** $CH_3(CH_2)_5CH=CH(CH_2)_7COH$ (with =O on carbonyl)

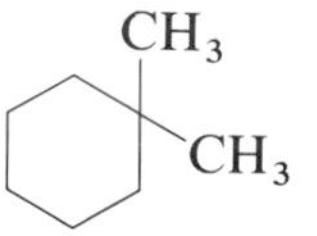

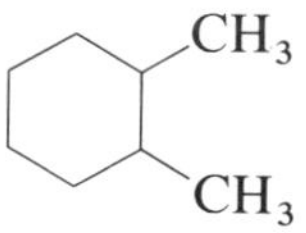

f. HOCCH=CHCOH (with two =O carbonyls)

12.14 Draw structural formulas for all compounds of molecular formula C_5H_{10} that are:
a. alkenes that do not show cis-trans isomerism.
b. alkenes that do show cis-trans isomerism.
c. cycloalkanes that do not show cis-trans isomerism.
d. cycloalkanes that do show cis-trans isomerism.

12.15 Draw structural formulas for the four isomeric chloropropenes, C_3H_5Cl.

Reactions of alkenes; addition (Sections 12.5A–12.5E)

12.16 Draw structural formulas for the major product of these alkene addition reactions:

a. $CH_3C=CHCH_3 + H_2O \xrightarrow{H_2SO_4}$ (with CH_3 substituent)

b. $CH_3C=CHCH_3 + HBr \longrightarrow$ (with CH_3 substituent)

$$\text{CH}_3$$

c. 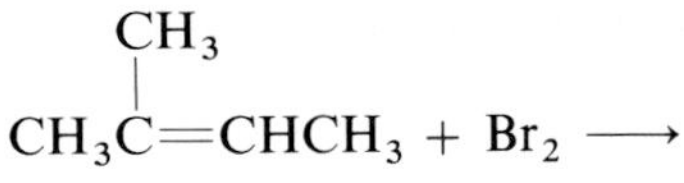 $\text{CH}_3\overset{|}{\text{C}}{=}\text{CHCH}_3 + \text{Br}_2 \longrightarrow$

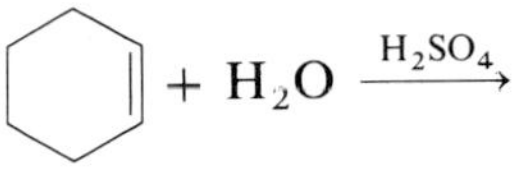

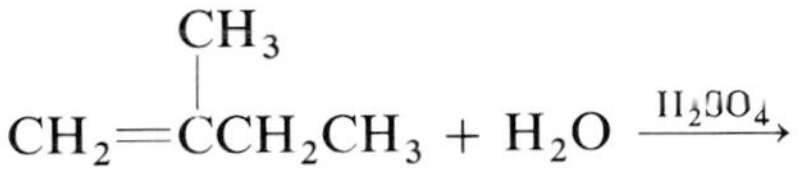

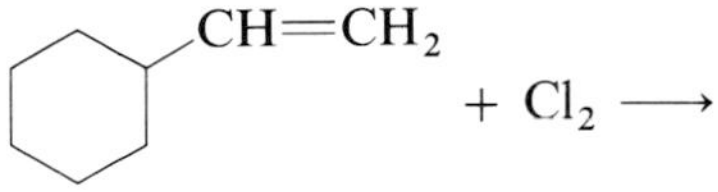

$$\text{CH}_3$$

d. $\text{CH}_3\overset{|}{\text{C}}{=}\text{CHCH}_3 + \text{H}_2 \xrightarrow{\text{Pt}}$

e. ⬡ $+ \text{H}_2\text{O} \xrightarrow{\text{H}_2\text{SO}_4}$

$$\text{CH}_3$$

f. $\text{CH}_2{=}\overset{|}{\text{C}}\text{CH}_2\text{CH}_3 + \text{H}_2\text{O} \xrightarrow{\text{H}_2\text{SO}_4}$

g. ⬡—$\text{CH}{=}\text{CH}_2$ $+ \text{Cl}_2 \longrightarrow$

h. $\underset{\text{H}}{\overset{\text{CH}_3}{\diagdown}}\text{C}{=}\text{C}\underset{\text{H}}{\overset{\text{CH}_2\text{CH}_3}{\diagup}}$ $+ \text{HCl} \longrightarrow$

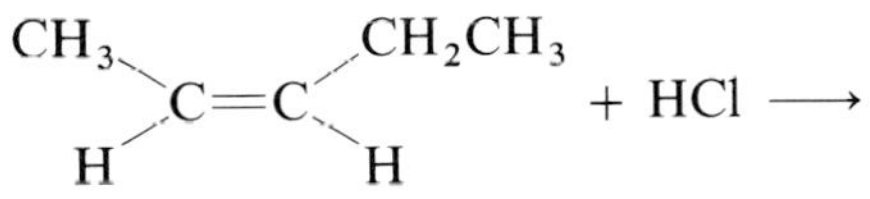

i. 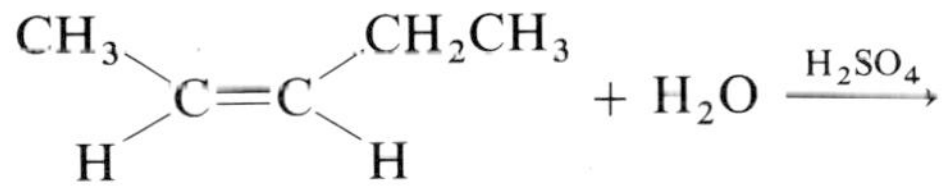 $\underset{\text{H}}{\overset{\text{CH}_3}{\diagdown}}\text{C}{=}\text{C}\underset{\text{H}}{\overset{\text{CH}_2\text{CH}_3}{\diagup}}$ $+ \text{H}_2\text{O} \xrightarrow{\text{H}_2\text{SO}_4}$

j. 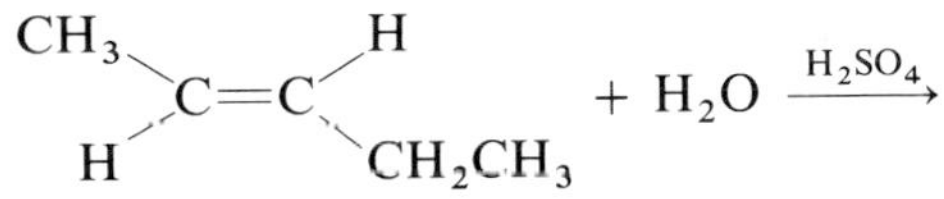 $\underset{\text{H}}{\overset{\text{CH}_3}{\diagdown}}\text{C}{=}\text{C}\underset{\text{CH}_2\text{CH}_3}{\overset{\text{H}}{\diagup}}$ $+ \text{H}_2\text{O} \xrightarrow{\text{H}_2\text{SO}_4}$

$$\text{CH}_3$$

k. 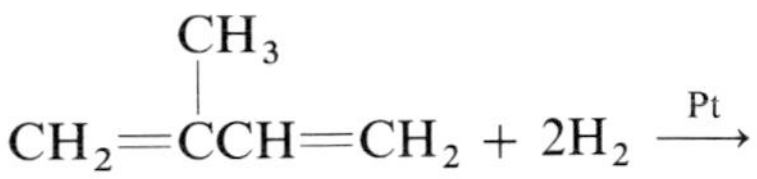 $\text{CH}_2{=}\overset{|}{\text{C}}\text{CH}{=}\text{CH}_2 + 2\text{H}_2 \xrightarrow{\text{Pt}}$

$$\text{H}_3\text{C} \quad \text{CH}_3$$

l. 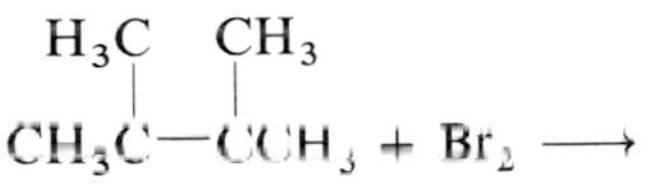 $\text{CH}_3\overset{|}{\text{C}}{-}\overset{|}{\text{C}}\text{CH}_3 + \text{Br}_2 \longrightarrow$

m. 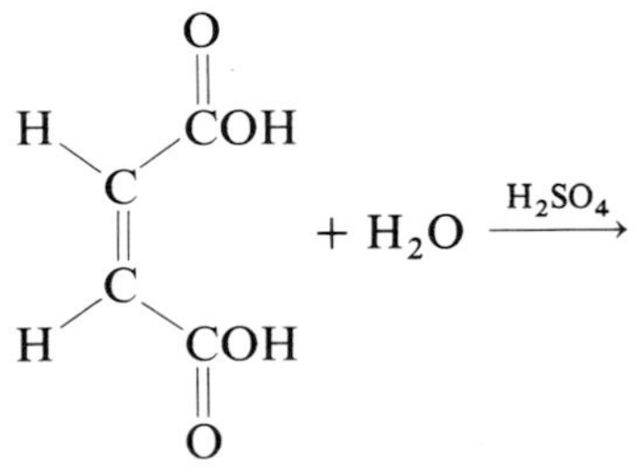 $\underset{\text{H}}{\overset{\text{H}}{}}\underset{\text{C}}{\overset{\text{C}\diagup^{\text{COH}}}{\diagdown\diagup}}$ $+ \text{H}_2\text{O} \xrightarrow{\text{H}_2\text{SO}_4}$

12.17 Draw the structural formula for an alkene or alkenes of molecular formula C_5H_{10} that will react to give the indicated compound as the major product. Note that in several parts of this problem (for example, part a), more than one alkene will give the same compound as the major product.

a. $C_5H_{10} + H_2O$ $\xrightarrow{H_2SO_4}$ $CH_3\overset{\overset{\displaystyle CH_3}{|}}{\underset{\underset{\displaystyle OH}{|}}{C}}CH_2CH_3$

b. $C_5H_{10} + Br_2$ $\longrightarrow$ $CH_3\overset{\overset{\displaystyle CH_3}{|}}{C}H\underset{\underset{\displaystyle Br}{|}}{C}H\underset{\underset{\displaystyle Br}{|}}{C}H_2$

c. $C_5H_{10} + H_2$ $\xrightarrow{Pt}$ $CH_3CH_2CH_2CH_2CH_3$

d. $C_5H_{10} + H_2O$ $\xrightarrow{H_2SO_4}$ $CH_3\underset{\underset{\displaystyle OH}{|}}{C}HCH_2CH_2CH_3$

e. $C_5H_{10} + HCl$ $\longrightarrow$ $CH_3\overset{\overset{\displaystyle CH_3}{|}}{\underset{\underset{\displaystyle Cl}{|}}{C}}CH_2CH_3$

12.18 Draw structural formulas for the carbocations formed by the reaction of H^+ with the following alkenes. Where two different carbocations are possible, state which is more stable.

a. $CH_3CH_2\overset{\overset{\displaystyle CH_3}{|}}{C}{=}CHCH_3 + H^+ \longrightarrow$

b. $CH_3CH_2CH{=}CHCH_3 + H^+ \longrightarrow$

c. 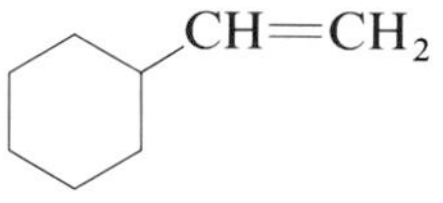 [cyclohexane ring with] $CH{=}CH_2$ $+ H^+ \longrightarrow$

d. 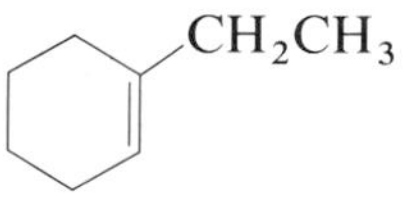 [cyclohexene ring with] CH_2CH_3 $+ H^+ \longrightarrow$

12.19 Write a reaction mechanism for the following alkene addition reactions. For each mechanism, identify all electrophiles and reactive intermediates.

a. $CH_3\overset{\overset{\displaystyle CH_3}{|}}{C}{=}CH_2 + HCl \longrightarrow CH_3\overset{\overset{\displaystyle CH_3}{|}}{\underset{\underset{\displaystyle Cl}{|}}{C}}CH_3$

$$\text{b. } CH_3\overset{\overset{\displaystyle CH_3}{|}}{C}=CH_2 + H_2O \xrightarrow{H_2SO_4} CH_3\overset{\overset{\displaystyle CH_3}{|}}{\underset{\underset{\displaystyle OH}{|}}{C}}CH_3$$

12.20 Terpin hydrate is prepared commercially by the addition of two moles of water to limonene in the presence of dilute sulfuric acid. Limonene is found in lemon, orange, caraway, dill, bergamot, and some other oils. Terpin hydrate is used medicinally as an expectorant for coughs. It may be given as a mixture of terpin hydrate and codeine. Propose a structure for terpin hydrate and a reasonable mechanism to account for the formation of the product you have predicted.

$$+\ 2H_2O \xrightarrow[H_2SO_4]{dilute} C_{10}H_{20}O_2$$

terpin hydrate

limonene

12.21 Reaction of 2-methylpropene with methanol in the presence of concentrate H_2SO_4 yields a product of molecular formula $C_5H_{12}O$.

$$CH_3\overset{\overset{\displaystyle CH_3}{|}}{C}-CH_2 + CH_3OH \xrightarrow{H_2SO_4} C_5H_{12}O$$

a. Propose a structural formula for $C_5H_{12}O$.
b. Propose a reaction mechanism for the formation of this product.

12.22 Show how you could distinguish between the members of the following pairs of compounds by a simple chemical test. In each case, tell what test you would perform and what you would expect to observe, and write an equation for each positive test.
a. cyclohexane and 1-hexene
b. 1-hexene and 2-chlorohexane
c. 2,3-dimethyl-2-butene and 1,1-dimethylcyclopentane

Reactions of alkenes; oxidation (Section 12.7)

12.23 Define oxidation (review Section 5.4).

12.24 Show by writing a balanced half-reaction that these reactions are oxidations:

$$\textbf{a. } \overset{\displaystyle CH_3}{\underset{\displaystyle CH_3}{}}\!\!\!>\!\!C=C\!\!<\!\!\overset{\displaystyle CH_3}{\underset{\displaystyle CH_3}{}} \longrightarrow \overset{\displaystyle CH_3}{\underset{\displaystyle CH_3}{}}\!\!\!>\!\!C=O + O=C\!\!<\!\!\overset{\displaystyle CH_3}{\underset{\displaystyle CH_3}{}}$$

$$\textbf{b. } CH_3CH_2CH=CHCH_2CH_3 \longrightarrow 2CH_3CH_2\overset{\overset{\displaystyle O}{\|}}{C}OH$$

c. 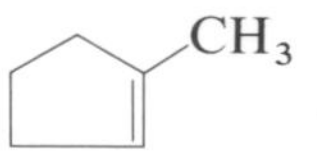 (cyclopentene with CH_3 substituent) $\longrightarrow$ $CH_3\overset{O}{\underset{\|}{C}}CH_2CH_2CH_2\overset{O}{\underset{\|}{C}}OH$

12.25 Draw structural formulas for the products of oxidation of these alkenes:

a. $CH_3CH_2CH{=}\overset{CH_3}{\underset{|}{C}}CH_2CH_3 \xrightarrow{\text{oxidation}}$

b. 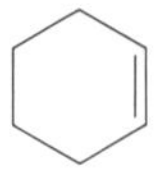 (cyclohexene) $\xrightarrow{\text{oxidation}}$

c. 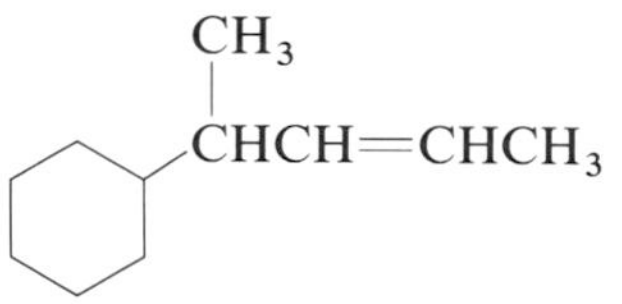 (cyclohexyl-$\overset{CH_3}{\underset{|}{C}}HCH{=}CHCH_3$) $\xrightarrow{\text{oxidation}}$

d. $CH_3CH_2CH{=}CHCH_2CH_2\overset{O}{\underset{\|}{C}}OH \xrightarrow{\text{oxidation}}$

12.26 Draw the structural formula for an alkene of given molecular formula that can be oxidized by hot potassium permanganate to give the indicated products.

a. $C_6H_{12} \xrightarrow{\text{oxidation}} CH_3CH_2\overset{O}{\underset{\|}{C}}OH + CH_3\overset{O}{\underset{\|}{C}}CH_3$

b. $C_6H_{12} \xrightarrow{\text{oxidation}} CH_3\overset{O}{\underset{\|}{C}}OH + CH_3CH_2CH_2\overset{O}{\underset{\|}{C}}OH$

c. $C_7H_{12} \xrightarrow{\text{oxidation}} CH_3\overset{O}{\underset{\|}{C}}CH_2CH_2CH_2\overset{O}{\underset{\|}{C}}CH_3$

d. $C_8H_{14} \xrightarrow{\text{oxidation}} HO\overset{O}{\underset{\|}{C}}CH_2\overset{CH_3}{\underset{\underset{CH_3}{|}}{C}}CH_2CH_2\overset{O}{\underset{\|}{C}}OH$

e. $C_9H_{16} \xrightarrow{\text{oxidation}}$ (cyclohexane)$={=}O + CH_3\overset{O}{\underset{\|}{C}}CH_3$

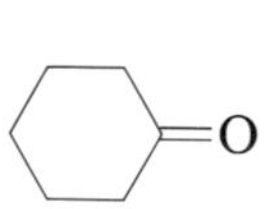

f. $C_9H_{16} \xrightarrow{\text{oxidation}}$ (cyclohexane)$-\overset{O}{\underset{\|}{C}}OH + CH_3\overset{O}{\underset{\|}{C}}OH$

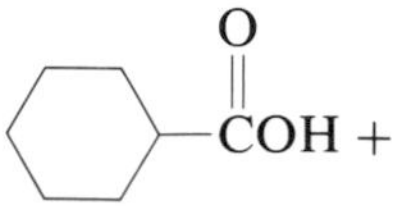

Reactions of alkenes; polymeriza-tion (Section 12.8)

12.27 Following is a structural formula for a section of polypropylene derived from three propylene monomers.

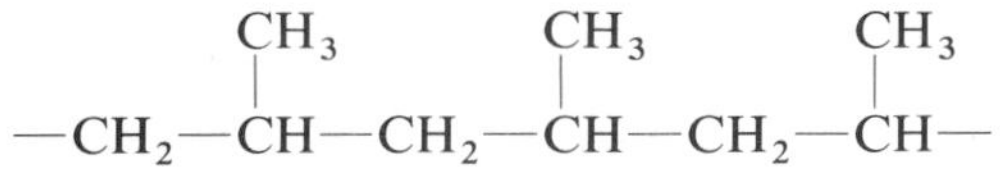

$$-CH_2-\underset{\underset{CH_3}{|}}{CH}-CH_2-\underset{\underset{CH_3}{|}}{CH}-CH_2-\underset{\underset{CH_3}{|}}{CH}-$$

a section of polypropylene

Draw structural formulas for comparable three-unit sections of:
a. polyvinyl chloride   **b.** Saran
c. Teflon   **d.** Plexiglas

12.28 Natural rubber is a polymer derived from the monomer 2-methyl-1,3-butadiene (isoprene). The repeating unit in this polymer is

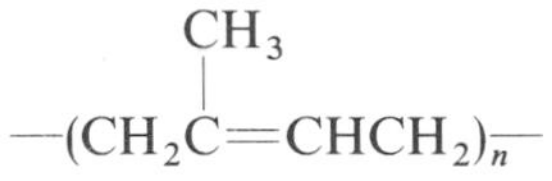

$$-(CH_2\underset{\underset{CH_3}{|}}{C}=CHCH_2)_n-$$

natural rubber

a. Draw the structural formula for a section of natural rubber, showing three repeating monomer units.
b. Draw the structural formula of the product of oxidation and cleavage of the carbon-carbon double bond in natural rubber, and name the two new functional groups in the product.
c. The smog prevalent in Los Angeles contains oxidizing agents. How could you account for the fact that this type of smog attacks natural rubber (automobile tires, and the like) but does not affect poly-ethylene or polyvinyl chloride?

Aromatic hydrocarbons (Section 12.9)

12.29 For each circled atom, predict bond angles formed by the attached atoms. Use the valence-shell electron-pair repulsion model to make these predictions.

a. 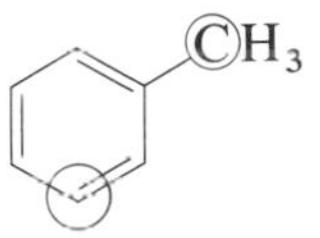 ⬡—(C)H₃

b. Br—⬡—(C)(=O)—CH₃

c. ⬡—(C)H=CH₂

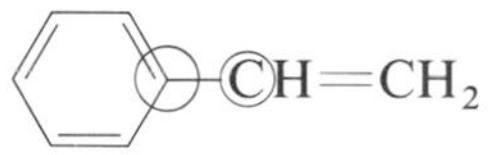

12.30 For each circled atom in Problem 12.29, identify which atomic orbitals are used to form each sigma bond and which to form each pi bond.

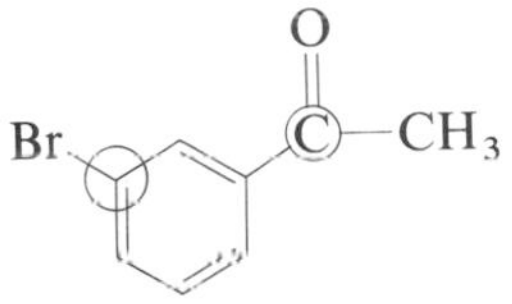

12.31 Name the compounds.

a. 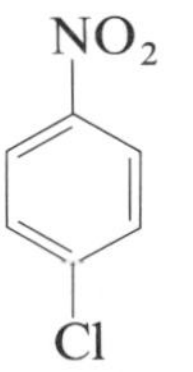 NO₂ / Cl (benzene ring)

b. 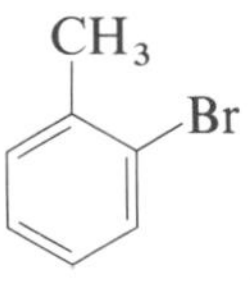 CH₃ / Br (benzene ring)

c.  CH₃ / F (benzene ring)

d.

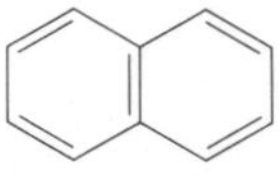

e.

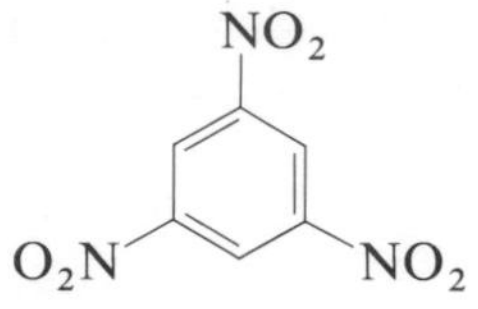

$CH_3CHCH{=}CHCH_3$

f.

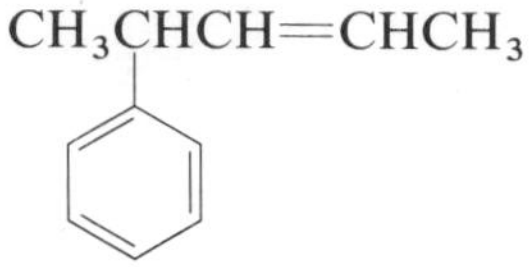

$CH{=}CH_2$

g.

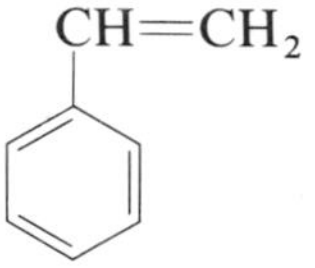

$CH_3CHCH_2CH{=}CH_2$

h.

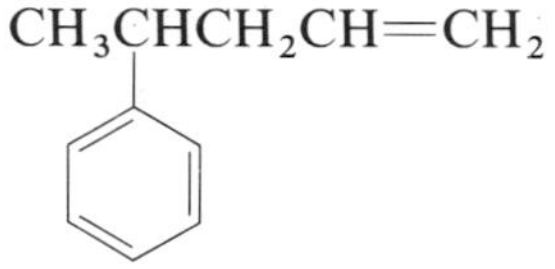

CH_3

i.

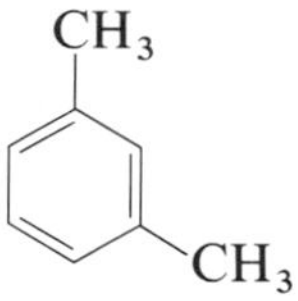

CH_3

Cl

j.

Cl

$CH_2CH_2CH_3$

k.

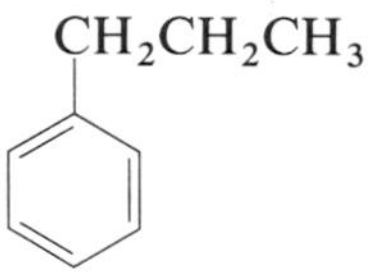

CH_3

l.

NO_2

12.32 Draw structural formulas for these molecules:

a. *m*-dibromobenzene
b. 2,4,6-trinitrotoluene (TNT)
c. *p*-chloroiodobenzene
d. 2-ethyl-4-isopropyltoluene
e. *p*-xylene
f. 2-ethylnaphthalene
g. *p*-diiodobenzene
h. 2-phenyl-2-pentene
i. phenanthrene
j. anthracene
k. isopropylbenzene (cumene)

Ethylene

The U.S. chemical industry produces more ethylene, on a pound-per-pound basis, than any other organic chemical. Reports on this and other key chemicals can be found regularly in the weekly publication *Chemical & Engineering News* (*C&EN*). A report on ethylene and its accompanying graph (Figure VI-1) follows.

Ethylene

How it is made: thermal (steam) cracking of hydrocarbons ranging from natural gas-derived ethane to oil-derived gas oil (fuel oil).

Major derivatives: polyethylenes 45%, ethylene oxide 20%, vinyl chloride 15%, styrene 10%.

Major end uses: fabricated plastics 65%, antifreeze 10%, fibers 5%, solvents 5%.

Commercial value: $4.60 billion total production in 1985.

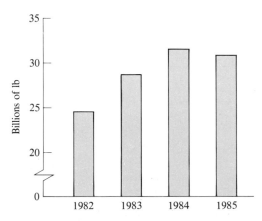

Figure VI-1 Production levels of ethylene.

Of the estimated 250 billion pounds of organic chemicals produced each year in the United States, approximately 100 billion pounds are derived from ethylene. Clearly in terms of its volume and the volume of the chemicals derived from it, ethylene is the organic chemical industry's most important building block. Our focus is on how this vital starting material is produced, its principal end uses, and consumer products derived from it.

First, how do we obtain ethylene? More than 90% of all organic chemicals used by the chemical industry are derived from petroleum and natural gas. However, ethylene is not found in either of these resources. If we do not find ethylene in nature, then how do we make it from the raw materials available to us? The answer is not an easy one and it differs from one part of the world to another depending on availability of raw materials and economic demand. As we shall see presently, how we make ethylene today may be different from how we will be forced to make it in the future.

Ethylene is produced by cracking of hydrocarbons. In the United States where there are vast reserves of natural gas, the main process for ethylene production has been thermal cracking, often in the presence of steam, of the small quantities of ethane, propane, and butane that can be recovered from natural gas. (Recall from Section 11.10A that natural gas is approximately 80% methane and 10% ethane.) For this reason, ethylene-generating plants constructed in the past have been concentrated near sites of natural gas reserves. In the United States, for example, many are located on the Gulf Coast of Texas and Louisiana.

When the thermal (steam) cracking of ethane is written as a balanced equation, it seems simple enough:

$$CH_3—CH_3 \xrightarrow{\text{thermal cracking}} CH_2=CH_2 \;+\; H_2$$

Actually the reaction is complicated, and several other substances are produced along with ethylene. For example, for every billion pounds of ethylene produced from ethane, there are also

Figure VI-2 Catalytic-cracking facilities, such as this refinery at Port Arthur, Texas, account for more than 80% of total ethylene production in the United States.

obtained 36 million pounds of propylene and 35 million pounds of butadiene as co-products. Although these quantities of starting materials and products may seem enormous to you, they reflect the scale on which the U.S. chemical industry operates. Although other low-molecular-weight alkanes can be cracked to give ethylene, thermal cracking of ethane gives the highest-percentage and highest-purity ethylene. Shown in Figure VI-2 is an ethylene-cracking plant in Port Arthur, Texas.

In the United States, natural gas is currently the main source of the raw materials for manufacturing ethylene. Approximately 10% of the natural gas consumed each year is used for this purpose. In Europe and Japan, however, supplies of natural gas are much more limited. As a result, those countries depend almost entirely on catalytic cracking of petroleum-derived naphtha for their ethylene.

Now that we know how ethylene is made, let us turn to the second question: How do we use it? Each year ethylene is the starting material for the synthesis of almost 100 billion pounds of chemicals and polymers. As you can see from Table VI-1, its major derivatives are polyethylene (45%), ethylene oxide and ethylene glycol (20%), vinyl chloride (15%), and styrene (10%).

We will concentrate on just one important derivative of ethylene, namely, the fabricated polyethylene plastics, which account for approx-

Table VI-1 Principal derivatives and end uses of ethylene.

Principal Derivatives of Ethylene	Structural Formula	1985 Production (Billions of lb)	Major End Uses
polyethylene	$—(CH_2—CH_2)_n—$	12.0	fabricated plastics
ethylene oxide/ ethylene glycol	$CH_2—CH_2,\; CH_2—CH_2$ $\underset{O}{}\quad \underset{OH}{}\;\underset{OH}{}$	9.17	antifreeze, polyester textile fibers, solvents
vinyl chloride	$CH_2=CHCl$	6.72	polyvinyl chloride-fabricated plastics
styrene	⬡$—CH=CH_2$	6.61	polystyrene, fabricated plastics, and synthetic rubbers

imately 45% of all ethylene used in this country. The first commercial process for ethylene polymerization used peroxide catalysts at temperatures of 500°C and pressures of 1000 atm, producing a polymer known as low-density polyethylene (LDPE). Low-density polyethylene is a soft, tough plastic. It has a density between 0.91 and 0.94 g/cm³ and a melting point of about 115°C. Because LDPE's melting point is only slightly above 100°C, it is not used for products that will be exposed to boiling water. Low-density polyethylene is about 50–60% crystalline. Although polymers do not crystallize in the conventional sense, they often have regions where their chains are precisely ordered relative to each other and interact by noncovalent forces. Such regions are called crystallites. When we say that low-density polyethylene is 50–60% crystalline, we mean that this percentage is composed of crystallites.

The main end use of low-density polyethylene is film for packaging such consumer items as baked goods, vegetables, and other produce; for coatings for cardboard and paper; and perhaps most important, for trash bags.

An alternative method of ethylene polymerization uses catalysts composed of titanium chloride and organoaluminum compounds. With catalysts of this type, ethylene can be polymerized under conditions as low as 60°C and 20 atm pressure. Polyethylene produced in this manner has a density of 0.96 g/cm³ and is called high-density polyethylene (HDPE). High-density polyethylene has a higher degree of crystallinity (90%) than LDPE and a higher melting point (135°C). It is best described as a hard, tough plastic. The physical properties and cost of HDPE relative to other materials make it ideal for the production of plastic bottles, lids, caps, and so on. It is also molded into housewares such as mixing bowls and refrigerator and freezer containers.

Approximately 45% of all high-density polyethylene used in the United States is blow-molded, mostly into containers. The process of blow-molding an HDPE bottle is illustrated in Figure VI-3.

Approximately 65% of all low-density polyethylene is used to manufacture films. These LDPE films are fabricated by a variation of the

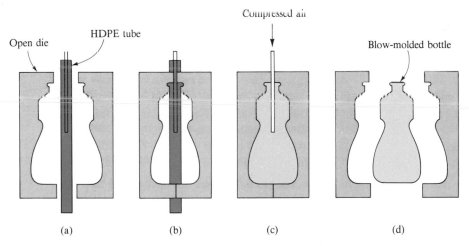

Figure VI-3 Blow-molding a high-density polyethylene bottle. (a) A short length of HDPE tubing is inserted into an open die, (b) the die is closed, sealing the bottom of the tube, and the unit is heated, (c) compressed air is forced into the warm polyethylene/die assembly and the tubing is blown up to take the shape of the mold, (d) the die is opened and there is the bottle!

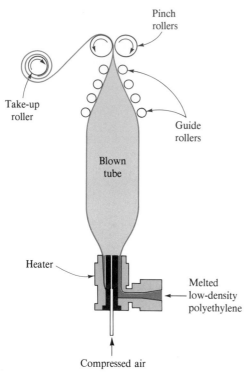

Pinch rollers

Take-up roller

Guide rollers

Blown tube

Heater

Melted low-density polyethylene

Compressed air

Figure VI-4 Fabrication of LDPE film.

blow-molding technique illustrated in Figure VI-4. A tube of LDPE, along with a jet of compressed air, is forced through an opening and blown into a giant, thin-walled bubble. The film is then cooled and taken up onto a roller. This double-walled film can be slit down the side to give LDPE film, or it can be sealed at points along its length to give LDPE trash bags.

Clearly our dependence on polyethylene is enormous, and it will continue to be so since our society is so industrialized.

Sources

American Chemical Society. 1973. *Chemistry in the Economy.* Washington, D.C.

Bilmeyer, F. W., Jr. 1971. *Textbook of Polymer Science*, 2d ed. New York: Wiley.

Fernelius, Y. C., Wittcoff, H. A., and Varnerid, R. E., eds. 1979. Ethylene: The Organic Chemical Industry's Most Important Building Block. *J. Chem. Ed.* 56:385–387.

Webber, D. *C&EN*'s Top 50 Chemical Products. *Chem. Eng. News*, 21 April 1986.

Wittcoff, H. A., and Reuben, B. G. 1980. *Industrial Organic Chemicals in Perspective*. New York: Wiley.

Terpenes

A wide variety of substances in the plant and animal world contain one or more carbon-carbon double bonds. In this essay, we will focus on one group of natural alkenes, the terpene hydrocarbons. The characteristic structural feature of a terpene is a carbon skeleton that can be divided into two or more units that are identical with the carbon skeleton of isoprene. This generalization is known as the isoprene rule. In discussing terpenes and the isoprene rule, it is common to refer to the head and tail of an isoprene unit. The tail of an isoprene unit is the carbon atom farther from the methyl branch.

$$CH_2=\overset{\overset{\displaystyle CH_3}{|}}{C}-CH=CH_2$$

isoprene

an isoprene unit

There are several important reasons for looking at this group of organic compounds. First, the number of terpenes found in bacteria, plants, and animals is staggering. Second, terpenes provide a glimpse at the wondrous diversity that nature generates from even a relatively simple carbon skeleton. Third, terpenes illustrate an important principle of the molecular logic of living systems: In building what might seem to be complex molecules, living systems piece together small subunits to produce complex but logically designed skeletal frameworks. In this mini-essay, we will show how to identify the skeletal framework of terpenes.

Probably the terpenes most familiar to you, at least by odor, are components of the so-called essential oils obtained by steam distillation or ether extraction of various parts of plants. Essential oils contain relatively low molecular weight substances that are largely responsible for characteristic plant fragrances. Many essential oils, particularly those from flowers, are used in perfumes.

An example of a terpene obtained from an essential oil is myrcene, $C_{10}H_{16}$, obtained from bayberry wax and from oils of bay and verbena. Its parent chain of eight carbon atoms contains three double bonds and two one-carbon branches [Figure VII-1(a)]. Figure VII-1(b) shows only the carbon skeleton of myrcene. As you can see from the position of the dashed lines in Figure VII-1(b), myrcene can be divided into two isoprene units linked head to tail. Head-to-tail linkages of isoprene units are vastly more common in nature than the alternative head-to-head or tail-to-tail patterns.

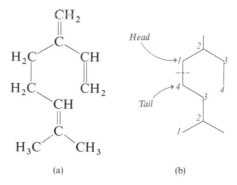

(a)   (b)

Figure VII-1 (a) The structure and (b) carbon skeleton of myrcene, a terpene of two isoprene units (10 carbon atoms).

geraniol
(roses and other
flowers)

an aggregating pheromone
of bark beetles

limonene
(oil of lemon
and orange)

menthol
(peppermint)

α-pinene
(turpentine)

camphor

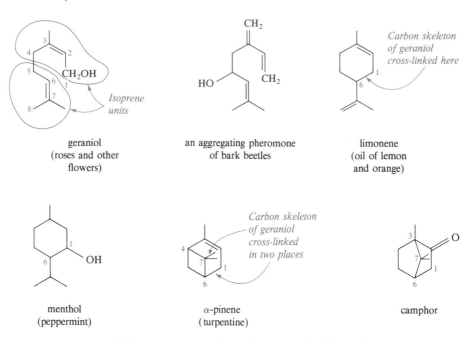

Figure VII-2 Several terpenes of two isoprene units (10 carbon atoms).

Figure VII-2 shows structural formulas for six more terpenes. Geraniol and the aggregating pheromone of bark beetles of the Ips family (see Mini-Essay X, "Pheromones") have the same carbon skeleton as myrcene but different locations of carbon-carbon double bonds. In addition, each has an —OH group. In the last four terpenes shown in Figure VII-2, the framework of carbon atoms present in myrcene, geraniol, and the bark beetle pheromone is cross-linked to form cyclic structures. To help you identify the points of cross-linkage and ring formation, the carbon atoms of the geraniol skeleton are numbered 1 through 8. Bond formation between carbon atoms 1 and 6 of the geraniol skeleton gives the carbon skeletons of limonene and menthol; and formation of bonds between carbons 1,6 and 4,7 gives the carbon skeleton of alpha-pinene; and between 1,6 and 3,7, the carbon skeleton of camphor.

Shown in Figure VII-3 are structural formulas for several terpenes of 15 carbon atoms. For reference, the carbon atoms of the parent chain of farnesol are numbered 1 through 12. Bond formation between carbon atoms 1 and 6 of this skeleton gives the carbon skeleton of zingi-

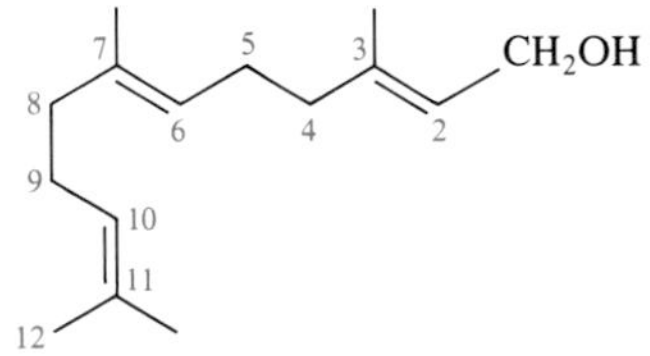

farnesol
(lily of the valley)

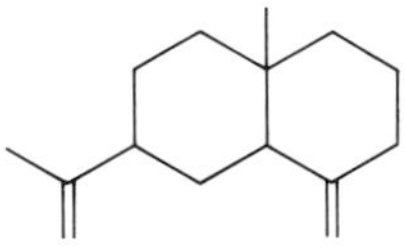

β-selinene
(celery)

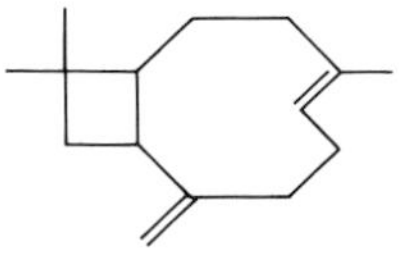

caryophyllene
(cloves)

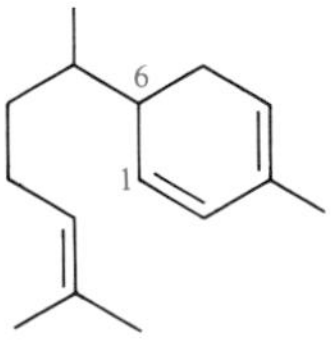

zingiberene
(ginger)

Figure VII-3 Several terpenes of three isoprene units (15 carbon atoms).

berene. You might try to discover for yourself what patterns of cross-linking give the carbon skeletons of beta-selinene and caryophyllene.

Shown in Figure VII-4 are structural formulas for vitamin A, a terpene of four isoprene units, and beta-carotene, a terpene of eight isoprene units. The four isoprene units of vitamin A are linked head to tail and cross-linked at one point to form a six-membered ring. The function of vitamin A is discussed in Section 20.6A. Beta-carotene can be divided into two 20-carbon terpenes, each identical to the carbon skeleton of vitamin A, and then these two 20-carbon units joined tail to tail. The function of beta-carotene is also discussed in Section 20.6A.

We have presented only a few of the terpenes that abound in nature, but these examples should be enough to suggest to you their wide-spread distribution in living systems, the biological individuality that plants and animals achieve through their synthesis, and the structural pattern (the isoprene rule) that underlies this apparent diversity in structural formula. In the future, when you encounter molecules of 10, 15, 20, and more carbon atoms derived from living systems, you might study their structural formulas to see whether they are terpenes.

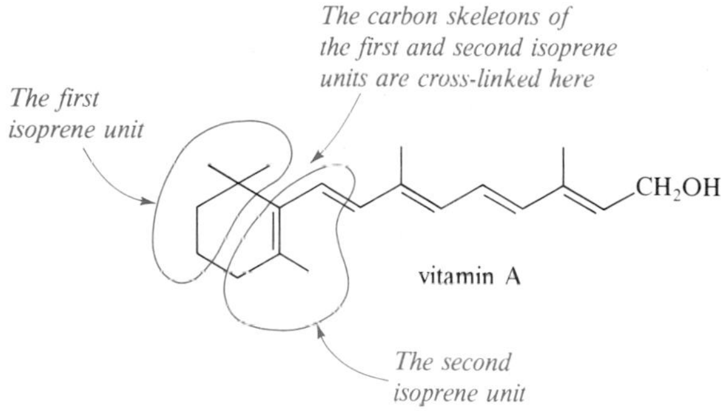

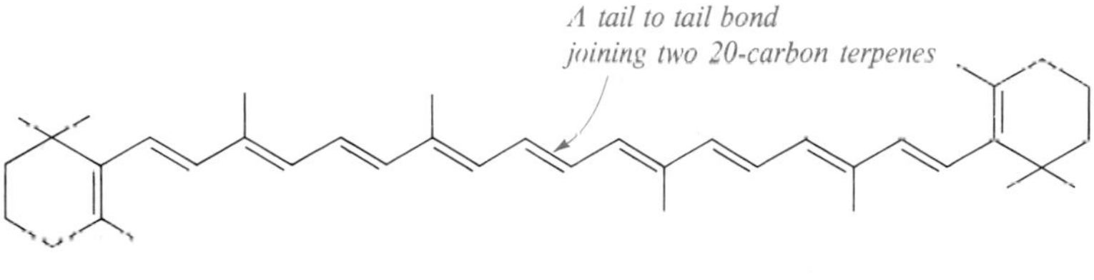

Figure VII-4 Vitamin A, a terpene of 20-carbon atoms (4 isoprene units) and beta-carotene, a terpene of 40-carbon atoms (8 isoprene units)

13

Alcohols, Ethers, Phenols, and Thiols

In this chapter, we will cover the physical and chemical properties of three classes of oxygen-containing compounds and one class of sulfur-containing compounds. Alcohols and phenols both contain an —OH group. The difference between them is that in an alcohol, —OH is bonded to an alkyl group, whereas in a phenol, it is bonded to a benzene ring. A thiol is like an alcohol in structure except that —OH is replaced by —SH:

$$CH_3CH_2OH \qquad \text{an alcohol} \qquad \text{a phenol} \qquad CH_3CH_2SH \qquad CH_3CH_2OCH_2CH_3$$

an alcohol   a phenol   a thiol   an ether

13.1 Structure of Alcohols and Ethers

The characteristic structural feature of an alcohol is a **hydroxyl (—OH) group** bonded to a saturated carbon atom (Section 10.2A). The oxygen atom of an alcohol is sp^3-hybridized. Two sp^3 hybrid orbitals of oxygen form sigma bonds to atoms of carbon and hydrogen, and the remaining hybrid orbitals each hold an unshared pair of electrons. Figure 13.1 shows a Lewis structure of methanol,

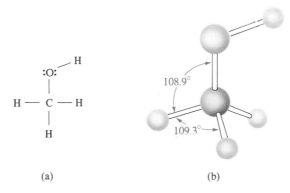

(a)   (b)

Figure 13.1 Structure of methanol, CH_3OH: (a) Lewis structure; (b) ball-and-stick model.

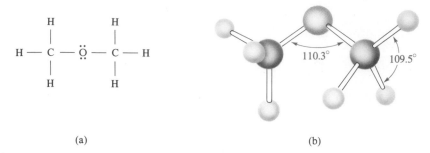

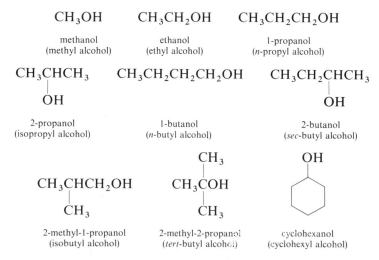

(a)   (b)

Figure 13.2 The structure of dimethyl ether, CH_3OCH_3: (a) Lewis structure; (b) ball-and-stick model.

CH_3OH, the simplest alcohol. The measured H—O—C bond angle in methanol is 108.9°, a value very close to the predicted tetrahedral angle of 109.5°. Also shown in Figure 13.1 is a ball-and-stick model of methanol.

The characteristic structural feature of an ether is an atom of oxygen bonded to two carbon chains (Section 10.2A). In an ether, sp^3 hybrid orbitals of oxygen form sigma bonds to the two hydrocarbon chains. Each of the remaining sp^3 hybrid orbitals contains an unshared pair of electrons. Figure 13.2 shows a Lewis structure and a three-dimensional representation of dimethyl ether, CH_3OCH_3, the simplest ether. The C—O—C bond angle in dimethyl ether is 110.3°, a value close to the predicted tetrahedral angle of 109.5°.

13.2 Nomenclature

A. Alcohols

In the IUPAC system, the longest chain of carbon atoms containing the —OH group is selected as the parent compound. To show that the compound is an

CH_3OH CH_3CH_2OH $CH_3CH_2CH_2OH$

methanol   ethanol   1-propanol
(methyl alcohol)   (ethyl alcohol)   (*n*-propyl alcohol)

CH_3CHCH_3 $CH_3CH_2CH_2CH_2OH$ $CH_3CH_2CHCH_3$
| |
OH   OH

2-propanol   1-butanol   2-butanol
(isopropyl alcohol)   (*n*-butyl alcohol)   (*sec*-butyl alcohol)

CH_3CHCH_2OH CH_3COH OH
| |
CH_3 CH_3

2-methyl-1-propanol   2-methyl-2-propanol   cyclohexanol
(isobutyl alcohol)   (*tert*-butyl alcohol)   (cyclohexyl alcohol)

Figure 13.3 Names and structural formulas of several low-molecular-weight alcohols.

alcohol, the suffix -e is changed to -ol (Section 11.5), and a number is added to show the location of the —OH group.

Common names for **alcohols** are derived by naming the alkyl group attached to —OH and then adding the word *alcohol*. Figure 13.3 gives IUPAC names, and in parentheses, common names for several low-molecular-weight alcohols.

Example 13.1

Write IUPAC names for these alcohols:

a.
$$CH_3—\overset{\displaystyle CH_3}{\underset{\displaystyle OH}{CH}}—CH_2—CH—CH_3$$

b. (cyclohexane ring with OH and CH₃ groups)

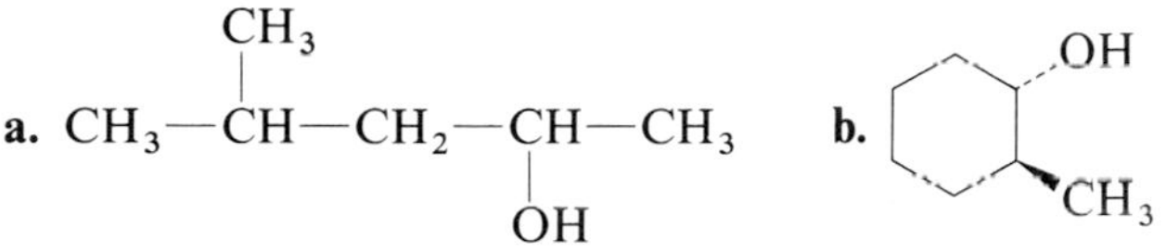

Solution

a. The longest chain that contains the —OH group is five carbon atoms, and it must be numbered so —OH is given the lowest possible number. The IUPAC name of this alcohol is 4-methyl-2-pentanol.

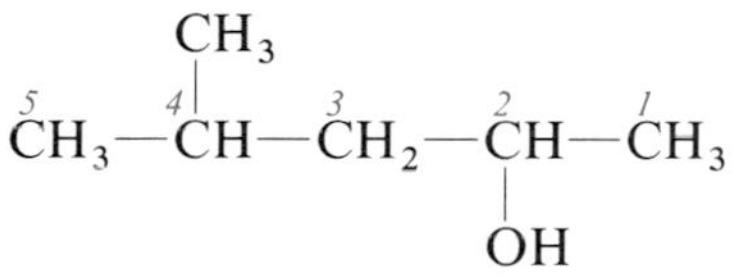

$$\overset{5}{C}H_3—\overset{4}{C}H—\overset{3}{C}H_2—\overset{2}{\underset{\displaystyle OH}{C}}H—\overset{1}{C}H_3$$
with CH₃ on carbon 4

4-methyl-2-pentanol

b. In cyclic alcohols, the carbon atoms of the ring are numbered from the carbon bearing the —OH group. Because the —OH is automatically on carbon 1, there is no need to give a number to show its location. In this compound, the hydroxyl and methyl groups are trans to each other, as shown by the dashed line (back of the plane of the paper) for —OH, and the solid wedge (in front of the plane of the paper) for the —CH₃ group. The name of this alcohol is *trans*-2-methylcyclohexanol.

Problem 13.1

Give IUPAC names for these alcohols:

a.
$$CH_3—CH_2—\underset{\displaystyle CH_2—CH_3}{CH}—CH_2—OH$$

b. (cyclopentane ring with CH₃ and OH groups)

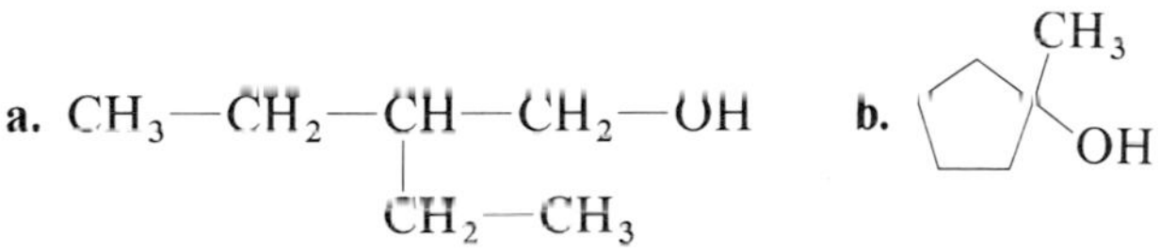

Alcohols are classified as **primary (1°)**, **secondary (2°)**, or **tertiary (3°)**, depending on whether the —OH group is on a primary carbon, a secondary carbon, or a tertiary carbon. General formulas of 1°, 2°, and 3° alcohols are given in Figure 13.4.

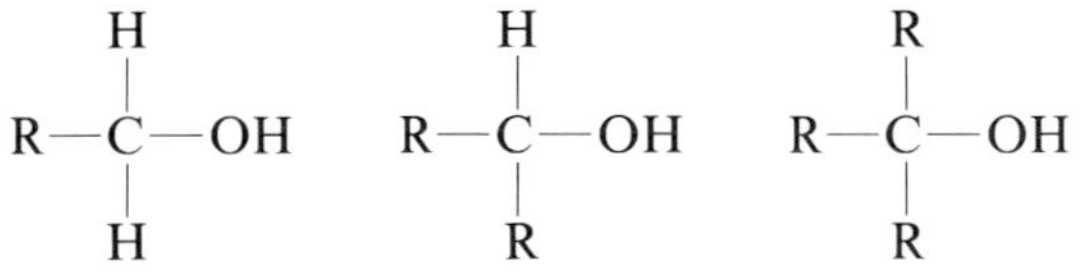

$$R—\overset{\displaystyle H}{\underset{\displaystyle H}{C}}—OH \qquad R—\overset{\displaystyle H}{\underset{\displaystyle R}{C}}—OH \qquad R—\overset{\displaystyle R}{\underset{\displaystyle R}{C}}—OH$$

primary (1°)   secondary (2°)   tertiary (3°)

Figure 13.4 Classification of alcohols: primary, secondary, and tertiary.

Example 13.2

Classify these alcohols as primary, secondary, or tertiary:

a. CH_3—$\underset{\underset{CH_3}{|}}{CH}$—OH

b. (cyclopentane)—$\underset{\underset{CH_3}{|}}{CH}$—OH

c. CH_3—$\underset{\underset{CH_3}{\overset{\overset{CH_3}{|}}{|}}}{C}$—OH

d. (benzene)—CH_2OH

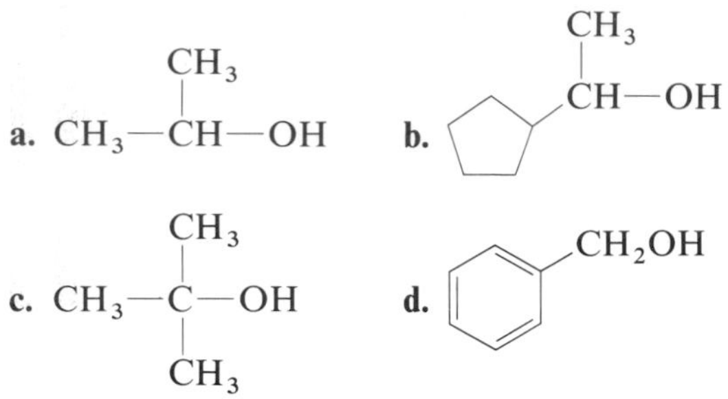

Solution

a. Because the carbon bearing the —OH group has two attached alkyl groups, it is a secondary carbon, and the alcohol is a secondary alcohol.
b. Because the carbon bearing the —OH group has one attached cycloalkyl group and one alkyl group, it is a secondary (2°) carbon, and the alcohol is a secondary (2°) alcohol.
c. A tertiary (3°) alcohol.
d. A primary (1°) alcohol.

Problem 13.2

Classify these alcohols as primary, secondary, or tertiary:

a. CH_3—$\underset{\underset{CH_3}{\overset{\overset{CH_3}{|}}{|}}}{C}$—$CH_2$—OH

b. (cyclopropane)—OH

c. $CH_2{=}CH$—CH_2—OH

d. (cyclopentane with OH and CH_3)

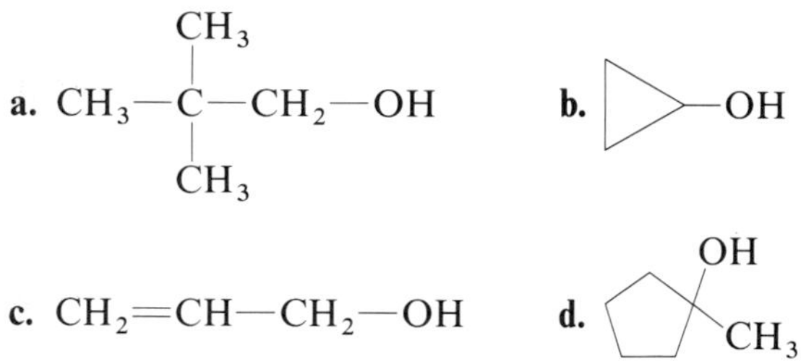

In the IUPAC system, compounds containing two hydroxyl groups are called **diols**, those containing three hydroxyl groups are called **triols**, and so on. Note that in IUPAC names for these compounds, the final -*e* (the suffix) of the parent name is retained.

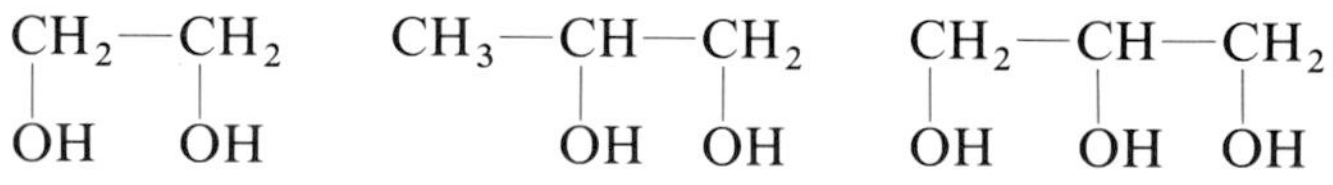

$$\underset{\underset{OH \quad OH}{|\qquad|}}{CH_2{-}CH_2} \qquad \underset{\underset{OH \quad OH}{|\qquad|}}{CH_3{-}CH{-}CH_2} \qquad \underset{\underset{OH \quad OH \quad OH}{|\qquad|\qquad|}}{CH_2{-}CH{-}CH_2}$$

1,2-ethanediol	1,2-propanediol	1,2,3-propanetriol
(ethylene glycol)	(propylene glycol)	(glycerol, glycerine)

Common names for compounds containing two hydroxyl groups on adjacent carbons are often referred to as **glycols** (Section 12.7A). Ethylene glycol and propylene glycol are synthesized from ethylene and propylene respectively, hence their common names.

Compounds containing —OH and C=C groups are called unsaturated (because of the presence of the carbon-carbon double bond) alcohols. In the IUPAC system, they are named as alcohols and the parent chain is numbered to give the —OH group the lowest possible number. That the carbon chain contains a double bond is shown by changing the infix from -*an*- to -*en*-, and that it is an alcohol is indicated by changing the suffix from -*e* to -*ol* (Section 11.5). Numbers must be used to show the location of both the carbon-carbon double bond and the hydroxyl group.

Example 13.3

Write IUPAC names for these unsaturated alcohols:

a. CH_2=CH—CH_2—OH   b. CH_3—CH_2—CH=CH—CH—CH_3
                                                                                 |
                                                                                OH

Solution

a. Because the chain contains three carbons, the parent name is propane. The chain is numbered so that the —OH group is on carbon 1 and the double bond is between carbons 2 and 3. The IUPAC name of this primary, unsaturated alcohol is 2-propen-1-ol. Its common name is allyl alcohol.

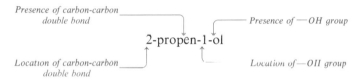

b. Because the parent chain contains six carbons, this compound is named as a derivative of hexane.

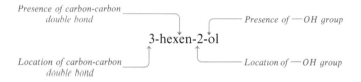

Problem 13.3

Write IUPAC names for these unsaturated alcohols:

a. CH_3—CH=CH—CH_2—OH   b.

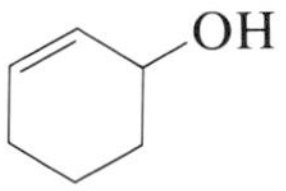

B. Ethers

In the IUPAC system, **ethers** are named by selecting the longest carbon chain as the parent compound and naming the —OR group as an alkoxy substituent. Following are IUPAC names for two low-molecular-weight ethers.

$$CH_3CH_2CH_2CH_2CHCH_2CH_2CH_3$$
$$\underset{\displaystyle OCH_3}{|}$$

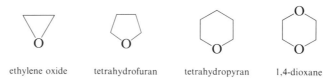

4-methoxyoctane   *trans*-2-ethoxycyclohexanol

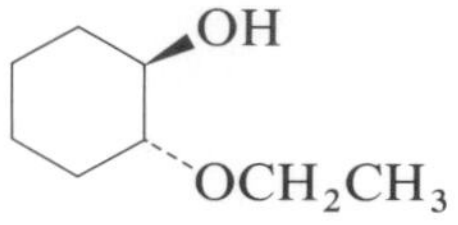

Common names are derived by specifying the alkyl groups attached to oxygen in alphabetical order and adding the word *ether*. Chemists almost invariably use common names for low-molecular-weight ethers. For example, while ethoxyethane is the IUPAC name for $CH_3CH_2OCH_2CH_3$, it is rarely called that but rather, diethyl ether, ethyl ether, or even more commonly, simply ether.

Heterocyclic ethers, that is, cyclic compounds in which the ether oxygen is one of the atoms in a ring, are given special names:

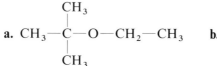

ethylene oxide   tetrahydrofuran    tetrahydropyran   1,4-dioxane

Example 13.4

Give common names for these ethers:

a. $CH_3-\underset{\displaystyle \underset{CH_3}{|}}{\overset{\displaystyle \overset{CH_3}{|}}{C}}-O-CH_2-CH_3$ b. 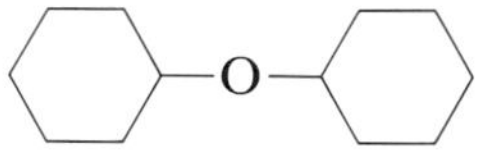 ⬡—O—⬡

c. $CH_2{=}CH-OCH_3$

Solution

a. *tert*-butyl ethyl ether. The IUPAC name of this ether is 2-ethoxy-2-methylpropane.
b. Its common name is dicyclohexyl ether. Its IUPAC name is cyclohexoxycyclohexane.
c. Groups attached to oxygen are methyl and vinyl (Section 12.2B). Therefore, its common name is methyl vinyl ether. Its IUPAC name is methoxyethene.

Problem 13.4

Name these ethers:

a. $CH_3-\underset{\displaystyle \underset{CH_3}{|}}{CH}-CH_2-O-CH_2-CH_3$ b. 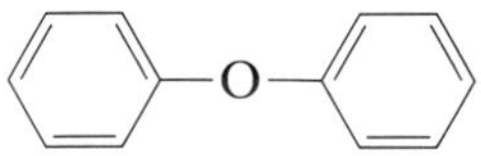 ⬡—O—⬡

c. $CH_3-O-\underset{\displaystyle \underset{CH_3}{|}}{\overset{\displaystyle \overset{CH_3}{|}}{C}}-CH_3$

13.3 Physical Properties of Alcohols and Ethers

A. Polarity of Alcohols

Because of the presence of the —OH group, alcohols are polar compounds. Oxygen is more electronegative than either carbon or hydrogen (Figure 4.3), and therefore there are partial positive charges on carbon and hydrogen and a partial negative charge on oxygen, as illustrated in Figure 13.5.

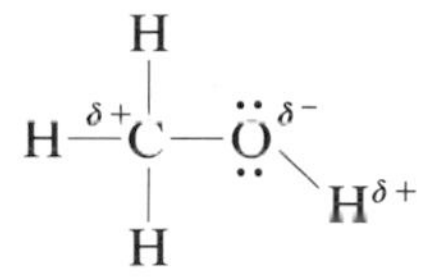

Figure 13.5 Polarity of the C—O—H bonds in alcohols.

The attraction between the positive end of one dipole and the negative end of another is called **dipole-dipole interaction**. When the positive end of one of the dipoles is a hydrogen bonded to a very electronegative atom, the interaction between dipoles is given the special name of **hydrogen bonding**. Figure 13.6 shows the association of ethanol molecules by hydrogen bonding between the partially negative oxygen atom of one alcohol and the partially positive hydrogen atom of another.

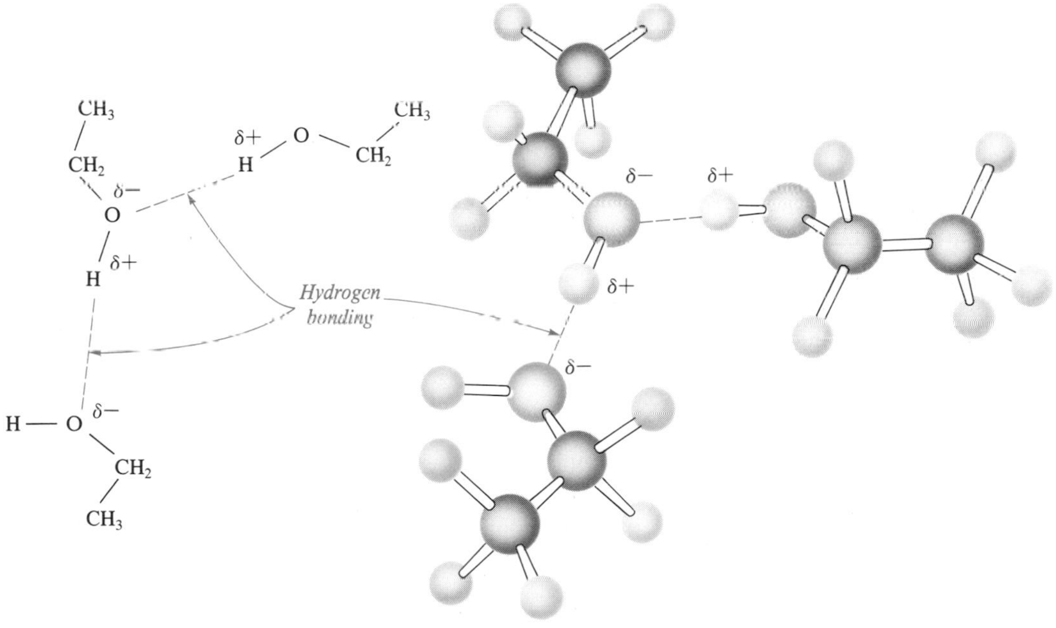

Figure 13.6 The association of ethanol in the liquid state: (a) Lewis structures; (b) ball-and-stick models. Each O—H can participate in up to three hydrogen bonds (one through hydrogen and two through oxygen). Only two of the three possible hydrogen bonds per molecule are shown in this figure.

B. Polarity of Ethers

Ethers are also polar molecules; oxygen bears a partial negative charge and each attached carbon bears a partial positive charge (Figure 13.7).

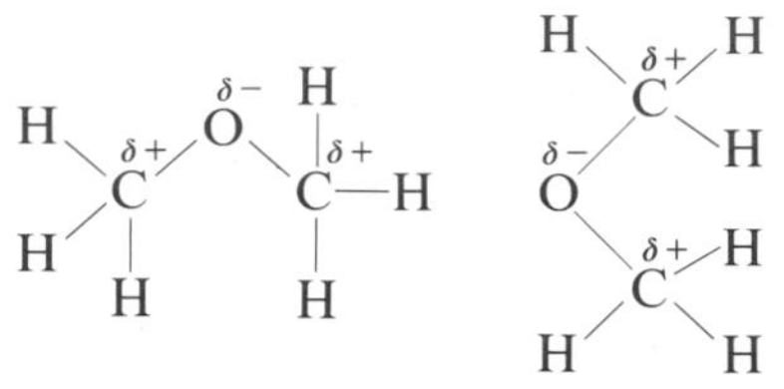

Figure 13.7 Polarity of C—O—C bonds in ethers.

Association of ether molecules by hydrogen bonding is not possible, since there is no partially positive hydrogen atom attached to oxygen to participate in hydrogen bonding. There is still the possibility, however, for ether molecules to associate by interaction between a partially positive carbon of one molecule and the partially negative oxygen of another. In fact, this type of interaction is very slight. Because each partially positive carbon is surrounded by four other atoms, it is not possible for oppositely charged dipoles to come close enough to interact. Thus, although ether molecules are polar, there is very little association between them in the pure state.

C. Relation between Structure and Physical Properties

Listed in Table 13.1 are boiling points and solubilities in water for several groups of alcohols, ethers, and hydrocarbons of similar molecular weights. Of the three classes of compounds compared in Table 13.1, alcohols have the highest boiling points because of hydrogen bonding between polar —OH groups. Ethers have boiling points close to those of nonpolar hydrocarbons of comparable molecular weight.

The effect of hydrogen bonding is illustrated dramatically by comparing the boiling points of ethanol (bp 78°C) and its structural isomer dimethyl ether (bp −24°C). The boiling points of these two compounds are different because polar O—H groups are present in the alcohol. Alcohol molecules interact by hydrogen bonding; ether molecules do not. Compare also the boiling points of 1-propanol (97°C) and ethyl methyl ether (11°C); of 1-butanol (117°C) and diethyl ether (35°C). The presence of additional hydroxyl groups in a molecule further increases the significance of hydrogen bonding, as can be seen by comparing the boiling points of hexane (bp 69°C), 1-pentanol (bp 138°C), and 1,4-butanediol (bp 230°C), all of which have approximately the same molecular weight. Because of increased dispersion forces between all the atoms, including the hydrocarbon portions, of the molecules, boiling points of alcohols and ethers increase with

Table 13.1
Boiling points
and solubilities
in water of
several groups of
alcohols, ethers,
and hydrocarbons
of similar
molecular
weight.

Structural Formula	Name	Molecular Weight	bp (°C)	Solubility in Water
CH_3OH	methanol	32	65	infinite
CH_3CH_3	ethane	30	−89	insoluble
CH_3CH_2OH	ethanol	46	78	infinite
CH_3OCH_3	dimethyl ether	46	−24	7 g/100 g
$CH_3CH_2CH_3$	propane	44	−42	insoluble
$CH_3CH_2CH_2OH$	1-propanol	60	97	infinite
$CH_3CH_2OCH_3$	ethyl methyl ether	60	11	soluble
$CH_3CH_2CH_2CH_3$	butane	58	0	insoluble
$CH_3CH_2CH_2CH_2OH$	1-butanol	74	117	8 g/100 g
$CH_3CH_2OCH_2CH_3$	diethyl ether	74	35	8 g/100 g
$CH_3CH_2CH_2CH_2CH_3$	pentane	72	36	insoluble
$CH_3CH_2CH_2CH_2CH_2OH$	1-pentanol	88	138	2.3 g/100 g
$CH_3CH_2CH_2CH_2OCH_3$	butyl methyl ether	88	71	slightly
$HOCH_2CH_2CH_2CH_2OH$	1,4-butanediol	90	230	infinite
$CH_3OCH_2CH_2OCH_3$	ethylene glycol dimethyl ether	90	84	infinite
$CH_3CH_2CH_2CH_2CH_2CH_3$	hexane	88	69	insoluble

increasing molecular weight. To see this, compare the boiling points of ethanol,
1-propanol, and 1-butanol.

Because alcohols and ethers can interact by hydrogen bonding with water,
they are more soluble in water than alkanes of comparable molecular weight
(Figure 13.8). Methanol, ethanol, and 1-propanol are soluble in water in all

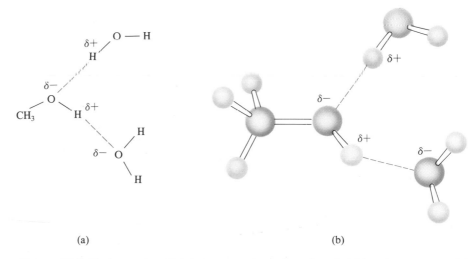

(a)   (b)

Figure 13.8 Hydrogen bonding between water and methanol: (a) Lewis structures; (b)
ball-and-stick models.

proportions. As molecular weight increases, the physical properties of alcohols and ethers become more like the physical properties of hydrocarbons of comparable molecular weight. Alcohols of higher molecular weight are much less soluble in water because of the increase in size of the hydrocarbon portion of the molecule. For example, 1-decanol is insoluble in water but soluble in ethanol and in nonpolar hydrocarbon solvents, such as benzene and hexane.

Example 13.5

Arrange the following compounds in order of increasing boiling point. Explain the basis for your answer.

$$CH_3—CH_2—OH \qquad CH_3—CH_2—Cl \qquad CH_3—CH_2—CH_3$$

☐ *Solution*

Propane and ethanol have similar molecular weights. Propane is a nonpolar hydrocarbon and the only interactions between molecules in the pure liquid are dispersion forces (review Sections 6.6 and 11.8). Ethanol is a polar compound and there is extensive hydrogen bonding between ethanol molecules in the pure liquid. Therefore, ethanol has a higher boiling point than propane. Chloroethane has a higher molecular weight than ethanol and is a polar molecule. However, because it cannot associate by hydrogen bonding, chloroethane has a lower boiling point than ethanol. In order of increasing boiling point, the compounds are

$$CH_3CH_2CH_3 \qquad CH_3CH_2Cl \qquad CH_3CH_2OH$$

| bp − 42°C | bp 12°C | bp 78°C |
| (mw 44.1) | (mw 64.5) | (mw 46.1) |

Problem 13.5

Arrange the compounds in order of increasing boiling point. Explain the basis for your answer.

$$CH_3OCH_2CH_2OCH_3 \qquad HOCH_2CH_2OH \qquad CH_3OCH_2CH_2OH$$

Example 13.6

Arrange the following compounds in order of increasing solubility in water. Explain the basis of your answer.

$$CH_3CH_2CH_2CH_2CH_2CH_3 \qquad CH_3OCH_2CH_2OCH_3 \qquad CH_3CH_2OCH_2CH_3$$

☐ *Solution*

Water is a polar solvent. Hexane, C_6H_{14}, a nonpolar hydrocarbon, has the lowest solubility in water. Both diethyl ether and ethylene glycol dimethyl ether (1,2-dimethoxyethane) are polar compounds due to the presence of C—O—C bonds, and each interacts with water molecules by hydrogen bonding. Because ethylene glycol dimethyl ether has more sites within the molecule for hydrogen bonding, it is more soluble in water than diethyl ether. The water solubilities of these substances are given in Table 13.1.

$$CH_3CH_2CH_2CH_2CH_2CH_3 \qquad CH_3CH_2OCH_2CH_3 \qquad CH_3OCH_2CH_2OCH_3$$

insoluble   8 g/100 g water   soluble in all proportions

Problem 13.6

Arrange the following compounds in order of increasing solubility in water.

$$ClCH_2CH_2Cl \qquad CH_3CH_2CH_2OH \qquad CH_3CH_2OCH_2CH_3$$

13.4 Reactions of Alcohols

Alcohols undergo various important reactions including (1) dehydration to alkenes and (2) oxidation to aldehydes, ketones, and carboxylic acids. Therefore, alcohols are valuable starting materials for the synthesis of other classes of organic compounds.

A. Dehydration to an Alkene

An alcohol can be converted to an alkene by elimination of a molecule of water from adjacent carbon atoms. Elimination of a molecule of water is called **dehydration**. In the laboratory, dehydration is most commonly brought about by heating the alcohol with either 85% phosphoric acid or concentrated sulfuric acid at temperatures of 100–200°C. For example, acid-catalyzed dehydration of ethanol gives ethylene:

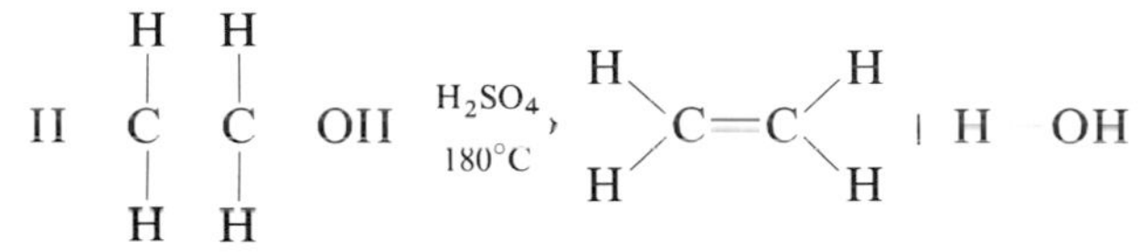

In the process, two sigma bonds (C—H and C—OH) are broken, and one pi bond (C=C) and one sigma bond (H—OH) are formed. Dehydration of cyclohexanol in the presence of 85% phosphoric acid yields cyclohexene:

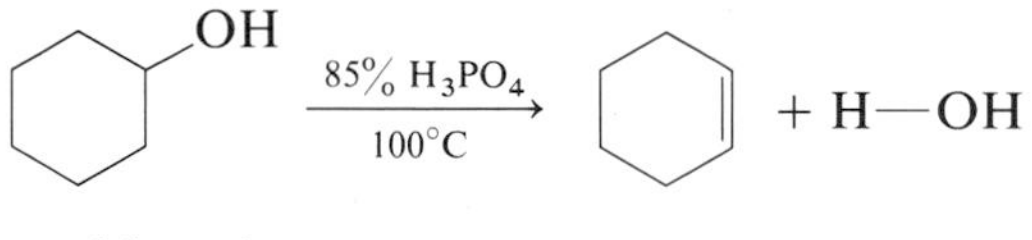

cyclohexanol   cyclohexene

Long before anyone understood the mechanism of acid-catalyzed dehydration of alcohols, it was recognized that when isomeric alkenes are obtained in an elimination reaction, the alkene having the greater number of substituents on the double bond generally predominates. For example, acid-catalyzed dehydration of 2-butanol gives 80% 2-butene and 20% 1-butene

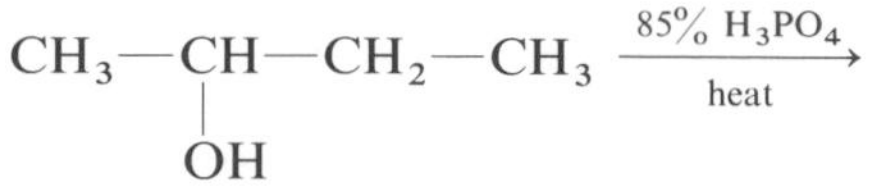

$$CH_3-CH-CH_2-CH_3 \xrightarrow[\text{heat}]{85\% \; H_3PO_4}$$

$$\underset{\text{OH}}{|}$$

2-butanol

$$CH_3-CH=CH-CH_3 + CH_2=CH-CH_2-CH_3 + HOH$$

2-butene   1-butene
(80%)   (20%)

Example 13.7

Draw structural formulas for the alkenes formed on acid-catalyzed dehydration of the following alcohols. Predict which is the major product and which the minor product.

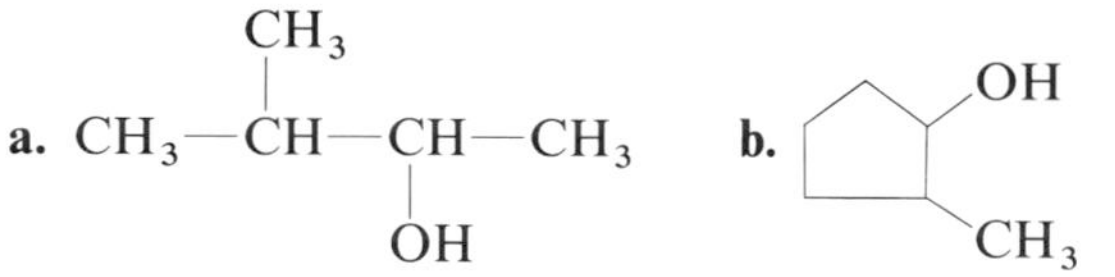

$$\text{a. } CH_3-\underset{\underset{OH}{|}}{\overset{\overset{CH_3}{|}}{CH}}-CH-CH_3 \qquad \text{b.}$$

Solution

a. Dehydration of 3-methyl-2-butanol causes loss of —H and —OH from carbons 1 and 2, to produce 3-methyl-1-butene, and from carbons 2 and 3, to produce 2-methyl-2-butene.

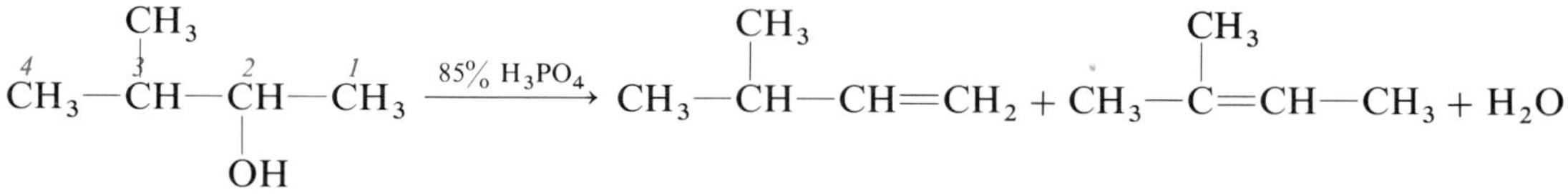

$$\overset{4}{CH_3}-\overset{3}{\underset{\underset{OH}{|}}{CH}}-\overset{2}{CH}-\overset{1}{CH_3} \xrightarrow{85\% \; H_3PO_4} CH_3-\overset{\overset{CH_3}{|}}{CH}-CH=CH_2 + CH_3-\overset{\overset{CH_3}{|}}{C}=CH-CH_3 + H_2O$$

3-methyl-2-butanol   3-methyl-1-butene   2-methyl-2-butene
                               (minor product)   (major product)

The product 3-methyl-1-butene has one alkyl substituent (an isopropyl group) on the double bond, whereas 2-methyl-2-butene has three alkyl substituents (three methyl groups) on the double bond. Therefore, the prediction is that 2-methyl-2-butene is the major product and 3-methyl-1-butene is the minor product.

b.

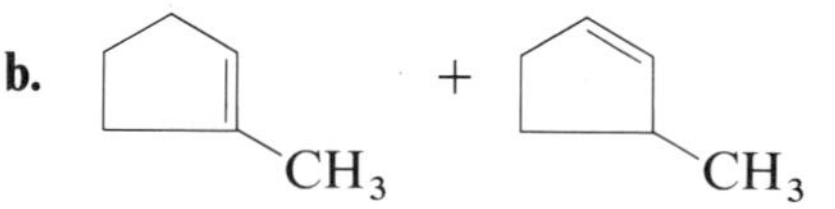

1-methylcyclopentene   3-methylcyclopentene
(major product)   (minor product)

The major product, 1-methylcyclopentene, has three alkyl substituents on the carbon-carbon double bond. The minor product, 3-methylcyclopentene, has only two substituents on the double bond.

Problem 13.7

Draw structural formulas for the alkenes formed on acid-catalyzed dehydration of the following alcohols. For each, predict which is the major product and which the minor product.

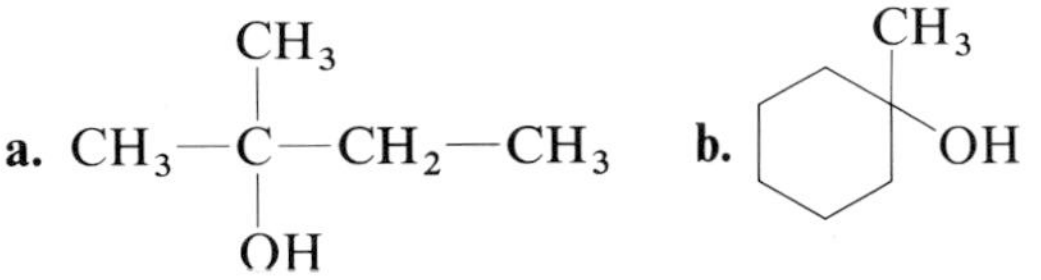

a.
$$CH_3-\overset{\overset{\displaystyle CH_3}{|}}{\underset{\underset{\displaystyle OH}{|}}{C}}-CH_2-CH_3$$

b.
a cyclohexane ring with CH_3 and OH substituents on the same carbon

In Section 12.5D we discussed a mechanism for acid-catalyzed hydration of alkenes to alcohols. This mechanism involves reaction of H^+ and an alkene, to form a carbocation intermediate, and then reaction of the carbocation with a molecule of water, to give the alcohol. The mechanism for acid-catalyzed dehydration of an alcohol to an alkene is the reverse of this mechanism. In step 1, as shown by the curved arrow, an unshared pair of electrons on oxygen forms a new bond to H^+, to form an oxonium ion.

Step 1

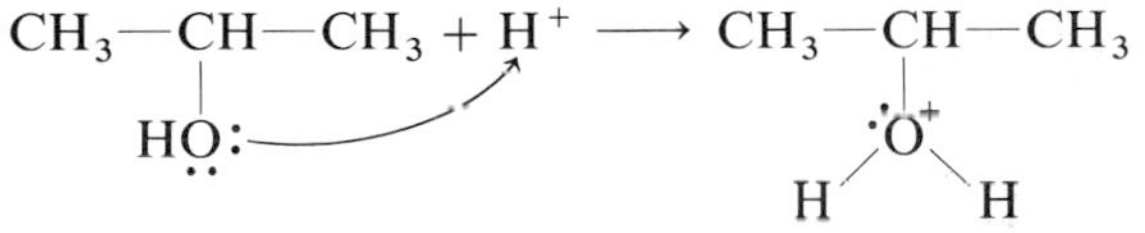

$$CH_3-\overset{\overset{}{|}}{\underset{\underset{\displaystyle H\overset{..}{\overset{..}{O}}:}{|}}{CH}}-CH_3 + H^+ \longrightarrow CH_3-\overset{\overset{}{|}}{\underset{\underset{\displaystyle \underset{H}{\diagup}\overset{+}{\overset{..}{O}}\underset{H}{\diagdown}}{}}{CH}}-CH_3$$

an oxonium ion

In step 2, the C—O bond is broken and the pair of electrons forming this bond goes to oxygen, to form a molecule of water and a secondary carbocation.

Step 2

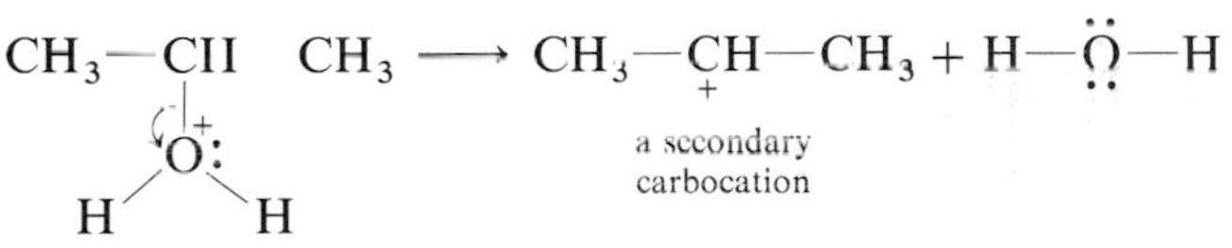

$$CH_3-\overset{\overset{}{|}}{\underset{\underset{\displaystyle \underset{H}{\diagup}\overset{+}{\overset{..}{O}:}\underset{H}{\diagdown}}{}}{CH}}\ CH_3 \longrightarrow CH_3-\overset{+}{CH}-CH_3 + H-\overset{..}{\underset{..}{O}}-H$$

a secondary carbocation

Finally, in step 3, a C—H bond on a carbon adjacent to the carbocation breaks to form H^+, and the pair of electrons of the C—H bond forms the pi bond of the alkene.

Step 3

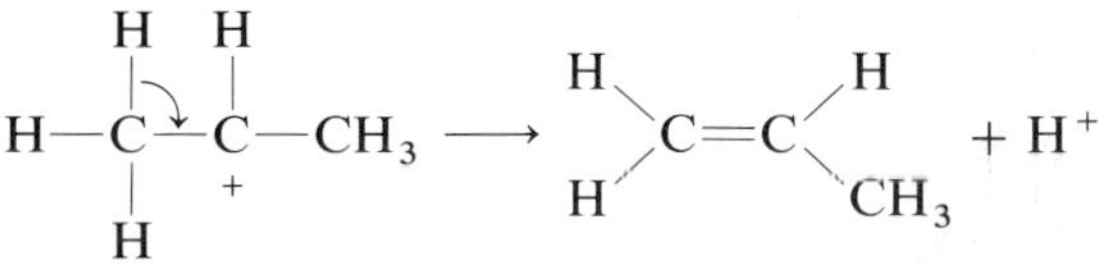

$$H-\overset{\overset{\displaystyle H\ \ H}{|\ \ |}}{\underset{\underset{\displaystyle H}{|}}{C}}\overset{}{\underset{+}{C}}-CH_3 \longrightarrow \overset{H}{\underset{H}{\diagup}}C=C\overset{H}{\underset{CH_3}{\diagdown}} + H^+$$

Because the reactive intermediate in acid-catalyzed dehydration is a carbocation, the relative ease of dehydration of alcohols parallels the ease of formation of carbocations. Tertiary alcohols are dehydrated more readily than secondary alcohols because a tertiary carbocation is formed more readily than a secondary carbocation. For the same reason, secondary alcohols undergo acid-catalyzed dehydration more readily than primary alcohols. Thus, the ease of dehydration of alcohols is

$$3° \text{ alcohols} > 2° \text{ alcohols} > 1° \text{ alcohols}$$

Because hydration-dehydration reactions are reversible, alkene formation and alcohol dehydration are competing processes and the following equilibrium exists:

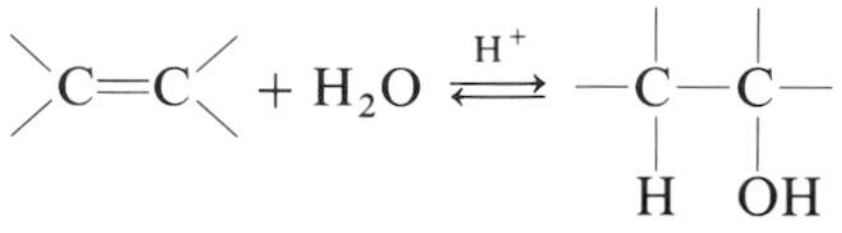

$$\underset{\text{alkene}}{\ce{>C=C<}} + H_2O \underset{}{\overset{H^+}{\rightleftharpoons}} \underset{\text{alcohol}}{-\overset{|}{\underset{|}{C}}-\overset{|}{\underset{|}{C}}-}$$
$$\qquad\qquad\qquad\quad H \quad OH$$

Large amounts of water favor alcohol formation, whereas experimental conditions in which water is removed favor alkene formation. Depending on the conditions, it is possible to use the hydration-dehydration equilibrium to prepare either alcohols or alkenes, each in high yields.

B. Oxidation to Aldehydes, Ketones, or Carboxylic Acids

1. Primary Alcohols

A primary alcohol can be oxidized to either an aldehyde or a carboxylic acid depending on the experimental conditions. In oxidation of a primary alcohol to a carboxylic acid, the aldehyde is an intermediate, as shown in the following equation:

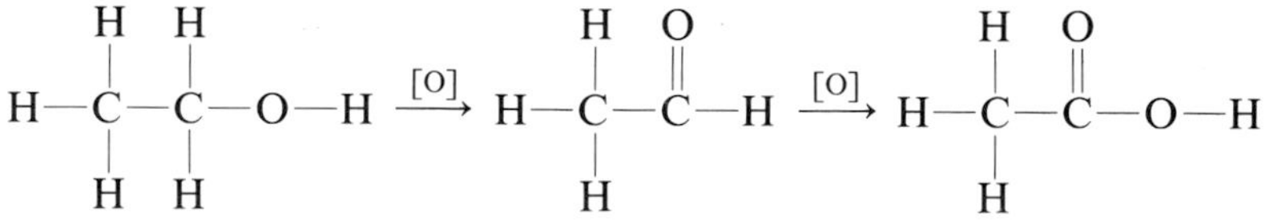

a primary alcohol → an aldehyde → a carboxylic acid

Inspection of balanced half-reactions shows that each transformation in this series is a two-electron oxidation.

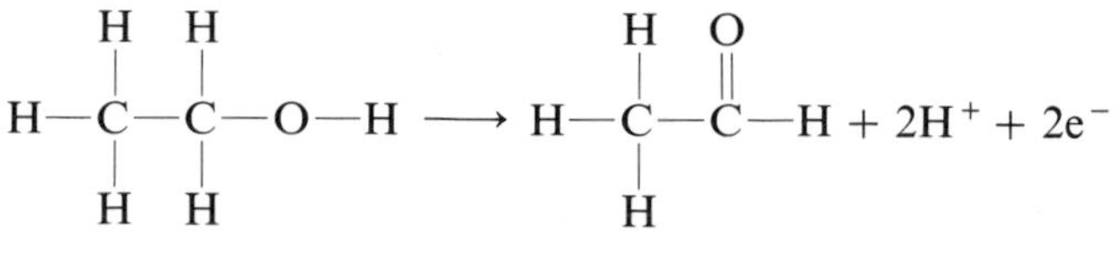

$$\cdots \longrightarrow \cdots + 2H^+ + 2e^-$$

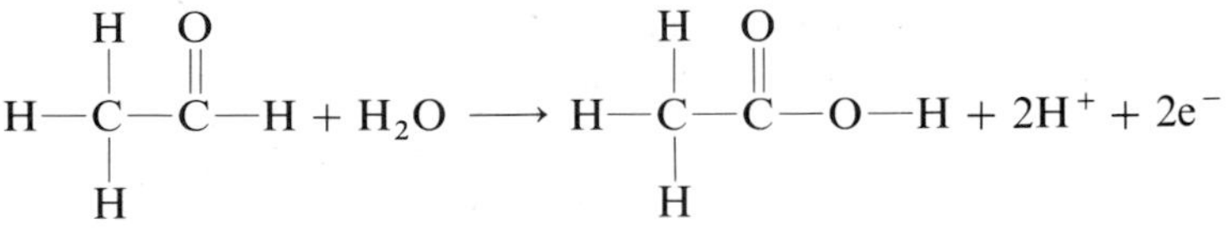

$$H-\underset{\underset{H}{|}}{\overset{\overset{H}{|}}{C}}-\overset{\overset{O}{\|}}{C}-H + H_2O \longrightarrow H-\underset{\underset{H}{|}}{\overset{\overset{H}{|}}{C}}-\overset{\overset{O}{\|}}{C}-O-H + 2H^+ + 2e^-$$

The most common oxidizing agent in the laboratory for converting primary alcohols to aldehydes or carboxylic acids is potassium dichromate, $K_2Cr_2O_7$. It is prepared by dissolving potassium dichromate in aqueous sulfuric acid and then mixing this solution with the organic alcohol dissolved in acetone. Generally, oxidation is rapid and yields of aldehyde are good. Green chromium(III) salts precipitate and can be separated by pouring off the acetone solution.

Oxidation of a primary alcohol to an aldehyde by potassium dichromate is illustrated by oxidation of 1-propanol (n-propyl alcohol) to propanal:

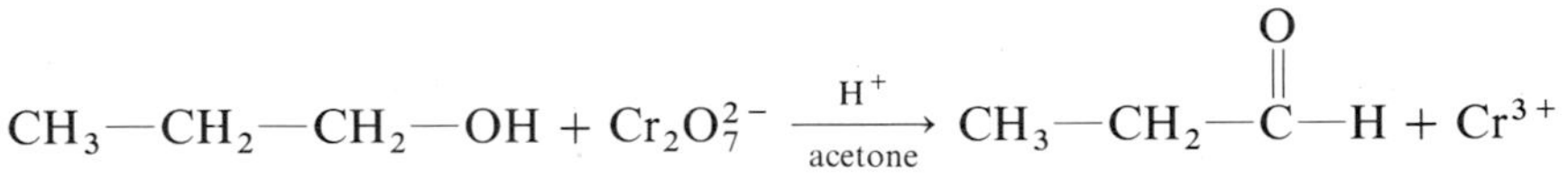

$$CH_3-CH_2-CH_2-OH + Cr_2O_7^{2-} \xrightarrow[acetone]{H^+} CH_3-CH_2-\overset{\overset{O}{\|}}{C}-H + Cr^{3+}$$

1-propanol   (orange)   propanal   (green)
(a 1° alcohol)   (an aldehyde)

Aldehydes are easily oxidized to carboxylic acids in a reaction that involves conversion of the aldehyde C—H bond to a C—OH bond:

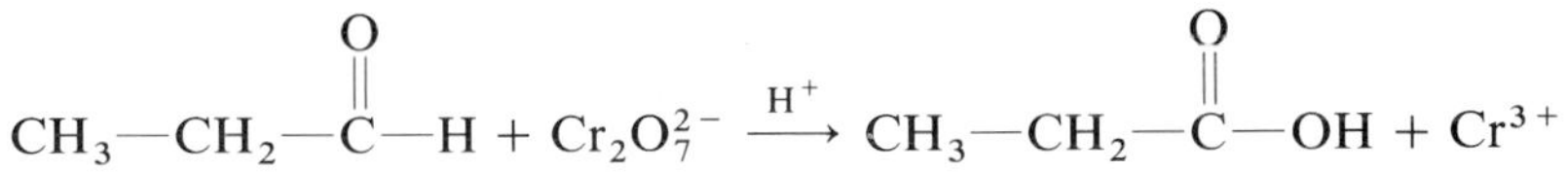

$$CH_3-CH_2-\overset{\overset{O}{\|}}{C}-H + Cr_2O_7^{2-} \xrightarrow{H^+} CH_3-CH_2-\overset{\overset{O}{\|}}{C}-OH + Cr^{3+}$$

propanal   propanoic acid
(an aldehyde)   (a carboxylic acid)

The product of oxidation of a primary alcohol depends on the solvent, the temperature, and other reaction conditions. We will not be concerned with these types of experimental details, noting only that either an aldehyde or a carboxylic acid can be obtained if proper conditions are chosen.

2. Secondary Alcohols

Secondary alcohols are oxidized to ketones:

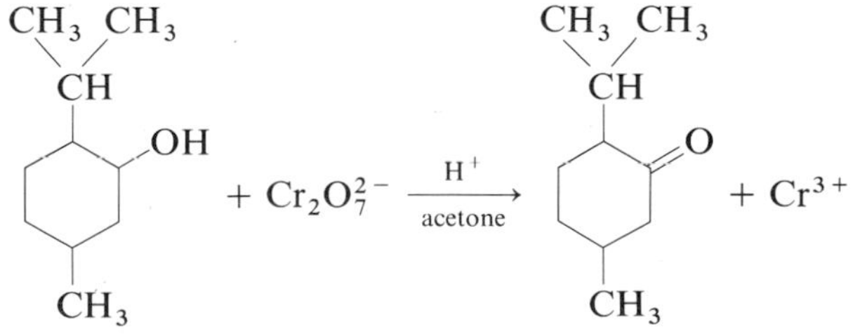

menthol   menthone
(a 2° alcohol)   (a ketone)

3. Tertiary Alcohols

Tertiary alcohols are resistant to oxidation, because the carbon bearing the —OH has no hydrogen atom on it. It is already bonded to three other carbon atoms and therefore cannot form a carbon-oxygen double bond.

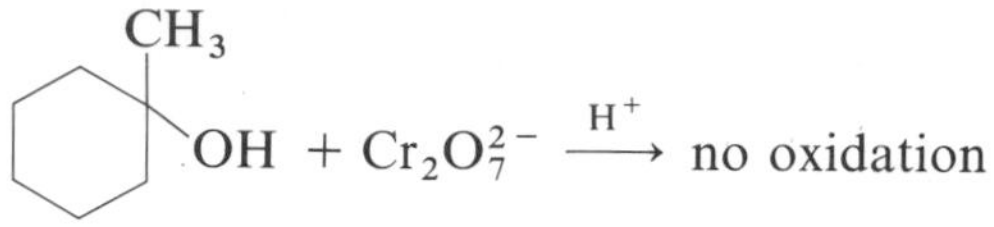

$$\text{(cyclohexane ring)}\overset{CH_3}{\underset{OH}{}} + Cr_2O_7^{2-} \xrightarrow{H^+} \text{no oxidation}$$

13.5 Alcohols of Industrial Importance

A. Methanol

By far the most important alcohol, at least in terms of bulk, is methanol. In 1985, production of methanol in the United States was just over 6 billion pounds. Virtually all methanol is manufactured by reaction of carbon monoxide and hydrogen.

$$CO + 2H_2 \xrightarrow{catalyst} CH_3OH$$
$$\text{methanol}$$

The major derivative of methanol is formaldehyde, prepared on an industrial scale by air oxidation. In a typical oxidation, air and methanol are passed over a zinc oxide–chromium oxide catalyst at elevated temperature and pressure:

$$2CH_3OH + O_2 \xrightarrow{catalyst} 2H-\overset{\overset{\displaystyle O}{\|}}{C}-H + 2H_2O$$
$$\text{methanol} \qquad\qquad \text{methanal} \\ \text{(formaldehyde)}$$

The most important end use of formaldehyde is in the manufacture of adhesives for plywood and particle board, and of a variety of polymers.

B. Ethylene Glycol

Over 4.7 billion pounds of ethylene glycol was manufactured in the United States in 1985. Starting material for its synthesis is ethylene, itself derived from refining either natural gas or petroleum. In the manufacture of ethylene glycol, a mixture of ethylene and air is passed over a silver catalyst. Reaction of ethylene oxide with water gives ethylene glycol:

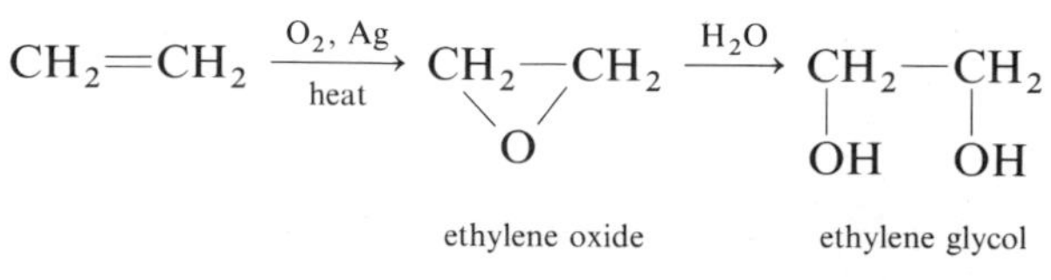

$$CH_2{=}CH_2 \xrightarrow[\text{heat}]{O_2,\ Ag} CH_2\overset{\diagdown\ \diagup}{\underset{O}{}}CH_2 \xrightarrow{H_2O} \underset{\underset{OH}{|}}{CH_2}-\underset{\underset{OH}{|}}{CH_2}$$
$$\text{ethylene oxide} \qquad\qquad\quad \text{ethylene glycol}$$

Ethylene glycol has two important uses: as an antifreeze in automobile radiators and as the monomer used along with terephthalic acid for the synthesis of polyester fibers (Dacron) and films (Mylar).

C. Ethanol

Ethanol, or simply "alcohol" in nonscientific language, has been prepared since antiquity by fermentation of sugars and starches, catalyzed by yeast:

$$C_6H_{12}O_6 \xrightarrow{\text{alcoholic fermentation}} 2CH_3CH_2OH + 2CO_2$$

glucose   ethanol

The sugars for this fermentation come from a variety of sources, including grains (hence the name *grain alcohol*), grape juice, various vegetables, and agricultural wastes, including corn stalks. The immediate product of fermentation is a water solution containing up to 15% alcohol. This alcohol can be concentrated by distillation. Beverage alcohol may contain traces of flavor derived from the source (grapes in brandy, grains in whiskeys) or may be essentially flavorless (like vodka).

Synthetic ethanol (1.1 billion pounds in 1985) is made by acid-catalyzed hydration of ethylene over a phosphoric acid catalyst:

$$CH_2{=}CH_2 + H_2O \xrightarrow{\text{catalyst}} CH_3{-}CH_2{-}OH$$

ethanol
(ethyl alcohol)

Ordinary commercial alcohol is a mixture of 95% alcohol and 5% water. **Absolute ethanol**, or 100% ethanol, is prepared from 95% ethanol by techniques that remove water from the mixture.

D. 2-Propanol

After methanol and ethylene glycol, the largest-volume alcohol produced by the US chemical industry is 2-propanol (isopropyl alcohol), manufactured by acid-catalyzed hydration of propene:

$$CH_3{-}CH{=}CH_2 + H_2O \xrightarrow{H_2SO_4} CH_3{-}\underset{\underset{\displaystyle OH}{|}}{CH}{-}CH_3$$

propene   2-propanol
(propylene)   (isopropyl alcohol)

Some 2-propanol is used in 70% aqueous solution as rubbing alcohol. However, the bulk of it is oxidized to acetone, which finds wide use as a solvent.

$$2CH_3-\overset{\overset{\displaystyle OH}{|}}{CH}-CH_3 + O_2 \xrightarrow{\text{catalyst}} 2CH_3-\overset{\overset{\displaystyle O}{\|}}{C}-CH_3 + 2H_2O$$

2-propanone
(acetone)

13.6 Ethers

A. Reactions of Ethers

Ethers resemble hydrocarbons in their resistance to chemical reactions. They do not react with oxidizing agents such as potassium permanganate or potassium dichromate. They are not affected by most strong acids or bases at moderate temperatures. It is precisely this resistance to chemical reaction and good solvent properties that make ethers such good solvents.

B. Ethers and Anesthesia

Before the middle 1800s, surgery was performed only when absolutely necessary, because there was no truly effective general anesthetic. More often than not, patients were drugged, hypnotized, or simply tied down. In 1772, Joseph Priestley isolated nitrous oxide, N_2O, a colorless gas, and in 1799 Sir Humphrey Davy demonstrated its anesthetic effect, naming it laughing gas. In 1844, an American dentist, Horace Wells, introduced nitrous oxide into general dental practice. However, one patient awakened prematurely, screaming with pain, and another died. Wells was forced to withdraw from practice, became embittered and depressed, and committed suicide at age 33. In the same period, a Boston chemist, Charles Jackson, anesthetized himself with diethyl ether and persuaded a dentist, William Morton, to use it. Subsequently, they persuaded a surgeon, John Warren, to give a public demonstration of surgery under anesthesia. The operation was completed successfully, and soon general anesthesia by diethyl ether became routine for general surgery.

Diethyl ether is easy to use and causes excellent muscle relaxation. Blood pressure, pulse rate, and respiration are usually only slightly affected. Its chief drawbacks are its irritating effect on the respiratory passages and its aftereffect of nausea. Further, when mixed with air in the right proportions, it is explosive! Modern operating theaters are often a maze of sophisticated electrical equipment, including cautery devices, which are frequently used throughout most surgical procedures. During prolonged ether anesthesia, concentrations of the gas in a patient's fatty tissue, abdominal cavity, and bladder can reach explosive levels. An electrical spark could quite literally produce an explosion. Precautionary measures to guard against such accidents became so cumbersome that the incentive was strong to develop alternative, nonflammable, and nonexplosive anesthetics.

One such alternative is the halogenated hydrocarbon 1-bromo-1-chloro-2,2,2-trifluoroethane, or as it is more commonly known, halothane:

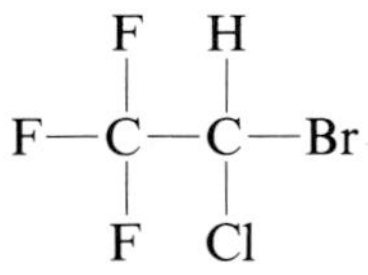

$$\underset{\substack{\text{1-bromo-1-chloro-2,2,2-trifluoroethane} \\ \text{(halothane)}}}{F-\overset{\displaystyle \overset{F}{|}}{\underset{\displaystyle \underset{F}{|}}{C}}-\overset{\displaystyle \overset{H}{|}}{\underset{\displaystyle \underset{Cl}{|}}{C}}-Br}$$

Halothane has distinct advantages over diethyl ether in that it is nonflammable and nonexplosive, and causes minimum discomfort to the patient. Although some cases of liver damage have been reported, halothane's record as a safe anesthetic is impressive.

Both diethyl ether and now halothane have been replaced by an even newer type of inhalation anesthetic, namely halogenated ethers. The most widely used of these are marketed under the trade names Enflurane and Isoflurane:

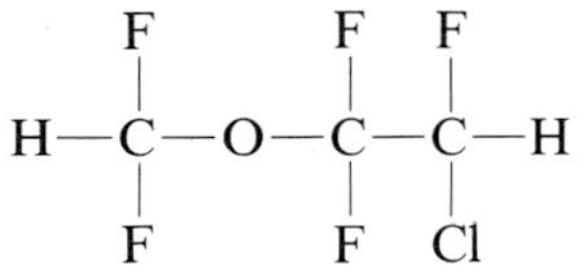

$$\underset{\text{Enflurane}}{H-\overset{\displaystyle \overset{F}{|}}{\underset{\displaystyle \underset{F}{|}}{C}}-O-\overset{\displaystyle \overset{F}{|}}{\underset{\displaystyle \underset{F}{|}}{C}}-\overset{\displaystyle \overset{F}{|}}{\underset{\displaystyle \underset{Cl}{|}}{C}}-H} \qquad \underset{\text{Isoflurane}}{H-\overset{\displaystyle \overset{F}{|}}{\underset{\displaystyle \underset{F}{|}}{C}}-O-\overset{\displaystyle \overset{H}{|}}{\underset{\displaystyle \underset{Cl}{|}}{C}}-\overset{\displaystyle \overset{F}{|}}{\underset{\displaystyle \underset{F}{|}}{C}}-F}$$

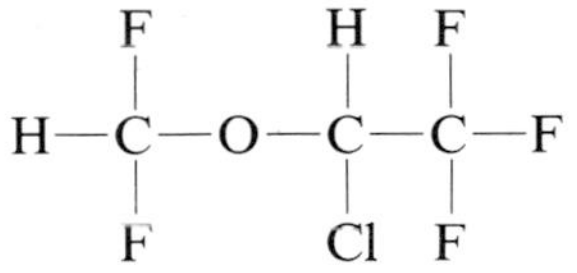

13.7 Phenols

A. Structure and Nomenclature

The characteristic structural feature of a **phenol** is the presence of a hydroxyl group bonded directly to a benzene or other aromatic ring. Following is the structural formula of phenol, the simplest member of this class of compounds:

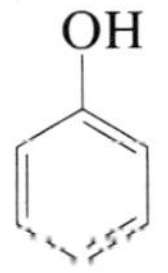

OH

phenol

Other phenols are named either as derivatives of the parent hydrocarbon or by common names.

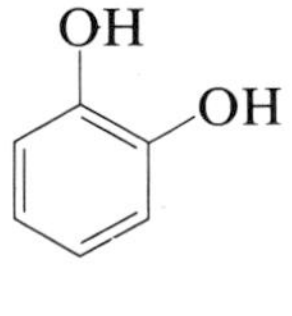

| 1,2-dihydroxy-benzene (catechol) | 1,3-dihydroxy-benzene (resorcinol) | 1,4-dihydroxy-benzene (hydroquinone) | 3-methylphenol (*m*-cresol) |

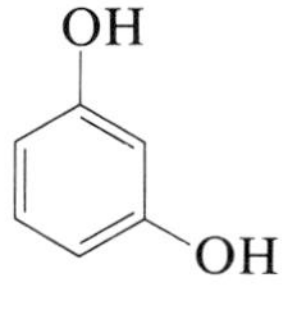

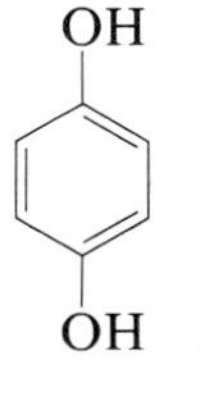

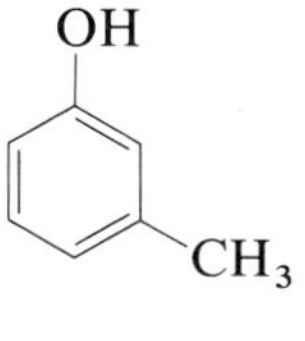

Phenols are widely distributed in nature. Phenol itself and the isomeric cresols (*ortho*-, *meta*-, and *para*-cresol) are found in coal tar and petroleum. Thymol and vanillin are important constituents of thyme and vanilla beans.

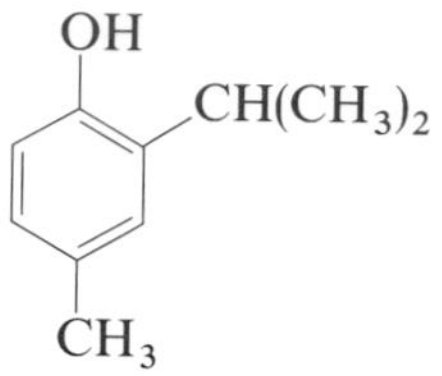

thymol 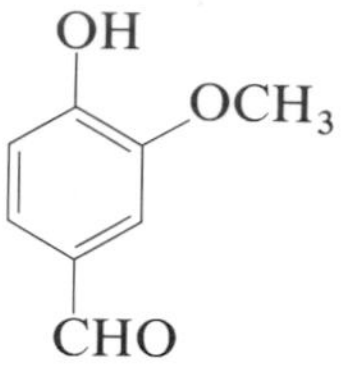   vanillin

Phenol, or carbolic acid, as it was once called, is a low-melting solid that is only slightly soluble in water. In sufficiently high concentrations, it is corrosive to all kinds of cells. In dilute solutions, it has some antiseptic properties, and was used for the first time in the nineteenth century by Joseph Lister for antiseptic surgery. Its medical use is now limited. It has been replaced by antiseptics that are more powerful and have fewer undesirable side effects. Among these is *n*-hexylresorcinol, a substance widely used in household preparations (Sucrets and mouthwashes) as a mild antiseptic and disinfectant:

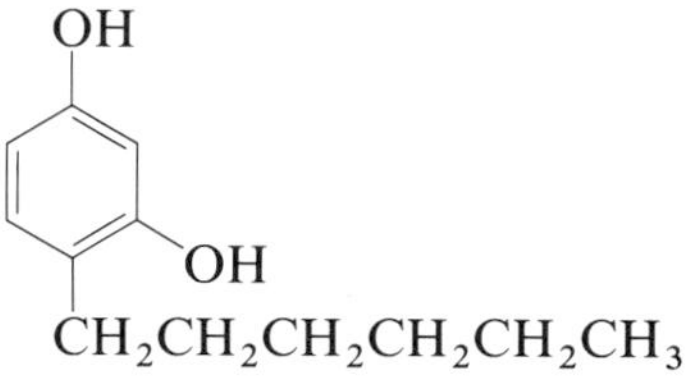

n-hexylresorcinol

B. Acidity of Phenols

Phenols and alcohols both contain a hydroxyl group, —OH. However, phenols are grouped as a separate class of compounds because their chemical properties are different from those of alcohols. One of the most important of these differences is that phenols are significantly more acidic than alcohols. The acid dissociation constant is approximately 10^6 times larger for phenol than for ethanol.

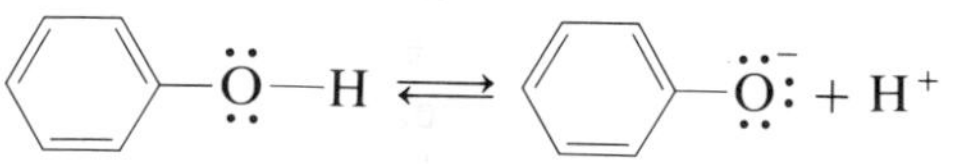

$$K_a = 1.3 \times 10^{-10} \qquad pK_a = 9.89$$

$$CH_3CH_2-\ddot{O}-H \rightleftharpoons CH_3CH_2-\ddot{O}{:}^- + H^+ \qquad K_a = 1.0 \times 10^{-16} \qquad pK_a = 16.0$$

Another way to compare the relative acid strengths of ethanol and phenol is to look at the hydrogen ion concentration and pH of a 0.1M aqueous solution of each (Table 13.2). For comparison, the hydrogen ion concentration and the pH of 0.1M HCl are also included.

Table 13.2
Relative acidities
of 0.1M ethanol,
phenol, and HCl.

Dissociation Equation	[H$^+$]	pH
$CH_3CH_2OH \rightleftharpoons CH_3CH_2O^- + H^+$	10^{-7}	7.0
$C_6H_5OH \rightleftharpoons C_6H_5O^- + H^+$	3.3×10^{-6}	5.4
$HCl \longrightarrow Cl^- + H^+$	0.1	1.0

In aqueous solution, alcohols are neutral substances and the hydrogen ion concentration of 0.1M ethanol is the same as that of pure water. A 0.1M solution of phenol is slightly acidic and has a pH of 5.4. By contrast, 0.1M HCl, a strong acid (completely ionized in aqueous solution), has a pH of 1.0.

Because phenols are weak acids, they react with strong bases such as NaOH, to form salts. However, phenols do not react with weaker bases, such as sodium bicarbonate.

| phenol (stronger acid) | sodium hydroxide (stronger base) | sodium phenoxide (weaker base) | water (weaker acid) |

That phenols are weakly acidic whereas alcohols are neutral provides a very convenient way to separate phenols from water-insoluble alcohols. Suppose that we want to separate phenol from cyclohexanol. Each is only slightly soluble in water, and therefore they can not be separated on the basis of their water solubility. However, they can be separated on the basis of their differences in acidity. First, the mixture of the two is dissolved in diethyl ether or some other water-immiscible solvent. Next, the ether solution is placed in a separatory funnel and shaken with dilute NaOH. Under these conditions, phenol reacts with NaOH and is converted to sodium phenoxide, a water-soluble salt. The upper layer in the separatory funnel is now diethyl ether, containing only dissolved cyclohexanol. The lower aqueous layer contains dissolved sodium phenoxide. The layers are separated and distillation of the ether (bp 35°C) leaves pure cyclohexanol (bp 161°C). Acidification of the aqueous phase with 0.1M HCl or other strong acid converts sodium phenoxide to phenol, which is water-insoluble and can be separated and recovered in pure form. These experimental steps are summarized in the accompanying flow chart.

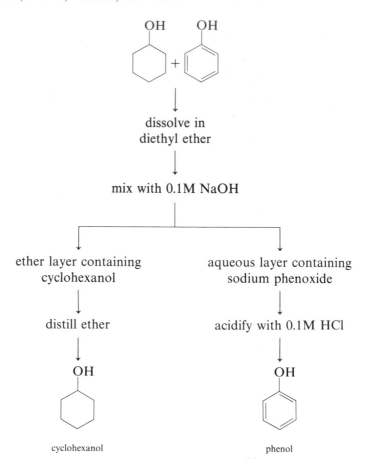

13.8 Thiols and Sulfides

A. Structure

Sulfur analogs of alcohols are called **thiols** (*thi-* from the Greek *theion*, sulfur), or in the older literature, mercaptans. The characteristic structural feature of a thiol is a **sulfhydryl (—SH) group** bonded to a carbon chain. Figure 13.9 shows a Lewis structure and a ball-and-stick representation of methanethiol, CH_3SH, the simplest thiol. The C—S—H bond angle in methanethiol is 100.3°.

B. Nomenclature

In the IUPAC system, thiols are named by selecting as the parent compound the longest chain of carbon atoms that contains the —SH group. To show that the compound is a thiol, the final *-e* in the name of the parent chain is retained and the suffix *-thiol* is added. A number must be used to locate the —SH group on the parent chain.

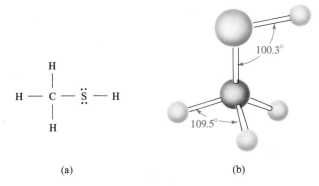

H
|
H — C — $\overset{\cdots}{\underset{\cdots}{S}}$ — H
|
H

(a)

100.3°

109.5°

(b)

Figure 13.9 Structure of methanethiol, CH_3SH: (a) Lewis structure; (b) ball-and-stick model.

In the common system of nomenclature, thiols are known as **mercaptans**. Common names for simple thiols are derived by naming the alkyl groups attached to —SH and then adding the word *mercaptan*. Listed in Figure 13.10 are IUPAC names, and in parentheses, common names, for several low-molecular-weight thiols.

$$CH_3{-}CH_2{-}SH \qquad CH_3{-}CH_2{-}CH_2{-}CH_2{-}SH \qquad CH_3{-}\underset{\underset{CH_3}{|}}{CH}{-}CH_2{-}SH$$

ethanethiol   1-butanethiol   2-methyl-1-propanethiol
(ethyl mercaptan)   (*n*-butyl mercaptan)   (isobutyl mercaptan)

$$CH_3{-}CH_2{-}\underset{\underset{SH}{|}}{CH}{-}CH_3 \qquad HS{-}CH_2{-}CH_2{-}SH$$

2-butanethiol   1,2-ethanedithiol
(*sec*-butyl mercaptan)   (ethylene mercaptan)

Figure 13.10 Names and structural formulas for several low-molecular-weight thiols.

In compounds containing other functional groups of higher priority, the presence of an —SH group is indicated by the prefix *mercapto-*.

$$HS{-}CH_2{-}CH_2{-}OH$$

2-mercaptoethanol

Sulfur analogs of ethers are named by using the word **sulfide** to show the presence of the —S— group. Following are common names of two thioethers:

$$CH_3{-}S{-}CH_3 \qquad CH_3{-}CH_2{-}S{-}\underset{\underset{CH_3}{|}}{CH}{-}CH_3$$

dimethyl sulfide   ethyl isopropyl sulfide

The characteristic structural feature of a **disulfide** is the presence of an —S—S— group. Common names of disulfides are derived by listing the names of the alkyl or aryl groups attached to sulfur and adding the word *disulfide*.

$$CH_3—S—S—CH_3$$

dimethyl disulfide

C. Physical Properties of Thiols

The physical properties of thiols are different from those of alcohols primarily because of the large difference in polarity of the O—H bond compared with the S—H bond. The electronegativities of sulfur and hydrogen are almost identical, and the S—H bond is nonpolar covalent. In comparison, the electronegativity difference between oxygen and hydrogen is 0.9 unit $(3.0 - 2.1)$, and the O—H bond is polar covalent.

$$CH_3—S \overset{\nearrow}{-} H \qquad CH_3 \overset{\delta-}{-} O \overset{\delta+}{\underset{\nearrow}{-}} H$$

a nonpolar covalent bond   a polar covalent bond

Because of the very low polarity of the S—H bond, thiols show little association by hydrogen bonding. Consequently, they have lower boiling points and are less soluble in water and in other polar solvents than alcohols of comparable molecular weights. Table 13.3 gives names and boiling points for several low-molecular-weight thiols. Shown for comparison are boiling points of alcohols of the same number of carbon atoms.

Thiol	bp (°C)	Alcohol	bp (°C)
methanethiol	6	methanol	65
ethanethiol	35	ethanol	78
1-butanethiol	98	1-butanol	117

In Section 13.3, we illustrated the importance of hydrogen bonding in alcohols by comparing the boiling points of ethanol (bp 78°C) and its structural isomer dimethyl ether (bp −24°C). By comparison, the boiling point of ethanethiol is 35°C, and the boiling point of its structural isomer dimethyl sulfide is 37°C.

$$CH_3—CH_2—SH \qquad CH_3—S—CH_3$$

ethanethiol   dimethyl sulfide
(bp 35°C)   (bp 37°C)

That the boiling points of these isomers are almost identical indicates little or no association by hydrogen bonding between thiols in the pure liquid.

The most outstanding physical characteristic of low-molecular-weight thiols is their stench. The scent of skunks is due primarily to two thiols, 3-methyl-1-butanethiol and 2-butene-1-thiol:

$$\begin{array}{c} CH_3 \\ | \\ CH_3CHCH_2CH_2SH \end{array} \qquad CH_3CH{=}CHCH_2SH$$

3-methyl-1-butanethiol   2-butene-1-thiol

Further, traces of low-molecular-weight thiols are added to natural gas (which has no detectable odor) so that gas leaks can be detected by the smell of the thiol.

D. Acidity of Thiols

Hydrogen sulfide is a stronger acid than water.

$$H_2O \rightleftharpoons HO^- + H^+ \qquad pK_a = 15.7$$

$$H_2S \rightleftharpoons HS^- + H^+ \qquad pK_a = 7.04$$

Similarly, thiols are stronger acids than alcohols are. Compare, for example, the acid dissociation constants of ethanol and ethanethiol in dilute aqueous solution.

$$CH_3{-}CH_2{-}OH \rightleftharpoons CH_3{-}CH_2{-}O^- + H^+ \qquad pK_a = 15.9$$

$$CH_3{-}CH_2{-}SH \rightleftharpoons CH_3\ CH_2\ S^- + H^+ \qquad pK_a = 8.5$$

Thiols are sufficiently strong acids that when they are dissolved in aqueous sodium hydroxide, they are converted completely to alkylsulfide salts:

$$CH_3{-}CH_2{-}SH + Na^+OH^- \longrightarrow CH_3{-}CH_2{-}S^-Na^+ + H{-}OH$$

(stronger acid)   (stronger base)   sodium ethylsulfide (weaker base)   (weaker acid)

To name salts of thiols, give the name of the cation first and then the name of the alkyl group to which is attached the suffix *-sulfide*. For example, the sodium salt derived from ethanethiol is named sodium ethylsulfide.

Like hydrogen sulfide and hydrosulfide salts, thiols form water insoluble salts with most heavy metals:

$$Hg^{2+} + 2RSH \longrightarrow Hg(SR)_2 + 2H^+$$

In fact, the common name of this class of sulfur-containing compounds is derived from the Latin *mercurium captans*, which means mercury-capturing. Reaction with Pb(II) is often used as a qualitative test for the presence of a sulfhydryl group. Treatment of a thiol with a saturated solution of lead(II) acetate, $Pb(OAc)_2$, usually gives a yellow solid and is a positive test for the presence of a thiol.

$$R{-}SH + Pb^{2+} \longrightarrow Pb(S{-}R)_2 + 2H^+$$

(yellow precipitate)

E. Oxidation of Thiols and Sulfides

Many of the chemical properties of thiols and sulfides are related to the fact that a divalent sulfur atom is easily oxidized to several higher oxidation states. Thiols are oxidized by mild oxidizing agents such as iodine, I_2, to **disulfides**:

$$R{-}S{-}H + H{-}S{-}R + I_2 \longrightarrow R{-}S{-}S{-}R + 2H^+ + 2I^-$$

$$\text{thiols} \qquad\qquad\qquad \text{a disulfide}$$

They are also oxidized to disulfides by molecular oxygen. In fact, thiols are so susceptible to oxidation that they must be protected from contact with air during storage.

$$R{-}S{-}H + H{-}S{-}R + \tfrac{1}{2}O_2 \longrightarrow R{-}S{-}S{-}R + H_2O$$

Disulfide bonds are an important structural feature of many biomolecules, including proteins (Chapter 21).

Oxidation of sulfides of the type R—S—R gives molecules called sulfoxides, probably the most familiar of which is dimethyl sulfoxide, abbreviated DMSO. This is a colorless, odorless liquid with a slightly bitter taste and a sweet after-taste. It solidifies at 18.5°C and boils at 189°C. Because DMSO is a byproduct of wood-pulp processing, its principal suppliers are companies associated with the paper industry. Dimethyl sulfoxide is also manufactured by air oxidation of dimethyl sulfide in the presence of oxides of nitrogen:

$$2CH_3{-}S{-}CH_3 + O_2 \xrightarrow{\text{oxides of nitrogen}} 2CH_3{-}\overset{\overset{\textstyle O}{\|}}{S}{-}CH_3$$

$$\text{dimethyl sulfide} \qquad\qquad\qquad \text{dimethyl sulfoxide}$$

It is a polar liquid, and an excellent solvent for polar organic molecules.

Key Terms and Concepts

absolute ethanol (13.5C)

acidity of phenols (13.7B)

acidity of thiols (13.8D)

alcohol (introduction and 13.2)

dehydration of alcohols (13.4A)

diol (13.2A)

dipole-dipole interaction (13.3A)

disulfide (13.8B)

ether (13.2B and 13.6)

ethers and anesthesia (13.6B)

glycol (13.2A)

hydrogen bonding (13.3A)

hydroxyl group (13.1)

mercaptan (13.8B)

nomenclature of alcohols (13.2A)

nomenclature of ethers (13.2B)

nomenclature of sulfides (13.8B)

nomenclature of thiols (13.8B)

oxidation of alcohols (13.4B)

oxidation of thiols (13.8E)

phenol (introduction and 13.7)   sulfide (13.8B)
primary alcohol (13.2A)   tertiary alcohol (13.2A)
secondary alcohol (13.2A)   thiol (13.8A)
sulfhydryl group (13.8A)   triol (13.2A)

Key Reactions

1. Acid-catalyzed dehydration of alcohols to alkenes (Section 13.4A).
2. Oxidation of primary alcohols to aldehydes (Section 13.4B).
3. Oxidation of primary alcohols to carboxylic acids (Section 13.4B).
4. Oxidation of secondary alcohols to ketones (Section 13.4B).
5. Phenols are weak acids and ionize in aqueous solution (Section 13.7B).
6. Reaction of phenols with NaOH and other strong bases to form water-soluble salts (Section 13.7B).
7. Thiols are weak acids and ionize in aqueous solution (Section 13.8D).
8. Reaction of thiols with NaOH and other strong bases to form water-soluble salts (Section 13.8D).
9. Reaction of thiols with Hg(II) and other heavy metal ions to form water-insoluble salts (Section 13.8D).
10. Oxidation of thiols by O_2 or I_2 to disulfides (Section 13.8E).

Problems

Structure and nomenclature of alcohols and ethers (Sections 13.1 and 13.2)

13.8   Name the following compounds.

a. $CH_3CH_2CH_2OH$

b. $HOCH_2CH_2CH_2CH_2OH$

c. $CH_2{=}\overset{\underset{\displaystyle |}{CH_3}}{C}CH_2CH_2OH$

d. $CH_3\overset{\underset{\displaystyle |}{CH_3}}{C}HO\overset{\underset{\displaystyle |}{CH_3}}{C}HCH_3$

e. $CH_3OCH_2CH_2OH$

f. $CH_3(CH_2)_8CH_2OH$

g. (cyclohexene ring with OCH₃)

h. (cyclohexane ring with OH and OH)

i. (benzene ring)$-O\overset{\underset{\displaystyle |}{CH_3}}{C}HCH_3$

j. (benzene ring)$-CH_2CH_2OH$

k. $CH_3\overset{\underset{\displaystyle |}{CH_3}}{C}H\underset{\underset{\displaystyle OH}{|}}{C}HCH_3$

l. $CH_3\underset{\underset{\displaystyle HO}{|}}{C}H\underset{\underset{\displaystyle OH}{|}}{C}HCH_3$

$$\underset{\substack{\text{OH}\\|}}{\text{m. CH}_3\text{CHCH}_2\text{Cl}} \qquad\qquad \underset{\substack{\text{CH}_3\\|\\\text{CH}_3\text{CH}_2}}{\text{n. CH}_3\text{CH}_2\text{CCH}_2\text{OH}}$$

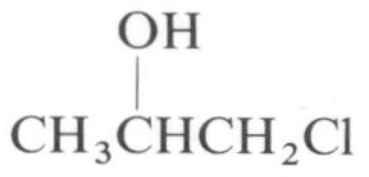

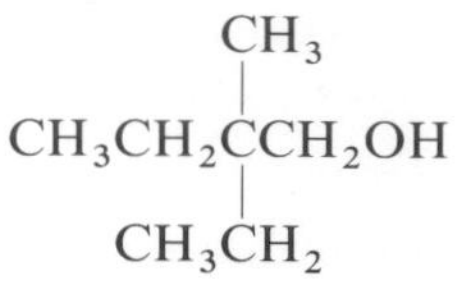

13.9   Write structural formulas for these compounds:

   a. isopropyl methyl ether   **b.** propylene glycol
   c. 2-methyl-2-propylpropane-1,3-diol **d.** 1-chloro-2-hexanol
   e. 5-methyl-2-hexanol   **f.** 2,5-dimethylcyclohexanol
   g. 2,2-dimethyl-1-propanol   **h.** *tert*-butyl alcohol
   i. methyl cyclopropyl ether   **j.** ethylene glycol
   k. methyl phenyl ether   **l.** *trans*-2-ethylcyclohexanol

13.10 Name and draw structural formulas for the eight isomeric alcohols of molecular formula $C_5H_{12}O$. Classify each as primary, secondary, or tertiary.

13.11 Name and draw structural formulas for the six isomeric ethers of molecular formula $C_5H_{12}O$.

Physical properties of alcohols and ethers (Section 13.3)

13.12 In the following compounds: (1) Circle each hydrogen atom that is capable of hydrogen bonding. (2) Put a square around each atom capable of hydrogen bonding to a partially positive hydrogen atom.

a. 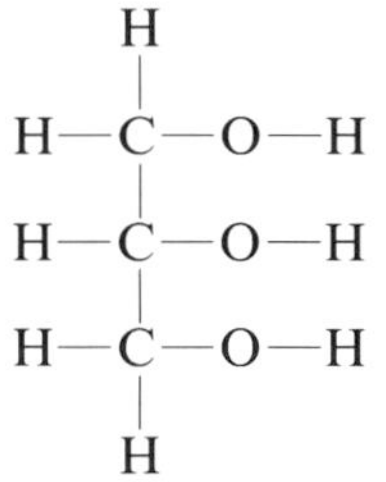
$$\begin{array}{c}\text{H}\\|\\\text{H}-\text{C}-\text{O}-\text{H}\\|\\\text{H}-\text{C}-\text{O}-\text{H}\\|\\\text{H}-\text{C}-\text{O}-\text{H}\\|\\\text{H}\end{array}$$

b.
$$\begin{array}{ccc}\text{H}&&\text{H}\\|&&|\\\text{H}-\text{O}-\text{C}&-&\text{C}-\text{S}-\text{H}\\|&&|\\\text{H}&&\text{H}\end{array}$$

c.
$$\begin{array}{c}\text{H}\\|\\\text{H}-\text{C}-\!\!\bigcirc\!\!-\text{O}-\text{H}\\|\\\text{H}\end{array}$$

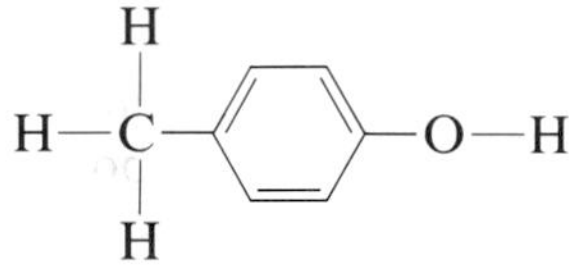

d. 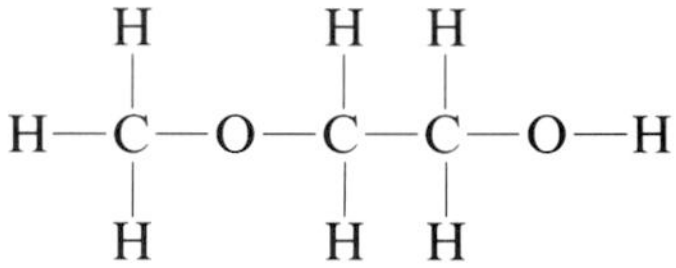
$$\begin{array}{ccc}\text{H}&\text{H}&\text{H}\\|&|&|\\\text{H}-\text{C}-\text{O}-\text{C}&-&\text{C}-\text{O}-\text{H}\\|&|&|\\\text{H}&\text{H}&\text{H}\end{array}$$

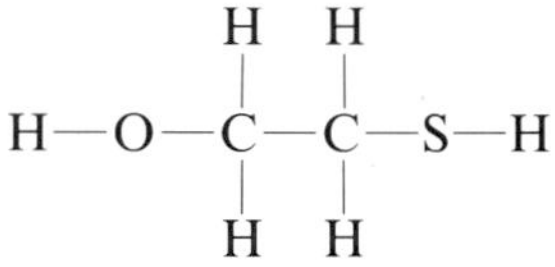

13.13 Arrange the compounds of each of the sets in order of decreasing boiling points. Explain your reasoning.

   a. $CH_3CH_2CH_3$ $CH_3CH_2CH_2CH_2CH_2CH_2CH_3$
        $CH_3CH_2CH_2CH_2CH_3$
   b. N_2H_4 H_2O_2 CH_3CH_3
   c. CH_3CO_2H CH_3CH_2OH CH_3OCH_3
   d. 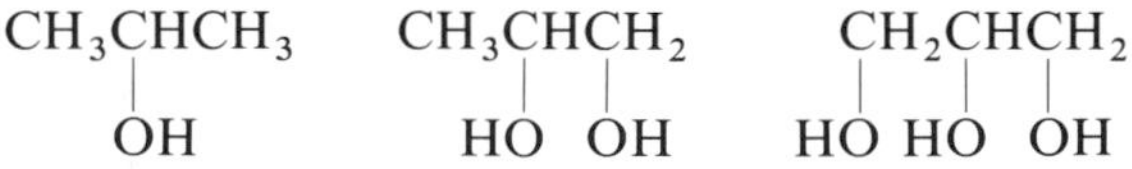 $\underset{\substack{|\\\text{OH}}}{\text{CH}_3\text{CHCH}_3}$ $\underset{\substack{|\ \ |\\\text{HO OH}}}{\text{CH}_3\text{CHCH}_2}$ $\underset{\substack{|\ \ |\ \ |\\\text{HO HO OH}}}{\text{CH}_2\text{CHCH}_2}$

13.14 Arrange the compounds in each set in order of decreasing solubility in water. Explain your reasoning.

a. ethanol, butane, diethyl ether

b. 1-hexanol, 1,2-hexanediol, hexane

13.15 Account for the fact that the boiling point of 1-butanol is higher than that of its structural isomer, diethyl ether.

$$CH_3CH_2CH_2CH_2OH \qquad CH_3CH_2OCH_2CH_3$$

1-butanol
(bp 117°C)

diethyl ether
(bp 35°C)

13.16 Why does ethanol (mw 46, bp 78°C) have a boiling point over 43° higher than that of ethanethiol (mw 62, bp 35°C)?

$$CH_3CH_2OH \qquad CH_3CH_2SH$$

ethanol
(bp 78°C)

ethanethiol
(bp 35°C)

13.17 Propanoic acid and methyl acetate are structural isomers. Both are liquid at room temperature. The boiling point of one of these liquids is 57°C; of the other, 141°C.

$$\overset{\displaystyle O}{\overset{\displaystyle \|}{CH_3CH_2C}}OH \qquad \overset{\displaystyle O}{\overset{\displaystyle \|}{CH_3C}}OCH_3$$

propanoic acid

methyl acetate

a. Which compound has the boiling point of 141°C? Of 57°C? Explain your reasoning.

b. Which compound is more soluble in water? Explain your reasoning.

13.18 Compounds that contain NH bonds show association by hydrogen bonding. Do you expect this association to be stronger or weaker than that in compounds containing OH bonds? (*Hint*: Remember the table of relative electronegativities, Figure 4.3.)

Preparation of alcohols (Review Section 12.5C)

13.19 Write structural formulas for the alkenes of the given molecular formula that undergo acid-catalyzed hydration to give the alcohol shown as the major product.

a. $C_3H_6 + H_2O \xrightarrow{H_2SO_4} CH_3\overset{\displaystyle OH}{\overset{\displaystyle |}{C}}HCH_3$

(1 alkene)

b. $C_4H_8 + H_2O \xrightarrow{H_2SO_4} CH_3\overset{\displaystyle CH_3}{\underset{\displaystyle CH_3}{\overset{\displaystyle |}{\underset{\displaystyle |}{C}}}}OH$

(1 alkene)

$$\text{c.} \quad C_4H_8 + H_2O \xrightarrow{H_2SO_4} CH_3\overset{\overset{\displaystyle OH}{|}}{C}HCH_2CH_3$$

(3 alkenes)

$$\text{d.} \quad C_7H_{12} + H_2O \xrightarrow{H_2SO_4}$$

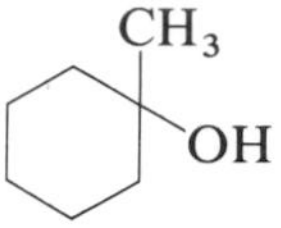

(2 alkenes)

13.20   Propose a mechanism for the acid-catalyzed hydration

$$CH_3\overset{\overset{\displaystyle CH_3}{|}}{C}=CHCH_3 + H_2O \xrightarrow{H_2SO_4} CH_3\overset{\overset{\displaystyle CH_3}{|}}{\underset{\underset{\displaystyle OH}{|}}{C}}CH_2CH_3$$

Reactions of
alcohols
(Section 13.4)

13.21   Draw structural formulas for the alkene or alkenes formed from acid-catalyzed dehydration of the following alcohols. Where two or more alkenes are formed, predict which is the major product and which the minor product.

a. $CH_3CH_2CH_2OH$

b. $CH_3CH_2\overset{\overset{\displaystyle}{|}}{C}HCH_3$ with OH below

c. (cyclopentane with CH$_3$ and OH)

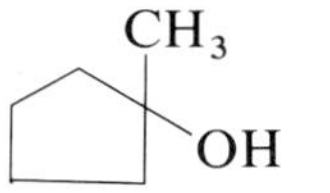

d. 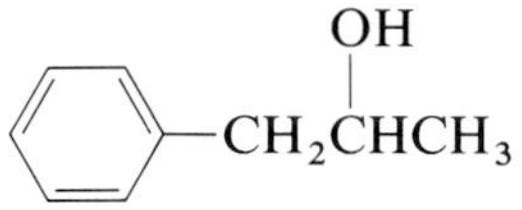 (benzene)$-CH_2\overset{\overset{\displaystyle OH}{|}}{C}HCH_3$

e. $HOCH_2CH_2CH_2CH_2OH$

f. $CH_3\overset{\overset{\displaystyle CH_3}{|}}{\underset{\underset{\displaystyle OH}{|}}{C}}CH_2CH_3$

13.22   Propose a mechanism for the acid-catalyzed dehydration of cyclohexanol to give cyclohexene and water.

13.23   Predict the relative ease with which the following alcohols undergo acid-catalyzed dehydration. Draw a structural formula for the major products of each dehydration.

a. $CH_3\overset{\overset{\displaystyle OH}{|}}{C}H\overset{\overset{\displaystyle}{|}}{C}HCH_2CH_3$ with CH$_3$ below

b. $CH_3CH_2\overset{\overset{\displaystyle OH}{|}}{\underset{\underset{\displaystyle CH_3}{|}}{C}}CH_2CH_3$

c. $HOCH_2CH_2\overset{\overset{\displaystyle}{|}}{C}HCH_2CH_3$ with CH$_3$ below

13.24 One of the reactions in the metabolism of glucose is the isomerization of citric acid to isocitric acid. The isomerization is catalyzed by the enzyme aconitase.

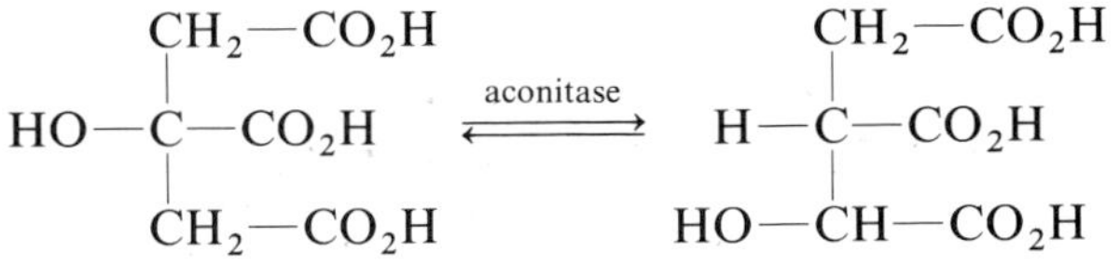

$$
\begin{array}{ccc}
\text{CH}_2\text{—CO}_2\text{H} & & \text{CH}_2\text{—CO}_2\text{H} \\
| & \xrightleftharpoons{\text{aconitase}} & | \\
\text{HO—C—CO}_2\text{H} & & \text{H—C—CO}_2\text{H} \\
| & & | \\
\text{CH}_2\text{—CO}_2\text{H} & & \text{HO—CH—CO}_2\text{H}
\end{array}
$$

citric acid   isocitric acid

Propose a reasonable mechanism to account for this isomerization. (*Hint:* Within its structure, aconitase has groups that can function as acids.)

13.25 Write structural formulas for the major organic product or products of the following oxidations.

a. 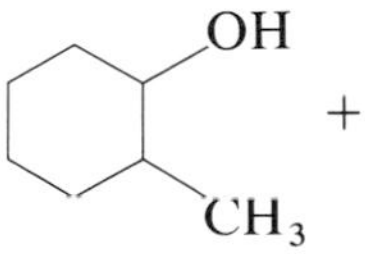 (cyclohexane with OH and CH$_3$) $+\ \text{Cr}_2\text{O}_7^{2-}\ \xrightarrow[\text{heat}]{\text{H}^+}$

b. $\text{HOCH}_2\text{CH}_2\text{CH}_2\text{CH}_2\text{CH}_2\text{CH}_2\text{OH} + \text{Cr}_2\text{O}_7^{2-}\ \xrightarrow[\text{heat}]{\text{H}^+}$

c. $\text{CH}_3\text{CH}_2\text{OH} + \text{O}_2$ (excess) $\xrightarrow{\text{(combustion)}}$

d. 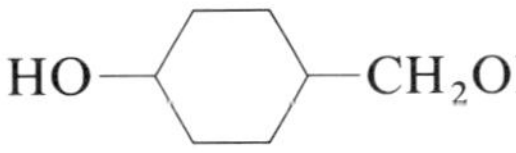 $\text{HO—}\langle\rangle\text{—CH}_2\text{OH} + \text{Cr}_2\text{O}_7^{2-}\ \xrightarrow[\text{heat}]{\text{H}^+}$

e. 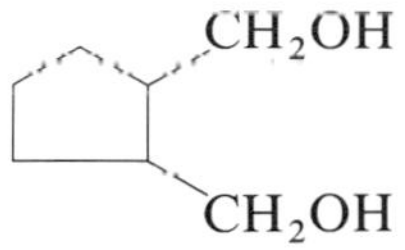 (cyclopentane with CH$_2$OH and CH$_2$OH) $+\ \text{Cr}_2\text{O}_7^{2-}\ \xrightarrow[\text{heat}]{\text{H}^+}$

13.26 The following reactions are important in the metabolism of either fats or carbohydrates. State which are oxidations, which reductions, and which neither oxidation nor reduction.

a. $\text{CH}_3(\text{CH}_2)_{12}\text{CH}_2\text{CH}_2\text{CO}_2\text{H} \longrightarrow \text{CH}_3(\text{CH}_2)_{12}\text{CH}=\text{CHCO}_2\text{H}$

b. $\text{CH}_3(\text{CH}_2)_{12}\text{CH}=\text{CHCO}_2\text{H} \longrightarrow \text{CH}_3(\text{CH}_2)_{12}\overset{\overset{\text{OH}}{|}}{\text{CH}}\text{CH}_2\text{CO}_2\text{H}$

c. 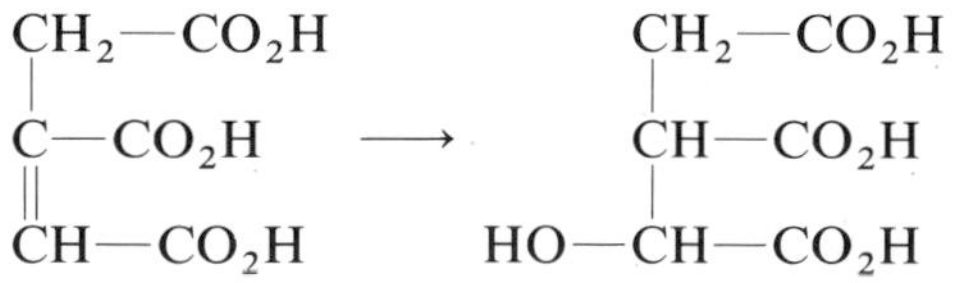
$$
\begin{array}{ccc}
\text{CH}_2\text{—CO}_2\text{H} & & \text{CH}_2\text{—CO}_2\text{H} \\
| & & | \\
\text{C—CO}_2\text{H} & \longrightarrow & \text{CH—CO}_2\text{H} \\
\| & & | \\
\text{CH—CO}_2\text{H} & & \text{HO—CH—CO}_2\text{H}
\end{array}
$$

aconitic acid   isocitric acid

d.

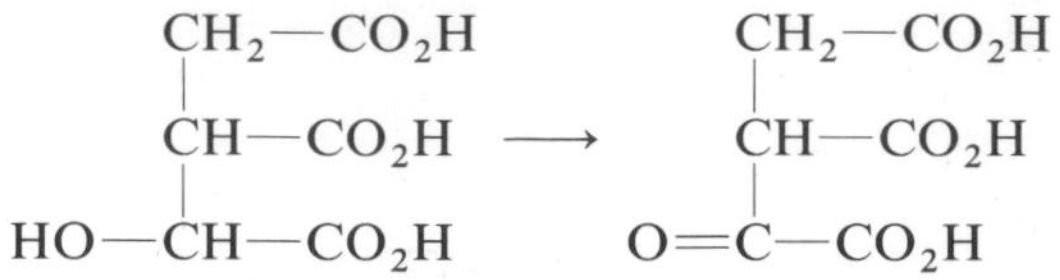

$$\begin{array}{cc}
CH_2-CO_2H & CH_2-CO_2H \\
| & | \\
CH-CO_2H & \longrightarrow & CH-CO_2H \\
| & | \\
HO-CH-CO_2H & O=C-CO_2H \\
\text{isocitric acid} & \text{oxalosuccinic acid}
\end{array}$$

e.

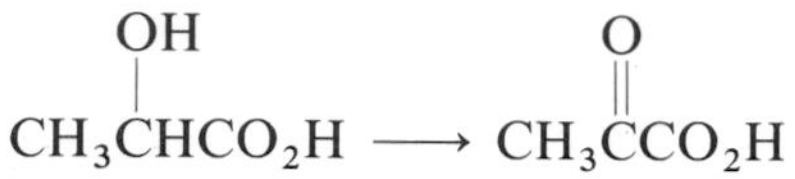

$$\begin{array}{cc}
OH & O \\
| & \parallel \\
CH_3CHCO_2H & \longrightarrow & CH_3CCO_2H \\
\text{lactic acid} & \text{pyruvic acid}
\end{array}$$

13.27 The following conversions can be carried out in one step. Show the reagent you would use to bring about each conversion.

a.

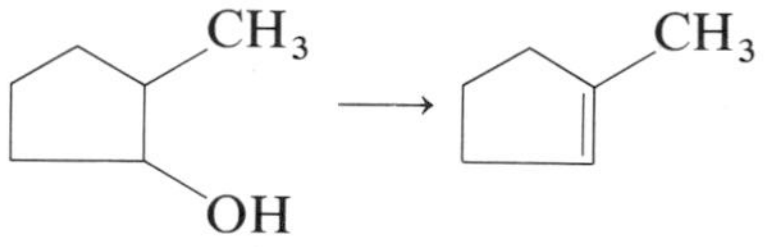

b.

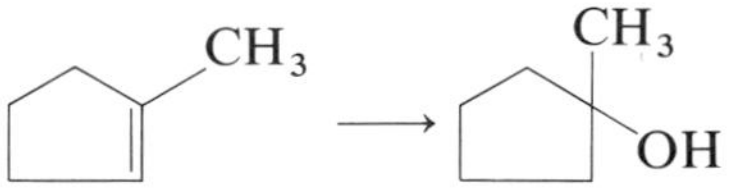

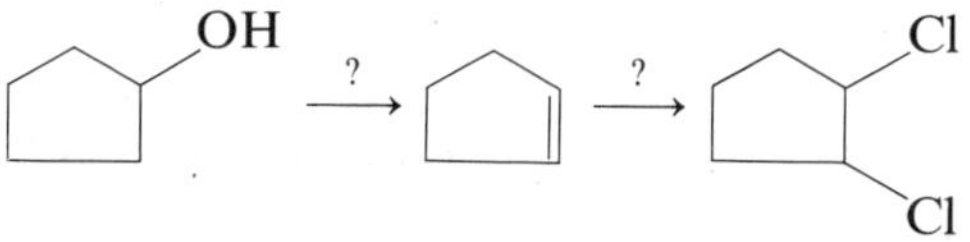

c.

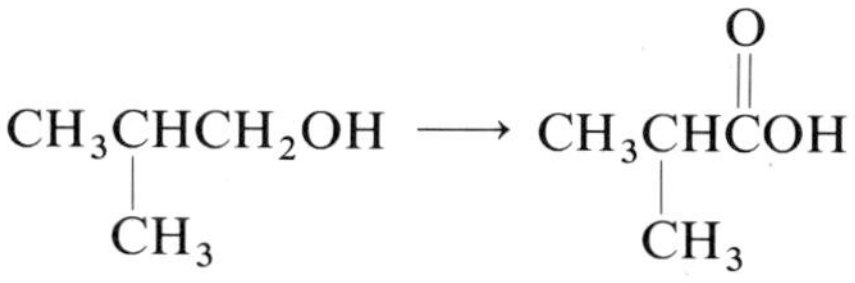

$$\begin{array}{cc}
 & O \\
 & \parallel \\
CH_3CHCH_2OH & \longrightarrow & CH_3CHCOH \\
| & | \\
CH_3 & CH_3
\end{array}$$

d.

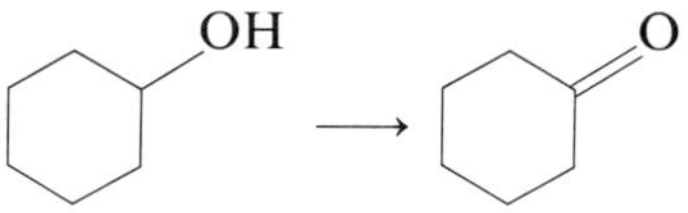

e.

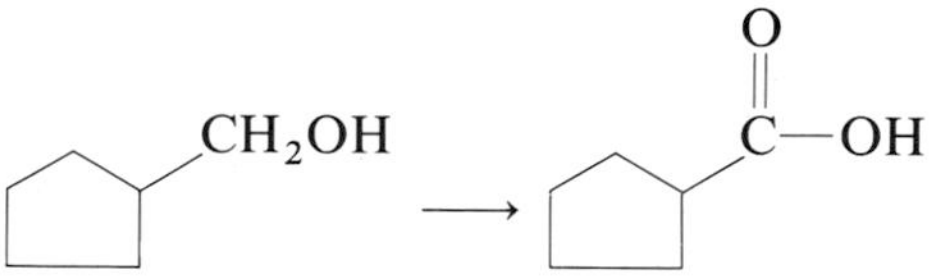

13.28 Following is a series of conversions in which a starting material is converted to the indicated product in two steps. State the reagent or reagents you would use to bring about each conversion.

a.

$$CH_3CH=CH_2 \xrightarrow{?} \overset{OH}{\underset{|}{CH_3CHCH_3}} \xrightarrow{?} \overset{O}{\overset{\parallel}{CH_3CCH_3}}$$

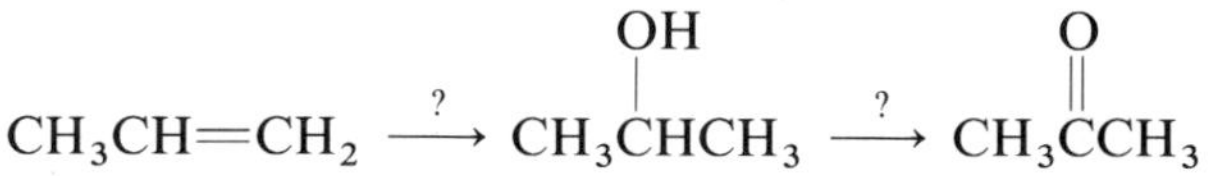

b.

c.

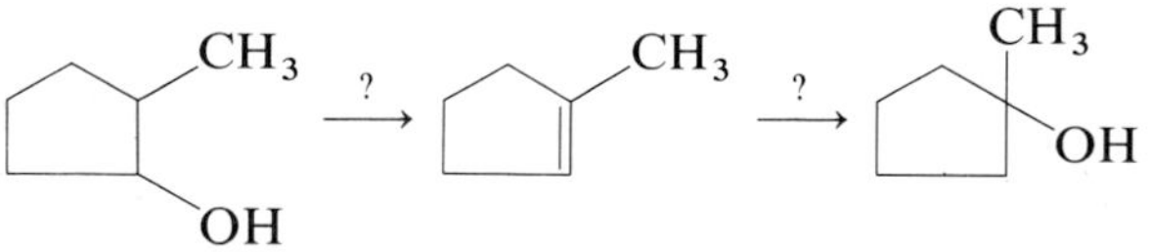

d.

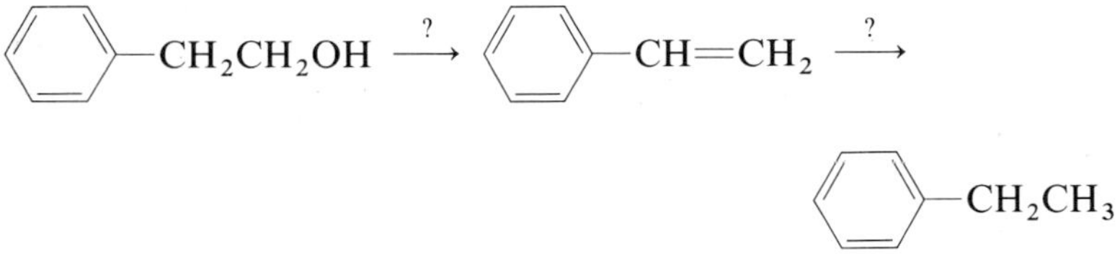

13.29 The following conversions can be carried out in two steps. Show reagents you would use and the structural formula of the intermediate formed in each conversion.

a. 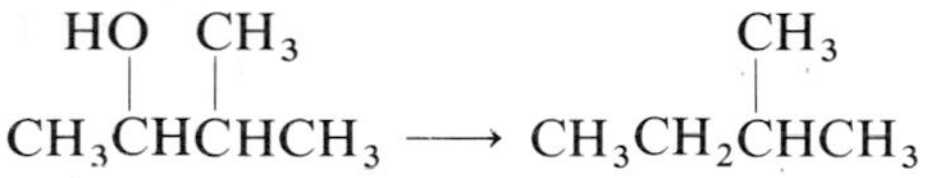
$$\underset{\overset{|}{\text{HO}}\ \overset{|}{\text{CH}_3}}{\text{CH}_3\text{CHCHCH}_3} \longrightarrow \underset{\overset{|}{\text{CH}_3}}{\text{CH}_3\text{CH}_2\text{CHCH}_3}$$

b. 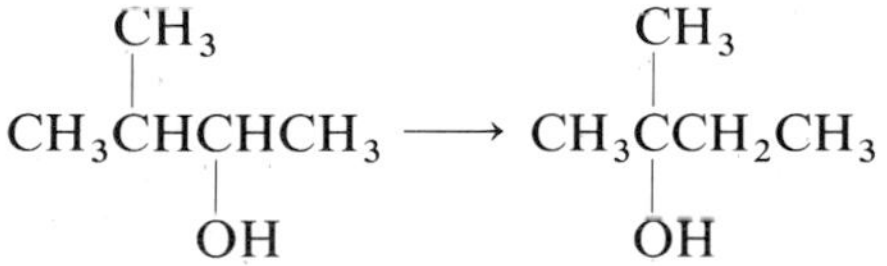
$$\underset{\overset{|}{\text{CH}_3}}{\text{CH}_3\text{CHCHCH}_3}\underset{\overset{|}{\text{OH}}}{} \longrightarrow \underset{\overset{|}{\text{CH}_3}}{\text{CH}_3\text{CCH}_2\text{CH}_3}\underset{\overset{|}{\text{OH}}}{}$$

c. 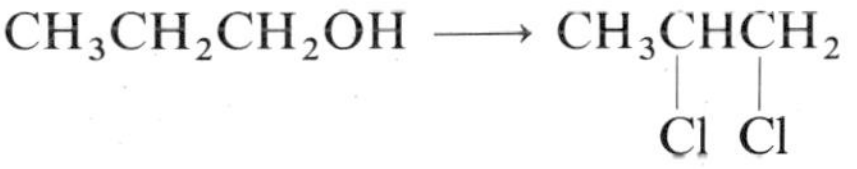
$$\text{CH}_3\text{CH}_2\text{CH}_2\text{OH} \longrightarrow \underset{\overset{|\ \ |}{\text{Cl Cl}}}{\text{CH}_3\text{CHCH}_2}$$

d.

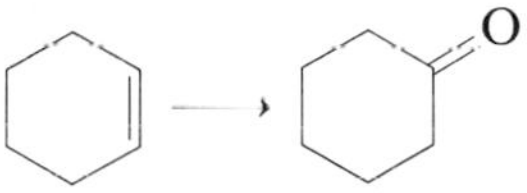

Phenols
(Section 13.7)

13.30 Name the following compounds.

a. 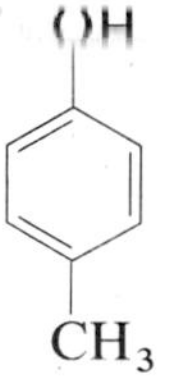   **b.** 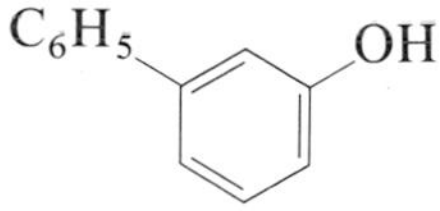   **c.**

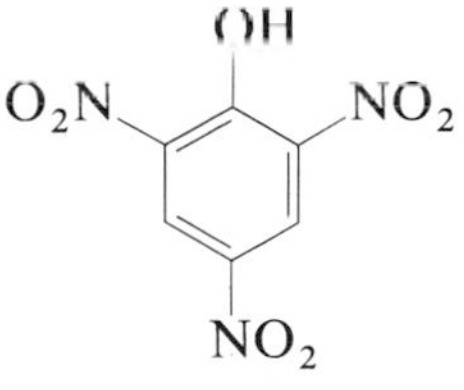

13.31 Write structural formulas for these compounds:
a. 2,4-dimethoxyphenol   **b.** sodium phenoxide
c. 2-isopropyl-4-methylphenol   **d.** *m*-cresol

13.32 Following is the structural formula of a compound known by the common name butylated hydroxytoluene (BHT). This substance is used as a preservative in food and animal feed and also as an antioxidant in soaps and petroleum products.

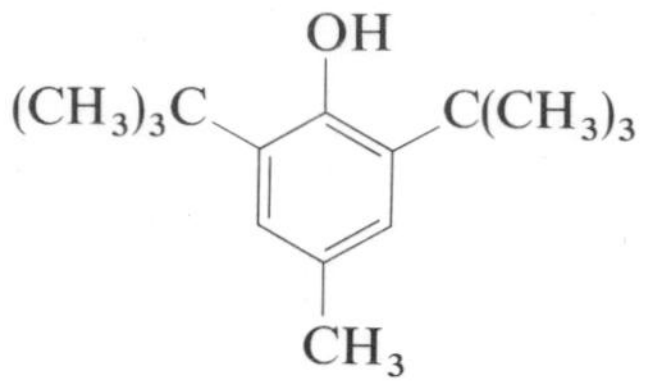

butylated hydroxytoluene
(BHT)

a. Write the IUPAC name of BHT. (*Hint:* Name it as a trisubstituted phenol.)

b. It is common to add 0.0001% BHT to anhydrous diethyl ether as an antioxidant. Calculate the number of milligrams of BHT in 1 L of diethyl ether.

c. The molecular weight of BHT is 220.3 g/mol. Calculate the number of moles of BHT in 1 pt of stabilized diethyl ether.

d. Another common antioxidant is butylated hydroxyanisole (BHA). Knowing what you do about the structure of BHT, propose a structural formula for BHA.

13.33 Identify all functional groups in the following compounds:

a.

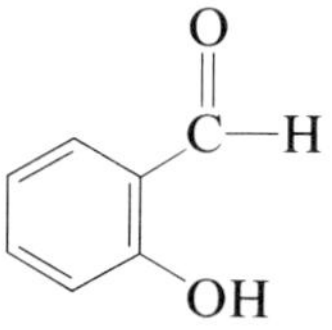

salicylaldehyde

b.

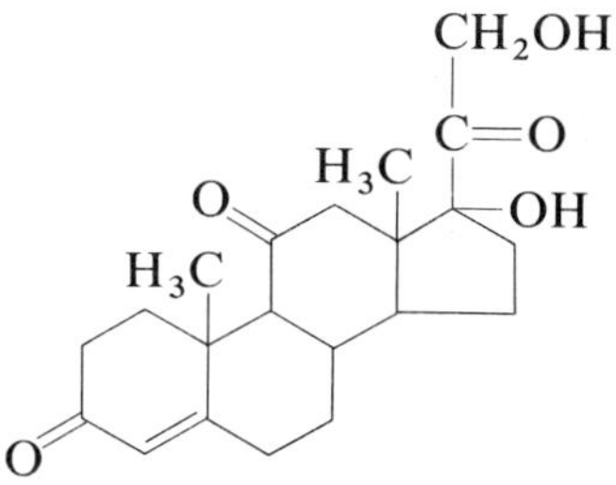

cortisone

c.

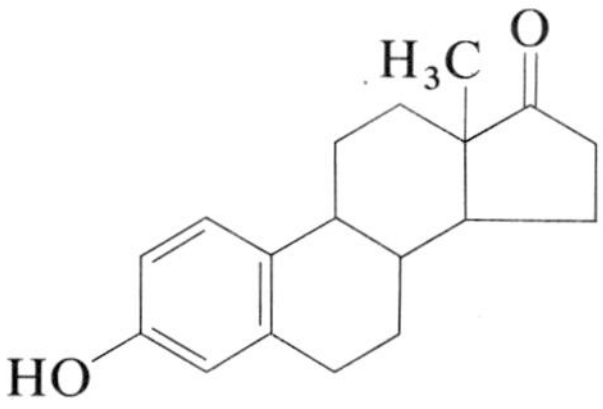

estrone
(a female sex hormone)

d.

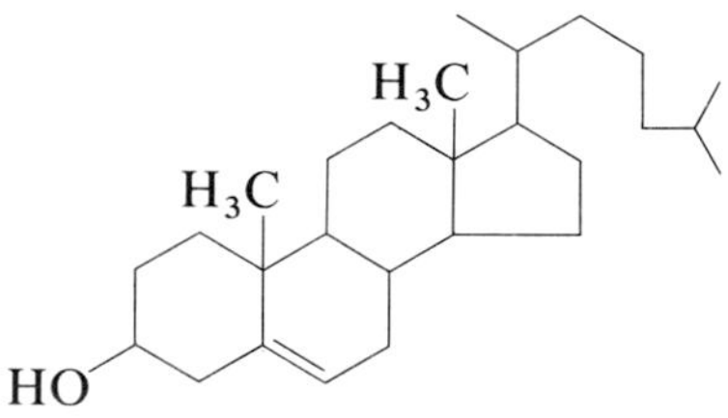

cholesterol

e.

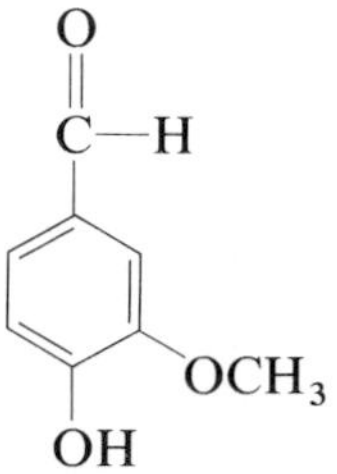

vanillin

13.34 Complete the reactions. Where you predict no reaction, write N.R.

a. 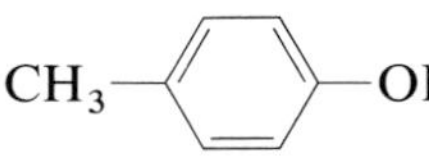 CH$_3$—⟨benzene⟩—OH + NaOH $\longrightarrow$

b. 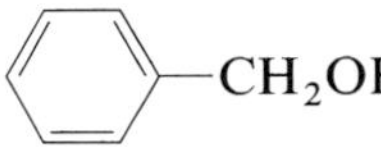 ⟨benzene⟩—CH$_2$OH + NaOH $\longrightarrow$

13.35 Show how you could distinguish between the following pairs of compounds by a simple chemical test. In each case, tell what test you would perform and what you would expect to observe, and write an equation for each positive test.

a. 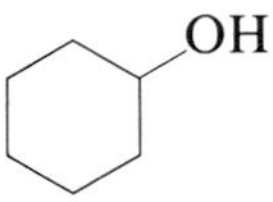 ⟨cyclohexane-OH⟩   and   ⟨benzene-OH⟩

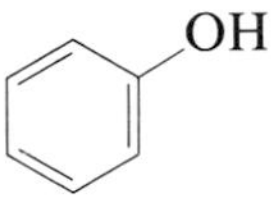

b.  ⟨cyclohexane⟩   and   ⟨cyclohexane-OH⟩

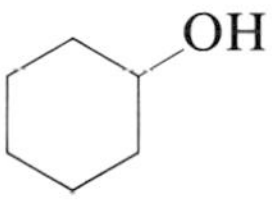

c.  ⟨cyclohexadiene⟩   and   ⟨cyclohexene⟩

d. 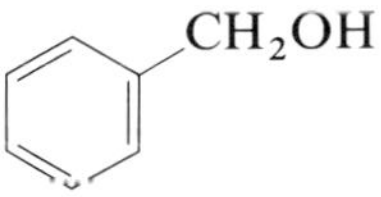 ⟨benzene-CH$_2$OH⟩   and   ⟨benzene with CH$_3$ and OH⟩

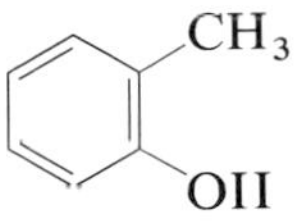

Thiols,
sulfides, and
disulfides
(Section 13.8)

13.36 Name the compounds:

a. CH$_3$CH$_2$SH

b. CH$_3$CHCH$_2$CH$_2$SH
     |
     CH$_3$

c. CH$_3$\,C=C\,H with H and CH$_2$SH

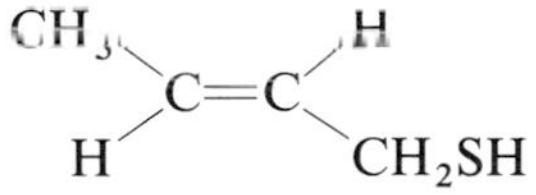

d. HOCH$_2$CH$_2$SH

13.37 Draw structural formulas for these compounds:
a. 2-pentanethiol   b. cyclopentanethiol
c. 1,2-ethanedithiol   d. diisobutyl sulfide
e. diisobutyl disulfide   f. 2,3-dimercapto-1-propanol

13.38 Write a balanced half-reaction for the conversion of two molecules of a thiol to a disulfide, and show that this conversion is a two-electron oxidation.

13.39 Draw structural formulas for the major organic products of the following reactions:

a. CH$_3$(CH$_2$)$_6$CH$_2$SH + NaOH $\longrightarrow$

b. $HSCH_2CH_2CH_2SH + \frac{1}{2}O_2 \longrightarrow$

c. $CH_3CH{=}CHCH_2CH_2SH + H_2 \xrightarrow{\text{Pt}}$

13.40 Penicillamine can be used to treat lead poisoning. Write an equation for the reaction of penicillamine with Pb^{2+} and explain how penicillamine might be used to counteract lead poisoning.

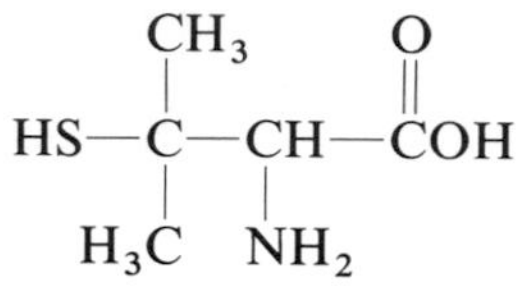

penicillamine

13.41 One treatment for mercury poisoning uses 2,3-dimercapto-1-propanol, a substance that forms a water-soluble complex with Hg(II) ion, which is then excreted in the urine. Draw a structural formula for this water-soluble complex.

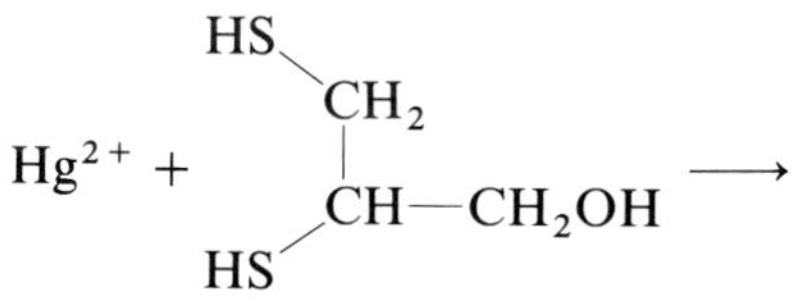

2,3-dimercapto-1-propanol

Amines

14.1 Structure, Classification, and Nomenclature

Amines are derivatives of ammonia in which one or more hydrogens are replaced by alkyl or aromatic groups. The most important chemical property of amines is their basicity. As we have seen, carbon, hydrogen, and oxygen are the three most common elements in organic compounds. Because of the wide distribution of amines in the biological world, nitrogen is the fourth most common component of organic materials.

A. Classification

Amines are classified as primary, secondary, or tertiary, depending on the number of carbon atoms bonded to nitrogen. In a **primary amine**, one hydrogen of ammonia is replaced by carbon. In a **secondary amine**, two hydrogens are replaced by carbons; and in a **tertiary amine**, three hydrogens are replaced by carbons. Following are structural formulas for a primary, a secondary, and a tertiary amine:

$$
\begin{array}{cccc}
\text{H} & \text{H} & \text{H} & \text{CH}_3 \\
| & | & | & | \\
\text{H—N:} & \text{CH}_3\text{—N:} & \text{CH}_3\text{—N:} & \text{CH}_3\text{—N:} \\
| & | & | & | \\
\text{H} & \text{H} & \text{CH}_3 & \text{CH}_3 \\
\text{ammonia} & \text{methylamine} & \text{dimethylamine} & \text{trimethylamine} \\
 & \text{(a 1° amine)} & \text{(a 2° amine)} & \text{(a 3° amine)}
\end{array}
$$

Alcohols are also classified as primary, secondary, or tertiary (Section 13.2A) but the basis for classification is different from that for amines. Classification of alcohols depends on the number of carbon atoms attached to the carbon bearing the —OH group.

$$CH_3 - \overset{\overset{\displaystyle CH_3}{|}}{\underset{\underset{\displaystyle CH_3}{|}}{C}} \overset{\curvearrowleft}{-} OH$$

This is a tertiary carbon

a tertiary alcohol

$$CH_3 - \overset{\overset{\displaystyle CH_3}{|}}{\underset{\underset{\displaystyle CH_3}{|}}{C}} \overset{\curvearrowleft}{-} NH_2$$

Only one carbon attached directly to nitrogen

a primary amine

Amines are further divided into aliphatic and aromatic amines. In aliphatic amines, all the carbons attached directly to nitrogen are derived from alkyl groups; in aromatic amines, one or more of the groups attached to nitrogen are aromatic rings.

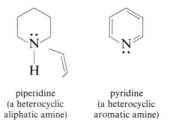

aniline
(a 1° aromatic amine)

N-methylaniline
(a 2° aromatic amine)

benzyldimethylamine
(a 3° aliphatic amine)

Amines in which the nitrogen atom is part of a ring are classified as hetero-cyclic amines. When a nitrogen atom replaces an atom of carbon in an aromatic ring, the amine is classified as a heterocyclic aromatic amine. Following are struc-tural formulas for two cyclic amines, one classified as a heterocyclic aliphatic amine and the other as a heterocyclic aromatic amine:

piperidine
(a heterocyclic
aliphatic amine)

pyridine
(a heterocyclic
aromatic amine)

B. Nomenclature

1. IUPAC System

In IUPAC nomenclature, the longest chain of carbon atoms that contains the **amino group** is taken as the parent and —NH_2 is considered a substituent, like —Cl, —NO_2, and so on. Its presence is indicated by the prefix *amino-*, and a number is used to show its location. If more than one alkyl group is attached to nitrogen, the one containing the longest chain of carbon atoms is taken as the parent; other substituents on nitrogen are named as alkyl groups and are preceded by *N-* to show that they are bonded to the nitrogen atom of the amine.

In these and the following examples, IUPAC names are given first. Instead of showing the same structural formulas again under "Common Names," we have listed common names, where they exist, here in parentheses under IUPAC names. As you will discover in your reading, common names for most amines are much more widely used than IUPAC names.

$$CH_3CH_2\!\!-\!\!NH_2 \qquad\qquad \underset{\underset{CH_3}{|}}{CH_3CHCH_2CH_2}\!\!-\!\!NH_2 \qquad\qquad \underset{\underset{CH_3}{|}}{CH_3CH_2CH_2CHCH_2}\!\!-\!\!NH\!\!-\!\!CH_3$$

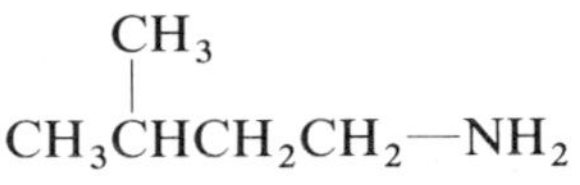

aminoethane   1-amino-3-methylbutane   *N*-methyl-1-amino-2-methylpentane
(ethylamine)   (isopentylamine)

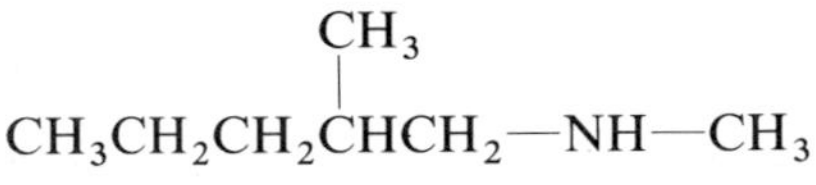

Compounds containing two or more amino groups are named by prefixes *di-*, *tri-*, and so on, to show multiple substitution and by numbers to show the location of each substituent. Following are structural formulas for three diamines. The first, 1,6-diaminohexane is one of two raw materials for the synthesis of Nylon 66. The second two amines are products of the decomposition of animal matter, as their alternative, common names surely suggest.

$$H_2NCH_2CH_2CH_2CH_2CH_2CH_2NH_2 \qquad\qquad H_2NCH_2CH_2CH_2CH_2CH_2NH_2$$

1,6-diaminohexane   1,5-diaminopentane
(hexamethylenediamine)   (pentamethylenediamine;
                               cadaverine)

$$H_2NCH_2CH_2CH_2CH_2NH_2$$

1,4-diaminobutane
(tetramethylenediamine;
putrescine)

If the —NH_2 group is one of two or more substituents, it is shown by the prefix *amino-*, as in the following examples:

$$H_2NCH_2CH_2OH \qquad\qquad H_2N\!\!-\!\!\langle\bigcirc\rangle\!\!-\!\!OH$$

2-aminoethanol   4-aminophenol
(ethanolamine)   (*p*-aminophenol)

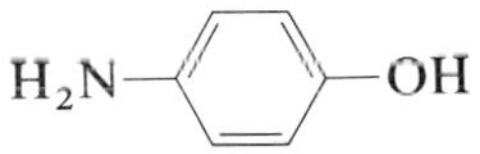

The compound $C_6H_5NH_2$ is named aniline, which becomes the parent name for its derivatives. Several simple derivatives of aniline are known almost exclusively by their common names, for example, toluidine (the ortho isomer is shown below).

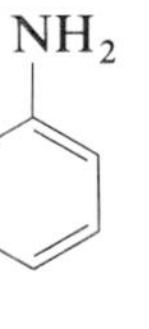

aniline 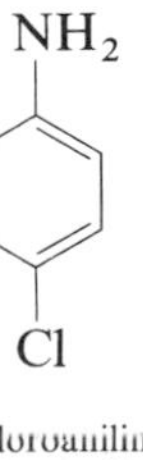   4-chloroaniline   2-methylaniline
            (*p*-chloroaniline)   (*o*-methylaniline;
                                   o-toluidine)

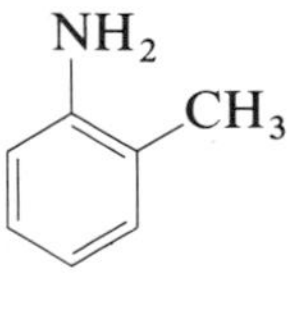

When a nitrogen atom has four organic groups attached to it (any combination of aliphatic or aromatic), the compound is named as an ammonium salt, as in the following examples:

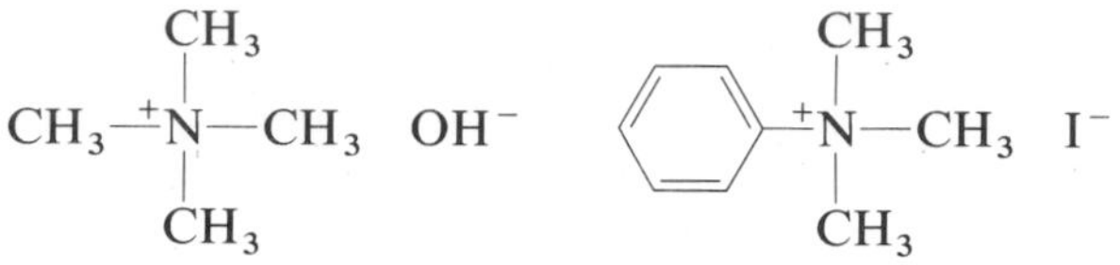

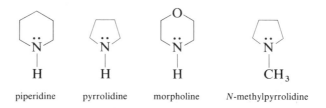

tetramethyl ammonium
hydroxide

phenyl trimethyl ammonium
iodide

Heterocyclic amines all have common names that the IUPAC has accepted. Structural formulas for the three most common **heterocyclic aliphatic amines** are shown below. Note that when there is an additional substituent on the nitrogen atom of the parent molecule, its location is indicated by *N*-.

piperidine   pyrrolidine   morpholine   *N*-methylpyrrolidine

Finally there are groups of **heterocyclic aromatic amines** whose common names have been retained by the IUPAC. Structural formulas and names for the most common of these are shown:

pyridine   pyrimidine   pyrrole   imidazole

2. Common Names

Common names for simple aliphatic amines are derived by listing the alkyl group or groups attached to nitrogen in alphabetical order, continuously in one long word, ending with the suffix -*amine*:

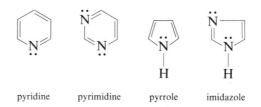

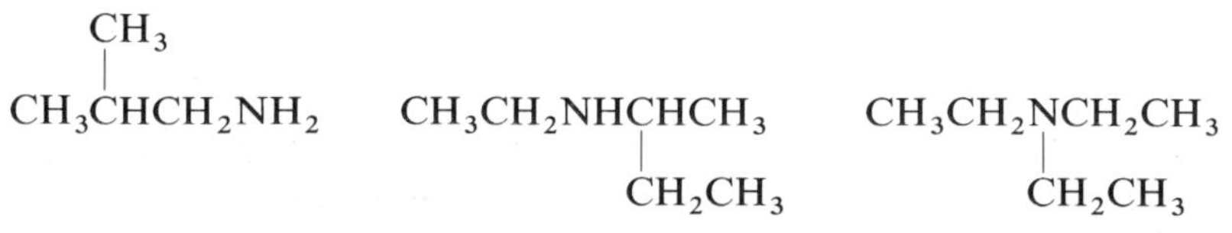

isobutylamine   *sec*-butylethylamine   triethylamine

Give each compound an IUPAC name and where possible, a common name also.

Example 14.1

a. $CH_3CH_2NHCH_3$

b. $CH_3CHCH_2CH_2CH_2CH_3$
  |
  $N(CH_3)_2$

c.

NH$_2$ attached to pyridine ring

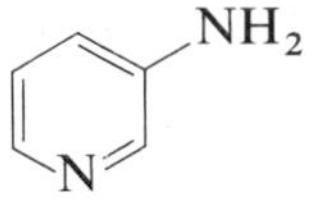

d. $CH_3CHCHCH_3$
  | |
  HO NH_2

☐ *Solution*

a. IUPAC: *N*-methyl-1-aminoethane. Common: ethylmethylamine.
b. IUPAC: *N,N*-dimethyl-2-aminohexane. Common: none.
c. IUPAC: 3 aminopyridine. Common: β-pyridylamine. In this common name, the pyridine ring is shown as a substituent on the amine group. We have little occasion to use this type of common name.
d. IUPAC: 3-amino-2-butanol. Common: none.

Problem 14.1

Give IUPAC and, where possible, common names for the following:

a. 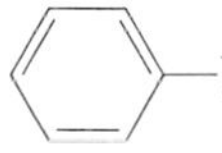 〈benzene ring〉—N(CH$_3$)$_2$

b. $CH_3CH_2CHCH_3$
  |
  NH_2

c. $H_2NCH_2CH_2CH_2OH$

14.2 Physical Properties

Amines are polar compounds and both primary and secondary amines can form intermolecular **hydrogen bonds**.

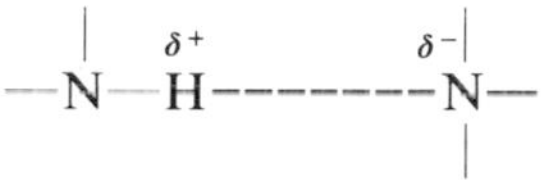

$$-N-H\text{-------}N-$$
with δ^+ over H and δ^- over N

However, because the difference in electronegativity is not so great between nitrogen and hydrogen $(3.0 - 2.1 = 0.9)$ as between oxygen and hydrogen $(3.5 - 2.1 = 1.4)$, an $N-H\text{------}N$ hydrogen bond is not nearly so strong as an $O-H\text{------}O$ hydrogen bond. The boiling points of ethane, methylamine, and methanol, all compounds of comparable molecular weight, are

	Mol. Wt.	bp (°C)
CH_3CH_3	30	−88
CH_3NH_2	31	−7
CH_3OH	32	65

Ethane is a nonpolar hydrocarbon, and the only interactions between molecules in the pure liquid are very weak dispersion forces. Therefore, it has the

Table 14.1 Physical properties of selected amines.

Name	Structure	mp (°C)	bp (°C)	Solubility (g/100 g H_2O)	Density of Liquid at 20°C (g/mL)
ammonia	NH_3	−78	−33	90	(a gas)
methylamine	CH_3NH_2	−95	−6	very	(a gas)
ethylamine	$CH_3CH_2NH_2$	−81	17	infinite	(a gas)
propylamine	$CH_3(CH_2)_2NH_2$	−83	48	soluble	0.717
isopropylamine	$(CH_3)_2CHNH_2$	−95	32	infinite	0.889
n-butylamine	$CH_3(CH_2)_3NH_2$	−49	78	infinite	0.741
dimethylamine	$(CH_3)_2NH$	−93	7	very	(a gas)
diethylamine	$(CH_3CH_2)_2NH$	−48	56	very	0.706
trimethylamine	$(CH_3)_3N$	−117	3	very	(a gas)
triethylamine	$(CH_3CH_2)_3N$	−114	89	soluble	0.727
cyclohexylamine	$C_6H_{11}NH_2$	−17	145	soluble	0.819
aniline	$C_6H_5NH_2$	−6	184	3.7	1.02
benzylamine	$C_6H_5CH_2NH_2$	—	185	infinite	0.981
pyridine	C_5H_5N	−42	116	infinite	0.982

lowest boiling point of the three. Both methylamine and methanol are polar molecules and interact in the pure liquid by hydrogen bonding. Hydrogen bonding is weaker in methylamine than in methanol, and therefore methylamine has a lower boiling point than methanol.

All classes of amines form hydrogen bonds with water and therefore are more soluble in water than hydrocarbons of comparable molecular weight are. Most low-molecular-weight amines are completely soluble in water. The higher-molecular-weight amines are only moderately soluble. Boiling points and solubilities in water for several amines are listed in Table 14.1.

14.3 Reactions of Amines

In this chapter, we will discuss only two reactions characteristic of amines, namely their basicity and their reaction with acids. Amines also react with other functional groups including aldehydes, ketones, carboxylic acids, and esters. We will discuss reactions of amines with these functional groups in following chapters.

A. Basicity of Amines

Like ammonia, all primary, secondary, and tertiary amines are weak bases, and aqueous solutions of amines are basic. The following reactions are written using curved arrows to emphasize that when an amine acts as a base, the unshared pair of electrons on nitrogen forms a new bond to hydrogen, and an H—O bond of water breaks to form hydroxide ion.

$$H-\overset{\overset{\displaystyle H}{|}}{\underset{\underset{\displaystyle H}{|}}{N}}: + H-\overset{..}{\underset{..}{O}}-H \rightleftharpoons H-\overset{\overset{\displaystyle H}{|}}{\underset{\underset{\displaystyle H}{|}}{N}}^{+}H + \ ^{-}:\overset{..}{\underset{..}{O}}-H$$

ammonia	ammonium hydroxide

$$CH_3-\overset{\overset{\displaystyle H}{|}}{\underset{\underset{\displaystyle H}{|}}{N}}: + H-\overset{..}{\underset{..}{O}}-H \longrightarrow CH_3-\overset{\overset{\displaystyle H}{|}}{\underset{\underset{\displaystyle H}{|}}{N}}^{+}H + \ ^{-}:\overset{..}{\underset{..}{O}}-H$$

methylamine	methylammonium hydroxide

The equilibrium constant for the reaction of methylamine with water to give methylammonium hydroxide is called a **base dissociation constant** and is given the symbol K_b.

$$K_b = \frac{[CH_3NH_3^+][OH^-]}{[CH_3NH_2]}$$

Values of K_b for some primary, secondary, and tertiary aliphatic amines and for some aromatic amines are given in Table 14.2. All aliphatic amines, whether primary, secondary, or tertiary have about the same base strength as ammonia. Aromatic amines such as aniline are significantly less basic than aliphatic amines. The K_b of aniline is less than the K_b of cyclohexylamine by a factor of one million (10^6).

Table 14.2
Basicity of several aliphatic and aromatic amines.

Name	Structural Formula	K_b	pK_b	pK_a
ammonia	NH_3	1.8×10^{-5}	4.74	9.26
methylamine	CH_3NH_2	4.4×10^{-4}	3.36	10.64
ethylamine	$CH_3CH_2NH_2$	6.3×10^{-4}	3.20	10.80
diethylamine	$(CH_3CH_2)_2NH$	3.1×10^{-4}	3.51	10.49
triethylamine	$(CH_3CH_2)_3N$	1.0×10^{-4}	4.00	10.00
cyclohexylamine	⬡—NH_2	5.5×10^{-4}	3.26	10.74
aniline	⬡—NH_2	4.2×10^{-10}	9.37	4.63
pyridine	⬡N	1.8×10^{-9}	8.74	5.26

cyclohexylamine   cyclohexylammonium hydroxide

$K_b = 5.5 \times 10^{-4}$

aniline   anilinium hydroxide

$K_b = 4.2 \times 10^{-10}$

Salts of aliphatic amines are named by changing the suffix *-amine* to *-ammonium* and adding the name of the anion in the salt. Salts of aromatic amines are named by dropping the terminal *-e* and adding *-ium* followed by the name of the anion in the salt.

Until very recently, it was customary to list only K_b or pK_b for amines. Now it is becoming more and more common, particularly in biochemistry, to list only K_a and pK_a values for amines. The K_a and pK_a values are used almost exclusively in discussing the acid-base properties of amino acids and proteins (Chapter 21). For this reason, Table 14.2 also gives pK_a values for amines. Values for pK_a and pK_b are related by the following equation:

$$pK_a + pK_b = 14$$

We can illustrate the differences between pK_b and pK_a by the following equations:

$$CH_3NH_2 + H_2O \rightleftharpoons CH_3NH_3^+ + OH^- \quad K_b = 4.4 \times 10^{-4} \quad pK_b = 3.36$$
$$CH_3NH_3^+ \rightleftharpoons CH_3NH_2 + H^+ \quad K_a = 2.3 \times 10^{-11} \quad pK_a = 10.64$$

Whereas pK_b measures directly the strength of CH_3NH_2 as a base, pK_a measures the strength of $CH_3NH_3^+$ as an acid. For perspective you might compare the pK_a values for acetic acid and the methylammonium ion:

$$CH_3CO_2H \rightleftharpoons CH_3CO_2^- + H^+ \quad K_a = 1.8 \times 10^{-5} \quad pK_a = 4.74$$
$$CH_3NH_3^+ \rightleftharpoons CH_3NH_2 + H^+ \quad K_a = 2.3 \times 10^{-11} \quad pK_a = 10.64$$

By using K_a values for a carboxylic acid and an amine, we can compare their acidities directly, because in each case we are looking at the dissociation constant of an acid to form a base and a proton. It is obvious from the above data that acetic acid is a much stronger acid than the methylammonium ion.

B. Reaction of Amines with Acids

All amines, whether soluble or insoluble in water, react quantitatively with acids to form salts. In the following amine examples, curved arrows are used to show the flow of electrons from the base to the acid.

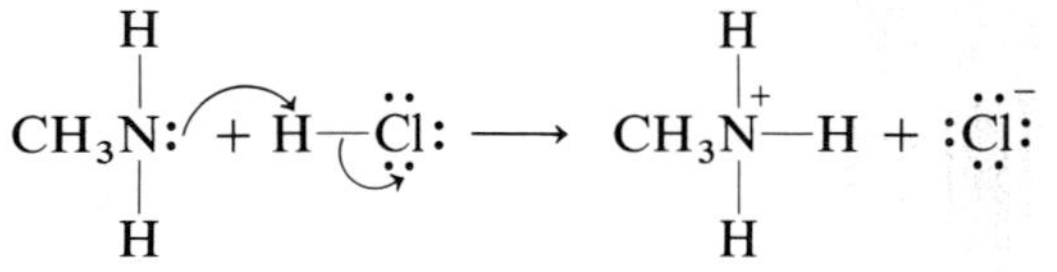

$$CH_3\overset{\overset{\displaystyle H}{|}}{\underset{\underset{\displaystyle H}{|}}{N}}: + H{-}\ddot{C}l: \longrightarrow CH_3\overset{\overset{\displaystyle H}{|}}{\underset{\underset{\displaystyle H}{|}}{\overset{+}{N}}}{-}H + :\ddot{\underset{\cdot\cdot}{C}}l:^-$$

methylamine   methylammonium chloride
(methylamine hydrochloride)

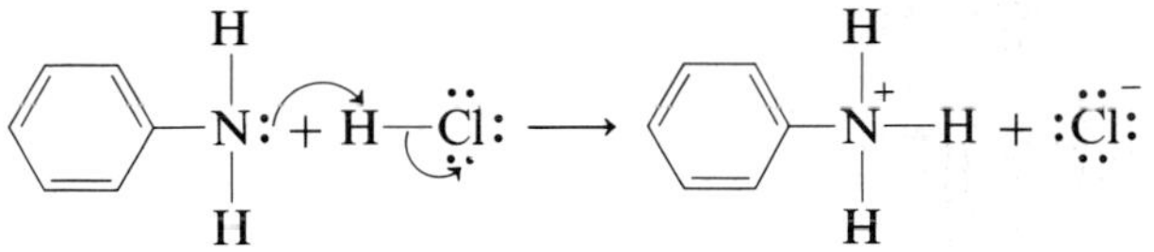

aniline   anilinium chloride
(aniline hydrochloride)

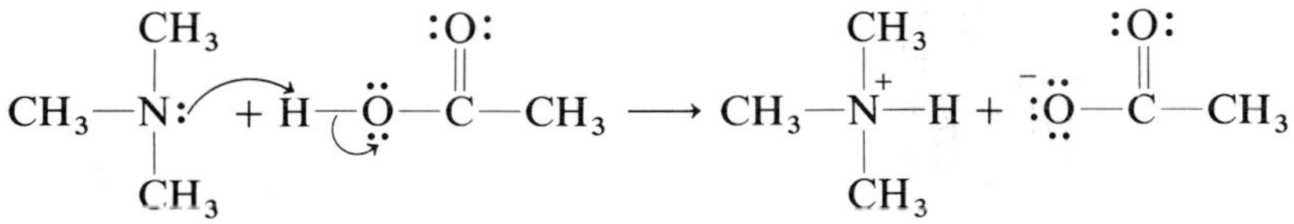

$$CH_3{-}\overset{\overset{\displaystyle CH_3}{|}}{\underset{\underset{\displaystyle CH_3}{|}}{N}}: + H{-}\overset{:O:}{\underset{}{\overset{\|}{\ddot{O}{-}C}}}{-}CH_3 \longrightarrow CH_3{-}\overset{\overset{\displaystyle CH_3}{|}}{\underset{\underset{\displaystyle CH_3}{|}}{\overset{+}{N}}}{-}H + :\ddot{O}{-}\overset{:O:}{\overset{\|}{C}}{-}CH_3$$

trimethylamine   acetic acid   trimethylammonium acetate

Example 14.2

Complete the acid-base reactions and name the salt formed.

a. $(CH_3CH_2)_2NH + HCl \longrightarrow$

b.  ⬡ₙ + $CH_3CO_2H \longrightarrow$

Solution

a. Diethylamine is a secondary aliphatic amine and reacts with HCl to form the salt diethylammonium chloride:

$$(CH_3CH_2)_2NH + HCl \longrightarrow (CH_3CH_2)_2NH_2^+ \; Cl^-$$

diethylamine   diethylammonium chloride

b. Pyridine is a heterocyclic aromatic amine and reacts with acetic acid to form the salt pyridinium acetate:

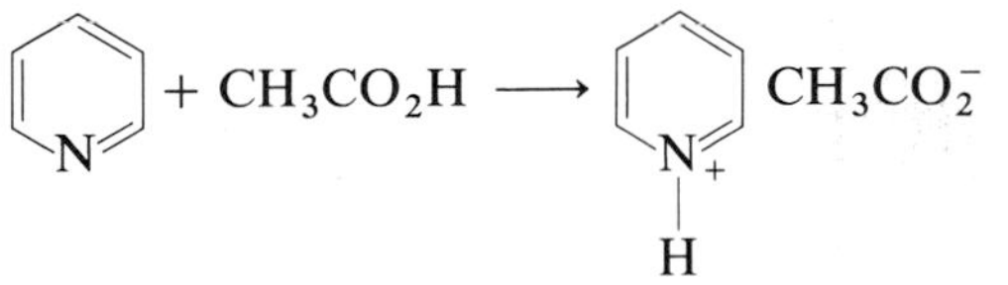

$$\text{(pyridine)} + CH_3CO_2H \longrightarrow \text{(pyridinium)} \; CH_3CO_2^-$$

pyridine   acetic acid   pyridinium acetate

Problem 14.2

Complete the acid-base reactions and name each salt formed.

a. $(CH_3CH_2)_3N + HCl \longrightarrow$

b. 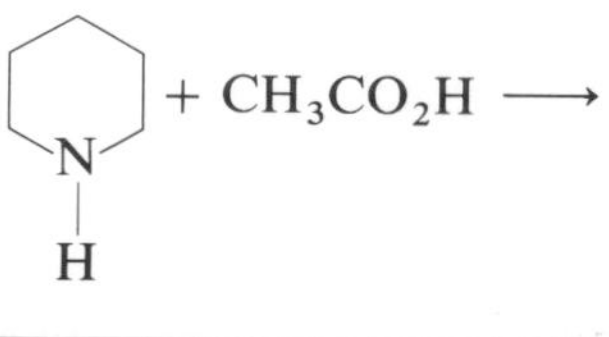 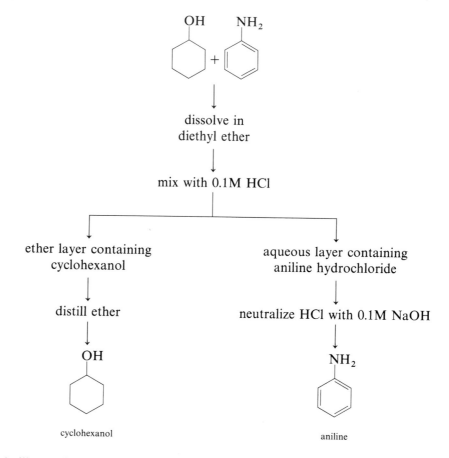 + CH$_3$CO$_2$H $\longrightarrow$

The basicity of amines and the solubility of amine salts in water can be used to distinguish between amines and nonbasic, water-insoluble compounds and also to separate them. The flow chart shows the separation of aniline from cyclohexanol.

dissolve in
diethyl ether

mix with 0.1M HCl

ether layer containing
cyclohexanol

aqueous layer containing
aniline hydrochloride

distill ether

neutralize HCl with 0.1M NaOH

cyclohexanol

aniline

Aniline and cyclohexanol are only slightly soluble in water and therefore cannot be separated on the basis of their water solubilities. However, both dissolve in diethyl ether. When an ether solution of the two compounds is shaken with 0.1M HCl, aniline reacts to form a water-soluble salt, aniline hydrochloride. Cyclohexanol remains in the ether layer. Separation of the ether layer and distillation of the ether gives cyclohexanol. Neutralization of the HCl in the aqueous layer with 0.1M NaOH converts aniline hydrochloride to free aniline, which then separates as a water-insoluble layer and can be recovered.

14.4 Some Natural and Synthetic Amines

Structural formulas for various natural amines of both plant and animal origin are shown in Figure 14.1. These molecules are chosen to illustrate something of the structural diversity and range of physiological activity of amines, their value as drugs, and their importance in nutrition.

Coniine from the water hemlock is highly toxic. It can cause weakness, labored respiration, paralysis, and eventually death. This is the toxic substance in "poison hemlock," used by Socrates to commit suicide. Nicotine is one of the principal heterocyclic amines of the tobacco plant. In small doses, nicotine is a stimulant. However, in larger doses it causes depression, nausea, and vomiting. In still larger doses, nicotine is a poison. Solutions of nicotine in water are often used as insecticides. Note that nicotinic acid, an oxidation product of nicotine, is one of the water-soluble vitamins humans need for proper nutrition. Ingested or inhaled nicotine does not give rise to nicotinic acid in the body, because humans have no enzyme systems capable of catalyzing this conversion. Smoking will not supply any vitamins! Quinine, isolated from the bark of the cinchona tree in South America, has long been used to treat malaria.

Histamine, formed by decarboxylation of the amino acid histidine (Table 21.1), is a toxic substance present in all tissues of the body, combined in some manner with proteins. Histamine is produced extensively during hypersensitive, allergic reactions, and the symptoms of this release are unfortunately familiar to most of us, particularly those who suffer from hay fever or other seasonal allergies. The search for antihistamines—drugs that inhibit the effects of histamine— has led to the synthesis of several drugs whose trade names are well known. Structural formulas for three of the most widely used antihistamines are shown in Figure 14.2. Note the structural similarity in these three drugs; each has two aromatic rings and a dimethylaminoethyl group, $-CH_2CH_2N(CH_3)_2$. Dexbrompheniramine is the most potent.

Serotonin and acetylcholine are both neurotransmitters important in human physiology—serotonin in parts of the central nervous system mediating affective behavior, acetylcholine in certain motor neurons responsible for causing contraction of voluntary muscles. Acetylcholine is stored in synaptic vesicles and released in response to electric activity in the neuron. It diffuses across the synapse and interacts with postsynaptic receptor sites on a neighboring neuron, to cause membrane depolarization and transmission of a nerve impulse. After interaction with a postsynaptic receptor site, acetylcholine is deactivated through hydrolysis to choline and acetate ion, an action catalyzed by the enzyme acetylcholinesterase. Choline itself has no activity as a neurotransmitter.

$$CH_3 \overset{CH_3}{\underset{CH_3}{\overset{|}{\underset{|}{N}}}}{}^+CH_2CH_2O\overset{O}{\overset{||}{C}}CH_3 + H_2O \xrightarrow{\text{acetylcholinesterase}} CH_3 \overset{CH_3}{\underset{CH_3}{\overset{|}{\underset{|}{N}}}}{}^+CH_2CH_2OH + {}^-O\overset{O}{\overset{||}{C}}CH_3$$

acetylcholine   choline   acetate

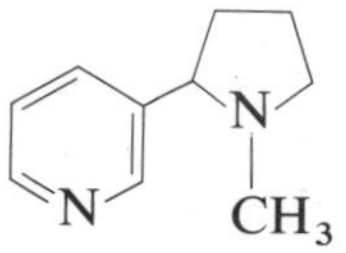

nicotine
(from tobacco)

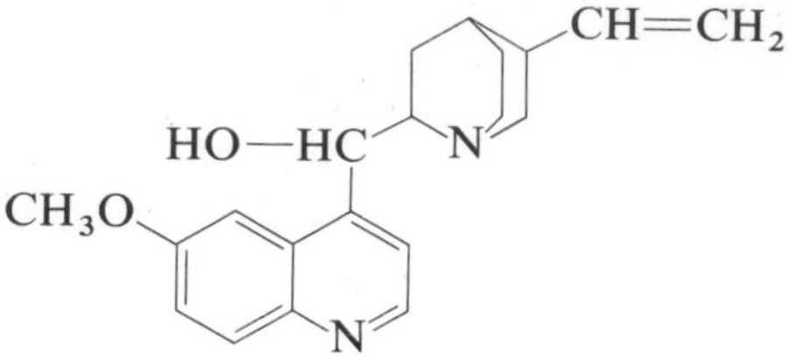

quinine

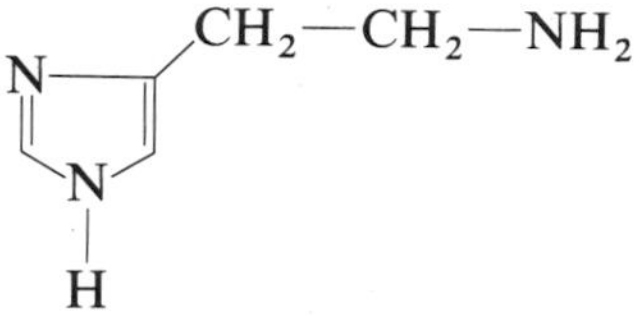

histamine

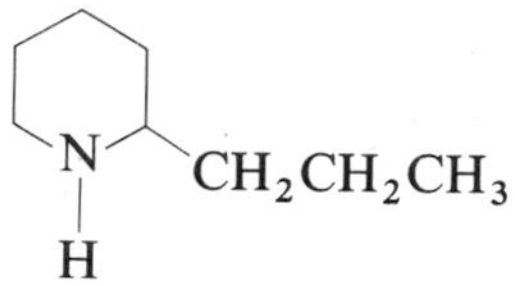

coniine
(from poison hemlock)

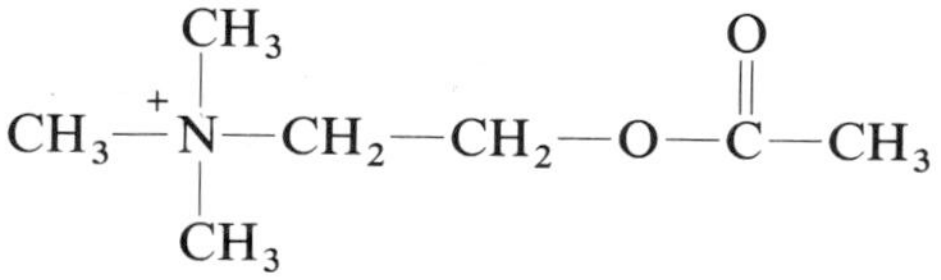

acetylcholine

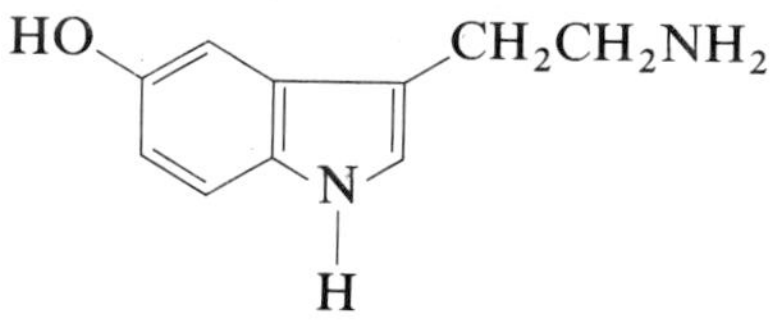

serotonin
(5-hydroxytryptamine)

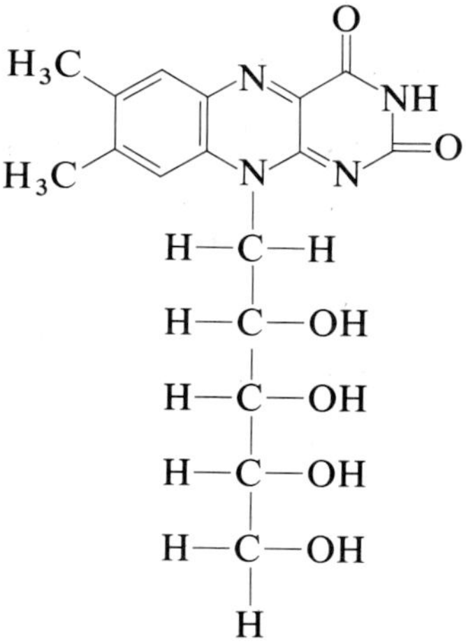

riboflavin
or vitamin B$_2$

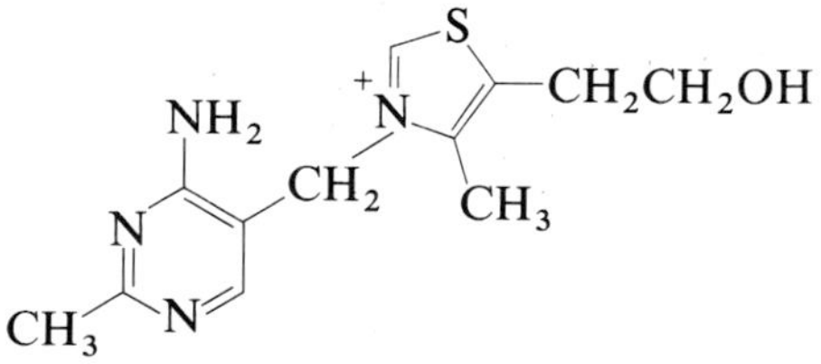

thiamine
or vitamin B$_1$

Figure 14.1 Several amines of plant and animal origin.

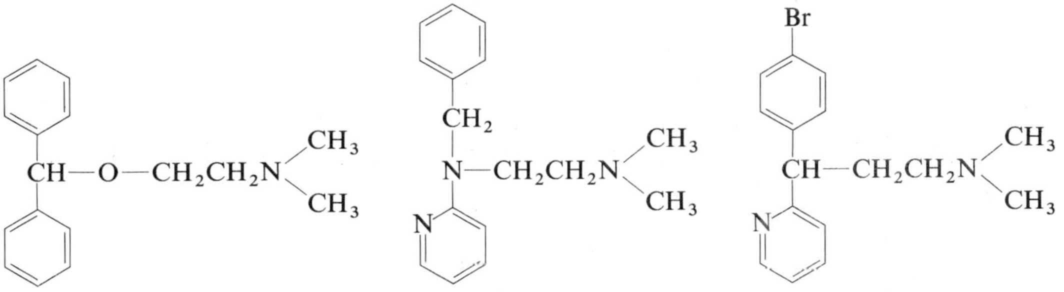

diphenylhydramine
(Benadryl)

tripelennamine
(Pyribenzamine)

dexbrompheniramine
(Disomer)

Figure 14.2 Three synthetic antihistamines.

Several other classes of synthetic compounds affect acetylcholine-mediated nerve transmission. Among the most widely known of these are the so-called nerve gases and related compounds that are now or have been used as insecticides. The nerve gases diisopropyl fluorophosphate (DFP) and Tabun are both potent inhibitors of acetylcholinesterase, and a few milligrams of either can kill a person in a few minutes through paralysis and respiratory failure.

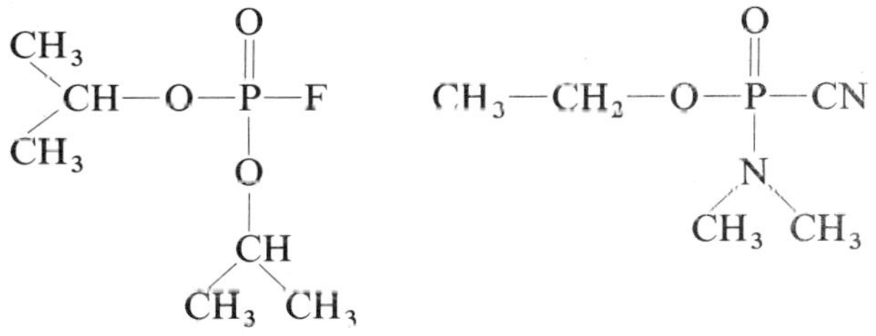

diisopropyl fluorophosphate
(DFP)

Tabun

Several water-soluble vitamins contain cyclic amines. Riboflavin (Figure 14.1) contains a fused three-ring amine called flavin. One of the nitrogen atoms of this ring system contains a five-carbon chain derived from the sugar D-ribose, hence the name riboflavin. Thiamine (vitamin B_1) contains a substituted pyrimidine ring and also a five-membered ring containing one atom each of nitrogen and sulfur. Pyridoxine, vitamin B_6, contains a substituted pyridine ring.

Key Terms and Concepts

amino group (14.1B)

base dissociation
   constant (14.3A)

basicity of amines (14.3A)

heterocyclic aliphatic amine (14.1B1)

heterocyclic aromatic amine (14.1B1)

hydrogen bonds (14.2)

nomenclature of amines (14.1B)

primary amine (14.1A)

secondary amine (14.1A)

tertiary amine (14.1A)

Key Reactions

1. Aliphatic and aromatic amines are weak bases and ionize in aqueous solution (Section 14.3A).

2. Aliphatic and aromatic amines react with HCl and other strong acids to give water-soluble salts (Section 14.3B).

Problems

Structure, nomenclature, and classification of amines (Section 14.1)

14.3 Write structural formulas for the following compounds. In addition, classify each as a primary amine, secondary amine, tertiary amine, aromatic amine, or ammonium salt.
   a. diethylamine   b. aniline
   c. cyclohexylamine   d. pyrrole
   e. pyridine   f. tetramethylammonium iodide
   g. 2-aminoethanol (ethanolamine)
   h. 2-aminopropanoic acid (alanine)
   i. pyrimidine   j. trimethylammonium chloride
   k. *p*-methoxyaniline   l. triethylamine
   m. *N*-methylaniline   n. *p*-chloroaniline
   o. 1,4-diaminobenzene   p. *p*-aminophenol
   q. pyridine 3-carboxylic acid (nicotine)

14.4 Give an acceptable name for these compounds:

a.

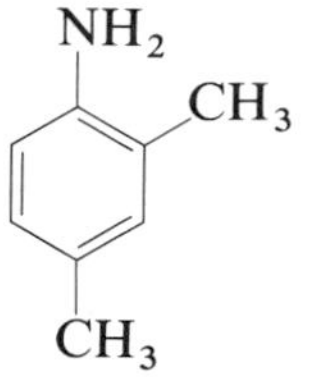

b.

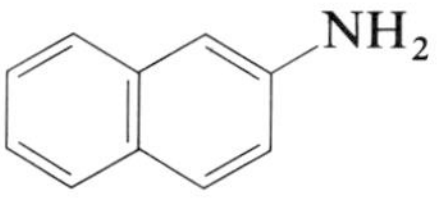

c. 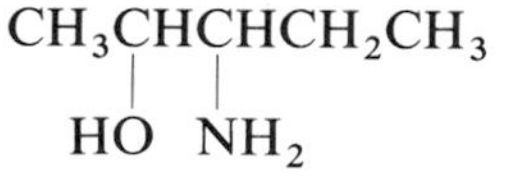 $CH_3CHCHCH_2CH_3$
        | |
       HO NH_2

d. 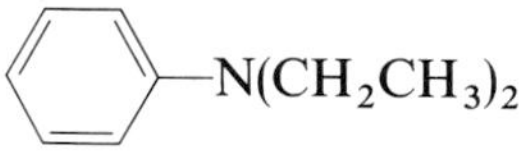 $-N(CH_2CH_3)_2$

e. $CH_3CH_2CH_2CH_2NH_2$ f. $(CH_3CH_2)_2NCH_3$

14.5 Draw structural formulas for the eight isomeric amines of molecular formula $C_4H_{11}N$. Name each and label each as primary, secondary, or tertiary.

Physical properties of amines (Section 14.2)

14.6 Draw structural formulas to illustrate hydrogen bonding between the circled atoms.

a. 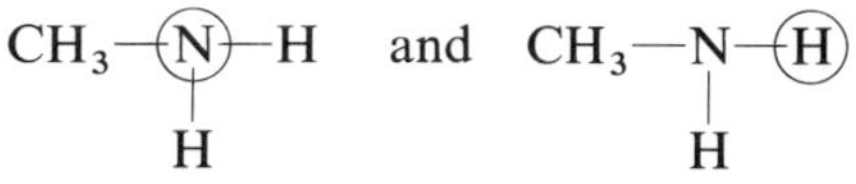 CH_3—Ⓝ—H   and CH_3—N—Ⓗ
        | |
        H   H

b. 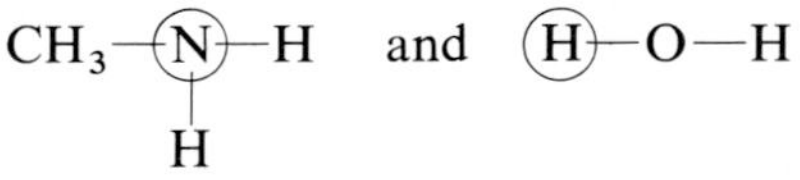 CH$_3$—Ⓝ—H   and   Ⓗ—O—H
          |
          H

c. 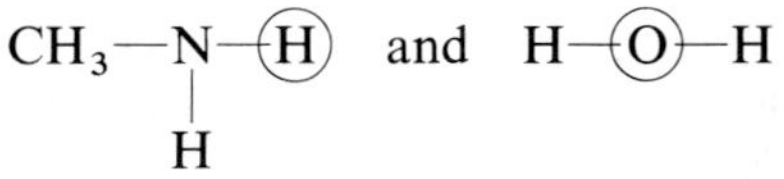 CH$_3$—N—Ⓗ   and   H—Ⓞ—H
          |
          H

14.7   Both 1-aminobutane and 1-butanol are liquids at room temperature. One of these compounds has a boiling point of 117°C, the other a boiling point of 78°C. Which compound has which boiling point? Explain your reasoning.

14.8   Arrange the following compounds in order of increasing boiling point:

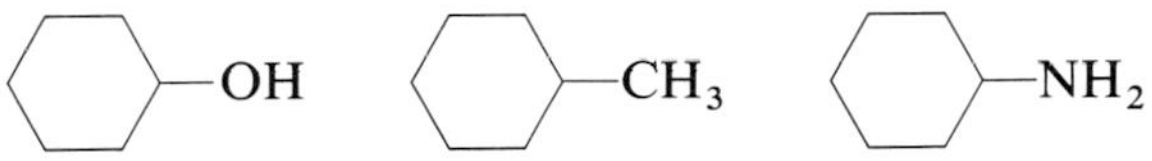

⬡—OH   ⬡—CH$_3$ ⬡—NH$_2$

cyclohexanol   methylcyclohexane   cyclohexylamine

Reactions
of amines
(Section 14.3)

14.9   Name and write the structural formula for the salts formed by reaction of the following with HCl.

a. CH$_3$CH$_2$NH$_2$ **b.** 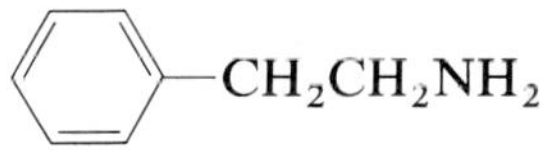 ⬡—CH$_2$CH$_2$NH$_2$

c. 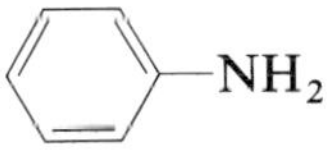 ⬡—NH$_2$ **d.** 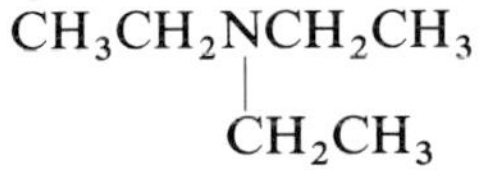 CH$_3$CH$_2$NCH$_2$CH$_3$
                              |
                              CH$_2$CH$_3$

14.10   Select the stronger base of each pair.

a. CH$_3$CH$_2$NH$_2$ or   ⬡—NH$_2$

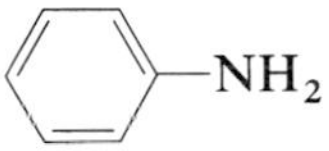

b. 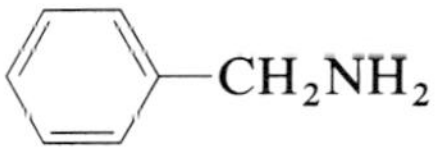 ⬡—CH$_2$NH$_2$ or   ⬡—NH$_2$

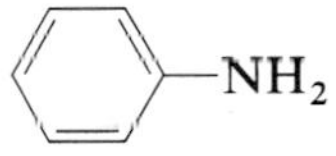

c. 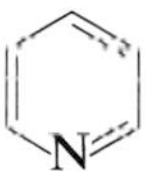 ⬡N   or   ⬡—NH$_2$

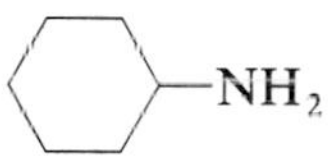

d. 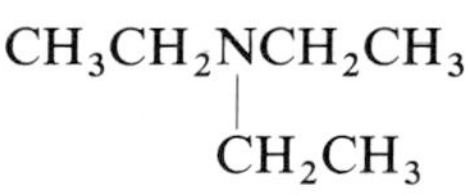 CH$_3$CH$_2$NCH$_2$CH$_3$ or   ⬡—N⟨CH$_2$CH$_3$ / CH$_2$CH$_3$
            |
            CH$_2$CH$_3$

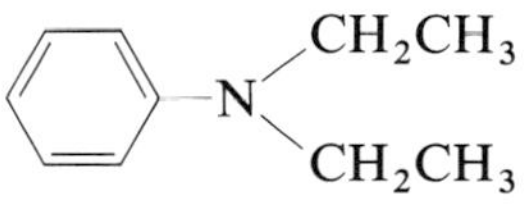

14.11   Arrange the compounds of each set in order of increasing basicity.

a. 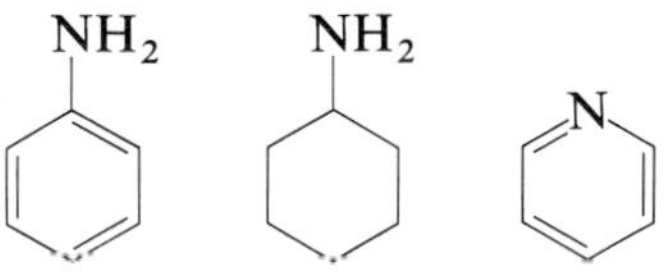   NH$_2$ NH$_2$
        ⬡   ⬡   ⬡N

        (i)   (ii)   (iii)

b.

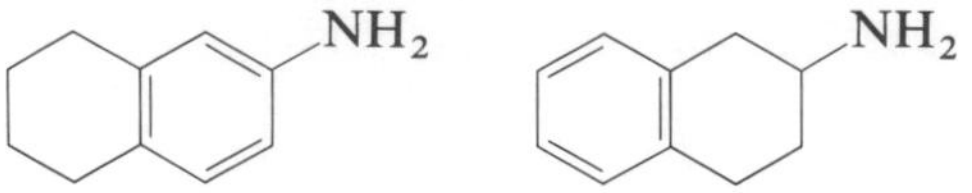

(i)   (ii)

14.12 Suppose you are given a mixture of the following three compounds. Describe a procedure you could use to separate and isolate each in a pure form.

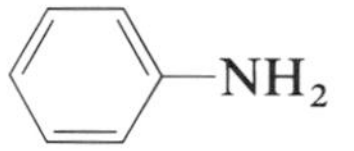

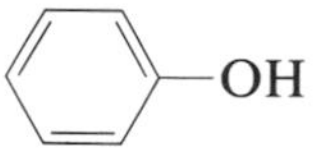

aniline   phenol   1-hexanol

$CH_3CH_2CH_2CH_2CH_2CH_2OH$

14.13 Alanine (2-aminopropanoic acid) is one of the important amino acids in proteins. Is the structural formula of alanine better represented by (i) or (ii)? Explain.

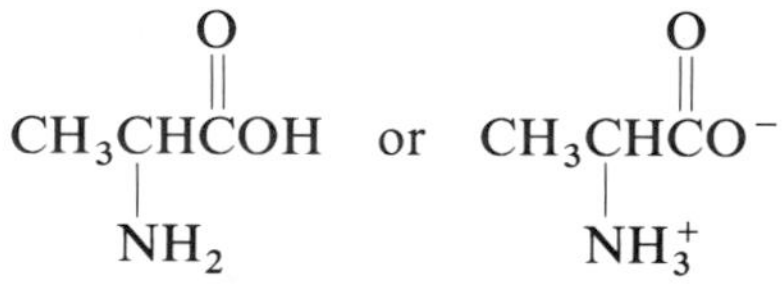

$$CH_3\overset{O}{\overset{\|}{C}H}COH \quad \text{or} \quad CH_3\overset{O}{\overset{\|}{C}H}CO^-$$

$$\underset{NH_2}{} \qquad\qquad \underset{NH_3^+}{}$$

(i)   (ii)

14.14 Describe a simple chemical test by which you could distinguish between the compounds of each of the following pairs. In each case, state what test you would perform and what you would expect to observe, and write a balanced equation for each positive test.
a. phenol and aniline
b. cyclohexylamine and cyclohexanol
c. trimethylacetic acid and 2,2-dimethyl-1-aminopropane

Alkaloids

Alkaloids are nitrogen-containing compounds of plant origin, which are physiologically active when administered to humans. Examples of alkaloids are morphine from opium poppies, quinine from the bark of cinchona trees, cocaine from coca leaves, and nicotine from tobacco plants. It is estimated that alkaloids are present in 10–20% of all vascular plants.

The field of alkaloid chemistry is both vast and complex, and we shall examine only a few members of this class. In so doing, we shall try to portray the ranges of structural diversity and physiological activity that characterize alkaloids and to indicate how important these natural products are in chemotherapy and psychopharmacology.

Atropine and Cocaine

One subgroup of alkaloids consists of the tropane alkaloids, the characteristic structural feature of which is tropane, a six-membered piperidine ring with a two-carbon bridge stretching between carbons 2 and 6. Atropine from deadly nightshade (*Atropa belladonna*) is used in dilute solutions to dilate the pupil of the eye before opthalamic examination and eye surgery.

atropine

cocaine

Cocaine is a tropane alkaloid isolated from the leaves of the South American coca plant (*Erythroxylon coca*). It was first isolated in pure form in 1880 and soon thereafter its property as a local anesthetic was noted. It was introduced into medicine in 1884 by two young Viennese physicians, Sigmund Freud and Karl Koller. Unfortunately, the use of cocaine can create a dependence, as Freud himself observed when he used it to wean a colleague from morphine and thereby produced one of the first known cocaine addicts.

After determining cocaine's structure, chemists could ask the tantalizing questions: How is the structure of cocaine related to its physiological activity? Is it possible to separate the anesthetic effects from the habituation? If these questions could be answered, then it should be possible to prepare synthetic alkaloidlike drugs that incorporate only those structural elements essential for anesthetic function, simultaneously eliminating the undesirable effects. With cocaine, chemists have duplicated the essential structural features: its benzoate ester, its basic nitrogen, and something of its carbon arrangement. This search resulted in the synthesis of procaine

(Novocaine) in 1905; it almost immediately replaced cocaine in dentistry and surgery. Lidocaine (Xylocaine) was introduced in 1948 and today is one of the most widely used local anesthetics. More recently, mepivacaine (Carbocaine) was also introduced.

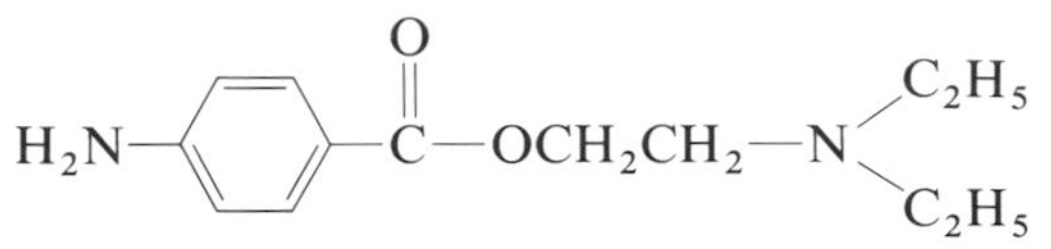

procaine

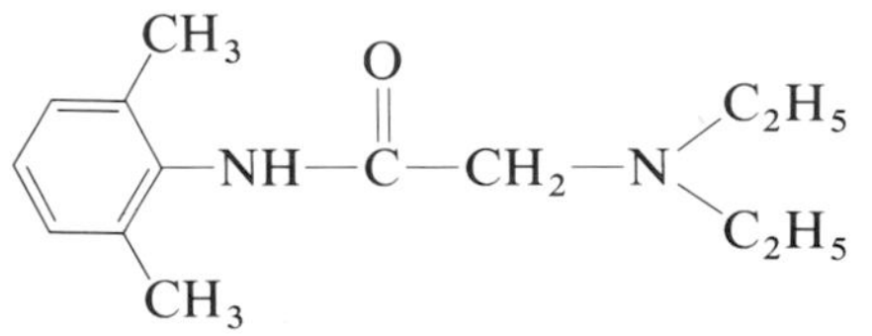

lidocaine

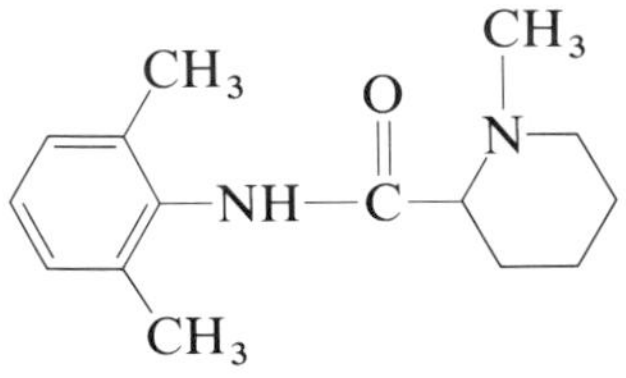

mepivacaine

Thus, seizing on clues provided by nature, chemists have been able to synthesize drugs far more suitable for a specific function than anything known to be produced by nature itself.

Morphine

Of all the alkaloids, probably the most widely known and completely studied are the so-called morphine alkaloids. Opium, the source of morphine alkaloids, is obtained from the opium poppy (*Papaver somniferum*) by cutting the unripe seed capsule. The milky juice that exudes is dried and powdered to make the opium of commerce, which contains well over twenty alkaloids including about 15% morphine and 0.5% codeine.

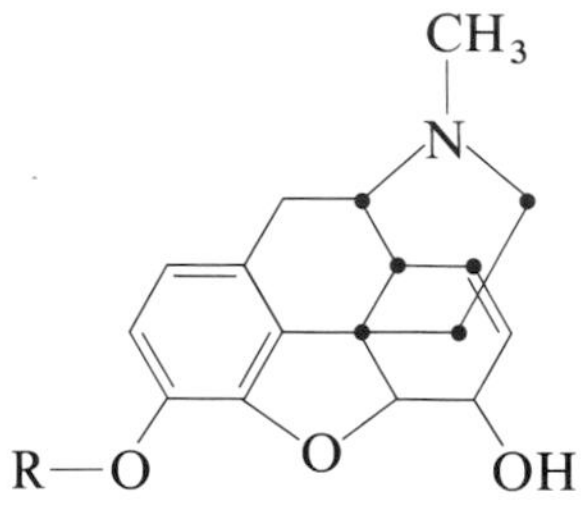

R = H in morphine
R = CH_3 in codeine

The two —OH groups of morphine are particularly important because many semisynthetic derivatives can be made by modifications of either or both of these groups. For example, codeine is methylmorphine, the methyl substituent being on the phenolic —OH group. Diacetylmorphine, or heroin, is made from morphine by acetylation of both —OH groups.

For the relief of severe pain of virtually every kind, morphine and its synthetic analogs remain the most potent drugs known. In 1680, Thomas Sydenham, an English physician, wrote: "Among the remedies which it has pleased Almighty God to give man to relieve his suffering, none is so universal and so efficacious as opium." Even today, morphine, the alkaloid that gives opium its

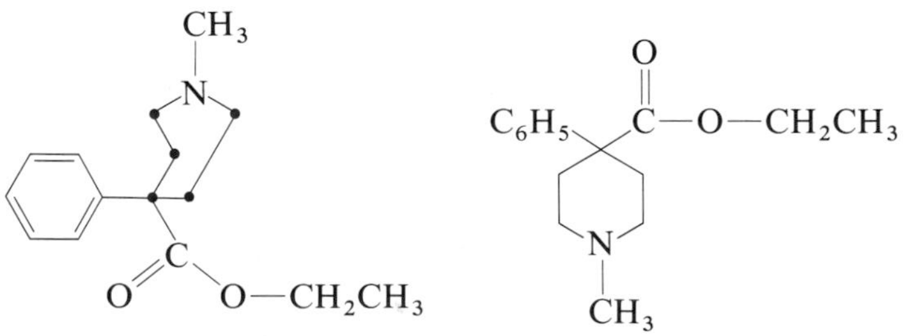

Figure VIII-1 Meperidine (Demerol) drawn in two different representations, the first of which suggests a structural similarity to morphine.

analgesic action, remains the standard against which newer analgesics are measured.

We can ask the same type of question about morphine as we did of cocaine, namely, Is it possible, using the structural features of morphine as a guide, to design drugs that possess the desirable analgesic effects of morphine and yet are free from the undesirable side effects of respiratory depression, hallucinogenic activity, and addiction? With this in mind, chemists have created numerous synthetic analgesics related in structure to morphine, the oldest and perhaps best known of which is meperidine (Demerol, Figure VIII-1). Meperidine was at first thought to be free of many of the morphinelike undesirable side effects. It is now clear, however, that meperidine is definitely addictive. In spite of much determined research, there are as yet no agents as effective as morphine against severe pain that are also entirely free from the risks of addiction. Still, the hope remains that some day the ideal analgesic will be prepared.

How and in what regions of the brain does morphine act? In 1973 scientists demonstrated that there are specific receptors for morphine and other opiates; these sites are clustered mainly in the brain's limbic system, an area involved with emotion and pain perception. It was further shown that these opioid receptors do not interact with any known neurotransmitters. Why then, scientists asked, does the human brain have receptors specific for morphine? Could it be that the brain produces its own opiates? In 1974, scientists discovered that opiatelike compounds are indeed present in the brain, and in 1975 Solomon Snyder at Johns Hopkins University isolated the first known brain opioids, and named them enkephalins, meaning "in the brain." Other brain opiates have since been isolated and named endorphins. The human endorphin anodynin is about as potent an analgesic as morphine. Scientists have yet to understand the role of these natural brain opioids. Perhaps when we do understand their biochemistry and function, we will discover clues that lead us toward the synthesis of more potent but less addictive analgesics.

Indole Alkaloids

During the last four decades, several indole alkaloids have received much attention, not only from chemists but from pharmacologists, psychologists, and physicians. This interest has evolved mainly from the discovery of the remarkable physiological properties of reserpine. The story of reserpine begins long ago. For at least 3000 years, the people of India have used the root of the climbing shrub *Rauwolfia serpentina* as a folk remedy to treat various afflictions. It is called *sarpagandha* in Sanskrit, referring to its use as an antidote for snakebite; it is called *chandra*, meaning "moon" in Hindi, referring to its calming effect on certain forms of insanity.

The modern story of rauwolfia began in the late 1920s, when Indian scientists undertook to study it and other botanical preparations used by native practitioners. By 1931, chemists had isolated a crystalline powder from dry rauwolfia root, and physicians reported that use of this powder brought relief in cases of acute insomnia accompanied by fits of insanity. According to one report: "Symptoms such as headache, a sense of heat, and insomnia disappear quickly and blood pressure can be reduced in a matter of weeks . . . ." Further clinical testing verified the potency of the ancient snakeroot remedy, and soon rauwolfia became an important drug in India for treating high blood pressure and certain forms of mental illness.

In 1949, Dr. Rustrom Jal Vakil, a physician at the King Edward Memorial Hospital in Bombay, reported in the *British Medical Journal* on his research with rauwolfia therapy for patients with high blood pressure. These studies were read by Dr. Robert Wilkins, director of the Hypertension Clinic at Massachusetts Memorial Hospital, who decided to try rauwolfia to see whether it would help certain of his patients who were not responding to other medication. In 1952 he confirmed reports from India of its mildly hypotensive (blood pressure–lowering) effect. He reported further that rauwolfia has a sedative action different from that of any other drug known at the time. Unlike barbiturates and other

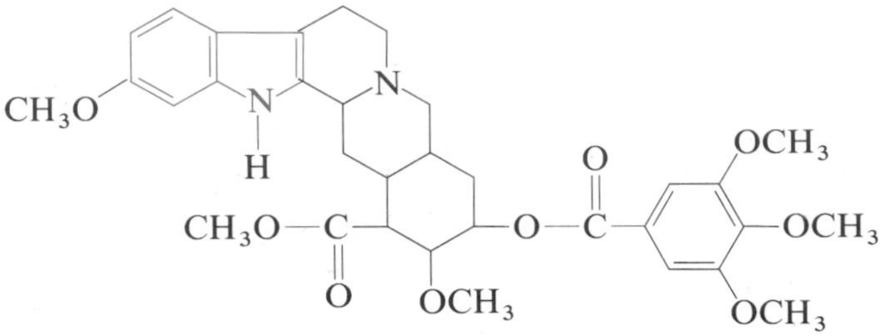

Figure VIII-2 Reserpine, a rauwolfia alkaloid. The indole ring is shown in color.

standard sedatives, rauwolfia does not produce grogginess, stupor, or lack of coordination. Patients on rauwolfia therapy appeared to be relaxed, quiet, and tranquil. Reports such as this generated interest among psychiatrists, and soon rauwolfia was recognized as an entirely new class of drug for the treatment of mental illness. It was the first of the so-called tranquilizers. (See Mini-Essay IX, "Biogenic Amines and Emotion.")

In 1952 chemists isolated the active compound from rauwolfia and named it reserpine. Reserpine, which proved to be 10,000 times more effective than the same weight of crude snakeroot extract, contains an indole nucleus as part of five fused rings. See Figure VIII-2.

In 1954, the first full year of reserpine therapy, two dozen companies in the United States were preparing rauwolfia products and by 1960, the cost of prescriptions for these totaled $30 million per year. Thus, in slightly more than two de-

cades, rauwolfia had advanced from a folk remedy to a widely used and highly effective drug for the treatment of high blood pressure and certain forms of mental illness.

Along with reserpine and reserpinelike alkaloids, another group of alkaloids, either containing the indole nucleus or containing structural features suggesting the indole nucleus, has been under intense research (Figure VIII-3). All characteristically produce behavioral aberrations—hallucinations, delusions, disturbances in thinking, and changes in mood.

The principal source of lysergic acid from which lysergic acid diethylamide (LSD) is made is ergot, a fungus that grows parasitically on rye. Mescaline is obtained from the cactus known as peyote, or mescal (*Lophophora williamsii*) and is named for the Mescalero Apaches of the Great Plains, who developed a religious rite in which its use was common. Because mescaline does not

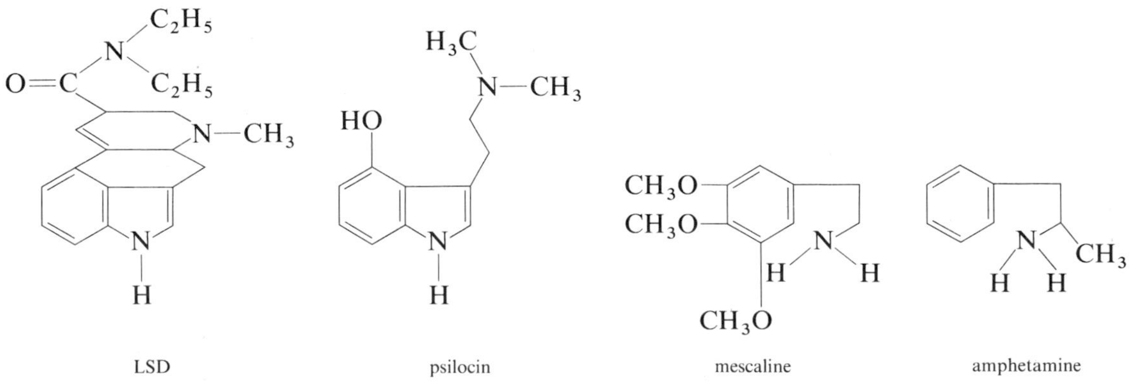

Figure VIII-3 Structural relations among several psychotomimetic drugs. The indole ring appears in LSD and psilocin. Mescaline and amphetamine are drawn so as to suggest an indole nucleus.

contain the indole nucleus, it does not properly belong to the class of indole alkaloids. Yet there is a suggestive chemical similarity and certainly strong pharmacological similarity between it and the indole psychotomimetics. Psilocin is the hallucinogenic principal of *Psilocybe aztecorum*, the narcotic mushroom of the Aztecs.

Serotonin and Norepinephrine

Of the various amines found in the brain, studies of serotonin, dopamine, and norepinephrine have been very important in currently evolving psychopharmacological concepts. Each compound functions in the central nervous system as a neurotransmitter.

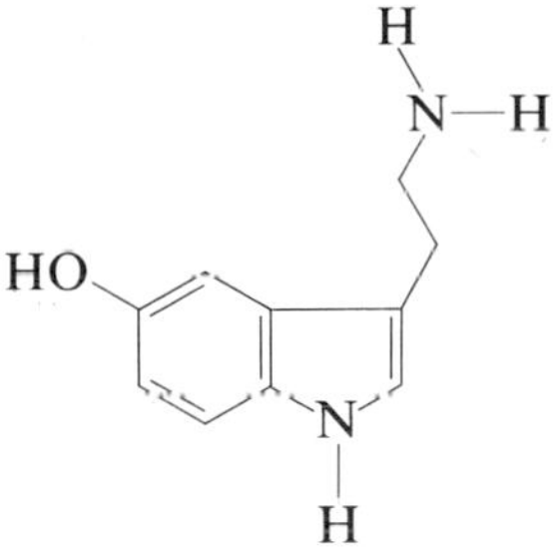

serotonin

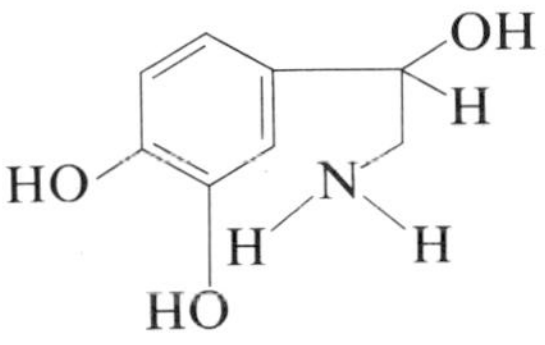

norepinephrine

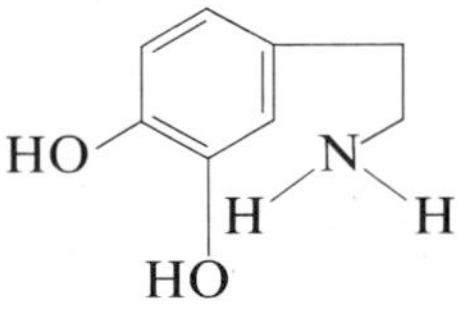

dopamine

An examination of the molecular structures of the psychotomimetic drugs reveals certain striking similarities between them and serotonin, dopamine, and norepinephrine. One theory holds that all known hallucinogens exert the effects they do because they can assume a conformation that simulates a structural characteristic of one or more of these three neurotransmitters.

The interest aroused by the discoveries of drugs that act selectively to affect mood and behavior has focused attention on possible chemical bases for disturbances in behavior. Underlying this effort is the hope that research on brain biochemistry will benefit the understanding and treatment of mental disease.

Sources

Goodman, L. S., and Gilman, A. 1980. *The Pharmacological Basis of Therapeutics*, 6th ed. New York: Macmillan.

Guillemin, R. 1978. Peptides in the brain: The new endocrinology of the neuron. *Science* 202:390.

Snyder, S. H. 1978. The brain's own opiates. *Chem. & Eng. News* 55:26.

Biogenic Amines and Emotion

Over the past several decades, much study has been given to biochemical correlates of emotion. Initial research in this field concentrated largely on levels of chemical modulators in blood and excretion of hormones and metabolites in the urine. The historic studies of Walter Cannon after 1900 suggested that epinephrine (adrenaline) is secreted in response to stimuli that produce fear and rage reactions in animals. In the ensuing years, studies in both animals and humans clearly indicated an increased secretion of epinephrine as well as norepinephrine in various types of stress, including parachute jumping, competitive sports, aggressive behavior, and viewing emotion-laden movies.

An area of more interest, but one far less amenable to direct experimental observation, is the pattern of biochemical changes that takes place in the brain itself in relation to emotional states. The reasons are obvious. It is far easier to examine blood levels of chemical modulators or the excretion of hormones and metabolites in the urine than to examine the biochemistry of neurons themselves. Yet it has been possible to do just this, in a limited way, in the past four decades. The catecholamines norepinephrine and dopamine (each derived from the parent molecule catechol) and the indole amine serotonin have received the most attention. We shall concentrate on norepinephrine and dopamine because more is known about them than any other class of neurotransmitters.

Biosynthesis of Norepinephrine and Dopamine

Norepinephrine and dopamine are limited to certain cells in the central nervous system where they are present in the cytoplasm, the axon, and synaptic vesicles. Synthesis of norepinephrine and dopamine begins with the amino acid tyrosine (Chapter 21). Oxidation of tyrosine, catalyzed by the enzyme tyrosine hydroxylase, forms dihydroxyphenylalanine (DOPA), which in turn undergoes loss of CO_2, catalyzed by DOPA decarboxylase, to give dihydroxyphenylethylamine (dopamine). Oxidation of dopamine, catalyzed by dopamine beta-hydroxylase, gives norepinephrine (Figure IX-1).

Norepinephrine and dopamine are protected from further reaction by being bound in synaptic vesicles. When an action potential arrives at a nerve ending, its neurotransmitters are released and they pass through the presynaptic membrane into the synaptic cleft. There they interact with specific receptor sites on the postsynaptic membrane.

Once a neurotransmitter has interacted with a receptor site on the next nerve cell, its further interaction must be prevented. Otherwise its effects would continue for too long and precise control of nerve function would be lost. Dopamine and norepinephrine are rapidly inactivated in two ways: (1) by reuptake through the presynaptic membranes into synaptic vesicles, and (2) by enzyme-catalyzed transformation in the synapse itself. A substantial fraction of each neurotransmitter is returned to synaptic vesicles for reuse. Some of each, however, undergoes oxidation catalyzed by the enzyme monoamine oxidase (MAO), in which the $-CH_2NH_2$ group is converted to a $-CO_2H$ group. The resulting carboxylic acid leaves via the blood and is excreted in the urine. Norepinephrine within synapses is metabolized principally by methyla-

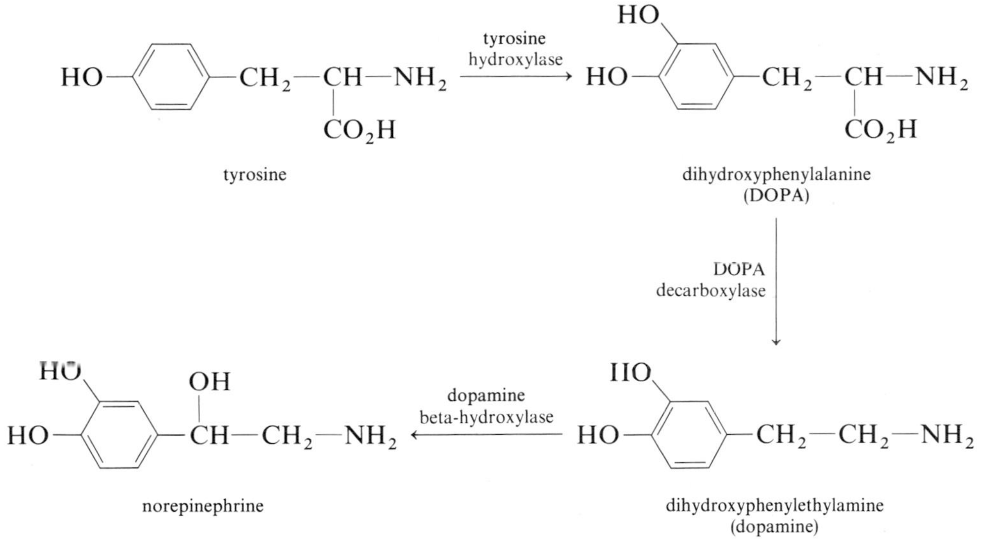

Figure IX-1 Biosynthesis of norepinephrine and dopamine from tyrosine.

tion catalyzed by the enzyme catecholamine-O-methyl transferase (COMT). The —OH on carbon 3 of the catechol ring is converted to —OCH_3. This product also enters the bloodstream and eventually is excreted in the urine (Figure IX-2).

Dopamine and Parkinson's Disease

An understanding of how dopamine acts as a neurotransmitter has led to an effective treatment for the crippling affliction Parkinson's disease. In 1959, the Swedish pharmacologist Arvid Carlsson discovered that when rats are given large doses of reserpine, they develop Parkinson-like tremors. He further discovered that there is an associated decrease in dopamine in the brain's caudate nucleus, a center involved with coordination and integration of fine muscle movement. Soon thereafter, George Cotzias of Brookhaven National Laboratory discovered that DOPA counteracts dopamine deficiency in Parkinson patients and effectively relieves symptoms of the disease. Today, even more effective anti-Parkinson drugs have been developed. The story of unraveling the biochemistry of dopa-

mine is a success story of how basic research can lead to a new treatment for a disease.

Psychopharmacology

Although interest in the psychological effects of drugs is almost as old as mankind, the use of drugs to treat psychiatric disorders has become widespread only since the mid-1950s, initiated largely by the great wave of enthusiasm for the use of reserpine for treating mania and excitement (see Mini-Essay VIII, "Alkaloids").

Almost simultaneously, scientists discovered the remarkable antipsychotic properties of chlorpromazine. Henri Laborit, a French physician, was looking for drugs to calm patients before surgery. He tried chlorpromazine (Thorazine), a drug synthesized by the French pharmaceutical company Specia in a search for newer and more effective antihistamines. Testing of chlorpromazine as an antihistamine was not pursued because initial trials showed that it was too sedating. However, Laborit discover that for his purposes, the drug was ideal, and he went on to suggest to his colleagues that they try it on heretofore unmanageable patients in mental institutions. Much to their surprise, psychiatrists

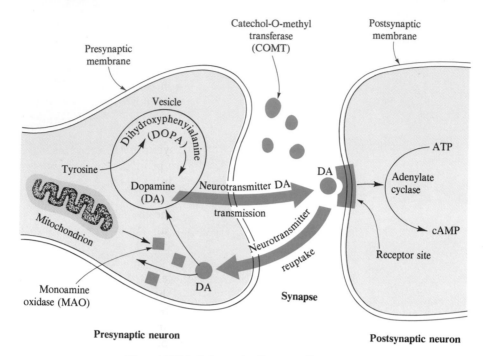

Figure IX-2 Schematic diagram of a synapse.

discovered that the drug calmed schizophrenics and seemed to relieve their symptoms. Chlorpromazine drugs produce sedation, emotional quieting, and relaxation, without clouding consciousness or intellectual functioning.

Chlorpromazine quickly usurped the position of reserpine when it became clear that chlorpromazine is easier to control and more effective than reserpine. Within a few years, chlorpromazine and its derivatives became one of the most

widely used drugs in medicine. It is estimated that between 1955, when it was first introduced, and 1965 at least 50 million patients received the drug (Figure IX-3).

The Catecholamine Hypothesis of Affective Illnesses

In attempts to correlate these observations with the underlying biochemistry, scientists have pro-

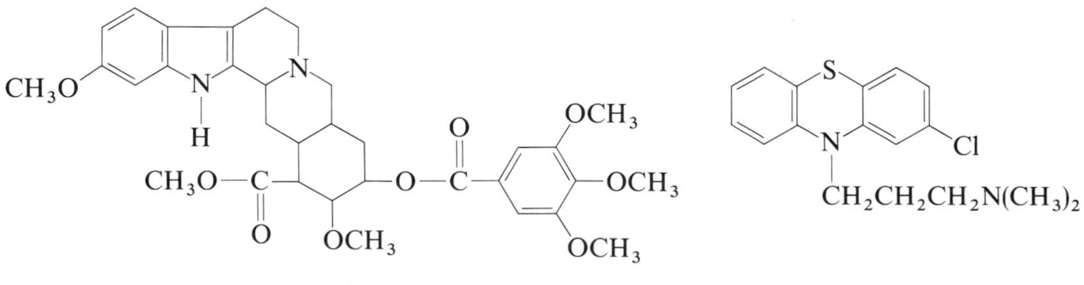

reserpine

chlorpromazine

Figure IX-3 Tranquilizers. Reserpine depletes synaptic vesicles of norepinephrine. Chlorpromazine impairs norepinephrine-receptor interaction.

posed the "catecholamine hypothesis" of affective illness. In outline, it has been proposed that:

1. Depression is caused by a functional decrease in either norepinephrine or dopamine; the major antidepressants act either by increasing the amount of norepinephrine or dopamine, or both, released into synapses or by enhancing their accumulation at appropriate receptor sites.
2. Mania is caused by a functional increase in either norepinephrine or dopamine; the major tranquilizing drugs act either by depleting the supply of available norepinephrine or dopamine, or both, or by reducing the effectiveness of their interaction at specific receptor sites.

What is the evidence for the hypotheses that norepinephrine or dopamine have anything to do with emotional states? Research on both animals and people suggests that reserpine, by some mechanism not yet understood, acts on synaptic vesicles and impairs their ability to store norepinephrine and dopamine. As a consequence, catecholamine neurotransmitters are released; they diffuse freely through the cytoplasm and onto mitochondrial-bound MAO, where they are oxidized to inactive compounds and eventually excreted in the urine. Thus, instead of being stored in synaptic vesicles for later release on nerve stimulation, catecholamine supplies are prematurely depleted. Even though there is continuing synthesis, the depletion may last for days or even weeks.

The weight of evidence suggests that the principal action of chlorpromazine is on norepinephrine and dopamine receptor sites rendering them incapable of responding. The result is similar to a decrease in supply of the neurotransmitters. Thus, although both reserpine and chlorpromazine are powerful tranquilizers, the mechanism of action of each is different.

Discovery of the tranquilizing effects of reserpine and chlorpromazine was followed within a few years by the discovery that iproniazid, a drug developed for the treatment of tuberculosis, had mood-elevating effects on tuberculosis patients.

The norepinephrine hypothesis was reinforced with the finding that iproniazid is a powerful inhibitor of monoamine oxidase (MAO), the enzyme responsible for metabolic degradation of norepinephrine, dopamine, and other brain monoamines. Inhibition of MAO permits an increase in the concentration of catecholamine neurotransmitters at nerve endings and presumably at synapses as well. This accumulation is thought to produce the antidepressant action of the drug in the human body. Elucidation of the structure of iproniazid sparked research efforts to synthesize new compounds with even greater clinical effectiveness. Among those synthesized and marketed was isocarboxazid (Marplan).

Imipramine and closely related tricyclic compounds are the drugs most widely used today to treat depression. It is interesting that imipramine (an antidepressant) has a ring structure that differs from that of chlorpromazine (a tranquilizer) only in replacement of the atom of sulfur in the middle ring by a two-carbon ethylene bridge. The mechanism by which imipramine functions as an antidepressant is not fully understood. It is thought, however, that it favors accumulation of norepinephrine at receptor sites by inhibiting uptake of intercellular norepinephrine. Thus imipramine artificially increases the concentration of norepinephrine at receptor sites and thereby potentiates its action. Antidepressants are shown in Figure IX-4.

In summary, a significant body of experimental evidence is at least consistent with the hypothesis that the effects of the major tranquilizers and antidepressants are related to their effects on norepinephrine and dopamine and that these catecholamine neurotransmitters are important in mental and behavioral states. But by no means does this evidence prove the hypothesis. For one thing, it is estimated that to date scientists have isolated and identified only a fraction of all central-nervous-system neurotransmitters. It would be remarkable indeed if the few studied to date are the most important ones involved in mediation of emotions.

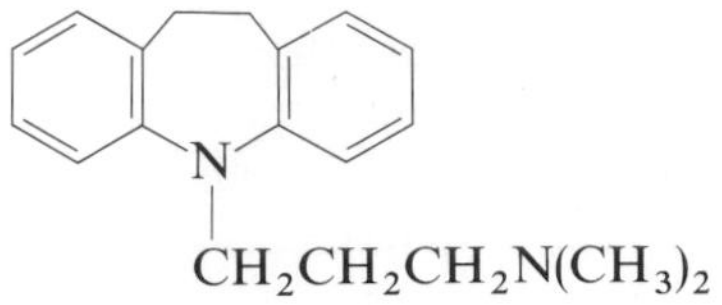

imipramine

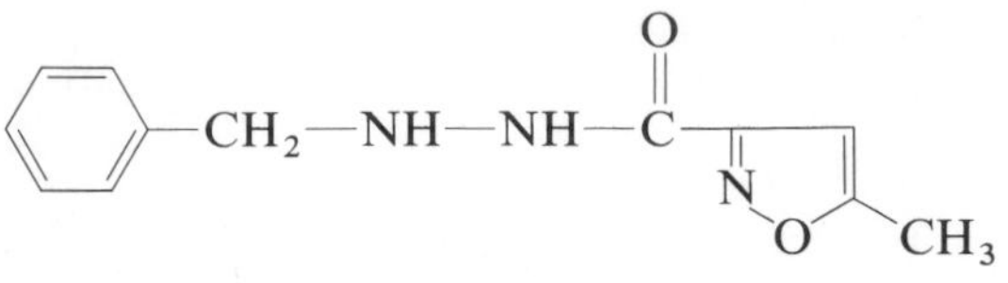

isocarboxazid

Figure IX-4 Antidepressants. Imipramine (Tofranil), an inhibitor of reuptake of norepinephrine. Isocarboxazid (Marplan), an inhibitor of monoamine oxidase.

Further, it is unlikely that norepinephrine or dopamine, or for that matter any other single neurotransmitter, is entirely responsible for a specific emotional state. Rather, it is more likely that other factors are important too—the interaction of certain amines at particular sites within the central nervous system, and environmental and psychological determinants.

Finally we must be wary of oversimplification in a subject as complex and multifaceted as human behavior.

Sources

Baldessarine, R. J. 1957. The basis for amine hypotheses in affective disorders. *Arch. Gen. Psychiatry* 32:285.

Cooper, J. R., Bloom, F. E., and Roth, R. H. 1978. *The Biochemical Basis of Neuropharmacology.* New York: Oxford University Press.

Krassner, M. B. 1983. Brain chemistry. *Chem. & Eng. News* 61:22.

Schildkraut, J. J., and Kety, S. S. 1967. Biogenic amines and emotion. *Science* 156:21.

15

Aldehydes and Ketones

In Chapter 12 we studied the physical and chemical properties of compounds containing carbon-carbon double bonds. In this and the following two chapters, we will study the physical and chemical properties of compounds containing the **carbonyl group** (C=O). Because the carbonyl group is the central structural feature of aldehydes, ketones, carboxylic acids, and their functional derivatives, it is one of the most important functional groups in organic chemistry. The chemical properties of this group are straightforward, and an understanding of its few characteristic reaction themes leads very quickly to an understanding of a wide variety of reactions in organic and biochemistry.

15.1 The Structure of Aldehydes and Ketones

A. Characteristic Structural Features

The characteristic structural feature of an **aldehyde** is the presence of a carbonyl group bonded to a hydrogen atom (Section 10.2B). In methanal (formaldehyde), the simplest aldehyde, the carbonyl group is bonded to two hydrogen atoms. In other aldehydes, it is bonded to one hydrogen atom and one carbon atom. Following are Lewis structures for methanal and ethanal. Under each in parentheses is its common name.

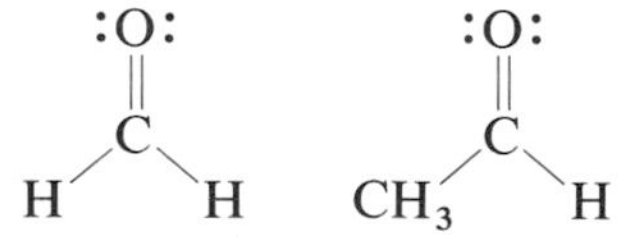

methanal
(formaldehyde)

ethanal
(acetaldehyde)

The characteristic structural feature of a **ketone** is a carbonyl group bonded to two carbon atoms (Section 10.2B). Following is a Lewis structure for 2-propanone (acetone), the simplest ketone.

:O:
‖
C
CH₃   CH₃

2-propanone
(acetone)

B. Covalent Bonding in Aldehydes and Ketones

In forming bonds to three other atoms, carbon uses sp^2 hybrid orbitals. The carbon-oxygen double bond consists of one sigma bond formed by overlap of sp^2 atomic orbitals of carbon and oxygen, and one pi bond formed by the overlap of parallel $2p$ orbitals. The two nonbonding pairs of electrons on oxygen lie in the remaining sp^2 orbitals of oxygen. Figure 15.1(b) shows an orbital-overlap diagram of the covalent bonding in formaldehyde. From the sp^2 hybridization of the carbonyl carbon, bond angles about this atom are predicted to be 120°. Actual bond angles in formaldehyde are shown in Figure 15.1(a).

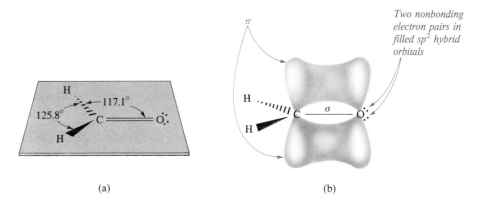

(a)   (b)

Figure 15.1 Covalent bonding in formaldehyde: (a) Lewis structure showing observed bond angles, and (b) covalent bond formation by overlap of atomic orbitals.

15.2 Nomenclature of Aldehydes and Ketones

A. IUPAC Nomenclature

The IUPAC system of nomenclature for aldehydes and ketones follows the familiar pattern of selecting as the parent compound the longest chain of carbon atoms that contains the functional group. The aldehyde group is shown by changing the suffix -e of the parent name to -al (Section 11.5). Because the aldehyde group can appear only at the end of a hydrocarbon chain and because numbering must start with it as carbon 1, its position is unambiguous and therefore there is no need to use a number to locate it. Following are IUPAC names for several low-molecular-weight aldehydes.

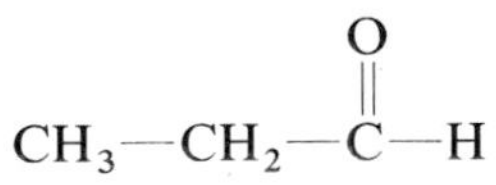

$$CH_3-CH_2-\overset{\overset{\textstyle O}{\|}}{C}-H \qquad CH_3-\underset{\underset{\textstyle CH_3}{|}}{CH}-CH_2-\overset{\overset{\textstyle O}{\|}}{C}-H \qquad CH_3-CH_2-\underset{\underset{\textstyle CH_3}{|}}{CH}-\overset{\overset{\textstyle O}{\|}}{C}-H$$

| propanal | 3-methylbutanal | 2-methylbutanal |

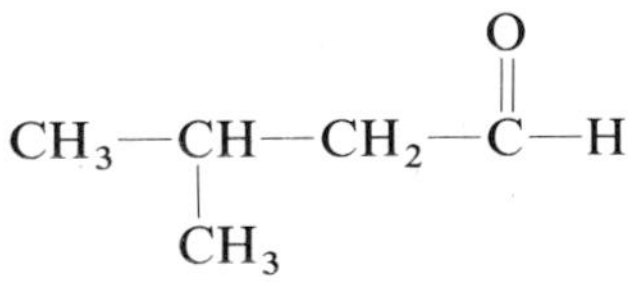

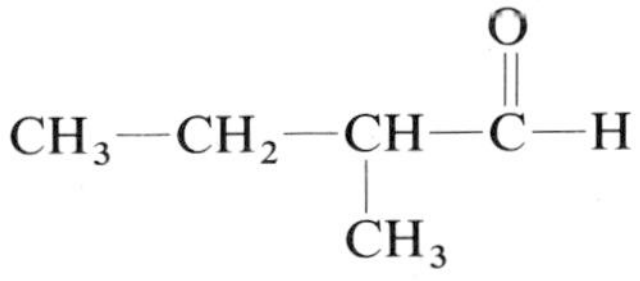

For unsaturated aldehydes (that is, those also containing an alkene), the presence of the carbon-carbon double bond is indicated by the infix -*en*-, as shown in the following examples. As with other molecules with both an infix and a suffix, the location of the suffix determines the numbering pattern.

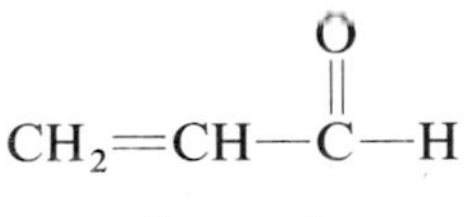

$$CH_2{=}CH-\overset{\overset{\textstyle O}{\|}}{C}-H \qquad CH_3-\underset{\underset{\textstyle CH_3}{|}}{C}{=}CH-CH_2-CH_2-\underset{\underset{\textstyle CH_3}{|}}{C}{=}CH-\overset{\overset{\textstyle O}{\|}}{C}-H$$

| 2-propenal | 3,7-dimethyl-2,6-octadienal |

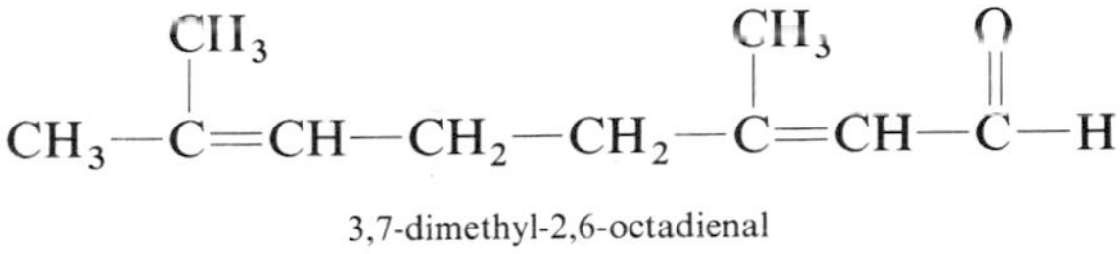

Among the aldehydes for which the IUPAC system retains common names are benzaldehyde and cinnamaldehyde.

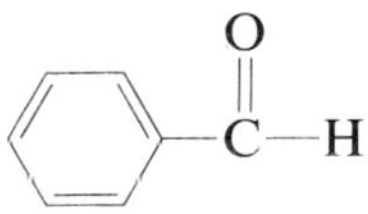

| benzaldehyde | cinnamaldehyde |

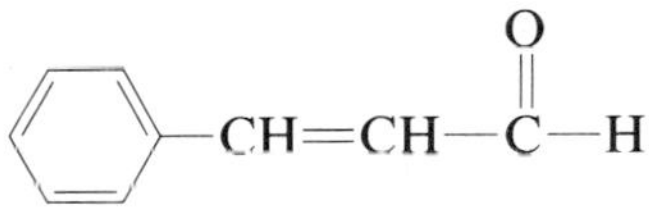

In the IUPAC system, ketones are named by selecting as the parent compound the longest chain that contains the carbonyl group and then indicating the presence of the carbonyl group by changing the suffix from -*e* to -*one*. The parent chain is numbered from the direction that gives the carbonyl group the lowest number. The IUPAC system retains the common names acetone and acetophenone.

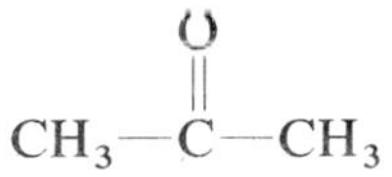

$$CH_3-\overset{\overset{\textstyle O}{\|}}{C}-CH_3 \qquad CH_3-\overset{\overset{\textstyle O}{\|}}{C}-CH_2-CH_3 \qquad CH_3-CH_2-\overset{\overset{\textstyle O}{\|}}{C}-\underset{\underset{\textstyle CH_3}{|}}{CH}-CH_2-CH_3$$

| 2-propanone (acetone) | 2-butanone | 4-methyl-3-hexanone |

| 2-methylcyclohexanone | acetophenone | p-chloroacetophenone |

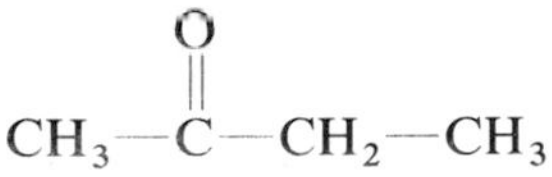

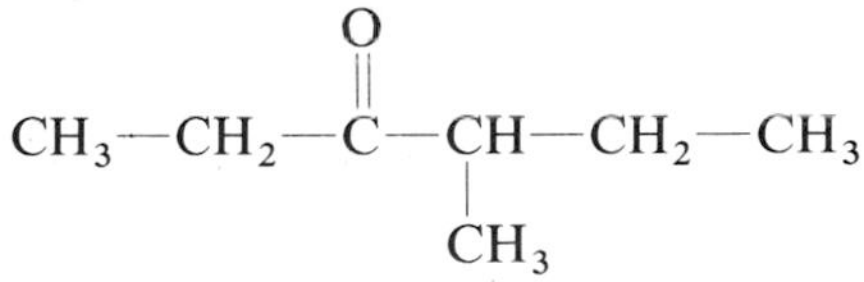

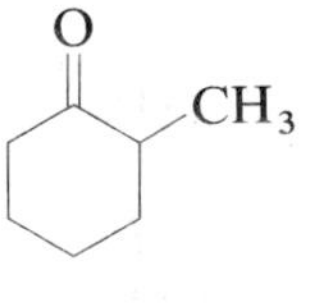

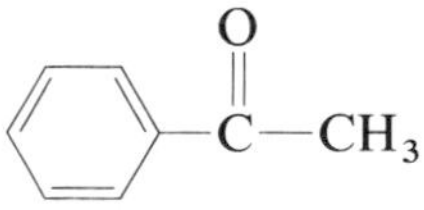

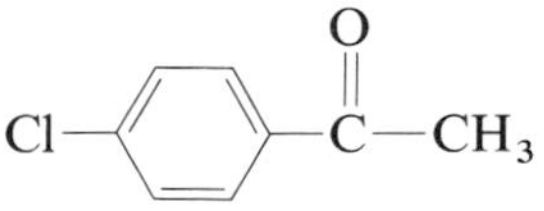

Example 15.1

Give IUPAC names for these compounds:

a. 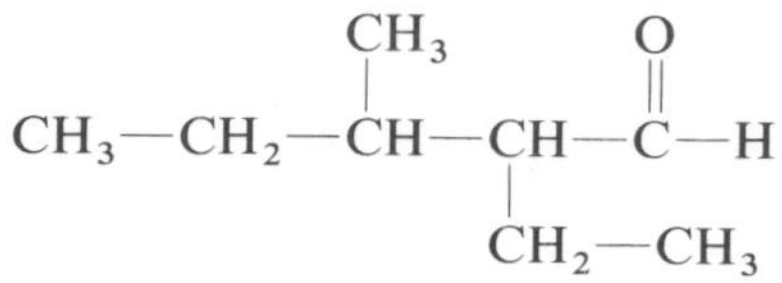
CH3
O
CH3—CH2—CH—CH—C—H
CH2—CH3

b. 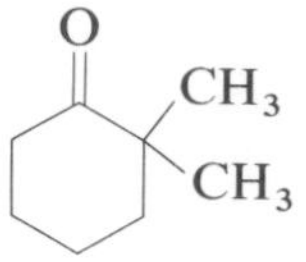
O
CH3
CH3

c. 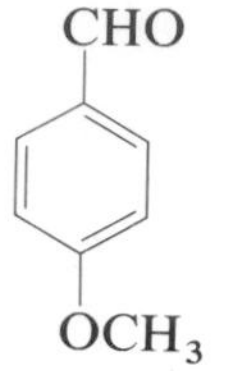
CHO
OCH3

☐ *Solution*

a. In this molecule, the longest chain is six carbons, but the longest chain that contains the aldehyde is five carbons. Therefore the parent chain is pentane.

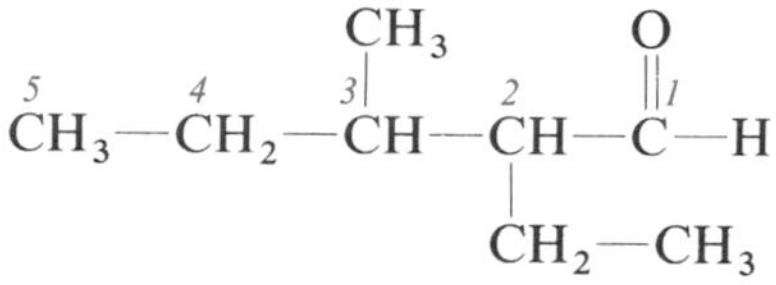
CH3
O
5 4 3 2 1
CH3—CH2—CH—CH—C—H
CH2—CH3

2-ethyl-3-methylpentanal

b. Number the six-membered ring beginning with the carbon bearing the carbonyl group. The IUPAC name is 2,2-dimethylcyclohexanone.

c. This molecule is derived from benzaldehyde. Its IUPAC name is 4-methoxybenzaldehyde. It may also be named *p*-methoxybenzaldehyde.

Problem 15.1

Give IUPAC names for the following.

a. 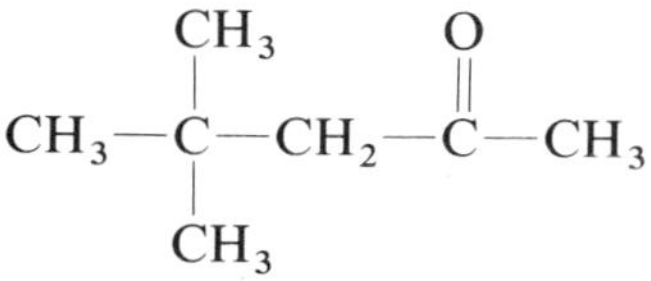
CH3
O
CH3—C—CH2—C—CH3
CH3

b. 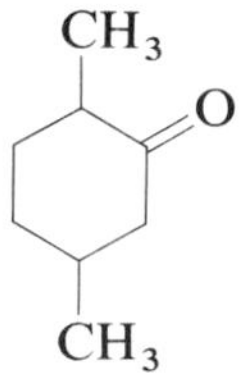
CH3
O
CH3

c. 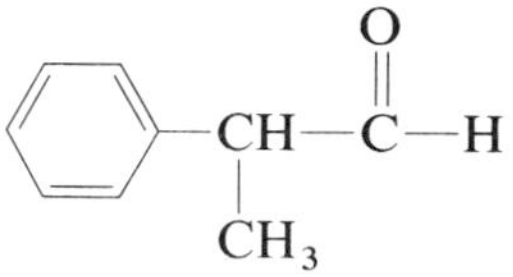
O
CH—C—H
CH3

B. IUPAC Names for More Complex Aldehydes and Ketones

For naming compounds that contain more than one functional group, that is, more than one that might be indicated by a suffix, the IUPAC system has established what is known as an order of precedence of functions. The order of precedence for the functional groups we will deal with most often is given in Table 15.1. There you will find how to indicate a given functional group if it has the highest precedence, and also how to show its presence if it has a lower precedence.

Following are several examples illustrating precedence rules.

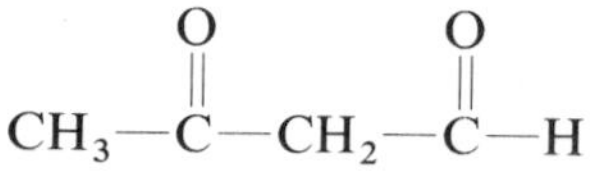
O
O
CH3—C—CH2—C—H

3-oxobutanal

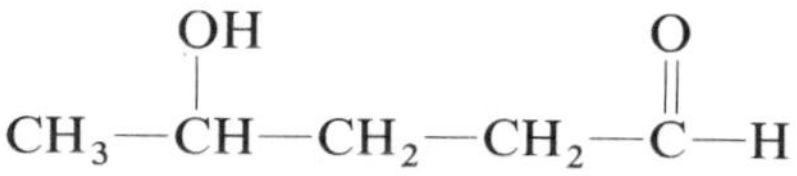
OH
O
CH3—CH—CH2—CH2—C—H

4-hydroxypentanal

Table 15.1
Order of precedence of several functional groups.

Functional Group	Suffix If Highest Precedence	Prefix If Lower Precedence
$\overset{\displaystyle O}{\underset{\displaystyle \|}{-C-OH}}$	oic acid	
$\overset{\displaystyle O}{\underset{\displaystyle \|}{-C-H}}$	al	oxo
$\overset{\displaystyle O}{\underset{\displaystyle \|}{-C-}}$	one	oxo
—OH	ol	hydroxy
—NH$_2$	amine	amino
—SH	thiol	mercapto

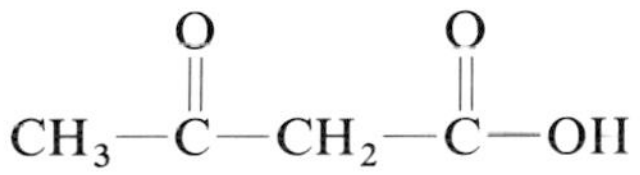

(decreasing precedence)

$$CH_3-\overset{O}{\overset{\|}{C}}-CH_2-\overset{O}{\overset{\|}{C}}-OH$$
3-oxobutanoic acid

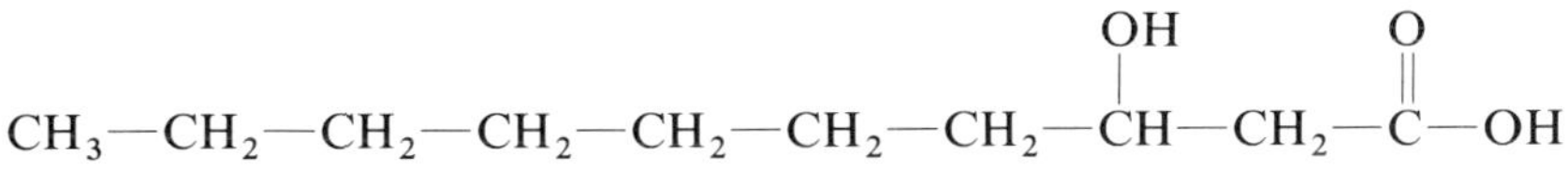

$$CH_3-CH_2-CH_2-CH_2-CH_2-CH_2-CH_2-\overset{OH}{\overset{\|}{CH}}-CH_2-\overset{O}{\overset{\|}{C}}-OH$$
3-hydroxydecanoic acid

C. Common Names

The common name for an aldehyde is derived from the common name of the corresponding carboxylic acid by changing the suffix -ic to -aldehyde. Because we have not yet studied common names for carboxylic acids, we cannot at this point give common names to aldehydes. However, we can illustrate how common names are derived by reference to a few common names you are familiar with. The common name formaldehyde is derived from formic acid, and the name acetaldehyde is derived from acetic acid:

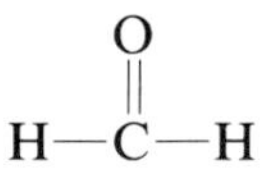

$$H-\overset{O}{\overset{\|}{C}}-H \qquad H-\overset{O}{\overset{\|}{C}}-OH \qquad CH_3-\overset{O}{\overset{\|}{C}}-H \qquad CH_3-\overset{O}{\overset{\|}{C}}-OH$$

formaldehyde 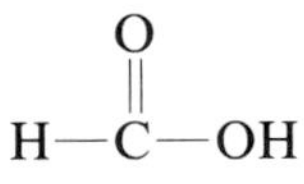   formic acid 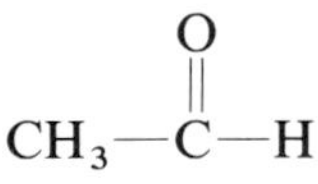   acetaldehyde 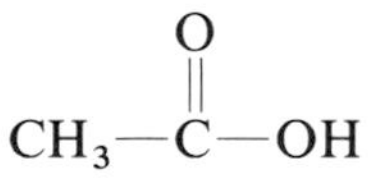   acetic acid

Common names for ketones are derived by naming the two alkyl or aryl groups attached to the carbonyl group, followed by the word *ketone*, as shown in the following examples. Note that each alkyl or aryl group is listed in alphabetical order as a separate word followed by the word *ketone*.

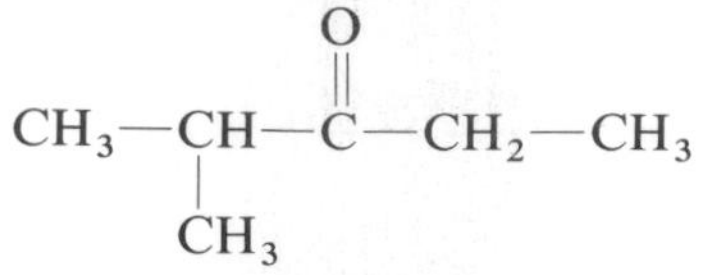

ethyl isopropyl ketone 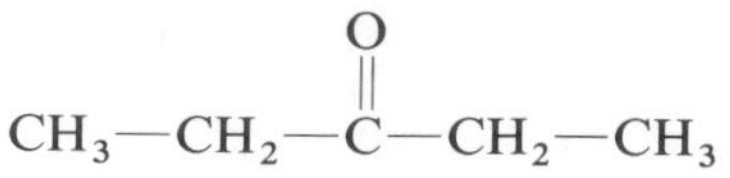   diethyl ketone 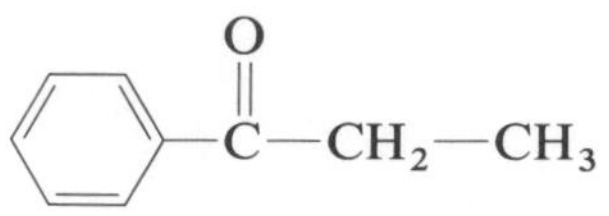   ethyl phenyl ketone

15.3 Physical Properties of Aldehydes and Ketones

Oxygen is more electronegative than carbon (3.5 compared with 2.5); therefore, the carbon-oxygen double bond is polar covalent. The oxygen atom of a carbonyl group bears a partial negative charge and the carbon atom a partial positive charge, as illustrated here for formaldehyde:

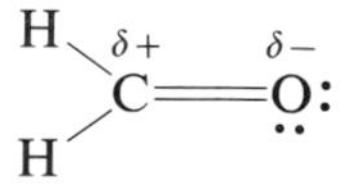

Alternatively, the **carbonyl group** may be pictured as a hybrid of two major contributing structures. Structure (b) places a negative charge on the more electronegative oxygen atom and a positive charge on the less electronegative carbon atom.

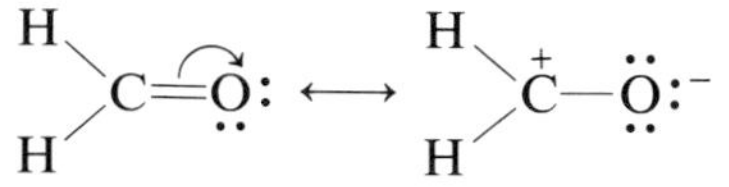

Because aldehydes and ketones are polar compounds and can interact in the pure state by dipole-dipole interaction, they have higher boiling points than

Table 15.2
Boiling points of compounds of comparable molecular weight.

Compound	Structural Formula	Mol. Wt.	bp (°C)
pentane	$CH_3CH_2CH_2CH_2CH_3$	72	36
methyl propyl ether	$CH_3CH_2CH_2OCH_3$	74	39
butanal	$CH_3CH_2CH_2\overset{\displaystyle O}{\overset{\|}{C}}H$	72	76
2-butanone	$CH_3CH_2\overset{\displaystyle O}{\overset{\|}{C}}CH_3$	72	80
1-butanol	$CH_3CH_2CH_2CH_2OH$	74	117
propanoic acid	$CH_3CH_2\overset{\displaystyle O}{\overset{\|}{C}}OH$	74	151

nonpolar compounds of comparable molecular weight. Table 15.2 lists boiling points of six compounds of comparable molecular weight.

Pentane, a nonpolar hydrocarbon, has the lowest boiling point. Although methyl propyl ether is a polar compound, there is little association between molecules in the liquid state. Hence it has a boiling point only slightly higher than that of pentane. Both butanal and 2-butanone are polar compounds, and because of the association between a partially positive carbon of one molecule and a partially negative oxygen of another, their boiling points are higher than the boiling points of pentane and methyl propyl ether. Aldehydes and ketones have no partially positive hydrogen atom attached to oxygen and cannot associate by hydrogen bonding. Therefore, they have lower boiling points than those of alcohols and carboxylic acids, compounds that can associate by hydrogen bonding.

Aldehydes and ketones can interact with water molecules as hydrogen-bond acceptors (Figure 15.2), and therefore low-molecular-weight aldehydes and ketones are more soluble in water than are nonpolar compounds of comparable molecular weight. Listed in Table 15.3 are values for boiling point and solubility in water for several low-molecular-weight aldehydes and ketones.

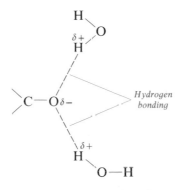

Figure 15.2 Hydrogen bonding between a carbonyl oxygen and water molecules.

Table 15.3
Physical properties of selected aldehydes and ketones.

Name	Structural Formula	bp (°C)	Solubility (g/100 g water)
formaldehyde	$HCHO$	−21	infinite
acetaldehyde	CH_3CHO	20	infinite
propanal	CH_3CH_2CHO	49	16
butanal	$CH_3CH_2CH_2CHO$	76	7
hexanal	$CH_3(CH_2)_4CHO$	129	slight
acetone	CH_3COCH_3	56	infinite
2-butanone	$CH_3CH_2COCH_3$	80	26
2-pentanone	$CH_3CH_2CH_2COCH_3$	101	5

15.4 Reactions of Aldehydes and Ketones

A carbonyl group, because of its polarity, reacts with both electrophiles and nucleophiles:

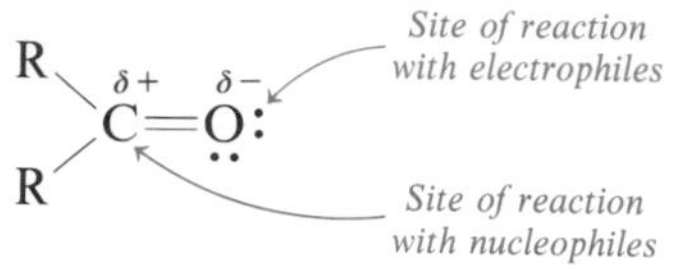

$$
\begin{array}{c}
R \\
\diagdown \\
\overset{\delta+}{C}=\overset{\delta-}{\ddot{O}}: \\
\diagup \\
R
\end{array}
\quad
\begin{array}{l}
\textit{Site of reaction} \\
\textit{with electrophiles}
\end{array}
$$

Site of reaction with nucleophiles

A **nucleophile** is any atom or group of atoms with an unshared pair of electrons that can be shared with another atom or group of atoms to form a new covalent bond. One of the most common reaction themes of the carbonyl group is **nucleophilic addition**, a reaction in which a nucleophile adds to the carbonyl carbon, to form a tetrahedral carbonyl addition compound. In the following general reaction, the nucleophilic reagent is written as H—Nu: to emphasize the presence of the unshared pair of electrons in the nucleophile.

Nucleophilic Addition

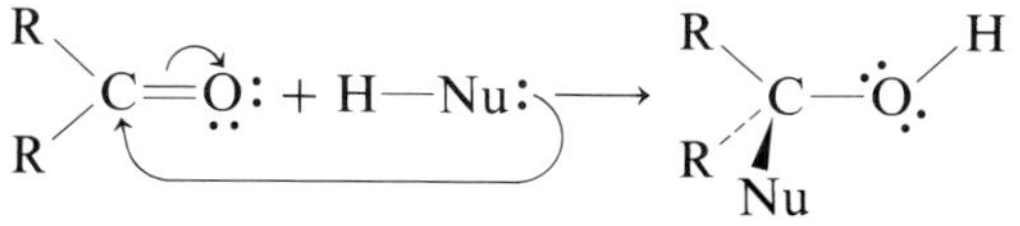

$$
\begin{array}{c}
R \\
\diagdown \\
C=\ddot{O}: + H—Nu: \longrightarrow \\
\diagup \\
R
\end{array}
\qquad
\begin{array}{c}
R \qquad H \\
\diagdown \qquad \diagup \\
C—\ddot{O}: \\
\diagup \diagdown \\
R \quad Nu
\end{array}
$$

tetrahedral carbonyl
addition compound

The most common electrophilic reagent in carbonyl addition reactions is the proton, H^+. Reaction of a carbonyl group with a proton gives a resonance-stabilized cation:

Electrophilic Addition

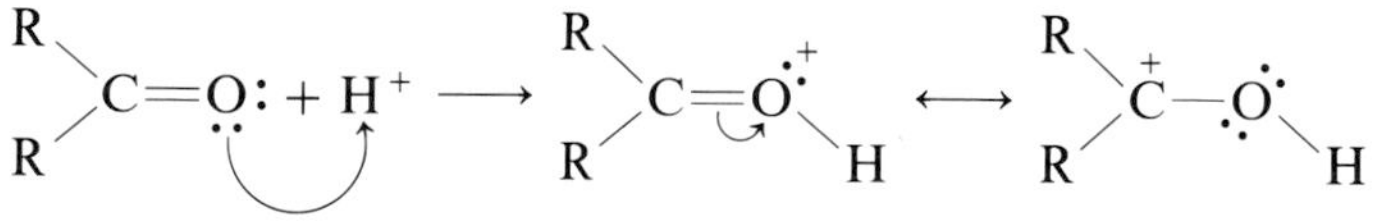

$$
\begin{array}{c}
R \\
\diagdown \\
C=\ddot{O}: + H^+ \longrightarrow \\
\diagup \\
R
\end{array}
\qquad
\begin{array}{c}
R \\
\diagdown \\
C=\overset{+}{\ddot{O}} \\
\diagup \quad \diagdown \\
R \qquad H
\end{array}
\longleftrightarrow
\begin{array}{c}
R \\
\diagdown \\
\overset{+}{C}—\ddot{O} \\
\diagup \quad \diagdown \\
R \qquad H
\end{array}
$$

resonance-stabilized cation

Protonation increases the electron deficiency of the carbonyl carbon and makes it even more reactive toward nucleophiles.

A. Addition of Water

Addition of water to the carbonyl group of an aldehyde or ketone forms a 1,1-diol. Note that in this designation, the numbers 1,1- do not refer to an IUPAC numbering system, but indicate that the two hydroxyl groups are on the same carbon. They are also called hydrates:

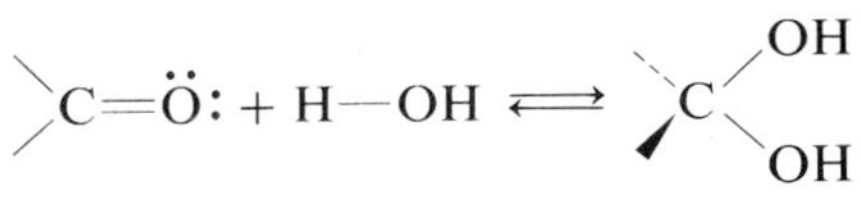

$$\underset{/}{\overset{\backslash}{C}}{=}\ddot{O}\text{:} + H{-}OH \rightleftharpoons \underset{\diagup}{\overset{\backslash}{C}}\underset{\backslash OH}{\overset{\diagup OH}{}}$$

a 1,1-diol
(a hydrate)

When formaldehyde is dissolved in water at 20°C, it is more than 99% hydrated. The equilibrium constant for this reaction is approximately 10^3.

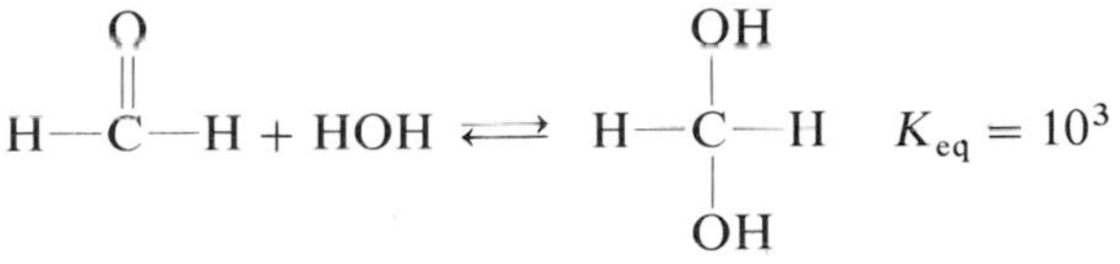

$$H{-}\overset{\overset{\displaystyle O}{\|}}{C}{-}H + HOH \rightleftharpoons H{-}\overset{\overset{\displaystyle OH}{|}}{\underset{\underset{\displaystyle OH}{|}}{C}}{-}H \quad K_{eq} = 10^3$$

greater than 99%

For acetaldehyde and most other aldehydes, equilibrium constants for hydration are approximately 1. For example, under experimental conditions comparable with those described for formaldehyde, acetaldehyde is approximately 58% hydrated.

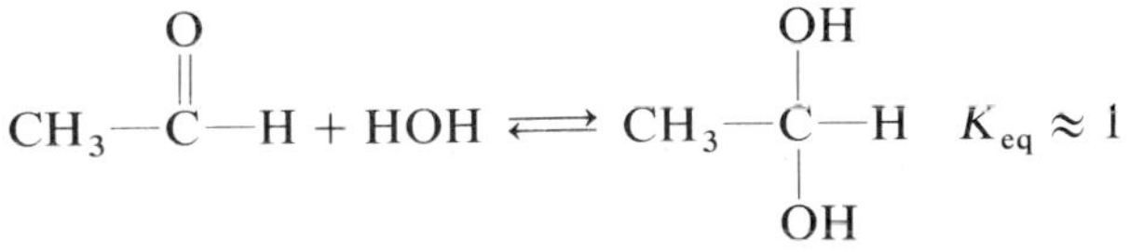

$$CH_3{-}\overset{\overset{\displaystyle O}{\|}}{C}{-}H + HOH \rightleftharpoons CH_3{-}\overset{\overset{\displaystyle OH}{|}}{\underset{\underset{\displaystyle OH}{|}}{C}}{-}H \quad K_{eq} \approx 1$$

58%

For most simple ketones, equilibrium constants for hydration are 10^{-3} or less. Thus, in aqueous solutions, ketones are almost entirely in the keto form instead of the hydrate.

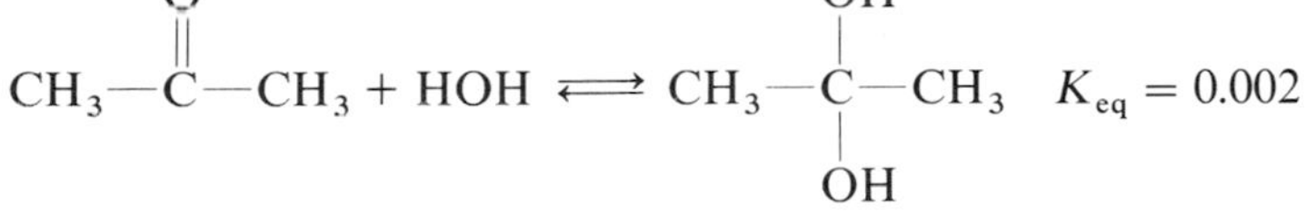

$$CH_3{-}\overset{\overset{\displaystyle O}{\|}}{C}{-}CH_3 + HOH \rightleftharpoons CH_3{-}\overset{\overset{\displaystyle OH}{|}}{\underset{\underset{\displaystyle OH}{|}}{C}}{-}CH_3 \quad K_{eq} = 0.002$$

very low

We can interpret the position of equilibria for carbonyl hydration by the relative sizes of atoms and groups of atoms bonded to the carbonyl carbon. Bond angles about a carbonyl carbon are approximately 120°; those for the same carbon in a hydrate are approximately 109.5°. Thus in hydration, there is a crowding as the groups attached to the carbonyl carbon are brought closer together in space. In formaldehyde, the two groups brought closer are hydrogen atoms; in acetaldehyde they are methyl and hydrogen; and in acetone they are two methyl groups. Because the increase in crowding is greatest for ketones, compared with aldehydes, equilibrium constants for their hydration are much smaller than for aldehydes.

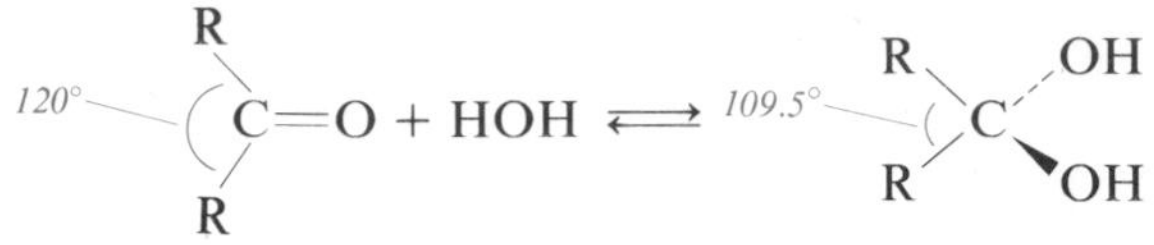

$$
\underset{120°}{\overset{R}{\underset{R}{\big\backslash}}} C{=}O + HOH \;\rightleftharpoons\; \underset{109.5°}{\overset{R}{\underset{R}{\big\backslash}}} C \overset{OH}{\underset{OH}{\big\diagup}}
$$

B. Addition of Alcohols: Formation of Acetals and Ketals

Alcohols add to aldehydes and ketones in the manner described for addition of water. Addition of one molecule of alcohol to an aldehyde forms a **hemiacetal** (a half-acetal). The comparable reaction with a ketone forms a **hemiketal** (a half-ketal).

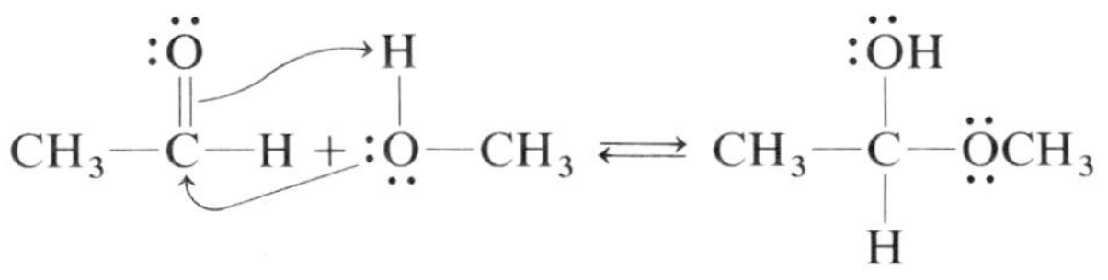

$$
CH_3{-}\overset{\overset{\displaystyle :\ddot{O}}{\|}}{C}{-}H + :\ddot{O}{-}CH_3 \;\rightleftharpoons\; CH_3{-}\underset{\underset{\displaystyle H}{|}}{\overset{\overset{\displaystyle :\ddot{O}H}{|}}{C}}{-}\ddot{O}CH_3
$$

(a hemiacetal)

$$
CH_3{-}\overset{\overset{\displaystyle :\ddot{O}}{\|}}{C}{-}CH_3 + :\ddot{O}{-}CH_2CH_3 \;\rightleftharpoons\; CH_3{-}\underset{\underset{\displaystyle CH_3}{|}}{\overset{\overset{\displaystyle :\ddot{O}H}{|}}{C}}{-}\ddot{O}CH_2CH_3
$$

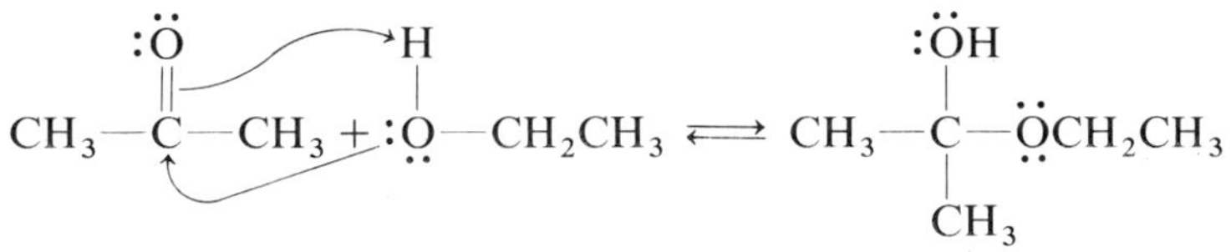

(a hemiketal)

Following are the characteristic structural features of a hemiacetal and a hemiketal. In each instance, the R group may be alkyl or aryl.

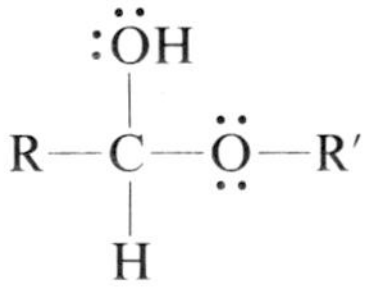

$$
R{-}\underset{\underset{\displaystyle H}{|}}{\overset{\overset{\displaystyle :\ddot{O}H}{|}}{C}}{-}\ddot{O}{-}R' \qquad R{-}\underset{\underset{\displaystyle R''}{|}}{\overset{\overset{\displaystyle :\ddot{O}H}{|}}{C}}{-}\ddot{O}{-}R'
$$

a hemiacetal   a hemiketal
(characteristic   (characteristic
structural feature)   structural feature)

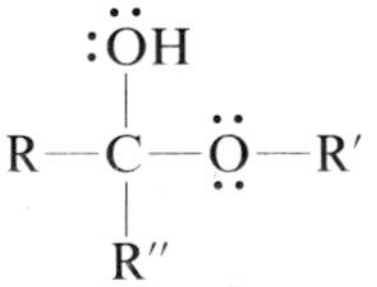

Hemiacetals and hemiketals are only minor components of an equilibrium mixture except in one very important type of molecule. When a hydroxyl group is part of the same molecule that contains the carbonyl group, and a five- or six-membered ring can form, the compound exists almost entirely in the cyclic hemiacetal or cyclic hemiketal form.

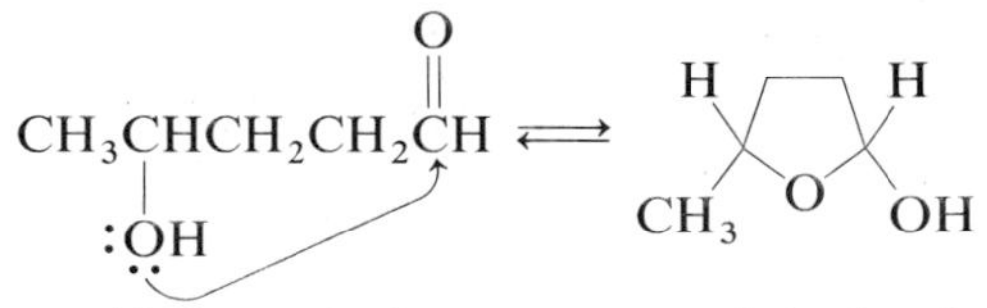

4-hydroxypentanal
(minor)

a cyclic hemiacetal
(major form present
at equilibrium)

Hemiacetals and hemiketals react further with alcohols to form **acetals** and **ketals** plus a molecule of water. Each of these reactions is acid-catalyzed.

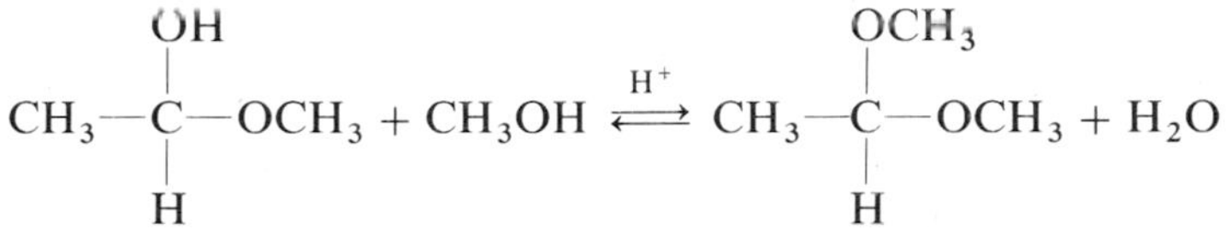

(a hemiacetal)

1,1-dimethoxyethane
(a dimethyl acetal)

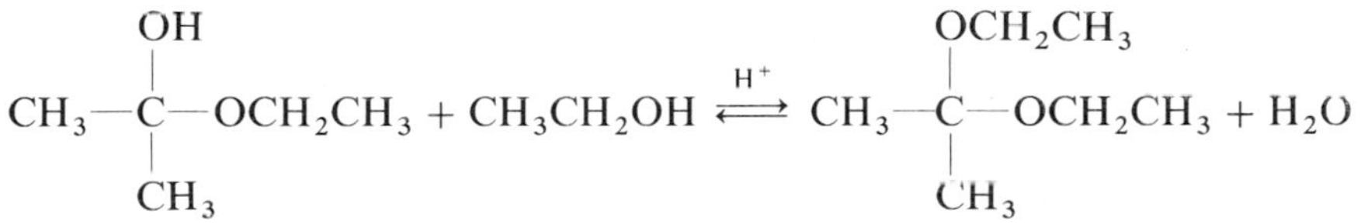

(a hemiketal)

2,2-diethoxypropane
(a diethyl ketal)

Following are general formulas showing the characteristic structural feature of an acetal and a ketal:

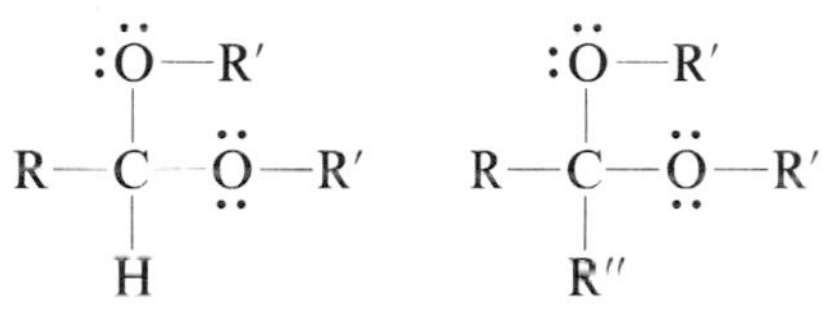

an acetal
(characteristic
structural feature)

a ketal
(characteristic
structural feature)

Acetal and ketal formation are equilibrium reactions, and to obtain high yields, it is necessary to remove water from the reaction mixture so as to favor product formation.

Example 15.2

For the following, show the reaction of each carbonyl compound with one molecule of alcohol to form a hemiacetal or hemiketal, and then with a second molecule of alcohol to form an acetal or ketal. Note that in part (b), ethylene glycol is a diol and one molecule provides both —OH groups.

a. 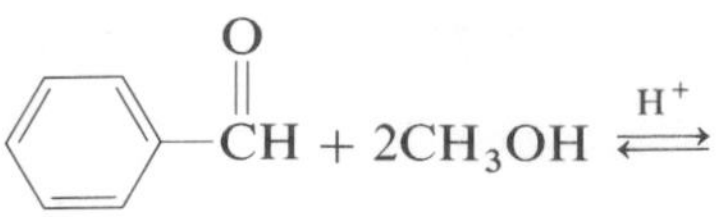 [benzaldehyde structure] $-CH + 2CH_3OH \xrightleftharpoons{H^+}$

b.  [cyclohexanone structure] $=O + HOCH_2CH_2OH \xrightleftharpoons{H^+}$

☐ *Solution*

a. 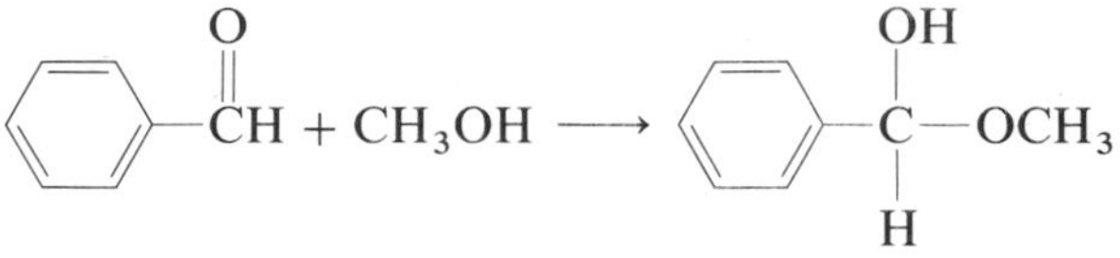 [benzaldehyde structure] $-CH + CH_3OH \longrightarrow$ [product] $C-OCH_3$ with OH and H

a hemiacetal

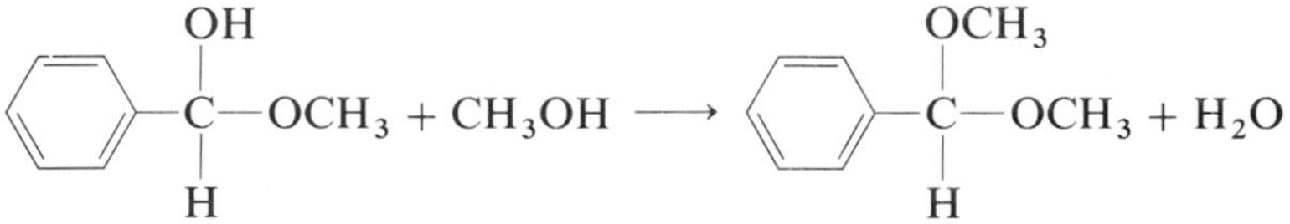

[structure] $C-OCH_3 + CH_3OH \longrightarrow$ [structure] $C-OCH_3 + H_2O$ with OCH₃ and H

an acetal

b. 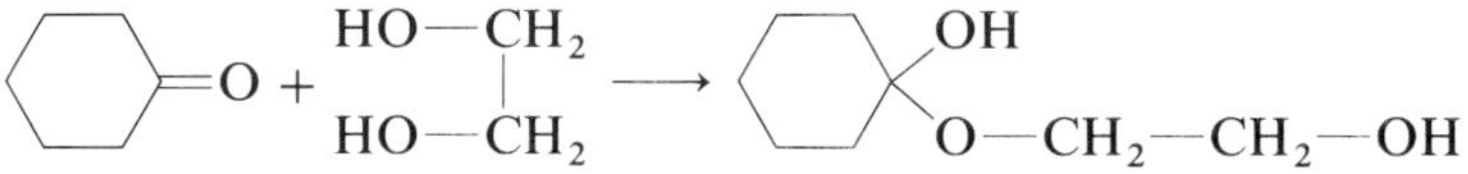 [cyclohexanone] $=O +$ $\begin{matrix} HO-CH_2 \\ | \\ HO-CH_2 \end{matrix} \longrightarrow$ [product with OH and $O-CH_2-CH_2-OH$]

a hemiketal

[structure with OH and $O-CH_2-CH_2-OH$] $\longrightarrow$ [cyclic structure $O-CH_2$ / $O-CH_2$] $+ H_2O$

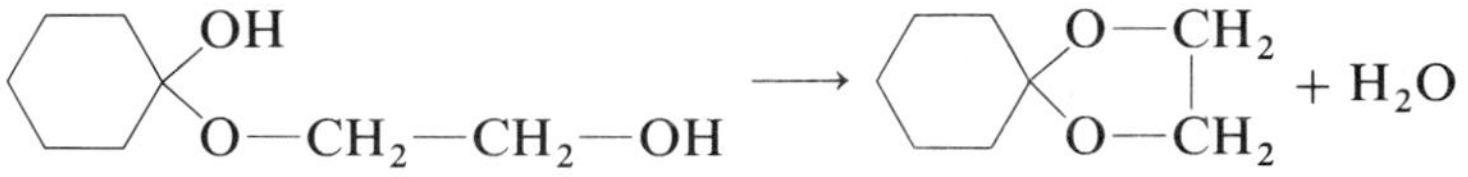

a cyclic ketal

Problem 15.2

The reaction of an acetal or ketal with water to form an aldehyde or a ketone and two molecules of alcohol is called hydrolysis. Following are structural formulas for one ketal and one acetal. Draw the structural formulas for the products of hydrolysis of each.

a. 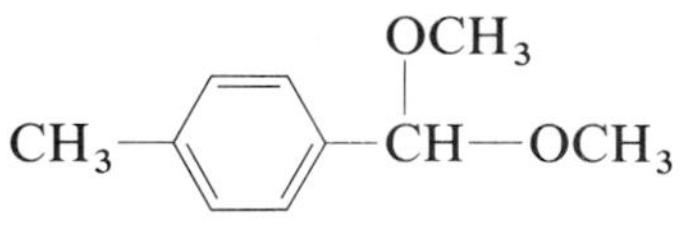 CH_3-[benzene ring]$-CH-OCH_3$ with OCH_3 above

b. 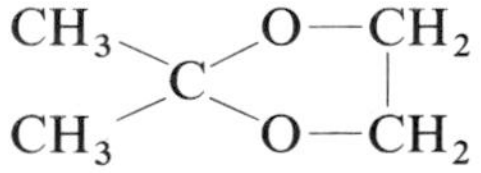 $\begin{matrix} CH_3 \\ \\ CH_3 \end{matrix} C \begin{matrix} O-CH_2 \\ | \\ O-CH_2 \end{matrix}$

As noted earlier, formation of acetals and ketals is catalyzed by acid. Their hydrolysis in water is also catalyzed by acid. Both acetals and ketals, however, are stable and unreactive in aqueous base.

In practice, formation of acetals and ketals is often carried out using the alcohol as the solvent and anhydrous acid, often dry HCl (hydrogen chloride gas), dissolved in the alcohol. Because the alcohol is both a reactant and solvent, it is present in large molar excess, which forces the position of equilibrium to the right and favors acetal/ketal formation.

C. Addition of Ammonia and Its Derivatives

Ammonia and amines of the type $R—NH_2$ react with the carbonyl group of aldehydes and ketones in the presence of an acid catalyst to give products that contain a carbon-nitrogen double bond, as shown below. A molecule containing a carbon-nitrogen double bond is called an **imine**, or alternatively, a **Schiff base**. The characteristic structural feature of an imine is a C=N group. Following are examples of conversion of an aldehyde and a ketone to imines.

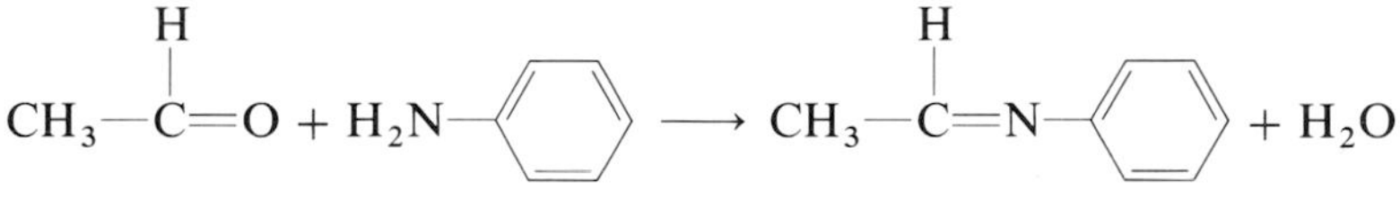

an imine
(a Schiff base)

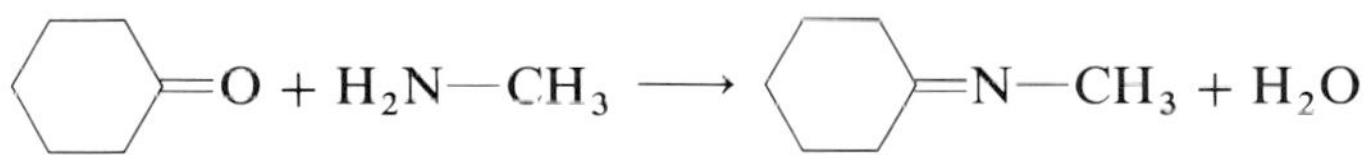

an imine
(a Schiff base)

The mechanism of imine formation can be divided into two steps. In step 1, the nitrogen atom of ammonia or the amine adds to the carbonyl carbon to form a tetrahedral carbonyl addition compound. In step 2, loss of water gives the imine.

Step 1: Formation of a tetrahedral carbonyl addition compound

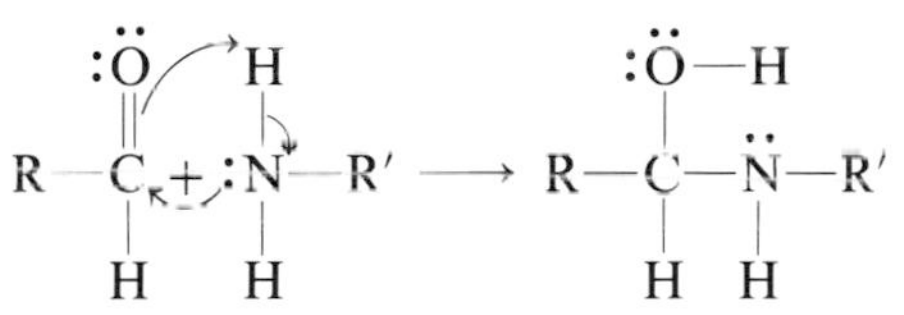

tetrahedral carbonyl
addition intermediate

Step 2: Loss of water

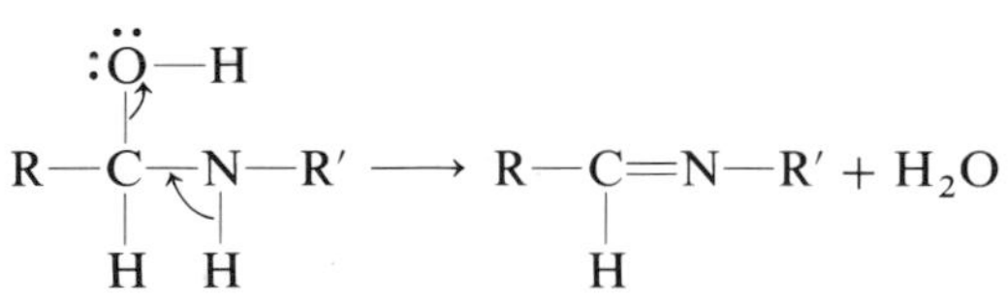

an imine
(a Schiff base)

As one example of the importance of imines in biological systems, the active form of vitamin A aldehyde (retinal) is bound to the protein opsin in the form of an imine. The —NH_2 group for imine formation is provided by the side chain of the amino acid lysine (Section 21.1). The imine formed by combination of vitamin A aldehyde and opsin is called rhodopsin, or alternatively, visual purple.

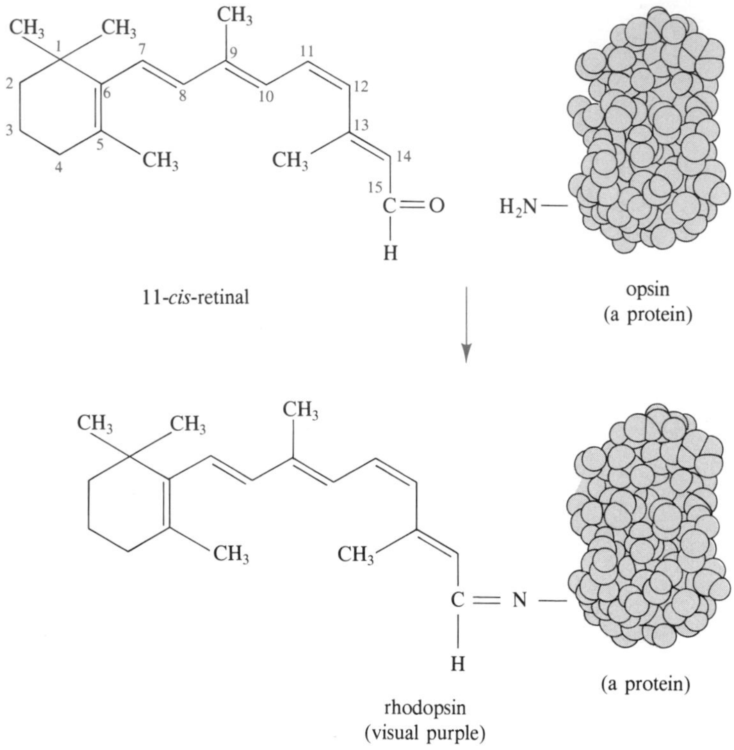

11-*cis*-retinal

opsin
(a protein)

rhodopsin
(visual purple)

(a protein)

**Example
15.3**

For the following, write structural formulas for the tetrahedral carbonyl addition compound and the imine (Schiff base) formed from it by loss of water.

a. 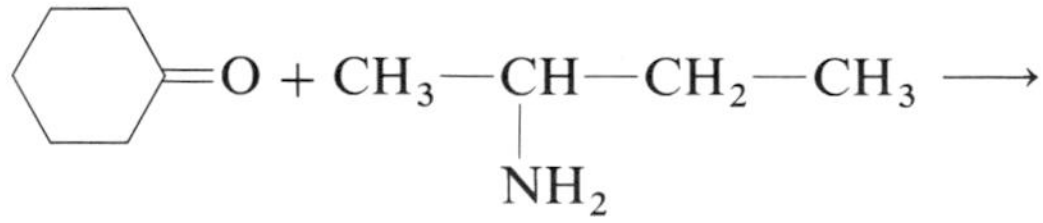 ⬡=O + CH_3—$\overset{\underset{\textstyle NH_2}{|}}{CH}$—$CH_2$—$CH_3$ ⟶

b. 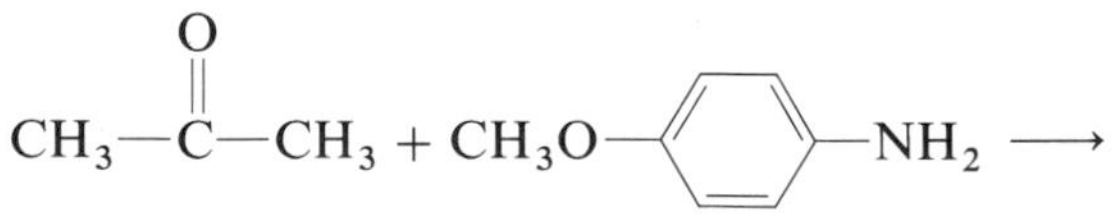 CH_3—$\overset{\overset{\textstyle O}{\|}}{C}$—$CH_3$ + CH_3O—⬡—NH_2 ⟶

☐ *Solution*

Following are structural formulas for the tetrahedral carbonyl addition compound and the imine.

a.

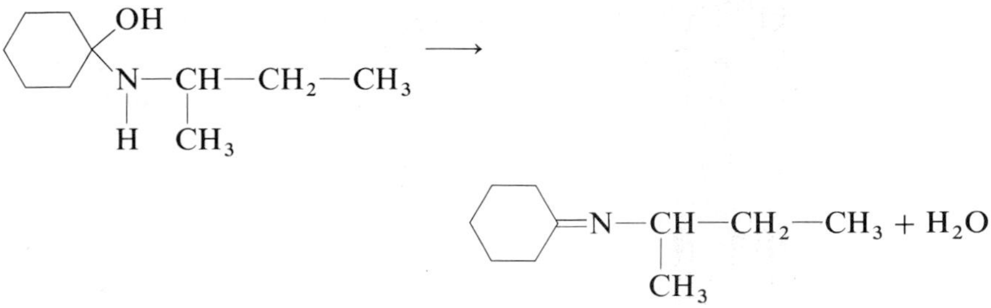

$$\underset{\substack{| \\ \text{H} \quad \text{CH}_3}}{\overset{\overset{\displaystyle \text{OH}}{|}}{\bigcirc}}\text{N}-\text{CH}-\text{CH}_2-\text{CH}_3 \longrightarrow$$

$$\bigcirc\!\!=\!\!\text{N}-\underset{\substack{| \\ \text{CH}_3}}{\text{CH}}-\text{CH}_2-\text{CH}_3 + \text{H}_2\text{O}$$

b.

$$\underset{\text{CH}_3}{\overset{\text{CH}_3}{\diagdown}}\underset{\substack{| \\ \text{H}}}{\overset{\overset{\displaystyle\text{OH}}{\diagup}}{\text{C}}}\text{N}-\bigcirc\!\!-\!\text{OCH}_3 \longrightarrow$$

$$\underset{\text{CH}_3}{\overset{\text{CH}_3}{\diagdown}}\text{C}\!=\!\text{N}-\bigcirc\!\!-\!\text{OCH}_3 + \text{H}_2\text{O}$$

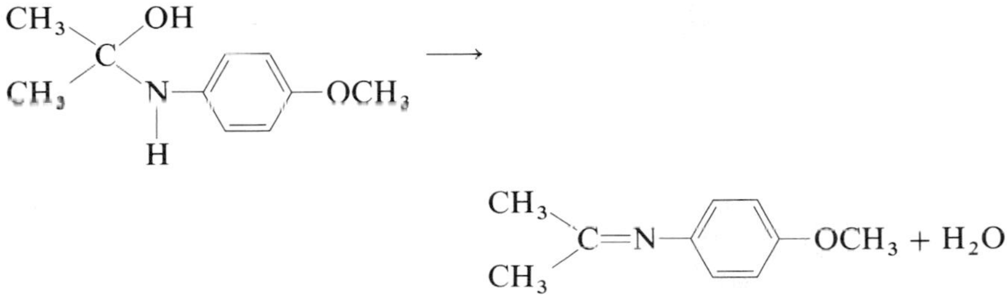

Problem 15.3

The reaction of an imine (a Schiff base) with water to form an amine and an aldehyde or ketone is called hydrolysis. Write structural formulas for the products of hydrolysis of the following imines.

a.

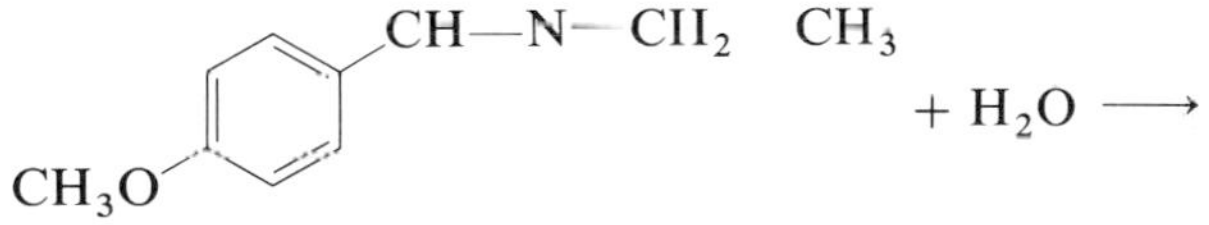

$$\text{CH}_3\text{O}-\bigcirc\!\!-\!\text{CH}-\text{N}-\text{CH}_2 \quad \text{CH}_3 \qquad + \text{H}_2\text{O} \longrightarrow$$

b.

$$\bigcirc\!\!-\!\text{CH}_2-\text{N}\!=\!\bigcirc + \text{H}_2\text{O} \longrightarrow$$

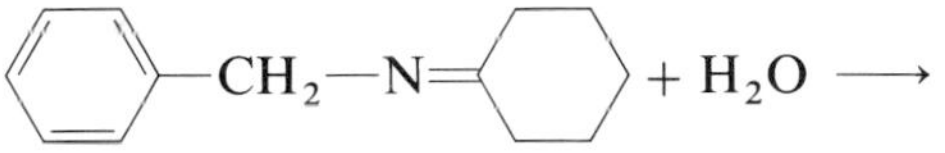

15.5 Oxidation of Aldehydes and Ketones

A. Oxidation of Aldehydes

Aldehydes are oxidized to carboxylic acids by a wide variety of oxidizing agents. In fact, they are one of the most easily oxidized of all functional groups. **Oxidation of an aldehyde** to a carboxylic acid is a two-electron oxidation, as shown by the balanced half-reaction

$$\underset{\substack{\| \\ }}{\overset{\overset{\displaystyle\text{O}}{\|}}{\text{R}-\text{C}-\text{H}}} + \text{H}_2\text{O} \longrightarrow \underset{}{\overset{\overset{\displaystyle\text{O}}{\|}}{\text{R}-\text{C}-\text{O}-\text{H}}} + 2\text{H}^+ + 2\text{e}^-$$

Oxidizing agents commonly used to oxidize aldehydes are potassium permanganate and chromic acid.

Aldehydes are also oxidized to carboxylic acids by silver(I) dissolved in ammonium hydroxide (**Tollens reagent**). The reagent is prepared by dissolving silver nitrate in water, adding sodium hydroxide to precipitate silver(I) as Ag_2O, and then adding ammonium hydroxide to redissolve silver(I) as the silver–ammonia complex ion. When a few drops of this test solution is added to an aldehyde, the aldehyde is oxidized to a carboxylate anion and silver(I) is reduced to metallic silver. If the Tollens test is done properly, silver precipitates as a smooth, mirrorlike deposit, hence the name silver-mirror test.

$$R-\overset{\overset{O}{\|}}{C}-H + Ag^+ \xrightarrow{NH_4OH} R-\overset{\overset{O}{\|}}{C}-O^- + Ag$$

precipitates
as silver mirror

Silver(I) is rarely used now because silver is expensive and because other, more convenient methods exist for oxidizing aldehydes. This oxidation, however, is still used to silver mirrors.

Copper(II) is also used for the oxidation of aldehydes to carboxylic acids. One copper-containing oxidizing agent is known as Benedict's solution, another as Fehling's solution. We will discuss oxidation by copper(II) in Section 19.2D within the context of oxidation of monosaccharides.

B. Oxidation of Ketones

Ketones are not normally oxidized by either potassium dichromate or potassium permanganate. At higher temperatures, however, they can be oxidized further with cleavage of one of the bonds to the carbonyl group. The most useful synthetic application of ketone oxidation is that of symmetrical cyclic ketones. For example, cyclohexanone is oxidized to hexanedioic acid (adipic acid), one of the two monomers required for the synthesis of the polymer Nylon 66. In the industrial process, the oxidizing agent is nitric acid.

$$\text{(cyclohexanone)} + HNO_3 \longrightarrow HO\overset{\overset{O}{\|}}{C}CH_2CH_2CH_2CH_2\overset{\overset{O}{\|}}{C}OH + \text{oxides of nitrogen}$$

hexanedioic acid
(adipic acid)

15.6 Reduction of Aldehydes and Ketones

A. Catalytic Reduction (Catalytic Hydrogenation)

Aldehydes are reduced to primary alcohols and ketones to secondary alcohols by hydrogen in the presence of a heavy metal catalyst, most often finely divided palladium, platinum, nickel, ruthenium, or a copper-chromium complex. Reductions are generally possible at temperatures of 25–100°C and at pressures of hydrogen of 1–5 atm. Sometimes, however, it is necessary to use much higher pressures of hydrogen. Under suitable conditions, cyclohexanone is reduced to cyclohexanol, and 3-hydroxybutanal is reduced to 1,3-butanediol:

cyclohexanone   cyclohexanol

$$CH_3-\underset{\underset{OH}{|}}{CH}-CH_2-\underset{\underset{\|}{O}}{C}-H + H_2 \xrightarrow{Ni} CH_3-\underset{\underset{OH}{|}}{CH}-CH_2-CH_2OH$$

3-hydroxybutanal   1,3-butanediol

The advantage of catalytic reduction (hydrogenation) of aldehydes and ketones is that it is simple to carry out, yields are generally very high, and isolation of the final product is very easy. The disadvantage is that some other functional groups are also reduced under these conditions, for example, carbon-carbon double and triple bonds; this can be seen in the commercial synthesis of 1-butanol from 2-butenal:

$$CH_3-CH=CH-\underset{\underset{\|}{O}}{C}-H + 2H_2 \xrightarrow{Ni} CH_2-CH_2-CH_2-CH_2OH$$

2-butenal   1-butanol
(crotonaldehyde)   (n-butyl alcohol)

B. Metal Hydride Reductions

By far the most common laboratory reagents for reducing aldehydes and ketones to alcohols are sodium borohydride, lithium aluminum hydride (LAH), and their derivatives. These compounds behave as sources of hydride ion.

$$Na^+ \quad H-\underset{\underset{H}{|}}{\overset{\overset{H}{|}}{B}}{}^-\!-H \qquad Li^+ \quad H-\underset{\underset{H}{|}}{\overset{\overset{H}{|}}{Al}}{}^-\!-H \qquad H:^-$$

sodium   lithium aluminum   hydride
borohydride   hydride (LAH)   ion

Lithium aluminum hydride is a very powerful reducing agent; it reduces not only aldehydes and ketones rapidly but also other functional groups such as carboxylic acids (Section 16.5C) and their functional derivatives (Section 17.6A). Sodium borohydride is a much more selective reducing agent; it reduces only aldehydes and ketones rapidly.

Reductions with sodium borohydride are usually effected in aqueous methanol, diethyl ether, or tetrahydrofuran. The initial product of reduction is a metal alkoxide, which on reaction with water is converted to an alcohol and sodium and borate salts. One mole of sodium borohydride reduces four moles of aldehyde.

$$4CH_3\overset{\overset{\displaystyle O}{\|}}{C}H + NaBH_4 \longrightarrow (CH_3CH_2O)_4B^-Na^+ \xrightarrow{H_2O} 4CH_3CH_2OH$$

metal alkoxide

Unlike sodium borohydride, lithium aluminum hydride reacts violently with water, methanol, and other solvents containing —OH groups, to liberate hydrogen gas and form metal hydroxides. Therefore, reductions of aldehydes and ketones with this reagent must be carried out in nonhydroxylic solvents, usually diethyl ether or tetrahydrofuran. The stoichiometry for lithium aluminum hydride reductions is the same as for sodium borohydride reductions, namely 1 mol of lithium aluminum hydride per 4 mol of aldehyde/ketone:

$$4R\overset{\overset{\displaystyle O}{\|}}{-}\overset{}{C}{-}R + LiAlH_4 \xrightarrow{ether} (R_2CHO)_4Al^-Na^+ \xrightarrow{H_2O} 4R\overset{\overset{\displaystyle OH}{|}}{-}CH{-}R$$

The key step in metal hydride reductions of aldehydes or ketones is transfer of a hydride ion from the reducing agent to the carbonyl carbon, to form a tetrahedral carbonyl addition compound.

$$Na^+ \quad H\overset{\overset{\displaystyle H}{|}}{\underset{\underset{\displaystyle H}{|}}{-}B^-}-H + R\overset{\overset{\displaystyle :\ddot{O}:}{\|}}{-}C{-}R \longrightarrow R\overset{\overset{\displaystyle :\ddot{O}-BH_3^-\ Na^+}{|}}{\underset{\underset{\displaystyle H}{|}}{-}C}-R$$

a metal alkoxide

Hydride transfer from boron or aluminum is repeated three times until all reducing equivalents have been used. In reduction of an aldehyde or ketone to an alcohol, only the hydrogen atom attached to carbon comes from the hydride reducing agent; the hydrogen atom attached to oxygen comes from water during hydrolysis of the metal alkoxide salt.

$$R\overset{\overset{\displaystyle O{-}H}{|}}{\underset{\underset{\displaystyle H}{|}}{-}C}-R$$

This hydrogen comes from water during hydrolysis

This hydrogen comes from the hydride reducing agent

Lithium aluminum hydride and sodium borohydride are reagents used in the laboratory to reduce aldehydes and ketones to alcohols. As we shall see in

Section 25.4B, nicotinamide adenine dinucleotide, a biological reducing agent, also reduces aldehydes and ketones by transfer of a hydride ion. Thus, hydride ion reductions are common in both the laboratory and the biological world.

15.7 Properties of Alpha-Hydrogens

A. Acidity of Alpha-Hydrogens

A carbon atom adjacent to a carbonyl group is called an α-carbon (alpha-carbon), and hydrogen atoms attached it are called α-hydrogens (alpha-hydrogens)

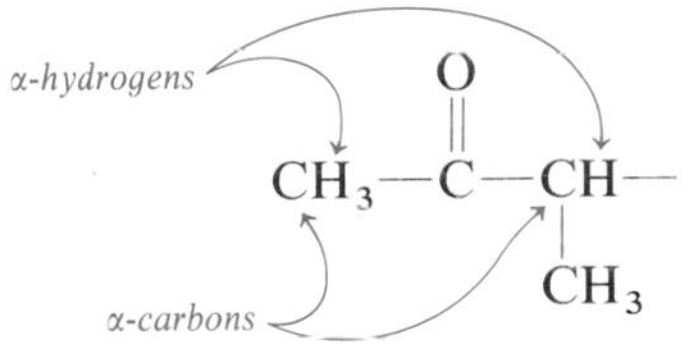

Because carbon and hydrogen have comparable electronegativities, there is normally no appreciable polarity to a C—H bond and no tendency for it to ionize; that is, a hydrogen atom attached to carbon shows no acidity. However, the situation is different for α-hydrogens. In the presence of a very strong base, an α-hydrogen can be removed to form an anion, as shown in the following equation:

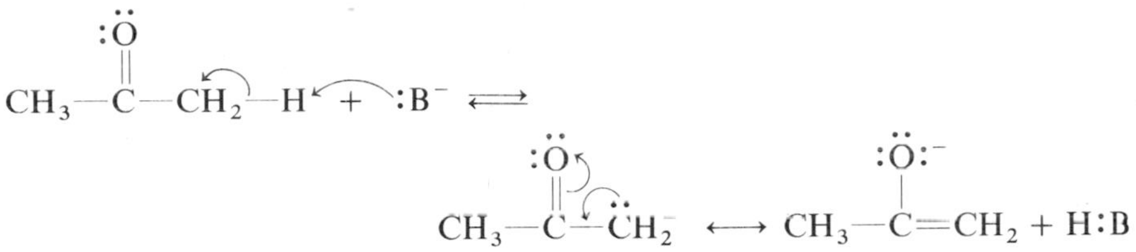

(a resonance-stabilized anion)

Two factors contribute to the increased acidity of α-hydrogens relative to other C—H bonds. First, the presence of the adjacent polar covalent C=O bond polarizes the electron pair of the C—H bond, so the hydrogen can be removed as a proton by a strong base. Second, and more important, is the resonance stabilization of the resulting anion, which can be written as a hybrid of two major contributing structures.

When the resonance-stabilized anion reacts with a proton, it may do so either on oxygen or on the α-carbon. Protonation on carbon gives the original molecule in what is called the keto form. Protonation on oxygen gives an **enol** (*en-* to show that it is an alkene and *-ol* to show it is an alcohol). The resonance-stabilized anion is called an enolate anion. Keto and enol forms have the same molecular formula but different structural formulas; therefore they are structural isomers.

$$CH_3-\overset{\overset{\displaystyle :\ddot{O}}{\|}}{C}-CH_2-H \xrightleftharpoons{\text{H}-\text{B}} CH_3-\overset{\overset{\displaystyle :\ddot{O}}{\|}}{C}-CH_2^- \longleftrightarrow CH_3-\overset{\overset{\displaystyle :\ddot{O}:^-}{|}}{C}=CH_2 \xrightarrow{\text{H}-\text{B}}$$

keto form   (an enolate anion)

$$CH_3-\overset{\overset{\displaystyle :\ddot{O}H}{|}}{C}=CH_2$$

enol form

B. Keto-Enol Tautomerism

Under ordinary conditions, all aldehydes and ketones are in equilibrium with the corresponding enol forms. Interconversion of these isomers is catalyzed by acids and bases, but even the surface of ordinary laboratory glassware is acidic enough to catalyze this interconversion. Interconversion of keto and enol forms is an example of **tautomerism**, the rearrangement of a proton and a double bond. Keto-enol interconversion is the most common form of tautomerism.

For most simple aldehydes and ketones, the position of equilibrium in keto-enol tautomerism lies on the side of the keto form simply because a carbon-oxygen double bond is stronger than a carbon-carbon double bond. Thus, for acetaldehyde and acetone, the keto form predominates by more than 99% at equilibrium.

$$CH_3-\overset{\overset{\displaystyle O}{\|}}{C}-H \rightleftharpoons CH_2=\overset{\overset{\displaystyle HO}{|}}{C}-H \qquad CH_3-\overset{\overset{\displaystyle O}{\|}}{C}-CH_3 \rightleftharpoons CH_3-\overset{\overset{\displaystyle OH}{|}}{C}=CH_2$$

(> 99%)   (> 99%)

For certain types of molecules, the enol form is the major and in some cases the only form present at equilibrium. For example, in molecules where the α-carbon is flanked by two carbonyl groups, as in 2,4-pentanedione, the position of equilibrium shifts in favor of the enol form. The reason for this shift in position of equilibrium is that the enol is stabilized by hydrogen bonding between O—H and the other carbonyl oxygen.

(20%)   (80%)

Phenols (Section 13.7) may be looked on as highly stable enols. The enol form in this equilibrium is, of course, favored by the gain in resonance stabilization of the aromatic ring.

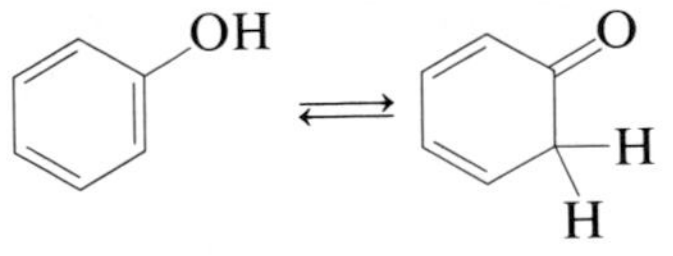

enol form   keto form

Write two enol forms for these compounds:

Example 15.4

a. 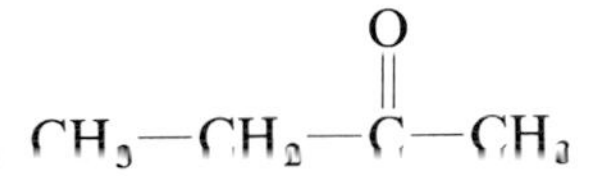 $CH_3-CH_2-\overset{O}{\overset{\|}{C}}-CH_3$ b.

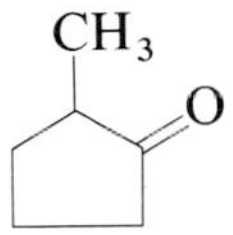

□ *Solution*

a. 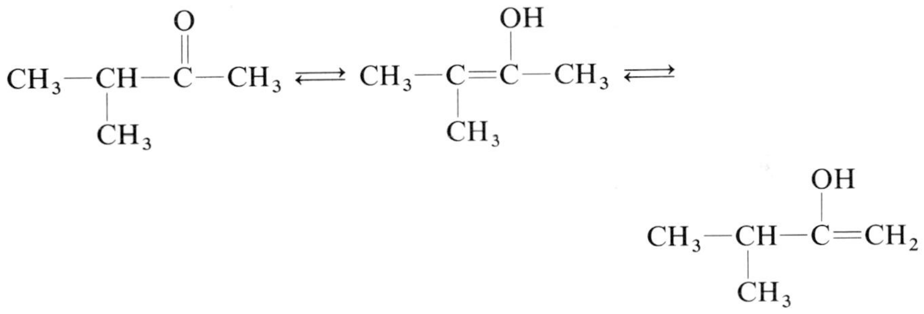 $CH_3-\overset{}{\underset{\underset{CH_3}{|}}{CH}}-\overset{O}{\overset{\|}{C}}-CH_3 \rightleftharpoons CH_3-\overset{OH}{\overset{|}{C}}=\overset{}{\underset{\underset{CH_3}{|}}{C}}-CH_3 \rightleftharpoons$

$CH_3-\overset{}{\underset{\underset{CH_3}{|}}{CH}}-\overset{OH}{\overset{|}{C}}=CH_2$

b.

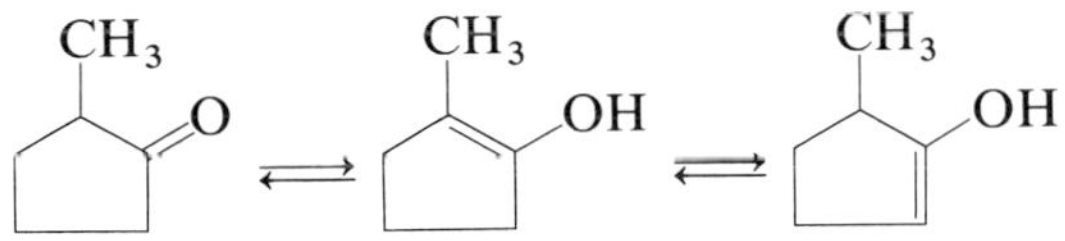

Problem 15.4

Following are enol forms. Draw the structural formula for the corresponding keto form.

a. 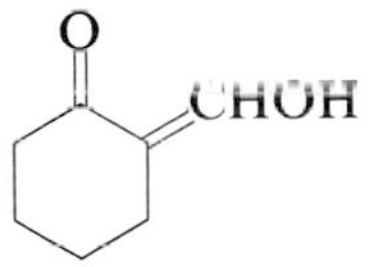   b. 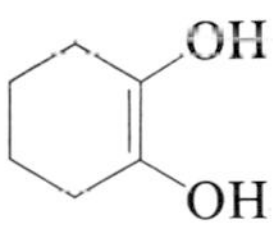   c.

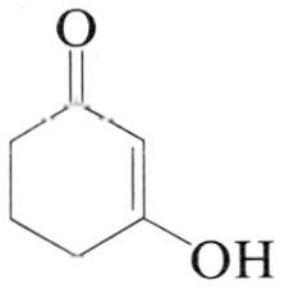

15.8 The Aldol Condensation

Unquestionably the most important reaction of an anion derived from the α-carbon of an aldehyde or ketone is nucleophilic addition to the carbonyl group of another carbonyl-containing compound, as illustrated by the following reactions. While such reactions may be catalyzed by either acid or base, base catalysis is more common.

$$CH_3-\overset{O}{\overset{\|}{C}}-H + CH_3-\overset{O}{\overset{\|}{C}}-H \xrightarrow{\text{NaOH}} CH_3-\overset{\overset{\beta}{OH}}{\underset{}{\overset{|}{CH}}}-\overset{\alpha}{CH_2}-\overset{O}{\overset{\|}{C}}-H$$

3-hydroxybutanal
(aldol)
(a β-hydroxyaldehyde)

$$CH_3-\overset{O}{\overset{\|}{C}}-CH_3 + CH_3-\overset{O}{\overset{\|}{C}}-CH_3 \xrightarrow{\text{NaOH}} CH_3-\underset{\underset{CH_3}{|}}{\overset{\overset{\beta}{OH}}{\overset{|}{C}}}-\overset{\alpha}{CH_2}-\overset{O}{\overset{\|}{C}}-CH_3$$

4-hydroxy-4-methyl-2-pentanone
(a β-hydroxyketone)

These reactions are called **aldol condensations**. The name aldol shows that the product contains both an aldehyde (*ald-*) and an alcohol (*-ol*). The product of the aldol condensation of acetaldehyde itself is called aldol. The name *condensation* tells that these reactions join, or condense, two molecules. The characteristic structural feature of a product of an aldol condensation is the presence of a β-hydroxyaldehyde or a β-hydroxyketone.

Chemists have proposed a three-step mechanism for base-catalyzed aldol condensations, the key step in which is *nucleophilic addition* of an α-carbanion from one carbonyl-containing compound to the carbonyl group of another, to form a **tetrahedral carbonyl addition compound**. This mechanism is illustrated by the aldol condensation between two molecules of acetaldehyde.

Step 1: Formation of anion at an α-carbon

$$H-\overset{..}{\underset{..}{O}}:^- + H-CH_2-\overset{\overset{..}{O}:}{\overset{\|}{C}}-H \longrightarrow$$

$$H_2O + {}^-\overset{..}{C}H_2-\overset{\overset{..}{O}:}{\overset{\|}{C}}-H \longleftrightarrow CH_2=\overset{:\overset{..}{O}:^-}{\overset{|}{C}}-H$$

resonance-stabilized
enolate anion

Step 2: Nucleophilic addition of the anion from one aldehyde or ketone to the carbonyl group of another, to form a tetrahedral carbonyl addition compound

$$CH_3-\overset{:\overset{..}{O}}{\overset{\|}{C}}-H + {}^-\overset{..}{C}H_2-\overset{\overset{..}{O}:}{\overset{\|}{C}}-H \longrightarrow CH_3-\overset{:\overset{..}{O}:^-}{\overset{|}{CH}}-CH_2-\overset{\overset{..}{O}:}{\overset{\|}{C}}-H$$

Step 3: Reaction of the oxygen anion with a proton donor

$$CH_3-\overset{:\overset{..}{O}:^-}{\overset{|}{CH}}-CH_2-\overset{\overset{..}{O}:}{\overset{\|}{C}}-H + H-OH \longrightarrow CH_3-\overset{:\overset{..}{O}H}{\overset{|}{CH}}-CH_2-\overset{\overset{..}{O}:}{\overset{\|}{C}}-H + OH^-$$

The ingredients in the key step of an aldol condensation are an anion and a carbonyl acceptor. In self-condensation, both roles are played by one kind of molecule. Mixed aldol condensations are also possible, like the mixed aldol condensation between acetone and formaldehyde. Formaldehyde cannot function as an anion because it has no α-hydrogen, but can function as a particularly good anion acceptor because of the unhindered nature of its carbonyl group. Acetone forms an anion, but its carbonyl group, bonded to two alkyl groups, is a poorer anion acceptor than the carbonyl group of formaldehyde. Consequently, mixed aldol condensation between acetone and formaldehyde gives 4-hydroxy-2-butanone:

$$CH_3-\overset{\overset{\displaystyle O}{\|}}{C}-CH_3 + H-\overset{\overset{\displaystyle O}{\|}}{C}-H \xrightarrow{\text{NaOH}} CH_3-\overset{\overset{\displaystyle O}{\|}}{C}-CH_2-\overset{\overset{\displaystyle OH}{|}}{CH_2}$$

4-hydroxy-2-butanone

In mixed aldol condensations, where the difference in reactivity between the two carbonyl-containing compounds is not appreciable, mixtures of products result. For example, in the condensation between equimolar concentrations of propanal and butanal, both α-carbons are similar, and so are the carbonyls. Consequently, aldol condensation between these two aldehydes gives a mixture of all four possible aldol condensation products:

$$CH_3CH_2\overset{\overset{\displaystyle O}{\|}}{CH} \quad + \quad CH_3CH_2CH_2\overset{\overset{\displaystyle O}{\|}}{CH}$$

self-condensation   mixed condensation   self-condensation

$$CH_3CH_2\overset{\overset{\displaystyle OH}{|}}{\underset{\underset{\displaystyle CH_3}{|}}{CH}}CH\overset{\overset{\displaystyle O}{\|}}{CH} + CH_3CH_2CH_2\overset{\overset{\displaystyle OH}{|}}{\underset{\underset{\displaystyle CH_3}{|}}{CH}}CH\overset{\overset{\displaystyle O}{\|}}{CH} + CH_3CH_2\overset{\overset{\displaystyle OH}{|}}{\underset{\underset{\displaystyle CH_2CH_3}{|}}{CH}}CH\overset{\overset{\displaystyle O}{\|}}{CH} + CH_3CH_2CH_2\overset{\overset{\displaystyle OH}{|}}{\underset{\underset{\displaystyle CH_2CH_3}{|}}{CH}}CH\overset{\overset{\displaystyle O}{\|}}{CH}$$

β-hydroxyaldehydes and β-hydroxyketones are very easily dehydrated, and often the conditions necessary for aldol condensation (acid or base catalysis) are enough to cause dehydration. Alternatively, warming the aldol product in dilute mineral acid leads to dehydration. The major product from dehydration of an aldol condensation product is one in which the double bond is in conjugation with the carbonyl group; that is, the product is an α,β-unsaturated aldehyde or ketone.

$$CH_3\overset{\overset{\displaystyle OH}{|}}{CH}-CH_2\overset{\overset{\displaystyle O}{\|}}{C}-H \xrightarrow{\text{HCl}} CH_3-\overset{\beta}{CH}=\overset{\alpha}{CH}-\overset{\overset{\displaystyle O}{\|}}{C}-H + H_2O$$

3-hydroxybutanal   2-butenal
(aldol)   (crotonaldehyde)

Example 15.5

Name and draw structural formulas for the products of the following aldol condensation products and for the unsaturated compounds produced by dehydration.

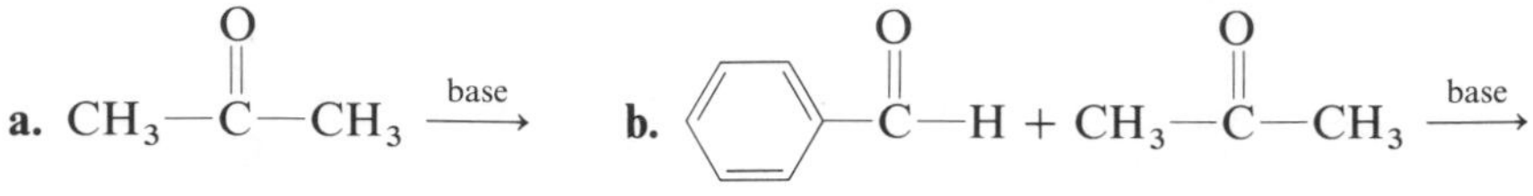

a. $CH_3-\overset{\overset{\displaystyle O}{\|}}{C}-CH_3 \xrightarrow{\text{base}}$ b. $\overset{\overset{\displaystyle O}{\|}}{C}-H + CH_3-\overset{\overset{\displaystyle O}{\|}}{C}-CH_3 \xrightarrow{\text{base}}$

☐ *Solution*

a. $CH_3-\overset{\overset{\displaystyle OH}{|}}{\underset{\underset{\displaystyle CH_3}{|}}{C}}-CH_2-\overset{\overset{\displaystyle O}{\|}}{C}-CH_3 \longrightarrow CH_3-\overset{\underset{\displaystyle CH_3}{|}}{C}=CH-\overset{\overset{\displaystyle O}{\|}}{C}-CH_3 + H_2O$

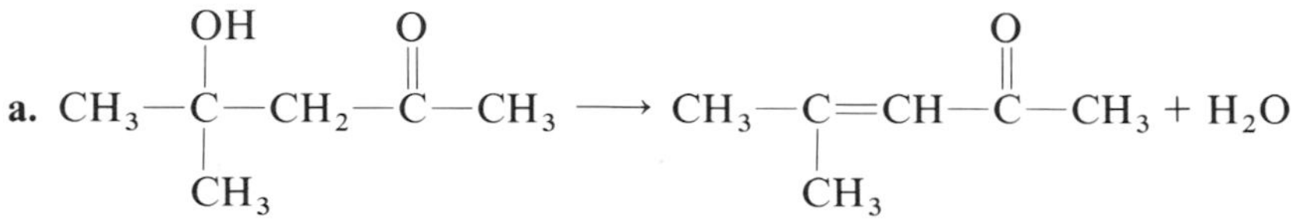

4-hydroxy-4-methyl-2-pentanone   4-methyl-3-penten-2-one

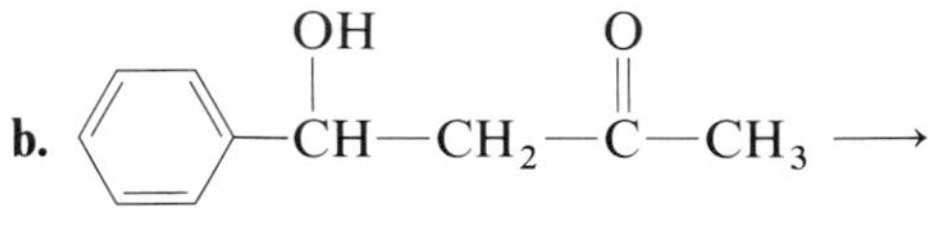

b. $\overset{\overset{\displaystyle OH}{|}}{CH}-CH_2-\overset{\overset{\displaystyle O}{\|}}{C}-CH_3 \longrightarrow$

4-hydroxy-4-phenyl-2-butanone

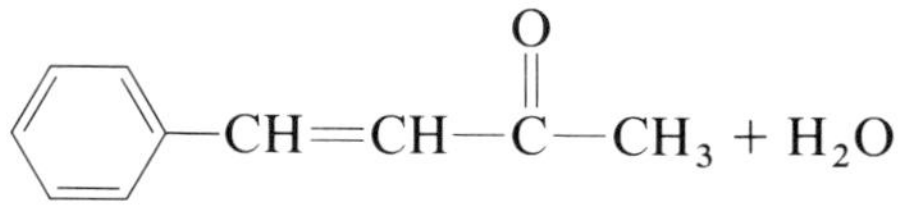

 $-CH=CH-\overset{\overset{\displaystyle O}{\|}}{C}-CH_3 + H_2O$

4-phenyl-3-buten-2-one

Problem 15.5

Draw structural formulas for the two carbonyl-containing compounds that on aldol condensation give the following:

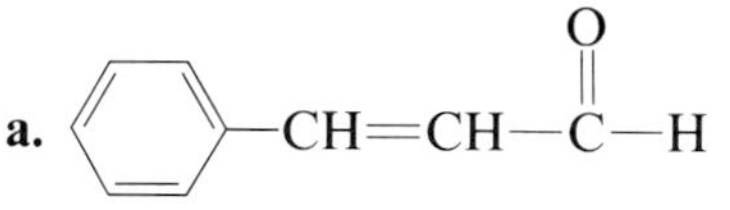

a. $-CH=CH-\overset{\overset{\displaystyle O}{\|}}{C}-H$ b. $CH_3(CH_2)_6CH=\overset{\underset{\displaystyle CH_2(CH_2)_4CH_3}{|}}{C}CH$

cinnamaldehyde

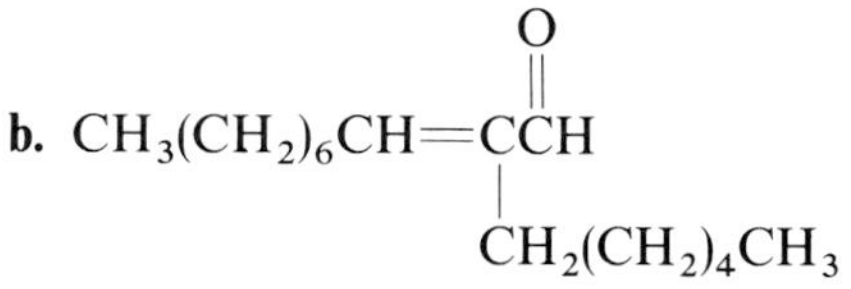

The double bonds of alkenes, aldehydes, and ketones can be reduced to single bonds. Hence aldol condensation is often used for preparing saturated alcohols. For example, acetaldehyde is converted to 1-butanol by the following series of steps: aldol condensation, dehydration, and catalytic reduction of both the carbon-carbon and the carbon-oxygen double bonds:

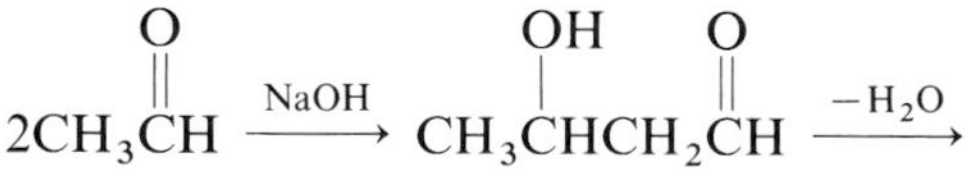

$2CH_3\overset{\overset{\displaystyle O}{\|}}{CH} \xrightarrow{\text{NaOH}} CH_3\overset{\overset{\displaystyle OH}{|}}{CH}CH_2\overset{\overset{\displaystyle O}{\|}}{CH} \xrightarrow{-H_2O}$

3-hydroxybutanal

$CH_3CH=CHCH \xrightarrow{2H_2/Ni} CH_3CH_2CH_2CH_2OH$

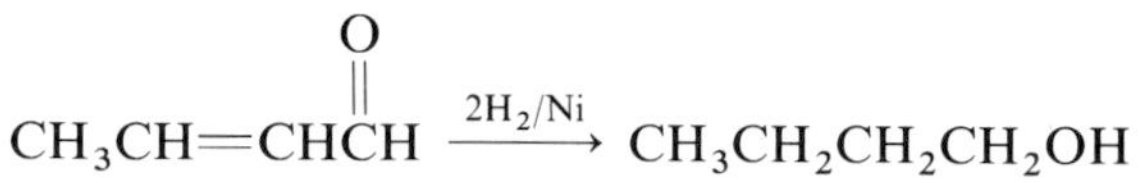

2-butenal   1-butanol

Alternatively, if the β-hydroxyaldehyde is isolated, the aldehyde may be reduced by hydrogen in the presence of a metal catalyst, LiAlH$_4$, or NaBH$_4$ to give 1,3-butanediol, or the aldehyde may be oxidized, to give 3-hydroxybutanoic acid.

$$\underset{\text{OH}}{\overset{}{|}}\; \underset{\text{O}}{\overset{}{||}}$$

CH$_3$CHCH$_2$CH $\xrightarrow{\text{NaBH}_4}$ CH$_3$CHCH$_2$CH$_2$OH

1,3-butanediol

CH$_3$CHCH$_2$CH $\xrightarrow{\text{oxidation}}$ CH$_3$CHCH$_2$COH

3-hydroxybutanoic acid

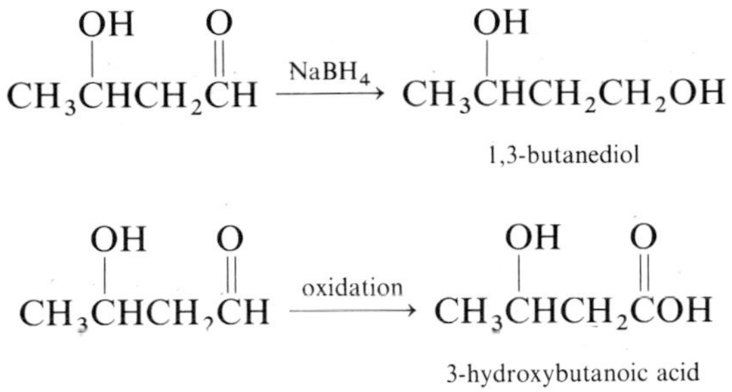

**Example
15.6**

Show reagents and conditions to illustrate how the following products can be synthesized from the given starting materials. Use an aldol condensation at some step in each synthesis.

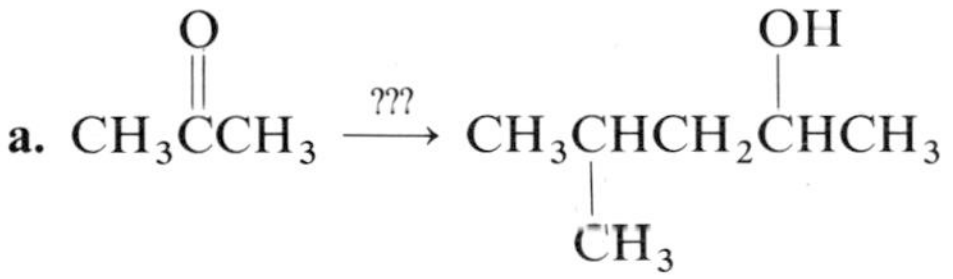

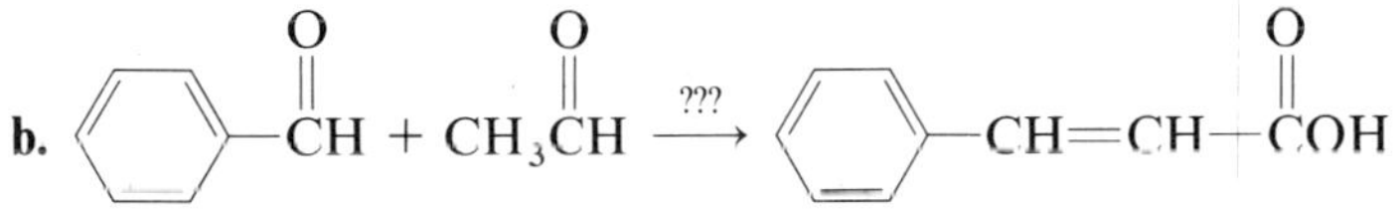

a. CH$_3$CCH$_3$ $\xrightarrow{???}$ CH$_3$CHCH$_2$CHCH$_3$ (with OH and CH$_3$ substituents)

b. C$_6$H$_5$—CH + CH$_3$CH $\xrightarrow{???}$ C$_6$H$_5$—CH=CH—COH

Solution

a. Aldol condensation of acetone in the presence of NaOH or other strong base gives 4-hydroxy-4-methyl-2-pentanone. Warming this β-hydroxyketone in acid leads to dehydration, to form 4-methyl-3-penten-2-one. Catalytic reduction of this α,β-unsaturated ketone by hydrogen in the presence of a heavy metal catalyst reduces both double bonds and gives the desired product.

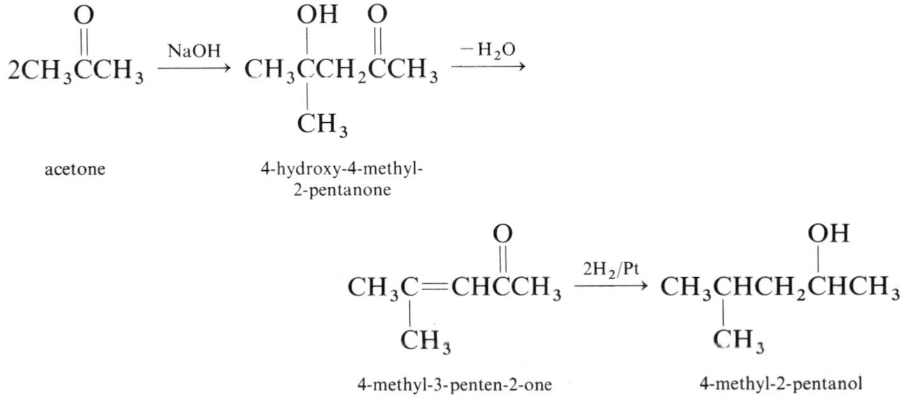

2CH$_3$CCH$_3$ $\xrightarrow{\text{NaOH}}$ CH$_3$CCH$_2$CCH$_3$ (with OH, O, CH$_3$) $\xrightarrow{-\text{H}_2\text{O}}$

acetone

4-hydroxy-4-methyl-2-pentanone

CH$_3$C=CHCCH$_3$ (with CH$_3$) $\xrightarrow{2\text{H}_2/\text{Pt}}$ CH$_3$CHCH$_2$CHCH$_3$ (with OH, CH$_3$)

4-methyl-3-penten-2-one   4-methyl-2-pentanol

b. Mixed aldol condensation between benzaldehyde and acetaldehyde gives 3-hydroxy-3-phenylpropanal. Dehydration of this α,β-unsaturated aldehyde gives cinnamaldehyde. Finally, oxidation of the aldehyde with silver nitrate in ammonium hydroxide (Tollens reagent) gives cinnamic acid:

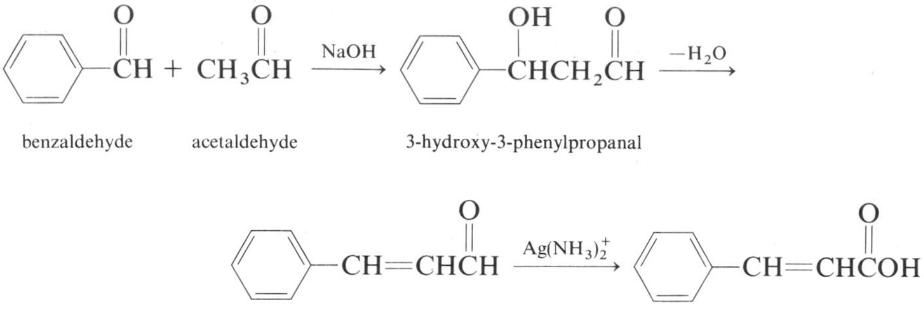

benzaldehyde   acetaldehyde   3-hydroxy-3-phenylpropanal

cinnamaldehyde   cinnamic acid

Problem 15.6

Show reagents and conditions to illustrate how the following products can be obtained from the given starting materials. Use an aldol condensation at some stage in each synthesis.

a. $CH_3CH_2\overset{O}{\underset{||}{C}}H \xrightarrow{??} CH_3CH_2CH_2\underset{\underset{CH_3}{|}}{C}HCH_2OH$

b. $CH_3CH_2CH_2\overset{O}{\underset{||}{C}}H \longrightarrow CH_3CH_2CH_2CH=\underset{\underset{CH_2CH_3}{|}}{C}\overset{O}{\underset{||}{C}}OH$

Key Terms and Concepts

acetal (15.4B)
aldehyde (15.1A)
aldol condensation (15.8)
carbonyl group (introduction)
enol (15.7A)
hemiacetal (15.4B)
hemiketal (15.4B)
imine (15.4C)
ketal (15.4B)
ketone (15.1A)

nucleophile (15.4)
nucleophilic addition (15.4)
oxidation of aldehydes (15.5A)
reduction of aldehydes and ketones (15.6)
Schiff base (15.4C)
tautomerism (15.7B)
tetrahedral carbonyl addition compound (15.8)
Tollens reagent (15.5A)

Key Reactions

    1. Addition of water: hydration (Section 15.4A).

    2. Addition of alcohols: formation of acetals and ketals (Section 15.4B).

    3. Addition of ammonia and amines: formation of Schiff bases (Section 15.4C).

    4. Oxidation of aldehydes to carboxylic acids (Section 15.5A).

    5. Oxidation and cleavage of ketones to two carboxylic acids (Section 15.5B).

    6. Catalytic reduction of aldehydes and ketones to alcohols (Section 15.6A).

    7. Metal hydride reduction of aldehydes and ketones to alcohols (Section 15.6B).

    8. Keto enol tautomerism (Section 15.7B).

    9. Aldol condensation of aldehydes and ketones (Section 15.8).

    10. Dehydration of the products of aldol condensations (Section 15.8).

Problems

Structure and nomenclature of aldehydes and ketones (Sections 15.1 and 15.2)

15.7   Name the following compounds:

a. CH_3CHCH with O double bond and CH_3 substituent

b. $CH_3CH_2CH_2CCH_2CH_2CH_3$ with O double bond

c. (cyclopentanone with CH_3 substituent)

d. $CH_3CH=CHCH$ with O double bond

e. $HOCH_2CCH_2OH$ with O double bond

f. CH_2CHCH with O double bond, HO and OH substituents

g. $CH_3OCH_2CH_2CH$ with O double bond

h. CH_3O—(benzene ring)—CCH_3 with O double bond

i. $CH_3CCH_2CCH_3$ with OH and O double bond, CH_3 substituent

j. $CH_3CH_2CHCH_2CHCH_2OH$ with OH and CH_3 substituents

k. $CH_3CH_2CH_2CH=CHCH_2CH_2CH$ with O double bond

l. (cyclopentane ring with two O groups)

15.8   Write structural formulas for these compounds:

    a. cycloheptanone   **b.** benzaldehyde

    c. 3,3-dimethyl-2-butanone   **d.** 2,4-pentanedione

    e. hexanal   **f.** 2-decanone

    g. *o*-hydroxybenzaldehyde

    h. 3-methoxy-4-hydroxybenzaldehyde (vanillin from the vanilla bean)

    i. 3-phenylpropenal (from oil of cinnamon)

15.9   Name and draw structural formulas for all:

    a. aldehydes of formula C_4H_8O **b.** aldehydes of formula $C_5H_{10}O$

    c. ketones of formula C_4H_8O **d.** ketones of formula $C_5H_{10}O$

Reactions of aldehydes and ketones (Sections 15.4–15.6)

15.10   Complete the following reactions. Where you predict no reaction, write N.R.

    a. $CH_3CH_2CH_2\overset{\displaystyle O}{\overset{\|}{C}}H + H_2 \xrightarrow{Pt}$

    b. 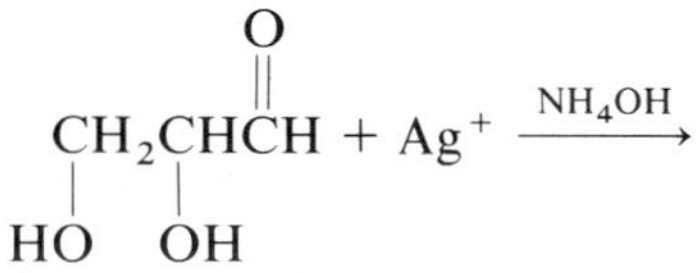 $\underset{\underset{HO\;\;\;OH}{|\;\;\;\;\;|}}{CH_2CH}\overset{\displaystyle O}{\overset{\|}{C}}H + Ag^+ \xrightarrow{NH_4OH}$

    c. $CH_3\underset{\underset{OH}{|}}{CH}CH_2\overset{\displaystyle O}{\overset{\|}{C}}CH_3 + K_2Cr_2O_7 \xrightarrow{H^+}$

    d. $CH_3\underset{\underset{OH}{|}}{CH}CH_2\overset{\displaystyle O}{\overset{\|}{C}}CH_3 + H_2 \xrightarrow{Pt}$

    e. 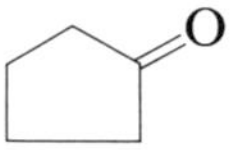 (cyclopentanone) $+ Ag^+ \xrightarrow{NH_4OH}$

    f. 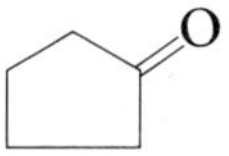 (cyclopentanone) $+ H_2 \xrightarrow{Pt}$

    g. $CH_3CH_2CH_2\overset{\displaystyle O}{\overset{\|}{C}}H + 1CH_3CH_2OH \longrightarrow$

    h. $CH_3CH_2CH_2\overset{\displaystyle O}{\overset{\|}{C}}H + 2CH_3CH_2OH \xrightarrow{H^+}$

    i. 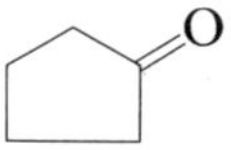 (cyclopentanone) $+ 1CH_3CH_2OH \longrightarrow$

    j. 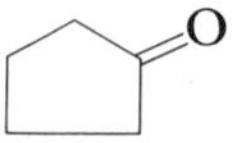 (cyclopentanone) $+ 2CH_3CH_2OH \xrightarrow{H^+}$

k. 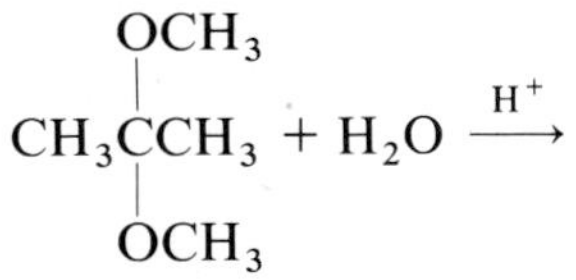 $CH_3\overset{\overset{\displaystyle OCH_3}{|}}{\underset{\underset{\displaystyle OCH_3}{|}}{C}}CH_3 + H_2O \xrightarrow{\;H^+\;}$

l. 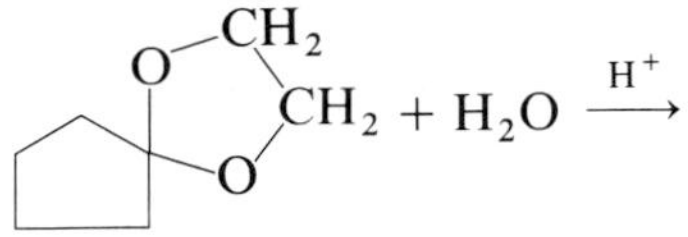 $+ H_2O \xrightarrow{\;H^+\;}$

m. 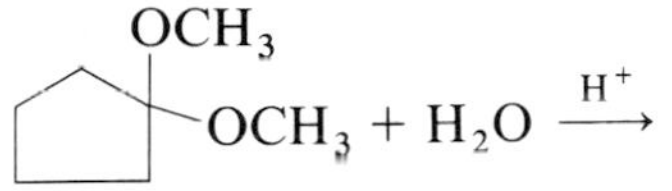 $+ H_2O \xrightarrow{\;H^+\;}$

n. 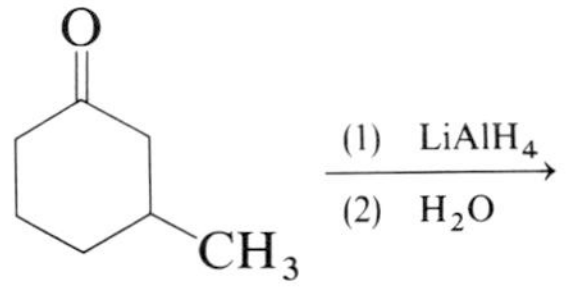 $\xrightarrow[\text{(2)}\;\;H_2O]{\text{(1)}\;\;LiAlH_4}$

15.11 Show how you could distinguish between the following pairs of compounds by a simple chemical test. In each case, tell what test you would perform and what you would expect to observe, and write an equation for each positive test.

a. benzaldehyde and acetophenone
b. benzaldehyde and benzyl alcohol

c.

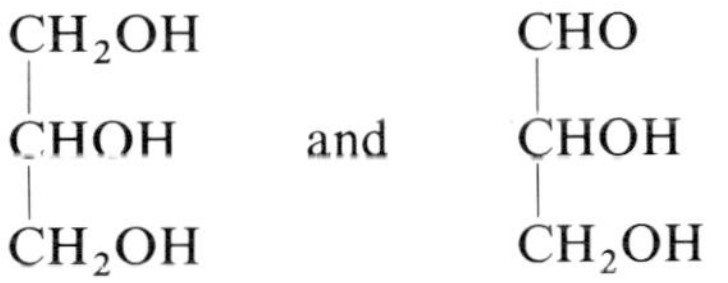

$$CH_2OH \qquad\qquad CHO$$
$$| \qquad\qquad\qquad |$$
$$CHOH \qquad \text{and} \qquad CHOH$$
$$| \qquad\qquad\qquad |$$
$$CH_2OH \qquad\qquad CH_2OH$$

glycerol   glyceraldehyde

15.12 The compound 4-hydroxypentanal forms a five-member cyclic hemiacetal (Section 15.4B) that reacts with a molecule of methanol to form a five-member cyclic acetal. Draw structural formulas for the five-member cyclic hemiacetal and the five-member cyclic acetal.

15.13 5-hydroxyhexanal readily forms a six-member hemiacetal:

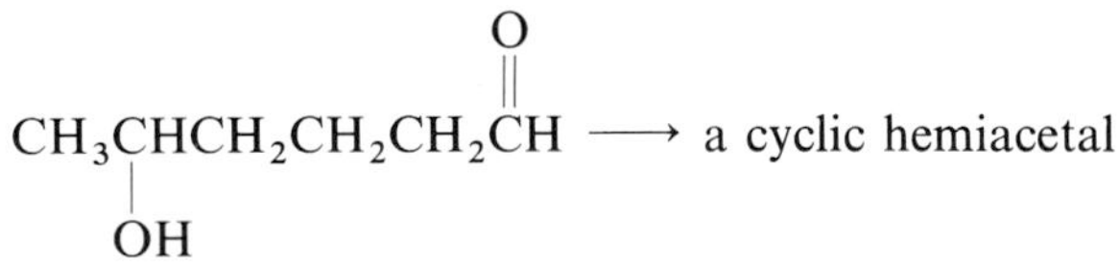

$$CH_3\underset{\underset{\displaystyle OH}{|}}{CH}CH_2CH_2CH_2\overset{\overset{\displaystyle O}{\|}}{C}H \longrightarrow \text{a cyclic hemiacetal}$$

5-hydroxyhexanal

a. Draw a structural formula for this cyclic hemiacetal.
b. How many cis-trans isomers are possible for this cyclic hemiacetal?
c. Draw planar hexagon representations for each cis and trans isomer.

d. Draw a chair conformation for the cyclic hemiacetal in which the hydroxyl and methyl groups are equatorial. Is this a cis or a trans isomer?

15.14 Acetaldehyde reacts with ethylene glycol in the presence of a trace of sulfuric acid, to give a cyclic acetal of formula $C_4H_8O_2$. Draw a structural formula for this acetal.

15.15 The following conversions can be carried out in either one step or two. Show reagents you would use to bring about each conversion, and draw structural formulas for the intermediate formed in any conversion that requires two steps.

a.

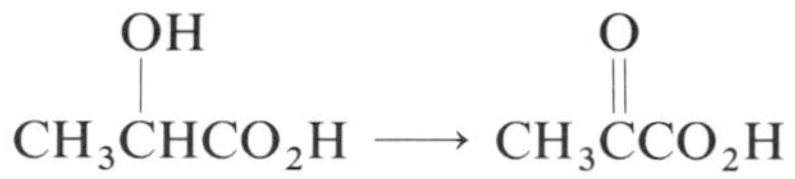

$$\underset{\substack{| \\ \text{OH}}}{CH_3CHCO_2H} \longrightarrow \underset{\substack{\| \\ O}}{CH_3CCO_2H}$$

b.

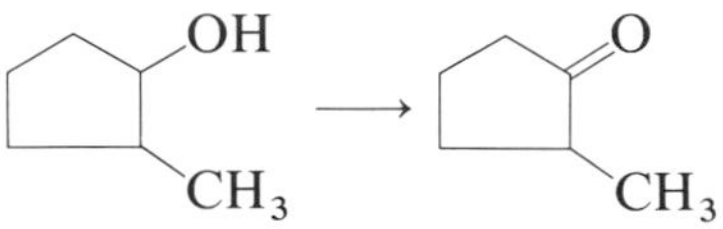

c.

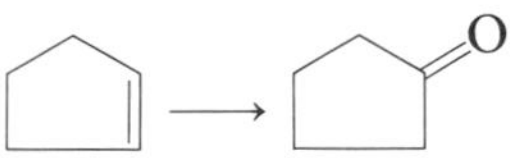

d.

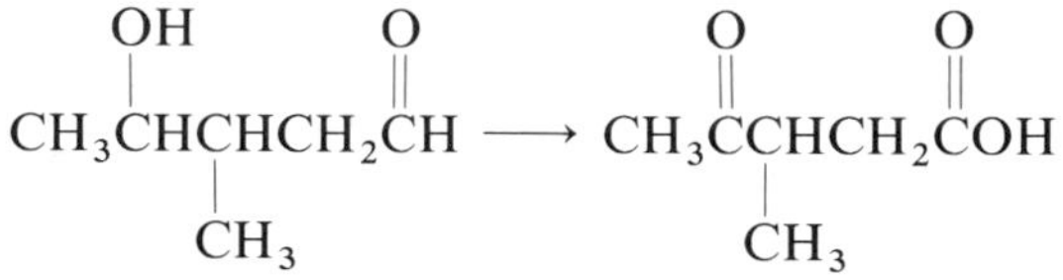

$$\underset{\substack{| \\ OH \quad\quad O \quad\quad\quad | \\ CH_3}}{CH_3CHCHCH_2CH} \longrightarrow \underset{\substack{O \quad\quad O \\ | \\ CH_3}}{CH_3CCHCH_2COH}$$

e.

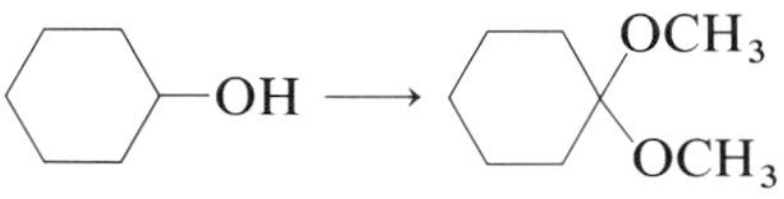

f.

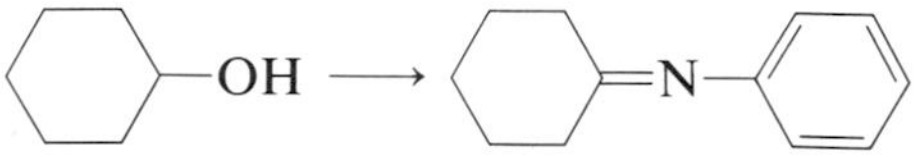

g.

$$CH_3CH=CH_2 \longrightarrow \underset{\substack{\| \\ O}}{CH_3CCH_3}$$

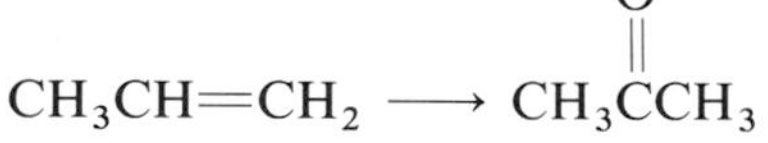

15.16 Pyridoxal phosphate is one of the metabolically active forms of vitamin B_6. Draw structural formulas for the Schiff bases formed by reaction of pyridoxal phosphate with the primary amines of (a) tyrosine and (b) glutamic acid.

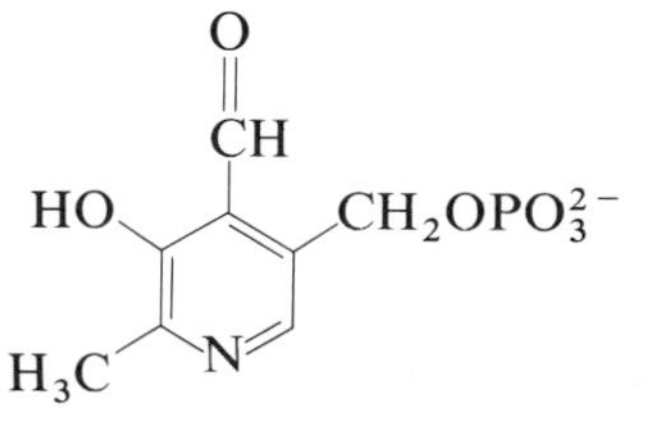

pyridoxal phosphate

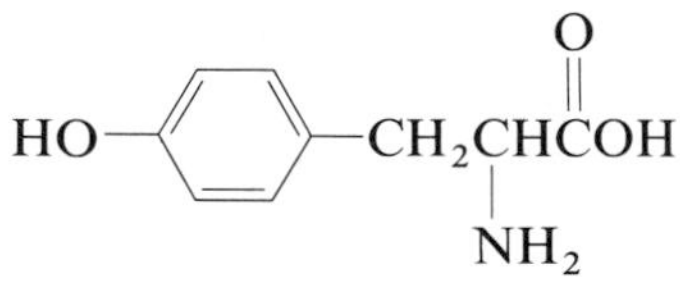

tyrosine

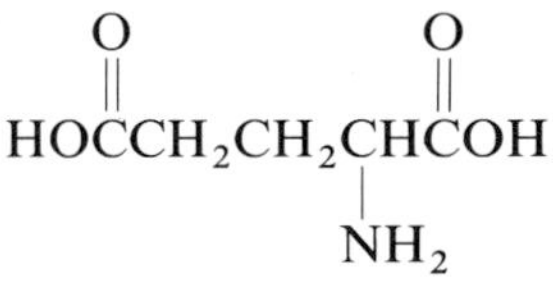

glutamic acid

15.17 Another of the metabolically active forms of vitamin B$_6$ is pyridoxamine phosphate. Draw structural formulas for the Schiff bases formed by reaction of pyridoxamine phosphate with the ketones of (a) pyruvic acid and (b) oxaloacetic acid.

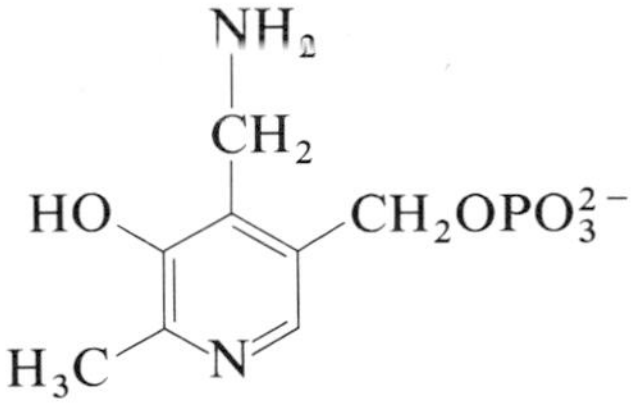

pyridoxamine phosphate

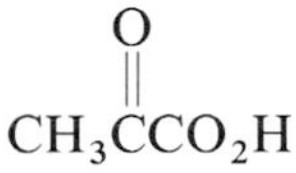

pyruvic acid

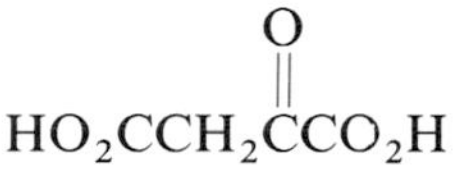

oxaloacetic acid

Reactions of aldehydes and ketones— tautomerism (Section 15.7)

15.18 What is meant by the term *keto-enol tautomerism*?

15.19 Draw the indicated number of enol structures for the following aldehydes and ketones. Draw them to show bond angles of approximately 120° about the carbon-carbon double bond of each enol form.

$$\textbf{a. } CH_3CH_2CH_2\overset{\displaystyle O}{\overset{\|}{C}}H \qquad \textbf{b. } CH_3CH_2\overset{\displaystyle O}{\overset{\|}{C}}CH_3 \qquad \textbf{c.}$$

(1 enol form)

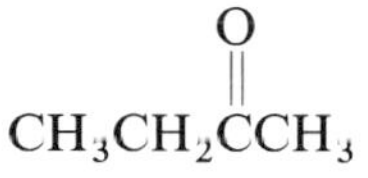

(2 enol forms)

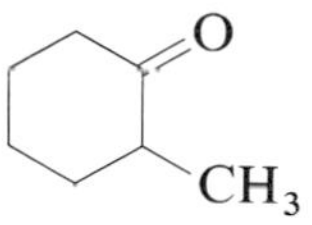

(2 enol forms)

15.20 The following are enols. Draw structural formulas for the keto form of each.

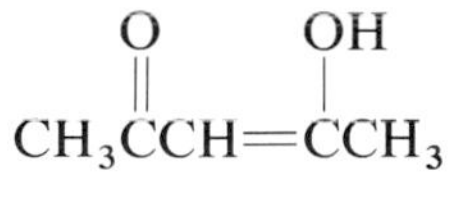

15.21 The following compound is an enediol, a compound with two hydroxyl groups on a carbon-carbon double bond. Draw structural formulas for the two carbonyl-containing compounds with which the enediol is in equilibrium.

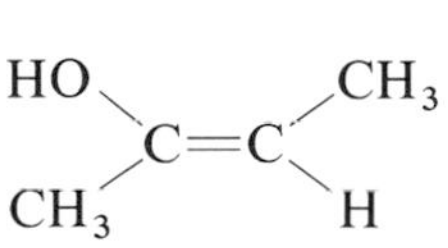

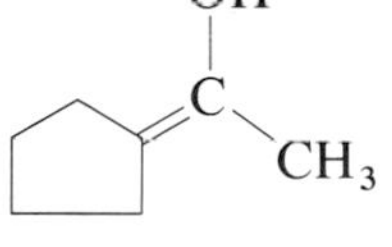

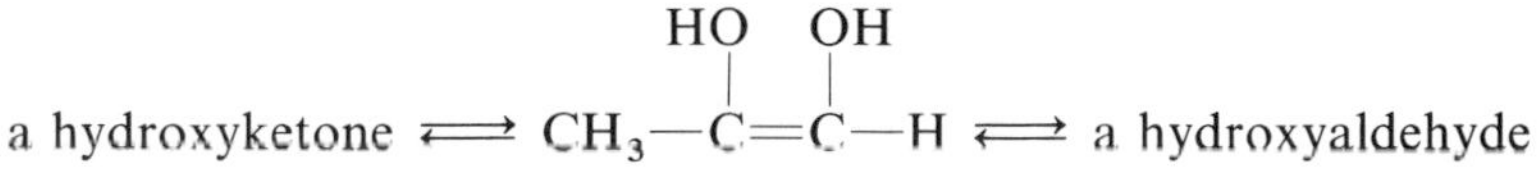

$$\text{a hydroxyketone} \rightleftharpoons CH_3-\overset{\overset{\displaystyle HO}{|}}{C}=\overset{\overset{\displaystyle OH}{|}}{C}-H \rightleftharpoons \text{a hydroxyaldehyde}$$

an enediol

15.22 How could you account for the conversion of glyceraldehyde, in dilute aqueous NaOH, to an equilibrium mixture of glyceraldehyde and dihydroxyacetone?

$$
\begin{array}{ccccc}
\text{CHO} & & \text{CHO} & & \text{CH}_2\text{OH} \\
| & \xrightleftharpoons[\text{base}]{\text{dilute}} & | & & | \\
\text{CHOH} & & \text{CHOH} & + & \text{C}=\text{O} \\
| & & | & & | \\
\text{CH}_2\text{OH} & & \text{CH}_2\text{OH} & & \text{CH}_2\text{OH}
\end{array}
$$

glyceraldehyde glyceraldehyde dihydroxyacetone

The aldol condensation (Section 15.8)

15.23 Draw structural formulas for the products of the following aldol condensations and for the unsaturated compounds formed by loss of water from the aldol condensation product:

a. $2\text{CH}_3\text{CH}_2\overset{\overset{\text{O}}{\|}}{\text{CH}} \xrightarrow{\text{base}}$

b. $2 \ \bigcirc\!\!-\!\overset{\overset{\text{O}}{\|}}{\text{C}}\text{CH}_2\text{CH}_3 \xrightarrow{\text{base}}$

c. $2 \ \text{(cyclohexanone)} \xrightarrow{\text{base}}$

15.24 Draw structural formulas for the products of these mixed aldol condensations and for the unsaturated compounds formed by loss of water from the mixed aldol condensation product:

a. $\bigcirc\!\!-\!\overset{\overset{\text{O}}{\|}}{\text{CH}} + \text{CH}_3\overset{\overset{\text{O}}{\|}}{\text{C}}\!-\!\bigcirc \xrightarrow{\text{base}}$

b. $\text{(cyclohexanone)} + \text{HCH} \xrightarrow{\text{base}}$ (with HCHO)

15.25 Show reagents and conditions to illustrate how the following products can be synthesized from the indicated starting materials by way of an aldol condensation:

a. $\text{CH}_3\overset{\overset{\text{O}}{\|}}{\text{CH}} \xrightarrow{\text{??}} \text{CH}_3\text{CH}_2\text{CH}_2\text{CH}_2\text{OH}$

b. $\text{CH}_3\overset{\overset{\text{O}}{\|}}{\text{CH}} \xrightarrow{\text{??}} \text{CH}_3\text{CH}=\text{CH}\overset{\overset{\text{O}}{\|}}{\text{C}}\text{OH}$

c. $\text{CH}_3\overset{\overset{\text{O}}{\|}}{\text{C}}\text{CH}_3 \xrightarrow{\text{??}} \text{CH}_3\overset{\overset{\text{OH}}{|}}{\underset{\underset{\text{CH}_3}{|}}{\text{C}}}\text{CH}_2\overset{\overset{\text{OH}}{|}}{\text{CH}}\text{CH}_3$

Pheromones

Chemical communication abounds in nature: the clinging, penetrating odor of the skunk's defensive spray; the hound, nose to the ground, in pursuit of prey; the female dog's making known her sexual availability; the female moth's attracting males from great distances for mating. As biologists and chemists cooperate to extend our knowledge of other animals, it is becoming increasingly clear that chemical communication is the primary mode of communication in most animals.

Before 1950, the isolation of enough biologically active material to permit us to decipher any chemical communications seemed an insurmountable task. Rapid progress in instrumental techniques, however, particularly in chromatography and spectroscopy, has now made it possible to isolate and carry out structural determinations on as little as a few micrograms of material. Even with these advances, isolating and identifying the components of pheromones remains a challenge to technical and experimental expertise. For example, obtaining a mere 12 milligrams of gypsy moth sex attractant required processing 500,000 virgin female moths, each yielding only 0.02 microgram of attractant. In other insect species, it is not uncommon to process at least 20,000 insects to get enough material for chemical identification.

The term *pheromone* (from the Greek *pherin*, to carry, and *horman*, to excite) is the accepted name for chemicals secreted by an organism of one species to evoke a response in another member of the same species. We will look at insect pheromones, because these have been the most widely studied. Pheromones are generally divided into two classes: primer and releaser pher-omones, depending on mode of action. Primer pheromones cause important physiological changes that affect an organism's development and later behavior. The most clearly understood primer pheromones regulate caste systems in social insects (bees, ants, and termites). A typical colony of honey bees (*Apis mellifera*) consists of one queen, several hundred drones (males), and thousands of workers (underdeveloped females). The queen bee is the only fully developed female in the colony. She secretes a "queen substance," which prevents the development of workers' ovaries and promotes the construction of royal colony cells for the rearing of new queens. One of the components of the primer pheromone in the queen substance has been identified as 9-keto-*trans*-2-decenoic acid (Figure X-1). This same substance also serves as a sex pheromone, attracting drones to the queen during her mating flight.

Releaser pheromones produce rapid, reversible changes in behavior, such as sexual attraction and stimulation, aggregation, trail marking, territorial and home-range marking, and other social behaviors. Some of the earliest observations of releaser pheromones were recorded in the alarm pheromones of the honey bee. Beekeepers, and perhaps some of the rest of us too, are well aware that the sting of one bee often causes swarms of angry workers to attack the same spot. When a worker stings an intruder, it discharges, along with venom, an alarm pheromone, which evokes the aggressive attack of other bees. One component of this alarm pheromone is isoamyl acetate, a sweet-smelling substance with an odor like that of banana oil (Figure X-2).

450A

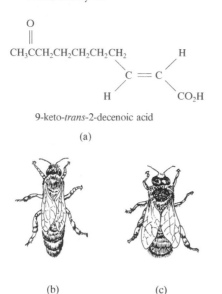

$$CH_3CCH_2CH_2CH_2CH_2CH_2$$
O (above first C)

9-keto-*trans*-2-decenoic acid

(a)

(b)   (c)

Figure X-1 (a) 9-keto-*trans*-2-decenoic acid, a component of the queen substance, (b) *Apis millifera*, a queen bee, and (c) a drone.

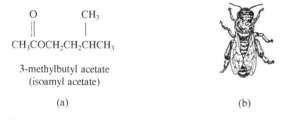

$$CH_3COCH_2CH_2CHCH_3$$

3-methylbutyl acetate
(isoamyl acetate)

(a)   (b)

Figure X-2 (a) 3-methylbutyl acetate (isoamyl acetate), a component of the alarm pheromone of the honey bee, and (b) a worker (female).

Of all classes of pheromones, sex and aggregating pheromones have received the greatest attention in both the scientific community and the popular press. Larvae of certain insects that release these classes of pheromones, particularly the moths and beetles, are among the world's most serious agricultural and forestland pests.

Sex pheromones are commonly referred to as sex attractants, but this term is misleading because it implies only attraction. Actually, the behavior elicited by sex pheromones is much more complex. Low levels of sex pheromone sti-

mulation cause orientation and flight of a male toward a female (or in some species, flight of a female toward a male). If the level of stimulation is high enough, copulation follows.

One of the aggregating pheromones recently identified and studied is that of the *Ips* genus of bark beetles. *Ips paraconfusus*, an insect especially destructive to ponderosa pines in the Sierra Nevada range of California, lives in the soil during the winter. In the early spring when the temperature begins to rise, a few males emerge from the ground and seek out ponderosa pines in which to construct breeding chambers. The few males bore into trees, and during this process, a pheromone produced in their hind gut is emitted, triggering a massive secondary invasion of both males and females. As these bark beetles bore into ponderosa pine, they infect the trees with fungal spores, and it is the fungal-spore infection that actually kills the trees. After fertilization and hatching, *Ips* larvae grow and develop behind the bark. In autumn, they leave the tree and return to the soil to begin another life cycle.

Investigation of the aggregating pheromone of *Ips paraconfusus* led to isolation and identification of three components (Figure X-3), all of which are terpene alcohols. Ipsenol and ipsdienol have carbon skeletons identical to that of myrcene (see Mini-Essay VII, "Terpenes") and differ only in the presence of a carbon-carbon double bond. The third component, *cis*-verbenol, has a carbon skeleton identical to that of alpha-pinene (see Mini-Essay VII, "Terpenes"). It has been shown more recently that *Ips paraconfusus* syn-

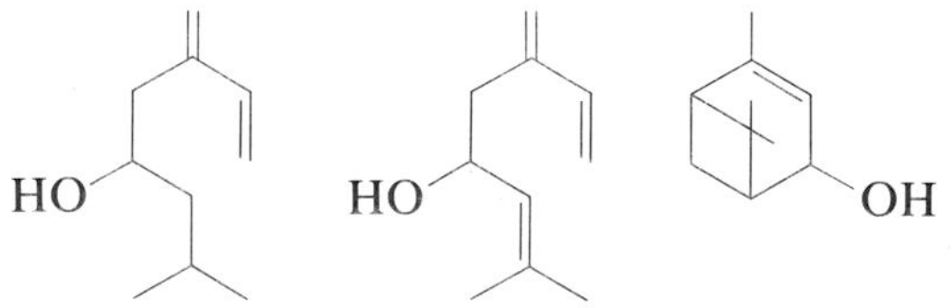

HO   HO   OH

ipsenol   ipsdienol   *cis*-verbenol

Figure X-3 Components of the aggregating pheromone of the bark beetle *Ips paraconfusus*. A mixture of all three is necessary for attraction of males and females in the field.

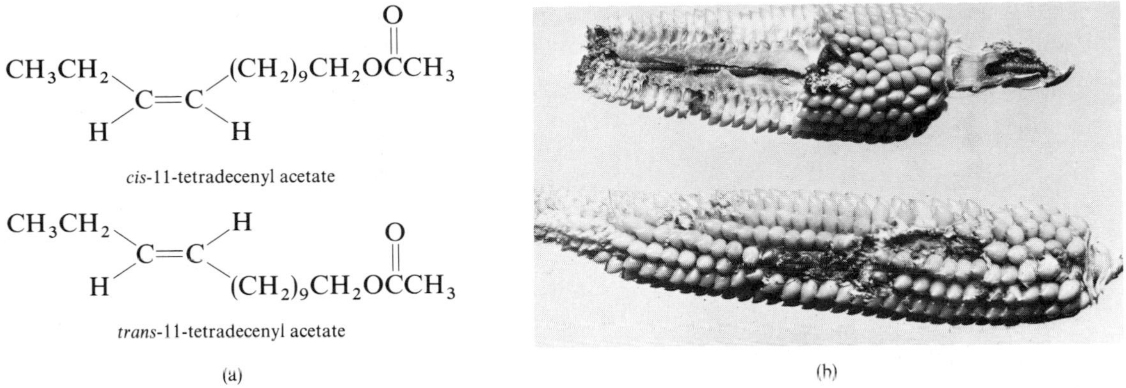

$$CH_3CH_2 \quad (CH_2)_9CH_2OCCH_3$$

cis-11-tetradecenyl acetate

trans-11-tetradecenyl acetate

(a)   (b)

Figure X-4 (a) 11-tetradecenyl acetate, a component of the sex pheromone of the European corn borer. (b) Corn infested with European corn borers.

thesizes verbenol from the alpha-pinene it encounters in the thick resin that flows from an injured ponderosa pine.

Several groups of scientists have studied the components of the sex pheromone of both Iowa and New York strains of the European corn borer. Females of these closely related species secrete the same sex attractant, 11-tetradecenyl acetate (Figure X-4). Males of the Iowa strain show maximum response to a mixture containing about 96% of the cis isomer and 4% of the trans isomer. When the pure cis isomer is used alone, males are only weakly attracted. Males of the New York strain show an entirely different response pattern. They respond maximally to a mixture containing 3% of the cis isomer and 97% of the trans isomer. There is evidence that optimum response to a narrow range of stereo-isomers as we see here, or to a mixture of components as in *Ips paraconfusus*, is widespread in nature; also, at least some species of insects maintain species isolation, at least for mating and reproduction, by the stereochemistry of their pheromones.

Within the last decade, scientists have developed several practical applications of pheromone systems to monitor and control selected insect pests. First, pheromone-baited traps can be placed in the field to monitor populations of selected insect pests. In this way, changes in population levels can be determined and large or potentially large areas of infestation defined. The great value of this information is that large-scale spraying of conventional insecticides can be drastically reduced or even avoided in areas where populations are below threshold levels. Several companies here and abroad are marketing pheromone-baited traps to monitor population levels of such insect pests as the Japanese beetle, the gypsy moth, the boll weevil, and the Mediterranean fruit fly.

Second, pheromones can be used for mass-trapping and population suppression of particular insect pests. Probably the largest single effort to date involving trapping and population suppression was undertaken in Norway and Sweden, to prevent a potentially catastrophic infestation of *Ips typographus*, a bark beetle largely confined to the coniferous forests of Europe and Asia and particularly attracted to the commercially valuable Norway spruce. The aggregation pheromone of *Ips typographus* consists of three components (Figure X-5).

In the three years before 1979, severe drought in Norway and Sweden affected a huge number of spruce trees, and in that year bark beetles killed or severely damaged an estimated 5 million trees. The governments of Norway and Sweden initiated a large-scale program to control *Ips typographus*; in the summer of 1979 they placed about a million pheromone-baited traps in infested forests. The beetle catch that year was

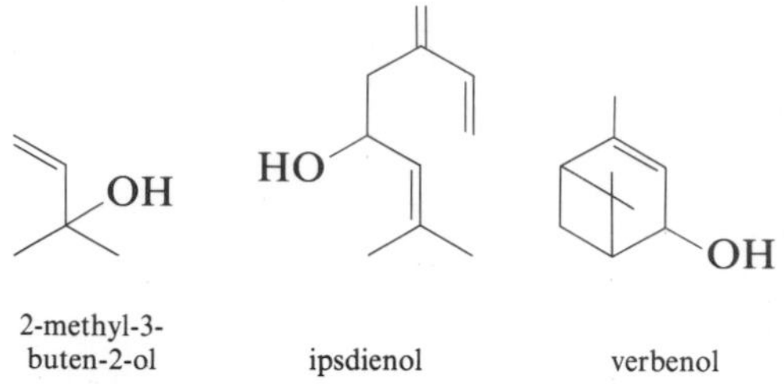

2-methyl-3-buten-2-ol   ipsdienol   verbenol

Figure X-5 The three components of the aggregating pheromone of the bark beetle *Ips typographus.*

estimated at 2.9 million. The program was repeated in 1980, with an estimated catch in Norway alone of 4.5 billion beetles. Although tree mortality during these years remained high, the feared catastrophic infestation of *Ips typographus* did not occur.

In a third use of pheromones in the field, insects can be lured to traps and treated there with insecticides, insect juvenile hormones or juvenile hormone analogs, or species-specific pathogenic organisms, all of which are then spread throughout the local population of that particular pest when the treated insects are released.

In a fourth use, specific pheromones can be spread throughout the air to disrupt mating or aggregation. Clearly, this means of population control and suppression requires an understanding of the growth and behavior patterns of the particular pest and also good timing.

From this information on pheromones, it should be clear that they are becoming an integral part of more environmentally sound means of insect pest control.

Sources

Klun, J. A., et al. 1973. Insect sex pheromones: Minor amounts of opposite geometrical isomer critical to attraction. *Science* 181:661.

O'Sullivan, D.A. 1979. Pheromone lures help control bark beetles. *Chem. & Eng. News.*

Shorey, H. H. 1976. *Animal Communication by Pheromones.* New York: Academic Press.

Silverstein, R. M. 1981. Pheromones: Background and potential use in pest control. *Science* 213:1326.

16

Carboxylic Acids

The most important chemical property of carboxylic acids, another class of organic compounds containing the carbonyl group, is their acidity. Further, carboxylic acids form numerous important derivatives, including esters, amides, and anhydrides. In this chapter we will concentrate on carboxylic acids themselves and, in the following chapter, on derivatives of carboxylic acids.

16.1 Structure of Carboxylic Acids

The characteristic structural feature of a carboxylic acid is the presence of a **carboxyl group** (Section 10.2C). Shown in Figure 16.1 is a Lewis structure for formic acid, the simplest organic compound containing a carboxyl group. Also shown is a ball-and-stick model. Predicted bond angles of the carboxyl group are 120° about the carbonyl carbon and 109.5° about the hydroxyl oxygen. Observed bond angles in formic acid are close to the predicted angles.

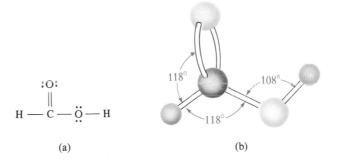

(a)   (b)

Figure 16.1 The structure of formic acid. (a) Lewis structure; (b) ball-and-stick model, showing observed bond angles.

16.2 Nomenclature of Carboxylic Acids

A. IUPAC Names

The IUPAC system of nomenclature for carboxylic acids selects as the parent compound the longest chain of carbon atoms that contains the carboxyl group.

The carboxyl group is indicated by changing the suffix -*e* of the parent compound to -*oic acid* (Section 11.5). Because the carbon of the carboxyl group is always carbon 1 of the parent compound, there is no need to give it a number. Following are structural formulas and IUPAC names for several carboxylic acids. Note that the IUPAC system retains the common names formic acid and acetic acid.

$$\overset{O}{\overset{\|}{HCOH}} \qquad CH_3\overset{O}{\overset{\|}{COH}} \qquad CH_3CH_2\overset{O}{\overset{\|}{COH}} \qquad CH_3\overset{CH_3}{\overset{|}{CH}}CH_2\overset{O}{\overset{\|}{COH}}$$

methanoic acid (formic acid)   ethanoic acid (acetic acid)   propanoic acid   3-methylbutanoic acid

If the carboxylic acid contains a carbon-carbon double bond, the infix is changed from -*an*- to -*en*- to indicate a double bond. The position of the double bond is shown by a number, just as for simple alkenes. Following are structural formulas for two carboxylic acids, each also containing carbon-carbon double bonds. In parentheses is the common name of each acid.

$$CH_2{=}CH{-}\overset{O}{\overset{\|}{COH}} \qquad \text{⬡}{-}CH{=}CH{-}\overset{O}{\overset{\|}{COH}}$$

2-propenoic acid (acrylic acid)   3-phenyl-2-propenoic acid (cinnamic acid)

In the IUPAC system, a carboxyl group takes precedence over most other functional groups, including the hydroxyl group and also the carbonyl group of aldehydes and ketones (Table 15.1). In a substituted carboxylic acid, the presence of an —OH group is indicated by the prefix *hydroxy*-; the presence of a carbonyl group of an aldehyde or ketone is indicated by the prefix *oxo*-, as illustrated in the following examples.

$$CH_3\overset{OH}{\overset{|}{CH}}CH_2CH_2CH_2\overset{O}{\overset{\|}{COH}} \qquad CH_3\overset{O}{\overset{\|}{C}}CH_2CH_2CH_2\overset{O}{\overset{\|}{COH}}$$

5-hydroxyhexanoic acid   5-oxohexanoic acid

Dicarboxylic acids are named by adding the suffix -*dioic acid* to the name of the parent compound that contains both carboxyl groups. The IUPAC system retains certain common names including oxalic, malonic, succinic, and tartaric acids. In Table 16.1 are structural formulas, IUPAC names, and common names for the most common dicarboxylic acids found in the biological world. The name oxalic acid is derived from one of its sources in the biological world, namely plants of the genus *Oxalis*, one of which is rhubarb. Oxalic acid is used as a cleansing agent for automobile radiators, as a laundry bleach, and in textile finishing and cleaning. Tartaric acid is a byproduct of fermentation of grape juice to wine. It is collected as the potassium salt and sold under the name cream of tartar. Adipic acid is one of the two monomers required for the synthesis of

Table 16.1
Dicarboxylic acids.

Structural Formula	IUPAC Name	Common Name
$\underset{\text{HOC—COH}}{\overset{\text{O} \quad \text{O}}{\parallel \quad \parallel}}$	ethanedioic acid	oxalic acid
$\underset{\text{HOCCH}_2\text{COH}}{\overset{\text{O} \quad \text{O}}{\parallel \quad \parallel}}$	propanedioic acid	malonic acid
$\underset{\text{HOCCH}_2\text{CH}_2\text{COH}}{\overset{\text{O} \qquad \text{O}}{\parallel \qquad \parallel}}$	butanedioic acid	succinic acid
HOC—CH—CH—COH with O (double bonds) and HO, OH below	2,3-dihydroxy-butanedioic acid	tartaric acid
$\underset{\text{HOCCH}_2\text{CH}_2\text{CH}_2\text{COH}}{\overset{\text{O} \qquad \text{O}}{\parallel \qquad \parallel}}$	pentanedioic acid	glutaric acid
$\underset{\text{HOCCH}_2\text{CH}_2\text{CH}_2\text{CH}_2\text{COH}}{\overset{\text{O} \qquad\qquad \text{O}}{\parallel \qquad\qquad \parallel}}$	hexanedioic acid	adipic acid

the polymer Nylon 66. In 1985, the U.S. chemical industry produced 1.63 billion pounds of adipic acid, solely for the synthesis of Nylon 66.

Tri- and higher carboxylic acids are named by using the suffixes *-tricarboxylic acid*, *-tetracarboxylic acid*, and so on. An example of a tricarboxylic acid is 2-hydroxy-1,2,3-propanetricarboxylic acid, whose common name, citric acid, is also retained by the IUPAC system. Citric acid is important in a metabolic pathway known as the tricarboxylic acid (TCA) cycle, or the citric acid or the Krebs cycle (Section 25.5).

$$
\begin{array}{c}
\text{O} \\
\parallel \\
\text{O} \quad \text{CH}_2\text{COH} \\
\parallel \quad \mid \\
\text{HOC—C—OH} \\
\mid \\
\text{CH}_2\text{COH} \\
\parallel \\
\text{O}
\end{array}
$$

2-hydroxy-1,2,3-propane-
tricarboxylic acid
(citric acid)

The simplest aromatic carboxylic acid is benzoic acid. Derivatives are named by using numbers and prefixes to show the presence and location of substituents. Certain aromatic carboxylic acids have common names by which they are more usually known. For example, 2-hydroxybenzoic acid is more often called salicylic acid, a name derived from the fact that this carboxylic acid was first isolated from the bark of the willow, a tree of the genus *Salix*.

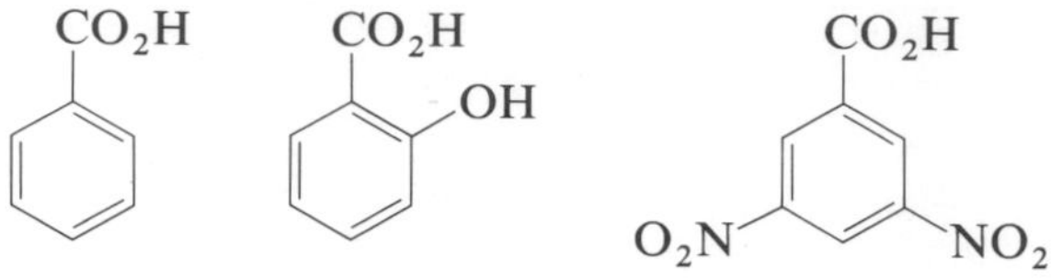

benzoic
acid

2-hydroxybenzoic
acid
(salicylic acid)

3,5-dinitrobenzoic
acid

Aromatic dicarboxylic acids are named using the suffix *-dicarboxylic acid*. Following are structural formulas for 1,2-benzenedicarboxylic acid and 1,4-benzenedicarboxylic acid. Each of these carboxylic acids has a common name by which it is more usually known—phthalic acid and terephthalic acid. The mono-potassium salt of phthalic acid (potassium hydrogen phthalate, or KHP) is widely used as a standard in preparing solutions for acid-base titrations.

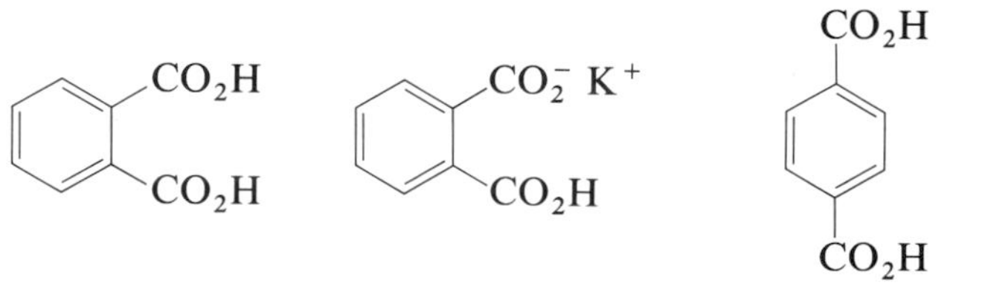

1,2-benzenedicarboxylic
acid
(phthalic acid)

potassium hydrogen
phthalate
(KHP)

1,4-benzenedicarboxylic
acid
(terephthalic acid)

Terephthalic acid is one of the two organic components required for synthesizing the textile fiber known as Dacron polyester, or Dacron. The U.S. chemical industry produced over 6 billion pounds of terephthalic acid in 1985. The raw material for its synthesis is *p*-xylene, a compound derived exclusively from the refining of petroleum. Oxidation of *p*-xylene by nitric acid gives terephthalic acid:

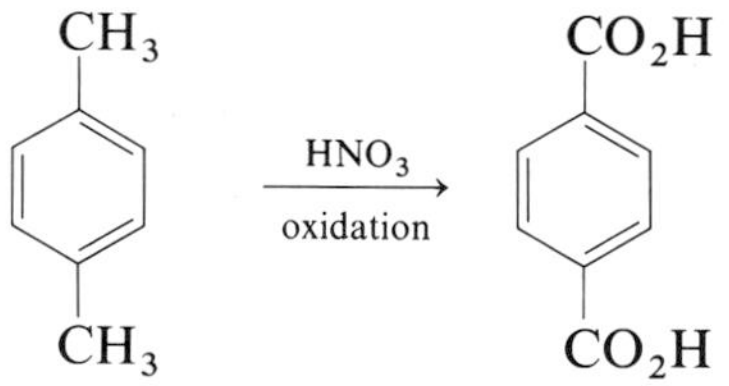

$$\xrightarrow[\text{oxidation}]{\text{HNO}_3}$$

p-xylene
(a product of
petroleum refining)

terephthalic acid

B. Common Names

Aliphatic carboxylic acids, many of which were known long before the development of structural theory and IUPAC nomenclature, were named according to their source or for some characteristic property. Formic acid was so named because it was first isolated from ants (Latin, *formica*). Acetic acid is a component of vinegar (Latin, *acetum*). Propionic acid was the first acid to be classified as a fatty acid (Greek, *pro*, first, and *pion*, fat). Butyric acid was first isolated from butter (Latin, *butyrum*). Oxalic acid was first isolated from a plant of the genus *Oxalis*. Valeric acid was first isolated from a plant of the genus *Valeriana*, native to Eurasia, widely cultivated in gardens and generally known as garden heliotrope. Several of the unbranched carboxylic acids most often found in the biological world along with their IUPAC and common names are listed in Table 16.2.

Table 16.2 Several carboxylic acids, and their common names and derivation.

Structure	IUPAC Name	Common Name	Derivation
HCO_2H	methanoic acid	formic acid	Latin: *formica*, ant
CH_3CO_2H	ethanoic acid	acetic acid	Latin: *acetum*, vinegar
$CH_3CH_2CO_2H$	propanoic acid	propionic acid	Greek: *propion*, first fatty acid
$CH_3(CH_2)_2CO_2H$	butanoic acid	butyric acid	Latin: *butyrum*, butter
$CH_3(CH_2)_3CO_2H$	pentanoic acid	valeric acid	Latin: *valeriana*, a flowering plant
$CH_3(CH_2)_4CO_2H$	hexanoic acid	caproic acid	Latin: *caper*, goat
$CH_3(CH_2)_6CO_2H$	octanoic acid	caprylic acid	Latin: *caper*, goat
$CH_3(CH_2)_8CO_2H$	decanoic acid	capric acid	Latin: *caper*, goat
$CH_3(CH_2)_{10}CO_2H$	dodecanoic acid	lauric acid	Latin: *laurus*, laurel
$CH_3(CH_2)_{12}CO_2H$	tetradecanoic acid	myristic acid	Greek: *muristikos*, fragrant
$CH_3(CH_2)_{14}CO_2H$	hexadecanoic acid	palmitic acid	Latin: *palma*, palm tree
$CH_3(CH_2)_{16}CO_2H$	octadecanoic acid	stearic acid	Greek: *stear*, solid fat
$CH_3(CH_2)_{18}CO_2H$	eicosanoic acid	arachidic acid	Greek: *arachne*, spider

When common names are used, Greek letters *alpha, beta, gamma,* and *delta* are often attached to locate substituents. The alpha position is the one next to the carboxyl group and an alpha substituent in a common name is equivalent to a 2 substituent in a IUPAC name. Following are two examples of the use of Greek letters to show the position of substituents. In each example, the IUPAC name is given first, followed by the common names. 2-aminopropanoic acid (alanine) is one of the 20 alpha–amino acids from which proteins are constructed (Chapter 21).

$$\overset{\delta}{C}-\overset{\gamma}{C}-\overset{\beta}{C}-\overset{\alpha}{C}-\overset{\overset{\textstyle O}{\|}}{C}OH \qquad \underset{\underset{\textstyle OH}{|}}{CH_2CH_2CH_2}\overset{\overset{\textstyle O}{\|}}{C}OH \qquad \underset{\underset{\textstyle NH_2}{|}}{CH_3CH}\overset{\overset{\textstyle O}{\|}}{C}OH$$

4-hydroxybutanoic acid
(γ-hydroxybutyric acid)

2-aminopropanoic acid
(α-aminopropionic acid;
alanine)

In common names, the presence of a ketone in a substituted carboxylic acid is indicated by the prefix *keto-*, as illustrated by the common name β-ketobutyric acid.

$$\underset{\substack{\text{3-oxobutanoic acid} \\ \text{(β-ketobutyric acid;} \\ \text{acetoacetic acid)}}}{CH_3\overset{\overset{O}{\|}}{C}CH_2\overset{\overset{O}{\|}}{C}OH} \qquad \underset{\text{an aceto group}}{CH_3\overset{\overset{O}{\|}}{C}-}$$

In practice, 3-oxobutanoic acid is known by two common names, *β-ketobutyric acid* and *acetoacetic acid*. The latter name, which is more common in the biological literature, is derived from the frequent reference to CH_3CO- as an aceto group. Thus, in the common nomenclature, 3-oxobutanoic acid is a substituted acetic acid and the name of the substituent is *aceto-*.

Example 16.1

Give IUPAC names for the following. Where possible, also give common names.

a. $CH_3\overset{\overset{CH_3}{|}}{CH}CO_2H$

b. $Cl-\overset{\overset{Cl}{|}}{\underset{\underset{Cl}{|}}{C}}-CO_2H$

c. $H_2N-\!\!\left\langle\!\!\bigcirc\!\!\right\rangle\!\!-CO_2H$

d. $CH_3\overset{\overset{HO}{|}}{CH}CH_2CO_2H$

Solution

a. The longest carbon chain is three atoms. The IUPAC name of this carboxylic acid is 2-methylpropanoic acid. The common name of the parent hydrocarbon is isobutane; therefore, the common name of this carboxylic acid is isobutyric acid.

b. Trichloroacetic acid. Acetic acid is retained by the IUPAC system. It is not necessary to use the numbers 2,2,2- to show the location of the three chlorine atoms because they can only be on the second carbon of the two-carbon chain. Trichloroacetic acid is often used in the clinical chemistry laboratory to precipitate proteins before analyzing blood or other biological fluids for other components.

c. 4-aminobenzoic acid. Its common name is *para*-aminobenzoic acid, or as it is often abbreviated, PABA. This substance is a growth factor needed by most microorganisms for the synthesis of folic acid (Section 22.6C). It is also used as a sunscreen in many tanning lotions.

d. 3-hydroxybutanoic acid. Its common name is beta-hydroxybutyric acid. This substituted carboxylic acid is one of three substances known as ketone bodies (Section 26.5).

Problem 16.1

Give IUPAC names for these compounds:

a. 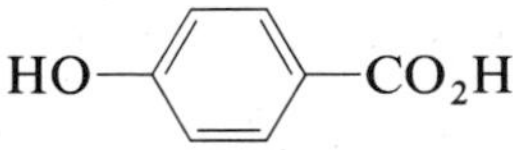 HO—⟨benzene ring⟩—CO₂H

b. CH₃CHCH₂CO₂H
      |
      CH₃

c. HO₂CCHCO₂H
        |
        CH₃

d. CH₃(CH₂)₈CH=CHCO₂H

16.3 Physical Properties

Because the carboxyl group contains three polar covalent bonds, carboxylic acids are polar compounds. The carbonyl oxygen and the hydroxyl oxygen bear partial negative charges, and the carbonyl carbon and hydroxyl hydrogen bear partial positive charges, as shown in Figure 16.2.

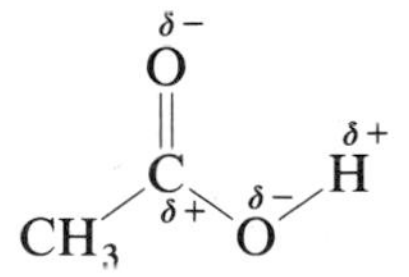

$$\begin{array}{c} \overset{\delta-}{O} \\ \parallel \\ CH_3 \overset{\delta+}{\underset{\delta+}{C}} \overset{\delta-}{O} \overset{\delta+}{H} \end{array}$$

Figure 16.2 Polarity of the carboxyl group.

Carboxylic acids can participate in hydrogen bonding through both C=O and OH groups, as shown in Figure 16.3 for acetic acid.

Because carboxylic acids are even more extensively hydrogen-bonded than alcohols, their boiling points are higher relative to alcohols of comparable

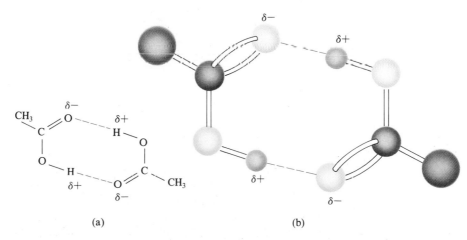

(a)   (b)

Figure 16.3 Hydrogen bonding between acetic acid molecules in pure liquid acetic acid. (a) Lewis structures; (b) ball-and-stick model.

molecular weight. For example, propanoic acid and 1-butanol have almost identical molecular weights, but because of more extensive hydrogen bonding, propanoic acid has a boiling point 24° higher than that of 1-butanol.

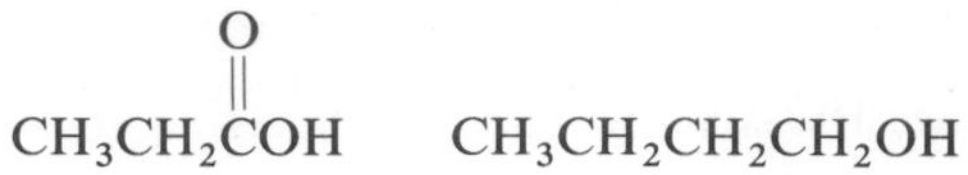

$$\text{CH}_3\text{CH}_2\overset{\displaystyle \overset{\text{O}}{\|}}{\text{C}}\text{OH} \qquad \text{CH}_3\text{CH}_2\text{CH}_2\text{CH}_2\text{OH}$$

<table>
<tr><td align="center">propanoic acid;
(propionic acid;
mw 74, bp 141°C)</td><td align="center">1-butanol
(n-butyl alcohol;
mw 74, bp 117°C)</td></tr>
</table>

Carboxylic acids also interact with water molecules by hydrogen bonding through both the carboxyl oxygen and the hydroxyl group:

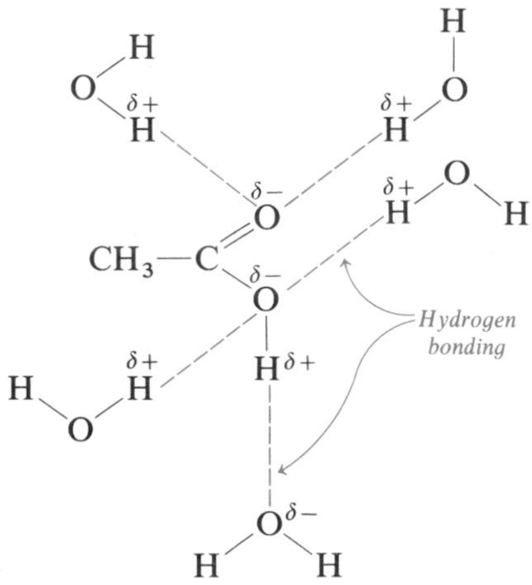

Because of these hydrogen-bonding interactions, carboxylic acids are more soluble in water than alkanes, ethers, alcohols, aldehydes, or ketones of comparable molecular weight. For example, propanoic acid (mw 74) is infinitely soluble in water, whereas the solubility of 1-butanol (mw 74) is only 8 g/100 g water.

As shown in Table 16.3, carboxylic acids with one to four carbon atoms are infinitely soluble in water. As molecular weight increases further, water solubility decreases. We can account for this trend in water solubility in the following

Table 16.3
Physical properties of some monocarboxylic acids.

Name	Structural Formula	mp (°C)	bp (°C)	Solubility in Water (g/100 g water)
formic acid	HCO_2H	8	100	infinite
acetic acid	CH_3CO_2H	16	118	infinite
propanoic acid	$CH_3CH_2CO_2H$	−22	141	infinite
butanoic acid	$CH_3(CH_2)_2CO_2H$	−6	164	infinite
hexanoic acid	$CH_3(CH_2)_4CO_2H$	−3	205	1.0
decanoic acid	$CH_3(CH_2)_8CO_2H$	32	—	insoluble

way. A carboxylic acid consists of two distinct parts, a polar hydrophilic carboxyl group, and except for formic acid, a nonpolar hydrophobic hydrocarbon chain. (**Hydrophilic** means "having an affinity for water; capable of dissolving in water." **Hydrophobic** means "tending not to combine with water; incapable of dissolving in water.") The hydrophilic carboxyl group increases water solubility; the hydrophobic hydrocarbon chain decreases water solubility.

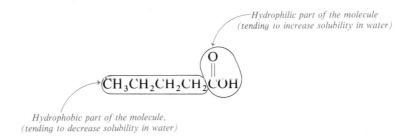

The first four aliphatic carboxylic acids are infinitely soluble in water because the hydrophobic effect of the hydrocarbon chain is more than counterbalanced by the hydrophilic character of the carboxyl group. As the size of the hydrophobic hydrocarbon chain increases relative to the size of the hydrophilic carboxyl group, water solubility decreases. The solubility of hexanoic acid in water is only 1.0 g per 100 g water. Decanoic acid is insoluble in water.

Example 16.2

Arrange the compounds in order of increasing boiling point:

a. CH$_3$CH$_2$CH$_2$COH

butanoic acid

b. CH$_3$CH$_2$CH$_2$CH$_2$CH

pentanal

c. CH$_3$CH$_2$CH$_2$CH$_2$CH$_2$OH

1-pentanol

☐ *Solution*

All three compounds are polar molecules of comparable molecular weight. Pentanal has no polar —OH group, cannot participate in hydrogen bonding in the pure liquid, and has the lowest boiling point. 1-Pentanol participates in hydrogen bonding through the polar —OH group and is next in boiling point. Butanoic acid participates in hydrogen bonding through both the polar C=O group and the —OH group; it has the highest boiling point.

pentanal	1-pentanol	butanoic acid
(mw 82; bp 103°C)	(mw 84; bp 137°C)	(mw 86; bp 164°C)

**Problem
16.2**

Arrange in order of increasing solubility in water:

a. $CH_3CH_2OCH_2CH_3$ **b.** $CH_3CH_2CH_2\overset{\displaystyle O}{\overset{\displaystyle \|}{C}}OH$ **c.** $CH_3(CH_2)_8\overset{\displaystyle O}{\overset{\displaystyle \|}{C}}OH$

diethyl ether   butanoic acid   decanoic acid

16.4 Preparation of Carboxylic Acids

A. Oxidation of Primary Alcohols

Oxidation of a primary alcohol (Section 13.4B) yields a carboxylic acid. In the laboratory, the most common oxidizing agents are potassium dichromate and potassium permanganate.

$$CH_3(CH_2)_5CH_2OH + Cr_2O_7^{2-} \xrightarrow{\text{H}_3\text{O}^+} CH_3(CH_2)_5\overset{\displaystyle O}{\overset{\displaystyle \|}{C}}OH + Cr^{3+}$$

1-heptanol
(*n*-heptyl alcohol)   heptanoic acid

$$HOCH_2CH_2CH_2CH_2OH + MnO_4^- \xrightarrow{\text{H}_3\text{O}^+} HO\overset{\displaystyle O}{\overset{\displaystyle \|}{C}}CH_2CH_2\overset{\displaystyle O}{\overset{\displaystyle \|}{C}}OH + Mn^{2+}$$

1,4-butanediol   butanedioic acid
(succinic acid)

B. Oxidation of Aldehydes

Aldehydes are oxidized to carboxylic acids by potassium permanganate, potassium dichromate, and even such weak oxidizing agents as Ag(I) and Cu(II), as described in Section 15.5A. In the following oxidation, silver ion is reduced to silver metal. Note that under these conditions, neither the primary nor the secondary alcohol of the starting material is oxidized.

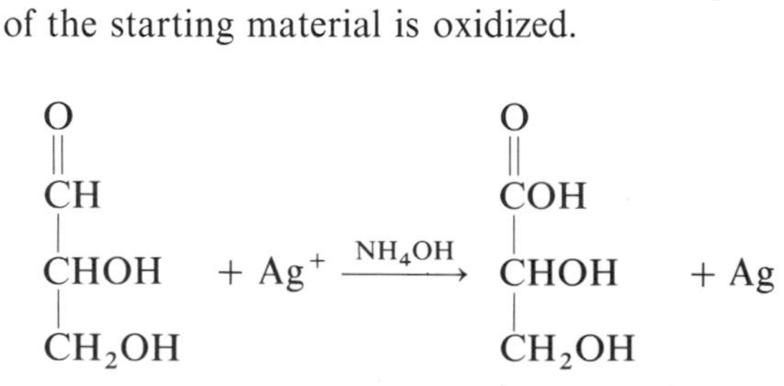

$$\begin{array}{ccc}
\overset{\displaystyle O}{\overset{\displaystyle \|}{C}}H & & \overset{\displaystyle O}{\overset{\displaystyle \|}{C}}OH \\
| & & | \\
CHOH & + \; Ag^+ \; \xrightarrow{\text{NH}_4\text{OH}} & CHOH \quad + \; Ag \\
| & & | \\
CH_2OH & & CH_2OH
\end{array}$$

2,3-dihydroxy-
propanal
(glyceraldehyde)   2,3-dihydroxy-
propanoic acid
(glyceric acid)

C. Oxidation of Alkenes

Oxidation of disubstituted alkenes of the type RCH=CHR by potassium dichromate or potassium permanganate causes cleavage of the carbon-carbon double bond and formation of two carboxylic acids:

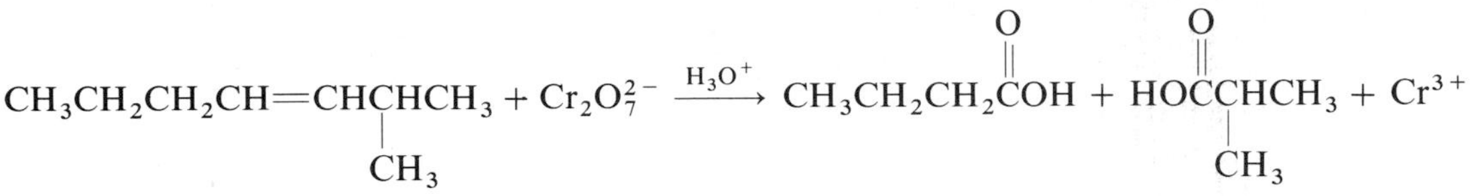

$$CH_3CH_2CH_2CH=CHCHCH_3 + Cr_2O_7^{2-} \xrightarrow{H_3O^+} CH_3CH_2CH_2\overset{\overset{\displaystyle O}{\|}}{C}OH + HO\overset{\overset{\displaystyle O}{\|}}{C}CHCH_3 + Cr^{3+}$$
$$\qquad\qquad | \qquad\qquad\qquad\qquad\qquad\qquad\qquad\qquad\qquad\quad |$$
$$\qquad\qquad CH_3 \qquad\qquad\qquad\qquad\qquad\qquad\qquad\qquad\qquad CH_3$$

2-methyl-3-heptene   butanoic acid   2-methyl-
(butyric acid)   propanoic acid
(isobutyric acid)

Oxidation of cyclohexene cleaves the carbon-carbon double bond and yields adipic acid, a dicarboxylic acid:

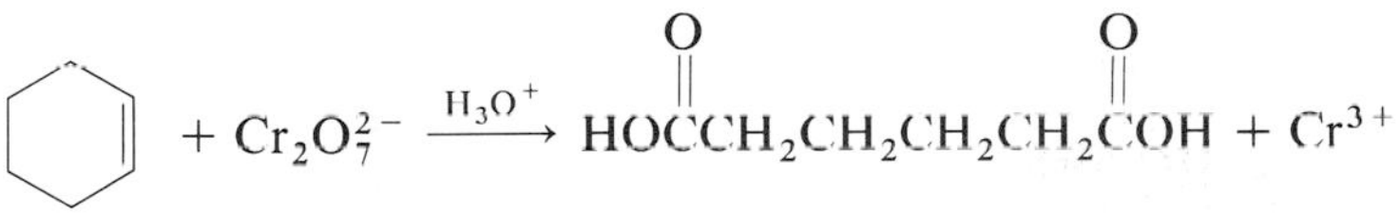

$$\bigcirc \!\!\!\!\!\!\!\! = \quad + Cr_2O_7^{2-} \xrightarrow{H_3O^+} HO\overset{\overset{\displaystyle O}{\|}}{C}CH_2CH_2CH_2CH_2\overset{\overset{\displaystyle O}{\|}}{C}OH + Cr^{3+}$$

cyclohexene   hexanedioic acid
(adipic acid)

Oxidation of a trisubstituted alkene yields a ketone and a carboxylic acid. For example, oxidation of 3-methyl-3-heptene gives

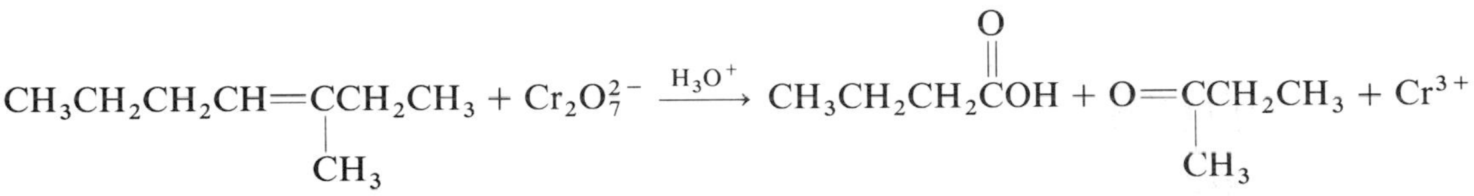

$$CH_3CH_2CH_2CH=CCH_2CH_3 + Cr_2O_7^{2-} \xrightarrow{H_3O^+} CH_3CH_2CH_2\overset{\overset{\displaystyle O}{\|}}{C}OH + O=CCH_2CH_3 + Cr^{3+}$$
$$\qquad\qquad\qquad | \qquad\qquad\qquad\qquad\qquad\qquad\qquad\qquad\qquad\qquad\qquad |$$
$$\qquad\qquad\qquad CH_3 \qquad\qquad\qquad\qquad\qquad\qquad\qquad\qquad\qquad\qquad\quad CH_3$$

3-methyl-3-heptene   butanoic acid   2-butanone
(butyric acid)   (ethyl methyl ketone)

Example 16.3

Draw structural formulas for the products of these oxidations:

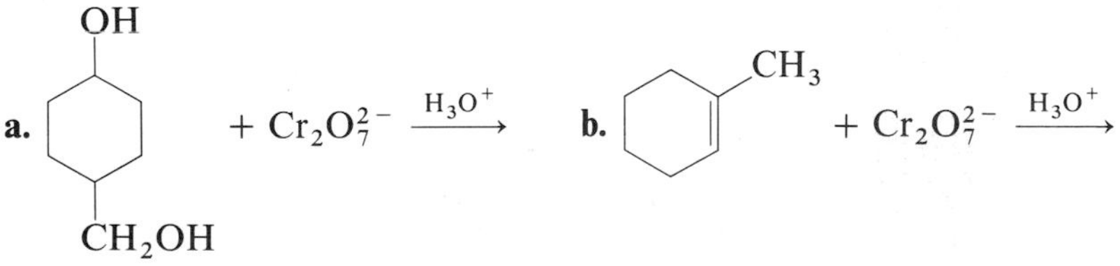

a. (cyclohexane ring with OH at top and CH_2OH at bottom) $+ Cr_2O_7^{2-} \xrightarrow{H_3O^+}$ **b.** (cyclohexene ring with CH_3) $+ Cr_2O_7^{2-} \xrightarrow{H_3O^+}$

Solution

a. The starting material contains both a primary alcohol and a secondary alcohol. In the presence of potassium dichromate, the primary alcohol is oxidized to a carboxylic acid and the secondary alcohol to a ketone:

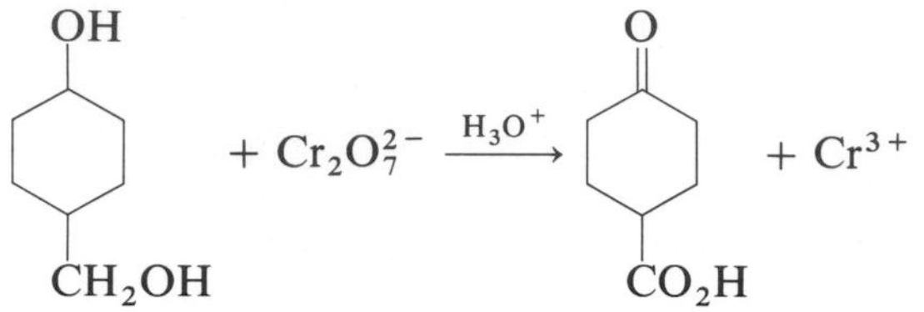

b. Oxidation of 1-methylcyclohexene yields a ketone and a carboxylic acid. The structural formula of the product is drawn below in two different ways: the first to emphasize where the ring is cleaved, the second to show the molecule as a chain of seven carbon atoms.

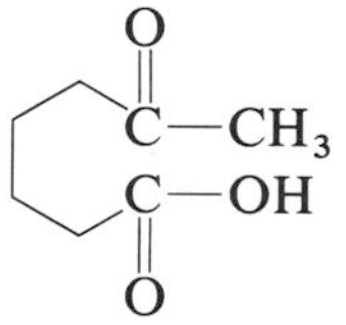

Problem 16.3

Draw structural formulas for the products of these oxidations:

a. $CH_3\overset{\overset{\displaystyle CH_3}{|}}{C}{=}CHCH_2CH_2CH{=}\overset{\overset{\displaystyle CH_3}{|}}{C}CH_3 + Cr_2O_7^{2-} \xrightarrow{H_3O^+}$

b. $HOCH_2CH_2CH_2CH_2\overset{\overset{\displaystyle O}{\|}}{C}H + Cr_2O_7^{2-} \xrightarrow{H_3O^+}$

16.5 Reactions of Carboxylic Acids

A. Acidity

Carboxylic acids ionize in water, to give acidic solutions. However, carboxylic acids are different in acidity from inorganic acids such as HCl, HBr, HNO_3, and H_2SO_4. Because these inorganic acids are 100% ionized in aqueous solution, they are classified as strong (meaning completely ionized) acids.

$$HCl \xrightarrow{H_2O} H^+ + Cl^-$$

Carboxylic acids are only slightly ionized in aqueous solution and therefore are classified as weak acids. When a carboxylic acid ionizes in water, an equilibrium is established between the carboxylic acid, the carboxylate ion, and H^+, as illustrated for the ionization of acetic acid:

$$CH_3\overset{\overset{\displaystyle O}{\|}}{C}OH \underset{H_2O}{\rightleftarrows} CH_3\overset{\overset{\displaystyle O}{\|}}{C}O^- + H^+ \qquad K_a = \frac{[H^+][CH_3CO_2^-]}{[CH_3CO_2H]} = 1.8 \times 10^{-5}$$

The equilibrium constant for this ionization K_a is called an acid dissociation constant (Section 9.5). The value of the acid dissociation constant for acetic acid is 1.8×10^{-5}, a typical value for simple carboxylic acids.

The ionization illustrated above is for acetic acid in water. A practical example of this equilibrium is vinegar, a 5% solution of acetic acid in water. Expressed in other units, the concentration of acetic acid in vinegar is approximately 50 g/L, or 0.83 mol/L. The hydrogen ion concentration in this solution is 3.8×10^{-3} mol/L, and its pH is approximately 2.4. By comparison, the concentration of hydrogen ion in 0.83M HCl is 0.83M, and the pH of this solution is 0.081.

The other class of organic acids we have studied so far are the phenols (Section 13.7B). The difference in acidity between HCl and weak organic acids such as acetic acid and phenol can be seen by comparing the hydrogen ion concentrations and pH of a 0.1M solution of each of these acids in water, as shown in Table 16.4. Hydrochloric acid is a strong acid and 100% ionized in aqueous solution. By comparison, acetic acid and phenol are weak acids, and only slightly ionized in water. Carboxylic acids, however, are much stronger acids than phenols. It is carboxylic acids that give most common biological materials their acid pH. One exception is human gastric (stomach) juice, whose acidity is due to hydrochloric acid. Shown in Table 16.5 are approximate pH values for some biological materials and foods and beverages.

Table 16.4
Relative acid strengths of 0.1M HCl, acetic acid, and phenol.

Acid	K_a	Ionization in Water	$[H^+]$	pH
HCl	very large	100%	0.1M	1.0
CH_3CO_2H	1.8×10^{-5}	1.3%	0.0013M	2.9
 ⬡—OH	3.3×10^{-10}	0.0033%	3.3×10^{-6}	5.5

Table 16.5
Approximate pH values for some foods, beverages, and biological materials.

Substance	pH	Substance	pH
blood plasma (human)	7.3–7.5	grapefruit	3.0–3.3
saliva (human)	6.5–7.5	lemons	2.2–2.4
stomach fluids (human)	1.0–3.0	oranges	3.0–4.0
milk (human)	6.6–7.6	potatoes	5.6–6.0
apples	2.9–3.3	skin (human)	4.5–5.5
bananas	4.5–4.7	soft drinks	2.4–4.0
beans	5.0–6.0	tomatoes	4.0–4.4
beer	4.0–5.0	vinegar	2.4–3.4
cheese	4.8–6.4	water, drinking	6.5–8.0
cider	2.9–3.3	wines	2.8–3.8
eggs	7.6–8.0		

B. Reaction with Bases

All carboxylic acids, whether soluble or insoluble in water, react quantitatively with NaOH, KOH, and other strong bases, to form salts.

benzoic acid
(only slightly
soluble in water)

sodium benzoate
(very soluble
in water)

Carboxylic acids also react with ammonia, and with primary, secondary, and tertiary amines to form salts.

benzoic acid
(only slightly
soluble in water)

ammonium benzoate
(very soluble
in water)

Sodium, potassium, and ammonium salts of carboxylic acids are ionic compounds and are much more soluble in water than the carboxylic acids from which they are derived. Benzoic acid, for example, is only very slightly soluble in water at room temperature. By contrast, the solubility of ammonium benzoate is 20 g/100 g water and of sodium benzoate is 66 g/100 g water.

Salts of carboxylic acids are named like the salts of inorganic acids; the cation is named first and then the anion. The name of the anion is derived from the carboxylic acid by dropping the suffic -*ic acid* and adding the suffix -*ate*, as illustrated by these examples:

Carboxylic Acid	Anion	Salt
$CH_3CH_2CO_2H$	$CH_3CH_2CO_2^-$	$(CH_3CH_2CO_2^-)_2Ca^{2+}$
propanoic acid (propionic acid)	propanoate (propionate)	calcium propanoate (calcium propionate)
$CH_3(CH_2)_{14}CO_4H$	$CH_3(CH_2)_{14}CO_2^-$	$CH_3(CH_2)_{14}CO_2^- \, Na^+$
hexadecanoic acid (palmitic acid)	hexadecanoate (palmitate)	sodium hexadecanoate (sodium palmitate)

Calcium propanoate is often added to bread and other baked goods "to retard spoilage." Hexadecanoic acid (palmitic acid) is one of the most abundant long-chain carboxylic acids in the biological world. Its concentration in palm oil is particularly high, hence its common name, palmitic acid. Because sodium hexadecanoate (sodium palmitate) is relatively abundant in animal fats, from which natural soaps are made, it is an important component of natural soaps (Section 20.2).

Example 16.4

Name these salts:

a. $CH_3CO_2^-(CH_3)_3NH^+$ b. 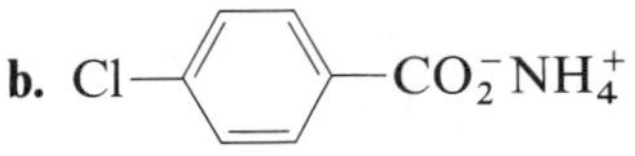 $Cl-\langle\!\!\!\bigcirc\!\!\!\rangle-CO_2^-NH_4^+$

Solution

a. The carboxylic acid is acetic acid and its anion is acetate ion. The cation is derived from trimethylamine and is named trimethylammonium ion. The name of the salt is trimethylammonium acetate.
b. The acid is 4-chlorobenzoic acid or *p*-chlorobenzoic acid. The name of this salt is ammonium 4-chlorobenzoate, or ammonium *p*-chlorobenzoate.

Problem 16.4

Draw structural formulas for these salts:

a. potassium 2-methylpropanoate (potassium isobutyrate)
b. calcium hexadecanoate (calcium palmitate)

Carboxylic acids also react with weaker bases such as sodium bicarbonate and sodium carbonate, to form salts. In these reactions, the carboxylic acid is converted to a sodium salt; bicarbonate and carbonate ions are converted to carbonic acid, H_2CO_3, which spontaneously breaks down to form carbon dioxide and water:

$$2CH_3\overset{O}{\overset{\|}{C}}OH + Na_2CO_3 \longrightarrow 2CH_3\overset{O}{\overset{\|}{C}}O^-Na^+ + CO_2 + H_2O$$

acetic   sodium   sodium
acid   carbonate   acetate

$$\begin{array}{c} \overset{O}{\overset{\|}{C}}O^-K^+ \\ | \\ H-C-OH \\ | \\ HO-C-H \\ | \\ \underset{O}{\underset{\|}{C}}OH \end{array} + NaHCO_3 \longrightarrow \begin{array}{c} \overset{O}{\overset{\|}{C}}O^-K^+ \\ | \\ H-C-OH \\ | \\ HO-C-H \\ | \\ \underset{O}{\underset{\|}{C}}O^-Na^+ \end{array} + CO_2 + H_2O$$

potassium hydrogen   potassium sodium
tartrate   tartrate
(cream of tartar)

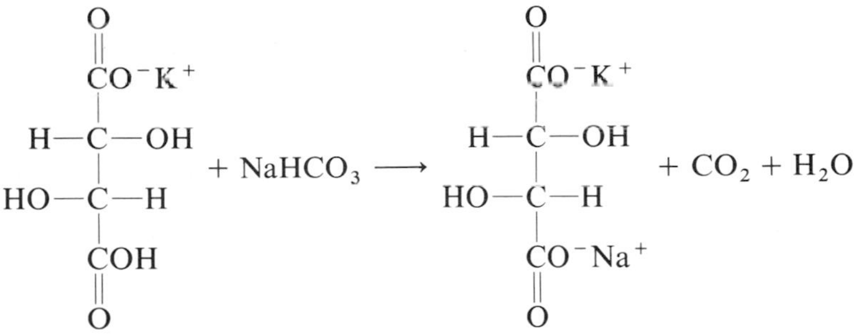

By this last reaction, you can see why sodium carbonate or sodium bicarbonate or both are used in baking. Baking powder is a combination of sodium carbonate or sodium bicarbonate and potassium hydrogen tartrate. When water is added, the acid and base in baking powder react, to liberate carbon dioxide, which forms bubbles in the batter or dough and causes it to "rise." Baking soda (sodium bicarbonate) can also be mixed with vinegar (a solution of acetic acid in water) or with lemon juice or orange juice (a solution containing citric acid) to produce carbon dioxide. Other recipes call for mixing baking soda with sour cream, which contains 2-hydroxypropanoic acid, known almost exclusively by its common name, lactic acid. Lactic acid and sodium bicarbonate react, to produce a salt plus carbon dioxide and water:

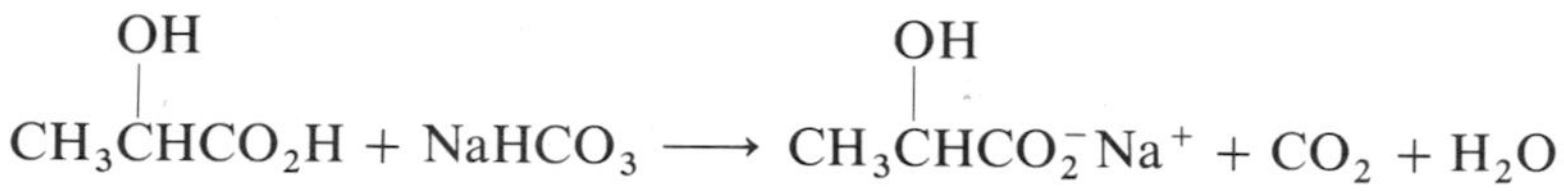

$$\underset{\substack{\text{2-hydroxypropanoic}\\ \text{acid}\\ \text{(lactic acid)}}}{CH_3\overset{\displaystyle OH}{\overset{|}{C}}HCO_2H} + NaHCO_3 \longrightarrow \underset{\substack{\text{sodium 2-hydroxy-}\\ \text{propanoate}\\ \text{(sodium lactate)}}}{CH_3\overset{\displaystyle OH}{\overset{|}{C}}HCO_2^-\,Na^+} + CO_2 + H_2O$$

Example 16.5

Complete and balance the acid-base equations:

a.  $CH_3\overset{\displaystyle HO}{\overset{|}{C}}H\overset{\displaystyle O}{\overset{||}{C}}OH + NaOH \longrightarrow$

b. $CH_3\overset{\displaystyle O}{\overset{||}{C}}CH_2CH_2CH_2\overset{\displaystyle O}{\overset{||}{C}}OH + NaHCO_3 \longrightarrow$

c. $HO\overset{\displaystyle O}{\overset{||}{C}}CH_2CH_2\overset{\displaystyle O}{\overset{||}{C}}OH + Na_2CO_3 \longrightarrow$

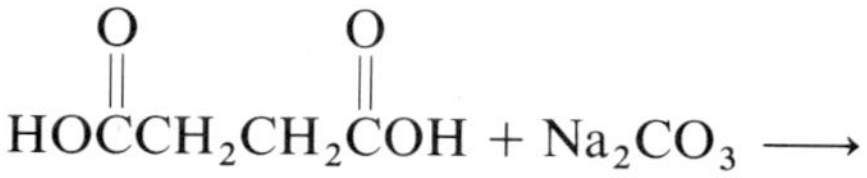

☐ *Solution*

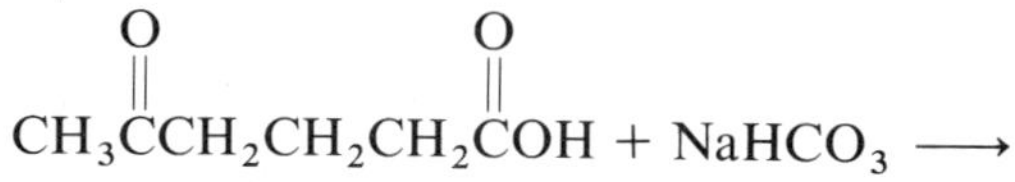

a. 2-hydroxypropanoic acid (lactic acid) is a monocarboxylic acid and reacts in a 1:1 molar ratio with sodium hydroxide, to form sodium lactate and water:

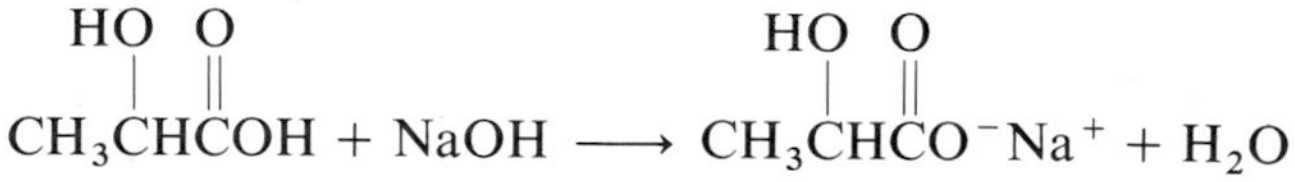

$$\underset{\substack{\text{2-hydroxy-}\\ \text{propanoic acid}\\ \text{(lactic acid)}}}{CH_3\overset{\displaystyle HO}{\overset{|}{C}}H\overset{\displaystyle O}{\overset{||}{C}}OH} + NaOH \longrightarrow \underset{\substack{\text{sodium 2-hydroxy-}\\ \text{propanoate}\\ \text{(sodium lactate)}}}{CH_3\overset{\displaystyle HO}{\overset{|}{C}}H\overset{\displaystyle O}{\overset{||}{C}}O^-Na^+} + H_2O$$

b. 5-oxohexanoic acid is also a monocarboxylic acid and reacts in a 1:1 molar ratio with sodium bicarbonate, to form a sodium salt, carbon dioxide, and water:

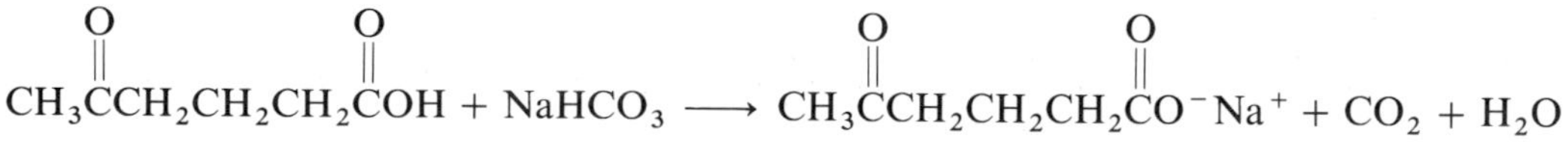

$$\underset{\text{5-oxohexanoic acid}}{CH_3\overset{\displaystyle O}{\overset{||}{C}}CH_2CH_2CH_2\overset{\displaystyle O}{\overset{||}{C}}OH} + NaHCO_3 \longrightarrow \underset{\text{sodium 5-oxohexanoate}}{CH_3\overset{\displaystyle O}{\overset{||}{C}}CH_2CH_2CH_2\overset{\displaystyle O}{\overset{||}{C}}O^-Na^+} + CO_2 + H_2O$$

c. Butanedioic acid (succinic acid) is a dicarboxylic acid and reacts with sodium carbonate in a 1:1 molar ratio:

$$\underset{\substack{\text{butanedioic acid}\\\text{(succinic acid)}}}{\text{HOCCH}_2\text{CH}_2\text{COH}} + \text{Na}_2\text{CO}_3 \longrightarrow \underset{\substack{\text{sodium butanedioate}\\\text{(sodium succinate)}}}{\text{Na}^+ \; {}^-\text{OCCH}_2\text{CH}_2\text{CO}^-\text{Na}^+} + \text{CO}_2 + \text{H}_2\text{O}$$

Problem 16.5

Complete and balance these acid-base reactions.

a. $\text{CH}_3\text{CH}_2\text{CH}{=}\text{CHCO}_2\text{H} + \text{NaOH} \longrightarrow$

b. $2\langle\ \rangle{-}\text{CO}_2\text{H} + \text{Na}_2\text{CO}_3 \longrightarrow$

c. HO—C—CO₂H + 3NaHCO₃ ⟶

with CH₂—CO₂H groups above and below

citric acid

C. Reduction

Carboxyl groups are among the most difficult organic functional groups to reduce. They are not affected by catalytic hydrogenation under conditions that easily reduce aldehydes and ketones to alcohols, say, temperatures of 25–100°C and pressures of hydrogen of 1–5 atm (Section 15.6A). Thus it is possible to reduce aldehydes or ketones to alcohols in the presence of carboxylic acids:

$$\underset{\text{5-oxohexanoic acid}}{\text{CH}_3\text{CCH}_2\text{CH}_2\text{CH}_2\text{COH}} + \text{H}_2 \xrightarrow[\text{25°C, 2 atm}]{\text{Pt}} \underset{\text{5-hydroxyhexanoic acid}}{\text{CH}_3\text{CHCH}_2\text{CH}_2\text{CH}_2\text{COH}}$$

It is, however, possible to reduce carboxylic acids to primary alcohols, using the metal hydride reducing agent lithium aluminum hydride, LiAlH_4 (Section 15.6B). With this reagent, terephthalic acid is reduced to a diol:

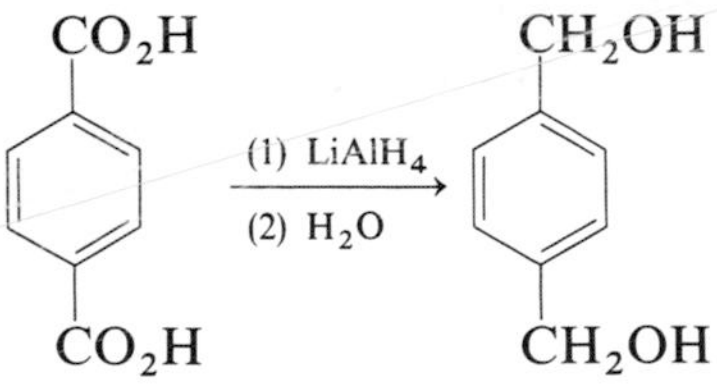

$$\underset{\substack{\text{terephthalic}\\\text{acid}}}{\overset{\text{CO}_2\text{H}}{\underset{\text{CO}_2\text{H}}{\bigcirc}}} \xrightarrow[\text{(2) H}_2\text{O}]{\text{(1) LiAlH}_4} \overset{\text{CH}_2\text{OH}}{\underset{\text{CH}_2\text{OH}}{\bigcirc}}$$

Recall (Section 15.6B) that LiAlH_4 also reduces aldehydes and ketones to alcohols but does not reduce alkenes or alkynes.

■

Example 16.6

Draw structural formulas for the products formed by reduction of the following with lithium aluminum hydride.

a. $CH_3\overset{\overset{\displaystyle CH_3}{|}}{C}=CHCH_2CH_2\overset{\overset{\displaystyle O}{||}}{C}OH$ b. $H\overset{\overset{\displaystyle O}{||}}{C}CH_2CH_2CH_2\overset{\overset{\displaystyle O}{||}}{C}OH$

☐ *Solution*

a. $CH_3\overset{\overset{\displaystyle CH_3}{|}}{C}=CHCH_2CH_2CH_2OH$ b. $HOCH_2CH_2CH_2CH_2CH_2OH$

■

Problem 16.6

Draw the structural formula for a compound of given molecular formula that after reduction by lithium aluminum hydride gives the following molecules:

a. $C_6H_8O_2 \xrightarrow[\text{(2) } H_2O]{\text{(1) } LiAlH_4} HO\text{—}\langle\bigcirc\rangle\text{—}OH$.

b. $C_6H_{10}O_4 \xrightarrow[\text{(2) } H_2O]{\text{(1) } LiAlH_4} HOCH_2CH_2CH_2CH_2CH_2CH_2OH$

■

D. Decarboxylation of Beta-Ketoacids and Beta-Dicarboxylic Acids

Carboxylic acids that have a carbonyl group on the carbon atom beta to the carboxyl group lose CO_2 on heating. This reaction causes loss of the carboxyl group and is called decarboxylation. For example, when 3-oxobutanoic acid is heated, it decarboxylates, to give acetone and carbon dioxide:

This carbonyl group is beta to the carboxyl group

$$CH_3-\overset{\overset{\displaystyle O}{||}}{\underset{\beta}{C}}-\overset{\alpha}{C}H_2-\overset{\overset{\displaystyle O}{||}}{C}-OH \xrightarrow{\text{heat}} CH_3-\overset{\overset{\displaystyle O}{||}}{C}-CH_3 + CO_2$$

3-oxobutanoic acid
(β-ketobutyric acid;
acetoacetic acid)

acetone

3-oxobutanoic, or acetoacetic acid as it is more commonly named in biochemistry, and its reduction product, 3-hydroxybutanoic acid (β-hydroxybutyric acid) are synthesized in the liver by partial oxidation of fatty acids; they are known collectively as ketone bodies. (We will discuss the synthesis and metabolism of ketone bodies in Section 26.5.) The concentration of ketone bodies in the blood of healthy, well-fed humans is approximately 0.01 mM/L. However, in starvation or diabetes mellitus, the concentration of ketone bodies may increase to as much as 500 times normal. Under these conditions, the concentration of 3-oxobutanoic acid (acetoacetic acid) increases to the point where it undergoes spontaneous decarboxylation, to form acetone and carbon dioxide. Acetone is not metabolized by humans and is excreted through the kidneys and lungs. The odor of acetone is responsible for the characteristic "sweet smell" on the breath of severely diabetic patients.

Decarboxylation on heating is a unique property of 3-oxocarboxylic acids (β-ketocarboxylic acids), and is not observed with other classes of ketoacids.

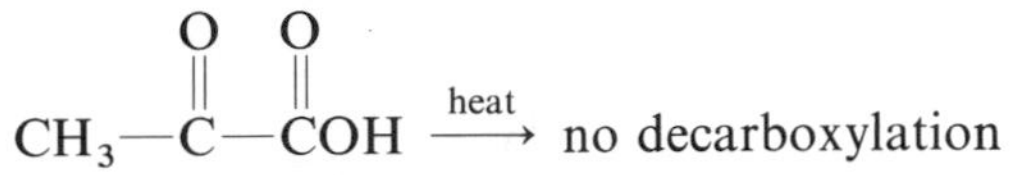

$$CH_3-\overset{\overset{\displaystyle O}{\|}}{C}-\overset{\overset{\displaystyle O}{\|}}{C}OH \xrightarrow{\text{heat}} \text{no decarboxylation}$$

2-oxopropanoic acid
(pyruvic acid)

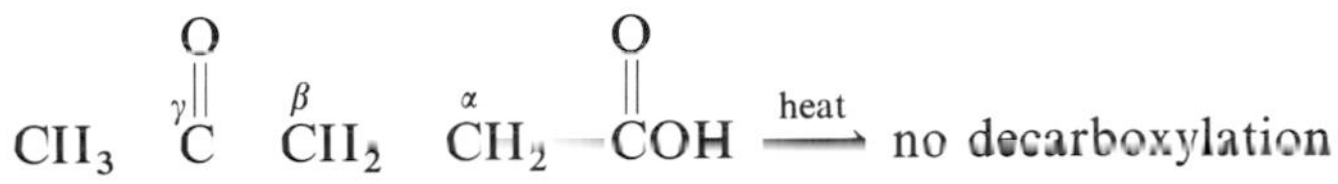

$$CH_3 \quad \overset{\overset{\displaystyle O}{\underset{\gamma}{\|}}}{C} \quad \overset{\beta}{CH_2} \quad \overset{\alpha}{CH_2} - \overset{\overset{\displaystyle O}{\|}}{C}OH \xrightarrow{\text{heat}} \text{no decarboxylation}$$

4-oxopentanoic acid
(γ-ketovaleric acid)

The mechanism for decarboxylation of β-ketoacids is illustrated by the decarboxylation of 3-oxobutanoic acid. The reaction is thought to involve a cyclic six-membered transition state, which by rearrangement of electron pairs, leads to the enol form of acetone and carbon dioxide. The enol form of acetone is in equilibrium with the keto form.

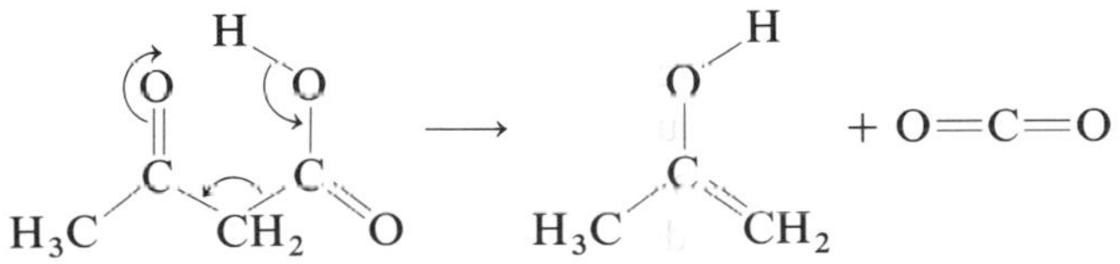

3-ketobutanoic acid   enol form
of acetone

Another important decarboxylation of a β-ketoacid in the biological world occurs during the oxidation of foodstuffs in the tricarboxylic acid cycle (Section 25.5). One of the intermediates in this cycle is 1-oxo-1,2,3-propanetricarboxylic acid, known almost exclusively by its common name, oxalosuccinic acid. Oxalosuccinic acid undergoes spontaneous decarboxylation to produce 2-oxopentanedioic acid (α-ketoglutaric acid). Only one of the three carboxyl groups of oxalosuccinic acid has a carbonyl group in the β-position to it. It is this carboxyl group that is lost as CO_2.

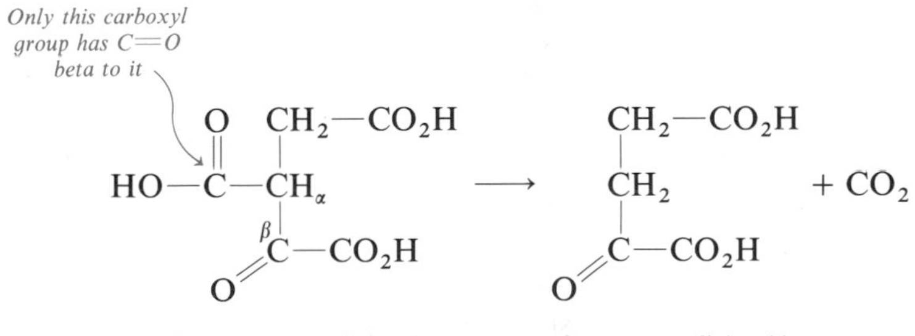

Only this carboxyl group has C=O beta to it

1-oxo-1,2,3-propanetrioic acid   2-oxopentanedioic acid
(oxalosuccinic acid)   (α-ketoglutaric acid)

Key Terms and Concepts

carboxyl group (16.1)   hydrophobic (16.3)

hydrophilic (16.3)   beta-ketoacid (16.5D)

Key Reactions

1. Carboxylic acids are weak acids and ionize in water to give acidic solutions (Section 16.5A).

2. Reaction with NaOH and other strong bases to give water-soluble salts (Section 16.5B).

3. Metal hydride reduction to primary alcohols (Section 16.5C).

4. Decarboxylation of β-ketoacids (Section 16.5D).

Problems

Structure and nomenclature of carboxylic acids (Sections 16.1 and 16.2)

16.7   Name the compounds:

a. $CH_3CHCH_2CH_2CO_2H$
        |
        OH

b. $C_6H_5CH_2CH_2CH_2CO_2H$

c. $ClCH_2CO_2H$

d. CH_3CHCO_2H
        |
        CH_3

e. 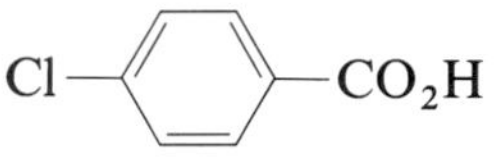 Cl—⟨benzene ring⟩—CO_2H

f. 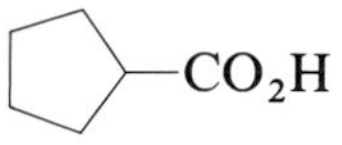 ⟨cyclopentane ring⟩—CO_2H

g. $C_6H_5CO_2^-\ Na^+$

h. $CH_3CH_2CH_2CH_2CO_2^-NH_4^+$

i. $HO_2CCH_2CH_2CH_2CH_2CO_2H$

j. CF_3CO_2H

k. $(CH_3CH_2CO_2^-)_2\ Ca^{2+}$

l. $CH_3(CH_2)_7CH{=}CH(CH_2)_7CO_2H$

16.8   Draw structural formulas for these compounds:

a. 3-hydroxybutanoic acid

b. sodium oxalate

c. trichloroacetic acid

d. 4-aminobutanoic acid

e. sodium hexadecanoate

f. calcium octanoate

g. potassium phenylacetate

h. octanoic acid

i. 2-aminopropanoic acid (alanine)

j. 2-hydroxypropanoic acid (lactic acid)

k. *p*-methoxybenzoic acid

l. potassium 2,4-hexadienoate (the food preservative, potassium sorbate)

Physical properties of carboxylic acids (Section 16.3)

16.9 Draw structural formulas to illustrate hydrogen bonding between the circled atoms.

a. 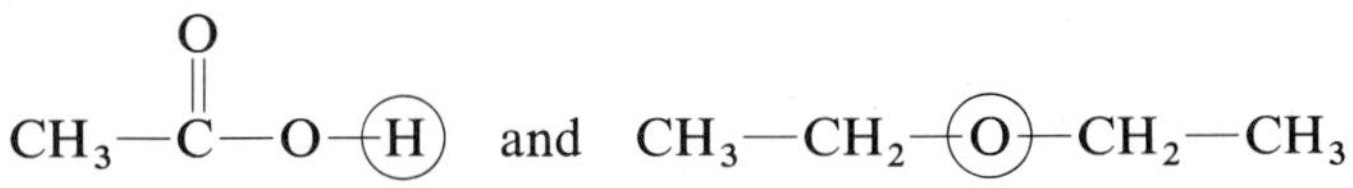 $CH_3—\overset{\overset{\displaystyle O}{\|}}{C}—O—\boxed{H}$ and $CH_3—CH_2—\boxed{O}—CH_2—CH_3$

b. $CH_3—\overset{\overset{\displaystyle \boxed{O}}{\|}}{C}—O—H$ and $CH_3—CH_2—O—\boxed{H}$

c. (cyclohexane ring)$—\overset{\overset{\displaystyle O}{\|}}{C}—O—\boxed{H}$ with ring substituent $\boxed{O}—H$

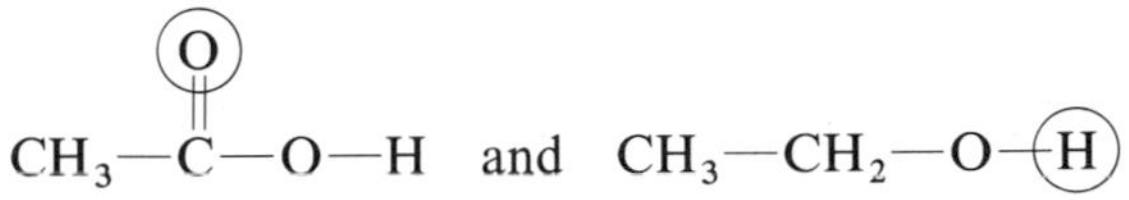

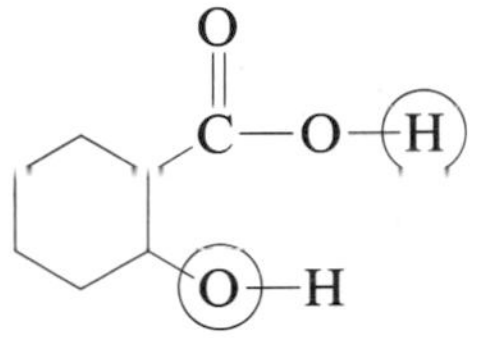

d. 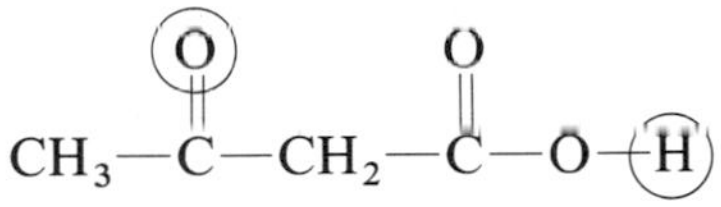 $CH_3—\overset{\overset{\displaystyle \boxed{O}}{\|}}{C}—CH_2—\overset{\overset{\displaystyle O}{\|}}{C}—O—\boxed{H}$

16.10 Arrange the compounds of each set in order of increasing boiling points.

a. $CH_3CH_2\overset{\overset{\displaystyle O}{\|}}{C}OH$ $CH_3CH_2CH_2CH_2OH$ $CH_3CH_2OCH_2CH_3$

b. $CH_3(CH_2)_8CO_2H$ (benzene ring)$—OII$ $CH_3(CH_2)_4CO_2H$

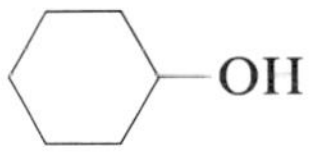

Preparation of carboxylic acids (Section 16.4)

16.11 Complete the following reactions:

a. $CH_3(CH_2)_4CH_2OH + Cr_2O_7^{2-} \xrightarrow[\text{heat}]{H_2O, H^+}$

b. 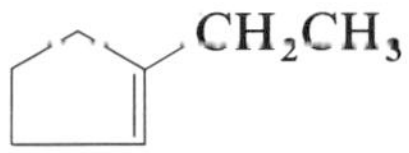 (cyclopentene ring with CH_2CH_3 substituent) $+ Cr_2O_7^{2-} \xrightarrow[\text{heat}]{H_2O, H^+}$

c. 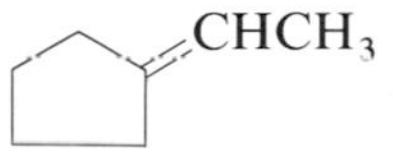 (cyclopentane ring with $CHCH_3$ substituent) $+ Cr_2O_7^{2-} \xrightarrow[\text{heat}]{H_2O, H^+}$

d. $CH_3(CH_2)_7CH=CH(CH_2)_7\overset{\overset{\displaystyle O}{\|}}{C}OH + Cr_2O_7^{2-} \xrightarrow[\text{heat}]{H_2O, H^+}$

e. 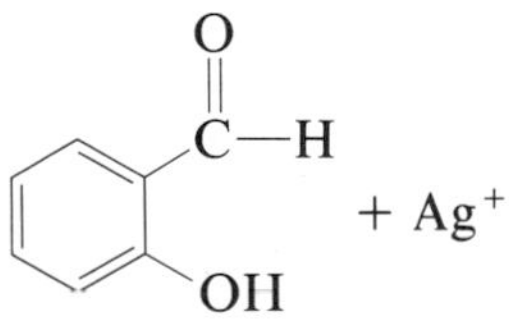 (benzene ring with $\overset{\overset{\displaystyle O}{\|}}{C}—H$ and OII substituents) $+ Ag^+ \xrightarrow{NH_4OH}$

salicylaldehyde

f. 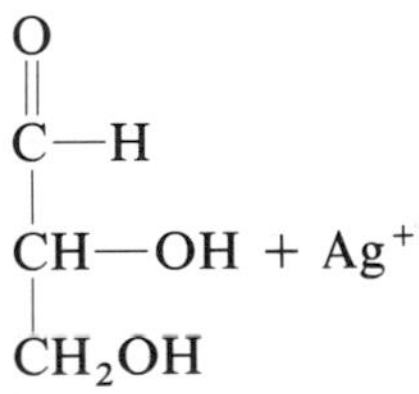 $\overset{\overset{\displaystyle O}{\|}}{\underset{\underset{\displaystyle CH_2OH}{CH—OH}}{C—H}} + Ag^+ \xrightarrow{NH_4OH}$

glyceraldehyde

16.12 Draw the structural formula of a compound of the given molecular formula that on oxidation gives the carboxylic acid or dicarboxylic acid shown.

a. $C_6H_{14}O \xrightarrow{\text{oxidation}} CH_3(CH_2)_4\overset{\overset{\displaystyle O}{\|}}{C}OH$

b. $C_6H_{12}O \xrightarrow{\text{oxidation}} CH_3(CH_2)_4\overset{\overset{\displaystyle O}{\|}}{C}OH$

c. $C_6H_{14}O_2 \xrightarrow{\text{oxidation}} HO\overset{\overset{\displaystyle O}{\|}}{C}CH_2CH_2CH_2CH_2\overset{\overset{\displaystyle O}{\|}}{C}OH$

d. $C_6H_{10} \xrightarrow{\text{oxidation}} HO\overset{\overset{\displaystyle O}{\|}}{C}CH_2CH_2CH_2CH_2\overset{\overset{\displaystyle O}{\|}}{C}OH$

Reactions of carboxylic acids (Section 16.5)

16.13 Arrange the compounds in order of increasing acidity:

a. 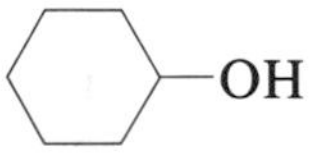 ⬡—OH   **b.** 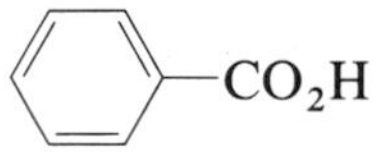 ⬡—CO$_2$H   **c.** 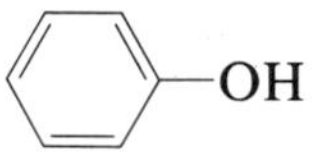 ⬡—OH

16.14 Complete these reactions. Where there is no reaction, write N.R.

a. $CH_3CO_2H + NaOH \longrightarrow$

b. 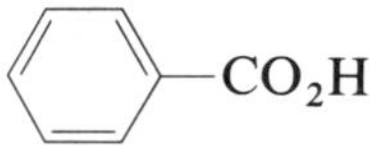 ⬡—$CO_2H + NaOH \longrightarrow$

c. $CH_3(CH_2)_{14}CO_2Na + H_2SO_4 \longrightarrow$

d. $CH_3CH_2CH_2CO_2H + NaHCO_3 \longrightarrow$

e. 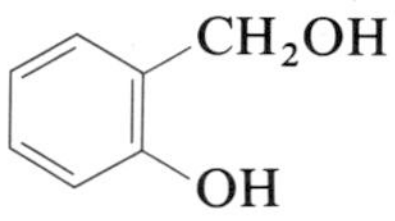 ⬡(with CH_2OH and OH) $+ NaOH \longrightarrow$

f. 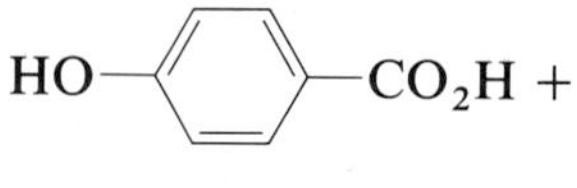 HO—⬡—$CO_2H + NaHCO_3 \longrightarrow$

g. $CH_3CH_2\overset{\overset{\displaystyle O}{\|}}{C}\underset{\underset{\displaystyle CH_3}{|}}{C}H\overset{\overset{\displaystyle O}{\|}}{C}OH \xrightarrow{\text{heat}}$ **h.** $HO\overset{\overset{\displaystyle O}{\|}}{C}CH_2\overset{\overset{\displaystyle OO}{\|\|}}{C}OH \xrightarrow{\text{heat}}$

16.15 Show how you could distinguish between the following pairs of compounds by a simple chemical test. In each case, tell what test you would perform and what you would expect to observe, and write an equation for each positive test.
a. acetic acid and acetaldehyde
b. hexanoic acid and 1-hexanol
c. benzoic acid and phenol
d. sodium salicylate and salicylic acid

e. oleic acid and stearic acid (see Table 20.1 for structural formulas of these fatty acids)

f. phenylacetic acid and acetophenone (methyl phenyl ketone)

16.16 Decarboxylation is a general reaction for any molecule that has a carbonyl group on the carbon atom beta to a carboxylic acid. One such example is malonic acid, which on heating loses carbon dioxide:

$$\underset{\text{malonic acid}}{HOCCH_2COH} \xrightarrow{\text{heat}} \text{a carboxylic acid} + CO_2$$

a. Draw a structural formula for the carboxylic acid formed on decarboxylation of malonic acid.

b. Do you expect that succinic acid would undergo the same type of decarboxylation?

16.17 The following conversions can be carried out in either one step or two. Show the reactants you would use and draw structural formulas for the intermediate formed in any conversion that requires two steps.

a. $CH_3(CH_2)_6CH \longrightarrow CH_3(CH_2)_6COH$ (with carbonyl O above each)

b.  ⬠ $\longrightarrow$ $HOCCH_2CH_2CH_2COH$

1,5-pentanedicarboxylic acid
(glutaric acid)

c. 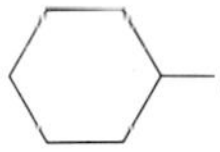 ⬡—OH $\longrightarrow$ $HOCCH_2CH_2CH_2CH_2COH$

1,6-hexanedicarboxylic acid
(adipic acid)

d. $HOCCH_2CH_2COH \longrightarrow Na^+ \ ^-OCCH_2CH_2CO^- \ Na^+$

1,4-butanedioic acid   sodium 1,4-butanedioate
(succinic acid)   (sodium succinate)

e. $HO_2CCH_2CH_2CO_2H \longrightarrow HOCH_2CH_2CH_2CH_2OH$

f.
$$\begin{array}{ccc} CHO & & CO_2H \\ | & & | \\ CHOH & & CHOH \\ | & \longrightarrow & | \\ CHOH & & CHOH \\ | & & | \\ CH_2OH & & CH_2OH \end{array}$$

g. $CH_3(CH_2)_6CH_2OH \longrightarrow CH_3(CH_2)_6CO_2^- \ NH_4^+$

Prostaglandins

The prostaglandins are a group of natural substances, all having the 20-carbon skeleton of prostanoic acid:

prostanoic acid

Prostaglandins and prostaglandin-derived materials have been found in virtually all human tissues examined thus far, and they are intimately involved in a host of bodily processes. For example, they are involved in both the induction of the inflammatory response and in its relief. The medical significance of these facts becomes obvious when we realize that more than 5 million Americans suffer from rheumatoid arthritis, an inflammatory disease. Prostaglandins are also involved in almost every phase of reproductive physiology.

The discovery of prostaglandins and determination of their structure began in 1930, when Raphael Kurzrok and Charles Lieb, gynecologists practicing in New York, observed that human seminal fluid stimulates contraction of isolated human uterine muscle. A few years later in Sweden, Ulf von Euler confirmed this report and noted that human seminal fluid also produces contraction of intestinal smooth muscle and lowers blood pressure when injected into the bloodstream. Von Euler proposed the name prostaglandin for the mysterious substance or substances responsible for such diverse effects, because at the time it was believed that they originated in the prostate gland. We now know

that prostaglandin production is by no means limited to the prostate gland. However, the name has stuck. By 1960, several prostaglandins had been isolated in pure crystalline form and their structural formulas had been determined. Structural formulas for three common prostaglandins are given in Figure XI-1.

Prostaglandins are abbreviated PG, with an additional letter and numerical subscript to indicate the type and series. The various types differ in the functional groups present in the five-membered ring. Those of the A type are alpha,beta-unsaturated ketones; those of the E type are beta-hydroxyketones; and those of the F type are 1,3-diols. The subscript alpha in the F type indicates that the hydroxyl group at carbon 9 is below the plane of the five-membered ring and on the same side as the hydroxyl at carbon 11. The various series of prostaglandins differ in the number of double bonds on the two side chains. Those of the 1 series have only one double bond; those of the 2 series have two double bonds; and those of the 3 series have three double bonds.

Concurrently with investigations of the chemical structure of prostaglandins, clinical scientists began to study the biochemistry of these remarkable compounds and their potential as drugs. Initially, research was hampered by the high cost and great difficulty of isolating and purifying them. If they could not be isolated easily, could they be synthesized instead? The first totally synthetic prostaglandins became available in 1968, when both Dr. John Pike of the Upjohn Company and Professor E. J. Corey of Harvard University announced laboratory syntheses of several prostaglandins and pro-

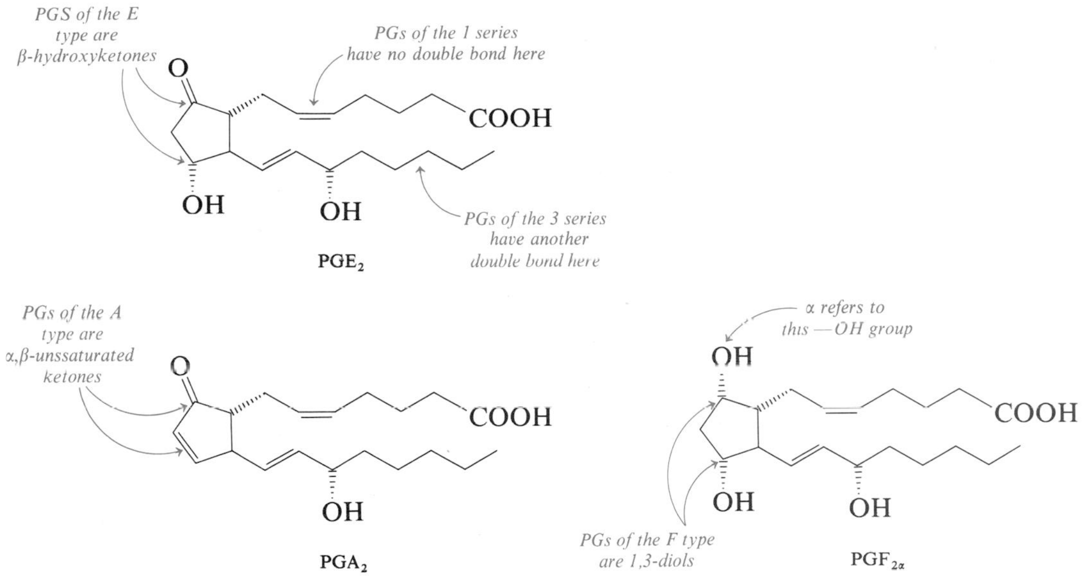

PGS of the E type are β-hydroxyketones

PGs of the 1 series have no double bond here

O

OH   OH

COOH

PGs of the 3 series have another double bond here

PGE₂

PGs of the A type are α,β-unsaturated ketones

O

OH

COOH

PGA₂

PGs of the F type are 1,3-diols

α refers to this —OH group

OH

OH   OH

COOH

PGF₂ₐ

Figure XI-1 Prostaglandins PGA₁, PGE₂, and PGF₂ₐ.

staglandin analogs. However, costs were still high. Then, in 1969, the price of prostaglandins dropped dramatically with the discovery that the gorgonian sea whip or sea fan, *Plexaura homomalla*, a coral that grows on reefs off the coast of Florida and in the Caribbean, is a rich source of prostaglandinlike materials (Figure XI-2). The concentration of PG-like substances in this marine organism is about 100 times the normal concentration found in most mammalian sources. In the laboratory, the PG-like compounds were extracted and then transformed to prostaglandins and prostaglandin analogs. Now, however, there is no need to depend on this natural source, because chemists have developed highly effective and stereospecific laboratory schemes for synthesizing almost any prostaglandin or prostaglandinlike substance.

Prostaglandins are not stored as such in tissues; instead, they are synthesized in response to specific environmental or physiological triggers. Starting materials for prostaglandin synthesis are unsaturated fatty acids of twenty carbon atoms. Those of the 2 series are derived from

Figure XI-2 Found in the Caribbean Sea, *Plexaura homomalla*, known as the sea whip or gorgonian, contains the highest concentration of prostaglandinlike compounds so far found in nature. Before economical laboratory syntheses of prostaglandins became possible, Upjohn extracted the rare substances from this coral.

arachidonic acid (5,8,11,14-eicosatetraenoic acid), an unsaturated fatty acid containing four carbon-carbon double bonds. Steps in the biochemical pathways by which arachidonic acid is converted to several key prostaglandins are summarized in Figure XI-3. Arachidonic acid is drawn in this figure to show the relation between its structural formula and that of the prostaglandins derived from it.

A key step in the biosynthesis of prostaglandins of the 2 series is reaction of arachidonic acid with two molecules of oxygen, O_2, to form PGG_2.

Enzyme-catalyzed reduction of PGG_2 gives PGH_2, a key intermediate from which all other prostaglandins of the 2 series are synthesized. Within minutes, it is converted to other prostaglandin and prostaglandin-derived compounds. Shown in Figure XI-3 is the biosynthesis of types A, E, F, G, and H. There are other types, also derived from the key intermediate PGH_2. One of these is thromboxane A_2. Precisely which prostaglandins are produced depends on the enzymes present in the particular tissue.

Now that we have seen how the body synthesizes prostaglandins, let us look at several functions of these substances in the body. First is participation of prostaglandins in blood clotting. There are three distinct phases to the physiological mechanisms that operate within the body to stop bleeding from a ruptured blood vessel. The first phase, called platelet aggregation, is initiated at the site of the injury by agents such as thrombin. During platelet aggregation, blood platelets become sticky and form a platelet plug at the site of the injury. If damage is minor and the blood vessel is small, this platelet plug may be sufficient to stop loss of blood from the vessel. If it is not sufficient, the platelets are stimulated to release a group of substances (the platelet-release reaction), which in turn promote a second wave of platelet aggregation and constriction of the injured vessel. The third phase is the triggering of the actual blood coagulation.

We have learned within the past few years that among the substances released in platelet release reactions is thromboxane A_2. This pros-

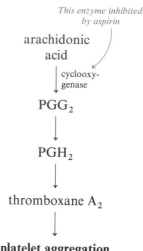

This enzyme inhibited by aspirin

arachidonic acid

↓ cyclooxy-genase

PGG_2

↓

PGH_2

↓

thromboxane A_2

↓

platelet aggregation

taglandin-derived molecule is a very potent vasoconstrictor and the key substance that triggers platelet aggregation. Just as we have known for some time that thrombin stimulates the second, irreversible phase of platelet aggregation, we have also known that aspirin and aspirinlike drugs, such as indomethacin, inhibit this second phase. How these drugs are able to do this remained a mystery until it was discovered that aspirin inhibits cyclooxygenase, the enzyme that initiates the synthesis of thromboxane A_2.

There is now good evidence that the ability of aspirin to reduce inflammation is also related to its ability to inhibit prostaglandin synthesis. Further research on the prostaglandins may help us understand even more about inflammatory diseases such as rheumatoid arthritis, asthma, and other allergic responses.

The first recorded observations on the biological activity of prostaglandins were those of gynecologists Kurzrok and Lieb. The first widespread clinical application of these substances was also by gynecologists and obstetricians. The observation that prostaglandins stimulate contraction of uterine smooth muscle led to the suggestion that these substances could be used for termination of second-trimester pregnancy. One problem with the use of natural prostaglandins for this purpose is that they are very rapidly degraded within the body. Therefore, their use

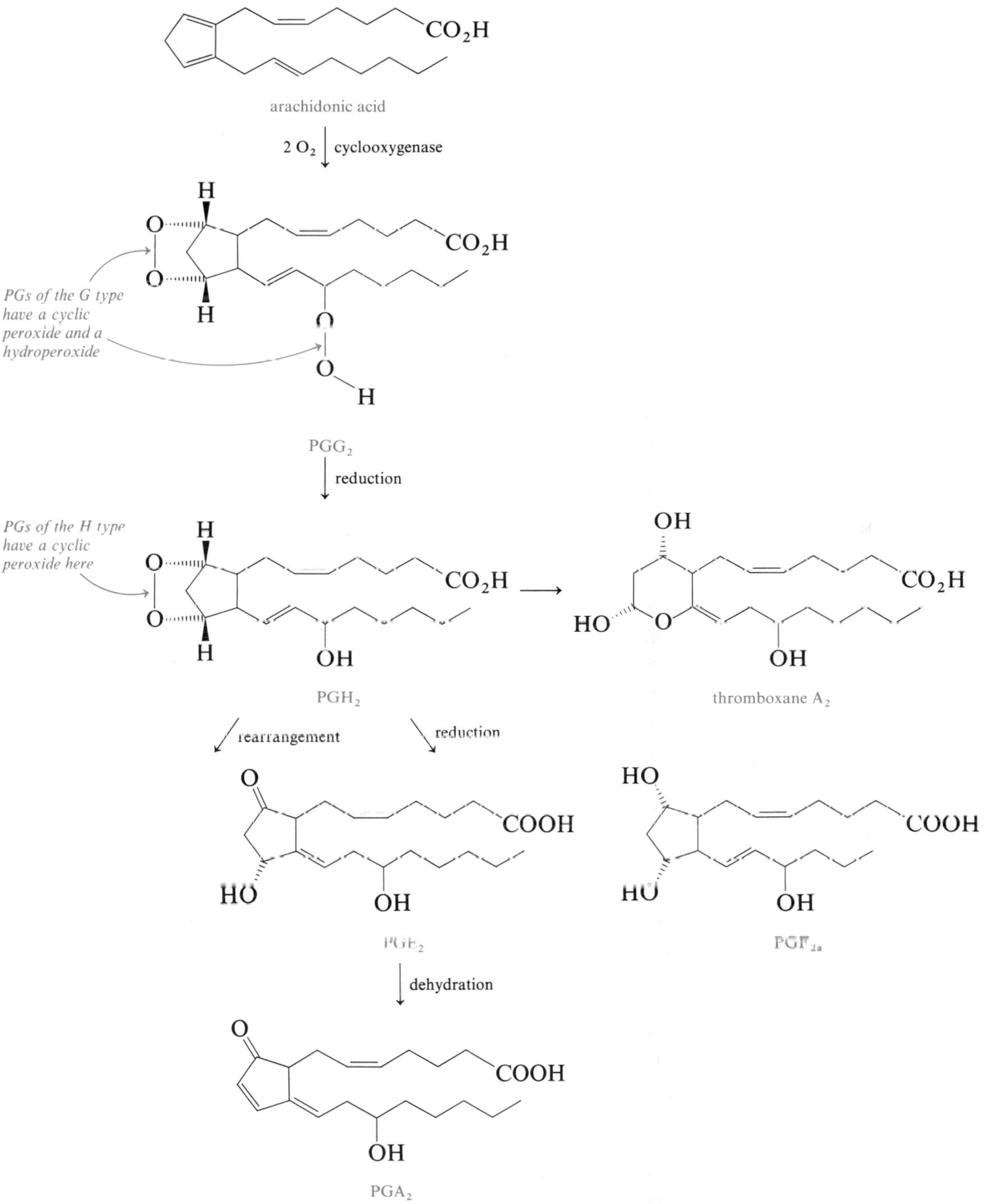

arachidonic acid

$2\ O_2$ | cyclooxygenase

PGs of the G type have a cyclic peroxide and a hydroperoxide

PGG_2

reduction

PGs of the H type have a cyclic peroxide here

PGH_2

thromboxane A_2

rearrangement

reduction

PGE_2

$PGF_{2\alpha}$

dehydration

PGA_2

Figure XI-3 Biosynthesis of several prostaglandins from arachidonic acid.

required repeated administration over a period of hours. In the search for less rapidly degrading prostaglandins, a number of semisynthetic prostaglandin analogs were prepared. One of the most effective was 15-methyl prostaglandin $F_{2\alpha}$, which is longer-acting and has 10 to 20 times the potency of $PGF_{2\alpha}$.

An extra methyl group at carbon 15

15-methyl prostaglandin $F_{2\alpha}$

The potential clinical use of prostaglandins and prostaglandin analogs for termination of second-trimester pregnancy was explored in a study designed and conducted by the World Health Organization Task Force on the Use of Prostaglandins for the Regulation of Fertility. This multicenter, multinational study, entitled "Prostaglandins and Abortion," is described in the *American Journal of Obstetrics and Gynecology* (1977). It concludes that a single intra-amniotic injection of 15-methyl $PGF_{2\alpha}$ is a safe and effective way of terminating second-trimester pregnancy.

We have looked at only a few aspects of the biosynthesis and importance in human physiology of prostaglandins. From even this brief study, it should be clear that we are only beginning to understand the chemistry and biochemistry of this group of compounds. And it should also be clear that the enormous prostaglandin research effort now under way offers great promise for even deeper insights into human physiology and for the development of new and highly effective drugs for clinical use.

Sources

Bergstrom, S. 1967. Prostaglandins: Members of a new hormonal system. *Science* 157:382.

Bergstrom, S., Carlson, L. A., and Weeks, J. R. 1968. The prostaglandins: A family of biologically active lipids. *Pharm. Rev.* 20:1.

Goodman, L. S., and Gilman A. 1980. *The Pharmacological Basis of Therapeutics*. 6th ed. New York: Macmillan.

Kuehl, F. A., and Egan, R. W. 1980. Prostaglandins, arachidonic acid, and inflammation. *Science* 210: 978–984.

Needleman, P., et al. 1976. Prostaglandins and abortion. *Nature* 261:558–560.

Ramwell, P. W., ed. 1973. *The Prostaglandins*. Vol. 1. New York: Plenum Press.

Samuelsson, B., et al. 1975. Prostaglandins. *Ann. Rev. Biochem.* 44:669–695.

World Health Organization. 1977. Prostaglandins and abortion. *Am. J. Gyn.* 129:593–606.

Derivatives of Carboxylic Acids

Anhydrides, **esters**, and **amides** are all functional derivatives of carboxylic acids. A general formula for the characteristic structural feature of each of these derivatives is

$$
\underset{\text{an anhydride}}{R-\overset{\overset{\displaystyle O}{\|}}{C}-O-\overset{\overset{\displaystyle O}{\|}}{C}-R} \qquad
\underset{\text{an ester}}{R-\overset{\overset{\displaystyle O}{\|}}{C}-O-R} \qquad
\underset{\text{an amide}}{R-\overset{\overset{\displaystyle O}{\|}}{C}-NH_2}
$$

In each of these functional groups, the —OH of the carboxyl group has been replaced by another group of atoms. One way to relate the structural formulas of these functional groups to the structural formula of a carboxylic acid is to imagine a reaction in which the —OH from the carboxyl and —H from an acid, an alcohol, or an amine is removed as water and the remaining atoms are joined in the following ways:

Removed as water

$$
\underset{\substack{\text{a carboxylic}\\\text{acid}}}{CH_3-\overset{\overset{\displaystyle O}{\|}}{C}-(OH\ +\ H)}\underset{\substack{\text{a carboxylic}\\\text{acid}}}{-O-\overset{\overset{\displaystyle O}{\|}}{C}-CH_3} \longrightarrow \underset{\text{an anhydride}}{CH_3-\overset{\overset{\displaystyle O}{\|}}{C}-O-\overset{\overset{\displaystyle O}{\|}}{C}-CH_3} + \underset{\text{water}}{H-OH}
$$

Removed as water

$$
\underset{\substack{\text{a carboxylic}\\\text{acid}}}{CH_3-\overset{\overset{\displaystyle O}{\|}}{C}-(OH\ +\ H)}\underset{\text{an alcohol}}{-OCH_3} \longrightarrow \underset{\text{an ester}}{CH_3-\overset{\overset{\displaystyle O}{\|}}{C}-OCH_3} + \underset{\text{water}}{H-OH}
$$

Removed as water

$$
\underset{\substack{\text{a carboxylic}\\\text{acid}}}{CH_3-\overset{\overset{\displaystyle O}{\|}}{C}-(OH\ +\ H)}\underset{\text{ammonia}}{-NH_2} \longrightarrow \underset{\text{an amide}}{CH_3-\overset{\overset{\displaystyle O}{\|}}{C}-NH_2} + \underset{\text{water}}{H-OH}
$$

The equations are shown only to illustrate the relation between a carboxylic acid and the three functional groups we shall study. They are not meant to illustrate methods for the synthesis of these functional groups.

17.1 Nomenclature

A. Anhydrides

The characteristic structural feature of an organic anhydride is the presence of a —CO—O—CO— group. Two examples of symmetrical anhydrides, that is, anhydrides derived from just one carboxylic acid, are

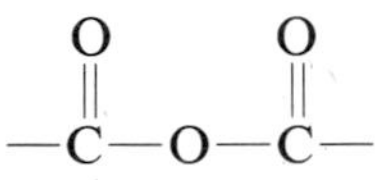

characteristic structural feature 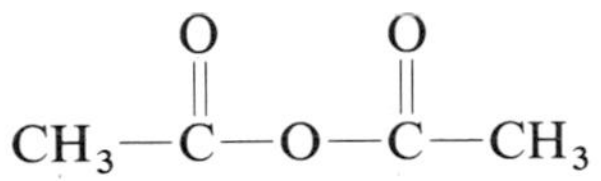   acetic anhydride 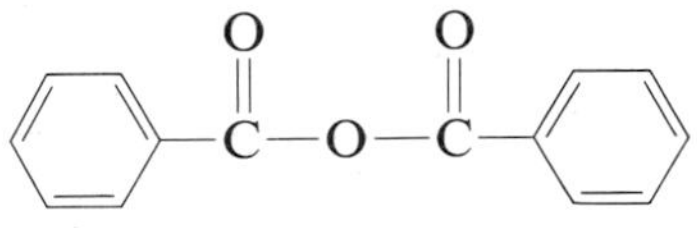   benzoic anhydride

In the IUPAC system, anhydrides are named by adding the word *anhydride* to the name of the parent acid. The anhydride derived from two molecules of acetic acid is named acetic anhydride; that derived from two molecules of benzoic acid is named benzoic anhydride.

Phosphoric acid also forms anhydrides with the following characteristic structural feature:

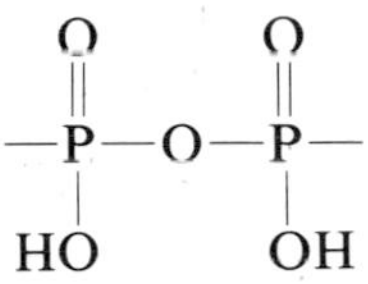

characteristic structural feature of a phosphate anhydride 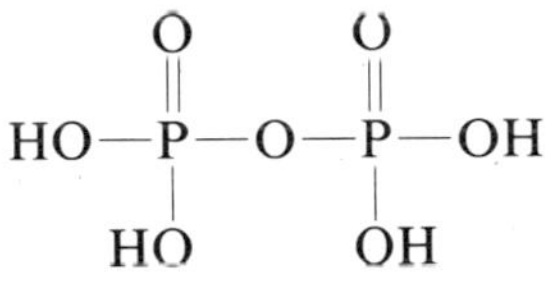   phosphoric anhydride (pyrophosphoric acid) 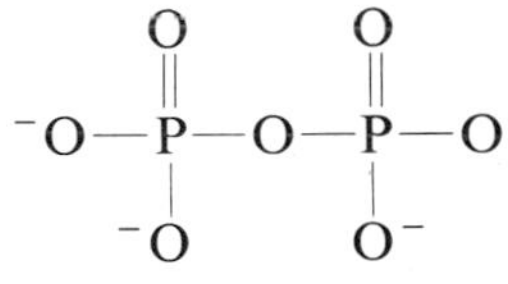   pyrophosphate

The anhydride derived from two molecules of phosphoric acid is named phosphoric anhydride, or more commonly, pyrophosphoric acid. Phosphoric anhydride, like phosphoric acid, is a strong acid. At pH 7, it is completely ionized and has a net charge of -4. The anion is named pyrophosphate. Pyrophosphate and other anhydrides of phosphoric acid are especially important in the biological world.

B. Esters

In the IUPAC system, an ester is named as a derivative of the carboxylic acid from which it is derived. The alkyl or aryl group attached to oxygen is named first. Then the acid is named by dropping the suffix -*ic acid* and adding the

Table 17.1
Example showing the derivation of ester names.

	Alkyl Group Attached to Oxygen	Name of Carboxylic Acid	Name of Ester
$\overset{\text{O}}{\overset{\|}{\text{CH}_3\text{C}}}\text{OCH}_2\text{CH}_3$	ethyl	acetic acid	ethyl acetate
$\text{C}_6\text{H}_5\text{—}\overset{\text{O}}{\overset{\|}{\text{C}}}\text{OCHCH}_3 \; (\text{CH}_3)$	isopropyl	benzoic acid	isopropyl benzoate
$\overset{\text{O}}{\overset{\|}{\text{CH}_2\text{C}}}\text{OCH}_2\text{CH}_3$ $\overset{}{\underset{\text{O}}{\overset{\|}{\text{CH}_2\text{C}}}}\text{OCH}_2\text{CH}_3$	diethyl	butanedioic acid (succinic acid)	diethyl butanedioate (diethyl succinate)

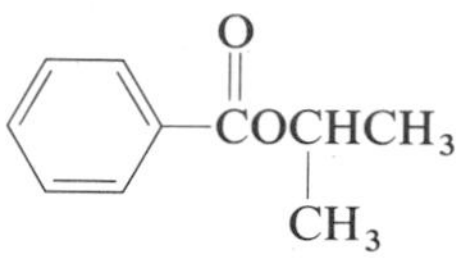

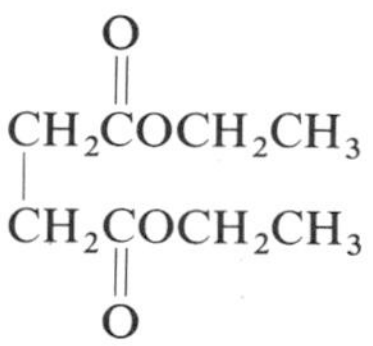

suffix -*ate*. In Table 17.1, names of esters are derived in a stepwise manner. First is given the name of the alkyl or aryl group attached to oxygen, then the IUPAC and common names of the acid from which the ester is derived, and finally the name of the ester.

Example 17.1

Name the following esters.

a. 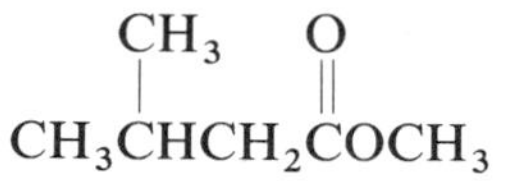 $\text{CH}_3\overset{\text{CH}_3}{\underset{\|}{\text{CH}}}\text{CH}_2\overset{\text{O}}{\overset{\|}{\text{C}}}\text{OCH}_3$ b. $\text{H}\overset{\text{O}}{\overset{\|}{\text{C}}}\text{OCHCH}_2\text{CH}_3 \;(\text{CH}_3)$

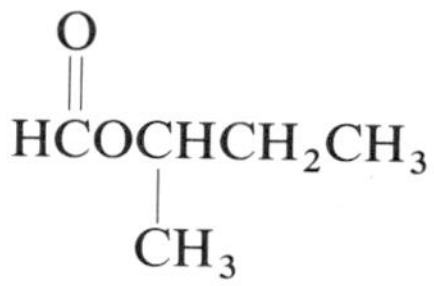

c. $\text{CH}_3\overset{\text{O}}{\overset{\|}{\text{C}}}\text{CH}_2\overset{\text{O}}{\overset{\|}{\text{C}}}\text{OCH}_2\text{CH}_3$

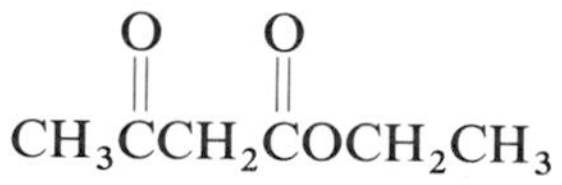

Solution

Each name is derived in a stepwise manner. First the name of the alkyl group attached to oxygen, then the IUPAC name (and where appropriate, common name as well) of the acid, and finally the name of the ester.

Alkyl Group Attached to Oxygen	Name of Carboxylic Acid	Name of Ester
a. methyl	3-methylbutanoic acid (isovaleric acid)	methyl 3-methylbutanoate (methyl isovalerate)
b. *sec*-butyl	formic acid	*sec*-butyl formate
c. ethyl	3-oxobutanoic acid (β-ketobutyric acid; acetoacetic acid)	ethyl 3-oxobutanoate (ethyl β-ketobutyrate; ethyl acetoacetate)

Problem 17.1

Name the following esters.

a. 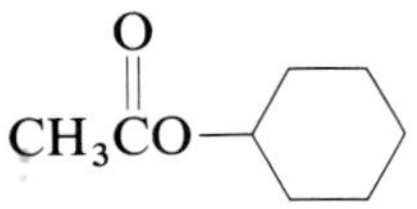 CH$_3$CO—⬡   (cyclohexyl)

b. 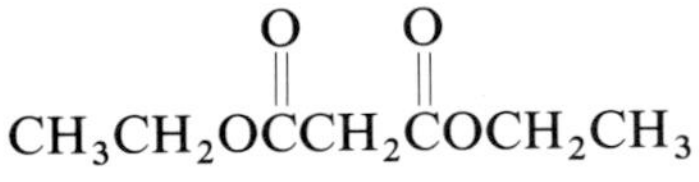 CH$_3$CH$_2$OCCH$_2$COCH$_2$CH$_3$

c. 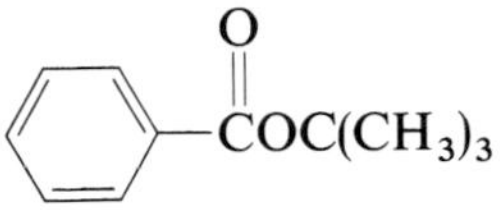 ⬡—COC(CH$_3$)$_3$

Esters of phosphoric acid are especially important in the biological world. Phosphoric acid has three —OH groups and can form mono-, di-, and triesters. These are named by giving the name or names of the groups attached to oxygen followed by the word *phosphate*. Examples are:

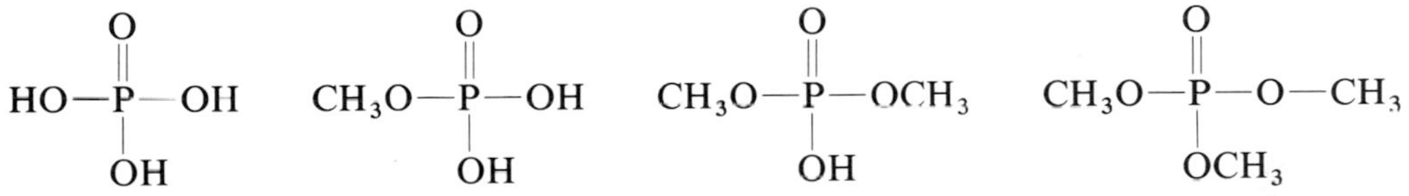

$$HO-\overset{O}{\underset{OH}{P}}-OH \qquad CH_3O-\overset{O}{\underset{OH}{P}}-OH \qquad CH_3O-\overset{O}{\underset{OH}{P}}-OCH_3 \qquad CH_3O-\overset{O}{\underset{OCH_3}{P}}-O-CH_3$$

phosphoric acid   methyl phosphate (a monoester)   dimethyl phosphate (a diester)   trimethyl phosphate (a triester)

In more complex phosphate esters, it is often easier to name the organic molecule itself and indicate the presence of a phosphate ester by adding the word *phosphate* as shown in the following examples. Glyceraldehyde 3-phosphate is an intermediate in glycolysis. Pyridoxal, more commonly called vitamin B$_6$, is metabolically active only after it is converted to its phosphate ester, pyridoxal phosphate.

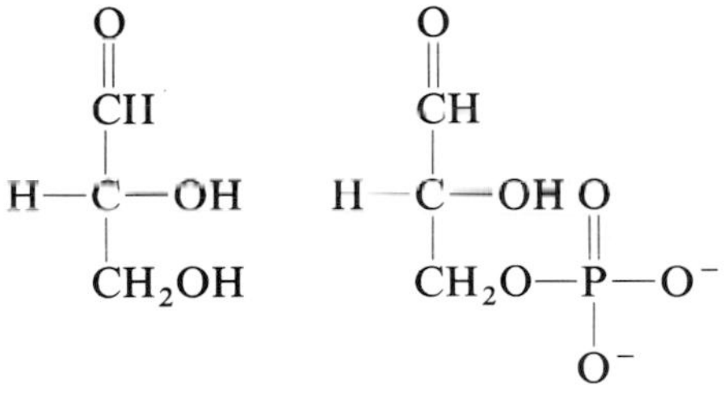

glyceraldehyde

glyceraldehyde 3-phosphate

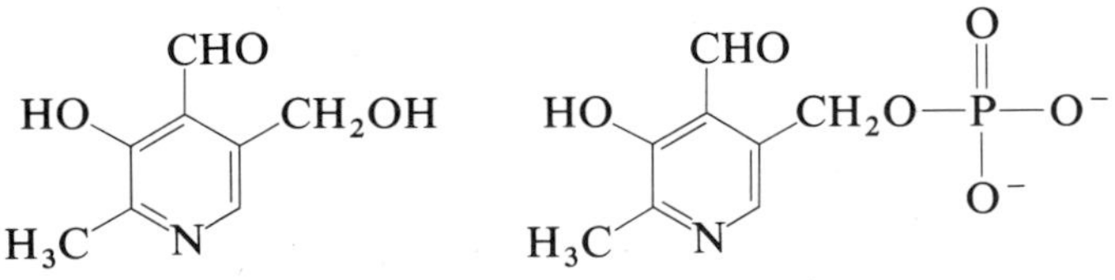

pyridoxal (vitamin B$_6$)

pyridoxal phosphate

In drawing structural formulas for phosphate anhydrides and esters found in biological systems, we will show the state of ionization at pH 7.4, the pH of normal blood plasma. At this pH, the two remaining hydrogen atoms of each phosphate group in the above esters are completely ionized, each having, therefore, a net charge of -2.

C. Amides

Amides are named as derivatives of their specific carboxylic acid by dropping the suffix *-oic acid* from the IUPAC name or *-ic acid* from the common name and adding *-amide*. In the examples, the IUPAC name is given first, and then in parentheses where appropriate, the common name.

$$CH_3-\overset{\overset{\displaystyle O}{\|}}{C}-NH_2 \qquad CH_3-\underset{\underset{\displaystyle CH_3}{|}}{CH}-\overset{\overset{\displaystyle O}{\|}}{C}-NH_2 \qquad \underset{}{\bigcirc}-\overset{\overset{\displaystyle O}{\|}}{C}-NH_2$$

acetamide   2-methylpropanamide   benzamide

(isobutyramide)

If a hydrogen atom of an amide is replaced by an alkyl or an aryl group, the substituent is named and its location on nitrogen is indicated by *N-*. Two substituents on an amide nitrogen are named and indicated by *N,N-*:

$$H-\overset{\overset{\displaystyle O}{\|}}{C}-\underset{\underset{\displaystyle CH_3}{|}}{N}-CH_3 \qquad CH_3CH_2CH_2\overset{\overset{\displaystyle O}{\|}}{C}-NH-\bigcirc$$

N,N-dimethylformamide   *N*-phenylbutanamide

Example 17.2

Name these amides:

a. $CH_3\overset{\overset{\displaystyle O}{\|}}{C}NHCH_3$ b. $CH_3\underset{\underset{\displaystyle }{}}{\overset{\overset{\displaystyle CH_3}{|}}{CH}}CH_2\overset{\overset{\displaystyle O}{\|}}{C}NH_2$

c. $H_2N\overset{\overset{\displaystyle O}{\|}}{C}CH_2CH_2CH_2CH_2\overset{\overset{\displaystyle O}{\|}}{C}NH_2$

Solution

Each is named below in a stepwise manner, just as we did for esters in Example 17.1.

Group Attached to Nitrogen	Name of the Carboxylic Acid	Name of the Amide
a. *N*-methyl	acetic acid	*N*-methylacetamide
b. _____	3-methylbutanoic acid (isovaleric acid)	3-methylbutanamide (isovaleramide)
c. _____	hexanedioic acid (adipic acid)	hexanediamide (adipamide)

Problem 17.2

Name the following amides:

a. $CH_3\overset{\displaystyle O}{\overset{\displaystyle \|}{C}}NH$—⬡

b. $CH_3(CH_2)_6\overset{\displaystyle O}{\overset{\displaystyle \|}{C}}NH_2$

c. (structure: benzene ring with $\overset{\displaystyle O}{\overset{\displaystyle \|}{C}}NH_2$ and OH substituents)

17.2 Esters of Nitrous and Nitric Acids

Several esters of nitric acid and nitrous acid have been used as drugs for more than a hundred years. Esters of nitric acid are named nitrates. Glyceryl nitrate, usually known as nitroglycerine, is a triester of glycerol.

HO—NO$_2$

$$CH_2—OH$$
$$CH—OH$$
$$CH_2—OH$$

$$CH_2—O—NO_2$$
$$CH—O—NO_2$$
$$CH_2—O—NO_2$$

nitric acid   1,2,3-propanetriol   glyceryl nitrate
                     (glycerol or glycerine)   (nitroglycerine)

Esters of nitrous acid are named nitrites. The structural formula of 3-methylbutyl nitrite, more often known as isopentyl nitrite or isoamyl nitrite, is

HO—NO

$$\overset{\displaystyle CH_3}{CH_3CHCH_2CH_2—OH}$$

$$\overset{\displaystyle CH_3}{CH_3CHCH_2CH_2—O—NO}$$

nitrous acid   3-methyl-1-butanol   3-methyl-1-butyl nitrite
                (isopentyl alcohol; isoamyl alcohol)   (isopentyl nitrite; isoamyl nitrite)

The most important medical use of nitroglycerine and isoamyl nitrite is relaxation of the smooth muscle of blood vessels and dilation of all large and small arteries of the heart. Both esters are used in treating angina pectoris, a heart disease characterized by spasms of the coronary artery and agonizing chest pains.

17.3 Physical Properties of Esters and Amides

Esters are polar compounds and are attracted to each other in the pure state by a combination of dipole-dipole interactions between polar —COO— groups and dispersion forces between nonpolar hydrocarbon chains. Most esters are insoluble in water because of the more dominant, hydrophobic character of the hydrocarbon portions of the molecule. Esters are soluble in polar organic solvents such as diethyl ether and acetone.

The low-molecular-weight esters have pleasant odors. The characteristic fragrances of many flowers and fruits is due to the presence of esters, either singly or more often, in mixtures. Fragrances associated with several esters are:

Ester	Fragrance
ethyl formate	artificial rum flavor
methyl butanoate	apples
ethyl butanoate	pineapples
octyl acetate	oranges

Amides are also polar molecules, and because of the polar character of the C=O and N—H bonds, hydrogen bonding is possible between a partially positive hydrogen of one amide group and a partially negative oxygen of another.

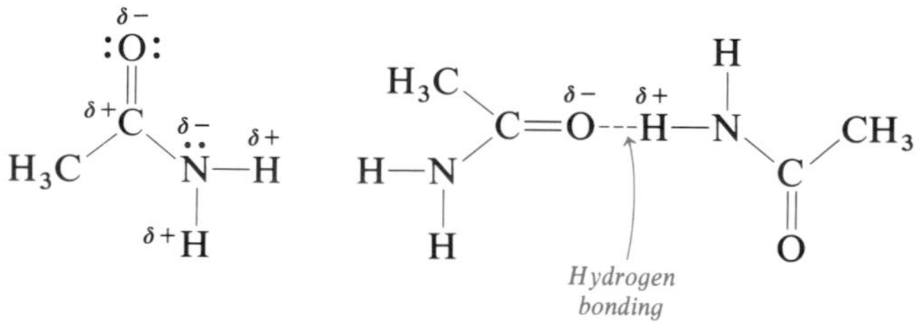

Hydrogen bonding

Because of this polarity and association by hydrogen bonding, amides have higher boiling points and are more soluble in water compared with esters of similar molecular weight. Virtually all amides are solids at room temperature.

17.4 Reactions of Anhydrides, Esters, and Amides

The basic reaction theme common to the carbonyl group of aldehydes, ketones, carboxylic acids, anhydrides, esters, and amides is nucleophilic addition to the carbonyl group. In aldehydes and ketones, the carbonyl addition product is often isolated as such. For example, in aldol condensations (Section 15.8), the carbonyl group undergoing reaction is transformed to an alcohol, and this nucleophilic addition product is the final product of the reaction:

$$CH_3\overset{\overset{O}{\|}}{C}H + CH_3\overset{\overset{O}{\|}}{C}H \xrightarrow[\substack{\text{aldol} \\ \text{condensation}}]{\text{NaOH}} CH_3\overset{\overset{OH}{|}}{C}HCH_2\overset{\overset{O}{\|}}{C}H$$

3-hydroxybutanal
(aldol)

In other reactions of aldehydes and ketones, a carbonyl addition product is formed but then undergoes loss of H_2O, to yield a new functional group. For example, reaction of an aldehyde or a ketone with a primary amine forms a carbonyl addition product that then loses a molecule of water, forming an imine (a Schiff base); in this reaction, a C=O group is transformed to a C=N— group (Section 15.4C).

$$CH_3CH + H_2N-\bigcirc \longrightarrow \left[CH_3C-N-\bigcirc \right] \longrightarrow CH_3C=N-\bigcirc + H_2O$$

a tetrahedral carbonyl   an imine
addition intermediate   (a Schiff base)

With the new functional groups to be studied in this chapter, the carbonyl addition product collapses to regenerate the carbonyl group.

$$R-C-X + H-Nu: \longrightarrow \left[R-C-Nu \right] \longrightarrow R-C \quad Nu + H-X$$

tetrahedral carbonyl
addition intermediate

The effect of this reaction is for a new atom or group of atoms to be substituted for one already attached to the carbonyl group. That is why we characterize these reactions as **nucleophilic substitution at a carbonyl carbon**.

17.5 Preparation of Esters: Fischer Esterification

A carboxylic acid can be converted to an ester by being heated with an alcohol in the presence of an acid catalyst, usually concentrated sulfuric acid, dry hydrogen chloride, or an ion-exchange resin in the acid form. Conversion of a carboxylic acid and an alcohol to an ester in the presence of an acid catalyst is called **Fischer esterification**. As an example, reaction of acetic acid and ethanol in the presence of concentrated sulfuric acid gives ethyl acetate and water:

$$CH_3COH + HOCH_2CH_3 \underset{}{\overset{H^+}{\rightleftharpoons}} CH_3COCH_2CH_3 + HOH$$

acetic acid   ethanol   ethyl acetate

Acid-catalyzed esterification is reversible, and generally at equilibrium the quantities of both ester and alcohol are appreciable. If 60.1 g (1.0 mol) of acetic acid and 60.1 g (1.0 mol) of 1-propanol are heated under reflux in the presence of a few drops of concentrated sulfuric acid until equilibrium is reached, the reaction mixture will contain about 0.67 mol each of propyl acetate and water, and about

0.33 mol each of acetic acid and 1-propanol. At equilibrium, about 67% of the acid and alcohol has converted to the desired ester.

$$CH_3\overset{O}{\overset{\|}{C}}OH + HOCH_2CH_2CH_3 \underset{}{\overset{H^+}{\rightleftharpoons}} CH_3\overset{O}{\overset{\|}{C}}OCH_2CH_2CH_3 + H_2O$$

	acetic acid	1-propanol	propyl acetate	water
initial:	1.00 mol	1.00 mol	0.00 mol	0.00 mol
equilibrium:	0.33 mol	0.33 mol	0.67 mol	0.67 mol

By careful control of reaction conditions, direct esterification can be used to prepare esters in high yields. For example, if the alcohol is inexpensive compared with the acid, a large excess of it can be used to drive the reaction to the right and achieve a high conversion of carboxylic acid to its ester. Or it may be possible to take advantage of a situation in which the boiling points of the reactants and ester are higher than the boiling point of water. In this case, heating the reaction mixture somewhat above 100°C removes water as it is formed and shifts the position of equilibrium toward the production of a higher yield of ester.

Fischer esterification is but one of the general methods for preparing esters. Another is reaction of an alcohol or phenol with an anhydride (Section 17.7).

Example 17.3

Name and draw structural formulas for the esters produced in these reactions:

a.

$$+ CH_3OH \overset{H^+}{\rightleftharpoons}$$

b. $$HO\overset{O}{\overset{\|}{C}}CH_2\overset{O}{\overset{\|}{C}}OH + 2CH_3CH_2OH \overset{H^+}{\rightleftharpoons}$$

Solution

a.

$$+ CH_3OH \overset{H^+}{\rightleftharpoons}$$

$$+ H_2O$$

2-hydroxybenzoic acid   methanol   methyl 2-hydroxybenzoate
(salicylic acid)   (methyl salicylate; oil of wintergreen)

b. $$HO\overset{O}{\overset{\|}{C}}CH_2\overset{O}{\overset{\|}{C}}OH + 2CH_3CH_2OH \overset{H^+}{\rightleftharpoons} CH_3CH_2O\overset{O}{\overset{\|}{C}}CH_2\overset{O}{\overset{\|}{C}}OCH_2CH_3 + H_2O$$

propanedioic acid   ethanol   diethyl propanedioate
(malonic acid)   (diethyl malonate)

Problem 17.3

Name and draw structural formulas for the esters formed in these reactions:

a.

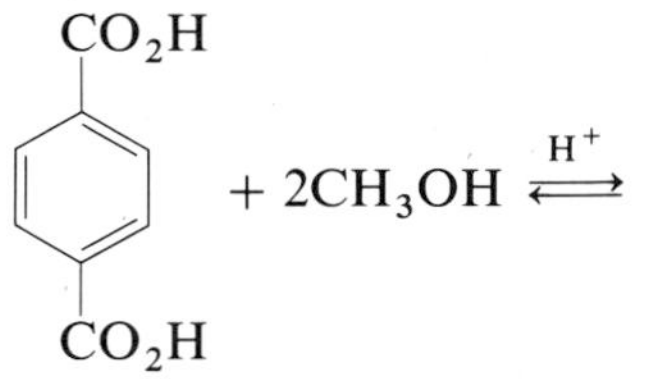

$$CO_2H$$ (on benzene ring, para) $+ 2CH_3OH \overset{H^+}{\rightleftharpoons}$

with CO_2H groups at para positions

b. $CH_3CO_2H + CH_3CH_2CH_2CH_2CH_2OH \overset{H^+}{\rightleftharpoons}$

Following is a mechanism for acid catalyzed esterification. Protonation of the carbonyl oxygen in step 1 gives a carbocation with a positive charge on the carbonyl carbon. Reaction of this ion in step 2 with a pair of electrons on the oxygen atom of the alcohol gives an oxonium ion, which loses H^+ in step 3, to give a tetrahedral carbonyl addition intermediate. Reaction of an —OH of this intermediate with H^+ in step 4, followed by loss of a molecule of water in step 5, gives a new carbocation, which then loses H^+ in step 6, to give the ester.

Step 1: Reaction of the carbonyl oxygen with H^+ to give a carbocation

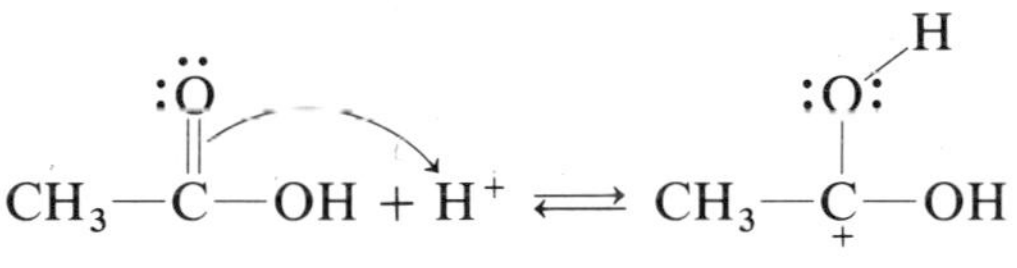

$$CH_3-\overset{\overset{\ddot{O}}{\|}}{C}-OH + H^+ \rightleftharpoons CH_3-\overset{\overset{:\ddot{O}-H}{|}}{\underset{+}{C}}-OH$$

a carbocation

Step 2: Reaction of an unshared pair of electrons from oxygen to form an oxonium ion

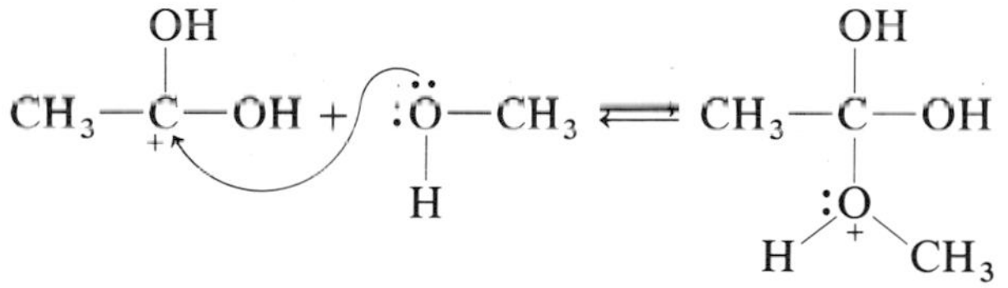

$$CH_3-\overset{\overset{OH}{|}}{\underset{+}{C}}-OH + :\ddot{O}-CH_3 \rightleftharpoons CH_3-\overset{\overset{OH}{|}}{\underset{\overset{:O}{H \overset{+}{\diagdown} CH_3}}{C}}-OH$$
$$\qquad\qquad\qquad\quad H$$

an oxonium ion

Step 3: Loss of H^+ to form a tetrahedral carbonyl addition intermediate

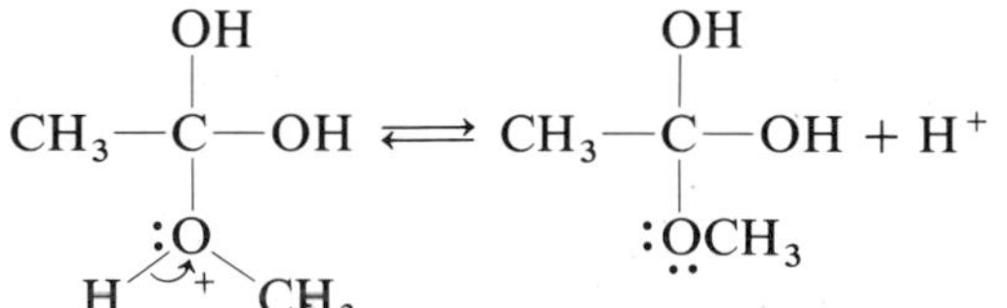

$$CH_3-\overset{\overset{OH}{|}}{\underset{\overset{:O}{H\overset{+}{\diagdown}CH_3}}{C}}-OH \rightleftharpoons CH_3-\overset{\overset{OH}{|}}{\underset{:\ddot{O}CH_3}{C}}-OH + H^+$$

tetrahedral carbonyl addition intermediate

Step 4: Reaction of an —OH of the tetrahedral carbonyl addition intermediate with H^+ to give a new oxonium ion

$$CH_3-\overset{\overset{\displaystyle OH}{|}}{\underset{\underset{\displaystyle OCH_3}{|}}{C}}-\ddot{O}H + H^+ \; \rightleftharpoons \; CH_3-\overset{\overset{\displaystyle OH}{|}}{\underset{\underset{\displaystyle OCH_3}{|}}{C}}-\overset{+}{\ddot{O}}\overset{\displaystyle H}{\underset{\displaystyle H}{<}}$$

a new oxonium ion

Step 5: Loss of H_2O from this oxonium ion to form a carbocation

$$CH_3-\overset{\overset{\displaystyle OH}{|}}{\underset{\underset{\displaystyle OCH_3}{|}}{C}}-\overset{+}{\ddot{O}}\overset{\displaystyle H}{\underset{\displaystyle CH_3}{<}} \; \rightleftharpoons \; CH_3-\overset{\overset{\displaystyle OH}{|}}{\underset{\underset{\displaystyle OCH_3}{|}}{\overset{+}{C}}} \; + \; H_2\ddot{O}:$$

a carbocation

Step 6: Loss of H^+ from the carbocation to give the ester

$$CH_3-\underset{\underset{\displaystyle OCH_3}{|}}{\overset{+}{C}} \;\; :\overset{\displaystyle H}{\underset{}{\ddot{O}}} \;\; \rightleftharpoons \;\; CH_3-\underset{\underset{\displaystyle OCH_3}{|}}{\overset{\overset{\displaystyle :\ddot{O}}{\|}}{C}} \;\; + \; H^+$$

an ester

This mechanism is a specific example of the more general mechanism we proposed in Section 17.4 for nucleophilic substitution at a carbonyl carbon. A key step in Fischer esterification is formation of a tetrahedral carbonyl addition intermediate:

$$CH_3-\overset{\overset{\displaystyle O}{\|}}{C}-OH + \overset{\overset{\displaystyle H}{|}}{O}-CH_3 \; \rightleftharpoons \; \left[CH_3-\underset{\underset{\displaystyle OCH_3}{|}}{\overset{\overset{\displaystyle O^{\diagup H}}{|}}{C}}-OH \right] \; \rightleftharpoons \; CH_3-\overset{\overset{\displaystyle O}{\|}}{C}-OCH_3 + H_2O$$

tetrahedral carbonyl
addition intermediate

The six-step mechanism we have proposed for Fischer esterification predicts that the oxygen atom of the alcohol is incorporated into the ester and that the oxygen atom appearing in the water molecule is derived from one of the two oxygen atoms of the carboxyl group. This prediction has been tested in the following way. Oxygen in nature is a mixture of three isotopes.

Isotope	Natural Abundance
oxygen-16	99.76%
oxygen-17	0.037%
oxygen-18	0.204%

Through the use of modern techniques for separating isotopes, it is possible to prepare compounds significantly enriched in oxygen-18. Such compounds are said to be isotopically enriched, or isotopically labeled. One easily prepared compound now commercially available is isotopically labeled methanol. When methanol enriched with oxygen-18 is caused to react with benzoic acid containing only naturally occurring amounts of oxygen-18, all the isotope enrichment (the isotope label) is found in the ester.

$$
\text{C}_6\text{H}_5-\overset{\overset{\text{O}}{\|}}{\text{C}}-\text{OH} + \text{H}-\overset{18}{\text{O}}\text{CH}_3 \rightleftharpoons \text{C}_6\text{H}_5-\overset{\overset{\text{O}}{\|}}{\text{C}}-\overset{18}{\text{O}}\text{CH}_3 + \text{H}_2\text{O}
$$

labeled methanol   labeled ester

Example 17.4

Draw structural formulas for the tetrahedral carbonyl addition intermediates formed in these acid-catalyzed esterifications:

a. $\text{CH}_3\text{CH}_2\overset{\overset{\text{O}}{\|}}{\text{C}}\text{OH} + \text{HOCH}_2\text{CH}_3 \overset{\text{H}^+}{\longrightarrow} \text{CH}_3\text{CH}_2\overset{\overset{\text{O}}{\|}}{\text{C}}\text{OCH}_2\text{CH}_3 + \text{H}_2\text{O}$

b. $\text{C}_6\text{H}_5-\overset{\overset{\text{O}}{\|}}{\text{C}}\text{OH} + \text{H}-\overset{18}{\text{O}}\text{CH}_3 \overset{\text{H}^+}{\longrightarrow} \text{C}_6\text{H}_5-\overset{\overset{\text{O}}{\|}}{\text{C}}-\overset{18}{\text{O}}\text{CH}_3 + \text{H}_2\text{O}$

Solution

a. $\text{CH}_3\text{CH}_2\overset{\overset{\text{O}}{\|}}{\text{C}}\text{OH} + \text{HOCH}_2\text{CH}_3 \overset{\text{H}^+}{\longrightarrow} \left[\text{CH}_3\text{CH}_2\overset{\overset{\text{OH}}{|}}{\underset{\underset{\text{OH}}{|}}{\text{C}}}-\text{OCH}_2\text{CH}_3 \right]$

b. $\text{C}_6\text{H}_5-\overset{\overset{\text{O}}{\|}}{\text{C}}\text{OH} + \text{H}-\overset{18}{\text{O}}\text{CH}_3 \overset{\text{H}^+}{\longrightarrow} \left[\text{C}_6\text{H}_5-\overset{\overset{\text{OH}}{|}}{\underset{\underset{\text{OH}}{|}}{\text{C}}}-\overset{18}{\text{O}}\text{CH}_3 \right]$

Problem 17.4

Draw structural formulas for the tetrahedral carbonyl addition intermediates formed in the following acid-catalyzed esterifications:

a. $\text{H}\overset{\overset{\text{O}}{\|}}{\text{C}}\text{OH} + \text{HO}\underset{\underset{\text{CH}_3}{|}}{\text{CHCH}_3} \overset{\text{H}^+}{\longrightarrow} \text{H}\overset{\overset{\text{O}}{\|}}{\text{C}}\text{O}\underset{\underset{\text{CH}_3}{|}}{\text{CHCH}_3} + \text{H}_2\text{O}$

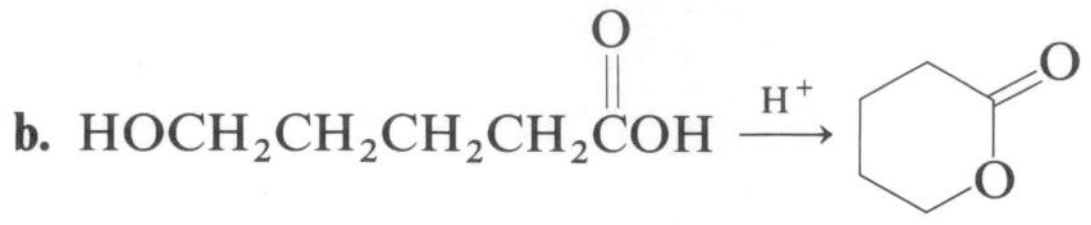

b. $HOCH_2CH_2CH_2CH_2\overset{\displaystyle O}{\overset{\|}{C}}OH \xrightarrow{H^+}$

17.6 Reactions of Esters

Of the three classes of carboxylic acid derivatives so far discussed, esters are intermediate in reactivity. Under most conditions, they are less reactive than anhydrides, but more reactive than amides.

A. Reduction

Esters are reduced by hydrogen in the presence of a heavy metal catalyst to two alcohols, one derived from the carboxyl portion of the ester, the other from the alkyl or aryl group. Such reductions often require high pressures of hydrogen gas and high temperatures. Esters are also reduced smoothly and easily by lithium aluminum hydride at room temperature:

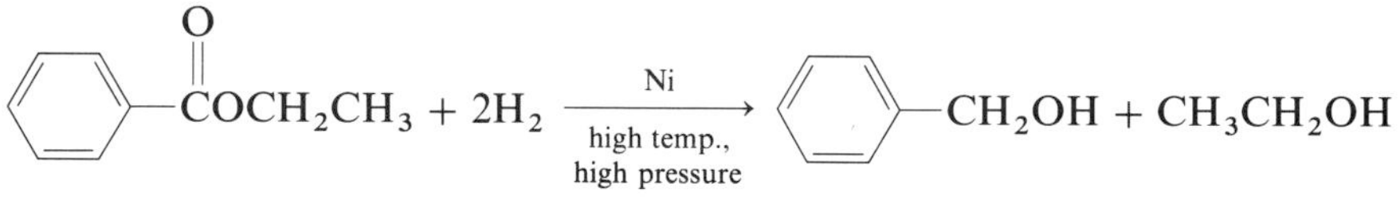

ethyl benzoate   benzyl alcohol   ethanol

$$CH_3O\overset{\displaystyle O}{\overset{\|}{C}}(CH_2)_4\overset{\displaystyle O}{\overset{\|}{C}}OCH_3 \xrightarrow[\text{(2) } H_2O]{\text{(1) LiAlH}_4} HOCH_2(CH_2)_4CH_2OH + 2CH_3OH$$

dimethyl hexanedioate   1,6-hexanediol   methanol
(dimethyl adipate)

B. Hydrolysis

Esters are normally unreactive with water. However, in the presence of either aqueous acid (most commonly HCl or H_2SO_4) or aqueous base (most commonly NaOH or KOH), they are split into a carboxylic acid and an alcohol.

1. Hydrolysis in Aqueous Acid

Following is an equation for acid-catalyzed hydrolysis of ethyl acetate to give acetic acid and ethanol:

$$CH_3\overset{\displaystyle O}{\overset{\|}{C}}OCH_2CH_3 + H_2O \underset{}{\overset{H^+}{\rightleftharpoons}} CH_3\overset{\displaystyle O}{\overset{\|}{C}}OH + CH_3CH_2OH$$

Because the mechanism we proposed in Section 17.5 for acid-catalyzed esterification is reversible, formation of the same tetrahedral carbonyl addition intermediate accounts equally well for acid-catalyzed hydrolysis.

$$CH_3\overset{O}{\overset{\|}{C}}{-}OCH_2CH_3 + H{-}OH \rightleftharpoons \left[CH_3\overset{OH}{\underset{OH}{\overset{|}{\underset{|}{C}}}}{-}OCH_2CH_3 \right] \rightleftharpoons CH_3\overset{O}{\overset{\|}{C}}OH + CH_3CH_2OH$$

$$\xrightarrow{\hspace{2cm}\text{hydrolysis}\hspace{2cm}}$$
$$\xleftarrow{\hspace{2cm}\text{esterification}\hspace{2cm}}$$

If acid-catalyzed hydrolysis is carried out in a large excess of water, the position of equilibrium is shifted in favor of formation of a carboxylic acid and an alcohol.

2. Hydrolysis in Aqueous Base

Esters are hydrolyzed in aqueous base to a carboxylate anion and an alcohol. Alkaline hydrolysis of esters is often referred to as **saponification**, a name derived from the Latin root *sapon-*, soap (Section 20.2). For saponification, one mole of base is required for each mole of ester, as illustrated in the equation,

$$CH_3\overset{O}{\overset{\|}{C}}OCH_2CH_3 + NaOH \xrightarrow[\text{(saponification)}]{H_2O} CH_3\overset{O}{\overset{\|}{C}}O^-Na^+ + CH_3CH_2OH$$

For all practical purposes, hydrolysis of an ester in aqueous base is irreversible, because the carboxylate anion, once formed, has no tendency to react with an alcohol.

Example 17.5

Complete and balance the following equations. Be certain to show each product as it would be ionized under the conditions specified in the problem.

a. $CH_3\overset{O}{\overset{\|}{C}}O$—⬡ $\xrightarrow{\begin{array}{c}\text{hydrolysis in}\\\text{aqueous acid}\end{array}}$

b. $CH_3\overset{O}{\overset{\|}{C}}OCH_2CH_2O\overset{O}{\overset{\|}{C}}CH_3$ $\xrightarrow[\text{(saponification)}]{\begin{array}{c}\text{hydrolysis in}\\\text{aqueous NaOH}\end{array}}$

☐ *Solution*

a. The products of hydrolysis of an ester in aqueous acid are a carboxylic acid and an alcohol, in this case acetic acid and cyclohexanol:

$$CH_3\overset{O}{\overset{\|}{C}}O\text{—}⬡ + H_2O \xrightarrow{H^+} CH_3\overset{O}{\overset{\|}{C}}OH + HO\text{—}⬡$$

cyclohexyl acetate　　　　　　　acetic acid　　cyclohexanol

b. This compound is a diester. Hydrolysis in aqueous NaOH requires two moles of NaOH per mole of ester and gives two moles of sodium acetate and one mole of ethylene glycol:

$$CH_3\overset{O}{\overset{\|}{C}}OCH_2CH_2O\overset{O}{\overset{\|}{C}}CH_3 + 2NaOH \longrightarrow 2CH_3\overset{O}{\overset{\|}{C}}O^-Na^+ + HOCH_2CH_2OH$$

sodium acetate   1,2-ethanediol
(ethylene glycol)

Problem 17.5

Complete and balance the following equations. Be certain to show each product as it would be ionized under the conditions specified in the problem.

a.

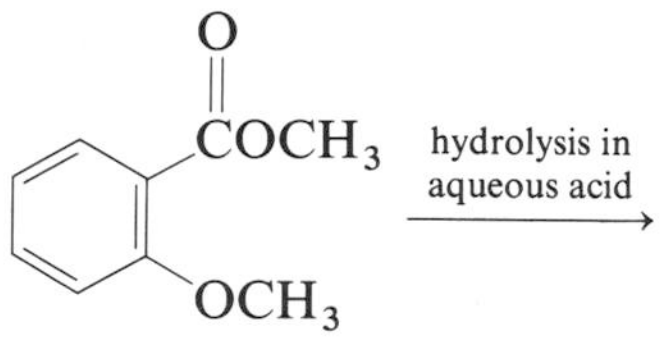

$$\xrightarrow{\text{hydrolysis in aqueous acid}}$$

b. $CH_3\overset{O}{\overset{\|}{C}}CH_2CH_2CH_2\overset{O}{\overset{\|}{C}}OCH_2CH_3 \xrightarrow[\text{(saponification)}]{\text{hydrolysis in aqueous NaOH}}$

C. Reaction with Ammonia and Amines: Formation of Amides

Reaction with ammonia converts an ester to an amide. This reaction is similar to hydrolysis (splitting apart by water). Because the "splitting" agent in this case is ammonia, the reaction is called **ammonolysis**. Ammonia is a strong nucleophile and adds directly to the carbonyl carbon to form a tetrahedral carbonyl addition intermediate, which in turn collapses to lose a molecule of alcohol and form an amide:

$$CH_3\overset{O}{\overset{\|}{C}}OCH_2CH_3 + NH_3 \longrightarrow \left[CH_3\overset{OH}{\underset{NH_2}{\overset{|}{\underset{|}{C}}}}-OCH_2CH_3 \right] \longrightarrow CH_3\overset{O}{\overset{\|}{C}}NH_2 + CH_2CH_2OH$$

ethyl acetate   tetrahedral carbonyl addition intermediate   acetamide

Although ammonolysis is an equilibrium reaction, the position of the equilibrium lies very far to the right; the concentration of ester present at equilibrium is so small that it may be regarded as zero. Thus, it is possible to prepare an amide from an ester; it is not possible to prepare an ester from an amide.

Another example of ammonolysis of an ester is the laboratory synthesis of barbituric acid and barbiturates. Heating urea (the diamide of carbonic acid) and diethyl malonate at 110°C in the presence of sodium ethoxide (the sodium salt of ethanol) gives barbituric acid:

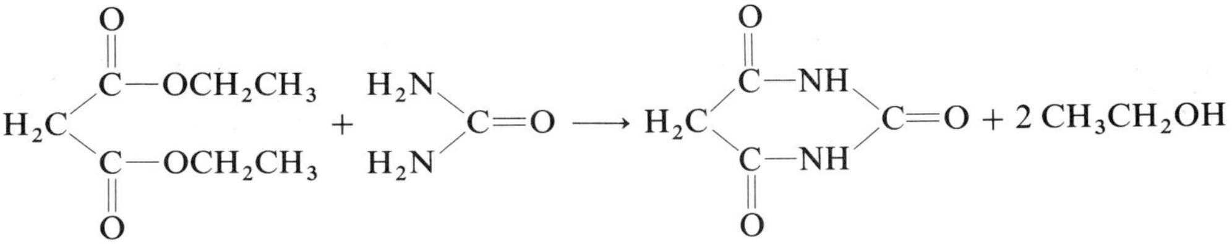

diethyl malonate   urea   barbituric acid

Mono- and disubstituted malonic esters yield substituted barbituric acids known as barbiturates.

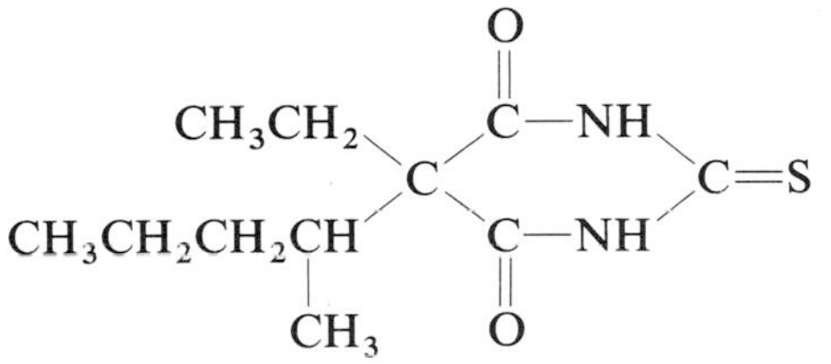

thiopental
(Penthothal)

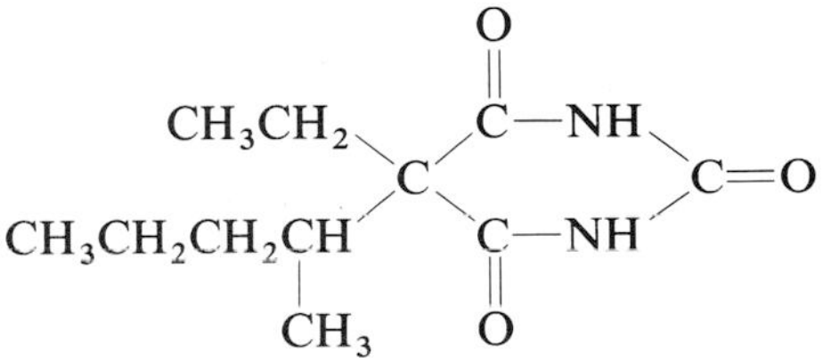

pentobarbital
(Nembutal)

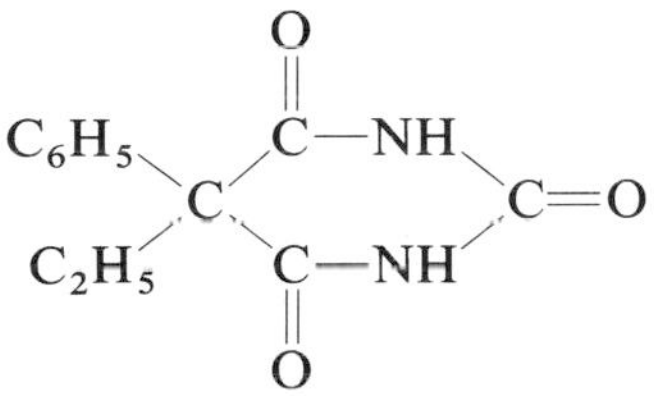

phenobarbital
(Luminal)

Barbiturates produce effects ranging from mild sedation to deep anesthesia, and even death, depending on the dose and the particular barbiturate. Sedation, long- or short-acting, depends on the structure of the barbiturate. Phenobarbital is long-acting, whereas pentobarbital acts for only about three hours. Thiopental is very fast-acting and is used as an anesthetic for producing deep sedation quickly.

Example 17.6

Complete equations for these ammonolysis reactions. The stoichiometry of each is given in the problem.

a. $\overset{O}{\overset{\|}{H C}} OCH_2CH_3 + NH_3 \longrightarrow$

b. $CH_3CH_2 O \overset{O}{\overset{\|}{C}} OCH_2CH_3 + 2NH_3 \longrightarrow$

a. The starting material is ethyl formate. Reaction with a mole of ammonia gives formamide:

$$\underset{\text{ethyl formate}}{\overset{\overset{\displaystyle O}{\parallel}}{HCOCH_2CH_3}} + NH_3 \longrightarrow \underset{\text{formamide}}{\overset{\overset{\displaystyle O}{\parallel}}{HCNH_2}} + HOCH_2CH_3$$

b. Reaction of one mole of diethyl carbonate with two moles of ammonia gives urea:

$$\underset{\text{diethyl carbonate}}{\overset{\overset{\displaystyle O}{\parallel}}{CH_3CH_2OCOCH_2CH_3}} + 2NH_3 \longrightarrow \underset{\text{urea}}{\overset{\overset{\displaystyle O}{\parallel}}{H_2NCNH_2}} + 2CH_3CH_2OH$$

Problem 17.6

Write equations for these ammonolysis reactions:

a. 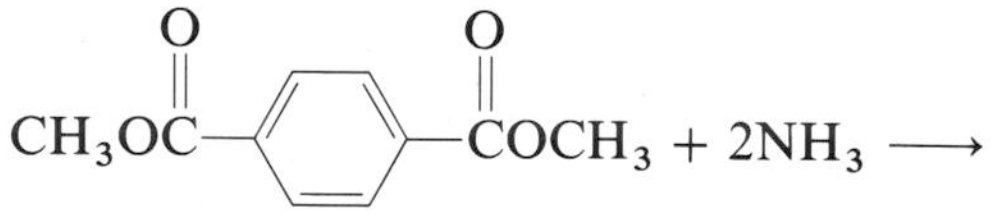 $CH_3O\overset{\overset{\displaystyle O}{\parallel}}{C}$—⟨benzene ring⟩—$\overset{\overset{\displaystyle O}{\parallel}}{C}OCH_3 + 2NH_3 \longrightarrow$

diethyl terephthalate

b. 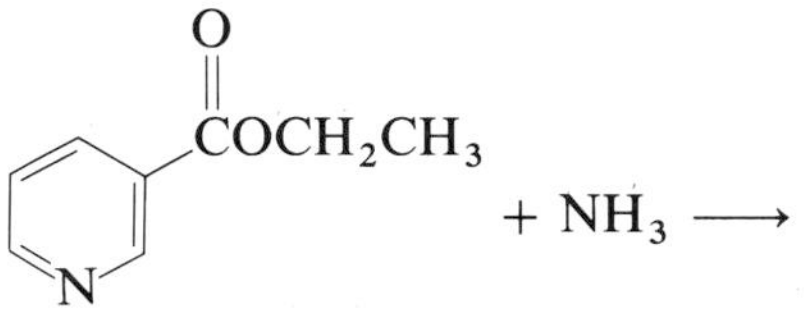 ⟨pyridine ring with N⟩$\overset{\overset{\displaystyle O}{\parallel}}{C}OCH_2CH_3 \quad + NH_3 \longrightarrow$

ethyl nicotinate

17.7 Reactions of Anhydrides

Of the three classes of functional derivatives of carboxylic acid we have studied, acid anhydrides are by far the most reactive. Anhydrides react with water to form carboxylic acids, with alcohols to form esters, and with ammonia and primary and secondary amines to form amides. Thus, acid anhydrides are valuable starting materials for preparing these other functional groups.

A. Hydrolysis

In hydrolysis, an anhydride is cleaved, forming two molecules of carboxylic acid, as illustrated by the hydrolysis of acetic anhydride:

$$\underset{\text{acetic anhydride}}{CH_3-\overset{\overset{\displaystyle O}{\parallel}}{C}-O-\overset{\overset{\displaystyle O}{\parallel}}{C}-CH_3} + H_2O \longrightarrow \underset{\text{acetic acid}}{CH_3-\overset{\overset{\displaystyle O}{\parallel}}{C}-OH} + \underset{\text{acetic acid}}{HO-\overset{\overset{\displaystyle O}{\parallel}}{C}-CH_3}$$

Acetic anhydride and other low-molecular-weight anhydrides react so readily with water that they must be protected from moisture during storage.

B. Reaction with Alcohols: Formation of Esters

Anhydrides react with alcohols to give one molecule of ester and one molecule of a carboxylic acid. Thus, reaction of an alcohol with an anhydride is a useful method for the synthesis of esters.

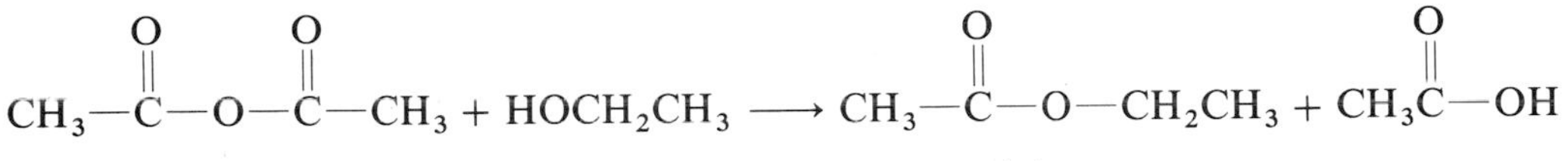

$$CH_3-\overset{O}{\overset{\|}{C}}-O-\overset{O}{\overset{\|}{C}}-CH_3 + HOCH_2CH_3 \longrightarrow CH_3-\overset{O}{\overset{\|}{C}}-O-CH_2CH_3 + CH_3\overset{O}{\overset{\|}{C}}-OH$$

acetic anhydride   ethyl acetate

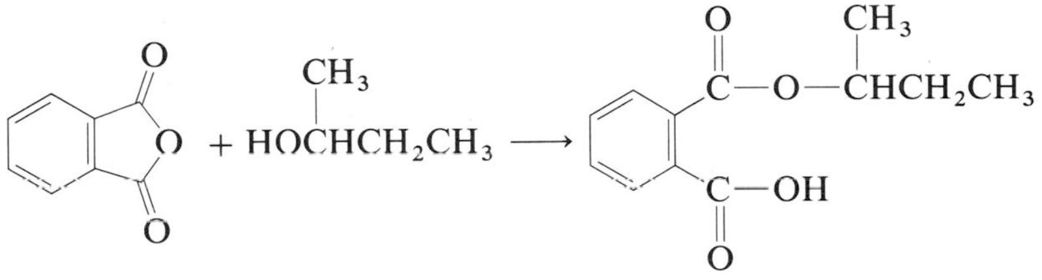

phthalic anhydride   *sec*-butyl hydrogen phthalate

Aspirin is prepared by reaction of acetic anhydride with the phenolic —OH group of salicylic acid. The CH_3CO— group is commonly called an acetyl group, a name derived from acetic acid by dropping the *-ic* from the name of the acid and adding *-yl*. Therefore, the chemical name of the product formed by reaction of acetic anhydride and salicylic acid is acetyl salicylic acid.

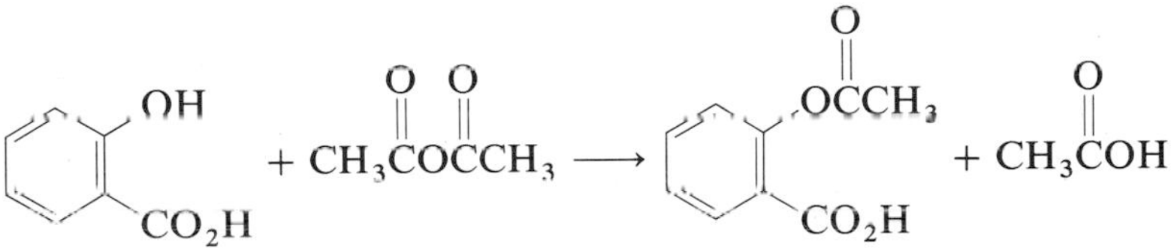

salicylic acid   acetyl salicylic
                                          (aspirin)

Aspirin is one of the few drugs produced on an industrial scale. In 1977, the United States produced 35 million pounds of it. Aspirin has been used since the turn of the century for relief of minor pain and headaches and for the reduction of fever. Compared with other drugs, aspirin is safe and well tolerated. However, it does have side effects. Because of its relative insolubility and acidity, it can irritate the stomach wall. These effects can be partially overcome by using its more soluble sodium salt instead. Because of these side effects, there has been increasing use of newer nonprescription analgesics, such as acetaminophen and Ibuprofen.

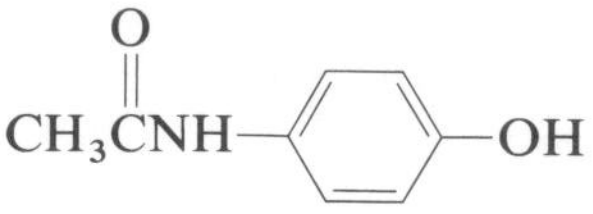

N-acetyl-4-aminophenol
(acetaminophen)

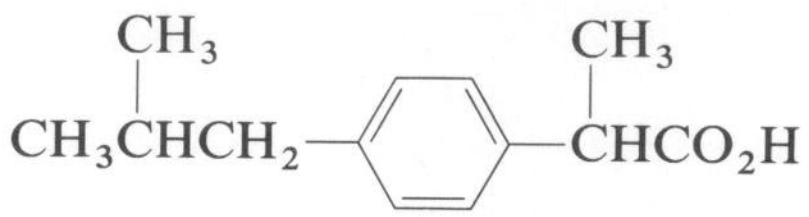

2-(4-isobutylphenyl)-propanoic acid
(Ibuprofen)

Ibuprofen was introduced in the United Kingdom in 1969 by the Boots Company as an anti-inflammatory agent for the treatment of rheumatoid arthritis and allied conditions. The Upjohn Company introduced it in the United States in 1974, and it is now marketed in over 120 countries. As an analgesic, it is approximately 28 times more potent than aspirin, and it is approximately 20 times more potent as a fever-reducing agent.

C. Reaction with Ammonia and Amines: Formation of Amides

Acid anhydrides react with ammonia, as well as with primary and secondary amines, to form amides. For complete conversion of an acid anhydride to an amide, two moles of amine are required, the first to form the amide and the second to neutralize the carboxylic acid byproduct. Reaction of an acid anhydride with an amine is one of the most common laboratory methods for synthesizing amides.

$$\underset{\text{acetic anhydride}}{CH_3-\overset{\overset{\displaystyle O}{\|}}{C}-O-\overset{\overset{\displaystyle O}{\|}}{C}-CH_3} + 2NH_3 \longrightarrow \underset{\text{acetamide}}{CH_3-\overset{\overset{\displaystyle O}{\|}}{C}-NH_2} + \underset{\text{ammonium acetate}}{CH_3-\overset{\overset{\displaystyle O}{\|}}{C}-O^-\ NH_4^+}$$

$$\underset{\text{acetic anhydride}}{CH_3\overset{\overset{\displaystyle O}{\|}}{C}O\overset{\overset{\displaystyle O}{\|}}{C}CH_3} + \underset{\text{dimethylamine}}{HN(CH_3)_2} \longrightarrow \underset{N,N\text{-dimethylacetamide}}{CH_3\overset{\overset{\displaystyle O}{\|}}{C}N(CH_3)_2} + \underset{\text{dimethylammonium acetate}}{CH_3\overset{\overset{\displaystyle O}{\|}}{C}O^-\ H_2\overset{+}{N}(CH_3)_2}$$

Example 17.7

Complete the following reactions. The stoichiometry of each is shown in the problem.

a. $2CH_3\overset{\overset{\displaystyle O}{\|}}{C}O\overset{\overset{\displaystyle O}{\|}}{C}CH_3 + HOCH_2CH_2OH \longrightarrow$

b. 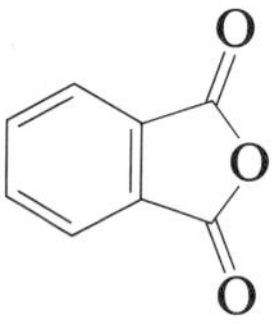 $+ 2CH_3CH_2NH_2 \longrightarrow$

☐ *Solution*   **a.** Ethylene glycol is a diol and reacts with two moles of acetic anhydride to produce a diester:

$$2CH_3\overset{O}{\overset{||}{C}}O\overset{O}{\overset{||}{C}}CH_3 + HOCH_2CH_2OH \longrightarrow CH_3\overset{O}{\overset{||}{C}}OCH_2CH_2O\overset{O}{\overset{||}{C}}CH_3 + 2CH_3\overset{O}{\overset{||}{C}}OH$$

acetic anhydride   ethylene glycol   (a diester)

b. Phthalic anhydride reacts with two moles of ethylamine, the first to form the amide bond of the product and the second to form the ethylammonium salt of the remaining carboxyl group.

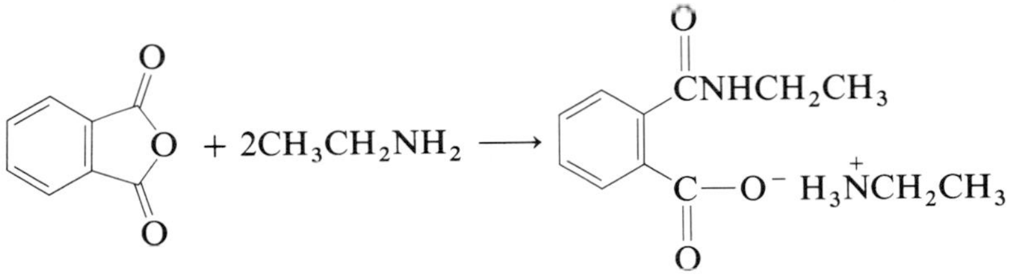

phthalic anhydride   ethylammonium *N*-ethylphthalamide

Problem 17.7

Write equations to show how you could prepare the following compounds by reaction of an anhydride with an alcohol or a phenol.

a. 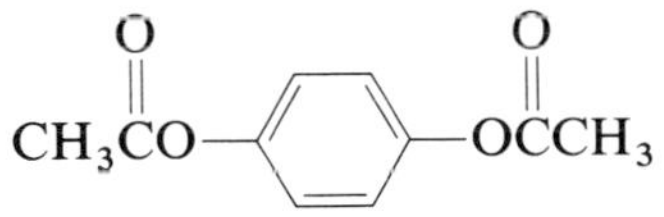 $CH_3\overset{O}{\overset{||}{C}}O\!\!-\!\!\bigcirc\!\!-\!\!O\overset{O}{\overset{||}{C}}CH_3$ **b.** $CH_3\overset{CH_3}{\overset{|}{C}}\!\!=\!\!CHCH_2O\overset{O}{\overset{||}{C}}CH_3$

17.8 Reactions of Amides

Amides are by far the least reactive of the functional groups we are considering. Their only important reaction for our purposes is hydrolysis brought about by heating the amide under reflux with concentrated aqueous acid (most commonly HCl) or aqueous base (most commonly NaOH or KOH). Because amides are so resistant to hydrolysis, it is often necessary to treat them under these conditions for several hours to bring about reaction.

Amides are hydrolyzed in aqueous acid to a carboxylic acid and an ammonium ion or an amine salt:

$$H\!\!-\!\!\overset{O}{\overset{||}{C}}\!\!-\!\!NH_2 + H_2O + HCl \longrightarrow H\!\!-\!\!\overset{O}{\overset{||}{C}}\!\!-\!\!O\!\!-\!\!H + NH_4^+\ Cl^-$$

formamide   formic acid   ammonium chloride

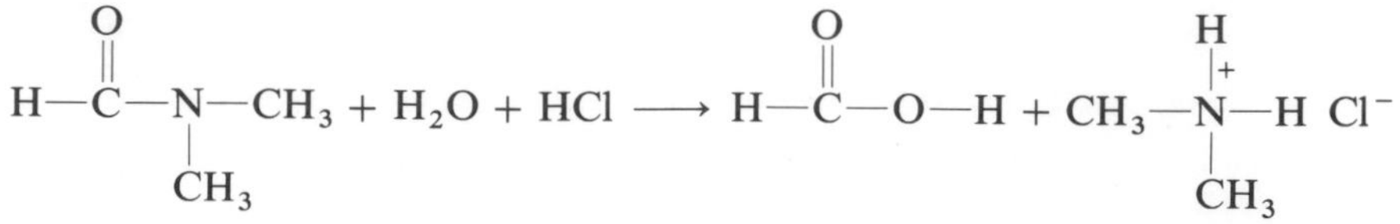

$$H-\overset{\overset{\displaystyle O}{\|}}{C}-\underset{\underset{\displaystyle CH_3}{|}}{N}-CH_3 + H_2O + HCl \longrightarrow H-\overset{\overset{\displaystyle O}{\|}}{C}-O-H + CH_3-\overset{\overset{\displaystyle H}{|+}}{\underset{\underset{\displaystyle CH_3}{|}}{N}}-H \ Cl^-$$

N,N-dimethyl-   formic acid   dimethylammonium
formamide   chloride

In aqueous base, the products of amide hydrolysis are ammonia or free amine and a carboxylate salt:

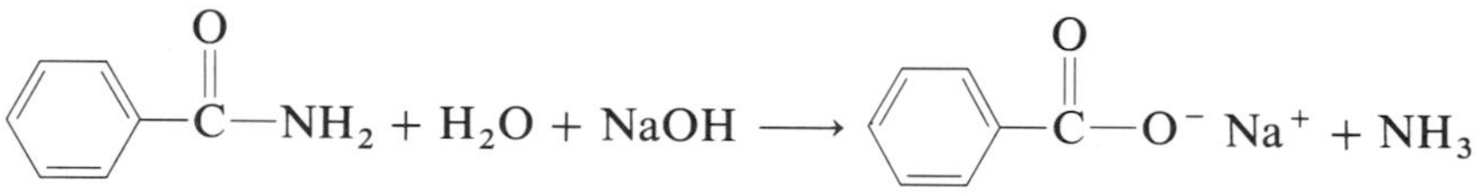

$$C_6H_5-\overset{\overset{\displaystyle O}{\|}}{C}-NH_2 + H_2O + NaOH \longrightarrow C_6H_5-\overset{\overset{\displaystyle O}{\|}}{C}-O^-\ Na^+ + NH_3$$

benzamide   sodium benzoate

$$CH_3(CH_2)_{16}\overset{\overset{\displaystyle O}{\|}}{C}-NHCH_3 + H_2O + NaOH \longrightarrow CH_3(CH_2)_{16}\overset{\overset{\displaystyle O}{\|}}{C}-O^-\ Na^+ + CH_3NH_2$$

N-methyloctadecanamide   sodium octadecanoate
(*N*-methylpalmitamide)   (sodium palmitate;
                                                 a natural soap)

Thus, in hydrolysis of amides, one mole of either acid or base is required for each mole of amide hydrolyzed.

Example 17.8

Complete equations for hydrolysis of the following amides in concentrated aqueous HCl. Show all products as they would exist under these conditions and indicate in your equation the number of moles of HCl required for hydrolysis of each amide.

$$\textbf{a. } CH_3\overset{\overset{\displaystyle O}{\|}}{C}NH_2 \qquad \textbf{b. } CH_3O-C_6H_4-NH\overset{\overset{\displaystyle O}{\|}}{C}CH_3$$

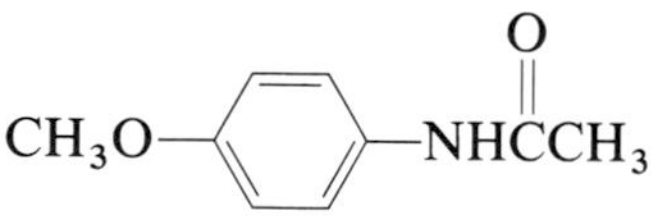

☐ *Solution*

a. Hydrolysis of acetamide gives acetic acid and ammonia. Ammonia is a base and in aqueous HCl is protonated to form an ammonium ion. The product is shown here as ammonium chloride:

$$CH_3\overset{\overset{\displaystyle O}{\|}}{C}NH_2 + H_2O + HCl \longrightarrow CH_3\overset{\overset{\displaystyle O}{\|}}{C}OH + NH_4^+\ Cl^-$$

b. CH_3O—⟨benzene ring⟩—$\overset{\overset{\displaystyle O}{\|}}{N}HCCH_3 + H_2O + HCl \longrightarrow$

N-acetyl-4-methoxyaniline
(*N*-acetyl-*p*-methoxyaniline)

CH_3O—⟨benzene ring⟩—$NH_3^+\ Cl^- + CH_3\overset{\overset{\displaystyle O}{\|}}{C}OH$

4-methoxyanilinium chloride
(*p*-methoxyanilinium chloride)

Problem 17.8

Complete the equations for hydrolysis of the following amides in concentrated aqueous NaOH. Show all products as they would exist under these conditions and indicate in your equation the number of moles of NaOH required for hydrolysis of each amide.

a. $CH_3\overset{\overset{\displaystyle O}{\|}}{C}NH_2$ b. CH_3O—⟨benzene ring⟩—$\overset{\overset{\displaystyle O}{\|}}{N}HCCH_3$

17.9 The Claisen Condensation: Synthesis of Beta-Ketoesters

The **Claisen condensation** involves condensation of the α-carbon of one molecule of ester with the carbonyl carbon of a second molecule of ester. For example, when ethyl acetate is heated with sodium ethoxide in ethanol, the α-carbon of one molecule of ethyl acetate forms a new carbon-carbon bond with the carbonyl group of a second molecule of ethyl acetate, and $—OCH_2CH_3$ is displaced.

*New carbon-carbon
bond formed in the
Claisen condensation*

$CH_3\overset{\overset{\displaystyle O}{\|}}{C}OCH_2CH_3 + CH_3\overset{\overset{\displaystyle O}{\|}}{C}OCH_2CH_3 \xrightarrow[CH_3CH_2OH]{CH_3CH_2O^-Na^+} CH_3\overset{\overset{\displaystyle O}{\|}}{C}—CH_2\overset{\overset{\displaystyle O}{\|}}{C}OCH_2CH_3 + CH_3CH_2OH$

*Carbonyl group
to which
α-carbon adds*   *α-carbon*

ethyl 3-oxobutanoate
(ethyl acetoacetate)

Thus, the Claisen condensation is another example of the general mechanism of nucleophilic substitution at a carbonyl carbon (Section 17.4).

The characteristic structural feature of the product of a Claisen condensation is a ketone on carbon 3 of an ester chain. In common nomenclature, carbon 3 of the carboxylic acid chain is called the beta-carbon (β-carbon). Thus, products of Claisen condensations are often called **β-ketoesters**.

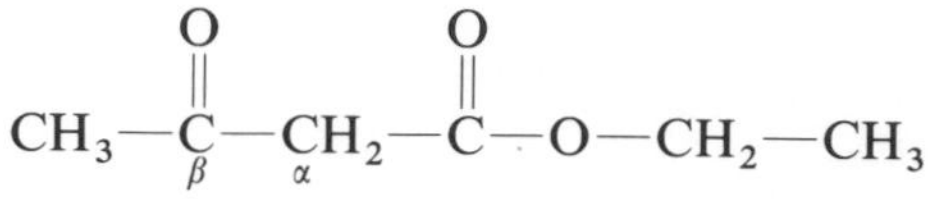

$$CH_3-\underset{\beta}{\overset{\overset{\displaystyle O}{\|}}{C}}-\underset{\alpha}{CH_2}-\overset{\overset{\displaystyle O}{\|}}{C}-O-CH_2-CH_3$$

a beta-ketoester

Claisen condensation of two molecules of ethyl propanoate gives the following beta-ketoester. In this reaction, the structural formulas of the two ester molecules are written to emphasize that the step forming the new carbon-carbon bond involves the α-carbon of one ester and the carbonyl carbon of the other.

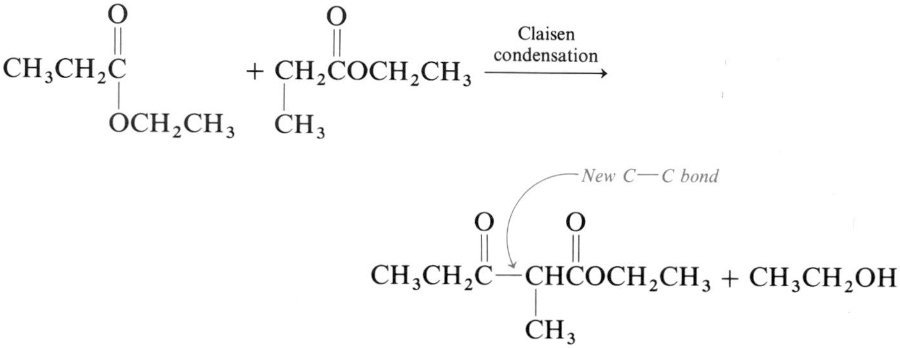

$$CH_3CH_2\overset{\overset{\displaystyle O}{\|}}{\underset{\underset{\displaystyle OCH_2CH_3}{|}}{C}} \quad + \quad \overset{\overset{\displaystyle O}{\|}}{\underset{\underset{\displaystyle CH_3}{|}}{CH_2COCH_2CH_3}} \xrightarrow{\begin{array}{c}\text{Claisen}\\\text{condensation}\end{array}}$$

New C—C bond

$$CH_3CH_2\overset{\overset{\displaystyle O}{\|}}{C}-\underset{\underset{\displaystyle CH_3}{|}}{CH}\overset{\overset{\displaystyle O}{\|}}{C}OCH_2CH_3 + CH_3CH_2OH$$

ethyl 2-methyl-3-oxopentanoate
(a beta-ketoester)

The mechanism for the Claisen condensation is similar to the three-step mechanism we proposed for the aldol condensation (Section 15.8). Both begin in step 1 by formation of an anion on an α-carbon. This is followed in step 2 of the Claisen condensation by addition of this anion to the carbonyl carbon of another ester, to form a tetrahedral carbonyl addition intermediate. Collapse of this intermediate in step 3 gives the beta-ketoester.

Step 1: Reaction of an α-hydrogen with base to form an anion

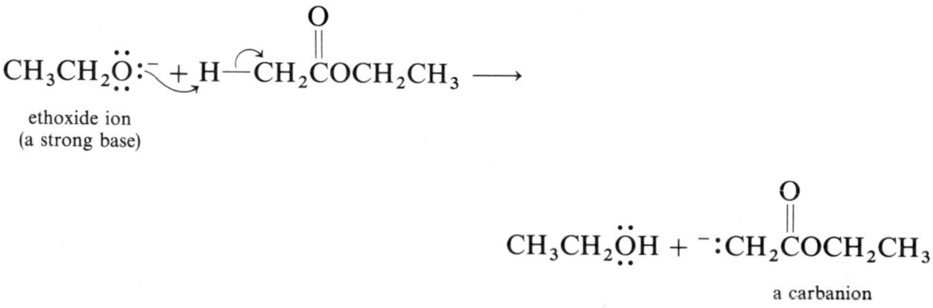

$$CH_3CH_2\ddot{\overset{..}{O}}\colon^- + H-CH_2\overset{\overset{\displaystyle O}{\|}}{C}OCH_2CH_3 \longrightarrow$$

ethoxide ion
(a strong base)

$$CH_3CH_2\ddot{\overset{..}{O}}H + {}^-\colon CH_2\overset{\overset{\displaystyle O}{\|}}{C}OCH_2CH_3$$

a carbanion

Step 2: Addition of the carbanion to a carbonyl carbon to form a tetrahedral carbonyl addition intermediate

$$CH_3\overset{\overset{\displaystyle :\ddot{O}}{\|}}{\underset{\underset{\displaystyle OCH_2CH_3CH_2CH_3}{|}}{C}} + :CH_2COCH_2CH_3 \longrightarrow CH_3\overset{\overset{\displaystyle :\ddot{O}:^-}{|}}{\underset{\underset{\displaystyle OCH_2CH_3}{|}}{C}}-CH_2\overset{\overset{\displaystyle O}{\|}}{C}OCH_2CH_3$$

tetrahedral carbonyl
addition intermediate

Step 3: Collapse of the tetrahedral carbonyl addition intermediate to give the beta-ketoester and regenerate ethoxide ion

$$CH_3\overset{\overset{\displaystyle :\ddot{O}:^-}{|}}{\underset{\underset{\displaystyle :OCH_2CH_3}{|}}{C}}CH_2\overset{\overset{\displaystyle O}{\|}}{C}OCH_2CH_3 \longrightarrow CH_3\overset{\overset{\displaystyle :\ddot{O}}{\|}}{C}CH_2\overset{\overset{\displaystyle O}{\|}}{C}OCH_2CH_3 + CH_3CH_2\ddot{O}:^-$$

Note that ethoxide ion is a catalyst in this reaction; it is used as a reactant in step 1 but regenerated as a product in step 3.

In the case of mixed Claisen condensations—that is, a condensation between two different esters—a mixture of four possible products is possible unless there is an appreciable difference in reactivity between one ester and the other. One such difference is if one of the esters has no α-hydrogens and therefore cannot serve as an anion. Examples of esters without α-hydrogens are ethyl formate, ethyl benzoate, and diethyl carbonate:

$$\overset{\overset{\displaystyle O}{\|}}{HCOCH_2CH_3} \qquad \overset{\overset{\displaystyle O}{\|}}{COCH_2CH_3} \qquad CH_3CH_2\overset{\overset{\displaystyle O}{\|}}{OCOCH_2CH_3}$$

ethyl formate   ethyl benzoate   diethyl carbonate

Example 17.9

Draw structural formulas for the products of the following Claisen condensations.

a.
$$\overset{\overset{\displaystyle O}{\|}}{COCH_2CH_3} + CH_3\overset{\overset{\displaystyle O}{\|}}{C}OCH_2CH_3 \xrightarrow{\text{base}}$$

b.
$$\overset{\overset{\displaystyle O}{\|}}{HCOCH_2CH_3} + CH_3CH_2\overset{\overset{\displaystyle O}{\|}}{C}OCH_2CH_3 \xrightarrow{\text{base}}$$

☐ *Solution*

a. Ethyl benzoate has no α-hydrogens and therefore can function only as an anion acceptor in a Claisen condensation. Ethyl acetate has three α-hydrogens and forms an anion, which then completes the reaction.

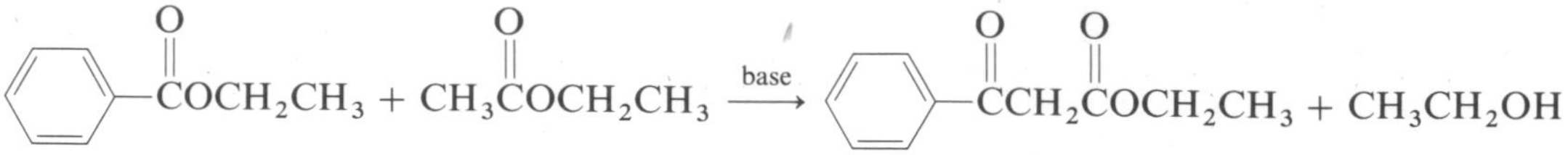

ethyl benzoate — ethyl acetate — ethyl 3-oxo-3-phenylpropanoate (a beta-ketoester)

b. Ethyl formate has no α-hydrogens and can function only as a carbanion acceptor for the anion formed on the α-carbon of ethyl propanoate.

$$\underset{\text{ethyl formate}}{HC(=O)OCH_2CH_3} + \underset{\text{ethyl propanoate}}{CH_3CH_2C(=O)OCH_2CH_3} \xrightarrow{\text{base}} \underset{\text{(a beta-ketoester)}}{HC(=O)CH(CH_3)C(=O)OCH_2CH_3} + CH_3CH_2OH$$

Problem 17.9

Following are structural formulas for two beta-ketoesters. Show how each could be formed by a Claisen condensation.

a. $CH_3CH_2CH_2C(=O)CH(CH_2CH_3)C(=O)OCH_2CH_3$

b.

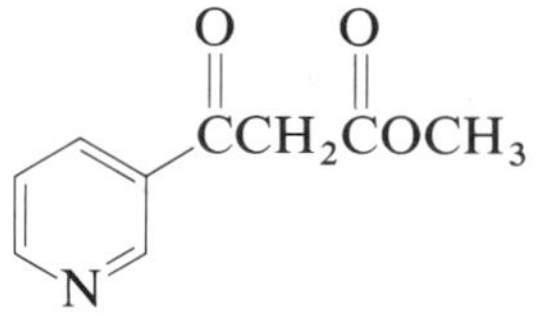

Key Terms and Concepts

amide (introduction)
ammonolysis (17.6C)
anhydride (introduction)
β-ketoester (17.9)
Claisen condensation (17.9)
ester (introduction)
Fischer esterification (17.5)
nucleophilic substitution at a carbonyl carbon (17.4)
saponification (17.6B)

Key Reactions

1. Acid-catalyzed esterification: Fischer esterification (Section 17.5).
2. Catalytic reduction of esters to two alcohols (Section 17.6A).
3. Metal hydride reduction of esters to two alcohols (Section 17.6A).
4. Hydrolysis of esters in aqueous acid to a carboxylic acid and an alcohol (Section 17.6B).
5. Hydrolysis of esters in aqueous base to a carboxylate salt and an alcohol (Section 17.6B).
6. Reaction of esters with ammonia and amines: formation of amides (Section 17.6C).

7. Hydrolysis of anhydrides (Section 17.7A).

8. Reaction of anhydrides with alcohols: formation of esters (Section 17.7B).

9. Reaction of anhydrides with ammonia and amines: formation of amides (Section 17.7C).

10. Hydrolysis of amides in aqueous acid to a carboxylic acid and an ammonium salt (Section 17.8).

11. Hydrolysis of amides in aqueous base to a carboxylate salt and ammonia or an amine (Section 17.8).

12. Claisen condensation: formation of β-ketoesters (Section 17.9).

Problems

Structure and nomenclature of esters, amides, and anhydrides (Section 17.1)

17.10   Name the compounds:

a. $CH_3CH_2\overset{O}{\overset{\|}{C}}O\overset{CH_3}{\underset{|}{C}}HCH_3$

b. $CH_3\overset{O}{\overset{\|}{C}}NH_2$

c. ⬡$-\overset{O}{\overset{\|}{C}}-O-\overset{O}{\overset{\|}{C}}-$⬡

d. $CH_2{=}CH\overset{O}{\overset{\|}{C}}OCH_3$

e. $CH_3CH_2CH_2CH_2\overset{O}{\overset{\|}{C}}NHCH_3$

f. $H_2N\overset{O}{\overset{\|}{C}}NH_2$

g. $CH_3CH_2\overset{O}{\overset{\|}{C}}OC_6H_5$

h. $CH_3O\overset{O}{\overset{\|}{C}}CH_2CH_2\overset{O}{\overset{\|}{C}}OCH_3$

i. (cyclohexane with $\overset{O}{\overset{\|}{}}OCCH_3$)

j. (cyclohexene with $\overset{O}{\overset{\|}{}}OCCH_3$)

17.11   Draw structural formulas for the following compounds:

a. phenyl benzoate	**b.** diethyl carbonate
c. benzamide	**d.** cyclobutyl butanoate
e. methyl 3-methylbutanoate	**f.** isopropyl 3-methylhexanoate
g. diethyl oxalate	**h.** ethyl *cis*-2-pentenoate
i. *N*-phenylacetamide	**j.** *N,N*-dimethylacetamide
k. acetic anhydride	**l.** *N*-phenylbutanamide
m. diethyl malonate	**n.** formamide
o. ethyl 3-hydroxybutanoate	**p.** methyl formate
q. trimethyl citrate	**r.** *p*-nitrophenyl acetate
s. ethyl *p*-hydroxybenzoate	**t.** ethyl *p*-aminobenzoate

*Physical
properties of
esters,
amides, and
anhydrides
(Section 17.3)*

17.12 Draw structural formulas for the nine isomeric esters of molecular formula $C_5H_{10}O_2$. Give each an IUPAC name.

17.13 Acetic acid and methyl formate are structural isomers. Both are liquids at room temperature. One has a boiling point of 32°C, the other a boiling point of 118°C. Which compound has which boiling point? Explain your reasoning.

$$\underset{\text{acetic acid}}{\overset{\overset{\displaystyle O}{\|}}{CH_3COH}} \qquad \underset{\text{methyl formate}}{\overset{\overset{\displaystyle O}{\|}}{HCOCH_3}}$$

17.14 Draw structural formulas to show hydrogen bonding between the circled atoms.

$$CH_3-\overset{\overset{\displaystyle \textcircled{O}}{\|}}{C}-\underset{\underset{\displaystyle H}{|}}{N}-H \quad \text{and} \quad CH_3-\overset{\overset{\displaystyle O}{\|}}{C}-\underset{\underset{\displaystyle H}{|}}{N}-\textcircled{H}$$

17.15 Following are melting and boiling points for acetamide and ethyl acetate.

$$\underset{\substack{\text{acetamide} \\ \text{(mp 82.3°C; bp 221°C)}}}{\overset{\overset{\displaystyle O}{\|}}{CH_3CNH_2}} \qquad \underset{\substack{\text{ethyl acetate} \\ \text{(mp } -83.6\text{°C; bp 77°C)}}}{\overset{\overset{\displaystyle O}{\|}}{CH_3COCH_2CH_3}}$$

a. What is the physical state (solid, liquid, or gas) of each compound at room temperature?

b. How could you account for the considerably higher boiling point of acetamide relative to ethyl acetate?

17.16 **a.** Write an equation for the equilibrium established when acetic acid and 1-propanol are heated under reflux in the presence of a few drops of concentrated sulfuric acid.

b. Using the data in Section 17.5, calculate the equilibrium constant for this reaction.

17.17 If 15 g of salicylic acid is caused to react with excess methanol, how many grams of methyl salicylate (oil of wintergreen) could be formed?

salicylic acid   methyl salicylate

17.18 When a carboxylic acid contains more than one —COOH group and the alcohol contains more than one —OH group, then under appropriate experimental conditions, hundreds of molecules can be linked to give a polyester. Dacron is a polyester of terephthalic acid and ethylene glycol:

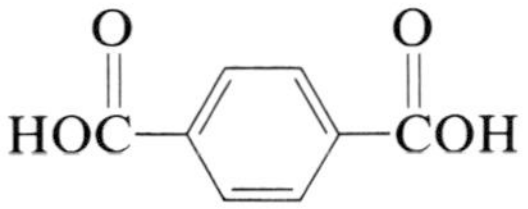

terephthalic acid   ethylene glycol

a. Formulate a structure of Dacron polyester. Be certain to show in principle how several hundred molecules can be hooked together to form the polyester.
b. Write an equation for the chemistry involved when a drop of concentrated hydrochloric acid makes a hole in a Dacron polyester shirt or blouse.
c. From what starting materials do you think the condensation fiber Kodel polyester is made?

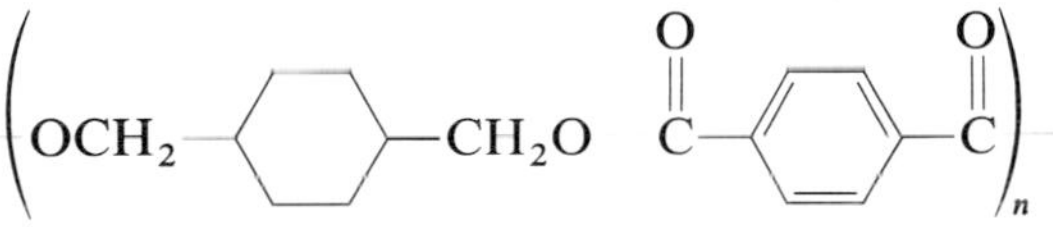

Kodel polyester

Reactions of esters, amides, and anhydrides (Sections 17.6–17.8)

17.19 Complete the equations for the hydrolysis of the following esters, amides, and anhydrides.

$$\text{a. } CH_3\overset{\overset{\displaystyle O}{\|}}{C}OCH_2CH_3 + H_2O \longrightarrow$$

$$\text{b. } CH_3\overset{\overset{\displaystyle O}{\|}}{C}O\underset{\underset{\displaystyle CH_2O\overset{\overset{\displaystyle O}{\|}}{C}CH_3}{|}}{\overset{\overset{\displaystyle CH_2O\overset{\overset{\displaystyle O}{\|}}{C}CH_3}{|}}{C}H} + 3H_2O \longrightarrow$$

$$\text{c. } CH_3CH_2\overset{\overset{\displaystyle O}{\|}}{C}OCH_2CH_2O\overset{\overset{\displaystyle O}{\|}}{C}CH_2CH_3 + 2H_2O \longrightarrow$$

$$\text{d. } CH_3CH_2O\overset{\overset{\displaystyle O}{\|}}{C}CH_2CH_2\overset{\overset{\displaystyle O}{\|}}{C}OCH_2CH_3 + 2H_2O \longrightarrow$$

e. $CH_3\overset{\displaystyle O}{\overset{\|}{C}}SCH_2CH_3 + H_2O \longrightarrow$

f. $CH_3CH_2O\overset{\displaystyle O}{\overset{\|}{C}}OCH_2CH_3 + 2H_2O \longrightarrow$

g. 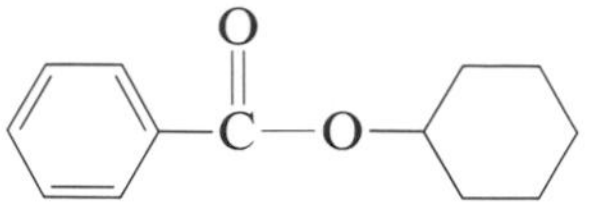 [phenyl]$-\overset{\displaystyle O}{\overset{\|}{C}}-O-$[cyclohexyl] $+ H_2O \longrightarrow$

h. 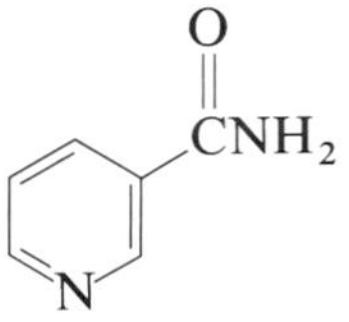 [pyridine-$\overset{\displaystyle O}{\overset{\|}{C}}NH_2$] $+ H_2O \longrightarrow$ i. $H_2N\overset{\displaystyle O}{\overset{\|}{C}}NH_2 + 2H_2O \longrightarrow$

j. $CH_3\overset{\displaystyle O}{\overset{\|}{C}}NHCH_2CH_2CH_3 + H_2O \longrightarrow$

k. $CH_3CH_2\overset{\displaystyle O}{\overset{\|}{C}}O\overset{\displaystyle O}{\overset{\|}{C}}CH_2CH_3 + H_2O \longrightarrow$

l. 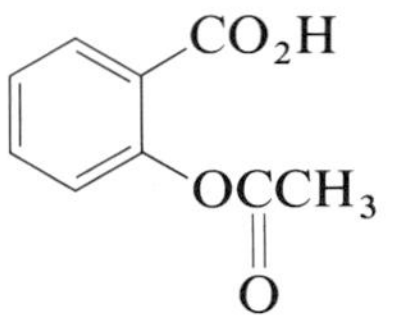 [benzene with CO_2H and $O\overset{\displaystyle O}{\overset{\|}{C}}CH_3$] $+ H_2O \longrightarrow$ m. 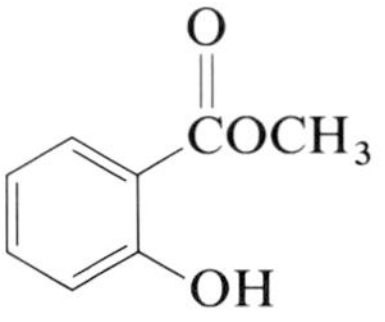 [benzene with $\overset{\displaystyle O}{\overset{\|}{C}}OCH_3$ and OH] $+ H_2O \longrightarrow$

17.20   The structural formula of choline is

$$CH_3-\overset{\displaystyle CH_3}{\underset{\displaystyle CH_3}{\overset{+}{N}}}-CH_2-CH_2-OH + CH_3\overset{\displaystyle O}{\overset{\|}{C}}O\overset{\displaystyle O}{\overset{\|}{C}}CH_3 \longrightarrow \text{acetylcholine}$$

choline

a. Name each functional group in choline.

b. Draw a structural formula for acetylcholine, a molecule synthesized in the laboratory by reaction of choline with acetic anhydride. Acetylcholine is an important neurotransmitter in the central nervous system.

17.21   Following are structural formulas of two drugs widely used in clinical medicine. The first is a tranquilizer. Miltown is one of the several trade names for this substance. The second drug, phenobarbital, is a long-acting sedative, a hypnotic, and a central-nervous-system depressant. Phenobarbital is used to treat mild hypertension (high blood pressure) and temporary emotional strain. Predict the products of hydrolysis in aqueous acid of each of these compounds.

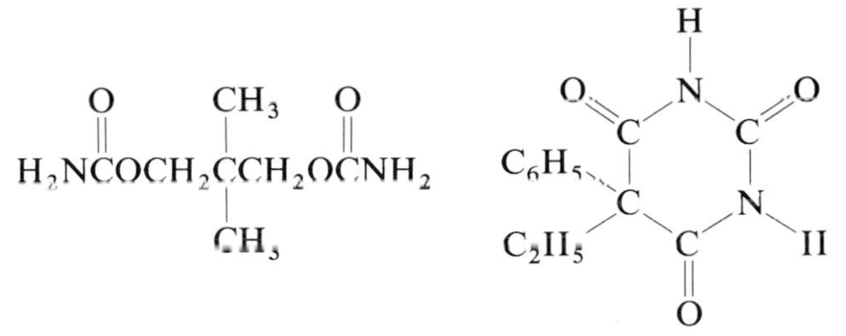

$$
\underset{\text{Miltown}}{\underset{\underset{\text{CH}_3}{|}}{\text{H}_2\text{NCOCH}_2\overset{\overset{\text{CH}_3}{|}}{\text{C}}\text{CH}_2\text{OCNH}_2}}
\qquad
\underset{\text{phenobarbital}}{\text{phenobarbital structure}}
$$

Miltown   phenobarbital

17.22   Explain why it is preferable to hydrolyze esters in aqueous base rather than in aqueous acid.

17.23   Complete the following reactions:

a. $CH_3CH_2\overset{O}{\overset{\|}{C}}OCH_3 + NH_3 \longrightarrow$

b. 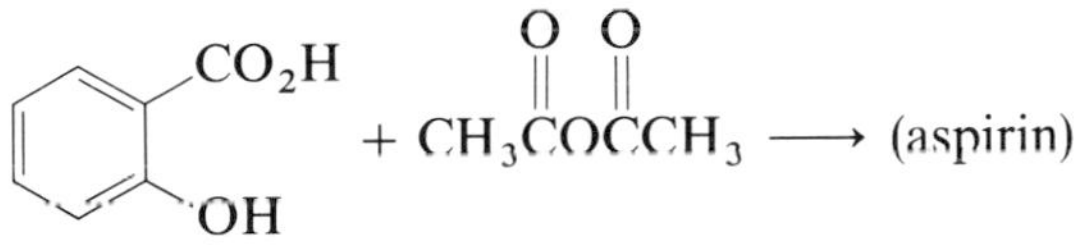 [benzene ring with CO$_2$H and OH] $+ CH_3\overset{O}{\overset{\|}{C}}O\overset{O}{\overset{\|}{C}}CH_3 \longrightarrow$ (aspirin)

c. CH_3CH_2O—[benzene ring]—$NH_2 + CH_3\overset{O}{\overset{\|}{C}}O\overset{O}{\overset{\|}{C}}CH_3 \longrightarrow$

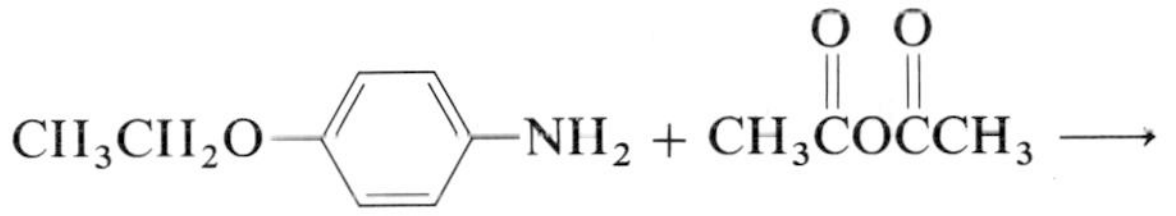

(phenacetin, a pain reliever)

d. 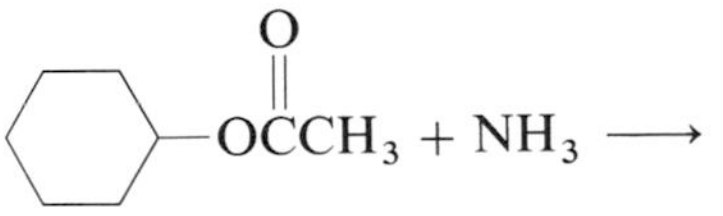 [cyclohexane ring]—$O\overset{O}{\overset{\|}{C}}CH_3 + NH_3 \longrightarrow$

e. 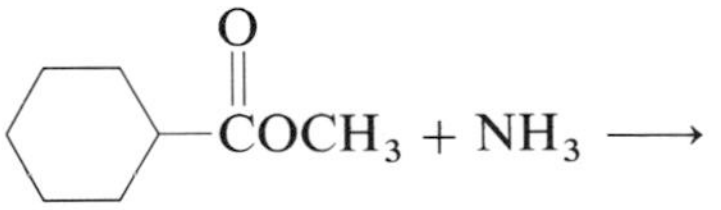 [cyclohexane ring]—$\overset{O}{\overset{\|}{C}}OCH_3 + NH_3 \longrightarrow$

f. 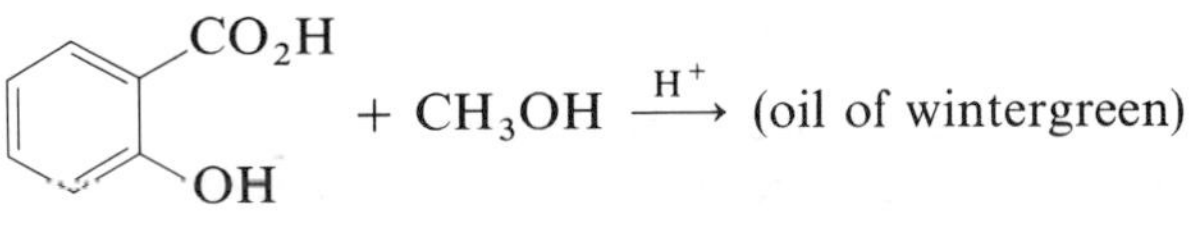 [benzene ring with CO$_2$H and OH] $+ CH_3OH \xrightarrow{H^+}$ (oil of wintergreen)

g. $2CH_3\overset{\overset{O}{\|}}{C}O\overset{\overset{O}{\|}}{C}CH_3 + HOCH_2CH_2OH \longrightarrow$

h. $CH_3\overset{\overset{O}{\|}}{C}OCH_3 + CH_3NH_2 \longrightarrow$

i. $CH_3\overset{\overset{O}{\|}}{C}OCH_3 + (CH_3)_2NH \longrightarrow$

17.24 Draw structural formulas for the products of complete hydrolysis of the following phosphate esters, amides, and anhydrides. In each case, name the functional group undergoing hydrolysis.

a. 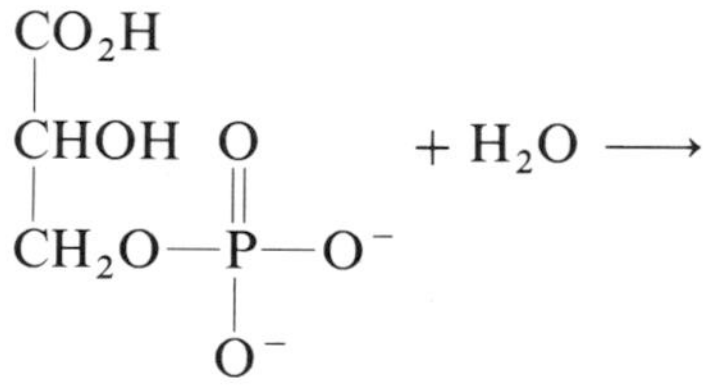
$$
\begin{array}{c}
CO_2H \\
| \\
CHOH \quad O \\
| \qquad \| \\
CH_2O-P-O^- \\
| \\
O^-
\end{array}
\quad + H_2O \longrightarrow
$$

b. $CH_3\overset{\overset{O}{\|}}{C}-O-\underset{\underset{O^-}{|}}{\overset{\overset{O}{\|}}{P}}-O^- + H_2O \longrightarrow$

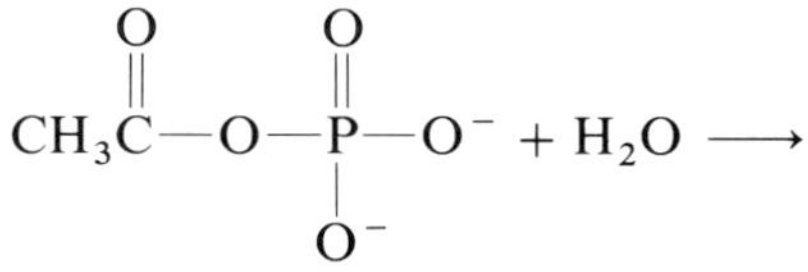

c. $^-O-\underset{\underset{O^-}{|}}{\overset{\overset{O}{\|}}{P}}-O-\underset{\underset{O^-}{|}}{\overset{\overset{O}{\|}}{P}}-O^- + H_2O \longrightarrow$

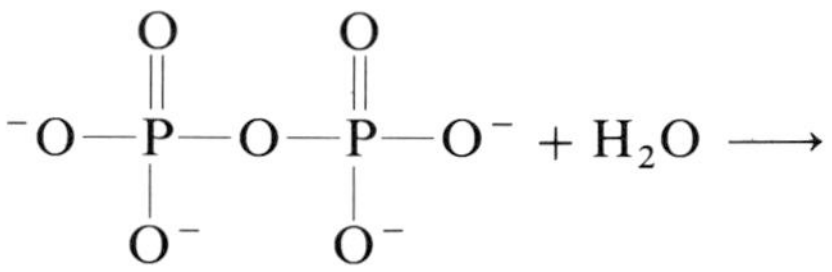

d. 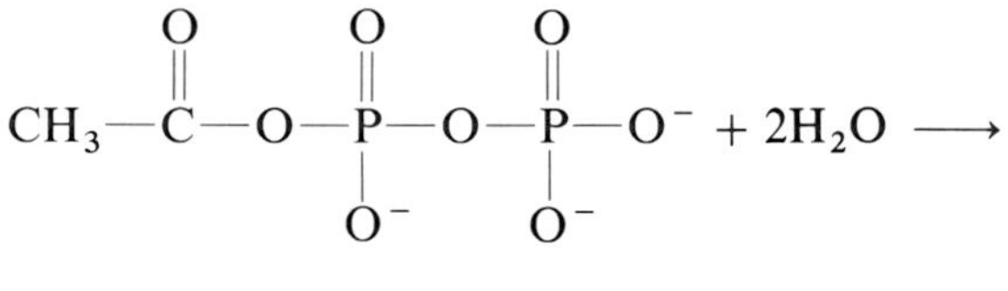 $CH_3-\overset{\overset{O}{\|}}{C}-O-\underset{\underset{O^-}{|}}{\overset{\overset{O}{\|}}{P}}-O-\underset{\underset{O^-}{|}}{\overset{\overset{O}{\|}}{P}}-O^- + 2H_2O \longrightarrow$

e. 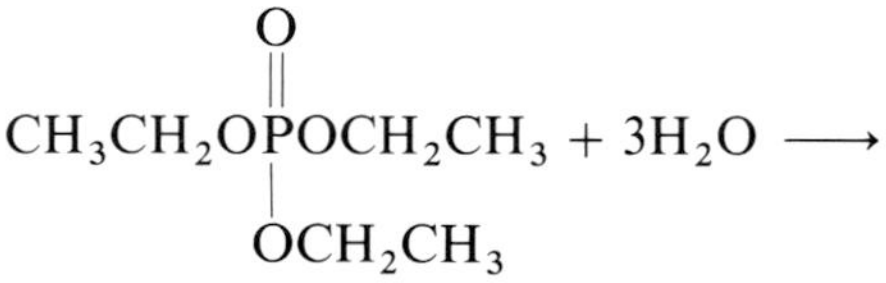 $CH_3CH_2O\underset{\underset{OCH_2CH_3}{|}}{\overset{\overset{O}{\|}}{P}}OCH_2CH_3 + 3H_2O \longrightarrow$

17.25 Show how you could distinguish between the following pairs of compounds by a simple chemical test. In each case, tell what test you would perform and what you would expect to observe, and write an equation for each positive test.
   a. isopropyl formate and 2-methylpropanoic acid (isobutyric acid)
   b. butanoic acid and butanamide
   c. methyl hexanoate and hexanal

d. 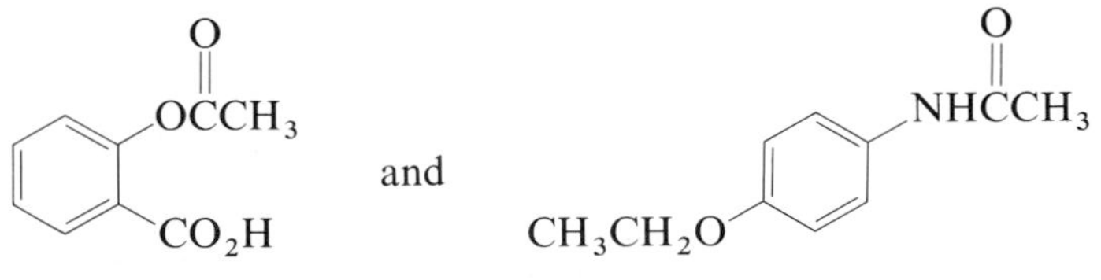 and

aspirin   phenacetin

17.26 The following conversions can be done in either one step or two. Show the reagents you would use and draw structural formulas for any intermediate involved in a two-step reaction. Use any necessary inorganic and organic compounds in addition to the indicated starting material.

a. $CH_3CH_2CH_2CH_2CH_2OH \longrightarrow CH_3CH_2CH_2CH_2\overset{\overset{\text{O}}{\|}}{C}OH$

b. $CH_3CH_2CH_2CH_2OH \longrightarrow CH_3CH_2CH_2\overset{\overset{\text{O}}{\|}}{C}OCH_2CH_2CH_2CH_3$

c. $CH_3CH_2CH_2CH_2OH \longrightarrow CH_3CH_2CH{=}CH_2$

d. $CH_3CH_2CH_2CH_2OH \longrightarrow CH_3CH_2\underset{\underset{\text{OH}}{|}}{C}HCH_3$

e.

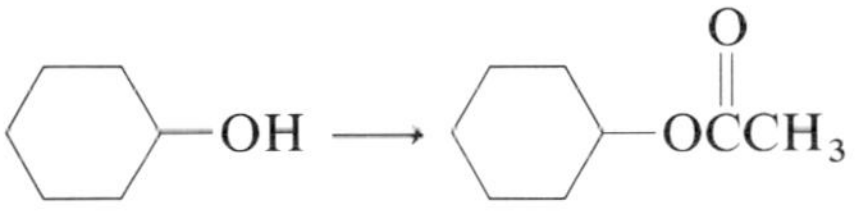

f. $H\overset{\overset{\text{O}}{\|}}{O}CCH_2CH_2CH_2CH_2\overset{\overset{\text{O}}{\|}}{C}OH \longrightarrow CH_3O\overset{\overset{\text{O}}{\|}}{C}CH_2CH_2CH_2CH_2\overset{\overset{\text{O}}{\|}}{C}OCH_3$

g. $2CH_3\overset{\overset{\text{O}}{\|}}{C}CH_3 \longrightarrow CH_3\underset{\underset{\text{CH}_3}{|}}{\overset{\overset{\text{OH}}{|}}{C}}CH_2\overset{\overset{\text{O}}{\|}}{C}CH_3$

h. 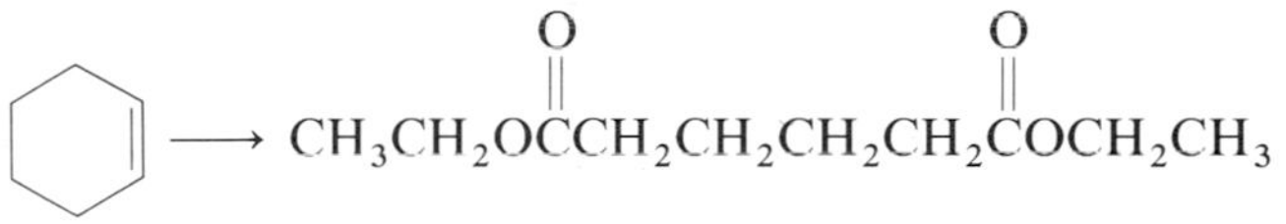 $\longrightarrow CH_3CH_2O\overset{\overset{\text{O}}{\|}}{C}CH_2CH_2CH_2CH_2\overset{\overset{\text{O}}{\|}}{C}OCH_2CH_3$

i.

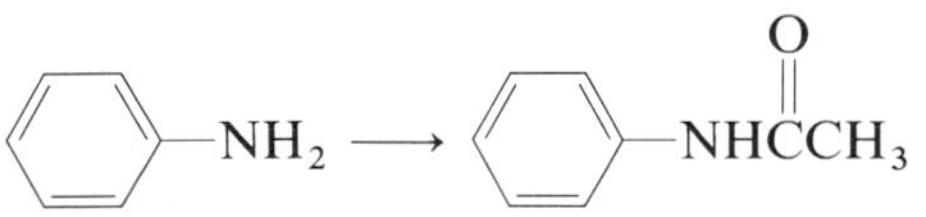

j. $CH_3CH_2CH_2OH \longrightarrow (CH_3CH_2CO_2^-)_2\ Ca^{2+}$

The Claisen condensation (Section 17.9)

17.27 What is the characteristic structural feature of the product of a Claisen condensation?

17.28 What is the characteristic structural feature of the product of an aldol condensation?

17.29 Draw structural formulas for the products of the following Claisen condensations.

a. $\underset{\displaystyle \quad}{CH_3CH_2\overset{\displaystyle O}{\overset{\displaystyle \|}{C}}OCH_2CH_3}$ $\xrightarrow[CH_3CH_2OH]{CH_3CH_2O^-\ Na^+}$

b. 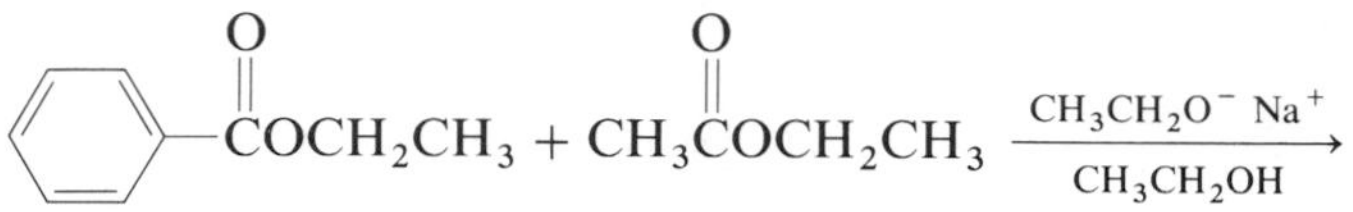 $\text{(phenyl)}-\overset{\displaystyle O}{\overset{\displaystyle \|}{C}}OCH_2CH_3 + CH_3\overset{\displaystyle O}{\overset{\displaystyle \|}{C}}OCH_2CH_3$ $\xrightarrow[CH_3CH_2OH]{CH_3CH_2O^-\ Na^+}$

17.30 Write equations to show how ethyl propanoate could be converted to these compounds:

a. $CH_3CH_2\overset{\displaystyle O}{\overset{\displaystyle \|}{C}}\underset{\displaystyle CH_3}{\overset{\displaystyle }{C}}H\overset{\displaystyle O}{\overset{\displaystyle \|}{C}}OCH_2CH_3$

b. $CH_3CH_2\overset{\displaystyle O}{\overset{\displaystyle \|}{C}}\underset{\displaystyle CH_3}{\overset{\displaystyle }{C}}H\overset{\displaystyle O}{\overset{\displaystyle \|}{C}}OH$

c. $CH_3CH_2\overset{\displaystyle O}{\overset{\displaystyle \|}{C}}CH_2CH_3$

Nylon and Dacron

After World War I, many chemists recognized the need for developing a basic knowledge of polymer chemistry. One of the most creative of these pioneers was Wallace M. Carothers. In the early 1930s, Carothers and his associates at E. I. du Pont de Nemours & Co., Inc., began fundamental research into the reactions of aliphatic dicarboxylic acids and dialcohols. From adipic acid and ethylene glycol, they obtained a polyester of high molecular weight that could be drawn into fibers. However, melting points of these first polyester fibers were too low for them to be used as textile fibers, and they were not investigated further. Carothers then turned his attention to the reactions of dicarboxylic acids and diamines, and in 1934 synthesized Nylon 66,

to-one salt, called nylon salt. Nylon salt is then heated in an autoclave to 250°C. As the temperature increases in the closed system, the internal pressure rises to about 15 atm. Under these conditions, $-CO_2^-$ groups from adipic acid and $-NH_3^+$ groups from hexamethylenediamine react to form amides. Water is a byproduct. As polymerization proceeds and more water is formed, steam and alcohol vapors are continuously bled from the autoclave to maintain a constant internal pressure. The temperature is gradually raised to about 275°C, and when all water vapor is removed, the internal pressure of the reaction vessel falls to 1 atm. Nylon 66 formed under these conditions melts at 250–260°C and has a molecular weight range of 10,000–20,000.

$$\underset{\text{adipic acid}}{HOC(CH_2)_4COH} + \underset{\substack{\text{hexamethylene-}\\\text{diamine}\\\text{(HMDA)}}}{H_2N(CH_2)_6NH_2} \longrightarrow$$

$$\underset{\text{nylon salt}}{^-OC(CH_2)_4CO^-\,H_3\overset{+}{N}(CH_2)_6NH_3^+} \xrightarrow{\text{heat}} \underset{\text{Nylon 66}}{\left[C(CH_2)_4CNH(CH_2)_6NH\right]_n} + H_2O$$

the first purely synthetic fiber. Nylon 66 is so named because it is synthesized from two different organic starting materials, each of six carbon atoms.

In the synthesis of Nylon 66, hexanedioic acid (adipic acid) and 1,6-diaminohexane (hexamethylene diamine, HMDA) are dissolved in aqueous ethanol, and they react to form a one-

In the first stage of fiber production, crude Nylon 66 is melted, spun into fibers, and cooled to room temperature. Next melt-spun fibers are drawn at room temperature (cold-drawn) to about four times their original length. As the fibers are drawn, crystalline regions are oriented in the direction of the fiber axis and hydrogen bonds are formed between carbonyl oxygens of

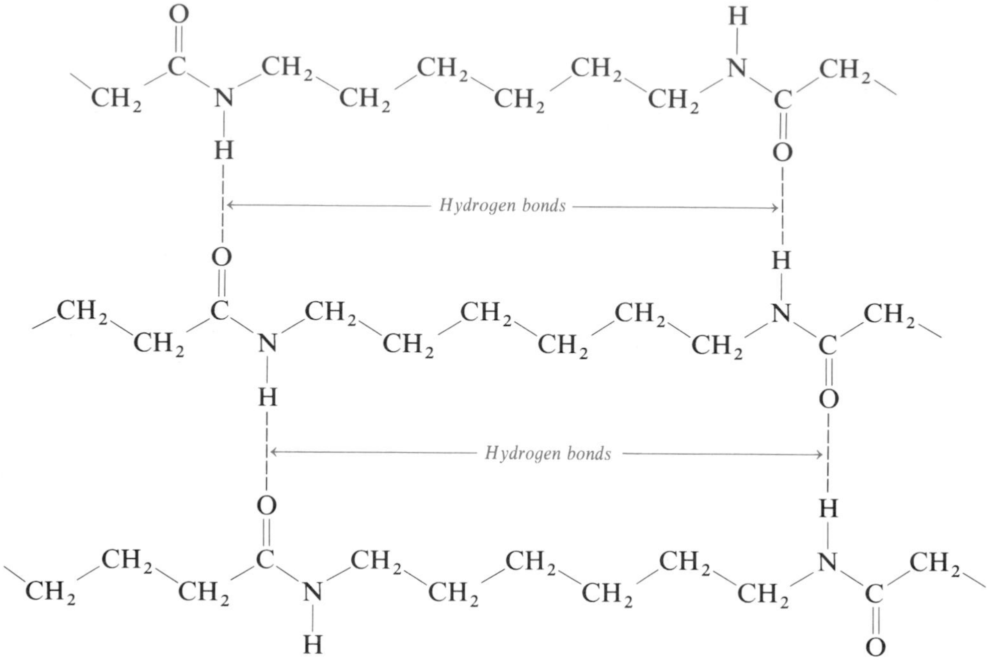

Figure XII-1 The structure of cold-drawn Nylon 66. Hydrogen bonds between adjacent chains hold molecules together.

one chain and amide hydrogens of another chain (Figure XII-1). The effects of orientation of polyamide molecules on the physical properties of the fiber are dramatic; both tensile strength and

Catalytic reduction of benzene to cyclohexane followed by air oxidation yields a mixture of cyclohexanol and cyclohexanone. Oxidation of this mixture by nitric acid gives adipic acid.

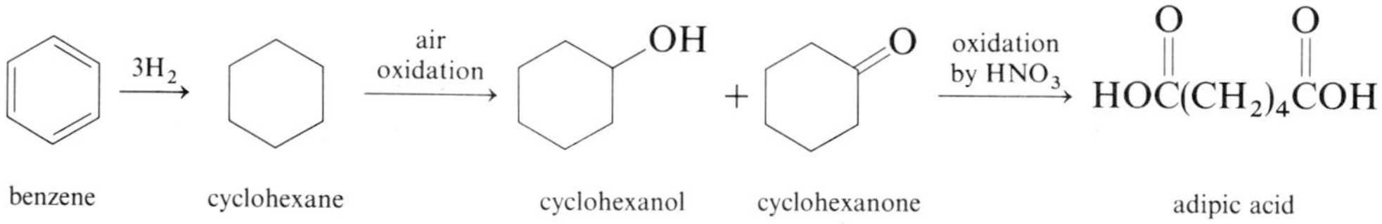

stiffness are increased markedly. Cold-drawing is important in synthetic fiber production.

When Du Pont's management decided to begin production of Nylon 66, only adipic acid was commercially available. The raw material base for the production of adipic acid was benzene.

Adipic acid was in turn the starting material for the synthesis of hexamethylenediamine. Reaction of adipic acid with ammonia gives a diammonium salt, which when heated gives adipamide. Catalytic reduction of adipamide gives hexamethylenediamine.

$$\underset{\text{adipic acid}}{HOC(CH_2)_4COH} \xrightarrow{2NH_3} \underset{\text{diammonium adipate}}{NH_4^+ \; {}^-OC(CH_2)_4CO^- \; NH_4^+} \xrightarrow{\text{heat}}$$

$$\underset{\text{adipamide}}{H_2NC(CH_2)_4CNH_2} \xrightarrow{4H_2} \underset{\text{HMDA}}{H_2N(CH_2)_6NH_2}$$

At the time, benzene was derived largely from coal, and both nitric acid and ammonia were derived from nitrogen present in air (air is approximately 80% N_2). Thus, Du Pont could rightly claim that Nylon 66 was derived from coal, air, and water.

two moles of sodium cyanide, to form 1,4-dicyano-2-butene. Reaction of this intermediate with hydrogen in the presence of a catalyst reduces both the carbon-carbon double bond and the carbon-nitrogen triple bonds and gives hexamethylenediamine.

$$\underset{\text{butadiene}}{CH_2{=}CHCH{=}CH_2} \xrightarrow{Cl_2} \underset{\substack{\text{1,4 dichloro-2-}\\\text{butene}}}{ClCH_2CH{=}CHCH_2Cl} \xrightarrow{NaCN}$$

$$\underset{\substack{\text{1,4-dicyano-2-}\\\text{butene}}}{N{\equiv}CCH_2CH{=}CHCH_2C{\equiv}N} \xrightarrow{5H_2} \underset{\text{hexamethylenediamine}}{H_2N(CH_2)_6NH_2}$$

Following World War II, Du Pont embarked on a great expansion of its Nylon 66 capacity, a move that demanded a similar expansion in facilities for producing hexamethylenediamine. The problem facing management was whether to continue to make this key starting material from benzene or to search for a more economical raw-material base and a more economical synthesis. Within a few years, Du Pont developed a new synthesis of hexamethylenediamine, using butadiene as a starting material. Recall that butadiene is a coproduct of thermal cracking of ethane and other light hydrocarbons extracted from natural gas. It is also obtained from catalytic cracking and re-forming of naphtha and other petroleum fractions.

Reaction of butadiene with chlorine under carefully controlled conditions forms 1,4-dichloro-2-butene, which is, in turn, reacted with

By the early 1950s, almost all hexamethylenediamine was being made from butadiene derived from petroleum and natural gas. The starting material for the production of adipic acid was benzene and still is. Today, however, benzene is derived almost entirely from catalytic cracking and re-forming of petroleum. Thus, the raw-material base for the synthesis of Nylon 66 has shifted from coal, air, and water to petroleum and natural gas.

Nylon 66 has been the primary nylon fiber synthesized in the United States and Canada, while that synthesized in many other parts of the world, particularly Germany, Italy and Japan is Nylon 6. The manufacture of Nylon 6 uses only one starting material, caprolactam, a six-carbon cyclic amide. The raw material base for the synthesis of caprolactam is benzene. During the synthesis of Nylon 6, caprolactam is partially hydrolyzed and heated to 250°C to drive off water and bring about polymerization.

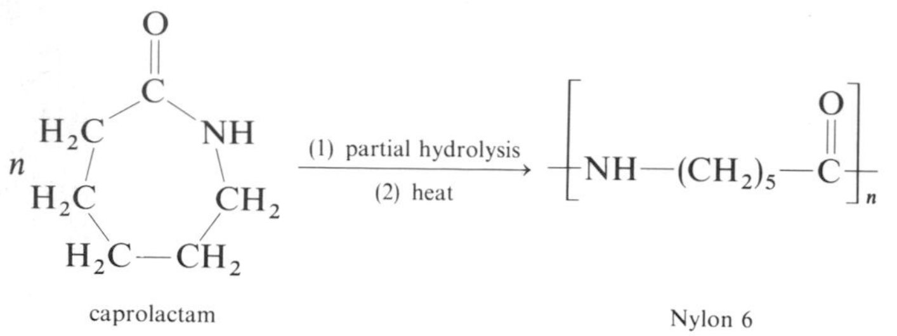

ties, and polyester condensations were reexamined. Recall that Carothers and his associates

caprolactam   Nylon 6

Why is Nylon 66 the primary nylon fiber produced in the United States and Canada and Nylon 6 the primary nylon fiber produced in Germany, Italy, and Japan? The answer lies chiefly in the availability of raw materials. In the United States and Canada, butadiene is readily available from thermal cracking of light hydrocarbons extracted from natural gas, itself a vast natural resource. Because natural gas is not so plentiful in Europe and Japan, these countries are forced to depend on petrochemicals as a raw material base for their synthesis of nylon. It is more economical for them to synthesize Nylon 6 from caprolactam than to synthesize Nylon 66 from adipic acid and hexamethylenediamine.

By the 1940s, scientists were beginning to understand some of the relationships between molecular structure and bulk physical properties, and polyester condensations were reexamined. Recall that Carothers and his associates had already concluded that the polyester fibers from aliphatic dicarboxylic acids and ethylene glycol were not suitable for textile use because they were too low-melting. Winfield and Dickson at the Calico Printers Association in England reasoned, correctly as it turned out, that a greater resistance to rotation in the polymer backbone would stiffen the polymer, raise its melting point, and thereby lead to a more acceptable polyester fiber. To create stiffness in the polymer chain, they used terephthalic acid, an aromatic dicarboxylic acid (Figure XII-2).

The crude polyester is first spun into fibers and then cold-drawn to form a textile fiber with the trade name Dacron polyester. The outstanding feature of Dacron polyester is its stiffness (about four times that of Nylon 66), very high strength, and a remarkable resistance to creasing

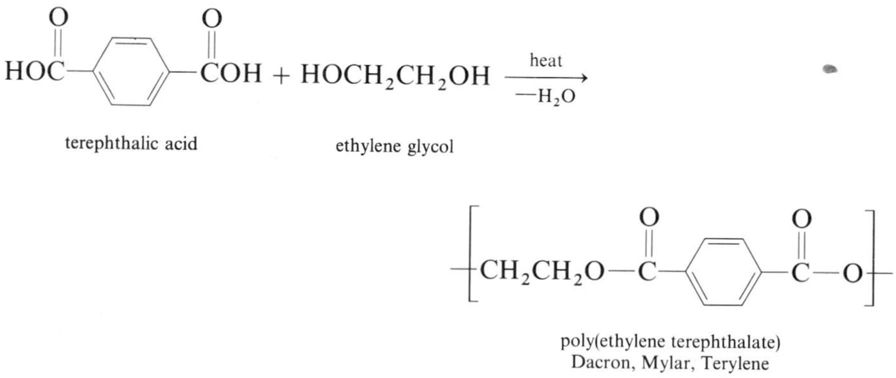

terephthalic acid   ethylene glycol

poly(ethylene terephthalate)
Dacron, Mylar, Terylene

Figure XII-2 The synthesis of Dacron polyester.

and wrinkling. Because Dacron polyesters are harsh to the touch (because of their stiffness), they are usually blended with cotton or wool to make acceptable textile fibers. Crude polyester is also fabricated into films and marketed under the trade name Mylar.

Ethylene glycol is prepared by air oxidation of ethylene followed by hydrolysis. Terephthalic acid is obtained by oxidation of *p*-xylene, an aromatic hydrocarbon obtained along with benzene and toluene from catalytic cracking and re-forming of naphtha and other petroleum fractions (Figure XII-3).

synthesized from terephthalic acid and 1,4-diaminobenzene; this was marketed under the trade name Kevlar (Figure XII-4). One of the remarkable features of Kevlar is its extremely light weight compared with other materials of similar strength. For example, a 3-in. cable woven of Kevlar has a strength equal to that of a similarly woven 3-in. steel cable. But whereas the steel cable weighs about 20 lb/ft, a comparable Kevlar cable weighs only 4 lb/ft. Kevlar now finds use in such things as anchor cables for offshore drilling rigs and reinforcement fibers for automobile tires. Kevlar can also be woven

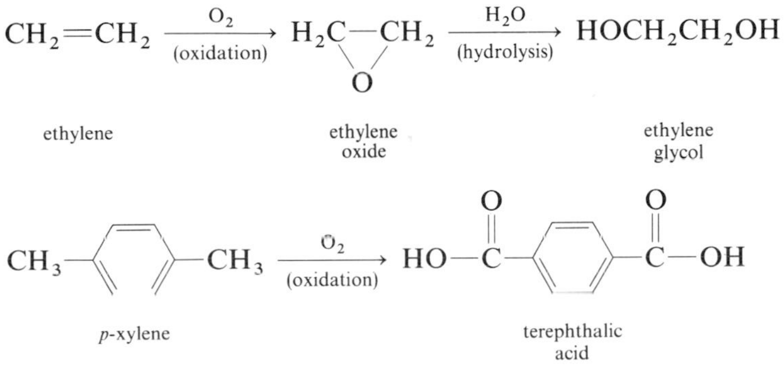

$$CH_2{=}CH_2 \xrightarrow[\text{(oxidation)}]{O_2} H_2C{-}CH_2 \xrightarrow[\text{(hydrolysis)}]{H_2O} HOCH_2CH_2OH$$

ethylene   ethylene oxide   ethylene glycol

p-xylene   terephthalic acid

Figure XII-3 The starting materials for the synthesis of Dacron polyester and Mylar are derived from petroleum and natural gas.

In 1981 production of man-made fibers in the United States exceeded 10 billion pounds. Heading the list were polyester fibers (4.8 billion pounds) and polyamide fibers (2.7 billion pounds).

The fruits of the research into the relations between molecular structure and physical properties of polymers, and of advances in fabrication techniques are nowhere better illustrated than by the polyaromatic amides (aramids) introduced by Du Pont in the early 1960s. Researchers reasoned that a polyamide composed of aromatic rings would be stiffer and stronger than a polyamide such as Nylon 66 or Nylon 6. In early 1960, Du Pont introduced a polyaromatic amide fiber

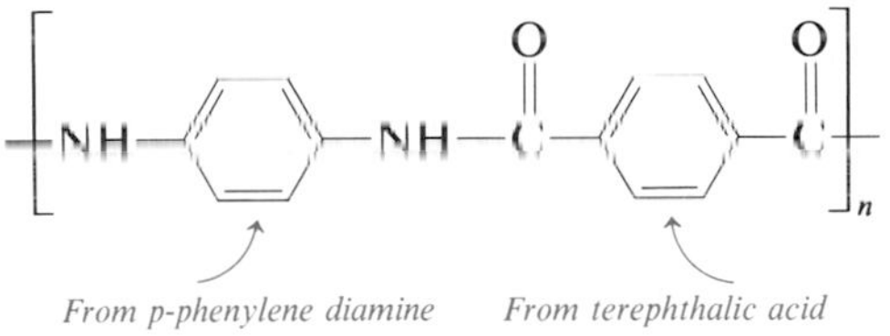

From p-phenylene diamine   *From terephthalic acid*

Figure XII-4 Kevlar, an aramid polymer.

into a fabric that stretches almost like a trampoline when struck by a bullet, absorbing the impact. Today there is a rapidly growing market among VIP's for Kevlar-lined vests, jackets, and raincoats (Figure XII-5).

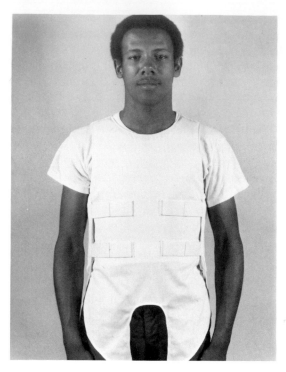

Figure XII-5 A Kevlar-lined bulletproof vest.

Sources

Anderson, B. C., Barton, L. R., and Collette, J. W. 1980. Trends in polymer development. *Science* 208:807–812.

Deanin, R. D. 1979. *New Industrial Polymers.* Washington, D.C.: American Chemical Society.

Encyclopedia of Polymer Science and Technology. 1976. New York: Wiley.

Witcoff, H. A., and Reuben, B. G. 1980. *Industrial Organic Chemicals in Perspective.* New York: Wiley.

18

Optical Isomerism

18.1 Review of Isomerism

Thus far, we have encountered three types of isomerism.

1. Structural isomers have the same molecular formula but a different order of attachment of their atoms (Section 11.2). Examples of structural isomers are pentane and 2-methylbutane; cyclohexane and 1-hexene; and ethanol and dimethyl ether.

$$CH_3CH_2CH_2CH_2CH_3 \quad \text{and} \quad CH_3\overset{\overset{\displaystyle CH_3}{|}}{C}HCH_2CH_3$$

pentane   2-methylbutane

and $CH_2{=}CHCH_2CH_2CH_2CH_3$

cyclohexane   1-hexene

$$HOCH_2CH_3 \qquad \text{and} \qquad CH_3OCH_3$$

ethanol   dimethyl ether

2. Conformational isomers have the same molecular formula and the same order of attachment of atoms, but a different arrangement of their atoms in space. Further, they are readily interconvertible by rotation about carbon-carbon single bonds (Section 11.6). Examples of conformational isomers are the eclipsed and staggered forms of butane.

eclipsed butane   and   staggered butane

3. Cis-trans isomers, like conformational isomers, have the same molecular formula and the same order of attachment of atoms, but different orientation of atoms in space. Unlike conformational isomers, cis-trans isomers cannot be interconverted by rotation about carbon-carbon single bonds. We have encountered cis-trans isomerism in two different types of molecules—cycloalkanes and alkenes. All cycloalkanes with different substituents on two or more carbon atoms of the ring show cis-trans isomerism (Section 11.7). Examples are the cis and trans isomers of 1,4-dimethylcyclohexane.

cis-1,4-dimethylcyclohexane   trans-1,4-dimethylcyclohexane

All alkenes in which each carbon of the double bond has two different substituents show cis-trans isomerism (Section 12.3). Examples are the cis and trans isomers of 2-butene.

cis-2-butene   trans-2-butene

A fourth type of isomerism is known as **optical isomerism**. It is called optical isomerism because of the effects these isomers have on the plane of polarized light (Section 18.4). The structural feature responsible for optical isomerism is chirality.

18.2 Molecules with One Chiral Center

A. Chiral Molecules and Enantiomers

Every object in nature has a **mirror image**. Shown in Figure 18.1 are stereo-representations of a lactic acid molecule and its mirror image. All bond angles about the central carbon are approximately 109.5° and the four bonds from this carbon create the shape of a regular tetrahedron (Section 4.5C). The question is, What is the relation between these two structural formulas? Do they represent the same compound or different compounds? The answer is that they represent different compounds. The lactic acid molecule drawn in Figure 18.1(a) can be turned any direction in space, but so long as no bonds are broken and rearranged, only two of the four groups attached to the central carbon can be made to coincide with those in 18.1(b), as shown in Figure 18.2.

The mirror images of lactic acid differ from each other just as a right hand differs from a left hand. They are related by reflection, but **not superposable** on

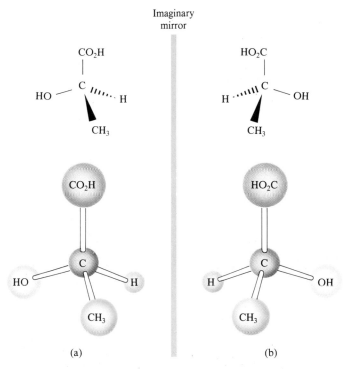

Figure 18.1 Stereorepresentations and ball-and-stick models of (a) a lactic acid molecule and (b) its mirror image. In these drawings, — represents a bond in the plane of the page, ◀ represents a bond projecting in front of the plane of the page, and ⅲⅲ represents a bond projecting behind the plane of the page.

each other. (Superposable objects can be placed one over the other so that all like parts coincide).

Objects that are not identical with their mirror images are said to be **chiral** (pronounced ki-ral, to rhyme with spiral; from the Greek *cheir*, hand). All chiral molecules show optical isomerism. In the molecules we will deal with in this chapter, chirality and hence optical isomerism arise because there is at least one carbon atom in the molecule that has four different groups attached to it. A carbon atom that has four different groups attached to it is called a chiral carbon, or alternatively, an **asymmetric carbon**.

Example 18.1

Which of these molecules contain chiral (asymmetric) carbons?

a. $CH_3CH_2CH_2CH_2OH$

b. $CH_3CH_2\overset{\displaystyle OH}{\overset{\displaystyle |}{C}}HCH_3$

c. (cyclohexane with CH_3)

d. $CH_3CH{=}CHCH_2CH_3$

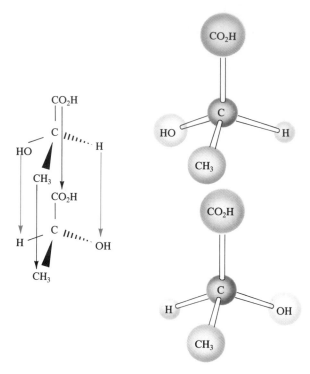

Figure 18.2 A molecule of lactic acid and its mirror image are not superposable on each other. No matter how the mirror image is turned in space, only two of the four groups attached to the central carbon can be made to coincide.

$$
\begin{array}{cc}
& O \\
& \| \\
\text{e. } & CH_3CCH_2CH_2CH_2CH_3
\end{array}
\qquad
\begin{array}{c}
O \\
\| \\
\text{f. } CH_3CCH_2CHCH_2CH_3 \\
\qquad\qquad\quad | \\
\qquad\qquad\quad CH_3
\end{array}
$$

Solution   To be chiral (asymmetric), a carbon atom must have four different groups attached to it.

a. 1-butanol. There is no chiral (asymmetric) carbon atom in this molecule.

b. 2-butanol. Carbon 2 has four different groups attached to it and is therefore a chiral (asymmetric) carbon atom.

$$
\begin{array}{c}
OH \qquad \text{\textit{A chiral carbon atom}} \\
| \\
CH_3-CH_2-C-CH_3 \\
| \\
H
\end{array}
$$

c. Methylcyclohexane. No chiral carbon atoms.

d. 2-pentene. No chiral carbon atoms.

e. 2-hexanone. No chiral carbon atoms.

f. 4-methyl-2-hexanone contains one chiral carbon atom.

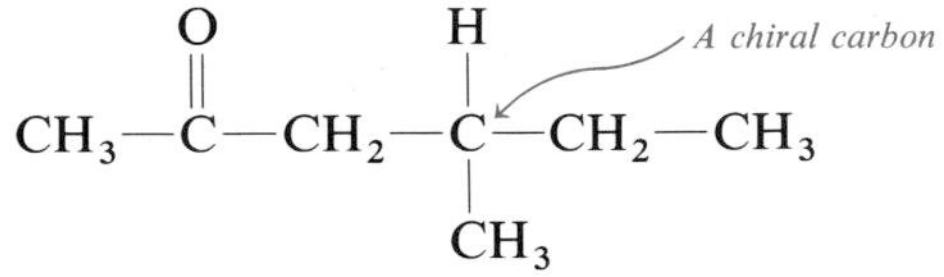

$$CH_3-\overset{\overset{\displaystyle O}{\|}}{C}-CH_2-\overset{\overset{\displaystyle H}{|}}{\underset{\underset{\displaystyle CH_3}{|}}{C}}-CH_2-CH_3 \quad \textit{A chiral carbon}$$

Problem 18.1

Which molecules contain chiral (asymmetric) carbons?

a. 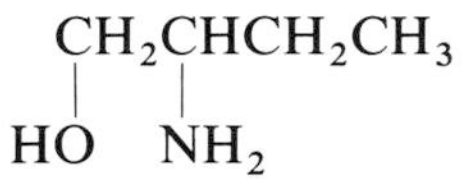 $CH_2CHCH_2CH_3$
    $\quad\quad|\quad\;\;|$
    $\quad\;\;HO\;\;NH_2$

b. 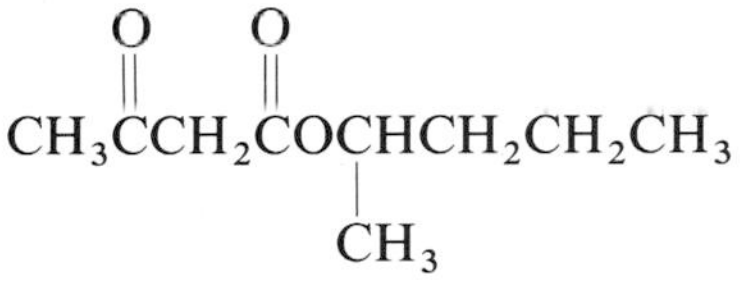 $CH_3\overset{\overset{\displaystyle O}{\|}}{C}CH_2\overset{\overset{\displaystyle O}{\|}}{C}OCHCH_2CH_2CH_3$
    $\quad\quad\quad\quad\quad\quad\quad\quad|$
    $\quad\quad\quad\quad\quad\quad\quad\;\;CH_3$

c. $CH_3CH_2\overset{\overset{\displaystyle OH}{|}}{C}HCH{=}CH_2$

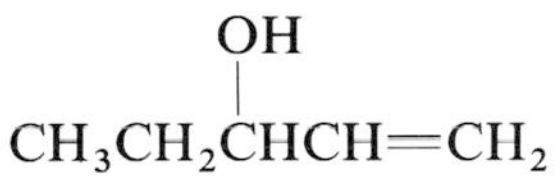

d.

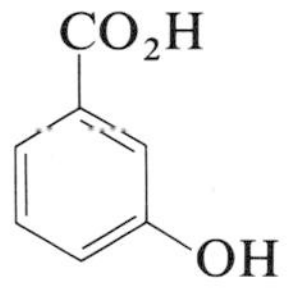

We use the term **enantiomer** (Greek, *enantios*, opposite, and *meros*, parts) to refer to molecules that are not superposable on their mirror images. Enantiomers always come in pairs; the molecule and its nonsuperposable mirror image. Many of the properties of enantiomers are identical; they have the same melting points, the same boiling points, the same solubility in solvents. Yet they are isomers, and we must expect them to show some differences in their properties. One important difference is their effect on the plane of polarized light.

Example 18.2

Draw stereorepresentations for the enantiomers of:

a. 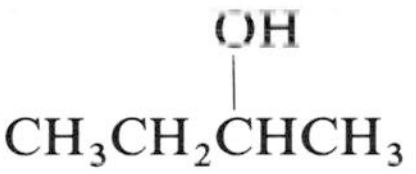 $CH_3CH_2\overset{\overset{\displaystyle OH}{|}}{C}HCH_3$

b. 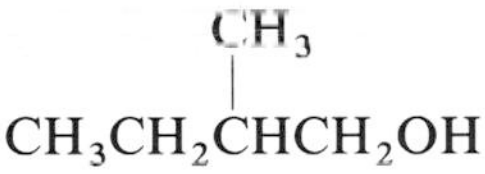 $CH_3CH_2\overset{\overset{\displaystyle CH_3}{|}}{C}HCH_2OH$

Solution

First locate and draw the chiral (asymmetric) carbon atom and the four bonds from it arranged to show the tetrahedral geometry. Next, draw the four groups attached to the chiral carbon. Finally, draw the nonsuperposable mirror image.

a. 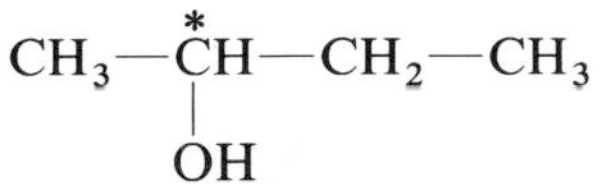 $CH_3-\overset{*}{\overset{\displaystyle |}{\underset{\underset{\displaystyle OH}{|}}{C}}}H-CH_2-CH_3$

Mirror

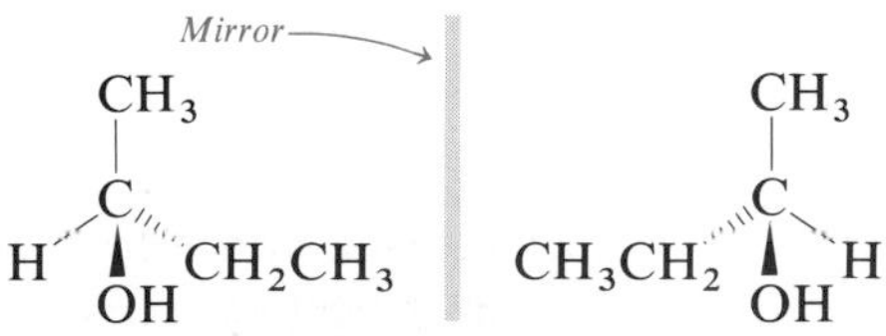

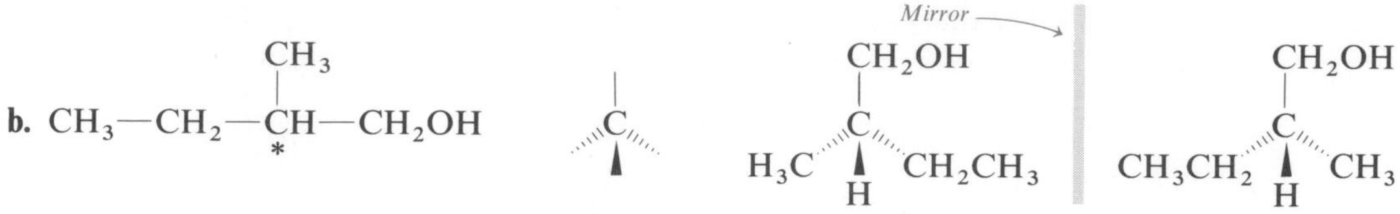

b. CH_3—CH_2—$\overset{*}{CH}$—CH_2OH

with CH_3 group at top

(the chiral carbon
atom marked by an
asterisk)

tetrahedral
geometry of
the chiral
carbon

Mirror

CH_2OH

H_3C —C— CH_2CH_3
        H

CH_2OH

CH_3CH_2 —C— CH_3
           H

a pair of enantiomers
(nonsuperposable mirror images)

**Problem
18.2**

Draw stereorepresentations for the enantiomers of:

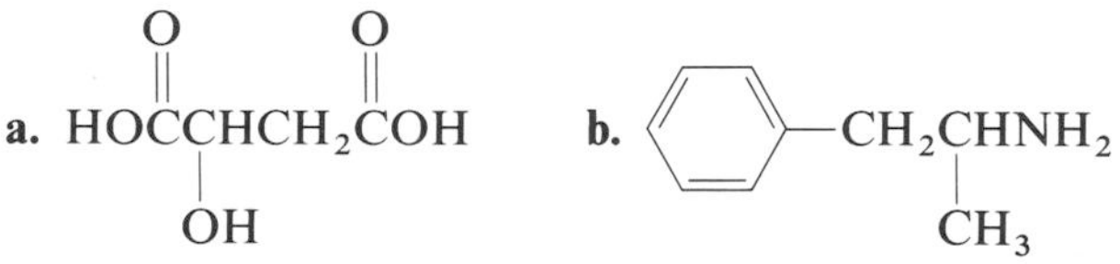

a. $\overset{O}{\overset{\|}{HOC}}CH\overset{O}{\overset{\|}{CH_2COH}}$
   $\underset{OH}{|}$

malic acid

b. ⬡—$CH_2\overset{}{CHNH_2}$
        $\underset{CH_3}{|}$

amphetamine

B. Achiral Molecules

For all molecules that contain a single chiral carbon atom, the mirror images are nonsuperposable and the compounds show enantiomerism. For achiral (without chirality) compounds, however, the molecule and its mirror image are superposable. Consider, for example, the amino acid glycine. Figure 18.3 shows stereorepresentations of (a) glycine and (b) its mirror image. The question is, What is the relation between the two? Are they superposable or nonsuperposable? The answer is that they are superposable. One way to see this is to turn (b) by 180° about the C—CO$_2$H bond. When this is done, it is possible to place (b) on top of (a) in such a way that all like groups coincide. Molecules that are superposable on their mirror images are identical and therefore do not show chirality; they are achiral (without handedness); achiral molecules do not show optical isomerism.

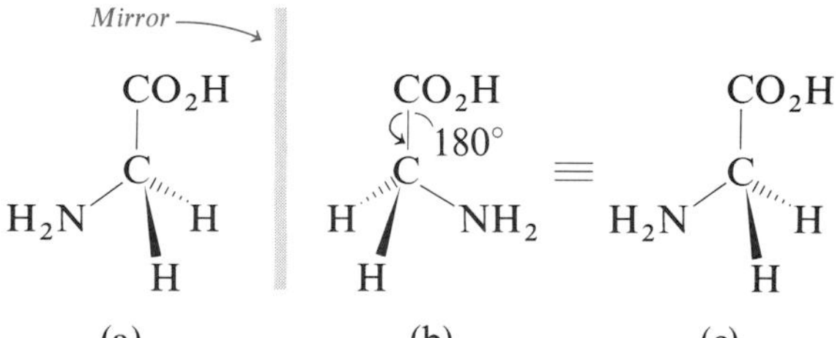

Mirror

CO_2H

H_2N —C— H
        H

(a)

CO_2H
  ↶ 180°
H —C— NH_2
     H

(b)

≡

CO_2H

H_2N —C— H
        H

(c)

Figure 18.3 Stereorepresentations of (a) glycine and (b) its mirror image. If (b) is turned by 180° about the C—CO$_2$H bond (c), it becomes superposable on and hence identical to (a). Glycine does not show chirality.

C. Plane of Symmetry

A **plane of symmetry** is defined as a plane (often visualized as a mirror) cleaving an object in such a way that one side of the object is the mirror image of the other. Illustrated in Figure 18.4 are planes of symmetry in a chair and a cup. The

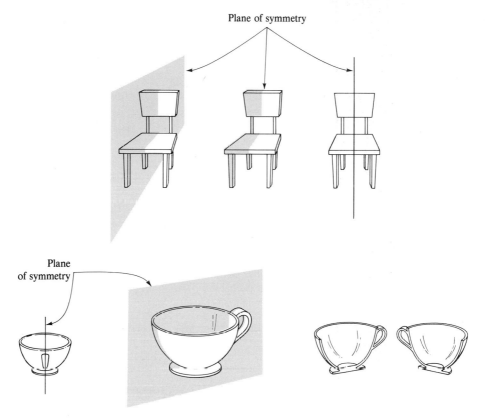

Figure 18.4 Planes of symmetry in a chair and a cup. The plane of symmetry in each object divides it so that one side is the mirror image of the other side.

plane of symmetry in the chair passes vertically through it and divides it so that one half is the mirror reflection of the other half. In the cup, the plane of symmetry passes through the handle.

Shown in Figure 18.5 is a stereorepresentation of glycine. The plane of symmetry in this molecule runs through the axis of the C—C—N bonds.

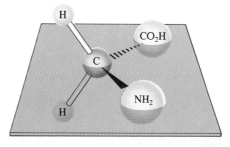

Figure 18.5 A stereorepresentation of glycine. The plane of symmetry in this molecule runs through the axis of the C—C—N bonds.

18.3 How to Predict Optical Isomerism

There are three methods you can use to determine whether a molecule shows optical isomerism.

1. The first and most direct test is to build a model of the molecule and one of its mirror image. If the two are superposable and therefore identical, then the molecule does not show optical isomerism; it has no enantiomer. If the two are nonsuperposable, the molecule shows optical isomerism; it can exist as a pair of enantiomers.

2. A second test is to look for a plane of symmetry. If the molecule has a plane of symmetry, it and its mirror image are superposable. It has no enantiomer and does not show optical isomerism. If there is no plane of symmetry, the molecule has a nonsuperposable mirror image; it can exist as a pair of enantiomers and shows optical isomerism.

3. A third and perhaps the simplest test is to look for a chiral (asymmetric) carbon atom. If the molecule has a chiral carbon atom, it has a nonsuperposable mirror image and shows optical isomerism.

You should arrive at the same answer from whichever test you apply. For example, if you conclude from test 3 that a molecule is chiral and shows optical isomerism, then you should arrive at the same conclusion from both tests 1 and 2 and vice versa.

Example 18.3

Which of the following molecules show optical isomerism? For each that does, label the chiral carbon and draw stereorepresentations for the pair of enantiomers. For each that does not, draw a stereorepresentation to show the plane of symmetry.

$$\overset{\displaystyle OH}{\underset{\displaystyle |}{}}$$

a. $CH_2\!=\!CHCHCH_2CH_3$

$$\overset{\displaystyle OH}{\underset{\displaystyle |}{}}$$

b. $CH_3CH_2CHCH_2CH_3$

$$\overset{\displaystyle OH}{\underset{\displaystyle |}{}}$$

c. $CH_3CH_2CHCH_2CH_2OH$

Solution

Both (a) and (c) have chiral carbon atoms and show optical isomerism. Compound (b) has no chiral carbon and does not show optical isomerism.

Mirror

a. $CH_2\!=\!CH$ ... CH_2CH_3 ... CH_3CH_2 ... $CH\!=\!CH_2$

Chiral carbon atom

b. CH_3CH_2 ... CH_2CH_3

The plane of symmetry bisects the molecule through the O—C—H bonds

c.

$$CH_2CH_3$$

$$HO \overset{C}{\underset{H}{|}} CH_2CH_2OH$$

$$CH_2CH_3$$

$$HOCH_2CH_2 \overset{C}{\underset{H}{|}} OH$$ — *Chiral carbon atom*

Problem 18.3

Which of the following molecules show optical isomerism? For each that does, label the chiral carbon and draw stereorepresentations for the pair of enantiomers. For each that does not, draw a stereorepresentation to show the plane of symmetry.

a. CH_3CHCO_2H
$\qquad\quad |$
$\qquad\quad NH_2$

b.

$$OH$$
$$|$$
$$CHCH_3$$

c.

$$CH_3$$
$$OH$$

18.4 How Optical Isomerism Is Detected in the Laboratory

A. Plane-Polarized Light

Ordinary light consists of waves vibrating in all planes perpendicular to its path (Figure 18.6). Certain materials, such as Polaroid sheet, a plastic film containing properly oriented crystals of an organic substance embedded in it, selectively transmit light waves vibrating in one specific plane. Light that vibrates in only one specific plane is said to be **plane-polarized**.

If you place a polarizing disc in the path of plane-polarized light so that its polarizing axis is parallel to the axis of the plane-polarized light, the maximum

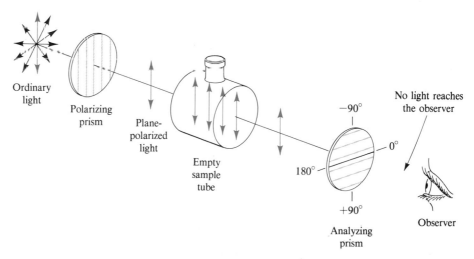

Figure 18.6 Schematic diagram of a polarimeter with the sample tube empty.

intensity of light passes through to you. If, however, the axis of the polarizing lens is perpendicular (that is, at an angle of 90°) to the axis of the polarized light, the minimum of polarized light passes through to you.

No doubt you are familiar with the effect of polarizing sheets on light from your experiences with sunglasses or camera filters made of this material. Polaroid sunglasses are particularly effective in blocking glare from water, windows, and other reflective surfaces. Glare is largely light polarized by the surface from which it is reflected, and if you rotate your head so that the polarizing axis of your Polaroid sunglasses is perpendicular to the axis of the polarized light, the glare will not pass through the lens.

B. The Polarimeter

A **polarimeter** consists of a light source, a polarizing prism, a sample tube, and an analyzing prism (Figure 18.6). If the sample tube is empty, the intensity of light reaching an observer is the maximum when the polarizing axes of the two prisms are parallel. If the analyzing prism is turned either clockwise or counterclockwise, less light is transmitted. When the axis of the analyzing prism is at right angles to the axis of the polarizing prism, the field of view is dark. This position is taken as 0° on the optical scale.

A polarimeter is used in the laboratory to detect and measure optical activity. One of the effects of an optically active compound is that it has the ability to rotate the plane of plane-polarized light, as can be observed in the following way. First, an empty sample tube is placed in the polarimeter and the analyzing prism is adjusted so that no light passes through to the observer, that is, it is set to 0°. When a solution of optically active compound is placed in the sample tube, a certain amount of light is observed now to pass through the analyzing

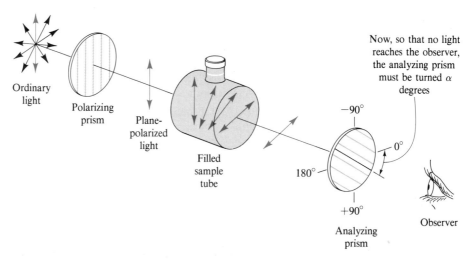

Figure 18.7 Schematic diagram of a polarimeter with the sample tube containing a solution of an optically active compound. The analyzing prism has been turned clockwise by α degrees to restore the dark field.

prism; the optically active compound has rotated the plane of light from the polarizing prism, so it is now no longer at an angle of 90° to the analyzing prism. Turning the analyzing prism a few degrees either clockwise or counterclockwise restores darkness to the field of view (Figure 18.7). The number of degrees α through which the analyzing prism must be turned to restore darkness to the field of view is called the **observed rotation**. If the analyzing prism must be turned to the right (clockwise) to restore darkness, then we say that the compound is **dextrorotatory** (Latin, *dexter*, on the right side). If the analyzing prism must be turned to the left (counterclockwise), then the compound, we say, is **levorotatory** (Latin, *laevus*, on the left side). In either case, the compound is optically active. Because of this effect of chiral compounds on the plane of polarized light, they are said to be **optically active** and to show **optical isomerism**.

C. Specific Rotation

Specific rotation $[\alpha]$ is defined as the rotation caused by a compound at a concentration of 1 g/mL in a sample tube 10 cm long. Specific rotation depends on the temperature and the wavelength of the light source, and these values must be reported as a part of the measurement. The most common light source is the D line of sodium, the same line that is responsible for the yellow color of excited sodium vapor lamps. It is common in reporting either observed or specific rotation to indicate a dextrorotatory compound by a positive sign ($+$) and a levorotatory compound by a negative sign ($-$). By these conventions, the specific rotation of sucrose (table sugar) dissolved in water at 25°C, with the D line of sodium as the light source, is reported in the following way:

$$[\alpha]_D^{25°C} - +66.5° \text{ (H}_2\text{O)}$$

Enantiomers are different compounds and have different properties; and one important difference is their optical activity. One member of a pair of enantiomers is dextrorotatory and the other is levorotatory. For each, the number of degrees of the specific rotation is the same, but the sign is different, as illustrated by the dextro- and levorotatory isomers of 2-butanol.

$$\text{CH}_3-\overset{\overset{\displaystyle \text{OH}}{\displaystyle |}}{\underset{\underset{\displaystyle \text{H}}{\displaystyle |}}{\text{C}}}-\text{CH}_2-\text{CH}_3$$

($+$)-2-butanol $[\alpha]_D^{20°C} = +13.9°$
($-$)-2-butanol $[\alpha]_D^{20°C} = -13.9°$

18.5 Racemic Mixtures

Lactic acid (Figure 18.1) was one of the first optically active compounds detected. It was originally isolated in 1780 from sour milk and found to be optically inactive; its specific rotation was 0°. In 1807, lactic acid was isolated from muscle tissue. It was found to be dextrorotatory and was designated (+)-lactic acid. We have already demonstrated that lactic acid shows optical isomerism. How can it be, then, that lactic acid from fermentation of milk is optically inactive while the lactic acid from muscle is optically active and dextrorotatory? The answer is that optically inactive lactic acid from fermentation of milk contains equal numbers of dextrorotatory and levorotatory molecules, and therefore has a rotation of 0°. A mixture containing equal amounts of a pair of enantiomers is called a **racemic mixture**.

18.6 Molecules with Two or More Chiral Centers

A. Enantiomers and Diastereomers

Compounds that contain two or more chiral (asymmetric) carbons can exist in more than two optical isomers. The maximum number of optical isomers is 2^n, where n is the number of chiral carbons. Consider, as an example, 2,3,4-trihydroxybutanal, a molecule that contains two chiral carbons, marked by asterisks:

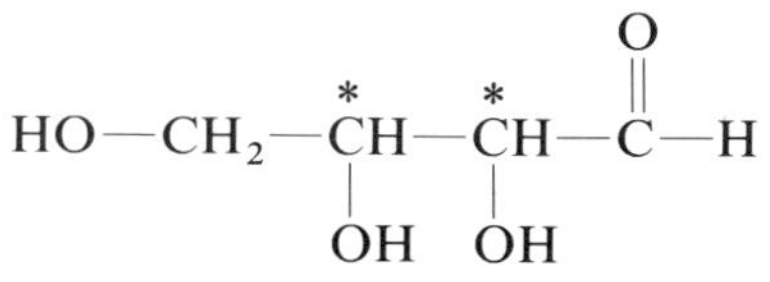

$$HO-CH_2-\overset{*}{C}H-\overset{*}{C}H-\overset{\overset{O}{\|}}{C}-H$$
$$\qquad\qquad \underset{OH}{|}\ \ \underset{OH}{|}$$

2,3,4-trihydroxybutanal

There are $2^2 = 4$ optical isomers of this compound, each of which is drawn in Figure 18.8. Formulas A and B are nonsuperposable mirror images and represent one pair of enantiomers. Formulas C and D are also nonsuperposable mirror images and represent a second pair of enantiomers. We can describe the optical isomers of this compound by saying that they consist of two pairs of enantiomers.

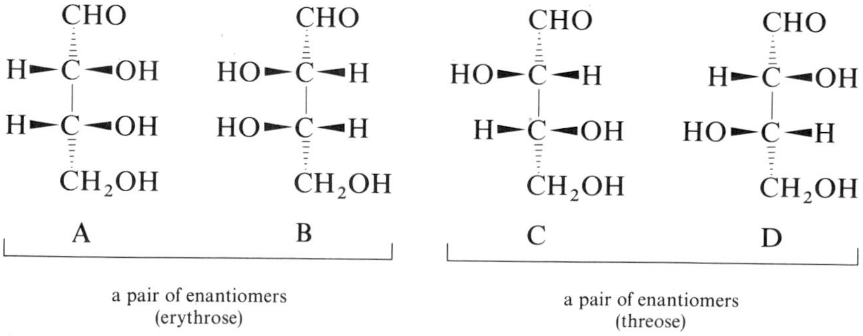

CHO	CHO	CHO	CHO
H►C◄OH	HO►C◄H	HO►C◄H	H►C◄OH
H►C◄OH	HO►C◄H	H►C◄OH	HO►C◄H
CH$_2$OH	CH$_2$OH	CH$_2$OH	CH$_2$OH
A	B	C	D

a pair of enantiomers (erythrose)   a pair of enantiomers (threose)

Figure 18.8 The four optical isomers of 2,3,4-trihydroxybutanal, a compound with two chiral carbons.

We know what the relation is between A and B, and between C and D; they are enantiomers. But how do we describe the relation between A and C and between A and D? The answer is that they are diastereomers. **Diastereomers** are optical isomers that are not mirror images of each other. Thus, for 2,3,4-trihydroxybutanal, A is the diastereomer of C and D; C is the diastereomer of A and B; and so on. Diastereomers have different physical and chemical properties and are sometimes given different names. The diastereomers of 2,3,4-trihydroxybutanal are given the common names erythrose and threose.

B. Meso Compounds

Certain molecules have special symmetry properties that reduce the number of optical isomers to fewer than what is predicted by the 2^n rule. One such example is tartaric acid. Both carbons 2 and 3 of this molecule are chiral (each has four different groups attached to it), and the 2^n rule predicts four optical isomers. In fact, only three optical isomers of this formula are known (Figure 18.9). Formulas E and F are nonsuperposable mirror images and represent a pair of enantiomers. Formulas G and H are mirror images of each other but are superposable. One way to see the superposability of G and H is to turn H by 180° in the plane of the page. When this is done, H can be made to lie on top of G, and all like groups coincide. Therefore, G and H are the same molecule and do not represent a pair of enantiomers.

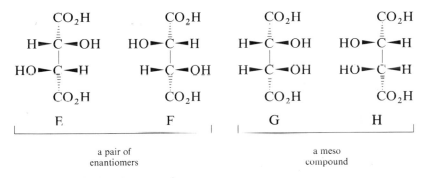

a pair of enantiomers	a meso compound

Figure 18.9 The three optical isomers of tartaric acid.

A structure that contains two or more chiral carbons but is superposable on its mirror image is called a **meso compound**. A meso compound is said to be an optical isomer even though it has no effect on the plane of polarized light. The physical properties of the three optical isomers of tartaric acid are given in Table 18.1.

Table 18.1 Physical properties of the optical isomers of tartaric acid.

Acid	mp (°C)	$[\alpha]_D^{25°}$
(+)-tartaric acid	170	+12°
(−)-tartaric acid	170	−12°
meso-tartaric acid	140	0°

18.7 Significance of Chirality in the Biological World

Except for inorganic salts and a relatively few low-molecular-weight organic molecules, most molecules in living organisms, both plant and animal, are chiral. Although these molecules can exist as a mixture of optical isomers, almost invariably only one optical isomer is found in nature. There are, of course, instances where more than one optical isomer is found, but these rarely exist together in the same biological system.

We can generalize further that only one enantiomer can be metabolized by an organism. Louis Pasteur discovered in 1858–1860, as one example of this phenomenon, that when *Penicillium glaucum*, a green mold found in aging cheese and rotting fruit, is grown in a solution containing racemic tartaric acid, the solution slowly becomes levorotatory. Pasteur concluded that the microorganism preferentially metabolizes (+)-tartaric acid. If the process is interrupted at the right time, (−)-tartaric acid can be crystallized from solution in pure form. If the process is allowed to continue, however, the microorganism eventually metabolizes (−)-tartaric acid as well. Thus while both enantiomers are metabolized by *Penicillium glaucum*, the (+)-enantiomer is metabolized much more rapidly.

A. Chirality in the Biological World

The generalization that only one enantiomer is found in a given biological system and one enantiomer is metabolized in preference to the other should be enough to convince us that we live in a chiral world. At least it is chiral at the molecular level. Essentially all chemical reactions in the biological world take place in a chiral environment. Perhaps the most conspicuous examples of chirality among biological molecules are the enzymes, all of which have multiple centers of chirality. An illustration is chymotrypsin, an enzyme that functions very efficiently in the intestine of animals at pH 7–8 in catalyzing the digestion of proteins. Chymotrypsin contains 251 separate chiral carbon atoms. The number of possible optical isomers is 2^{251}, a number large beyond comprehension. Fortunately nature does not squander its precious energies and resources unnecessarily; only one of these optical isomers is produced and used by any given organism.

B. How an Enzyme Distinguishes between a Molecule and Its Enantiomer

Enzymes catalyze biological reactions by first adsorbing on their surfaces the molecule or molecules about to undergo reaction. These molecules may be held on the enzyme surface by a combination of hydrogen bonds, ionic bonds, dispersion forces, or even covalent bonds. Thus, whether the molecules about to undergo reaction are chiral or not, they are held in a chiral environment.

It is generally agreed that an enzyme with specific binding site for three of the four substituents on a chiral carbon can distinguish between a molecule and its enantiomer or diastereomer. Assume for example that an enzyme involved in catalyzing a reaction of glyceraldehyde has three binding sites, one specific for —H, another specific for —OH, and the third specific for —CHO. Assume further that the three sites are arranged on the enzyme surface as shown in Figure 18.10. The enzyme can "recognize" (+)-glyceraldehyde (the natural or biologically active form) and distinguish it from (−)-glyceraldehyde, because the correct enantiomer can be adsorbed with three groups attached to their appropriate binding sites; the other enantiomer can, at best, bind to only two of these sites.

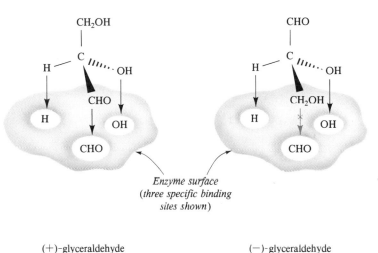

(+)-glyceraldehyde   (−)-glyceraldehyde

Figure 18.10 A schematic diagram of an enzyme surface capable of interacting with (+)-glyceraldehyde at three specific binding sites, but with (−)-glyceraldehyde at only two of these sites.

Since interactions between molecules in living systems take place in a chiral environment, it should be no surprise that a molecule and its enantiomer have different physiological properties. It should be no surprise that *Penicillium glaucum* selectively metabolizes (+)-tartaric acid compared with (−)-tartaric acid; or that (+)-leucine tastes sweet, and its enantiomer (−)-leucine has a bitter taste.

(+)-leucine
$[\alpha]_D^{25°C} = +10.42°$

(−)-leucine
$[\alpha]_D^{25°C} = -10.42°$

That the interactions between molecules in the biological world are very specific in stereochemistry is not surprising, but just how these interactions take place at the molecular level with such precision and efficiency is one of the great puzzles that modern science has only recently begun to unravel.

Key Terms and Concepts

asymmetric carbon (18.2A)

chiral (18.2A)

cis-trans isomerism (introduction)

conformational isomerism
   (introduction)

dextrorotatory (18.4B)

diastereomer (18.6A)

enantiomer (18.2A)

levorotatory (18.4B)

meso compound (18.6B)

mirror image (18.2A)

nonsuperposable mirror image (18.2A)

observed rotation (18.4B)

optical activity (18.4B)

optical isomerism (introduction and
   18.4B)

plane of symmetry (18.2C)

plane-polarized light (18.4A)

polarimeter (18.4B)

racemic mixture (18.5)

specific rotation (18.4C)

structural isomerism (introduction)

Problems

Molecules with one chiral center (Sections 18.2 and 18.3)

18.4   Draw mirror images for the following:

a.   b. $H \blacktriangleright \overset{\text{CHO}}{\underset{\text{CH}_2\text{OH}}{C}} \blacktriangleleft OH$ c. $H_2N \blacktriangleright \overset{\text{CO}_2\text{H}}{\underset{\text{CH}_3}{C}} \blacktriangleleft H$

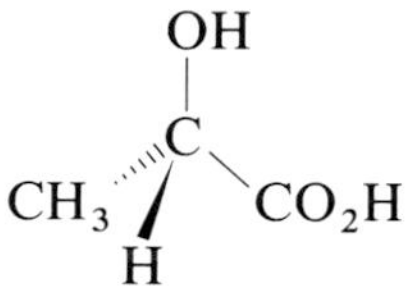

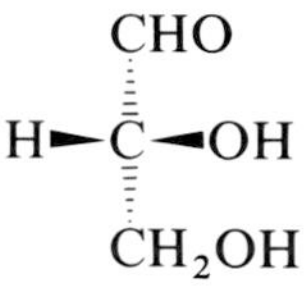

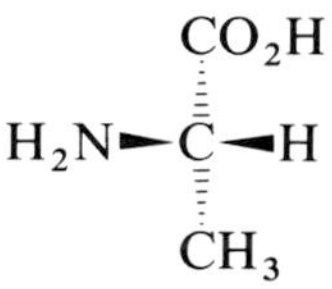

d. 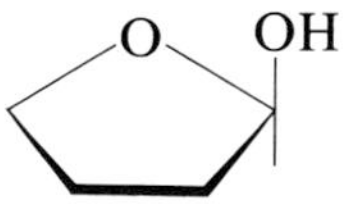   e.    f.

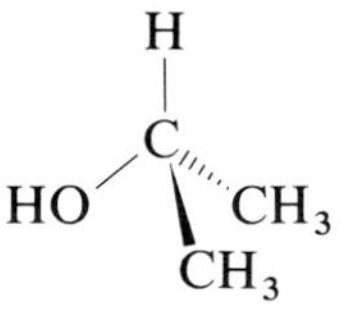

18.5   Following are several stereorepresentations of lactic acid. Take (a) as a reference structure. Which of the stereorepresentations are identical to (a) and which are mirror images of (a)?

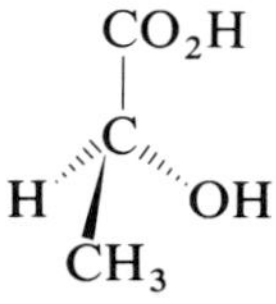

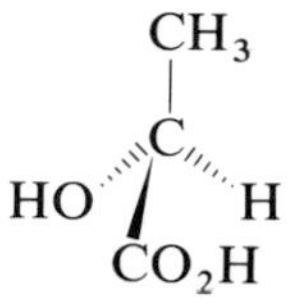

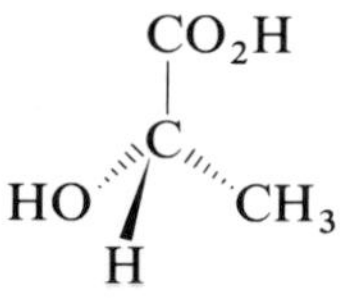

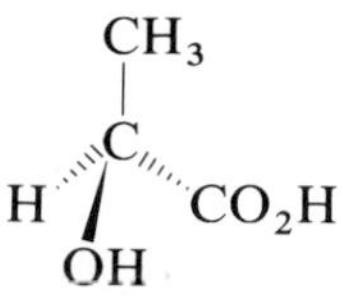

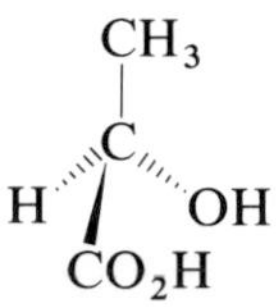

18.6 Which of the following molecules contain a chiral carbon? For each that does, draw stereorepresentations for both enantiomers.

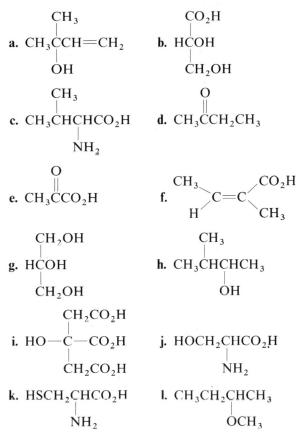

a. CH₃CCH=CH₂ with CH₃ above and OH below

b. HCOH with CO₂H above and CH₂OH below

c. CH₃CHCHCO₂H with CH₃ above and NH₂ below

d. CH₃CCH₂CH₃ with O (double bond) above

e. CH₃CCO₂H with O (double bond) above

f. CH₃/H—C=C—CO₂H/CH₃

g. HCOH with CH₂OH above and CH₂OH below

h. CH₃CHCHCH₃ with CH₃ above and OH below

i. HO—C—CO₂H with CH₂CO₂H above and CH₂CO₂H below

j. HOCH₂CHCO₂H with NH₂ below

k. HSCH₂CHCO₂H with NH₂ below

l. CH₃CH₂CHCH₃ with OCH₃ below

18.7 Draw the structural formula of at least one alkene of molecular formula C₅H₉Br that shows:
a. neither cis-trans isomerism nor optical isomerism.
b. cis trans isomerism but not optical isomerism
c. optical isomerism but not cis-trans isomerism.
d. both cis-trans isomerism and optical isomerism.

Molecules with two or more chiral carbons (Section 18.6)

18.8 Mark each chiral carbon in the molecules with an asterisk:

a. 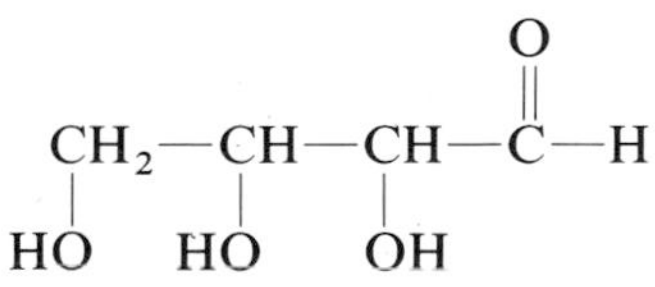 CH₂—CH—CH—C—H with HO, HO, OH below and O (double bond) above the C

b. H—C—CO₂H with CH₂CO₂H above and HO—CH—CO₂H below

c. CH₃CH₂CHCHCOH with CH₃ and O above and NH₂ below

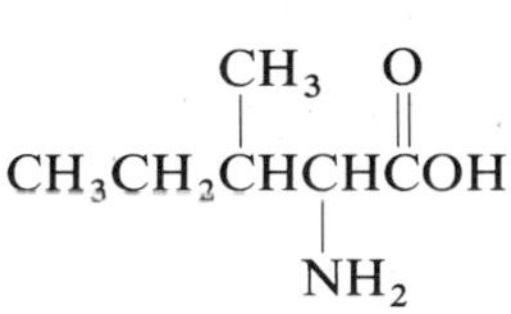

d. 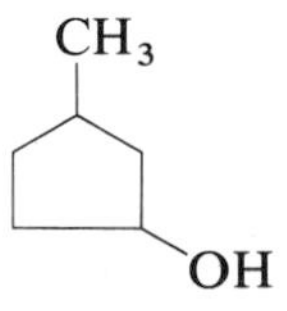 cyclopentane ring with CH₃ and OH substituents

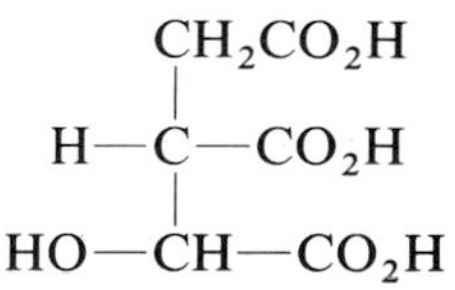

e.

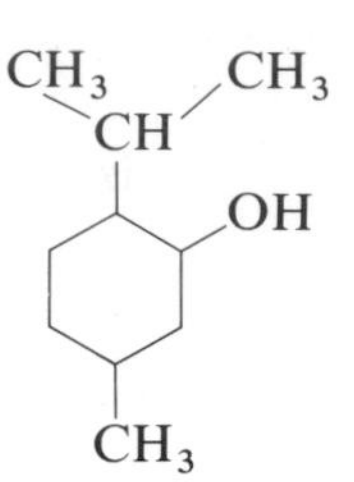

f.

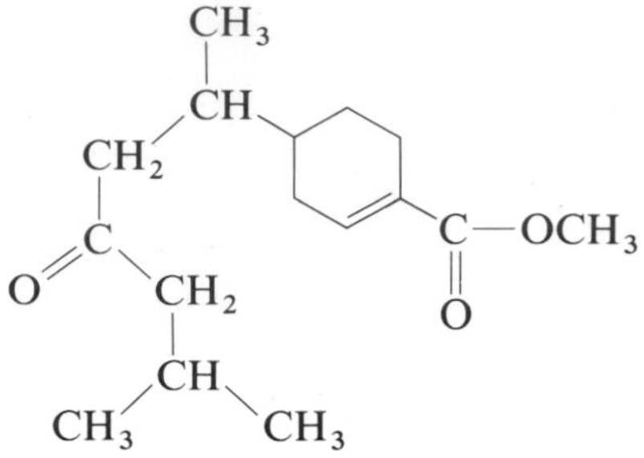

g.

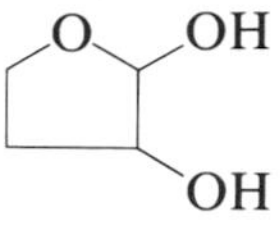

h.

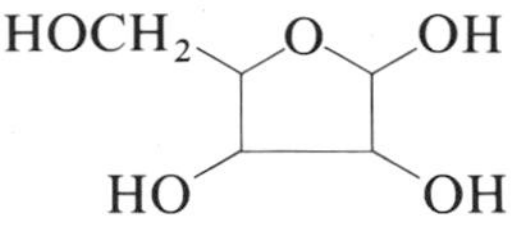

i.

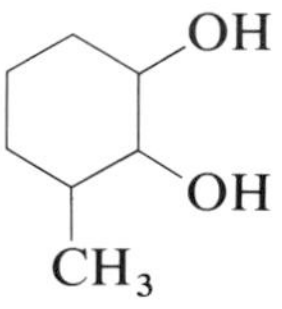

j.

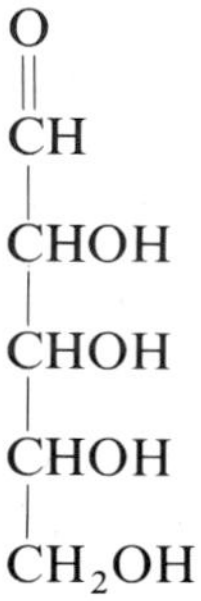

$$O$$
$$\|$$
$$CH$$
$$|$$
$$CHOH$$
$$|$$
$$CHOH$$
$$|$$
$$CHOH$$
$$|$$
$$CH_2OH$$

k.

$$CH_2OH$$
$$|$$
$$C=O$$
$$|$$
$$CHOH$$
$$|$$
$$CHOH$$
$$|$$
$$CH_2OH$$

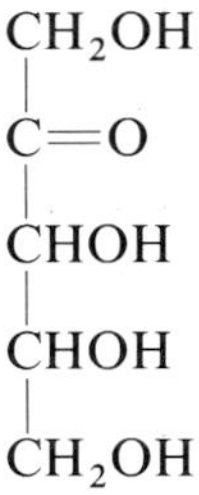

18.9   **a.** How many optical isomers are possible for each molecule in Problem 18.8?

b. How many pairs of enantiomers are possible for each molecule in Problem 18.8?

18.10   4-hydroxypentanal forms a five-member cyclic hemiacetal (Section 15.4B):

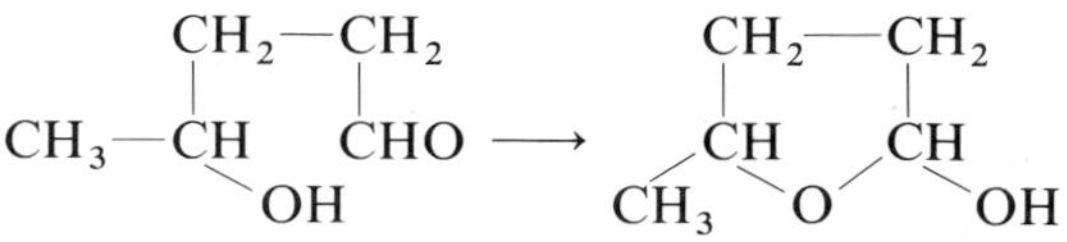

4-hydroxypentanal   a cyclic hemiacetal

How many stereoisomers are possible for this cyclic hemiacetal? Draw stereorepresentations of each.

18.11 5-hydroxyhexanal readily forms a six-member cyclic hemiacetal:

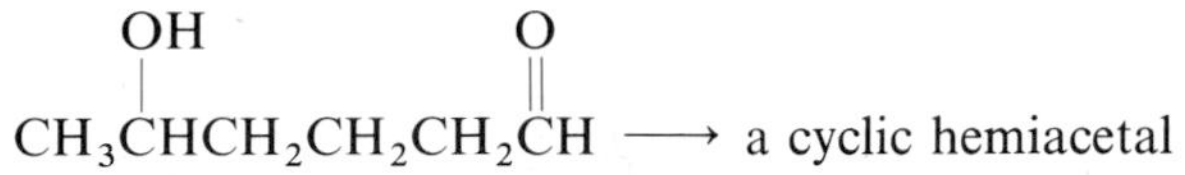

$$\underset{\text{5-hydroxyhexanal}}{CH_3\overset{\overset{\displaystyle OH}{|}}{C}HCH_2CH_2CH_2\overset{\overset{\displaystyle O}{\|}}{C}H} \longrightarrow \text{a cyclic hemiacetal}$$

a. Draw a structural formula for the cyclic hemiacetal.
b. How many stereoisomers are possible for 5-hydroxyhexanal?
c. How many stereoisomers are possible for the cyclic hemiacetal?
d. Draw planar hexagon representations for each stereoisomer of the cyclic hemiacetal.

18.12 Glucose, a polyhydroxyaldehyde, forms a six-member cyclic hemiacetal in which the oxygen on carbon 5 of the chain reacts with the aldehyde on carbon 1.

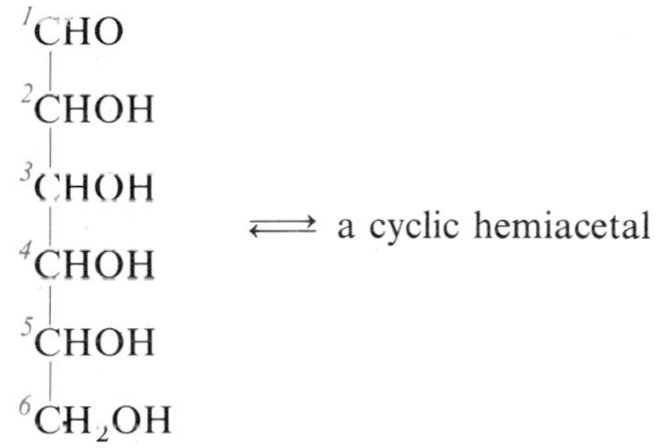

$$\begin{array}{l} {}^{1}CHO \\ {}^{2}CHOH \\ {}^{3}CHOH \\ {}^{4}CHOH \\ {}^{5}CHOH \\ {}^{6}CH_2OH \end{array} \quad \rightleftharpoons \text{a cyclic hemiacetal}$$

glucose
(open-chain form)

a. How many chiral carbon atoms are there in the open-chain form of glucose? How many stereoisomers are possible for a molecule of this structure?
b. Draw a structural formula for the cyclic hemiacetal of glucose (do not worry about showing stereochemistry).
c. How many chiral carbon atoms are there in the cyclic hemiacetal formed by glucose? How many stereoisomers are possible for the cyclic hemiacetal?

18.13 Explain the difference in molecular structure between *meso*-tartaric acid and racemic tartaric acid.

18.14 Which of the following are meso compounds?

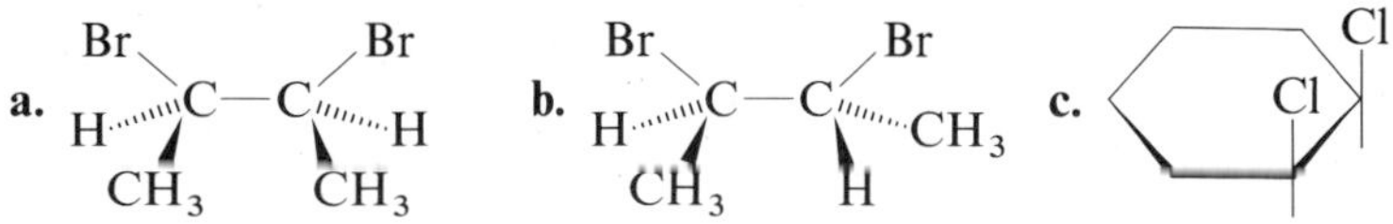

d.

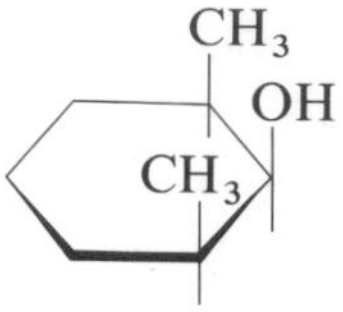

CH_3
OH
CH_3

e.

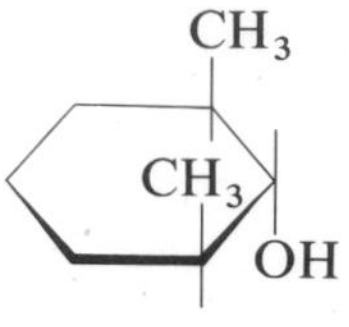

CH_3
CH_3
OH

f.

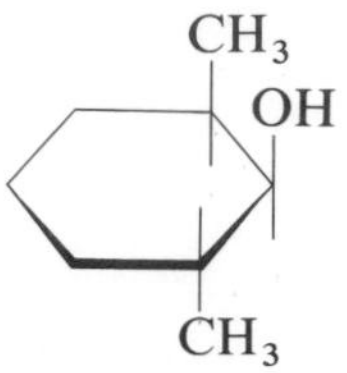

CH_3
OH
CH_3

g.

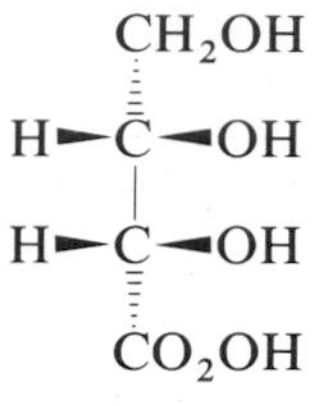

CH_2OH
H—C—OH
H—C—OH
CO_2OH

h.

CH_2OH
HO—C—H
H—C—OH
CH_2OH

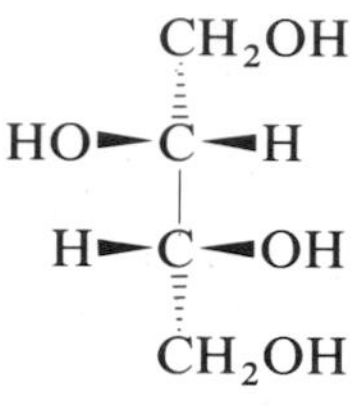

i.

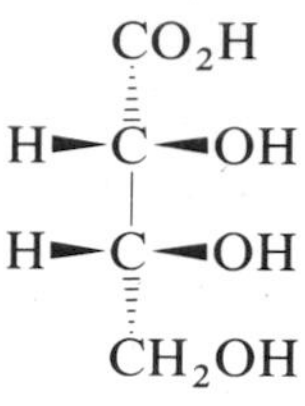

CO_2H
H—C—OH
H—C—OH
CH_2OH

j.

CO_2H
H—C—OH
HO—C—H
CH_2OH

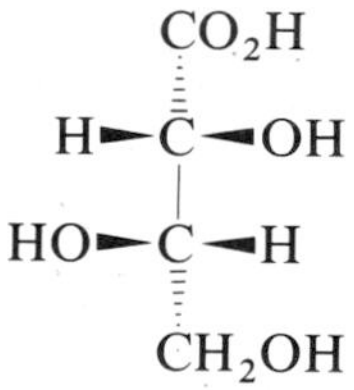

18.15 Inositol is a growth factor for animals and microorganisms. It is used medically for treating cirrhosis of the liver, hepatitis, and fatty infiltration of the liver. The most prevalent natural form is *cis*-1,2,3,5-*trans*-4,6-cyclohexanehexol. In this cis-trans designation, the —OH groups on carbons 2, 3, and 5 are cis to the —OH on carbon 1; the —OH groups on carbons 4 and 6 are trans to the —OH on carbon 1. Draw a stereorepresentation of the natural isomer (show the cyclohexane ring as a planar hexagon) and determine whether it shows enantiomerism or is a meso compound.

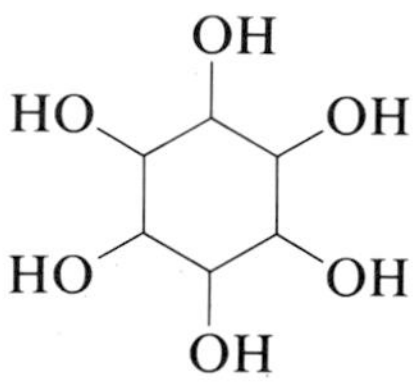

OH
HO
OH
HO
OH
OH

inositol

18.16 Draw all stereoisomers for the following compounds. Classify them into pairs of enantiomers or meso compounds.

a.  $CH_3CHCHCH_3$
H_2N OH

b. 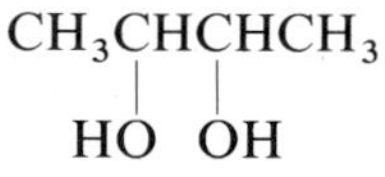 $CH_3CHCHCH_3$
HO OH

c. 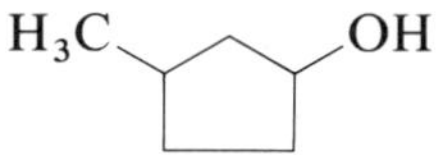 H_3C OH

d. 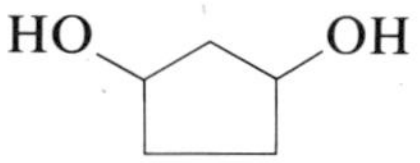 HO OH

18.17 Draw the four stereoisomers of grandisol, a sex hormone secreted by the hind gut of the male boll weevil (*Anthonomus grandis*).

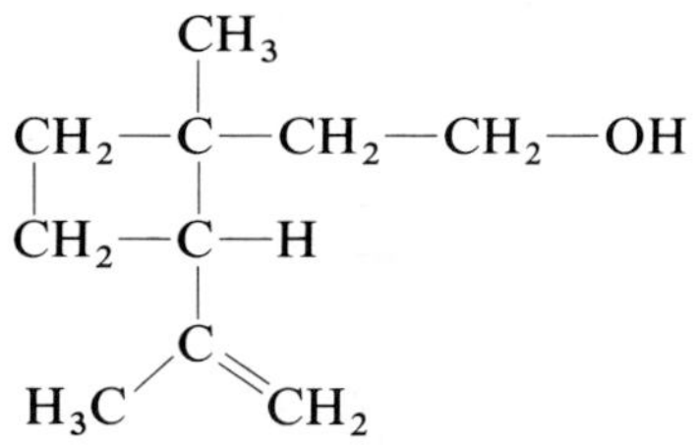

$$CH_2—\underset{\underset{\displaystyle CH_2—\underset{\displaystyle \underset{H_3C}{}C}{C}—H}{\overset{\displaystyle \overset{CH_3}{|}}{C}}—CH_2—CH_2—OH$$

grandisol

Significance of
chirality in
the biological
world (Section
18.7)

18.18   How can you explain the following observations:
   a. An enzyme is able to distinguish between a pair of enantiomers, and catalyze a biochemical reaction of one enantiomer but not of its mirror image.
   b. The microorganism *Penicillium glaucum* metabolizes (+)-tartaric acid preferentially over (−)-tartaric acid.

19

Carbohydrates

Carbohydrates are the most abundant organic molecules in plants and animals. They perform many vital functions—as storehouses of chemical energy (glucose, starch, glycogen); as components of supportive structures in plants (cellulose) and bacterial cell walls (mucopolysaccharides); and as essential components of nucleic acids (D-ribose and 2-deoxy-D-ribose), thereby affecting mechanisms for the genetically controlled development and growth of living cells. Further, plasma membranes of animal cells have bound to them numerous relatively small carbohydrates that mediate interactions between cells. For example, A, B, and O blood types are determined by specific membrane-bound carbohydrates.

Carbohydrates are often referred to as **saccharides**, because of the sweet taste of the simpler members of the family, the sugars (Latin, *saccharum*, sugar). The name carbohydrate is derived from the fact that many members of this class have the formula $C_n(H_2O)_m$; hence, their name "hydrates of carbon." Two examples of carbohydrates whose molecular formulas can be written alternatively as hydrates of carbon are:

Carbohydrate	Molecular Formula	Molecular Formula as Hydrate of Carbon
glucose (blood sugar)	$C_6H_{12}O_6$	$C_6(H_2O)_6$
sucrose (table sugar)	$C_{12}H_{22}O_{11}$	$C_{12}(H_2O)_{11}$

Not all carbohydrates have this general formula, however. Some also contain nitrogen. But the term carbohydrate has become firmly rooted in chemical nomenclature, and although it is not completely accurate, it persists as the name of this class of compounds.

At the molecular level, carbohydrates are polyhydroxyaldehydes, polyhydroxyketones, or compounds that yield either polyhydroxyaldehydes or polyhydroxyketones after hydrolysis. Complex carbohydrates are polymers of monosaccharides joined by acetal bonds (Section 15.4B). Therefore, the chemistry of carbohydrates is essentially the chemistry of two functional groups—

hydroxyl groups and carbonyl groups—and of acetal bonds formed between these two functional groups.

However, that carbohydrates have only two types of functional groups belies the complexity of their chemistry. All but the most simple carbohydrates contain multiple centers of chirality. For example, glucose, the most common carbohydrate in the biological world, contains one aldehyde, four secondary alcohols, one primary alcohol, and five centers of chirality. Dealing with molecules of this complexity presents enormous challenges to organic chemists and biochemists alike.

19.1 Monosaccharides

A. Structure

Monosaccharides are the monomers from which all more complex carbohydrates are constructed. They have the general formula $C_nH_{2n}O_n$, where n varies from 3 to 8. The suffix *-ose* indicates that a molecule is a carbohydrate, and the prefixes *tri-*, *tetra-*, *penta-* and so on, indicate the number of carbon atoms in the chain.

triose: $C_3H_6O_3$ hexose: $C_6H_{12}O_6$
tetrose: $C_4H_8O_4$ heptose: $C_7H_{14}O_7$
pentose: $C_5H_{10}O_5$ octose: $C_8H_{16}O_8$

There are only two trioses, glyceraldehyde and dihydroxyacetone. Glyceraldehyde contains two —OH groups and an aldehyde; dihydroxyacetone contains two —OH groups and a ketone. An aldehyde is shown to be present in a monosaccharide by the prefix *aldo-*, and a ketone by *keto-*. Thus glyceraldehyde belongs to the class of monosaccharides known as aldotrioses and dihydroxyacetone to the class known as ketotrioses.

CHO   CH₂OH
| |
CHOH   C=O
| |
CH₂OH   CH₂OH

glyceraldehyde   dihydroxyacetone
(an aldotriose)   (a ketotriose)

Often the designations *aldo-* and *keto-* are omitted, and these molecules are referred to simply as trioses. While these designations do not tell the nature of the carbonyl group, at least they indicate that the monosaccharide contains three carbon atoms.

B. Nomenclature

Glyceraldehyde is a common name; the IUPAC name for this monosaccharide is 2,3-dihydroxypropanal. Similarly, dihydroxyacetone is a common name; its IUPAC name is 1,3-dihydroxypropanone. However, the common names for these and other monosaccharides are so firmly rooted in the literature of organic chemistry and biochemistry, that they are used almost exclusively whenever these compounds are referred to. Therefore, throughout our discussions of the chemistry of carbohydrates, we will use the names most common to chemistry and biochemistry.

C. Chirality of Monosaccharides

Dihydroxyacetone has no chiral carbon and does not show optical isomerism. Glyceraldehyde, however, contains one chiral carbon and can exist as a pair of enantiomers (Figure 19.1). The configuration IA is named D-glyceraldehyde and its enantiomer, IB, is named L-glyceraldehyde.

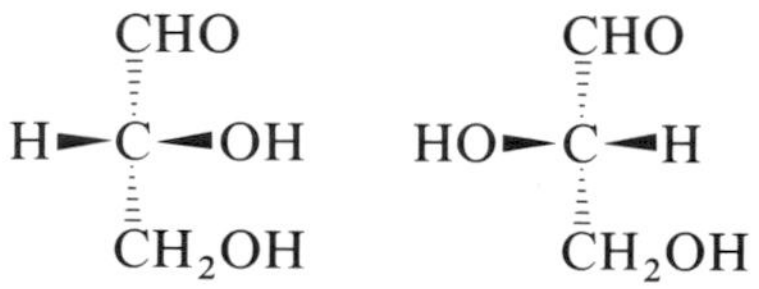

$$
\begin{array}{cc}
\text{CHO} & \text{CHO} \\
\text{H}\!\blacktriangleright\!\text{C}\!\blacktriangleleft\!\text{OH} & \text{HO}\!\blacktriangleright\!\text{C}\!\blacktriangleleft\!\text{H} \\
\text{CH}_2\text{OH} & \text{CH}_2\text{OH}
\end{array}
$$

D-glyceraldehyde   L-glyceraldehyde
$[\alpha]_D^{25} = +13.5°$ $[\alpha]_D^{25} = -13.5°$
IA   IB

Figure 19.1 The enantiomers of glyceraldehyde.

In the three-dimensional formulas in Figure 19.1, the configuration of each atom or group of atoms bonded to the chiral carbon is indicated by a combination of dashed and solid wedges. Structural formulas for monosaccharides can also be drawn as **Fischer projections**. According to this convention, the carbon chain is written vertically with the most highly oxidized carbon atom at the "top." Horizontal lines show groups projecting above the plane of the page; vertical lines show groups projecting behind the plane of the page. Applying these rules gives the following Fischer projections for the enantiomers of glyceraldehyde:

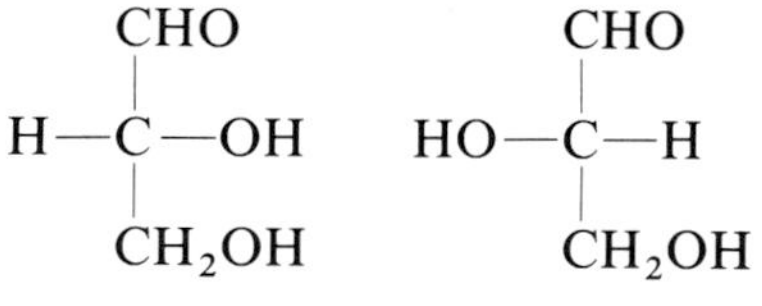

$$
\begin{array}{cc}
\text{CHO} & \text{CHO} \\
\text{H}\!-\!\text{C}\!-\!\text{OH} & \text{HO}\!-\!\text{C}\!-\!\text{H} \\
\text{CH}_2\text{OH} & \text{CH}_2\text{OH}
\end{array}
$$

D-glyceraldehyde   L-glyceraldehyde

At times there is confusion about whether a structural formula is or is not a Fischer projection. The problem arises because Fischer projections can be mistaken for Lewis structures, and whereas Fischer projection formulas do show stereochemistry about chiral carbons, Lewis structures do not. Therefore, the original Fischer convention has been modified to avoid this potential problem. In this modification, all chiral carbon atoms are represented by crossing points of bonds; chiral carbons are not shown. Following are representations of D- and

L-glyceraldehyde according to this convention. We shall use this convention throughout.

$$
\begin{array}{cc}
\text{CHO} & \text{CHO} \\
\text{H}\!-\!\!\!\boxed{}\!\!\!-\text{OH} & \text{HO}\!-\!\!\!\boxed{}\!\!\!-\text{H} \\
\text{CH}_2\text{OH} & \text{CH}_2\text{OH}
\end{array}
$$

D-glyceraldehyde   L-glyceraldehyde

(drawn according to the modified Fischer convention)

D-glyceraldehyde and L-glyceraldehyde serve as reference points for the assignment of configuration to all other aldoses and ketoses. Those that have the same configuration as D-glyceraldehyde about the chiral carbon farthest from the aldehyde or ketone are called **D-monosaccharides**; those that have the same configuration as L-glyceraldehyde about the chiral carbon farthest from the aldehyde or ketone are called **L-monosaccharides**.

In 1891, when Emil Fischer proposed the use of D and L to specify absolute configurations in monosaccharides, it was known that glyceraldehyde exists as a pair of enantiomers and that one of them has a specific rotation of $+13.5°$; the other, a specific rotation of $-13.5°$. The question Fischer and others faced was, Which enantiomer has which specific rotation? Is the specific rotation of D-glyceraldehyde $+13.5°$ or $-13.5°$? Because there was no experimental way to answer the question at that time, Fischer did the only thing he could—he guessed. He guessed that IA is the absolute configuration of the dextrorotatory enantiomer and named it D-glyceraldehyde (D for dextrorotatory). He named the other enantiomer L-glyceraldehyde (L for levorotatory). Fischer could have been wrong, but by a stroke of good fortune, he wasn't. In 1952, his assignment of absolute configuration was proved correct by a special application of X-ray crystallography. Thus, Fischer projections of monosaccharides give absolute configurations of all chiral centers.

The following aldohexose contains 4 chiral carbon atoms, marked by asterisks, and according to the 2^n rule, it can exist as 16 optical isomers (8 pairs of enantiomers):

$$
\begin{array}{c}
\text{CHO} \\
*\text{CHOH} \\
*\text{CHOH} \\
*\text{CHOH} \\
*\text{CHOH} \\
\text{CH}_2\text{OH}
\end{array}
$$

an aldohexose
[16 optical isomers (8 pairs
of enantiomers) are possible]

Table 19.1 Configurational relationships between the isomeric D-aldotetroses, D-aldopentoses, and D-aldohexoses derived from D-glyceraldehyde.

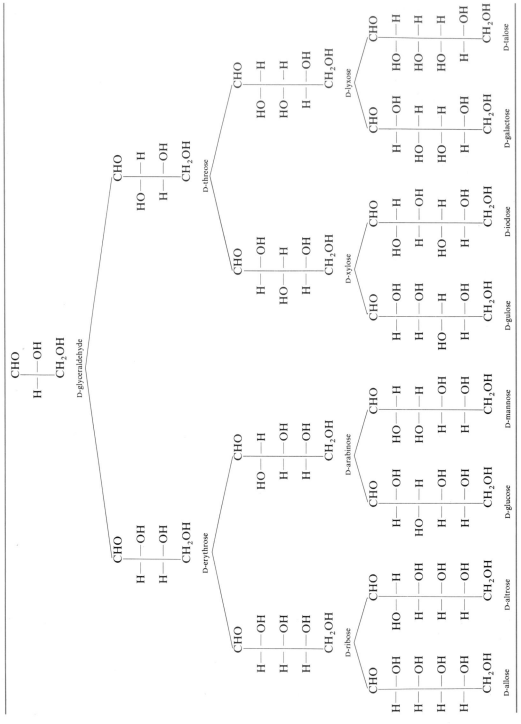

In Table 19.1 you will find Fischer projection formulas for eight of the optical isomers of this aldohexose. The other eight optical isomers are the enantiomers of those shown, that is, they are L-allose, L-altrose, L-glucose, and so on.

Shown in Tables 19.1 and 19.2 are names and Fischer projection formulas for all D-tetroses, D-pentoses, and D-hexoses. Each name consists of three parts. The letter D specifies the absolute configuration at the penultimate carbon; prefixes such as *rib-*, *arabin-*, and *gluc-* specify the configuration of all other chiral centers relative to that of the penultimate carbon; and *-ose* shows that the molecule belongs to the class called carbohydrates.

Table 19.2
Configurational relationships between the D-ketopentoses and D-ketohexoses derived from dihydroxyacetone and D-erythrulose.

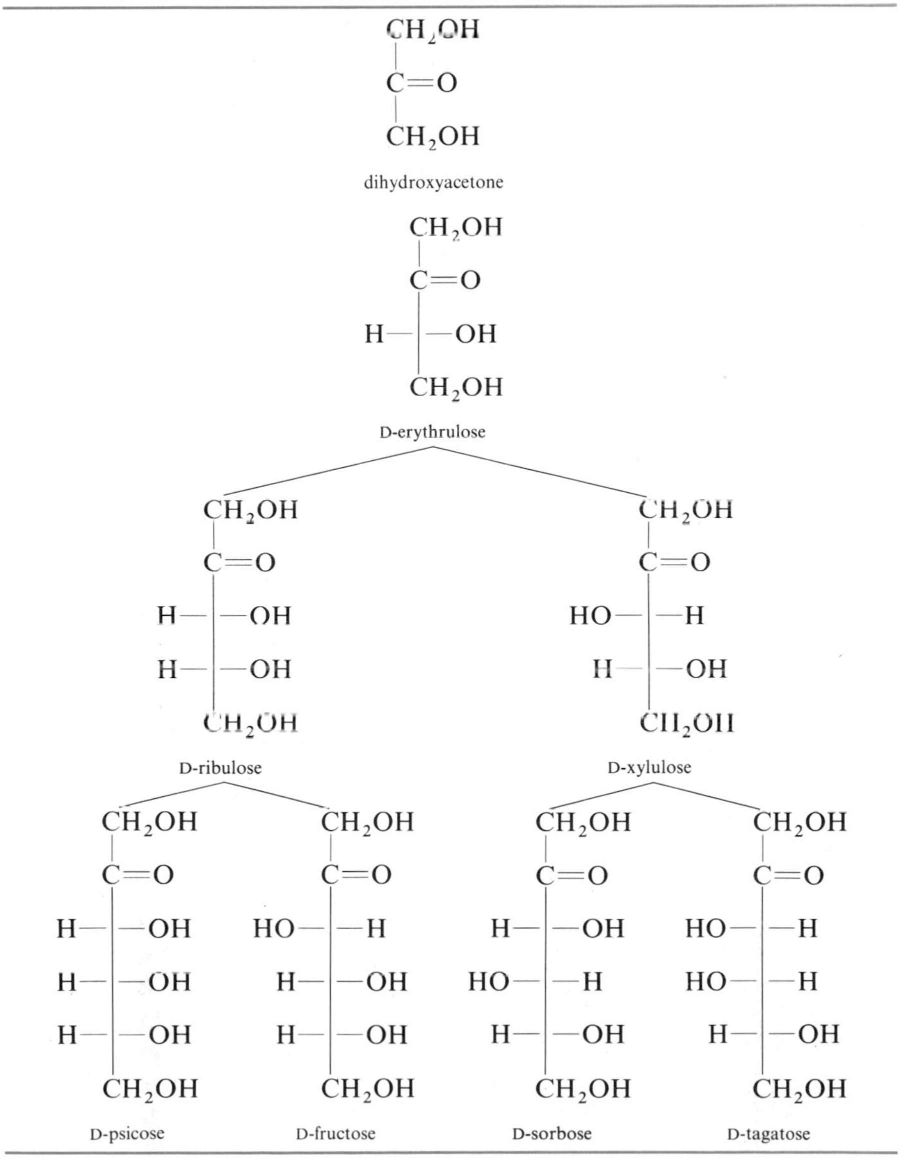

D-ribose and 2-deoxy-D-ribose (below), the most abundant pentoses in the biological world, are essential building blocks of nucleic acids: D-ribose in ribonucleic acids (RNAs) and 2-deoxy-D-ribose in deoxyribonucleic acids (DNAs).

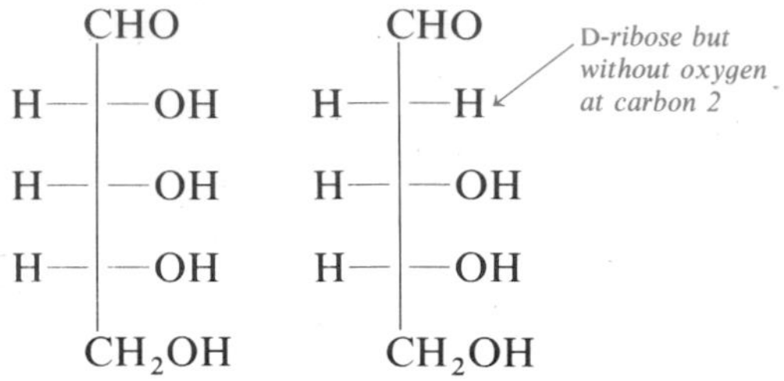

D-ribose but without oxygen at carbon 2

D-ribose   2-deoxy-D-ribose

The three most abundant hexoses in the biological world are D-glucose, D-galactose, and D-fructose. The first two are D-aldohexoses; the third is a D-ketohexose. Note that D-galactose differs from D-glucose only in the configuration at carbon 4. Compounds that have multiple chiral centers but differ from each other in the configuration at only one of these chiral centers are called epimers. Thus, D-glucose and D-galactose are epimers.

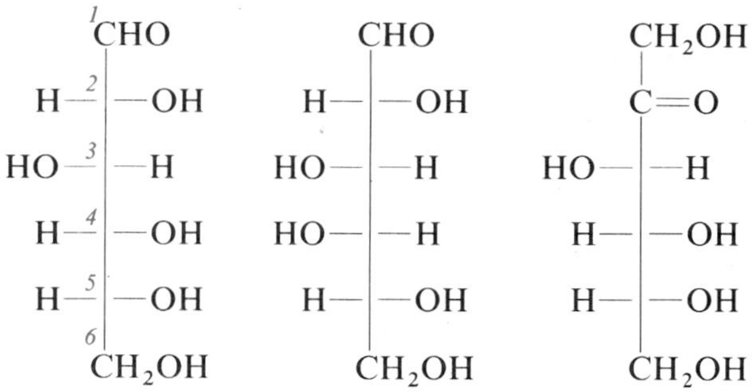

D-glucose

D-galactose
(C-4 isomer of
D-glucose)

D-fructose

Glucose, by far the most common hexose, is also known as dextrose because it is dextrorotatory. Other names for this monosaccharide are grape sugar, blood sugar, and corn sugar, names that indicate its sources in an uncombined state. Human blood normally contains 65–110 mg of glucose per 100 mL.

Fructose is found combined with glucose in the disaccharide sucrose (table sugar, Section 19.4C). D-galactose is found combined with glucose in the disaccharide lactose (milk sugar). Lactose is found only in milk.

Example 19.1

a. Draw Fischer projections for all aldoses of four carbon atoms.
b. Show which are D-monosaccharides, which are L-monosaccharides, and which are enantiomers.
c. Refer to Table 19.1 and write names for the aldotetroses you have drawn.

Solution   Following are Fischer projections for the four possible aldotetroses. The designations D and L refer to the arrangement of groups attached to the penultimate carbon, which in aldotetroses is carbon 3. In the Fischer projection of a D-aldotetrose, the —OH on carbon 3 is on the right; for an L-aldotetrose, it is on the left.

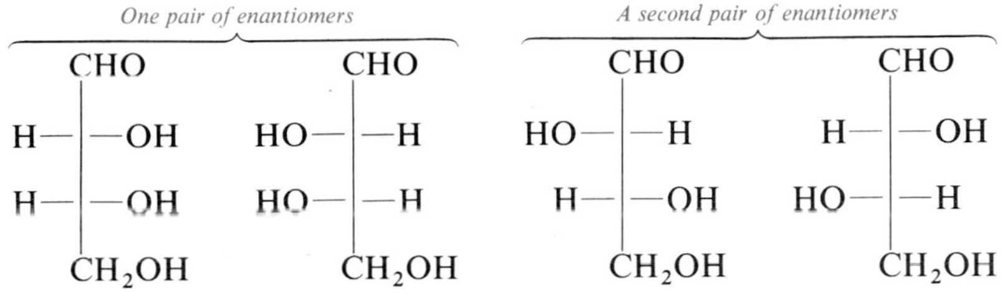

One pair of enantiomers		*A second pair of enantiomers*	
CHO	CHO	CHO	CHO
H——OH	HO——H	HO——H	H——OH
H——OH	HO——H	H——OH	HO——H
CH$_2$OH	CH$_2$OH	CH$_2$OH	CH$_2$OH
a D-aldose	an L-aldose	a D-aldose	an L-aldose
(D-erythose)	(L-erythrose)	(D-threose)	(L-threose)

Problem 19.1

a. Draw Fischer projections for all 2-ketoses with five carbon atoms.
b. Show which are D-ketopentoses, which are L-ketopentoses, and which are enantiomers.
c. Refer to Table 19.2 and write names for the ketopentoses you have drawn.

D. Amino Sugars

Amino sugars contain an —NH$_2$ group in place of an —OH group. Only three amino sugars are common in nature: D-glucosamine, D-mannosamine, and D-galactosamine.

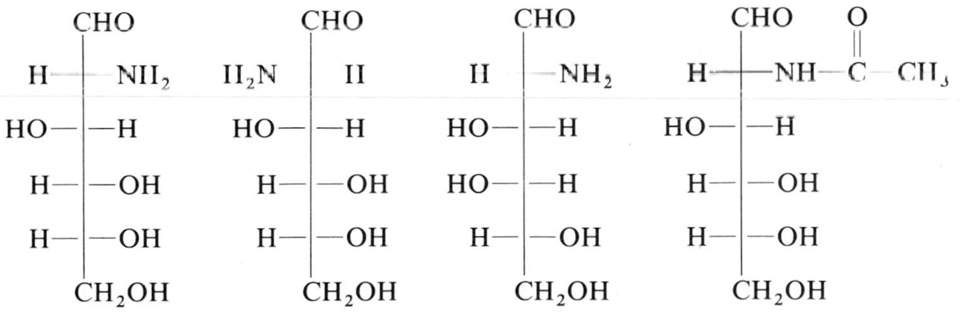

CHO	CHO	CHO	CHO
H——NH$_2$	H$_2$N——H	H——NH$_2$	H——NH—C—CH$_3$ (O‖)
HO——H	HO——H	HO——H	HO——H
H——OH	H——OH	HO——H	H——OH
H——OH	H——OH	H——OH	H——OH
CH$_2$OH	CH$_2$OH	CH$_2$OH	CH$_2$OH
D-glucosamine	D-mannosamine (C-2 isomer of D-glucosamine)	D-galactosamine (C-4 isomer of D-glucosamine)	N-acetyl-D-glucosamine

N-acetyl-D-glucosamine, a derivative of D-glucosamine, is a component of many polysaccharides, including chitin, the hard shell-like exoskeleton of lobsters, crabs, shrimp, and other crustaceans.

E. Cyclic Structure of Monosaccharides

Aldehydes and ketones react with alcohols to form hemiacetals and hemiketals. Cyclic hemiacetals and hemiketals form very readily when hydroxyl and carbonyl groups are part of the same molecule. For example, 4-hydroxypentanal forms a five-membered cyclic hemiacetal. Note that 4-hydroxypentanal contains one chiral center and that in hemiacetal formation, a second chiral center is generated.

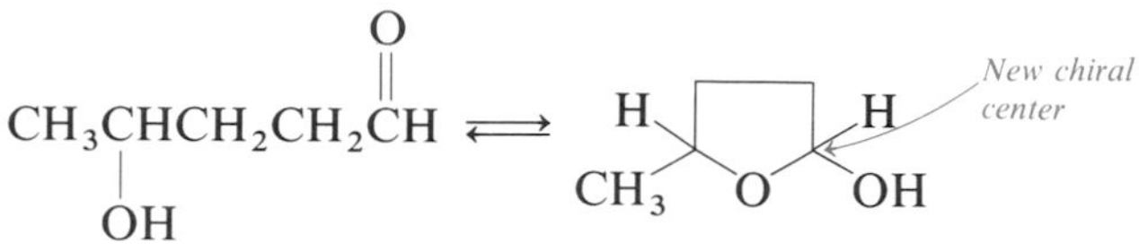

4-hydroxypentanal
(minor form present
at equilibrium)

a cyclic hemiacetal
(major form present
at equilibrium)

Monosaccharides have hydroxyl and carbonyl groups in the same molecule and they too form cyclic hemiacetals and hemiketals.

D-glucose can be isolated in two crystalline forms called α and β, which have different chemical and physical properties. One of the most easily measured physical properties of these isomers is their optical rotation. One form has a specific rotation of $+112°$, the other a specific rotation of $+19°$. These α and β isomers are formed by reaction between the —OH on carbon 5 and the carbonyl group on carbon 1, to give a pair of six-member cyclic hemiacetals. The carbonyl carbon at which cyclic hemiacetal formation takes place is given the special name **anomeric carbon**. The diastereomers thus formed are given the special name anomers.

In the terminology of carbohydrate chemistry, α indicates that the —OH on the newly created anomeric carbon is trans to the terminal —CH$_2$OH (carbon 6 in glucose). The term beta (β) indicates that the —OH on the anomeric carbon is cis to the terminal —CH$_2$OH. Structural formulas for α-D-glucose and β-D-glucose are drawn in Figure 19.2 as strain-free chair conformations. Also drawn is the open-chain, or free aldehyde, form with which the cyclic hemiacetals are

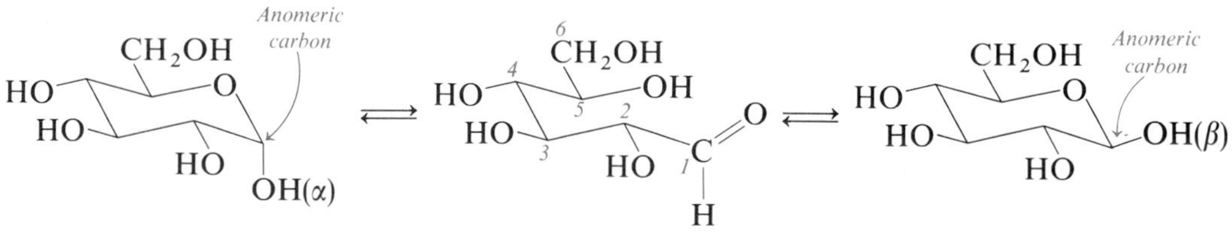

α-D-glucopyranose
(α-D-glucose:
mp 146°C
$[\alpha] = +112°$)

open-chain, or
free aldehyde, form
of D-glucose

β-D-glucopyranose
(β-D-glucose; mp 190°C
$[\alpha] = +19°$)

Figure 19.2 The cyclic hemiacetal forms of D-glucose.

in equilibrium in aqueous solution. The equilibrium constant for hemiacetal formation is greater than 190, which means that at equilibrium, little free aldehyde is present. Note that in the chair conformations of α- and β-D-glucose, substituents on carbons 2, 3, and 4 of each ring are equatorial (Section 11.6B). The —OH on the anomeric carbon of α-D-glucose is axial; the —OH on the anomeric carbon of β-D-glucose is equatorial.

The size of a monosaccharide hemiacetal or hemiketal ring is shown by reference to the molecules pyran and furan.

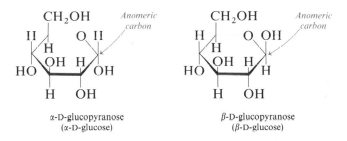

pyran   furan

Six-member hemiacetal or hemiketal rings are shown by the infix *-pyran-*, and five-member hemiacetal or hemiketal rings are shown by the infix *-furan-*. Thus, the alpha and beta anomers of D-glucose are properly named α-D-glucopyranose and β-D-glucopyranose. However, for convenience they are often named simply α-D-glucose and β-D-glucose.

Structural formulas showing these cyclic hemiacetals can also be drawn as planar hexagons (Figure 19.3). Such representations are called **Haworth structures**, after English chemist Walter N. Haworth (Nobel laureate, 1937).

CH₂OH   *Anomeric carbon*   CH₂OH   *Anomeric carbon*

α-D-glucopyranose
(α-D-glucose)

β-D-glucopyranose
(β-D-glucose)

Figure 19.3 Haworth structures for the cyclic hemiacetal forms of D-glucose.

In Haworth structures of aldohexopyranoses, the —OH on the anomeric carbon is below the plane of the ring (trans to the terminal —CH₂OH) in the α-anomer and above the plane of the ring (cis to the terminal —CH₂OH) in the β-anomer.

Other monosaccharides also form cyclic hemiacetals and hemiketals. Following are structural formulas for those formed by D-fructose. Cyclization (in this case hemiketal formation) between the carbonyl group on carbon 2 and the hydroxyl on carbon 5 gives a pair of anomers called α-D-fructofuranose and β-D-fructofuranose. Fructose also forms a pair of **pyranoses** by cyclization between the carbonyl group and the hydroxyl on carbon 6. Structural formulas of these compounds along with approximate percentages of each at equilibrium in aqueous solution are shown in Figure 19.4. In the **furanose** forms, the most common in the biological world, the —OH on the anomeric carbon is below the plane of the ring in the α-anomer and above the plane of the ring in the β-anomer.

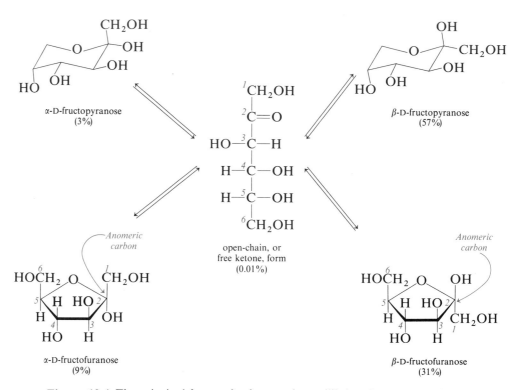

Figure 19.4 The principal forms of D-fructose in equilibrium in aqueous solution.

Example 19.2

D-galactose forms a cyclic hemiacetal containing a six-member ring. Draw chair and Haworth structures for α-D-galactopyranose and β-D-galactopyranose. Label the anomeric carbon in each cyclic hemiacetal.

☐ *Solution*

One way of drawing structures for the six-member cyclic hemiacetals of D-galactose is to use the α and β forms of D-glucopyranose as reference, and to remember, or discover by looking at Table 19.1, that D-galactose differs from D-glucose only in the configuration at carbon 4; that is, it is the epimer of glucose at carbon 4. Another way of arriving at the correct pyranose form is to build a molecular model of D-galactose, twist it to create the required hemiacetals, and examine the models to discover how each ring substituent is oriented in space. Chair structures for the alpha and beta anomers of D-galactose are drawn below, along with the open-chain form with which they are in equilibrium in aqueous solution.

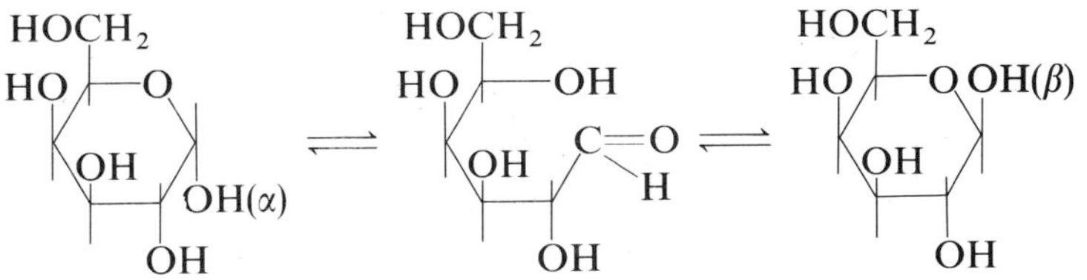

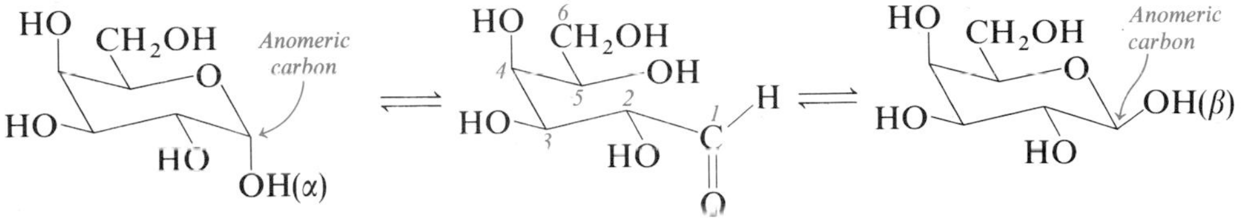

α-D-galactopyranose
([α] = +191°)

open-chain form

β-D-galactopyranose
([α)] = −53°)

Problem 19.2

D-mannose forms a cyclic hemiacetal containing a six-member ring. Draw chair and Haworth structures for α-D-mannopyranose and β-D-mannopyranose. Label the anomeric carbon atom in each.

The most prevalent forms of D-ribose and other pentoses in the biological world are furanoses. Shown in Figure 19.5 are structural formulas for α-D-ribofuranose (α-D-ribose) and β-2-deoxy-D-ribofuranose (β-2-deoxy-D-ribose). Units of D-ribose and 2-deoxy-D-ribose in nucleic acids and most other biological molecules are found almost exclusively in the β configuration.

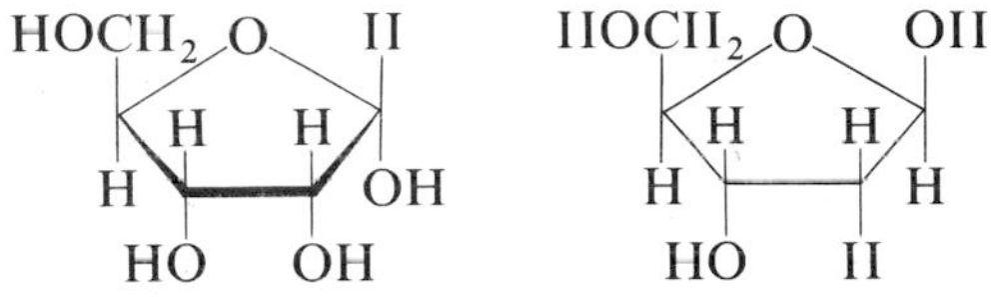

α-D-ribofuranose

β-D-2-deoxy-D-ribofuranose

Figure 19.5 Furanose forms of D-ribose and 2-deoxy-D-ribose.

F. Mutarotation

The α- and β-anomers of monosaccharides are interconvertible in aqueous solution and the change in specific rotation that accompanies this interconversion is known as **mutarotation**. As an example, a freshly prepared solution of α-D-glucose shows an initial rotation of +112°, which gradually decreases to +52° as α-D-glucose reaches an equilibrium with β-D-glucose. The equilibrium mixture consists of 64% β-D-glucose and 36% α-D-glucose. A solution of β-D-glucose also undergoes mutarotation, during which the specific rotation changes from an initial value of +19° to the same equilibrium value of +52°.

Mutarotation is common to all carbohydrates that exist in α and β forms. Shown in Table 19.3 are specific rotations for the α and β forms of D-galactose and D-mannose, along with equilibrium values for the specific rotation of each after mutarotation.

Table 19.3
Specific rotations of the α and β forms of D-galactose and D-mannose before and after mutarotation.

Monosaccharide	Specific Rotation		Specific Rotation after Mutarotation
α-D-galactose	$+190.7°$	$\longrightarrow$	$+80.2°$
β-D-galactose	$+52.8°$	$\longrightarrow$	$+80.2°$
α-D-mannose	$+29.3°$	$\longrightarrow$	$+14.5°$
β-D-mannose	$-16.3°$	$\longrightarrow$	$+14.5°$

G. Physical Properties

Monosaccharides are colorless, crystalline solids, and because hydrogen bonding is possible between polar —OH groups and water, all monosaccharides are very soluble in water. They are only slightly soluble in alcohol and insoluble in nonhydroxylic solvents, such as ether, chloroform, and benzene.

Although all monosaccharides are sweet to the taste, some are sweeter than others (Table 19.4). Of the monosaccharides, D-fructose tastes the sweetest, even more than sucrose (table sugar). The sweet taste of honey is due largely to D-fructose, and of corn syrup, to D-glucose. Molasses is a byproduct of table-sugar manufacture. In the production of table sugar, sugar cane or sugar beet is boiled with water and then cooled. As the mixture cools, sucrose crystals separate and are collected. Subsequent boilings and coolings yield a dark, thick syrup known as molasses.

Table 19.4
Relative sweetness. Sucrose is taken as a standard and assigned the value 100.

Monosaccharides	Disaccharides	Other Carbohydrate Sweetening Agents
D-fructose 174	sucrose (table sugar) 100	honey 97
D-glucose 74	lactose (milk sugar) 0.16	molasses 74
D-xylose 0.40		corn syrup 74
D-galactose 0.22		

19.2 Reactions of Monosaccharides

A. Formation of Glycosides (Acetals)

Reaction of a monosaccharide hemiacetal or hemiketal (Section 19.1E) with an alcohol forms an acetal or a ketal, as illustrated by the reaction of β-D-gluco-pyranose (β-D-glucose) with methanol:

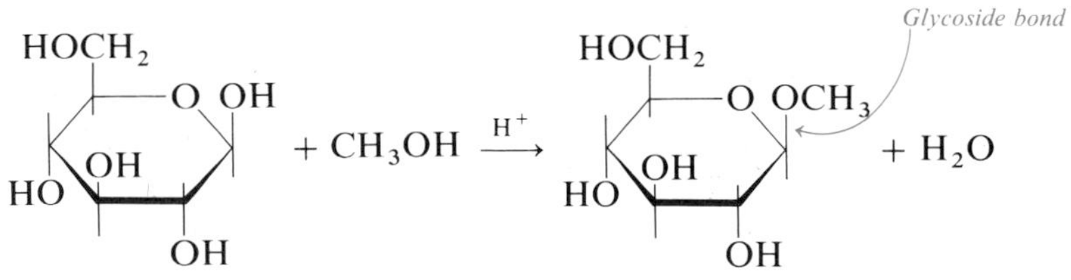

β-D-glucopyranose
(β-D-glucose)

methyl β-D-glucopyranoside
(methyl β-D-glycoside)

A cyclic acetal or ketal derived from a monosaccharide is called a **glycoside**, and the bond from the anomeric carbon to the —OR group is called a **glycoside bond**.

Glycosides are named by listing the alkyl or aryl group attached to oxygen, and following this by the name of the carbohydrate involved. The name of a particular glycoside is derived by dropping the terminal -*e* from the name of the monosaccharide and adding -*ide*. For example, glycosides derived from D-glucose are named D-glucosides; those derived from D-ribose are named D-ribosides. In Haworth structures, the —OR on an anomeric carbon of a glycoside is below the plane of the ring in an α-anomer and above the plane of the ring in a β-anomer. In chair conformations, the —OR on an anomeric carbon is axial in an α-anomer and equatorial in a β-anomer.

Example 19.3

Draw structural formulas for these glycosides. In each, label the anomeric carbon and the glycoside bond.

a. methyl β-D-ribofuranoside (methyl β-D-riboside)
b. methyl α-D-galactopyranoside (methyl α-D-galactoside)

Solution

a. D-ribose forms a five-member cyclic hemiacetal that reacts with methanol to form a cyclic acetal. The —OCH₃ group on the anomeric carbon is above the plane of the ring (on the same side as the terminal —CH₂OH group) in a β-ribofuranoside.

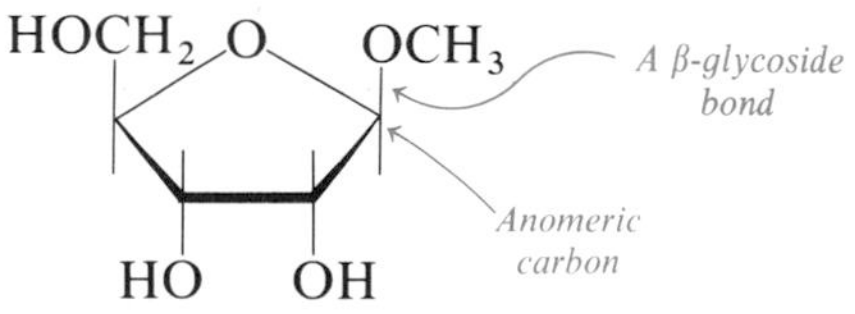

methyl β-D-ribofuranoside
(methyl β-D-riboside)

b. D-galactose forms a six-member cyclic hemiacetal that reacts with methanol to form a cyclic acetal. The —OCH₃ group is below the plane of the ring (trans to the terminal —CH₂OH group) in an α-D-galactopyranoside. Fol-

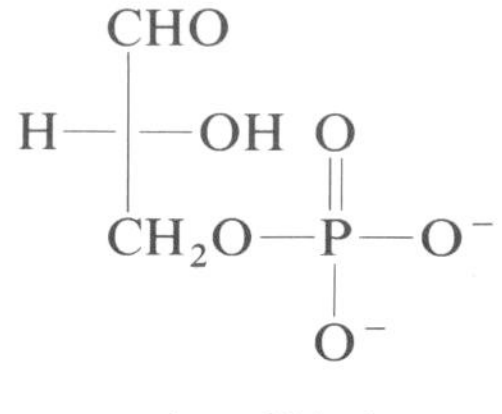

D-glyceraldehyde
3-phosphate
(net charge −2)

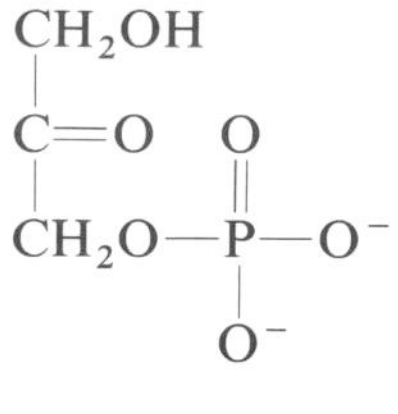

dihydroxyacetone
phosphate
(net charge −2)

Phosphate esters are also formed by monosaccharide cyclic hemiacetals and hemiketals. Following is a structural formula for β-D-glucose 1-phosphate. Glucose is in the form of a six-membered cyclic hemiacetal with the —OH on the anomeric carbon β (above the plane of the ring). The phosphate ester is formed by the —OH on carbon 1. Also shown is a structural formula for β-D-ribose 5-phosphate. Ribose is in the form of a five-membered cyclic hemiacetal with the —OH on the anomeric carbon above the plane of the ring. The phosphate ester is formed by the —OH on carbon 5 of ribose.

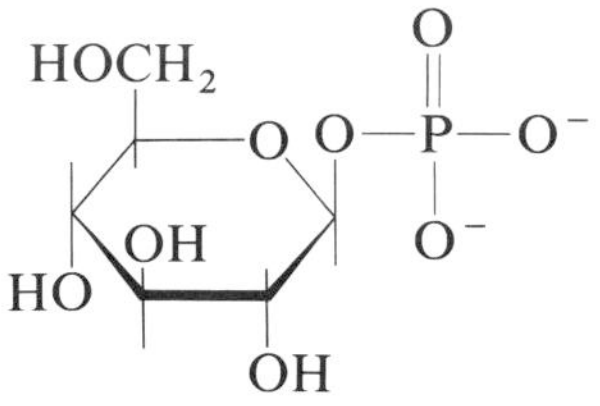

β-D-glucose 1-phosphate
(net charge −2)

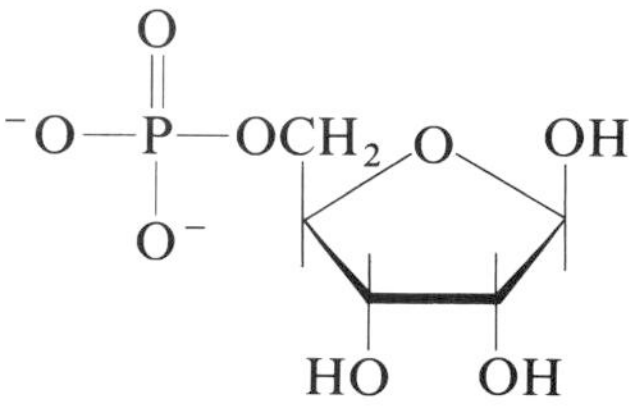

β-D-ribose 5-phosphate
(net charge −2)

Example 19.5

Draw structural formulas for the following monosaccharide phosphate esters and state the net charge on each at pH 7.

a. α-D-glucose 1-phosphate
b. β-D-fructose 1,6-diphosphate. Show fructose first as a five-membered cyclic hemiketal, then in a second structural formula as an open-chain, or free ketone, form (Figure 19.4).

☐ *Solution*

a. Draw glucose as a six-membered cyclic hemiacetal with the —OH on the anomeric carbon below the plane of the ring. Show the phosphate ester bond between the oxygen atom of carbon 1 and phosphoric acid. At pH 7, the net charge on this ester is −2.

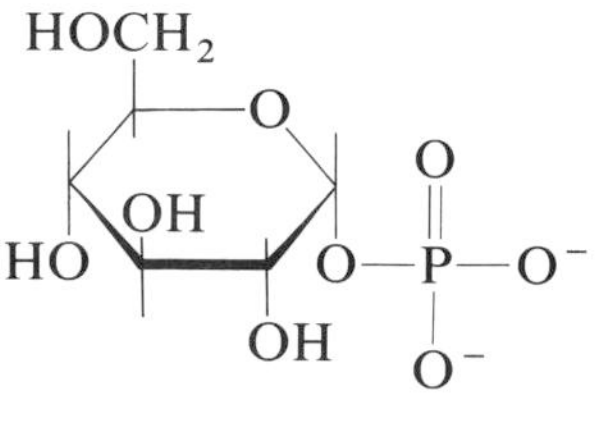

b. At pH 7, the net charge on this diester is -4.

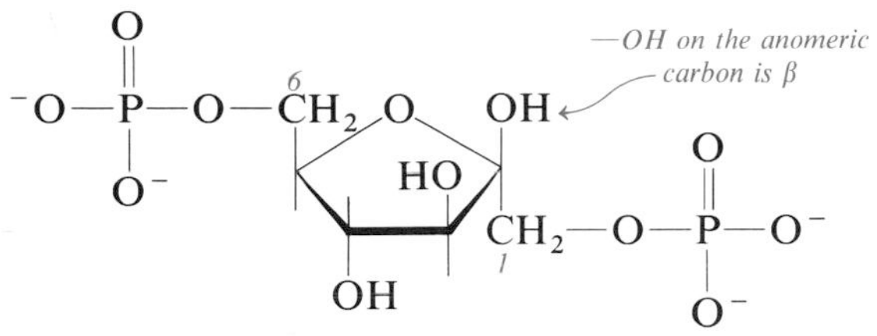

—OH on the anomeric carbon is β

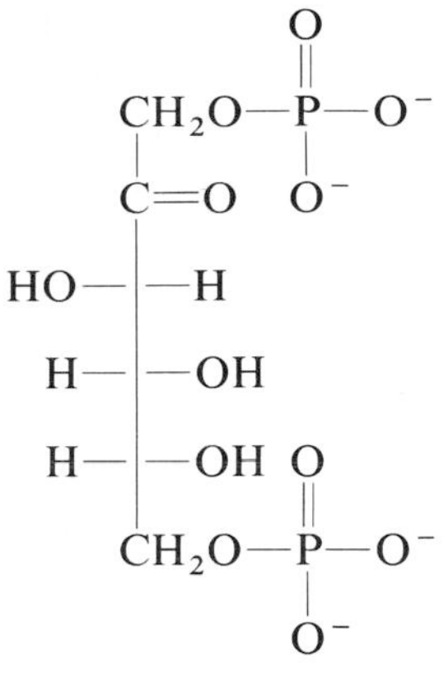

Problem 19.5

Draw structural formulas for these esters:

a. β-D-glucose 6-phosphate
b. β-D-ribose 1,5-diphosphate

C. Reduction

The carbonyl group of a monosaccharide can be reduced to an alcohol by various reducing agents, including $NaBH_4$ and hydrogen in the presence of a metal catalyst. Reduction products are known as alditols. Reduction of D-glucose gives D-glucitol, more commonly known as sorbitol.

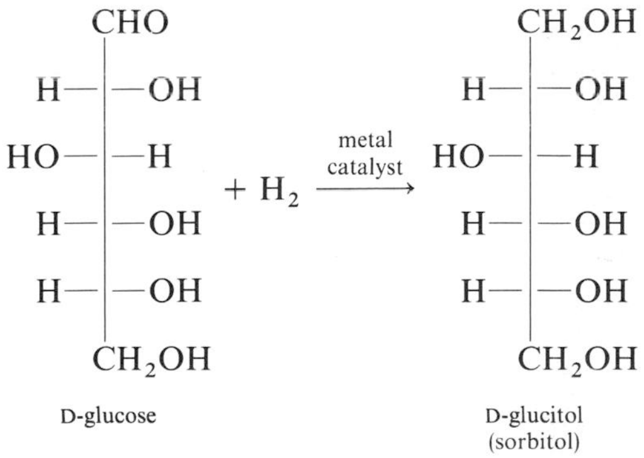

D-glucose

D-glucitol
(sorbitol)

Sorbitol is found throughout the plant world. It is often used as a non-glucose-containing sweetener for foods and candies for diabetics. Also common in the biological world are erythritol and D-mannitol.

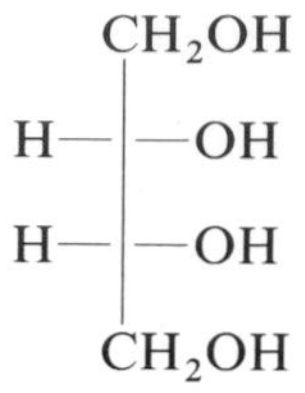

$$
\begin{array}{cc}
 & \text{CH}_2\text{OH} \\
 & \text{HO} \long!\!\!-\text{H} \\
\text{CH}_2\text{OH} & \text{HO} \long!\!\!-\text{H} \\
\text{H} \longrightarrow\!\!\text{OH} & \text{H} \longrightarrow\!\!\text{OH} \\
\text{H} \longrightarrow\!\!\text{OH} & \text{H} \longrightarrow\!\!\text{OH} \\
\text{CH}_2\text{OH} & \text{CH}_2\text{OH} \\
\text{erythritol} & \text{D-mannitol}
\end{array}
$$

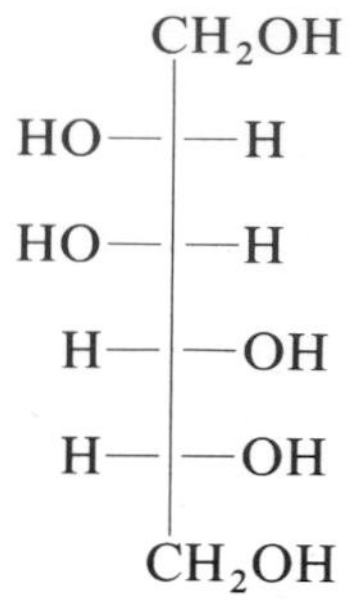

At one time, xylitol was used as a sweetening agent in "sugarless" gum, candy, and sweet cereals. It has been removed from the market, however, because tests showed it to be potentially carcinogenic.

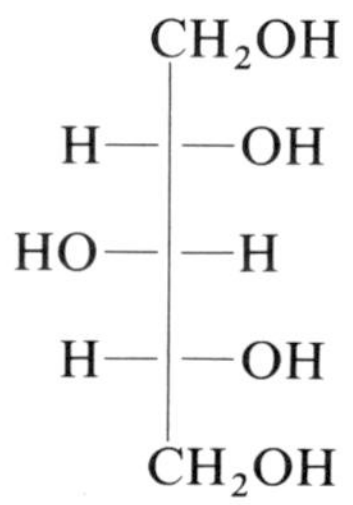

$$
\begin{array}{c}
\text{CH}_2\text{OH} \\
\text{H} \longrightarrow\!\!\text{OH} \\
\text{HO} \longleftarrow\!\!\text{H} \\
\text{H} \longrightarrow\!\!\text{OH} \\
\text{CH}_2\text{OH}
\end{array}
$$

xylitol

D. Oxidation of Monosaccharides

Monosaccharides (and carbohydrates in general) are classified as reducing or nonreducing according to their behavior toward Cu(II) (Benedict's solution) or toward Ag(I) in ammonium hydroxide (Tollens solution). Tollens solution is prepared by dissolving silver nitrate in ammonium hydroxide (Section 15.5A). A positive Tollens test is indicated by precipitation of metallic silver in the form of a silver mirror:

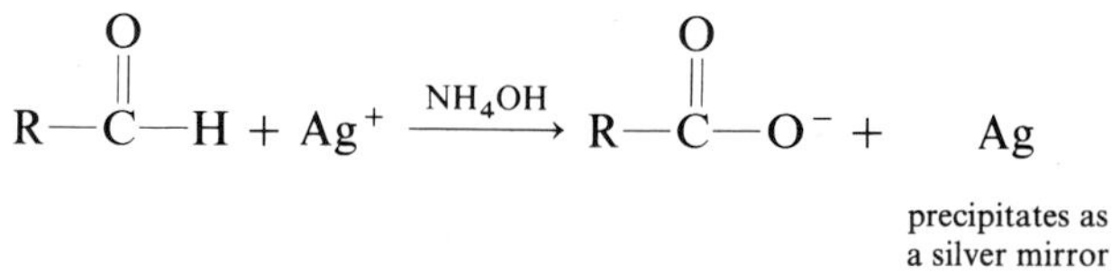

$$
\text{R}-\overset{\overset{\text{O}}{\|}}{\text{C}}-\text{H} + \text{Ag}^+ \xrightarrow{\text{NH}_4\text{OH}} \text{R}-\overset{\overset{\text{O}}{\|}}{\text{C}}-\text{O}^- + \quad \text{Ag}
$$

precipitates as
a silver mirror

Benedict's solution is prepared by adding copper(II) sulfate to a solution of sodium carbonate and sodium citrate. The function of citrate is to buffer the pH of the solution and to form a complex ion with copper(II). A positive test is indicated by formation of copper(I) oxide, which precipitates as a brick-red solid.

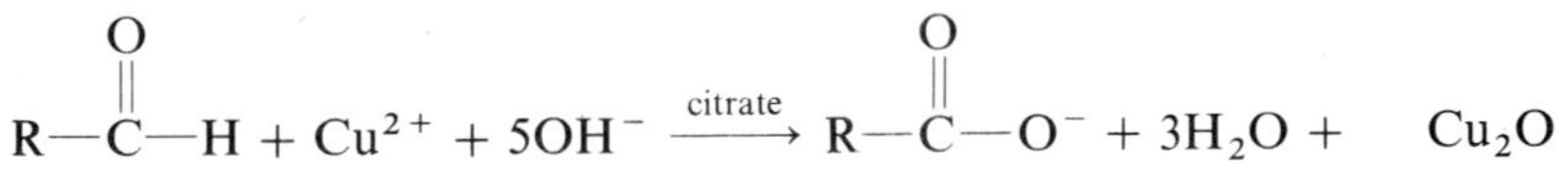

$$R-\overset{\overset{\displaystyle O}{\|}}{C}-H + Cu^{2+} + 5OH^{-} \xrightarrow{\text{citrate}} R-\overset{\overset{\displaystyle O}{\|}}{C}-O^{-} + 3H_2O + \quad Cu_2O$$

precipitates as a
brick-red solid

Carbohydrates that reduce copper(II) ion to Cu_2O or silver(I) to metallic silver are classified as **reducing carbohydrates**. Those that do not reduce these reagents are classified as **nonreducing carbohydrates**. The chemical basis for this classification depends on two things. First, all monosaccharides contain either an aldehyde or an α-hydroxyketone; second, in dilute base, the conditions of these tests, ketoses are in equilibrium with aldoses via enediol intermediates (Problems 15.21 and 15.22).

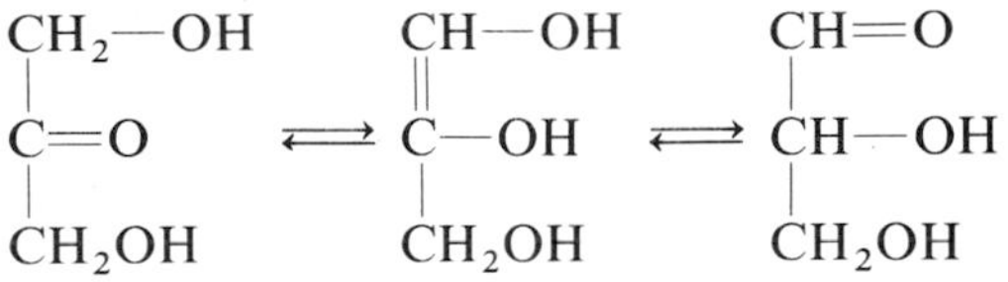

$$
\begin{array}{ccc}
CH_2-OH & CH-OH & CH{=}O \\
| & \| & | \\
C{=}O & C-OH & CH-OH \\
| & | & | \\
CH_2OH & CH_2OH & CH_2OH
\end{array}
$$

$$\text{a ketose} \quad \rightleftharpoons \quad \text{an enediol} \quad \rightleftharpoons \quad \text{an aldose}$$

Oxidation of an aldose or 2-ketose by Benedict's or Tollens solutions yields a monocarboxylic acid known as an aldonic acid. For example, D-glucose is oxidized to D-gluconic acid:

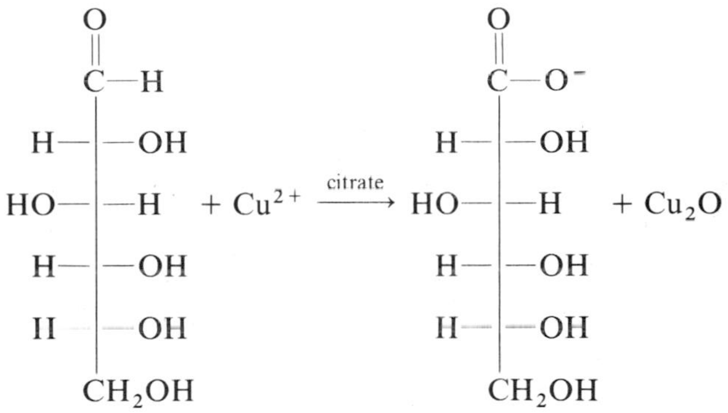

$$
\begin{array}{ccc}
\overset{\overset{\displaystyle O}{\|}}{C}-H & & \overset{\overset{\displaystyle O}{\|}}{C}-O^{-} \\
H-\!\!-OH & & H-\!\!-OH \\
HO-\!\!-H \quad + Cu^{2+} & \xrightarrow{\text{citrate}} & HO-\!\!-H \quad + Cu_2O \\
H-\!\!-OH & & H-\!\!-OH \\
II-\!\!-OH & & H-\!\!-OH \\
CH_2OH & & CH_2OH
\end{array}
$$

D-glucose / anion derived from D-gluconic acid

19.3 L-Ascorbic Acid (Vitamin C)

L-ascorbic acid (vitamin C) resembles a monosaccharide in its structural formula. In fact, it is synthesized both biochemically and industrially from D-glucose. Let us examine the individual steps in the biosynthesis of this vitamin (1) to see how D-glucose, a D-monosaccharide, is converted to L-ascorbic acid and (2) to see the types of reactions involved.

All steps in the biochemical synthesis of L-ascorbic acid are enzyme-catalyzed. As we look at them, we will be concerned only with recognizing types of reactions (oxidation, reduction, and the like), not with the particular enzymes or oxidizing and reducing agents involved in each reaction.

Oxidation of carbon 6 of D-glucose followed by reduction of the aldehyde at carbon 1 gives L-gulonic acid. This acid is of the L-series, not because of inversion of configuration at the penultimate carbon of D-glucose but because of the rules for writing Fischer projections. Carbon 1 of what was D-glucose is now —CH$_2$OH and carbon 6 is now —CO$_2$H. According to the Fischer convention, the carbon chain must be turned in the plane of the page and renumbered so that the carbonyl group (the most highly oxidized carbon) is uppermost and appears as carbon 1. When this is done, the —OH group on the penultimate carbon is now on the left and therefore the resulting monosaccharide belongs to the L series. If you compare the orientations of the —OH groups on carbons 2, 3, and 4 with that of the —OH group on carbon 5, and then refer to Table 19.1, you will discover that the monosaccharide you are now dealing with has the name gulose. The acid is therefore called gulonic acid since it is a carboxylic acid.

In the following step, L-gulonic acid is converted to a cyclic ester by reaction of the —OH on carbon 4 with the —CO$_2$H group. Cyclic esters are given the special name lactone. Therefore, the product formed in this reaction is called L-gulonolactone. Because humans, other primates, and guinea pigs lack the enzyme system necessary to convert L-gulonic acid to L-gulonolactone, they cannot synthesize ascorbic acid. Oxidation of the secondary alcohol at carbon 3, followed by enolization, gives L-ascorbic acid (vitamin C).

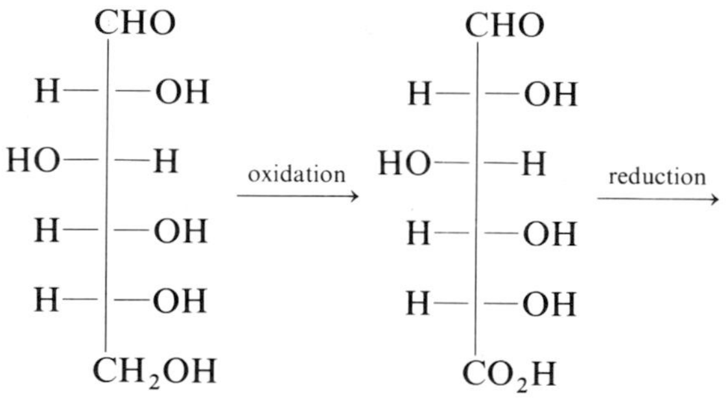

D-glucose   →(oxidation)→   D-gluconic acid   →(reduction)→

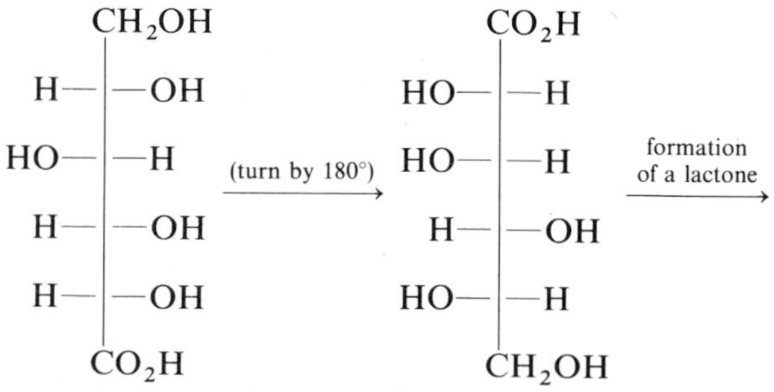

→(turn by 180°)→   L-gulonic acid   →(formation of a lactone)→

CH$_2$OH   CH$_2$OH   CH$_2$OH

H——ÒH   oxidation   H——OH   enolization   H——OH

O.   O.   O.

OH HO$=$O $\longrightarrow$ OH $=$O $\longrightarrow$ $=$O

                                                  O   HO   OH

L-gulonolactone   L-ascorbic acid
                                                                       vitamin C

L-ascorbic acid is very easily oxidized to L-dehydroascorbic acid, a diketone.
Both L-ascorbic acid and L-dehydroascorbic acid are physiologically active and
are found together in most body fluids. Activity is lost if the lactone is hydrolyzed
to a carboxylic acid.

CH$_2$OH   CH$_2$OH

H——OH   H——OH

O.   oxidation   O.

$=$O $\underset{\text{reduction}}{\overset{\text{oxidation}}{\rightleftharpoons}}$ $=$O

HO   OH   O   O

L-ascorbic acid   L-dehydroascorbic acid

Approximately 30 million pounds of vitamin C is synthesized per year in the
United States, starting from D-glucose. Within the drug industry, only aspirin
exceeds vitamin C in quantity produced.

19.4 Disaccharides and Oligosaccharides

Most carbohydrates in nature contain more than one monosaccharide unit.
Those that contain two units are called **disaccharides**, those that contain three
units are called **trisaccharides**, and so on. The more general term **oligosaccharide**
is often used for carbohydrates that contain from 4 to 10 monosaccharides.
Carbohydrates containing larger numbers of monosaccharides are called **polysaccharides**.

In a disaccharide, two monosaccharide units are joined by a glycoside bond
between the anomeric carbon of one unit and an —OH of the other. Three
important disaccharides are maltose, lactose, and sucrose.

A. Maltose

Maltose derives its name from its presence in malt liquors, the juice from
sprouted barley, and other cereal grains. Maltose consists of two molecules of
D-glucose joined by a glycoside bond between carbon 1 (the anomeric carbon)
of one glucose and carbon 4 of the second glucose. Because the oxygen atom

on the anomeric carbon of the first glucose unit is alpha, the bond joining the two glucose units is called an α-1,4-glycoside bond. Following are Haworth and chair formulas for β-maltose, so named because the —OH on the anomeric carbon of the rightmost glucose unit is beta.

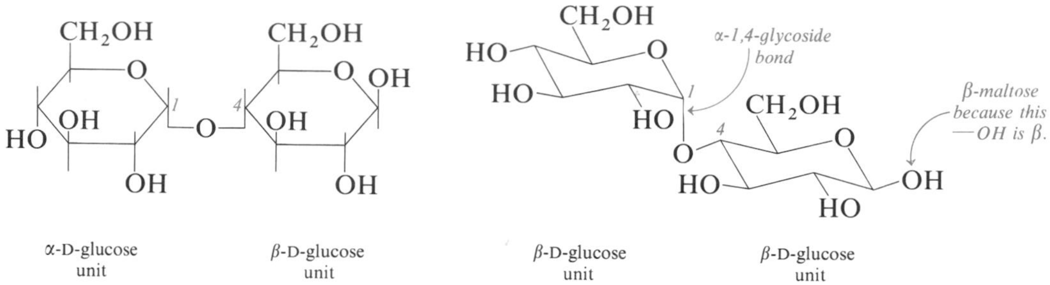

β-maltose (from the hydrolysis of starch)

Maltose is a reducing sugar, because the anomeric carbon on the right unit of D-glucose is in equilibrium with the free aldehyde and can be oxidized to a carboxylic acid.

B. Lactose

Lactose is the principal sugar present in milk. It makes up about 5–8% of human milk and 4–6% of cow's milk. Hydrolysis of lactose yields D-glucose and D-galactose. In lactose, a unit of D-galactopyranose is joined by a β-glycoside bond to carbon 4 of D-glucopyranose. Lactose is a reducing sugar.

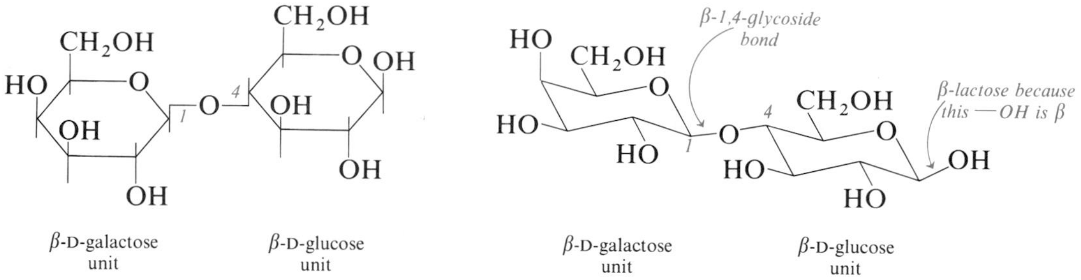

β-lactose (from the milk of mammals)

C. Sucrose

Sucrose (table sugar) is the most abundant disaccharide in the biological world. It is obtained principally from the juice of sugar cane and sugar beets. In sucrose, carbon 1 of D-glucose is joined to carbon 2 of D-fructose by an α-1,2-glycoside bond. Glucose is in a six-member (pyranose) ring form and fructose is in a five-member (furanose) ring form. Because the anomeric hemiacetal carbons of both glucose and fructose are involved in formation of the glycoside bond, sucrose is a nonreducing sugar.

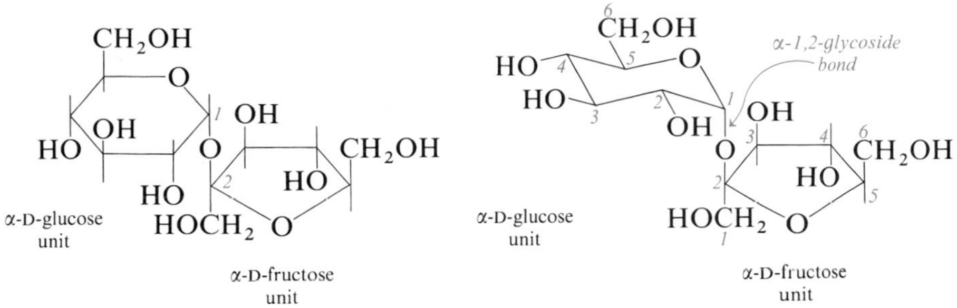

sucrose (cane or beet sugar)

Example 19.6

Draw Haworth and chair formulas for the alpha anomer of a disaccharide in which two units of D-glucopyranose are joined by an α-1,6-glycoside bond.

Solution

First draw the structural formula of α-D-glucopyranose. Then connect the anomeric carbon of this monosaccharide to carbon 6 of a second D-glucopyranose glucose unit by an α-glycoside bond. The resulting molecule is either alpha or beta, depending on the orientation of the —OH group on the reducing end of the disaccharide.

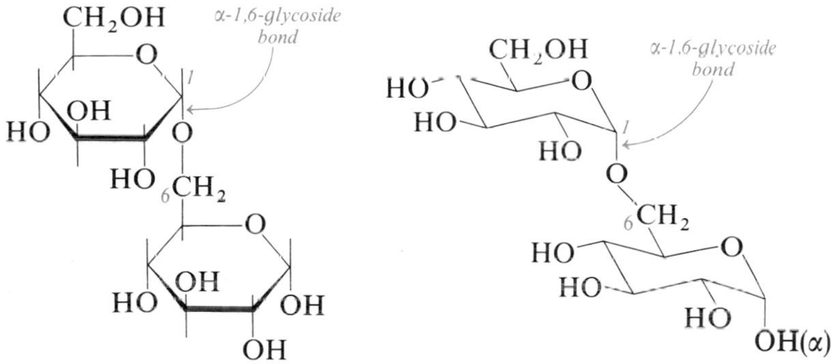

Problem 19.6

Draw Haworth and chair formulas for the beta anomer of a disaccharide in which two units of D-glucopyranose are joined by a β-1,6-glycoside bond.

D. Blood Group Substances

Plasma membranes of animal cells have large numbers of relatively small carbohydrates bound to them. In fact, it appears that the outsides of most plasma membranes are literally "sugar-coated." These membrane-bound carbohydrates are a part of the mechanism by which cell types recognize each other, and in effect act as biochemical markers (antigenic determinants). Typically, these membrane-bound carbohydrates contain from 4 to 20 monosaccharides, among which only a few kinds predominate. These include D-galactose (Gal), D-mannose (Man), L-fucose (Fuc), *N*-acetyl-D-glucosamine (NAGlu) and *N*-acetyl-D-galactosamine (NAGal). L-fucose is a 6-deoxymonosaccharide.

$$
\begin{array}{c}
\text{CHO} \\
\text{HO}\!-\!\!-\!\text{H} \\
\text{H}\!-\!\!-\!\text{OH} \\
\text{H}\!-\!\!-\!\text{OH} \\
\text{HO}\!-\!\!-\!\text{H} \\
\text{CH}_3
\end{array}
$$

An L-monosaccharide because —OH on carbon 5 is on the left.

Carbon 6 is —CH₃ rather than —CH₂OH

L-fucose

Among the first discovered and best understood of these membrane-bound carbohydrates are the so-called blood group substances. Although blood group substances are found chiefly on the surface of erythrocytes, they are also found on proteins and lipids in other parts of the body. In the ABO system, first described in 1900, individuals are classified according to four blood types: A, B, AB, and O. Blood from individuals of the same type can be mixed without clumping (agglutination) of erythrocytes. However, if serum of type A blood is mixed with type B blood, or vice versa, the erythrocytes will clump. Serum from a type O individual causes clumping of both type A and type B blood. At the cellular level, the chemical basis for this classification is a relatively small, membrane-bound carbohydrate. Following is the composition of the tetrasaccharide found on erythrocytes of individuals with type A blood. The configurations of the glycoside bonds between the monosaccharides and of the bond between the tetrasaccharide and an —OH on the erythrocyte surface are shown in parentheses.

N-acetyl-D-galactosamine $\xrightarrow{(\alpha\text{-}1,4)}$ D-galactose $\xrightarrow{(\beta\text{-}1,3)}$ *N*-acetyl-D-glucosamine $\xrightarrow{(\beta\text{-}1,\ldots)}$ cell wall

(NAGal)   (Gal)   (NAGlu)

$\uparrow$ $(\alpha\text{-}1,2)$

L-fucose

(Fuc)

This tetrasaccharide has several distinctive features. First, it contains a monosaccharide of the "unnatural," or L series, namely L-fucose. Second, it contains D-galactose to which two other monosaccharides are bonded, one by an α-1,2-glycoside bond, the other by an α-1,4-glycoside bond. This last monosaccharide is what determines the ABO classification. In blood of type A, the chain terminates in *N*-acetyl-D-galactosamine (NAGal); in type B blood, it terminates instead in D-galactose (Gal); and in type O blood, it is missing completely. The saccharides of type AB blood contain both tetrasaccharides.

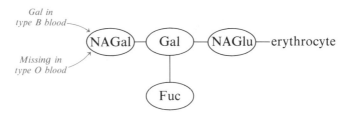

the biochemical marker (antigenic determinant) for type A blood

19.5 Polysaccharides

A. Starch: Amylose and Amylopectin

Starch is the reserve carbohydrate for plants. It is found in all plant seeds and tubers and is the form in which glucose is stored for later use by plants. Starch can be separated into two principal polysaccharides, amylose and amylopectin. While the starch from each plant is unique, most starches contain 19–25% amylose and 75–80% amylopectin. Complete hydrolysis of both amylose and amylopectin yields only D-glucose. X-Ray diffraction studies show that amylose is composed of continuous, unbranched chains of up to 4000 D-glucose monomers joined by α-1,4-glycoside bonds (Figure 19.7).

Amylopectin has a highly branched structure and contains two types of glycoside bonds. It contains the same type of chains of D-glucose joined by α-1,4-glycoside bonds as amylose does, but chain lengths vary from only 24 to 30 units. (See Figure 19.8.) In addition, there is considerable branching from this linear network. At branch points, new chains are started by α-1,6-glycoside bonds between carbon 1 of one glucose unit and carbon 6 of another glucose unit. In fact, amylopectin has such a branched structure that it is hardly possible to distinguish between main chains and branch chains.

Why are carbohydrates stored in plants as polysaccharides rather than monosaccharides, a more directly usable form of energy? The answer has to do with osmotic pressure (Section 7.6D), which is proportional to molar concentration, not the molecular weight of a solute. If we assume that 1000 molecules of glucose are assembled in one starch macromolecule, then we can predict that a solution containing 1 g of starch per 10 mL will have only $\frac{1}{1000}$ the osmotic pressure of a solution of 1 g of glucose in the same volume of solution. This feat of packaging is of tremendous advantage because it reduces the strain on various membranes enclosing such macromolecules.

B. Glycogen

Glycogen is the reserve carbohydrate for animals. Like amylopectin, glycogen is a nonlinear polymer of D-glucose joined by α-1,4- and α-1,6-glycoside bonds,

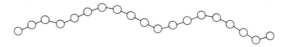

amylose
(long unbranched chains of glucose units
joined by α-1,4-glycoside bonds)

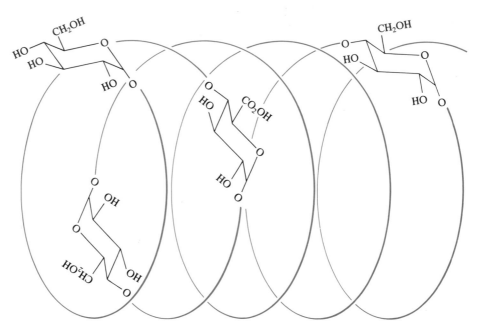

Figure 19.7 Amylose is a linear polymer of up to 4000 monomers of D-glucose joined by α-1,4,-glycoside bonds.

CH₂OH

α-1,6-glycosidic linkage

CH₂OH

O

CH₂

CH₂OH

α-1,4-glycosidic linkages

amylopectin

Figure 19.8 Amylopectin is a highly branched polymer with chains of 24–30 units of D-glucose joined by α-1,4-glycoside bonds and branch points created by α-1,6-glycoside bonds.

but it has a lower molecular weight and an even more highly branched structure (Figure 19.9). The total amount of glycogen in the body of a well-nourished adult is about 350 g, divided almost equally between liver and muscle.

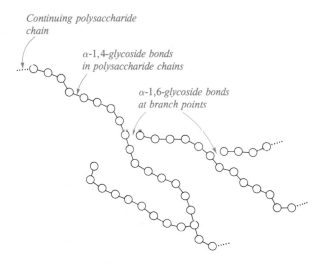

Figure 19.9 Glycogen is a highly branched polymer of D-glucose joined by α-1,4-glycoside bonds. Branch points created by α-1,6-glycoside bonds contain 12–18 units of glucose.

C. Cellulose

Cellulose, the most widely distributed skeletal polysaccharide, constitutes almost half the cell wall material of wood. Cotton is almost pure cellulose. Cellulose is a linear polymer of D-glucose monomers joined by β-1,4-glycoside bonds (Figure 19.10). It has an average molecular weight of 400,000, corresponding to approximately 2800 glucose units. Cellulose fibers consist of bundles of parallel polysaccharide chains held together by hydrogen bonding between hydroxyl groups on adjacent chains. This arrangement of parallel chains in bundles and the resulting hydrogen bonding gives cellulose fibers their high mechanical strength.

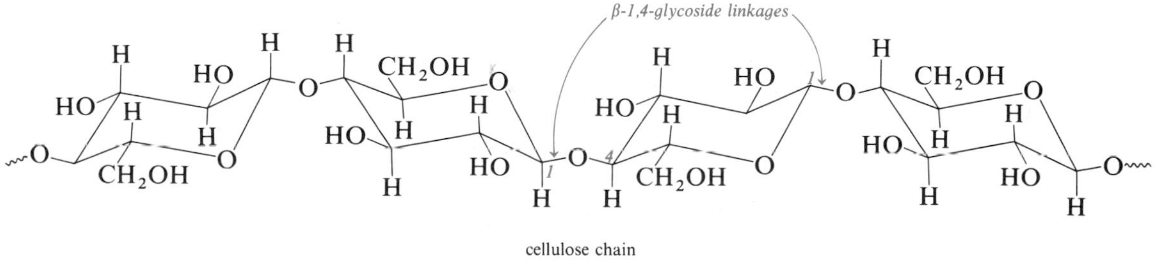

cellulose chain

Figure 19.10 Cellulose is a linear polymer of up to 3000 units of D-glucose joined by β-1,4-glycoside bonds.

Humans and other animals cannot use cellulose as a food. The reason is that our digestive systems do not contain β-glycosidases, enzymes that catalyze hydrolysis of β-glycoside bonds. They contain only α-glycosidases; hence, the polysaccharides we use as sources of glucose are starch and glycogen. On the other hand, many bacteria and microorganisms do contain β-glycosidases and can digest cellulose. Termites are fortunate in having such bacteria in their intestines and can use wood as their principal food. Ruminants (cud-chewing animals) can also digest grasses and wood because β-glycosidase-containing microorganisms are present in their alimentary systems.

D. Textile Fibers from Cellulose

Cotton, an important textile fiber, is almost pure cellulose. However, cotton represents only an insignificant fraction of the cellulose in the biological world. Both rayon and acetate rayon are made from chemically modified and regenerated cellulose and were the first man-made textile fibers to become commercially important.

In the production of **rayon**, cellulose is converted to a water-soluble derivative by reaction with carbon disulfide to form an alkali-soluble xanthate ester. A solution of cellulose xanthate is then extruded through a spinnerette, a metal disc with many tiny holes, into dilute sulfuric acid to hydrolyze the xanthate esters and precipitate free, or "regenerated," cellulose. Regenerated cellulose extruded as a filament is called viscose rayon thread; extruded as a sheet, it is called cellophane.

$$R-\overset{..}{\underset{..}{O}}H + \overset{..}{\underset{..}{S}}{=}C{=}\overset{..}{\underset{..}{S}} \xrightarrow{\text{NaOH}} R-\overset{..}{\underset{..}{O}}-\overset{\overset{:\overset{..}{S}:}{\|}}{C}-\overset{..}{\underset{..}{S}}:^- \text{Na}^+$$

carbon
disulfide

sodium salt of
a xanthate ester

In the industrial synthesis of acetate rayon, cellulose is acetylated with acetic anhydride. Acetylated cellulose is then dissolved in a suitable solvent, precipitated, and drawn into fibers known as acetate rayon. Cellulose acetate, acetylated to the extent of about 80%, became commercial in Europe about 1920 and in the United States a few years later. Cellulose triacetate, which has about 97% of the hydroxyls converted to acetate esters, became commercial in the United States in 1954. Today, acetate fibers rank fourth in production in the United States, surpassed only by Dacron polyester, Nylon, and rayon fibers.

one glucose unit of a
fully acetylated cellulose

Key Terms and Concepts

amino sugar (19.1D)

anomeric carbon (19.1E)

Benedict's solution (19.2D)

blood group substances (19.4D)

carbohydrate (introduction)

disaccharide (19.4)

Fischer projection formula (19.1C)

furanose (19.1E)

glycoside (19.2A)

N-glycoside (19.2A)

glycoside bond (19.2A)

Haworth structure (19.1E)

monosaccharide (19.1A)

D-monosaccharide (19.1C)

L-monosaccharide (19.1C)

mutarotation (19.1F)

nonreducing carbohydrate (19.2D)

oligosaccharide (19.4)

polysaccharide (19.4 and 19.5)

pyranose (19.1E)

rayon (19.5D)

reducing carbohydrate (19.2D)

saccharide (introduction)

Key Reactions

1. Formation of cyclic hemiacetals and hemiacetals (Section 19.1E).

2. Reaction of monosaccharides with alcohols: formation of glycosides (Section 19.2A).

3. Reaction of monosaccharides with heterocyclic aromatic amines to form *N*-glycosides (Section 19.2A).

4. Reduction of monosaccharides to alditols (Section 19.2C).

5. Oxidation of monosaccharides to aldonic acids: reducing sugars (Section 19.2D).

Problems

Structure of monosaccharides (Section 19.1)

19.7 The term carbohydrate is derived from "hydrates of carbon." Show the origin of this term by reference to the molecular formulas of D-ribose, D-fructose, and lactose.

19.8 Explain the meaning of the designations D and L as used to specify the stereochemistry (configuration) of monosaccharides.

19.9 List the rules for drawing Fischer projection formulas.

19.10 Table 19.1 shows a Fischer projection formula of D-arabinose. Draw a Fischer projection formula of L-arabinose, a natural aldopentose of the "unnatural" L-configuration.

19.11 **a.** Build a molecular model of D-glucose in the open-chain form.

b. Using this molecular model, show the reaction of the —OH on carbon 5 with the aldehyde of carbon 1 to form a cyclic hemiacetal. Show that either alpha-D-glucose or beta-D-glucose can be formed, depending on the direction from which the —OH group interacts with the aldehyde group.

19.12 Explain the conventions alpha and beta as used to designate the stereochemistry of cyclic forms of monosaccharides.

19.13 Explain the phenomenon of mutarotation with reference to carbohydrates. How is mutarotation detected?

19.14 A solution of alpha-D-glucose has a specific rotation of $+112°$; a beta-D-glucose solution has a specific rotation of $+19°$. On mutarotation, the specific rotation of each solution changes to an equilibrium value of $+52°$. Calculate the percentage of beta-D-glucose in the equilibrium mixture.

Reactions of monosaccharides (Section 19.2)

19.15 There are four isomeric D-aldopentoses (Table 19.1). Suppose the aldehyde in each is reduced to a primary alcohol. Which yield optically inactive alditols? Which yield optically active alditols?

19.16 An important technique for establishing relative configurations among isomeric aldoses is to convert both terminal carbon atoms to the same functional group. This can be done by either selective oxidation or selective reduction. As a specific example, nitric acid oxidation of D-erythrose gives *meso*-tartaric acid. Oxidation of D-threose under similar conditions gives D-tartaric acid.

$$\text{D-threose} \xrightarrow[\text{oxidation}]{\text{HNO}_3} \text{D-tartaric acid}$$

$$\text{D-erythrose} \xrightarrow[\text{oxidation}]{\text{HNO}_3} \textit{meso-}\text{tartaric acid}$$

Using this information, show which of the following structural formulas is D-erythrose and which is D-threose. Check your answer by referring to Table 19.1.

```
        CHO                    CHO
a.  H——|——OH      b.  HO——|——H

    H——|——OH          H——|——OH

       CH₂OH                 CH₂OH
```

19.17 Classify the following as reducing or nonreducing sugars.
a. alpha-D-glucose   **b.** beta-D-ribose
c. 2-deoxy-D-ribose   **d.** alpha-methyl-D-glucoside

19.18 Treatment of D-glucose in dilute aqueous base at room temperature yields an equilibrium mixture of D-glucose, D-mannose, and D-fructose. How might you account for this conversion? (*Hint*: Review Section 15.7B and your answers to Problems 15.21 and 15.22.)

19.19 Ketones are not oxidized by mild oxidizing agents. However, both dihydroxyacetone and fructose give a positive Benedict's test and are classified as reducing sugars. How could you explain that these ketoses are reducing sugars? (*Hint:* These tests are done in dilute aqueous base.)

19.20 L-fucose is one of several monosaccharides commonly found in the surface polysaccharides of animal cells. This 6-deoxyaldohexose is synthesized from D-mannose in a series of eight steps, shown below.

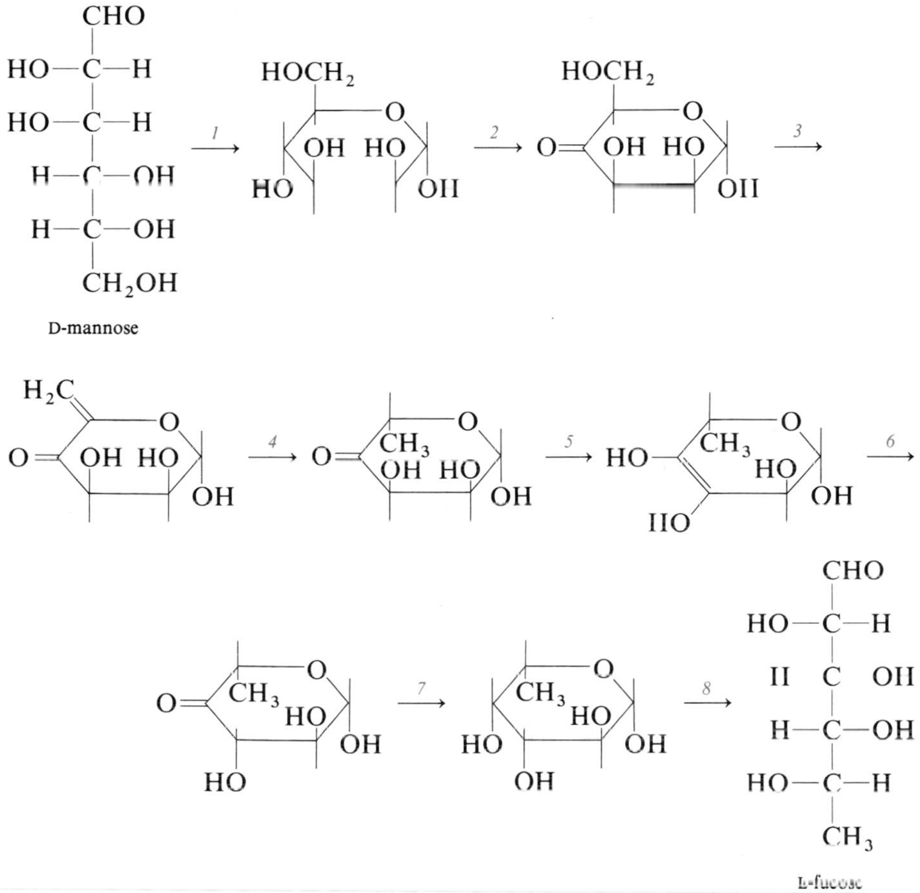

D-mannose

L-fucose

a. Describe the type of reaction (oxidation, reduction, hydration, and so on) involved in each step.

b. Explain why this monosaccharide belongs to the L series even though it is derived biochemically from a D sugar.

19.21 Draw structural formulas for the following phosphate esters.
a. beta-D-galactose 6-phosphate
b. beta-D-ribose 3-phosphate
c. beta-2-deoxy-D-ribose 5-phosphate
d. beta-D-ribose 1,3-diphosphate
e. glycerol 1-phosphate

19.22 The backbone of ribonucleic acid (RNA) consists of units of beta-D-ribose joined by phosphate ester bonds between the hydroxyl on carbon

3 of one ribose and the hydroxyl on carbon 5 of another ribose. Draw the structural formula of two units of beta-D-ribose joined in this manner.

(beta-D-ribose)—(phosphate)—(beta-D-ribose)

Disaccharides and oligosac- charides (Section 19.4)

19.23 Classify the following as reducing or nonreducing sugars.
  a. sucrose   **b.** lactose
  c. alpha-methyl-lactoside   **d.** maltose
  e. beta-methyl-maltoside

19.24 Trehalose, a disaccharide consisting of two glucose units joined by an alpha-1,1-glycoside bond, is found in young mushrooms and is the chief carbohydrate in the blood of certain insects.

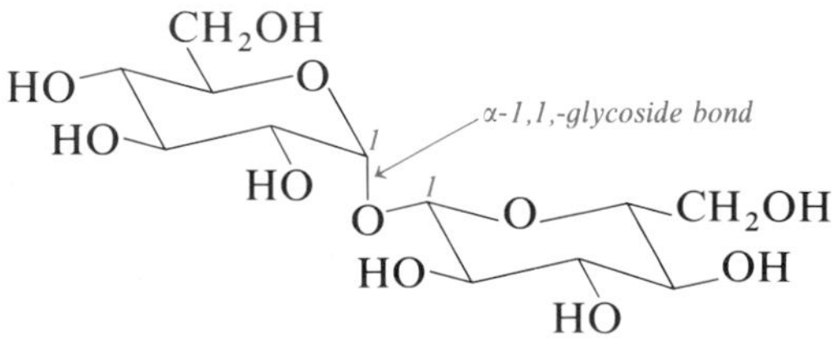

From its structural formula, would you expect trehalose (a) to be a reducing sugar? (b) to undergo mutarotation?

19.25 Raffinose is the most abundant trisaccharide in nature.
  a. Name the three monosaccharide units in raffinose.
  b. There are two glycoside bonds in raffinose. Describe each as you have already done for other disaccharides.
  c. Would you expect raffinose to be a reducing sugar?
  d. Would you expect raffinose to undergo mutarotation?

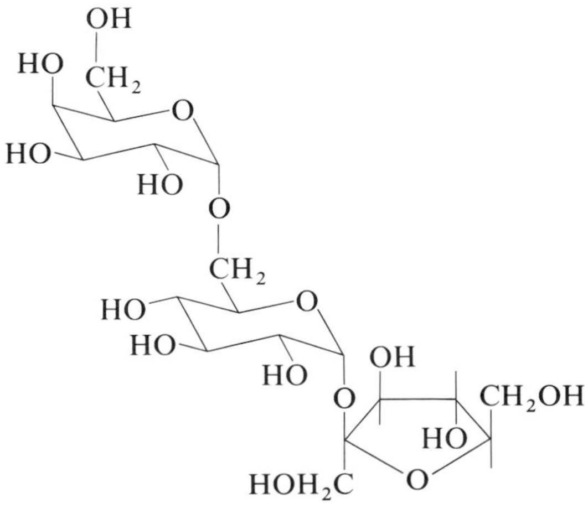

raffinose

19.26 Following is the Fischer projection formula for *N*-acetyl-D-glucosamine. This substance forms a six-member cyclic hemiacetal.

$$\underset{\text{N-acetyl-D-glucosamine}}{\begin{array}{c} \text{CHO} \quad \overset{\text{O}}{\underset{\parallel}{}} \\ \text{H}\!-\!\!-\!\text{NH}\!-\!\overset{}{\text{CCH}}_3 \\ \text{HO}\!-\!\!-\!\text{H} \\ \text{H}\!-\!\!-\!\text{OH} \\ \text{H}\!-\!\!-\!\text{OH} \\ \text{CH}_2\text{OH} \end{array}}$$

N-acetyl-D-glucosamine

a. Draw Haworth and chair structures for the alpha and beta forms of this monosaccharide.

b. Draw Haworth and chair structures for the disaccharide formed by joining two units of *N*-acetyl-D-glucosamine by a beta-1,4-glycoside bond. (If you have done this correctly, you have drawn the structural formula of the repeating dimer of chitin, the polysaccharide component of the shells of lobster and other crustaceans.)

Polysac-
charides
(Section 19.5)

19.27 What is the main difference in structure between cellulose and starch? Why are humans unable to digest cellulose?

19.28 Propose a likely structure for the following polysaccharides.

a. Alginic acid, isolated from seaweed, is used as a thickening agent in ice cream and other foods. Alginic acid is a polymer of D-mannuronic acid units joined by beta-1,4-glycoside bonds.

b. Pectic acid is the main constituent of pectin, which is responsible for the formation of jellies from fruits and berries. Pectic acid is a polymer of D-galacturonic acid units joined by α-1,4-glycoside bonds.

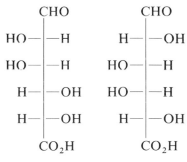

D-mannuronic acid   D-galacturonic acid

Clinical Chemistry— The Search for Specificity

The analytical procedure most often performed in the clinical chemistry laboratory is the determination of glucose in blood, urine, or other biological fluid. The need for a rapid and reliable test for blood glucose stems from the high incidence of the disease diabetes mellitus. There are approximately 2 million known diabetics in the United States, and it is estimated that another 2 million more are undiagnosed.

Diabetes mellitus is characterized by insufficient blood levels of the polypeptide hormone insulin (Section 21.6F). If insulin is deficient, glucose cannot enter muscle and liver cells, which in turn leads to increased levels of blood glucose (hyperglucosemia), impaired metabolism of fats and proteins, ketosis, and possibly diabetic coma. Thus, it is critical for the early diagnosis and effective management of this disease to have a rapid and reliable procedure for determining blood glucose.

Over the past 70 years, many such tests have been developed. We will discuss four of these, each chosen to illustrate something of the problems involved in developing suitable clinical laboratory tests and how these problems can be solved. Furthermore, these tests will illustrate the use of both chemical and enzymatic techniques in the modern clinical chemistry laboratory.

The first widely used glucose test was based on the activity of glucose as a reducing sugar. Specifically, the aldehyde group of glucose is oxidized by ferricyanide ion to a carboxyl group. In the process Fe(III) in ferricyanide ion is reduced to Fe(II) in ferrocyanide ion (Figure XIII-1). The reaction is carried out in the pres-

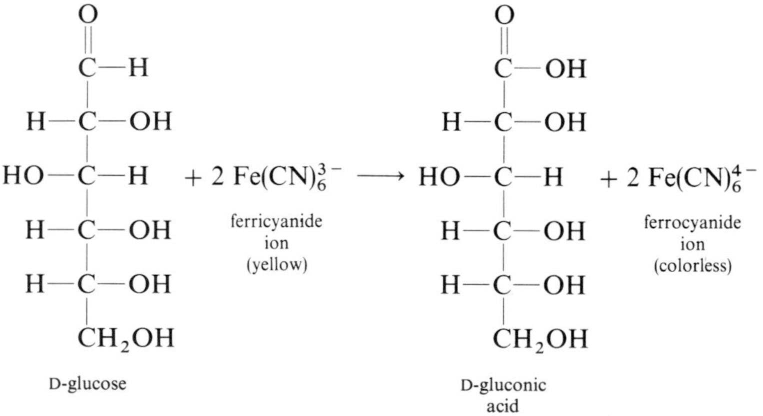

$$3 Fe(CN)_6^{4-} + 4 Fe^{3+} \longrightarrow Fe_4[Fe(CN)_6]_3$$

ferrocyanide ion   Prussian blue

Figure XIII-1 The first widely used glucose test was based on the ability of glucose to reduce Fe(III) in ferricyanide ion to Fe(II) in ferrocyanide ion. This in turn reacts with excess Fe(III) to form Prussian blue.

ence of excess Fe(III). Under these conditions, the ferrocyanide ion reacts further with Fe(III) to form ferric ferrocyanide, more familiar as Prussian blue. The concentration of glucose in the test sample is measured spectrophotometrically. In this test, the absorbance of Prussian blue is directly proportional to the concentration of glucose in the test sample.

Although this method can be used to measure glucose concentration, it has the disadvantage that ferricyanide also oxidizes several other reducing substances found in blood, including ascorbic acid, uric acid, certain amino acids, and phenols. In addition, any other aldoses present in blood also reduce ferricyanide. All these substances are said to give false positive results. The ferricyanide and other oxidative tests first developed often gave values as much as 30% or higher over the so-called true glucose value.

A more satisfactory approach in the search for specificity lay in attacking the problem in a completely different way, namely, by taking advantage of a chemical reactivity of glucose other than its property as a reducing sugar. One of the most successful and widely used of these nonoxidative methods involves reaction of glucose with o-toluidine to form a blue-green Schiff base. The absorbance of this Schiff base can be measured spectrophotometrically at 625 nm and is directly proportional to glucose concentration (Figure XIII-2).

The o-toluidine method can be applied directly to serum, plasma, cerebrospinal fluid, and urine, and to samples as small as 20 microliters (20×10^{-6} L). In addition, it does not give false positive results with other reducing substances, since the procedure itself does not involve oxidation. However, galactose and mannose, and to a lesser extent lactose and xylose, are potential sources of false positive results, because they also react with o-toluidine to give colored Schiff bases. This, however, is generally not a problem, since these mono- and disaccharides are normally present in serum and plasma only in very low concentrations.

In recent years the search for even greater specificity in glucose determinations has led to the introduction of enzyme-based glucose assay procedures. What was needed was an enzyme that catalyzes a specific reaction of glucose but not comparable reactions of any other substance normally present in biological fluids. The enzyme glucose oxidase meets these requirements. It catalyzes the oxidation of beta-D-glucose to D-gluconic acid (Figure XIII-3). Glucose oxidase is specific for beta-D-glucose. Therefore, complete oxidation of any sample containing both beta-D-glucose and alpha-D-glucose requires conversion of the alpha form to the beta form. Fortunately, this interconversion is rapid and complete in the short time required for the test. Molecular oxygen, O_2, is the oxidizing agent in

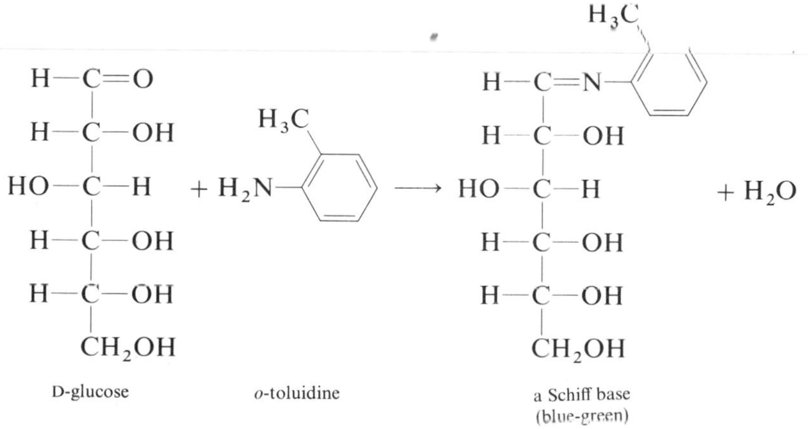

Figure XIII-2 For many years, the o-toluidine test was the standard clinical chemistry laboratory test for glucose.

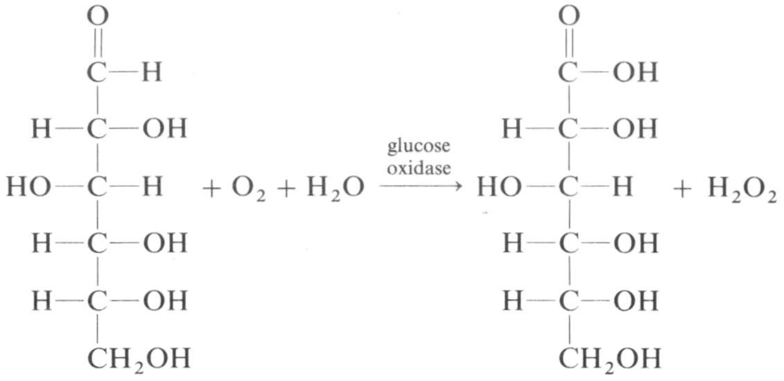

Figure XIII-3 The glucose oxidase method is the most specific test yet developed for measuring glucose concentration in biological fluids.

this reaction; it is reduced to hydrogen peroxide, H_2O_2, which in turn is used to oxidize another substance whose concentration can be determined spectrophotometrically. In one procedure, hydrogen peroxide is caused to react with iodide ion, to form molecular iodine, I_2:

$$2I^- + H_2O_2 + 2H^+ \longrightarrow I_2 + 2H_2O$$

The absorbance at 420 nm is used to calculate iodine concentration and then glucose concentration. In another procedure, hydrogen peroxide is used to oxidize o-toluidine to a colored product in a reaction catalyzed by the enzyme peroxidase. The concentration of the colored oxidation product is determined spectrophotometrically.

$$o\text{-toluidine} + H_2O_2 \xrightarrow{\text{peroxidase}}$$

$$\text{(colored products)} + H_2O$$

Several commercially available test kits use the glucose oxidase reaction for qualitative determination of glucose in urine. One of these, Clinistix (produced by the Ames Co., Elkhart, Ind.), consists of a filter-paper strip impregnated with glucose oxidase, peroxidase, and o-toluidine. The test end of the paper is dipped in urine, removed, and examined after 10 sec. A blue color

develops if the concentration of glucose in the urine exceeds about 1 mg/mL.

Recall that the first assay method we looked at in this mini-essay was also an oxidative procedure. However, it gave positive errors in the presence of other reducing substances. In a sense, the search for specificity has now come full circle, because now the most highly specific and accurate assay, and the one which is said to give "true" glucose values, is also an oxidative method. Unlike the earlier, ferricyanide method, however, this newer, oxidative method is highly specific because it is catalyzed by beta-D-glucose oxidase.

Any determination of glucose in blood or a 24-hr urine sample reflects glucose levels during the sample period only. There is now a simple, convenient laboratory method that can be used to monitor long-term glucose levels. This method depends on the measurement of the relative amounts of hemoglobin and certain hemoglobin derivatives normally present in blood. Hemoglobin A (HbA) is the main type of hemoglobin present in normal red blood cells. In addition, there are several lesser components, including glycosylated hemoglobins (HbA$_1$). Glycosylated hemoglobins (see Figure XIII-4) are synthesized within red blood cells in two steps. In step 1, the

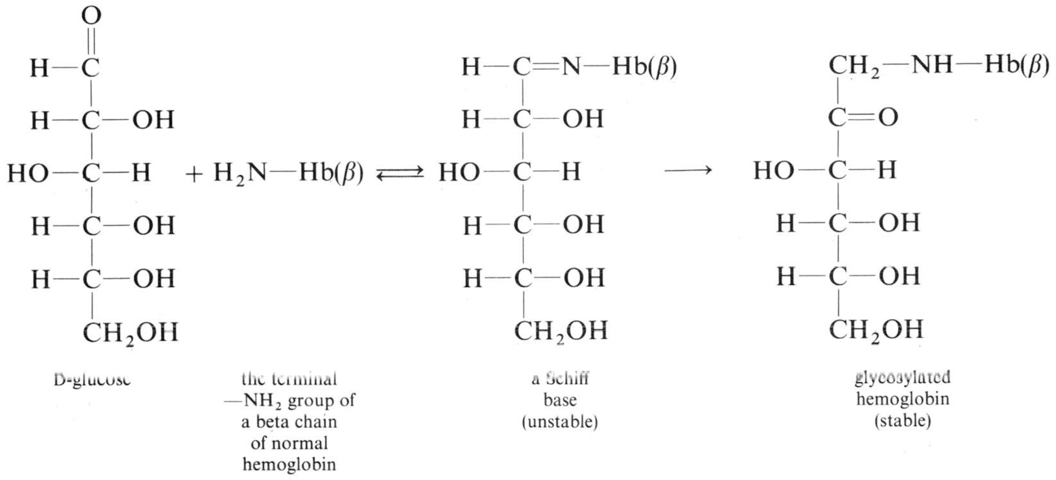

$$
\begin{array}{c}
\underset{D\text{-glucose}}{
\begin{array}{c}
\text{O} \\
\parallel \\
\text{H--C} \\
\text{H--C--OH} \\
\text{HO--C--H} \\
\text{H--C--OH} \\
\text{H--C--OH} \\
\text{CH}_2\text{OH}
\end{array}}
\; + \;
\text{H}_2\text{N--Hb}(\beta)
\;\rightleftharpoons\;
\underset{\begin{array}{c}a\ \text{Schiff}\\ \text{base}\\ \text{(unstable)}\end{array}}{
\begin{array}{c}
\text{H--C}=\text{N--Hb}(\beta) \\
\text{H--C--OH} \\
\text{HO--C--H} \\
\text{H--C--OH} \\
\text{H--C--OH} \\
\text{CH}_2\text{OH}
\end{array}}
\;\longrightarrow\;
\underset{\begin{array}{c}\text{glycosylated}\\ \text{hemoglobin}\\ \text{(stable)}\end{array}}{
\begin{array}{c}
\text{CH}_2\text{--NH--Hb}(\beta) \\
\text{C}=\text{O} \\
\text{HO--C--H} \\
\text{H--C--OH} \\
\text{H--C--OH} \\
\text{CH}_2\text{OH}
\end{array}}
\end{array}
$$

the terminal
—NH$_2$ group of
a beta chain
of normal
hemoglobin

Figure XIII-4 Formation of glycosylated hemoglobin.

free —NH$_2$ of the beta chain of hemoglobin reacts with the carbonyl group of glucose to form a Schiff base (Section 15.4C). Step 1 is reversible. In a slower, irreversible second step, the Schiff base undergoes a type of keto-enol tautomerism (Section 15.7B) to form a glyco-

sylated hemoglobin. A glycosylated hemoglobin molecule is shown schematically in Figure XIII-5.

Because this slow, reversible second step occurs continuously throughout the 120-day life span of a typical red blood cell, levels of glycosylated hemoglobin with a red blood cell pop-

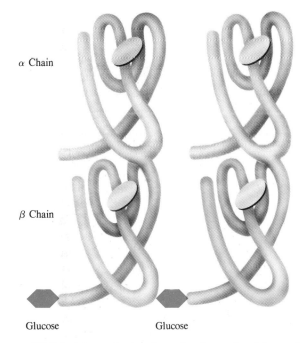

α Chain

β Chain

Glucose   Glucose

Figure XIII-5 Schematic drawing of a glycosylated hemoglobin.

ulation reflect the average blood glucose levels during that period.

Normal levels of glycosylated hemoglobins usually fall within the range 4.5–8.5% of total hemoglobin. In cases of uncontrolled or poorly controlled diabetes, the percentage of glycosylated hemoglobins may rise to two or three times these values. Conversely, once long-term blood-glucose levels have been achieved, glycosylated hemoglobins gradually fall to within normal ranges. Thus, the level of glycosylated hemoglobin can be used to give a picture of the average blood glucose level over the previous 8 to 10 weeks.

Sources

Bunn, H. F. 1981. Evaluation of glycosylated hemoglobin in diabetic patients. *Diabetes* 30:613.

Garet, M. C., Blouquit, Y., Molko, F., and Rosa, J. 1979. HbA$_1$—A review of its structure, biosynthesis, clinical significance, and methods of assay. *Biomedicine* 30:234.

Henry, R. J., Cannon, D. O., and Winkleman, J. W., eds. 1974. *Clinical Chemistry, Principles and Techniques.* 2d ed. New York: Harper and Row.

Tietz, N., ed. 1976. *Fundamentals of Clinical Chemistry.* Philadelphia: W. B. Saunders.

Lipids

Lipids are a heterogeneous class of natural organic compounds, grouped together not by the presence of a distinguishing functional group or structural feature, but rather on the basis of common solubility properties. Lipids are all insoluble in water and very soluble in one or more organic solvents, including diethyl ether, chloroform, benzene, and acetone. In fact, these four solvents are often referred to as lipid-solvents, or fat-solvents. Proteins, carbohydrates, and nucleic acids are largely insoluble in these solvents.

In this chapter we will describe the structure and biological function of representative members of the five major types of lipids: fats and oils, phospholipids, the fat-soluble vitamins, steroids, and waxes. In addition, we will describe the structure of biological membranes.

20.1 Fats and Oils

You certainly are familiar with fats and oils because you encounter them every day in such things as milk, butter, oleomargarine, and corn oil and other liquid vegetable oils, and also in many other foods. Fats and oils are triesters of glycerol and are called **triglycerides**. Triglycerides are the most abundant lipids. Complete hydrolysis of triglyceride yields one molecule of glycerol and three molecules of fatty acid:

$$\underset{\substack{\text{a triglyceride} \\ \text{(a fat or oil)}}}{\begin{array}{c} \text{O} \\ \| \\ \text{R}-\text{C}-\text{O}-\text{CH} \end{array} \begin{array}{c} \overset{\text{O}}{\overset{\|}{}} \\ \text{CH}_2-\text{O}-\text{C}-\text{R} \\ \\ \text{CH}_2-\text{O}-\text{C}-\text{R} \\ \| \\ \text{O} \end{array}} + 3\text{H}_2\text{O} \xrightarrow{\text{hydrolysis}} \underset{\text{glycerol}}{\begin{array}{c} \text{CH}_2-\text{OH} \\ | \\ \text{CH}-\text{OH} \\ | \\ \text{CH}_2-\text{OH} \end{array}} + \underset{\text{fatty acids}}{3\text{R}-\overset{\text{O}}{\overset{\|}{\text{C}}}-\text{OH}}$$

A. Fatty Acids

Fatty acids are monocarboxylic acids obtained from the hydrolysis of triglycerides. Over 70 different fatty acids have been isolated from various cells and tissues. Given in Table 20.1 are common names and structural formulas for several of the most abundant fatty acids.

Table 20.1
Some natural fatty acids.

Carbon Atoms	Structural Formula	Common Name	mp (°C)
Saturated fatty acids			
12	$CH_3(CH_2)_{10}CO_2H$	lauric acid	44
14	$CH_3(CH_2)_{12}CO_2H$	myristic acid	58
16	$CH_3(CH_2)_{14}CO_2H$	palmitic acid	63
18	$CH_3(CH_2)_{16}CO_2H$	stearic acid	70
20	$CH_3(CH_2)_{18}CO_2H$	arachidic acid	77
Unsaturated fatty acids			
16	$CH_3(CH_2)_5CH=CH(CH_2)_7CO_2H$	palmitoleic acid	−1
18	$CH_3(CH_2)_7CH=CH(CH_2)_7CO_2H$	oleic acid	16
18	$CH_3(CH_2)_4(CH=CHCH_2)_2(CH_2)_6CO_2H$	linoleic acid	−5
18	$CH_3CH_2(CH=CHCH_2)_3(CH_2)_6CO_2H$	linolenic acid	−11
20	$CH_3(CH_2)_4(CH—CHCH_2)_4(CH_2)_2CO_2H$	arachidonic acid	−49

We can generalize as follows about the most abundant fatty acid components of higher plants and animals.

1. Nearly all fatty acids have an even number of carbon atoms, most between 12 and 20 carbon atoms, in an unbranched chain. Those having 16 or 18 carbon atoms are by far the most abundant in nature.
2. The three most abundant fatty acids are palmitic, stearic, and oleic acids.
3. As the number of carbon atoms in a saturated fatty acid increases, its melting point increases.
4. Unsaturated fatty acids have lower melting points than their saturated counterparts.
5. The greater the degree of unsaturation in a fatty acid, the lower its melting point.
6. In most unsaturated fatty acids, cis isomers predominate; trans isomers are rare.

Because fatty acids have long hydrocarbon chains, they are insoluble in water. They do interact with water in a particular way, however. If a drop of fatty acid is placed on the surface of water, it spreads out to form a thin film one molecule thick (a monomolecular layer), with the polar carboxyl groups dissolved in the water and the nonpolar hydrocarbon chains forming a hydrocarbon layer on the surface of the water (Figure 20.1).

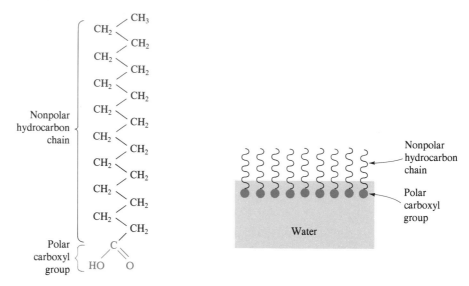

Figure 20.1 Interaction of fatty acid molecules with water to form a monomolecular layer.

B. Structure of Triglycerides

A triglyceride in which all three fatty acids are identical is called a simple triglyceride. Simple triglycerides are rare in nature; mixed triglycerides are much more common. Following is the structural formula of a mixed triglyceride formed from glycerol and molecules of stearic, oleic, and palmitic acids, the three most abundant fatty acids:

C. Physical Properties of Triglycerides

The physical properties of a triglyceride depend on its fatty acid components. In general, the melting point of a triglyceride increases as the number of carbons in its hydrocarbon chains increases and decreases as the degree of unsaturation increases. Triglycerides rich in oleic acid, linoleic acid, and linolenic and other unsaturated fatty acids are generally liquid at room temperature and are called **oils**. Triglycerides rich in palmitic, stearic, and other saturated fatty acids are generally semisolids or solids at room temperature and are called **fats**. Table

Table 20.2
Distribution of
saturated and
unsaturated fatty
acids in some
triglycerides.
Percentages are
given for the
most abundant
fatty acids; others
are present in
lesser amounts.

Source	% Triglyceride in Edible Portion	% Fatty Acids by Weight		
		Saturated	Oleic	Linoleic
Animal fat				
beef	5–37	48.0	49.6	2.5
butter	81	54.2	27.7	36
fish (tuna)	4	24	25	0.5
milk (whole)	4	57	33	3
pork	52	37	42	10
Vegetable oil				
coconut oil	100	76.2	7.5	0.5
corn oil	100	14.6	49.6	34.3
peanut oil	100	13.8	56.0	26
soybean oil	100	13.4	28.9	50.7
cottonseed oil	100	27.2	22.9	47.8

20.2 lists the percentage composition in grams of fatty acid per 100 grams of triglyceride for several common fats and oils. Notice that beef tallow is approximately 48.0% saturated and 53.1% unsaturated fatty acids by weight. Vegetable oils such as corn oil, soybean oil, and wheat germ oil are all approximately 80% by weight unsaturated fatty acids. Butter fat is distinctive in that it contains significant amounts of lower-molecular-weight fatty acids.

The lower melting points of triglycerides rich in unsaturated fatty acids (vegetable oils, as compared with animal fats) are related to differences in three-dimensional shape between the hydrocarbon chains of unsaturated and of saturated fatty acid components. Shown in Figure 20.2 is the structural formula of tripalmitin and a space-filling model of this saturated triglyceride. Notice that the three saturated hydrocarbon chains of tripalmitin lie parallel to each other and that the molecule has an ordered, compact shape. Dispersion forces between these hydrocarbon chains are strong. Because of this compact nature and the interaction by dispersion forces, triglycerides rich in saturated fatty acids have melting points above room temperature.

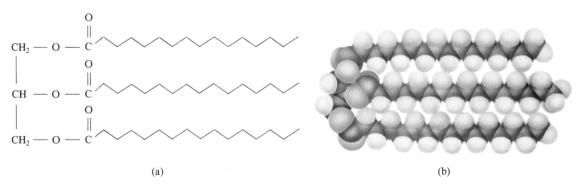

(a) (b)

Figure 20.2 A saturated triglyceride, tripalmitin: (a) structural formula; (b) space-filling model.

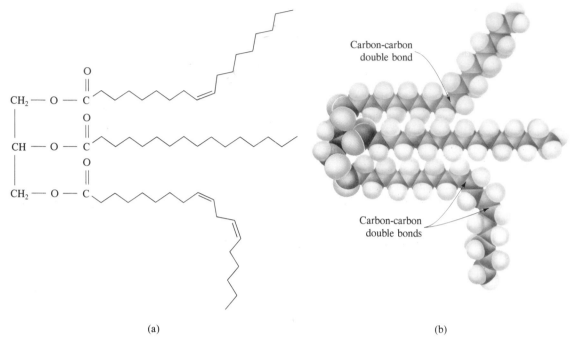

(a)   (b)

Figure 20.3 An unsaturated triglyceride: (a) structural formula; (b) space-filling model.

The three-dimensional shape of an unsaturated triglyceride is quite different from the shape of a saturated triglyceride. Figure 20.3 shows the structural formula of a triglyceride derived from one molecule each of palmitic acid, oleic acid, and linoleic acid. Notice the cis configuration about the double bonds in the hydrocarbon chains of oleic and linoleic acids. Also shown in Figure 20.3 is a space-filling model of this unsaturated triglyceride. An unsaturated triglyceride has a far less ordered structure than a saturated triglyceride, and because unsaturated triglycerides do not pack together so closely and compactly, dispersion forces between them are not so great as the dispersion forces between saturated triglycerides. Consequently, unsaturated triglycerides have lower melting points than the triglycerides that are more highly saturated.

Example 20.1

Following is the fatty acid composition by percentage of two triglycerides. Predict which triglyceride has the lower melting point.

	% Fatty Acid by Weight				
Triglyceride	Palmitic	Stearic	Palmitoleic	Oleic	Linoleic
A	24.0	8.4	5.0	46.9	10.2
B	9.8	2.4	0.4	28.9	50.7

Solution   Triglyceride A is composed of approximately 32% saturated fatty acids and 62% unsaturated fatty acids. Triglyceride B is composed of 12% saturated fatty acids and 80% unsaturated fatty acids. Of the unsaturated fatty acids in B, more than 50% are linoleic acid, a fatty acid with two double bonds. Predict that triglyceride B has a lower melting point because of its higher degree of unsaturation. The fatty acid composition of triglyceride A is typical of human depot fat (mp 15°C). Triglyceride B is soybean oil (mp − 16°C).

Problem 20.1

Why do beef tallow and corn oil, both composed of approximately 50% oleic acid, have such different melting points?

D. Rancidity

On exposure to air, most triglycerides develop an unpleasant odor and flavor, and are said to become rancid. In part, **rancidity** is the result of slight hydrolysis of the fat and oil, causing production of low-molecular-weight fatty acids. The odor of rancid butter is due largely to the presence of butanoic acid formed by the hydrolysis of butterfat. These same low-molecular-weight fatty acids can be formed by air oxidation of unsaturated fatty-acid side chains. The rate of rancidification varies with individual triglycerides, largely because of the presence of certain natural substances called antioxidants, which inhibit the process. One of the most common lipid antioxidants is vitamin E (Section 20.6C).

E. Reduction of Fats and Oils

For various reasons, partly convenience and partly dietary preference, conversion of oils to fats has become an important industry. The process is called **hardening** and involves reaction of an oil with hydrogen in the presence of a catalyst and **reduction** of some of the carbon-carbon double bonds of a triglyceride. If all double bonds are reduced (saturated with hydrogen), the resulting triglyceride is hard and brittle. In practice, the degree of hardening is carefully controlled to produce fat of a desired consistency. The resulting fats are sold for kitchen use (Crisco, Spry, and others). Oleomargarine and other butter substitutes are prepared by hydrogenation of cottonseed, soybean, corn, or peanut oils. The resulting product is often churned with milk and artificially colored to give it a flavor and a consistency resembling those of butter.

20.2 Soaps and Detergents

A. Structure and Preparation of Soaps

Soaps are potassium or sodium salts of fatty acids. Their preparation by boiling lard or other animal fat with potash is one of the most ancient organic reactions known. Potash (*pot* plus *ash*), so named because it is the solid residue obtained by extracting wood ashes with water and then evaporating the water in iron pots, is a mixture of potassium carbonate and potassium hydroxide. The reaction that takes place is **saponification** (hydrolysis in alkali) of the triglyceride, to give glycerol and potassium salts of fatty acids:

$$
\underset{\text{a triglyceride}}{
\begin{array}{c}
\quad\quad\quad\quad\quad O \\
\quad\quad\quad\quad\quad \| \\
\quad\quad\quad CH_2\!-\!O\!-\!C\!-\!R \\
O \quad\quad\quad | \\
\| \quad\quad\quad\quad | \\
R\!-\!C\!-\!O\!-\!CH \\
\quad\quad\quad\quad | \\
\quad\quad\quad CH_2\!-\!O\!-\!C\!-\!R \\
\quad\quad\quad\quad\quad \| \\
\quad\quad\quad\quad\quad O
\end{array}}
\;+\;3KOH\;
\xrightarrow[\text{(saponification)}]{\text{hydrolysis}}\;
\underset{\text{glycerol}}{
\begin{array}{c}
CH_2\!-\!OH \\
| \\
CH\!-\!OH \\
| \\
CH_2\!-\!OH
\end{array}}
\;+\;3\underset{\text{a potassium soap}}{
\begin{array}{c}
O \\
\| \\
R\!-\!C\!-\!O^-\,K^-
\end{array}}
$$

In Europe, soap manufacture started in Marseilles in the Middle Ages but by no means was it a commonly available product. However, by the late 1700s, manufacture of soap was widespread throughout Europe and North America, and had become a big industry. As the soap as well as the glass and paper industries prospered, more and more wood had to be burned to provide the potash, and it seemed for a time that the forests of Europe might be threatened. Fortunately, through a new technology called the LeBlanc process, sodium carbonate (soda) became commercially available on a large scale and could in turn be used to produce sodium hydroxide. The change from potassium hydroxide to sodium hydroxide meant a change from potassium soaps to sodium soaps.

The most common triglycerides used today are from beef tallow (from meat-packing plants) and from coconut palm oil. After hydrolysis is complete, sodium chloride is added to precipitate the soap as thick curds. The water layer is then drawn off and glycerol is recovered by vacuum distillation. The crude soap contains sodium chloride, sodium hydroxide, and also other impurities. These are removed by boiling the curd in water and reprecipitating with more sodium chloride. After several such purifications, the soap can be used without further processing as an inexpensive industrial soap. Fillers such as pumice may be added to make a scouring soap. Other treatments transform the crude soap into pH-controlled cosmetic soaps, medicated soaps, and the like.

B. How Soaps Clean

Soap owes its remarkable cleansing properties to its ability to act as an emulsifying agent. Regarded from one end, the organic portion of a natural soap is a polar, negatively charged, hydrophilic carboxylate group that interacts with surrounding water molecules by ion-dipole interactions. Regarded from the other end, it is a long, nonpolar, hydrophobic hydrocarbon chain that does not interact at all with surrounding water molecules. Because the long hydrocarbon chains of natural soaps are insoluble in water, they tend to cluster in such a way as to minimize their contact with surrounding water molecules. The polar carboxylate groups, on the other hand, tend to remain in contact with the surrounding water molecules. The problem, then, is how to shield the hydrophobic hydrocarbon chains from contact with water but keep the hydrophilic carboxylate groups in contact with water. The solution is to cluster soap molecules into **micelles**. In soap micelles, the charged carboxylate groups form a negatively

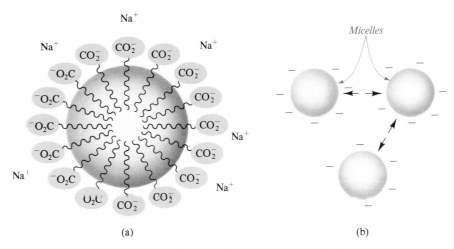

Figure 20.4 Soap micelles. (a) Diagram of a soap micelle showing nonpolar (hydrophobic) hydrocarbon chains clustered in the interior of the micelle and polar (hydrophilic) carboxylate groups spread on the surface of the micelle. (b) Soap micelles repel each other because of the negative charges on their surfaces.

charged surface and the nonpolar hydrocarbon chains lie buried within the center (Figure 20.4).

Most of the things we commonly think of as dirt, such as grease, oil, and fat stains are nonpolar and insoluble in water. When soap and this type of dirt are mixed together, as in a washing machine, the nonpolar hydrocarbon ends of soap micelles "dissolve" the nonpolar dirt molecules. In effect, new soap micelles are formed, this time with nonpolar dirt molecules in the center (Figure 20.5). In this way, nonpolar organic grease, oil, and dirt are dissolved and washed away in the polar wash water.

Soaps are not without their disadvantages. First, they are salts of weak acids, and in the presence of mineral acids, they are converted to free fatty acids. Whereas soaps are soluble in water as micelles, the free fatty acids are insoluble and form a scum. For this reason, soaps cannot be used in acidic solution.

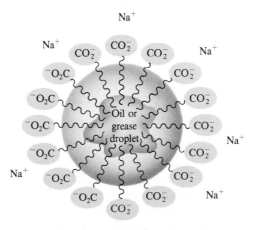

Figure 20.5 Soap micelles with a "dissolved" oil droplet.

$$CH_3(CH_2)_{16}CO_2^- \ Na^+ + HCl \longrightarrow CH_3(CH_2)_{16}CO_2H + NaCl$$

soluble in water   insoluble in

as micelles   water

Second, soaps form insoluble salts when used in water containing calcium, magnesium, or iron ions (hard water):

$$2CH_3(CH_2)_{16}CO_2^- \ Na^+ + Ca^{2+} \longrightarrow [CH_3(CH_2)_{16}CO_2^-]_2Ca^{2+} + 2Na^+$$

soluble in water   a water-insoluble

as micelles   calcium salt

These Ca(II), Mg(II), and Fe(III) fatty acid salts create problems, including rings around the bathtub, films that spoil the luster of hair, and grayness and roughness that build up on textiles after repeated washing.

C. Synthetic Detergents

Once the cleansing action of soaps was understood, the design criteria for a **synthetic detergent** could be established: a molecule with a long hydrocarbon chain, preferably 12 to 20 carbon atoms, and a polar group at one end of the molecule that does not form insoluble salts with Ca(II), Mg(II), or other ions present in hard water. Chemists recognized that the essential characteristics of a soap could be produced in a molecule containing a sulfate group instead of a carboxylate group. Calcium, magnesium, and iron salts of alkyl sulfate esters are much more soluble in water than comparable salts of fatty acids are.

The first synthetic detergent was made from 1-dodecanol (lauryl alcohol) by combining it with sulfuric acid to form a sulfate ester, followed by neutralization with sodium hydroxide to form sodium dodecyl sulfate (SDS):

$$CH_3(CH_2)_{10}CH_2OH + HO\overset{\overset{\displaystyle O}{\|}}{\underset{\underset{\displaystyle O}{\|}}{S}}OH \longrightarrow CH_3(CH_2)_{10}CH_2O\overset{\overset{\displaystyle O}{\|}}{\underset{\underset{\displaystyle O}{\|}}{S}}OH + H_2O$$

1-dodecanol   1-dodecyl hydrogen sulfate

(lauryl alcohol)   (lauryl hydrogen sulfate)

$$CH_3(CH_2)_{10}CH_2O\overset{\overset{\displaystyle O}{\|}}{\underset{\underset{\displaystyle O}{\|}}{S}}OH + NaOH \longrightarrow CH_3(CH_2)_{10}CH_2O\overset{\overset{\displaystyle O}{\|}}{\underset{\underset{\displaystyle O}{\|}}{S}}O^- \ Na^+ + H_2O$$

sodium dodecyl sulfate (SDS)

(sodium lauryl sulfate)

The physical resemblance between this synthetic detergent and natural soaps is obvious—a long nonpolar (hydrophobic) hydrocarbon chain and a highly polar (hydrophilic) end group. Large-scale commercial production of SDS was not possible because bulk quantities of 1-dodecanol were lacking. However, because of high foaming properties, SDS is used in numerous specialized applications, including many shampoos and cosmetics. It is also used in biochemistry to denature proteins and to disrupt biological membranes.

Currently, the most important synthetic detergent is dodecylbenzene sulfonate. Its preparation starts with dodecene, made by polymerizing four molecules of propylene (a byproduct of the petroleum refining industry). Next, benzene and the dodecene are reacted to form dodecylbenzene, and this is followed by sulfonation with sulfuric acid. The sulfonic acid is neutralized with NaOH and the product mixed with builders and spray-dried to give a smooth-flowing powder. The most common builders are sodium tripolyphosphate and sodium silicate.

$$4CH_3CH{=}CH_2 \xrightarrow{H_3PO_4} C_{12}H_{24} \xrightarrow[AlCl_3]{benzene} CH_3(CH_2)_{10}CH_2{-}\hspace{-0.3em}\bigcirc\hspace{-0.3em} \xrightarrow{H_2SO_4}$$

propylene   propylene   dodecylbenzene
           tetramer

$$CH_3(CH_2)_{10}CH_2{-}\hspace{-0.3em}\bigcirc\hspace{-0.3em}{-}\overset{O}{\underset{O}{\overset{\|}{\underset{\|}{S}}}}OH \xrightarrow{NaOH} CH_3(CH_2)_{10}CH_2{-}\hspace{-0.3em}\bigcirc\hspace{-0.3em}{-}\overset{O}{\underset{O}{\overset{\|}{\underset{\|}{S}}}}O^-\,Na^+$$

sodium dodecylbenzene sulfonate

Alkylbenzene sulfonate detergents were introduced in the 1950s, and today they command close to 90% of the market once held by natural soaps.

Among the common additives to the most detergent preparations are foam stabilizers, bleaches, and optical brighteners. A common foam stabilizer added to liquid soaps but not laundry detergents (for obvious reasons—think of a top-loading washing machine with foam spewing up over the lid!) is the amide prepared from dodecanoic acid (lauric acid) and 2-aminoethanol (ethanolamine). The most common bleach is sodium perborate tetrahydrate, which decomposes at temperatures above 50°C to give hydrogen peroxide, the actual bleaching agent.

$$CH_3(CH_2)_{10}\overset{O}{\overset{\|}{C}}NHCH_2CH_2OH \qquad NaBO_3{\cdot}4H_2O$$

N-hydroxyethyldodecanamide   sodium perborate
(a foam stabilizer)   (a bleach)

Also added to laundry detergents are optical brighteners, also called optical bleaches, that are absorbed onto fabrics and fluoresce with a blue color, offsetting any yellowing due to aging of the fabric. Quite literally, these optical brighteners produce a "whiter-than-white" appearance. You most certainly have observed the effects of optical brighteners if you have ever been in the presence of black lights and seen the glow of "white" T-shirts, blouses, and the like.

20.3 Phospholipids

Phospholipids are the second most abundant kind of natural lipids. They are found almost exclusively in plant and animal membranes, which typically consist of about 40–50% phospholipids and 50–60% protein.

The most abundant phospholipids contain glycerol and fatty acids, as the simple fats do. They also contain phosphoric acid and a low-molecular-weight alcohol. The most common of these low-molecular-weight alcohols are choline, ethanolamine, serine, and inositol. In the following formulas, the —OH involved in formation of the phosphate ester is shown in color. Further, each molecule is shown as it would be ionized at pH 7.4.

$$HOCH_2CH_2 \overset{CH_3}{\underset{CH_3}{\overset{|}{\underset{|}{N^+}}}} CH_3 \qquad HOCH_2CH_2NH_2 \qquad HOCH_2 \overset{}{\underset{NH_3^+}{\overset{|}{C}H}} CO_2^-$$

choline   2-aminoethanol   serine   inositol
                       (ethanolamine)

The most abundant phospholipids in higher plants and animals are the **lecithins** and the **cephalins**.

$$\overset{O}{\underset{RCO}{\overset{\|}{}}} - \overset{CH_2O - \overset{O}{\overset{\|}{C}}R}{\underset{CH_2O - \overset{O}{\overset{\|}{P}} - OCH_2CH_2^+ \overset{CH_3}{\underset{CH_3}{N}CH_3}}{\underset{O^-}{}}}$$

a lecithin
(a phospholipid
containing choline)

$$\overset{O}{\underset{RCO}{\overset{\|}{}}} - \overset{CH_2O - \overset{O}{\overset{\|}{C}}R}{\underset{CH_2O - \overset{O}{\overset{\|}{P}} - OCH_2CH_2NH_3^+}{\underset{O^-}{}}}$$

a cephalin
(a phospholipid
containing ethanolamine)

Lecithins are phosphate esters of choline and cephalins are phosphate esters of ethanolamine. Lecithin and cephalin are shown as they would be ionized at pH 7.4. At this pH, each of these molecules has a net charge of zero. The fatty acids most common in these membrane phospholipids are palmitic and stearic acids (both fully saturated) and oleic acid (one double bond in the hydrocarbon chain).

20.4 Biological Membranes

A. Composition

Membranes are an important feature of cell structure and are vital for all living organisms. Some of the most important functions of membranes can be illustrated by considering the **cell membrane**.

1. Cell membranes are mechanical barriers that separate the contents of cells from their environment.
2. Cell membranes control the passage of molecules and ions into and out of cells. For example, essential nutrients are transported into cells and metabolic wastes out of cells through their membranes. Cell membranes also help to regulate the concentrations of molecules and ions within cells.
3. Cell membranes provide structural support for certain proteins. Some of these proteins are "receptors" for hormone-carried "messages"; others are specific enzyme complexes.

The cell membrane is but one of the membranes possessed by most cells. Several other types of membranes found within a typical cell are shown in Figure 20.6.

The subcellular membranes shown in Figure 20.6 have functions similar to those of the cell membrane itself. For example, the nuclear membrane separates the nucleus from the rest of the cell. The inner membranes of the mitochondria contain the enzymes that catalyze the reactions of the final states of respiration (Chapter 24). The endoplasmic reticulum contains enzymes that carry out numerous synthetic reactions. The rough endoplasmic reticulum supports ribosomes and the enzymes that catalyze the synthesis of proteins from amino acids. The smooth endoplasmic reticulum contains hydroxylation enzymes, steroid synthesis enzymes, and enzymes for drug metabolism. Lysosomes contain enzymes that digest substances brought into the cell. Membranes are more than impervious, mechanical barriers separating the cell and its organelles from the environment. They are highly specialized structures that perform many tasks with great precision and accuracy.

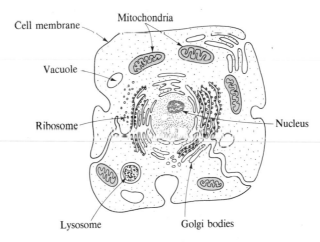

Figure 20.6 Diagram of a cell.

B. Structure

The determination of the detailed molecular structure of membranes is one of the most challenging problems in biochemistry today. Despite intensive research, many aspects of membrane structure and activity still are not understood. Before we discuss a model for membrane structure, let us first consider the shapes of phospholipid molecules and the organization of phospholipid molecules in aqueous solution.

Shown in Figure 20.7 is a structural formula and space-filling model of a lecithin, an important membrane phospholipid. Lecithin and other phospholipids are elongated, almost rodlike, molecules, with the nonpolar (hydrophobic) hydrocarbon chains lying essentially parallel to one another and with the polar (hydrophilic) phosphate ester group pointing in the opposite direction.

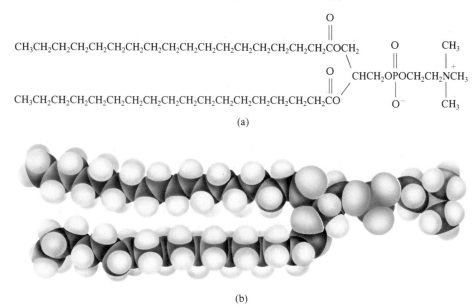

(a)

(b)

Figure 20.7 A lecithin: (a) structural formula; (b) space-filling model.

To understand what happens when phospholipid molecules are placed in aqueous medium, recall from Section 20.2B that soap molecules placed in water form micelles in which polar head groups interact with water molecules and nonpolar hydrocarbon tails cluster within the micelle and are removed from contact with water. One possible arrangement for phospholipids in water also is micelle formation (Figure 20.8).

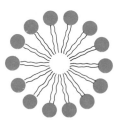

Figure 20.8 Proposed micelle formation of phospholipids in an aqueous medium.

Another arrangement that satisfies the requirement that polar groups interact with water and nonpolar groups cluster together to exclude water is a **lipid bilayer**. A schematic diagram of a lipid bilayer is shown in Figure 20.9. The

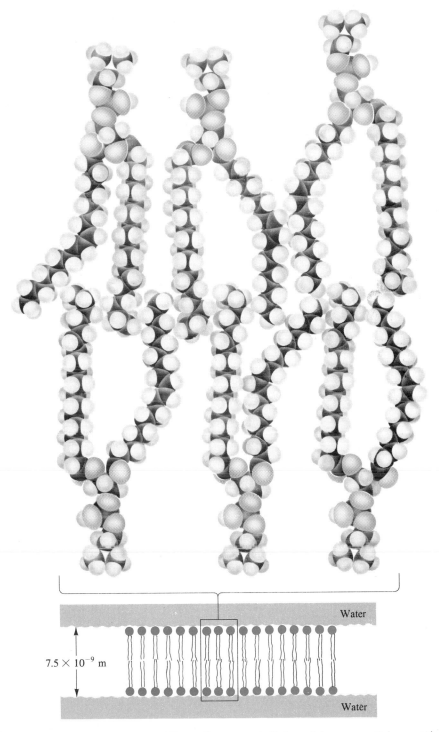

Figure 20.9 A section of lipid bilayer (lower part). Enlarged (upper part) is a section of six phospholipid molecules in the bilayer. Note in the enlargement that 50% of the hydrocarbon chains are unsaturated.

favored structure for phospholipids in aqueous solution is a lipid bilayer instead of a micelle, because micelles can grow only to a limited size before holes begin to appear in the outer polar surface. Lipid bilayers can grow to an almost infinite extent and provide a boundary surface for a cell or organelle, whatever its size.

It is important to realize that self-assembly of phospholipid molecules into a bilayer is a spontaneous process driven by two types of noncovalent forces: (1) hydrophobic interactions that result when nonpolar hydrocarbon chains cluster together and exclude water molecules, and (2) electrostatic interactions and hydrogen bonding that result when polar head groups interact with water molecules.

Lipid bilayers are highly impermeable to ions and most polar molecules because of their structural characteristics and because it takes a great deal of energy to transport an ion or a polar molecule through the nonpolar interior of the bilayer. Water, however, passes readily in and out of a lipid bilayer. Glucose passes through lipid bilayers 10^4 times more slowly than water, and sodium ion 10^9 times more slowly than water.

The most satisfactory current model for the arrangement of proteins and phospholipids in plant and animal membranes is the **fluid-mosaic model**. According to this model, membrane phospholipids form a lipid bilayer and membrane proteins are embedded in this bilayer. Some proteins are exposed to the aqueous environment on the outer surface of the membrane; others provide channels that penetrate the membrane from the outer to the inner surface; and still others are embedded within the lipid bilayer. Four possible protein arrangements are shown schematically in Figure 20.10.

The fluid-mosaic model is consistent with the evidence provided by chemical analysis and electron-microscope pictures of cell membranes. However, this model does not explain just how membrane proteins act as pumps and gates for the transport of ions and molecules across the membrane, or how they act as receptors for hormone-borne messages and communications between one cell and another. Nor does it explain how enzymes bound on membrane surfaces catalyze reactions. All these questions are active areas of research today.

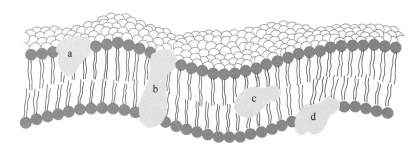

Figure 20.10 Fluid-mosaic model of a biological membrane, showing the lipid bilayer and membrane proteins oriented (a) on the outer surface of the membrane, (b) penetrating the entire thickness of the membrane, (c) embedded within the membrane, and (d) on the inner surface of the membrane.

20.5 Steroids

Steroids are a group of lipids that contain as a characteristic structural feature four fused carbon rings: 3 six-member rings designated A, B, and C; and 1 five-member ring designated D. Further, the parent compound from which all steroids are derived possesses methyl groups at the A/B and C/D ring junctions and a side chain of eight carbon atoms attached to ring D (Figure 20.11).

The steroid nucleus is found in many extremely important biomolecules, all of which are derived from cholesterol. In a sense, then, cholesterol can be called the parent steroid.

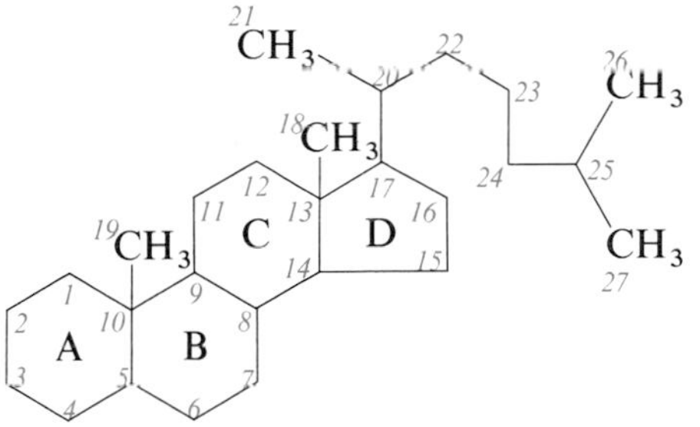

Figure 20.11 Letter designations and numbering system for steroids.

A. Cholesterol

Cholesterol is a white, water-insoluble compound found in varying amounts in practically all living organisms except bacteria. It is synthesized in the liver, intestine, and other tissues. Of these, synthesis in the liver is quantitatively the most important. Cholesterol contains multiple centers of chirality and possibilities for cis-trans isomerism about the five- and six-membered rings. The isomer that nature produces and the one that is involved in animal metabolism has somewhat the character of a staircase with risers and treads. It can be described as roughly planar with both angular methyl groups above the plane of the molecule.

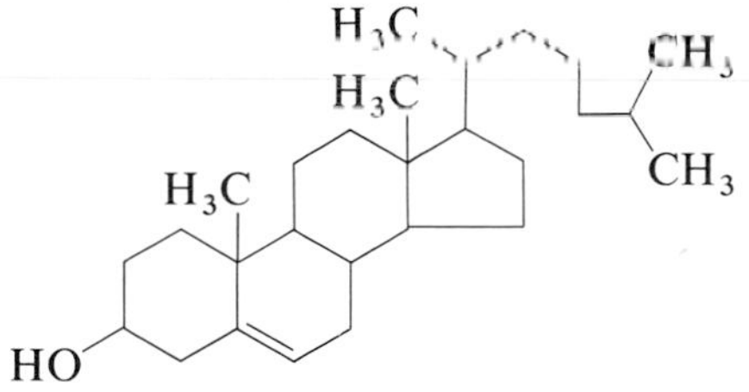

cholesterol

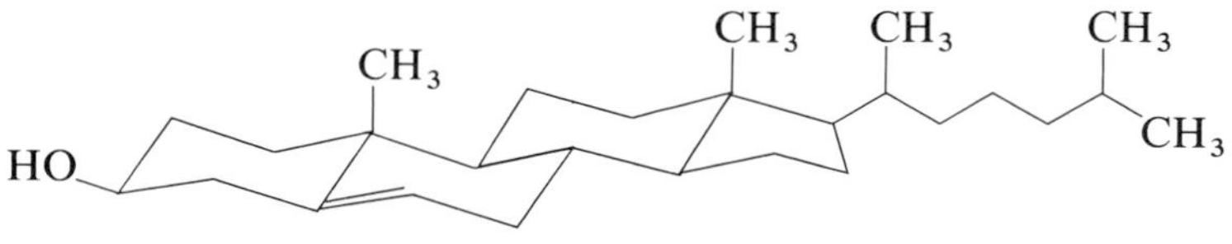

cholesterol is roughly planar with both angular methyl groups above the plane of the molecule

Cholesterol is a vital part of human metabolism because it is:

1. An essential component of biological membranes. The total body content of cholesterol in a healthy adult is about 140 g, of which 120 g is present in biological membranes. In humans, for example, membranes of the central and peripheral nervous systems contain about 10% cholesterol by dry weight.
2. The precursor for the biosynthesis of bile acids, steroid hormones, and vitamin D.

Because measuring the concentration of cholesterol in serum is easy, much information has been collected in attempts to correlate serum cholesterol levels with various diseases. Human blood plasma contains an average of 50 mg of free cholesterol per 100 mL and about 200 mg of cholesterol esterified with fatty acids. One of the diseases associated with increased concentrations of cholesterol is arteriosclerosis, or hardening of the arteries, among the most common of the diseases of aging. With increasing age, humans normally develop decreased capacity to metabolize fat, and therefore, cholesterol concentration in membranes increases. Because of the roughly planar shape and hydrophobic character of cholesterol, it is able to fit between the hydrophobic fatty acid chains of phospholipids, with its polar —OH group on the surface of the membrane in contact with polar parts of the phospholipids and with the aqueous environment. Because cholesterol has a very ordered and rigid structure, its increased concentration in membranes decreases their fluidity and makes them more susceptible to stress and rupture. This is particularly evident in membranes of the coronary artery. The correlation between elevated blood cholesterol levels and coronary artery disease is due, at least partly, to increased incorporation of cholesterol in coronary membranes and their resulting increased fragility.

Arteriosclerosis accompanied by a buildup of cholesterol and other lipids on the inner surfaces of arteries is known as **atherosclerosis**; the condition causes a decrease in the diameter of the channels through which blood must flow. This decreased diameter, together with increased turbulence, leads to a greater probability of clot formation. If a blood vessel is blocked by a clot, cells may be deprived of oxygen and die. Death of tissue in this way is called infarction.

Infarction can occur in any tissue, and the clinical symptoms depend on which vessels and tissues are involved. Myocardial infarction involves the myocardium, or heart muscle tissue. (For a discussion of an important laboratory method for diagnosis of myocardial infarction, see Mini-Essay XV, "Clinical Enzymology—The Search for Specificity.")

B. Adrenocorticoid Hormones

The cortex of the adrenal gland synthesizes two main classes of hormones, called **adrenocorticoid hormones**: (1) mineralocorticoid hormones, which affect water and electrolyte balance, and (2) glucocorticoid hormones, which affect carbohydrate and protein metabolism.

Aldosterone, the most effective mineralocorticoid hormone secreted by the adrenal cortex, acts on kidney tubules to stimulate resorption of sodium ions, thus regulating water and electrolyte metabolism. An adult on a diet with normal sodium content produces about 0.1 mg of aldosterone per day.

aldosterone
(a mineralocorticoid hormone
secreted by the adrenal cortex)

Cortisol is the principal glucocorticoid hormone of the adrenal cortex, which secretes about 25 mg of this substance per day. Cortisol affects the metabolism of carbohydrates, proteins, and fats; water and electrolyte balance; and inflammatory processes within the body. In the presence of cortisol, the synthesis of protein in muscle tissue is depressed, protein degradation is increased, and the supply of free amino acids is increased in both muscle cells and blood plasma. The liver, in turn, is stimulated to use the carbon skeletons of certain amino acids for the synthesis of glucose and glycogen. Thus, cortisol and other glucocorticoid hormones act to increase the supply of glucose and liver glycogen at the expense of body protein. Cortisol also has some mineralocorticoid action; it promotes resorption of sodium ions and water retention by the tubules of the kidney. However, it is far less potent as a mineralocorticoid than aldosterone is.

cortisol

cortisone

prednisolone

Cortisol and its oxidation product, cortisone, are probably best known for their use in clinical medicine as remarkably effective anti-inflammatory agents. They are used in the treatment of a host of inflammatory diseases, including acute attacks of rheumatoid arthritis and bronchial asthma, and inflammation of the eye, colon, and other organs. Laboratory research has produced a series of semisynthetic steroid hormones, including prednisolone, that are even more potent than cortisone in treating inflammatory diseases. Many of these semisynthetic hormones have the additional advantage over cortisone in not stimulating sodium retention and fluid accumulation.

C. Sex Hormones

Of the male sex hormones, or androgens, testosterone is the most important. It is produced in the testes from cholesterol. The chief function of testosterone is to promote normal growth of the male reproductive organs and development of the characteristic deep voice, pattern of facial and body hair, and musculature.

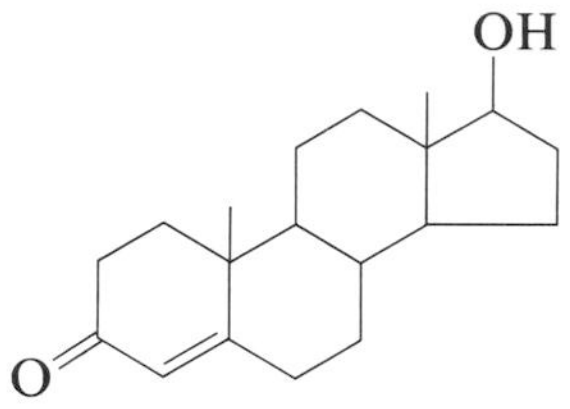

testosterone

The use of anabolic steroids among certain types of athletes to build muscle mass and strength, particularly for explosive sports, is common knowledge. Testosterone itself produces these effects but it is not active when taken orally because it is metabolized to an inactive steroid in the liver. Two laboratory modifications of testosterone have produced a synthetic steroid that does have these effects and at the same time has little of the virilizing effects of testosterone. Dianabol is synthesized by introduction of a methyl group on carbon 20 of ring D and a second carbon-carbon double bond in ring A.

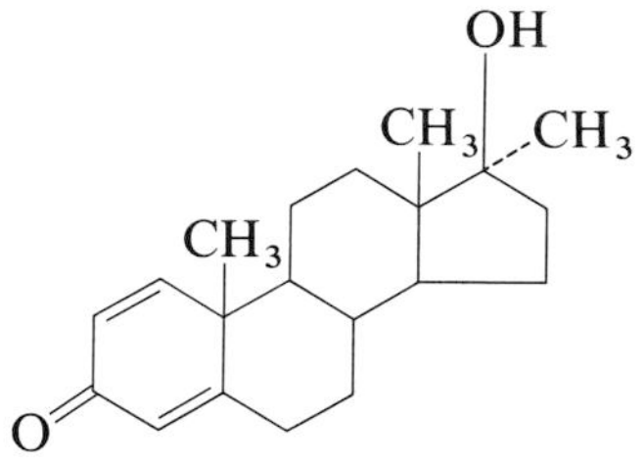

dianabol
(a synthetic anabolic steroid used to
increase muscle mass and strength)

It is thought that many male and female athletes take as much as 100 mg per day of dianabol while in training. Like any other drug, dianabol has its side effects, among which are increased sterility, impotence, and the risk of diabetes, coronary heart disease, and cancer. Increased awareness of these side effects coupled with routine urinalyses of athletes at big competitions, it is hoped, will help to prevent abuse of dianabol and other anabolic steroids.

Two types of female sex hormones are particularly important—progesterone, and a group of hormones known as estrogens. Changing rates of secretion of these hormones cause the periodic change in the ovaries and uterus known as the menstrual cycle. Immediately following menstrual flow, increased estrogen secretion causes growth of the uterus lining and ripening of ova. Estradiol is one of the most important of the estrogens, which are responsible for development of the female secondary sex characteristics.

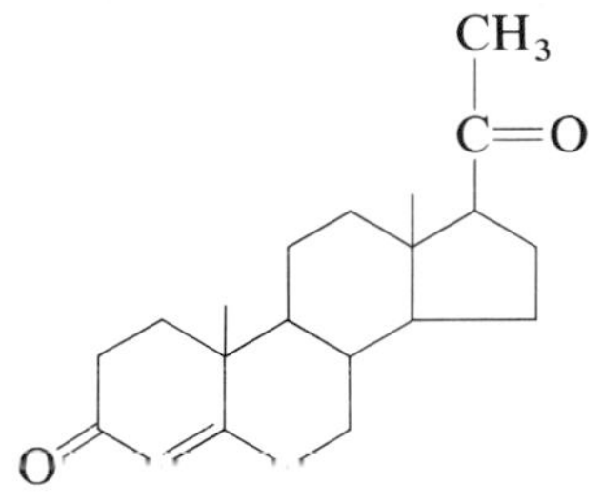

progesterone 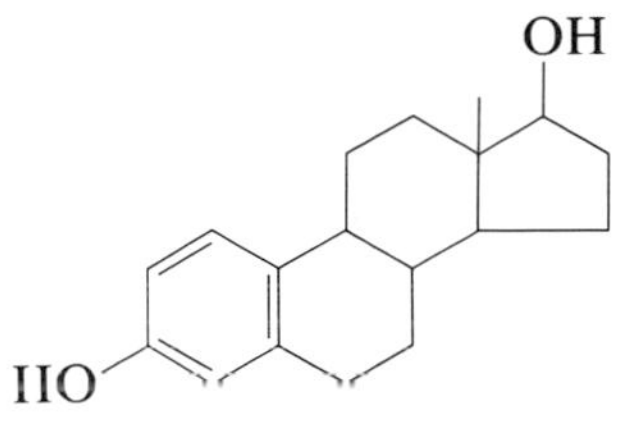   estradiol

Progesterone is synthesized in the ovaries from cholesterol. Its secretion just before ovulation keeps ova from ripening and also prepares the uterus for implantation and maintenance of a fertilized egg. If conception does not occur, progesterone production decreases and menstruation occurs. If fertilization and implantation do occur, production of progesterone continues, helping to maintain the pregnancy. One of the consequences of continued progesterone production is prevention of ovulation during pregnancy.

Once the role of progesterone in inhibiting ovulation was understood, its potential as a possible contraceptive drug was realized. Unfortunately, progesterone itself is relatively ineffective when taken orally, and injection often produces local irritation. As a result of massive research programs, many synthetic steroids that could be administered orally became available in the early 1960s. When taken regularly, these drugs prevent ovulation, yet allow most women a normal menstrual cycle. Some of the most effective contain a progesteronelike analog, such as ethynodiol diacetate, combined with a smaller amount of an estrogenlike material. The small amount of estrogen prevents irregular menstrual flow ("breakthrough bleeding") during prolonged use of contraceptive pills.

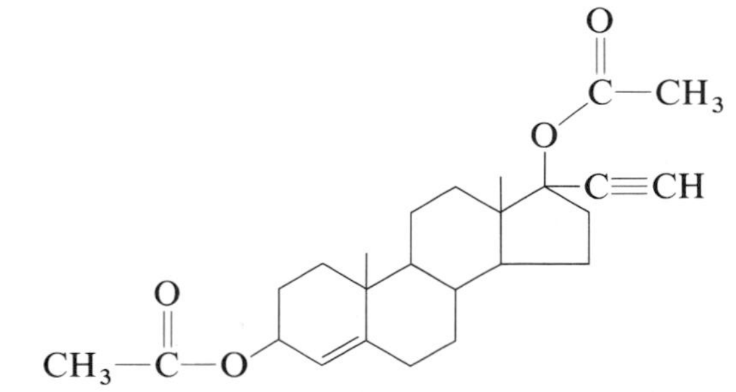

ethynodiol diacetate
(progesterone analog widely
used in oral contraceptives)

D. Bile Acids

Bile acids are synthesized in the liver from cholesterol and then stored in the gallbladder. During digestion, the gallbladder contracts and supplies bile to the small intestine by way of the bile duct. The primary bile acid in humans is cholic acid:

cholic acid
(an important constituent of human bile)

Bile acids have several important functions. First, they are products of the breakdown of cholesterol and thus are a principal pathway for the elimination of cholesterol from the body via the feces. Second, because bile acids can emulsify fats in the intestine, they aid in the digestion and absorption of dietary fats. Third, they can dissolve cholesterol by the formation of cholesterol–bile salt micelles or cholesterol–lecithin–bile salt micelles. In this way cholesterol, whether it is from the diet, synthesized in the liver, or removed from circulation by the liver, can be made soluble.

20.6 Fat-Soluble Vitamins

Vitamins are organic molecules required in trace amounts for normal metabolism but not able to be synthesized either at all or in amounts adequate for healthy growth. Therefore, because they cannot be synthesized, they must be supplied in the diet. This implies that they must be synthesized somewhere in the biological world, which of course they are. The main sources of vitamins for humans and all other animals are plants and microorganisms. We will concentrate on those vitamins that humans need. With one exception, all vitamins required by humans are also required by other mammals. The exception is vitamin C, which is needed only by primates and guinea pigs.

Vitamins are divided into two classes, depending on solubility characteristics; those that are fat-soluble and those that are water-soluble. Most of the twelve recognized water-soluble vitamins are components of coenzymes whose structure and functions we shall examine subsequently (Section 22.2C, and the following chapters on metabolism). Names and sources of the four **fat-soluble vitamins** and the serious clinical conditions that result from a deficiency of each are summarized in Table 20.3.

Table 20.3
Fat-soluble vitamins required by humans and serious clinical symptoms that result from their deficiency.

Vitamin	Source	Clinical Conditions Resulting from Deficiency
A	egg yolk, green and yellow vegetables, fruits, liver, and dairy products	night blindness, keratinization of mucous membranes
D	dairy products, action of sunlight on skin	rickets
E	green leafy vegetables	fragile red blood cells
K	leafy vegetables, intestinal bacteria	failure of blood clotting

A. Vitamin A

Vitamin A, or retinol, is a primary alcohol of molecular formula $C_{20}H_{30}O$. Vitamin A alcohol occurs only in the animal world, where the best sources are cod-liver oil and other fish-liver oils, animal livers, and dairy products. Vitamin A in the form of a precursor, or provitamin, is found in the plant world in pigments called carotenes. The most common of these, β-carotene ($C_{40}H_{56}$), has an orange-red color and is used as a food coloring. The carotenes have no vitamin A activity but are cleaved by enzymes in the intestine at the central carbon-carbon double bond, to give two molecules of retinol, which is then stored in the liver.

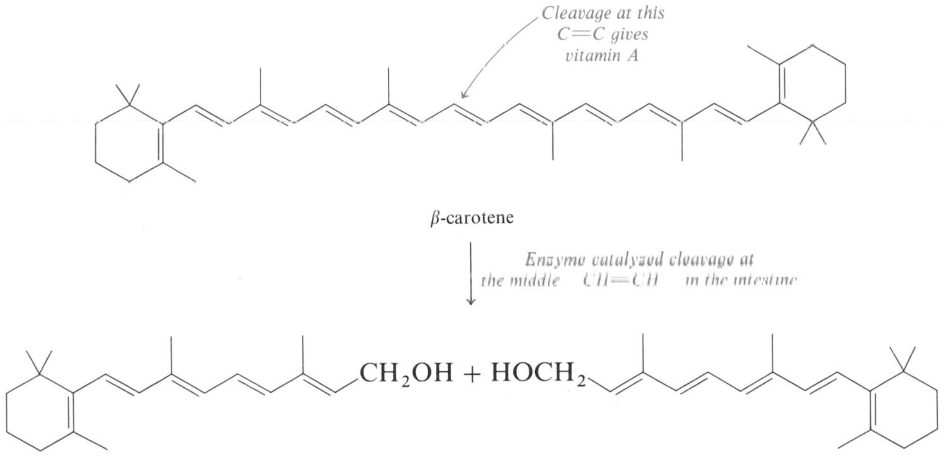

Cleavage at this C=C gives vitamin A

β-carotene

Enzyme catalyzed cleavage at the middle CH=CH in the intestine

CH_2OH + $HOCH_2$

all *trans*-retinol
(vitamin A)

Probably the most understood role of vitamin A is its participation in the **visual cycle** in rod cells. The eye contains two types of photoreceptors: rod cells, the agents for black and white vision in dim light (night vision); and cone cells, agents for color vision in brighter light. Each rod cell contains several million molecules of a protein called opsin. When the primary amine on the side chain of a lysine (one of the 20 amino acid components of proteins) in opsin reacts with the aldehyde group of 11-*cis*-retinal, an imine (Schiff base) called rhodopsin is formed. Neither opsin nor 11-*cis*-retinal absorbs visible light, but rhodopsin absorbs very strongly in the visible region of the spectrum.

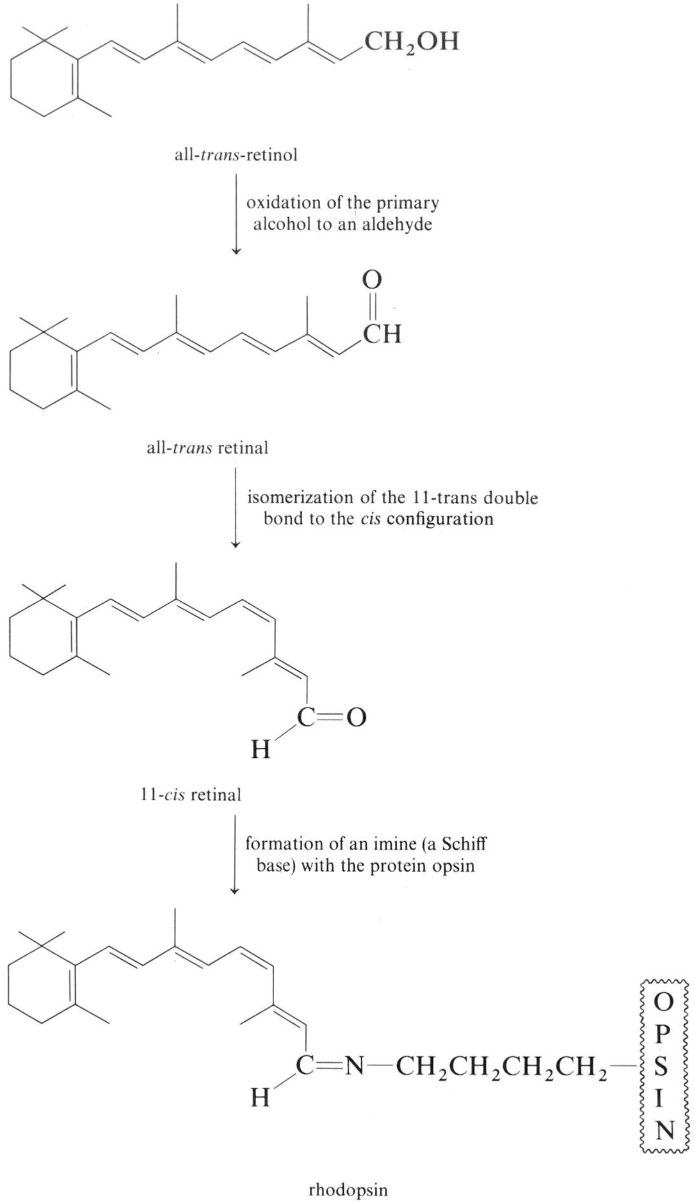

all-*trans*-retinol

oxidation of the primary
alcohol to an aldehyde

all-*trans* retinal

isomerization of the 11-trans double
bond to the *cis* configuration

11-*cis* retinal

formation of an imine (a Schiff
base) with the protein opsin

rhodopsin

The primary event in dark, or night, vision is interaction of a photon of light with a molecule of rhodopsin (Figure 20.12). Absorption of light causes photo-isomerization of 11-*cis*-retinal to all-*trans*-retinal. This change in shape in the retinal portion of rhodopsin brings about a change in conformation of opsin, which in some way not yet understood, generates an impulse in the optic nerve and sends a signal to the visual cortex in the brain. This entire process takes place in about one-millionth of a second and is accompanied by hydrolysis of rhodopsin to free all-*trans*-retinal and opsin. The visual cycle is completed by the following sequence of enzyme-catalyzed reactions: reduction of all-*trans*-retinal to all-*trans*-retinol, isomerization to 11-*cis*-retinol, oxidation to 11-*cis*-retinal, and reaction with opsin to regenerate rhodopsin.

Although the first symptom of vitamin A deficiency is night blindness, other clinical conditions develop too, indicating that vitamin A has other roles in the body besides photoreception. Probably its most important action is on epithelial cells, particularly those of the mucous membranes of the eye, respiratory tract,

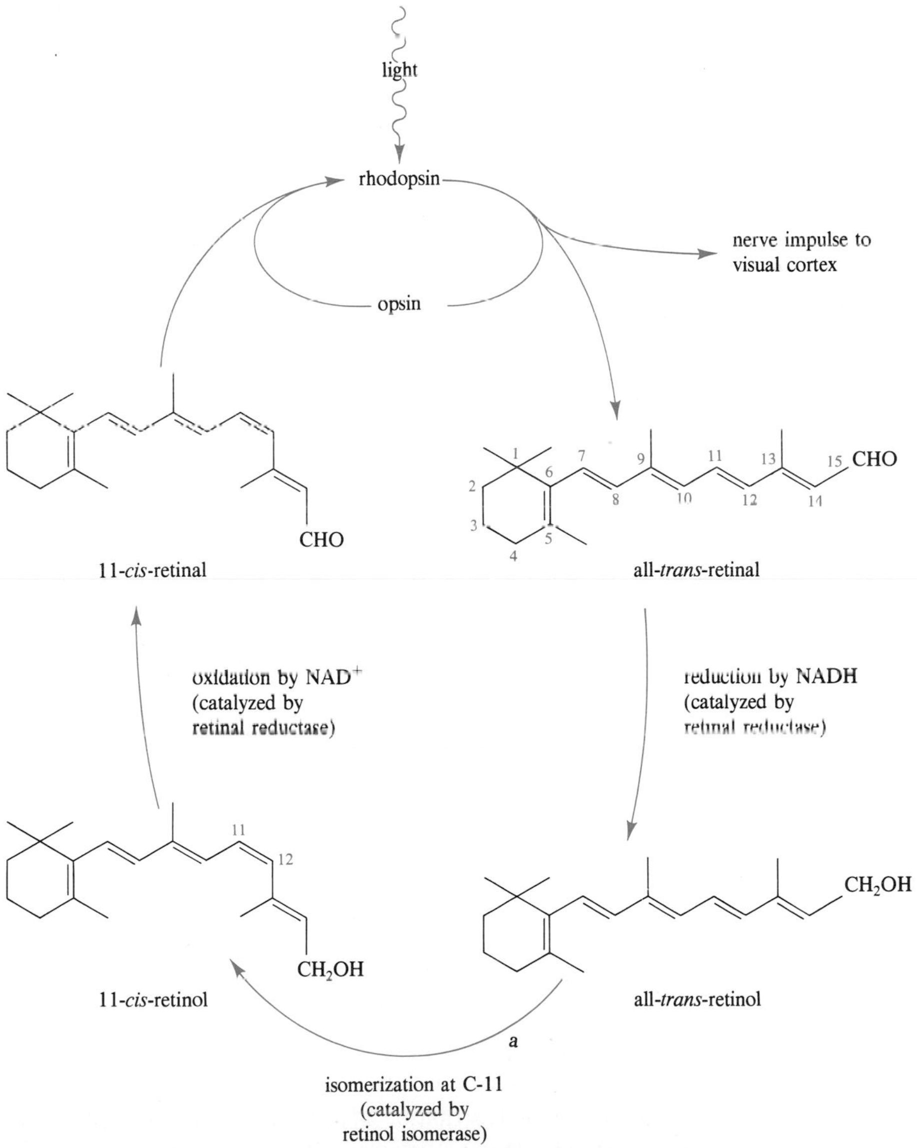

Figure 20.12 The visual cycle in rod cells. Similar cycles occur in cone cells.

and genitourinary tract. Without adequate supplies of vitamin A, these mucous membranes become hard and dry, a process known as keratinization. If untreated, keratinization of the cornea can lead to blindness. The mucous membranes of the respiratory, digestive, and urinary tracts also become keratinized in vitamin A deficiency, and become susceptible to infection.

B. Vitamin D

The term vitamin D is a generic name for a group of structurally related compounds produced by the action of ultraviolet light on certain provitamins. Vitamin D_3 (cholecalciferol) is produced in the skin of mammals by the action of sunlight on 7-dehydrocholesterol. When the skin has normal exposure to sunlight, enough 7-dehydrocholesterol is converted to vitamin D_3 so no dietary vitamin D is necessary. Only when the skin does not manufacture enough vitamin D_3 is there a need to supplement the diet with artificially fortified foods or multivitamins.

Vitamin D_3 has little or no biological activity, but must be metabolically activated before it can function in its target tissues. In the liver, vitamin D_3 is oxidized at carbon 25 of the side chain to form 25-hydroxyvitamin D_3. Although 25-hydroxyvitamin D_3 is the most abundant form in the circulatory system, it has only modest biological activity and undergoes further oxidation in the kidneys to form 1,25-dihydroxyvitamin D_3, the active form of the vitamin.

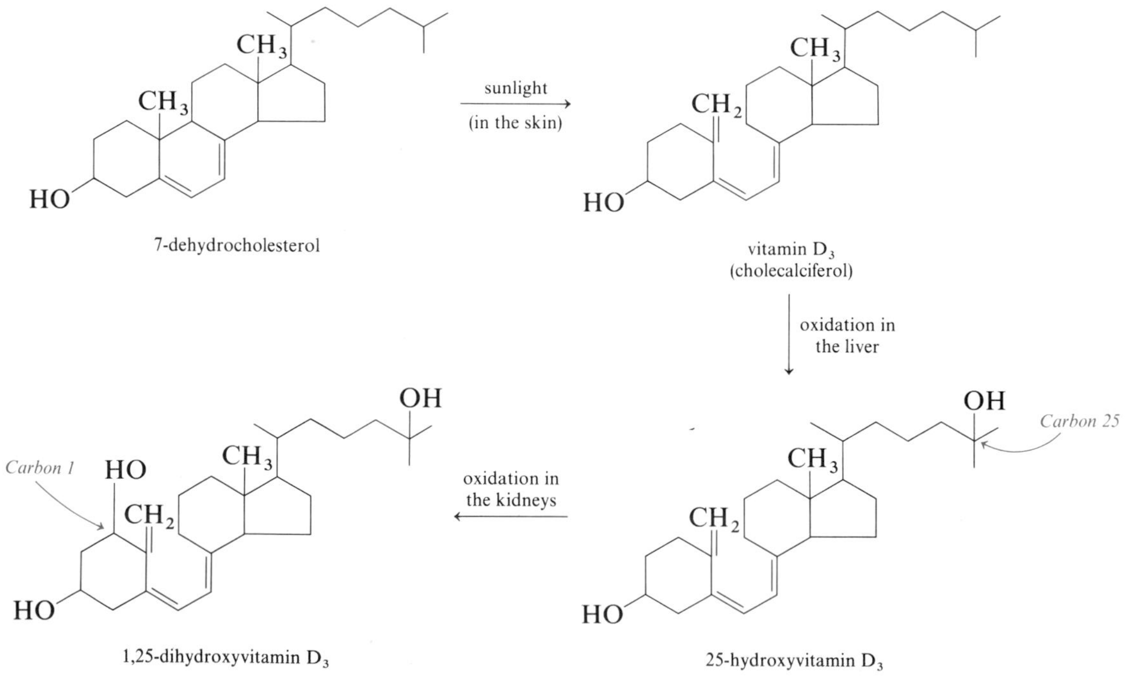

7-dehydrocholesterol

sunlight (in the skin)

vitamin D_3 (cholecalciferol)

oxidation in the liver

Carbon 25

25-hydroxyvitamin D_3

oxidation in the kidneys

Carbon 1

1,25-dihydroxyvitamin D_3

The principal function of vitamin D metabolites is to regulate calcium metabolism. 1,25-dihydroxyvitamin D_3 acts in the small intestine to facilitate absorption of calcium and phosphate ions; it acts in the kidneys to stimulate reabsorption of filtered calcium ions; and it acts in bone to stimulate demineralization and release calcium and phosphate ions into the bloodstream. A deficiency of vitamin D in childhood is associated with rickets, a mineral-metabolism disease that leads to bowlegs, knock-knees, and enlarged joints.

C. Vitamin E

Vitamin E is a group of eight structurally related compounds called tocopherols. Of these, α-tocopherol has the greatest potency. Vitamin E occurs in fish oil, in other oils such as cottonseed and peanut oil, and in green, leafy vegetables. The richest source of vitamin E is wheat germ oil.

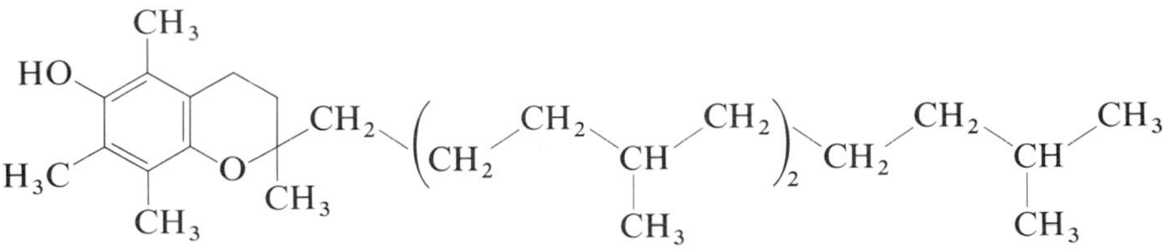

vitamin E (α-tocopherol)

Deficiency of vitamin E in laboratory animals causes infertility, hence the derivation of the name of this vitamin from the Greek, *tocopherol*, promoter of childbirth. Deficiency in humans leads to premature destruction of erythrocytes and anemia. However, because vitamin E is present in green, leafy vegetables, rice, and so on, deficiency in humans is rare. Vitamin E is also an antioxidant in that it inhibits the oxidation of vitamin A, unsaturated fatty acids, phospholipids, and other unsaturated compounds by molecular oxygen. There is speculation that increased dosages of vitamin E may decrease the rate of aging, possibly by decreasing the rate of oxidation of susceptible biomolecules by molecular oxygen.

D. Vitamin K

Vitamin K exists in two principal forms, each consisting of two fused rings and a long, branched side chain of four or five isoprene units. The K_1 vitamins are synthesized in plants, particularly green, leafy vegetables, and they have a double bond only in the isoprene unit closest to the aromatic rings. The K_2 vitamins are synthesized by microorganisms in the large intestine and have double bonds in each of the isoprene units. Because of the combination of dietary intake and microbiological synthesis, deficiency of vitamin K in humans is rare.

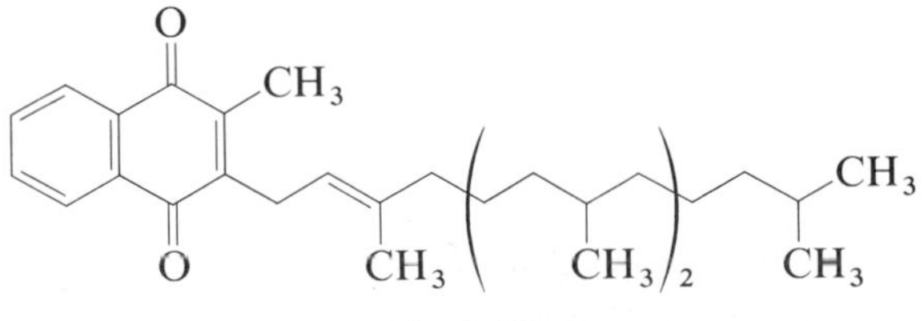

vitamin K_1
(from green, leafy plants)

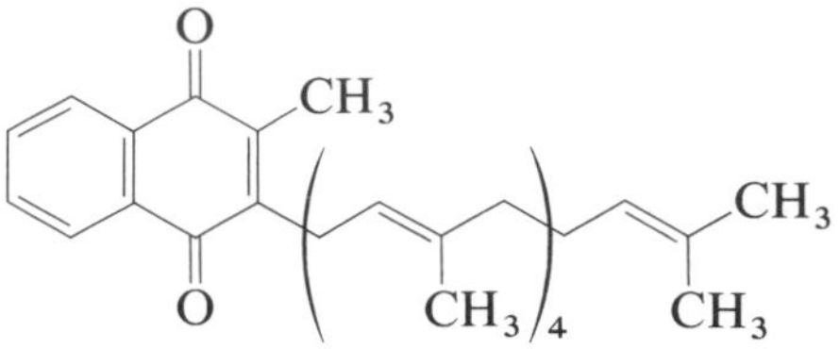

vitamin K$_2$
(from microorganisms in the large intestine)

The only known role of vitamin K is in blood-clotting; a deficiency of vitamin K leads to a slowing of clot formation.

20.7 Waxes

Waxes are esters of fatty acids and alcohols, each having from 16 to 34 carbon atoms. Carnauba wax coats the leaves of the carnauba palm, a native of Brazil; it is largely myricyl cerotate. Beeswax, secreted from the wax glands of the bee, is largely myricyl palmitate.

$$CH_3(CH_2)_{24}\overset{O}{\overset{||}{C}}O(CH_2)_{29}CH_3 \qquad CH_3(CH_2)_{14}\overset{O}{\overset{||}{C}}O(CH_2)_{29}CH_3$$

myricyl cerotate
(major component of carnauba wax)

myricyl palmitate
(major component of beeswax)

Waxes are harder, more brittle, and less greasy to the touch than fats. Applications are found in polishes, cosmetics, ointments, and other pharmaceutical preparations.

Key Terms and Concepts

adrenocorticoid hormones (20.5B)

atherosclerosis (20.5A)

bile acid (20.5D)

biological membrane (20.4)

detergents (20.2C)

cell membrane (20.4A)

cephalin (20.3)

fat (20.1C)

fat-soluble vitamins (20.6)

fatty acid (20.1A)

fluid-mosaic model (20.4B)

hardening of oils (20.1E)

lecithin (20.3)

lipid (introduction)

lipid bilayer (20.4B)

micelle (20.2B)

oil (20.1C)

phospholipid (20.3)

rancidity (20.1D)

reduction of triglycerides (20.1E)

saponification (20.2A)

sex hormone (20.5C)

soap (20.2A)

steroid (20.5)

synthetic detergent (20.2C)   visual cycle (20.6A)
triglyceride (20.1)   waxes (20.7)

Key Reactions

1. Saponification of triglycerides: preparation of natural soaps (Section 20.2A).
2. Reaction of natural soaps in "hard water" to form water-insoluble salts (Section 20.2B).

Problems

Fats and oils (Section 20.1)

20.2 List six important functions of lipids in the human body. Name a lipid representing each function.

20.3 How many isomers (including stereoisomers) are possible for a triglyceride containing one molecule each of palmitic, stearic, and oleic acids?

20.4 What is meant by the term *hardening* as applied to fats and oils?

20.5 Saponification number is defined as the number of milligrams of potassium hydroxide required to saponify 1 g of a fat or oil. Calculate the saponification number of tristearin, of molecular weight 890.

20.6 The saponification number of butter is approximately 230; of oleomargarine, approximately 195. Calculate the average molecular weight of butter fat and of oleomargarine.

Fatty acids (Section 20.1)

20.7 Examine the structural formulas for lauric, palmitic, stearic, oleic, linoleic, and arachidonic acids. For each that shows cis-trans isomerism, state the total number of such isomers possible.

20.8 Compare saturated fatty acids and monosaccharides with respect to their solubility in water; in ether.

20.9 By using structural formulas, illustrate how fatty-acid molecules interact with water to form a monomolecular layer on the surface of water.

20.10 Draw structural formulas for the products formed by reaction of 9-octadecenoic acid (oleic acid) with the following.
  a. Br_2 **b.** H_2/Pt/3 atm pressure   **c.** $NaOH/H_2O$
  d. $NaHCO_3/H_2O$ **e.** $LiAlH_4$, followed by H_2O

Soaps and detergents (Section 20.2)

20.11 By using structural formulas, show how a soap "dissolves" fats, oils, and grease.

20.12 Show by balanced equations the reaction of a soap with (a) hard water, and (b) acidic solution.

20.13 Characterize the structural features necessary to make a good detergent. Illustrate by structural formulas two different classes of synthetic detergents. Name each example.

20.14 Following are structural formulas for a cationic detergent and a nonionic detergent. How do you account for the detergent properties of each?

$$C_6H_5CH_2\overset{\overset{\displaystyle CH_3}{|}}{\underset{\underset{\displaystyle C_8H_{17}}{|}}{N^+}}-CH_3Cl^-$$

benzyldimethyloctylammonium
chloride
(a cationic detergent)

$$CH_3(CH_2)_{14}\overset{\overset{\displaystyle O}{||}}{C}OCH_2\overset{\overset{\displaystyle CH_2OH}{|}}{\underset{\underset{\displaystyle CH_2OH}{|}}{C}}CH_2OH$$

pentaerythrityl palmitate
(a nonionic detergent)

*Phospholipids
(Section 20.3)*

20.15 Draw structural formulas for the products of complete hydrolysis of a lecithin; a cephalin.

*Steroids
(Section 20.5)*

20.16 Draw the structural formula of cholesterol; label all chiral carbons and state the total number of stereoisomers possible for cholesterol.

20.17 Esters of cholesterol and fatty acids are normal constituents of blood plasma. The fatty acids esterified with cholesterol are generally unsaturated. Draw the structural formula for cholesteryl oleate.

20.18 Cholesterol is an important component of the lipid fraction of cell membranes. How do you think a cholesterol molecule might be oriented in a biological membrane?

20.19 Examine the structural formulas of testosterone, a male sex hormone; of progesterone, a female sex hormone. What are the similarities in structure between the two? What are the differences?

20.20 Describe how a combination of progesterone and estrogen analogs functions as an oral contraceptive.

20.21 Examine the structural formula of cholic acid and account for the ability of this and other bile acids to emulsify fats and oils.

*Fat-soluble
vitamins
(Section 20.6)*

20.22 Examine the structural formula of vitamin A and state the number of cis-trans isomers possible for this molecule.

20.23 In fish-liver oils, vitamin A is present as esters of fatty acids. The most common of these esters is vitamin A palmitate. Draw its structural formula.

20.24 Describe the symptoms of severe vitamin A deficiency.

20.25 Examine the structural formulas of vitamins A, D_3, E, and K_2. From their structural formulas, would you expect them to be more soluble in water or in olive oil? Would you expect them to be soluble in blood plasma?

20.26 Explain why vitamin E is added to some processed foods.

*Biological
membranes
(Section 20.4)*

20.27 Two of the chief noncovalent forces directing the organization of biomolecules in aqueous solution are the tendencies to (1) arrange polar groups so that they interact with water by hydrogen bonding, and (2) arrange nonpolar groups so that they are shielded from water. Show how these forces direct micelle formation by soap molecules and lipid bilayer formation of phospholipids.

Describe the main features of the fluid-mosaic model of the structure of biological membranes.

Table 21.1

Nonpolar si

NH_3^+

H—CH—C

glycine (gly)

H_3C

CH_3—CH_2

L-iso

CH

L-phenyl

Polar unchar

HO—CH_2—

L-serine

HS—CH_2—

L-cysteine

CH

N   NH

L-histid

Tab
Som
acid:
in p
antil

Polar charged

O
‖
$^-$O—C—CH

L-aspartic

$H_3\overset{+}{N}$—CH_2—

21

Amino Acids and Proteins

Amino acids are compounds whose chemistry is built on that of amines and carboxylic acids. That amino acids are difunctional presents a special challenge to chemists, because in dealing with a reaction of the carboxyl group, we must also be aware of reactions the amino group might undergo, and vice versa.

Proteins are derived from amino acids. In studying these substances, we observe at first hand one of the principles of the molecular logic of living systems, namely, that in constructing macromolecules (biopolymers), living systems begin with small, readily available subunits (monomers). The monomer units from which proteins are derived are amino acids.

21.1 Amino Acids

A. Structure

Amino acids are compounds that contain both a carboxyl group and an amino group. While many types of amino acids are known, the α-amino acids are the most significant in the biological world because they are the units from which proteins are constructed. A general structural formula for an α-amino acid is shown in Figure 21.1. Although Figure 21.1(a) is a common way of writing structural formulas for amino acids, it is not accurate, since it shows an acid (—CO_2H) and a base (—NH_2) within the same molecule. These acidic and basic groups react with each other to form a dipolar ion or internal salt [Figure 21.1(b)]. The internal salt of an amino acid is given the special name of **zwitterion**. A zwitterion has no net charge; it contains one positive charge and one negative charge.

$$\underset{\underset{NH_2}{|}}{R-CH-}\overset{\overset{O}{\|}}{C}-OH \qquad \underset{\underset{NH_3^+}{|}}{R-CH-}\overset{\overset{O}{\|}}{C}-O^-$$

(a)   (b)

Figure 21.1 General formula for an α-amino acid: (a) un-ionized form; (b) dipolar ion.

591

components of cell walls of certain bacteria. A variety of D-amino acids have been found in peptide antibiotics, a few of which are listed in Table 21.3.

21.2 Acid-Base Properties of Amino Acids

A. Ionization of Amino Acids

Given in Table 21.4 are pK_a values for ionizable groups of the 20 protein-derived amino acids. There are several things to notice from the data in this table.

Table 21.4
pK_a values for ionizable groups of amino acids.

Amino Acid	α-CO$_2$H Group	α-NH$_3^+$ Group	Side Chain
alanine	2.35	9.87	
arginine	2.01	9.04	12.48
asparagine	2.02	8.80	
aspartic acid	2.10	9.82	3.86
cysteine	1.86	10.25	8.00
glutamic acid	2.10	9.47	4.07
glutamine	2.17	9.13	
glycine	2.35	9.78	
histidine	1.77	9.10	6.10
isoleucine	2.32	9.76	
leucine	2.33	9.74	
lysine	2.18	8.95	10.53
methionine	2.28	9.20	
phenylalanine	2.58	9.24	
proline	2.00	10.60	
serine	2.21	9.15	
threonine	2.09	9.10	
tryptophan	2.38	9.39	
tyrosine	2.20	9.11	10.07
valine	2.29	9.72	

1. *Acidity of α-carboxyl groups.* The average pK_a value for an α-carboxyl group is 2.16. If you compare this value with that for acetic acid ($pK_a = 4.74$) and other simple carboxylic acids (Section 16.5), you will see that the α-carboxyl group of an amino acid is a considerably stronger acid.

$$\alpha-\overset{\overset{\textstyle O}{\|}}{C}OH \rightleftharpoons \alpha-\overset{\overset{\textstyle O}{\|}}{C}O^- + H^+ \qquad K_a = 6.9 \times 10^{-3} \qquad pK_a = 2.16$$

an α-carboxyl
group
(stronger acids than
simple carboxylic acids)

2. *Acidity of side chain carboxyl groups.* The side chain carboxyl groups of aspartic and glutamic acids are only slightly stronger acids than acetic acid.

3. *Basicity of α-amino groups.* The average pK_a value for an α-amino group is 9.56, a value very close to that for primary aliphatic amines (Section 14.3A).

$$\alpha\text{-NH}_3^+ \; \rightleftharpoons \; \alpha\text{-NH}_2 + \text{H}^+ \qquad K_a = 2.75 \times 10^{-10} \qquad pK_a = 9.56$$

an α-amino
group
(comparable in
strength to simple
amine salts)

4. *Basicity of the guanidine group of arginine.* The nitrogen-containing side chain of arginine is called a guanidine group and is a much stronger base than the amino group of lysine or other primary aliphatic amines. Consequently, the guanidine group of arginine is 100% protonated, with a charge of +1, at physiological pH.

$$\text{R}-\text{NH}-\overset{\overset{\displaystyle \text{NH}_2^+}{\|}}{\text{C}}-\text{NH}_2 \; \rightleftharpoons \; \text{R}-\text{NH}-\overset{\overset{\displaystyle \text{NH}}{\|}}{\text{C}}-\text{NH}_2 + \text{H}^+ \qquad K_a = 3.3 \times 10^{-13} \qquad pK_a = 12.48$$

the guanidine
group on the side
chain of arginine
(a weaker acid than
simple amine salts)

(a stronger base
than simple amines)

5. *Basicity of the imidazole group of histidine.* The five-membered nitrogen-containing ring on the side chain of histidine is called an imidazole group (Section 14.1B). The imidazole group is a weaker base than simple aliphatic amines. Alternatively, the protonated form of the imidazole group is a stronger acid than the protonated form of a simple amine.

$$K_a = 7.9 \times 10^{-7} \qquad pK_a = 6.10$$

the imidazole
ring of histidine
(a stronger acid than
simple amine salts)

B. Ionization of Amino Acids as a Function of pH

We have just considered the principal ionizable groups of amino acids separately. Let us now consider how the interaction of ionizable groups within a particular amino acid affects the properties of that amino acid. Each weak acid dissociates to give its conjugate base and H^+, and has its own acid dissociation constant, K_a.

$$\text{HA} \; \rightleftharpoons \; \text{A}^- + \text{H}^+ \qquad K_a = \frac{[\text{conjugate base}][\text{H}^+]}{[\text{weak acid}]}$$

weak
acid

conjugate
base

Taking the logarithm of the acid dissociation equation, and then rearranging it gives the Henderson-Hasselbalch equation (Section 9.9).

Henderson-Hasselbalch Equation

$$pH = pK_a + \log \frac{[\text{conjugate base}]}{[\text{weak acid}]}$$

The Henderson-Hasselbalch equation provides a particularly direct way of calculating the ratio of conjugate base to weak acid at any pH. Shown in Table 21.5 are values of this ratio for a weak acid with a dissociation constant pK_a. Also shown is the percentage of molecules present as undissociated weak acid at pH values higher and lower than the value of pK_a by one and two units.

Table 21.5
Ratio of conjugate base to weak acid as a function of pH.

pH	[Conj. Base]/[Weak Acid]	% Present as Weak Acid
$pK_a + 2$	100/1	0.990%
$pK_a + 1$	10/1	9.09%
pK_a	1/1	50.0%
$pK_a - 1$	1/10	90.9%
$pK_a - 2$	1/100	99.0%

Given the data in Table 21.5, we can generalize as follows:

1. If the pH of a solution is 2.0 or more units higher (more basic) than the pK_a of an ionizable group, then the group is more than 99% in the conjugate base form.
2. If the pH of a solution is 1.0 unit higher (more basic) than the pK_a of an ionizable group, then the group is approximately 90% in the conjugate base form and 10% in the acid form.
3. If the pH of a solution is equal to the pK_a of an ionizable group, then the group is 50% in the acid form and 50% in the conjugate base form.
4. If the pH of a solution is 1.0 unit lower (more acidic) than the pK_a of an ionizable group, then the group is approximately 10% in the conjugate base form and 90% in the acid form.
5. If the pH of a solution is 2.0 or more units lower (more acidic) than the pK_a of an ionizable group, then the group is more than 99% in the acid form.

Example 21.1

Draw a structural formula for L-serine and estimate what the net charge on this amino acid is at pH 3.0, 7.0, and 10.0.

☐ *Solution*

The pK_a of the α-carboxyl group of serine is 2.21. At pH of 3.0, which is 0.79 unit higher than its pK_a, the carboxyl group is approximately 90% in the ionized form and bears a negative charge. The pK_a of the α-amino group is 9.15. At pH 3.0, which is approximately 6 units lower than the pK_a of the ionizable group, the α-amino group is completely in the protonated form and bears a positive charge. The same type of calculations can be repeated at pH 7.0 and 10.0. Results are shown on these structural formulas:

| | pH = 3.0 | pH = 7.0 | pH = 10.0 |
| | net charge = + | net charge = 0 | net charge = − |

Problem 21.1

Draw a structural formula for lysine and estimate what the net charge is on each functional group at pH 3.0, 7.0, and 10.0.

C. Titration of Amino Acids

Values of pK_a for the ionizable groups of amino acids are usually obtained by acid-base **titration** and measuring the pH of the solution as a function of added base (or added acid, depending on how the titration is done). In an example of this experimental procedure, consider a solution containing 1.0 mol of glycine to which enough strong acid has been added so that both the carboxyl and the amino groups are fully protonated. Next, this solution is titrated with 1.0 M NaOH; the volume of base added and the pH of the resulting solution are recorded and then plotted as shown in Figure 21.3. The most acidic group and the one to react first with added sodium hydroxide is the carboxyl group. When exactly 0.5 mol of NaOH has been added, the carboxyl group is half-neutralized. At this point, the dipolar ion has a concentration equal to that of the positively charged ion, and the pH equals the pK_a of the carboxyl group.

$$[\overset{+}{H_3N}-CH_2-CO_2H] = [\overset{+}{H_3N}-CH_2-CO_2^-] \quad \text{where pH} = pK_{a\text{-}CO_2H}$$

positive ion
(cation)

dipolar ion
(no net charge)

The endpoint of the first part of the titration is reached when 1.0 mol of sodium hydroxide has been added. At this point, the predominant species in solution is the dipolar ion, and the observed pH of the solution is 6.07. The next section of the curve represents titration of the $-NH_3^+$ group. When another 0.5 mol of sodium hydroxide has been added (bringing the total to 1.5 mol), half the $-NH_3^+$ groups are neutralized and converted to $-NH_2$. At this point, the concentrations of the dipolar ion and the negatively charged ion are equal, and the observed pH is 9.78, the pK_a of the amino group of glycine.

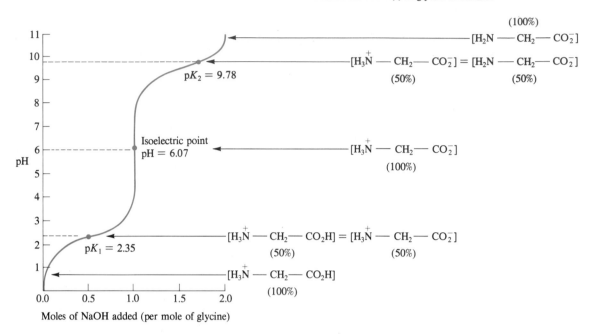

Figure 21.3 Titration of glycine with sodium hydroxide.

$$[\overset{+}{H_3N}-CH_2-CO_2^-] = [H_2N-CH_2-CO_2^-] \quad \text{where pH} = pK_{\alpha\text{-}CO_2H}$$

dipolar ion
(no net charge)　　　　　　negative ion
　　　　　　　　　　　　　　(anion)

The second endpoint of the titration is reached when a total of 2.0 mol of sodium hydroxide has been added and glycine is converted entirely to an anion.

D. Isoelectric Point

Titration curves such as that for glycine permit us to determine pK_a values for the ionizable groups of an amino acid. They also permit us to determine another important property, namely, isoelectric point, abbreviated pI. **Isoelectric point** for an amino acid is defined as the pH at which the majority of the molecules in solution have no net charge, that is, a net charge of zero. By examining the titration curve, you can see that the isoelectric point for glycine is 6.07, halfway between the pK_a values for the α-carboxyl and α-amino groups.

$$pI = \tfrac{1}{2}(pK_{\alpha\text{-}CO_2H} + pK_{\alpha\text{-}NH_3^+})$$
$$= \tfrac{1}{2}(2.35 + 9.78) = 6.07 \quad \text{(isoelectric point for glycine)}$$

Calculation of the isoelectric points for amino acids such as aspartic and glutamic acids (with carboxyl side chains) or lysine and arginine (with basic side chains) can be done similarly. For aspartic and glutamic acids, the isoelectric point occurs at a pH at which the net charge on the two carboxyl groups is -1

and balances the charge of $+1$ on the α-amino group. For glutamic acid, the isoelectric point is

$$pI = \tfrac{1}{2}(pK_{\alpha\text{-CO}_2\text{H}} + pK_{\text{chain-CO}_2\text{H}})$$
$$= \tfrac{1}{2}(2.10 + 4.07) = 3.09 \quad \text{(isoelectric point for glutamic acid)}$$

For lysine and arginine, the isoelectric point occurs at a pH at which the net charge on the α-amino group and the amino side chain is $+1$, balancing the charge of -1 on the α-carboxyl group. For lysine, the isoelectric point is

$$pI = \tfrac{1}{2}(pK_{\alpha\text{-NH}_3^+} + pK_{\text{chain-NH}_3^+})$$
$$= \tfrac{1}{2}(8.95 + 10.53) = 9.74 \quad \text{(isoelectric point for lysine)}$$

Isoelectric points for amino acids with ionizable side chains are given in Table 21.6.

Table 21.6
Isoelectric points for amino acids with ionizable side chains.

Amino Acid	Ionizable Side-Chain Group	pI (Isoelectric Point)
aspartic acid	carboxyl	2.98
glutamic acid	carboxyl	3.09
histidine	imidazole	7.60
cysteine	sulfhydryl	5.10
tyrosine	phenol	6.16
lysine	amine	9.74
arginine	guanine	10.76

Given a value for the isoelectric point of an amino acid, one can estimate the charge on that amino acid at any pH. For example, the charge on tyrosine is zero at pH 6.16 (its isoelectric point). A small fraction of tyrosine molecules are positively charged at pH 6.0 (0.16 unit lower than its pI) and virtually all are positively charged at pH 4.16 (2 units lower than its pI). As another example, at pH 9.74, the net charge on lysine is zero. At pH values lower than 9.74, an increasing fraction of lysine molecules are positively charged.

E. Electrophoresis

Electrophoresis is a process of separating compounds on the basis of their electrical charges. Electrophoretic separations can be carried out using paper, starch, agar, certain plastics, and cellulose acetate as solid supports. In paper electrophoresis, a paper strip saturated with an aqueous buffer of predetermined pH serves as a bridge between two electrode vessels. Next, a sample of amino acids is applied as a spot. When an electric potential is then applied to the electrode vessels, amino acids migrate toward the electrode carrying the charge opposite to their own. Molecules having a high charge density move more rapidly than those with a lower charge density. Any molecule already at its isoelectric point remains at the origin.

After electrophoretic separation is complete, the strip is dried and sprayed with a dye to make the separated components visible. The most common dye for amino acids is ninhydrin, a triketone with a benzene ring fused to a five-membered ring. In aqueous solution, the middle carbonyl group of the five-membered ring is almost fully hydrated, to give a compound called ninhydrin hydrate:

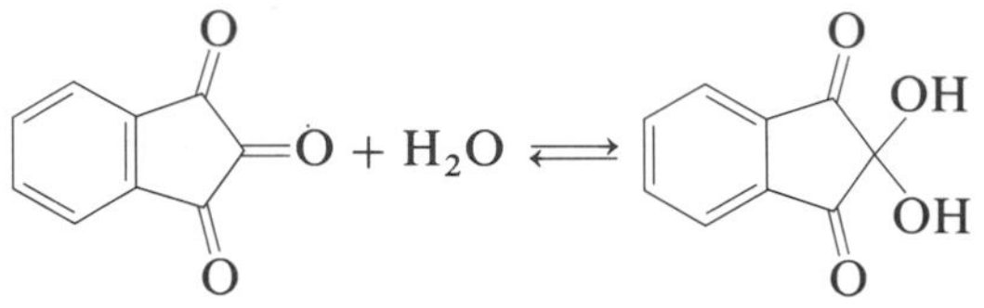

ninhydrin   ninhydrin hydrate

Ninhydrin reacts with α-amino acids to produce an aldehyde, carbon dioxide, and a purple anion with an absorption maximum at 580 nm:

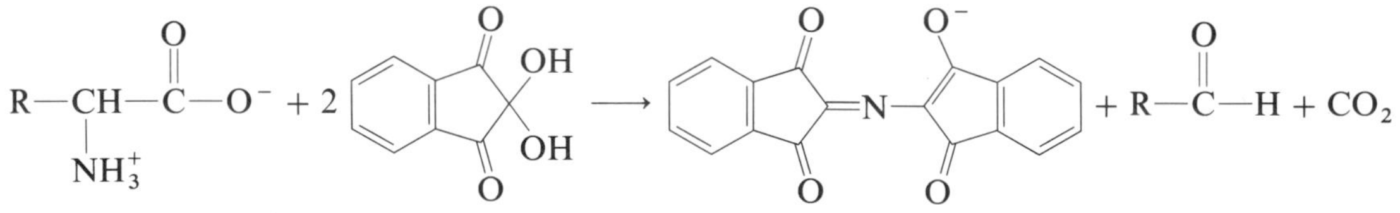

an α-amino   ninhydrin   anion
acid   hydrate   (purple)

Example 21.2

The isoelectric point of tyrosine is 6.16. Toward which electrode will tyrosine migrate during paper electrophoresis at pH 7.0?

☐ *Solution*

When the pH of the solution equals 6.16, the isoelectric pH of tyrosine, tyrosine molecules bear no net charge and will remain where spotted on the paper. At pH 7.0, which is slightly more basic than tyrosine's isoelectric pH, tyrosine molecules will bear a small net negative charge and will move toward the positive electrode.

Problem 21.2

The isoelectric point of histidine is 7.60. Toward which electrode will histidine migrate on paper electrophoresis at pH 7.0?

Example 21.3

Electrophoresis of a mixture of lysine, histidine, and cysteine is carried out at pH 7.60. Describe the behavior of each amino acid under these conditions.

☐ *Solution*

The isoelectric point of histidine is 7.60. At this pH, histidine has a net charge of zero and does not move from the origin. The pI of cysteine is 5.10; at pH

7.60, cysteine has a net negative charge and moves toward the positive electrode. The pI of lysine is 9.74; at pH 7.60 lysine has a net positive charge and moves toward the negative electrode (Figure 21.4).

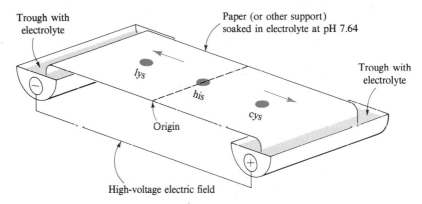

Figure 21.4 Electrophoresis of a mixture of histidine, lysine, and cysteine at pH 7.60.

Problem 21.3

Describe the behavior of a mixture of glutamic acid, arginine, and valine on paper electrophoresis at pH 6.0.

21.3 Polypeptides and Proteins

In 1902, Emil Fischer proposed that proteins are long chains of amino acids joined together by amide bonds between the α-carboxyl group of one amino acid and the α-amino group of another. For these amide bonds, Fischer proposed the special name **peptide bond**. Figure 21.5 shows the peptide bond formed between glycine and alanine in the dipeptide glycylalanine.

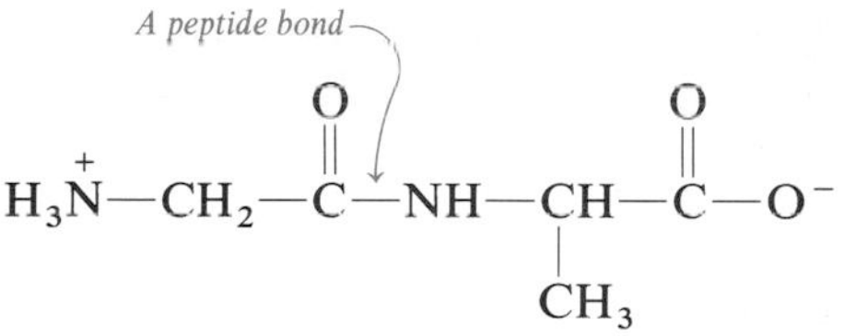

A peptide bond

$$\overset{+}{H_3N}-CH_2-\overset{\overset{\displaystyle O}{\|}}{C}-NH-CH-\overset{\overset{\displaystyle O}{\|}}{C}-O^-$$
$$\underset{CH_3}{|}$$

Figure 21.5 The peptide bond in glycylalanine.

A molecule containing two amino acids joined by an amide bond is called a dipeptide. Those containing larger numbers of amino acids are called tripeptides, tetrapeptides, pentapeptides, and so on. Molecules containing 10 or more amino acids are generally called polypeptides. Proteins are biological macromolecules of molecular weight 5000 or greater, consisting of one or more polypeptide chains.

By convention, polypeptides are written from the left, beginning with the amino acid having the free H_3N^+— group and proceeding to the right toward the amino acid with the free —CO_2^- group. The amino acid with the free H_3N^+— group is called the **N-terminal amino acid** and that with the free —CO_2^- group is called the **C-terminal amino acid**. The structural formula for a polypeptide sequence may be written out in full, or the sequence of amino acids may be indicated using the standard abbreviation for each.

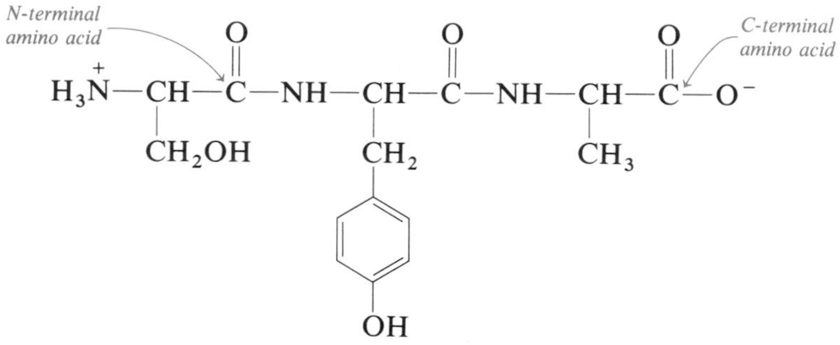

ser-tyr-ala
(seryltyrosylalanine)

Polypeptides are named by listing each amino acid in order, from the N-terminal end of the chain to the C-terminal end. The name of the C-terminal amino acid is given in full. The name of each other amino acid in the chain is derived by dropping the suffix -*ine* or -*ic acid* and adding -*yl*. For example, if the order of amino acids from the N-terminal end is serine-tyrosine-alanine (ser-tyr-ala), the name of the tripeptide is seryltyrosylalanine.

Example 21.4

Name and draw a structural formula for the tripeptide gly-ser-asp. Label the N-terminal amino acid and the C-terminal amino acid. What is the net charge on this tripeptide at pH 6.0?

☐ *Solution*

In writing the formula for this tripeptide, begin with glycine on the left. Then connect the α-carbonyl of glycine to the α-amino group of serine by a peptide bond. Finally, connect the α-carbonyl of serine to the α-amino group of aspartic acid by another peptide bond. If you have done this correctly, the backbone of the peptide chain should be a repeating sequence of nitrogen–alpha carbon–carbonyl. The net charge on this tripeptide at pH 6.0 is −1.

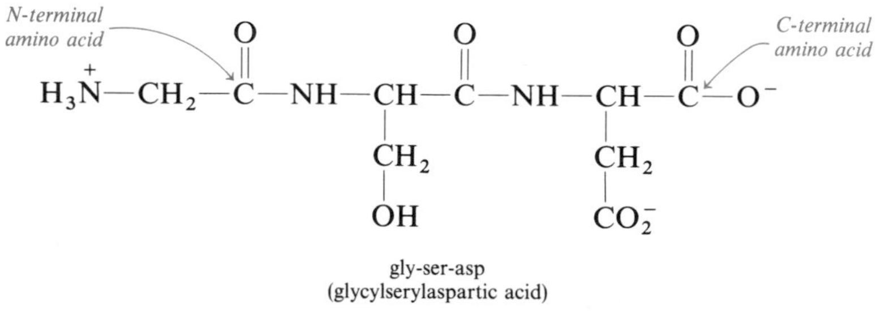

gly-ser-asp
(glycylserylaspartic acid)

Problem 21.4

Name and draw a structural formula for lys-phe-ala. Label the N-terminal amino acid and the C-terminal amino acid. What is the net charge on this tripeptide at pH 6.0?

21.4 Amino Acid Analysis

The first step in analyzing a polypeptide is hydrolysis and quantitative determination of its amino acid composition. Recall that amide bonds are very resistant to hydrolysis (Section 17.8). Hydrolysis of polypeptides requires heating in 6M HCl at 110°C for 24–70 hr, or heating in 2–4M NaOH at comparable temperatures and for comparable times. Once the polypeptide is hydrolyzed, the resulting mixture of amino acids is analyzed by ion-exchange chromatography. Amino acids are detected as they emerge from the column by reaction with ninhydrin (Section 21.2E). Current procedures for hydrolysis of polypeptides and analysis of amino acid mixtures have been refined to the point where it is possible to obtain amino acid composition from as little as 50 nanomoles $(50 \times 10^{-9}$ mol) of polypeptide. Figure 21.6 shows the analysis of a polypeptide

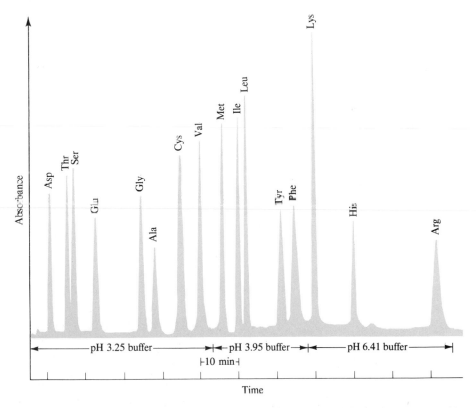

Figure 21.6 Analysis of a mixture of amino acids by ion-exchange chromatography.

hydrolysate by ion exchange chromatography. Note that during hydrolysis, the side-chain amides of asparagine and glutamine are hydrolyzed, and these amino acids are detected as glutamic acid and aspartic acid. For each glutamine or asparagine hydrolyzed, there is an equivalent amount of ammonia formed.

21.5 Primary Structure of Polypeptides and Proteins

Primary (1°) structure of polypeptides and proteins refers to the sequence of amino acids in a polypeptide chain. In this sense, primary structure is a complete description of all covalent bonding in a polypeptide or protein.

It is difficult to appreciate the incredibly large number of different polypeptides that can be constructed from the 20 amino acids, where the number of amino acids in a polypeptide can range from under ten to well over a hundred. With only three amino acids, there are 27 different tripeptides possible. For glycine, alanine, and serine, the 27 tripeptides are:

gly-gly-gly	ser-ser-ser	ala-ala-ala
gly-gly-ser	ser-ser-gly	ala-ala-gly
gly-gly-ala	ser-ser-ala	ala-ala-ser
gly-ser-gly	ser-gly-ser	ala-gly-ala
gly-ala-gly	ser-ala-ser	ala-ser-ala
gly-ser-ala	ser-gly-ala	ala-gly-ser
gly-ala-ser	ser-ala-gly	ala-ser-gly
gly-ser-ser	ser-gly-gly	ala-gly-gly
gly-ala-ala	ser-ala-ala	ala-ser-ser

For a polypeptide containing one each of the 20 different amino acids, the number of possible polypeptides is $20 \times 19 \times 18 \times \cdots \times 2 \times 1$, or about 2×10^{18}. With larger polypeptides and proteins, the possible combinations become truly countless!

21.6 Three-Dimensional Shapes of Polypeptides and Proteins

A. Geometry of a Peptide Bond

In the late 1930s, Linus Pauling began a series of studies designed to learn more about the three-dimensional shapes of proteins. One of his first discoveries was that a peptide bond itself is planar. As shown in Figure 21.7, the four atoms of a peptide bond and the two alpha-carbons joined to it all lie in the same plane.

Had you been asked earlier to predict the **geometry of a peptide bond**, you probably would have reasoned in the following way. There are three bundles of electron density around the carbonyl carbon; therefore predict bond angles of 120° about the carbonyl carbon. There are four bundles of electron density around the amide nitrogen; therefore predict bond angles of 109.5° about this atom. These predictions agree with the observed bond angles of approximately

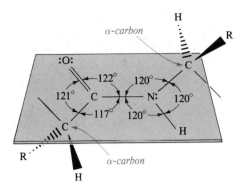

Figure 21.7 Planarity of a peptide bond. Bond angles about the carbonyl carbon and the amide nitrogen are approximately 120°.

120° about the carbonyl carbon. However, a bond angle of 120° about the amide nitrogen is unexpected. To account for this observed geometry, Pauling proposed that a peptide bond is more accurately represented as a resonance hybrid of two important contributing structures:

Contributing structure I shows C=O double bond and a C—N single bond. Structure II shows a C—O single bond and a C=N double bond. If structure I is the major contributor to the hybrid, the C—N—C bond angle would be nearer 109.5°. If, on the other hand, structure II is the major contributor, the C—N—C bond angle would be nearer 120°. The fact, first observed by Pauling, is that the C—N—C bond angle is very near 120°, which means that the peptide bond is planar and structure II is the major contributor to the resonance hybrid.

Two configurations are possible for the atoms of a planar peptide bond. In one configuration, the two α-carbons are cis to each other; in the other, they are trans to each other:

The trans configuration is more favorable because the bulky α-carbons are farther from each other than they are in the cis configuration. Virtually all peptide bonds in natural proteins have the trans configuration.

B. Secondary Structure

Secondary (2°) structure refers to ordered arrangements (conformations) of amino acids in localized regions of a polypeptide, or protein, molecule. The first studies of polypeptide conformations were also carried out by Linus Pauling and Robert Corey, beginning in 1939. They assumed that in conformations of greatest stability, (1) all atoms in a peptide bond lie in the same plane, and (2) each amide group is hydrogen-bonded between the N—H of one peptide bond and the C=O of another, as shown in Figure 21.8.

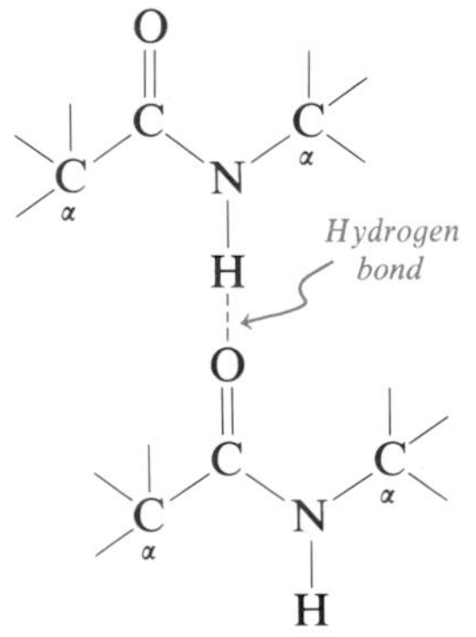

Figure 21.8 Hydrogen bonding between amide groups.

On the basis of model-building, Pauling and Corey proposed that two folding patterns should be particularly stable: the **α-helix** and the antiparallel **β-pleated sheet**. In the α-helix pattern shown in Figure 21.9, a polypeptide chain is coiled in a spiral. As you study the α-helix in Figure 21.9(c), note the following:

1. The helix is coiled in a clockwise, or right-handed, manner. Right-handed means that if you turn the helix clockwise, it twists away from you. In this sense, a right-handed helix is analogous to the right-hand thread of a common wood or machine screw.
2. There are 3.6 amino acids per turn of the helix.
3. Each peptide bond is trans and planar.
4. The N—H group of each peptide bond points roughly upward, parallel to the axis of the helix; and the C=O of each peptide bond points roughly downward, also parallel to the axis of the helix.
5. The carbonyl group of each peptide bond is hydrogen-bonded to the N—H group of the peptide bond four amino acid units away from it. Hydrogen bonds are shown as dotted lines.
6. All R— groups point outward from the helix.

Almost immediately after Pauling proposed the α-helix structure, other researchers proved the presence of α-helix in keratin, the protein of hair and wool.

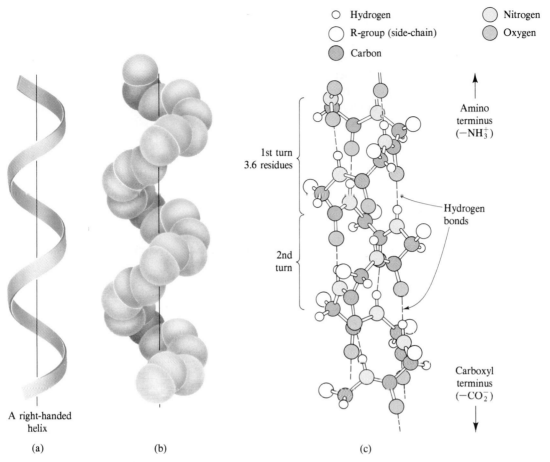

○ Hydrogen

○ R-group (side-chain)

● Carbon

◐ Nitrogen

◐ Oxygen

1st turn
3.6 residues

2nd
turn

Amino
terminus
$(-NH_3^+)$

Hydrogen
bonds

Carboxyl
terminus
$(-CO_2^-)$

A right-handed
helix

(a)   (b)   (c)

Figure 21.9 (a) A right-handed α-helix. (b) Space-filling model of the carbon-nitrogen backbone of an α-helix. (c) Ball-and-stick model of an α-helix showing intrachain hydrogen bonding. There are 3.6 amino acid residues per turn.

It soon became obvious that the α-helix is one of the fundamental folding patterns of polypeptide chains.

β-Pleated sheets consist of extended polypeptide chains with neighboring chains running in opposite (antiparallel) directions. Unlike the α-helix arrangement, N—H and C=O groups lie in the plane of the sheet and are roughly perpendicular to the long axis of the sheet. The C=O group of each peptide bond is hydrogen-bonded to the N—H group of a peptide bond of a neighboring chain.

As you study the section of β-pleated sheet shown in Figure 21.10, note the following:

1. The two polypeptide chains lie adjacent to each other and run in opposite (antiparallel) directions.

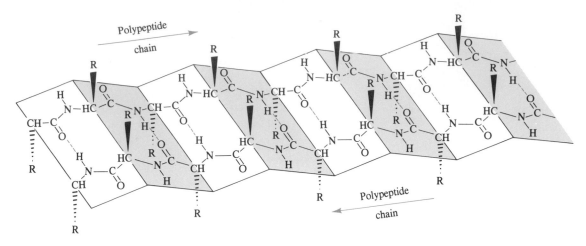

Figure 21.10 β-Pleated sheet conformation with two polypeptide chains running in opposite (antiparallel) directions. Hydrogen bonding between chains is indicated by dotted lines.

2. Each peptide bond is trans and planar.
3. The polypeptide is a chain of flat or planar sections connected at amino acid α-carbons.
4. The C=O and N—H groups of peptide bonds from adjacent chains point at each other and are in the same plane, so hydrogen bonding is possible between adjacent polypeptide chains.
5. The R— groups on any one chain alternate, first above the plane of the sheet and then below the plane of the sheet.

The pleated sheet conformation is stabilized by hydrogen bonding between N—H groups of one chain and C=O groups of an adjacent chain. By comparison, the α-helix is stabilized by hydrogen bonding between N—H and C=O groups within the same polypeptide chain.

The term secondary structure is used to describe α-helix, β-pleated sheet, and other types of periodic conformations in localized regions of polypeptide or protein molecules.

C. Tertiary Structure

Tertiary (3°) structure refers to the overall folding pattern and arrangement in space of all atoms in a single polypeptide chain. Actually, there is no sharp dividing line between secondary and tertiary structure. Secondary structure refers to the spatial arrangement of amino acids close to one another on a polypeptide chain, and tertiary structure refers to the three-dimensional arrangement of all atoms of a polypeptide chain.

Disulfide bonds (Section 13.8E) are important in maintaining tertiary structure. Disulfide bonds are formed between side chains of cysteine by oxidation of two thiol groups (—SH) to form a disulfide bond (—S—S—), as shown:

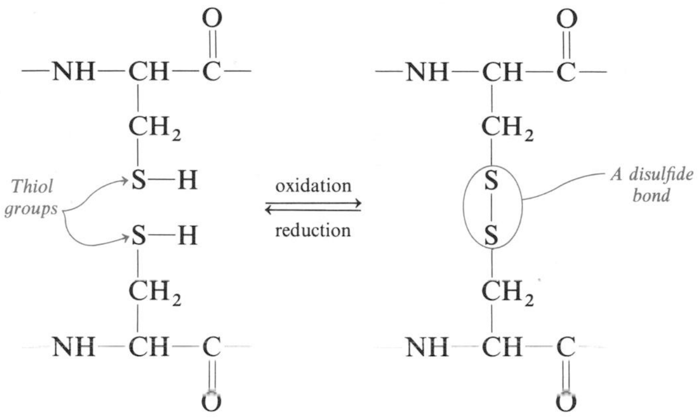

$$
\begin{array}{c}
\text{—NH—CH—C—} \\
\qquad\qquad\| \\
\qquad\qquad\text{O} \\
\text{CH}_2 \\
\text{S—H} \\
\text{S—H} \\
\text{CH}_2 \\
\text{NH—CH—C—}
\end{array}
\quad
\xrightleftharpoons[\text{reduction}]{\text{oxidation}}
\quad
\begin{array}{c}
\text{—NH—CH—C—} \\
\text{CH}_2 \\
\text{S} \\
\text{S} \\
\text{CH}_2 \\
\text{NH—CH—C—}
\end{array}
$$

Thiol groups

A disulfide bond

Treatment of a disulfide bond with a reducing agent regenerates the thiol groups.

Scientists have now determined the primary structure for several hundred polypeptides and proteins, and the secondary and tertiary structure of scores of these are also known. Let us look at the three-dimensional structure of myoglobin, for example, a protein found in skeletal muscle and particularly abundant in diving mammals such as seals, whales, and porpoises. Myoglobin and its structural relative, hemoglobin (Figure 21.12), are the oxygen transport and storage molecules of vertebrates. Hemoglobin binds molecular oxygen in the lungs and transports it to myoglobin in muscles. Myoglobin stores molecular oxygen until it is needed for metabolic oxidation.

Myoglobin consists of a single polypeptide chain of 153 amino acids. The complete amino acid sequence (primary structure) of the chain is known. Myoglobin also contains a single heme unit. Determination of the three-dimensional structure of myoglobin represented a milestone in the study of molecular architecture. J. C. Kendrew, for his contribution to this research, shared the Nobel Prize in chemistry in 1963. The secondary and tertiary structure of myoglobin are shown in Figure 21.11. The single polypeptide chain is folded into a complex, almost boxlike shape.

A more detailed analysis has revealed the exact location of all atoms of the peptide backbone and also the location of all side chains. The important structural features of myoglobin are:

1. The backbone consists of eight relatively straight sections of α-helix, each separated by a bend in the polypeptide chain. The longest section of α-helix has 23 amino acids, the shortest has 7. Some 75% of the amino acids are found in these eight regions of α-helix.

2. Hydrophobic side chains, such as those of phenylalanine, alanine, valine, leucine, isoleucine, and methionine, are clustered in the interior of the molecule, where they are shielded from contact with water. Hydrophobic interactions between nonpolar side chains are important in directing the folding of the polypeptide chain of myoglobin into this compact, three-dimensional shape.

3. The outer surface of myoglobin is coated with hydrophilic side chains, such as those of lysine, arginine, serine, glutamic acid, histidine, and glutamine, which

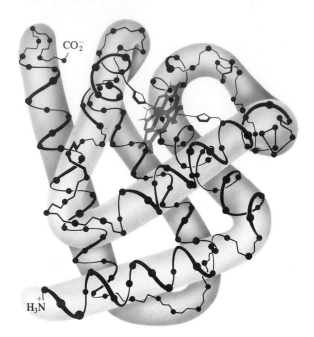

Figure 21.11 The three-dimensional structure of myoglobin. The heme group is shown in color. The N-terminal amino acid (indicated by $-NH_3^+$) is at the lower left and the C-terminal amino acid (indicated by $-CO_2^-$) is at the upper left.

interact with the aqueous environment by hydrogen bonding. The only polar side chains that point to the interior of the myoglobin molecule are those of two histidines. These side chains can be seen in Figure 21.11 as five-membered rings pointing inward toward the heme group.

4. Oppositely charged amino acids close to each other in the three-dimensional structure interact by electrostatic attractions called salt linkages. An example of a salt linkage is the attraction of the side chains of lysine ($-NH_3^+$) and glutamic acid ($-CO_2^-$).

The tertiary structures of several other globular proteins have also been determined. It is clear that globular proteins contain α-helix and β-pleated sheet structures, and also that the relative amounts of each vary widely. Lysozyme, with 129 amino acids in a single polypeptide chain, has only 25% of its amino acids in α-helix regions. Cytochrome, with 104 amino acids in a single polypeptide chain, has no α-helix structure but does contain several regions of β-pleated sheet. Yet, whatever the proportions of α-helix, β-pleated sheet, or other periodic structure, virtually all nonpolar side chains of globular proteins are directed toward the interior of the molecule, while polar side chains are on the surface of the molecule and are in contact with the aqueous environment. Thus the same type of hydrophobic/hydrophilic interactions that are responsible for formation of soap micelles (Section 20.2B) and phospholipid bilayers (Section 20.4B) are responsible for the three-dimensional shapes of globular proteins.

Example 21.5

With which of the following amino acid side chains can the side chain of threonine form hydrogen bonds?

a. valine   **b.** asparagine   **c.** phenylalanine
d. histidine   **e.** tyrosine   **f.** alanine

☐ *Solution*

The side chain of threonine contains a hydroxyl group that can participate in hydrogen bonding in two ways: oxygen has a partial negative charge and can function as a hydrogen bond acceptor; hydrogen has a partial positive charge and can function as a hydrogen bond donor. Therefore, the side chain of threonine can function as a hydrogen bond acceptor for the side chains of tyrosine, asparagine, and histidine. The side chain of threonine can also function as a hydrogen bond donor for the side chains of tyrosine, asparagine, and histidine.

Problem 21.5

At pH 7.4, with what amino acid side chains can the side chain of lysine form salt linkages?

D. Quaternary Structure

Most proteins of molecular weight greater than 50,000 consist of two or more noncovalently linked polypeptide chains. The arrangement of protein monomers in an aggregation is known as a **quaternary (4°) structure**. A good example is hemoglobin, a protein that consists of four separate protein monomers: two α-chains of 141 amino acids each and two β-chains of 146 amino acids each. The quaternary structure of hemoglobin is shown in Figure 21.12.

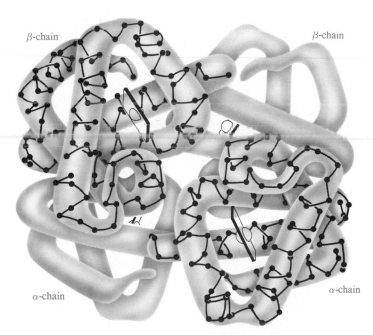

Figure 21.12 The quaternary structure of hemoglobin, showing the four subunits packed together. The flat disks represent four heme units.

The chief factor stabilizing the aggregation of protein subunits is hydrophobic interaction. When separate monomers fold into compact three-dimensional shapes to expose polar side chains to the aqueous environment and shield non-polar side chains from water, there are still hydrophobic "patches" on the surface, in contact with water. These patches can be shielded from water if two or more monomers assemble so their hydrophobic patches are in contact. The molecular weights, numbers of subunits, and biological functions of several proteins with quaternary structure are shown in Table 21.7.

Table 21.7 Quaternary structure of selected proteins.

Protein	Mol. Wt.	Number of Subunits	Subunit Mol. Wt.	Biological Function
insulin	11,466	2	5,733	a hormone regulating glucose metabolism
hemoglobin	64,500	4	16,100	oxygen transport in blood plasma
alcohol dehydrogenase	80,000	4	20,000	an enzyme of alcoholic fermentation
lactate dehydrogenase	134,000	4	33,500	an enzyme of anaerobic glycolysis
aldolase	150,000	4	37,500	an enzyme of anaerobic glycolysis
fumarase	194,000	4	48,500	an enzyme of the tricarboxylic acid cycle
tobacco mosaic virus	40,000,000	2200	17,500	plant virus coat

E. Denaturation

Globular proteins found in living organisms are remarkably sensitive to changes in environment. Relatively small changes in pH, temperature, or solvent composition, even for only a short period, may cause them to become denatured. **Denaturation** causes physical change, the most observable result of which is loss of biological activity. Except for cleavage of disulfide bonds, denaturation stems from changes in secondary, tertiary, or quaternary structure through disruption of noncovalent interactions, such as hydrogen bonds, salt linkages, and hydrophobic interactions. Common denaturing agents include the following:

1. Heat. Most globular proteins become denatured when heated above 50–60°C. For example, boiling or frying an egg causes egg-white protein to become denatured, forming an insoluble mass.

2. Large changes in pH. Adding concentrated acid or alkali to a protein in aqueous solution causes changes in the charged character of ionizable side chains and interferes with salt linkages. For example, in certain clinical chemistry tests where it is necessary first to remove any protein material, trichloroacetic acid (a strong organic acid) is added to denature and precipitate any protein present.

3. Detergents. Treating a protein with sodium dodecylsulfate (SDS, Section 20.2C), a detergent, causes the native conformation to unfold and exposes the nonpolar protein side chains to the aqueous environment. These side chains are then stabilized by hydrophobic interaction with hydrocarbon chains of the detergent.

4. Organic solvents such as alcohols, acetone, or ether.

5. Mechanical treatment. Most globular proteins are denatured in aqueous solution if they are stirred or shaken vigorously. An example is whipped egg whites.

6. Urea and guanidine hydrochloride cause disruption of protein hydrogen bonding and hydrophobic interactions. Because urea is a small molecule with a high degree of polarity, it is very soluble in water. A solution of 8M urea (480 g urea/L of water) is commonly used to denature proteins. Guanidine is a derivative of urea in which $C=O$ is replaced by $=NH$. Guanidine is a strong base and reacts with HCl and to form the salt guanidine hydrochloride.

$$
\underset{\text{urea}}{\overset{\displaystyle\overset{O}{\underset{\|}{}}}{H_2N-C-NH_2}}
\qquad
\underset{\text{guanidine}}{\overset{\displaystyle\overset{NH}{\underset{\|}{}}}{H_2N-C-NH_2}}
\qquad
\underset{\substack{\text{guanidine}\\\text{hydrochloride}}}{\overset{\displaystyle\overset{NH_2^+\ Cl^-}{\underset{\|}{}}}{H_2N-C-NH_2}}
$$

Denaturation can be partial or complete. It can also be reversible or irreversible. For example, the hormone insulin can be denatured with 8M urea and then the three disulfide bonds reduced to —SH groups. If urea is then removed and the disulfide bonds re-formed by oxidation, the resulting molecule has less than 1% of its former biological activity. In this case, denaturation is both complete and irreversible. Consider another example, ribonuclease, an enzyme that consists of a single polypeptide chain of 124 amino acids folded into a compact, three-dimensional structure partly stabilized by four disulfide bonds. Treatment of ribonuclease with urea causes the molecule to unfold, and the disulfide bonds can then be reduced to thiol groups. At this point, the protein is completely denatured—it has no biological activity. If urea is removed from solution and the thiol groups reoxidized to disulfide bonds, the protein regains its full biological activity. In this instance, denaturation has been complete but reversible.

F. 1° Structure Determines 2°, 3°, and 4° Structure

The primary structure of a protein is determined by information coded within genes. Once the primary structure of a polypeptide is established, the structure itself directs the folding of the polypeptide chain into a three-dimensional structure. In other words, information inherent in the primary structure of a protein determines its secondary, tertiary, and quaternary structures.

If the three-dimensional shape of a polypeptide or protein is determined by its primary structure, how can we account for the observation that denaturation is reversible for some proteins and not others?

The reason for this difference in behavior from one protein to another is that some proteins, like ribonuclease, are synthesized as single polypeptide chains, which then fold into unique three-dimensional structures with full biological activity. Others, like insulin, are synthesized as larger molecules that are not biologically active at first but "activated" later by specific enzyme-catalyzed peptide-bond cleavage. Insulin is synthesized in the beta cells of the pancreas as a single polypeptide chain of 84 amino acids. This molecule, called proinsulin, has no biological activity. When insulin is needed, a section of 33 amino acids is hydrolyzed from proinsulin in an enzyme-catalyzed reaction to produce the active hormone (Figure 21.13). Bovine insulin contains 51 amino acids in two polypeptide chains. The A chain contains 21 amino acids and has glycine (gly) at the —NH$_3^+$ terminus and asparagine (asn) at the —CO$_2^-$ terminus. The B chain contains 30 amino acids with phenylalanine (phe) at the —NH$_3^+$ terminus and alanine (ala) at the —CO$_2^-$ terminus.

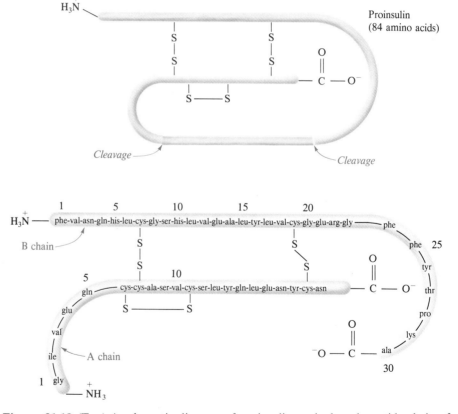

Figure 21.13 (Top) A schematic diagram of proinsulin, a single polypeptide chain of 84 amino acids. (Bottom) The amino acid sequence of bovine insulin.

Because the information directing the original folding of the single polypeptide chain of proinsulin is not present in the A and B chains of the active hormone, refolding of the denatured protein is irregular and denaturation is irreversible.

Zymogens are enzymes produced as inactive proteins, which are then activated by cleavage of one or more of the polypeptide bonds. The process of producing a protein in an inactive, storage form is common. For example, the digestive enzymes trypsin and chymotrypsin are produced in the pancreas as inactive proteins, named trypsinogen and chymotrypsinogen. There is a logical and simple reason for the synthesis of zymogens. In the case of trypsin and chymotrypsin, their function is to catalyze the hydrolysis of dietary proteins reaching the intestinal track. Proteins there are hydrolyzed to their component amino acids and then absorbed through the wall of the intestine into the bloodstream. If trypsin and chymotrypsin were produced as active enzymes, they might well catalyze their own hydrolysis as well as that of other proteins in the pancreas—in effect, a "self-destruct" system. But nature has protected against this happening by synthesizing and storing zymogens instead.

21.7 Fibrous Proteins

Fibrous proteins are stringy, physically tough macromolecules composed of rodlike polypeptide chains joined together by several types of cross-linkages to form stable, insoluble structures. The two main classes of fibrous proteins are the keratins of skin, wool, claws, horn, scales, and feathers, and the collagens of tendons and hides.

A. The Alpha-Keratins

Hair and wool are very flexible and also elastic, so when tension is released, the fibers revert to their original length. At the molecular level, the fundamental structural unit of hair is a polypeptide wound into an α-helix conformation (Figure 21.14). Several levels of structural organization are built from the simple α-helix. First, three strands of α-helix are twisted together to form a larger cable called a protofibril. Protofibrils are then wound into bundles to form an 11-strand cable called a microfibril. These, in turn, are embedded in a larger matrix that ultimately forms a hair fiber (Figure 21.14). When hair is stretched, hydrogen bonds along turns of each α-helix are elongated. The main force causing stretched hair fibers to return to their original length is re-formation of hydrogen bonds in the α-helices.

Microfibril   Protofibril   α-Helix

Figure 21.14 Detailed structure of a hair fiber.

The α-keratins of horns and claws have essentially the same structure as hair but with a much higher concentration of cysteine and a greater degree of disulfide cross-linking between individual helices. These additional disulfide bonds greatly increase resistance to stretching and produce the hard keratins of horn and claw.

B. Collagen Triple Helix

Collagens are constituents of skin, bone, teeth, blood vessels, tendons, cartilage, and connective tissue. They are the most abundant protein in higher vertebrates and make up almost 30% of total body mass in humans. Table 21.8 lists the collagen content of several tissues. Note that bone, the Achilles tendon, skin, and the cornea of the eye are largely collagen.

Table 21.8 Collagen content of some body tissues.

Tissue	Collagen (% Dry Weight)
bone, mineral-free	88
Achilles tendon	86
skin	72
cornea	68
cartilage	46–63
ligament	17
aorta	12–24

Because collagen is abundant and widely distributed in vertebrates and because it is associated with a variety of diseases and problems of aging, more is known about this fibrous protein than about any other. Collagen molecules are very large and have a distinctive amino acid composition. One-third of all amino acids in collagen are glycine, and another 21% are either hydroxylysine or hydroxyproline (Section 21.1D). Both hydroxylated amino acids are formed after their parent amino acids (L-proline and L-lysine) and incorporated in collagen molecules. Because cysteine is almost entirely absent, there are no disulfide cross-links in collagen. When collagen fibers are boiled in water, they are converted to insoluble gelatins.

The polypeptide chains of collagen fold into a conformation that is particularly stable and unique to collagen. In this conformation, three protein strands wrap around each other to form a left-handed superhelix called the **collagen triple helix**. This unit, called tropocollagen, looks much like a three-stranded rope (Figure 21.15).

The hydroxyl groups of hydroxyproline and hydroxylysine residues help to maintain the triple helix structure by forming hydrogen bonds between adjacent chains. Fibers in which proline and lysine groups have not been hydroxylated are far less stable than fibers in which these groups have been hydroxylated. One of the important functions of vitamin C is in hydroxylation of collagen. Without adequate supplies of vitamin C, collagen metabolism is impaired, giving

Figure 21.15 Collagen triple helix.

rise to scurvy, a condition in which tropocollagen fibers do not form stable, physically tough fibers. Scurvy produces skin lesions, fragile blood vessels, and bleeding gums.

Collagen fibers are formed when many tropocollagen molecules line up side by side in a regular pattern and are then cross-linked by newly formed covalent bonds. Most covalent cross-linking involves the side chains of lysines. The extent and type of cross-linking vary with age and physiological condition. For example, the collagen of rat Achilles tendon is highly cross-linked, and collagen of the more flexible tendon of rat tail is less highly cross-linked. Further, it is not clear when, if ever, the process of cross-linking is completed. Some believe it continues throughout life, producing increasingly stiffer skin, blood vessels, and other tissues, which then contribute to the medical problems of aging and the aged.

21.8 Plasma Proteins: Examples of Globular Proteins

Human blood consists of a fluid portion (plasma) and cellular components. The cellular components, which make up 40–45% of the volume of whole blood, consist of red blood cells (erythrocytes), white blood cells (leukocytes), and blood platelets. Human plasma consists largely of water (90–92%) in which are dissolved various inorganic ions and a heterogeneous mixture of organic molecules, the largest groups of which are the **plasma proteins**. The earliest method of separating plasma proteins into fractions used ammonium sulfate to "salt out" different types of proteins. The fraction precipitated from plasma 50% saturated with ammonium sulfate was called **globulin**. The fraction not precipitated at this salt concentration but precipitated from plasma saturated with ammonium sulfate was called **albumin**. Today, electrophoresis is the most common method of separating proteins of biological fluids into fractions, especially in the clinical laboratory, where it is used routinely to measure proteins in human plasma, urine, and cerebrospinal fluid. It is estimated that between 15 and 20 million plasma-protein electrophoretic analyses are carried out each year in the United States and Canada.

In plasma-protein electrophoresis, a sample of plasma is applied as a narrow line to a cellulose acetate strip. The ends of the strip are then immersed in a buffer of pH 8.8, and a voltage is applied to the strip. At pH 8.8, plasma proteins have net negative charges and migrate toward the positive electrode. After a predetermined time, the cellulose acetate strip is removed, dried, and sprayed with a dye that selectively stains proteins. The separated protein fractions then appear on the developed strip as spots [Figure 21.16(a)]. The amount of protein in each spot is determined using a densitometer to measure intensity versus width of each spot. The concentration of protein in each spot is proportional to the area under each peak.

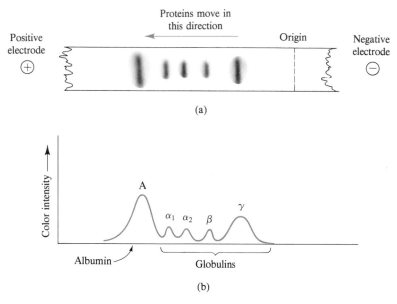

Figure 21.16 Separation of serum proteins by electrophoresis. (a) A sample is applied as a narrow line at the origin. After electrophoresis at pH 8.8, the paper is dried and stained. (b) A plot of color intensity of each spot.

Electrophoresis on cellulose acetate separates serum proteins into five large fractions: one albumin fraction and four globulin fractions. The four globulin fractions are arbitrarily designated α_1, α_2, β, and γ according to their electrophoretic mobilities. Serum albumin has an isoelectric point of about 4.9 and migrates farthest toward the positive electrode. Gamma-globulin has an isoelectric point of about 7.4 and migrates the shortest distance. Shown in Table 21.9 are the concentrations of the five large protein fractions of human serum.

Table 21.9
Concentrations of the important human serum proteins as determined by electrophoresis.

Fraction	(g/100 mL)	Total Protein (%)
albumin	3.5–5.0	52–67
globulins		
α_1	0.1–0.4	2.5–4.5
α_2	0.5–1.1	6.6–13.6
β	0.6–1.2	9.1–14.7
γ	0.5–1.5	9.0–21.6

The primary function of albumins is to regulate the osmotic pressure of blood. In addition, albumins are important in transporting fatty acids and certain drugs such as aspirin and digitalis. The α_1 and α_2 fractions transport other biomolecules, such as fats, steroids, and phospholipids and various other lipids. The α_1 fraction also contains antitrypsin, a protein that inhibits the protein-digesting enzyme trypsin. The α_2 fraction contains haptoglobulin, which binds any hemoglobin released from destroyed red blood cells, and ceruloplasmin, the principal copper-containing protein of the body. The α_2 fraction also contains prothrombin, an inactive form of the blood-clotting enzyme thrombin. The β fraction contains a variety of specific transport proteins, as well as substances involved in blood clotting.

The γ-globulin fraction consists primarily of **antibodies (immunoglobulins)**, whose function is to combat **antigens** (foreign proteins) introduced into the body. Specific antibodies are formed by the immune system in response to specific antigens. The response is the basis for immunization against such infectious diseases as polio, tetanus, and diphtheria. An antibody consists of a combination of heavy (high-molecular-weight) and light (low-molecular-weight) polypeptide chains held together by disulfide bonds (Figure 21.17). Each antibody has two identical binding sites that react with specific antigens to form an insoluble complex called precipitin (Figure 21.18). Formation of precipitin deactivates the antigen and permits its removal and breakdown by white blood cells.

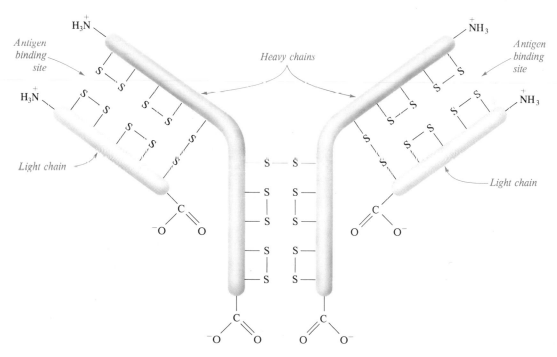

Figure 21.17 The three-dimensional shape of an antibody.

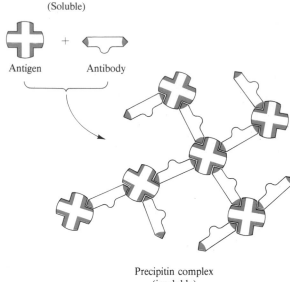

Figure 21.18 The action of an antibody and its specific antigen to form an inactive precipitin complex. The precipitated antigen-antibody complex is then ingested and broken down by white blood cells.

Key Terms and Concepts

albumin (21.8)

amino acid (21.1A)

antibody (21.8)

antigen (21.8)

chirality of amino acids (21.1B)

collagen (21.7B)

collagen triple helix (21.7B)

denaturation (21.6E)

electrophoresis (21.2E)

fibrous protein (21.7)

geometry of a peptide bond (21.6A)

globular protein (21.8)

globulins (21.8)

α-helix (21.6B)

immunoglobulin (21.8)

ionization of amino acids (21.2A)

isoelectric point (21.2D)

α-keratin (21.7A)

peptide bond (21.3)

plasma protein (21.8)

β-pleated sheet (21.6B)

primary structure (21.5)

quaternary structure (21.6D)

secondary structure (21.6B)

C-terminal amino acid (21.3)

N-terminal amino acid (21.3)

tertiary structure (21.6C)

titration of amino acids (21.2C)

zwitterion (21.1A)

Problems

*Amino acids
(Section 21.1)*

21.6 Explain the meaning of the designation L as it is used to indicate the stereochemistry (configuration) of amino acids found in proteins.

21.7 How do L-serine and D-glyceraldehyde compare in configuration about the chiral carbon? L-serine and L-glyceraldehyde?

21.8 **a.** Which amino acid found in proteins has no chiral carbon?
b. Which amino acids found in proteins have two chiral carbons?

21.9 How many stereoisomers are possible for:
a. L-4-hydroxyproline   **b.** L-5-hydroxylysine   **c.** ornithine
d. citrulline   **e.** thyroxine

Acid-base properties of amino acids (Section 21.2)

21.10 For amino acids with nonionizable side chains, the value of pI (the isoelectric point) can be calculated from the equation

$$pI = \tfrac{1}{2}(pK_a \text{ of } \alpha\text{-}CO_2H + pK_a \text{ of } \alpha\text{-}NH_3^+)$$

Given the following values of pK_a, calculate the isoelectric point of each amino acid listed.

	pK_a of α-CO$_2$H	pK_a of α-NH$_3^+$
Glycine	2.35	9.78
Serine	2.21	9.15

21.11 For amino acids with a side-chain $-CO_2H$ group, the value of pI can be calculated from the equation

$$pI = \tfrac{1}{2}(pK_a \text{ of } \alpha\text{-}CO_2H + pK_a \text{ of side-chain } -CO_2H)$$

Given the following values of pK_a, calculate the pI of the following amino acids. Compare these values with those given in Table 21.6.

	pK_a of α-CO$_2$H	pK_a of α-NH$_3^+$	pK_a of Side-Chain $-CO_2H$
Asparatic acid	2.10	9.82	3.86
Glutamic acid	2.10	9.47	4.07

21.12 For amino acids with side-chain amino groups, the value of pI can be calculated from the equation

$$pI = \tfrac{1}{2}(pK_a \text{ of } \alpha\text{-}NH_3^+ + pK_a \text{ of side-chain amino group})$$

Given the following values of pK_a, calculate the pI of each amino acid. Compare these values with those given in Table 21.6.

	pK_a of α-CO$_2$H	pK_a of α-NH$_3^+$	pK_a of Side-Chain Amino Group
Lysine	2.18	8.95	10.53
Arginine	2.01	9.04	12.48

21.13 For the following amino acids, draw a structural formula for the form you expect would predominate at pH 1.0, 6.0, and 12.0. Refer to Section 21.2D and Problems 21.10–21.12 for values of pI.
a. alanine   **b.** tyrosine   **c.** aspartic acid   **d.** arginine

21.14   **a.** Estimate the pH at which the solubility of alanine in water is a minimum.

b. Why does the solubility of alanine increase as the pH is increased?

c. Why does the solubility of alanine increase as the pH is decreased?

21.15   Which of the following amino acids will migrate toward the (+) electrode and which will migrate toward the (−) electrode on electrophoresis at pH 6.0? at pH 8.6?

a. tyrosine   **b.** arginine   **c.** cysteine
d. aspartic acid   **e.** asparagine   **f.** histidine

Primary structure of polypeptides and proteins (Section 21.3)

21.16   What is the characteristic structural feature of a peptide bond?

21.17   Write a structural formula for the tripeptide glycylserylaspartic acid. Write a structural formula for an isomeric tripeptide. Calculate the net charge on each tripeptide at pH 6.0.

21.18   Write the structural formula for the tripeptide lys-asp-val. Calculate the net charge on this tripeptide at pH 6.0.

21.19   How many tetrapeptides can be constructed from the 20 amino acids
a. if each of the amino acids is used only once in the tetrapeptide?
b. if each amino acid can be used up to four times in the tetrapeptide?

21.20   Write an equation for the oxidation of two molecules of cysteine by O_2 to form a disulfide bond.

21.21   Following is the structural formula of glutathione (GSH), one of the most common small peptides in animals, plants, and bacteria.

$$\overset{+}{H_3}N-CH-CH_2-CH_2-\overset{\displaystyle O}{\overset{\|}{C}}-NH-CH-\overset{\displaystyle O}{\overset{\|}{C}}-NH-CH_2-\overset{\displaystyle O}{\overset{\|}{C}}-O^-$$

$$CO_2^- \qquad\qquad CH_2$$

$$SH$$

glutathione (GSH)

a. Name the amino acids in this tripeptide.

b. What is unusual about the peptide bond formed between the first two amino acids in this tripeptide?

c. Write an equation for the reaction of two molecules of glutathione with O_2 to form a disulfide bond.

Three-dimensional shapes of polypeptides and proteins (Section 21.5)

21.22   Using structural formulas, show how the theory of resonance accounts for the fact that a peptide bond is planar.

21.23   In constructing models of polypeptide chains, Linus Pauling assumed that for maximum stability, (1) all amide bonds are trans and coplanar, and (2) there is a maximum of hydrogen bonding between amide groups. Examine the alpha-helix (Figure 21.9) and the beta-pleated sheet (Figure 21.10) and convince yourself that in each conformation, amide bonds are planar and each carbonyl oxygen is hydrogen-bonded to an amide hydrogen.

21.24 Examine the alpha-helix conformation. Are the amino acid side chains arranged all inside the helix or all outside the helix, or are they randomly oriented?

21.25 Draw structural formulas to illustrate the noncovalent interactions indicated:
  a. Hydrogen bonding between the side chains of thr and asn.
  b. Salt linkage between the side chains of lys and glu.
  c. Hydrophobic interactions between the side chains of two phenyl-alanines.

21.26 Consider a typical globular protein in an aqueous medium of pH 6.0. Which of the following amino acid side chains would you expect to find on the outside and in contact with water? which on the inside and shielded from contact with water?
  a. glutamic acid   **b.** glutamine   **c.** arginine
  d. serine   **e.** valine   **f.** phenylalanine
  g. lysine   **h.** isoleucine   **i.** threonine

21.27 Which of the following peptides and proteins migrate to the (+) electrode and which migrate to the (−) electrode on electrophoresis at pH 6.0? at pH 8.6?
  a. ala-glu-ile   **b.** gly-asp-lys   **c.** val-ala-leu
  d. tyr-trp-arg   **e.** thyroglobulin (pI 4.6)   **f.** hemoglobin (pI 6.8)

21.28 The following proteins have approximately the same molecular weight and size. The pI of each is given.

carboxypeptidase   pI 6.0
pepsin   pI 1.0
human growth hormone   pI 6.9
ovalbumin   pI 4.6

  a. State whether each is positively charged, negatively charged, or uncharged at pH 6.0.
  b. Draw a diagram showing the results of electrophoresis of a mixture of the four at pH 6.0.

21.29 Examine the primary structure of bovine insulin (Figure 21.13) and list all asp, glu, lys, arg, and his in the molecule. Predict whether insulin has an isoelectric point nearer that of the acidic amino acids (pI 2.0–3.0), the neutral amino acids (pI 5.5–6.5), or the basic amino acids (pI 9.5–11.0).

21.30 Following is the primary structure of glucagon, a polypeptide hormone that helps to regulate glycogen metabolism. Glucagon is secreted by the alpha cells of the pancreas during the fasting state, when blood glucose levels are decreasing. This hormone stimulates the enzymes that catalyze

1   *5*   *10*   *15*
his-ser-glu-gly-thr-phe-thr-ser-asp-tyr-ser-lys-tyr-leu-asp-ser-arg-arg-

              20   *25*   *29*
      ala-gln-asp-phe-val-gln-trp-leu-met-asn-thr

glucagon

the hydrolysis of glycogen to glucose and thus helps to maintain blood glucose levels within a normal concentration range. Glucagon contains 29 amino acids and has a molecular weight of approximately 3500.

a. Estimate the net charge on glucagon at pH 6.0.

b. Predict whether the isoelectric point of glucagon would be nearer the isoelectric point of the acidic amino acids (pI 2.0–3.0), the neutral amino acids (pI 5.5–6.5), or the basic amino acids (pI 9.5–11.0).

21.31 Myoglobin and hemoglobin are globular proteins. Myoglobin consists of a single polypeptide chain of 153 amino acids. Hemoglobin is composed of four polypeptide chains, two of 141 amino acids and two of 146 amino acids. The three-dimensional structures of myoglobin and hemoglobin polypeptide chains are similar, yet myoglobin exists as a monomer in aqueous solution, while the four polypeptide chains of hemoglobin self-assemble to form a tetramer. Which polypeptide chains, those of myoglobin or hemoglobin, would have a higher percentage of nonpolar amino acids?

21.32 What is irreversible denaturation and how does it differ from reversible denaturation?

21.33 After water, proteins are the chief constituents of most tissues. Often in the analysis of lesser constituents, it is necessary first to remove all proteins. The most common reagents for this purpose are 0.5M trichloroacetic acid, ethanol, or acetone. Explain the basis for using these reagents to deproteinize a solution.

21.34 Is the following statement true or false? Explain your answer. "The principal factor directing the folding of globular proteins in an aqueous environment is hydrogen bonding between polar side chains and water molecules."

21.35 Suppose proinsulin is treated with a disulfide reducing agent in the presence of 8M urea. These reagents are then removed from solution and the denatured protein is allowed to refold in the presence of an oxidizing agent that converts thiols to disulfides. Do you expect that proinsulin after this treatment would have the same conformation as the original molecule or a different conformation? Explain your answer.

Fibrous proteins (Section 21.7)

21.36 What is the most characteristic type of secondary structure in the protein of (a) hair; (b) hooves; (c) collagen.

21.37 What is meant by the following statement? "An alpha-helix is flexible and it is also elastic."

21.38 What is the function of collagen? Describe (a) the macroscopic physical properties of collagen, and (b) the molecular structure of collagen.

Plasma proteins (Section 21.8)

21.39 Of the five main types of serum proteins, which has the highest isoelectric point? Which has the lowest isoelectric point?

21.40 Explain the process of "salting out."

21.41 What is the primary function of serum albumin?

21.42 What is the principal function of the proteins of the gamma-globulin fraction?

Abnormal Human Hemoglobins

There are an estimated 30 billion red blood cells (erythrocytes) in the bloodstream of an adult, each packed with about 270 million molecules of hemoglobin. For sheer numbers, hemoglobin is one of the most plentiful proteins in the body. Hemoglobin's function is to pick up molecular oxygen in the lungs and deliver it to all parts of the body for metabolic oxidation. Normal adult hemoglobin (HbA) is composed of four polypeptide chains: two alpha chains, each of 141 amino acids; and two beta chains, each of 146 amino acids. Each polypeptide chain surrounds one heme group that binds oxygen reversibly. The tetrameric structure of hemoglobin is stabilized principally by hydrophobic interactions. Shown in Figure XIV-1 is the three-dimensional shape of a single beta chain. The N-terminal amino

acid is indicated by $-NH_3^+$ and the C-terminal amino acid by $-CO_2^-$. The three-dimensional structure of hemoglobin A was determined by Max Perutz. For this pioneering work he shared in the Nobel Prize in 1963.

It is so-called abnormal human hemoglobins that have attracted particular attention because of the diseases associated with them. The best known of these diseases is sickle-cell anemia, a name derived from the characteristic sickle shape of affected red blood cells when they are deoxygenated. When combined with oxygen, red blood cells of persons with sickle-cell anemia have the flat, disclike conformation of normal erythrocytes. However, when oxygen pressure is reduced, affected cells become distorted and considerably more rigid and inflexible than normal cells (Figure XIV-2).

Because sickled cells are larger than some of the blood channels through which they must pass, they tend to become wedged in capillaries, thereby blocking flow of blood. Surprisingly little is known about why some organs and tissues are affected more than others by the disease, the normal age at which the disease starts, and male versus female susceptibility. Some persons afflicted with sickle-cell anemia die at an early age, often due to childhood infections complicated by the disease. Others lead long, productive lives.

In 1949, Linus Pauling made a discovery that opened the way to an understanding of this disease at the molecular level. He observed that normal adult hemoglobin (HbA) differs significantly from sickle-cell hemoglobin (HbS). At pH 6.9, HbA has a net negative charge and HbS has a net positive charge. On paper electrophoresis at this pH, HbA moves toward the positive

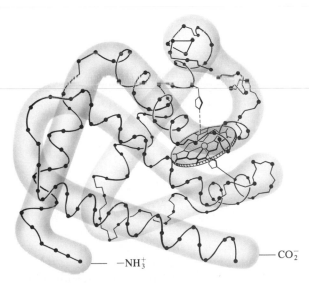

$-NH_3^+$ $-CO_2^-$

Figure XIV-1 The beta chain of hemoglobin.

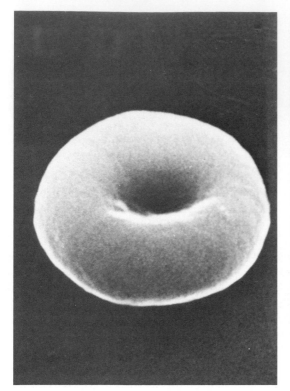 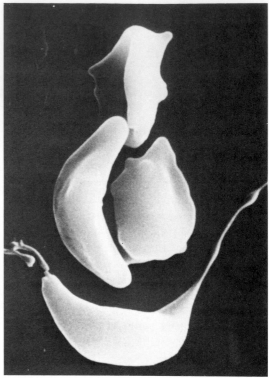

Figure XIV-2 Normal red blood cells (left) magnified × 6750 and cells that have sickled (right) after discharging oxygen. Magnified × 8700.

electrode and HbS toward the negative electrode. Vernon Ingram pursued this discovery, and in 1956 showed that sickle-cell hemoglobin differs from normal hemoglobin only in the amino acid at the sixth position of the beta chain. Alpha chains of both are identical, but glutamic acid at position 6 of each beta chain of HbA is replaced by valine in HbS. As a result of the valine–glutamic acid substitution, two negatively charged, hydrophilic side chains are replaced by two uncharged, hydrophobic side chains.

How is the substitution of HbS for HbA in red blood cells related to the process of sickling? We know that HbS functions perfectly normally in transporting molecular oxygen from the lungs to cells. In this regard it is indistinguishable from HbA. However, when it gives up its oxygen, HbS tends to form polymers that separate from solution in crystalline form. There is now good evidence that the basic unit of crystalline HbS polymer is a double-stranded fiber stabilized by hydrophobic interactions, including that between valine at position 6 of one beta chain and a hydrophobic patch on another HbS molecule. Double-stranded HbS polymer molecules then interact to form multistranded cablelike structures. This is a remarkable phenomenon: polymerization of HbS is facilitated by the presence of valine at beta-6, but comparable polymerization of HbA is prevented by the presence of glutamic acid at beta-6.

Now that scientists understand sickle-cell anemia at the molecular level, the challenge is to devise specific medical treatments to prevent, or at least inhibit, the sickling process. One strategy being actively pursued is the search for substances that inhibit the polymerization of HbS by disrupting or preventing hydrophobic interactions of beta-6 valines.

Sickle-cell anemia is a genetic disease. Persons with an HbS gene from only one parent are said to have sickle-cell trait. About 40% of the hemoglobin in these individuals is HbS. Generally no ill effects are associated with sickle-cell trait except under extreme conditions. Persons with HbS genes from both parents are said to have sickle-cell disease, and all their hemoglobin is HbS. The mutant gene coding for HbS occurs in about 10% of black Americans and in about 20% of African blacks. The gene is also present in significant numbers of the populations of countries bordering the Mediterranean Sea and parts of India.

That there seems to be so much natural selection pressure against the HbS gene raises questions of why it has persisted so long in the gene pool and why sickle-cell trait is so common in populations of specific parts of the world. Of several explanations offered, the most likely, first advanced in 1949, is that sickle-cell trait provides some protection against *Plasmodium falciparum*, the parasite responsible for the most severe form of malaria. The falciparum parasite lives part of its life cycle in red blood cells and grows equally well in oxygenated cells containing either HbS or HbA. However, when infected cells containing HbS are deoxygenated and they sickle, the parasites living in them are killed. Not all infected HbS cells sickle at any one time, but the approximately 40% that do sufficiently reduce the severity of the malaria and prevent death.

The dramatic success in discovering the genetic and molecular basis for sickle-cell anemia spurred interest in searching for other abnormal hemoglobins. To date, several hundred have been isolated and the changes in primary structure have been determined. In most, there is but a single amino acid residue change in either the alpha or the beta chain, and each substitution is consistent with the change of a single nucleotide in one DNA codon (Section 23.11A). Several abnormal hemoglobins are listed in Table XIV-1.

Although most of the abnormal hemoglobins differ from HbA by only a single amino acid substitution, several have been discovered in which there are either insertions or deletions of amino acids. For example, in hemoglobin-Leiden, discovered in 1968, glutamic acid at position 6 in each beta chain is missing altogether. In hemoglobin–Gun Hill (Figure XIV-3), discovered in 1967 in a 41-year-old man and one of his three daughters, there is a deletion of five amino acids in each beta chain. Thus, each beta chain is shortened to 141 amino acids. In hemoglobin-Grady (Figure XIV-3), discovered in 1974 in a 25-year-old woman and her father, there is insertion of three amino acids in each alpha chain. Thus, each alpha chain is elongated to144 amino acid residues.

Table XIV-1

Abnormal human hemoglobins. Many of these names are derived from the location of their discovery.

Hemoglobin Variant	Amino Acid Substitution		
	Position	From	To
alpha-chain			
J-Paris	12	ala	asp
G-Philadelphia	68	asn	lys
M-Boston	58	his	tyr
Dakar	112	his	gln
beta-chain			
S	6	glu	val
J-Trinidad	16	gly	asp
E	26	glu	lys
M-Hamburg	63	his	tyr

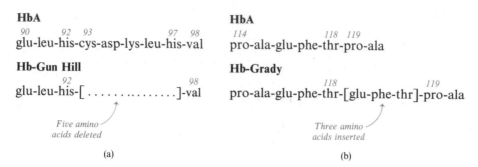

Figure XIV-3 Some abnormal human hemoglobins; (a) a deletion mutation and (b) an insertion mutation.

Sources

Dayhoff, M. O. 1972. *Atlas of Protein Sequence and Structure*. Vol. 5. Washington, D. C.; National Biomedical Foundation.

Ingram, B. 1957. Gene mutations in human hemoglobin: The chemical difference between normal and sickle-cell hemoglobin. *Nature* 180:326.

Maugh, T. H. 1981. A new understanding of sickle cell emerges. *Science* 211:265–267.

Morimoto, H.; Lehmann, H.; and Perutz, M. F. 1971. Molecular pathology of human hemoglobins. *Nature* 232:408.

22 Enzymes

Living cells are unique in their ability to carry out complex reactions with remarkable specificity and remarkable speed. The agents responsible for this property of living matter are a group of protein biocatalysts called **enzymes**, each designed to catalyze a specific reaction or type of reaction. James Sumner, in 1926, was the first to isolate an enzyme in pure crystalline form. The enzyme was urease, which catalyzes the hydrolysis of urea to ammonia and carbon dioxide:

$$\underset{\text{urea}}{H_2N-\overset{\overset{\displaystyle O}{\|}}{C}-NH_2} + H_2O \xrightarrow{\text{urease}} 2NH_3 + CO_2$$

All enzymes, it is now clear, are proteins, and the one feature that distinguishes them from other proteins is that they are catalysts.

Practically speaking, enzyme technology has been with us for centuries. The use of enzymes for fermentation of fruit juices and grains to make alcoholic beverages is a long-practiced art. Cheese was and still is made by treating milk with renin, an enzyme obtained from the lining of calf stomachs. The active ingredient in commercially available meat tenderizers is an enzyme extracted from papaya plants.

Understanding enzymes and their properties is essential to understanding metabolism, metabolic diseases, and therapies for treating metabolic diseases, as well as many of the enzyme-based bioassays currently in use in the clinical chemistry laboratory.

22.1 Nomenclature and Classification of Enzymes

In the early work on metabolism, the numerous enzymes discovered were generally named according to their function; the suffix-*ase* was added to the name of the substrate whose degradation the enzyme catalyzed. Examples are urease, which catalyzes the hydrolysis of urea to carbon dioxide and ammonia, and arginase, an enzyme of the urea cycle (Section 27.3), which catalyzes the hydrolysis of arginine to urea and ornithine.

$$
\underset{\text{arginine}}{\underset{\overset{|}{\text{NH}_3^+}}{\overset{\overset{\text{NH}_2^+}{\|}}{\text{H}_2\text{NCNHCH}_2\text{CH}_2\text{CH}_2\text{CHCO}^-}}} + \text{H}_2\text{O} \xrightarrow{\text{arginase}} \underset{\text{urea}}{\overset{\overset{\text{O}}{\|}}{\text{H}_2\text{NCNH}_2}} + \underset{\text{ornithine}}{\underset{\overset{|}{\text{NH}_3^+}}{\overset{\overset{\text{O}}{\|}}{\text{H}_3^+\text{NCH}_2\text{CH}_2\text{CH}_2\text{CHCO}^-}}}
$$

The practice of naming enzymes according to their function was soon extended to enzymes involved in nondegradative reactions and also to the type of reaction catalyzed. For example, enzymes catalyzing oxidations became known as oxidases (for instance, glucose oxidase). Others became classified as reductases, isomerases, synthetases (for instance, triose phosphate isomerase, citrate synthetase), and so on. Growth of this unsystematic nomenclature presented many problems, including more than one name for a single enzyme.

To overcome these difficulties, the International Union of Biochemistry in 1961 adopted the recommendations of its **Enzyme Commission** (EC) for a systematic nomenclature and classification of enzymes. For each enzyme, the EC proposed a systematic name and a unique numerical designation. In the Enzyme Commission classification, enzymes are divided into the following six large classes:

1. Oxidoreductases, which catalyze oxidation-reduction reactions.
2. Transferases, which catalyze the transfer of a group of atoms from one substrate to another or from one part of a substrate to another.
3. Hydrolases, which catalyze hydrolysis of esters, anhydrides, amides, imines, and the like.
4. Lyases, which catalyze nonhydrolytic removal of groups to form a double bond (for example, removal of HOH from an alcohol to form an alkene) or addition of groups to a double bond (for example, addition of HOH to an alkene to form an alcohol).
5. Isomerases, which catalyze isomerizations.
6. Ligases, which catalyze covalent bond formation coupled with hydrolysis of adenosine triphosphate (ATP) or similar nucleoside triphosphate.

However, because systematic names and numerical designations are often cumbersome, the Enzyme Commission also recommends a single, unique common name for each enzyme. Many of these common names are derived by naming the substrate and the type of reaction, and including the suffix -*ase*. An example is the common name of the enzyme that catalyzes the oxidation of lactate to pyruvate. Oxidations of this type, in which hydrogen atoms are removed from adjacent atoms, are often called dehydrogenations. In this enzyme-catalyzed reaction, the oxidizing agent is nicotinamide adenine dinucleotide (NAD^+).

$$\underset{\text{lactate}}{CH_3\overset{\overset{\displaystyle OH}{|}}{C}HCO_2^-} + NAD^+ \xrightarrow{\text{LDH}} \underset{\text{pyruvate}}{CH_3\overset{\overset{\displaystyle O}{||}}{C}CO_2^-} + NADH + H^+$$

Substrate: lactate
Reaction type: dehydrogenation
Common name: lactate dehydrogen(ation) + *ase* = lactate dehydrogenase
Abbreviation: LDH

Because of the simplicity and wide use of these Enzyme Commission–recommended common names, we shall use them throughout the text.

There is a further problem to be dealt with in enzyme nomenclature and classification—namely, that a single organism or even a single cell may produce two or more enzymes that catalyze the same reaction. Such enzymes are termed isoenzymes, or isozymes. For example, lactate dehydrogenase (LDH) occurs as five isoenzymes, designated LDH_1, LDH_2, LDH_3, LDH_4, and LDH_5. (For further discussion of the isoenzymes of LDH and their use in diagnosis of myocardial infarction, see Mini-Essay XV, "Clinical Enzymology—The Search for Specificity.") Although isoenzymes are similar in structure and physical properties, they do show certain differences. The property by which they are most commonly detected, separated, and identified is their behavior on electrophoresis. Because most isoenzymes have slightly different sizes, shapes, and net charges, they migrate at different rates. The Enzyme Commission has recommended that isoenzymes be designated by arabic numerals 1, 2, 3, . . . , with the lowest number given to the form that migrates most rapidly toward the anode during electrophoresis.

22.2 Cofactors, Prosthetic Groups, and Coenzymes

The enzymes that act as biocatalysts show considerable diversity of structure. Many enzymes are simple proteins, which means that the protein itself is the true catalyst. Other enzymes catalyze reactions of their substrates only when specific nonprotein molecules or metal ions are present. A cofactor is any nonprotein molecule or ion that is essential for the enzyme-catalyzed reaction. A prosthetic group can be defined similarly. The distinction between a cofactor and a prosthetic group is one of degree. A nonprotein molecule or ion that is very tightly bound to an enzyme is called a **prosthetic group**; one that is more loosely bound is called a **cofactor**. Since this is not an exact definition, it is entirely possible that what is a cofactor for one enzyme may be a prosthetic group for another. In the following discussion, we will concentrate on the types of nonprotein molecules and ions required for enzyme activity rather than the precise terminology for each.

A coenzyme is a true substrate for an enzyme-catalyzed reaction, and because it is a substrate, it undergoes a chemical change during the particular enzyme-catalyzed reaction. Unlike other substrates, a modified coenzyme is recycled by another metabolic pathway, and therefore can be used over and over for the same reaction or type of reaction.

A. Metal Ions

Metal ions function primarily by forming complexes with an enzyme proper or with other nonprotein groups required by the enzyme for catalytic activity. In some cases, metal ions appear to be only loosely associated with an active enzyme and can be removed easily from it. In other instances, metal ions are integral parts of the enzyme structure and are retained throughout isolation and purification procedures. As an example, virtually all reactions that involve adenosine triphosphate (ATP) and the hydrolysis of phosphate anhydride bonds require Mg^{2+} as a cofactor. In these reactions, the positively charged cation coordinates with the negatively charged oxygens of the phosphate groups. As another example, carbonic anhydrase requires one Zn^{2+} per molecule of enzyme for activity.

In recent years, we have come to realize that many other metals, some of them required only in trace amounts, are also essential for proper enzyme function in humans; hence, they are required for good health. In many instances, we have little or no understanding of how these metal ions function or why they are essential.

B. Prosthetic Groups

One important class of prosthetic groups comprises the hemes. The structure of heme consists of four substituted pyrrole rings joined by one-carbon bridges into a larger ring called porphyrin [Figure 22.1(a)]. Shown in Figure 22.1(b) is the heme group found in hemoglobin and myoglobin. Note that there is a metal atom in the center of the heme group. In hemoglobin and myoglobin, an iron atom occurs as Fe^{2+}. A magnesium ion, Mg^{2+}, embedded in a porphyrin ring is an integral part of chlorophyll.

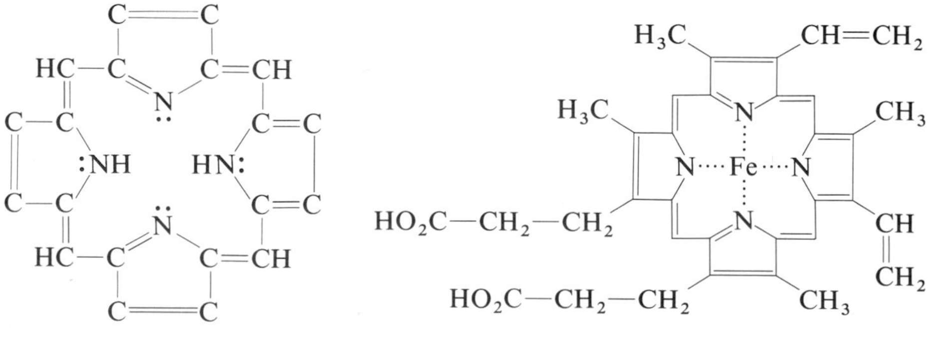

(a)   (b)

Figure 22.1 Heme coenzymes: (a) the porphyrin ring system; (b) the heme prosthetic group of hemoglobin, myoglobin, and certain enzymes.

C. Coenzymes and Vitamins

A **coenzyme** is a small organic molecule that binds reversibly to an enyme and functions as a second substrate for the enzyme. For example, the enzyme lactate dehydrogenase (LDH) requires nicotinamide adenine dinucleotide (NAD^+) for activity:

$$\underset{\text{lactate}}{CH_3\overset{\overset{\displaystyle OH}{|}}{C}HCO_2^-} + NAD^+ \xrightarrow[\text{dehydrogenase}]{\text{lactate}} \underset{\text{pyruvate}}{CH_3\overset{\overset{\displaystyle O}{\|}}{C}CO_2^-} + NADH + H^+$$

It should be obvious why NAD^+ is required—the organic molecule NAD^+ oxidizes lactate to pyruvate and in the process is reduced to NADH. Other metabolic pathways, chief among them electron transport and oxidative phosphorylation reoxidize NADH to NAD^+, so this vital coenzyme can be used over and over for further substrate oxidations.

Humans and many other organisms cannot synthesize certain coenzymes, and therefore, they must obtain from their diet either the coenzyme itself or a substance from which the coenzyme can be synthesized. These so-called essential coenzymes or coenzyme precursors are vitamins. Vitamins are divided into two classes, based on physical properties: those that are water-soluble and those that are fat-soluble. As might be expected, water-soluble vitamins are highly polar, hydrophilic substances, while fat-soluble vitamins are nonpolar, hydrophobic substances. Most water-soluble vitamins are either coenzymes themselves or small molecules from which coenzymes are synthesized within the body.

Table 22.1 lists the nine water-soluble vitamins required in human diets, the coenzyme derived from each, and the function of each coenzyme.

Table 22.1 Nine water-soluble vitamins, the coenzymes derived from each, and their biological function.

Vitamin	Coenzyme	Function of Coenzyme
B_3, nicotinic acid	nicotinamide adenine dinucleotide	oxidation-reduction
B_2, riboflavin	flavin adenine dinucleotide flavin mononucleotide	oxidation-reduction
C, ascorbic acid	———	oxidation-reduction
B_1, thiamine	thiamine pyrophosphate	decarboxylation
B_6, pyridoxine	pyridoxal phosphate	transfer of $-NH_2$ groups
pantothenic acid	coenzyme A	transfer of CH_3CO- groups
folic acid	tetrahydrofolic acid	transfer of $-CH_3$, $-CH_2OH$, and $-CHO$ groups
biotin	biocytin	transfer of $-CO_2H$ groups
B_{12}, cobalamin	coenzyme B_{12}	transfer of $-CO-SCoA$ groups

Table 22.2
Chief nutritional sources of the water-soluble vitamins and clinical symptoms that result from their deficiency.

Vitamin	Source	Effects of Deficiency
B_3, nicotinic acid	liver, lean meats, cereals, and legumes	pellagra; dermatitis; nervous and digestive problems
B_2, riboflavin	most foods; milk and meat products are especially rich	cornea vascularization; lesions of the skin, especially on the face
C, ascorbic acid	plants, especially rapidly growing fruits and vegetables	scurvy; failure to form connective tissue
B_1, thiamine	fresh vegetables, husks of cereal grains, liver and other organ meats	beriberi; neuritis; heart failure; mental disturbances
B_6, pyridoxine	meats, cereal grains, lentils	nervous disorders; dermatitis; lesions on the face
pantothenic acid	most foods, especially liver, meat, cereals, milk, fresh vegetables	vomiting; abdominal distress; insomnia
folic acid	organ meats, fresh green vegetables	anemia
biotin	yeast, meats, dairy products, grains, fruits and vegetables; intestinal bacteria	scaly skin; muscle pains; weakness; depression
B_{12}, cobalamin	meat and milk products	pernicious anemia

Table 22.2 lists the chief nutritional sources of each water-soluble vitamin and the clinical symptoms that result from their deficiency.

22.3 Mechanism of Enzyme Catalysis

A. Formation of Enzyme-Substrate Complex

Enzymes function as catalysts in much the same way as common inorganic or organic laboratory catalysts. A catalyst, whatever the kind, combines with a reactant to "activate" it. In enzyme-catalyzed reactions, reactants are referred to as substrates (S). In the first and critical step in all enzyme catalysis, enzyme and substrate combine to form an activated complex called an **enzyme-substrate (ES) complex**. This complex then undergoes a chemical change to form an enzyme-product complex from which one product or more then dissociate and regenerate the enzyme.

$$E + S \rightleftharpoons ES$$
(enzyme-substrate
complex)

$$ES \longrightarrow EP$$
(enzyme-product
complex)

$$EP \longrightarrow E + P$$

Interactions between an enzyme and a substrate generally involve noncovalent forces such as ion-ion or ion-dipole interactions, hydrogen bonding, and dispersion forces. In some cases, however, actual covalent bonds are formed between the enzyme and substrate. Whatever the types of interaction between enzyme and substrate and between enzyme and product, they must be sufficiently weak that the enzyme-product complex can break apart to liberate product and regenerate the enzyme.

B. Active Site

Virtually all enzymes are globular proteins, and even the simplest have molecular weights ranging from 12,000 to 40,000, meaning that they consist of 100–400 amino acids. It has been proposed that, because enzymes are so large compared with molecules whose reactions they catalyze, substrate and enzyme interact over only a small region of the enzyme surface, called the **active site**. It is at this site that substrate is bound, the reaction catalyzed, and product or products released.

To date, numerous enzymes have been isolated in pure crystalline form and studied by X-ray crystallography. In all cases in which the three-dimensional structure of an enzyme has been determined and the interactions between it and its substrate studied, the active site has been found to be a portion of the enzyme surface with a unique arrangement of amino acid side chains. X-ray crystallography studies suggest that as few as 10 amino acids may be involved at the active site.

In 1890, Emil Fischer likened the binding of an enzyme and its substrate to the interaction of a lock and key. According to this lock-and-key model, shown schematically in Figure 22.2, enzyme (the lock) and substrate (the key) have complementary shapes and fit together. Recall from our discussion of the significance of chirality in the biological world (Section 18.7) that we accounted for the remarkable ability of enzymes to distinguish between enantiomers by proposing that an enzyme and its substrate must interact through at least three specific binding sites on the surface of the enzyme. Groups on the enzyme surface that participate in binding enzyme and substrate to form an enzyme-substrate complex are called binding groups. In Figure 22.2, these three binding sites are labeled *a*, *b*, and *c*. The complementary regions on the substrate are labeled *a'*, *b'*, and *c'*.

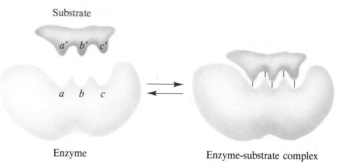

Substrate

Enzyme

Enzyme-substrate complex

Figure 22.2 Lock-and-key model of the interaction between enzyme and substrate.

Once a substrate molecule is recognized and bound to the active site of the enzyme, certain functional groups in the active site called catalytic groups participate directly in the making and breaking of chemical bonds. In this sense, the active site on an enzyme is a unique combination of binding groups and catalytic groups.

C. Catalytic Efficiency

Enzymes can effect enormous increases in the rates of chemical reactions. An example is peroxidase, an enzyme that catalyzes the decomposition of hydrogen peroxide to oxygen and water:

$$2H_2O_2 \xrightarrow{\text{peroxidase}} 2H_2O + O_2$$

hydrogen peroxide

Many biological oxidations use molecular oxygen as the oxidizing agent, and in some of these, oxygen is reduced to hydrogen peroxide, a substance that is very toxic and must be decomposed rapidly to prevent damage to cellular compo-

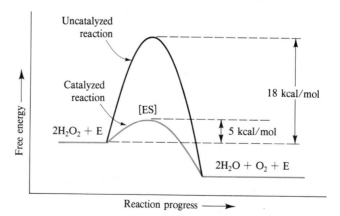

Figure 22.3 Energy changes for the uncatalyzed and peroxidase-catalyzed decomposition of hydrogen peroxide.

nents. As shown in Figure 22.3, the energy of activation for the uncatalyzed decomposition of hydrogen peroxide is 18 kcal/mol. Peroxidase provides an alternative pathway with an energy of activation of only 5.0 kcal/mol. Since the rate of a chemical reaction depends on the energy of activation, the lower the energy of activation for a reaction, the higher the rate. This seemingly small decrease in energy of activation (from 18 kcal/mol to 5 kcal/mol) corresponds to an increase in rate of reaction of almost 10^{10}!

A second example is carbonic anhydrase, an enzyme present in most tissues but in especially high concentration in erythrocytes; it catalyzes the reversible reaction between carbon dioxide and water to produce carbonic acid. The rate of hydration of carbon dioxide is normally very low but is increased almost 10^7 times by carbonic anhydrase:

$$CO_2 + H_2O \underset{\text{anhydrase}}{\overset{\text{carbonic}}{\rightleftharpoons}} H_2CO_3$$

carbon   carbonic
dioxide   acid

D. How Enzymes Increase Rates of Biochemical Reactions

It is helpful, in thinking about rates of chemical reactions, to think about the following factors. To react, molecules must:

1. Collide.
2. Collide so the groups participating in the reaction are properly oriented to each other.
3. Collide with enough energy to allow bond breaking and bond making.

There are four main effects by which enzymes increase the rates of chemical reactions, all of which are related to the preceding requirements. Even though all four effects are involved in virtually every enzyme-catalyzed reaction, the balance between them may be entirely different in one reaction over another. Therefore, the order in which they are described should not be taken as a ranking of their importance.

1. Proximity

We can best appreciate the effects of proximity by referring to an example, namely the oxidation of lactate by NAD^+ catalyzed by lactate dehydrogenase (LDH). In this oxidation, the two different substrates must be brought close enough together to react. Because of the relatively low concentrations of each in a cell or other biological medium, the chance of their coming together in solution and reacting is very small. However, since LDH can bind both lactate and NAD^+, the chance that these two molecules are close enough to react (in effect, collide) becomes very high. Thus, an enzyme "collects" substrates from solution, thereby increasing the effective concentration of one relative to the other and in this way making reactions more likely.

2. Orientation

Not only do substrates have to come together (collide) to react, but they must do so with the proper orientation. For complex molecules in solution, the chances of a collision in which the reactive portions of each substrate are properly aligned may be very slight. With enzymes, however, substrates are oriented with great precision at the active site and therefore properly positioned for reaction.

3. Strain and Induced Fit

The lock-and-key model for enzyme catalysis that Emil Fischer proposed in 1890 is an overly simplified and undoubtedly inaccurate model for the interaction between enzyme and substrate. Much experimental evidence, including X-ray crystallographic pictures of actual enzyme-substrate complexes, suggests that when enzyme and substrate react to form an enzyme-substrate complex, the conformation of both enzyme and substrate change. The change in conformation of the enzyme in response to binding of substrate is called induced fit (see Figure 22.4). As the conformation of the enzyme changes in response to binding substrate, strain (most commonly distortion of bond angles and bond lengths) is induced in the substrate, thus reducing the energy required to convert substrate to product. In other words, inducing strain in the substrate makes it less stable and thereby reduces the energy of activation required for conversion of substrate to product.

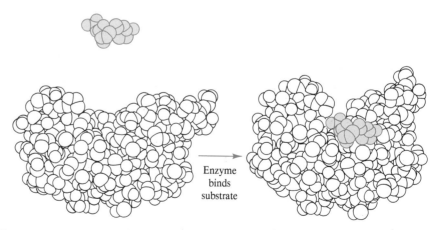

Figure 22.4 As an enzyme and substrate interact, the conformation of the enzyme changes to bind the substrate tightly.

4. Catalytic Functional Groups at the Active Site

Many of the laboratory organic reactions we studied earlier were catalyzed by either acid (H^+) or base (OH^-). In most biological media, the concentration of these ions is very low. One big exception, of course, is gastric secretions, in which the concentration of hydrogen ion may be as high as 0.1M (pH = 1.0). Enzymes at their active sites contain functional groups such as the $—CO_2H$ side chains of aspartate and glutamate, which can function very effectively as hydrogen ion donors. Similarly, they contain functional groups such as the $—NH_2$ of lysine and the $—CO_2^-$ groups of aspartate and glutamate, which can function very effectively as hydrogen ion acceptors. Thus, although the concentration of acid or base may not be high in solution, the effective concentration of proton acceptors or proton donors at the active site of an enzyme may be very high.

In summary, enzymes are remarkably effective catalysts because they can bring molecules together so that reactive groups are properly positioned to interact, and so that functional groups at the active site can provide both proton donors and proton acceptors, also properly positioned to bring about reaction.

22.4 Factors That Affect Rate of Enzyme-Catalyzed Reactions

The rate of an enzyme-catalyzed reaction depends on many factors, the most important of which are concentration of the enzyme, concentration of the substrate, pH, temperature, and presence of enzyme inhibitors. Let us look at each of these factors in detail.

A. Concentration of Enzyme

In an enzyme-catalyzed reaction, concentration of the enzyme is very low compared with concentration of the substrate; under these conditions, rate of reaction is directly proportional to concentration of enzyme. For example, if concentration of the enzyme is doubled, the rate of conversion of substrate to product is also doubled. The effect of enzyme concentration on rate of reaction is shown in Figure 22.5.

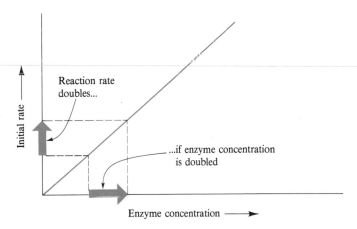

Figure 22.5 The effect of enzyme concentration on the rate of conversion of substrate to product.

B. Concentration of Substrate

To understand the effect of substrate concentration on the rate of an enzyme-catalyzed reaction, let us consider a series of experiments, each using the same concentration of enzyme but a different initial concentration of substrate.

Suppose we mix a given concentration of enzyme and substrate and then measure the initial rate of the reaction. In a second experiment, we mix the same concentration of enzyme but this time increase the concentration of substrate and again measure the initial reaction rate. This process is repeated, each time with the same enzyme concentration but a different substrate concentration. Figure 22.6 shows the relation between initial reaction rate and concentration of substrate. In region (a), an increase in initial substrate concentration causes a 1:1 increase in reaction rate; doubling the concentration of substrate doubles the reaction rate. Beyond region (a), an increase in initial substrate concentration also increases the reaction rate, but the effect becomes progressively smaller. Finally, in region (b), an increase in initial substrate concentration has no effect whatsoever on the reaction rate.

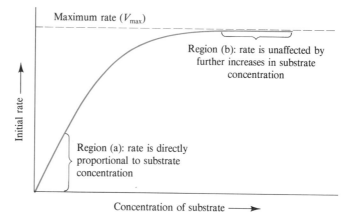

Figure 22.6 Dependence of initial rate of an enzyme-catalyzed reaction on concentration of the substrate.

C. Michaelis-Menton Equation

The shape of the curve shown in Figure 22.6 for the dependence of reaction rate on substrate concentration is one long familiar to mathematicians, namely, a hyperbola. The first to recognize this relation for enzyme-catalyzed reactions and put it in mathematical form were Lenore Michaelis and Maude Menton. In 1913, they proposed the following equation (that of a hyperbola) for enzyme kinetics. Although others have since refined and extended their work, the equation remains known as the **Michaelis-Menton equation**.

The Michaelis-Menton Equation

$$\text{Rate} = \frac{V_{max} \times [S]}{[S] + K_m}$$

The two constants in the equation are determined experimentally (Figure 22.7). The rate V_{max} is the maximum possible for a given enzyme concentration. The value K_m is the substrate concentration when the rate of the enzyme-catalyzed reaction is one-half the maximum rate.

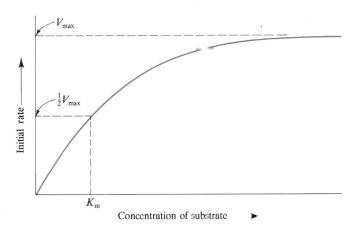

Figure 22.7 The value K_m is the concentration of substrate required to give an initial reaction rate of $\frac{1}{2}V_{max}$.

1. Significance of V_{max}

At V_{max}, all enzyme molecules have formed enzyme-substrate complexes and are operating continuously, catalyzing the conversion of substrate to product. We say that at this point the enzyme is saturated. Thus, values of V_{max} can be used to compare the maximum activity of one enzyme with that of another enzyme that might catalyze the same reaction.

2. Significance of K_m

The substrate concentration K_m required to convert one-half of all enzyme molecules to enzyme-substrate complexes is a measure of the affinity of enzyme for substrate. A small value for K_m means that a relatively low concentration of substrate is needed to saturate the enzyme; the enzyme has a high affinity for its substrate. On the contrary, a large value for K_m means that a relatively high concentration of substrate is needed to saturate the enzyme; the enzyme has a low affinity for its substrate.

Example 22.1

Following are data for five experiments, each using the same concentration of enzyme but a different initial concentration of substrate. Also given is the initial reaction rate for each substrate concentration. In these reactions, rate is measured as milligrams of substrate per milliliter of solution reacting per minute.

Initial Substrate Concentration (mol/L)	Initial Reaction Rate (mg/mL/min)
15.0×10^{-5}	0.38
10.0×10^{-5}	0.33
5.0×10^{-5}	0.25
3.3×10^{-5}	0.20
2.5×10^{-5}	0.166

a. Prepare a graph of initial rate versus substrate concentration and estimate V_{max}, $\frac{1}{2}V_{max}$, and K_m.

b. For this enzyme-catalyzed reaction, the initial rate is 0.166 mg/mL/min when the substrate concentration is 2.5×10^{-5}M. What will be the initial rate at this substrate concentration if the enzyme concentration is doubled?

☐ *Solution*

a. In the accompanying graph, substrate concentration is plotted on the horizontal axis and initial reaction rate on the vertical axis. From this graph, estimate that V_{max} is approximately 0.41 mg of substrate reacting per milliliter of solution per minute. With this value, $\frac{1}{2}V_{max}$ is approximately 0.22 mg/mL/min and K_m is approximately 3.5×10^{-5}M. For this enzyme, a substrate concentration of 3.5×10^{-5} mol/L is required to convert half of all enzyme molecules to enzyme-substrate complexes.

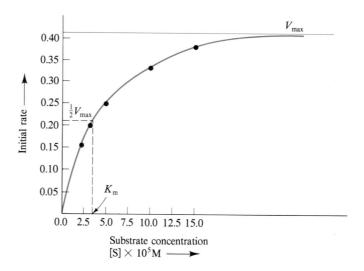

b. The rate of an enzyme-catalyzed reaction is directly proportional to the enzyme concentration. If the enzyme concentration is doubled, the initial rate doubles and the new initial rate becomes 0.332 mg/mL/min.

Problem 22.1

The initial rates of an enzyme-catalyzed reaction at five different substrate concentrations follow. Rate is given in units of micromoles of substrate reacting per minute.

Initial Substrate Concentration (mol/L)	Initial Reaction Rate (μmol/min)
2.0×10^{-3}	14
3.0×10^{-3}	18
4.0×10^{-3}	22
10.0×10^{-3}	31
12.0×10^{-3}	33

a. Prepare a graph of initial rate versus initial substrate concentration, and estimate V_{max}, $\frac{1}{2}V_{max}$, and K_m.
b. From your graph, estimate what the initial rate is when the substrate concentration is 6×10^{-3}M.
c. If the enzyme concentration is doubled, what will the new initial rate be when $[S] = 6 \times 10^{-3}$M?

D. pH

The catalytic activity of all enzymes is affected by the pH of the solution in which the reaction occurs. Often, small changes in pH cause large changes in the ability of a given enzyme to function as a biocatalyst. Shown in Figure 22.8 is a typical plot of enzyme activity versus pH. Notice that enzyme activity is a maximum in a narrow pH range and decreases at both higher and lower pHs.

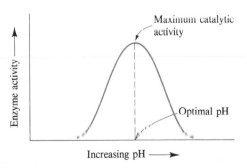

Figure 22.8 The dependence of enzyme activity on pH.

The pH corresponding to maximum enzyme activity is called the optimal pH. Most enzymes have maximum catalytic activity around pH 7, the pH of most biological fluids. Many enzymes, however, have maximum activity at considerably higher or lower pHs. For example, pepsin, a digestive enzyme of the stomach, has maximum activity around pH 1.5, the pH of gastric fluids. Table 22.3 lists optimal pH values for several enzymes.

Variations in enzyme activity with changes in pH depend on several factors, some or all of which may exist at the same time. First, changes in pH may cause partial denaturation of the enzyme protein. Second, catalytic activity may

Table 22.3
Optimal pH
values for several
enzymes.

Enzyme	Optimal pH
pepsin	1.5
acid phosphatase	4.7
α-glucosidase	5.4
urease	6.7
α-amylase (pancreatic)	7.0
carboxypeptidase	7.5
succinate dehydrogenase	7.6
trypsin	7.8
alkaline phosphatase	9.5
arginase	9.7

be possible only when certain amino acid side chains at the active site are in the correct states of ionization. Suppose, for example that for catalysis by a particular enzyme, the side chains of both lysine and a glutamic acid at the active site must be ionized (lys-NH_3^+ and glu-CO_2^-), as shown in Figure 22.9(b). This combination of ionization states is possible only in a particular pH range. At lower pH values (more acidic), catalytic activity decreases because the carboxyl of glutamate is protonated to $-CO_2H$ [Figure 22.9(a)]. At higher pH values (more basic), catalytic activity decreases because the side chain of lysine is deprotonated to $-NH_2$ [Figure 22.9(c)]. The effect of pH on catalytic activity may be much more complex than what is shown in Figure 22.9, particularly if the states of ionization of several amino acid side chains and of the substrate itself are important.

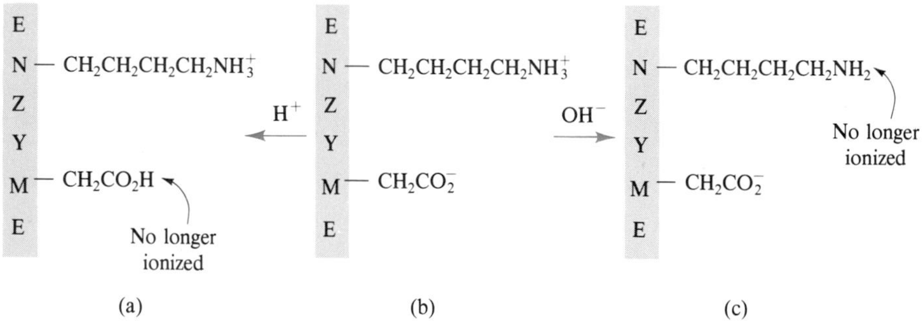

Figure 22.9 Dependence of catalytic activity on the ionization of amino acid side chains. (a) Below the optimal pH there is decreased or no catalytic activity. (b) At the optimal pH there is maximum catalytic activity. (c) Above the optimal pH there is decreased or no catalytic activity.

Example 22.2

Assume that one of the interactions binding a particular substrate to an enzyme is hydrogen bonding between a carbonyl group of the substrate and the $-OH$ group of tyrosine.

$$\text{(enzyme)} - \underset{}{\bigcirc} - \text{O} - \overset{\delta+}{\text{H}} ----- \overset{\delta-}{\text{O}} = \text{C} \overset{\text{CH}_2 \cdots}{\underset{\text{CH}_2 \cdots}{}} \text{(substrate)}$$

What is the reason that the rate of this enzyme-catalyzed reaction is greatest below pH 8.1 but decreases at pHs greater (more basic) than 8.1? (The pK_a of the side chain of tyrosine is 10.1.)

Solution

For binding to occur between a carbonyl group of the substrate and the —OH group of tyrosine, it is essential to have the side chain of tyrosine in the un-ionized form. At pH 8.1 (two pH units more acidic than the pK_a of this group), the side chain is completely in the acid (—OH) form, and the rate is a maximum. As pH increases, the side chain becomes partially ionized, and at pH 10.1, the side chain is 50% ionized. The ionized form cannot participate in hydrogen bonding to bind substrate, and therefore the rate of reaction decreases.

Problem 22.2

For a particular enzyme-catalyzed reaction involving the side chain of histidine, the optimal pH is 4.0. Activity of the enzyme decreases above pH 4.0. Does the active form of this enzyme require the side chain of histidine to be in the acid form or in the conjugate base form? Explain.

E. Temperature

A fourth factor affecting the rate of an enzyme-catalyzed reaction is temperature. Just as there is an optimal pH for an enzyme-catalyzed reaction, so too is there an optimal temperature. Most enzymes have optimal temperatures in the range 25–37°C. Figure 22.10 shows a typical plot of enzyme activity as a function of temperature. Enzyme activity first increases with temperature because of an increase in the number of collisions between enzyme and substrate and an increase in the energy of these collisions. At higher temperatures, enzyme activity

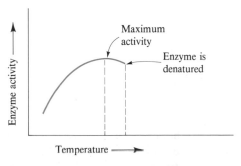

Figure 22.10 Dependence of enzyme activity on temperature.

decreases rapidly due to heat denaturation of the enzyme protein. The activity of most enzymes can be destroyed by heat treatment. There are, of course, exceptions, among which are the enzymes of bacteria living in hot springs at temperatures of 60–80°C.

F. Competitive Inhibition of Enzyme Activity

An **inhibitor** is any compound that can decrease the rate of an enzyme-catalyzed reaction. In fact, it is remarkably easy to inhibit enzymes. Certainly the denaturing agents like urea, guanidine hydrochloride, or detergents decrease the activity of enzymes because they bring about massive changes in the three-dimensional structure of the enzyme protein itself (Section 21.6E). Most often, these changes are irreversible and inhibition is irreversible. Some compounds, however, inhibit enzyme activity in such a way that the inhibition can be reversed, either by removing the offending compound or increasing the concentration of the substrate of the enzyme.

Understanding reversible enzyme inhibition is important for those in the health sciences. Many medicines act at the molecular level by inhibiting one or more enzymes, thereby decreasing the rates of the reactions these enzymes catalyze. For discussion of one particularly well understood example of how a drug works at the molecular level to inhibit a particular enzyme-catalyzed reaction, see Mini-Essay XVI, "The Penicillins." The penicillins and also many other classes of drugs are administered to patients to decrease the flow of molecules through a particular metabolic pathway.

From a study of the effects of inhibitors on the rates of enzyme-catalyzed reactions and on both V_{max} and K_m, several types of reversible inhibition have been distinguished. **Competitive inhibition** is the most common type.

A competitive inhibitor binds to the active site of an enzyme and thus "competes" with substrate for the active site. Most often, competitive inhibitors are very closely related in structure to the enzyme substrate. Consider, as an example, the enzyme fumarase, which catalyzes the hydration of fumarate to malate:

fumarate   L-malate

Shown in Figure 22.11 are structural formulas for several competitive inhibitors of fumarase. Note the structural similarities between these inhibitors and fumarate.

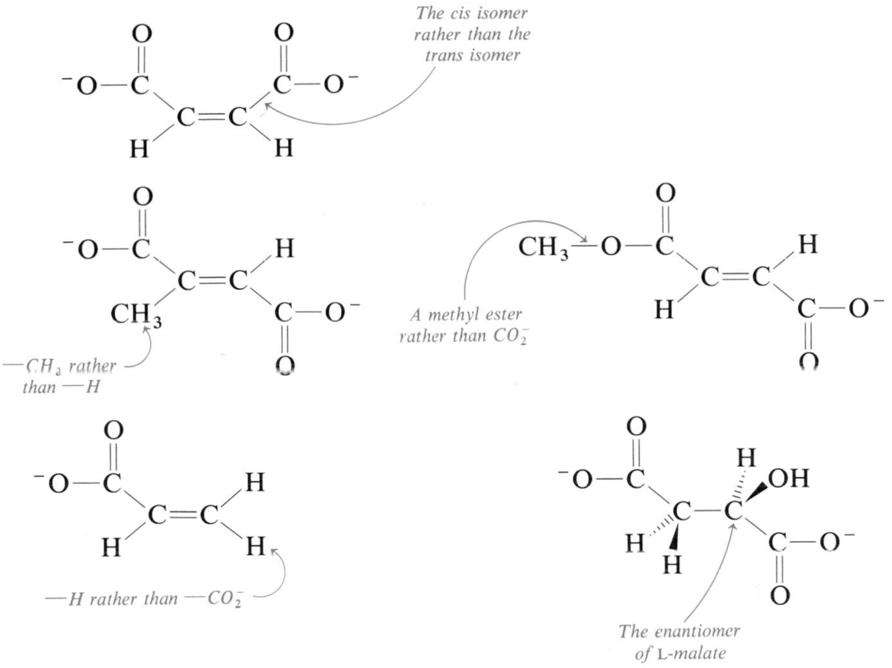

Figure 22.11 Several competitive inhibitors of the enzyme fumarase.

The nature of competitive inhibition is shown schematically in Figure 22.12. Part (a) of this figure shows an enzyme in the presence of both inhibitor and substrate. The two compete for the active site, and the inhibitor is shown forming an enzyme-inhibitor complex that blocks the active site for further catalytic activity.

A characteristic feature of competitive inhibition is that it can be reversed by increasing the concentration of substrate. We can account for this by looking at the two equilibria involved in a solution containing enzyme, substrate, and inhibitor. The first [Figure 22.12(a)] is between enzyme plus inhibitor, to form an enzyme-inhibitor complex. The second [Figure 22.12(b)] is between enzyme plus substrate, to form an enzyme-substrate complex. If we increase the concentration of substrate, then according to Le Chatelier's principle (Section 8.5), we also increase the concentration of enzyme-substrate complex at the expense of enzyme-inhibitor complex. The reversal of competitive inhibition is shown schematically in Figure 22.12(b).

Competitive inhibition can be detected by studying the rate of an enzyme-catalyzed reaction in the presence and in the absence of a competitive inhibitor. As shown in Figure 22.13, V_{max} is unchanged in the presence of a competitive inhibitor. However, K_m is increased, because a greater concentration of substrate is required to achieve one-half enzyme saturation in the presence of the inhibitor.

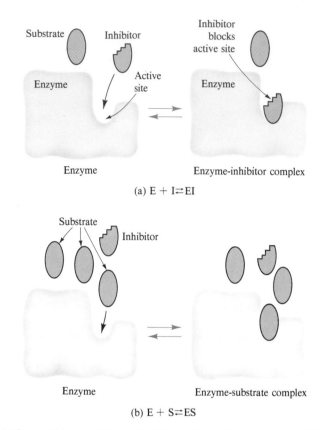

(a) E + I ⇌ EI

(b) E + S ⇌ ES

Figure 22.12 Competitive inhibition. (a) Formation of an enzyme-inhibitor complex. (b) When substrate is increased, the concentration of ES is increased and the concentration of EI is decreased, thus reversing the effect of the inhibitor.

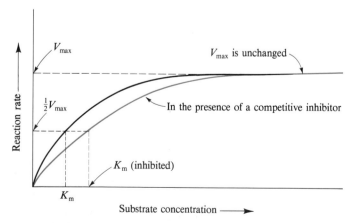

Figure 22.13 An example of competitive inhibition. When a competitive inhibitor is present, V_{max} is unchanged but K_m is increased.

22.5 Regulation of Enzyme Activity

Enzymes bring about enormous increases in the rates of chemical reactions, thus making possible life as we know it. But this is only part of the story of their importance for living systems. Not only can they increase rates of chemical reactions, but their activity can be regulated. As a consequence, rates of individual reactions can be controlled and integrated into separate metabolic pathways, which in turn are integrated into an overall metabolic system for the entire organism.

Regulation of enzyme activity is accomplished by two biological mechanisms. In the first, **allosteric regulation** (feedback control), the activity of key enzymes is altered by interaction of the enzyme with molecules produced within the cell itself. The result of this interaction may be either inhibition of activity or stimulation of activity. In the second biological mechanism, **genetic control**, the concentration of key enzymes is regulated by the rate of enzyme (protein) synthesis.

A. Allosteric Regulation—Feedback Control

The molecules responsible for regulating cellular metabolism are a special group of enzymes called **allosteric enzymes** (Greek, *allos*; other, plus *steros*, space). Regulation of metabolism through control of the activity of allosteric enzymes is immensely beneficial to an organism because through this control, the concentration of metabolites can be maintained within very narrow limits. Thus cells prevent unnecessary accumulation not only of the final product of a metabolic sequence but also of intermediates along the pathway. The evolution of **regulatory enzymes** was an essential step in achieving efficient use of cellular resources and in the evolution from single cells to multicellular organisms.

Following are the characteristics of an allosteric enzyme.

1. All allosteric enzymes have quaternary structure; that is, they are composed of two or more polypeptide chains.
2. All allosteric enzymes have two or more binding sites: an active site specific for substrate, and a regulatory site specific for a regulator molecule.
3. The regulatory site is distinct from the active site both in location on the enzyme and in shape. Because it is different from the active site, a regulatory site can bind molecules quite different in size and shape from the natural substrate for the enzyme.
4. Binding of a molecule at the regulatory site brings about a change in the three-dimensional shape of the enzyme protein, and in particular, of the active site. Molecules that increase enzyme activity are called allosteric activators; those that bring about a decrease in enzyme activity are called allosteric inhibitors.

To better understand the significance of an allosteric enzyme, suppose a cell needs a constant supply of molecule E, which is synthesized in a series of enzyme-catalyzed steps starting with molecule A. The simplest way for the concentration of E to be regulated within the cell is for E to be synthesized in a process that its own concentration regulates as shown here.

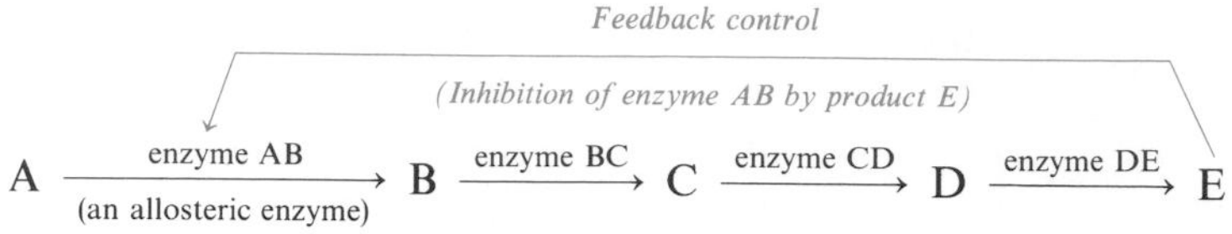

Feedback control

(Inhibition of enzyme AB by product E)

$$A \xrightarrow[\text{(an allosteric enzyme)}]{\text{enzyme AB}} B \xrightarrow{\text{enzyme BC}} C \xrightarrow{\text{enzyme CD}} D \xrightarrow{\text{enzyme DE}} E$$

If the concentration of E rises above that needed by the cell, it inhibits enzyme AB, the first enzyme in the sequence of steps that leads to the formation of E. On the other hand, if the concentration of E falls below that needed by the cell, inhibition of enzyme AB is decreased, thereby allowing increase in the rate of synthesis of E.

The first example of regulation of enzyme activity by **feedback control** was discovered in 1957 and involves the synthesis of isoleucine in the bacterium *E. coli*. This synthesis begins with threonine, and in a series of five sequential steps, each catalyzed by a different enzyme (E1, E2, . . . , E5), gives isoleucine. The concentration of isoleucine within the cell is regulated by the activity of isoleucine as an inhibitor of threonine deaminase, the first enzyme in this multistep synthesis.

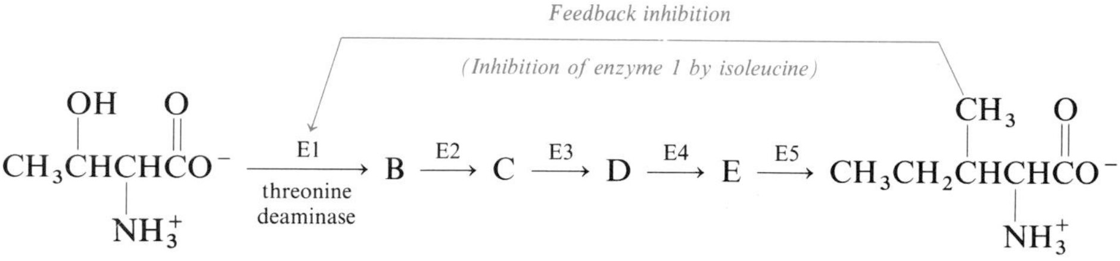

Feedback inhibition

(Inhibition of enzyme 1 by isoleucine)

threonine

isoleucine

Because many of the examples in which allosteric regulation has been studied involve inhibition of a first, or at least an early, step in a metabolic pathway, allosteric regulation has become associated with inhibition. This is not the total picture, however. There are many examples in which allosteric regulation brings about activation of a metabolic pathway.

Allosteric modification of enzyme activity is significant because regulatory and catalytic sites have evolved separately. One important consequence is that allosteric regulators of a particular metabolic pathway may be products of entirely different pathways within the cell or even compounds produced outside the cell (like hormones). This special feature of allosteric regulation has permitted development of remarkably sensitive mechanisms for controlling metabolism within cells and within the organism as a whole.

B. Genetic Control

Genetic control of enzyme activity involves regulation of the rate of protein biosynthesis by induction and repression. The first demonstrated example of **enzyme induction** grew out of studies in the 1950s on the metabolism of the bacterium *E. coli*. Beta-galactosidase, an enzyme required for the utilization of lactose, catalyzes hydrolysis of lactose to D-galactose and D-glucose.

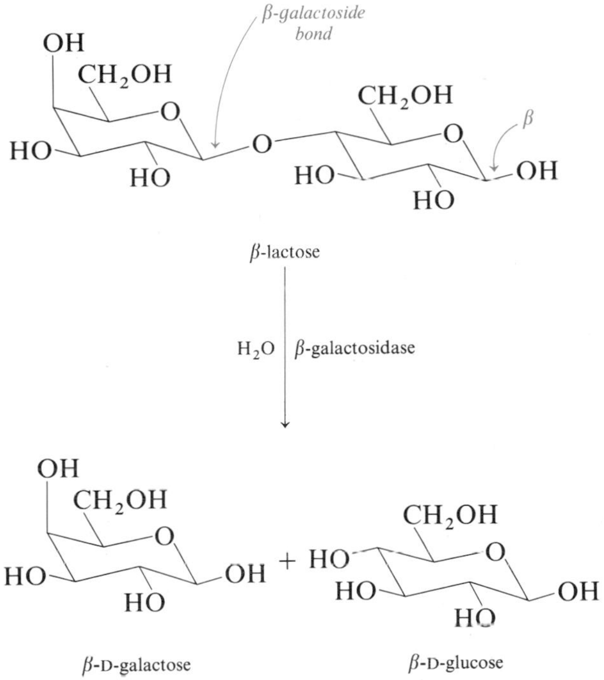

β-lactose

H₂O | β-galactosidase

β-D-galactose   β-D-glucose

When lactose is absent from the growth medium, no β-galactosidase is present in *E. coli*. If, however, lactose is added to the medium, within minutes the bacterium begins to produce this enzyme (Figure 22.14); lactose induces the synthesis of β-galactosidase. If lactose is then removed from the growth medium, production of β-galactosidase stops. Genetic control of enzyme activity is biologically significant because it allows an organism to adapt quickly to changes in its environment.

22.6 Enzymes and the Health Sciences

Our study of the structure and properties of enzymes so far has been descriptive, and in the case of enzyme kinetics, mathematical. This background has an important relation to the health sciences. The fact is, enzymology is an essential part of the everyday life of clinicians.

A. Enzymes in the Diagnosis of Diseases

Enzymes can be used as diagnostic tools because certain enzymes, such as those involved in blood coagulation, are normal constituents of plasma; their concentration in plasma is high compared with their concentration in cells. Other enzymes are normally present almost exclusively in cells and are released into the blood and other biological fluids only as a result of routine destruction of

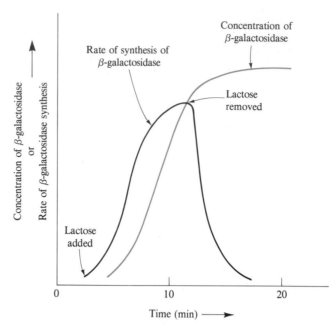

Figure 22.14 Beta-galactosidase, an inducible enzyme. Synthesis of β-galactosidase begins within minutes after lactose is added to the growth medium and ceases shortly after lactose is removed from the growth medium.

cells. Plasma levels of these enzymes are a million times or more lower than their cell levels. However, plasma concentrations of cellular enzymes may be elevated significantly in cases of cell injury and destruction (a damaged heart or skeletal muscle), or uncontrolled growth (as in cancer). Changes in plasma concentrations of appropriately chosen enzymes can be examined and used to detect cell damage; thus the site of damage or uncontrolled cell proliferation is suggested. Further, the degree of elevation of plasma concentration can often be used to determine the extent of cellular damage. Measurement of enzyme concentrations in blood plasma and other biological fluids has become a critical diagnostic tool, particularly for diseases of the heart, liver, pancreas, skeletal muscle, and bone, and for malignant diseases. In fact, certain enzyme deter-

Table 22.4
Some enzymes used in diagnostic enzymology.

Enzyme	Principal Clinical Condition in Which Enzyme Determination Is Used
lactate dehydrogenase (LDH)	heart or skeletal muscle damage
alkaline phosphatase	liver and bone disease
acid phosphatase	cancer of the prostate
serum glutamate oxaloacetate transaminase (SGOT)	heart and liver disease
creatine phosphokinase (CK)	myocardial infarction and muscle diseases
α-amylase	pancreatitis

minations are performed so often that they have become routine in the clinical chemistry laboratory. Several of these enzymes are listed in Table 22.4. For discussion of the use of assays for lactate dehydrogenase (LDH) and creatine phosphokinase (CK) as an invaluable tool for the diagnosis of myocardial infarction, see Mini-Essay XV.

B. Enzymes as Laboratory Reagents

Many diseases are characterized by changes in the concentrations of specific compounds. The problem for the clinical chemistry laboratory is measuring the concentrations of these compounds in the presence of thousands of other compounds that might react similarly and therefore give either false positive or false negative results. Enzymes, because of their specificity, are ideal reagents for this type of determination. For example, the concentration of glucose in blood is normally 60–110 mg/100 mL. It is important for the diagnosis and effective treatment of patients with diabetes mellitus and other forms of hyperglycemia (abnormally high levels of blood glucose) to be able to determine blood glucose levels rapidly and accurately. It is likewise important to be able to determine blood glucose levels rapidly and accurately for those with hypoglycemia (abnormally low levels of blood glucose). The most common reagent in today's clinical chemistry laboratory for measuring glucose in blood and other biological fluids is the enzyme glucose oxidase. This enzyme is entirely specific for glucose and catalyzes the oxidation of glucose to gluconic acid and hydrogen peroxide:

$$\text{Glucose} + \text{O}_2 \xrightarrow{\text{glucose oxidase}} \text{gluconic acid} + \text{H}_2\text{O}_2$$

(For a more detailed discussion of the use of glucose oxidase as a reagent for the determination of glucose, see Mini-Essay XIII, "Clinical Chemistry—The Search for Specificity.")

C. Enzymes as Sites for the Action of Drugs

The pharmaceutical industry tries to produce drugs, either from natural sources or laboratory synthesis, that will counteract diseases (specific metabolic disorders). Because scientists have only an imperfect understanding of the underlying metabolic disorders responsible for most diseases, design of drugs is on a less rational basis than what would be desirable. In fact, many of today's most widely used drugs have been discovered quite by accident. Through research, scientists have been able to learn a great deal about their mechanisms of action at the molecular level. The sulfa drugs furnish a good example.

Sulfonic acids form amides in which the —OH is replaced by —NH$_2$. Following are structural formulas for benzenesulfonic acid and its amide, benzenesulfonamide. Also shown is the structural formula of p-aminobenzenesulfonamide, more familiar as sulfanilamide.

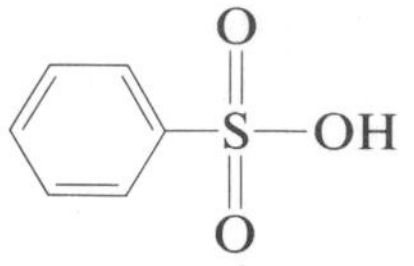

benzenesulfonic
acid
benzenesulfonamide 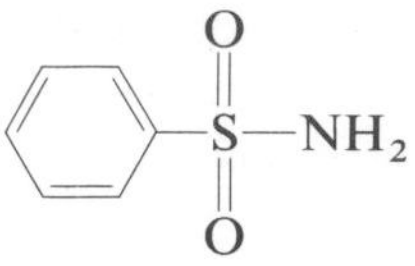
p-aminobenzenesulfonamide 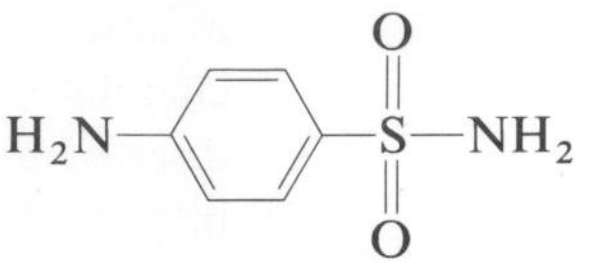
(sulfanilamide)

The discovery of the medical uses of sulfanilamide and its derivatives was a milestone in the history of chemotherapy because it represents one of the first rational investigations of synthetic organic molecules as potential drugs to fight infection. Sulfanilamide was first prepared in 1908 in Germany, but not until 1932 was its possible therapeutic value realized. In that year, the dye Prontosil was prepared. During research over the next two years, the German scientist G. Domagk observed Prontosil's remarkable effectiveness in curing streptococcal and staphylococcal infections in mice and other experimental animals. Domagk further discovered that Prontosil is rapidly reduced in cells to sulfanilamide and that sulfanilamide, not Prontosil, is the actual antibiotic. His discoveries were honored in 1939 by a Nobel Prize in medicine.

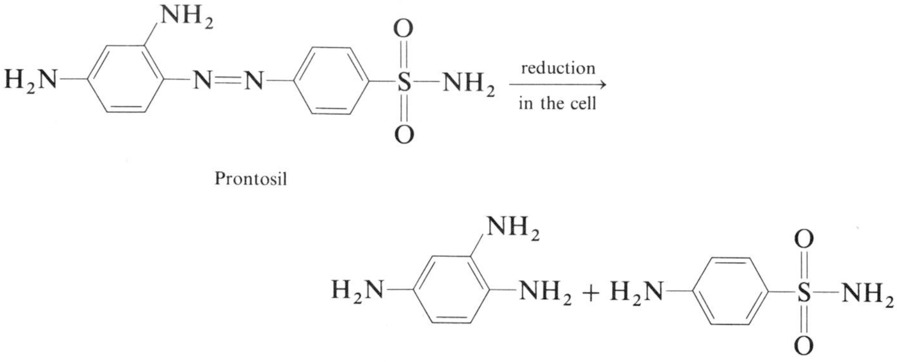

Prontosil

sulfanilamide

The key to understanding the action of sulfanilamide came in 1940 with the observation that inhibition of bacterial growth by sulfanilamide can be reversed by adding large amounts of p-aminobenzoic acid (PABA) to the growth medium. From this experiment, it was recognized that p-aminobenzoic acid is a growth factor for certain bacteria, and that in some way not then understood, sulfanilamide interferes with the bacteria's ability to use PABA. As you can see in the following structural formulas, obvious similarities in structure exist between p-aminobenzoic acid and sulfanilamide:

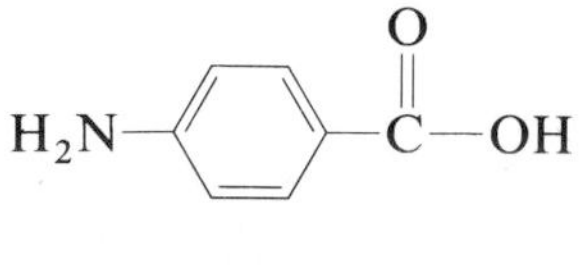

p-aminobenzoic acid
(PABA)
sulfanilamide

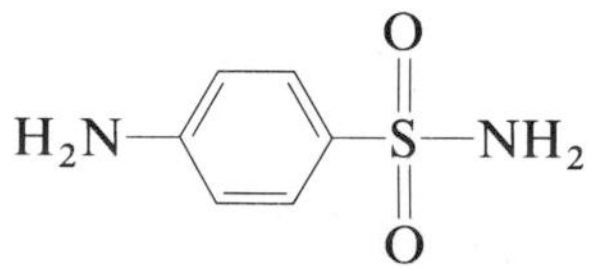

In the search for even better sulfa drugs, literally thousands of derivatives of sulfanilamide have been synthesized in the laboratory. Two of the most effective sulfa drugs are sulfathiazole and sulfadiazine:

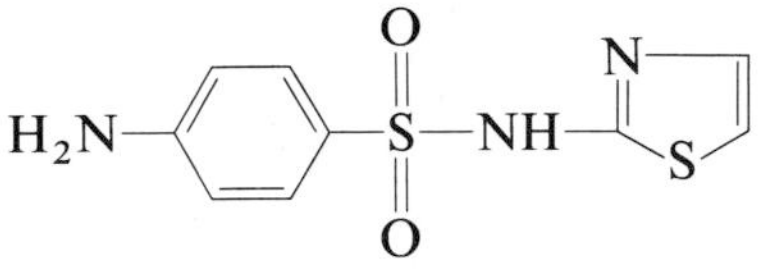

sulfathiazole 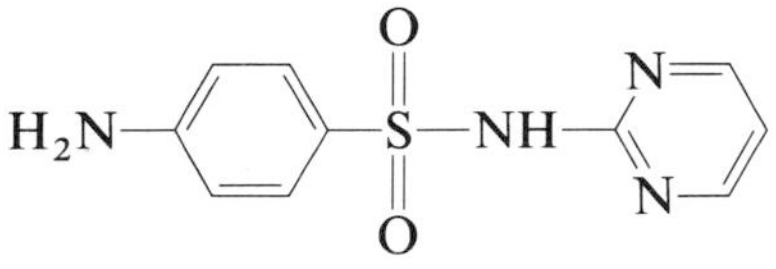   sulfadiazine

It now appears that sulfa drugs inhibit one or more of the enzyme-catalyzed steps in the synthesis of folic acid from *p*-aminobenzoic acid. Sulfanilamide can combat bacterial infections in humans without harming the patient because although humans also require folic acid, they do not make it from *p*-aminobenzoic acid. For humans, folic acid is a vitamin (Section 22.2C) and must be supplied in the diet.

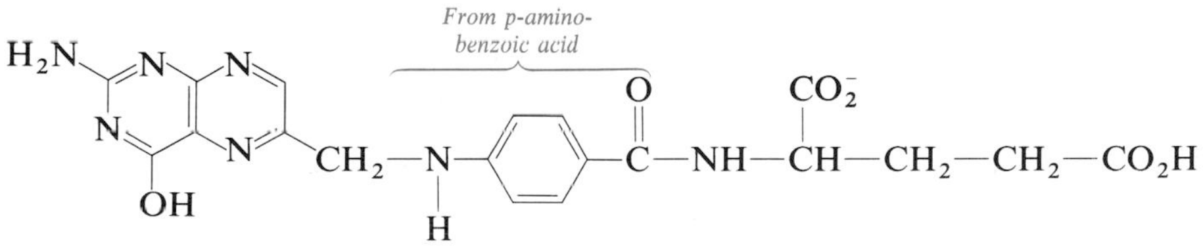

folic acid

Sulfa drugs, the first of the new "wonder drugs," were found to be effective in treating tuberculosis, pneumonia, and diphtheria, and they helped usher in a new era in public health in the United States in the 1930s. During World War II, they were routinely sprinkled on wounds to prevent infection. As a historical footnote, sulfa drugs were very soon eclipsed by an even newer class of wonder drugs for fighting bacterial infection, namely, the penicillins. (See Mini-Essay XVI, "The Penicillins.")

Key Terms and Concepts

active site (22.3B)
allosteric enzyme (22.5A)
allosteric regulation (22.5A)
clinical enzymology (22.6)
coenzyme (22.2C)
cofactor (22.2)
competitive inhibition (22.4F)
enzyme (introduction)
enzyme induction (22.5B)
enzyme-substrate complex (22.3A)

feedback control (22.5A)
genetic control (22.5B)
inhibitor (22.4F)
Enzyme Commission (22.1)
K_m (22.4C2)
metal ion cofactor (22.2A)
Michaelis-Menton equation (22.4C)
prosthetic group (22.2)
regulatory enzyme (22.5A)
V_{max} (22.4C1)

Problems

22.3   Name three groups of enzyme cofactors.

22.4   What is the name given to cofactors that are permanently bound to an enzyme?

22.5   What is the relation between coenzymes and water-soluble vitamins?

22.6   Of the water-soluble vitamins, (a) which are coenzymes themselves? (b) which precursors from which coenzymes are synthesized in the body?

22.7   Is the following statement true or false? "Enzymes increase the rate at which a reaction reaches equilibrium but do not change the position of equilibrium for the reactions they catalyze." Explain.

22.8   For an uncatalyzed reaction and an enzyme-catalyzed reaction, compare (a) rate of formation of products; (b) the position of equilibrium (equilibrium constant) for the reaction.

22.9   List three characteristics of enzymes that make them superior catalysts compared with their nonbiological laboratory counterparts.

22.10 Binding of substrate to the surface of an enzyme can involve a combination of ionic interactions, hydrogen bonding, and dispersion forces. By what type of interaction or interactions might the side chains of the following amino acids bind a lecithin to form an enzyme-substrate complex?

   a. phenylalanine   **b.** serine   **c.** glutamic acid
   d. lysine   **e.** valine

22.11 Of the 20 protein-derived amino acids, the side chains of the following are most often involved as catalytic groups at the active site of an enzyme. What is the net charge on the side chain of each amino acid at pH 7.4?

   a. cys   **b.** his   **c.** ser   **d.** asp   **e.** glu   **f.** lys

22.12 The following precautions are commonly observed when storing and handling solutions of enzymes. Explain the importance of each.

   a. Enzyme solutions are stored at a low temperature, usually at 0°C or below.
   b. The pH of most enzyme solutions is kept near 7.0.
   c. Enzyme solutions are prepared by dissolving the enzyme in water distilled from all-glass apparatus; ordinary tap water is never used.
   d. When an enzyme is being dissolved in aqueous solution, it is dissolved with as little stirring as possible. Vigorous stirring or shaking is never used to hasten the dissolving.

22.13 Refer to Figure 22.6 and explain why in region (a), an increase in substrate concentration has a direct increase on reaction velocity. Also explain why in region (b), an increase in substrate concentration does not affect the reaction velocity.

22.14 What does it mean to say that an enzyme is saturated?

22.15 The value V_{max} for an enzyme-catalyzed reaction is 3 mg/mL/min. At what rate is product formed when only one-third of the enzyme molecules have substrate bound to them?

22.16 Following are the initial velocities of an enzyme-catalyzed reaction at six different substrate concentrations. Velocity is given in units of milligrams of product formed per milliliter of solution per minute.

[S] (mol/L)	Velocity (mg/mL/min)
0.5×10^{-3}	1.5×10^{-3}
1.0×10^{-3}	3.0×10^{-3}
1.5×10^{-3}	4.4×10^{-3}
2.0×10^{-3}	5.0×10^{-3}
3.0×10^{-3}	5.8×10^{-3}
4.0×10^{-3}	6.2×10^{-3}

  a. Prepare a graph of initial velocity versus substrate concentration, and from your graph, estimate V_{max}, $\frac{1}{2}V_{max}$, and K_m.
  b. At what substrate concentration will the initial velocity be 2.5×10^{-3} mg/mL/min?
  c. What percentage of enzyme is in the form of an enzyme-substrate complex when the initial velocity is 2.0×10^{-3} mg/mL/min?

22.17 Lysozyme catalyzes the hydrolysis of glycoside bonds of the polysaccharide components of certain types of bacterial cell walls. The catalytic activity of this enzyme is at a maximum at pII 5.0. The active site of lysozyme contains the side chains of asp and glu, and for maximum catalytic activity, the side chain of glu must be in the acid, or protonated, form and the side chain of asp in the conjugate base, or deprotonated, form. Explain why the velocity of lysozyme-catalyzed reactions decreases as the pH becomes more acidic than the optimal pH. Also explain why reaction velocity decreases as the pH becomes more basic than the optimal pH.

22.18 An enzyme isolated from yeast has an optimal temperature of 40°C. Explain why the velocity of the reaction catalyzed by this enzyme (a) decreases as the temperature is lowered to 0°C; (b) decreases as the temperature is increased above 40°C.

22.19 Following are equations for the ionization of the side chains of histidine and cysteine, along with the pK_a of each.

$$CH_2-S-H \rightleftharpoons CH_2-S^- + H^+ \qquad pK_a = 8.0$$

(This form required for maximum activity)

Assume that both histidine and cysteine are catalytic groups for a particular enzyme. Assume also that for maximum activity, the side chain of histidine must be in the protonated form and the side chain of cysteine must be in the deprotonated form. Estimate the pH at which the catalytic activity of this enzyme is the maximum, and sketch a pH-activity graph.

22.20 Various enzymes and their K_m values follow. Which enzyme has the highest affinity for substrate? Which has the lowest affinity for substrate?

Enzyme	K_m
sucrase	1.6×10^{-2}M
β-glucosidase	6×10^{-3}M
enolase	7×10^{-5}M
catalase	1.17M

22.21 Following is the initial velocity versus substrate concentration for an enzyme-catalyzed reaction and for the same reaction in the presence of an inhibitor. Inhibitor concentration is constant.

[S] (mol/L)	Velocity (mmol/min)	Velocity (Inhibited) (mmol/min)
1.0×10^{-4}	0.14	0.088
1.25×10^{-4}	0.16	0.105
1.67×10^{-4}	0.19	0.13
2.5×10^{-4}	0.24	0.18
5.0×10^{-4}	0.31	0.26
10.0×10^{-4}	0.38	0.36

a. Prepare a graph of initial velocity versus substrate concentration for the uninhibited reaction.
b. On the same graph, plot initial velocity versus substrate concentration for the inhibited reaction.
c. Is this inhibition competitive or noncompetitive?
d. Can the effects of this inhibitor be overcome? If so, how?

Regulation of enzyme activity (Section 22.5)

22.22 Name two biological mechanisms for regulating enzyme activity.

22.23 What is meant by the term regulatory enzyme?

22.24 What is meant by enzyme induction?

22.25 A metabolic pathway is shown, in which substance A is converted to B, and then B can be converted to substance D or substance F, depending on the needs of the cell at any particular time.

$$A \xrightarrow{\text{I}} B \overset{\text{II}}{\underset{\text{III}}{\diagup\diagdown}} \begin{array}{c} C \longrightarrow \longrightarrow \longrightarrow D \\ E \longrightarrow \longrightarrow \longrightarrow F \end{array}$$

a. Which of these steps commits B to the synthesis of D?

b. Which step commits B to the synthesis of F?

c. Assume that D is an allosteric inhibitor of the enzyme catalyzing reaction B → C; explain how this relation can regulate the concentration of D.

d. Assume that both D and F are allosteric inhibitors of the enzyme catalyzing reaction A → B; show how this relation can regulate the concentration of B, C, and E.

Clinical Enzymology—
The Search for Specificity

A 35-year-old, muscular man complains of severe chest pains and is admitted to the hospital. He lifts heavy objects all day in the course of his work. Is his chest pain due to overexertion that particular day, a temporary muscle spasm, a heart attack, or some other cause? The attending physician must rely on several types of information in making a correct diagnosis: patient history; the clinical pattern of the chest pains; electrocardiogram findings; and the rise and fall in the concentration of certain blood-serum enzymes. Today enzyme assays can be used to determine with virtually 100% certainty whether a patient has or has not had a heart attack and also the extent of damage to cardiac muscle tissue. To understand the basis for these enzyme tests, we must know what kinds of enzymes are normally found in serum and what isoenzymes are.

Serum Enzymes

Two kinds of enzymes are normally found in serum, functional enzymes and nonfunctional enzymes. Functional enzymes are secreted into the circulatory system, where they have clearly defined physiological roles. An example is

and blood only as a result of normal tissue breakdown. What makes the presence of nonfunctional enzymes significant is that their level in serum increases dramatically any time there is cellular injury or increased breakdown due to:

1. Localized trauma, such as a blow, a surgical procedure, or even an intramuscular injection.
2. Inadequate flow of blood to a particular tissue or area.
3. Any condition, such as cancer, in which there is an increase in cell growth accompanied by a corresponding increase in cell destruction.

Isoenzymes

Many enzymes exist in multiple forms, and while all forms of a particular enzyme catalyze the same reaction or reactions, they often do so at different rates. The term *isoenzyme* is used to distinguish between multiple forms of the same enzyme. Two of the most extensively studied sets of isoenzymes are those of lactate dehydrogenase and of creatine kinase.

Lactate dehydrogenase (LDH) catalyzes the following reversible reaction:

$$\underset{\text{lactate}}{CH_3\overset{\overset{\displaystyle OH}{|}}{C}HCO_2^- + NAD^+} \underset{\text{dehydrogenase}}{\overset{\text{lactate}}{\rightleftharpoons}} \underset{\text{pyruvate}}{CH_3\overset{\overset{\displaystyle O}{\|}}{C}CO_2^- + NADH + H^+}$$

thrombin, an enzyme involved in blood clotting. Nonfunctional enzymes have no apparent role in serum. They are largely confined to cells and appear in the surrounding extracellular fluids

In the forward reaction, lactate is oxidized by NAD^+, and in the reverse reaction, pyruvate is reduced by NADH. High levels of LDH are found in the liver, the skeletal and heart muscles,

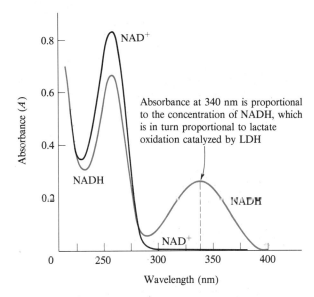

Figure XV-1 Absorbance versus wavelength for NADH and NAD$^+$.

kidneys, and erythrocytes. When extracts of these or other types of tissues are subjected to electrophoresis at pH 8.0, lactate dehydrogenase can be separated into five isoenzymes. By convention, the isoenzyme moving most rapidly toward the positive electrode is called LDH$_1$ and that moving most slowly is called LDH$_5$. The LDH isoenzymes are not visible to the eye. So that their locations can be determined, the elec-

trophoresis strip is incubated with lactate and NAD$^+$. At sites on the strip where LDH is present, NAD$^+$ is reduced to NADH. Figure XV-1 shows a plot of absorbance versus wavelength for NAD$^+$ and NADH. Notice that only NADH absorbs radiation between 300 and 400 nm. In the clinical laboratory, absorbance at 340 nm is used to detect NADH.

Figure XV-2(a) shows a typical LDH isoenzyme pattern. In the preparation of this strip, the sample is spotted at the right and the direction of migration is toward the positive electrode at the left.

The five LDH isoenzymes are all tetramers composed of different combinations of two polypeptide chains. One chain is designated H because it is found in highest concentration in heart muscle LDH. The other, found in highest concentration in skeletal muscle, is designated M. The fastest-moving LDH isoenzyme is a tetramer of four H chains and the slowest is a tetramer of four M chains. The other three are hybrids of H and M chains.

Table XV-1 shows the distribution of LDH isoenzymes in several human tissues. Notice that each type of tissue has a distinct isoenzyme pattern. Liver and skeletal muscle, for example, contain particularly high percentages of LDH$_5$. Also notice that heart muscle and skeletal muscle have different ratios of LDH$_1$/LDH$_2$.

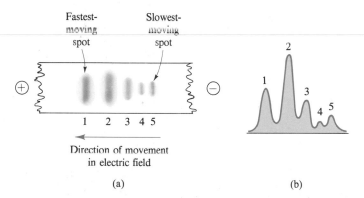

Figure XV-2 An LDH isoenzyme assay. (a) The patterns of LDH isoenzymes in normal serum. (b) A densitometer plot showing the relative concentrations of each isoenzyme. The area under each peak is proportional to the concentration of isoenzyme.

Table XV-1
Percentage
distribution of
LDH isoenzymes
in several tissues.

Tissue	LDH_1 (H_4)	LDH_2 (H_3M)	LDH_3 (H_2M_2)	LDH_4 (HM_3)	LDH_5 (M_5)
serum	25	35	20	10	10
heart	40	35	20	5	0
kidney	35	30	25	10	0
liver	0	5	10	15	70
brain	25	35	30	10	0
skeletal muscle	0	0	10	30	60

Because LDH is widely distributed throughout the body, elevated serum levels of LDH are associated with a broad serum of diseases: anemias involving hemolysis of red blood cells, acute liver diseases, congestive heart failure, pulmonary embolism, and muscular diseases, such as muscular dystrophy. This broad distribution makes an LDH assay a good initial test. If LDH activity is elevated, then an isoenzyme assay can be used to pinpoint the location and type of disease more accurately.

Creatine kinase (CK) catalyzes the transfer of a phosphate group from creatine phosphate to ADP (Section 24.6C). You should note that although the current name for this enzyme is creatine kinase, until recently the preferred name was creatine phosphokinase (CPK). It is likely that you will encounter both names and both abbreviations in your readings.

$$^-O-\overset{\overset{\displaystyle O}{\|}}{\underset{\underset{\displaystyle O^-}{|}}{P}}-NH-\overset{\overset{\displaystyle NH_2^+}{\|}}{\underset{\underset{\displaystyle CH_3}{|}}{C}}-N-CH_2-CO_2^- + ADP \xrightarrow{\text{creatine kinase}} H_2N-\overset{\overset{\displaystyle NH_2^+}{\|}}{\underset{\underset{\displaystyle CH_3}{|}}{C}}-N-CH_2-CO_2^- + ATP$$

creatine phosphate   creatine

Creatine kinase consists of three isoenzymes, each of which is a dimer formed by combinations of B and M polypeptide chains. The B subunit is so named because it was first isolated from brain tissue. The M subunit was first isolated from skeletal muscle tissue. Table XV-2 shows the percentage distribution of CK isoenzymes in several tissues. Notice that heart muscle is the only tissue containing a high percentage of CK-MB isoenzyme.

Table XV-2
Percentage
distribution of
creatine kinase
(CK) isoenzymes
in several
human tissues.

Tissue	CK_1 (B_2)	CK_2 (MB)	CK_3 (M_2)
serum	0	0	100
heart	0	40	60
lung	90	0	10
bladder	95	0	5
brain	90	0	10
skeletal muscle	0	0	100

Enzyme Profile of a Heart Attack

During a heart attack (myocardial infarction, or MI) a coronary artery is partially or completely blocked, reducing the flow of oxygen-rich blood to the heart muscle it serves. If the muscle is damaged because of oxygen starvation, cells die and release their contents into the surrounding extracellular fluid. Eventually, the cell contents find their way into the bloodstream. The levels of LDH begin to rise appproximately 6–24 hr following a heart attack and frequently reach two to three times normal serum levels. Peak LDH serum activity is usually reached within 2–3 days and may remain elevated for up to two weeks. Many types of cell and tissue damage lead to elevation in serum LDH activity. What is unique about the pattern that follows heart

damage is what happens to the ratio LDH_1/LDH_2. According to the data in Table XV-1 normal serum contains approximately 25% LDH_1 and 35% LDH_2. Thus, in normal serum, the LDH_1/LDH_2 ratio is less than 1. In heart tissue, the LDH_1/LDH_2 ratio is greater than 1. Thus, following a heart attack, there is an elevation in LDH_1 activity in the serum and the LDH_1/LDH_2 ratio "flips"; that is, it changes from less than 1 to greater than 1. In 80% of patients with heart attacks, a flipped LDH_1/LDH_2 ratio appears within 24–48 hr following the attack. Although a flipped LDH_1/LDH_2 ratio is not always seen following a heart attack, there is almost invariably a significant increase in LDH_1 activity. For this reason, several companies have developed enzyme assay tests that are highly specific for LDH_1 only. Figure XV-3 shows an LDH isoenzyme pattern after a mild heart

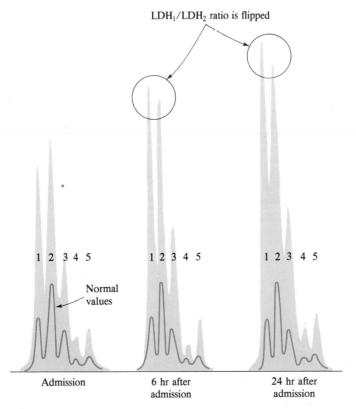

Figure XV-3 LDH isoenzyme assay following a heart attack.

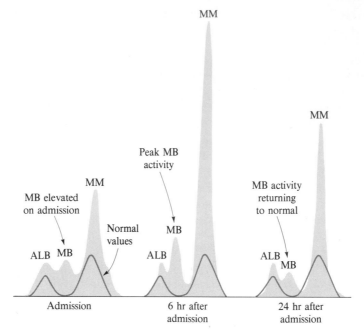

Figure XV-4 Creatine kinase (CK) isoenzyme patterns following a heart attack. The peak labeled ALB is serum albumin and is used as a reference and calibration point.

attack. Note that the LDH_1/LDH_2 ratio is flipped at 12 and 24 hr following admission to the hospital.

Serum levels of creatine kinase also rise after many types of cell and tissue damage. As shown in Table XV-2, heart muscle is the only human tissue with a high percentage of CK-MB isoenzyme, and for this reason, the serum CK isoenzyme pattern following heart damage is unique. Serum CK-MB begins to rise approximately 4–8 hr after myocardial infarction and reaches a peak at about 24 hr. Because CK iso-

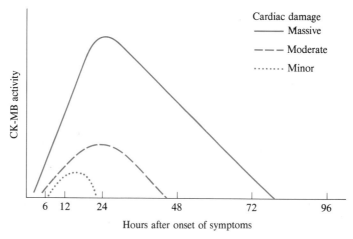

Figure XV-5 Typical plots of serum creatine kinase–MB activity following heart damage.

enzymes are degraded rapidly, CK levels soon begin to drop and return to normal within a few days after the attack. Figure XV-4 shows a creatine kinase isoenzyme pattern following a heart attack. Note that all samples, including the one on admission, are positive for CK-MB. The second sample shows greatest activity, and the third shows CK-MB returning to normal.

It is often possible to determine the extent of heart damage from the CK-MB pattern. Shown in Figure XV-5 is a plot of CK-MB activity following minor, moderate, and massive heart damage. Notice that when the heart damage is massive, CK-MB appears in the serum sooner, its activity rises higher, and it returns more slowly to normal, compared with lesser attacks.

What about our 35-year-old man admitted to the hospital with chest pain? Enzyme assays over the next 48 hr showed increased levels of LDH and CK enzymes. Isoenzyme assays, however, showed no elevation in CK-MB and no significant change in the $LDH_1/LDII_2$ ratio. Therefore, his pains were associated with trauma to skeletal muscle and there was no indication of heart damage.

The Penicillins

The most successful of all antibiotics are the penicillins, the first of the so-called miracle drugs. These truly remarkable drugs are almost completely harmless to all living organisms except for certain classes of bacteria. As a result of extensive research on the structure, chemistry, and mechanism of antibacterial activity of penicillins, it is safe to say that we have a clearer understanding of the penicillins than of almost any other class of antibiotic.

The discovery of penicillin was purely accidental. In 1928, the Scottish bacteriologist Alexander Fleming (later to become Sir Alexander Fleming) reported:

> While working with staphylococcal variants, a number of culture plates were set aside on the laboratory bench and examined from time to time. In the examinations, these plates were necessarily exposed to the air and they became contaminated with various microorganisms. It was noticed that around a large colony of contaminating mold, the staphylococcal colonies became transparent and were obviously undergoing lysis .... I was sufficiently interested in the antibacterial substance produced by the mold to pursue the matter.

Because the contaminating mold was *Penicillium notatum*, Fleming named the antibacterial substance penicillin. Despite several attempts, he was unable to isolate and purify an active form of it. Nonetheless, he continued to maintain his cultures of the mold.

The outbreak of war in Europe in 1939 stimulated an intensive search for new drugs, and in Great Britain the potential of Fleming's penicillin was reinvestigated. Howard Florey, an Australian experimental pathologist, and Ernst Chain, a Jewish chemist who had fled Nazi Germany, worked together on the project. Using the newly discovered technique of freeze-drying (lyophilization), they succeeded in isolating penicillin from Fleming's cultures. Within a few months, larger quantities of purified penicillin were available, and many of its physical, chemical, and antibacterial properties had been determined. Florey and Chain published, in 1940, a report of treatment of bacterial infection in mice, and two years later, a report on treatment of humans. By 1943, pharmaceutical companies in Britain and the United States were producing penicillin on a large scale and it was authorized for use by the military. The following year, penicillin became available for civilian use, and in 1945 Fleming, Florey, and Chain were awarded the Noble Prize in medicine and physiology. Thus, in less than two decades, penicillin had progressed from a chance observation in a research laboratory to a drug that has been recognized as one of the greatest contributions of medical science in the service of humanity.

Preliminary investigations of the structure of penicillin presented a confusing picture until it was discovered that *P. notatum* produces different kinds of penicillin, depending on the composition of the medium in which the mold is grown. Initially, six different penicillins were recognized, all of which proved to be derivatives of 6-aminopenicillanic acid (Figure XVI-1). Of the six, penicillin G (benzylpenicillin) became the most widely used and the standard against which others were judged.

The structural formula of penicillins consists of a five-member ring fused to a four-member ring. The four-member ring is a cyclic amide, the special name for which is lactam. Because the nitrogen atom of this lactam is on the carbon

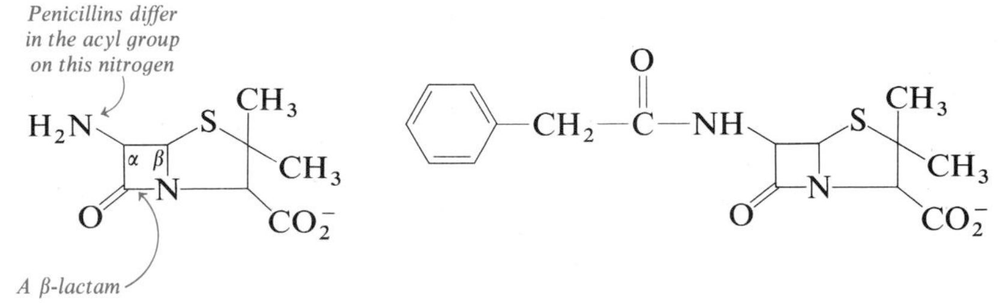

6-aminopenicillanic acid

penicillin G or benzylpenicillin

Figure XVI-1 The penicillins.

atom beta to the carbonyl group, the general name of this type of ring is beta-lactam.

The penicillins undergo a variety of chemical reactions, some of which are very complex. We will concentrate on just two of these, each chosen because it has important consequences for the medical use of these antibiotics. Treatment of penicillin with aqueous HCl brings about hydrolysis of the amide bond of the highly strained beta-lactam and cleavage of the five-member ring also (Figure XVI-2). Both penaldic acid and penicillamine are devoid of antibacterial activity. Because penicillin G is rapidly inactivated by this type of hydrolysis in the acid conditions of the stomach, it cannot be given orally; it must be given by intramuscular injection.

The second important reaction of the penicillins is selective hydrolysis of the beta-lactam ring catalyzed by a group of enzymes called beta-lactamases (Figure XVI-3). The product of this enzyme-catalyzed hydrolysis is penicilloic acid. Like penaldic acid and penicillamine, penicilloic acid has no antibacterial activity. The main basis for the natural resistance of certain bacteria to penicillins is their ability to synthesize beta-lactamases and thereby inactivate penicillins with which they come in contact.

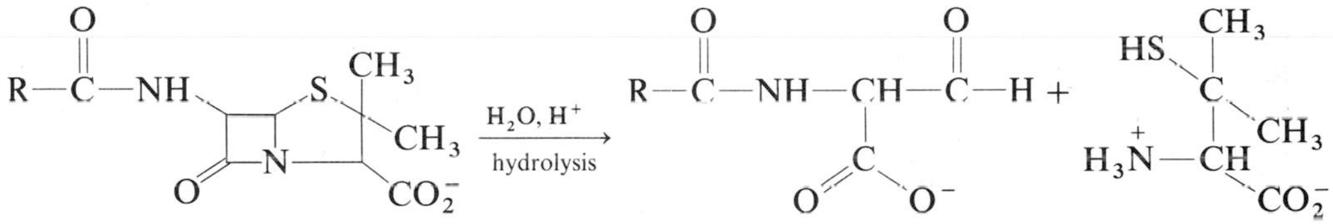

penicillin | penaldic acid | penicillamine

Figure XVI-2 Acid-catalyzed hydrolysis of penicillin. Neither penaldic acid nor penicillamine has any antibacterial activity.

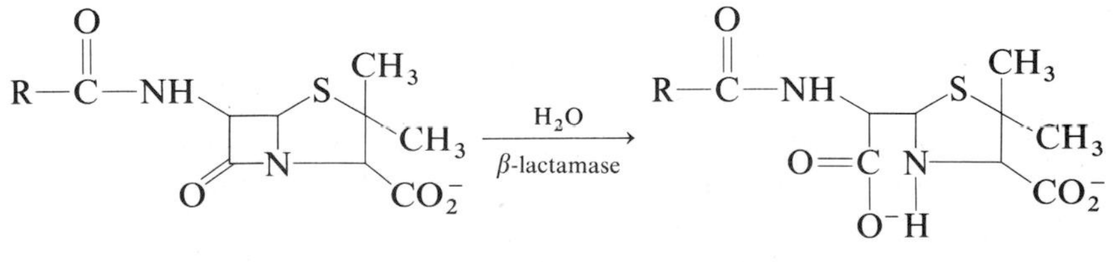

penicillin | penicilloic acid

Figure XVI-3 Selective hydrolysis of the beta-lactam ring catalyzed by beta-lactamase.

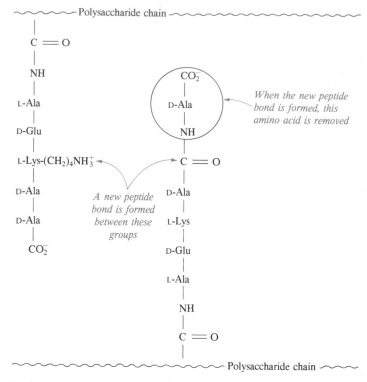

Figure XVI-4 Certain types of bacterial cell walls are constructed of long polysaccharide chains to which are attached short polypeptide chains. In the final stage of cell-wall construction, cross-linking of the polypeptide chains creates an enormous bag-shaped macromolecule.

The penicillins owe their antibacterial activity to a common mechanism that inhibits the biosynthesis of a vital part of bacterial cell walls. Within certain types of bacterial cells, osmotic pressure is as high as 10–20 atm, and without the support of a cell wall, the bacterial cell would rupture. One of the simplest types of bacterial cell walls is constructed of long polysaccharide chains to which are attached short polypeptide chains (Figure XVI-4).

The final reactions in construction of a bacterial cell wall are formation of amide bonds between adjacent polypeptide chains (Figure XVI-4). Through this type of peptide bond interchange, polysaccharide chains are cross-linked, to form one enormous bag-shaped macromolecule.

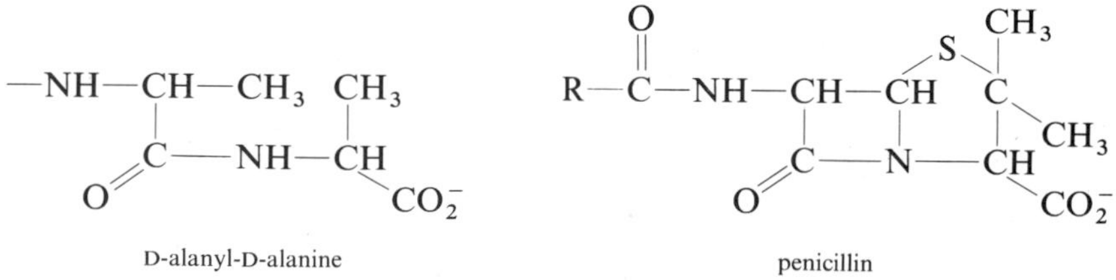

D-alanyl-D-alanine

penicillin

Figure XVI-5 Structural formulas of D-alanyl-D-alanine and penicillin, drawn to suggest a structural similarity between the two.

It is formation of the final cross-linked macromolecule that penicillin inhibits. Numerous hypotheses have been proposed to explain just how this occurs. One hypothesis is that the penicillins have a structure like D-alanyl-D-alanine, the terminal amino acids of the short polypeptide chains that must be cross-linked. The similarity is illustrated in Figure XVI-5. Penicillin is thought to bind selectively to the active site of the enzyme complex that catalyzes peptide bond interchange in the final step of cell-wall construction. Hence, at the molecular level, penicillin's antibacterial activity seems to be selective enzyme inhibition.

That this pattern of cell-wall construction is unique to certain forms of bacteria and not found in mammalian cells no doubt accounts for the lack of toxicity of penicillins to humans. However, the use of penicillins does have its problems. A significant percentage of the population have become hypersensitive to the drug and experience severe allergic reaction. The factor responsible for the allergic reaction is not penicillin itself but certain degradation products, particularly 6-aminopenicillanic acid (Figure XVI-1).

The susceptibility of penicillin G to hydrolysis by acid and the emergence of beta-lactamase-producing strains of bacteria have provided incentive for researchers to develop more effective penicillins. As a result of such effort, by 1974 over 20,000 semisynthetic penicillins had been prepared. At present, the three most widely pre-

broader spectrum and attacks both Gram-negative and Gram-positive bacteria. Penicillin VK is more resistant to acid hydrolysis than penicillin G and can be given orally. Methicillin is about 1000 times more resistant to the action of beta-lactamases than penicillin G and is used to treat infections caused by "penicillin-resistant" organisms.

Soon after the penicillins were introduced into medical practice, resistant strains began to appear, and they have proliferated ever since. Many argue that the widespread, unnecessary use of penicillins is the primary reason why resistant strains have emerged. One of the most serious is *Neisseria gonorrhoeae*; this strain causes a gonorrhea that is very difficult to treat. One approach to resistant strains is to synthesize newer, more effective beta-lactamase antibiotics, of which one class is the cephalosporins (Figure XVI-7). The first cephalosporin was iso-

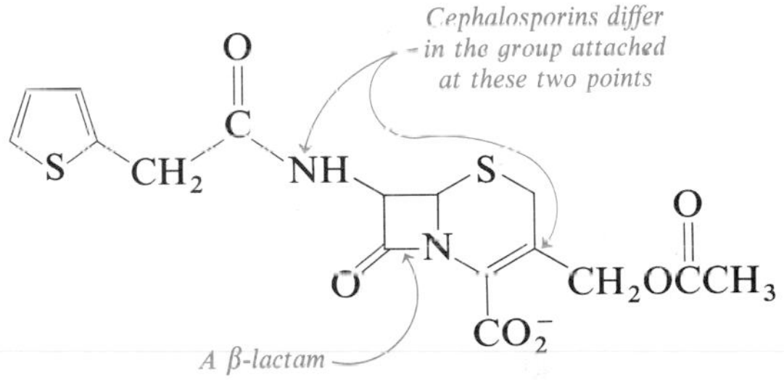

Figure XVI-7 Cephalothin, one of the first of a new generation of beta-lactam antibiotics.

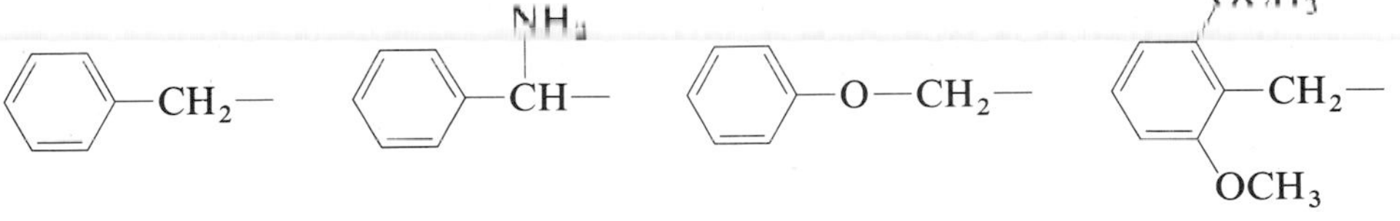

Figure XVI-6 Structural relations between penicillin G and three widely used semisynthetic penicillins.

scribed penicillins are ampicillin, penicillin VK, and penicillin G. The side chains of these three and of methicillin are shown in Figure XVI-6.

Penicillin G is most effective against Gram-negative bacteria. Ampicillin is a antibiotic of

lated from the fungus *Cephalosporium acremonium*. Several cephalosporins have already been approved for clinical use, and approval of at least a dozen others is pending. Clinical studies indicate that this class of beta-lactam antibiotics has a broader spectrum of activity than the penicillins and at the same time a greater resistance to hydrolysis by beta-lactamases. Cephalosporins now account for approximately 35% of all antibiotic prescriptions.

The cephalosporins contain a beta-lactam ring fused to a six-member ring containing atoms of sulfur and nitrogen and a carbon-carbon double bond. As a family, cephalosporins differ from one another in the acyl group attached to the —NH_2 group of the beta-lactam ring and in the substituent on carbon 3 of the six-member ring.

An entirely different approach to the treatment of beta-lactam-resistant infections is to use either a penicillin or a cephalosporin combined with a compound that inhibits the activity of beta-lactamases. One such compound, clavulanic acid, has virtually no antibiotic activity by itself but is a powerful, irreversible inhibitor of beta-lactamases. Note that clavulanic acid itself is a beta-lactam (Figure XVI-8). With this combination of drugs, it now appears possible to in-

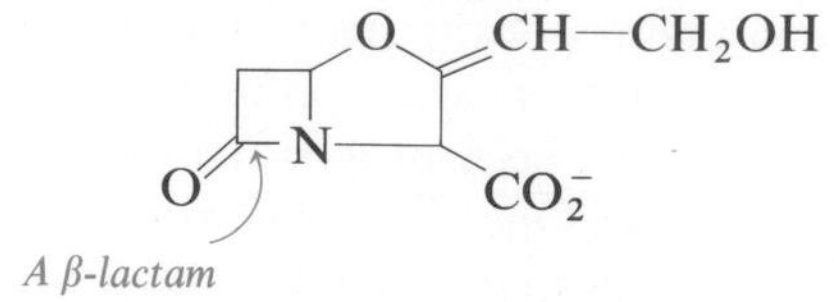

A β-lactam

Figure XVI-8 Clavulanic acid, a powerful inhibitor of beta-lactamases.

terfere not only with an infectious organism's essential biochemistry but also with its first line of defense against attack by drugs.

The penicillins and cephalosporins are among the most important anti-infective agents and almost certainly will continue to be so. Because the possibilities for substituting different groups on the essential ring structures of each are almost limitless, even more effective beta-lactam antibiotics are yet to be discovered. So, too, it is probable that in response to these drugs, even newer drug-resistant strains of bacteria will emerge.

23 Nucleic Acids and the Synthesis of Proteins

Nucleic acids are the third broad class of biopolymers that, like proteins and polysaccharides, are vital components of living materials. In this chapter we will look at the structure of nucleosides and nucleotides, and the manner in which these small building blocks are bonded together to form nucleic acids. Then, we will consider the three-dimensional structure of nucleic acids. Finally, we will examine the manner in which genetic information coded on deoxyribonucleic acids is expressed in protein biosynthesis.

23.1 Components of Deoxyribonucleic Acids (DNAs)

Controlled hydrolysis breaks DNA molecules into three components: (1) phosphoric acid; (2) 2-deoxy-D-ribose; and (3) heterocyclic aromatic amine bases. The bases fall into two classes: those derived from pyrimidine and those derived from purine. Following are structural formulas of the four bases most abundant in DNA, along with formulas for their parent bases.

pyrimidine   cytosine (C)   thymine (T)

purine   adenine (A)   guanine (G)

23.2 Nucleosides

A nucleoside is a glycoside in which nitrogen 9 of a purine base or nitrogen 1 of a pyrimidine base is bonded to 2-deoxy-D-ribose by a β-*N*-glycoside bond (Section 19.2A). In structural formulas for nucleosides and nucleotides, atoms of the purine and pyrimidine bases are designated by unprimed numbers; primed numbers are used to designate atoms of 2-deoxy-D-ribose. Two nucleosides, 2′-deoxyadenosine and 2′-deoxycytidine, are shown in Figure 23.1. The other two nucleosides found in DNA are 2′-deoxythymidine and 2′-deoxyguanosine.

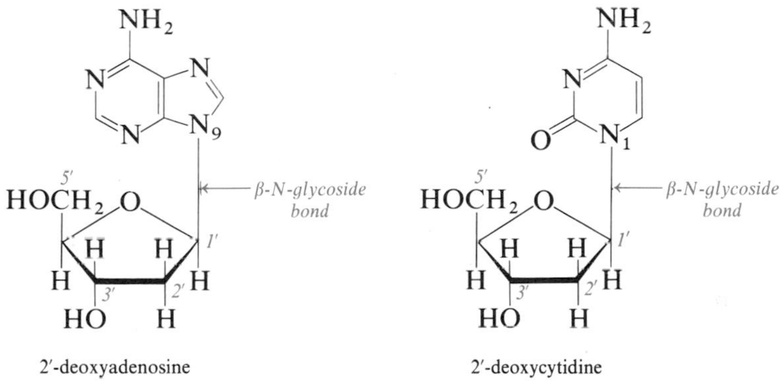

Figure 23.1 Nucleosides: 2′-deoxyadenosine and 2′-deoxycytidine.

23.3 Nucleotides

A nucleotide is a nucleoside monophosphate ester in which a molecule of phosphoric acid is esterified with a free hydroxyl group of 2-deoxy-D-ribose. Nucleoside monophosphates are illustrated in Figure 23.2 by the 5′-monophosphate

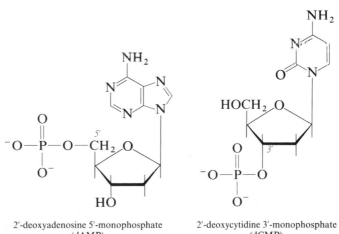

2′-deoxyadenosine 5′-monophosphate
(dAMP)

2′-deoxycytidine 3′-monophosphate
(dCMP)

Figure 23.2 Nucleotides (nucleoside monophosphate esters).

ester of 2′-deoxyadenosine and the 3′-monophosphate ester of 2′-deoxycytidine. Note that at pH 7.0, the two protons of a monophosphate ester are ionized, giving this group a net charge of −2.

Mononucleotides are commonly named as phosphate esters (for example, deoxyadenosine 5′-monophosphate) or as acids (for example, deoxyadenylic acid), or by four-letter abbreviations (for example, dAMP). In these four-letter abbreviations, the letter *d* indicates 2-deoxy-D-ribose, the second letter indicates the nucleoside, and the third and fourth letters indicate that the molecule is a monophosphate (MP) ester. Table 23.1 lists names for the principal mononucleotides derived from DNA.

Table 23.1
Names of the major mononucleotides derived from DNA.

As a Monophosphate	As an Acid	By a Four-Letter Abbreviation
deoxyadenosine monophosphate	deoxyadenylic acid	dAMP
deoxyguanosine monophosphate	deoxyguanidylic acid	dGMP
deoxycytidine monophosphate	deoxycytidylic acid	dCMP
deoxythymidine monophosphate	deoxythymidylic acid	dTMP

All nuceloside monophosphates can be further phosphorylated to form nucleoside diphosphates and nucleoside triphosphates. In diphosphates and triphosphates, the second and third phosphate groups are joined by anhydride bonds. At pH 7.0, all protons of diphosphate and triphosphate groups are fully ionized, giving them net charges of −3 and −4, respectively.

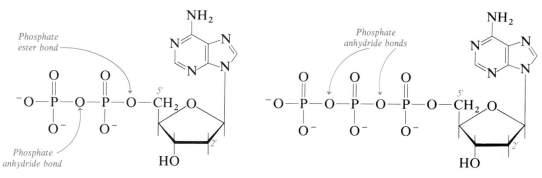

2′-deoxyadenosine 5′-diphosphate (dADP)

2′-deoxyadenosine 5′-triphosphate (dATP)

Example 23.1

☐ *Solution*

Draw structural formulas for these mononucleotides.

a. 2′-deoxycytidine 5′-monophosphate (dCMP)
b. 2′-deoxyguanosine 5′-triphosphate (dGTP)

a. Cytosine is joined by a β-*N*-glycoside bond between N-1 of cytosine and C-1 of the cyclic hemiacetal form of 2-deoxy-D-ribose. The 5′-hydroxyl of the pentose is bonded to phosphate by an ester bond.

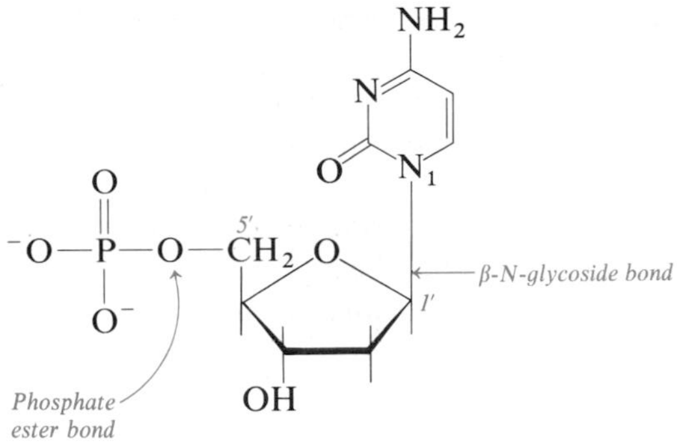

β-*N-glycoside bond*

Phosphate ester bond

b. Guanine is joined by a *β-N*-glycoside bond between N-9 of guanine and C-1 of the cyclic hemiacetal form of 2-deoxy-D-ribose. The 5'-hydroxyl group of the pentose is joined to three phosphate groups by a combination of one ester bond and two anhydride bonds.

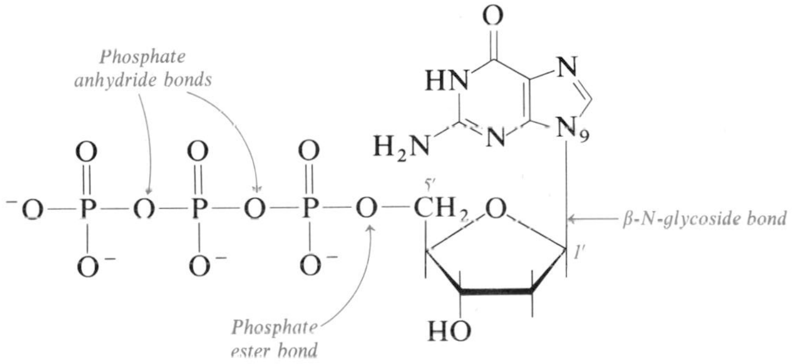

Phosphate anhydride bonds

β-*N-glycoside bond*

Phosphate ester bond

Problem 23.1

Draw structural formulas for (a) dTTP and (b) dGMP.

23.4 Structure of DNA

A. Primary Structure: The Covalent Backbone

Deoxyribonucleic acids (DNAs) consist of a backbone of alternating units of deoxyribose and phosphate, in which the 3'-hydroxyl of one deoxyribose is joined to the 5'-hydroxyl of the next deoxyribose by a phosphodiester bond (Figure 23.3). This pentose-phosphate backbone is constant throughout an entire DNA molecule. A heterocyclic base—adenine, guanine, thymine, or cytosine—is attached to each deoxyribose by a *β-N*-glycoside bond.

The sequence of bases in a DNA molecule is indicated by single-letter abbreviations for each base, beginning from the free 5'-hydroxyl end of the chain. According to this convention, the base sequence of the section of DNA shown

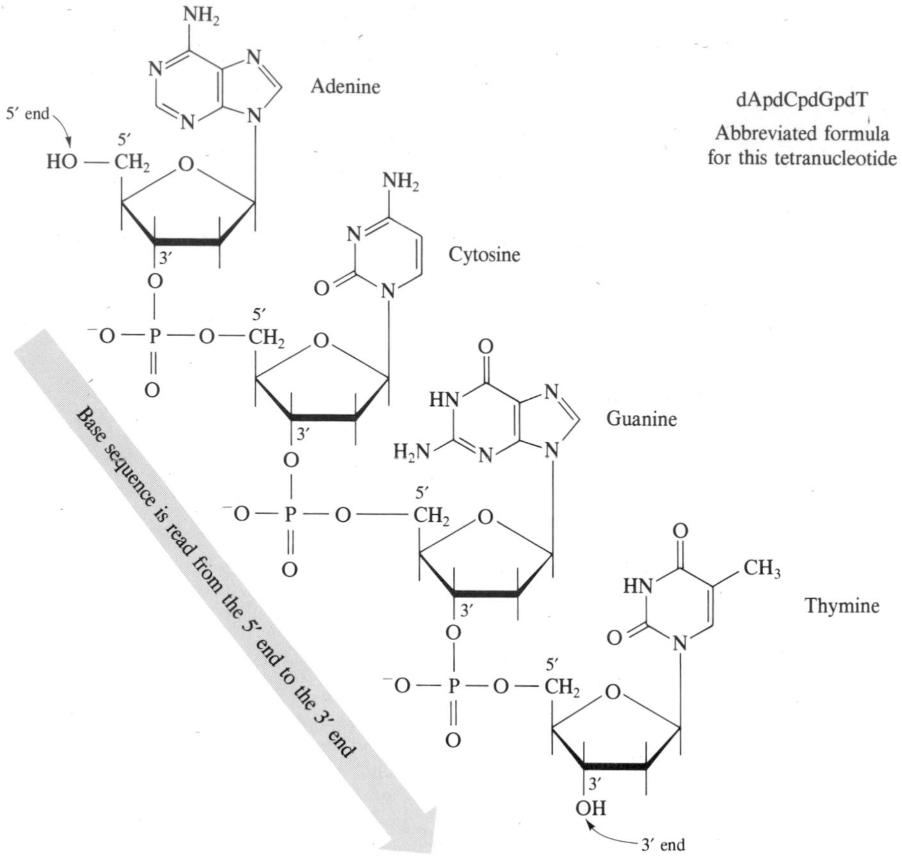

Figure 23.3 Partial structural formula of a deoxyribonucleic acid (DNA), showing a tetranucleotide sequence. In this abbreviated sequence, the bases of the tetranucleotide are read from the 5′ end of the chain to the 3′ end, as indicated by the arrow.

in Figure 23.3 is written dApdCpdGpdT, where the letter d indicates that each nucleoside monomer is derived from deoxyribose and the letter p indicates a phosphodiester bond in the backbone of the molecule. Alternatively, the base sequence can be written ACGT, a notation that emphasizes the order of the heterocyclic amine bases in the molecule.

Example 23.2

Draw a complete structural formula for a section of DNA containing the base sequence pdApdC.

☐ *Solution*

The first letter in the shorthand formula of this dinucleotide is p, indicating that the 5′-hydroxyl is bonded to phosphate by an ester bond. The last letter, C, shows that the 3′-hydroxyl is free, not esterified with phosphate.

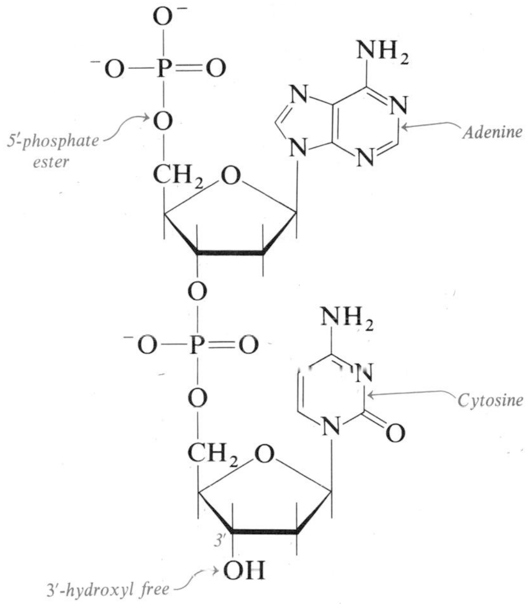

Draw a complete structural formula for a section of DNA containing the base sequence dCpdTpdGp.

Problem 23.2

B. Base Composition

By 1950, it was clear that DNA molecules consist of chains of alternating units of deoxyribose and phosphate linked by phosphodiester bonds, with a base attached to each deoxyribose by a β-N-glycoside bond. However, the precise sequence of bases along the chain of any particular DNA molecule was completely unknown. At one time, it was thought that the four principal bases occurred in equal ratios and perhaps repeated in a regular pattern along the pentose-phosphate backbone of the molecule. However, more precise determinations of base sequence by Erwin Chargaff revealed that the bases do not occur in equal ratios (Table 23.2).

Table 23.2 Comparison of base composition (in mole percentage) of DNA from several organisms.

Organism	A	G	C	T	A/T	G/C	Purines/Pyrimidines
human	30.9	19.9	19.8	29.4	1.05	1.00	1.04
sheep	29.3	21.4	21.0	28.3	1.03	1.03	1.03
sea urchin	32.8	17.7	17.3	32.1	1.02	1.02	1.03
marine crab	47.3	2.7	2.7	47.3	1.00	1.00	1.00
yeast	31.3	18.7	17.1	32.9	0.95	1.09	1.00
E. coli	24.7	26.0	26.0	23.6	1.04	1.01	1.03

From consideration of data such as shown in Table 23.2, the following conclusions emerged.

1. The mole-percentage base composition of DNA in any organism is the same in all cells and is characteristic of the organism.
2. The mole-percentage of adenine and of thymine are equal, and the mole-percentage of guanine and of cytosine are equal:

$$\%[\text{adenine}] = \%[\text{thymine}]$$
$$\%[\text{cytosine}] = \%[\text{guanine}]$$

3. The mole-percentage of purine bases (A + G) and of pyrimidine bases (C + T) are equal:

$$\%[\text{purines}] = \%[\text{pyrimidines}]$$

C. Molecular Dimensions of DNAs

Additional information on the structure of DNA emerged when X-ray diffraction photographs of DNA fibers taken by Rosalind Franklin and Maurice Wilkens were analyzed. These photographs showed that DNA molecules are long, fairly straight, and not more than a dozen atoms thick. Furthermore, even though the base composition of DNAs isolated from different organisms varies over a wide range, DNA molecules themselves are remarkably uniform in thickness. Herein lies one of the chief problems to be solved. How could the molecular dimensions of DNAs be so regular even though the relative percentages of the various bases differ so widely?

D. The Double Helix

With this accumulated information, the stage was set for the development of a hypothesis about DNA conformation. In 1953, F. H. C. Crick, a British physicist, and James D. Watson, an American biologist, postulated a precise model of the three-dimensional structure of DNA. The model not only accounted for many of the observed physical and chemical properties of DNA but also suggested a mechanism by which genetic information could be repeatedly and accurately replicated. Watson, Crick, and Wilkins shared the 1962 Nobel Prize in physiology and medicine for "their discoveries concerning the molecular structure of nucleic acids, and its significance for information transfer in living material."

The heart of the Watson-Crick model is the postulate that a molecule of DNA consists of two antiparallel polynucleotide strands coiled in a right-handed manner about the same axis to form a **double helix**. To account for the observed base ratios and the constant thickness of DNA, Watson and Crick postulated that purine and pyrimidine bases project inward toward the axis of the helix and are always paired in a very specific manner.

According to scale models, the dimensions of a thymine-adenine base pair are identical to the dimensions of a cytosine-guanine base pair, and the length of each pair is consistent with the thickness of a DNA strand (Figure 23.4). This fact gives rise to the principle of **complementarity**. In DNA, adenine is always

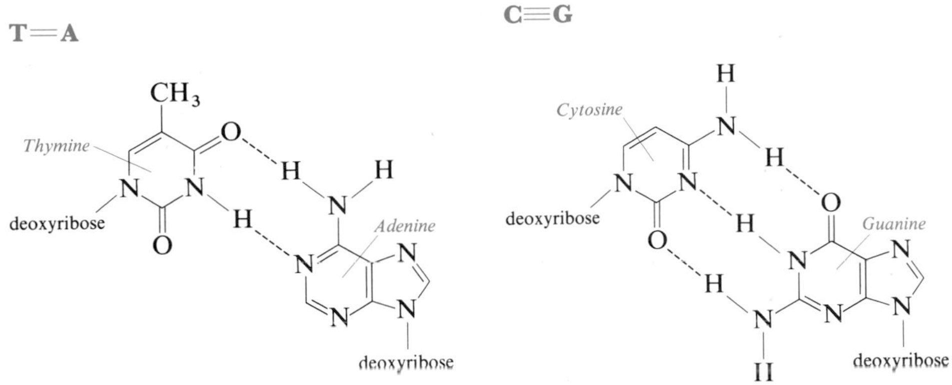

$$C\equiv G$$

$$T=A$$

Figure 23.4 Hydrogen-bonded interaction between thymine and adenine and between cytosine and guanine. The first pair is abbreviated T═A (showing two hydrogen bonds) and the second pair is abbreviated C≡G (showing three hydrogen bonds).

paired by hydrogen bonding with thymine; hence, adenine and thymine are complementary bases. Similarly, guanine and cytosine are complementary bases. A significant finding arising from Watson and Crick's model-building is that no other base pairing is consistent with the observed thickness of a DNA molecule. A pair of pyrimidine bases is too small to account for the observed thickness, while a pair of purine bases is too large. Thus, according to the Watson-Crick model, the repeating units in a double-stranded DNA molecule are not single bases of differing dimensions, but base pairs of identical dimensions.

To account for the periodicity observed from X-ray data, Watson and Crick postulated that base pairs are stacked one on top of the other, with a distance of 3.4×10^{-8} cm between base pairs. Exactly ten base pairs are stacked in one complete turn of the helix. There is one complete turn of the helix every 34×10^{-8} cm (Figure 23.5).

Example 23.3

One strand of a DNA molecule has a base sequence of 5'-ACTTGCCA-3'. Write the base sequence for the complementary strand.

☐ *Solution*

Remember that base sequence is always written from the 5' end of the strand to the 3' end, that A is always paired by hydrogen bonding with its complement T, and that G is always paired by hydrogen bonding with its complement C. In double-stranded DNA, the strands run in opposite (antiparallel) directions, so the 5' end of one strand is associated with the 3' end of the other strand. Hydrogen bonds between base pairs are shown by dashed lines.

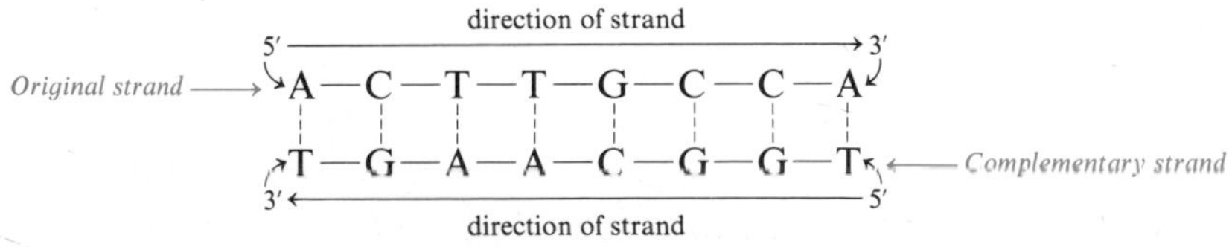

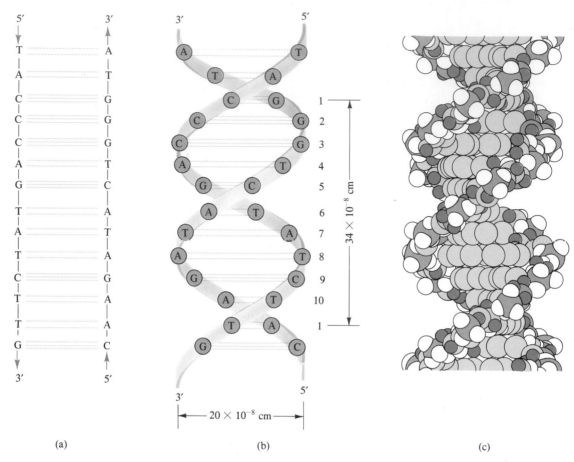

(a) (b) (c)

Figure 23.5 Abbreviated representation of the Watson-Crick double-helix model of DNA. (a) Two complementary antiparallel polynucleotide strands and the hydrogen bonds between complementary base pairs. (b) The strands are twisted in a double helix of thickness 20×10^{-8} cm and a repeat distance of 34×10^{-8} cm along the axis of the double helix. There are 10 base pairs per complete turn of the helix. (c) A space-filling model of a section of DNA double helix.

The complement of 5'-ACTTGCCA-3' is shown under it in the solution. Writing this strand poses a communication problem. DNA strands are always written from 5' to 3' end. Therefore, if the original strand is 5'-ACTTGCCA-3', its complement is 5'-TGGCAAGT-3'.

Problem 23.3

Write the complementary base sequence for 5'-CCGTAGGA-3'.

23.5 DNA Replication

At the time Watson and Crick proposed their model for the conformation of DNA, biologists had already amassed much evidence that DNA is the hereditary, or genetic, material. Detailed studies had revealed that during cell division, there was exact duplication of DNA. The challenge posed to molecular biologists was, How does the genetic material duplicate itself with such unerring fidelity?

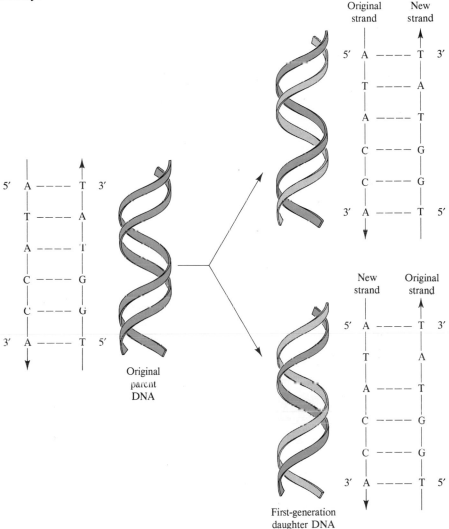

Figure 23.6 Schematic diagram of semiconservative replication. The double helix uncoils and each chain of the parent serves as a template for the synthesis of its complement. Each "daughter" DNA contains one strand from the original DNA and one newly synthesized strand.

One of the exciting things about the double-helix model is that it immediately suggested how DNA might produce an exact copy of itself. The double helix consists of two parts, one the complement of the other. If the two strands separate and each serves as a template for the construction of its own complement, then each new double strand will be an exact replica of the original DNA. Because each new double-stranded DNA molecule contains one strand from the parent molecule and one newly synthesized, **daughter strand**, the process is called **semiconservative replication** (see page 667, Figure 23.6). Although Figure 23.6 shows the result of DNA replication, the actual process is much more complicated than shown. In *E. coli*, replication is thought to proceed by four main steps. While there are variations from species to species, replication in other organisms follows a similar process.

A. Initiation of Replication

Replication starts at a specific point on a chromosome, where unwinding proteins catalyze uncoiling of the DNA helix. During the unwinding, hydrogen bonds between complementary base pairs are broken and purine and pyrimidine bases in the center of double-stranded DNA are exposed (Figure 23.7). The point of unwinding is called a **replication fork.**

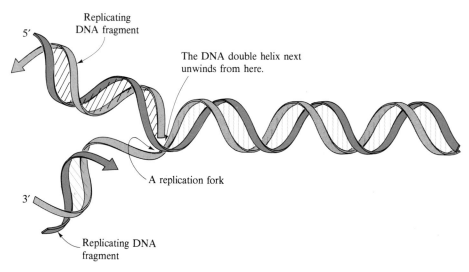

Replicating
DNA fragment

5′

The DNA double helix next
unwinds from here.

A replication fork

3′

Replicating DNA
fragment

Figure 23.7 Unwinding of DNA, creating a replication fork.

B. Formation of DNA Segments

In step 2, DNA replication proceeds along both branches of the exposed DNA template from the 3′ end toward the 5′ end. Because the two unwound DNA strands run in opposite directions, DNA synthesis proceeds toward the replication fork on one strand and away from the replication fork on the other. Addition of mononucleotides to growing DNA daughter strands is catalyzed by DNA polymerase, an enzyme that recognizes the 3'-hydroxyl end of the growing daughter strand and positions the proper complementary deoxynucleoside triphosphate to pair by hydrogen bonding with the next base pair on the template. Finally, the 3'-hydroxyl of the daughter strand displaces pyrophosphate from the 5' end of the next nucleoside triphosphate, to form a phosphodiester bond, and the daughter strand becomes elongated by one nucleotide (Figure 23.8).

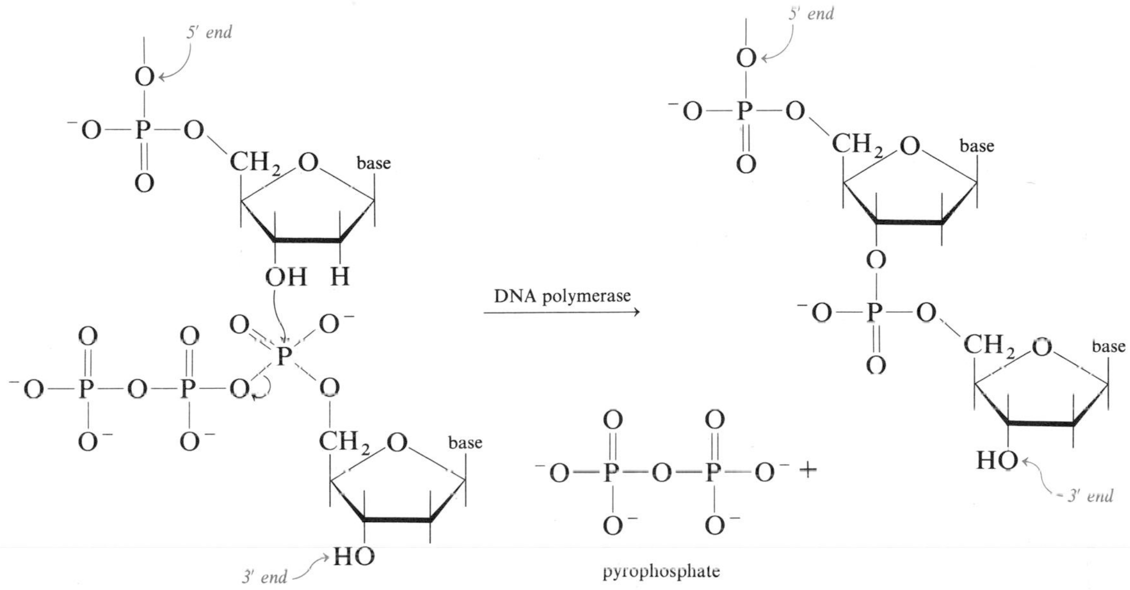

Figure 23.8 Formation of a phosphodiester bond and elongation of a **daughter** strand by one nucleotide.

C. Creation of a New Replication Fork and Continuation of DNA Synthesis

In step 3, a new section of DNA is unwound, creating a second replication fork, and replication is repeated. According to this mechanism, one daughter strand is synthesized as a continuous strand from the 3' end of the DNA template toward the first replication fork and then toward each newly created replication fork as further sections of double helix are unwound. The second daughter strand is synthesized as a series of fragments, each as long as the distance from one replication fork to the next. Breaks created at replication forks are called **nicks** (Figure 23.9) and the DNA fragments separated by nicks are called **Okazaki fragments**, after the biochemist who first discovered them. The isolation of Okazaki fragments is evidence that replication of DNA is not a continuous process.

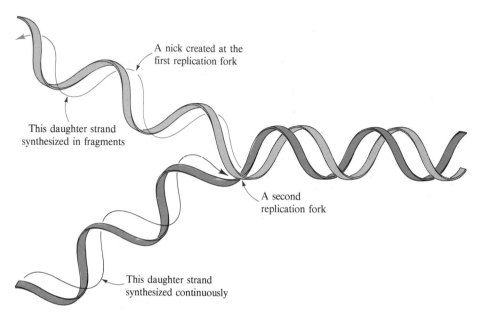

A nick created at the first replication fork

This daughter strand synthesized in fragments

A second replication fork

This daughter strand synthesized continuously

Figure 23.9 Synthesis of DNA daughter strands toward and away from a replication fork.

D. Completion of the DNA Strand

In step 4, an enzyme called DNA ligase closes nicks, to form a completed daughter strand.

23.6 Ribonucleic Acids (RNAs)

Ribonucleic acids (RNAs) are similar to deoxyribonucleic acids in that they, too, consist of long, unbranched chains of nucleotides joined by phosphodiester bonds between the 3′-hydroxyl of one pentose and the 5′-hydroxyl of the next. Thus, they have much the same structure as DNA (Figure 23.3). However, three main differences in structure exist between RNA and DNA:

1. The pentose unit of RNA is D-ribose rather than 2-deoxy-D-ribose.
2. The pyrimidine bases in RNA are uracil and cytosine rather than thymine and cytosine.
3. RNA is single-stranded rather than double-stranded.

Following are structural formulas of β-D-ribose and uracil.

β-D-ribose

uracil
(U)

Ribonucleic acids are distributed throughout the cell; they are present in the nucleus, in the cytoplasm, and in subcellular particles called mitochondria. Furthermore, cells contain three types of RNA: ribosomal RNA, transfer RNA, and messenger RNA. These three types of RNA differ in molecular weight and, as their names imply, they perform different functions within the cell.

A. Ribosomal RNAs

Ribosomal RNAs (rRNA) have molecular weights of 0.5–1.0 million and comprise up to 85–90% of total cellular ribonucleic acid. The bulk of rRNAs are found in the cytoplasm in subcellular particles called **ribosomes**, which contain about 60% RNA and 40% protein. Complete ribosomes (refered to as 70S ribosomes) can be dissociated into two subunits of unequal size, known as 50S subunits and 30S subunits (Figure 23.10). The designation S stands for Svedberg units. Values of S are derived from rates of sedimentation during centrifugation and are used to estimate molecular weight and compactness of ribosomal particles. A large value of S indicates a high molecular weight; a small value indicates a low molecular weight. The 50S ribosomal subunit is about twice the size of the 30S subunit and further dissociates into 23S and 5S subunits and approximately 30 different polypeptides (Figure 23.10). The smaller 30S subunit dissociates into a single 16S subunit and about 20 different polypeptides.

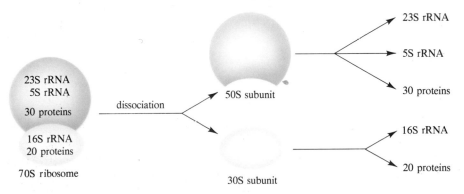

Figure 23.10 Dissociation of a complete ribosome into subunits.

Many of the proteins bound to ribosomes have a high precentage of lysine and arginine, and at the pH of cells, the side chains of these amino acids have net positive charges. It is likely that interactions between positively charged amino acid side chains and negatively charged phosphate groups of RNA are an important factor in stabilizing larger ribosomal particles.

B. Transfer RNA

Transfer RNA (tRNA) molecules have the lowest molecular weight of all nucleic acids. They consist of 75–80 nucleotides in a single chain; this chain is folded into a three-dimensional structure, stabilized by hydrogen bonding between complementary base pairs. Nearly all tRNA chains have G at the 5′ end and CCA at the 3′ end. The three-dimensional shapes of a number of tRNAs have been determined, typical of which is that of yeast phenylalanine tRNA (Figure 23.11).

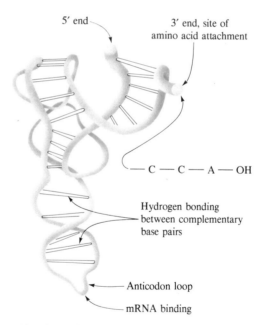

Figure 23.11 The three-dimensional shape of yeast phenylalanine tRNA.

The function of tRNA is to carry amino acids to the sites of protein synthesis on ribosomes. For this purpose, an amino acid is joined to the 3′ end of its specific tRNA by an ester bond, formed between the α-carboxyl group of the amino acid and the 3′-hydroxyl group of ribose. An amino acid thus bound to tRNA is said to be activated, because it is prepared for the synthesis of a peptide bond.

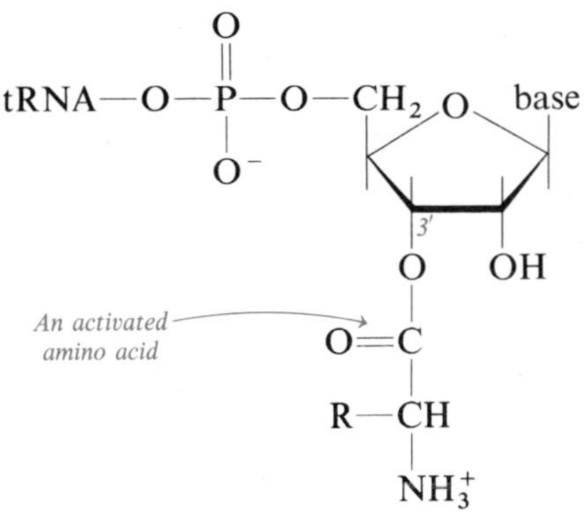

C. Messenger RNA

Messenger RNA (mRNA) is present in cells in relatively small amounts and is very short-lived. It is single-stranded, has an average molecular weight of several hundred thousand, and has a base composition much like that of the DNA of the organism from which it is isolated. The name messenger RNA derives from the function of this type of RNA, which is made in cell nuclei on a DNA template and carries coded genetic information to the ribosomes for the synthesis of new proteins (Section 23.9).

23.7 Transcription of Genetic Information: mRNA Biosynthesis

Messenger RNA is synthesized from DNA in a manner similar to the replication of DNA. Double-stranded DNA is unwound, and a complementary strand of mRNA is synthesized along one strand of the DNA template, beginning from the 3′ end. The synthesis of mRNA from a DNA template is called **transcription**, because genetic information contained in a sequence of bases of DNA is transcribed into a complementary sequence of bases in mRNA.

Example 23.4

☐ *Solution*

Following is a base sequence from a portion of DNA. Write the sequence of bases of the mRNA synthesized, using this section of DNA as a template.

3′-A-G-C-C-A-T-G-T-G-A-C-C-5′

RNA synthesis begins at the 3′ end of the DNA template and proceeds toward the 5′ end. The complementary mRNA strand is formed using the bases C, G, A, and U. Uracil (U) is the complement of adenine (A) on the DNA template.

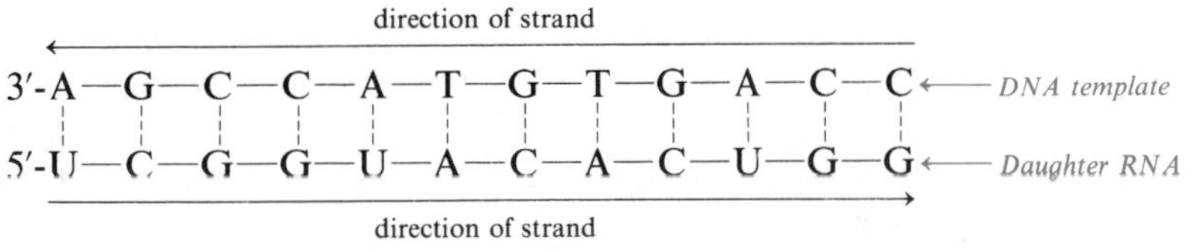

direction of strand

3′-A—G—C—C—A—T—G—T—G—A—C—C ←—— *DNA template*

5′-U—C—G—G—U—A—C—A—C—U—G—G ←—— *Daughter RNA*

direction of strand

To write the base sequence of the DNA template, start from the 5′ end. If the DNA template is

5′-C-C-A-G-T-G-T-A-C-C-G-A-3′

then the complementary mRNA strand is

5′-U-C-G-G-U-A-C-A-C-U-G-G-3′

Problem 23.4

Following is a base sequence from a portion of DNA. Write the sequence of bases in the mRNA synthesized using this section of DNA as a template.

5′-T-C-G-G-T-A-C-A-C-T-G-G-3′

23.8 Genetic Code

A. Triplet Nature of the Code

It was clear by the early 1950s that the sequence of bases in DNA molecules constitutes a store of genetic information, and that the sequence of bases directs the synthesis of mRNA and of proteins. However, the statement that the sequence of bases in DNA directs the synthesis of proteins presented the following problem: How can a molecule containing only four variable units (adenine, cytosine, guanine, and thymine) direct the synthesis of molecules containing up to 20 units (the 20 common protein-derived amino acids)? How can an alphabet of 4 letters code for the order of letters in the 20-letter alphabet that occurs in proteins?

An obvious answer is that not one base but a combination of bases codes for each amino acid. If the code consists of nucleotide pairs, there are $4^2 = 16$ combinations, a more extensive code, but still not extensive enough to code for 20 amino acids. If the code consists of nucleotides in groups of three, $4^3 = 64$ combinations are possible, more than enough to code for the primary sequence of a protein. This appears to be a very simple solution to a system that must have taken eons of evolutionary trial and error to develop. Yet proof now exists, from comparison of gene (nucleic acid) and protein (amino acid) sequences, that nature does indeed use this simple 3-letter, or triplet, code to store genetic information. A triplet of nucleotides is called a **codon**.

B. Deciphering the Genetic Code

The next question is, Which of the 64 triplets code for which amino acids? In 1961, Marshall Nirenberg provided a simple experimental approach to the problem, based on the observation that synthetic polynucleotides direct polypeptide synthesis in much the same manner as natural mRNAs do. Nirenberg incubated ribosomes, amino acids, tRNAs, and appropriate protein-synthesizing enzymes. With only these components, there was no polypeptide synthesis. However, when he added synthetic polyuridylic acid (poly U), a polypeptide of high molecular weight was synthesized. What was more important, the synthetic poly-nucleotide contained only phenylalanine. With this discovery, the first element of the **genetic code** was deciphered: the triplet UUU codes for phenylalanine.

Similar experiments were carried out with different synthetic polyribonucleo-tides. It was found, for example, that polyadenylic acid (poly A) leads to the synthesis of polylysine, and that polycytidylic acid (poly C) leads to the synthesis of polyproline.

Codon on mRNA	Amino Acid
UUU	phenylalanine
AAA	lysine
CCC	proline

By 1966, all 64 codons had been deciphered (Table 23.3).

Table 23.3 The genetic code: mRNA codons and the amino acid whose incorporation each codon directs.

UUU	Phe	UCU	Ser	UAU	Tyr	UGU	Cys
UUC	Phe	UCC	Ser	UAC	Tyr	UGC	Cys
UUA	Leu	UCA	Ser	UAA	Stop	UGA	Stop
UUG	Leu	UCG	Ser	UAG	Stop	UGG	Trp
CUU	Leu	CCU	Pro	CAU	His	CGU	Arg
CUC	Leu	CCC	Pro	CAC	His	CGC	Arg
CUA	Leu	CCA	Pro	CAA	Gln	CGA	Arg
CUG	Leu	CCG	Pro	CAG	Gln	CGG	Arg
AUU	Ile	ACU	Thr	AAU	Asn	AGU	Ser
AUC	Ile	ACC	Thr	AAC	Asn	AGC	Ser
AUA	Ile	ACA	Thr	AAA	Lys	AGA	Arg
AUG	Met	ACG	Thr	AAG	Lys	AGG	Arg
GUU	Val	GCU	Ala	GAU	Asp	GGU	Gly
GUC	Val	GCC	Ala	GAC	Asp	GGC	Gly
GUA	Val	GCA	Ala	GAA	Glu	GGA	Gly
GUG	Val	GCG	Ala	GAG	Glu	GGG	Gly

C. Properties of the Genetic Code

Several features of the genetic code are evident from a study of Table 23.3.

1. Only 61 triplets code for amino acids. The remaining three (UAA, UAG, and UGA) are signals for chain terminations; that is, they signal to the protein-synthesizing machinery of the cell that the primary sequence of the protein is complete. The three-chain termination triplets are indicated in Table 23.3 by Stop.

2. The code is degenerate, which means that several amino acids are coded for by more than one triplet. If you count the number of triplets coding for each

amino acid, you will find that only methionine and tryptophan are coded for by just one triplet. Leucine, serine, and arginine are coded for by six triplets, and the remaining amino acids are coded for by two, three, or four triplets.

3. For the 15 amino acids coded for by two, three, or four triplets, the degeneracy is only in the last base of the triplet. For example, glycine is coded for by the triplets GGA, GGG, GGC, and GGU. In the codons for these 15 amino acids, it is only the third letter of the codon that varies.

4. There is no ambiguity in the code, meaning that each triplet codes for one and only one amino acid.

We must ask one last question about the genetic code: Is the code universal—that is, is it the same for all organisms? Every bit of experimental evidence available today from the study of viruses, bacteria, and higher animals, including humans, indicates that the code is universal. Furthermore, that it is the same for all these different organisms means that it has been the same over billions of years of evolution.

Example 23.5

During transcription, a portion of mRNA is synthesized with the following base sequence:

5'-AUG-GUA-CCA-CAU-UUG-UGA-3'

a. Write the base sequence of the DNA from which this portion of mRNA was synthesized.

b. Write the primary structure of the polypeptide coded for by this section of mRNA.

Solution

a. During transcription, mRNA is synthesized from a DNA strand, beginning from the 3' end of the DNA template. The DNA strand must be complementary to the newly synthesized mRNA strand.

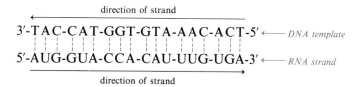

```
                      direction of strand
          ←─────────────────────────────────────
          3'-T A C-C A T-G G T-G T A-A A C-A C T-5' ←── DNA template
             | | | | | | | | | | | | | | | | | | |
          5'-A U G-G U A-C C A-C A U-U U G-U G A-3' ←── RNA strand
          ─────────────────────────────────────→
                      direction of strand
```

b. The sequence of amino acids is shown below the mRNA strand.

5'-AUG-GUA-CCA-CAU-UUG-UGA-3'

met -val -pro -his -leu -stop

The codon UGA codes for termination of a growing polypeptide chain; therefore, the sequence given in this problem codes for a pentapeptide only.

Problem 23.5

The following section of DNA codes for oxytocin, a polypeptide hormone.

mRA synthesis begins here

3'-ACG-ATA-TAA-GTT-TTA-ACG-GGA-GAA-CCA-ACT-5'

a. Write the base sequence of the mRNA synthesized from this section of DNA.

b. Given the sequence of bases in part (a), write the amino acid sequence of oxytocin.

23.9   Translation of Genetic Information: Biosynthesis of Polypeptides

The biosynthesis of polypeptides is usually described in three main processes: initiation of the polypeptide chain, elongation, and termination of the completed chain. These processes, along with the substances required for each, are summarized in Table 23.4.

Table 23.4
Main processes in polypeptide synthesis.

Process	Substances Required
initiation	tRNA carrying *N*-formylmethionine, mRNA, 30S and 50S subunits, GTP, protein-initiating factors
elongation	amino acyl tRNAs, protein elongation factors, GTP
termination	termination codon on mRNA, protein termination factors

A. Initiation of Polypeptide Synthesis

In bacteria, all polypeptide chains are initiated with the amino acid *N*-formylmethionine (fMet). *N*-formylmethionine is bound to a specific tRNA molecule and given the symbol tRNA$_{fMet}$.

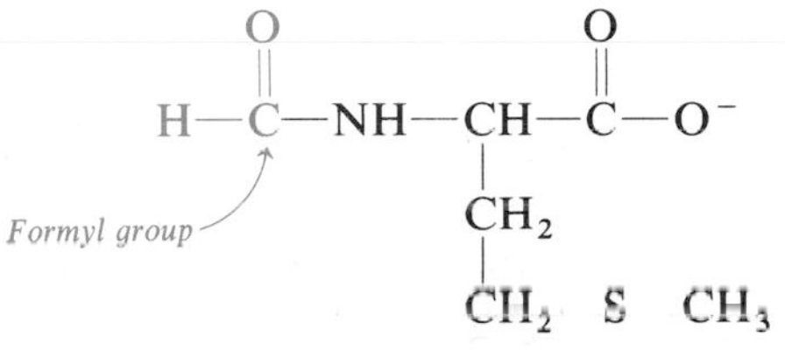

$$H-\overset{\overset{\displaystyle O}{\|}}{C}-NH-CH-\overset{\overset{\displaystyle O}{\|}}{C}-O^{-}$$

Formyl group

CH$_2$

CH$_2$ S   CH$_3$

N-formylmethionine
(fMet)

Many bacterial polypeptides do have *N*-formylmethionine as the *N*-terminal amino acid. However, for most bacterial proteins, *N*-formylmethionine, either by itself or with several other amino acids at the *N*-terminal end of the chain, is cleaved to give the native protein.

The first step in initiation is alignment of mRNA on a 30S ribosomal subunit so that the initiating codon is located at a specific site on the ribosome, called the P site. The initiating codon is most commonly AUG, the one for methionine. Next, tRNA carrying *N*-formylmethionine (fMet) binds to the initiating codon, and this complex, in turn, binds a 50S ribosomal subunit, to give a unit called an initiation complex (Figure 23.12).

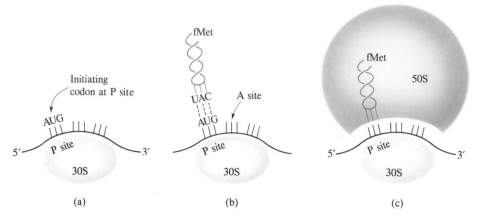

Figure 23.12 Formation of an initiation complex. (a) Alignment of mRNA on a 30S ribosomal subunit so that AUG, the initiating codon, is located at the P site. (b) Binding of tRNA carrying *N*-formylmethionine (fMet) to the initiating codon. (c) Association of the 50S ribosomal subunit to give an initiation complex.

B. Elongation of the Polypeptide Chain

Elongation of a polypeptide chain consists of three steps that are repeated over and over until the entire polypeptide chain is synthesized. In the first step, a "charged" tRNA (one carrying an amino acid esterified at the 3′ end of a tRNA chain) binds to the A site of an initiating complex (Figure 23.13).

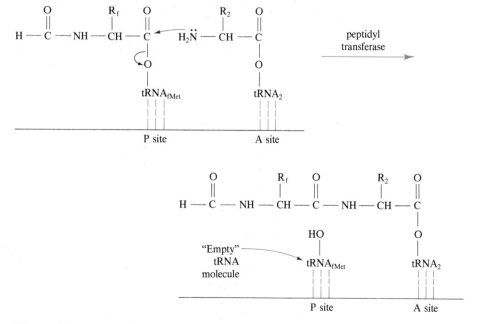

Figure 23.13 Formation of a peptide bond between an amino acid at the P site and another at the A site.

The second step is formation of a peptide bond between the carboxyl group of the tRNA-bound amino acid at the P site and the amino group of the tRNA-bound amino acid at the A site. Peptide bond formation is catalyzed by the enzyme peptidyl transferase. After a new peptide bond is formed, the tRNA attached to the P site is "empty" and the growing polypeptide chain is now attached to the tRNA bound to the A site.

The third step in the elongation cycle involves release of the empty tRNA from the P site and translocation of the growing polypeptide chain from the A site to the P site.

The three steps in the elongation cycle are shown schematically in Figure 23.14 for the synthesis of the tripeptide fMet-arg-phe from fMet-arg.

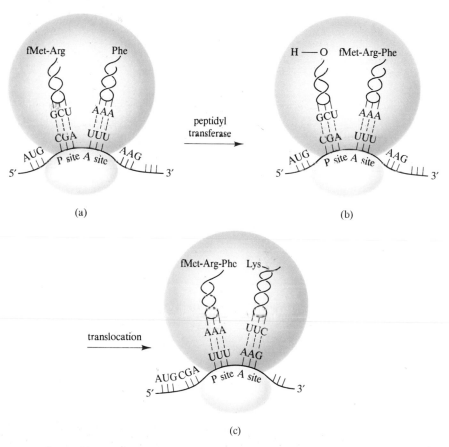

Figure 23.14 Chain elongation. (a) The growing polypeptide chain bound to arg-tRNA is aligned at the P site, and phe-tRNA is aligned at the A site. (b) Peptidyl transferase catalyzes peptide bond formation between the carbonyl group of arginine and the amino group of phenylalanine, and the growing polypeptide chain is transferred to phe-tRNA. (c) As a result of translocation, phe-tRNA is moved to the P site, and the next amino acid in the primary sequence, lys-tRNA, is aligned at the A site.

C. Termination of Polypeptide Synthesis

Polypeptide synthesis continues through the chain elongation cycle until the ribosome complex reaches a stop codon (UAA, UAG, or UGA) on mRNA. There, a specific protein called a termination factor binds to the stop codon and catalyzes hydrolysis of the completed polypeptide chain from tRNA. The "empty" ribosome then dissociates, ready to bind to another strand of mRNA and fMet-tRNA to form another initiation complex.

Figure 23.15 shows several ribosome complexes moving along a single strand of mRNA and illustrates that several identical polypeptide chains can be synthesized simultaneously from a single mRNA molecule. Figure 23.15 also shows that as a polypeptide chain grows, it folds spontaneously into its native three-dimensional conformation.

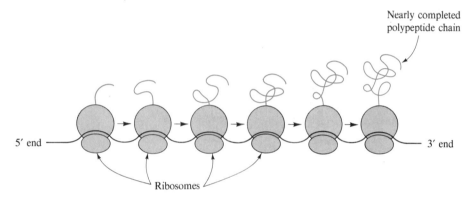

Figure 23.15 Simultaneous elongation of several identical polypeptide chains on a single strand of mRNA. The growing polypeptide chains spontaneously assume their natural three-dimensional conformation.

23.10 Inhibition of Protein Synthesis and the Action of Antibiotics

Several widely used antibiotics, including tetracycline, streptomycin, chloramphenicol, and puromycin (Figure 23.16), act by inhibiting protein synthesis in bacteria at the ribosomal level. Although the general process of protein synthesis described in Section 23.9 operates universally, some details of the processes in bacteria and animals are different. Because of these differences, many antibiotics inhibit protein synthesis in bacteria while having little or no effect on host cells.

The tetracyclines are a family of antibiotics of which all have the tetracyclic ring structure shown in Figure 23.16 but different groups attached to this ring pattern. Tetracyclines, because of their broad activity as antimicrobials, are among the most widely used antibiotics. Tetracyclines prevent binding of charged tRNAs to 30S ribosomal subunits and thereby disrupt protein synthesis.

Chloramphenicol binds specifically to the A site of a 50S ribosomal subunit and thereby prevents charged tRNAs from binding to it. Chloramphenicol is also a broad-spectrum antibiotic. However, in some persons it causes serious,

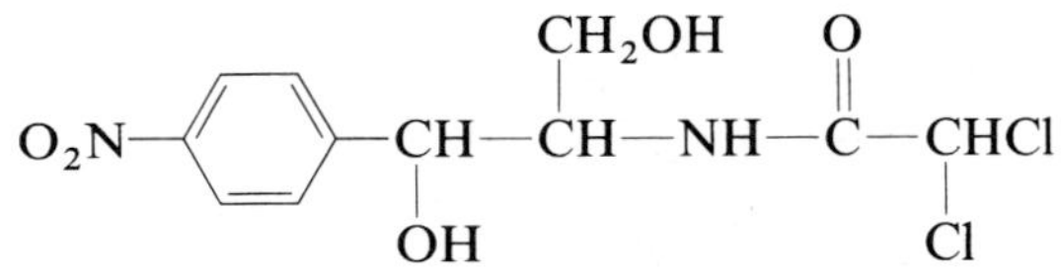

chloramphenicol (binds to the
A site and inhibits binding of
charged tRNAs)

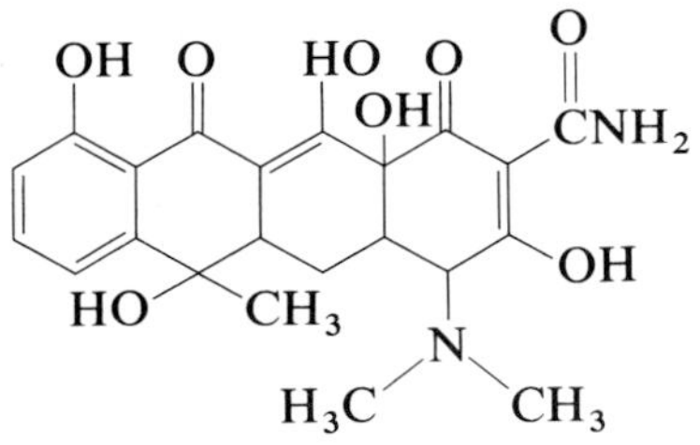

tetracycline (inhibits binding
of charged tRNAs to the 30S
ribosomal subunit)

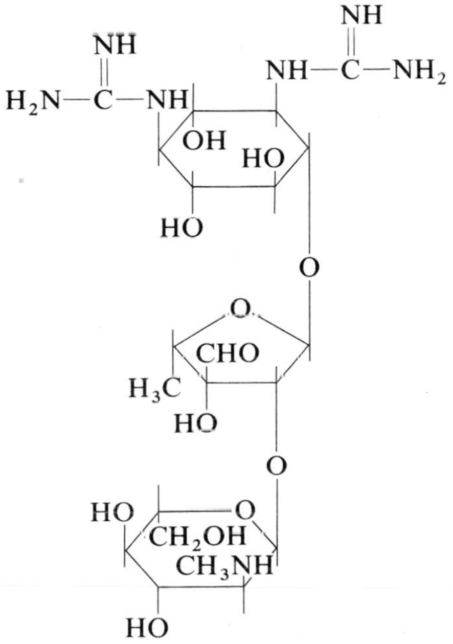

streptomycin (binds to proteins
of the 30S ribosomal subunit and
causes misreading of mRNA code)

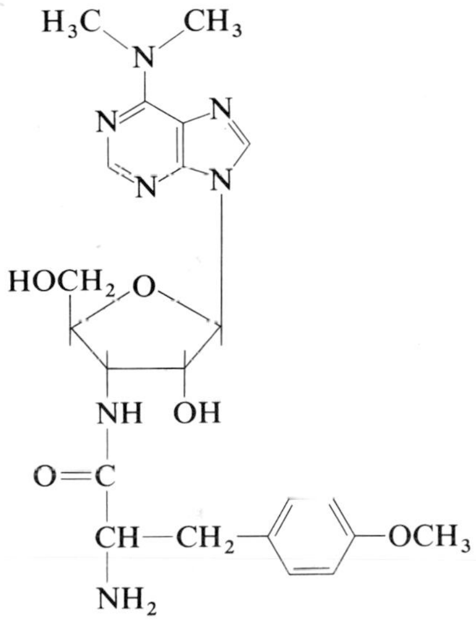

puromycin (is inserted in the
growing polypeptide chain and
causes premature termination
of polypeptide synthesis)

Figure 23.16 Structural formulas for four antibiotics and their effects on protein synthesis in bacteria.

often toxic, side effects. For this reason, its use has been restricted largely to treatment of acute infections for which other antibiotics are ineffective or to cases in which, for medical reasons, other antibiotics cannot be used.

Puromycin is a structural analog of a charged tRNA molecule (one bearing an amino acid esterified to the 3′-hydroxyl of the terminal nucleotide) and binds to the A site during chain elongation. There, the enzyme peptidyl transferase catalyzes formation of a peptide bond between a growing polypeptide chain and the amino group of puromycin; at this point, further chain elongation ceases. Thus, puromycin causes premature termination of polypeptide synthesis.

Streptomycin binds with proteins of the 30S ribosomal subunit and interferes with interactions between mRNA codons and tRNAs. This interference gives rise to errors in reading the mRNA code and causes incorrect amino acids to be inserted into the growing polypeptide chain.

23.11 Mutations

A **mutation** is any change or alteration in the sequence of heterocyclic aromatic amine bases on DNA molecules. At the molecular level, mutation in its simplest form is a change in a single base pair in a DNA molecule. Such mutations are called **point mutations** and can be divided into three groups: (1) base-pair substitutions, (2) base-pair insertions, and (3) base-pair deletions. A point mutation in DNA is transmitted to mRNA during transcription and is ultimately expressed as a protein with an altered primary structure.

A. Base-Pair Substitutions

A point mutation leading to the substitution of one base for another in a section of double-stranded DNA affects only one codon, as illustrated in Figure 23.17.

Substituted base pair

Strand I: 3′-ACG-TTA-GCG-CCA-5′   Strand I: 3′-ACG-TTG-GCG-CCA-5′

Strand II: 5′-TGC-AAT-CGC-GGT-3′   Strand II: 5′-TGC-AAC-CGC-GGT-3′

(a)   (b)

Figure 23.17 A portion of DNA (a) before a base-pair substitution, and (b) after.

Example 23.6

Refer to the DNA sequence in Figure 23.17.

a. Write the sequence of bases in the mRNA transcribed from the 3′ end of strand I of the original DNA. Also write the sequence of amino acids coded for by this section of mRNA. Remember that protein synthesis begins at the 5′ end of mRNA.

b. Do the same for strand I as it is after mutation and compare the two amino acid sequences.

Solution

a. Original DNA: 3′-ACG-TTA-GCG-CCA-5′

mRNA: 5′-UGC-AAU-CGC-GGU-3′

Amino acids: cys   asn   arg   gly

b. Mutant DNA: 3′-ACG-TTG-GCG-CCA-5′

mRNA: 5′-UGC-AAC-CGC-GGU-3′

Amino acids: cys   asn   arg   gly

This point mutation does not cause any change in the amino acid sequence. Both AAU and AAC code for asparagine.

Following is a segment of DNA showing five triplets.

$$3'\text{-GAC-TCC-GAT-CGC-GAT-}5'$$

a. Write the sequence of bases in the mRNA transcribed from the 3' end of this section of DNA; write the amino acid sequence coded for by the complementary mRNA.

b. Assume that a point mutation changes the fifth base from the 3' end of the DNA strand from C to T. Write the mRNA sequence transcribed after this mutation and the amino acid sequence it codes for.

B. Base-Pair Insertion and Deletion

An insertion mutation involves addition of one or more base pairs to a DNA strand. A deletion mutation, on the contrary, involves removal of one or more base pairs. Both types of mutations change the reading frame of all bases after the mutation point; thus, all amino acids in the primary structure following the mutation are affected. Shown in Figure 23.18 is a section of double-stranded DNA and the same section after insertion of one base pair.

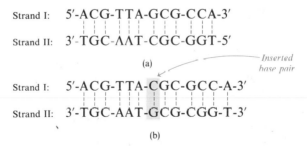

Figure 23.18 Insertion mutation. A section of double-stranded DNA (a) before insertion of a base pair, and (b) after.

Example 23.7

Following is a section of a single strand of DNA showing four triplets, the section of mRNA transcribed from the 3' end of this DNA template, and the amino acid sequence coded for by this section of mRNA. Insert A after TTA in the DNA template, write the sequence of bases in the mRNA produced by transcription from the mutant DNA, and write the amino acid sequence the new mRNA codes for.

☐ *Solution*

Inserting A at the position indicated gives the following DNA template, mRNA, and amino acid sequence. Except for the first amino acid, the entire sequence is modified.

Inserted base

DNA template: 3′-TTA-AGG-TTG-TTG-G-5′

mRNA: 5′-AAU-UCC-AAC-AAC-C-3′

Amino acids: asn   ser   asn   asn

■ **Problem 23.7**

Consider the DNA strand sequence 3′-GAT-GGG-ATG-TCT-5′.

a. Write the base sequence of the complementary strand of mRNA and the amino acid sequence it codes for.
b. Delete T from GAT in the DNA strand and write the new mRNA sequence and the amino acid sequence it codes for.

C. Mutations and Mutagens

Replication of DNA occurs with astounding fidelity! From time to time, however, mutations do occur. Mutations that occur without any external environmental influence are termed spontaneous mutations. From studies with bacteria, it has been estimated that the frequency of spontaneous mutation is one error for every 10^9 to 10^{10} base pairs copied—a remarkably low number, but one important for evolution.

A second and much more prevalent cause for mutations involves environmental factors. Any environmental factor that brings about a mutation is called a **mutagen**. Common mutagens are ultraviolet light, X-rays, and chemicals. Consider, as an example of a chemical mutagen, 5-bromouracil, a compound used to treat certain types of skin cancer. Because its bromine atom is about the same size as the methyl group of thymine and in the same position, 5-bromouracil can substitute for thymine during replication.

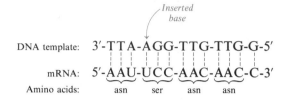

thymine   5-bromouracil   5-bromouracil
                       (keto form)   (enol form)

The mutagenicity of 5-bromouracil arises because the bromine atom makes the enol form of this compound (which base-pairs with guanine) more stable than the keto form (which instead base-pairs with adenine).

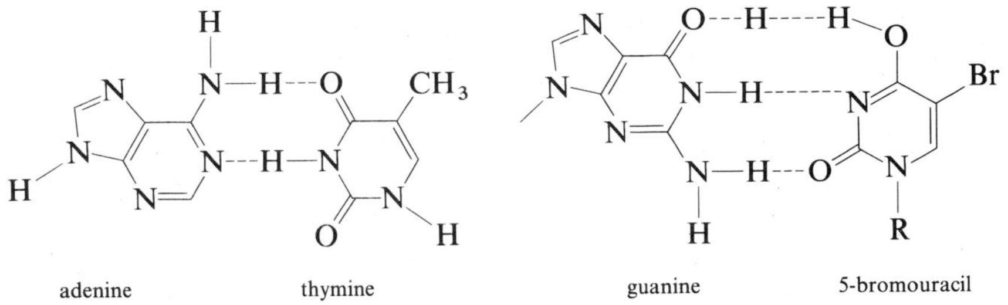

adenine   thymine   guanine   5-bromouracil

Thus, the chemical mutagenicity of 5-bromouracil can be laid to its incorporation in place of thymine and base-pairing with guanine instead of adenine.

Other chemical mutagens react with the heterocyclic aromatic amine bases and alter them chemically in ways that disrupt normal base-pairing. Among the most potent chemical mutagenic agents are nitrous acid and compounds derived from it by reaction with secondary amines. Following are structural formulas for nitrous acid and N,N-dimethylnitrosamine, the product formed by reaction of dimethylamine and nitrous acid:

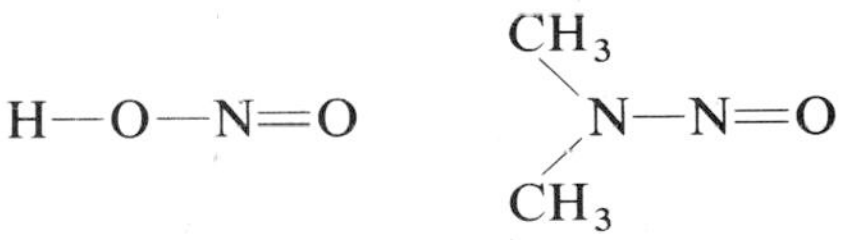

nitrous acid   N,N-dimethylnitrosamine

Nitrous acid and nitrosamines react with heterocyclic aromatic amines of DNA to convert a C—NH$_2$ group to a C=O group, which in turn changes hydrogen bonding and base-pairing. Following is shown the reaction between cytosine and nitrous acid, to give uracil. Cytosine base-pairs with guanine, but uracil base-pairs with adenine.

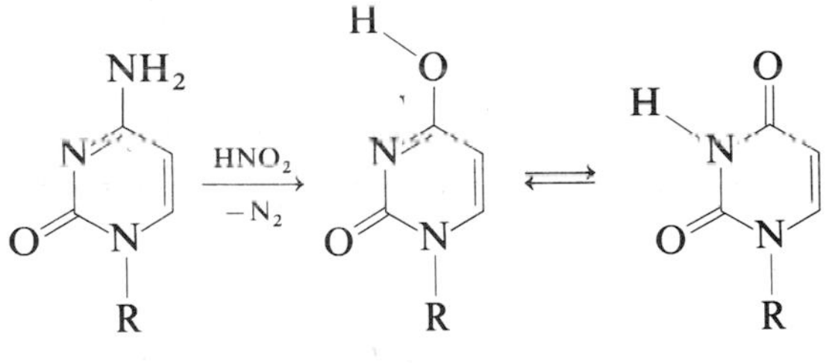

cytosine   uracil   uracil
(base-pairs   (enol form)   (keto form; base-pairs
with guanine)   with adenine)

5-bromouracil and nitrous acid are relatively specific in the mutations they cause. Other mutagens have broader and less specific properties. Fortunately, cells have several mechanisms available to repair altered (damaged) DNA, so the site of altered base-pairing can be repaired quickly and efficiently. Otherwise, an organism would soon be killed by the combination of spontaneous and environmentally caused mutations.

D. The Ames Test and Chemical Carcinogens

In view of the increasing number of chemicals being produced and released into our environment, it is important for a rapid and reliable test for mutagenicity to be available. The need for such a test is made even more critical because most chemical carcinogens (cancer-causing chemicals) are also mutagens. It must be emphasized that there is not a one-to-one correlation between mutagenicity and carcinogenicity; most carcinogens are mutagens, but not all mutagens are carcinogens.

The standard test for mutagenicity, developed by Bruce Ames and known as the **Ames test**, is based on the following observations:

1. A mutant of the bacterium *Salmonella typhimurium* lacks the ability to make histidine. Thus for it, histidine is an essential amino acid and must be supplied in the growth medium. Furthermore, this mutant has been made especially sensitive to mutagens by inactivation of several of its DNA repair mechanisms.
2. Mutagens cause this histidine-dependent strain to revert to its wild form, which can synthesize histidine from the growth medium; for the wild strain, histidine is not an essential amino acid.
3. Several compounds that are carcinogenic in animals are not carcinogenic in bacteria. The explanation for this observation is that these noncarcinogenic chemicals undergo chemical modification in the liver of animals and are there transformed to compounds that are carcinogenic.

In the Ames test, a histidine-requiring strain of *Salmonella typhimurium* is plated on agar with enough histidine in the growth medium to support a few rounds of cell division. Also present in the growth medium is a rat-liver microsomal fraction. A control plate has only growth medium, the histidine-dependent bacteria, and rat-liver microsomal fraction. The experimental plate has these same components plus the chemical to be tested. If no more wild colonies grow on the experimental plate than on the control plate (only equal numbers of spontaneous mutations), then the test chemical is not classified as a mutagen. If, however, significantly more wild colonies grow on the experimental plate, then the test chemical is reported to be a mutagen. By examining the relative growth rates stimulated by various test chemicals, one can establish their relative mutagenicities.

The Ames test has now been used for thousands of compounds, including industrial chemicals, pesticides, food additives, hair dyes, and cosmetics. Surprisingly, many compounds previously thought to be safe have been found to give positive Ames tests and have thus been identified as chemical mutagens.

At present, tests for mutagenicity are relatively simple and done on bacteria, whereas tests for carcinogenicity are complex and time-consuming and require testing with laboratory animals. Therefore the Ames test for mutagenicity has become a preliminary screening for potential carcinogenicity. It must be emphasized again that a positive Ames test does not demonstrate that the mutagen is also a carcinogen. However, the correlation is high between a positive Ames test and carcinogenicity.

Key Terms and Concepts

Ames test (23.11D)
base composition of DNA (23.4B)
codon (23.8A)
complementarity (23.4D)
daughter strand (23.5)
deoxyribonucleic acids (DNA) (23.1)
double helix (23.4D)
genetic code (23.8B)
messenger RNA (23.6C)
mutagen (23.11C)
mutation (23.11)
nicks (23.5C)
nucleoside (23.2)

nucleotide (23.3)
Okazaki fragment (23.5C)
point mutation (23.11)
replication (23.5)
replication fork (23.5A)
ribonucleic acids (RNAs) (23.6)
ribosomal RNAs (23.6A)
ribosome (23.6A)
semiconservative replication (23.5)
transcription (23.7)
transfer RNA (23.6B)
translation (23.9)

Problems

*Nucleosides
and
nucleotides
(Sections 23.2
and 23.3)*

23.8   Examine the structure of purine. Would this molecule be planar or puckered? Would it exist as several interconvertible conformations (like cyclohexane) or be rigid and inflexible? Explain the basis for your answer.

23.9   An important drug in the chemotherapy of leukemia is 6-mercaptopurine, a sulfur analog of adenine. Draw a structural formula for 6-mercaptopurine.

23.10 Explain the difference in structure between a nucleoside and a nucleotide.

23.11 Name and draw structural formulas for the following. In each label the *N*-glycoside bond:
   a. a nucleoside composed of beta-D-ribose and adenine.
   b. a nucleoside composed of beta-D-ribose and uracil.
   c. a nucleoside composed of beta-2-deoxy-D-ribose and cytosine.

23.12 Name and draw structural formulas for the following. Label all *N*-glycoside bonds, ester bonds, and anhydride bonds.
   a. ADP   **b.** dGMP   **c.** GTP

23.13 Calculate what the net charge on the following would be at pH 7.4.
   a. ATP   **b.** 2′-deoxyadenosine   **c.** GMP

23.14 Cyclic-AMP (adenosine-3′,5′-cyclic monophosphate), first isolated in 1959, is involved in many diverse biological processes as a regulator of metabolic and physiological activity. In it, a single phosphate group is esterified with both the 3′- and 5′ hydroxyls of adenosine. Draw the structural formula for this substance.

23.15 Following are sequences for several polynucleotides. Write structural formulas for each. Calculate what the net charge on each would be at pH 7.4.

   a. dApdGpdA   **b.** pppdCpdT   **c.** pdGpdCpdCpdTpdA

23.16 Compare the alpha-helix found in proteins with the double helix of DNA in regard to the following points.

   a. The units that repeat in the backbone of the chain.

   b. The projection in space of the backbone substituents (R groups in the case of amino acids; purine and pyrimidine bases in the case of DNA) relative to the axis of the helix.

23.17 List the postulates of the Watson-Crick model of DNA structure. This model is based on certain experimental observations of base composition and molecular dimensions. Describe these observations and show how the model accounts for each.

23.18 Explain the role of hydrophobic interaction in stabilizing (a) soap micelles; (b) lipid bilayers; (c) double-stranded DNA.

23.19 What type of bond or interaction holds monomers together in (a) proteins? (b) nucleic acids? (c) polysaccharides?

23.20 In terms of hydrogen bonding, which is more stable, an A—T base pair or a G—C base pair?

23.21 At high temperatures, nucleic acids become denatured; that is, they unwind into disordered single strands. Account for the fact that, the higher the content of G—C base pairs, the higher the temperature required to denature a given molecule of DNA.

23.22 Regarding the DNA triplet ATC, is its complement TAG or GAT? Explain.

23.23 What is the meaning of the adjective *semiconservative* in the term semi-conservative replication?

23.24 From what direction is a DNA strand read during formation of its complement?

23.25 What is an Okazaki fragment? Explain how isolation and identification of Okazaki fragments provide evidence that the synthesis of DNA is not a continuous process.

23.26 Compare DNA and RNA on the following points:

   a. monosaccharide units   **b.** principal purine and pyrimidine bases

   c. primary structure   **d.** location in the cell

   e. function in the cell

23.27 Compare ribosomal RNA, messenger RNA, and transfer RNA on (a) molecular weight; (b) function in protein synthesis.

23.28 Draw a diagram of an mRNA-ribosome initiation complex and label the following:

   a. 30S subunit   **b.** 50S subunit   **c.** 5′ and 3′ ends of mRNA

23.29 For the DNA strand sequence

5′-ACC-GTT-GCC-AAT-G-3′

(a) write the sequence of its DNA complement, and (b) of its mRNA complement.

The genetic code (Section 23.8)

23.30 Consider the mRNA sequence 5'-AGG-UCC-CAG-3'.
  a. What tripeptide is synthesized if the code is read from the 5' end to the 3' end?
  b. What tripeptide is synthesized if the code is read from the 3' end to the 5' end?
  c. Calculate what the net charge on each tripeptide would be at pH 7.4.
  d. Which way is the code read in the cell and which tripeptide is synthesized?

23.31 What peptide sequences are coded for by the following mRNA sequences? (Each is written in the 5' ⟶ 3' direction.)
  a. GCU-GAA-UGG   b. UCA-GCA-AUC
  c. GUC-GAG-GUG   d. GCU-UCU-UAA

23.32 Complete the table.

DNA	DNA Complement	mRNA Complement	Amino Acid Coded for
TGC	———	———	———
CAG	———	———	———
———	ACG	———	———
———	GTA	———	———
———	———	GUC	———
———	———	UGC	———
———	———	CAC	———

23.33 The alpha-chain of human hemoglobin has 141 amino acids in a single polypeptide chain.
  a. Calculate the minimum number of bases on DNA necessary to code for the alpha-chain. Include in your calculation the bases necessary for specifying termination of polypeptide synthesis.
  b. Calculate the length in centimeters of DNA containing this number of bases.

Translation of genetic information: biosynthesis of polypeptides (Section 23.9)

23.34 a. Draw the structural formula of *N*-formylmethionine.
  b. Draw structural formulas for the products of hydrolysis of the amide bond in *N*-formylmethionine. Show each product as it would be ionized at pH 7.0.

23.35 Each of the following reactions involves ammonolysis of an ester. Draw the structural formula of the amide produced in each reaction.

a. 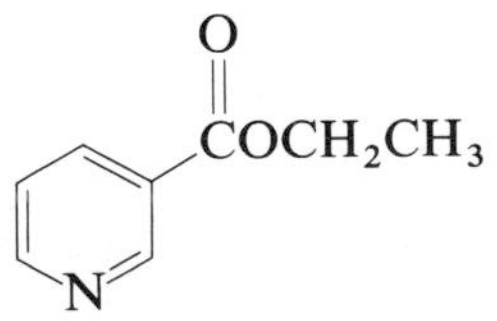 [pyridine ring]—$COCH_2CH_3$ + NH_3 ⟶ nicotinamide + CH_3CH_2OH

$$\text{b. } CH_3CH_2O\overset{\overset{\displaystyle O}{\|}}{C}OCH_2CH_3 + 2NH_3 \longrightarrow \text{urea} + 2CH_3CH_2OH$$

$$\text{c. } H_2C\overset{\overset{\displaystyle \overset{O}{\|}}{COCH_2CH_3}}{\underset{\underset{\displaystyle O}{\|}}{COCH_2CH_3}} + H_2N\overset{\overset{\displaystyle O}{\|}}{C}NH_2 \longrightarrow \text{barbituric acid} + 2CH_3CH_2OH$$

23.36   Show that the reaction catalyzed by peptidyl transferase is an example of ammonolysis of an ester.

23.37   Are polypeptide chains synthesized from the *N*-terminal amino acid toward the C-terminal amino acid or vice versa?

Mutations (Sections 23.11)

23.38   Following in (a) is an mRNA sequence written from the 5′ end to the 3′ end. Below it are three substitution mutations, one insertion mutation, and one deletion mutation. For what polypeptide sequence does the normal mRNA code, and what is the effect of each mutation on the resulting polypeptide?
  a. Normal: 5′-UCC-CAG-GCU-UAC-AAA-GUA-3′
  b. Substitution of A for C: 5′-UCC-AAG-GCU-UAC-AAA-GUA-3′
  c. Substitution of A for C: 5′-UCC-CAG-GCU-UAA-AAA-GUA-3′
  d. Substitution of A for C: 5′-UCA-CAG-GCU-UAC-AAA-GUA-3′
  e. Insertion of A: 5′-UCC-CAG-GCU-AUA-CAA-AGU-A-3′
  f. Deletion of A: 5′-UCC-CAG-GCU-UCA-AAG-UA-3′

23.39   In HbS, the abnormal human hemoglobin found in individuals with sickle-cell anemia, glutamic acid at position 6 of the beta chain, is replaced by valine.
  a. List the two codons for glutamic acid and the four codons for valine.
  b. Show that a glutamic acid codon can be converted to a valine codon by a single substitution mutation.

24 Flow of Energy in the Biological World

All living organisms need a constant supply of energy to support maintenance of cell structure and growth; in this sense, energy is the key to life itself. We will learn how cells extract energy from foodstuffs and how this energy is used in chemical, mechanical, and osmotic work.

24.1 Metabolism and Metabolic Pathways

Metabolism is defined as the sum of all chemical reactions an organism uses to grow, feed, move, excrete wastes, and communicate. Metabolism has two main components, catabolism and anabolism. **Catabolism** includes all reactions leading to the breakdown of biomolecules. **Anabolism** includes all reactions leading to the synthesis of biomolecules. In general, catabolism produces energy and anabolism consumes energy.

All reactions of a cell or organism are organized into orderly, carefully regulated sequences known as **metabolic pathways**. Each metabolic pathway consists of a series of consecutive steps that convert a starting material to an end product. The range of metabolic pathways in even a one-celled organism such as the bacterium *E. coli* is enormous. To support growth, a culture medium for *E. coli* needs to contain only glucose as a source of carbon atoms and energy, inorganic salts as sources of nitrogen and phosphorus, and a few other simple substances. Growth of *E. coli* under these conditions means that each cell has the metabolic pathways needed to extract energy from the culture medium and use it to synthesize all the carbohydrates, lipids, proteins, enzymes, coenzymes, nucleic acids, and other biomolecules necessary for maintenance and development. The ability of *E. coli* to grow under these conditions is truly remarkable, especially when you consider the complexity of some of the biomolecules found in living systems.

Fortunately for those who study the biochemistry of living systems, many similarities are found among the chief metabolic pathways in humans, *E. coli*, and for that matter, most other organisms. The number of individual reactions is large, but the number of different kinds of reactions is small. For example, the basic features of how different cells extract energy from foodstuffs and use it to synthesize other biomolecules, and even the means of self-regulation, are surprisingly similar. Because of these similarities, scientists can study the metabolism of simple organisms and then use these results to help understand the corresponding metabolic pathways in more complex organisms, including humans. We shall concentrate on human biochemistry, but much of what we say about human metabolism can be applied equally well to the metabolism of most other organisms.

24.2 Flow of Energy in the Biosphere

The uniqueness of living systems rests in their ability to capture energy from the environment, to store it, at least temporarily, and to use it to power the vast number of vital biological processes. The energy for all biological processes comes ultimately from the sun, whose enormous energy is derived from the fusion of hydrogen atoms, converting them to helium:

$$2\text{H}\cdot \xrightarrow{\text{nuclear fusion}} \text{He}{:} + \text{energy}$$

A portion of this energy streams toward us as sunlight and is absorbed by chlorophyll pigments in plants. There, this energy drives **photosynthesis**, the im-

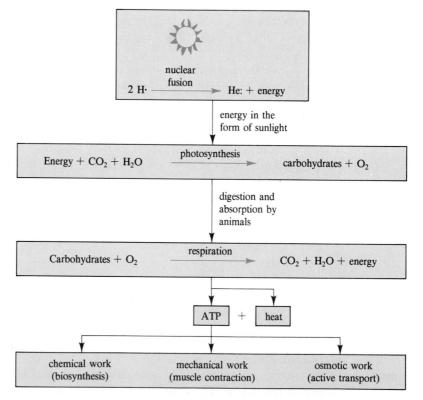

Figure 24.1 The flow of energy in the biosphere. (Adapted from David S. Page, *Principles of Biological Chemistry*, 2d ed. Boston: Willard Grant Press, 1981.)

mediate product of which is glucose:

$$6CO_2 + 6H_2O + energy \xrightarrow{\text{photosynthesis}} C_6H_{12}O_6 + 6O_2$$
$$\text{glucose}$$

In secondary steps, plants convert glucose to other carbohydrates, triglycerides, and proteins, all chemical storage forms of energy. Animals get these energy-rich molecules either directly or indirectly from plants.

During **respiration**, both plants and animals oxidize these energy-rich compounds to carbon dioxide and water. Respiration is accompanied by the release of energy:

$$\begin{array}{c}\text{glucose and other} \\ \text{storage forms of} \\ \text{energy}\end{array} + O_2 \xrightarrow{\text{respiration}} CO_2 + H_2O + energy$$

A portion of the energy derived from respiration is transformed to adenosine triphosphate (ATP), a carrier of energy that can be used directly in performing biological work. The remainder of the energy of respiration is liberated as heat. Steps in the flow of energy in the biosphere are summarized in Figure 24.1.

24.3 ATP: The Central Carrier of Energy

A. Concept of Free Energy

Energy changes for reactions taking place in biological systems are commonly reported as changes in **free energy** ΔG^0. A change in free energy measures the maximum work that can be obtained from a given reaction or process. The symbol ΔG^0 stands for the change in free energy per mole of reactant when the reaction is carried out at standard temperature and 1 atm pressure.

Reactions that result in a decrease in free energy are said to be **exergonic**. Exergonic reactions include the oxidation of carbohydrates, fats, and proteins. The following equation shows that oxidation of glucose to carbon dioxide and water results in a decrease in free energy of 686,000 cal/mol of glucose:

$$C_6H_{12}O_6 + 6O_2 \longrightarrow 6CO_2 + 6H_2O \qquad \Delta G^0 = -686,000 \text{ cal/mol}$$
$$\text{glucose}$$

Because exergonic reactions bring about a decrease in free energy, they are said to be spontaneous, which means that they proceed to the right as written; at equilibrium, the concentration of products is greater than concentration of reactants. The more negative the value of ΔG^0, the greater the concentration of products relative to reactants.

It is important to remember that although a negative value of ΔG^0 means that a reaction is spontaneous as written, it gives us no indication of the rate at which the reaction occurs. For example, ΔG^0 is negative for conversion of glucose and oxygen to carbon dioxide and water; this tells us that the reaction is spontaneous as written. Yet we know that in the absence of heat or appropriate catalysts, no reaction occurs.

Reactions that occur with an increase in free energy are said to be **endergonic**, which means that the reaction proceeds to the left as written; at equilibrium, the concentration of reactants is greater than concentration of products. The more positive the value of ΔG^0, the greater the concentration of reactants relative to products. The following equation shows that photosynthesis occurs with an increase in free energy.

$$6CO_2 + 6H_2O \longrightarrow \underset{\text{glucose}}{C_6H_{12}O_6} + 6O_2 \qquad \Delta G^0 = +686,000 \text{ cal/mol}$$

Because endergonic reactions occur with an increase in free energy, they are not spontaneous; at equilibrium very little product is formed unless energy is supplied to drive the reaction to the right. As shown in Figure 24.1, the energy to drive photosynthesis is supplied by sunlight. The relations between the sign of ΔG^0 and spontaneity are summarized in Figure 24.2.

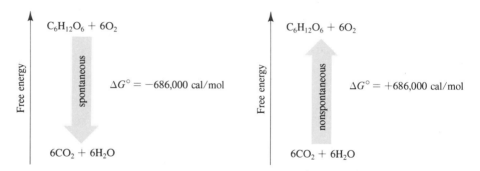

Figure 24.2 Conversion of glucose and oxygen to carbon dioxide and water occurs with a decrease in free energy; it is a spontaneous reaction. Conversion of carbon dioxide and water to glucose and oxygen occurs with an increase in free energy; it is not a spontaneous reaction.

B. ATP, a High-Energy Compound

The central role of **adenosine triphosphate (ATP)** in the transfer of energy in the biological world depends on the triphosphate end of the molecule. The structure of ATP is shown in Figure 24.3. At pH 7.4, all protons of the triphosphate group are ionized, giving ATP a charge of -4. In cells, ATP is most often present with Mg^{2+} in a 1:1 complex with a charge of -2. Figure 24.4 shows abbreviated structural formulas of ATP, adenosine diphosphate (ADP), and adenosine monophosphate (AMP). In these formulas, only phosphate ester and anhydride bonds are shown.

The key to understanding how ATP affects the flow of energy in the biological world is knowing that it can transfer a phosphoryl group, $-PO_3^{2-}$, to another molecule. For example, during hydrolysis of ATP in water, a phosphoryl group is transferred from ATP to water. The products of this hydrolysis are ADP and phosphate ion.

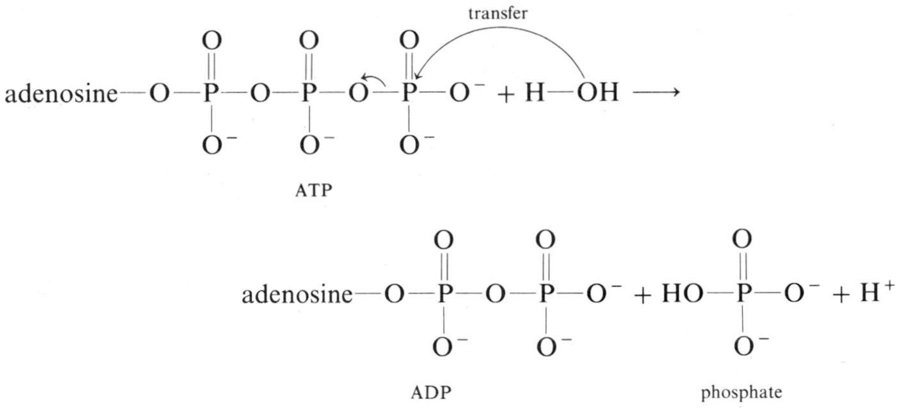

Transfer of a phosphoryl group from ATP to water is accompanied by a decrease in free energy, as shown in the following equation:

$$ATP^{4-} + HOH \qquad ADP^{3-} + HPO_4^{2-} + H^+ \qquad \Delta G^0 = -7{,}300 \text{ cal/mol}$$

Adenosine triphosphate is but one of the many phosphate-containing compounds common in biological systems. Several of these, along with the **free**

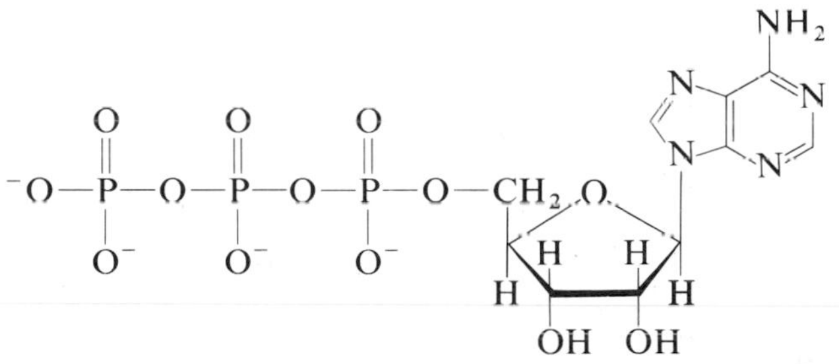

Figure 24.3 The structure of adenosine triphosphate (ATP).

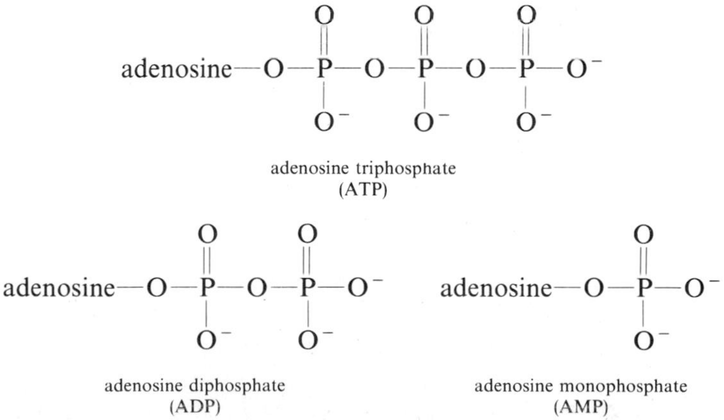

Figure 24.4 Abbreviated structural formulas for adenosine triphosphate (ATP), adenosine diphosphate (ADP), and adenosine monophosphate (AMP).

energy of hydrolysis of each, are listed in Table 24.1. Notice that ATP has a free energy of hydrolysis larger than that of simple phosphate esters such as glucose 6-phosphate. Because of the size of its free energy of hydrolysis, ATP is called a high-energy compound. **High-energy compounds** have free energies of hydrolysis of $-7,000$ cal/mol or greater; **low-energy compounds** have free energies of hydrolysis of less than $-7,000$ cal/mol. As you can see from Table 24.1, the line between high-energy and low-energy compounds is not sharp.

Table 24.1
Free energy of hydrolysis of some phosphate-containing compounds present in biological systems.

Compound	Products of Hydrolysis	ΔG^0 (cal/mol)
phosphoenolpyruvate + $H_2O \longrightarrow$ pyruvate + phosphate		$-14,800$
1,3-diphosphoglycerate + $H_2O \longrightarrow$ 3-phosphoglycerate + phosphate		$-11,800$
ATP + $H_2O \longrightarrow$ ADP + phosphate		$-7,300$
glucose 1-phosphate + $H_2O \longrightarrow$ glucose + phosphate		$-5,000$
fructose 6-phosphate + $H_2O \longrightarrow$ fructose + phosphate		$-3,800$
glucose 6-phosphate + $H_2O \longrightarrow$ glucose + phosphate		$-3,300$

Why does the hydrolysis of the phosphate anhydride bond of ATP have a ΔG^0 so much larger than that of the hydrolysis of a phosphate ester bond, say the bond in glucose 6-phosphate? The reason lies in the structure of ATP itself. At the pH of cells, the phosphate groups of ATP are fully ionized, giving ATP a net charge of -4. These negative charges are very close to each other and create an electrostatic strain within the molecule. Hydrolysis of the terminal phosphate anhydride gives inorganic phosphate and ADP, an ion with a net charge of -3. Thus, hydrolysis of ATP relieves some electrostatic strain. Be-

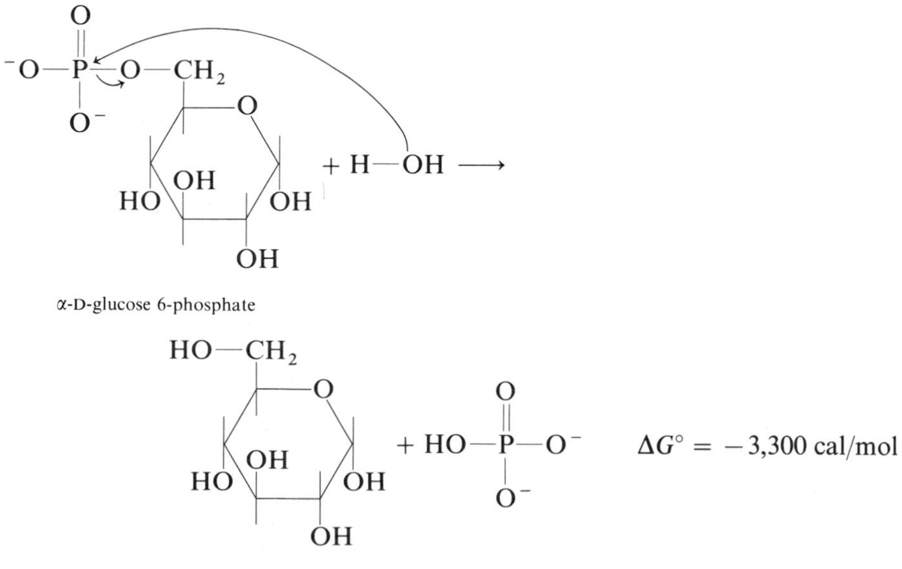

α-D-glucose 6-phosphate

$\Delta G^\circ = -3,300$ cal/mol

α-D-glucose   phosphate

cause there is no such electrostatic strain in phosphate esters such as glucose 6-phosphate or glucose 1-phosphate, their hydrolysis releases comparatively less energy.

C. Other High-Energy Compounds

Two other high-energy compounds are also listed in Table 24.1. Both are intermediates in glycolysis, the metabolic pathway by which glucose is converted to pyruvate. Hydrolysis of phosphoenolpyruvate, the final step in glycolysis, gives the enol form of pyruvate and inorganic phosphate. (For a review of keto and enol forms, see Section 15.7B.)

phosphoenolpyruvate — pyruvate (enol form)

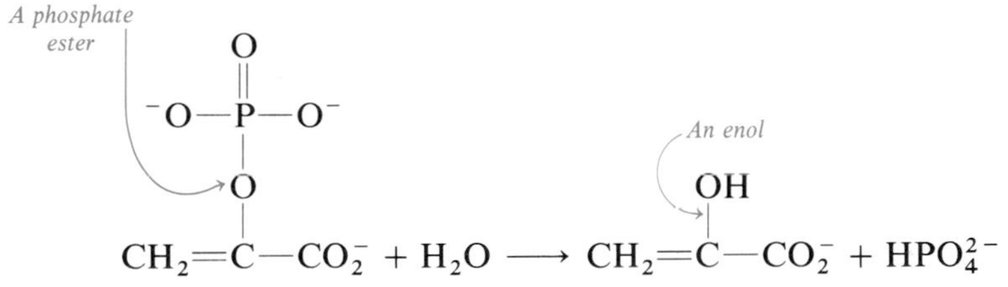

The equilibrium between the keto and enol forms of pyruvate lies almost completely on the side of the keto form; accordingly, conversion to the keto form is accompanied by a large decrease in free energy.

pyruvate (enol form) — pyruvate (keto form)

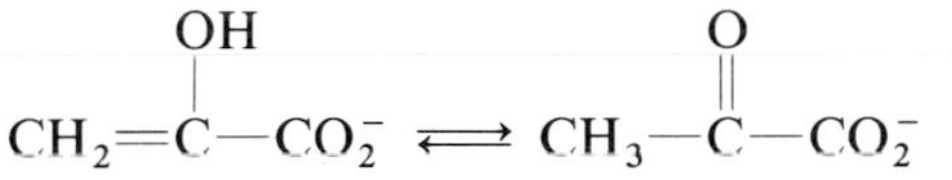

The other high-energy compound listed in Table 24.1 is 1,3-diphosphoglycerate.

1,3-diphosphoglycerate — 3-phosphoglycerate

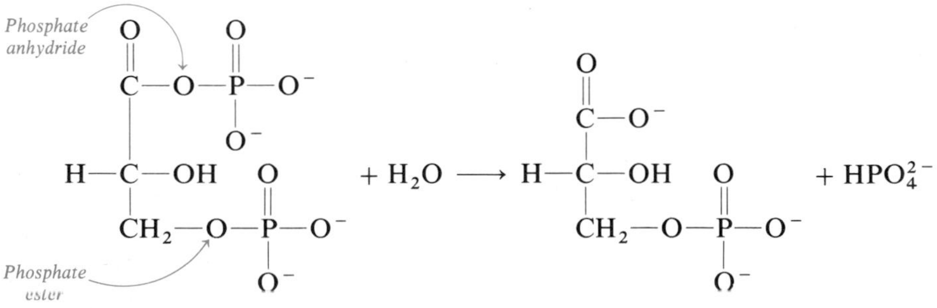

1,3-diphosphoglycerate contains a phosphate ester and a phosphate anhydride. Hydrolysis of the phosphate anhydride yields phosphate, 3-phosphoglycerate, and energy.

D. Central Role of ATP in Cellular Energetics

We have examined reactions involving transfer of a phosphoryl group to water. The same phosphate-containing compounds can, at least in principle, transfer a phosphoryl group to compounds of the type H—OR. Following is an equation for the transfer of a phosphoryl group from phosphoenolpyruvate to α-D-glucose to form pyruvate and α-D-glucose 6-phosphate. The flow of electrons in this reaction is shown by curved arrows.

phosphoenol-   α-D-glucose   pyruvate   α-D-glucose 6-phosphate
pyruvate

The change in free energy for this reaction can be calculated by (1) dividing the reaction into two separate equations for which changes in free energy are known; and (2) adding the separate equations and the free energy change for each.

$$\text{phosphoenolpyruvate} + \text{H—OH} \longrightarrow \text{pyruvate} + \text{HPO}_4^{2-} \qquad \Delta G^0 = -14{,}800 \text{ cal/mol}$$
$$\text{glucose} + \text{HPO}_4^{2-} \longrightarrow \text{glucose 6-phosphate} + \text{H—OH} \qquad \Delta G^0 = +\ 3{,}300 \text{ cal/mol}$$
$$\text{glucose} + \text{phosphoenol-} \longrightarrow \text{pyruvate} + \text{glucose 6-} \qquad \Delta G^0 = -11{,}500 \text{ cal/mol}$$
$$\qquad\qquad\text{pyruvate} \qquad\qquad\qquad\qquad \text{phosphate}$$

This calculation shows that transfer of a phosphoryl group from pyruvate to glucose occurs with a large decrease in free energy; it is a spontaneous reaction and proceeds to the right as written. Yet, although it is spontaneous, direct transfer of a phosphoryl group from phosphoenolpyruvate to glucose has not been observed in living systems. Rather, ATP is a common intermediate, or "medium of exchange," that links this and other high-energy phosphate donors to phosphate acceptors.

$$\text{phosphoenolpyruvate} + \text{ADP} \longrightarrow \text{pyruvate} + \text{ATP}$$
$$\text{glucose} + \text{ATP} \longrightarrow \text{glucose 6-phosphate} + \text{ADP}$$

So that you can appreciate how this means of phosphate transfer is valuable to cells, consider that virtually all reactions in living systems are enzyme-catalyzed.

Figure 24.5(a) shows the number of enzymes necessary to catalyze the transfer of phosphate from phosphoenolpyruvate (PEP), or 1,3-diphosphoglycerate (1,3-DPG), or ATP to five different phosphate acceptors. For the reactions in Figure 24.5(a), fifteen different enzymes are required. If ATP is used as a collector and a common donor of phosphate groups to other low-energy acceptors, only seven different enzymes are required [Figure 24.5(b)].

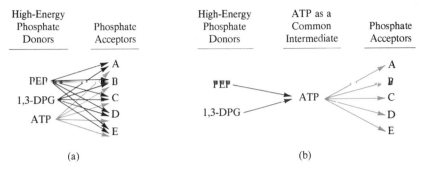

(a)   (b)

Figure 24.5 An illustration of the efficiency of using ATP as a common phosphate acceptor/donor. In (a), 15 different enzymes are required while in (b) only 7 are required.

24.4 Stages in Oxidation of Foodstuffs and Generation of ATP

The basic strategy used by all cells to extract energy from their surroundings is to oxidize foodstuffs and use a portion of the free energy released to convert ADP and HPO_4^{2-} to ATP. Oxidation of foodstuffs and the generation of ATP is accomplished in four stages.

A. Stage 1: Digestion and Absorption of Fuel Molecules

Stage 1, digestion of foods, involves hydrolysis of carbohydrates to monosaccharides, proteins to amino acids, and fats and oils to fatty acids and glycerol (Figure 24.6):

$$\text{polysaccharides} + H_2O \xrightarrow{\text{hydrolysis}} \text{monosaccharides}$$

$$\text{fats and oils} + H_2O \xrightarrow{\text{hydrolysis}} \text{fatty acids} + \text{glycerol}$$

$$\text{proteins} + H_2O \xrightarrow{\text{hydrolysis}} \text{amino acids}$$

Figure 24.6 Stage 1 in the oxidation of foodstuffs and generation of ATP: hydrolysis of complex fuel molecules to monosaccharides, fatty acids plus glycerol, and amino acids.

As a result of hydrolysis, the hundreds of thousands of different proteins, fats, oils, and carbohydrates ingested in the diet are converted to fewer than 30 lower-molecular-weight compounds, the most common of which are listed in Table 24.2.

Table 24.2
The 27 most common low-molecular-weight molecules derived from hydrolysis of carbohydrates, fats and oils, and proteins.

From Carbohydrates	From Fats and Oils	From Proteins
D-glucose	palmitic acid	20 amino acids
D-fructose	stearic acid	
D-galactose	oleic acid	
	glycerol	

B. Stage 2: Degradation of Fuel Molecules to Acetyl CoA

In stage 2 (Figure 24.7), the carbon skeletons of glucose, fructose, and galactose along with those of fatty acids, glycerol and several amino acids are converted to acetate in the form of a thioester named **acetyl coenzyme A**, or more commonly, acetyl CoA. The carbon skeletons of other amino acids are degraded to different small molecules, but eventually all go through the reactions of stage 3.

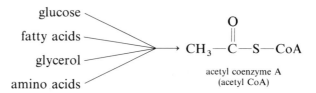

Figure 24.7 Stage 2 of the oxidation of foodstuffs and generation of ATP. The carbon skeletons of glucose, fatty acids, glycerol, and certain amino acids are degraded to the acetyl group of acetyl CoA.

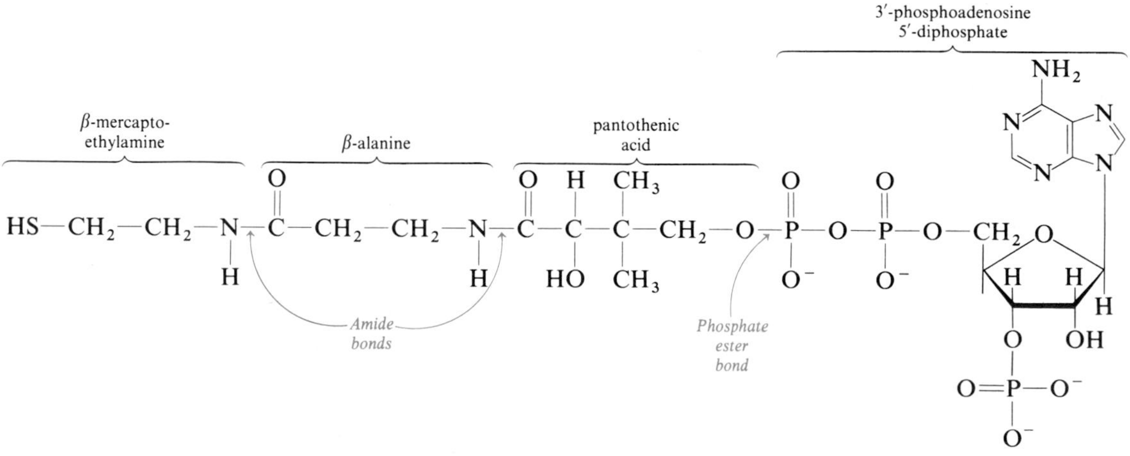

Figure 24.8 Coenzyme A. The acetylated form of this coenzyme, designated acetyl coenzyme A, or acetyl CoA, is the thioester of acetic acid and the terminal sulfhydryl group. Pantothenic acid is one of the vitamins of the B group.

Coenzyme A (Figure 24.8) is derived from four subunits. On the left is a two-carbon unit derived from beta-mercaptoethylamine, which is joined by an amide bond to the carboxyl group of beta-alanine. The amino group of beta-alanine is, in turn, joined by another amide bond to the carboxyl group of pantothenic acid, a vitamin of the B group (Section 22.2C). Finally, the —OH group of pantothenic acid is joined by an ester bond to the terminal phosphate of ADP. A key feature in the structure of coenzyme A is the presence of the terminal sulfhydryl group (—SH). Acetyl CoA is a thioester derived from the carboxyl group of acetic acid and the thiol group of coenzyme A.

C. Stage 3: The Krebs, or Tricarboxylic Acid, Cycle

Stage 3 consists of a series of reactions known alternatively as the **tricarboxylic acid (TCA) cycle**, the citric acid cycle, or the **Krebs cycle** (Figure 24.9). An important function of the tricarboxylic acid cycle is oxidation of the two-carbon acetyl group of acetyl CoA to two molecules of carbon dioxide.

$$\underset{\text{acetyl coenzyme A}}{CH_3-\overset{\displaystyle O}{\overset{\|}{C}}-S-CoA} \xrightarrow[\text{acid cycle}]{\text{tricarboxylic}} 2CO_2 + \underset{\text{coenzyme A}}{CoA-SH}$$

Figure 24.9 Stage 3 in the oxidation of foodstuffs and generation of ATP: the tricarboxylic acid cycle. The carbon atoms derived from stages 1 and 2 are oxidized to carbon dioxide.

The biological oxidizing agents for stage 3 are nicotinamide adenine dinucleotide (NAD^+) and flavin adenine dinucleotide (FAD). The former substance, NAD^+ (Figure 24.10), is the principal acceptor of electrons in the oxidation of fuel molecules.

The reactive group of NAD^+ is a pyridine ring, which accepts two electrons and one proton to form the reduced coenzyme NADH:

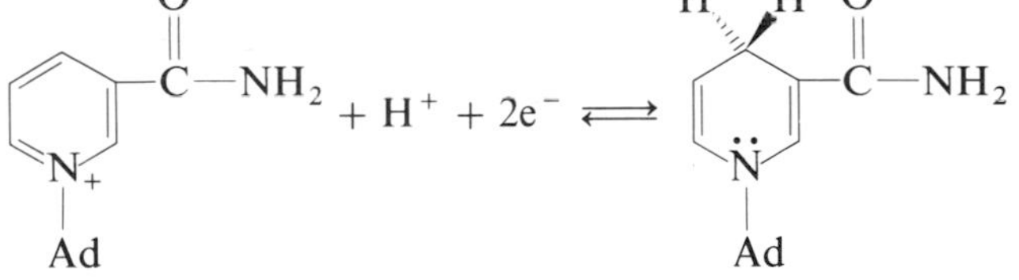

NAD^+ NADH

The second electron acceptor in the oxidation of fuel molecules is FAD (Figure 24.11). This molecule is composed of several subunits: a three-ring flavin group, a five-carbon group derived from D-ribose, and adenosine diphosphate.

The reactive group in FAD is a flavin group, which accepts two electrons and two protons to form the reduced coenzyme $FADH_2$.

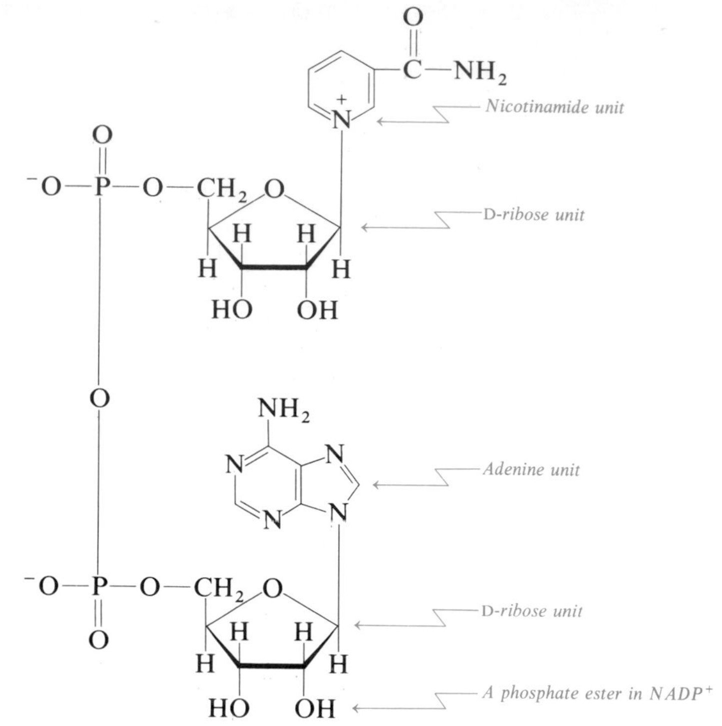

Figure 24.10 Nicotinamide adenine dinucleotide, NAD$^+$. Nicotinamide is one of the water-soluble vitamins. In nicotinamide adenine dinucleotide phosphate, NADP$^+$, the 2′ hydroxyl of D-ribose is esterified with phosphoric acid.

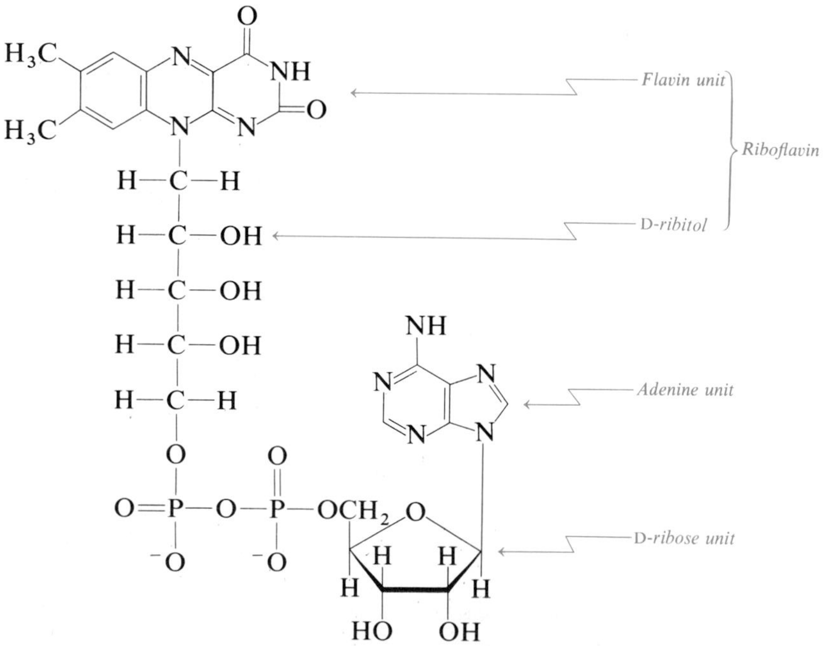

Figure 24.11 Flavin adenine dinucleotide, FAD. Riboflavin is one of the B vitamins.

$$+ 2H^+ + 2e^- \rightleftharpoons$$

FAD   FADH$_2$

All reactions of the tricarboxylic acid cycle (stage 3) and also of electron transport and oxidative phosphorylation (stage 4) take place within subcellular structures called **mitochondria** (singular, mitochondrion). To picture a mitochondrion (Figure 24.12), imagine two balloons, one larger than the other, and imagine that the larger balloon is extensively folded and stuffed inside the smaller balloon. Because the surface area of the inner membrane is so extensively and irregularly folded, it is approximately 10,000 times the area of the outer membrane. The folds of the inner membrane are called cristae, and the space that surrounds them is called the matrix. All enzymes required for catalysis of the tricarboxylic acid cycle are located within the mitochondria—some in the matrix, and others bound to the inner membrane.

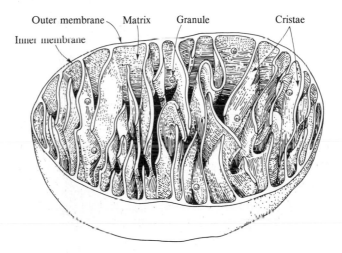

Outer membrane   Matrix   Granule   Cristae

Inner membrane

Figure 24.12 A mitochondrion. Both inner and outer membranes are phospholipid bilayers. The surface of the inner membrane is highly folded and several thousand times larger in surface area than the outer membrane.

D. Stage 4: Electron Transport and Oxidative Phosphorylation—A Central Pathway for Oxidation of Reduced Coenzymes and Generation of ATP

In stage 4, reduced coenzymes (NADH and FADH$_2$) accumulated from stages 2 and 3 are reoxidized by molecular oxygen; in effect, this is the aerobic phase of metabolism. Because reoxidation of NADH and FADH$_2$ is coupled with phosphorylation of ADP to ATP, stage 4 is called **oxidative phosphorylation**. The net reactions of stage 4 are shown in Figure 24.13.

$$2NADH + O_2 + 2H^+ \longrightarrow 2NAD^+ + 2H_2O$$
$$2FADH_2 + O_2 \longrightarrow 2FAD + 2H_2O$$
$$ADP + HPO_4^{2-} \longrightarrow ATP + H_2O$$

Figure 24.13 Stage 4 of the oxidation of foodstuffs and generation of ATP. Reoxidation of NADH and FADH$_2$ is coupled with phosphorylation of ADP to give ATP.

The four stages in the oxidation of foodstuffs and the generation of ATP are summarized in Figure 24.14.

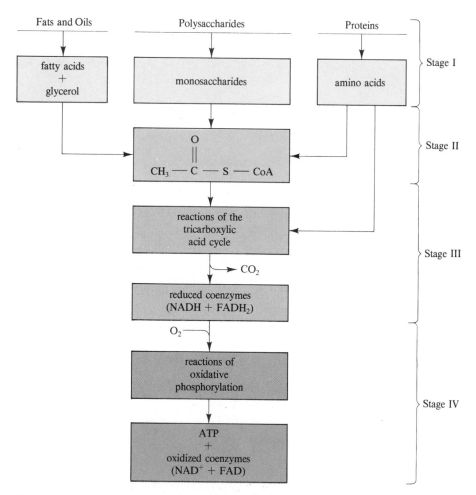

Figure 24.14 Summary of the four stages in the oxidation of foodstuffs and generation of ATP.

24.5 Electron Transport and Oxidative Phosphorylation: A Closer Look

A. Oxidation Part of Oxidative Phosphorylation

The final stage in oxidation of foodstuffs and generation of ATP involves re-oxidation of NADH and $FADH_2$ by molecular oxygen. As shown by the following equations, each oxidation is accompanied by a large decrease in free energy.

$$NADH + H^+ + \tfrac{1}{2}O_2 \longrightarrow NAD^+ + H_2O \qquad \Delta G^0 = -52{,}300 \text{ cal/mol}$$
$$FADH_2 + \tfrac{1}{2}O_2 \longrightarrow FAD + H_2O \qquad \Delta G^0 = -43{,}400 \text{ cal/mol}$$

We have written these equations as single reactions. Writing balanced half-reactions for the oxidation of NADH and $FADH_2$ and the reduction of oxygen to water allows a better appreciation of how cells bring about these oxidations.

Oxidation Half-Reactions

$$NADH \longrightarrow NAD^+ + H^+ + 2e^-$$
$$FADH_2 \longrightarrow FAD + 2H^+ + 2e^-$$

Reduction Half-Reaction

$$O_2 + 4H^+ + 4e^- \longrightarrow 2H_2O$$

Within mitochondria, the site of respiration, electrons are not passed directly from reduced coenzymes to molecular oxygen. Rather, they are passed from one acceptor to another and then to molecular oxygen by a pathway called the **electron transport** chain. All enzymes and cofactors required for electron transport are located on the inner membranes of mitochondria and are arranged in sequence so that electrons can be passed directly from one to the next. As illustrated in Figure 24.15, there are six intermediate carriers of electrons between NADH and molecular oxygen.

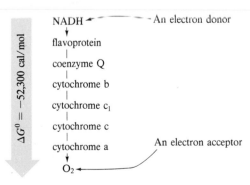

Figure 24.15 Six carriers of electrons separate NADH (an electron donor) from molecular oxygen (an electron acceptor) in the respiratory chain.

In the first step of the **respiratory chain**, a pair of electrons is transferred from NADH to a flavomononucleotide (FMN), a molecule similar in structure to riboflavin and FAD. This flavoprotein can exist in both oxidized (FMN) and reduced ($FMNH_2$) forms.

$$\underset{\text{(reduced form)}}{\text{NADH}} + H^+ + \underset{\text{(oxidized form)}}{\text{FMN}} \longrightarrow \underset{\text{(oxidized form)}}{NAD^+} + \underset{\text{(reduced form)}}{FMNH_2}$$

The second carrier of electrons in the respiratory chain is coenzyme Q (Figure 24.16). This molecule has a long hydrocarbon chain of 6–10 isoprene units, which anchors it firmly in the nonpolar environment of the inner membrane of the mitochondrion. As you can see from the balanced half-reaction in Figure 24.16, the oxidized form of coenzyme Q is a two-electron oxidizing agent. In the second step of the respiratory chain, two electrons are transferred from the flavoprotein reduced in step 1 to the oxidized form of coenzyme Q.

$$\underset{\text{(reduced form)}}{\text{flavoprotein}} + \underset{\text{(oxidized form)}}{\text{coenzyme Q}} \longrightarrow \underset{\text{(oxidized form)}}{\text{flavoprotein}} + \underset{\text{(reduced form)}}{\text{coenzyme Q}}$$

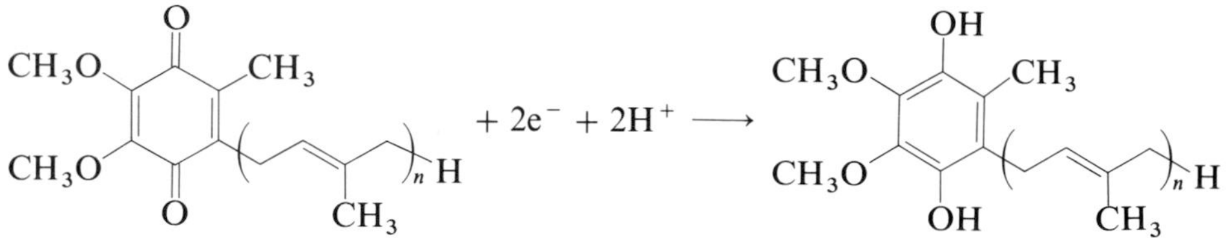

coenzyme Q (oxidized form)

coenzyme Q (reduced form)

Figure 24.16 Coenzyme Q. The nonpolar side chain of this molecule consists of six to ten ($n = 6$–10) isoprene units.

The remaining carriers of electrons in the respiratory chain are four structurally related proteins known as cytochromes. Cytochrome c, the most thoroughly studied of these electrons carriers, is a globular protein of molecular weight 12,400; it consists of a single polypeptide chain of 104 amino acids folded around a single heme group. The iron atom of all four cytochromes can exist in either Fe(II) or Fe(III) oxidation states. Thus, an atom of Fe(III) in a cytochrome molecule can accept an electron and be reduced to Fe(II), which in turn gives up an electron to reduce the next cytochrome in the chain.

In the final step of the respiratory chain, electrons are transferred from cytochrome a to a molecule of oxygen. In the following equation, cytochrome a is abbreviated as Cyt a.

$$\underset{\text{(reduced form)}}{2\text{Cyt a}(Fe^{2+})} + \tfrac{1}{2}O_2 + 2H^+ \longrightarrow \underset{\text{(oxidized form)}}{2\text{Cyt a}(Fe^{3+})} + H_2O$$

The seven steps in the transfer of electrons from NADH to O_2 are summarized in Figure 24.17. Notice that the free-energy decrease in four of these steps is larger than that required for phosphorylation of ADP ($\Delta G^0 = +7,300$ cal/mol).

Electrons from $FADH_2$ are also transported via the intermediates of the respiratory chain to molecular oxygen. Electrons from $FADH_2$, however, enter the chain at coenzyme Q (Figure 24.17). There are only five intermediates in the transport of electrons from coenzyme Q to molecular oxygen.

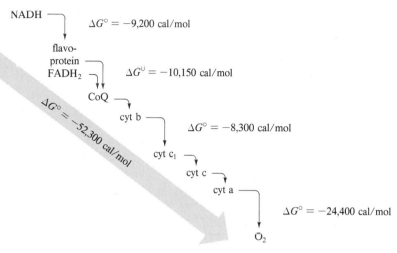

NADH

$\Delta G^\circ = -9,200$ cal/mol

flavo-
protein
$FADH_2$

$\Delta G^0 = -10,150$ cal/mol

CoQ

cyt b

$\Delta G^\circ = -8,300$ cal/mol

$\Delta G^\circ = -52,300$ cal/mol

cyt c_1

cyt c

cyt a

$\Delta G^\circ = -24,400$ cal/mol

O_2

Figure 24.17 Energetics of the flow of electrons from NADH and $FADH_2$ to molecular oxygen in the respiratory chain.

B. Phosphorylation Part of Oxidative Phosphorylation

Cells have evolved a mechanism that couples the energy-releasing oxidation of reduced coenzymes with the energy-requiring phosphorylation of ADP. For each mole of NADH entering the respiratory chain, three moles of ATP are formed. The overall equation for oxidation of NADH and phosphorylation of ADP can be written as the sum of the exergonic oxidation of NADH and the endergonic phosphorylation of ADP:

$$NADH + H^+ + \tfrac{1}{2}O_2 \longrightarrow NAD^+ + H_2O$$
$$\underline{3H^+ + 3ADP + 3HPO_4^{2-} \longrightarrow 3ATP + 3H_2O}$$
$$NADH + 4H^+ + \tfrac{1}{2}O_2 + 3ADP + 3HPO_4^{2-} \longrightarrow NAD^+ + 3ATP + 4H_2O$$

Coupling the oxidation and phosphorylation reactions conserves $\frac{22}{52}$, or approximately 42%, of the decrease in free energy during the reoxidation of NADH.

Reoxidation of $FADH_2$ is coupled with phosphorylation of two moles of ADP, and approximately 34% of the decrease in free energy is conserved as ATP.

$$FADH_2 + \tfrac{1}{2}O_2 \longrightarrow FAD + H_2O$$
$$\underline{2ADP + 2HPO_4^{2-} + 2H^+ \longrightarrow 2ATP + 2H_2O}$$
$$FADH_2 + \tfrac{1}{2}O_2 + 2ADP + 2HPO_4^{2-} + 2H^+ \longrightarrow FAD + 2ATP + 3H_2O$$

Although we have written equations for oxidation of reduced coenzymes and phosphorylation as separate reactions, it is more accurate to consider them a single (but very complex), coupled reaction. *Coupled* means that one is tightly linked to the other. If electron transport is prevented (for example, by lack of oxygen as a terminal acceptor of electrons), then no ATP is produced. On the other hand, if there is a shortage of ADP or inorganic phosphate, so phosphorylation cannot take place, then electron transport does not occur.

C. Coupling of Oxidation and Phosphorylation: The Chemiosmotic Theory

While it has been possible to learn a great deal about how both oxidation and phosphorylation proceed during respiration, it has proved difficult to explain how these two processes are coupled. Biochemists reasoned that they must share a common intermediate that, in effect, couples them. By analogy, a phosphoryl group cannot be transferred directly from phosphoenolpyruvate to glucose. Rather, ATP is a common intermediate that couples reactions between phosphoenolpyruvate and glucose, to form glucose 6-phosphate and pyruvate (Section 24.3D).

$$
\begin{array}{l}
\text{phosphoenolpyruvate} + \text{ADP} \longrightarrow \text{pyruvate} + \text{ATP} \\
\underline{\hspace{4em} \text{glucose} + \text{ATP} \longrightarrow \text{glucose 6-phosphate} + \text{ADP}} \\
\text{phosphoenolpyruvate} + \text{glucose} \longrightarrow \text{glucose 6-phosphate} + \text{pyruvate}
\end{array}
$$

It was assumed for many years that the common intermediate would be a chemical compound involved in both electron transport and ATP synthesis. But none could be discovered. More recently, the search for a common intermediate broadened with the realization that the "intermediate" need not be a covalent compound after all but some other form of stored chemical energy instead. The most widely accepted current model for coupling oxidation and phosphorylation was put forward in 1960 by Peter Mitchell, an English chemist. According to his **chemiosmotic theory**, as electrons are transferred along the respiratory chain during oxidation of reduced coenzymes, protons are transferred from inside the inner mitochondrial membrane to outside the membrane. It is the protons pumped outside that provide the driving force for ATP synthesis. As protons flow from the side of higher concentration outside the membrane toward the inside, they pass through a macromolecular structure called ATP synthase complex, where actual synthesis of ATP occurs.

Mitchell's theory stirred much controversy and was by no means widely accepted, even into the mid-1970s. Acceptance did develop, however, and in 1978 he was awarded the Nobel Prize in chemistry.

1. How the Proton Gradient Is Established

At the heart of the chemiosmotic theory is the concept of a "proton pump." Several electron-transport reactions in the respiratory chain involve protons as either reactants or products. Following are three such reactions, each written for simplicity as a balanced half-reaction:

$$\text{NADH} \longrightarrow \text{NAD}^+ + \text{H}^+ + 2e^-$$

$$\text{FADH}_2 \longrightarrow \text{FAD} + 2\text{H}^+ + 2e^-$$

$$\text{coenzyme Q} \longrightarrow \text{coenzyme Q} + 2\text{H}^+ + 2e^-$$

(reduced form)   (oxidized form)

Mitchell proposes that sites of these reactions are arranged on the inner surface of the mitochondrial membrane in such a way that protons as reactants are taken from inside the membrane and those given off as products are released outside the membrane. Equally important, only protons are pumped outside the membrane; negative ions are not pumped out simultaneously. Through operation of the proton pump, two types of gradients are created: (1) a concentration gradient, because there are more protons outside than inside the membrane; and (2) a charge gradient, with the outside of the membrane positively charged compared with the inside (Figure 24.18). The energy involved

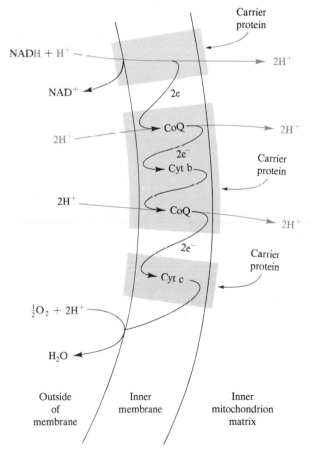

Figure 24.18 A key postulate in Mitchell's chemiosmotic hypothesis is that for each pair of electrons transferred from NADH to molecular oxygen, six hydrogen ions are pumped from the mitochondrial matrix through the inner membrane to the outside. Thus, there is established both a proton and a charge gradient between the inner mitochondrial matrix and the outer intermembrane space.

in both the concentration gradient and the charge gradient is involved in generating ATP.

2. How the Proton Gradient Is Coupled with ATP Synthesis

Mitchell proposes that ATP synthesis takes place at ATPase synthetase complexes located inside the inner mitochondrial membrane. Each complex consists of an F_1 system of five different proteins, which is joined to the inner membrane by an F_0 protein. One proposal is that as protons are propelled by the concentration and charge gradients back into mitochondria through the F_0 channel and into the F_1 system, they somehow cause a conformational change in the F_1 system, which in turn affects the enzyme ATP synthase in such a way that ADP and inorganic phosphate are converted to ATP (Figure 24.19). We know almost nothing about how a proton flux might be connected to a conformational change in the F_0–F_1 system or how that in turn might be connected with ATP synthesis.

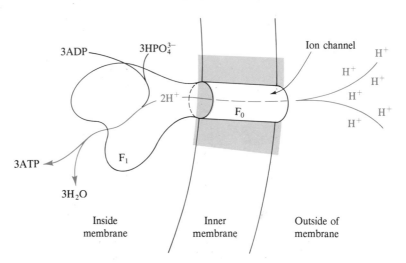

Figure 24.19 The chemiosmotic theory. Movement of protons through the F_0 channel, creation of a conformational change in the F_1 system and synthesis of ATP.

D. Inhibitors of Electron Transport and Oxidative Phosphorylation

1. Inhibition of Electron Transport in the Respiratory Chain

Numerous chemicals interfere with specific steps in the transfer of electrons in the respiratory chain. Because they inhibit electron transport, they also inhibit phosphorylation and production of ATP. One of the best-known of these chemicals is cyanide ion, a powerful inhibitor of cytochrome oxidase, the enzyme that catalyzes the transfer of electrons from cytochrome c to cytochrome a. Cyanide ion also complexes with the iron atom of cytochrome a, to form a complex that is unable to function as a carrier of electrons. The result of cyanide ion poisoning is a block in the flow of electrons from NADH and $FADH_2$ to molecular oxygen. Cyanide ion has the same effect on the cell as lack of oxygen; death is by asphyxiation.

Another inhibitor of electron transport is rotenone, a powerful inhibitor of NADH-dehydrogenase, the enzyme that catalyzes the transfer of electrons from NADH to a flavoprotein in the first step of respiration.

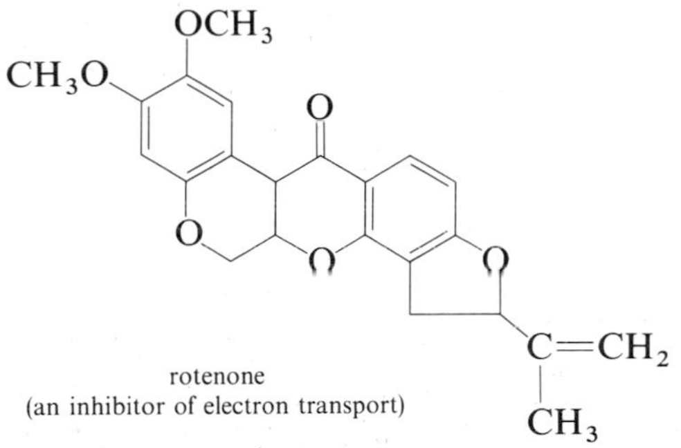

rotenone
(an inhibitor of electron transport)

Because rotenone passes readily into the breathing tubes of insects and is intensely toxic to these organisms, it is widely used as an insecticide. It is also toxic to fish, because it passes readily into their gills. Rotenone is not readily absorbed through the skin and therefore has a relatively low toxicity for humans and other vertebrates.

2. *Inhibitors of Oxidative Phosphorylation*

Other compounds have no effect on the transport of electrons but act to uncouple it from phosphorylation. Thus, reduced coenzymes are reoxidized by molecular oxygen, but there is no accompanying synthesis of ATP. One such uncoupling agent is 2,4-dinitrophenol, which appears to have its effect by increasing the permeability of the inner mitochondrial membrane to protons. With increased membrane permeability, both proton and charge gradients are reduced, thus decreasing the driving force for synthesis of ATP.

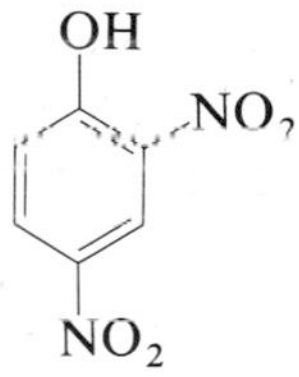

2,4-dinitrophenol
(uncouples electron
transport and phosphorylation)

24.6 Utilization of ATP for Cellular Work

As we have seen (Section 24.3), hydrolysis of the terminal phosphate anhydride bond of ATP occurs with a decrease in free energy. Cells are able to use a portion of this free energy to do three important types of work: **chemical work**, **mechanical work**, and **osmotic work**. Let us look in more detail at each type of work and see how it depends on ATP.

A. Chemical Work

The formation of peptide, glycoside, and ester bonds requires energy. For example, formation of a glycoside bond between glucose and fructose to form sucrose requires 5,500 cal for each mole of sucrose formed:

$$\text{glucose} + \text{fructose} \longrightarrow \text{sucrose} + H_2O \qquad \Delta G^0 = +5,500 \text{ cal/mol}$$

On the other hand, hydrolysis of ATP decreases free energy:

$$\text{ATP} + H_2O \longrightarrow \text{ADP} + HPO_4^{2-} \qquad \Delta G^0 = 7,300 \text{ cal/mol}$$

Adding these reactions gives a net reaction that occurs with a decrease in free energy and is spontaneous in the direction written:

$$
\begin{array}{ll}
\text{glucose} + \text{fructose} \longrightarrow \text{sucrose} + H_2O & \Delta G^0 = +5,500 \text{ cal/mol} \\
\underline{\text{ATP} + H_2O \longrightarrow \text{ADP} + HPO_4^{2-}} & \underline{\Delta G^0 = -7,300 \text{ cal/mol}} \\
\text{glucose} + \text{fructose} + \text{ATP} \longrightarrow \text{sucrose} + \text{ADP} + HPO_4^{2-} & \Delta G^0 = -1,800 \text{ cal/mol}
\end{array}
$$

If it were possible to capture a part of the free energy of the phosphate anhydride bond in ATP and channel it into glycoside bond formation, glucose and fructose could be converted to sucrose. Cells accomplish this by two sequential enzyme-catalyzed reactions involving a common intermediate:

$$
\begin{array}{l}
\text{glucose} + \text{ATP} \longrightarrow \text{glucose 1-phosphate} + \text{ADP} \\
\underline{\text{glucose 1-phosphate} + \text{fructose} \longrightarrow \text{sucrose} + HPO_4^{2-}} \\
\text{glucose} + \text{fructose} + \text{ATP} \longrightarrow \text{sucrose} + \text{ADP} + HPO_4^{2-}
\end{array}
$$

Glucose 1-phosphate is the common intermediate. Together, these sequential reactions have a net free-energy change of $-1,800$ cal/mol. Thus, a portion of the energy stored in ATP is captured in the form of a common intermediate and is then used to form a glycoside bond.

B. Osmotic Work: Transport across Membranes

The movement of molecules and ions across a membrane is called transport, and it is an essential process in all living organisms. Transport is of two types: passive and active. In **passive transport**, a molecule or an ion moves across a membrane from the side of high concentration to the side of lower concentration. Passive transport is spontaneous and requires no energy. In **active transport**, a molecule or an ion is moved across a membrane from the side of low concentration to the side of higher concentration. Active transport is nonspontaneous and requires energy. Figure 24.20 illustrates transport with and against a concentration gradient.

For an example of the results of active transport, compare the relative concentrations of ions and molecules in the intracellular and extracellular fluids of skeletal muscle tissue (Figure 24.21). Note that the concentrations of K^+, Mg^{2+},

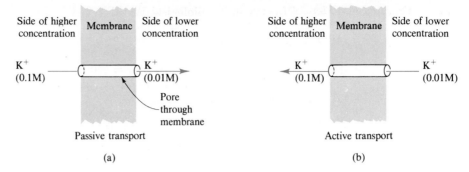

Figure 24.20 Transport across membranes. (a) In passive transport, molecules and ions flow with a concentration gradient. (b) In active transport, molecules and ions flow against a concentration gradient. Active transport is nonspontaneous and requires energy.

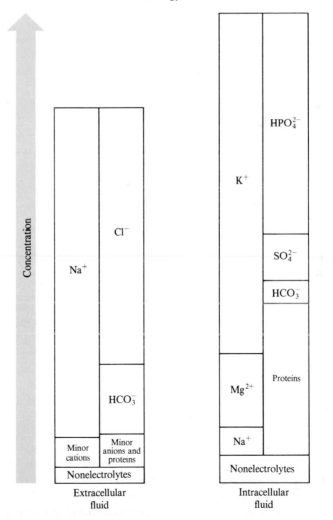

Figure 24.21 Relative concentrations of some molecules and ions in the intracellular and extracellular fluids of human skeletal muscle.

HPO_4^{2-}, and SO_4^{2-} are all much higher inside the cells of skeletal muscle than they are in the surrounding fluid. It requires energy to concentrate these ions within skeletal muscle cells.

At present, little is known about the mechanism of active transport. It is known, however, that active transport requires energy and that it is linked to the hydrolysis of high-energy phosphate bonds in ATP to give ADP and HPO_4^{2-}.

C. Mechanical Work: Muscle Contraction

Figure 24.22 is a schematic diagram of a section of skeletal muscle fiber. A fiber consists of two types of protein-containing filaments. One type of filament, containing the protein actin, consists of thin rods connected to a protein plate, or disc. Actin filaments connected to one plate do not make contact with those from an adjacent plate. A second type of filament, containing the protein myosin, consists of thicker rods that overlap actin filaments from adjacent plates.

Our best current model of muscle contraction is called the sliding filament model. During contraction, according to this model, actin filaments slide past myosin filaments, and in the process, the free ends of actin filaments are pulled close together. As actin filaments slide toward each other, they in turn pull the protein plates closer together, and the entire muscle fiber contracts. Contraction of muscle fibers is coupled with the hydrolysis of ATP to ADP and phosphate, but how these two processes are coupled is almost totally unknown.

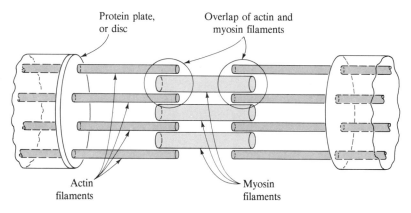

Figure 24.22 A schematic drawing of a skeletal muscle fiber.

Although ATP is the immediate source of energy to power contraction of skeletal muscle, it is not the form in which energy for muscle contraction is stored. In resting muscle, energy is stored as creatine phosphate, a high-energy compound containing a phosphate amide bond. Following is an equation for the hydrolysis of creatine phosphate. The free-energy change for this reaction is $-10,300$ cal/mol.

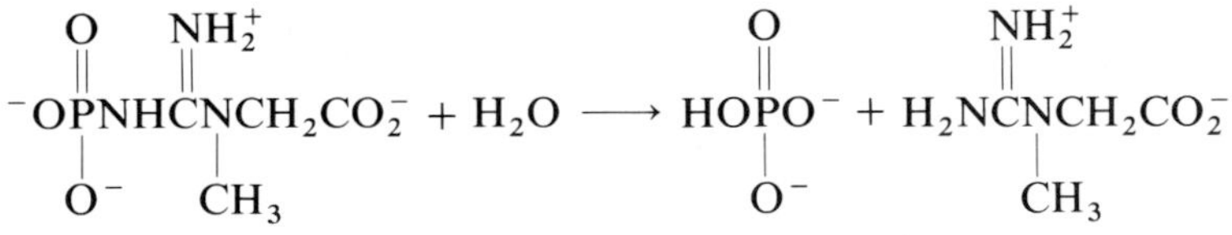

$$\underset{\substack{\text{creatine} \\ \text{phosphate}}}{\overset{\displaystyle O \quad\quad NH_2^+}{\underset{\displaystyle O^- \quad CH_3}{^-OPNHCNCH_2CO_2^-}}} + H_2O \longrightarrow \underset{\displaystyle O^-}{\overset{\displaystyle O}{HOPO^-}} + \underset{\substack{\displaystyle CH_3 \\ \text{creatine}}}{\overset{\displaystyle NH_2^+}{H_2NCNCH_2CO_2^-}} \qquad \Delta G^0 = -10{,}300 \text{ cal/mol}$$

The immediate chemical change on muscle contraction is hydrolysis of ATP and an increase in the concentration of ADP. In response, a phosphoryl group is transferred from creatine phosphate to ADP, and more ATP becomes available for muscle contraction. This reaction is catalyzed by the enzyme creatine kinase (CK):

$$\text{creatine phosphate} + \text{ADP} \underset{\text{kinase}}{\overset{\text{creatine}}{\rightleftarrows}} \text{creatine} + \text{ATP}$$

$$\xrightarrow{\quad\quad \text{active muscle} \quad\quad}$$

$$\xleftarrow{\quad\quad \text{resting muscle} \quad\quad}$$

During rest, the supply of ATP is regenerated, and in turn, used to regenerate the supply of creatine phosphate.

Key Terms and Concepts

acetyl coenzyme A (24.4B)	Krebs cycle (24.4C)
active transport (24.6B)	low-energy compound (24.4B)
adenosine triphosphate (ATP) (24.3B)	mechanical work (24.6C)
anabolism (24.1)	metabolic pathway (24.1)
catabolism (24.1)	metabolism (24.1)
chemical work (24.6A)	mitochondrion (24.4C)
chemiosmotic theory (24.5C)	osmotic work (24.6B)
electron transport (24.5D)	oxidative phosphorylation (24.4D)
endergonic (24.3A)	passive transport (24.6B)
exergonic (24.3A)	photosynthesis (24.2)
free energy ΔG^0 (24.3A)	respiration (24.2)
free energy of hydrolysis (24.3B)	respiratory chain (24.5A)
high-energy compound (24.3B)	tricarboxylic acid (TCA) cycle (24.4C)

Key Reactions

1. Hydrolysis of high-energy compounds: ATP, ADP, phosphoenolpyruvate, and 1,3-diphosphoglycerate (Sections 24.3B and C).

2. NAD^+ as a biological oxidizing agent: reduction of NAD^+ to NADH (Section 24.4C).

3. NADH as a biological reducing agent: oxidation of NADH to NAD^+ (Section 24.4C).

4. FAD as a biological oxidizing agent: reduction of FAD to $FADH_2$ (Section 24.4C).

5. $FADH_2$ as a biological reducing agent: oxidation of $FADH_2$ to FAD (Section 24.4C).

Problems

Concept of free energy (Sections 24.1–24.3)

24.1 What is meant by the term *free energy*? By ΔG^0?

24.2 How is the sign of ΔG^0 related to:
a. the rate of a chemical reaction?
b. the position of equilibrium of a chemical reaction?
c. the spontaneity of a chemical reaction?

24.3 Define the term *high-energy compound* as it is used in biochemistry.

24.4 Adenosine triphosphate (ATP) is a phosphorylating agent. Explain what change in structural formula takes place when a molecule is phosphorylated.

24.5 Write equations for phosphorylation of the following compounds. Assume that ATP is the phosphorylating agent and that it is converted to ADP. Write structural formulas for each phosphorylated product.
a. phosphorylation of glucose to give alpha-D-glucose 6-phosphate
b. phosphorylation of glycerol to give glycerol 1-phosphate
c. phosphorylation of fructose 6-phosphate to give alpha-D-fructose 1,6-diphosphate

24.6 Calculate ΔG^0 for the following reactions. Which are spontaneous as written? Which are not spontaneous as written?
a. phosphoenolpyruvate + ADP $\longrightarrow$ pyruvate + ATP
b. 1,3-diphosphoglycerate + ADP $\longrightarrow$ 3-phosphoglycerate + ATP
c. glucose + ATP $\longrightarrow$ glucose 6-phosphate + ADP
d. glucose 1-phosphate + ADP $\longrightarrow$ glucose + ATP
e. glucose 1-phosphate $\longrightarrow$ glucose 6-phosphate

24.7 The change in free energy for complete oxidation of glucose to carbon dioxide and water is $-686,000$ cal/mol of glucose.

$$C_6H_{12}O_6 + 6O_2 \longrightarrow 6CO_2 + 6H_2O \qquad \Delta G^0 = -686,000 \text{ cal/mol}$$

If all this decrease in free energy could be channeled by a cell into conversion of ADP and HPO_4^{2-} to ATP, how many moles of ATP could be formed per mole of glucose oxidized?

Stages in the oxidation of foodstuffs and generation of ATP (Section 24.4)

24.8 Outline the four stages by which cells extract energy from foodstuffs. Of these four stages, which are concerned primarily with each of these processes?

a. degradation of fuel molecules
b. generation of NADH and FADH$_2$
c. generation of ATP   d. consumption of O$_2$

24.9   Name the separate units from which pantothenic acid is constructed.

24.10   a. Write an abbreviated structural formula for NAD$^+$, showing the portion of the molecule that functions as an oxidizing agent.
        b. Write an abbreviated structural formula for NADH, showing the portion of the molecule that functions as a reducing agent.
        c. Which water-soluble vitamin is an essential part of NAD$^+$?
        d. Complete and balance the following half-reaction:

$$NAD^+ + H^+ \longrightarrow$$

24.11   Write balanced equations for the oxidation of the following by NAD$^+$. Note that for each oxidation, the organic product is also given.

a. $CH_3CH_2OH \xrightarrow{\text{oxidation}} CH_3\overset{\displaystyle O}{\overset{\|}{C}}H$

b. $CH_3\overset{\displaystyle OH}{\underset{|}{C}}HCO_2^- \xrightarrow{\text{oxidation}} CH_3\overset{\displaystyle O}{\overset{\|}{C}}CO_2^-$

c. $H-\overset{\displaystyle OH}{\underset{|}{\underset{\displaystyle |}{\overset{|}{C}}}}-CO_2^-$ $\xrightarrow{\text{oxidation}}$ $\overset{\displaystyle O}{\overset{\|}{C}}-CO_2^-$
   $\overset{|}{C}HCO_2^-$ $\overset{|}{C}HCO_2^-$
   $\overset{|}{C}H_2CO_2^-$ $\overset{|}{C}H_2CO_2^-$

d. $CH_3\overset{\displaystyle O}{\overset{\|}{C}}H \xrightarrow{\text{oxidation}} CH_3\overset{\displaystyle O}{\overset{\|}{C}}O^-$

24.12   Write the standard abbreviations for the oxidized and reduced forms of flavin adenine dinucleotide. Which water-soluble vitamin is an essential precursor for this molecule?

24.13   Write a balanced equation for the oxidation of succinate by FAD. The organic product is fumarate.

$$^-O_2CCH_2CH_2CO_2^- \xrightarrow{\text{oxidation}} \underset{H}{^-O_2C}\diagdown C=C \diagup \overset{H}{\underset{CO_2^-}{}}$$

succinate   fumarate

Electron transport and oxidative phosphorylation (Section 24.5)

24.14   What is the function of the respiratory chain?

24.15   The final stage in aerobic metabolism involves oxidative phosphorylation. What is oxidized? What is phosphorylated?

24.16   Four of the carriers of electrons in the electron transport chain are structurally related proteins. Name the prosthetic group associated with each of these proteins. What metal is associated with each prosthetic group?

24.17   Explain why cyanide poisoning has the same effect on a cell as a lack of oxygen.

Utilization of ATP for cellular work (Section 24.6)

24.18   Name the three important types of cellular work that require ATP.

24.19   What is meant by the term *coupled reaction*? Give an example of the coupling of two biochemical reactions by a common intermediate.

24.20   What is the role of creatine phosphate in skeletal muscle?

25

Metabolism of Carbohydrates

Glucose is the key food molecule for most organisms, and virtually all organisms catabolize glucose by the same set of metabolic pathways. This fact suggests that glucose metabolism became a central feature at an early stage in the evolution of living systems. We shall concentrate on the metabolic pathways by which cells extract energy from glucose.

25.1 Digestion and Absorption of Carbohydrates

A. Digestion and Absorption

The main function of dietary carbohydrate is as a source of energy. In a typical American diet, carbohydrates provide about 50–60% of daily energy needs. The remainder is supplied by fats and proteins. During **digestion of carbohydrates**, disaccharides and polysaccharides are hydrolyzed to monosaccharides, chiefly glucose, fructose, and galactose.

$$\text{polysaccharides} + n\text{H}_2\text{O} \xrightarrow[\substack{\text{(mouth and} \\ \text{intestine)}}]{\alpha\text{-amylases}} n \text{ maltose}$$

$$\text{maltose} + \text{H}_2\text{O} \xrightarrow[\text{(intestine)}]{\text{maltase}} \text{glucose} + \text{glucose}$$

$$\text{sucrose} + \text{H}_2\text{O} \xrightarrow[\text{(intestine)}]{\text{sucrase}} \text{glucose} + \text{fructose}$$

$$\text{lactose} + \text{H}_2\text{O} \xrightarrow[\text{(intestine)}]{\text{lactase}} \text{glucose} + \text{galactose}$$

Hydrolysis of starch begins in the mouth, catalyzed by the enzyme α-amylase, a component of saliva. There, starch is broken down to smaller polysaccharides and the disaccharide maltose (Section 19.4A). Hydrolysis of sucrose, lactose, maltose, and the remaining polysaccharides is completed in the small intestine, catalyzed by the enzymes maltase, sucrase, lactase, and intestinal α-amylase.

Lactose (Section 19.4B) is the principal carbohydrate in milk; human and cow's milk is about 5% lactose by weight. Human babies are born with the digestive enzymes necessary to hydrolyze lactose to glucose and galactose. Many individuals lose the ability to hydrolyze lactose, a condition known as lactose intolerance. For them, lactose passes through the digestive system to the large intestine. There it increases the osmotic pressure of intestinal fluids, which in turn interferes with reabsorption of water and leads to diarrhea. Further, intestinal bacteria ferment lactose to gases, chiefly carbon dioxide, methane, and hydrogen, which further irritate the intestinal lining and lead to nausea and vomiting. Lactose intolerance quite predictably develops around the age of four, especially in African, Asian, Middle Eastern, Mediterranean, and American Indian peoples.

B. Normal Blood Glucose Levels

Under normal conditions, the concentration of glucose in blood is between 60 and 100 mg per 100 mL. This level rises following a meal and then falls to fasting level, a point that usually is associated with the onset of hunger. If blood glucose falls below about 60 mg per 100 mL, the condition is known as **hypoglycemia**. In hypoglycemia, there is danger that cells of the central nervous system and other tissues that depend on glucose for nourishment may not receive adequate supplies of glucose. When blood glucose levels rise above about 160 mg per 100 mL, the condition is known as **hyperglycemia**.

The liver is the key organ for regulating the concentration of glucose in the blood. As glucose is absorbed after a meal, the liver counters this increase by removing glucose from the bloodstream. Glucose removed from blood is used by the liver in two ways: (1) it can be converted to glycogen or triglycerides and stored in the liver; or (2) it can be catabolized to generate ATP and heat. Thus, the concentration of glucose in the bloodstream represents a balance between cellular intake, storage, and catabolism.

C. Glucose Tolerance Test

Any defect in the regulation of blood glucose levels can be detected by a **glucose tolerance test**, which measures the ability of tissues to absorb glucose from the blood. One part of the test depends on the limited ability of the kidneys to reabsorb glucose as they filter and purify the blood. When blood glucose levels are lower than approximately 160–180 mg/100 mL, virtually all glucose is reabsorbed by the kidneys and returned to the bloodstream. However, when blood glucose levels exceed 160–180 mg/100 mL, the kidneys can no longer absorb the excess and it is passed into the urine. The condition in which glucose appears in the urine is called glycosuria and the blood glucose level at which this occurs is called the renal threshold.

A glucose tolerance test is done in the following way. After an overnight fast, the patient is given a single dose of glucose, typically 50–100 g in a fruit-flavored drink. Specimens of blood and urine are taken before the glucose is administered, and then at regular intervals for 3–4 hr after the test dose is taken. In normal individuals, the blood-glucose level increases within the first hour from 80 mg/100 mL to approximately 130 mg/100 mL; at the end of 2–3 hr, it returns to normal levels. For persons with diabetes, blood glucose begins at an elevated level and rises much higher after ingestion of the glucose test solution. Furthermore, the return to pretest levels is much slower than that observed in normal individuals. Figure 25.1 illustrates typical glucose-tolerance curves for a normal individual and one with mild diabetes.

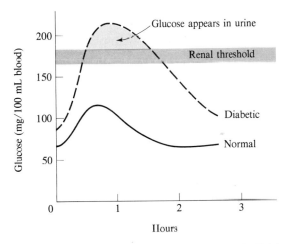

Figure 25.1 A typical glucose tolerance curve for a normal individual and one with mild diabetes mellitus.

25.2 Central Role of Glucose in Carbohydrate Metabolism

Because of the glucose requirements of cells, especially cells of the central nervous system, the body has developed a set of interrelated metabolic pathways designed to use glucose efficiently and to ensure an adequate supply of it in the bloodstream. Several of these pathways oxidize glucose to carbon dioxide and water and conserve a portion of the energy stored in glucose as ATP and other high-energy compounds. Other pathways "buffer" the concentration of glucose in the blood; that is, their job is to maintain blood-glucose levels within a narrow range. After an overview of the most important pathways of glucose metabolism, we shall study four of them (glycolysis, lactate fermentation, alcoholic fermentation, and the tricarboxylic acid cycle) in detail.

A. Glycolysis

Glycolysis is a series of ten consecutive reactions by which glucose is oxidized to two molecules of pyruvate. The oxidizing agent is NAD^+. Furthermore, two molecules of ATP are produced for each molecule of glucose oxidized to pyruvate. Following is the net reaction for glycolysis.

$$C_6H_{12}O_6 + 2NAD^+ + 2HPO_4^{2-} + 2ADP \xrightarrow{\text{glycolysis}} 2CH_3\overset{\overset{\displaystyle O}{\|}}{C}CO_2^- + 2NADH + 2ATP$$

glucose   pyruvate

B. Oxidation and Decarboxylation of Pyruvate

Following glycolysis, the carboxylate group of pyruvate is converted to carbon dioxide, and the remaining two carbons are converted to an acetyl group in the form of a thioester with coenzyme A. Several coenzymes including NAD^+ and coenzyme A are required for this metabolic pathway.

$$CH_3\overset{\overset{\displaystyle O}{\|}}{C}CO_2^- + NAD^+ + CoA \quad SH \xrightarrow[\text{of pyruvate}]{\substack{\text{oxidative} \\ \text{decarboxylation}}} CH_3\overset{\overset{\displaystyle O}{\|}}{C}-SCoA + CO_2 + NADH$$

pyruvate   acetyl CoA

C. The Tricarboxylic Acid Cycle

In the reactions of the tricarboxylic acid cycle, the two-carbon acetyl group of acetyl CoA is oxidized to two molecules of carbon dioxide:

$$CH_3\overset{\overset{\displaystyle O}{\|}}{C}-SCoA + 3NAD^+ + FAD + HPO_4^{2-} + ADP \xrightarrow{\text{TCA cycle}}$$

$$2CO_2 + 3NADH + FADH_2 + ATP + CoA-SH$$

The combination of glycolysis, oxidation of pyruvate to acetyl CoA, and the tricarboxylic acid cycle brings about complete oxidation of glucose to carbon dioxide and water and generates 2 moles of $FADH_2$, 10 moles of NADH, and 4 moles of ATP for each mole of glucose oxidized.

D. Oxidative Phosphorylation

Glycolysis, oxidation of pyruvate to acetyl coenzyme A, and the tricarboxylic acid cycle are completely anaerobic, meaning that they do not involve molecular oxygen. Rather, there is a buildup of reduced coenzymes. Oxidation of the accumulated NADH and $FADH_2$ is coupled with phosphorylation of ADP during electron transport and oxidative phosphorylation (Section 24.5). It is **oxidative phosphorylation** that generates the major share of the ATP produced during glucose catabolism:

$$10NADH + 2FADH_2 + 6O_2 + 32ADP + 32HPO_4^{2-} + 10H^+ \xrightarrow{\substack{\text{oxidative} \\ \text{phosphorylation}}}$$

$$10NAD^+ + 2FAD + 32ATP + 44H_2O$$

Example 25.1

Glucose is oxidized to carbon dioxide and water by a combination of three metabolic pathways. How many molecules of CO_2 are produced in each pathway?

☐ *Solution*

No CO_2 is produced during glycolysis. Two molecules of CO_2 are produced in the oxidation and decarboxylation of pyruvate to acetyl coenzyme A. The remaining four molecules of CO_2 are produced through the reactions of the tricarboxylic acid cycle.

Problem 25.1

a. During glycolysis, how many moles of NADH and $FADH_2$ are produced per mole of glucose converted to pyruvate?
b. During the conversion of pyruvate to acetyl CoA, how many moles of NADH are produced per mole of pyruvate?
c. During the tricarboxylic acid cycle, how many moles of NADH and $FADH_2$ are produced per mole of acetyl CoA entering the cycle?

E. Pentose Phosphate Pathway

The **pentose phosphate pathway** is an alternative pathway for the oxidation of glucose to carbon dioxide and water:

$$C_6H_{12}O_6 + 12NADP^+ + 6H_2O \xrightarrow{\substack{\text{pentose} \\ \text{phosphate} \\ \text{pathway}}} 6CO_2 + 12NADPH + 12H^+$$

glucose

At first glance, the pentose phosphate pathway appears to accomplish the same thing as a combination of glycolysis, oxidation of pyruvate to acetyl CoA, and the tricarboxylic acid cycle, namely, oxidation of glucose to carbon dioxide and water. While it is true that both sets of pathways bring about oxidation of glucose, there are important differences between them. The following reactions of the pentose phosphate pathway have been chosen to illustrate two of the most important differences. The first reaction of this pathway is oxidation of the aldehyde group of glucose 6-phosphate to a carboxylate group. Oxidation requires $NADP^+$ (Figure 24.10), which is a phosphorylated form of NAD^+, and the process is catalyzed by glucose 6-phosphate dehydrogenase. Next, oxidation of the secondary alcohol on carbon 3 of 6-phosphogluconate by a second molecule of $NADP^+$ gives a beta-ketoacid, which undergoes decarboxylation (Section 16.5D) to form ribulose 5-phosphate. In one of several reactions that follow, ribulose 5-phosphate is isomerized to ribose 5-phosphate.

These reactions are shown below using a convention widely used in biochemistry whenever there is a need to show reactants and products in a particularly compact manner. In this convention, a reactant may be shown at the tail of a curved arrow merging with the main arrow and a product may be shown at the head of an arrow branching off the main arrow. Curved arrows are used in the first and second equations to show that $NADP^+$ is the oxidizing agent and that it is reduced to NADPH. In the third reaction, a curved arrow is used to show that carbon dioxide is a product.

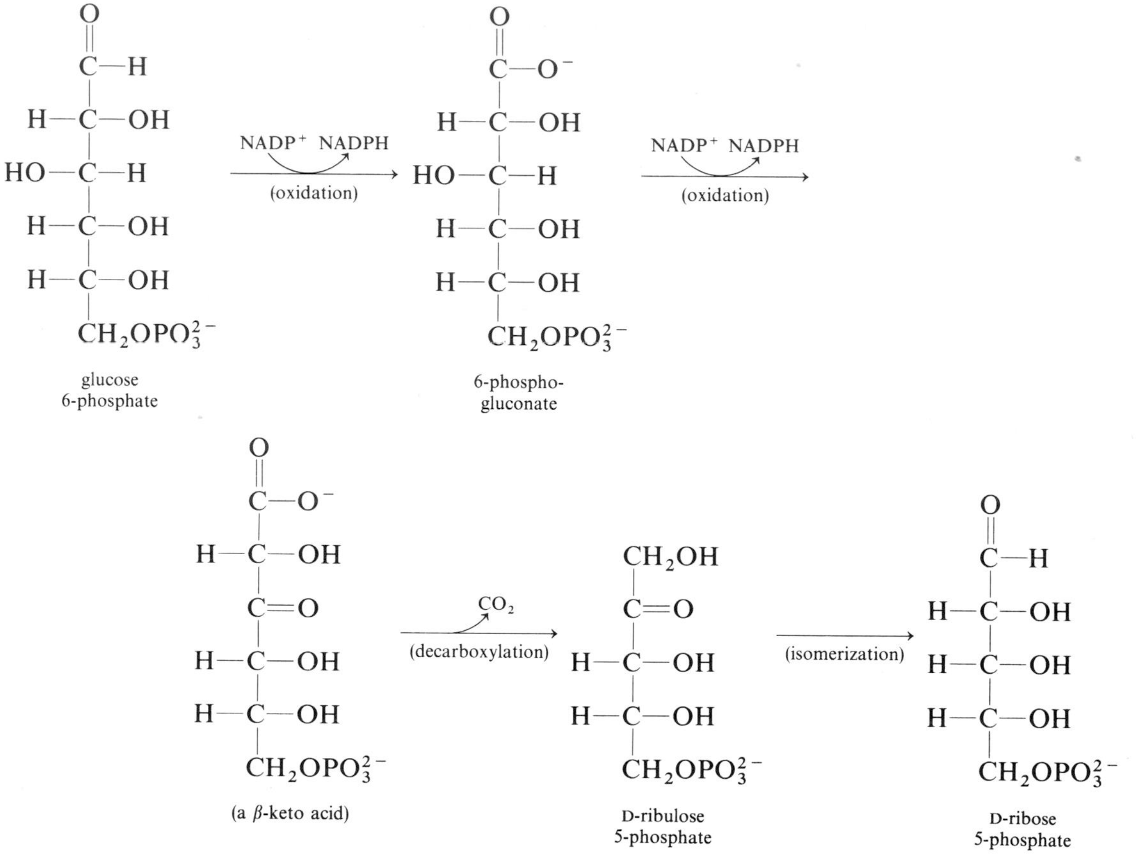

glucose
6-phosphate

6-phospho-
gluconate

(a β-keto acid)

D-ribulose
5-phosphate

D-ribose
5-phosphate

These four reactions of the pentose phosphate pathway illustrate two of its most important features. First, this metabolic pathway provides a pool of pentoses for the synthesis of nucleic acids. It also provides a pool of tetroses, not illustrated here. Second, it uses $NADP^+$ as an oxidizing agent and generates the reduced coenzyme NADPH. The major function of NADPH is as a reducing agent in the biosynthesis of other molecules. For example, adipose tissue, which has a high demand for reducing power to support the synthesis of fatty acids, is rich in $NADP^+$/NADPH. By comparison, glycolysis, oxidation of pyruvate, and the tricarboxylic acid cycle require NAD^+ and FAD as oxidizing agents, coenzymes that are reduced to NADH and $FADH_2$. These are in turn used for the generation of ATP through electron transport and oxidative phosphorylation (Section 24.5).

The pentose phosphate pathway is especially important for the normal functioning of red blood cells that depend on this pathway for a supply of NADPH, needed as a reducing agent to maintain iron atoms of hemoglobin in the Fe^{2+} state.

The activity of the pentose phosphate pathway is controlled by allosteric regulation of the first enzyme in the pathway, glucose 6-phosphate dehydrogenase. There is a genetic disease, **glucose 6-phosphate dehydrogenase deficiency,** that affects over 100 million people, mostly in Mediterranean and tropical areas. In this disease, operation of the pentose phosphate pathway is decreased due to a defect in glucose 6-phosphate dehydrogenase. As a result, concentrations of NADPH are lower than normal, erythrocyte membranes are fragile and rupture more easily than normal, and the average life span of erythrocytes is reduced. The clinical condition that results from glucose 6-phosphate dehydrogenase deficiency is called hemolytic anemia. Like sickle-cell anemia (see Mini-Essay XIV, "Abnormal Human Hemoglobins"), this disease appears to make individuals more resistant to certain malaria parasites.

F. Glycogenesis and Glycogenolysis

Glycogenesis and glycogenolysis are probably the most important metabolic pathways contributing to a relatively constant blood glucose level. When dietary intake of glucose exceeds immediate needs, humans and other animals convert the excess to glycogen (Section 19.5B), which is stored in liver and muscle tissue. In normal adults, the liver can store about 110 g of glycogen, and muscles about 255 g. The pathway that converts glucose to glycogen is called **glycogenesis**:

$$(C_6H_{10}O_5)_n + nH_2O \underset{\text{glycogenesis}}{\overset{\text{glycogenolysis}}{\rightleftharpoons}} nC_6H_{12}O_6$$

$$\underset{\text{glycogen}}{\phantom{(C_6H_{10}O_5)_n}} \qquad\qquad\qquad \underset{\text{glucose}}{\phantom{nC_6H_{12}O_6}}$$

Liver and muscle glycogen are storage forms of glucose. When there is need for additional blood glucose, glycogen is hydrolyzed and glucose released into the bloodstream. The pathway that hydrolyzes glycogen to glucose is called **glycogenolysis**. This process is stimulated by the pancreatic hormone glucagon (Problem 21.30). The counterbalancing actions of glucagon and insulin in regulating normal, resting levels of blood glucose are shown schematically in Figure 25.2.

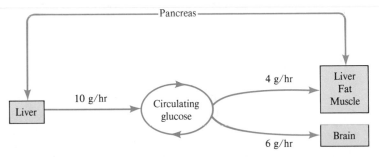

Figure 25.2 Under normal circumstances, the rate of glucagon-stimulated hydrolysis of glycogen and release of glucose into the bloodstream is balanced by insulin-stimulated uptake and metabolism of glucose by the brain and central nervous system, and muscle, adipose, and liver tissue.

G. Synthesis of Fatty Acids and Triglycerides

When carbohydrate intake is greater than the body's immediate needs for energy and its capacity to store glycogen, the excess is converted to fatty acids, which can be stored in almost unlimited quantities as triglycerides. To be stored as triglycerides, glucose is first catabolized to acetyl CoA, whose acetyl group provides the carbon atoms for the synthesis of fatty acids:

$$C_6H_{12}O_6 \longrightarrow \underset{\text{acetyl CoA}}{CH_3\overset{\displaystyle O}{\overset{\|}{C}}-SCoA} + 2CO_2$$

$$\underset{\text{glucose}}{} \qquad \qquad \updownarrow$$

$$\text{fatty acids}$$

Fatty acids are then combined with glycerol to form triglycerides. The synthesis of fatty acids from acetyl CoA represents a link between the metabolism of glucose and that of fatty acids. (We shall discuss the biochemistry of fatty acid synthesis and degradation in Chapter 26.)

H. Gluconeogenesis

The total supply of glucose in the form of liver and muscle glycogen and blood glucose can be depleted after about 12–18 hr of fasting. In fact, these stores of glucose often are not sufficient for the duration of an overnight fast between dinner and breakfast. Further, they also can be depleted in a short time during work or strenuous exercise. Without any way for additional supplies to be provided, nerve tissue, including the brain, would soon be deprived of glucose. Fortunately, the body has developed a metabolic pathway to overcome this problem.

Gluconeogenesis is the synthesis of glucose from noncarbohydrate molecules. During periods of low carbohydrate intake and when carbohydrate stores are being depleted rapidly, the carbon skeletons of lactate, glycerol (derived from the hydrolysis of fats), and certain amino acids are channeled into the synthesis of glucose.

$$\begin{matrix} \text{lactate} \\ \text{or} \\ \text{certain amino acids} \\ \text{or} \\ \text{glycerol} \end{matrix} \xrightarrow{\text{gluconeogenesis}} \text{glucose}$$

The major pathways in the metabolism of glucose are summarized in Figure 25.3.

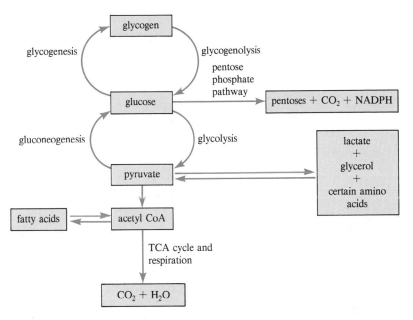

Figure 25.3 The flow of carbon atoms in the major metabolic pathways of glucose metabolism. The flow of energy (ATP generation and consumption) is not shown.

25.3 Glycolysis

A. Reactions of Glycolysis

Although writing the net reaction of **glycolysis** is simple (Section 25.2A), it took several decades of patient, intensive research by scores of scientists to discover the separate steps by which glucose is catabolized to pyruvate and to understand how this metabolic pathway is coupled with the production of ATP. By 1940, all the steps in glycolysis had been worked out. Glycolysis is frequently called the **Embden-Meyerhof pathway**, in honor of the two German biochemists, Gustav Embden and Otto Meyerhof, who contributed so greatly to our present knowledge of it.

All the reactions of glycolysis occur in the cytosol, and in a sense, the first reaction of glycolysis is transport of glucose across the cell membrane and into the cytosol. It is thought that transport involves combination of glucose with a carrier protein on the outer surface of the membrane, movement of this complex through the membrane, and release of glucose at the inner surface of the membrane. Because transport is from a high concentration outside the cell membrane toward a lower concentration inside the cell, the process is thought to be passive (Section 24.6B).

1. Phosphorylation of Glucose

The first step of glycolysis is phosphorylation of glucose by ATP to yield glucose 6-phosphate. Transfer of a phosphate group from ATP to an organic molecule is one of the basic reaction types in living systems, and any enzyme that catalyzes this type of reaction is called a kinase. The enzyme that catalyzes the transfer of a phosphate group from ATP to glucose (a hexose) is called hexokinase.

$$
\begin{array}{c}
\text{CHO} \\
\text{H}-\!\!-\text{OH} \\
\text{HO}-\!\!-\text{H} \\
\text{H}-\!\!-\text{OH} \\
\text{H}-\!\!-\text{OH} \\
\text{CH}_2\text{OH}
\end{array}
+ \text{ATP} \xrightarrow{\text{hexokinase}}
\begin{array}{c}
\text{CHO} \\
\text{H}-\!\!-\text{OH} \\
\text{HO}-\!\!-\text{H} \\
\text{H}-\!\!-\text{OH} \\
\text{H}-\!\!-\text{OH} \\
\text{CH}_2\text{OPO}_3^{2-}
\end{array}
+ \text{ADP}
$$

glucose   glucose 6-phosphate

Phosphorylation of glucose at this stage serves a very important function. Whereas glucose passes freely through membranes, phosphorylated intermediates normally do not pass through either cell or mitochondrial membranes. Thus, phosphorylation of glucose at this early stage confines it and all subsequent phosphorylated intermediates to the cytosol, where all glycolytic enzymes are located.

2. Isomerization of Glucose 6-Phosphate to Fructose 6-Phosphate

The second step of glycolysis, isomerization of glucose 6-phosphate to fructose 6-phosphate, is catalyzed by the enzyme phosphoglucoisomerase. This isomerization involves formation of an enediol intermediate (see Problem 15.21), which then forms the carbonyl group of the ketone in fructose 6-phosphate.

$$
\begin{array}{c}
\text{CHO} \\
\text{H}-\text{C}-\text{OH} \\
\text{HO}-\!\!-\text{H} \\
\text{H}-\!\!-\text{OH} \\
\text{H}-\!\!-\text{OH} \\
\text{CH}_2\text{OPO}_3^{2-}
\end{array}
\rightleftharpoons
\left[
\begin{array}{c}
\text{H}-\text{C}-\text{OH} \\
\| \\
\text{C}-\text{OH} \\
\text{HO}-\!\!-\text{H} \\
\text{H}-\!\!-\text{OH} \\
\text{H}-\!\!-\text{OH} \\
\text{CH}_2\text{OPO}_3^{2-}
\end{array}
\right]
\rightleftharpoons
\begin{array}{c}
\text{CH}_2\text{OH} \\
\text{C}=\text{O} \\
\text{HO}-\!\!-\text{H} \\
\text{H}-\!\!-\text{OH} \\
\text{H}-\!\!-\text{OH} \\
\text{CH}_2\text{OPO}_3^{2-}
\end{array}
$$

glucose 6-phosphate   (an enediol)   fructose 6-phosphate
(an aldohexose)   (a ketohexose)

3. Phosphorylation of Fructose 6-Phosphate

In the third step of glycolysis, a second mole of ATP is used to convert fructose 6-phosphate to fructose 1,6-diphosphate. This phosphorylation is catalyzed by phosphofructokinase, a allosteric enzyme whose activity is a key control point in the regulation of glycolysis. As will be discussed in Section 25.3C, the catalytic activity of this enzyme is regulated (increased as well as decreased) by a number of metabolites that are indicators of energy balance within the cell. Thus, through modulation of the catalytic activity of phosphofructokinase, glycolysis can be increased when there is demand for more ATP, or decreased when there is an adequate supply of ATP.

$$
\begin{array}{c}
\text{CH}_2\text{OH} \\
| \\
\text{C}=\text{O} \\
\text{HO}-\!\!|\!\!-\text{H} \\
\text{H}-\!\!|\!\!-\text{OH} \\
\text{H}-\!\!|\!\!-\text{OH} \\
| \\
\text{CH}_2\text{OPO}_3^{2-}
\end{array}
\;+\;\text{ATP}\;\xrightarrow{\text{phospho-fructokinase}}\;
\begin{array}{c}
\text{CH}_2\text{OPO}_3^{2-} \\
| \\
\text{C}=\text{O} \\
\text{HO}-\!\!|\!\!-\text{H} \\
\text{H}-\!\!|\!\!-\text{OH} \\
\text{H}-\!\!|\!\!-\text{OH} \\
| \\
\text{CH}_2\text{OPO}_3^{2-}
\end{array}
\;+\;\text{ADP}
$$

fructose
6-phosphate   fructose
1,6-diphosphate

4. Cleavage of Fructose 1,6-Diphosphate into Two Triose Phosphates

In the fourth step of glycolysis, fructose 1,6-diphosphate is cleaved to dihydroxyacetone phosphate and glyceraldehyde 3-phosphate by a reaction that is the reverse of an aldol condensation (Section 15.8). Recall that an aldol condensation involves addition of the alpha carbon of one carbonyl-containing compound to the carbonyl group of another to form a beta-hydroxyaldehyde or a beta-hydroxyketone. Among the functional groups in fructose 1,6-diphosphate is a ketone, and beta to it is a secondary alcohol. Because the cleavage of fructose 1,6-diphosphate is like the reverse of an aldol condensation, the enzyme that catalyzes this reaction is named aldolase.

$$
\begin{array}{c}
\text{CH}_2\text{OPO}_3^{2-} \\
| \\
\text{C}=\text{O} \\
\text{HO}-\!\!|\!\!-\text{H} \\
\text{H}-\!\!|\!\!-\text{OH} \\
\text{H}-\!\!|\!\!-\text{OH} \\
| \\
\text{CH}_2\text{OPO}_3^{2-}
\end{array}
\;\xrightarrow{\text{aldolase}}\;
\begin{array}{c}
\text{CH}_2\text{OPO}_3^{2-} \\
| \\
\text{C}=\text{O} \\
| \\
\text{CH}_2\text{OH} \\
+ \\
\text{H}-\text{C}=\text{O} \\
| \\
\text{H}-\text{C}-\text{OH} \\
| \\
\text{CH}_2\text{OPO}_3^{2-}
\end{array}
\quad
\begin{array}{l}
\text{dihydroxyacetone} \\
\text{phosphate} \\
\\
\\
\\
\\
\text{glyceraldehyde} \\
\text{3-phosphate}
\end{array}
$$

fructose 1,6-diphosphate

5. Isomerization of Dihydroxyacetone Phosphate to Glyceraldehyde 3-Phosphate

In the fifth step of glycolysis, dihydroxyacetone phosphate is converted to glyceraldehyde 3-phosphate by the same type of enediol intermediate we have already seen in the isomerization of glucose 6-phosphate to fructose 6-phosphate.

$$
\begin{array}{c}
\text{CH}_2\text{OH} \\
| \\
\text{C}=\text{O} \\
| \\
\text{CH}_2\text{OPO}_3^{2-}
\end{array}
\quad
\underset{\text{isomerase}}{\overset{\text{triose}}{\underset{\text{phosphate}}{\rightleftarrows}}}
\quad
\left[
\begin{array}{c}
\text{OH} \\
| \\
\text{C}-\text{H} \\
|| \\
\text{C}-\text{OH} \\
| \\
\text{CH}_2\text{OPO}_3^{2-}
\end{array}
\right]
\quad \rightleftarrows \quad
\begin{array}{c}
\text{O} \\
|| \\
\text{C}-\text{H} \\
| \\
\text{H}-\text{C}-\text{OH} \\
| \\
\text{CH}_2\text{OPO}_3^{2-}
\end{array}
$$

dihydroxyacetone phosphate (a ketotriose)   (an enediol)   glyceraldehyde 3-phosphate (an aldotriose)

6. Oxidation of the Aldehyde of Glyceraldehyde 3-Phosphate

In the sixth step, glyceraldehyde 3-phosphate is oxidized by NAD^+. In this reaction, catalyzed by glyceraldehyde 3-phosphate dehydrogenase, one phosphate ion is required. The immediate product of the aldehyde oxidation is the mixed anhydride, 1,3-diphosphoglycerate.

$$
\begin{array}{c}
\text{O} \\
|| \\
\text{C}-\text{H} \\
| \\
\text{H}-\text{C}-\text{OH} \\
| \\
\text{CH}_2\text{OPO}_3^{2-}
\end{array}
\; + NAD^+ + HPO_4^{2-}
\xrightarrow[\text{dehydrogenase}]{\text{glyceraldehyde 3-phosphate}}
\begin{array}{c}
\text{O} \\
|| \\
\text{C}-\text{OPO}_3^{2-} \\
| \\
\text{H}-\text{C}-\text{OH} \\
| \\
\text{CH}_2\text{OPO}_3^{2-}
\end{array}
\; + NADH
$$

A mixed anhydride

glyceraldehyde 3-phosphate   1,3-diphosphoglycerate

7. Transfer of a Phosphoryl Group to ADP to Form ATP

Transfer of a phosphoryl group from 1,3-diphosphoglycerate to ADP in the seventh step produces the first ATP generated in glycolysis. In this reaction, catalyzed by phosphoglycerate kinase, the anhydride bond of 1,3-diphosphoglycerate is exchanged for the terminal phosphate anhydride bond in ATP. This synthesis of ATP is known as substrate phosphorylation, to distinguish it from the oxidative phosphorylation of ADP that occurs during electron transport and oxidative phosphorylation in mitochondria.

$$
\begin{array}{c}
\text{O} \\
|| \\
\text{C}-\text{OPO}_3^{2-} \\
| \\
\text{H}-\text{C}-\text{OH} \\
| \\
\text{CH}_2\text{OPO}_3^{2-}
\end{array}
\; + ADP
\xrightarrow[\text{kinase}]{\text{phosphoglycerate}}
\begin{array}{c}
\text{O} \\
|| \\
\text{C}-\text{O}^- \\
| \\
\text{H}-\text{C}-\text{OH} \\
| \\
\text{CH}_2\text{OPO}_3^{2-}
\end{array}
\; + ATP
$$

1,3-diphosphoglycerate   3-phosphoglycerate

Let us stop and look at the energy balance to this point. Two molecules of ATP were consumed in the conversion of glucose to fructose 1,6-diphosphate.

Now, with the oxidation of two molecules of glyceraldehyde 3-phosphate to 3-phosphoglycerate (remember that the original glucose molecule has been split into 2 three-carbon fragments), two molecules of ATP have been generated. Thus, through the first seven steps of glycolysis, the energy debit and credit are balanced; there is neither profit nor loss.

8. Isomerization of 3-Phosphoglycerate to 2-Phosphoglycerate

In step 8, a phosphate group is transferred from the hydroxyl group of carbon 3 to the hydroxyl group on carbon 2. This isomerization is an exchange of phosphate esters between hydroxyl groups on glycerate. The reaction proceeds by enzyme-catalyzed transfer of a phosphate group from a phosphorylated enzyme, to form 2,3-diphosphoglycerate. The 3-phospho group of this intermediate is then transferred back to the enzyme, leaving 2-phosphoglycerate.

$$\begin{array}{c}CO_2^- \\ | \\ H-\!\!\!-\!\!OH \\ | \\ CH_2OPO_3^{2-}\end{array} + E\!-\!OPO_3^{2-} \xrightarrow{\text{phospho-glyceromutase}} \begin{array}{c}CO_2^- \\ | \\ H-\!\!\!-\!\!OPO_3^{2-} \\ | \\ CH_2OPO_3^{2-}\end{array} + E\!-\!OH$$

3-phosphoglycerate — 2,3-diphosphoglycerate

$$\begin{array}{c}CO_2^- \\ | \\ H-\!\!\!-\!\!OPO_3^{2-} \\ | \\ CH_2OPO_3^{2-}\end{array} + E\!-\!OH \xrightarrow{\text{phospho-glyceromutase}} \begin{array}{c}CO_2^- \\ | \\ H-\!\!\!-\!\!OPO_3^{2-} \\ | \\ CH_2OH\end{array} + E\!-\!OPO_3^{2-}$$

2,3-diphosphoglycerate — 2-phosphoglycerate

9. Dehydration of 2-Phosphoglycerate

In step 9, 2-phosphoglycerate is dehydrated by removal of H and OH from adjacent carbons, to form phosphoenolpyruvate. Because the product of this reaction contains an alcohol (as a phosphate ester) on a carbon-carbon double bond and is therefore an enol, the enzyme catalyzing the reaction is named enolase.

$$\begin{array}{c}CO_2^- \\ | \\ H-\!C\!-\!OPO_3^{2-} \\ | \\ CH_2OH\end{array} \xrightarrow{\text{enolase}} \begin{array}{c}CO_2^- \\ | \\ C\!-\!OPO_3^{2-} \\ \| \\ CH_2\end{array} + H_2O$$

2-phosphoglycerate — phosphoenolpyruvate

10. Transfer of a Phosphate Group from Phosphoenolpyruvate to ADP

The tenth and final step of glycolysis is what gives the energy profit. Phosphoenolpyruvate is a high-energy compound (Section 24.3C), and in this step, transfers its phosphate group to ADP, to form ATP. In the following equation, the terminal phospate group of ADP is written out to show how phosphate is transferred from phosphoenolpyruvate to ADP. Note that the name of the enzyme catalyzing this reaction, like all enzymes involving ADP and ATP, includes the word *kinase*.

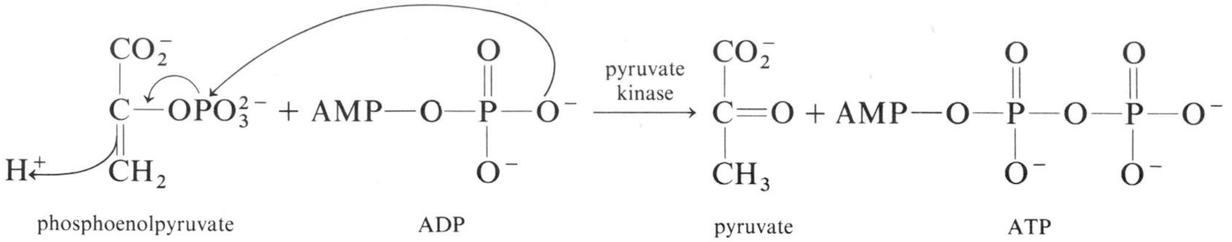

$$
\underset{\text{phosphoenolpyruvate}}{\overset{\text{CO}_2^-}{\underset{\text{CH}_2}{\overset{|}{\underset{|}{\text{C}}}}} \text{—OPO}_3^{2-}} + \underset{\text{ADP}}{\text{AMP—O—}\overset{\text{O}}{\underset{\text{O}^-}{\overset{||}{\text{P}}}}\text{—O}^-} \xrightarrow{\overset{\text{pyruvate}}{\text{kinase}}} \underset{\text{pyruvate}}{\overset{\text{CO}_2^-}{\underset{\text{CH}_3}{\overset{|}{\underset{|}{\text{C}}}}}\text{=O}} + \underset{\text{ATP}}{\text{AMP—O—}\overset{\text{O}}{\underset{\text{O}^-}{\overset{||}{\text{P}}}}\text{—O—}\overset{\text{O}}{\underset{\text{O}^-}{\overset{||}{\text{P}}}}\text{—O}^-}
$$

Because the carbon skeleton of glucose entering glycolysis is split into two triose phosphates, eventually giving two molecules of phosphoenolpyruvate, step 10 of glycolysis produces two molecules of ATP for each molecule of glucose entering the pathway.

The ten steps in the conversion of glucose to pyruvate, including those that consume NAD^+ and ATP as well as those that generate ATP, are summarized in Figure 25.4.

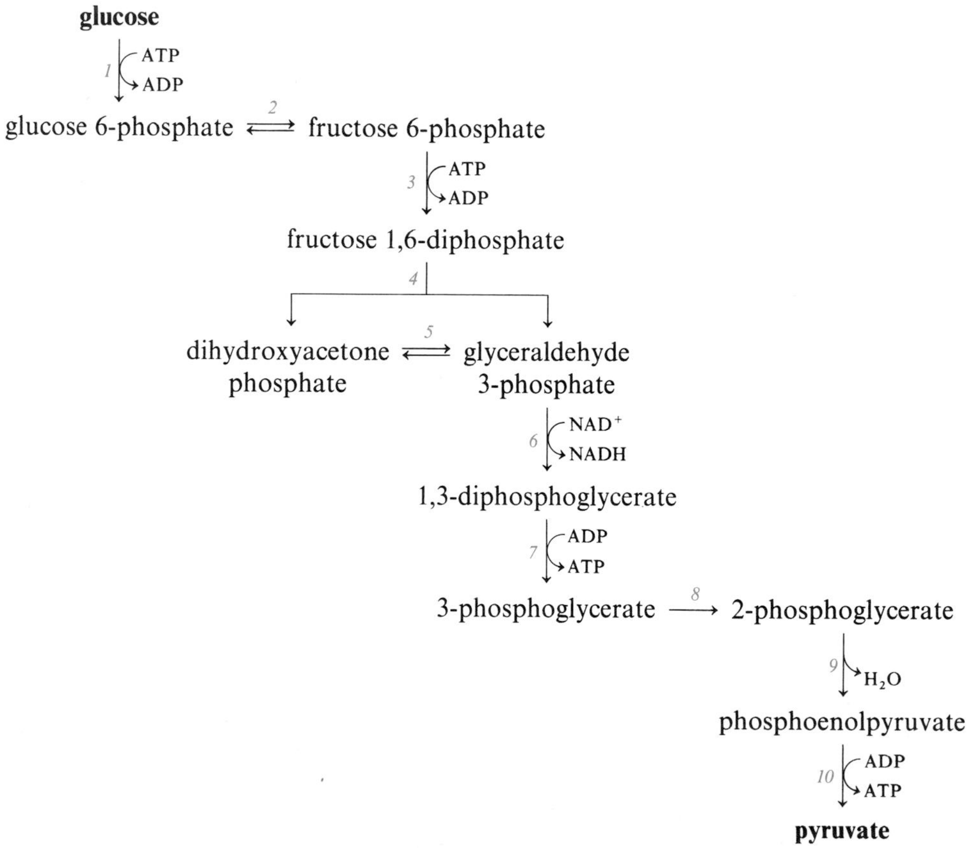

glucose

    1 ⌐ATP
       └ADP

glucose 6-phosphate ⇌² fructose 6-phosphate

    3 ⌐ATP
       └ADP

fructose 1,6-diphosphate

    4

dihydroxyacetone ⇌⁵ glyceraldehyde
phosphate   3-phosphate

    6 ⌐NAD^+
       └NADH

1,3-diphosphoglycerate

    7 ⌐ADP
       └ATP

3-phosphoglycerate →⁸ 2-phosphoglycerate

    9 └H_2O

phosphoenolpyruvate

    10 ⌐ADP
       └ATP

pyruvate

Figure 25.4 The ten steps of glycolysis.

Summing the energy balance for glycolysis, on the debit side two moles of ATP are required (steps 1 and 3) to convert glucose to fructose 1,6-diphosphate. On the credit side, two moles of ATP are produced in step 7 from reaction between 1,3-diphosphoglycerate and ADP, and another two moles in step 10 from reaction between phosphoenolpyruvate and ADP. Thus, there is a net profit of two moles of ATP per mole of glucose entering glycolysis.

Example 25.2

List all reactions of glycolysis that involve isomerization.

☐ *Solution*

An isomerization is a reaction in which a reactant and product are isomers of each other. There are three isomerizations in glycolysis:

Step 2: glucose 6-phosphate ⟶ fructose 6-phosphate
Step 5: dihydroxyacetone phosphate ⟶ glyceraldehyde 3-phosphate
Step 8: 3-phosphoglycerate ⟶ 2-phosphoglycerate

Problem 25.2

List all reactions of glycolysis that involve (a) oxidation; (b) cleavage of carbon-carbon bonds.

B. Entry of Fructose and Galactose into Glycolysis

Transformation of fructose into glycolytic intermediates takes place in the liver, and begins with phosphorylation of fructose by ATP, catalyzed by the enzyme fructokinase. Fructose 1-phosphate, the product, is then split into two trioses by the same type of reaction we have already seen in step 4 of glycolysis—in which fructose 1,6-diphosphate is cleaved into two trioses.

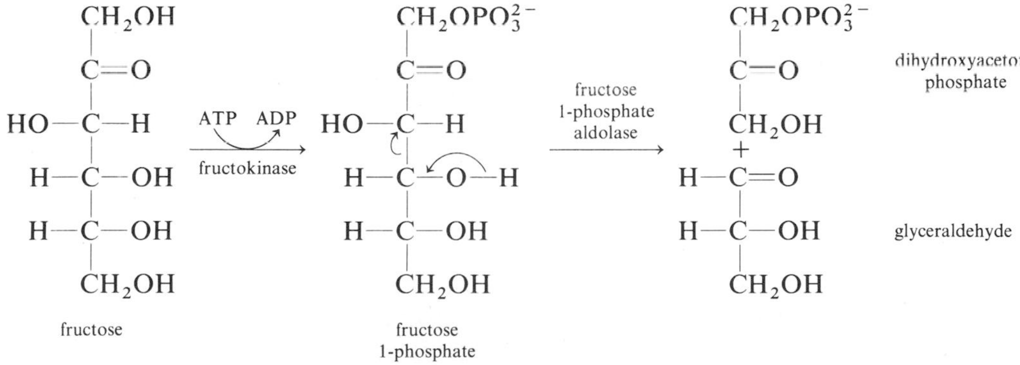

Dihydroxyacetone phosphate is a glycolytic intermediate and enters glycolysis at step 5. Glyceraldehyde is metabolized in several ways. It can be phosphorylated to glyceraldehyde 3-phosphate and then enter glycolysis. Alternatively, depending on the needs of the organism, it can be reduced to glycerol and then phosphorylated to glycerol phosphate, a metabolic intermediate required for the synthesis of phospholipids.

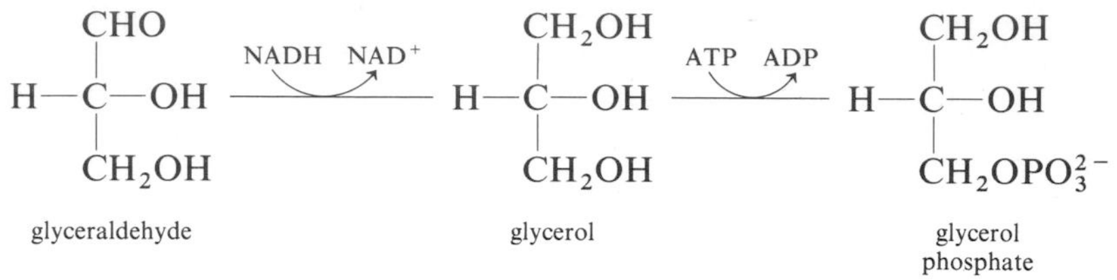

glyceraldehyde   glycerol   glycerol phosphate

As a result of a genetic disease, some humans lack the enzyme fructokinase and cannot metabolize fructose in the normal way. Fructose is instead excreted in the urine. Those who lack the enzyme fructose 1-phosphate aldolase have a much more serious problem. Because fructose 1-phosphate cannot be broken down to trioses, it accumulates in the liver and interferes with the activity of several enzyme systems, including those of gluconeogenesis. Kidney function is also disturbed. This condition is known as fructose intolerance. Vomiting and loss of appetite are early symptoms of **fructose intolerance**.

Galactose enters glycolysis by way of a series of reactions that convert it to glucose 6-phosphate:

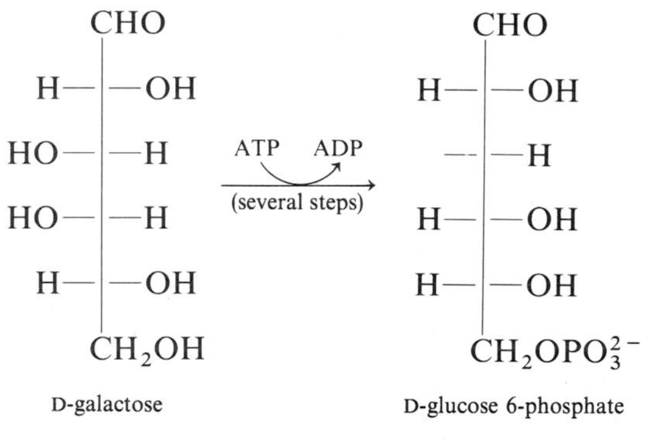

D-galactose   D-glucose 6-phosphate

The result of these steps is inversion of configuration at carbon 4 and phosphorylation of the hydroxyl group at carbon 6. Among humans, there is an inherited disease, **galactosemia**, which manifests itself by an inability to metabolize galactose. The genetic defect leading to galactosemia is the liver's failure to produce a key enzyme involved in the inversion of configuration at carbon 4 that converts galactose to glucose. In persons with this disease, galactose accumulates in the blood and various tissues, including those of the central nervous system, and causes damage to cells. Early symptoms are similar to those of lactose and fructose intolerance, namely diarrhea, nausea, and vomiting. Without treatment, an infant with galactosemia is likely to suffer irreversible brain damage and even death. If recognized in time, however, it can be treated simply.

Because milk is the only source of galactose, it is excluded from the infant's diet.

C. Regulation of Glycolysis

Within cells, the rate of glycolysis is controlled by the activity of two allosteric enzymes, hexokinase and phosphofructokinase. Hexokinase catalyzes the phosphorylation of glucose to glucose 6-phosphate:

Inhibited by
glucose 6-phosphate

$$\text{glucose} + \text{ATP} \xrightarrow{\text{hexokinase}} \text{glucose 6-phosphate} + \text{ADP}$$

Hexokinase represents a control point not only for glycolysis but also for other pathways in the metabolism of glucose. Unless glucose is first phosphorylated, it cannot enter glycolysis, the pentose phosphate pathway, or glycogenesis. Hexokinase is inhibited by a high concentration of glucose 6-phosphate, the end product of the reaction it catalyzes. Thus, phosphorylation of glucose is under self-control by feedback inhibition.

The second and more important control point for glycolysis is phosphofructokinase. Once glucose is converted to fructose 1,6-diphosphate, it is committed irreversibly to glycolysis. Because phosphorylation of fructose 6-phosphate represents a committed step, the enzyme that catalyzes it is ideally suited for being a regulatory enzyme. Phosphofructokinase is inhibited by high concentrations of ATP and citrate (an intermediate in the TCA) and it is activated by high concentrations of ADP and AMP.

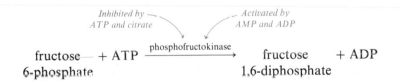

Inhibited by —   *Activated by*
ATP and citrate   *AMP and ADP*

$$\text{fructose 6-phosphate} + \text{ATP} \xrightarrow{\text{phosphofructokinase}} \text{fructose 1,6-diphosphate} + \text{ADP}$$

To understand the molecular logic behind these methods of enzyme regulation, remember that glycolysis provides fuel (in the form of acetyl CoA) for the tricarboxylic acid cycle, which in turn provides fuel (in the form of NADH and $FADH_2$) for respiration and oxidative phosphorylation. When a cell or organism is in a state of low energy demand (supplies of ATP are adequate for immediate energy needs), there is no need to commit glucose to carbohydrate degradation. Hence, the inhibition of phosphofructokinase by ATP. On the other hand, when a cell or organism is using a great deal of energy and the concentration of ATP decreases and of ADP and AMP increase, ADP and AMP become metabolic signals to speed the degradation of carbohydrates so that more ATP is produced.

25.4 Fates of Pyruvate

A key to understanding the fates of pyruvate is to recognize that it is produced by oxidation of glucose through the reactions of glycolysis. NAD^+ is the oxidizing agent and is reduced to NADH:

$$C_6H_{12}O_6 + 2NAD^+ \xrightarrow{\text{glycolysis}} 2CH_3\overset{\overset{\displaystyle O}{\|}}{C}CO_2^- + 2NADH$$

glucose   pyruvate

A continuing supply of NAD^+ is necessary for continued operation of glycolysis. Therefore, pyruvate is metabolized in ways that regenerate NAD^+.

A. Oxidation to Acetyl CoA

In most mammalian cells operating with a good supply of oxygen, O_2 is the terminal acceptor of electrons from NADH. During respiration, NADH is oxidized to NAD^+, oxygen is reduced to H_2O, and these processes are coupled with phosphorylation of ADP:

$$NADH + H^+ + \tfrac{1}{2}O_2 \xrightarrow{\text{respiration}} NAD^+ + H_2O$$

Thus, under aerobic conditions, where supplies of ATP and NAD^+ are furnished by electron transport and oxidative phosphorylation, pyruvate is transported into the mitochondria by a specific carrier protein and there oxidized to acetyl coenzyme A, a fuel for the tricarboxylic acid cycle.

$$CH_3\overset{\overset{\displaystyle O}{\|}}{C}CO_2^- + NAD^+ + CoA{-}SH \xrightarrow[\text{dehydrogenase}]{\text{pyruvate}} CH_3\overset{\overset{\displaystyle O}{\|}}{C}{-}SCoA + NADH + CO_2$$

pyruvate   acetyl CoA

Oxidation is catalyzed by pyruvate dehydrogenase, a multienzyme complex attached to the inner wall of the mitochondrion. Coenzymes required for oxidation of pyruvate to acetyl CoA are NAD^+, coenzyme A, lipoic acid, FAD, and thiamine pyrophosphate.

B. Reduction to Lactate: Lactate Fermentation

Under anaerobic conditions, when oxygen is not available to accept electrons, the electron carriers of the electron transport system (Section 24.5) become almost totally reduced. Consequently, even if NADH produced in the cytosol by glycolysis were transported into the mitochondria, there would be no way for it to be reoxidized to NAD^+. Yet, glycolysis must proceed, because it is the only way to generate ATP under anaerobic conditions. In vertebrates, the most important pathway for regeneration of NAD^+ under anaerobic conditions is reduction of pyruvate to lactate catalyzed by lactate dehydrogenase:

$$CH_3\overset{\overset{\displaystyle O}{\|}}{C}CO_2^- + NADH + H^+ \xrightarrow[\text{dehydrogenase}]{\text{lactate}} CH_3\overset{\overset{\displaystyle OH}{|}}{C}HCO_2^- + NAD^+$$

pyruvate   lactate

Adding the reduction of lactate to the net reaction of glycolysis gives an overall reaction for a metabolic pathway called **lactate fermentation**:

$$C_6H_{12}O_6 + 2ADP + HPO_4^{2-} \xrightarrow[\text{fermentation}]{\text{lactate}} 2CH_3\overset{\overset{\displaystyle OH}{|}}{C}HCO_2^- + 2ATP + 2H^+$$

glucose   lactate

While lactate fermentation allows glycolysis to continue in the absence of oxygen and generates some ATP, it also brings about an increase in the concentration of lactate, and perhaps more important, protons, in muscle tissue and in the bloodstream. This buildup of lactate and protons is associated with fatigue. When blood lactate reaches a concentration of about 0.4 mg/100 mL, muscle tissue becomes almost completely exhausted.

Most of the lactate formed in active skeletal muscle is transported by the bloodstream to the liver, where it is converted to glucose by the reactions of gluconeogenesis. This newly synthesized glucose is then returned to skeletal muscles for further anaerobic glycolysis and generation of ATP. In this way, a part of the metabolic burden of active skeletal muscle is shifted, at least temporarily, to the liver. Transport of lactate from muscle to the liver, resynthesis of glucose by gluconeogenesis, and return of glucose to muscle tissue is called the Cori cycle (Figure 25.5).

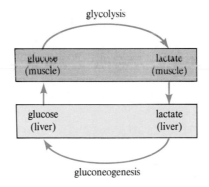

Figure 25.5 The Cori cycle.

C. Reduction to Ethanol: Alcoholic Fermentation

Yeast and several other organisms have developed an alternative pathway to regenerate NAD^+ under anaerobic conditions. In the first step of this pathway, pyruvate is decarboxylated to acetaldehyde:

$$CH_3\overset{\overset{\displaystyle O}{\|}}{C}CO_2^- + H^+ \xrightarrow[\text{decarboxylase}]{\text{pyruvate}} CH_3\overset{\overset{\displaystyle O}{\|}}{C}H + CO_2$$

pyruvate   acetaldehyde

The carbon dioxide produced in this reaction is responsible for the foam on beer and the carbonation of naturally fermented wines and champagnes. In a second step, acetaldehyde is reduced by NADH to ethanol:

$$CH_3\overset{\overset{\displaystyle O}{\|}}{C}H + NADH + H^+ \xrightarrow[\text{dehydrogenase}]{\text{alcohol}} CH_3CH_2OH + NAD^+$$

acetaldehyde   ethanol

Adding reactions for the decarboxylation of pyruvate and reduction of acetaldehyde to the net reaction of glycolysis gives the overall reaction for **alcoholic fermentation**:

$$C_6H_{12}O_6 + 2ADP + 2HPO_4^{2-} \xrightarrow[\text{fermentation}]{\text{alcoholic}} 2CH_3CH_2OH + 2CO_2 + 2ATP$$

glucose   ethanol

Note that both alcoholic fermentation and lactate fermentation represent ways in which cells can continue glycolysis under anaerobic conditions, that is, under conditions where NADH cannot be reoxidized by O_2.

Example 25.3

Under conditions of high oxygen concentration in muscle cells, which of the following compounds would be present in higher concentration?

a. NAD^+ or NADH   **b.** acetyl CoA or coenzyme A

☐ *Solution*

a. If there is an adequate supply of oxygen to cells, NADH can be oxidized to NAD^+, and therefore, NAD^+ will be present in higher concentration than NADH.

b. If NAD^+ is present in high concentrations, glycolysis can continue and pyruvate is produced. Pyruvate is, in turn, converted to acetyl CoA, and therefore, the concentration of acetyl CoA increases and of free coenzyme A decreases.

Problem 25.3

Under conditions of low oxygen concentration in muscle cells, which of the following compounds, do you predict, would be present in higher concentration?

a. acetyl CoA or lactate   **b.** lactate or pyruvate

25.5 The Tricarboxylic Acid Cycle

Under aerobic conditions, the central metabolic pathway for the oxidation of the carbon skeletons of not only carbohydrates but also of fatty acids and amino acids to carbon dioxide is the **tricarboxylic acid cycle (TCA)**, known alternatively as the citric acid cycle, or **Krebs cycle**. The last-mentioned name is in honor of Sir Adolph Krebs, the biochemist who in 1937 first proposed the cyclic nature of this pathway. The name *citric acid cycle* is little used today, because it gives undue importance to what is but one of the intermediates in this metabolic pathway. All enzymes of the TCA cycle are located within the mitochondria, most within the mitochondrial matrix.

Through the reactions of the TCA cycle, the carbon atoms of the acetyl group of acetyl CoA are oxidized to carbon dioxide. As you can see from the balanced half-reaction, this is an eight-electron oxidation.

$$CH_3\overset{\displaystyle O}{\overset{\displaystyle \|}{C}}-SCoA + 3H_2O \longrightarrow 2CO_2 + CoA-SH + 8H^+ + 8e^-$$

This oxidation is brought about by three molecules of NAD^+ and one molecule of FAD. Following are balanced half-reactions for the reduction of NAD^+ to NADH and FAD to $FADH_2$.

$$3NAD^+ + 3H^+ + 6e^- \longrightarrow 3NADH$$
$$FAD + 2H^+ + 2e^- \longrightarrow FADH_2$$
$$\overline{3NAD^+ + FAD + 5H^+ + 8e^- \longrightarrow 3NADH + FADH_2}$$

Adding the balanced half-reactions for the oxidation of the two-carbon acetyl group of acetyl CoA and the reduction of three moles of NAD^+ and one mole of FAD gives the net reaction of the tricarboxylic acid cycle:

$$CH_3\overset{\displaystyle O}{\overset{\displaystyle \|}{C}}SCoA + 3NAD^+ + FAD + 3H_2O \xrightarrow{\text{tricarboxylic acid cycle}}$$

$$2CO_2 + CoA-SH + 3NADH + FADH_2 + 3H^+$$

As we study the individual reactions of the TCA cycle, we shall concentrate on the four reactions that involve oxidations and produce reduced coenzymes, and the two that produce carbon dioxide.

A. Steps in the Tricarboxylic Acid Cycle

1. Formation of Citrate

The two-carbon acetyl group of acetyl coenzyme A enters the TCA cycle by carbonyl condensation between the alpha carbon of acetyl CoA and the carbonyl group of oxaloacetate. The product of this reaction is citrate, the tricarboxylic acid from which the cycle derives one of its names. In this reaction, catalyzed by citrate synthase, carbonyl condensation is coupled with hydrolysis of the thioester to form free coenzyme A:

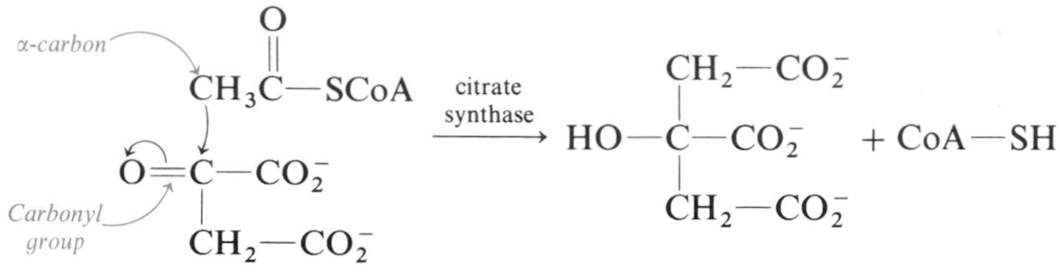

oxaloacetate   citrate

Oxaloacetate is in a sense a starting point of the TCA cycle, and it is also an endpoint. As we shall see, subsequent reactions of the cycle regenerate oxaloacetate, thus providing for entry of further acetyl groups into the cycle.

2. Isomerization of Citrate to Isocitrate

In the second reaction of the cycle, catalyzed by aconitase, citrate is converted to an isomer, isocitrate. It is thought that this isomerization is accomplished in two reactions, both catalyzed by aconitase. First, in a reaction analogous to acid-catalyzed dehydration of an alcohol (Section 13.4A), citrate undergoes enzyme-catalyzed dehydration to aconitate. Then, in a reaction analogous to acid-catalyzed hydration of an alkene (Section 12.5C), aconitate undergoes enzyme-catalyzed hydration to form isocitrate.

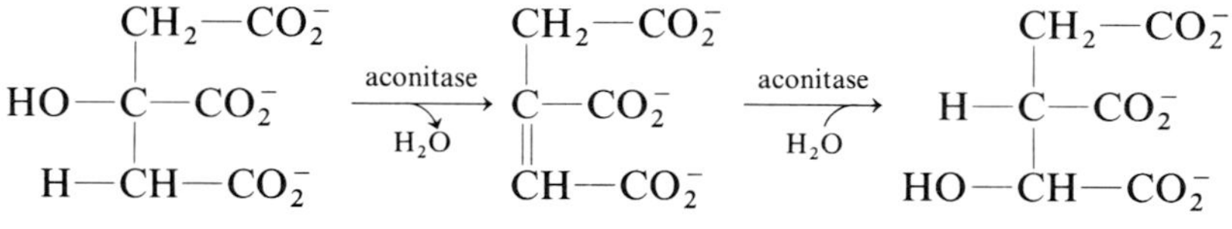

citrate   aconitate   isocitrate

3. Oxidation and Decarboxylation of Isocitrate

In step 3, the secondary alcohol of isocitrate is oxidized to a ketone by NAD^+ in a reaction catalyzed by isocitrate dehydrogenase. The product, oxalosuccinate, is a beta-ketoacid and undergoes decarboxylation (Section 16.5D) to produce alpha-ketoglutarate.

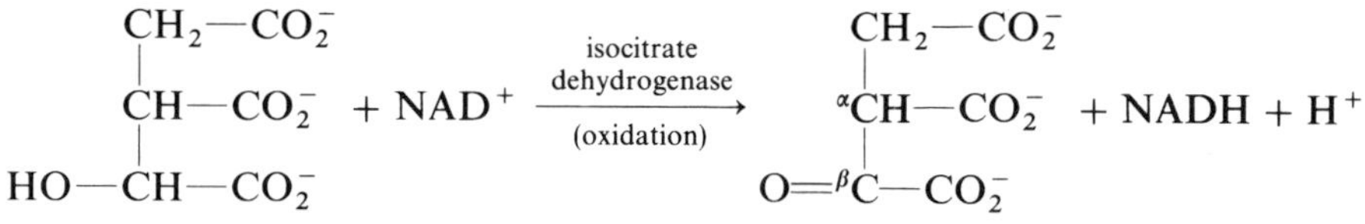

isocitrate   oxalosuccinate
         (a β-ketoacid)

$$\underset{\text{oxalosuccinate}}{\begin{array}{l} CH_2-CO_2^- \\ | \\ CH-CO_2^- \\ | \\ O=C-CO_2^- \end{array}} + H^+ \xrightarrow[\text{(decarboxylation)}]{\text{isocitrate dehydrogenase}} \underset{\alpha\text{-ketoglutarate}}{\begin{array}{l} CH_2-CO_2^- \\ | \\ CH_2 \\ | \\ O=C-CO_2^- \end{array}} + CO_2$$

4. Oxidation and Decarboxylation of Alpha-Ketoglutarate

The second molecule of carbon dioxide is generated by the TCA cycle in the same type of oxidative decarboxylation as that for the conversion of pyruvate to acetyl CoA and carbon dioxide (Section 25.4A). In oxidative decarboxylation of alpha-ketoglutarate, the carboxyl group is converted to carbon dioxide and the adjacent ketone is oxidized to a carboxyl group in the form of a thioester with coenzyme A.

$$\underset{\alpha\text{-ketoglutarate}}{\begin{array}{l} CH_2-CO_2^- \\ | \\ CH_2 \\ | \\ O=C-CO_2^- \end{array}} + NAD^+ + CoA-SH \xrightarrow{\alpha\text{-ketoglutarate dehydrogenase}} \underset{\substack{\text{succinyl coenzyme A} \\ \text{(succinyl CoA)}}}{\begin{array}{l} CH_2-CO_2^- \\ | \\ CH_2 \\ | \\ O=C-SCoA \end{array}} + NADH + CO_2$$

Then, in coupled reactions catalyzed by succinyl CoA synthetase, succinyl coenzyme A, HPO_4^{2-}, and guanosine diphosphate (GDP) react, to form succinate, guanosine triphosphate (GTP), and coenzyme A:

$$\underset{\text{succinyl CoA}}{\begin{array}{l} CH_2-CO_2^- \\ | \\ CH_2-C-SCoA \\ \quad\quad \| \\ \quad\quad O \end{array}} + GDP + HPO_4^{2-} \xrightarrow{\substack{\text{succinyl CoA} \\ \text{synthetase}}} \underset{\text{succinate}}{\begin{array}{l} CH_2-CO_2^- \\ | \\ CH_2-CO_2^- \end{array}} + GTP + CoA-SH$$

The terminal phosphate group of GTP can be transferred to ADP according to the reaction

$$GTP + ADP \rightleftharpoons GDP + ATP$$

Thus, one molecule of a high-energy compound (either GTP or ATP) is produced for each molecule of acetyl CoA entering the tricarboxylic acid cycle. This is the only reaction of the TCA cycle that conserves energy as ATP.

5. Oxidation of Succinate

In the third oxidation of the cycle, catalyzed by succinate dehydrogenase, succinate is oxidized to fumarate. The oxidizing agent is FAD, which is reduced to $FADH_2$. Succinate dehydrogenase is inhibited by such compounds as malonate (Section 22.4F).

$$\underset{\text{succinate}}{\underset{\displaystyle \begin{array}{c} CO_2^- \\ | \\ CH_2 \\ | \\ CH_2 \\ | \\ CO_2^- \end{array}}{}} + FAD \quad \xrightarrow[\text{dehydrogenase}]{\text{succinate}} \quad \underset{\text{fumarate}}{\underset{\displaystyle \begin{array}{c} H \quad CO_2^- \\ \diagdown C \diagup \\ \| \\ C \\ \diagup \diagdown \\ ^-O_2C \quad H \end{array}}{}} + FADH_2$$

6. Hydration of Fumarate

In the second hydration of the tricarboxylic acid cycle, fumarate is converted to L-malate in a reaction catalyzed by the enzyme fumarase:

$$\underset{\text{fumarate}}{\underset{\displaystyle \begin{array}{c} H \quad CO_2^- \\ \diagdown C \diagup \\ \| \\ C \\ \diagup \diagdown \\ ^-O_2C \quad H \end{array}}{}} + H_2O \quad \xrightarrow{\text{fumarase}} \quad \underset{\text{L-malate}}{\underset{\displaystyle \begin{array}{c} CO_2^- \\ | \\ HO-C-H \\ | \\ CH_2 \\ | \\ CO_2^- \end{array}}{}}$$

Fumarase shows a high degree of specificity; it recognizes only fumarate (a trans isomer) as a substrate and gives only L-malate (one member of a pair of enantiomers) as the product.

7. Oxidation of L-Malate

In the fourth and final oxidation of the TCA cycle, L-malate is oxidized by NAD^+ to oxaloacetate:

$$\underset{\text{L-malate}}{\underset{\displaystyle \begin{array}{c} CO_2^- \\ | \\ HO-C-H \\ | \\ CH_2 \\ | \\ CO_2^- \end{array}}{}} + NAD^+ \quad \xrightarrow[\text{dehydrogenase}]{\text{malate}} \quad \underset{\text{oxaloacetate}}{\underset{\displaystyle \begin{array}{c} CO_2^- \\ | \\ O=C \\ | \\ CH_2 \\ | \\ CO_2^- \end{array}}{}} + NADH + H^+$$

With production of oxaloacetate, the reactions of the tricarboxylic acid cycle are complete. Continued operation of the cycle requires two things: (1) a supply of carbon atoms in the form of acetyl groups from acetyl CoA, and (2) a supply of oxidizing agents in the form of NAD^+ and FAD. The TCA cycle is linked to glycolysis and the oxidation of pyruvate to get acetyl CoA as a fuel, and it is also linked to the breakdown of fatty acids and amino acids. For a supply of NAD^+ and FAD, the cycle depends on reactions of the electron transport system and oxidative phosphorylation. Recall (Section 24.5) that since oxygen is the final acceptor of electrons in the electron transport system, continued operation of the TCA cycle depends ultimately on an adequate supply of oxygen.

Another important feature of the cycle is best seen by returning to the balanced equation for the cycle (Section 25.2C):

$$CH_3\overset{\displaystyle O}{\overset{\displaystyle \|}{C}}-SCoA + 3NAD^+ + FAD + HPO_4^{2-} + ADP \xrightarrow{\text{TCA cycle}}$$

$$2CO_2 + 3NADH + FADH_2 + ATP + CoA-SH$$

The TCA cycle is truly catalytic; its intermediates do not enter into the balanced equation for this pathway, since they are neither destroyed nor synthesized in the net reaction. The only function of the TCA cycle is to accept acetyl groups from acetyl CoA, oxidize them to carbon dioxide, and at the same time produce a supply of reduced coenzymes as fuel for electron transport and oxidative phosphorylation. In fact, if any of the intermediates of the cycle is removed, then operation of the cycle ceases, because there is no way to regenerate oxalo acetate. As we shall see, however, the cycle is connected through several of its intermediates to other metabolic pathways. In practice, certain intermediates of the cycle can be used for the synthesis of other biomolecules, provided that another intermediate is supplied that in turn can be converted to oxaloacetate, making up for the intermediate withdrawn.

The reactions of the tricarboxylic acid cycle, including those that generate carbon dioxide, reduced coenzymes, and high-energy phosphates, are summarized in Figure 25.6. This figure also shows the central role of this cycle and its linkage to other metabolic pathways.

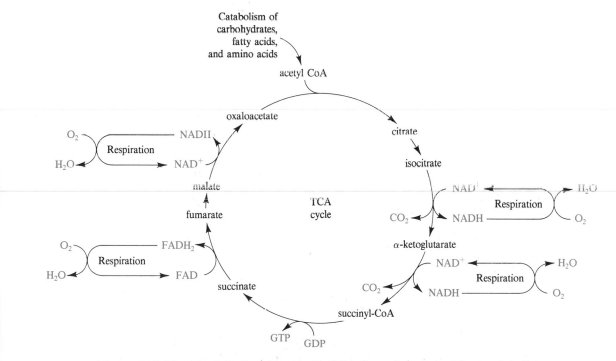

Figure 25.6 The tricarboxylic acid cycle. Fuel for the cycle is derived from catabolism of carbohydrates, fatty acids, and amino acids. For a continuing supply of NAD^+ and FAD, the TCA cycle depends on respiration and oxygen.

B. Control of the Tricarboxylic Acid Cycle

The chief points of control of the TCA cycle are two regulatory enzymes.

Enzyme Name	How Regulated
citrate synthetase	inhibited by ATP and NADH
isocitrate dehydrogenase	inhibited by ATP and NADH, activated by ADP

To appreciate the importance of these regulatory enzymes, remember that the main function of the TCA cycle is to provide fuel in the form of reduced coenzymes for electron transport and oxidative phosphorylation (Section 24.5). Under conditions where supplies of ATP are adequate for the immediate needs of cells, ATP interacts with citrate synthetase to reduce its affinity for acetyl coenzyme A. Thus, ATP acts as a negative modifier of citrate synthetase and inhibits entry of acetyl CoA into the TCA cycle. In this case, acetyl CoA is channeled into the synthesis of fatty acids and triglycerides (Section 26.5). Similarly, NADH, a product of the TCA cycle, acts as a negative modifier of citrate synthetase. Isocitrate dehydrogenase, the primary control point in the cycle, is also inhibited by ATP and NADH. Because the activity of this enzyme is increased by interaction with ADP, this substance is said to be a positive modifier of isocitrate dehydrogenase.

25.6 Energy Balance for Oxidation of Glucose to Carbon Dioxide and Water

Now that we have examined the biochemical pathways by which the carbon atoms of glucose are oxidized to carbon dioxide, let us look at the energy changes in these transformations. Complete oxidation of glucose to carbon dioxide occurs with a large decrease in free energy:

$$C_6H_{12}O_6 + 6O_2 \longrightarrow 6CO_2 + 6H_2O \qquad \Delta G^0 = -686,000 \text{ cal/mol}$$

The number of moles of ATP derived from aerobic catabolism of glucose are summarized in Table 25.1. Note that glycolysis takes place in the cytoplasm. For glucose catabolized in skeletal muscle, one ATP is required to transport each NADH produced by glycolysis from the cytosol to the mitochondrion, site of the TCA cycle, thus yielding 36 mol ATP per mole of glucose. In the liver and heart muscle, however, NADH is transported from the cytoplasm to the mitochondria by a different mechanism, which does not require expenditure of ATP. Thus, in the liver and heart muscle, 38 mol ATP is produced per mole of glucose.

We can write the net reaction and the associated energy changes for the complete oxidation of glucose as the sum of an exergonic oxidation of glucose to carbon dioxide and water and an endergonic phosphorylation of 36 moles of ADP.

Table 25.1 Yield of ATP from the complete oxidation of glucose to carbon dioxide and water in skeletal muscle.

Reaction	Process	Yield of ATP (moles)
Glycolysis		
glucose $\longrightarrow$ glucose 6-phosphate	phosphorylation	-1
fructose 6-phosphate $\longrightarrow$ fructose 1,6-diphosphate	phosphorylation	-1
glyceraldehyde 3-phosphate $\longrightarrow$ 1,3-diphosphoglycerate	oxidation by NAD^+	$+6$
transport of NADH from cytosol to mitochondrion	active transport	-2
1,3-diphosphoglycerate $\longrightarrow$ 3-phosphoglycerate	phosphorylation	$+2$
phosphoenolpyruvate $\longrightarrow$ pyruvate	phosphorylation	$+2$
Oxidation of pyruvate		
pyruvate $\longrightarrow$ acetyl CoA + CO_2	oxidation by NAD^+	$+6$
Tricarboxylic acid cycle		
isocitrate $\longrightarrow$ α-ketoglutarate + CO_2	oxidation by NAD^+	$+6$
α-ketoglutarate $\longrightarrow$ succinyl CoA + CO_2	oxidation by NAD^+	$+6$
succinyl CoA $\longrightarrow$ succinate	phosphorylation	$+2$
succinate $\longrightarrow$ fumarate	oxidation by FAD	$+4$
malate $\longrightarrow$ oxaloacetate	oxidation by NAD^+	$+6$
Net yield of ATP (skeletal muscle) per mole of glucose		$+36$

Exergonic Reaction

$$C_6H_{12}O_6 + 6O_2 \longrightarrow 6CO_2 + 6H_2O \qquad \Delta G^0 = -686{,}000 \text{ cal/mol}$$

Endergonic Reaction

$$36ADP + 36HPO_4^{2-} \longrightarrow 36ATP + 36H_2O \qquad \Delta G^0 = +263{,}000 \text{ cal/mol}$$

Overall Reaction

$$C_6H_{12}O_6 + 6O_2 + 36ADP + 36HPO_4^{2-} \longrightarrow$$
$$6CO_2 + 36ATP + 42H_2O \qquad \Delta G^0 = -423{,}000 \text{ cal/mol}$$

Can be used for biochemical work   *Liberated as heat*

The total energy conserved as a result of aerobic oxidation of 1 mol of glucose is 36 mol of ATP, or 263,000 cal/mol. The efficiency of energy conservation during glucose metabolism is

$$\frac{263{,}000}{686{,}000} \times 100 = 38\% \text{ free energy conserved as ATP}$$

It is an impressive feat for living cells to trap this amount of energy as ATP!

The decrease in free energy for lactate fermentation (glucose $\longrightarrow$ lactate) is 47,000 cal/mol, a much smaller value than that for aerobic oxidation of glucose to carbon dioxide. We can write the net reaction and associated energy changes for lactate fermentation as the sum of the exergonic conversion of glucose to lactate and the endergonic phosphorylation of ADP.

Exergonic Reaction

$$\text{Glucose} \longrightarrow \text{2 lactate} \qquad\qquad \Delta G^0 = -47,000 \text{ cal/mol}$$

Endergonic Reaction

$$2\text{ADP} + 2\text{HPO}_4^{2-} \longrightarrow 2\text{ATP} + 2\text{H}_2\text{O} \qquad\qquad \Delta G^0 = +14,600 \text{ cal/mol}$$

Overall Reaction

$$\text{Glucose} + 2\text{ADP} + 2\text{HPO}_4^{2-} \longrightarrow \text{2 lactate} + 2\text{ATP} + 2\text{H}_2\text{O} \qquad \Delta G^0 = -32,400 \text{ cal/mol}$$

Thus, the total energy conserved through lactate fermentation of 1 mol of glucose is 2 mol of ATP or 14,600 cal/mol.

$$\frac{14,600}{686,000} \times 100 = 2\% \text{ free energy conserved as ATP}$$

Lactate fermentation keeps glycolysis going, but at a cost. Only 2 mol of ATP are produced per mole of glucose by lactate fermentation, compared to 36 mol of ATP produced by complete oxidation of glucose to carbon dioxide and water. The same is true for alcoholic fermentation. Thus, in the use of fuel molecules for producing heat and ATP, aerobic catabolism of glucose is 18 times more efficient than either lactate or alcoholic fermentation.

Key Terms and Concepts

alcoholic fermentation (25.4C)

blood glucose levels (25.1B)

Cori cycle (25.4B)

digestion of carbohydrates (25.1A)

Embden-Meyerhoff pathway (25.3A)

fructose intolerance (25.3B)

galactosemia (25.3B)

gluconeogenesis (25.2H)

glucose 6-phosphate dehydrogenase deficiency (25.2E)

glucose tolerance test (25.1C)

glycogenesis (25.2F)

glycogenolysis (25.2F)

glycolysis (25.3)

hyperglycemia (25.1B)

hypoglycemia (25.1B)

Krebs cycle (25.5)

lactate fermentation (25.4B)

oxidative phosphorylation (25.2D)

pentose phosphate pathway (25.2E)

tricarboxylic acid cycle (25.5)

Key Reactions

1. Hydrolysis of disaccharides and polysaccharides to monosaccharides (Section 25.1A).
2. Net reaction of glycolysis (Section 25.2A).
3. Net reaction for oxidative decarboxylation of pyruvate (Section 25.2B).
4. Net reaction for the tricarboxylic acid cycle (Section 25.2C).
5. Net reaction for the pentose phosphate pathway (Section 25.2E).
6. Net reaction for glycogenolysis (Section 25.2F).
7. Net reaction for glycogenesis (Section 25.2F).
8. The 10 steps in glycolysis (Section 25.3A).
9. Entry of fructose and galactose into glycolysis (Section 25.3B).
10. Oxidative decarboxylation of pyruvate to acetyl CoA during aerobic respiration (Section 25.4A).
11. Reduction of pyruvate to lactate during lactate fermentation (Section 25.4B).
12. Reduction of pyruvate to ethanol during alcoholic fermentation (Section 25.4C).
13. The 7 steps of the tricarboxylic acid cycle (Section 25.5A).

Problems

Central role of glucose in carbohydrate metabolism (Section 25.2)

25.4 Match the names with the processes listed.
   a. glycolysis   **b.** gluconeogenesis
   c. glycogenolysis   **d.** glycogenesis
   _____ synthesis of glucose from noncarbohydrate molecules
   _____ breakdown of glucose to pyruvate
   _____ hydrolysis of glycogen to glucose
   _____ conversion of glucose to glycogen

25.5 How many moles of ATP are produced either directly or by oxidation of reduced coenzymes and phosphorylation of ADP when:
   a. 2 mol glucose is oxidized to CO_2?
   b. 2 mol glucose is oxidized to pyruvate?
   c. 2 mol glucose 6-phosphate is oxidized to 2 mol ribose 5-phosphate?
   d. 2 mol acetyl CoA is oxidized to fumarate?

25.6 When liver stores of glycogen are very low (in the morning or during vigorous exercise) and blood glucose levels are low, how can glucose be produced and energy supplied?

25.7 Name two important functions of the pentose phosphate pathway.

25.8 What is the difference in structural formula between NAD^+ and $NADP^+$?

25.9 The degradation of carbohydrates provides the cell with three things. energy; NADPH as a reducing agent for biosynthesis; and a pool of

intermediates for the biosynthesis of other molecules. Which of these three are produced by the following pathways?
a. conversion of glucose to lactate
b. tricarboxylic acid cycle
c. pentose phosphate pathway
d. conversion of glucose to ethanol

Glycolysis (Section 25.3)

25.10 Name one coenzyme required for glycolysis. From what vitamin is this coenzyme derived?

25.11 Number the carbon atoms of glucose 1 through 6 and show the fate of each atom in glycolysis.

25.12 Write equations for the two reactions of glycolysis that consume ATP.

25.13 Write equations for the two reactions of glycolysis that produce ATP.

25.14 Although glucose is the principal source of carbohydrates for glycolysis and other pathways, fructose and galactose are also metabolized for energy.
a. What is the main dietary source of fructose? of galactose?
b. Explain how the carbon skeleton of fructose enters glycolysis.
c. Explain how the carbon skeleton of galactose enters glycolysis.

25.15 Describe the genetic defect leading to (a) fructose intolerance; (b) galactosemia.

25.16 The feedback effects of ATP, ADP, and AMP are important in regulating both glycolysis and the tricarboxylic acid cycle. Explain the effect of ATP and ADP on (a) isocitrate dehydrogenase, a regulatory enzyme of the tricarboxylic acid cycle; (b) phosphofructokinase, a regulatory enzyme of glycolysis.

Fates of pyruvate (Section 25.4)

25.17 Number the carbon atoms of glucose 1 through 6 and show the fate of each in (a) alcoholic fermentation; (b) lactate fermentation.

25.18 In what ways are alcoholic fermentation and lactate fermentation similar? In what ways do they differ?

25.19 Write balanced half-reactions for the following conversions:
a. glucose $\longrightarrow$ pyruvate
b. glucose $\longrightarrow$ lactate
c. lactate $\longrightarrow$ pyruvate
d. pyruvate $\longrightarrow$ ethanol + carbon dioxide

25.20 What is the principal function of the Cori cycle?

25.21 From your knowledge of glycolysis, the fates of pyruvate, and the tricarboxylic acid cycle, propose a series of steps for the following biochemical conversions.
a. glycerol $\longrightarrow$ lactate
b. 3-phosphoglycerol $\longrightarrow$ ethanol + carbon dioxide
c. 3-phosphoglyceraldehyde $\longrightarrow$ glucose 6-phosphate
d. glycerol $\longrightarrow$ acetyl CoA
e. ethanol $\longrightarrow$ carbon dioxide

The tricarboxylic acid cycle (Section 25.5)

25.22 What is the main function of the TCA cycle?

25.23 Write equations for the step or steps in the TCA cycle that involve:

a. formation of a new carbon-carbon bond.

b. oxidation by NAD^+.

c. oxidation by FAD.

d. formation of a high-energy phosphate bond.

25.24 Why is GTP just as effective a high-energy compound as ATP?

25.25 What does it mean to say that the TCA cycle is catalytic? that it does not produce any new compounds?

25.26 The main control points of the TCA cycle are the regulatory enzymes, citrate synthetase, and isocitrate dehydrogenase.

a. Write an equation for the reaction catalyzed by each enzyme.

b. Each enzyme is inhibited by NADH and ATP. Explain the benefit to the cell of this means of regulation.

Energy balance for glucose metabolism (Section 25.6)

25.27 A maximum of 36 mol ATP can be formed as the result of complete metabolism of 1 mol glucose to carbon dioxide and water. How many of the 36 moles are formed in:

a. glycolysis?

b. the tricarboxylic acid cycle?

c. the electron transport system?

25.28 The total amount of energy that can be obtained from complete oxidation of glucose is 686,000 cal/mol. What fraction of this energy is conserved as ATP in alcoholic fermentation? (Note that although this fraction is small, it is enough for the survival of anaerobic cells.)

26

Metabolism of Fatty Acids

In this chapter, we shall discuss the metabolic pathways for the catabolism of fatty acids and show how these pathways are coupled with the generation of ATP. In addition, we shall discuss the biosynthesis of fatty acids and then compare and contrast the steps by which cells degrade and synthesize these vital molecules. Finally we will show some of the interrelationships between the metabolism of fatty acids and carbohydrates.

26.1 Fatty Acids as Sources of Energy

For available energy, fatty acids have the highest caloric value of any food. Following are balanced equations for the complete oxidation of glucose and palmitic acid, one of the most abundant fatty acids. As you can see by comparing the changes in free energy, complete oxidation of a gram of palmitic acid yields almost 2.5 times the energy obtained from a gram of glucose.

	ΔG^0 (cal/mol)	ΔG^0 (cal/g)
$C_6H_{12}O_6 + 6O_2 \longrightarrow 6CO_2 + 6H_2O$	$-686{,}000$	$-3{,}800$
glucose		
$CH_3(CH_2)_{14}CO_2H + 23O_2 \longrightarrow 16CO_2 + 16H_2O$	$-2{,}340{,}000$	$-9{,}300$
palmitic acid		

The yield of energy per gram is larger because the hydrocarbon chain of a fatty acid is more highly reduced than the oxygenated chain of a carbohydrate. This can be seen by comparing the number of moles of oxygen consumed per carbon atom. One mole of oxygen is consumed per carbon atom of glucose, while $\frac{23}{16}$, or 1.44, moles of oxygen are consumed per carbon atom of palmitic acid.

Fatty acids constitute about 40% of the calories in a typical American diet. Further, because they can be stored in large quantities, fatty acids as triglycerides are the most important storage form of energy. Adipose tissue contains specialized cells, called adipocytes, whose sole function is to store fats.

26.2 Hydrolysis of Triglycerides

The first phase of catabolism of fatty acids involves their release from triglycerides by **hydrolysis**, catalyzed by a group of enzymes called lipases:

$$\underset{\text{a triglyceride}}{\begin{array}{c} \text{O} \quad\ \text{CH}_2\text{O}-\overset{\overset{\text{O}}{\|}}{\text{C}}\text{R} \\ \overset{\|}{\text{RCO}}-\text{CH} \\ \qquad\ \text{CH}_2\text{O}-\underset{\underset{\text{O}}{\|}}{\text{C}}\text{R} \end{array}} + 3\text{H}_2\text{O} \xrightarrow{\text{lipase}} \underset{\text{glycerol}}{\begin{array}{c}\text{CH}_2\text{OH} \\ \text{CHOH} \\ \text{CH}_2\text{OH}\end{array}} + \underset{\text{fatty acids}}{3\overset{\overset{\text{O}}{\|}}{\text{RCO}}^-} + 3\text{H}^+$$

Fatty acids cannot be transported as such in the bloodstream since they are insoluble in water. Instead they are transported in combination with albumin, the most abundant of the serum proteins (Section 21.8).

Release of fatty acids from adipose tissue into the bloodstream is stimulated by several hormones, including epinephrine, adrenocorticotropic hormone, growth hormone, and thyroxine. Accumulation of fatty acids in adipose tissue and storage as triglycerides is stimulated by high levels of glucose and insulin in the bloodstream.

26.3 Essential Fatty Acids

Somewhat more than 50% of the fatty acids in human triglycerides are unsaturated. These unsaturated fatty acids have several vital functions. Their presence lowers the melting points of triglycerides (Section 20.1C) and ensures that triglyceride droplets stored in the body remain liquid at body temperature. For comparison, tripalmitin, a saturated triglyceride, has a melting point of 65°C. Similarly, the fluidity of biological membranes depends on the presence of unsaturated fatty acids in membrane phospholipids. Further, prostaglandins and related compounds are synthesized from unsaturated fatty acids, chiefly arachidonic acid (Table 20.1). (For discussion of the biosyntheses of several prostaglandins and their functions in the body, see Mini-Essay XI, "The Prostaglandins.")

It was discovered in 1929 that if fatty acids (in the form of fats) were withheld from the diet of rats, they soon began to suffer from retarded growth, scaly skin, kidney damage, and premature death, even though they were fed adequate supplies of energy in the form of carbohydrates and proteins. Adding unsaturated fatty acids (specifically linoleic, linolenic, and arachidonic acids) to their diet prevented these conditions in control animals. In humans, signs of unsaturated-fatty-acid deficiency include scaly and thickened skin and decrease in growth rate. Because of the natural occurrence of fatty acids in normal diets, deficiency diseases are generally seen only in infants fed on a formula that lacks these unsaturated fatty acids, and in hospital patients who are fed intravenously for prolonged periods.

Humans and other higher animals produce the enzymes necessary to catalyze the synthesis of saturated fatty acids and of oleic acid, an unsaturated fatty acid with a double bond between carbons 9 and 10. However, they cannot synthesize linoleic acid, an unsaturated fatty acid with double bonds between carbons 9 and 10, and 12 and 13. Because this unsaturated fatty acid must be obtained from the diet to have normal growth and well-being, it is classified as an **essential fatty acid**.

$$CH_3(CH_2)_7 \overset{10}{C}H = \overset{9}{C}H(CH_2)_7 CO_2H$$

oleic acid
(can be synthesized in the
liver by humans and higher animals)

$$CH_3(CH_2)_4 \overset{13}{C}H = \overset{12}{C}HCH_2 \overset{10}{C}H = \overset{9}{C}H(CH_2)_7 CO_2H$$

linoleic acid
(cannot be synthesized by
humans and higher animals)

Linolenic and arachidonic acids are also required for normal growth and development. However, these unsaturated fatty acids can be synthesized in the liver from linoleic acid, and therefore are not classified as essential fatty acids.

$$CH_3CH_2(CH = CHCH_2)_3(CH_2)_6 CO_2H$$

linolenic acid

$$CH_3(CH_2)_4(CH = CHCH_2)_4(CH_2)_2 CO_2H$$

arachidonic acid
(prostaglandins are synthesized)
from this unsaturated fatty acid)

Although no minimum daily requirement for linoleic acid and the other polyunsaturated fatty acids has been established, the Food and Nutrition Board suggests an intake of about 6 g per day for adults. For infants and premature babies, the requirements are higher.

Linoleic acid and other unsaturated fatty acids are especially abundant in plant oils. As little as one teaspoon of corn oil a day supplies all necessary unsaturated fatty acids.

26.4 Oxidation of Fatty Acids

The three major stages in **oxidation of fatty acids** are activation of free fatty acids in the cytoplasm by formation of a thioester with coenzyme A; transport across the inner mitochondrial membrane; and oxidation within mitochondria to carbon dioxide and water. Let us look at each stage separately.

A. Activation of Free Fatty Acids

As the first step in catabolism, a free fatty acid in the cytoplasm is converted to a thioester formed with coenzyme A. The product is called a fatty acyl CoA. Thioester formation is an endergonic reaction, and the energy to drive it is derived by coupling thioester formation with hydrolysis of ATP. In this coupled hydrolysis, ATP is converted to AMP and pyrophosphate. Within the cytoplasm, pyrophosphate is further hydrolyzed to two phosphate ions.

$$\Delta G^0$$
(cal/mol)

Endergonic Reaction

$$\text{RCO}^- + \text{HS}-\text{CoA} \longrightarrow \text{RC}-\text{SCoA} + \text{OH}^- \qquad +7{,}300$$

Exergonic Reactions

$$\text{ATP}^{4-} + \text{H}_2\text{O} \longrightarrow \text{AMP}^{2-} + {}^-\text{O}-\overset{\text{O}}{\underset{\text{O}^-}{\text{P}}}-\text{O}-\overset{\text{O}}{\underset{\text{O}^-}{\text{P}}}-\text{O}^- + 2\text{H}^+ \qquad -7{,}600$$

pyrophosphate

$${}^-\text{O}-\overset{\text{O}}{\underset{\text{O}^-}{\text{P}}}-\text{O}-\overset{\text{O}}{\underset{\text{O}^-}{\text{P}}}-\text{O}^- + \text{H}_2\text{O} \longrightarrow 2\text{HPO}_4^{2-} \qquad -8{,}000$$

pyrophosphate

Adding the one endergonic reaction and two exergonic reactions gives the overall equation for activation of a fatty acid:

$$\text{RCO}^- + \text{HS}-\text{CoA} + \text{ATP}^{4-} + 2\text{H}_2\text{O} \longrightarrow$$

$$\text{RC}-\text{SCoA} + 2\text{HPO}_4^{2-} + \text{AMP}^{2-} + \text{H}^+ \qquad \Delta G^0 = -8{,}300 \text{ cal/mol}$$

Because activation of fatty acids is coupled with hydrolysis of two high-energy phosphate anhydride bonds, the initial investment by a cell in fatty acid oxidation is equivalent to 2 moles of ATP for each mole of fatty acid oxidized.

B. Transport of Activated Fatty Acids into Mitochondria

Mitochondrial membranes do not contain a system for transporting fatty acid thioesters of coenzyme A. They do, however, contain a system for transporting fatty acids in the form of esters with the molecule carnitine. Functional groups in carnitine are a carboxylate group, a secondary alcohol, and a quaternary ammonium ion. Fatty acyl CoA and carnitine undergo a reaction in which the fatty acyl group is transferred from the sulfur atom of coenzyme A to the oxygen atom of the secondary alcohol of carnitine. This reaction is an example of exchange of ester groups between molecules.

$$
\underset{\displaystyle RC-SCoA}{\overset{\displaystyle O}{\parallel}} + HO-\underset{\substack{CH_2 \\ | \\ CH_2 \\ | \\ CH_3-\overset{+}{N}-CH_3 \\ | \\ CH_3}}{\overset{\substack{CO_2^- \\ | \\ CH_2 \\ |}}{CH}} \rightleftharpoons \underset{\displaystyle RCO}{\overset{\displaystyle O}{\parallel}}-\underset{\substack{CH_2 \\ | \\ CH_2 \\ | \\ CH_3-\overset{+}{N}-CH_3 \\ | \\ CH_3}}{\overset{\substack{CO_2^- \\ | \\ CH_2 \\ |}}{CH}} + HS-CoA
$$

carnitine   fatty acid ester
of carnitine

The fatty acid ester of carnitine is transported through the inner mitochondrial membrane, and there the reaction is reversed; the fatty acid ester and a molecule of coenzyme A react, to form a fatty acyl CoA and regenerate carnitine. The freed carnitine is then returned to the cytoplasm to repeat the cycle. The effect of these two reactions, one in the cytoplasm and the other in the mitochondria, is to transfer fatty acyl CoA from the cytoplasm into mitochondria.

C. Beta-Oxidation Spiral

Once an activated fatty acid is in a mitochondrion, its carbon chain is degraded two carbons at a time. The metabolic pathway by which this is accomplished is called beta-oxidation because in two separate steps, a beta carbon is oxidized.

1. Oxidation

In the first step of beta-oxidation, the carbon chain is oxidized and a double bond is formed between the alpha and beta carbons (carbons 2 and 3) of the hydrocarbon chain. The oxidizing agent, FAD, is reduced to $FADH_2$, which is subsequently oxidized in the respiratory chain (Section 24.5):

$$
R-CH_2-CH_2-\overset{\displaystyle O}{\overset{\displaystyle \parallel}{C}}-SCoA + FAD \longrightarrow
$$

a saturated thioester

$$
R-CH=CH-\overset{\displaystyle O}{\overset{\displaystyle \parallel}{C}}-SCoA + FADH_2
$$

an α,β-unsaturated thioester

2. *Hydration*

Next, in a reaction analogous to acid-catalyzed hydration of an alkene (Section 12.5C), water is added to the carbon-carbon double bond, to form a beta-hydroxythioester:

$$R—CH\!\!=\!\!CH—\overset{\displaystyle O}{\overset{\displaystyle \|}{C}}—SCoA + H_2O \longrightarrow R—\overset{\displaystyle OH}{\underset{\displaystyle |}{CH}}—CH_2—\overset{\displaystyle O}{\overset{\displaystyle \|}{C}}—SCoA$$

an α,β-unsaturated   a β-hydroxythioester
thioester

The effect of the first two reactions of beta-oxidation is conversion of a —CH$_2$— group on carbon 3 of the hydrocarbon chain to a —CHOH— group.

3. *Oxidation*

In the second oxidation of beta-oxidation, the secondary alcohol of the β-hydroxythioester is oxidized to a ketone. The oxidizing agent is NAD$^+$, which is reduced to NADH:

$$R—\overset{\displaystyle OH}{\underset{\displaystyle |}{CH}}—CH_2—\overset{\displaystyle O}{\overset{\displaystyle \|}{C}}—SCoA + NAD^+ \longrightarrow$$

a β-hydroxythioester

$$R—\overset{\displaystyle O}{\overset{\displaystyle \|}{C}}—CH_2—\overset{\displaystyle O}{\overset{\displaystyle \|}{C}}—SCoA + NADH$$

a β-ketothioester

4. *Cleavage of Acetyl Coenzyme A*

In the final step of beta-oxidation, reaction of the beta-ketothioester with a molecule of coenzyme A brings about cleavage of a carbon-carbon bond and gives a molecule of acetyl CoA and a fatty acyl CoA molecule now shortened by two carbon atoms:

$$R—\overset{\displaystyle O}{\overset{\displaystyle \|}{C}}\overset{\frown}{—}CH_2—\overset{\displaystyle O}{\overset{\displaystyle \|}{C}}—SCoA + CoA—SH \longrightarrow$$

a β-ketothioester

$$R—\overset{\displaystyle O}{\overset{\displaystyle \|}{C}}—SCoA + CH_3—\overset{\displaystyle O}{\overset{\displaystyle \|}{C}}—SCoA$$

a β-ketothioester,   acetyl CoA
now shortened
by two carbons

The same series of steps is then repeated on the shortened fatty acyl chain and another molecule of acetyl CoA is cleaved. This series of steps is continued until the entire chain is degraded to acetyl CoA. The steps of beta-oxidation are called a **spiral**, because after each series of four reactions, the carbon chain is shortened by two carbon atoms. Figure 26.1 illustrates beta-oxidation of the carbon chain of palmitic acid to 8 molecules of acetyl CoA.

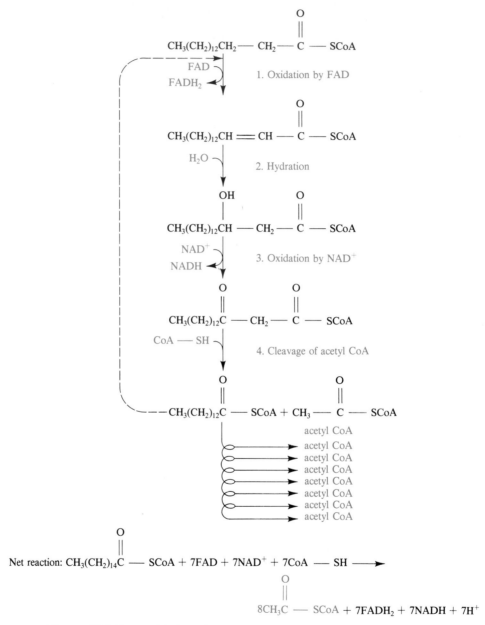

Figure 26.1 Beta-oxidation of palmitic acid to 8 molecules of acetyl CoA.

D. Energetics of Fatty Acid Oxidation

Now that we have examined the steps of beta-oxidation, let us calculate how much of the free energy available from complete oxidation of a fatty acid to carbon dioxide and water is conserved as ATP. Let us take palmitic acid as a specific example. Seven turns of beta-oxidation converts 1 mole of palmitic acid to 8 moles of acetyl CoA and generates 7 moles of $FADH_2$ and 7 moles of NADH. Reoxidation of each $FADH_2$ is coupled with formation of 2 ATP and reoxidation of each NADH is coupled with formation of 3 ATP (Section 24.5). Furthermore, oxidation of each acetyl CoA in the tricarboxylic acid cycle, followed by oxidation of all reduced coenzymes, generates another 12 ATP. Because 2 phosphate anhydride bonds (equivalent to 2 moles of ATP) are required to activate each mole of palmitic acid, 2 ATP must be subtracted. The ATP balance for the oxidation of 1 mole of palmitic acid is

$$
\begin{array}{ll}
14\ \text{ATP} & \text{from oxidation of 7 } FADH_2 \\
21\ \text{ATP} & \text{from oxidation of 7 NADH} \\
96\ \text{ATP} & \text{from oxidation of 8 acetyl CoA} \\
-2\ \text{ATP} & \text{from activation of palmitic acid} \\
\hline
129\ \text{ATP} &
\end{array}
$$

Coupling the exergonic oxidation of palmitic acid with the endergonic phosphorylation of ADP gives:

Exergonic Reaction

$$CH_3(CH_2)_{14}CO_2H + 23O_2 \longrightarrow 16CO_2 + 16H_2O \qquad \Delta G^0 = -2{,}340 \text{ kcal/mol}$$

Endergonic Reaction

$$129ADP + 129HPO_4^{2-} \longrightarrow 129ATP + 129H_2O \qquad \Delta G^0 = +940 \text{ kcal/mol}$$

Net Reaction

$$CH_3(CH_2)_{14}CO_2H + 23O_2 + 129ADP + 129HPO_4^{2-} \longrightarrow$$
$$16CO_2 + 145H_2O + 129ATP \qquad \Delta G^0 = -1{,}400 \text{ kcal/mol}$$

Thus we see that some $\frac{940}{2340}$, or 40%, of the standard free energy of oxidation of palmitate is conserved as ATP and can be used by cells for doing work. This fraction of energy conserved as ATP is comparable to that conserved in the complete oxidation of glucose to carbon dioxide and water (Section 25.6).

Example 26.1

Beta-oxidation of stearic acid, $CH_3(CH_2)_{16}CO_2H$, produces 9 moles of acetyl CoA, 8 moles of NADH, and 8 moles of $FADH_2$. Calculate the number of moles of ATP produced:

a. by oxidative phosphorylation of 8 moles of NADH.
b. by oxidative phosphorylation of 8 moles of $FADH_2$.
c. by oxidation of 9 moles of acetyl CoA through the reactions of the tricarboxylic acid cycle.
d. by oxidative phosphorylation of the NADH and $FADH_2$ produced during the oxidation of 9 moles of acetyl CoA in the tricarboxylic acid cycle.
e. in parts a–d combined.

☐ *Solution*

a. Three moles of ATP are produced by oxidative phosphorylation of each mole of NADH. Therefore, oxidative phosphorylation of 8 moles of NADH gives 24 moles of ATP.

b. Two moles of ATP are produced per mole of $FADH_2$. Therefore, oxidative phosphorylation of 8 moles of $FADH_2$ gives 16 moles of ATP.

c. The reactions of the tricarboxylic acid cycle produce 1 mole of GTP (which can be converted to ATP) per mole of acetyl CoA entering the cycle. Therefore, oxidation of 9 moles of acetyl CoA in the TCA cycle gives 9 moles of ATP.

d. Each turn of the TCA cycle gives 3 moles of NADH and 1 mole of $FADH_2$ per mole of acetyl CoA entering the cycle. Therefore, 9 moles of acetyl CoA give 27 moles of NADH and 9 moles of $FADH_2$. Oxidative phosphorylation of these reduced coenzymes gives $81 + 18 = 99$ moles of ATP.

e. Complete oxidation of 1 mole of stearic acid and oxidative phosphorylation of the resulting NADH and $FADH_2$ give a total of $24 + 16 + 9 + 99 = 148$ moles of ATP. Because two high-energy phosphate anhydride bonds are required in the activation of a fatty acid for beta-oxidation, the net yield per mole of stearic acid is 146 moles of ATP. Note that almost 65% of this ATP is produced by oxidative phosphorylation of NADH and $FADH_2$ generated through the tricarboxylic acid cycle.

The structural formula of myristic acid is

$$CH_3(CH_2)_{12}CO_2H$$

myristic acid

In the complete beta-oxidation of myristic acid to acetyl CoA:
a. How many moles of ATP are required?
b. How many moles of NADH and $FADH_2$ are produced?
c. How many moles of acetyl CoA are produced?

Problem 26.1

E. Oxidation of Propanoate

Thus far we have dealt with beta-oxidation of fatty acids with an even number of carbon atoms. These acids are degraded completely to acetyl CoA. While fatty acids with odd numbers of carbon atoms are not nearly so common, they do occur in nature. The final beta-oxidation product of an odd-numbered carbon chain is the thioester of propanoic acid. The IUPAC name of this ester is propanoyl CoA. Its common name is propionyl CoA (derived from the common name propionic acid). In normal human metabolism, the most important source of propanoyl CoA is not odd-chain fatty acids but the carbon skeletons of the branched-chain amino acids isoleucine and valine.

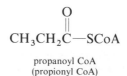

$$\overset{\overset{\displaystyle O}{\displaystyle \|}}{CH_3CH_2C}-SCoA$$

propanoyl CoA
(propionyl CoA)

Propanoyl CoA is converted to succinyl CoA, an intermediate in the TCA cycle. In the first reaction of this conversion, propanoyl CoA is carboxylated to give methylmalonyl CoA:

propanoyl CoA   methylmalonyl CoA

This reaction requires ATP as a source of energy to form the new carbon-carbon bond. It also requires the coenzyme biotin. Next, methylmalonyl CoA is iso-merized to succinyl CoA in an unusual reaction that requires vitamin B_{12} as a cofactor. In vitamin B_{12} deficiency, both propanoate and methylmalonate appear in the urine.

methylmalonyl CoA   succinyl CoA
(an intermediate
in the TCA cycle)

Studies using radioisotopes have revealed that this isomerization involves migration of the entire thioester group to the methyl carbon and exchange of a hydrogen atom for it.

The importance of vitamin B_{12} was first realized when it was discovered that liver extracts could be used to treat patients with pernicious anemia; this condition was so named because it does not respond to treatment with iron. Symptoms of pernicious anemia include tiredness, anorexia, headaches, and neurological disorders. The principle in liver extract that reverses pernicious anemia was isolated, purified, and crystallized in 1948, and its complete three-dimensional structure was worked out by Dorothy Hodgkin in 1956. For her work in determining the structure of this complex molecule, she received the Nobel Prize in chemistry in 1964.

Most cases of pernicious anemia are not due to lack of B_{12} in the diet, but to a deficiency of a substance called intrinsic factor, which is normally present in gastric juice. Intrinsic factor is necessary for absorption of B_{12} through the walls of the gastrointestinal tract and into the bloodstream. Because most B_{12}-deficiency diseases are due to a lack of intrinsic factor and reduced absorption of the vitamin, the most common means of administration of B_{12} is direct intramuscular injection.

26.5 Formation of Ketone Bodies

Acetoacetate, beta-hydroxybutyrate, and acetone are classed as ketone bodies. Note that the names we have given for the first two of these compounds are common names. Each also has an IUPAC name. However, as is so often the case in both organic chemistry and biochemistry, these and many other compounds are still known largely by their common names.

$$\underset{\substack{\text{3-hydroxybutanoate} \\ (\beta\text{-hydroxybutyrate})}}{CH_3\overset{\overset{\displaystyle OH}{|}}{C}HCH_2\overset{\overset{\displaystyle O}{\|}}{C}O^-} \qquad \underset{\substack{\text{3-oxobutanoate} \\ (\text{acetoacetate})}}{CH_3\overset{\overset{\displaystyle O}{\|}}{C}CH_2\overset{\overset{\displaystyle O}{\|}}{C}O^-} \qquad \underset{\text{acetone}}{CH_3\overset{\overset{\displaystyle O}{\|}}{C}CH_3}$$

Acetoacetate is so named because it is a derivative of acetate. The substituent group is $CH_3CO—$, which in the common system of nomenclature, is called an aceto group. Hence, the name acetoacetate.

Ketone bodies are products of human metabolism and are always present in blood plasma. However, under normal conditions, their concentration in plasma is low. In humans and most other animals, the liver is the only organ that produces any significant amounts of ketone bodies. Most tissues, with the notable exception of the brain, have the capacity to use them as energy sources.

Ketone bodies are synthesized from acetyl coenzyme A. In a series of three reactions, acetyl CoA is converted to acetoacetate:

$$\underset{\text{acetyl CoA}}{2CH_3\overset{\overset{\displaystyle O}{\|}}{C}—SCoA} + H_2O \xrightarrow[\text{steps}]{\text{three}} \underset{\text{acetoacetate}}{CH_3\overset{\overset{\displaystyle O}{\|}}{C}CH_2\overset{\overset{\displaystyle O}{\|}}{C}O^-} + 2CoA—SH + H^+$$

In one subsequent reaction, the ketone group of acetoacetate is reduced by NADH to a secondary alcohol. The product is beta-hydroxybutyrate.

$$\underset{\text{acetoacetate}}{CH_3\overset{\overset{\displaystyle O}{\|}}{C}CH_2\overset{\overset{\displaystyle O}{\|}}{C}O^-} + NADH + H^+ \xrightarrow{\text{(reduction)}} \underset{\beta\text{-hydroxybutyrate}}{CH_3\overset{\overset{\displaystyle OH}{|}}{C}HCH_2\overset{\overset{\displaystyle O}{\|}}{C}O^-} + NAD^+$$

In another reaction, acetoacetate loses carbon dioxide to give acetone. Recall that decarboxylation is a characteristic reaction of beta-ketoacids (Section 16.5D).

$$\underset{\text{acetoacetate}}{CH_3\overset{\overset{\displaystyle O}{\|}}{C}CH_2\overset{\overset{\displaystyle O}{\|}}{C}O^-} + H^+ \xrightarrow{\text{(decarboxylation)}} \underset{\text{acetone}}{CH_3\overset{\overset{\displaystyle O}{\|}}{C}CH_3} + CO_2$$

When the production of acetoacetate, beta-hydroxybutyrate, and acetone exceeds the capacity of the body to metabolize them, the condition is known as **ketosis**. Of the three ketone bodies, acetoacetic acid and beta-hydroxybutyric acid are the most significant because they are acids and must be buffered in the blood and most other body fluids to keep their accumulation from disrupting normal acid-base balance. The acidosis that results from the accumulation of ketone bodies is called **ketoacidosis**. During ketoacidosis, the effectiveness of hemoglobin in transporting oxygen is reduced. In the extreme, a deficiency in the supply of oxygen to the brain can produce a fatal coma. The presence of ketone bodies in the urine indicates an advanced state of ketoacidosis and provides a clear signal that immediate medical attention is essential.

Several abnormal conditions, including starvation, unusual diets, and diabetes mellitus lead to increased production of ketone bodies, to ketoacidosis, and to spilling of ketone bodies into the urine. After a short period of starvation, carbohydrate reserves become depleted and the cell or organism turns to beta-oxidation of fatty acids as a source of energy. Fatty acid degradation in the liver is increased, and in turn leads to an increase in the concentration of acetyl CoA. Under normal conditions, acetyl CoA in the liver can be channeled into three metabolic pathways: the tricarboxylic acid cycle, for oxidation to carbon dioxide and water; the synthesis of fatty acids and triglycerides, for storage in the liver; and finally, the synthesis of ketone bodies. During starvation and under conditions where carbohydrate metabolism is drastically reduced, the synthesis of pyruvate and other intermediates of the tricarboxylic acid cycle is also reduced. Therefore, the increased supply of acetyl CoA generated during starvation is channeled into the production of ketone bodies (Figure 26.2).

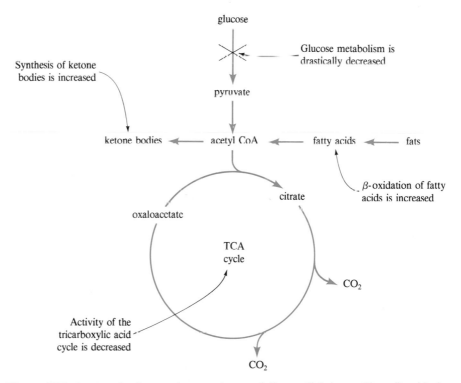

Figure 26.2 As a result of starvation, an abnormal diet, or diabetes mellitus, β-oxidation of fatty acids increases, the concentration of acetyl CoA increases, and more and more of it is channeled into the synthesis of ketone bodies.

26.6 Synthesis of Fatty Acids

In principle, fatty acids could be synthesized by reversal of beta-oxidation, that is, by addition of successive units of two-carbon acetyl groups to acetyl CoA and reduction of the resulting ketone groups to methylene groups. However, synthetic reactions are rarely the reverse of degradation reactions. As an example of this generalization, degradation and **synthesis of fatty acids** are quite different biochemical pathways both in mechanism and in location within the cell. Among the main differences are the following:

1. Synthesis of fatty acids takes place in the cytoplasm, whereas degradation takes place in mitochondria.
2. Synthesis involves two reductions, one of a ketone to a secondary alcohol and the other of a carbon-carbon double bond to a carbon-carbon single bond. In a sense, these two reductions are the reverse of two steps in the oxidation of fatty acid hydrocarbon chains. However, synthesis of fatty acids uses $NADPH/NADP^+$ for both reductions; by comparison, fatty acid oxidation uses $FAD/FADH_2$ for one oxidation and $NAD^+/NADH$ for the other.
3. Fatty acid chains are built up by successive addition of two-carbon units derived not from acetyl CoA but from malonyl CoA.

$$^-O-\overset{\overset{\displaystyle O}{\|}}{C}-CH_2-\overset{\overset{\displaystyle O}{\|}}{C}-SCoA$$

malonyl CoA

4. Coenzyme A is involved in degradation of fatty acids but not in their synthesis.

A. Formation of Malonyl CoA

Malonyl CoA is formed by carboxylation of acetyl CoA in a reaction that requires biotin as a cofactor and acetyl CoA carboxylase as an enzyme catalyst. You might compare this reaction with the carboxylation of propanoyl CoA to give methylmalonyl CoA (Section 26.4E).

$$O=C=O + CH_3-\overset{\overset{\displaystyle O}{\|}}{C}-SCoA \xrightarrow[\substack{\text{acetyl CoA} \\ \text{carboxylase}}]{\text{biotin}} \ ^-O-\overset{\overset{\displaystyle O}{\|}}{C}-CH_2-\overset{\overset{\displaystyle O}{\|}}{C}-SCoA + H^+$$

acetyl CoA   malonyl CoA

Acetyl CoA carboxylase is a regulatory enzyme, and the rate of fatty acid synthesis is controlled by modulation of its activity.

B. Synthesis of Fatty Acid Hydrocarbon Chains

Synthesis of fatty acid hydrocarbon chains is catalyzed by a multienzyme complex called fatty acid synthase. A key part of this enzyme complex is a low-molecular-weight protein called acyl carrier protein (ACP). Synthesis of a fatty acid chain begins with transfer of an acetyl group from the sulfur atom of coenzyme A to a sulfur atom of ACP. In effect, this reaction is the exchange of one sulfur ester for another. Next, the acetyl group is shifted to an adjacent sulfhydryl group on the enzyme complex. Then a malonyl group is transferred from the sulfur atom of coenzyme A to the first sulfhydryl group of ACP. The result of these reactions is positioning of one acetyl group and one malonyl group as thioesters at adjacent sites on fatty acid synthetase (Figure 26.3).

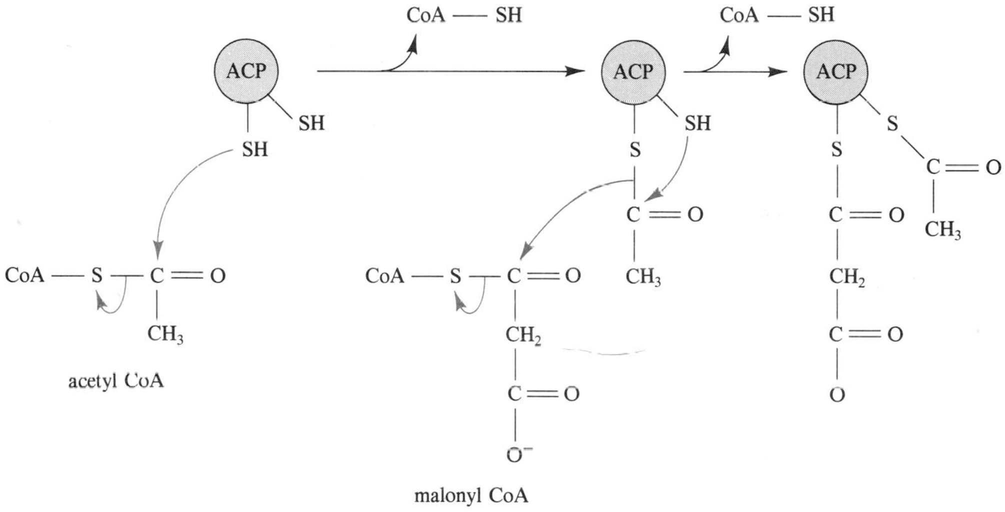

Figure 26.3 Binding of acetyl and malonyl groups to the acyl carrier protein (ACP).

At this point, a pair of two-carbon fragments are activated, one as acetyl-ACP and the other as malonyl-ACP. They next undergo a series of four reactions that cause elongation of the hydrocarbon chain by two atoms at a time. These four steps are condensation, reduction, dehydration, and reduction, each catalyzed by a separate enzyme component of the fatty acid synthase complex. To visualize the operation of this complex, think of ACP in the center of a circle, surrounded by the enzymes that catalyze each step of chain elongation. Further, think of ACP as turning within this enzyme complex, with the growing hydrocarbon chain as a flexible arm that gets longer and longer as the hydrocarbon chain is elongated. The relation of acyl carrier protein to the four enzyme systems of chain elongation is illustrated in Figure 26.4.

1. Condensation

The first step in chain elongation is formation of a carbon-carbon bond between the carbonyl group of acetyl-ACP and the beta-carbon of malonyl-ACP to give acetoacetyl-ACP:

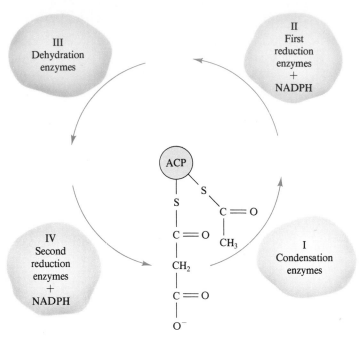

Figure 26.4 The relation between acyl carrier protein and the four enzyme systems responsible for chain elongation. In this arrangement, the growing chain is bound as a thioester to ACP and swings from one enzyme in the multienzyme complex to the next.

$$\underset{\text{acetyl-ACP}}{CH_3\overset{\displaystyle O}{\overset{\|}{C}}-S-ACP} + \underset{\text{malonyl-ACP}}{CH_2\overset{\displaystyle O}{\overset{\|}{C}}-S-ACP} \longrightarrow$$
$$\underset{\displaystyle CO_2^-}{}$$

$$\underset{\substack{\text{acetoacetyl-ACP} \\ \text{(a } \beta\text{-ketothioester)}}}{CH_3\overset{\displaystyle O}{\overset{\|}{C}}CH_2\overset{\displaystyle O}{\overset{\|}{C}}-S-ACP} + ACP-SH + CO_2$$

This enzyme-catalyzed formation of a new carbon-carbon bond is analogous to a Claisen condensation (Section 17.9) and forms a beta-ketothioester. Note that this condensation is coupled with the loss of carbon dioxide by decarboxylation. Thus, although carbon dioxide (actually bicarbonate) is required for fatty acid synthesis, it does not appear in the newly synthesized fatty acid.

2. Reduction of a Ketone to a Secondary Alcohol

In step 2, the beta–keto group of the growing fatty acid chain is reduced to a secondary alcohol:

$$\underset{\text{acetoacetyl-ACP}}{CH_3\overset{\overset{\displaystyle O}{\|}}{C}CH_2\overset{\overset{\displaystyle O}{\|}}{C}\text{—S—ACP}} + NADPH \longrightarrow$$

$$\underset{\substack{\beta\text{-hydroxybutyryl-ACP} \\ (a\ \beta\text{-hydroxythioester})}}{CH_3\overset{\overset{\displaystyle OH}{|}}{C}HCH_2\overset{\overset{\displaystyle O}{\|}}{C}\text{—S—ACP}} + NADP^+$$

The reducing agent is NADPH, consistent with the principal use of this coenzyme as a reducing agent in biosynthesis (Section 25.2E). Note that the carbon bearing the —OH group is chiral. Experiments have shown that the configuration of this chiral carbon is the opposite of the comparable chiral carbon involved in fatty acid oxidation (that is, it is the enantiomer).

3. Dehydration

In step 3, the beta-hydroxythioester is dehydrated, to form an α,β-unsaturated thioester in a reaction analogous to acid-catalyzed dehydration of an alcohol:

$$\underset{\beta\text{-hydroxybutyryl-ACP}}{CH_3\overset{\overset{\displaystyle OH}{|}}{C}HCH_2\overset{\overset{\displaystyle O}{\|}}{C}\text{—S—ACP}} \longrightarrow \underset{\substack{\text{crotonyl-ACP} \\ (a\ trans\ \alpha,\beta\text{-unsaturated} \\ \text{thioester})}}{\overset{\displaystyle H}{\underset{\displaystyle CH_3}{}}C=C\overset{\overset{\overset{\displaystyle O}{\|}}{C}\text{—S—ACP}}{\underset{\displaystyle H}{}}} + H_2O$$

The configuration about the double bond formed in step 3 is trans. By comparison, configurations in the unsaturated fatty acid components of triglycerides and phospholipids are entirely cis.

4. Reduction to a Carbon-Carbon Single Bond

In the final reaction of chain elongation, the carbon-carbon double bond of the growing chain is reduced to a carbon-carbon single bond. The reducing agent is another molecule of NADPH.

$$\underset{\text{crotonyl-ACP}}{\overset{\displaystyle H}{\underset{\displaystyle CH_3}{}}C=C\overset{\overset{\overset{\displaystyle O}{\|}}{C}\text{—S—ACP}}{\underset{\displaystyle H}{}}} + NADPH \longrightarrow$$

$$\underset{\text{butyryl-ACP}}{CH_3CH_2CH_2\overset{\overset{\displaystyle O}{\|}}{C}\text{—S—ACP}} + NADP^+$$

The thioester formed after steps 1–4 is shown in Figure 26.5. At this point, the acyl group of the four-carbon thioester is transferred to the adjacent —SH group and a second malonyl group is transferred to ACP.

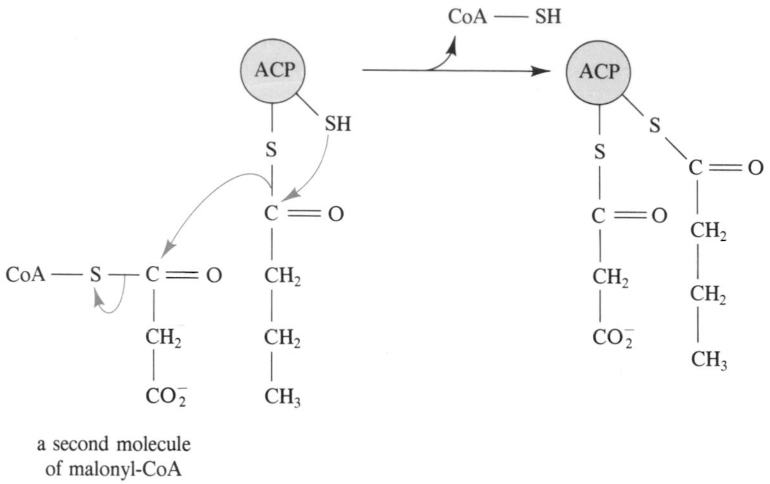

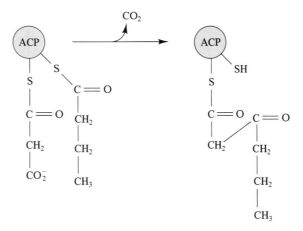

a second molecule
of malonyl-CoA

Figure 26.5 Preparation for a second cycle of chain elongation reactions.

The second cycle of chain elongation begins with formation of a carbon-carbon bond between the carbonyl carbon of the four-carbon thioester and the alpha carbon of malonyl-ACP (Figure 26.6).

Figure 26.6 The beginning of the second cycle of chain elongation reactions.

The cycle of condensation, reduction, dehydration, and reduction continues until the 16-carbon chain of palmitoyl-ACP is formed. At this point, the thioester of palmitoyl-ACP is hydrolyzed and palmitic acid is released from the multienzyme complex.

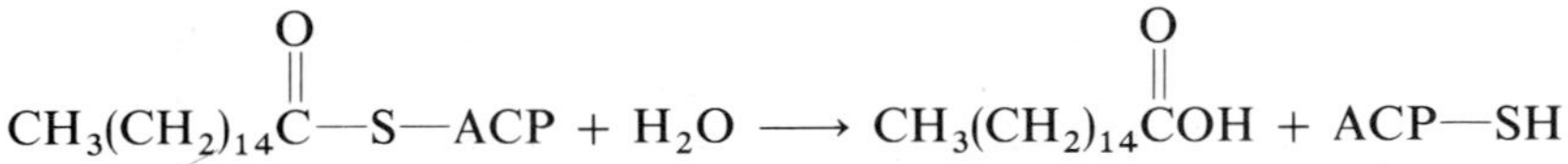

$$CH_3(CH_2)_{14}\overset{\displaystyle O}{\overset{\|}{C}}-S-ACP + H_2O \longrightarrow CH_3(CH_2)_{14}\overset{\displaystyle O}{\overset{\|}{C}}OH + ACP-SH$$

palmityl-ACP   palmitic acid
                                  (hexadecanoic acid)

Fatty acid synthesis catalyzed by fatty acid synthase yields only palmitic acid. Yet approximately 60% of the fatty acids of triglycerides and phospholipids contain fatty acids of 18 and 20 carbon atoms. The reactions of further chain elongation appear to be identical with those catalyzed by fatty acid synthase, but are catalyzed by other enzymes found associated with the endoplasmic reticulum.

C. Synthesis of Unsaturated Fatty Acids

A significant portion of fatty acids in human triglycerides are unsaturated and can be synthesized by oxidation of saturated fatty acids. Insertion of unsaturation is catalyzed by enzymes called fatty acid desaturase, as illustrated here by the conversion of stearic acid to oleic acid. Note that molecular oxygen, O_2, is the oxidizing agent and that in this reaction, both NADH and the saturated fatty acid chain are oxidized.

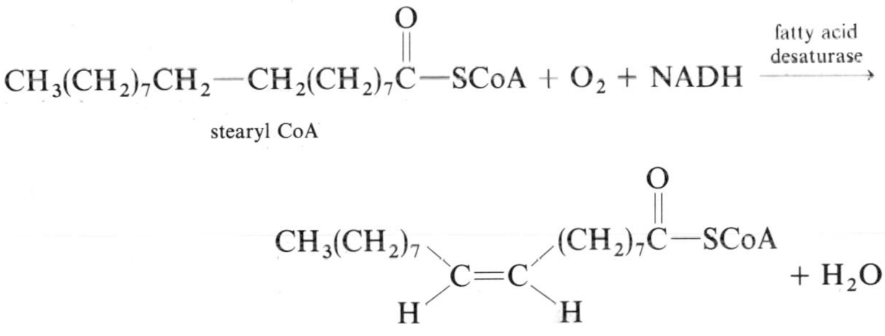

$$CH_3(CH_2)_7CH_2-CH_2(CH_2)_7\overset{\displaystyle O}{\overset{\|}{C}}-SCoA + O_2 + NADH \xrightarrow{\text{fatty acid desaturase}}$$

stearyl CoA

$$CH_3(CH_2)_7 \underset{H}{\overset{}{\diagdown}} C = C \underset{H}{\overset{(CH_2)_7\overset{\displaystyle O}{\overset{\|}{C}}-SCoA}{\diagup}} + H_2O + NAD^+$$

oleyl CoA

Mammalian fatty acid desaturases have three important characteristics:

1. Double bonds introduced in fatty acid chains have a cis configuration.
2. The enzymes are active on hydrocarbon chains of only 18 or fewer carbon atoms.
3. Double bonds can be introduced between carbons 4–5, 5–6, 6–7, and 9–10. What is important to note is that these desaturases cannot introduce double bonds beyond carbons 9–10.

Linoleic, linolenic, and arachidonic acids are polyunsaturated. Linoleic acid has double bonds between carbons 9–10 and 12–13. In linolenic acid, there are double bonds between carbons 9–10, 12–13, and 15–16; in arachidonic acid, they are between carbons 5–6, 8–9, 11–12, and 14–15. Because mammalian fatty acid desaturases cannot introduce double bonds beyond carbons 9–10, linoleic acid must be supplied in the diet. It in turn can be used for the synthesis of the other polyunsaturated fatty acids.

D. Synthesis of Fatty Acids from the Carbon Atoms of Glucose

There is a close relationship between the metabolism of glucose and the metabolism of fatty acids (see Figure 24.14). Specifically, the body has only a limited capacity to store glucose. However, it has a very large capacity to store fatty acids in the form of triglycerides. Through the metabolic pathways we have already covered, the carbon atoms of glucose can be used for the synthesis of fatty acids. The flow of carbon atoms from glucose to palmitic acid is traced in Figure 26.7.

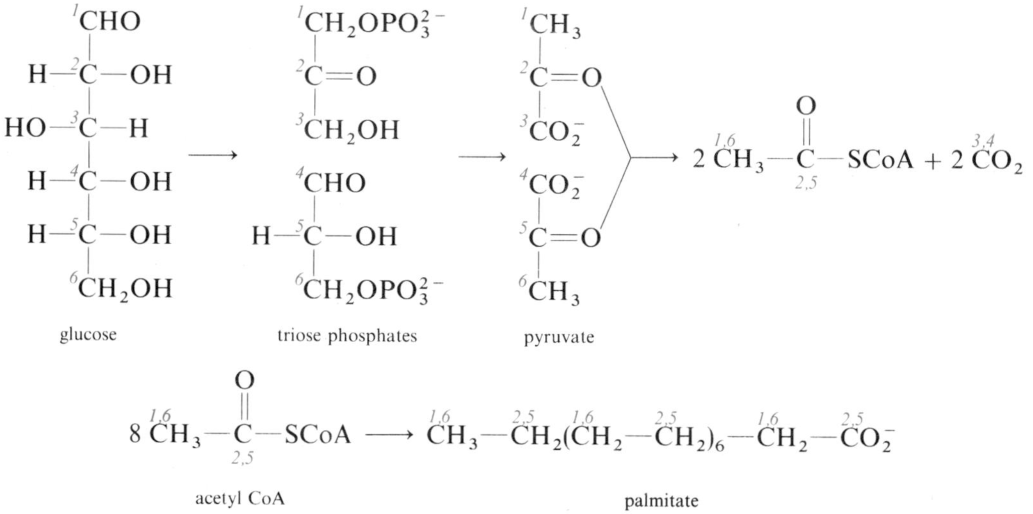

Figure 26.7 The synthesis of palmitate from glucose. The carbon atoms of glucose are numbered 1 through 6.

Cleavage of glucose during glycolysis produces one molecule each of 3-phosphoglyceraldehyde and dihydroxyacetone phosphate. Dihydroxyacetone phosphate is isomerized to 3-phosphoglyceraldehyde and both continue in glycolysis to form pyruvate. Oxidation and decarboxylation of pyruvate (Section 25.4A) give acetyl CoA and carbon dioxide. The carbonyl carbons of acetyl CoA are derived from carbons 2 and 5 of glucose, and the methyl carbons are derived from carbons 1 and 6 of glucose. Acetyl CoA in the form of malonyl CoA is the key building block for the synthesis of fatty acids including palmitic acid. As shown in Figure 26.7, carbon atoms 1, 2, 5, and 6 of glucose can become incorporated into the carbon skeleton of a fatty acid.

26.7 Synthesis of Cholesterol and Other Steroids

Cholesterol is a necessary component of biological membranes. Further, it is the molecule from which all other classes of steroids are derived, including bile acids and sex hormones. In Western society, cholesterol is usually obtained in the diet. If dietary sources are not sufficient, however, it can be synthesized. All nucleated cells have the ability to synthesize cholesterol, but in man, 80–95% of all cholesterol synthesis is done in the liver and intestine.

It was a challenge to biochemists to discover how this complex molecule is constructed. The availability of radioactive isotopes for research purposes, in particular carbon-14, gave scientists the probe they needed. They discovered that the carbon skeleton of cholesterol is derived entirely from acetate, and further, that the two-carbon acetate unit is not broken in the process. In other words, carbon atoms of cholesterol are derived in order from a methyl carbon and then the carbonyl carbon, then another methyl carbon and its carbonyl carbon, and so on. This pattern is but another demonstration that in putting together large and complex molecules, nature begins with small, readily available subunits and puts them together piece by piece. In the case of cholesterol and all other steroids, the readily available subunit is acetyl CoA, a molecule produced in the degradation of glucose and other monosaccharides, fatty acids, and, as we shall see in Chapter 27, also from amino acids.

The **synthesis of cholesterol** begins by condensation of two molecules of acetyl CoA to produce acetoacetyl CoA, in a reaction catalyzed by acetyl-CoA acetyl-transferase:

$$CH_3\overset{\overset{\displaystyle O}{\|}}{C}-SCoA + CH_3\overset{\overset{\displaystyle O}{\|}}{C}-SCoA \longrightarrow CH_3C CH_2\overset{\overset{\displaystyle O}{\|}}{C}-SCoA + CoA-SH$$

acetyl CoA   acetyl CoA   acetoacetyl CoA

At this point, either one or another of two enzyme systems is activated. One enzyme system leads to ketone bodies; acetoacetyl CoA is converted to acetoacetate and in turn to acetone and β-hydroxybutyrate. A second enzyme system catalyzes condensation of acetoacetyl CoA with a third molecule of acetyl CoA, to form 3-hydroxy-3-methylglutaryl-CoA (HMG-CoA):

$$CH_3\overset{\overset{\displaystyle O}{\|}}{C}CH_2\overset{\overset{\displaystyle O}{\|}}{C}-SCoA + CH_3\overset{\overset{\displaystyle O}{\|}}{C}-SCoA \longrightarrow$$

acetoacetyl CoA   acetyl CoA

$$^-O\overset{\overset{\displaystyle O}{\|}}{C}CH_2\underset{\underset{\displaystyle CH_3}{|}}{\overset{\overset{\displaystyle OH}{|}}{C}}CH_2\overset{\overset{\displaystyle O}{\|}}{C}-SCoA + CoA-SH$$

3-hydroxy-3-methylglutaryl-CoA

Once formed, 3-hydroxy-3-methylglutaryl CoA is reduced to mevalonate (the anion of mevalonic acid), and then, in several subsequent steps, converted to 3,3-dimethylallylpyrophosphate.

$$^-OCCH_2CCH_2CH_2OH \longrightarrow CH_3C=CHCH_2O-P-O-P-O^-$$

mevalonate   3,3-dimethylallylpyrophosphate

Each of these compounds is particularly important. Mevalonate is important because it is the first step that specifically commits the carbon skeletons of acetate to the synthesis of cholesterol. The enzyme that catalyzes this reaction, HMG-CoA reductase, is a regulatory enzyme. The compound 3,3-dimethylallyl-pyrophosphate is important because it contains the carbon skeleton of an iso-prene unit and is the basic building block from which all terpenes are derived—including vitamin A, the carotenes, the side chains of vitamins E and K, and co-enzyme Q. (For further discussion of terpenes, see Mini-Essay VII, "Terpenes.") All the remaining steps in the synthesis of cholesterol are well understood. However, we will not discuss them here.

Before we leave this section, let us stop for a moment to emphasize the cen-tral importance of acetyl CoA in metabolism. As we have indicated, it is pro-duced from the degradation of carbohydrates, fatty acids, and proteins. It is also the starting material for the synthesis of several classes of biomolecules including fatty acids, steroids, and terpenes.

Carbohydrates ⎤   O   ⎡→ Steroids
Fatty acids ————⟩→ CH_3C—SCoA ——⟨→ Fatty acids
Certain amino acids ⎦   ⎣→ Terpenes

Key Terms and Concepts

beta-oxidation spiral (26.4C)   ketosis (26.5)
essential fatty acids (26.3)   oxidation of fatty acids (26.4)
hydrolysis of triglycerides (26.2)   synthesis of cholesterol (26.7)
ketoacidosis (26.5)   synthesis of fatty acids (26.6)
ketone bodies (26.5)

Key Reactions

1. Activation of free fatty acids by conversion to a thioester of acetyl CoA (Section 26.4A).

2. The four reactions of the β-oxidation spiral (Section 26.4C).

3. Carboxylation of propanoyl CoA to methylmalonyl CoA (Section 26.4E).
4. Isomerization of methylmalonyl CoA to succinyl CoA (Section 26.4E).
5. Formation of ketone bodies from acetyl CoA (Section 26.5).
6. Carboxylation of acetyl CoA to form malonyl CoA (Section 26.6A).
7. The four steps in the cycle of synthesis of fatty acid hydrocarbon chains (Section 26.6B).

Problems

Fatty acids
as sources
of energy
(Section 26.1)

26.2 Compare carbohydrates and fatty acids as energy sources. How do you account for the difference between the amount of energy released on complete oxidation of each?

26.3 Write structural formulas for palmitic, oleic, and stearic acids, the three most abundant fatty acids.

Oxidation of
fatty acids
(Section 26.4)

26.4 A fatty acid must be activated before it can be metabolized in cells. Write a balanced equation for the reaction that activates palmitic acid.

26.5 Name three coenzymes necessary for the catabolism of fatty acids to acetyl CoA. What vitamin precursor is associated with each coenzyme?

26.6 Outline the four steps in the fatty acid oxidation spiral.

26.7 How much energy in the form of ATP is produced directly in the oxidation of palmitic acid to acetyl CoA?

26.8 Review the oxidation reactions in the catabolism of glucose and fatty acids. Prepare a list of (a) types of functional groups oxidized, and (b) the oxidizing agent used for each type. Compare the types of functional groups oxidized by FAD with those oxidized by NAD^+.

26.9 Calculate the number of moles of ATP produced when:
  a. palmitoyl CoA is oxidized to acetyl CoA and all the reduced coenzymes produced in the process are reoxidized by molecular oxygen.
  b. palmitoyl CoA is oxidized to CO_2 and all the reduced coenzymes produced in the process are reoxidized by molecular oxygen.

26.10 In patients with pernicious anemia, up to 50–90 mg of a dicarboxylic acid of molecular formula $C_4H_6O_4$ appear in the urine daily. Draw a structural formula for this dicarboxylic acid. How do you account for its formation?

26.11 The respiratory quotient (RQ) is used in studies of energy metabolism and exercise physiology. It is defined as the ratio of the volume of carbon dioxide produced to the volume of oxygen used:

$$RQ = \frac{\text{volume of } CO_2}{\text{volume of } O_2}$$

  a. Show that the RQ for glucose is 1.00. (*Hint*: Look at the balanced equation for the complete oxidation of glucose.)
  b. Calculate the RQ for triolein, a triglyceride of molecular formula $C_{57}H_{104}O_6$.

c. Calculate the RQ on the assumption that triolein and glucose are oxidized in equal molar amounts.

d. For an individual on a normal diet, the RQ is approximately 0.85. Would this value increase or decrease if ethanol were to supply an appreciable portion of caloric needs?

Formation of ketone bodies (Section 26.5)

26.12 What is the only organ in humans that produces significant amounts of ketone bodies?

26.13 Explain why ketone-body formation increases markedly when excessive amounts of fatty acids are oxidized and carbohydrate availability is limited.

26.14 Explain why the accumulation of ketone bodies leads to acidosis.

Synthesis of fatty acids (Section 26.6)

26.15 Starting with butyryl-ACP, show all steps in the synthesis of hexanoic acid. Name the type of reaction involved in each step.

$$
\begin{array}{c}
O \\
\parallel \\
CH_3CH_2CH_2CSACP
\end{array}
$$

butyryl-ACP

26.16 For the synthesis of stearic acid from acetyl-ACP:
a. How many moles of NADPH are required?
b. How many moles of malonyl-ACP are required?

26.17 During fatty acid synthesis, NADPH is oxidized to $NADP^+$. Name the metabolic pathway primarily responsible for regeneration of NADPH.

26.18 If glucose were the only source of acetyl CoA, how many moles of glucose would be required for the synthesis of one mole of palmitate? How many grams of glucose are required for the synthesis of one mole of palmitate?

26.19 Explain why almost all fatty acids have an even number of carbon atoms in an unbranched chain.

27

Metabolism of Amino Acids

In the broadest sense, amino acids have three vital functions in the human body. Amino acids are (1) building blocks for the synthesis of proteins; (2) sources of carbon and nitrogen atoms for the synthesis of other biomolecules; and (3) sources of energy. Compared with the metabolism of carbohydrates and fatty acids, the metabolism of amino acids is extremely complex. Unlike hexoses and fatty acids, which share common metabolic pathways (for example, glycolysis for hexoses and beta-oxidation for fatty acids), each amino acid is degraded and synthesized by a separate pathway. We shall not go into the details of the metabolic pathways for the degradation and synthesis of each amino acid, but instead examine the overall process. Of specific interest is how the carbon skeletons of amino acids are used as sources of energy and how amino acid nitrogen atoms are collected, converted to urea, and excreted.

27.1 Amino Acid Metabolism—An Overview

A. Amino Acids Are Used for the Synthesis of Body Proteins

The most important function of amino acids, at least in terms of total amino acid use, is as building blocks for the synthesis of proteins. It is estimated that approximately 75% of amino acid metabolism in a normal, healthy adult is devoted to this purpose. The maintenance of body proteins is not a simple matter. Tissue proteins are being hydrolyzed constantly through normal "wear and tear." At the same time, we eat proteins that are hydrolyzed in the gut to amino acids. The amino acids from food and from hydrolysis of tissue proteins combine to create what is called the **amino acid pool**, from which new proteins are synthesized.

The use of radioisotopes has given us some idea of the extent of turnover of body proteins and the amino acid pool. The **half-life** of liver proteins, for example, is about 10 days. This means that over a 10-day period, half the proteins in the liver are hydrolyzed to amino acids and replaced by equivalent proteins. The half-life of plasma proteins is also about 10 days, hemoglobin about 30 days, and muscle protein about 180 days. The half-life of collagen is much longer. Some proteins, particularly enzymes and polypeptide hormones, have much shorter half-lives. That of insulin, once it is released from the pancreas, is estimated to be only 7–10 minutes.

Clearly, the stability of body proteins is more apparent than real and represents a dynamic balance between degradation and synthesis. In spite of this turnover, the total amount of body protein remains relatively constant in most adults. This means that the quantity of amino acids required for the synthesis of body proteins and the quantity obtained from hydrolysis of body proteins are roughly equivalent. Therefore, the amino acid pool of most adults contains a surplus approximately equal to the amino acids obtained in the diet. This surplus is used for the synthesis of nonprotein compounds and as a source of fuel, or it is excreted.

B. Amino Acids as Sources of Carbon and Nitrogen for the Synthesis of Other Biomolecules

Tissues constantly draw on the amino acid pool for the synthesis of nonprotein biomolecules. These molecules include nucleic acids; porphyrins, such as those in the prosthetic groups of hemoglobin and myoglobin; choline and ethanolamine, which are building blocks of phospholipids; glucosamine and other amino sugars; and neurotransmitters, such as acetylcholine, dopamine, norepinephrine, and serotonin. Like proteins, these compounds are also being broken down and replaced constantly.

C. Amino Acids as Fuel

Unlike carbohydrates and fatty acids, amino acids in excess of immediate needs cannot be stored for later use. Their nitrogen atoms are converted to ammonium ions, urea, or uric acid, depending on the organism, and excreted. Their carbon skeletons are degraded to pyruvate, acetyl CoA, or one of the intermediates of the tricarboxylic acid cycle. The various metabolic pathways of amino acid metabolism are summarized in Figure 27.1.

D. Essential Amino Acids

Most dietary proteins contain all the amino acids humans need for synthesizing their proteins. They are often present in widely different proportions, however. For protein synthesis to take place, all the required amino acids must be present at the time of synthesis and in the correct proportions. Studies of protein synthesis have led to the concept of essential and nonessential amino acids. Nonessential amino acids are synthesized in the body at a rate equal to the needs of protein biosynthesis. Essential amino acids cannot be synthesized within the body fast enough to support normal protein synthesis.

In humans, the most widely used experimental procedure for classifying amino acids as essential or nonessential is nitrogen balance. A normal, healthy

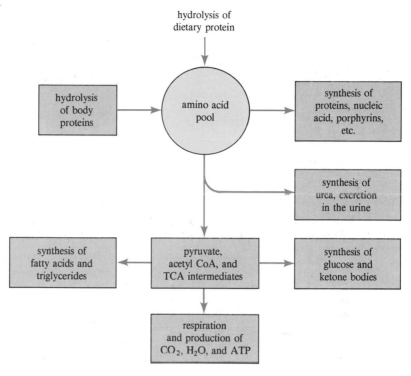

Figure 27.1 An overview of the metabolism of amino acids. Average daily turnover of amino acids is approximately 400 g.

adult, for whom the rate of nitrogen intake equals the rate of its loss in feces, urine, and sweat, is said to be in nitrogen balance. In periods of active growth or tissue repair, when more nitrogen is ingested than excreted, the individual is said to be in positive nitrogen balance. In the opposite condition, starvation or malnutrition, when body proteins are being used for fuel and more nitrogen is excreted than is taken in, the individual is said to be in negative nitrogen balance. Whether an amino acid is essential or nonessential can be determined by withholding it alone from the diet, supplying all other amino acids. If the absence of this amino acid from the diet brings about a negative nitrogen balance, the amino acid is classified as essential.

Of the 20 amino acids that the human body needs, adequate amounts of 12 can be synthesized by enzyme-catalyzed reactions starting from carbohydrates or lipids, and a source of nitrogen. For the remaining amino acids, either no biochemical pathways are available for their synthesis, or the available pathways do not provide adequate amounts for proper nutrition. Therefore, these eight amino acids must be supplied in the diet, and are called essential amino acids (Table 27.1).

Tyrosine is synthesized from phenylalanine in the body. Therefore, in Table 27.1, the requirements for tyrosine and phenylalanine are combined. Similarly, the sulfur-containing amino acids methionine and cysteine are combined.

Table 27.1
Essential amino acids required for humans.

Essential Amino Acid	Daily Requirement, mg/kg Body Weight		
	Infant (4–6 mo)	Child (10–12 yr)	Adult
histidine	33	—	—
isoleucine	83	28	12
leucine	135	42	16
lysine	99	44	12
total S-containing amino acids (methionine and cysteine)	49	22	10
total aromatic amino acids (phenylalanine and tyrosine)	141	22	16
threonine	68	28	8
tryptophan	21	4	3
valine	92	25	14

Histidine is essential for growth in infants and may be needed by adults also. Arginine is synthesized in the body, but the rate of internal synthesis is not adequate to meet the needs of the body during periods of rapid growth and protein synthesis. Therefore, 8, 9, or 10 amino acids are essential for humans, depending on age and state of health.

E. Biological Value of Dietary Proteins

It should now be clear that not all proteins are equivalent, at least for human nutrition. Some contain a more appropriate blend of essential amino acids than others do. One measure of the relative blend of essential amino acids for human nutrition is a protein's biological value, that is, the percentage that is absorbed and used to build body tissue. Some of the first information on the biological value of dietary proteins came from studies on rats. In one series of experiments, young rats were fed diets containing protein in the form of casein (a milk protein), gliadin (a wheat protein), or zein (a corn protein). With casein as the sole dietary source of protein, the rats remained healthy and grew normally. Those fed gliadin maintained their weight but did not grow much. Those fed zein not only failed to grow but lost weight, and if kept on this diet, eventually died. Because casein evidently supplies all required amino acids in the correct proportions needed for growth, it is called a complete protein. Analysis revealed that gliadin contains too little lysine, and that zein is low in both lysine and tryptophan. When a gliadin diet is supplemented with lysine, or the zein diet with lysine and tryptophan, test animals grew normally.

Table 27.2 shows the biological value for rats of some common dietary sources of protein. The proteins in egg are the best-quality natural protein. The proteins of milk have a biological value of 84, and meat and soybeans, about 74. The legumes, vegetables, and cereal grains are in the range 50–70.

Animal proteins generally contain a blend of essential amino acids similar to those that humans need. Many plant proteins, however, are low in one or more

Table 27.2
Biological value
for rats of some
common sources
of dietary proteins.

Food	Protein as % of Dry Solid	Biological Value of Protein, %
hen's egg, whole	48	94
cow's milk, whole	27	84
fish	72	83
beef	45	74
soybeans	41	73
rice, brown	9	73
potato, white	6	67
wheat, whole grain	14	65
corn, whole grain	11	59
dry beans, common	25	58

essential amino acids. Fortunately, not all plant proteins are deficient in the same amino acids. For example, beans and other legumes are low in methionine but adequate in lysine. Wheat and other cereal grains have just the opposite pattern; they are low in lysine but adequate in methionine. Thus it is possible, by eating wheat and beans together, to increase by 33% the usable protein you would get by eating either of these foods alone.

Estimates of recommended daily intake of protein have varied over the years as our understanding of the relation between diet and nutrition has advanced. In 1980, the Food and Nutrition Board of the National Academy of Sciences stated that a generous protein allowance for a healthy adult is 0.8 g of high-quality protein per kilogram of "ideal" body weight per day. For example, for a healthy 68-kg (150-lb) male of medium frame, the RDA is 0.8 × 68, or 54, g protein per day.

The provision of a diet adequate in protein and essential amino acids is a grave problem in the world today, especially in areas of Asia, Africa, and South America. The overriding dimension of this problem is poverty and an inability to select foods of adequate protein and caloric content. The best overall foods are the cereal grains, which provide not only calories but protein also. When these are supplemented with animal protein or a proper selection of plant protein, the diet is adequate for even the most vulnerable. However, as income decreases, there is less animal protein in the diet, and even cereal grains are often replaced by cheaper sources of calories, such as starches or tubers—foods that have either very little or no protein. The poorest 25% of the world's population consumes diets with caloric and protein content that fall dangerously below the calculated minimum daily requirements.

Those most apt to show symptoms of too little food, too little protein, or both, are young children in the years immediately following weaning. They fail to grow properly, and their tissues become wasted. This sickness is called marasmus, a name derived from a Greek word meaning "to waste away." Muscles become atrophied and the face develops a wizened "old man's" look. Another disease, kwashiorkor, leads to tragically high death rates among children. As long as a child is breast-fed, it is healthy. At weaning (often forced when a second child is born), the first child's diet is switched to starch or other inadequate sources of protein. Symptoms of the disease are edema, cessation of growth, severe body wasting, diarrhea, mental apathy, and a peeling of the skin that leaves areas of raw flesh. Those afflicted with the disease are doomed to short lives. Kwashiorkor was unknown in the medical literature until 1933, when it was described by Cicely Williams, who studied the condition while she was working among the tribes of West Africa. She gave it the name by which it was known in the African Ga tribe.

One solution to the problem of quantity and quality of protein has been to breed new varieties of cereal grains with higher protein content or better-quality protein, or both. Alternatively, cereals and their derived products can be supplemented (fortified) with amino acids in which they are deficient: principally lysine for wheat; lysine or lysine plus threonine for rice; and lysine plus tryptophan for corn. New methods of synthesis and fermentation now provide cheap sources of these amino acids, thus making the economics of food fortification entirely practical. In another attack on the problem of protein malnutrition, nutritionists have developed several high-protein, low-cost infant foods. Clearly, advances in food chemistry and technology have provided the means to eradicate hunger and malnutrition. What remains is for the world's political and social systems to put this knowledge into practice.

27.2 Hydrolysis (Digestion) of Dietary Proteins

Proteins ingested in the diet cannot be absorbed as such through the epithelial cells of the intestine and passed into the bloodstream. First, they must be hydrolyzed (digested) into amino acids, dipeptides, and tripeptides. Digestion of proteins begins in the stomach, where the highly acid gastric juices (pH approximately 1.0) cause denaturation of polypeptide chains, thus making them more susceptible to the catalytic activity of proteases (protein-hydrolyzing enzymes). The early stages of protein hydrolysis are catalyzed by four specific enzymes: pepsin, trypsin, chymotrypsin, and elastase. These and all other enzymes involved in the hydrolysis of dietary proteins are synthesized as inactive pro-enzymes, namely, pepsinogen, trypsinogen, chymotrypsinogen, and pro-elastase. Each pro-enzyme is larger than the active enzyme by one or more short sections of polypeptide, which effectively prevent the pro-enzyme from folding into a biologically active conformation. Pepsinogen is secreted directly into the stomach. There its extra polypeptide section, 42 amino acids long, is cleaved by hydrolysis of one peptide bond:

$$\text{Pepsinogen} + \text{H}_2\text{O} \xrightarrow[\text{(stomach)}]{\text{H}^+} \text{pepsin} + \text{polypeptide of 42 amino acids}$$

Trypsinogen, chymotrypsinogen, and pro-elastase are secreted by the pancreas into the small intestine. There trypsinogen is hydrolyzed to trypsin, which in turn catalyzes hydrolysis of remaining trypsinogen, chymotrypsinogen, and pro-elastase to their active forms.

$$\text{Trypsinogen} + H_2O \xrightarrow{\text{trypsin}} \text{trypsin} + \text{polypeptide}$$

$$\text{Chymotrypsinogen} + H_2O \xrightarrow{\text{trypsin}} \text{chymotrypsin} + \text{polypeptide}$$

$$\text{Pro-elastase} + H_2O \xrightarrow{\text{trypsin}} \text{elastase} + \text{polypeptide}$$

The four proteases hydrolyze larger polypeptides into a series of smaller polypeptides. Digestion is then continued by several other classes of enzymes, including the aminopeptidases and carboxypeptidases. Aminopeptidases catalyze the hydrolysis of amino acids from the *N*-terminal end of a polypeptide chain; carboxypeptidases do the same but from the *C*-terminal end of a polypeptide chain.

In the final stage of digestion, the water-soluble amino acids and di- and tripeptides are absorbed through the wall of the intestine and passed directly into the bloodstream.

27.3 Catabolism of Amino Acids

Since learning the different sequences of reactions by which each amino acid is synthesized and degraded, and covering pathways for even a few amino acids would be an advanced undertaking, we shall instead concentrate on the general principles of amino acid degradation, without referring to specific amino acids. As we shall see, the final stage in metabolism of the carbon skeletons of amino acids is the tricarboxylic acid cycle, which is why the metabolism of amino acids is very closely integrated with the metabolism of both carbohydrates and fatty acids.

A. Transamination

The loss of the alpha-amino group is the first stage in the metabolism of most amino acids. It is accomplished by two different reactions: transamination and oxidative deamination.

In **transamination**, an alpha amino group is transferred from a donor alpha-amino acid to an acceptor alpha-ketoacid. In the process, the acceptor alpha-ketoacid is transformed into a new alpha-amino acid. While several different alpha-ketoacids participate in transamination reactions, the most important are pyruvate and alpha-ketoglutarate. During the transamination phase of amino acid catabolism, all amino groups (except possibly those of lysine and threonine) are channeled into either alanine or glutamate.

Alanine Transaminase

$$\underset{\substack{\text{(an } \alpha\text{-amino} \\ \text{acid)}}}{\overset{\overset{\displaystyle NH_3^+}{\mid}}{RCHCO_2^-}} + \underset{\substack{\text{pyruvate} \\ \text{(a ketoacid)}}}{\overset{\overset{\displaystyle O}{\parallel}}{CH_3CCO_2^-}} \rightleftharpoons \underset{\substack{\text{(a new} \\ \alpha\text{-ketoacid)}}}{\overset{\overset{\displaystyle O}{\parallel}}{RCCO_2^-}} + \underset{\substack{\text{L-alanine} \\ \text{(a new } \alpha\text{-ketoacid)}}}{\overset{\overset{\displaystyle NH_3^+}{\mid}}{CH_3CHCO_2^-}}$$

Glutamate Transaminase

$$\underset{\substack{\text{(an } \alpha\text{-amino} \\ \text{acid)}}}{\overset{\overset{NH_3^+}{|}}{RCHCO_2^-}} + \underset{\substack{\alpha\text{-ketoglutarate} \\ \text{(an } \alpha\text{-ketoacid)}}}{\overset{\overset{O}{\|}}{^-O_2CCH_2CH_2CCO_2^-}} \rightleftharpoons \underset{\substack{\text{(a new} \\ \alpha\text{-ketoacid)}}}{\overset{\overset{O}{\|}}{RCCO_2^-}} + \underset{\substack{\text{L-glutamate} \\ \text{(a new } \alpha\text{-amino acid)}}}{\overset{\overset{NH_3^+}{|}}{^-O_2CCH_2CH_2CHCO_2^-}}$$

Example 27.1

Draw structural formulas for the starting materials and products of these transamination reactions:

a. tyrosine + alpha-ketoglutarate $\longrightarrow$ **b.** valine + pyruvate $\longrightarrow$

☐ *Solution*

a.

tyrosine   α-ketoglutarate

p-hydroxyphenylpyruvate   L-glutamate

b.

valine   pyruvate   2-keto-3-methyl-   L-alanine
                                      butanoate
                                      (α-ketoisovalerate)

Problem 27.1

Draw structural formulas for the starting materials and products of these transamination reactions:

a. phe + pyruvate $\longrightarrow$ **b.** his + α-ketoglutarate $\longrightarrow$

Transaminations are catalyzed by a specific group of enzymes called aminotransferases, or more commonly, transaminases. Though transaminases are found in all cells, their concentrations are particularly high in heart and liver tissues. Damage to either heart or liver leads to release of transaminases into the blood, and determination of serum levels of these enzymes can provide the clinician with valuable information about the extent of heart or liver damage. The two transaminases most commonly assayed for this purpose are serum glutamate oxaloacetate transaminase (SGOT) and serum glutamate pyruvate transaminase (SGPT).

For catalytic activity, all transaminases require pyridoxal phosphate, a coenzyme derived from pyridoxine, vitamin B$_6$ (Figure 27.2). In its role as a catalyst,

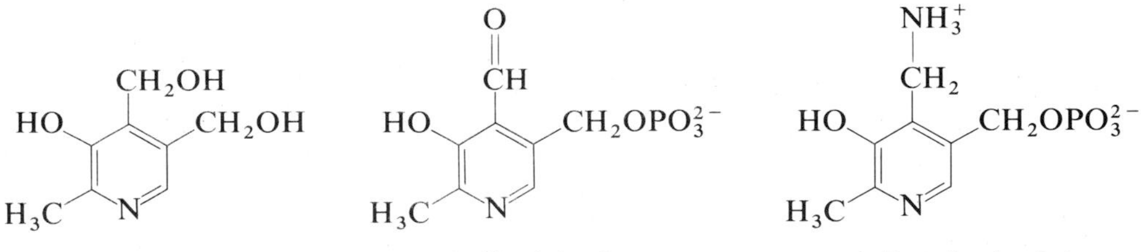

pyridoxine (vitamin B_6) | pyridoxal phosphate (PLP) | pyridoxamine phosphate (PMP)

Figure 27.2 Pyridoxine, or vitamin B_6. Pyridoxal phosphate (PLP) and pyridoxamine phosphate (PMP) are coenzymes derived from pyridoxine.

this coenzyme undergoes reversible transformations between an aldehyde (pyridoxal phosphate) and a primary amine (pyridoxamine phosphate). It first reacts as pyridoxal phosphate with an α-amino group, to form a Schiff base (Section 15.4C), which by rearrangement of two hydrogen atoms and the double bond, forms an isomeric Schiff base. This isomeric Schiff base then undergoes hydrolysis to give pyridoxamine and an α-ketoacid. The amino group of pyridoxamine then reacts with the keto group of a different α-ketoacid, to form another Schiff base, which after isomerization and hydrolysis, regenerates pyridoxal and a new α-amino acid. These reversible transformations are illustrated in Figure 27.3. To simplify the drawings, pyridoxal phosphate is abbreviated PP—CHO and pyridoxamine is abbreviated PP—CH_2NH_2.

Transaminations have two vital functions. First, they provide a means of readjusting the relative proportions of a number of amino acids to meet the particular needs of the organism; in most diets, the amino acid blend does not correspond precisely to what is needed. Second, transaminations collect the nitrogen atoms of all amino acids as glutamate, the primary source of nitrogen atoms for synthesis.

B. Oxidative Deamination

The second major pathway by which amino groups are removed from amino acids is **oxidative deamination** of glutamate in the liver, to form ammonium ion and alpha-ketoglutarate. The oxidation requires either NAD^+ or $NADP^+$ and is catalyzed by the enzyme glutamate dehydrogenase:

$$\underset{\text{glutamate}}{^-O_2CCH_2CH_2\overset{\overset{NH_3^+}{|}}{C}HCO_2^-} + NAD^+ + H_2O \xrightarrow[\text{dehydrogenase}]{\text{glutamate}}$$

$$\underset{\alpha\text{-ketoglutarate}}{^-O_2CCH_2CH_2\overset{\overset{O}{\|}}{C}CO_2^-} + NADH + NH_4^+ + H^+$$

In this way, amino groups collected from other amino acids are converted to ammonium ion.

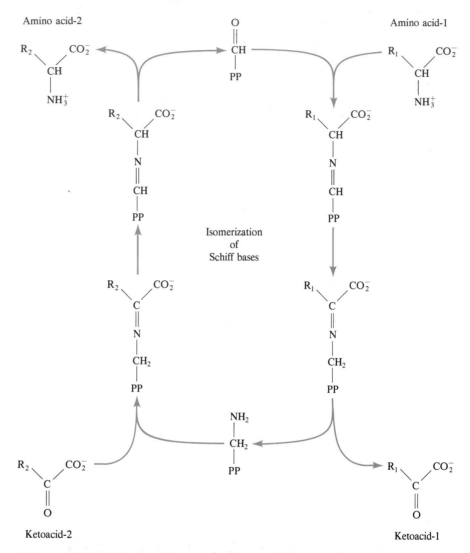

Figure 27.3 Mechanism of transamination catalyzed by pyridoxal/pyridoxamine phosphate.

Normal concentrations of ammonium ion in plasma are 0.025 to 0.04 mg/L. Ammonium ion is extremely toxic and must be eliminated. The main pathway by which ammonium ion is detoxified and eliminated in humans is formation of urea, a neutral nontoxic compound, followed by excretion in the urine.

C. Synthesis of Urea

Urea synthesis in mammals occurs exclusively in the liver. The metabolic pathway that catalyzes the formation of urea is called the urea cycle, or the Krebs-

Henseleit cycle, after Hans Krebs and Kurt Henseleit, who proposed it in 1932. This cycle accepts one carbon atom in the form of bicarbonate (or carbon dioxide) and two nitrogen atoms, one from ammonium ion and the other from aspartate, and in a five-step cycle, generates urea and fumarate. The net reaction of the **urea cycle** is shown in Figure 27.4.

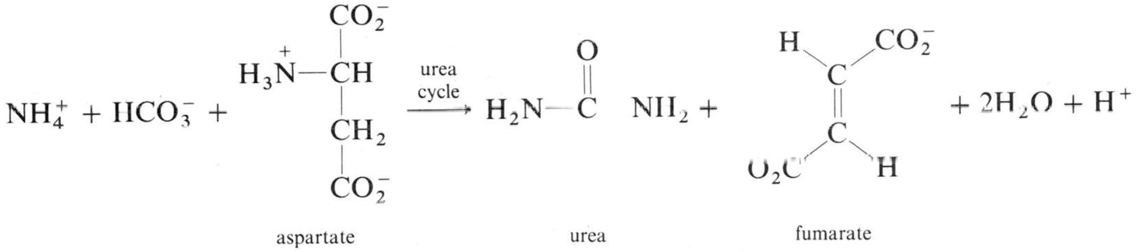

Figure 27.4 The net reaction of the urea cycle.

The five reactions of the urea cycle are shown in Figure 27.5. The first step in the formation of urea is synthesis of carbamoyl phosphate from bicarbonate, ammonium ion, and inorganic phosphate. This reaction is catalyzed by carbamoyl phosphate synthetase and is coupled with hydrolysis of two molecules of ATP to ADP. In step 2, carbamoyl phosphate reacts with ornithine, to form citrulline. The third step, condensation of citrulline with aspartate, is coupled with hydrolysis of a third molecule of ATP and incorporates a second nitrogen atom into the cycle. Cleavage of argininosuccinate produces arginine and fumarate (step 4). Finally, hydrolysis of arginine (step 5) yields one molecule of urea and regenerates ornithine.

Operation of the cycle requires a continuous supply of carbamoyl phosphate and aspartate. Carbamoyl phosphate is supplied by reaction of ammonium ion and bicarbonate. Aspartate is supplied from fumarate via reactions of the tricarboxylic acid cycle, followed by transamination. The conversion of fumarate to aspartate via oxaloacetate demonstrates the interrelation between the urea cycle and the tricarboxylic acid cycle (Figure 27.6).

Virtually all tissues produce NH_4^+, and ammonium ion is highly toxic, especially to the nervous system. In humans, the synthesis of urea in the liver is the only important route for detoxification and elimination of NH_4^+. Failure of the urea-synthesizing pathway for any reason, including liver malfunction or inherited defects in any of the five enzymes of the urea cycle, causes an increase of ammonium ion in the blood, liver, and urine, a condition that produces **ammonia intoxication**. Symptoms of ammonia intoxication are protein-induced vomiting, blurred vision, tremors, slurred speech, and ultimately, coma and death. In treating ammonia intoxication, it is essential to decrease the intake of dietary protein in order to decrease ammonium ion formation. Genetic defects in each of the five enzymes of the urea cycle do exist, but fortunately these inborn errors of metabolism are rare.

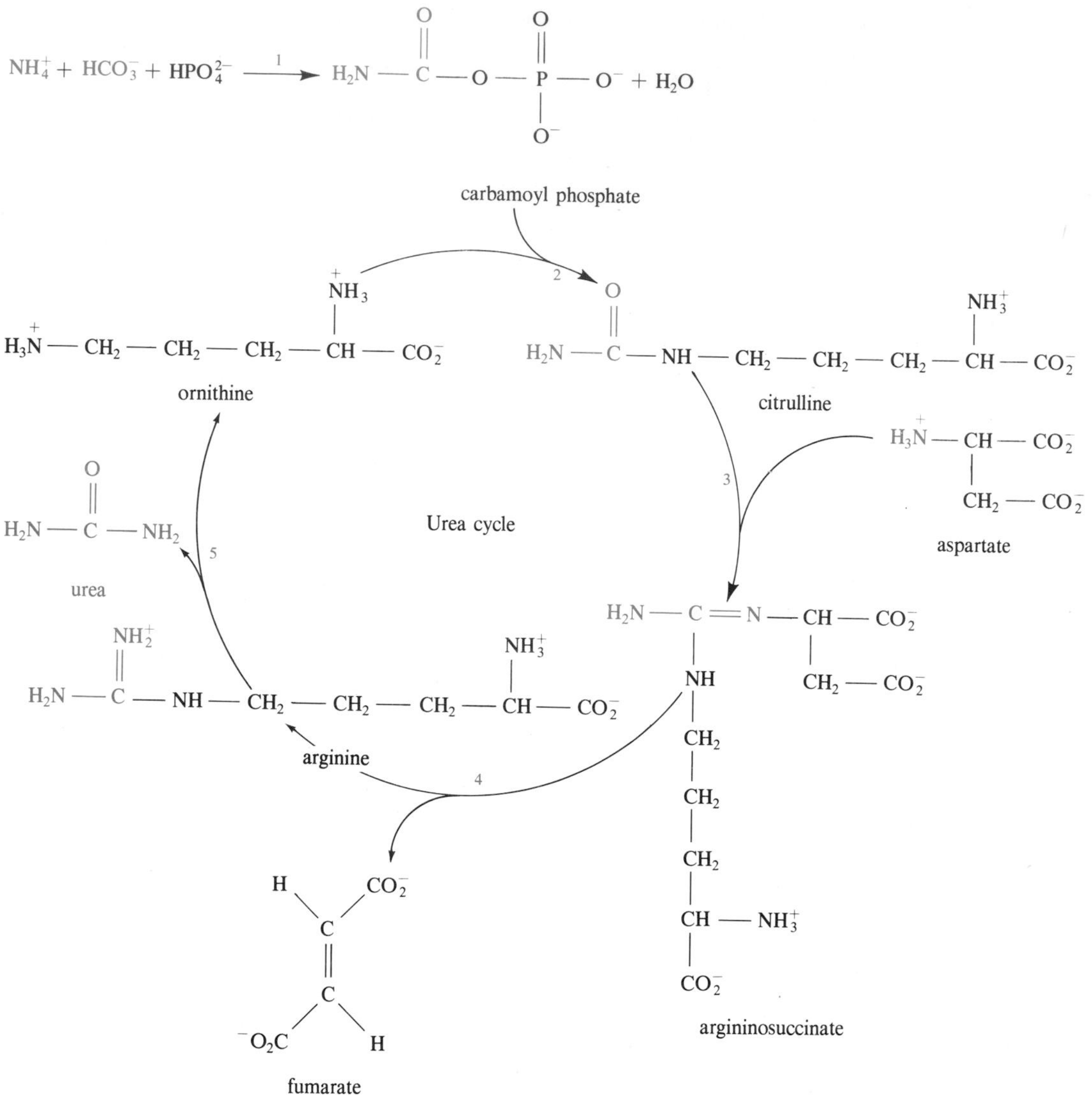

Figure 27.5 The urea cycle. The enzyme-catalyzed steps are numbered 1–5.

D. Fates of Carbon Skeletons of Amino Acids

By transamination, oxidative deamination, and a few other reactions, the carbon skeletons of amino acids are converted to one of six common intermediates, all of which we have seen at one time or another (Chapters 25 and 26, and this chapter). These common intermediates and the amino acids from which they are derived are summarized in Table 27.3. The central pathway for the oxidation of these common intermediates to carbon dioxide and water is the

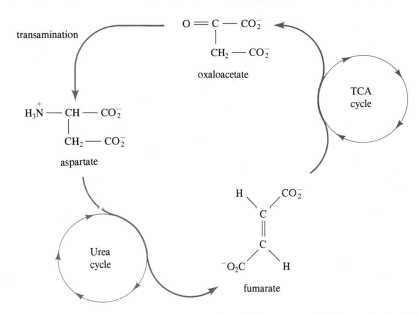

Figure 27.6 Aspartate, required for operation of the urea cycle, is synthesized from fumarate, a product of the urea cycle, via the tricarboxylic acid cycle, followed by transamination.

Table 27.3
Common intermediates derived from amino acids.

Common Intermediate	Name	Amino Acid Source
$CH_3\overset{O}{\overset{\|}{C}}CO_2^-$	pyruvate	alanine, glycine, serine, cysteine, tryptophan
$^-O_2CCH_2CH_2\overset{O}{\overset{\|}{C}}CO_2^-$	α-ketoglutarate	arginine, histidine, proline, glutamine, glutamate
$^-O_2CCH_2CH_2\overset{O}{\overset{\|}{C}}\,SCoA$	succinyl CoA	valine, isoleucine, methionine, threonine
fumarate structure	fumarate	phenylalanine, tyrosine
$^-O_2CCH_2\overset{O}{\overset{\|}{C}}CO_2^-$	oxaloacetate	asparagine, aspartate
$CH_3\overset{O}{\overset{\|}{C}}-SCoA$	acetyl CoA	leucine, phenylalanine, tyrosine, lysine, tryptophan, isoleucine

tricarboxylic acid cycle. The points at which these intermediates enter the cycle are shown in Figure 27.7.

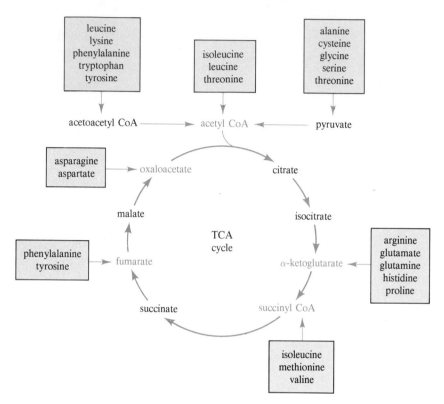

Figure 27.7 Pathways by which carbon skeletons from amino acid degradation enter the tricarboxylic acid.

E. Conversion to Glucose and Ketone Bodies

Amino acids degraded to pyruvate, alpha-ketoglutarate, succinyl CoA, fumarate, and oxaloacetate can be converted to phosphoenolpyruvate and then to glucose. These amino acids are said to be glycogenic, and the synthesis of glucose from them is called gluconeogenesis (Section 25.2H). **Glycogenic amino acids**, along with glycerol, provide alternative sources of glucose during periods of low carbohydrate intake or when stores are being rapidly depleted.

Amino acids degraded directly to acetyl CoA cannot be converted to glucose, since humans and other animals have no biochemical pathways for the synthesis of glucose from acetyl CoA. It is for this reason that fatty acids cannot serve as sources of carbon atoms for the synthesis of glucose. Acetyl CoA derived from the degradation of amino acids can be transformed to ketone bodies (Section 26.5). Amino acids that are degraded to acetyl CoA and then transformed to ketone bodies are said to be **ketogenic**.

The first experimental attempts to classify amino acids as glycogenic or ketogenic were carried out on test animals when the metabolic pathways for the degradation of individual amino acids were only poorly understood. In the earliest studies, laboratory dogs were made diabetic, either by selective chemical destruction of the insulin-producing ability of the pancreas, or by removal of the pancreas itself. Blood-glucose levels were then controlled by injecting insulin. These diabetic dogs excreted glucose in the urine even when glycogen and fat stores had been depleted and when they were fed a diet containing protein as the sole source of metabolic fuel. They also excreted urea, the means by which amino acid-derived nitrogen atoms are detoxified and eliminated. The molar ratio of glucose to urea indicates the extent to which the carbon skeletons of amino acids can be used for the synthesis of glucose. These studies revealed that in diabetic dogs, a maximum of 58 g glucose can be derived from 100 g protein. In other words, 58% of protein is glycogenic.

To determine which of the 20 amino acids were glycogenic, diabetic test animals were fed pure amino acids, one at a time. If glucose was excreted in the urine following such a feeding, the amino acid was classified as glycogenic. If acetoacetate, beta-hydroxybutyrate, or acetone was excreted, the amino acid was classified as ketogenic. Of the 20 protein-derived amino acids, only leucine is purely ketogenic. Six amino acids are both glycogenic and ketogenic, and the remaining thirteen amino acids are purely glycogenic. The glycogenic and ketogenic amino acids are:

Glycogenic		Glycogenic and Ketogenic	Ketogenic
alanine	glycine	isoleucine	leucine
arginine	histidine	lysine	
asparagine	methionine	phenylalanine	
aspartic acid	proline	threonine	
cysteine	serine	tryptophan	
glutamic acid	valine	tyrosine	
glutamine			

Key Terms and Concepts

amino acid pool (27.1A)

ammonia intoxication (27.3C)

glycogenic amino acids (27.3E)

ketogenic amino acids (27.3E)

oxidative deamination (27.3B)

protein half-life (27.1A)

transamination (27.3A)

urea cycle (27.3C)

Key Reactions

1. Reactions of pyridoxal phosphate/pyridoxamine phosphate in transamination (Section 27.3A).

2. Oxidative deamination of glutamate by NAD^+ (Section 27.3B).

3. Net reaction of the urea cycle (Section 27.3C).

4. The five reactions of the urea cycle (Section 27.3C).

Problems

27.2   List the three vital functions served by amino acids in the body.

27.3   Define the term half-life as it is applied in this chapter to tissue and plasma proteins.

27.4   Compare the degree to which carbohydrates, fats, and proteins can be stored in the body for later use.

27.5   What percentage of the total energy requirement of the average adult is supplied by carbohydrates? by fats? by proteins?

27.6   Complete the following reactions. Show structural formulas for products and reactants.

   a. leucine + oxaloacetate $\xrightarrow{\text{transaminase}}$

   b. alanine + alpha-ketoglutarate $\xrightarrow{\text{transaminase}}$

   c. glycine + pyruvate $\xrightarrow{\text{transaminase}}$

   d. glycine + pyridoxal phosphate $\xrightarrow{\text{transaminase}}$

   e. pyridoxamine phosphate + pyruvate $\xrightarrow{\text{transaminase}}$

27.7   **a.** Write an equation for the reaction catalyzed by the enzyme serum glutamate oxaloacetate transaminase (SGOT); for the reaction catalyzed by serum glutamate pyruvate transaminase (SGPT).

   b. Describe how an assay for the presence of these enzymes in blood can provide information about possible heart and liver damage.

27.8   In nutritional studies on rats, it has been found that certain alpha-ketoacids may substitute for essential amino acids. Shown here are structural formulas for three such alpha-ketoacids.

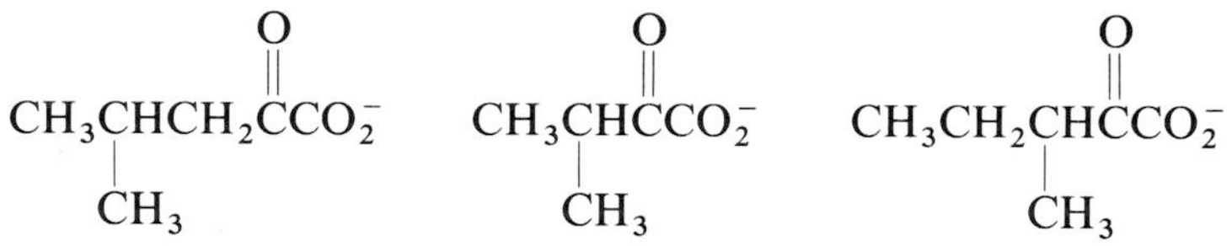

$$\underset{\text{(a)}}{\underset{\underset{CH_3}{|}}{CH_3CHCH_2\overset{\overset{O}{||}}{C}CO_2^-}} \qquad \underset{\text{(b)}}{\underset{\underset{CH_3}{|}}{CH_3CH\overset{\overset{O}{||}}{C}CO_2^-}} \qquad \underset{\text{(c)}}{\underset{\underset{CH_3}{|}}{CH_3CH_2CH\overset{\overset{O}{||}}{C}CO_2^-}}$$

   a. Account for substitution, in certain instances, of these alpha-ketoacids for essential amino acids.

   b. For which essential amino acid might each substitute?

27.9   The following reaction is the first step in the degradation of ornithine. Propose a metabolic pathway to account for this transformation.

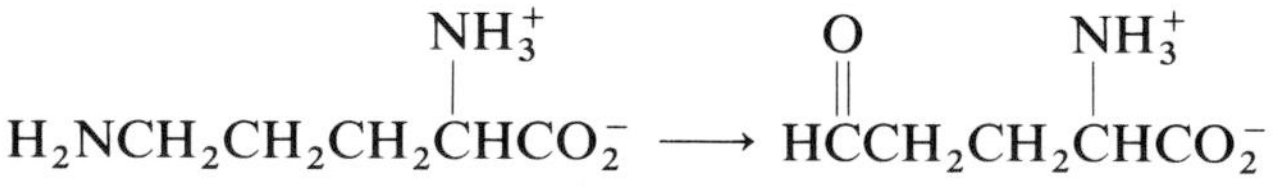

$$\underset{\text{ornithine}}{H_2NCH_2CH_2CH_2\overset{\overset{NH_3^+}{|}}{C}HCO_2^-} \longrightarrow \underset{\text{glutamate semialdehyde}}{\overset{\overset{O}{||}}{H}CCH_2CH_2\overset{\overset{NH_3^+}{|}}{C}HCO_2^-}$$

27.10   Write an equation for the oxidative deamination of glutamate.

27.11   What is the function of the urea cycle?

27.12   Using structural formulas, write an equation for the hydrolysis of arginine to ornithine and urea.

27.13   In what organ does the synthesis of urea take place?

27.14   Urea has two nitrogen atoms. What is the source of each? What is the source of the single carbon atom in urea?

27.15   Write a balanced equation for the net reaction of the urea cycle.

27.16   What is meant by ammonia intoxication?

27.17   List the five points at which carbon skeletons derived from amino acids enter the tricarboxylic acid cycle.

27.18   **a.** What does it mean to say that an amino acid is glycogenic?
        b. What does it mean to say that an amino acid is ketogenic?
        c. Is it possible for an amino acid to be both glycogenic and ketogenic? Explain.

27.19   Propose biochemical pathways to explain how the cell might carry out the following transformations. Name each type of reaction (for example, hydration, dehydration, oxidation, hydrolysis).
        a. phenylalanine $\longrightarrow$ phenylacetate
        b. 3-phosphoglycerate $\longrightarrow$ serine
        c. citrate $\longrightarrow$ glutamate
        d. ornithine $\longrightarrow$ glutamate
        e. methylmalonyl CoA $\longrightarrow$ oxaloacetate

27.20   Following is the metabolic pathway for the conversion of isoleucine to acetyl CoA and propionyl CoA. You have already studied each type of reaction shown here, though not necessarily in this chapter. For each step in this sequence, name the type of reaction and specify any coenzymes involved.

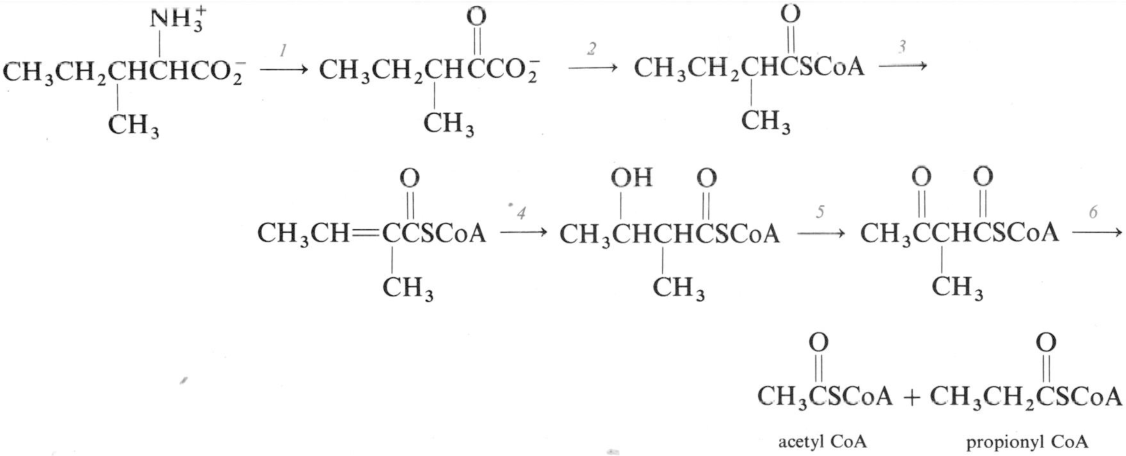

$$CH_3CH_2\underset{\underset{CH_3}{|}}{CH}\underset{\underset{NH_3^+}{|}}{CH}CO_2^- \xrightarrow{1} CH_3CH_2\underset{\underset{CH_3}{|}}{CH}\overset{\overset{O}{||}}{C}CO_2^- \xrightarrow{2} CH_3CH_2\underset{\underset{CH_3}{|}}{CH}\overset{\overset{O}{||}}{C}SCoA \xrightarrow{3}$$

$$CH_3CH{=}\underset{\underset{CH_3}{|}}{C}\overset{\overset{O}{||}}{C}SCoA \xrightarrow{4} CH_3\underset{\underset{CH_3}{|}}{\overset{\overset{OH}{|}}{CH}}CH\overset{\overset{O}{||}}{C}SCoA \xrightarrow{5} CH_3\overset{\overset{O}{||}}{C}\underset{\underset{CH_3}{|}}{CH}\overset{\overset{O}{||}}{C}SCoA \xrightarrow{6}$$

$$CH_3\overset{\overset{O}{||}}{C}SCoA + CH_3CH_2\overset{\overset{O}{||}}{C}SCoA$$

acetyl CoA   propionyl CoA

27.21   Following is the metabolic pathway for the conversion of proline to glutamate. Name the type of reaction involved in each step of this transformation and specify any coenzymes you think might be involved.

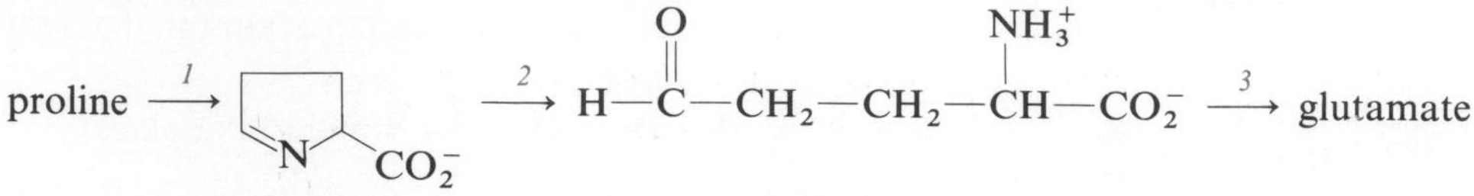

$$\text{proline} \xrightarrow{1} \underset{\underset{N}{}}{\boxed{}}\text{CO}_2^- \xrightarrow{2} \underset{\underset{\displaystyle H-\overset{\displaystyle\overset{O}{\|}}{C}-CH_2-CH_2-\overset{\overset{\displaystyle NH_3^+}{|}}{CH}-CO_2^-}{}}{} \xrightarrow{3} \text{glutamate}$$

27.22 Most substances in the biological world are built from just thirty or so smaller molecules. Review the biochemistry we have discussed in this textbook and make your own list of these thirty or so fundamental building blocks of nature.

Answers to In-Chapter Problems

Chapter 1

1.1 **a.** 10^{-12} Hz **b.** 10^{-6} Hz **c.** 10^6 Hz **1.2** **a.** 5.976×10^{27} g **b.** 7.382×10^9 km
1.3 **a.** 1.67×10^{-24} g **b.** 1.54×10^{-8} m
1.4 **a.** 1.10×10^5 **b.** 9.04×10^4 **c.** 6.10×10^{-7} **d.** 7.01×10^{-2} **1.5** 54 miles/hr
1.6 $2.1 \times 10^{-7}\%$ **1.7** 15.6 mL **1.8** 41 m **1.9** 325 mg **1.10** 73.6 L **1.11** 2.64 g/mL
1.12 1.46 cm^3 **1.13** **a.** 20°C **b.** 113°F **1.14** **a.** 378 K **b.** −43°C **1.15** a solid
1.16 1.67 kcal **1.17** 0.244 cal/g·°C

Chapter 2

2.1 **a.** metal, solid **b.** nonmetal **c.** metal, solid
2.2 **a.** N_2, nonmetal **b.** Ba, metal, solid **c.** Cr, metal, solid **d.** He, nonmetal, gas
2.3 C_2H_6O **2.4** 2 atoms carbon, 3 atoms hydrogen, 1 atom chlorine
2.5 15 protons, 15 electrons, 16 neutrons
2.6 uranium-238: 92 protons, 92 electrons, 146 neutrons
uranium-235: 92 protons, 92 electrons, 143 neutrons
2.7 cobalt-60: in the nucleus: 27 protons, 33 neutrons; outside the nucleus: 27 electrons
2.8 19.5 g **2.9** 0.204 g **2.10** 4.24×10^{25} atoms
2.11 $^{222}_{86}Rn \longrightarrow {}^{218}_{84}Po + {}^4_2\alpha$ **2.12** 8.6×10^{-10} g

Chapter 3

3.1 one s orbital holding 2 electrons; three p orbitals holding six electrons; five d orbitals holding
10 electrons; seven f orbitals holding 14 electrons
3.2 $3s4d6s4f5d$ **3.3** As: $1s^2 2s^2 2p^6 3s^2 3p^6 3d^{10} 4s^2 4p^3$
3.4 In the chlorine electron configuration, the third energy level is the highest occupied; chlorine is in the
third period of the periodic table. Chlorine has seven valence electrons; chlorine is in Column VII.
3.5 **a.** Sr: $[Kr]5s^2$ **b.** $[Ar]4s^2 3d^{10} 4p^3$ **3.6** **a.** K· **b.** ·Äs:
3.7 Cl < I < Na **3.8** **a.** Li $\longrightarrow$ Li$^+$ + e$^-$ **b.** Cs < Li < Cl
3.9 K($[Ar]4s^1$) $\longrightarrow$ K$^+$($[Ar]$ + e$^-$) Cl($[Ne]3s^2 3p^5$) + e$^-$ $\longrightarrow$ Cl$^-$($[Ar]$)$^-$
3.10 **a.** Ca + O$_2$ $\longrightarrow$ 2CaO; CaO + H$_2$O $\longrightarrow$ Ca(OH)$_2$
b. 2Cl$_2$ + 5O$_2$ $\longrightarrow$ 2Cl$_2$O$_5$; Cl$_2$O$_5$ + H$_2$O $\longrightarrow$ 2HClO$_3$

Chapter 4

4.1 **a.** CuCl$_2$ **b.** Ba(NO$_3$)$_2$ **c.** Mg$_3$(PO$_4$)$_2$
4.2 **a.** copper(II) oxide **b.** iron(II) sulfide **c.** strontium chloride

4.3   **a.** 110.3 amu   **b.** 148.3 amu   **4.4** 38.5 g CO_2 **4.5** 5.64×10^{20} atoms hydrogen

4.6   0.318 mol sulfuric acid   **4.7** 28.88% magnesium, 14.25% carbon, 56.92% oxygen

4.8   28.18% nitrogen   **4.9** 92.6% mercury   **4.10** N_2O_3 **4.11** $FeCl_2$ **4.12** $C_5H_{10}O_5$

4.13 $C_4H_4O_4$ **4.14** polar covalent; $^{\delta+}C$; $^{\delta-}N$

4.15   **a.** H:C̈:C̈l: **b.** :C::O: **c.** :S̈::C::S̈.

4.16   **a.** :O=C with O:⁻ groups   **b.** ⁻:Ö—H   **c.** :O=N—Ö:⁻ with :Ö: above

4.17   :Ö=Ö—Ö: ⟷ :Ö—Ö=Ö:

4.18   **a.** in CH_3, 109.5°; in CHO, 120°   **b.** 120°   **c.** 109.5°   **d.** 109.5°

4.19   **a.** polar   **b.** nonpolar   **c.** polar   **4.20** **a.** yes   **b.** yes   **c.** no

Chapter 5

5.1 $2Na + Cl_2 \longrightarrow 2NaCl$ **5.2** $2C_8H_{18} + 25O_2 \longrightarrow 16CO_2 + 18H_2O$

5.3   **a.** $2C + O_2 \longrightarrow 2CO$ **b.** $Li_2O + H_2O \longrightarrow 2LiOH$

5.4   **a.** $2Ag_2O \longrightarrow 4Ag + O_2$ **b.** $2AsH_3 \longrightarrow 2As + 3H_2$

5.5   **a.** $Zn + H_2SO_4 \longrightarrow H_2 + ZnSO_4$ **b.** $Hg + AgNO_3 \longrightarrow Ag + HgNO_3$

5.6   **a.** $Al(OH)_3 + 3HC_2H_3O_2 \longrightarrow Al(C_2H_3O_2)_3 + 3H_2O$

       b. $2KOH + H_2SO_4 \longrightarrow K_2SO_4 + 2H_2O$

5.7   **a.** $Ba(C_2H_3O_2)_2$; soluble   **b.** Ag_2S; insoluble   **c.** $(NH_4)_3PO_4$; soluble   **d.** $CaCO_3$; insoluble

5.8   **a.** $CrCl_3 + 3NaOH \longrightarrow Cr(OH)_3\downarrow + 3NaCl$

                             chromium(III)   sodium
                               hydroxide   chloride

       b. $H_2SO_4 + BaCl_2 \longrightarrow BaSO_4\downarrow + 2HCl$

                               barium   hydrochloric
                               sulfate   acid

5.9   **a.** Fe, +3; O, −2   **b.** Na, +1; Mn, +7; O, −2   **c.** N, +4; O, −2

5.10   **a.** not oxidation-reduction

       b. zinc is oxidized, is reducing agent; hydrogen ion is reduced, is oxidizing agent

5.11   copper is oxidized to Cu^{2+}, copper is reducing agent; Hg^{2+} is reduced to Hg, Hg^{2+} is oxidizing agent

5.12 $2NaI + Br_2 \longrightarrow 2NaBr + I_2$

       $2I^- \longrightarrow I_2 + 2e^-$

       $\underline{2e^- + Br_2 \longrightarrow 2Br^-}$

       $2I^- + Br_2 \longrightarrow I_2 + 2Br^-$

       $2NaI + Br_2 \longrightarrow I_2 + 2NaBr$

5.13 $C_7H_{16} + 11O_2 \longrightarrow 7CO_2 + 8H_2O$ $2C_3H_7OH + 10O_2 \longrightarrow 6CO_2 + 8H_2O$

5.14   13.8 g O_2 **5.15** 0.941 g Cl_2 **5.16** 1.25×10^{23} molecules of oxygen   **5.17** 43% yield

5.18   **a.** exothermic; reverse: $2NH_3(g) \longrightarrow N_2(g) + 3H_2(g)$, $\Delta H = +11.0$ kcal

       b. endothermic; reverse: $4HCl(g) + O_2(g) \longrightarrow 2H_2O(g) + 2Cl_2(g)$, $\Delta H = -27.8$ kcal

       c. exothermic; reverse: $3H_2O(l) + 2CO_2(g) \longrightarrow C_2H_5OH(l) + 3O_2(g)$, $\Delta H = +327$ kcal

5.19   −173 kcal   **5.20** −219 kcal

Chapter 6

6.1 1.67×10^5 Pa; 4.92×10^4 Pa   **6.2** 126 mL   **6.3** 1.38 L
6.4 4.8 L   **6.5** 0.179 g/L   **6.6** 1.16 g oxygen
6.7 0.195 atm oxygen; 0.004 atm carbon dioxide; 0.062 atm water (g); 0.741 atm nitrogen
6.8 0.526 cal/g·°C   **6.9** 5.33 kcal/mol   **6.10** 0.502 kcal   **6.11** 1.20 kcal

Chapter 7

7.1 3 g NaCl   **7.2** Dilute 400 mL ethyl alcohol to 1 L with water.
7.3 0.0562 mol glucose   **7.4** 11.0 g NaCl   **7.5** 12 mL 6.0M HCl   **7.6** 256 mL 0.195M HCl
7.7 0.78 mL 15M acetic acid   **7.8** 1.90 g magnesium   **7.9** 0.220M HCl
7.10 0.0958M acetic acid

Chapter 8

8.1

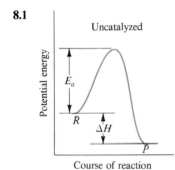
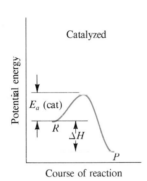

8.2 $K_{eq} = \dfrac{[NO_2]^2}{[NO]^2[O_2]}$

8.3 **a.** $K_{eq} = \dfrac{[H_2O][CO]}{[H_2][CO_2]}$
  b. Increased $[CO_2]$ will shift equilibrium to right; decreased $[H_2]$ will shift equilibrium to left.
8.4 Increased temperature will shift equilibrium to left.

8.5 **a.** $K_{eq} = \dfrac{[H_2]^2[O_2]}{[H_2O]^2}$ **b.** shift left   **c.** shift right
  d. no effect   **e.** only a change in temperature will affect the value of K_{eq}

Chapter 9

9.1 **a.** $HS^- + OH^- \longrightarrow S^{2-} + H_2O$
    The conjugate base of HS^- is S^{2-}, the sulfide ion; the conjugate acid of OH^- is water.
  b. $HS^- + HCl \longrightarrow H_2S + Cl^-$
    The conjugate acid of HS^- is hydrogen sulfide, H_2S; the conjugate base of HCl is the chloride ion, Cl^-.
9.2 Carbonic acid, H_2CO_3; carbonate ion. Hydroiodic acid, HI; iodide ion. Chloric acid, $HClO_3$; chlorate ion.
9.3 **a.** $H_2SO_4 + 2KOH \longrightarrow K_2SO_4 + 2H_2O$ **b.** $H_2SO_4 + HCO_3^- \longrightarrow H_2CO_3 + HSO_4^-$
  c. $H_2SO_4 + Fe \longrightarrow FeSO_4 + H_2$
9.4 **a.** $HBrO_3 \longrightarrow H^+ + BrO_3^-$ **b.** $HNO_2 \rightleftharpoons H^+ + NO_2^-$
  c. $H_2SO_3 \rightleftharpoons H^+ + HSO_3^-$; $HSO_3^- \rightleftharpoons H^+ + SO_3^{2-}$

9.5 $C_6H_8O_7 \rightleftharpoons H^+ + C_6H_7O_7^-$ $K_{eq} = \dfrac{[H^+][C_6H_7O_7^-]}{[C_6H_8O_7]}$

9.6 $[H^+] = 0.1M$ **9.7** $[H^+] = 4.2 \times 10^{-3}M$ **9.8** $[H^+] = 1.8 \times 10^{-4}M$
9.9   **a.** 3.30   **b.** $[H^+] = 6.9 \times 10^{-4}M$ **9.10** $pH = 5.04$ **9.11** $[H^+] = 1.0 \times 10^{-10}M; pH = 10$
9.12   **a.** $pH = 4.05$ **b.** $pH = 4.00$ **c.** $pH = 4.10$ **9.13**   From $pH = 4.74$ to $pH = 12.0$

Chapter 10

10.1
$$H-\overset{\overset{\displaystyle H}{|}}{\underset{\underset{\displaystyle H}{|}}{C}}-O-\overset{\overset{\displaystyle H}{|}}{\underset{\underset{\displaystyle H}{|}}{C}}-\overset{\overset{\displaystyle H}{|}}{\underset{\underset{\displaystyle H}{|}}{C}}-H$$
$CH_3-O-CH_2-CH_3$ or $CH_3OCH_2CH_3$

10.2
$$H-\overset{\overset{\displaystyle H}{|}}{\underset{\underset{\displaystyle H}{|}}{C}}-\overset{\overset{\displaystyle O}{\|}}{C}-\overset{\overset{\displaystyle H}{|}}{\underset{\underset{\displaystyle H}{|}}{C}}-\overset{\overset{\displaystyle H}{|}}{\underset{\underset{\displaystyle H}{|}}{C}}-\overset{\overset{\displaystyle H}{|}}{\underset{\underset{\displaystyle H}{|}}{C}}-H$$
$CH_3-C-CH_2-CH_2-CH_3$ or $CH_3COCH_2CH_2CH_3$

$$H-\overset{\overset{\displaystyle H}{|}}{\underset{\underset{\displaystyle H}{|}}{C}}-\overset{\overset{\displaystyle O}{\|}}{C}-\overset{\overset{\displaystyle H}{|}}{\underset{\underset{\displaystyle H-C-H}{|}}{C}}-\overset{\overset{\displaystyle H}{|}}{\underset{\underset{\displaystyle H}{|}}{C}}-H$$
$CH_3-C-CH-CH_3$ or $CH_3COCH(CH_3)_2$
with CH_3

$$H-\overset{\overset{\displaystyle H}{|}}{\underset{\underset{\displaystyle H}{|}}{C}}-\overset{\overset{\displaystyle H}{|}}{\underset{\underset{\displaystyle H}{|}}{C}}-\overset{\overset{\displaystyle O}{\|}}{C}-\overset{\overset{\displaystyle H}{|}}{\underset{\underset{\displaystyle H}{|}}{C}}-\overset{\overset{\displaystyle H}{|}}{\underset{\underset{\displaystyle H}{|}}{C}}-H$$
$CH_3-CH_2-C-CH_2-CH_3$ or $CH_3CH_2COCH_2CH_3$

10.3
$$H-\overset{\overset{\displaystyle H}{|}}{\underset{\underset{\displaystyle H}{|}}{C}}-\overset{\overset{\displaystyle H}{|}}{\underset{\underset{\displaystyle H}{|}}{C}}-\overset{\overset{\displaystyle H}{|}}{\underset{\underset{\displaystyle H}{|}}{C}}-\overset{\overset{\displaystyle O}{\|}}{C}-O-H$$
$CH_3-CH_2-CH_2-C-OH$ or $CH_3CH_2CH_2CO_2H$

$$H-\overset{\overset{\displaystyle H}{|}}{\underset{\underset{\displaystyle H}{|}}{C}}-\overset{\overset{\displaystyle H}{|}}{\underset{\underset{\displaystyle H-C-H}{|}}{C}}-\overset{\overset{\displaystyle O}{\|}}{C}-O-H$$
$CH_3-CH-C-OH$ or $CH_3CH(CH_3)CO_2H$
with CH_3

10.4   Following are molecular formulas for each compound: **a.** C_4H_6O **b.** C_4H_4O **c.** C_4H_6O **d.** C_4H_6O
Compounds (a), (c), and (d) have the same molecular formula but a different order of attachment of atoms, and therefore they are structural isomers. There are no structural isomers of compound (b) shown in this problem.

10.5   Labels on Lewis structures at the left (see page A5) point to atoms and show the hybridization of each atom. Labels on the middle diagrams point to bonds and show the type of bond, either sigma or pi. Labels on the right diagrams point to atoms and show predicted bond angles.

a. H—C—Ö—C—H   H—C—Ö—C—H   H—C—Ö—C—H
   (sp³)   (σ)   (109.5°)

b. H—C—C=C—H   H—C—C=C—H   H—C—C=C—H
   (sp³, sp²)   (σ, π)   (109.5°, 120°)

c. H—C—N—H   H—C—N—H   H—C—N—H
   (sp³)   (σ)   (109.5°)

Chapter 11

11.1 **a.** Structural isomers. In each, the longest chain is six carbon atoms. In the formula on the left, there are one-carbon branches on the third and fourth carbons of the chain. In the formula on the right, there are also two one-carbon branches but they are on the second and fourth carbons.

b. Identical. The longest chain is five carbon atoms with one-carbon branches on the second and third carbons of the chain.

11.2 There is one isomer with five carbons in the chain, one with four carbons in the longest chain and a one-carbon branch, and one with three carbons in the longest chain and two one-carbon branches.

$$CH_3-CH_2-CH_2-CH_2-CH_3 \qquad CH_3-\underset{\underset{CH_3}{|}}{CH}-CH_2-CH_3 \qquad CH_3-\underset{\underset{CH_3}{|}}{\overset{\overset{CH_3}{|}}{C}}-CH_3$$

11.3 **a.** 5-isopropyl-2-methyloctane   **b.** 4-isopropyl-4-propylheptane
11.4 **a.** 1-ethyl-1-methylcyclopropane   **b.** 1-tert-butyl-2-methylcyclopentane
11.5 **a.** eth-en-e combined to give ethene.   **b.** prop-yn-e combined to give propyne
c. but-an-oic acid combined to give butanoic acid   **d.** but-an-al combined to give butanal
e. cyclopent-an-one combined to give cyclopentanone
f. cyclohept-en-e combined to give cycloheptene
11.6 Following are the two eclipsed conformations of butane:

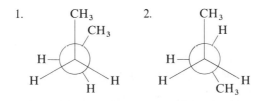

Of the two, (2) is the more stable because the two methyl groups are farther apart. Conformation (1) is less stable because in it the two methyl groups are closer together.

11.7 **a.** Methylcyclohexane does not show cis-trans isomerism because it has only one substituent on the ring.
b. 1,3-dimethylcyclopentane shows cis-trans isomerism.

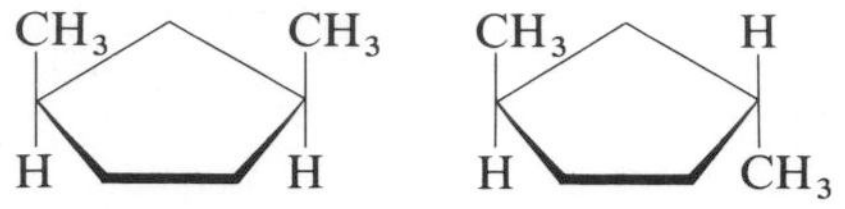

cis-1,3-dimethyl-
cyclopentane

trans-1,3-dimethyl-
cyclopentane

c. Because ethylcyclopentane has only one substituent on the ring, it does not show cis-trans isomerism.
d. 1-ethyl-2-methylcyclobutane shows cis-trans isomerism.

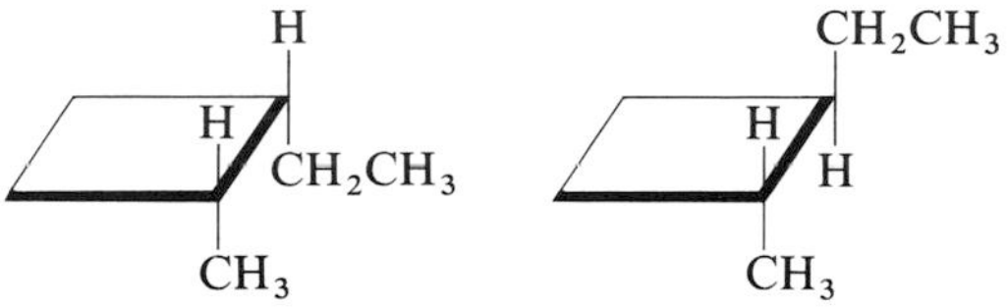

cis-1-ethyl-2-methyl-
cyclobutane

trans-1-ethyl-2-methyl-
cyclobutane

11.8 **a.** 2,2-dimethylpropane   2-methylbutane   pentane

(bp 9.5°C)   (bp 29°C)   (bp 36°C)

b. 2,2,4-trimethylpentane   3,3-dimethylheptane   nonane

(bp 99°C)   (bp 137°C)   (bp 151°C)

11.9 **a.**

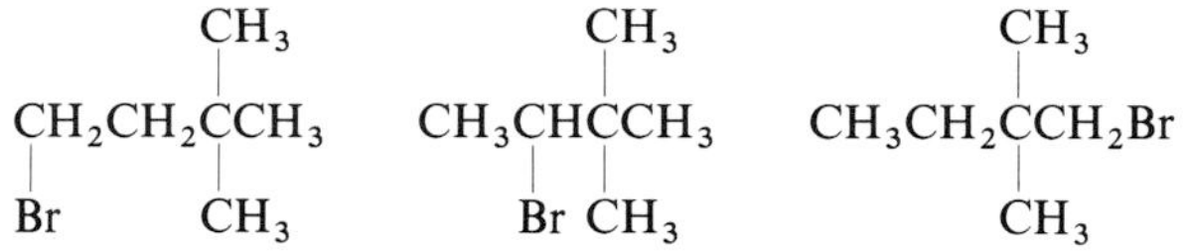

1-bromo-3,3-
dimethylbutane

3-bromo-2,2-
dimethylbutane

1-bromo-2,2-
dimethylbutane

b.

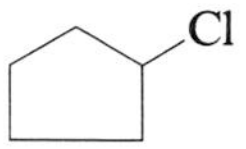

chlorocyclopentane
(cyclopentyl chloride)

Chapter 12

12.1 **a.** There are four alkenes with the carbon skeleton given in (a).

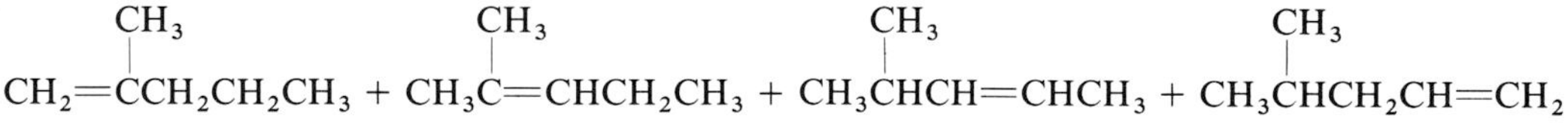

2-methyl-1-pentene   2-methyl-2-pentene   4-methyl-2-pentene   4-methyl-1-pentene

b. There are two alkenes with the carbon skeleton given in (b).

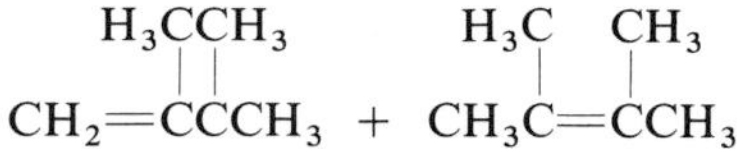

2,3-dimethyl-1-butene   2,3-dimethyl-2-butene
(tetramethylethylene)

c. There is only one alkene with the carbon skeleton given in (c).

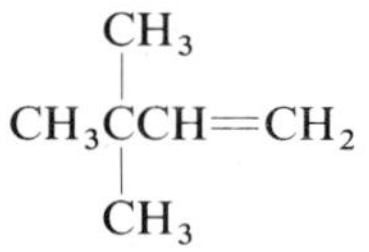

$$CH_3$$
$$CH_3CCH{=}CH_2$$
$$CH_3$$

3,3-dimethyl-1-butene
(*tert*-butylethylene)

12.2 Only part (c) shows cis-trans isomerism.

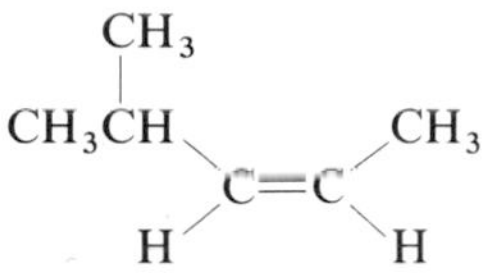

cis-4-methyl-2-pentene 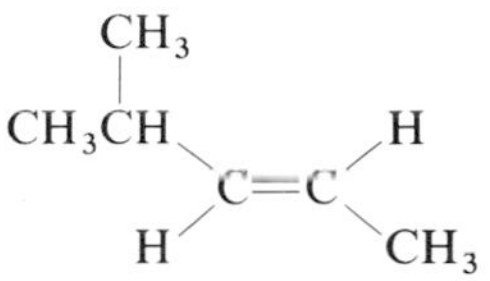   *trans*-4-methyl-2-pentene

12.3 **a.** 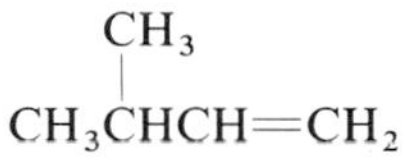 $CH_3CHCH{=}CH_2$ (with CH_3 substituent)   **b.** (1-methylcyclopentene structure with CH_3)

3-methyl-1-butene   1-methylcyclopentene

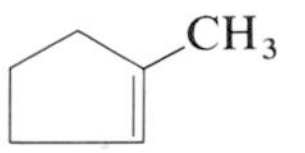

12.4 Following are names and structural formulas for the two possible addition products. For each part, the major product is given first.

a. 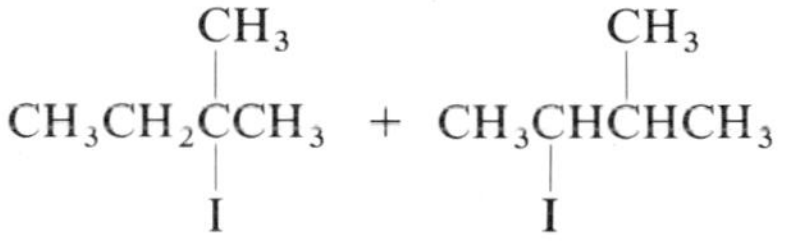 $CH_3CH_2CCH_3$ (with CH_3, I) $+$ $CH_3CHCHCH_3$ (with CH_3, I)   **b.** 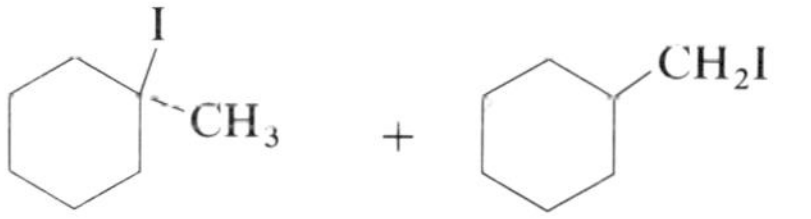 (1-iodo-1-methylcyclohexane structure, I, CH_3) $+$ (iodomethylcyclohexane structure, CH_2I)

2-iodo-2-methylbutane   2-iodo-3-methylbutane   1-iodo-1-methylcyclohexane   iodomethylcyclohexane
(major product)   (minor product)   (major product)   (minor product)

12.5 Only the major product is given. Note that both alkenes give the same alcohol as the major product.

a. 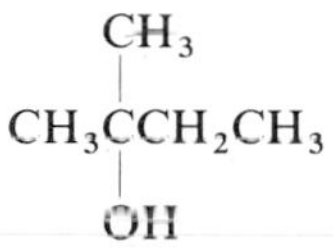 $CH_3CCH_2CH_3$ (with CH_3, OH)   **b.** $CH_3CCH_2CH_3$ (with CH_3, OH)

2-methyl-2-butanol   2-methyl-2-butanol

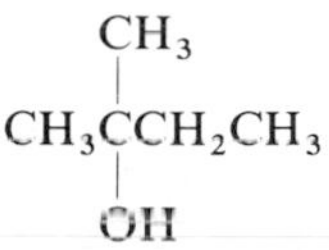

12.6 **a.** tertiary **b.** secondary **c.** primary; In order of increasing ease of formation, they are (c), (b), (a).

12.7 **a.**  (cyclohexylidene structure) $={=}CHCH_2CH_3$ **b.** 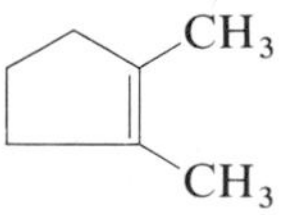 (cyclopentene structure with two CH_3 groups)

Chapter 13

13.1 **a.** 2-ethyl-1-butanol   **b.** 1-methylcyclopentanol
13.2 **a.** primary   **b.** secondary   **c.** primary   **d.** tertiary
13.3 **a.** 2-buten-1-ol   **b.** 3-cyclohexenol

13.4 **a.** ethyl isobutyl ether. Its IUPAC name is 1-ethoxy-2-methylpropane.   **b.** diphenyl ether
c. tertiary-butyl methyl ether or *tert*-butyl methyl ether or *t*-butyl methyl ether. Its IUPAC name is 2-methoxy-2-methylpropane.

13.5 $CH_3OCH_2CH_2OCH_3$ $CH_3OCH_2CH_2OH$ $HOCH_2CH_2OH$

(bp 84°C)   (bp 125°C)   (bp 198°C)

13.6 $ClCH_2CH_2Cl$ $CH_3CH_2OCH_2CH_3$ $CH_3CH_2CH_2OH$

slightly   8 g/100 g H_2O soluble in all
proportions

13.7 For each reaction, the major product is given first.

a. $CH_3\overset{\underset{|}{CH_3}}{C}{=}CHCH_3$ + $CH_2{=}\overset{\underset{|}{CH_3}}{C}CH_2CH_3$ **b.**

2-methyl-2-butene   2-methyl-1-butene   1-methylcyclohexene   methylenecyclohexane
(major product)   (minor product)   (major product)   (minor product)

Chapter 14

14.1 **a.** *N,N*-dimethylaniline   **b.** 2-aminobutane (*sec*-butylamine)   **c.** 3-amino-1-propanol

14.2 **a.** $CH_3CH_2\overset{\underset{|}{\underset{CH_2CH_3}{}}}{\overset{H}{N^+}}CH_2CH_3$ Cl^- or $(CH_3CH_2)_3\overset{+}{N}H\ Cl^-$ **b.**

triethylammonium chloride
(triethylamine hydrochloride)

piperidinium acetate

Chapter 15

15.1 **a.** 4,4-dimethyl-2-pentanone   **b.** 2,5-dimethylcyclohexanone
c. 2-phenylpropanal (2-phenylpropionaldehyde)

15.2 **a.** CH_3— —$\overset{\overset{O}{\|}}{C}$—H + $2CH_3OH$ **b.** $CH_3\overset{\overset{O}{\|}}{C}CH_3$ + $HOCH_2CH_2OH$

15.3 **a.** CH_3O— —$\overset{\overset{O}{\|}}{C}$—H + $H_2NCH_2CH_3$ **b.** —CH_2NH_2 + O=

15.4 **a.**   **b.**   **c.**

15.5 **a.** —$\overset{\overset{O}{\|}}{C}H$ + $CH_3\overset{\overset{O}{\|}}{C}H$ **b.** $2CH_3(CH_2)_6\overset{\overset{O}{\|}}{C}H$

15.6 **a.** $2CH_3CH_2\overset{\overset{\displaystyle O}{\|}}{C}H \xrightarrow[\text{(aldol)}]{\text{NaOH}} CH_3CH_2\overset{\overset{\displaystyle OH}{|}}{C}H\overset{\underset{\displaystyle CH_3}{|}}{C}H\overset{\overset{\displaystyle O}{\|}}{C}H \xrightarrow[-H_2O]{H^+}$

$CH_3CH_2CH=\overset{\underset{\displaystyle CH_3}{|}}{C}\overset{\overset{\displaystyle O}{\|}}{C}H \xrightarrow{2H_2/Pt} CH_3CH_2CH_2\overset{\underset{\displaystyle CH_3}{|}}{C}HCH_2OH$

b. $2CH_3CH_2CH_2\overset{\overset{\displaystyle O}{\|}}{C}H \xrightarrow[\text{(aldol)}]{\text{NaOH}} CH_3CH_2CH_2\overset{\overset{\displaystyle OH}{|}}{C}H\overset{\underset{\displaystyle CH_3CH_2}{|}}{C}H\overset{\overset{\displaystyle O}{\|}}{C}H \xrightarrow[-H_2O]{H^+}$

$CH_3CH_2CH_2CH=\overset{\underset{\displaystyle CH_3CH_2}{|}}{C}\overset{\overset{\displaystyle O}{\|}}{C}H \xrightarrow{Ag(NH_3)_2^+} CH_3CH_2CH_2CH=\overset{\underset{\displaystyle CH_3CH_2}{|}}{C}\overset{\overset{\displaystyle O}{\|}}{C}OH$

Chapter 16

16.1 **a.** 4-hydroxybenzoic acid (*p*-hydroxybenzoic acid)   **b.** 3-methylbutanoic acid (isovaleric acid)
c. 2-methylpropanedioic acid (methylmalonic acid)   **d.** 2-dodecenoic acid

16.2 $CH_3(CH_2)_8CO_2H$ $CH_3CH_2OCH_2CH_3$ $CH_3CH_2CH_2CO_2H$

slightly   8 g/100 g H_2O soluble in all
soluble   proportions

16.3 **a.** $CH_3\overset{\underset{\displaystyle }{}}{\overset{\overset{\displaystyle CH_3}{|}}{C}}=O + HO\overset{\overset{\displaystyle O}{\|}}{C}CH_2CH_2\overset{\overset{\displaystyle O}{\|}}{C}OH + O=\overset{\underset{\displaystyle CH_3}{|}}{C}CH_3$ **b.** $HO\overset{\overset{\displaystyle O}{\|}}{C}CH_2CH_2CH_2\overset{\overset{\displaystyle O}{\|}}{C}OH$

16.4 **a.** $CH_3\overset{\underset{\displaystyle CH_3}{|}}{C}H\overset{\overset{\displaystyle O}{\|}}{C}O^- K^+$ **b.** $[CH_3(CH_2)_{14}CO_2]_2 Ca^{2+}$

16.5 **a.** $CH_3CH_2CH-CHCO_2H + NaOH \longrightarrow CH_3CH_2CH-CHCO_2^- Na^+ + H_2O$

b. $2C_6H_5CO_2H + Na_2CO_3 \longrightarrow 2C_6H_5CO_2^- Na^+ + CO_2 + H_2O$

c. $HO-\overset{\overset{\displaystyle CH_2-CO_2H}{|}}{\underset{\underset{\displaystyle CH_2-CO_2H}{|}}{C}}-CO_2H + 3NaHCO_3 \longrightarrow HO-\overset{\overset{\displaystyle CH_2-CO_2^- Na^+}{|}}{\underset{\underset{\displaystyle CH_2-CO_2^- Na^+}{|}}{C}}-CO_2^- Na^+ + 3CO_2 + 3H_2O$

16.6 **a.** $O=\langle\hspace{-4pt}\bigcirc\hspace{-4pt}\rangle=O$ **b.** $HO\overset{\overset{\displaystyle O}{\|}}{C}CH_2CH_2CH_2CH_2\overset{\overset{\displaystyle O}{\|}}{C}OH$

Chapter 17

17.1 IUPAC names are given first. Common names, where appropriate, are given in parentheses.
a. cyclohexyl acetate   **b.** diethyl propanedioate (diethyl malonate)   **c.** *tert*-butyl benzoate

17.2   **a.** *N*-phenylacetamide   **b.** octanamide
     c. 2-hydroxybenzamide or *o*-hydroxybenzamide (salicylamide)

17.3   **a.** $CH_3OC{-}\langle\text{benzene}\rangle{-}COCH_3$ **b.** $CH_3COCH_2CH_2CH_2CH_2CH_3$

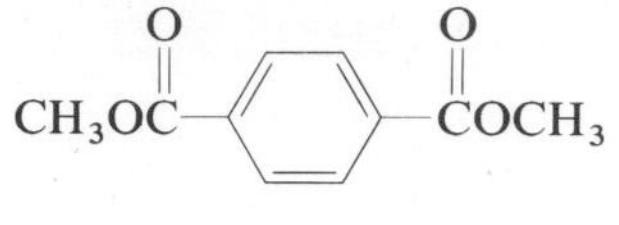

     dimethyl 1,4-benzenedicarboxylate   pentyl acetate
     (dimethyl terephthalate)   (amyl acetate)

17.4   **a.**   **b.**

17.5   **a.** $+ H_2O \xrightarrow{H^+}$ $+ CH_3OH$

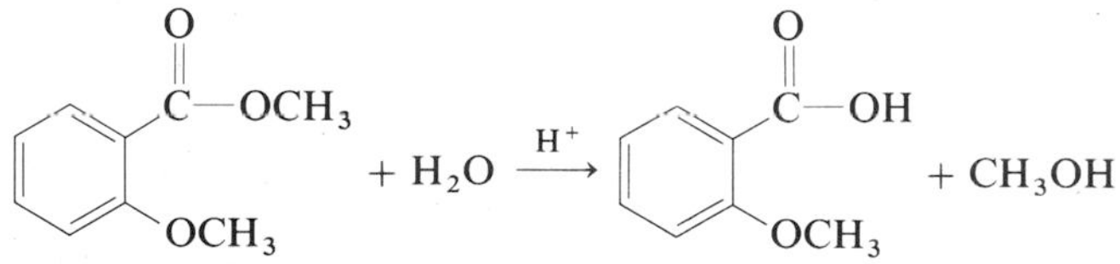

     b. $CH_3CCH_2CH_2CH_2COCH_2CH_3 + NaOH \longrightarrow CH_3CCH_2CH_2CH_2CO^- Na^+ + CH_3CH_2OH$

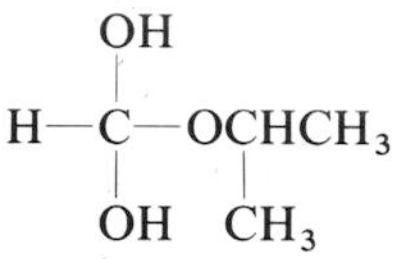

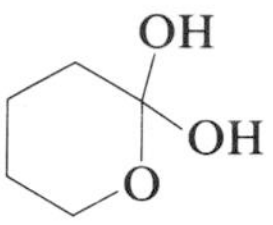

17.6   **a.** $CH_3OC{-}\langle\text{benzene}\rangle{-}COCH_3 + 2NH_3 \longrightarrow H_2NC{-}\langle\text{benzene}\rangle{-}CNH_2 + 2CH_3OH$

     b. $+ NH_3 \longrightarrow$ $+ CH_3CH_2OH$

17.7   **a.** $HO{-}\langle\text{benzene}\rangle{-}OH + 2CH_3COCCH_3 \longrightarrow CH_3CO{-}\langle\text{benzene}\rangle{-}OCCH_3 + 2CH_3COH$

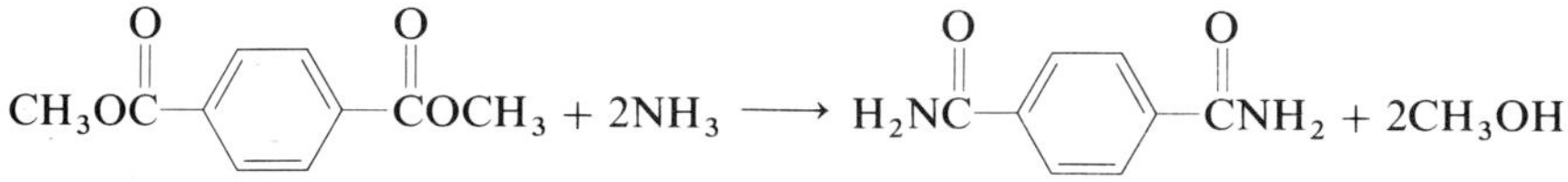

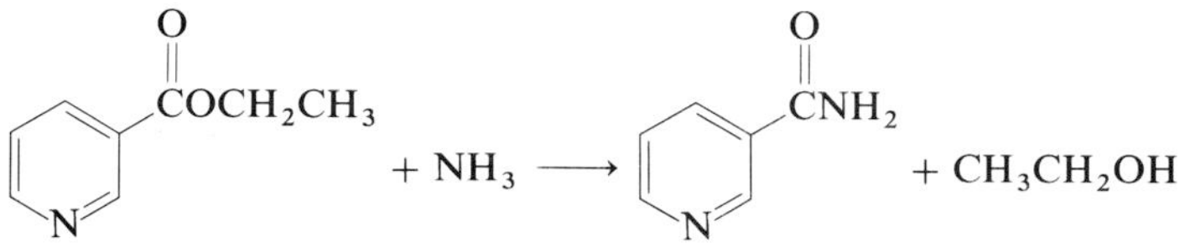

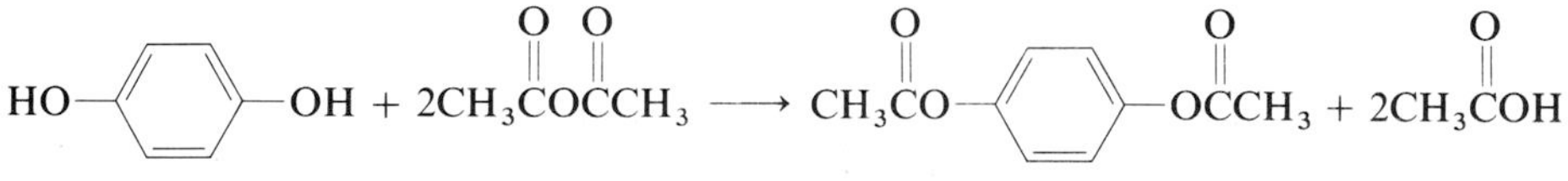

     b. $CH_3C{=}CHCH_2OH + CH_3COCCH_3 \longrightarrow CH_3C{=}CHCH_2OCCH_3 + CH_3COH$ (with CH_3 groups)

17.8   **a.** $CH_3CNH_2 + NaOH \xrightarrow{H_2O} CH_3CO^- Na^+ + NH_3$

     b. $CH_3O{-}\langle\text{benzene}\rangle{-}NHCCH_3 + NaOH \xrightarrow{H_2O} CH_3O{-}\langle\text{benzene}\rangle{-}NH_2 + CH_3CO^- Na^+$

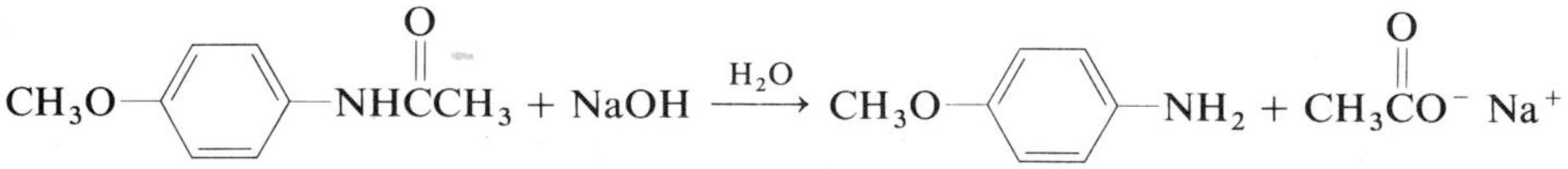

17.9   **a.** $2CH_3CH_2CH_2COCH_2CH_3 \xrightarrow{base} CH_3CH_2CH_2CCHCOCH_2CH_3 + CH_3CH_2OH$
                                              CH_2CH_3

b. (structure) + CH_3COCH_3 $\xrightarrow{\text{base}}$ (structure) + CH_3OH

Chapter 18

18.1 Compounds (a), (b) and (c) each contain one chiral (asymmetric) carbon, as shown by an asterisk on each structural formula.

a. $CH_2\overset{*}{C}HCH_2CH_3$ with HO and NH_2

b. $CH_3CCH_2CO\overset{*}{C}HCH_2CH_2CH_3$ with CH_3

c. $CH_3CH_2\overset{OH}{\underset{*}{C}}HCH{=}CH_2$

18.2 a. (mirror image pair of structures)   **b.** (mirror image pair of structures)

18.3 Compounds (a) and (b) are chiral and therefore show optical isomerism. Compound (c) has a plane of symmetry and is therefore achiral.

a. (mirror image pair of structures) — Chiral carbon atom

b. (mirror image pair of structures) — Chiral carbon atom

c. (cyclopentane structure with CH₃ and OH) The plane of symmetry bisects the $CH_3{-}C{-}OH$ bonds

Chapter 19

19.1 There are four 2-ketohexoses, shown here as two pairs of enantiomers:

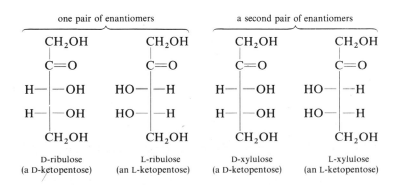

one pair of enantiomers		a second pair of enantiomers	
CH_2OH	CH_2OH	CH_2OH	CH_2OH
$C{=}O$	$C{=}O$	$C{=}O$	$C{=}O$
H——OH	HO——H	H——OH	HO——H
H——OH	HO——H	H——OH	HO——H
CH_2OH	CH_2OH	CH_2OH	CH_2OH
D-ribulose (a D-ketopentose)	L-ribulose (an L-ketopentose)	D-xylulose (a D-ketopentose)	L-xylulose (an L-ketopentose)

19.2 D-mannose differs in configuration from D-glucose only at carbon 2. Therefore the alpha and beta forms of D-mannose differ from those of D-glucose only in the orientation of the —OH on carbon 2. Following are chair and Haworth structures for alpha-D-mannose and beta-D-mannose:

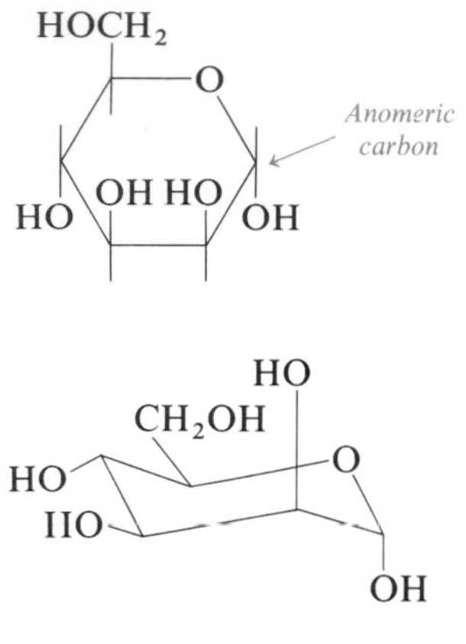

α-D-mannose 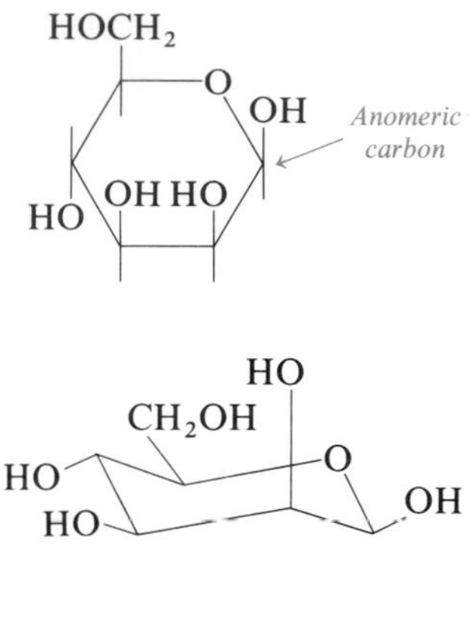   β-D-mannose

19.3 a.

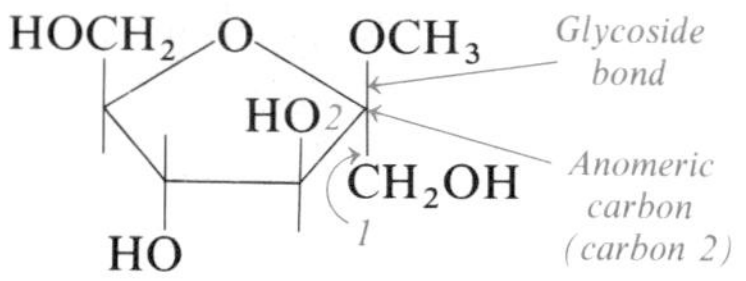

b.

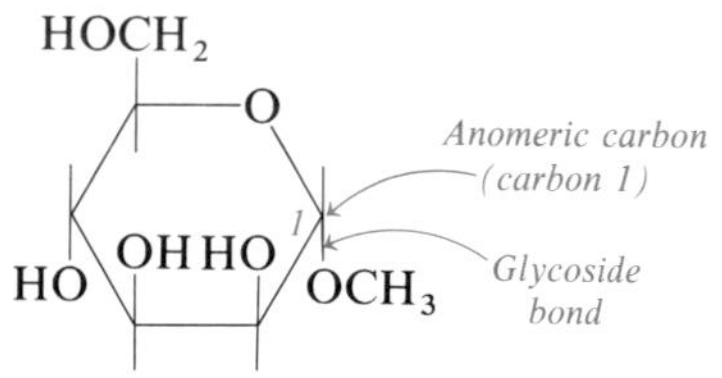

19.4 a.

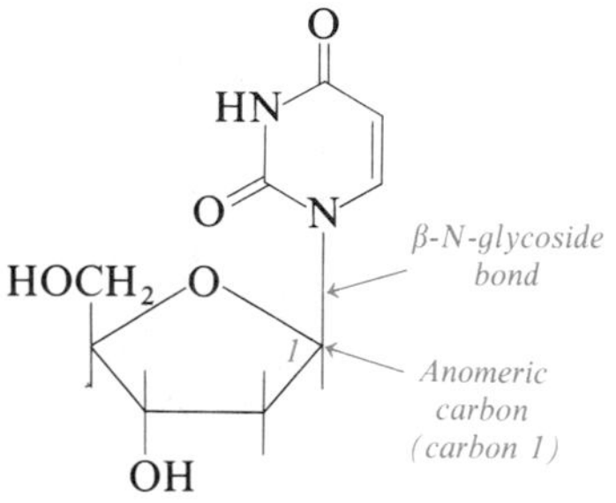

b.

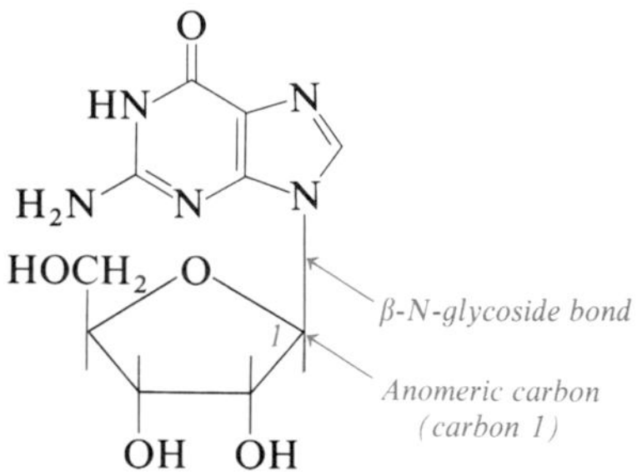

19.5 a.

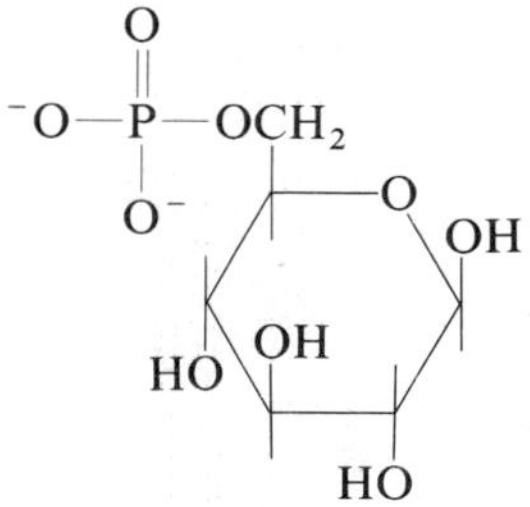

net charge is −2

b.

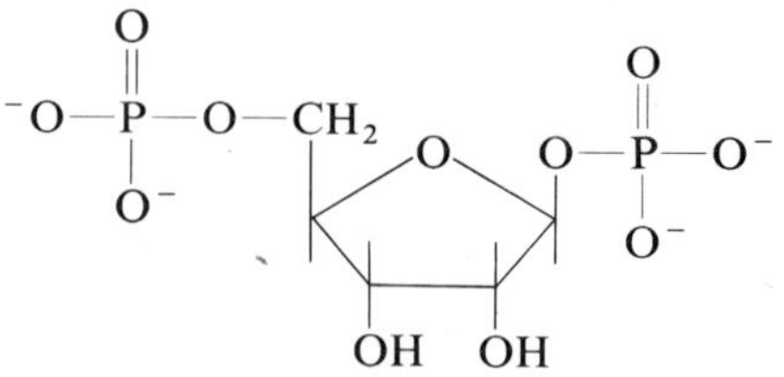

net charge is −4

19.6

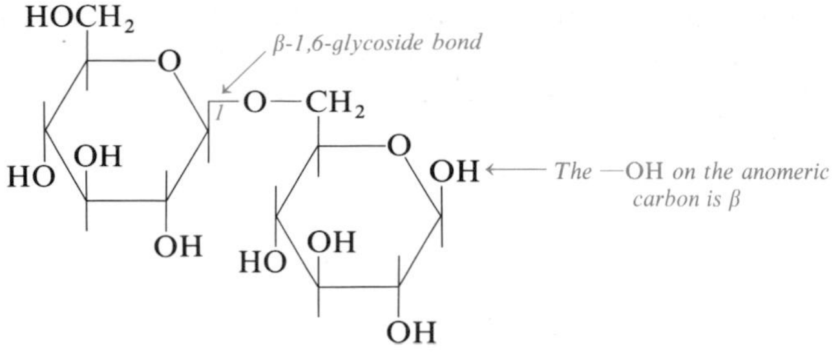
HOCH2
O
β-1,6-glycoside bond
O—CH2
HO
OH
OH
O
OH
The —OH on the anomeric carbon is β
HO
OH
OH

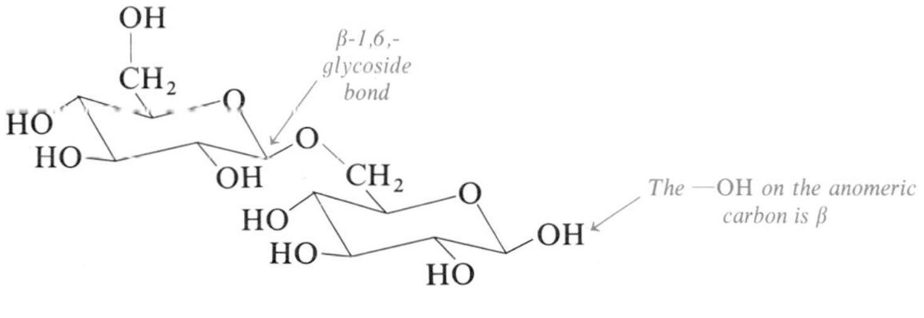
OH
CH2
O
HO
HO
β-1,6,-glycoside bond
O
OH
CH2
O
HO
HO
OH
HO
The —OH on the anomeric carbon is β

Chapter 20

20.1 Although the percentage of oleic acid is approximately the same for beef tallow and corn oil, the total percentages of unsaturated fatty acids are quite different; only 52.1% for beef tallow, but 85.1% for corn oil. The additional unsaturation is due largely to linoleic acid.

Chapter 21

21.1 Following is a structural formula showing the pK_a values (Table 21.4) rounded off to one decimal place of each ionizable group. Note that each ionizable group is shown in the protonated form.

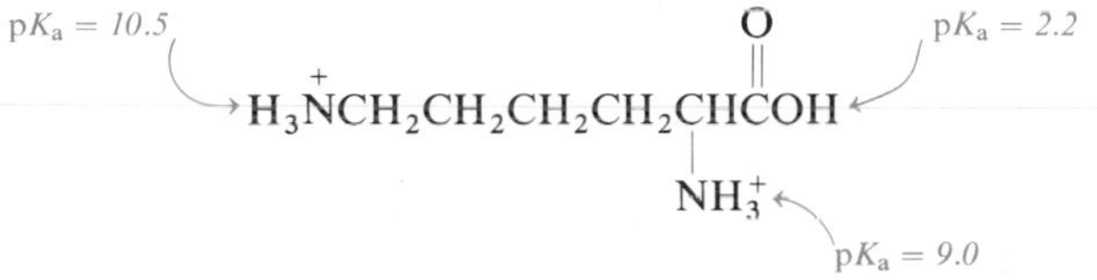
pKa = 10.5
pKa = 2.2
H3NCH2CH2CH2CH2CHCOH
NH3+
pKa = 9.0

The pK_a values for the alpha-carboxyl and alpha-amino groups are approximately the same as for serine (Example 21.1). The pK_a value for the side-chain amino group is 10.5. Therefore at pH 3.0 and 6.0, the side-chain amino group is completely in the protonated form and bears a charge of +1. A pH of 10.0 is 0.5 unit lower than the pK_a of the side-chain amine. By referring to Table 21.5, estimate that the degree of protonation is between 91% (pH = pK_a − 1) and 50% (pH = pK_a).

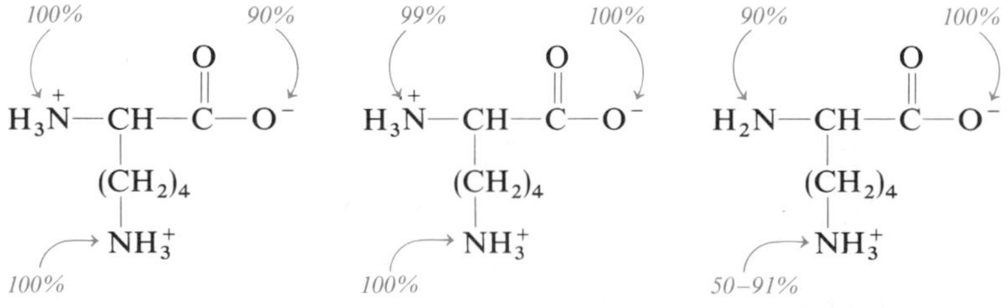
100%
90%
H3N—CH—C—O−
(CH2)4
NH3+
100%
99%
100%
H3N—CH—C—O−
(CH2)4
NH3+
100%
90%
100%
H2N—CH—C—O−
(CH2)4
NH3+
50–91%

pH = 3.0, net charge = ±1 | pH = 7.0, net charge = +1 | pH = 10.0, net charge = −0.5 to −0.09

21.2 A pH of 7.0 is 0.60 unit lower (more acidic) than the pI of histidine. Therefore, at this pH, histidine carries a net positive charge, and on electrophoresis, will migrate toward the negative electrode.

21.3 The isoelectric point of valine is 6.0, a value close to that for other amino acids containing an alpha-carboxyl and an alpha-amino group as the only ionizable groups. From Table 21.6, find that the isoelectric point for glutamic acid is 3.1 and for arginine is 10.8.

	Glutamic Acid	**Arginine**	**Valine**
pI	3.1	10.8	6.0
Net charge at pH 6.0	-1	$+1$	zero

On electrophoresis at pH 6.0, valine will not move from the origin. Glutamic acid will move toward the positive electrode and arginine toward the negative electrode.

21.4 Following is the structural formula for lys-phe-ala. The net charge on this tripeptide at pH 6.0 is $+1$.

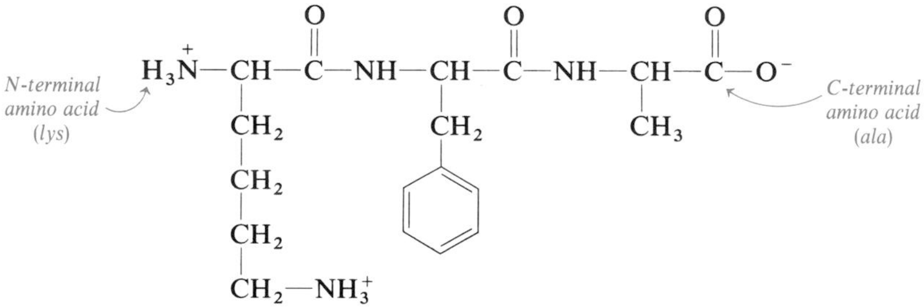

21.5 The side chain of lysine ($-NH_3^+$) can form salt linkages with the side chains of glutamic acid ($-CO_2^-$) and aspartic acid ($-CO_2^-$).

Chapter 22

22.1 **a.** $V_{max} = 38$ μmol/min; $\frac{1}{2}V_{max} = 19$ μmol/min; $K_m = 3.5 \times 10^{-3}$ M
b. initial velocity $= 26$ μmol/min   **c.** new initial velocity $= 52$ μmol/min

22.2 pK_a of the imidazole ring of histidine is 6.10 (Table 21.4). At pH 4.0, the imidazole is 100% in the protonated, or acid, form and bears a net charge of $+1$. Because the optimal pH of this enzyme is 4.0, it must be that the enzyme requires the histidine side chain in the protonated (acid) form.

Chapter 23

23.1 **a.** Deoxythymidine triphosphate

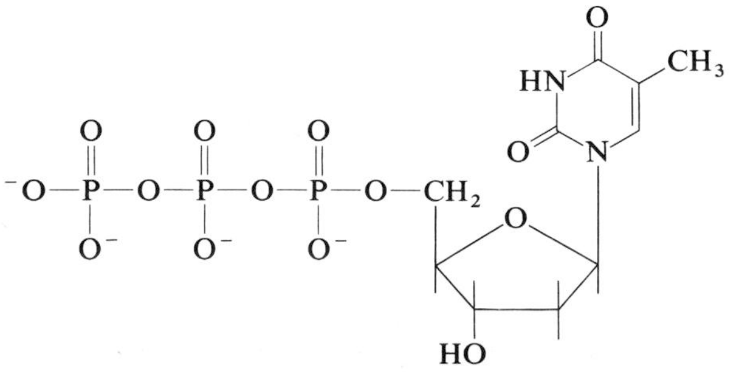

b. Deoxyguanosine monophosphate

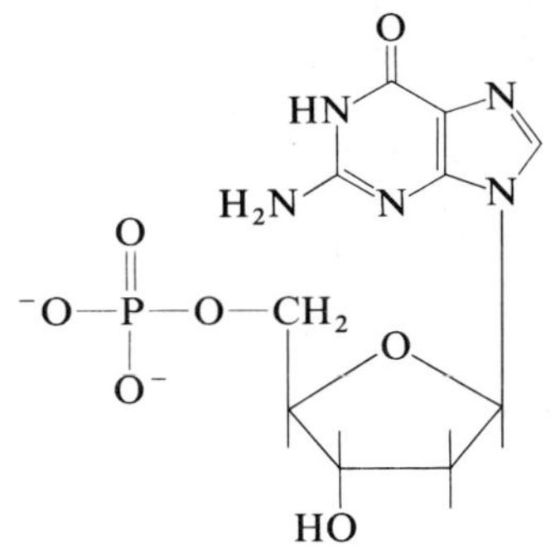

23.2

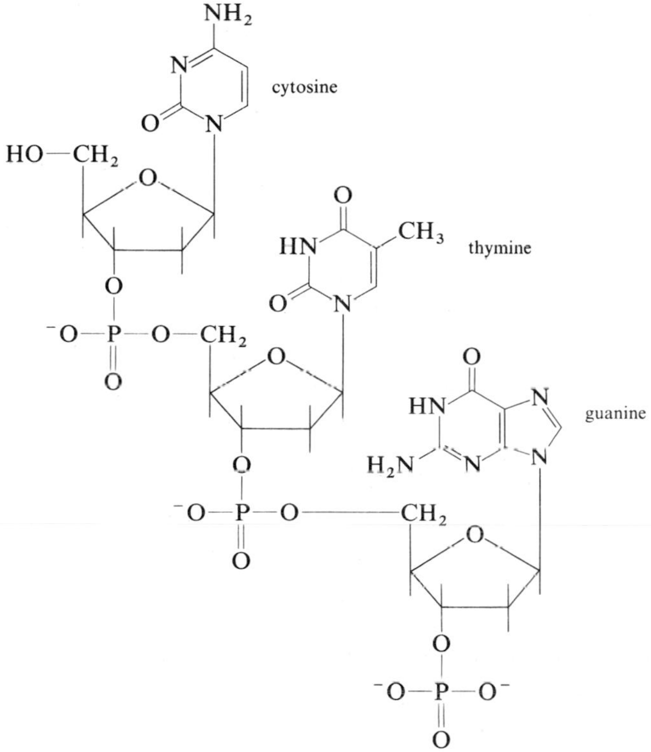

23.3 Following are the original and complementary strands.

Original strand: 5′-CCGTAGGA-3′
Complementary strand: 3′-GGCATCCT-5′

The complementary strand can be written alternatively as

5′-T-C-C-T-A-C-G-G-3′

23.4 Following is the original base sequence of DNA, and the sequence of bases in mRNA synthesized using the original sequence as a template.

Original DNA: 5′-TCGGTACACTGG-3′
Transcribed mRNA: 3′-AGCCAUGUGACC-5′

23.5 Following are DNA, its mRNA complement, and the primary structure of the polypeptide coded for by this section of mRNA.

Original DNA: 3′-ACG-ATA-TAA-GTT-TTA-ACG-GGA-GAA-CCA-ACT-5′
Transcribed mRNA: 5′-UGC-UAU-AUU-CAA-AAU-UGC-CCU-CUU-GGU-UGA-3′
Amino acid sequence: cys-tyr-ile-gln-asn-cys-pro-leu-gly-stop

23.6 a.   Original DNA: 3′-GAC-TCC-GAT-CGC-GAT-5′
Transcribed mRNA: 5′-CUG-AGG-CUA-GCG-CUA-3′
Amino acid sequence: leu-arg-leu-ala-leu

b.   Mutant DNA: 3′-GAC-TTC-GAT-CGC-GAT-5′
Transcribed mRNA: 5′-CUG-AAG-CUA-GCG-CUA-3′
Mutant amino acid sequence: leu-lys-leu-ala-leu

23.7 a.   Original DNA: 3′-GAT-GGG-ATG-TCT-5′
Transcribed mRNA: 5′-CUA-CCC-UAC-AGA-3′
Amino acid sequence: leu-pro-tyr-arg

b.   Mutant DNA: 3′-GAG-GGA-TGT-CT-5′
Transcribed mRNA: 5′-CUC-CCU-ACA-GA-3′
Mutant amino acid sequence: leu-pro-thr

Chapter 24

No in-chapter problems.

Chapter 25

25.1 a. 2 mol NADH per mole of glucose. No $FADH_2$ is produced.
b. 1 mol NADH per mole of pyruvate.   **c.** 3 mol NADH and 1 mol $FADH_2$ per mole of acetyl CoA.
25.2 a. There is only one oxidation, namely step 6: oxidation of 3-phosphoglyceraldehyde to 1,3-diphosphoglycerate.
b. Only one reaction involves cleavage of a carbon-carbon bond, namely step 4: conversion of fructose 1,6-diphosphate to dihydroxyacetone phosphate and 3-phosphoglyceraldehyde.
25.3 a. lactate   **b.** lactate

Chapter 26

26.1 a. Only 1 mol ATP is required, that in activation of myristic acid and its conversion to myristyl CoA. Note, however, that although only 1 mol ATP is required, two high-energy bonds are hydrolyzed to provide the necessary energy for converting myristic acid to its CoA ester.
b. 6 mol NADH and 6 mol $FADH_2$ **c.** 7 mol acetyl CoA

Chapter 27

27.1 a.

phenylalanine   pyruvate   phenylpyruvate   alanine

b.

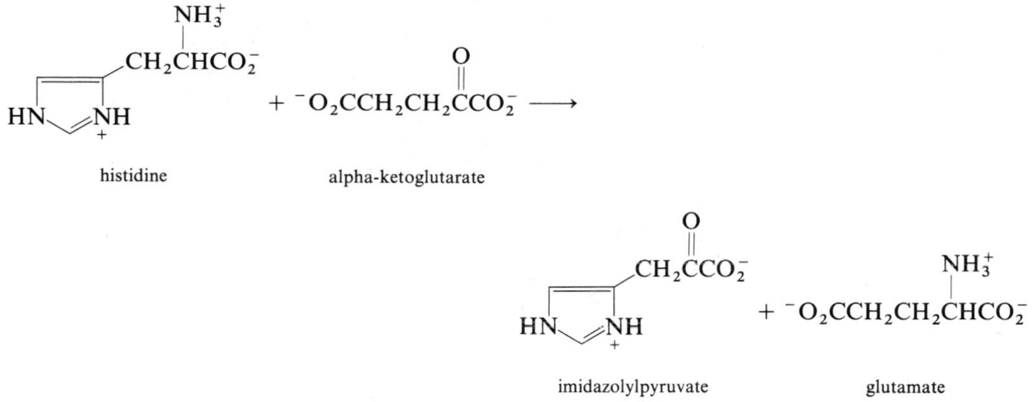

$$\underset{\text{histidine}}{\underset{\text{HN}\diagdown\text{NH}^+}{\overset{\overset{\overset{\text{NH}_3^+}{|}}{\text{CH}_2\text{CHCO}_2^-}}{\bigcirc}}} + {}^-\text{O}_2\text{CCH}_2\text{CH}_2\overset{\overset{\text{O}}{\|}}{\text{C}}\text{CO}_2^- \longrightarrow$$

histidine   alpha-ketoglutarate

$$\underset{\text{imidazolylpyruvate}}{\underset{\text{HN}\diagdown\text{NH}^+}{\overset{\overset{\overset{\text{O}}{\|}}{\text{CH}_2\overset{}{\text{C}}\text{CO}_2^-}}{\bigcirc}}} + \underset{\text{glutamate}}{{}^-\text{O}_2\text{CCH}_2\text{CH}_2\overset{\overset{\text{NH}_3^+}{|}}{\text{CHCO}_2^-}}$$

imidazolylpyruvate   glutamate

Index